Continued on inside back cover

The Riverside Anthology
of Short Fiction

Convention and Innovation

The Riverside Anthology of Short Fiction

Convention and Innovation

Dean Baldwin
Penn State Erie
The Behrend College

Houghton Mifflin Company   *Boston   New York*

To the memory of V. S. Pritchett;
To my many students in English 184, especially Adria, Jim, Kristi, Liane, Ron,
"Skorp," and Tina;
and to Vicki, Phil, Dorothy, Tanya, and Jim, with all my love.

Cover Art: (l) Burne-Jones, Sir Edward. *The Golden Stairs.* 1880. Oil on canvas. Tate
Gallery, London, Great Britain. (r) Marcel Duchamp. *Nude Descending a Staircase, No.*
2. 1912. Philadelphia Museum of Art. The Louis and Walter Arensberg Collection.

Sponsoring Editor: Jayne Fargnoli
Basic Book Editor: Martha Bustin
Senior Project Editor: Susan Westendorf
Production/Design Coordinator: Jennifer Meyer Dare
Senior Manufacturing Coordinator: Priscilla Bailey
Marketing Manager: Nancy Lyman

Printed in the U.S.A.

Library of Congress Catalog Card Number: 97-72437

ISBN: 0-395-81386-7

1 2 3 4 5 6 7 8 9-DC-01 00 99 98 97

Acknowledgments
ACHEBE, CHINUA "Vengeful Creditor" by Chinua Achebe. Copyright © 1973 by Chinua Achebe. Reprinted
by permission of the author. (continued on p. 1229)

❧ Contents

✒ *Preface*

The Riverside Anthology of Short Fiction has grown out of many years of teaching the short story to undergraduates and wishing for a collection that presented stories less like individual gemstones on display in a cabinet and more like fresh air and the world outside. For certainly stories form a vast and sustaining medium that connects us with the past and future, with places and situations familiar and foreign, with our own interior lives and with each other. The ninety-nine selections included in this volume have been chosen for their ability to spark this sense of stories as essential, various, and interrelated, and as age-old and ongoing. Canonical works illuminate fresh and seldom-anthologized stories, and vice versa. Examples of detective, romance, adventure, and horror stories juxtaposed with literary short stories reveal the creative tension between "high" and "popular" art. The contributions of women and of writers from diverse ethnic backgrounds are prominently featured, and a generous selection of stories from many parts of the non-English-speaking world balances a selection of those by American and British authors. Throughout all, the purpose of this book is to help students understand the richness and vitality of the short fiction genre, to connect with its encompassing pleasures, and to write about stories in an informed and involved way.

    The Riverside Anthology of Short Fiction also celebrates the interplay of convention and innovation. Students become attuned to common conventions of the genre, see how brilliantly these conventions can be deployed, and observe how the well-established ways of doing things often inspire innovations, which in time become new conventions. The theme of the interaction of convention and innovation has proven to be a useful way to bring extra depth and cohesion to the short-story course, or to be an interesting thread that can be added to other approaches taken to the course. It invites students to see fiction not as a "given" but as an art form partly made up of conventional elements that change over time in response to new perceptions of reality, aesthetics, and the function of art. Selections from other cultures also enable students to see how these conventions can be fruitfully adapted and reinterpreted.

KEY FEATURES

- **Sidebars on Topics Relevant to the Study of Short Fiction.** A unique feature of *The Riverside Anthology of Short Fiction* is the inclusion of seven short boxed essays that examine key topics and make reference to relevant stories within the collection. Four of these sidebars focus on important sub-genres—detective, romance, adventure, and horror stories—subjects already familiar to many students from popular culture. These sidebars consider the backgrounds, conventions, and literary dimensions of these story types and various approaches that may be taken toward them. The three other sidebars explore issues of social criticism, psychoanalytical criticism, and distinctions made between popular and literary short stories. Collectively the sidebars encourage critical reading and the making of connections among stories.

- **Introduction: "Convention and Innovation in the Short Story."** This brief essay introduces the idea of literary conventions—what they are; how they function; how writers use, vary, and react against them; and how they affect such elements of fiction as point of view, character, and plot. Often these familiar plots and devices are so accepted that we hardly notice them, yet the enjoyment and understanding of fiction can be significantly enhanced by "tuning in" to such conventional elements, as well as to innovations that work unexpected changes on the norm.

- **A Selection of Precursor Stories.** The first seven selections in this anthology illustrate some important early forms of short fiction: a story from Native American (Abenaki) oral tradition; one of Aesop's fables; a character sketch by Theophrastus; the Daedalus and Icarus myth from Ovid's *Metamorphoses;* the parable of the Good Samaritan; a romantic tale from Boccaccio's *Decameron;* and a fairy tale, "The Blue Beard." Much can be learned from considering the themes and techniques of these precursors and their echoes in later selections. The first section of *Part II: A Brief History of the Short Story* (at the end of the book) provides additional background, as needed, on these early and influential forms.

- **Breadth and Balance in the Stories.** The collection offers a wide variety of stories from a large number of peoples and cultures and a generous selection of both commonly anthologized authors and unusual and contemporary selections. The stories here reflect various aspects of the short-story genre—its international character, the diversity of its writers, its history, the interplay of convention and innovation, and representations of common fictional elements and themes. An alternate Table of Contents lists authors in alphabetical order, making all approaches easy to use.

- **Multiple Selections by Six Authors.** Edgar Allan Poe, Guy de Maupassant, Anton Chekhov, Katherine Mansfield, Eudora Welty, and Margaret Atwood are represented by two stories each, to encourage a closer study of these important writers and to facilitate comparisons.

- **Substantial but Nonintrusive Pedagogy.** Brief biographical headnotes appear before each story, and Questions for Discussion and Writing appear after each. In addition, the following sections may be found at the back of the book (after *Part I: The Stories*), to be used as needed:

Part II: A Brief History of the Short Story, including material on precursors to the short-story genre

Part III: Reading and Writing about Short Fiction, including Reading Fiction Actively; John Updike's story "Lucid Eye in Silvertown" (annotated and analyzed as part of a discussion on critical reading); The Elements of Fiction, with examples from the anthologized stories; and Writing about Short Fiction, with (1) a list of questions students can ask of any story, (2) a brief section on critical approaches, and (3) a sample paper that shows how one student worked through an assignment on Updike's story, from brainstorming to final draft.

Part IV: Reference, including A Glossary of Literary Terms, A Selective Bibliography for Students, and the Author/Title Index.

THE INSTRUCTOR'S RESOURCE MANUAL

The Instructor's Resource Manual is intended as a guide for both experienced and inexperienced teachers. The body of the Instructor's Resource Manual consists of individual essays on each of the stories. These essays offer critical insights into the stories and discussions of teaching strategies, and they are followed by both class discussion questions and a bibliography for further reading. The manual contains outlines for three ways of organizing a course using *The Riverside Anthology of Short Fiction:* by convention and innovation, by the elements of fiction, and by theme. It also offers teaching ideas on how to use the book's special features—its sidebars, chronological organization, and sections on reading analytically, writing about short fiction, and analyzing by elements.

ACKNOWLEDGMENTS

I owe a debt greater than I can repay to all those who have helped, directly and indirectly, with this project.

My thanks, first of all, to the editors at Houghton Mifflin—Jayne Fargnoli, George Kane, and Martha Bustin—for their heroic patience, cooperative spirit, and good advice. Susan Westendorf, Terri Teleen, and Nancy Lyman have also been extremely helpful throughout the process.

Thanks are due also to my friends and colleagues who helped at every stage, from reading manuscript to suggesting stories and tracking down information for footnotes: Michael Bott, Steve de Hart, Gregory Morris, Michael O'Shea, Allan Parker, Marjorie Podolsky, Brian Ryder, Roberta Salper, Soledad Traverso, Katheryn Wolfe, and especially the coauthor of the Instructor's Resource Manual, Allan Weiss.

Special mention must be made of the librarians and secretarial staff who bore with me patiently throughout the two years of preparation: Brenda Bane, Wendy Eidenmuller, Marie Goodenow, Norma Hartner, and Patty Mrowzowski.

Much of the credit for whatever virtues this book possesses must go to those who reviewed the manuscript at various stages in its preparation and who made invaluable corrections and suggestions:

Mariam Marty Clark, Auburn University

John Clifford, University of North Carolina—Wilmington

Susan Danielson, Portland State University

C. R. Embry, Truckee Meadows Community College

Donald B. Johns, University of California—Davis

Joe Lostracco, Austin Community College (Tex.)

Maureen Murphy, St. Louis Community College—Meramec

Michael J. O'Shea, Newberry College

Natalie Schroeder, University of Mississippi

Robert Solotaroff, University of Minnesota

Michelle Pagni Stewart, California State University—San Bernardino

Allan Weiss, York University (Canada)

I am also grateful to Penn State Erie, The Behrend College, for granting me a sabbatical, during which time I accomplished much of the work on this book.

Finally, I must acknowledge the patience of my beloved wife, who supported and encouraged me throughout this project.

D. B.

INTRODUCTION: CONVENTION AND INNOVATION IN THE SHORT STORY

> I have a notion that most of the revolutionary changes in the arts have taken place owing to the inability of an artist, or a group of artists, to conform to the usages of his time. He has been forced to originality because he could not express himself in current terms. —W. SOMERSET MAUGHAM

Every art form has its conventions—that is, those devices of content, style, or technique that make artistic communication possible. Landscape painting, for example, focuses on a picturesque scene, depicts it in accordance with the laws of visual perspective, and surrounds the object with a window-like frame. Dance has its language of movement, theater its conventions of dialogue and lighting, to name just a few. Sometimes, when a particular device becomes stale through overuse, we use the term "conventional" in a derogatory sense, but convention is essential to art, just as conventions of grammar, vocabulary, and syntax are essential to language.

Some conventions have become so common that they appear inevitable or even "natural." When we set the table for dinner, for example, we put the forks to the left of the plate, even though most people, being right-handed, reach across the plate to take up the fork. We perform both actions so automatically that it rarely occurs to us to question why the fork is placed on the left when most of us use it with our right hand. It is not until we see Europeans eating with the fork in the left hand and the knife in the right that we realize that the placement of eating utensils is an inherited tradition—entirely conventional. Similarly, movies are almost always accompanied by a sound track consisting not simply of dialogue and sound effects but also of appropriate music. Such music is so common in films that we often forget it is there, helping to guide and direct our responses to the action on the screen. The sound track seems like a "natural" accompaniment to filmed action, but of course in "real life" there is no sound track. We may be surrounded by music, voluntarily or involuntarily, but such music bears no necessary relation to our activities. The sound track, like the way we set the table for dinner, is an artistic convention.

At the other end of the scale, conventions may strike us as so unnatural or ludicrous that they prevent us from participating in and hence enjoying a particular art form. The dying character in an opera who sings a ten-minute aria after receiving a fatal wound may seem ludicrous to someone unfamiliar with the convention. In the early cowboy movies, the "good guys" wore white hats and were clean-shaven, whereas the "bad guys" wore black hats and were scruffy. These naive conventions were later discarded by more "realistic" films, which nevertheless retained many other conventions of the cowboy genre—the pretty saloon girl with the good heart, the quick-draw shoot-out, and the sheriff with a troubled past. Lovers of the western accept the conventions and may even revel in them, whereas others cannot enjoy the genre because for them the conventions seem arbitrary and artificial.

The basic fictional conventions are often called "elements" of fiction—point of view, character, setting, plot, style, figurative language, theme, and so on. This book treats these elements as labels for conventions that authors use and change as they seek to communicate with readers in new ways. One way to approach short fiction, then, is to realize that many of its methods are in fact conventions. For example, consider point of view.

POINT OF VIEW

From the earliest times, readers and listeners have granted narrators the privilege of knowing everything and anything. The narrator of the biblical Book of Job, for instance, is privy to conversations between God and Satan. How does he or she know such things? We don't even ask. For the sake of the story, we grant the narrator such knowledge. Moreover, omniscient narrators are permitted to know what all characters are thinking and what their motivations are, as well as the course of events past, present, and future. In reality, nobody possesses such knowledge, but for the sake of the story we accept omniscient narrators without questioning where they obtained their knowledge or authority.

Like omniscient narrators, first-person narrators are granted something none of us has—perfect memories for who did what and who said what to whom—down to precise detail and the exact wording of complicated sentences. W. Somerset Maugham acknowledges the artificiality of this convention:

> "This is merely a device to gain verisimilitude. It is one that has its defects, for it may strike the reader that the narrator could not know all the events he sets forth; and when he tells a story in the first person at one remove, when he reports, I mean, a story that someone tells him, it may very well seem that the speaker, a police officer, for example, or a sea-captain, could never have expressed himself with such facility and with such elaboration. Every convention has its disadvantages. These must be as far as possible disguised and what cannot be disguised must be accepted. The advantage of this one is its directness. It makes it possible for the writer to tell no more than he knows. Making no claim to omniscience, he can frankly say when a motive or an occurrence is unknown to him, and thus often give his story a plausibility that it might otherwise lack." [Quoted in Archer 88]

Both the omniscient narrator and the first-person narrator are conventions relating to point of view. One is not "better" than the other; good and bad stories have been written using each approach. Understanding how each convention works, however, what its strengths and limitations are, can increase our appreciation and understanding of fiction.

CHARACTER

Another way to look at conventions is to consider how they have been altered or even discarded as authors have sought new ways to convey their experiences and insights. To understand this idea more clearly, consider the idea of character. When the short story arose in the early years of the nineteenth century, writers typically focused on extraordinary characters—such as Poe's madmen or Irving's folkloristic heroes. Other authors of the time focused on idealized heroes and heroines, such as handsome and dashing noblemen, and beautiful, chaste heroines. Eventually, reaction set in, and writers began turning their attention to ordinary, more "realistic" characters—farmers, workers, clerks, bureaucrats. The emphasis shifted from the extraordinary to the mundane. In the process, fiction also began to treat sympathetically groups of people not previously included or considered only in very stereotypical ways: women, members of various racial and ethnic groups, children, the elderly, homosexuals, and others.

But it was not only the type of character that changed, but also the devices for probing and developing character. The heroes and heroines of sentimental romance defined themselves by what they said and did; by the end of the nineteenth century, characters were increasingly being analyzed for the motives behind their words and actions. The question of *what* became the question of *why*. In order to probe individual psyches, writers invented new devices (conventions) for representing psychological processes: interior monologues, symbolic dreams, stream of consciousness, and manipulation of exterior imagery and symbols, to name just a few.

It is important to note, however, that the idealized and stock characters of nineteenth-century fiction have not disappeared. In slightly altered form, they still dominate romance novels, best sellers, movies, television dramas, and comic books. Thus, new conventions do not necessarily drive out old ones. Highly conventional forms exist alongside innovative ones in every art form. Consider, for example, the variety of music available in a typical record store—from Gregorian chant to acid rock, delta blues to gangsta rap. This anthology attempts to convey something of this cultural mix by including both conventional and innovative stories during various periods of the short story's history.

GENRE

Yet another way to look at convention in fiction is to consider stories by genre: detective stories, horror stories, sports stories, western stories, love stories, science fiction, and adventure are among the many subgenres of fiction. Each of these involves a set of conventions. Readers know what to expect from each of these and sometimes react angrily if their expectations are not satisfied—if the criminal isn't caught and punished, for example, or if a love story doesn't end happily. Here again, however, writers and readers may become bored if the conventions remain unchanged. Tracing the innovations in a particular type of story over time can not only be a fascinating literary exercise but can also reveal a great deal about changing tastes, ideas, and values. To take an obvious example, love stories in the nineteenth century rarely dealt directly with sex. Sexual attraction was represented as longing or passion, but seldom as a physical force, and of course the details of physical love were at best suggested, perhaps by a kiss or a swoon, but never by direct description (except in another subgenre, pornography). Today, love stories commonly deal frankly with intimate details. These changes in the love story represent important cultural changes as well as literary ones. It is not simply that daring authors broke new ground and rebelled against previous conventions; in so doing, they both shaped and reflected the society around them.

Becoming alert to the conventions and innovations in any art form is an important step in understanding, appreciating, and enjoying that form. Seeing plot, for instance, as just one way among many to structure a story frees us from feeling that a story without plot is "pointless" or "formless," just as recognizing that music without melody can still yield pleasure. This anthology introduces a wide variety of fiction and fictional possibilities. Beyond that, it encourages a state of mind that understands and appreciates the full range of what short stories can offer—what they in all their diversity can say about and to us in all of ours.

Enjoy!

WORK CITED

Archer, Stanley. *W. Somerset Maugham: A Study of the Short Fiction*. New York: Twayne, 1993.

PART ONE

Stories

Gluskabe[1] and the Four Wishes
As retold by Joseph Bruchac

The Europeans who came to the "New World" nearly obliterated the rich oral traditions of Native Americans, first by conquest, then by suppression and religious conversion. Fortunately, however, the tales have not only survived but have helped such groups as the Abenaki preserve their cultural traditions, values, and sense of themselves as a people.

The present teller of these tales, Joseph Bruchac, is but one in a long line of storytellers, preserving the ancient tales for his own people and sharing them with others.

LONG AGO, GLUSKABE lived with his grandmother, Woodchuck, near the big water. Gluskabe is the one who defeated the monster which tried to keep all the water in the world for himself. He is the one who made the big animals grow small so they would be less dangerous to human beings.

When Gluskabe had done many things to make the world a better place for his children and his children's children, he decided it was time to rest. He went down to the big water, climbed into his magic canoe made of stone, and sailed away to a far island. Some say that the island is in the great lake the people call Petonbowk. Others say they went far to the east, beyond the coast of Maine.

They say the fog which rises out there is actually the smoke from Gluskabe's 10 pipe. It is said that for a time Gluskabe let it be known to the world that anyone who came to him would be granted one wish.

Once there were four Abenaki men who decided to make the journey to visit Gluskabe. One of them was a man who had almost no possessions. His wish was that Gluskabe would make it so that he owned many fine things. The second man was a man who was very vain. He was already quite tall, but he wore his hair piled up high on his head and stuffed moss in his moccasins so that he would be even greater in height. His wish was to be taller than all men. A third man was very afraid of dying. His wish was that he would live longer than any man. The fourth man was a man who spent much time hunting to provide food for his family and his village. But he 20 was not a very good hunter, even though he tried very hard. His wish was that he would become a good enough hunter to always give his people enough to eat.

The four of them set out in a canoe to find the island of Gluskabe. Their trip was not an easy one. The currents were strong and they had to paddle hard against them. The man who owned nothing knew a song to calm the waters and when he sang it the currents ceased and they were able to go on their way. Now a wind began to blow very hard, pushing them back towards shore. But the second man took out some tobacco and offered it to the wind and it became calm enough for them to continue on their way. Soon great whales began to come up near the

---

1. In Abenaki lore, Gluskabe is "the man who made himself from something"—the dust wiped from the hands of Tabaldak, creator of human beings. Tabaldak put Gluskabe in charge of the earth, with the power to change things. The Abenaki originally lived in the territory from Lake Champlain in New York State to Cape Breton Island, Canada.

boat and it seemed as if they would tip the boat over. But the man who was afraid 30
of dying had brought with him a small stone figure shaped like a whale. He
dropped it into the water as an offering and the whales dove beneath the surface
and were gone. Now the island of Gluskabe was very close, but they could not see
it because a fog came up over the ocean and covered everything. The fourth man,
who wanted to be a good hunter, took out his pipe and began to smoke it, making
an offering of his smoke so that Gluskabe would stop smoking his own pipe and
let the fog lift. Soon the fog rolled away and they saw the Island of Gluskabe was
there before them.

They left their boat on the shore and made their way to the place where
Gluskabe sat.   40

"Kuai!" Gluskabe said. "You have had to work hard to come here to see me.
You have earned the right to each make one wish."

"I wish to own many fine possessions," said the first man.

"My wish is to be taller than any other man," said the second.

"I want to live longer than any man," said the third.

"My desire is not so much for myself," said the fourth man. "I want to be a
good enough hunter to provide food for my family and my people."

Gluskabe looked at the fourth man and smiled. Then he took out four
pouches and gave one to each of the men. "In these you will find what you want.
But do not open them before you get home and in your own lodge."   50

The men all agreed and went back to their canoe. They crossed the waters
and reached the land. Then each of them started on his own way home. The first
man, who wanted many possessions, took the canoe, which had belonged to the
one who wanted to live longer than any man.

"Take this to go home in," said the man who wanted to live long, "I am going
to live forever, so it will be easy for me to get another canoe."

As the man who wanted many possessions paddled along he thought about
all that he would have. He would have fine clothing of buckskin, he would have
ornaments made of shells and bright stones, he would have stone axes and finely
made weapons, he would have a beautiful lodge to live in. As he thought of all the 60
things he would have he grew more and more anxious to see them. Finally, he
could wait no longer.

"It will not hurt anything if I just peek inside this pouch," he said. Then he
opened it just a crack to look inside. As soon as he did so all kinds of things began
to pour out of the pouch. Moccasins and shirts, necklaces and wampum belts,
axes and spears and bows and arrows. The man tried to close the pouch but he
could not do so. The things came pouring out and filled the canoe, covering the
man. They were so heavy that the canoe sank and the man, tangled in all his possessions, sank with them and drowned.

The second man, who wanted to be taller than all others, had walked along 70
for only a short time before he, too, became curious. He stopped on top of a high
ridge and took out the pouch. "How can this make me taller?" he said. "Perhaps
there is some kind of magic ointment in here that I can rub on myself to make me
grow. There would be nothing wrong with trying out just a little of it before I get
home." Then he opened the pouch. As soon as he did so he was transformed into
a pine, the tallest of the trees. To this day the pines stand taller than all others,

growing on the high ridges, and in the wind you may hear them whispering, bragging about their height, taller than all men.

The third man, too, did not go far before he became curious. "If I am going to live forever," he said, "then nothing will be able to hurt me. Thus there is no reason why I should not open this pouch." He opened it up. As soon as he did so he turned into a great boulder, one which would stand unchanged for thousands of seasons, longer than the life of any man.

The fourth man, though, did not think of himself as he traveled home. He had further to go than the others, but he did not stop. "Soon," he said to himself, "I will be able to feed my people." He went straight to his lodge and when he got inside he opened the pouch. But there was nothing inside it. Yet as he sat there, holding the open pouch, there came into his mind a great understanding. He realized the ways he must proceed to hunt animals. He began to understand how to prepare himself for a hunt and how to show the animals respect so that they would always allow him to hunt. It seemed he could hear someone speaking to him, more than one person. Then he realized what he was hearing. He was hearing the voices of the animals themselves, telling him about their ways. From that day on he was the best hunter among the people. He never took more game than was needed, yet he always provided enough to feed his people. His was truly the best of the gifts given by Gluskabe.

Questions for Discussion and Writing

1. Analyze the use of magic and the supernatural in this story. What part does each play in the story? How does the supernatural in this story differ from the supernatural in ghost or horror stories?

2. What values and attitudes does the tale encourage or teach? How relevant are these values to the present day?

ᖗ AESOP
(Sixth Century B.C.?)

TRANSLATED BY S. A. HANDFORD

The Town Mouse and the Country Mouse

The name of Aesop is permanently linked with the fable genre, but it is doubtful that such a person ever lived. Like Homer, the name assigned to the author of the great Greek epics, "Aesop" may be a convenient fiction.

What is beyond dispute is the enduring popularity and continuing influence of the fables attributed to Aesop. They are masterpieces of economy, sharp characterization, and insightful wit.

A FIELD-MOUSE INVITED a friend who lived in a town house to dine with him in the country. The other accepted with alacrity; but when he found that the fare consisted only of barley and other corn, he said to his host: "Let me tell you, my friend, you live like an ant. But I have abundance of good things to eat, and if you will come home with me you shall share them all." So the two of them went off at once; and when his friend showed him peas and beans, bread, dates, cheese, honey, and fruit, the astonished field-mouse congratulated him heartily and cursed his own lot. They were about to begin their meal when the door suddenly opened, and the timid creatures were so scared by the sound that they scuttled into chinks. When they had returned and were just going to take some dried figs, they saw   10 someone else come into the room to fetch something, and once more they jumped to take cover in their holes. At this the field-mouse decided that he did not care if he had to go hungry. "Good-bye, my friend," he said with a groan. "You may eat your fill and enjoy yourself. But your good cheer costs you dear in danger and fear. I would rather gnaw my poor meals of barley and corn without being afraid or having to watch anyone out of the corner of my eye."

  A simple life with peace and quiet is better than faring luxuriously and being tortured by fear.   [Sixth Century B.C.]

Questions for Discussion and Writing
1. Why is it especially apt to use mice as the main characters for this story? Would dogs or cats work equally well? Why or why not?
2. Does Aesop draw the correct moral from his tale? Does the story "prove" that country life is superior to city life? Explain.

৵ THEOPHRASTUS
(*Ca. 372–287* B.C.)

TRANSLATED BY J. M. EDMONDS

Garrulity

Originally named Tyrtamus, Theophrastus was given his nickname, which literally translates as "divinely speaking," by Aristotle (384–322 B.C.) in honor of his skill in conversation. He was born in Eresus on the Island of Lesbos, studied philosophy with a man named Leucippus, and eventually found his way to Athens, where he became a follower of Plato. After Plato's death, he joined Aristotle and succeeded him as the leader of his school in 322 B.C.

  Theophrastus wrote a number of important scientific treatises, but his most lasting work is his *Ethical Characters,* valuable not only for their witty characterizations but also for their vivid pictures of life in ancient Greece.

G ARRULITY, SHOULD YOU LIKE to define it, would seem to be an inability to control one's speech. The garrulous man is the sort who says to anyone he meets that he is talking nonsense—no matter what that man may tell him—and that he knows it all himself, and if he listens, he'll find out about it. And as the other tries to answer, he keeps interrupting and says, "Now don't forget what you intend to say!" and "Good of you to remind me of that!" and "How nice to be able to talk!" "That's something I left out!" and "You're quick to grasp the point!" and "I've been waiting all this time to see whether you would come around to my view!" He tries to give himself more openings like these, so that the man who meets him can't even catch his breath. 10

Once he has finished off individuals, he is apt to move against whole formations and put them to flight in the midst of their business. He goes into the schools and wrestling grounds and prevents the boys from making progress with their studies. That is how much he talks to their trainers and teachers.

When people say they must go, he is apt to keep them company, or see them back home. He reports what has happened in the assembly to people who ask him, but adds to his account as well the battle in the year of Aristophon and that of the Spartans under Lysander, and the speeches by which he himself gained a public reputation, and as he tells his story he interjects a condemnation of the masses, so that his hearers interrupt him, or doze off, or go away and leave before 20 he finishes.

When he is among them, he prevents jurors from reaching a verdict, an audience from watching the show, and dinner guests from getting anything to eat, and he remarks "it's hard for me to keep still," and how mobile the tongue is, and that he simply couldn't be quiet, not even if he might appear to chatter more than the swallows. He puts up with being mocked even by his own children when he wants them to go to bed right now, and they stop him by saying this: "Talk to us a little, so we can get to sleep."   [Fourth Century B.C.]

Questions for Discussion and Writing
1. Are the traits of the garrulous (overly talkative) man still recognizable today? What details have changed? Which ones have remained the same?
2. If Theophrastus were living today, what types of people might he satirize?

✎ OVID
(43 B.C.–A.D. 18)

TRANSLATED BY ROLFE HUMPHRIES

Daedalus and Icarus

The Latin poet Ovid (full name Publius Ovidius Naso) was born to an aristocratic family in the mountains of central Italy. His family sent him to Rome for his education, intending him for a career in law and politics, but although he occupied minor government posts, his passion was poetry.

He is known today primarily for two works, *The Art of Love,* which influenced the medieval idea of courtly love, and *The Metamorphoses,* from which

generations of authors drew their knowledge of Roman mythology. For
unknown reasons, Ovid was banished by Caesar Augustus in A.D. 8 and he died
in exile.

Homesick for homeland, Daedalus hated Crete
And his long exile there, but the sea held him.
"Though Minos blocks escape by land or water,"
Daedalus said, "surely the sky is open,
And that's the way we'll go. Minos' dominion
Does not include the air." He turned his thinking
Toward unknown arts, changing the laws of nature.
He laid out feathers in order, first the smallest,
A little larger next it, and so continued,
The way that pan-pipes rise in gradual sequence.   10
He fastened them with twine and wax, at middle,
At bottom, so, and bent them, gently curving,
So that they looked like wings of birds, most surely.
And Icarus, his son, stood by and watched him,
Not knowing he was dealing with his downfall,
Stood by and watched, and raised his shiny face
To let a feather, light as down, fall on it,
Or stuck his thumb into the yellow wax,
Fooling around, the way a boy will, always,
Whenever a father tries to get some work done.   20
Still, it was done at last, and the father hovered,
Poised, in the moving air, and taught his son:
"I warn you, Icarus, fly a middle course:
Don't go too low, or water will weigh the wings down,
Don't go too high, or the sun's fire will burn them.
Keep to the middle way. And one more thing,
No fancy steering by star or constellation,
Follow my lead!" That was the flying lesson,
And now to fit the wings to the boy's shoulders.
Between the work and warning the father found   30
His cheeks were wet with tears, and his hands trembled.
He kissed his son (*Good-bye,* if he had known it),
Rose on his wings, flew on ahead, as fearful
As any bird launching the little nestlings
Out of high nest into thin air. *Keep on,*
Keep on, he signals, *follow me!* He guides him
In flight—O fatal art!—and the wings move
And the father looks back to see the son's wings moving.
Far off, far down, some fisherman is watching
As the rod dips and trembles over the water,   40
Some shepherd rests his weight upon his crook,

Some ploughman on the handles of the ploughshare,
And all look up, in absolute amazement,
At those air-borne above. They must be gods!
They were over Samos, Juno's sacred island,
Delos and Paros toward the left, Lebinthus
Visible to the right, and another island,
Calymne, rich in honey. And the boy
Thought *This is wonderful!* and left his father,
Soared higher, higher, drawn to the vast heaven,
Nearer the sun, and the wax that held the wings   50
Melted in that fierce heat, and the bare arms
Beat up and down in air, and lacking oarage
Took hold of nothing. *Father!* he cried, and *Father!*
Until the blue sea hushed him, the dark water
Men call the Icarian now. And Daedalus,
Father no more, called "Icarus, where are you!
Where are you, Icarus? Tell me where to find you!"
And saw the wings on the waves, and cursed his talents,
Buried the body in a tomb, and the land
Was named for Icarus.   [10–15 A.D.] 60

Questions for Writing and Discussion

1. What details does Ovid use to convey character? How does he individualize Daedalus and Icarus?
2. How does Ovid heighten the emotional effect of the story? Point to specific details.

✒ ST. LUKE
(First Century A.D.)

REVISED STANDARD VERSION

The Good Samaritan

Little is known about the writer of the third Gospel. Tradition identifies him as the physician who accompanied St. Paul on several missionary journeys and assigns his birthplace as Antioch in Syria. A gentile who converted to Christianity, he is also regarded as the author of the Acts of the Apostles, the fifth book of the New Testament.

AND BEHOLD, a certain lawyer stood up, and tempted him, saying, Master, what shall I do to inherit eternal life?
He said unto him, What is written in the law? how readest thou?

And he answering said,
Thou shalt love the Lord thy God
with all thy heart, and with all thy soul,
and with all thy strength, and with all thy mind;
and thy neighbor as thyself.

And he said unto him, Thou hast answered right: this do, and thou shalt live.

But he, willing to justify himself, said unto Jesus, And who is my neighbor? 10

And Jesus answering said, A certain man went down from Jerusalem to Jericho, and fell among thieves, which stripped him of his raiment, and wounded *him,* and departed, leaving *him* half dead.

And by chance there came down a certain priest that way; and when he saw him, he passed by on the other side.

And likewise a Levite, when he was at the place, came and looked on *him,* and passed by on the other side.

But a certain Samaritan, as he journeyed, came where he was; and when he saw him, he had compassion on *him,*

and went to *him,* and bound up his wounds, pouring in oil and wine, and 20 set him on his own beast, and brought him to an inn, and took care of him.

And on the morrow when he departed, he took out two pence, and gave *them* to the host, and said unto him, Take care of him: and whatsoever thou spendest more, when I come again, I will repay thee.

Which now of these three, thinkest thou, was neighbor unto him that fell among the thieves?

And he said, He that showed mercy on him. Then said Jesus unto him, Go, and do thou likewise. [ca. 70 A.D.]

Questions for Writing and Discussion
1. Luke characterizes the lawyer by saying that he "stood up and tempted him" and was "willing to justify himself." How do these details relate to the story of the Good Samaritan?
2. How does the parable answer the lawyer's question, "And who is my neighbor?"

⤕ GIOVANNI BOCCACCIO
(1313–1375)

TRANSLATED BY G. H. McWILLIAMS

Fiametta's Story

Giovanni Boccaccio was one of the early leaders in what we now call the Italian Renaissance, that extraordinary burst of creativity that marked the end of the Middle Ages and the beginning of the modern world.

Born the illegitimate son of a Florentine banker and a French woman, he rebelled against the life his father wanted for him and turned to literature. His greatest work, *The Decameron,* grew out of the Black Death of 1348, which killed over half the population of Florence. *The Decameron* is one of the world's great collections of stories, exuberant in its variety, range of characters, and celebration of life.

ONCE FILOMENA HAD FINISHED, the queen, finding that there was no one left to speak apart from herself (Dioneo being excluded from the reckoning because of his privilege), smiled cheerfully and said:

It is now my own turn to address you, and I shall gladly do so, dearest ladies, with a story similar in some respects to the one we have just heard. This I have chosen, not only to acquaint you with the power of your beauty over men of noble spirit, but so that you may learn to choose for yourselves, whenever neces- sary, the persons on whom to bestow your largesse, instead of always leaving these matters to be decided for you by Fortune, who, as it happens, nearly always scat- ters her gifts with more abundance than discretion.   10

You are to know, then, that Coppo di Borghese Domenichi, who once used to live in our city and possibly lives there still, one of the most highly respected men of our century, a person worthy of eternal fame, who achieved his position of pre-eminence by dint of his character and abilities rather than by his noble lin- eage, frequently took pleasure during his declining years in discussing incidents from the past with his neighbours and other folk. In this pastime he excelled all others, for he was more coherent, possessed a superior memory, and spoke with greater eloquence. He had a fine repertoire, including a tale he frequently told concerning a young Florentine called Federigo, the son of Messer Filippo Alberighi, who for his deeds of chivalry and courtly manners was more highly 20 spoken of than any other squire in Tuscany. In the manner of most young men of gentle breeding, Federigo lost his heart to a noble lady, whose name was Monna Giovanna, and who in her time was considered one of the loveliest and most adorable women to be found in Florence. And with the object of winning her love, he rode at the ring, tilted, gave sumptuous banquets, and distributed a large num- ber of gifts, spending money without any restraint whatsoever. But since she was no less chaste than she was fair, the lady took no notice, either of the things that were done in her honour, or of the person who did them.

In this way, spending far more than he could afford and deriving no profit in return, Federigo lost his entire fortune (as can easily happen) and reduced himself 30 to poverty, being left with nothing other than a tiny little farm, which produced an income just sufficient for him to live very frugally, and one falcon of the finest breed in the whole world. Since he was as deeply in love as ever, and felt unable to go on living the sort of life in Florence to which he aspired, he moved out to Campi, where his little farm happened to be situated. Having settled in the coun- try, he went hunting as often as possible with his falcon, and, without seeking as- sistance from anyone, he patiently resigned himself to a life of poverty.

Now one day, while Federigo was living in these straitened circumstances, the husband of Monna Giovanna happened to fall ill, and, realizing that he was about to die, he drew up his will. He was a very rich man, and in his will he left 40 everything to his son, who was just growing up, further stipulating that, if his son should die without legitimate issue, his estate should go to Monna Giovanna, to whom he had always been deeply devoted.

Shortly afterwards he died, leaving Monna Giovanna a widow, and every summer, in accordance with Florentine custom, she went away with her son to a country estate of theirs, which was very near Federigo's farm. Consequently this young lad of hers happened to become friendly with Federigo, acquiring a passion for birds and dogs; and, having often seen Federigo's falcon in flight, he became fascinated by it and longed to own it, but since he could see that Federigo was deeply attached to the bird, he never ventured to ask him for it.   50

And there the matter rested, when, to the consternation of his mother, the boy happened to be taken ill. Being her only child, he was the apple of his mother's eye, and she sat beside his bed the whole day long, never ceasing to comfort him. Every so often she asked him whether there was anything he wanted, imploring him to tell her what it was, because if it was possible to acquire it, she would move heaven and earth to obtain it for him.

After hearing this offer repeated for the umpteenth time, the boy said:

'Mother, if you could arrange for me to have Federigo's falcon, I believe I should soon get better.'

On hearing this request, the lady was somewhat taken aback, and began to 60 consider what she could do about it. Knowing that Federigo had been in love with her for a long time, and that she had never deigned to cast so much as a single glance in his direction, she said to herself: 'How can I possibly go to him, or even send anyone, to ask him for this falcon, which to judge from all I have heard is the finest that ever flew, as well as being the only thing that keeps him alive? And how can I be so heartless as to deprive so noble a man of his one remaining pleasure?'

Her mind filled with reflections of this sort, she remained silent, not knowing what answer to make to her son's request, even though she was quite certain that the falcon was hers for the asking.

At length, however, her maternal instincts gained the upper hand, and she 70 resolved, come what may, to satisfy the child by going in person to Federigo to collect the bird, and bring it back to him. And so she replied:

'Bear up, my son, and see whether you can start feeling any better. I give you my word that I shall go and fetch it for you first thing tomorrow morning.'

Next morning, taking another lady with her for company, his mother left the house as though intending to go for a walk, made her way to Federigo's little cottage, and asked to see him. For several days, the weather had been unsuitable for hawking, so Federigo was attending to one or two little jobs in his garden, and when he heard, to his utter astonishment, that Monna Giovanna was at the frontdoor and wished to speak to him, he happily rushed there to greet her.   80

When she saw him coming, she advanced with womanly grace to meet him. Federigo received her with a deep bow, whereupon she said:

'Greetings, Federigo!' Then she continued: 'I have come to make amends for the harm you have suffered on my account, by loving me more than you ought to have done. As a token of my esteem, I should like to take breakfast with you this morning, together with my companion here, but you must not put yourself to any trouble.'

'My lady,' replied Federigo in all humility, 'I cannot recall ever having suffered any harm on your account. On the contrary I have gained so much that if ever I attained any kind of excellence, it was entirely because of your own great worth and the love I bore you. Moreover I can assure you that this visit which you have been generous enough to pay me is worth more to me than all the money I ever possessed, though I fear that my hospitality will not amount to very much.'

So saying, he led her unassumingly into the house, and thence into his garden, where, since there was no one else he could call upon to chaperon her, he said:

'My lady, as there is nobody else available, this good woman, who is the wife of the farmer here, will keep you company whilst I go and see about setting the table.'

Though his poverty was acute, the extent to which he had squandered his wealth had not yet been fully borne home to Federigo; but on this particular morning, finding that he had nothing to set before the lady for whose love he had entertained so lavishly in the past, his eyes were well and truly opened to the fact. Distressed beyond all measure, he silently cursed his bad luck and rushed all over the house like one possessed, but could find no trace of either money or valuables. By now the morning was well advanced, he was still determined to entertain the gentlewoman to some sort of meal, and, not wishing to beg assistance from his own farmer (or from anyone else, for that matter), his gaze alighted on his precious falcon, which was sitting on its perch in the little room where it was kept. And having discovered, on picking it up, that it was nice and plump, he decided that since he had nowhere else to turn, it would make a worthy dish for such a lady as this. So without thinking twice about it he wrung the bird's neck and promptly handed it over to his housekeeper to be plucked, dressed, and roasted carefully on a spit. Then he covered the table with spotless linen, of which he still had a certain amount in his possession, and returned in high spirits to the garden, where he announced to his lady that the meal, such as he had been able to prepare, was now ready.

The lady and her companion rose from where they were sitting and made their way to the table. And together with Federigo, who waited on them with the utmost deference, they made a meal of the prize falcon without knowing what they were eating.

On leaving the table they engaged their host in pleasant conversation for a while, and when the lady thought it time to broach the subject she had gone there to discuss, she turned to Federigo and addressed him affably as follows:

'I do not doubt for a moment, Federigo, that you will be astonished at my impertinence when you discover my principal reason for coming here, especially when you recall your former mode of living and my virtue, which you possibly mistook for harshness and cruelty. But if you had ever had any children to make you appreciate the power of parental love, I should think it certain that you would to some extent forgive me.

'However, the fact that you have no children of your own does not exempt me, a mother, from the laws common to all other mothers. And being bound to obey those laws, I am forced, contrary to my own wishes and to all the rules of decorum and propriety, to ask you for something to which I know you are very deeply attached—which is only natural, seeing that it is the only consolation, the only pleasure, the only recreation remaining to you in your present extremity of fortune. The gift I am seeking is your falcon, to which my son has taken so power- ful a liking, that if I fail to take it to him I fear he will succumb to the illness from which he is suffering, and consequently I shall lose him. In imploring you to give me this falcon, I appeal, not to your love, for you are under no obligation to me on that account, but rather to your noble heart, whereby you have proved yourself superior to all others in the practice of courtesy. Do me this favour, then, so that I may claim that through your generosity I have saved my son's life, thus placing him forever in your debt.'

When he heard what it was that she wanted, and realized that he could not oblige her because he had given her the falcon to eat, Federigo burst into tears in her presence before being able to utter a single word in reply. At first the lady thought his tears stemmed more from his grief at having to part with his fine fal- con than from any other motive, and was on the point of telling him that she would prefer not to have it. But on second thoughts she said nothing, and waited for Federigo to stop crying and give her his answer, which eventually he did.

'My lady,' he said, 'ever since God decreed that you should become the ob- ject of my love, I have repeatedly had cause to complain of Fortune's hostility to- wards me. But all her previous blows were slight by comparison with the one she has dealt me now. Nor shall I ever be able to forgive her, when I reflect that you have come to my poor dwelling, which you never deigned to visit when it was rich, and that you desire from me a trifling favour which she has made it impossi- ble for me to concede. The reason is simple, and I shall explain it in few words.

'When you did me the kindness of telling me that you wished to breakfast with me, I considered it right and proper, having regard to your excellence and merit, to do everything within my power to prepare a more sumptuous dish than those I would offer to my ordinary guests. My thoughts therefore turned to the fal- con you have asked me for and, knowing its quality, I reputed it a worthy dish to set before you. So I had it roasted and served to you on the trencher this morning, and I could not have wished for a better way of disposing of it. But now that I dis- cover that you wanted it in a different form, I am so distressed by my inability to grant your request that I shall never forgive myself for as long as I live.'

In confirmation of his words, Federigo caused the feathers, talons and beak to be cast on the table before her. On seeing and hearing all this, the lady re- proached him at first for killing so fine a falcon, and serving it up for a woman to eat; but then she became lost in admiration for his magnanimity of spirit, which no amount of poverty had managed to diminish, nor ever would. But now that her hopes of obtaining the falcon had vanished she began to feel seriously concerned for the health of her son, and after thanking Federigo for his hospitality and good intentions, she took her leave of him, looking all despondent, and returned to the child. And to his mother's indescribable sorrow, within the space of a few days, whether through his disappointment in not being able to have the falcon, or because he was in any case suffering from a mortal illness, the child passed from this life.

After a period of bitter mourning and continued weeping, the lady was re- 180 peatedly urged by her brothers to remarry, since not only had she been left a vast fortune but she was still a young woman. And though she would have preferred to remain a widow, they gave her so little peace that in the end, recalling Federigo's high merits and his latest act of generosity, namely to have killed such a fine falcon in her honour, she said to her brothers:

'If only it were pleasing to you, I should willingly remain as I am; but since you are so eager for me to take a husband, you may be certain that I shall never marry any other man except Federigo degli Alberighi.'

Her brothers made fun of her, saying:

'Silly girl, don't talk such nonsense! How can you marry a man who hasn't a 190 penny with which to bless himself?'

'My brothers,' she replied 'I am well aware of that. But I would sooner have a gentleman without riches, than riches without a gentleman.'

Seeing that her mind was made up, and knowing Federigo to be a gentleman of great merit even though he was poor, her brothers fell in with her wishes and handed her over to him, along with her immense fortune. Thenceforth, finding himself married to this great lady with whom he was so deeply in love, and very rich into the bargain, Federigo managed his affairs more prudently, and lived with her in happiness to the end of his days.   [1348–1353]

Questions for Writing and Discussion

1. How do you regard Federigo and his actions? Is he an admirable character or not? Explain.
2. This story revolves around a series of ironies, misunderstandings created when characters do not have the full picture or when characters know less than we the readers do about their situations. What is your reaction to the ironies in this story? Do they seem far-fetched, realistic, effective, moving? Give examples to support your answer.

ᴥ CHARLES PERRAULT
(1628–1703)

Fairy Tale: The Blue Beard

Like fables, fairy tales have long been associated with children's literature. "Cinderella," "Sleeping Beauty," "Snow White," and "Beauty and the Beast" are probably best known today through the highly sanitized Disney films. As "The Blue Beard" demonstrates, however, fairy tales are often violent or gory, and deal with our deepest fears: death, loss of parents, loss of identity, the unknown. They were originally told more for their sensationalism than for their morality.

The themes of female curiosity, multiple marriages, and murders apparently
have a wide appeal, for tales similar to "The Blue Beard" have been found in
many countries over a long period of time. This is the first version in English,
printed in 1729, a translation of Charles Perrault's (1628–1703) *Histoires ou
contes du temps passé* (1697).

T HERE WAS ONCE UPON a time a man who had several fine houses both in town
and country, a good deal of silver and gold plate, embroider'd furniture, and
coaches gilt all over with gold. But this same man had the misfortune to have a
Blue Beard, which made him so frightfully ugly that all the women and girls ran
away from him.

One of his neighbours, a lady of quality, had two daughters who were perfect
beauties. He desired of her one of them in marriage, leaving to her the choice of
which of them she would bestow upon him. They would neither of them have
him, and sent him backwards and forwards from one another, being resolved
never to marry a man that had a *Blue Beard.* That which moreover gave them the 10
greater disgust and aversion, was that he had already been marry'd to several
wives, and no body ever knew what were become of them.

The *Blue Beard,* to engage their affection, took them with my lady their
mother, and three or four other ladies of their acquaintance, and some young people of the neighbourhood, to one of his country seats, where they staid full eight
days. There was nothing now to be seen but parties of pleasure, hunting of all
kinds, fishing, dancing, feasts and collations[1]. No body went to bed, they past the
night in rallying and playing upon one another: In short, every thing so well succeeded, that the youngest daughter began to think, that the master of the house
had not a *Beard* so very *Blue,* and that he was a very civil gentleman.   20

As soon as they returned home the marriage was concluded. About a month
afterwards the *Blue Beard* told his wife, that he was obliged to take a journey into a
distant country for six weeks at least, about an affair of very great consequence,
desiring her to divert herself in his absence, send for her friends and acquaintance,
carry them into the country, if she pleased, and make good cheer wherever she
was: Here, said he, are the keys of the two great rooms that hold my best and richest furniture; these are of my silver and gold plate, which is not to be made use of
every day; these open my strong boxes, which hold my gold and silver money;
these my casket of jewels; and this is the masterkey that opens all my apartments:
But for this little one here, it is the key of the closet at the end of the great gallery 30
on the ground floor. Open them all, go into all and every one except that little
closet, which I forbid you, and forbid you in such a manner, that if you happen to
open it, there is nothing but what you may expect from my just anger and resentment. She promised to observe every thing he order'd her, who, after having embraced her, got into his coach and proceeded on his journey.

Her neighbours and good friends did not stay to be sent for by the new married lady, so great was their impatience to see all the rich furniture of her house,
not daring to come while the husband was there, because of his Blue Beard which

---

1. Meetings, get togethers.

frighten'd them. They ran through all the rooms, closets, wardrobes, which were all so rich and fine that they seemed to surpass one another. After that, they went up into the two great rooms where were the best and richest furniture; they could not sufficiently admire the number and beauty of the tapestry, beds, couches, cabinets, stands, tables and looking-glasses, in which you might see yourself from head to foot; some of them were framed with glass, others with silver and silver gilt, the finest and most magnificent as ever were seen: They never ceased to extol and envy the happiness of their friend, who in the mean time no ways diverted herself in looking upon all these rich things, because of the impatience she had to go and open the closet of the ground floor. She was so much pressed by her curiosity, that without considering that it was very uncivil to leave her company, she went down a back pair of stairs, and with such an excessive haste, that she had like to have broken her neck two or three times.

Being come to the closet door, she stopt for some time, thinking upon her husband's orders, and considering what unhappiness might attend her were she disobedient; but the temptation was so strong she could not overcome it: She took then the little key and opened it in a very great trembling. But she could see nothing distinctly, because the windows were shut; after some moments she began to observe that the floor was all covered over with clotted blood, on which lay the bodies of several dead women ranged against the walls. (These were all the wives that the *Blue Beard* had married and murder'd one after another.) She thought that she should have died for fear, and the key that she pulled out of the lock fell out of her hand: After having somewhat recover'd her surprise, she took up the key, locked the door and went up stairs into her chamber to recover herself, but she could not, so much was she frightened. Having observed that the key of the closet was stain'd with blood, she tried two or three times to wipe it off, but the blood would not come out; in vain did she wash it and even rub it with soap and sand, the blood still remained, for the key was a Fairy, and she could never quite make it clean; when the blood was gone off from one side, it came again on the other.

The *Blue Beard* returned from his journey the same evening, and said he had received letters upon the road, informing him that the affair he went about was finished to his advantage. His wife did all she could to convince him she was extremely glad of his speedy return. The next morning he asked for the keys, which she returned, but with such a trembling hand, that he easily guess'd what had happen'd. What is the matter, said he, that the key of the closet is not amongst the rest? I must certainly, said she, have left it above upon the table. Do not fail, said the *Blue Beard*, of giving it to me presently: After several goings backwards and forwards she was forced to bring him the key. The *Blue Beard* having very attentively consider'd it, said to his Wife, how comes this blood upon the key? I don't know, said the poor Woman paler than death. You don't know, replied the *Blue Beard*, I know very well, you were resolv'd to go into the closet, were you not? Very well, Madam, you shall go in, and take your place amongst the ladies you saw there.

Upon this she threw herself at her husband's feet, and begged his pardon with all the signs of a true repentance, and that she would never more be disobedient. She would have melted a rock, so beautiful and sorrowful was she; but the *Blue Beard* had a heart harder than the hardest rock! You must die, Madam, said he, and that presently. Since I must die, said she, looking upon him with her eyes all bathed in tears, give me some little time to say my prayers. I give you, said the *Blue Beard,* a quarter of an hour, but not one moment more.

When she was alone, she called out to her sister, and said to her, Sister *Anne,* for that was her name, go up, I desire thee, upon the top of the tower, and see if my brothers are not coming, they promised me that they would come to day, and 90 if thou seest them, give them a sign to make haste. Her sister *Anne* went up upon the top of the tower, and the poor afflicted lady cried out from time to time, *Anne, sister Anne, dost thou see nothing coming?* And sister *Anne* said, *I see nothing but the sun that makes a dust, and the grass that grows green.* In the mean while the *Blue Beard,* holding a great cutlass in his hand, cried out as loud as he could to his wife, Come down, presently, or I'll come up to you. One moment longer, if you please, said his wife, and immediately she cried out very softly, *Anne, sister Anne, dost thou see nothing coming?* And sister *Anne* said, *I see nothing but the sun that makes a dust, and the grass that grows green.* Come down quickly, cried the *Blue Beard,* or I'll come up to you. I am coming, answer'd his wife, and then she cried, *Anne, sister Anne,* 100 *dost thou see nothing coming?* I see, replied sister *Anne,* a great dust that comes on this side here. *Are they my brothers?* Alas! no, my dear sister, I see a flock of sheep. Will you not come down? cried the *Blue Beard.* One moment longer, said his wife, and then she cried out, *Anne, sister Anne, dost thou see nothing coming?* I see, said she, two horsemen coming, but they are yet a great way off. God be praised, said she immediately after, they are my brothers; I have made them a sign as well as I can to make haste. The *Blue Beard* cried out now so loud, that he made the whole house tremble.

The poor Lady came down and threw herself at his feet all in tears with her hair about her shoulders: This signifies nothing, says the *Blue Beard,* you must die; 110 then taking hold of her hair with one hand, and holding up the cutlass with the other, he was going to cut off her head. The poor lady turning about to him, and looking at him with dying eyes, desired him to afford her one little moment to recollect herself: No, no, said he, recommend thy self to God: for at this very instant there was such a loud knocking at the gate, that the *Blue Beard* stopt short of a sudden: They open'd the gate, and immediately enter'd two horsemen, who drawing their swords, ran directly to the *Blue Beard.* He knew them to be his wife's brothers, one a dragoon[2], the other a musqueteer, so that he ran away immediately to save himself: but the two brothers pursued him so close, that they overtook him before he could get to the steps of the porch, when they ran their swords 120 through his body and left him dead.

The poor lady was almost as dead as her husband, and had not strength enough to rise and embrace her brothers. The *Blue Beard* had no heirs, and so his wife became mistress of all his estate. She made use of one part of it to marry her sister *Anne* to a young gentleman who had loved her a long while, another part to buy captains commissions for her brothers, and the rest to marry herself to a very honest gentleman, who made her forget the ill time she had pass'd with the *Blue Beard.*   [1697]

---

2. A heavily armed soldier on horseback.

Questions for Discussion and Writing
1. Which events in the story seem poorly explained or inadequately motivated? Explain.
2. What does the story seem to say about female curiosity?

❧ ERNST THEODOR AMADEUS HOFFMANN
(1776–1822)

TRANSLATED BY L. J. KENT AND E. C. KNIGHT

The Sandman

E. T. A. Hoffmann's work is part of musical as well as literary history. Several of Hoffmann's stories were adapted by Jacques Offenbach (1819–1880) for his opera *The Tales of Hoffmann* (1881), and Piotr Ilyich Tchaikovsky's (1840–1893) ballet, *The Nutcracker* (1892), was inspired by Hoffmann's fantasy, "The Nutcracker and the Mouse King." Until recently, however, Hoffmann was often dismissed as a popular writer of Gothic thrillers. Today he is being read as a careful craftsman whose frightening, uncanny, and supernatural effects are conveyed in a remarkably realistic prose.

Hoffmann's childhood reads like a Victorian melodrama. His parents divorced when he was two, leaving him in the care of his neurotic mother, a grandmother, two aunts, and an eccentric uncle. Upstairs lived a woman who imagined herself the Virgin Mary and thought her son was Jesus Christ. If this household had any advantage, it was the musical training he received from his Uncle Doerffer, an enthusiastic amateur.

Hoffmann was attracted to the law as well as to music and literature, and in the miraculous year 1816 his many ambitions came to fruition, when he received an excellent judicial appointment, debuted as an opera composer, and published *The Devil's Elixir,* his first novel. It is Hoffmann's stories, however, particularly those in *Ritter Gluck* (1809), *Nightpieces* (1817) and *The Serapion Brethren* (1819), on which his reputation rests. Psychoanalytic criticism sees that he has created a window onto the unconscious in his visions, doppelgangers, automatons, madness, and dreams. His literary influence has been remarkable and long-lasting. Writers as diverse as Honoré de Balzac (1799–1850), Charles Dickens (1812–1870), Edgar Allan Poe (1809–1849), and Nikolai Gogol (1809–1852) were affected by his work, and through them subsequent generations of writers.

Hoffmann was in many ways the typical Romantic artist—passionate, patriotic, contemptuous of middle-class respectability, fascinated by the occult, imaginative, and bitterly opposed to injustice and pomposity. Yet he was also a successful and respected lawyer, judge, and civil servant. These contrasting character traits are reflected in fiction that is at once firmly realistic and fantastically imaginative.

NATHANAEL TO LOTHAR

YOU CERTAINLY MUST be disturbed because I have not written for such a long, long time. Mother, I am sure, is angry, and Klara will imagine that I am spending my time in dissipation, having completely forgotten my pretty angel whose image is so deeply imprinted on my heart. But it's not so; I think of you all every day and every hour, and my lovely Klärchen[1] appears to me in my sweet dreams, her bright eyes smiling at me as charmingly as when I was with you. Alas, how could I write to you in the tormented frame of mind that has disrupted all my thoughts! Something horrible has entered my life! Dark forebodings of some impending doom loom over me like black clouds that are impervious to every ray of friendly sunshine. I will now tell you what happened to me. I must tell you, but the mere thought of it makes me laugh like a madman. Oh, my dearest Lothar, how can I begin to make you realize, even vaguely, that what happened a few days ago really could have so fatal and disruptive an effect on my life? If you were here you could see for yourself; but now you will certainly think I am a crazy man who sees ghosts. In brief, this horrible thing I have experienced, the fatal effects of which I am vainly trying to shake off, is simply this: A few days ago, on October 30th, at twelve noon, a barometer dealer[2] came into my room and offered me his wares. I bought nothing and threatened to kick him down the stairs, whereupon he left of his own accord.

You will surmise that only associations of the strangest kind that are profoundly entangled in my life could have made this incident significant, and that the character of this wretched dealer must have had an evil influence on me. In fact, this is the case. I will, with all my strength, pull myself together and calmly and patiently tell you enough about my early youth so that everything will appear clearly and distinctly to your keen mind. But just as I am about to begin, I can hear you laugh, and I can hear Klara say: "This is all childish nonsense!" Laugh! I beg you, have a good laugh! But, my God, my hair is standing on end, and it is in mad despair that I ask you to laugh at me—as Franz Moor asked Daniel. But back to my story.

Except at the noon meal, my brothers and sisters and I saw little of our father during the day. His work must have kept him very busy. After supper, which was served at seven in the old-fashioned way, we all went into father's workroom and sat at a round table. Father smoked and drank a large glass of beer. He often told us marvelous stories, and he would get so carried away that his pipe would keep going out and I would relight it for him with a piece of burning paper, which I thought was great fun. But there were occasions when he'd put picture books in our hands and sit silently in his armchair, blowing out billows of smoke till we all seemed to be swimming in clouds. Mother was very sad on such evenings, and hardly had the clock struck nine when she would say: "Now, children, off to bed with you! The Sandman is coming, I can already hear him." And at these times I always really did hear something clumping up the stairs with a heavy, slow step; it must have been the Sandman. Once, this dull trampling step was especially fright-

1. Little Klara.
2. A peddler selling barometers, eyeglasses, binoculars, and other items made of glass.

ening; and as my mother led us away, I asked her: "Oh, Mama, who is this nasty Sandman who always drives us away from Papa? What does he look like?"

"My dear child, there is no Sandman," my mother answered. "When I tell you that the Sandman is coming, it only means that you are sleepy and can't keep your eyes open any longer, as though someone had sprinkled sand into them."

Mother's answer did not satisfy me, for in my childish mind I was certain that she denied that there was a Sandman only to keep us from being afraid of him—I had surely always heard him coming up the stairs. Full of curiosity to learn more about this Sandman and what his connection was with us children, I finally asked the old woman who took care of my youngest sister what kind of man the Sandman was.

"Oh, dear Thanael," she replied, "don't you know that yet? He is a wicked man who comes to children when they refuse to go to bed and throws handfuls of sand in their eyes till they bleed and pop out of their heads. Then he throws the eyes into a sack and takes them to the half-moon as food for his children, who sit in a nest and have crooked beaks like owls with which they pick up the eyes of human children who have been naughty."

A horrible picture of the cruel Sandman formed in my mind, and in the evenings, when I heard stumbling steps on the stairs, I trembled with fear and dread. My mother could get nothing out of me but the stammered, tearful cry: "The Sandman! The Sandman!" Then I ran into the bedroom and was tortured all night by the horrible apparition of the Sandman. I was old enough to realize that the nurse's tale of the Sandman and his children's nest in the half-moon couldn't be altogether true; nevertheless, the Sandman remained a frightful specter; and I was seized with utmost horror when I heard him not only mount the stairs, but violently tear open the door to my father's room and enter. Frequently, he stayed away for a long time; then he came many times in succession. This continued for years, and I never got used to this terrible phantom. My image of the horrible Sandman grew no paler. His intimacy with my father occupied my imagination more and more. An insurmountable reluctance prevented me from asking my father about him; but if only I—if only I could solve the mystery and get to see this fantastic Sandman with my own eyes—that was the desire that increased in me year by year. The Sandman had directed my thoughts toward marvels and wonders which can so easily take hold of a childish mind. I liked nothing better than to hear or read horrible tales about goblins, witches, dwarfs, and such; but at the head of them all was the Sandman, of whom I was always drawing hideous pictures, in charcoal, in chalk, on tables, cupboards, and walls.

When I was ten my mother moved me from the nursery into a small room that opened off the corridor and was close to my father's room. As always, on the stroke of nine, when the mysterious step could be heard in the house, we had to scurry out. From my room I could hear him enter my father's, and soon thereafter I seemed to detect a thin, strange-smelling vapor spreading through the house. As my curiosity to know the Sandman grew, so did my courage. When my mother had left, I would sneak out of my room into the corridor; but I could never discover anything, because the Sandman had already gone through the door by the time I got to a spot from which he would have been visible. Finally, driven by an

uncontrollable impulse, I determined to hide in my father's room itself to await the
Sandman.   90

I could tell one evening from my father's silence and my mother's sadness
that the Sandman was coming. I pretended, therefore, to be very tired, left the
room before nine o'clock, and hid in a dark corner close to the door. The front
door groaned. Slow, heavy, resounding steps crossed the hall to the stairs. My
mother hurried past me with the rest of the children. Softly, softly I opened the
door of my father's room. He was sitting as usual, silent and rigid, his back to the
door; he didn't notice me. I slipped quickly behind the curtain that covered an
open cupboard in which my father's clothes were hanging. Closer, ever closer resounded the steps—there was a strange coughing, scraping, and mumbling outside. My heart quaked with fear and expectation. Close, close to the door, there   100
was a sharp step; a powerful blow on the latch and the door sprang open with a
bang! Summoning up every drop of my courage, I cautiously peeped out. The
Sandman was standing in the middle of my father's room, the bright candlelight
full on his face. The Sandman, the horrible Sandman, was the old lawyer
Coppelius who frequently had dinner with us!

But the most hideous figure could not have filled me with deeper horror
than this very Coppelius. Picture a large, broad-shouldered man with a fat, shapeless, head, an ochre-yellow face, bushy gray eyebrows from beneath which a pair
of greenish cat's eyes sparkled piercingly, and with a large nose that curved over
the upper lip. The crooked mouth was frequently twisted in a malignant laugh, at   110
which time a pair of dark red spots would appear on his cheeks and a strange
hissing sound would escape from between clenched teeth. Coppelius invariably
appeared in an old-fashioned coat of ash gray, with trousers and vest to match, but
with black stockings and shoes with small agate buckles. His little wig barely extended past the crown of his head, his pomaded[3] curls stood high over his big red
ears, and a broad hair bag[4] stood stiffly out from his neck so that the silver clasp
which held his folded cravat was visible. His whole appearance was loathsome and
repulsive; but we children were most revolted by his huge, gnarled, hairy hands,
and we would never eat anything they had touched. He noticed this and took
pleasure in touching, under some pretext or other, some piece of cake or delicious   120
fruit that mother had slipped on our plates, so that, tears welling up in our eyes,
we were unable to enjoy the tidbit intended for us because of the disgust and abhorrence we felt. He did the same thing on holidays when each of us received a
glass of sweet wine from our father. He would pass his hand over it or would even
raise the glass to his blue lips and laugh demoniacally, and we could only express
our indignation by sobbing softly. He always called us "the little beasts"; and when
he was present, we were not to make a sound. How we cursed this horrible man
who deliberately and malevolently ruined our slightest pleasure! Mother seemed
to loath the repulsive Coppelius as much as we did; the moment he appeared, her
gaiety, her lightheartedness, and her natural manner were transformed into de-   130
jected brooding. Father behaved toward him as if he were a superior being whose
bad manners must be endured and who must be humored at any cost. Coppelius

---

3. Curls held in place by hair oil.
4. A bag, usually of silk, to contain the back hair of a wig.

needed only to hint, and his favorite dishes were cooked and rare wines were served.

When I now saw this Coppelius, then, the terrible conviction that he alone was the Sandman possessed me; but the Sandman was no longer the hobgoblin of the nurse's tale, the one who brought the eyes of children for his brood to feed upon in the owl's nest in the half-moon. No! He was a horrible and unearthly monster who wreaked grief, misery, and destruction—temporal and eternal— wherever he appeared.   140

I was riveted to the spot, spellbound. At the risk of being discovered and, as I could clearly anticipate, severely punished, I remained watching, my head stretched out through the curtain. My father greeted Coppelius ceremoniously. "To work!" Coppelius cried in a hoarse, jarring voice, throwing off his coat. Silently and gloomily my father took off his dressing gown, and both of them dressed in long black smocks. I did not see where these came from. My father opened the folding door of a wall cupboard, but what I had always believed was a cupboard was not. It was rather a black recess that housed a little hearth. Coppelius went to the hearth, and a blue flame crackled up from it. All kinds of strange utensils were about. God! As my old father now bent over the fire, he looked completely differ-   150 ent. His mild and honest features seemed to have been distorted into a repulsive and diabolical mask by some horrible, convulsive pain. He looked like Coppelius, who was drawing sparkling lumps out of the heavy smoke with the red-hot tongs he wielded and then hammering the coals furiously. It seemed as if I saw human faces on all sides—but eyeless faces, with horrible deep black cavities instead.

"Give me eyes! Give me eyes!" Coppelius ordered in a hollow booming voice. Overcome by the starkest terror, I shrieked and tumbled from my hiding place to the floor. Coppelius seized me. "Little beast! Little beast!" he bleated, bar- ing his teeth. He dragged me to my feet and flung me on the hearth, where the flames began singeing my hair. "Now we have eyes, eyes, a beautiful pair of chil-   160 dren's eyes!" he whispered. Pulling glowing grains from the fire with his naked hands, he was about to sprinkle them in my eyes when my father raised his hands entreatingly: "Master! Master!" he cried, "leave my Nathanael his eyes!" "Let the child keep his eyes and do his share of the world's weeping," Coppelius shrieked with a shrill laugh, "but now we must carefully observe the mechanism of the hands and feet." He thereupon seized me so violently that my joints cracked, un- screwed my hands and feet, then put them back, now this way, then another way. "There's something wrong here! It's better the way they were! The Old Man knew his business!" Coppelius hissed and muttered. But everything around me went pitch black; a sudden convulsive pain flashed through my nerves and bones—I   170 felt nothing more.

A gentle, warm breath passed across my face, and I awoke as from the sleep of death, my mother bending over me.

"Is the Sandman still here?" I stammered.

"No, my dearest child, he left long ago and will do you no harm," my mother said, kissing and cuddling her reclaimed darling.

Why should I bore you, my dear Lothar? Why should I go into such copious detail when so much remains to be said? Suffice it to say that I had been caught spying and had been manhandled by Coppelius. My fear and terror had brought

on a violent fever, which kept me ill for many weeks. "Is the Sandman still here?" 180
were my first words after regaining consciousness, the first sign of my recovery,
my deliverance. I have only to tell you now about the most horrible moment in all
the years of my youth; then you will be convinced that it is not because of faulty
vision that everything seems devoid of color to me, but that a somber destiny has
really hung a murky veil over my life, which I will perhaps tear through only
when I die.

Coppelius was not seen again; it was said that he had left the town.

It was about a year later, when we were once more sitting at the round table
as was our custom. Father was very cheerful and was telling us entertaining stories
about his youthful travels. As the clock struck nine, we suddenly heard the front 190
door groan on its hinges and, leaden steps resounded across the hall and up the
stairs.

"It's Coppelius," my mother said, growing pale.

"Yes, it is Coppelius," father repeated in a faint, broken voice. Tears welled in
mother's eyes.

"But Father, Father!" she cried, "must it be like this?"

"It is the last time!" he answered, "I promise you this is the last time he will
come here. Now go, take the children with you. Go, go to bed! Good night!"

I felt as if I had been turned into cold heavy stone—I couldn't catch my
breath! But as I stood there, motionless, my mother seized me by the arm. "Come, 200
Nathanael, do come!" I let myself be led to my room. "Calm yourself, calm yourself and go to bed!" my mother cried to me. "Go to bed and go to sleep. Sleep!"
But tormented by an indescribable fear, I couldn't close my eyes. The detestable
and loathsome Coppelius stood before me with fiery eyes, laughing at me malevolently. I tried in vain to obliterate his image from my mind. It must have been
about midnight when there was a terrifying explosion—like the firing of a cannon.
The entire house resounded with the detonation; there was a rattling and clattering past my door. The front door slammed shut violently.

"That is Coppelius!" I cried in terror, springing out of bed. Then there was a
shriek, a wail of heartrending grief. I rushed to my father's room. The door was 210
open, and suffocating smoke rolled toward me. The maid shrieked, "Oh, the master! Oh, the master!" My father lay dead in front of the smoking hearth, his face
charred black and his features hideously contorted; my brothers and sisters were
sobbing and moaning around him—my mother unconscious beside him!
"Coppelius, you vile Satan, you've murdered my father!" I cried, and lost consciousness.

When my father was placed in his coffin two days later, his features were
once more serene and gentle, as they had been in life. My soul drew consolation
from the thought that his alliance with the satanic Coppelius could not have thrust
him into everlasting perdition.   220

The explosion had awakened the neighbors; the tragedy was talked about
and reached the ears of the authorities, who wanted to proceed against Coppelius
and hold him accountable. But Coppelius had vanished from town without leaving a trace.

So, my dear friend, when I now tell you that this barometer dealer was the infamous Coppelius himself, you will not blame me for regarding this apparition as foreboding some frightful disaster. He was dressed differently, but Coppelius's figure and face are too deeply etched on my mind for me possibly to make a mistake. In addition, Coppelius has hardly changed his name. I have been told that he claims to be a Piedmontese skilled craftsman, Giuseppe Coppola.   230

I am determined, regardless of the consequences, to deal with him and to avenge my father's death.

Do not tell my mother anything of this loathsome monster's presence here. Give my love to dear, sweet Klara. I will write to her when I am in a calmer frame of mind. Farewell, etc., etc.

KLARA TO NATHANAEL

DESPITE IT'S BEING true that you have not written for a long time, I believe that I am still in your thoughts. You surely had me most vividly in mind when you intended sending your last letter to Lothar, because you addressed it to me instead. I opened the letter with delight and did not realize my error until I read: "Oh, my dearest Lothar." I should have stopped reading and given the letter to your   240 brother. Even though you have often reproached me, in your innocent, teasing manner, for being so serene and womanly in disposition that if the house were about to collapse I would quickly smooth a misplaced crease out of a curtain— like the woman in the story—before escaping; nevertheless, I can hardly tell you how deeply the beginning of your letter shocked me. I could barely breathe; everything swam before my eyes. Oh, my dearest Nathanael, what horrible thing has entered your life? To be parted from you, never again to see you—the thought pierced my breast like a red-hot dagger. I read on and on. Your description of the repulsive Coppelius horrifies me. For the first time I learned about the terrible, violent way your dear old father died. My brother Lothar, to whom I gave this letter,   250 tried with little success to calm me. The horrid barometer dealer Giuseppe Coppola followed my every step, and I am almost ashamed to admit that he even disturbed my normally sound and restful sleep with all kinds of horrible dream images. Soon, however—by the very next day, in fact—I saw everything differently. Do not be angry with me, my dearest one, if Lothar tells you that despite your strange presentiment that Coppelius will harm you, I am still cheerful and calm.

I will frankly confess that in my opinion all the fears and terrors of which you speak took place only in your mind and had very little to do with the true, external world. A loathsome character old Coppelius may have been, but what really   260 led to the abhorrence you children felt stemmed from his hatred of children.

Naturally, your childish mind associated the dreadful Sandman of the nurse's tale with old Coppelius—who would have been a monster particularly threatening to children even if you had not believed in the Sandman. The sinister business conducted at night with your father was probably nothing other than secret alchemical experiments, which would have displeased your mother because not only was a great deal of money being squandered, but, as is always the case with such experimenters, your father's mind was so imbued with an illusory desire for higher knowledge that he may have become alienated from his family. Your father, no doubt, was responsible for his own death through some carelessness or other, and Coppelius is not guilty of it. Let me tell you that yesterday I asked our neighbor, an experienced chemist, whether experiments of this kind could possibly lead to such a sudden lethal explosion. "Absolutely," he replied, and continued, at length and in detail, to tell me how such an accident could occur, mentioning so many strange-sounding names that I can't recall any of them. Now, you will be annoyed with your Klara and will say, "Such a cold nature is impervious to any ray of the mysterious which often embraces man with invisible arms. Like the simple child who rejoices over some glittering golden fruit that conceals a fatal poison, she sees only the bright surface of the world."

Oh, my dearest Nathanael, do you not believe that even in gay, easygoing, and carefree minds there may exist a presentiment of dark powers within ourselves that are bent upon our own destruction? But forgive me, simple girl that I am, if I presume to tell you what my thoughts really are about such inner conflicts. I will not, to be sure, find the right words; and you will laugh at me—not because what I say is foolish, but because I express my ideas so clumsily.

If there is a dark power that treacherously attaches a thread to our heart to drag us along a perilous and ruinous path that we would not otherwise have trod; if there is such a power, it must form inside us, from part of us, must be identical with ourselves; only in this way can we believe in it and give it the opportunity it needs if it is to accomplish its secret work. If our mind is firm enough and adequately fortified by the joys of life to be able to recognize alien and hostile influences as such, and to proceed tranquilly along the path of our own choosing and propensities, then this mysterious power will perish in its futile attempt to assume a shape that is supposed to be a reflection of ourselves. "It is also a fact," Lothar adds, "that if we have once voluntarily surrendered to this dark physical power, it frequently introduces in us the strange shapes which the external world throws in our way, so that we ourselves engender the spirit which in our strange delusion we believe speaks to us from that shape. It is the phantom of our own ego, whose intimate relationship, combined with its profound effect on our spirits, either flings us into hell or transports us to heaven." You see, dear Nathanael, that my brother Lothar and I have fully discussed the matter of dark powers and forces—a subject which I have outlined for you not without difficulty and which seems very profound to me. I do not completely understand Lothar's last words; I have only an inkling of his meaning, and yet it seems to be very true. I beg you to cast the hateful lawyer Coppelius and the barometer man Giuseppe Coppola from your thoughts. Be convinced that these strange figures are powerless; only your belief in their hostile influence can make them hostile in reality. If profound mental agitation did not speak out from every line in your letter, if your frame of mind did not distress me so deeply, I could joke about Sandman the lawyer and barometer dealer Coppelius. Cheer up, please! I have decided to be your guardian angel, and if ugly Coppola takes it into his head to plague you in your dreams, I will exorcise him with loud laughter. Neither he nor his revolting fists frighten me at all; as a lawyer he is not going to spoil my tidbits, nor, as a Sandman, harm my eyes.

Ever yours, my dearest beloved Nathanael, etc., etc., etc.

NATHANAEL TO LOTHAR

I AM VERY SORRY that Klara recently opened and read my letter to you through a mistake occasioned by my distraction. She has written me a very thoughtful and philosophical letter in which she proves, in great detail, that Coppelius and Coppola exist only in my mind and are phantoms of my ego that will vanish in a moment if I accept them as such. As a matter of fact, one would not think that Klara, with her bright, dreamy, childlike eyes, could analyze with such intelligence and pedantry. She refers to your views. The two of you have discussed me. No doubt you are giving her lessons in logic so that she is learning to sift and analyze everything very neatly. Do stop that! By the way, it is probably quite certain that the barometer dealer Giuseppe Coppola cannot possibly be the old lawyer Coppelius. I am attending lectures by the physics professor who just came here recently and who, like the famous naturalist, is called Spalanzani and is of Italian origin. He has known Coppola for many years; besides which, one can tell from his accent that he is really a Piedmontese. Coppelius was a German, but, it seems to me, not an honest one. I am still a little uneasy. You and Klara may still consider me a morbid dreamer; however, I cannot get rid of the impression that Coppelius's damned face makes on me. I am very happy that he has left the city, as Spalanzani told me. This professor is an eccentric fellow. A small, chubby man with big cheekbones, a thin nose, protruding lips, and small piercing eyes. But better than from any description, you can get a picture of him if you look at a picture of Cagliostro as painted by Chodowiecki in any Berlin pocket almanac.[5] Spalanzani looks just like that.

Recently, when I went up the steps, I noticed that the curtain that usually covers the glass door was not completely drawn across. I do not even know why I was curious enough to peek, but I did. A tall, very slender, beautifully dressed, beautifully proportioned young lady was sitting in the room in front of a small table, on which she had placed her outstretched arms, with hands clasped. She was sitting opposite the door, so I could see her divinely beautiful face. She did not seem to notice me; indeed, her eyes seemed fixed, I might almost say without vision. It seemed to me as if she were sleeping with her eyes open. I became very uneasy and therefore stole quietly away to the neighboring lecture room. Later, I discovered that the figure I had seen is Spalanzani's daughter, Olympia, whom he, for some strange reason, always keeps locked up so that no one can come near her. Perhaps, after all, there is something wrong with her; maybe she is an idiot, or something like that. But why do I write you about all this? I can tell you better and in greater detail when I see you. By the way, I am planning to visit you in two weeks. I must see my dear, sweet, lovely Klara again. The irritation which, I must confess, possessed me after the arrival of that disagreeable analytical letter will have vanished by then. For this reason I am not writing to her today. A thousand greetings, etc., etc., etc.

Gentle reader, nothing can be imagined that is stranger and more extraordinary than the fate that befell my poor friend, the young student Nathanael, which

---

5. There was such a picture in the Berlin Genealogical Calendar for 1789.

I have undertaken to relate to you. Have you, gentle reader, ever experienced any- thing that totally possessed your heart, your thoughts, and your senses to the ex- clusion of all else? Everything seethed and roiled within you; heated blood surged through your veins and inflamed your cheeks. Your gaze was peculiar, as if seek-   360 ing forms in empty space invisible to other eyes, and speech dissolved into gloomy sighs. Then your friends asked you: "What is it, dear friend? What is the matter?" And wishing to describe the picture in your mind with all its vivid colors, the light and the shade, you struggled vainly to find words. But it seemed to you that you had to gather together all that had occurred—the wonderful, the magnificent, the heinous, the joyous, the ghastly—and express it in the very first word so that it would strike like lightning. Yet, every word, everything within the realm of speech, seemed colorless, frigid, dead. You tried, tried again, stuttered and stam- mered, while the insipid questions asked by friends struck your glowing passion like icy blasts until it was almost extinguished. If, like an audacious painter, you   370 had initially sketched the outline of the picture within you in a few bold strokes, you would have easily been able to make the colors deeper and more intense until the multifarious crowd of living shapes swept your friends away and they saw themselves, as you see yourself, in the midst of the scene that had issued from your soul.

Sympathetic reader, no one, I must confess, asked me about the history of young Nathanael; you are, however, surely aware that I belong to that remarkable species of authors who, when they carry something within themselves as I have just described it, feels as if everyone who approaches—indeed, everyone in the whole world—is asking "What is it? Do tell us, dear sir!"   380

I was most strongly compelled to tell you about Nathanael's disastrous life. The marvelous and the extraordinary aspects of his life entirely captivated my soul; but precisely for this reason and because, my dear reader, it was essential at the beginning to dispose you favorably toward the fantastic—which is no mean matter—I tormented myself to devise a way to begin Nathanael's story in a manner at once creative and stirring: "Once upon a time," the nicest way to begin a story, seemed too prosaic. "In the small provincial town of S——, there lived"—was somewhat better, at least providing an opportunity for development toward the climax. Or, immediately, in medias res:[6] " 'Go to hell!' the student Nathanael cried,   390 his eyes wild with rage and terror, when the barometer dealer Giuseppe Coppola—" In fact, that is what I had written when I thought I noticed something humorous in Nathanael's wild look—but the story is not at all comic. There were no words I could find that were appropriate to describe, even in the most feeble way, the brilliant colors of my inner vision. I resolved not to begin at all. So, gentle reader, do accept the three letters, which my friend Lothar has been kind enough to communicate, as the outline of the picture to which I will endeavor to add ever more color as I continue with the story. As a good portrait painter, I may possibly succeed in making Nathanael recognizable even if the original is unknown to you; and you may feel as if you had seen him with your own eyes on very many occa- sions. Possibly, also, you will come to believe that real life is more singular and   400

6. Into the middle of things; i.e., into the middle of the story.

more fantastic than anything else and that all a writer can really do is present it as "in a glass, darkly."

To supply information necessary for the beginning, these letters must be supplemented by noting that soon after the death of Nathanael's father, Klara and Lothar, children of a distant relative who had likewise died and left them orphans, were taken in by Nathanael's mother. Klara and Nathanael soon grew strongly attached to each other, to which no one in the world could object; hence, when Nathanael left home to continue his studies at G——, they were engaged. His last letter is written from G——, where he is attending the lectures of the famous professor of physics Spalanzini.   410

I could now confidently continue with my story, but even at this moment Klara's face is so vividly before me that I cannot avert my eyes, just as I never could when she gazed at me with one of her lovely smiles. Klara could not be considered beautiful; all who profess to be judges of beauty agreed on that. Nevertheless, architects praised the perfect proportions of her figure, and painters considered her neck, shoulders, breasts almost too chastely formed. Yet on the other hand, they adored her glorious hair and raved about her coloring, which reminded them of Battoni's Magdalen.[7] One of them, a veritable romantic, elaborated an old comparison between her eyes and a lake by Ruïsdael,[8] in which the pure azure of a cloudless sky, the woodlands and flower-bedecked fields, and the whole bright and varied life of a lush landscape are reflected. Poets and musicians went even further and said, "That is nonsense about a lake and a mirror! Can we look at the girl without sensing heavenly music which flows into us from her glance and penetrates to the very soul until everything within us stirs awake and pulsates with emotion? And if we cannot then sing splendid tunes, we are not worth much; the smile flitting about her lips will tell us this clearly enough when we have the courage to speak out in her presence something that we profess to be a song when, in fact, it is only a disconnected jumble of notes strung together."   420

And this really was the case. Klara had the spirited imagination of a gay, innocent, unaffected child, the deep sympathetic feelings of a woman, and an understanding that was clear and discriminating. Dreamers and visionaries had bad luck with her; for despite the fact that she said little—she was not disposed to be talkative—her clear glance and her rare ironical smile asked, "Dear friends, how can you suppose that I will accept these fleeting and shadowy images for true shapes which are alive and breathe?" For this reason, many chided Klara for being cold, without feeling, and unimaginative; but others, those whose conception of life was clearer and deeper, were singularly enamored of this tenderhearted, intelligent, and childlike girl, though no one cared for her so much as Nathanael, who had a strong proclivity for learning and art. Klara clung to her lover with all of her soul, and when he parted from her, the first clouds passed over her life. With what delight she flew into his arms when he returned to his native town (as he had promised he would in his last letter to Lothar) and entered his mother's room. It turned out as Nathanael had believed it would: the instant he saw Klara again   430   440

---

7. "The Repentent Magdalen" by Pompeo Battoni (1708–1787), which Hoffman would have seen in Dresden.

8. Jacob van Ruisdael (1628–1682), a landscape painter of the Dutch school.

thoughts about the lawyer Coppelius or Klara's pedantic letter—all his depressions vanished.

Nevertheless, Nathanael was right when he wrote to his friend Lothar that the abhorrent barometer dealer Coppola had exercised a disastrous influence on his life. This was evident to everyone for even in the first few days of his visit Nathanael seemed completely changed; he surrendered to gloomy brooding and behaved in a manner more strange than they had known before. All of life, every- 450 thing, had become only a dream and a presentiment; he was always saying that any man, although imagining himself to be free, was in fact only the horrible plaything of dark powers, which it was vain to resist. Man must humbly submit to whatever fate has in store for him. He went so far as to insist that it was foolish to believe that man's creative achievements in art or science resulted from the expression of free will; rather, he claimed that the inspiration requisite for creation comes not from within us but results from the influence of a higher external principle.

To the clear-thinking Klara all this mystical nonsense was repugnant in the extreme, but it seemed pointless to attempt any refutation. It was only when Nathanael argued that Coppelius was the evil principle that had entered him and 460 possessed him at the moment he was listening behind the curtain, and that this loathsome demon would in some terrible way destroy their happiness, that Klara grew very serious and said, "Yes, Nathanael, you are right; Coppelius is an evil and malignant principle. His effect can be no less diabolical than the very powers of hell if they assume living form, but only if you fail to banish him from your mind and thoughts. He will exist and work on you only so long as you believe in him; it is only your belief that gives him power."

Nathanael was greatly angered because Klara said that the demon existed only in his own mind, and he wanted to begin a disquisition on the whole mystic doctrine of devils and sinister powers, but Klara terminated the conversation 470 abruptly by making a trivial remark, much to Nathanael's great annoyance. He thought that profound secrets were inaccessible to those with cold, unreceptive hearts, without being clearly aware that he included Klara among these inferior natures; and therefore he did not cease trying to initiate her into these secrets. Early in the morning, when Klara was helping to prepare breakfast, he would stand beside her and read to her from various occult books until she begged, "But my dear Nathanael, what if I have to accuse you of being the evil principle that is fatally influencing my coffee? For if I please you and drop everything to look into your eyes as you read, my coffee will boil over and no one will have breakfast." Nathanael slammed his book shut and rushed to his room indignantly. 480

Nathanael had formerly possessed a notable talent for writing delightful and amusing stories, to which Klara would listen with enormous pleasure; now, however, his tales were gloomy, unintelligible, and shapeless so that although Klara spared his feelings and did not say so, he probably felt how little they interested her. Above all, Klara disliked the tedious; and her uncontrollable drowsiness of spirit was betrayed by her glance and by her word. In truth, Nathanael's stories were really very boring. His resentment of Klara's cold, prosaic disposition increased; she could not conquer her dislike of his dark, gloomy, and dreary occultism; and so they drifted further and further apart without being conscious of it. Nathanael was forced to confess to himself that the ugly image of Coppelius 490 had faded in his imagination, and it often cost him great effort to present Coppelius in adequate vividness in his writing where he played the part of the sinister bogeyman. Finally it occurred to him to make his gloomy presentiment that Coppelius would destroy his happiness the subject of a poem. He portrayed himself and Klara as united in true love but plagued by some dark hand that occasionally intruded into their lives, snatching away incipient joy. Finally, as they stood at the altar, the sinister Coppelius appeared and touched Klara's lovely eyes, which sprang into Nathanael's own breast, burning and scorching like bleeding sparks. Then Coppelius grabbed him and flung him into a blazing circle of fire that spun round with the speed of a whirlwind and, with a rush, carried him away. The awesome noise was like a hurricane furiously whipping up the waves so that they rose up like white-headed black giants in a raging inferno. But through this savage tumult he could hear Klara's voice: "Can't you see me, dear one? Coppelius has deceived you. That which burned in your breast was not my eyes. Those were fiery drops of the blood from your own heart. Look at me. I have still got my own eyes." Nathanael thought: "It is Klara: I am hers forever." Then it was as though this thought had grasped the fiery circle and forced it to stop turning, while the raging noise died away in the black abyss. Nathanael looked into Klara's eyes; but it was death that, with Klara's eyes, looked upon him kindly. While Nathanael was composing his poem he was very calm and serene; he reworked and polished every line, and since he fettered himself with meter, he did not pause until everything in the poem was perfect and euphonious. But when it was finally completed and he read the poem aloud to himself, he was stricken with fear and a wild horror and he cried out, "Whose horrible voice is that?" Soon, however, he once more came to understand that it was really nothing more than a very successful poem, and he felt certain that it would arouse Klara's cold nature, although he did not clearly understand why Klara should be aroused by it or what would be accomplished by frightening her with these hideous visions that augured a terrible fate and the destruction of their love.

They were sitting in his mother's little garden. Klara was extremely cheerful because Nathanael had not plagued her with his dreams and foreboding for the three days he had devoted to writing the poem. Nathanael also chatted gaily about things that amused her, as he had in the past, so that Klara remarked, "Now I really do have you back again. Do you see how we have driven out the hateful Coppelius?"

Nathanael suddenly remembered that the poem he had intended to read to Klara was in his pocket. He took the sheets from his pocket and started reading while Klara, anticipating something boring as usual and resigning herself to the situation, calmly began knitting. But as the dark cloud of the poem grew ever blacker, the knitting in her hand sank and she stared fixedly into Nathanael's eyes. But Nathanael was carried inexorably away by his poem; passion flushed his cheeks a fiery red, and tears flowed from his eyes. When he finally finished, he uttered a groan of absolute exhaustion; he grasped Klara's hand and sighed, as though dissolving in inconsolable grief, "Alas! Klara, Klara!"

Klara pressed him tenderly to her bosom and said in a voice at once soft but very slow and somber, "Nathanael, my darling Nathanael, throw that mad, insane, stupid tale into the fire." Nathanael then sprang indignantly to his feet, thrust

Klara away, cried, "You damned, lifeless automaton," and ran off. Klara, deeply
hurt, wept bitter tears, sobbing, "He has never loved me because he does not un-   540
derstand me."

Lothar came into the arbor; Klara had to tell him everything that had happened. He loved his sister with all his soul, and every word of her complaint fell
like a fiery spark upon his heart so that the indignation that he had long felt toward the visionary Nathanael flared into furious rage. He ran to find Nathanael
and in harsh words reproached him for his insane behavior toward his beloved
sister. Nathanael, incensed, answered in kind, "Crazy, conceited fool!" and was answered by "Miserable commonplace idiot!" A duel was inevitable, and they agreed
to meet on the following morning behind the garden and to fight, in accordance
with the local student custom, with sharpened foils. They stalked about in silence   550
and gloom. Klara, who had overheard and seen the violent argument, and who
had seen the fencing masters bring the foils at dusk, suspected what was to happen. They both reached the dueling ground and cast off their coats in foreboding
silence, and with their eyes aglow with the lust of combat, they were about to attack when Klara burst through the garden door. Through her sobs she cried: "You
ferocious, cruel beasts! Strike me down before you attack each other. How am I to
live when my lover has slain my brother, or my brother has slain my lover?"

Lothar lowered his weapon and gazed in silence at the ground, but in
Nathanael's heart the affection he had once felt for lovely Klara in the happiest
days of youth reawoke with a lacerating sorrow. The murderous weapon fell from   560
his hand, and he threw himself at Klara's feet: "Can you ever forgive me, my one
and only, beloved Klara? Can you ever forgive me, my dear brother Lothar?"
Lothar was touched by his friend's profound grief, and all three embraced in reconciliation, with countless tears, vowing eternal love and fidelity.

Nathanael felt as if a heavy burden that had weighed him to the ground had
been lifted, as if by resisting the dark powers that had gripped him he had saved
his whole being from the threat of utter ruin. He spent three blissful days with his
dear friends and then returned to G——, where he intended to remain for another
year before returning to his native town forever.

Everything that referred to Coppelius was kept from Nathanael's mother, for   570
they knew that it was impossible for her to think of him without horror, since like
Nathanael, she believed him to be guilty of her husband's death.

Upon returning to his lodgings, Nathanael was completely astonished to find
that the whole house had been burned down; nothing remained amid the ruins
but the bare outer walls. Although the fire had started in the laboratory of the
chemist living on the ground floor and had then spread upwards, some of
Nathanael's courageous and energetic friends had managed, by breaking into his
room on the upper floor, to save his books and manuscripts and instruments.
They had carried them undamaged to another house and had rented a room there,
into which Nathanael immediately moved. It did not strike him as singular that he   580
now lived opposite Professor Spalanzini, nor did it seem particularly strange to
him when he discovered that by looking out of his window he could see where
Olympia often sat alone, so that he could clearly recognize her figure, although

her features were blurred and indistinct. It did finally occur to him that Olympia often sat for hours at a small table in the same position in which he had seen her when he had first discovered her through the glass door, doing nothing and incessantly gazing across in his direction. He was forced to confess to himself that he had never seen a lovelier figure, although, with Klara in his heart, he remained perfectly indifferent to the stiff and rigid Olympia; only occasionally did he glance up from his book at the beautiful statue—that was all.   590

He was writing to Klara when there was a soft tap at the door. At his call, the door opened and Coppola's repulsive face peered in. Nathanael was shaken to the roots. Remembering, however, what Spalanzini had said to him about his compatriot Coppola and what he had solemnly promised his sweetheart regarding the Sandman Coppelius, he felt ashamed of his childish fear of ghosts and forcibly pulled himself together and said as calmly as possible, "I don't want a barometer, my good friend, do go away."

Coppola, however, came right into the room and said in a hoarse voice, his mouth twisted in a hideous laugh, his little eyes flashing piercingly from beneath his long, gray eyelashes, "Oh, no barometer? No barometer! I gotta da eyes too. I   600
gotta da nice eyes!" Horrified, Nathanael cried, "Madman, how can you have eyes? Eyes?" But Coppola instantly put away his barometers and, thrusting his hands in his wide coat pockets, pulled out lorgnettes and eyeglasses and put them on the table. "So, glasses—put on nose, see! These are my eyes, nice-a eyes!" Saying this, he brought forth more and more eyeglasses from his pockets until the whole table began to gleam and sparkle. Myriad eyes peered and blinked and stared up at Nathanael, who could not look away from the table, while Coppola continued putting down more and more eyeglasses; and flaming glances crisscrossed each other ever more wildly and shot their blood-red rays into Nathanael's breast.

Overcome by an insane horror, Nathanael cried, "Stop, stop, you fiend!" He   610
seized Coppola by the arm even as Coppola was once more searching in his pocket for more eyeglasses, although the table was already covered with them. Coppola gently shook him off with a hoarse revolting laugh and with the words "Oh! None for you? But here are nice spyglasses." He swept the eyeglasses together and returned them to the pocket from which they had come and then produced from a side pocket a number of telescopes of all sizes. As soon as the eyeglasses were gone Nathanael grew calm again, and focusing his thoughts on Klara, he clearly saw that this gruesome illusion had been solely the product of his own mind and that Coppola was an honest optician and maker of instruments and far removed from being the ghostly double and revenant of the accursed Coppelius.   620
Besides, there was nothing at all remarkable about the spyglasses that Coppola was placing on the table now, or at least nothing so weird about them as about the eyeglasses. To make amends for his behavior, Nathanael decided actually to buy something, picked up a small, very beautifully finished pocket spyglass, and in order to test it, looked through the window. Never in his life had he come across a glass that brought objects before his eyes with such clarity and distinctness. He involuntarily looked into Spalanzini's room. Olympia, as usual, sat before the little table, her arms upon it, her hands folded. For the first time now he saw her exquisitely formed face. Only her eyes seemed peculiarly fixed and lifeless. But as he

continued to look more and more intently through the glass, it seemed as though 630
moist moonbeams were beginning to shine in Olympia's eyes. It seemed as if the
power of vision were only now starting to be kindled; her glances were inflamed
with ever-increasing life.

Nathanael leaned on the window as if enchanted, staring steadily upon
Olympia's divine beauty. The sound of a throat being cleared and a shuffling of feet
awakened him from his enchantment. Coppola was standing behind him. "*Tre
zechini*—three ducats," Coppola said. Nathanael had completely forgotten the optician. He quickly paid the sum requested. "Nice-a glass, no? Nice-a glass?"
Coppola asked in his hoarse and revolting voice, smiling maliciously. "Yes, yes,
yes," Nathanael answered irritably. "Goodbye, my friend." But only after casting 640
many peculiar sidelong glances at Nathanael did Coppola leave the room.
Nathanael heard him laughing loudly on the stairs. "Ah," thought Nathanael, "he's
laughing at me because I overpaid him for this little spyglass." But as he quietly
voiced these words he seemed to hear a deep sigh, like a dying man's, echoing
through the room. Terror stopped his breath. To be sure, it was he who had deeply
sighed; that was obvious. "Klara is absolutely right," he said to himself, "in calling
me an absurd visionary, yet it is ridiculous—more than ridiculous—that I am so
strangely distressed by the thought of having overpaid Coppola for the spyglass. I
see no reason for it." Then Nathanael sat down to finish his letter to Klara, but a
glance through the window showed him that Olympia still sat as before, and as 650
though impelled by an irresistible power, he jumped up, seized Coppola's spyglass, and could not tear himself away from the alluring vision of Olympia until
his friend Siegmund called for him to go to Professor Spalanzini's lecture. The curtain was tightly drawn across the fateful door so that he could not see Olympia;
nor could he see her for the next two days from his own room, despite the fact
that he scarcely ever left his window and, almost without interruption, gazed into
her room through Coppola's glass. Moreover, on the third day curtains were drawn
across the window, and Nathanael, in despair, driven by longing and ardent passion, rushed out beyond the city gates. Olympia's image hovered before him in the
air, emerged from the bushes, and peered up at him with great and lustrous eyes 660
from the shining brook. Klara's image had completely faded from his soul. He
thought of nothing but Olympia, and he lamented aloud, in a tearful voice, "Oh!
My lofty and lovely star of love, have you arisen only to disappear again and leave
me in the gloomy night of dark despair?"

As he was about to return home, he became aware of great noise and activity
in Spalanzini's house. The doors were open and various kinds of gear were being
carried in. The first-floor windows had been removed from their hinges, maids
with large dustmops were busily rushing about, sweeping and dusting, while inside the house carpenters and upholsterers were banging and hammering.
Nathanael stood absolutely still in the street, struck with amazement. Siegmund 670
then joined him and asked with a laugh: "Well, what do you think of our old
Spalanzini now?" Nathanael assured him that he could say nothing, since he knew
absolutely nothing about the professor, but that, much to his astonishment, he
had noticed the feverish activity that was taking place in the silent and gloomy
house. Siegmund told him that Spalanzini was going to give a great party, a concert and a ball, the next day and that half the university had been invited. Rumor

had it that Spalanzini was going to present his daughter Olympia to the public for the first time, after so long having carefully guarded her from every human eye.

Nathanael received an invitation, and at the appointed hour, when carriages were driving up and lights gleamed in the decorated rooms, he went to the profes- 680 sor's house with palpitating heart. The gathering was large and dazzling. Olympia appeared, elegantly and tastefully dressed. No one could help but admire her beautifully shaped face and her figure. On the other hand, there was something peculiarly curved about her back, and the wasplike thinness of her waist also appeared to result from excessively tight lacing. There was, further, something stiff and measured about her walk and bearing that struck many unfavorably, but it was attributed to the constraint she felt in society. The concert began. Olympia played the piano with great talent and also skillfully sang a *bravura* aria in a voice that was high-pitched, bell-like, almost shrill. Nathanael was completely enchanted; he was standing in the back row and could not precisely distinguish 690 Olympia's features in the dazzling candlelight. Surreptitiously, he took Coppola's glass from his pocket and looked at her. Oh! Then he perceived the yearning glance with which she looked at him, and he saw how every note achieved absolute purity in the loving glance that scorched him to his very soul. Her skillful roulades appeared to him to be the heavenly exaltations of a soul transfigured by love; and, finally, when the cadenza was concluded, the long trill echoed shrilly through the hall and he felt as if he were suddenly embraced by burning arms. No longer able to contain himself, rapture and pain mingling within him, he cried: "Olympia!" Everyone looked at him; many laughed. The cathedral organist pulled a gloomier face than before and simply said, "Now, now!"   700

The concert was over. The ball began. Oh, to dance with her! That was his one desire. But how could he summon up the courage to ask her, the queen of the ball, to dance with him? And yet, without really knowing how it happened, just as the dance began he found himself standing close to her and she had not yet been asked to dance. Barely able to stammer a few words, he grasped her hand. It was cold as ice. A deathly chill passed through him. Gazing into Olympia's eyes he saw that they shone at him with love and longing; and at that moment the pulse seemed to beat again in her cold hand, and warm life-blood to surge through her veins. In Nathanael's heart, too, passion burned with greater intensity. He threw his arms around the lovely Olympia and whirled her through the dance. He had 710 thought that he usually followed the beat of the music well, but from the peculiar rhythmical evenness with which she danced and which often confused him, he was aware of how faulty his own sense of time really was. Yet he would dance with no other partner, and he felt that he would murder anyone else who approached Olympia to ask her to dance. But this occurred only twice; to his amazement Olympia remained seated on each occasion until the next dance, when he did not fail to lead her out to the dance floor. If Nathanael had had eyes for anything but the lovely Olympia, there would inevitably have been a number of disagreeable quarrels; for it was obvious that the carefully smothered laughter which broke out among the young people in this corner and that, was directed toward the lovely 720 Olympia, whom they were watching curiously for an unknown reason. Heated by the quantity of wine he had drunk and by the dancing, Nathanael had cast off his characteristic shyness. He sat beside Olympia, her hand in his, and with fervor and passion he spoke of his love in words that no one could understand, neither he nor Olympia. But perhaps she did, for she sat with her eyes fixed upon his, sighing again and again, "Ah, ah, ah!" Whereupon Nathanael answered: "Oh, you magnificent and heavenly woman! You ray shining from the promised land of love! You deep soul, in which my whole being is reflected," and more of the same. But Olympia did nothing but continue to sigh, "Ah, ah!"

Professor Spalanzini passed the happy couple several times and smiled at them with a look of strange satisfaction. It seemed to Nathanael, although he was in a very different, higher world, that it was suddenly getting noticeably darker down here at Professor Spalanzini's. When he looked around him, it was with great consternation that he saw that only two lights were burning in the empty room and that they were about to go out. The music and the dancing had ceased long ago. "We must part, we must part!" he cried in wild despair, then kissed Olympia's hand. He bent down to her mouth; icy lips met his burning ones. Just as when, touching her cold hand, he had felt a shudder seize him, the legend of the dead bride flashed suddenly through his mind. But Olympia drew him close to her, and the kiss seemed to warm her lips into life. Professor Spalanzini walked slowly through the empty room, his steps echoing hollowly, and in the flickering light cast by the candles, his figure assumed a sinister and ghostly appearance.

"Do you love me? Do you love me, Olympia? Just one word! Do you love me?" Nathanael whispered.

But as she rose, Olympia only sighed, "Ah, ah!"

"Yes, you, my lovely, wonderful evening star," said Nathanael, "you have risen for me and will illuminate and transfigure my soul forever."

"Ah, ah!" Olympia replied as she walked away. Nathanael followed her; they stood before the professor.

"You had a most lively conversation with my daughter," the professor said with a smile. "If you enjoy talking with this silly girl you are welcome to come and do so."

Nathanael left, his heart ablaze with all of heaven.

Spalanzini's ball was the talk of the town for the next few days. Despite the fact that the professor had done everything to put on a splendid show, the wags found plenty of fantastic and peculiar things to talk about. Their favorite target was the rigid and silent Olympia, who, her beautiful appearance notwithstanding, was assumed to be hopelessly stupid, which was thought to be the reason Spalanzini had so long kept her concealed. Nathanael heard all this, not without inner fury, but he said nothing. "What would be the use," he thought, "of proving to these fellows that it was their own stupidity which precluded them from appreciating Olympia's profound and beautiful mind."

"Do me a favor, brother," Siegmund said to him one day, "and tell me how it is possible for an intelligent fellow like you to have fallen for that wax-faced, wooden puppet across the way?"

Nathanael was about to lose his temper, but he quickly gained control of himself and replied, "Tell me, Siegmund, how do you account for the fact that a man who is able to so readily discern beauty has not seen the heavenly charms of Olympia? Yet, thank heaven you are not my rival, for if you were a rival, the blood of one of us would be spilled."

Siegmund, seeing how things were with his friend, adroitly switched tactics, and after commenting that there was no point in arguing about the object of a person's love, he added, "It's very strange, however, that many of us have come to the same conclusion about Olympia. She seems to us—don't take this badly, my brother—strangely stiff and soulless. Her figure is symmetrical, so is her face, that's true enough, and if her eyes were not so completely devoid of life—the power of vision, I mean—she might be considered beautiful. Her step is peculiarly measured; all of her movements seem to stem from some kind of clockwork. Her playing and her singing are unpleasantly perfect, being as lifeless as a music box; it is the same with her dancing. We found Olympia to be rather weird, and we wanted to have nothing to do with her. She seems to us to be playing the part of a human being, and it's as if there really were something hidden behind all of this."

Nathanael did not surrender to the bitterness aroused in him by Siegmund's words; rather, mastering his resentment, he merely said, very gravely, "Olympia may indeed appear weird to you cold and unimaginative mortals. The poetical soul is accessible only to the poetical nature. Her adoring glances fell only upon *me* and irradiated my feelings and thoughts. I discover myself again only in Olympia's love. That she does not indulge in jabbering banalities like other shallow people may not seem right to you. It's true that she says little; but the few words she does utter are in a sacred language that expresses an inner world imbued with love, with the higher, spiritual knowledge gathered from a vision of the world beyond. But you have no feeling for these things; I am wasting my breath."

"God protect you, brother," said Siegmund very gently, almost sadly. "It does seem to me that you are moving in an evil direction. You may depend upon me if—no, I'll say nothing more." It suddenly dawned upon Nathanael that his cold, unimaginative friend Siegmund sincerely wished him very well, and so he warmly shook his outstretched hand.

Nathanael had completely forgotten that there was in the world a Klara whom he had once loved; his mother, Lothar—all had disappeared from his mind. He lived only for Olympia, beside whom he sat every day, hour after hour, carrying on about his love, about mutual sympathy kindled into life, and about their psychic affinity—and Olympia listened to all of this with great reverence. From deep within his desk, Nathanael dug up everything he had ever written—poems, fantasies, visions, romances, tales—and the number was increased daily by a plethora of hyperbolic sonnets, verses, and canzonets; and all of this he read to Olympia tirelessly for hours at a time. Never before had he had such a splendid listener. She neither embroidered nor knitted; she did not look out of the window nor feed a bird nor play with a lapdog or kitten; she did not twist slips of paper or anything else around her fingers; she had no need to disguise a yawn by forcing a cough. In brief, she sat for hours on end without moving, staring directly into his eyes, and her gaze grew ever more ardent and animated. Only when Nathanael at last stood up and kissed her hand and then her lips did she say, "Ah, ah!" and then add, "Goodnight, my dearest."

When Nathanael returned to his own room, he cried, "How beautiful, how profound is her mind! Only you, only you truly understand me." He trembled with rapture when he thought of the marvelous harmony which daily grew between him and Olympia; it seemed to him as if she expressed thoughts about his work and about all of his poetic gifts from the very depth of his own soul, as though she spoke from within him. This must, to be sure, have been the case, for Olympia never spoke any word other than those already recorded. But even in clear and sober moments, those, for example, which followed his awaking in the morning, when Nathanael was conscious of Olympia's utter passivity and taciturnity, he merely said, "What are words? Mere words! The glance of her heavenly eyes expresses more than any commonplace speech. Besides, how is it possible for a child of heaven to confine herself to the narrow circle demanded by wretched, mundane life?"

Professor Spalanzini appeared to be most pleased by the intimacy that had developed between his daughter and Nathanael, and he gave Nathanael many unmistakable signs of his delight. When, at great length, Nathanael ventured to hint delicately at a possible marriage with Olympia, the professor's face broke into a smile and he said that he would allow his daughter to make a perfectly free choice. Emboldened by these words, and with passion inflaming his heart, Nathanael determined to implore Olympia the very next day to put into plain words what her sweet and loving glances had told him—that she would be his forever. He searched for the ring his mother had given him when he had left. He intended to present it to Olympia as a symbol of his devotion and the joyous life with her that had flowered. While looking for the ring he came upon his letters from Klara and Lothar; he cast them aside indifferently, found the ring, put it in his pocket, and hurried with it across to Olympia.

While still on the stairs, he heard a singular hubbub that seemed to come from Spalanzini's study. There was a stamping, a rattling, pushing, a banging against the door, and, intermingled, curses and oaths, "Let go! Let go! Monster! Villain! Risking body and soul for it? Ha! Ha! Ha! Ha! That wasn't our arrangement! I, I made the eyes! I made the clockwork! Damned idiot, you and your damned clockwork! Dog of a clockmaker! Out! Let me go!" The voices causing this uproar belonged to Spalanzini and the abominable Coppelius. Nathanael rushed in, seized by a nameless dread. The professor was grasping a female figure by the shoulders, the Italian Coppola had her by the feet, and they were twisting and tugging her this way and that, contending furiously for possession of her. Nathanael recoiled in horror upon recognizing the figure as Olympia's. Flaring up in a wild rage, he was about to tear his beloved from the grasp of these madmen when Coppola, wrenching the figure from the professor's hand with the strength of a giant, struck the professor such a fearful blow with it that he toppled backwards over the table on which vials, retorts, flasks, and glass test tubes were standing—everything shattered into a thousand fragments. Then Coppola threw the figure over his shoulder and with a horrible, shrill laugh, ran quickly down the stairs, the figure's grotesquely dangling feet bumping and rattling woodenly on every step. Nathanael stood transfixed; he had only too clearly seen that in the deathly pale waxen face of Olympia there were no eyes, but merely black holes. She was a lifeless doll. Spalanzini was writhing on the floor; his head and chest and arm had been cut by the glass fragments and blood gushed from him as if from a fountain. But he summoned up all his strength: "After him, after him! What are you waiting for! Coppelius—Coppelius has stolen my best automaton. Worked

at it for twenty years—put everything I had into it—mechanism—speech—movement—all mine. The eyes—the eyes stolen from you! Damn him! Curse him! After
him! Get me Olympia! Bring back Olympia! There are the eyes!"

And now Nathanael saw something like a pair of bloody eyes staring up at
him from the floor. Spalanzini seized them with his uninjured hand and flung
them at Nathanael so that they hit his breast. Then madness racked Nathanael
with scorching claws, ripping to shreds his mind and senses.   870

"Whirl, whirl, whirl! Circle of fire! Circle of fire! Whirl round, circle of fire!
Merrily, merrily! Aha, lovely wooden doll, whirl round!"

With these words Nathanael hurled himself upon the professor and clutched
at his throat. He would have strangled him if several people who had been attracted by the noise had not rushed in and torn the raging Nathanael away, thus
saving the professor, whose wounds were then bandaged. As strong as he was,
Siegmund was unable to subdue the madman, who continued to scream in a horrible voice, "Wooden doll, whirl round!" and to flail about with clenched fists.
Finally, several men combined their strength and flung Nathanael to the ground
and tied him up. Nathanael's words turned into a heinous bellow, and in a raging   880
frenzy, he was taken away to the madhouse.

Before continuing my narration, gentle reader, of what further happened to
the unhappy Nathanael, I can assure you, in case you are interested in Spalanzini,
that skillful craftsman and maker of automatons, that his recovery from his
wounds was complete. He was, however, forced to leave the university because
Nathanael's story had caused a considerable scandal and because opinion generally
held that it was an inexcusable deceit to have smuggled a wooden doll into proper
tea circles, where Olympia had been such a success, and to have palmed it off as a
human. In fact, lawyers held that it was a subtle imposture and considered it felo-
nious because it had been so craftily devised and was directed against the public   890
so that, except for some astute students, it had gone undetected, notwithstanding
the fact that everyone now claimed wisdom and pointed to various details which
they said had struck them as suspicious. They did not, however, bring any clues to
light. Why, for example, would anyone have had his suspicions aroused by the fact
that Olympia, according to an elegant tea party-goer, had sneezed more often than
she had yawned? This elegant gentleman was of the opinion that the sneezing had
really been the sound of the concealed clockwork winding itself up—concomi-
tantly, there had always been an audible creaking—and so on. The professor of
poetry and rhetoric took a pinch of snuff, snapped the lid shut, cleared his throat,
and solemnly declared, "Most honorable ladies and gentlemen, do you not see the   900
point of it all? It is all an allegory, an extended metaphor. Do you understand?
Sapienti sat."[9]

But many honorable gentlemen were not reassured by this. The story of the
automaton had very deeply impressed them, and a horrible distrust of human figures in general arose. Indeed, many lovers insisted that their mistresses sing and
dance unrhythmically and embroider, knit, or play with a lapdog or something
while being read to, so that they could assure themselves that they were not in

9. "Fill yourselves with knowledge."

love with a wooden doll; above all else, they required the mistresses not only to listen, but to speak frequently in such a way that it would prove that they really were capable of thinking and feeling. Many lovers, as a result, grew closer than ever before; but others gradually drifted apart. "One really can't be sure about this," said one or another. At tea parties, people yawned with incredible frequency and never sneezed, in order to ward off all suspicion. Spalanzini, as has been noted, had to leave the place in order to escape criminal charges of having fraudulently introduced an automaton into human society. Coppola had also disappeared.

Nathanael awoke as from a deep and frightful dream, opened his eyes, and experienced an indescribable sensation of bliss warmly permeating his body. He lay on his own bed in his own room at home, Klara bending over him, his mother and Lothar standing nearby.

"At last, at last, my darling Nathanael, you have recovered from your terrible illness and are once more mine!" cried Klara with deep emotion, clasping him in her arms. Bright scalding tears streamed from his eyes, so overcome with mingled feelings of sorrow and delight was he, and he gasped, "Klara, my Klara!"

Then Siegmund, who had faithfully stood by his friend in his hour of need, entered the room; and Nathanael shook his hand. "My faithful brother, you have not deserted me."

Every vestige of insanity had disappeared and Nathanael soon recovered his strength again under the tender care of his mother, sweetheart, and friends. Good luck had, in the meantime, visited the house—an old miserly uncle, from whom they had expected nothing, had died and left not only a considerable fortune but a small estate that was pleasantly situated not far from the town. And there they resolved to go and live, Nathanael and Klara, whom he was to marry, and his mother and Lothar. Nathanael had grown more gentle and childlike than ever before, and for the first time could fully appreciate the heavenly purity of Klara's noble spirit. No one ever reminded him, even most remotely, of what had taken place. But when Siegmund said goodbye to him, he remarked, "By heaven, brother, I was on the wrong road. But an angel guided me to the path of light just in time. It was Klara." Siegmund would let him say nothing else for fear that the wounding memories of the past might flare up in him too vividly.

The time came when these four lucky people were to move into their property, and as they were walking through the streets at noon, after having made many purchases, the high tower of the town hall cast its huge shadow over the marketplace. "Oh!" said Klara, "Let us climb to the top once more and look at the distant mountains!" No sooner said than done. Nathanael and Klara climbed the tower; his mother and the servant went home. Lothar, not wishing to climb so many steps, remained below. There the two lovers stood arm in arm on the topmost gallery of the tower looking down into the fragrant woods beyond which the blue mountains rose up like a giant city.

"Just look at that strange little gray bush," Klara cried. "It really seems to be coming toward us." Nathanael automatically felt his side pocket, where he found Coppola's spyglass, and looked to one side. Klara was standing in front of the glass. Then there was a convulsive throbbing in his pulse. Deathly pale, he stared at Klara; but soon streams of fire flashed and spurted from his rolling eyes. He roared horrendously, like a hunted beast, leaped high into the air, and bursting with horrible laughter, he shrieked in a piercing voice, "Whirl wooden doll! Whirl wooden doll!" And seizing Klara with superhuman strength he tried to hurl her from the tower, but Klara, with a strength born of the agony of desperation, clung tightly to the railing. Lothar heard the madman raving, and he heard Klara's cry of terror. He was seized with a terrible foreboding and raced up the stairs. The door 960 leading to the second flight was shut. Klara's cries were growing fainter and fainter. Mad with rage and fear, he pushed against the door, which finally burst open. "Help! Save me, save me!" Her voice faded in the air. "She is dead, murdered by that madman," Lothar cried. The door leading to the gallery was also locked, but his desperation endowed him with the strength of a giant and he tore it from its hinges. Good God! Klara was in the grasp of Nathanael the madman, hanging in the air over the gallery railing, to which she barely clung with one hand. Quick as lightning, Lothar seized his sister and pulled her back, at the same instant smashing the madman in the face with his fist so hard that he reeled back and let go of his victim. 970

Lothar raced down the stairs with his unconscious sister in his arms. She was saved. Nathanael dashed around the gallery, leaping up in the air and shouting, "Circle of fire! Whirl round, circle of fire! Whirl round!" A crowd gathered quickly, attracted by the wild screaming; and in the midst of them there towered the gigantic figure of the lawyer Coppelius, who had just arrived in town and had come directly to the marketplace. Some wanted to go up and overpower the madman, but Coppelius laughed and said, "Ha, ha! Just wait; he'll come down on his own." And he looked up with the rest. Nathanael suddenly froze, leaned forward, caught sight of Coppelius, and with a shattering scream of "Ah, nice-a eyes, nice-a eyes!" jumped over the railing. 980

Nathanael lay on the pavement with his head shattered, but Coppelius had vanished in the crowd.

Many years later it was reported that Klara had been seen in a remote district sitting hand in hand with a pleasant-looking man in front of the door of a splendid country house, two merry boys playing around her. Thus it may be concluded that Klara eventually found that quiet, domestic happiness that her cheerful nature required and that Nathanael, with his lacerated soul, could never have provided her. [1816]

Questions for Discussion and Writing

1. Why does the young Nathanael think that the Sandman and Coppelius are the same person?
2. Who or what is Coppelius? Is he human, supernatural, imaginary?
3. Is Klara correct in saying, "All the fears and terrors of which you speak took place only in your mind and had very little to do with the true, external world"? Is it possible to separate "objective reality" from "subjective reality"?

4. Compare and contrast Klara and Olympia. Why does Nathanael fall in love first with the one and then with the other?

5. There is a great deal of imagery relating to eyes, sight, and vision in the story. What function does this imagery serve? Why is it there?

6. What are the major divisions in "The Sandman"? Is this a unified story, or is it two stories imperfectly joined together? Consider, too, the shifting point of view as part of this issue.

7. What is the theme of the story? Is it a satire on the Romantic imagination? How does it involve the myth of Pygmalion, who creates his own perfect woman? Does the theme involve reason versus emotion or subjectivity versus objectivity? Is it a study in madness? Explain how Hoffman has woven various themes together.

Sidebar: EXPLORING SUB-GENRES

The Horror Story

Since ancient times, literature has appealed to the strongest emotions, including fright or terror. Fear of the gods, the mob, the dark, the unknown, the dangerous, or of death itself has often been exploited by writers for various purposes and effects. Ancient myths often featured gruesome murders, incest, brutal revenge, and supernatural monsters; medieval knights battled giants, dragons, and witches; in the Renaissance, Shakespeare's *Hamlet* (1601) and *Macbeth* (1606), and John Webster's *Duchess of Malfi* (1613) exploited the gruesome, grotesque, and bloody. Popular ballads and fairy tales like "The Blue Beard" were often sensational and frightening in their violence and gore.

The invention of fiction that focuses exclusively on arousing terror, however, is usually credited to the English writer Horace Walpole (1717–1797), whose *The Castle of Otronto* (1764) is widely regarded as the first Gothic novel. Walpole's wildly inventive mixture of medieval castles, dungeons, secret passages, ghosts, and supernatural apparitions came at the height of the Age of Reason, captured the emerging Romantic imaginations of readers, and spawned a new genre of writing. Walpole's innovations became conventions: ancestral curses, inanimate objects that behave as if alive, subterranean passages, supernatural visitations, and perhaps most importantly the young woman pursued by dangers. Gradually, the term "Gothic" lost its specifically medieval associations and became attached to any fiction that exploits the macabre, with or without supernatural elements. Mary Shelley's *Frankenstein* (1818), for example, contains elements of the Gothic thriller, as well as what we now call science fiction.

The emergence of the short story is intimately connected with Gothic or horror stories. Nearly all the early writers of short stories—Hoffman, Irving, Poe, Hawthorne, and Gogol—exploited features of the Gothic and macabre. E. T. A. Hoffman's "The Sandman" is a compelling story of childhood fears, adult memories and feelings of guilt, psychological and physical terror, a mad scientist and his creation, and finally death. On the surface, it is a frightening tale of a young man who descends into madness and commits suicide, but to say that Nathanael goes mad explains very little. Why does Nathanael become obsessed with the Sandman? Why does he identify Coppelius with this imaginary figure? How do these childhood and adult terrors relate to his obsession with Olympia? What are the repeated references to eyes and sight meant to suggest? Guilt? A childhood trauma? The relationship between inward vision and outward reality? The more we look for clues as to why Nathanael goes mad, the more psychologically complex the story becomes. "The Sandman" permits a multitude of readings, all of which go beyond the superficially scary into the realms of the mind, spirit, and imagination.

Edgar Allan Poe was deeply influenced by German Romanticism in general and by the tales of Hoffman in particular. That influence appears in "The Tell-Tale Heart," but Poe does not simply imitate his model. Poe's story is more carefully unified and tightly controlled than Hoffman's. Hoffman's tale involves three narrators, covers the whole life of Nathanael, and complicates the focus by introducing Professor Spalanzini and Olympia. Poe's unity and economy concentrate the horror; there is no

The Nightmare (1781) by Swiss-born British painter Henry Fuseli (1741–1825). (Photograph © 1993 The Detroit Institute of Arts, Founders Society Purchase with funds from Mr. and Mrs. Bert L. Smokler and Mr. and Mrs. Lawrence A. Fleischman)

emotional respite from beginning to end; and by exploiting the possibility of madness and various suggestions of obsession and guilt (including a similar use of eye imagery), Poe loses none of Hoffman's psychological depth.

Many other writers after Hoffman and Poe exploited Gothic horror in their work: Hawthorne, Gogol, Bierce, H. H. Munro ("Saki"), Paz, O'Connor, Jackson, and Carter. The ghost story and other expressions of the uncanny were potent reactions as realism and scientific rationalism became more prevalent in the nineteenth century. Gogol's story ends with a ghostly visitation or apparition that suggests, as all such stories do, that the world may be more complex and less mechanistic than science suggests. Similarly, "The Lottery" incorporates mythic references and Freudian psychology in a tale that is at once believable and fantastic.

In the twentieth century, writers have taken what might be called the "evil as normal" approach. Octavio Paz's "Blue Bouquet" begins as a story of the everyday but then shocks us with an encounter that seems at once surreal, hallucinatory, mad, and plausible. Shirley Jackson's "The Lottery" follows a similar pattern by presenting what at first seems a placid New England village and then suddenly turning it into a terrifying place of ritual sacrifice. Angela Carter's "The Bloody Chamber" combines fairy tale with Gothic traditions in a particularly disturbing way. In addition to the physical dangers faced by the heroine is a sense of corruption and perversion, to which the heroine is drawn in spite of her innocence. Lilies, usually a symbol of purity or resurrection, become part of this supercharged atmosphere bordering on necrophilia.

The horror story raises numerous questions about us as individuals and as a culture. Why do we find pleasure in frightening stories that depict physical, psychic, or supernatural horror? Why do we assume that supernatural powers are our enemies? Why are the victims in horror stories so often women? With whom do we identify in horror stories—with the victims or with the aggressors? Does the horror genre appeal mainly to young men, and if so, what does this tell us? Do horror stories make us indifferent toward violence? What is their relation to the wars, murders, and genocide of the daily news?

Contemporary horror stories still employ some of the conventions Walpole invented over two hundred years ago. Now, as then, horror stories explore the irrational and inexplicable in a universe that sometimes may appear too rational, too dryly scientific. Perhaps their appeal lies in allowing us to explore the unknown and forbidden in physical and emotional safety and to escape momentarily the humdrum monotony of our daily lives. Some commentators say that evil is the ultimate subject of horror. The decline of religion and the rise of scientific rationalism have banished the traditional symbols and personifications of evil, but not evil itself. Perhaps for this reason the monsters that haunt our nightmares tell us a great deal about ourselves and the times in which we live.

ᴈ WASHINGTON IRVING
(1783–1859)

Rip Van Winkle
A Posthumous Writing of Deidrich Knickerbocker

Washington Irving has been called America's first professional writer to be internationally successful. He is also widely acclaimed as the author of the earliest
short stories written in America: "Rip Van Winkle," "The Legend of Sleepy
Hollow," and "The Spectre Bridegroom," all published in *The Sketch Book of
Geoffrey Crayon, Gent.* (1810–1820).

   Irving was one of eleven children of a successful hardware merchant who
fought on the rebel side in the Revolutionary War. Educated at private schools
and by voracious reading in his father's library, he began legal studies but soon
gave them up in favor of writing satirical sketches for his brother's newspaper.
These, along with sketches by his brothers and brother-in-law, resulted in a
collection, *Salmagundi* (1807–1808). Irving next wrote *A History of New York*,
published under the pseudonym Diedrich Knickerbocker (1809). A parody of
historical writing, it was greeted at the time as the first significant book by an
American.

   In spite of his literary success, Irving turned to the family's hardware business, and from 1816–1818 worked vainly to rescue its English branch in
Liverpool. The business collapsed, but while in England, Irving encountered
British Romanticism and met Sir Walter Scott (1771–1832), who encouraged
his work. *The Sketch Book,* Irving's collection of light essays and the three stories
already mentioned, was a huge international success. His artistic and financial
triumph was undermined by tragedy, however, when his fiancée Matilda
Hoffman died. Although Irving published many more books during his career,
his writing never regained the optimism and humor it had exhibited to that
time. Much of his energy was directed into diplomatic work, particularly in
Spain, and in writing history and biography. His influence on American literature, however, has been significant, as a contributor to the short story form and
as a creator of uniquely American archetypes and symbols.

"By Woden, God of Saxons,
From whence comes Wensday, that is Wodensday,
Truth is a thing that ever I will keep
Until thylke day in which I creep into
My sepulchre—"   —CARTWRIGHT

[THE FOLLOWING TALE was found among the papers of the late Diedrich
Knickerbocker, an old gentleman of New York, who was very curious, in the

Dutch History of the province, and the manners of the descendants from its primitive settlers. His historical researches, however, did not lie so much among books as among men; for the former are lamentably scanty on his favorite topics; whereas he found the old burghers, and still more, their wives, rich in that legendary lore, so invaluable to true history. Whenever, therefore, he happened upon a genuine Dutch family, snugly shut up in its low-roofed farmhouse under a spreading sycamore, he looked upon it as a little clasped volume of black-letter,[1] and studied it with the zeal of a bookworm.

The result of all these researches was a history of the province during the reign of the Dutch governors, which he published some years since. There have been various opinions as to the literary character of his work, and, to tell the truth, it is not a whit better than it should be. Its chief merit is its scrupulous accuracy, which, indeed, was a little questioned on its first appearance, but has since been completely established; and it is now admitted into all historical collections as a book of unquestionable authority.

The old gentleman died shortly after the publication of his work, and, now that he is dead and gone, it cannot do much harm to his memory to say that his time might have been much better employed in weightier labors. He, however, was apt to ride his hobby his own way; and though it did now and then kick up the dust a little in the eyes of his neighbors, and grieve the spirit of some friends for whom he felt the truest deference and affection, yet his errors and follies are remembered "more in sorrow than in anger,"* and it begins to be suspected that he never intended to injure or offend. But however his memory may be appreciated by critics, it is still held dear among many folk, whose good opinion is well worth having; particularly by certain biscuit bakers, who have gone so far as to imprint his likeness on their new year cakes, and have thus given him a chance for immortality almost equal to the being stamped on a Waterloo medal, or a Queen Anne's farthing.]

Rip Van Winkle
A Posthumous Writing of Deidrich Knickerbocker

WHOEVER HAS MADE a voyage up the Hudson must remember the Kaatskill mountains. They are a dismembered branch of the great Appalachian family, and are seen away to the west of the river, swelling up to a noble height, and lording it over the surrounding country. Every change of season, every change of weather, indeed every hour of the day, produces some change in the magical hues and shapes of these mountains; and they are regarded by all the good wives, far

---

1. Gothic-style print.
* Vide the excellent discourse of G. C. Verplanck, Esq., before the New York Historical Society [Irving's note].

and near, as perfect barometers. When the weather is fair and settled they are clothed in blue and purple, and print their bold outlines on the clear evening sky; but sometimes, when the rest of the landscape is cloudless, they will gather a hood of gray vapors about their summits, which, in the last rays of the setting sun, will glow and light up like a crown of glory.

At the foot of these fairy mountains the voyager may have descried the light smoke curling up from a village, whose shingle roofs gleam among the trees just where the blue tints of the upland melt away into the fresh green of the nearer landscape. It is a little village of great antiquity, having been founded by some of the Dutch colonists, in the early times of the province, just about the beginning of the government of the good Peter Stuyvesant (may he rest in peace!), and there were some of the houses of the original settlers standing within a few years, built of small yellow bricks brought from Holland, having latticed windows and gable fronts, surmounted with weathercocks.

In that same village, and in one of these very houses (which, to tell the precise truth, was sadly time-worn and weather-beaten), there lived many years since, while the country was yet a province of Great Britain, a simple, good-natured fellow, of the name of Rip Van Winkle. He was a descendant of the Van Winkles who figure so gallantly in the chivalrous days of Peter Stuyvesant[2] and accompanied him to the siege of Fort Christina. He inherited, however, but little of the martial character of his ancestors. I have observed that he was a simple, good-natured man; he was moreover a kind neighbor, and an obedient henpecked husband. Indeed, to the latter circumstance might be owing that meekness of spirit which gained him such universal popularity; for those men are most apt to be obsequious and conciliating abroad who are under the discipline of shrews at home. Their tempers, doubtless, are rendered pliant and malleable in the fiery furnace of domestic tribulation, and a curtain lecture is worth all the sermons in the world for teaching the virtues of patience and long-suffering. A termagant wife may, therefore, in some respects, be considered a tolerable blessing; and, if so, Rip Van Winkle was thrice blessed.

Certain it is that he was a great favorite among all the good wives of the village, who, as usual with the amiable sex, took his part in all family squabbles, and never failed, whenever they talked those matters over in their evening gossipings, to lay all the blame on Dame Van Winkle. The children of the village, too, would shout with joy whenever he approached. He assisted at their sports, made their playthings, taught them to fly kites and shoot marbles, and told them long stories of ghosts, witches, and Indians. Whenever he went dodging about the village, he was surrounded by a troop of them hanging on his skirts,[3] clambering on his back, and playing a thousand tricks on him with impunity; and not a dog would bark at him throughout the neighborhood.

The great error in Rip's composition was an insuperable aversion to all kinds of profitable labor. It could not be from the want of assiduity or perseverance; for he would sit on a wet rock, with a rod as long and heavy as a Tartar's lance, and fish all day without a murmur, even though he should not be encouraged by a sin-

---

2. Director general of New Netherland, 1647–1664.
3. His coat-tails.

gle nibble. He would carry a fowling-piece[4] on his shoulder, for hours together, trudging through woods and swamps, and up hill and down dale, to shoot a few squirrels or wild pigeons. He would never refuse to assist a neighbor even in the roughest toil, and was a foremost man at all country frolics for husking Indian corn, or building stone fences. The women of the village, too, used to employ him to run their errands, and to do such little odd jobs as their less obliging husbands would not do for them—in a word, Rip was ready to attend to anybody's business but his own; but as to doing family duty, and keeping his farm in order, he found it impossible.

In fact, he declared it was of no use to work on his farm; it was the most 60
pestilent little piece of ground in the whole country; everything about it went wrong, and would go wrong in spite of him. His fences were continually falling to pieces; his cow would either go astray, or get among the cabbages; weeds were sure to grow quicker in his fields than anywhere else; the rain always made a point of setting in just as he had some outdoor work to do; so that, though his patrimonial estate had dwindled away under his management, acre by acre, until there was little more left than a mere patch of Indian corn and potatoes, yet it was the worst conditioned farm in the neighborhood.

His children, too, were as ragged and wild as if they belonged to nobody. His son Rip, an urchin begotten in his own likeness, promised to inherit the habits, 70
with the old clothes of his father. He was generally seen trooping like a colt at his mother's heels, equipped in a pair of his father's cast-off galligaskins,[5] which he had much ado to hold up with one hand, as a fine lady does her train in bad weather.

Rip Van Winkle, however, was one of those happy mortals, of foolish, well-oiled dispositions, who take the world easy, eat white bread or brown, whichever can be got with least thought or trouble, and would rather starve on a penny than work for a pound. If left to himself, he would have whistled life away, in perfect contentment; but his wife kept continually dinning in his ears about his idleness, his carelessness, and the ruin he was bringing on his family.   80

Morning, noon, and night, her tongue was incessantly going, and everything he said or did was sure to produce a torrent of household eloquence. Rip had but one way of replying to all lectures of the kind, and that, by frequent use, had grown into a habit. He shrugged his shoulders, shook his head, cast up his eyes, but said nothing. This, however, always provoked a fresh volley from his wife, so that he was fain to draw off his forces, and take to the outside of the house—the only side which, in truth, belongs to a henpecked husband.

Rip's sole domestic adherent was his dog Wolf, who was as much henpecked as his master; for Dame Van Winkle regarded them as companions in idleness, and even looked upon Wolf with an evil eye, as the cause of his master's going so often 90
astray. True it is, in all points of spirit befitting an honorable dog, he was as courageous an animal as ever scoured the woods—but what courage can withstand the ever-during and all-besetting terrors of a woman's tongue? The moment Wolf entered the house, his crest fell, his tail drooped to the ground, or curled between

4. A gun for hunting birds.
5. Baggy stockings or breeches.

his legs, he sneaked about with a gallows air, casting many a sidelong glance at Dame Van Winkle, and at the least flourish of a broomstick or ladle he would fly to the door with yelping precipitation.

Times grew worse and worse with Rip Van Winkle, as years of matrimony rolled on: a tart temper never mellows with age, and a sharp tongue is the only edge tool that grows keener with constant use. For a long while he used to console 100 himself, when driven from home, by frequenting a kind of perpetual club of the sages, philosophers, and other idle personages of the village, which held its sessions on a bench before a small inn, designated by a rubicund portrait of his Majesty George the Third. Here they used to sit in the shade, of a long lazy summer's day, talking listlessly over village gossip, or telling endless sleepy stories about nothing. But it would have been worth any statesman's money to have heard the profound discussions which sometimes took place, when by chance an old newspaper fell into their hands from some passing traveler. How solemnly they would listen to the contents, as drawled out by Derrick Van Bummel, the schoolmaster, a dapper learned little man, who was not to be daunted by the most gigan- 110 tic word in the dictionary; and how sagely they would deliberate upon public events some months after they had taken place.

The opinions of this junto were completely controlled by Nicholas Vedder, a patriarch of the village, and landlord of the inn, at the door of which he took his seat from morning till night, just moving sufficiently to avoid the sun, and keep in the shade of a large tree; so that the neighbors could tell the hour by his movements as accurately as by a sun-dial. It is true, he was rarely heard to speak, but smoked his pipe incessantly. His adherents, however (for every great man has his adherents), perfectly understood him, and knew how to gather his opinions. When anything that was read or related displeased him, he was observed to smoke 120 his pipe vehemently, and to send forth short, frequent, and angry puffs; but when pleased, he would inhale the smoke slowly and tranquilly, and emit it in light and placid clouds, and sometimes taking the pipe from his mouth, and letting the fragrant vapor curl about his nose, would gravely nod his head in token of perfect approbation.

From even this stronghold the unlucky Rip was at length routed by his termagant wife, who would suddenly break in upon the tranquillity of the assemblage, and call the members all to naught; nor was that august personage, Nicholas Vedder himself, sacred from the daring tongue of this terrible virago, who charged him outright with encouraging her husband in habits of idleness. 130

Poor Rip was at last reduced almost to despair, and his only alternative to escape from the labor of the farm and the clamor of his wife was to take gun in hand and stroll away into the woods. Here he would sometimes seat himself at the foot of a tree, and share the contents of his wallet[6] with Wolf, with whom he sympathized as a fellow-sufferer in persecution. "Poor Wolf," he would say, "thy mistress leads thee a dog's life of it; but never mind, my lad, while I live thou shalt never want a friend to stand by thee!" Wolf would wag his tail, look wistfully in his master's face, and if dogs can feel pity, I verily believe he reciprocated the sentiment with all his heart.

6. Knapsack.

In a long ramble of the kind, on a fine autumnal day, Rip had unconsciously 140
scrambled to one of the highest parts of the Kaatskill mountains. He was after his
favorite sport of squirrel-shooting, and the still solitudes had echoed and reechoed with the reports of his gun. Panting and fatigued, he threw himself, late in
the afternoon, on a green knoll covered with mountain herbage that crowned the
brow of a precipice. From an opening between the trees, he could overlook all the
lower country for many a mile of rich woodland. He saw at a distance the lordly
Hudson, far, far below him, moving on its silent but majestic course, with the reflection of a purple cloud, or the sail of a lagging bark, here and there sleeping on
its glassy bosom, and at last losing itself in the blue highlands.

On the other side he looked down into a deep mountain glen, wild, lonely, 150
and shagged, the bottom filled with fragments from the impending cliffs, and
scarcely lighted by the reflected rays of the setting sun. For some time Rip lay
musing on this scene; evening was gradually advancing; the mountains began to
throw their long blue shadows over the valleys; he saw that it would be dark long
before he could reach the village; and he heaved a heavy sigh when he thought of
encountering the terrors of Dame Van Winkle.

As he was about to descend he heard a voice from a distance hallooing, "Rip
Van Winkle! Rip Van Winkle!" He looked around, but could see nothing but a
crow winging its solitary flight across the mountain. He thought his fancy must
have deceived him, and turned again to descend, when he heard the same cry ring 160
through the still evening air, "Rip Van Winkle! Rip Van Winkle!"—at the same
time Wolf bristled up his back, and giving a low growl, skulked to his master's
side, looking fearfully down into the glen. Rip now felt a vague apprehension
stealing over him: he looked anxiously in the same direction, and perceived a
strange figure slowly toiling up the rocks, and bending under the weight of something he carried on his back. He was surprised to see any human being in this
lonely and unfrequented place, but supposing it to be some one of the neighborhood in need of his assistance, he hastened down to yield it.

On nearer approach, he was still more surprised at the singularity of the
stranger's appearance. He was a short square built old fellow, with thick bushy 170
hair, and a grizzled beard. His dress was of the antique Dutch fashion—a cloth
jerkin[7] strapped round the waist—several pair of breeches, the outer one of ample
volume, decorated with rows of buttons down the sides, and bunches at the
knees. He bore on his shoulders a stout keg, that seemed full of liquor, and made
signs for Rip to approach and assist him with the load. Though rather shy and dis-
trustful of this new acquaintance, Rip complied with his usual alacrity, and, mutually relieving each other, they clambered up a narrow gully, apparently the dry bed
of a mountain torrent. As they ascended, Rip every now and then heard long
rolling peals, like distant thunder, that seemed to issue out of a deep ravine, or
rather cleft, between lofty rocks, toward which their rugged path conducted. He 180
paused for an instant, but supposing it to be the muttering of one of those transient thunder-showers which often take place in mountain heights, he proceeded.
Passing through the ravine, they came to a hollow, like a small amphitheater, surrounded by perpendicular precipices, over the brinks of which impending trees

7. Vest.

shot their branches, so that you only caught glimpses of the azure sky, and the bright evening cloud. During the whole time, Rip and his companion had labored on in silence; for though the former marveled greatly what could be the object of carrying a keg of liquor up this wild mountain, yet there was something strange and incomprehensible about the unknown that inspired awe, and checked familiarity.

On entering the amphitheater, new objects of wonder presented themselves. On a level spot in the center was a company of odd-looking personages playing at nine-pins. They were dressed in a quaint outlandish fashion: some wore short doublets,[8] others jerkins, with long knives in their belts, and most of them had enormous breeches, of similar style with that of the guide's. Their visages, too, were peculiar: one had a large head, broad face, and small piggish eyes; the face of another seemed to consist entirely of nose, and was surmounted by a white sugar-loaf hat,[9] set off with a little red cock's tail. They all had beards, of various shapes and colors. There was one who seemed to be the commander. He was a stout old gentleman, with a weather-beaten countenance; he wore a laced doublet, broad belt and hanger, high-crowned hat and feather, red stockings, and high-heeled shoes, with roses in them. The whole group reminded Rip of the figures in an old Flemish painting, in the parlor of Dominie Van Schaick, the village parson, and which had been brought over from Holland at the time of the settlement.

What seemed particularly odd to Rip, was, that though these folks were evidently amusing themselves, yet they maintained the gravest faces, the most mysterious silence, and were, withal, the most melancholy party of pleasure he had ever witnessed. Nothing interrupted the stillness of the scene but the noise of the balls, which, whenever they rolled, echoed along the mountains like rumbling peals of thunder.

As Rip and his companion approached them, they suddenly desisted from their play, and stared at him with such a fixed statue-like gaze, and such strange, uncouth, lackluster countenances, that his heart turned within him, and his knees smote together. His companion now emptied the contents of the keg into large flagons, and made signs to him to wait upon the company. He obeyed with fear and trembling; they quaffed the liquor in profound silence, and then returned to their game.

By degrees Rip's awe and apprehension subsided. He even ventured, when no eye was fixed upon him, to taste the beverage, which he found had much of the flavor of excellent Hollands. He was naturally a thirsty soul, and was soon tempted to repeat the draught. One taste provoked another, and he reiterated his visits to the flagon so often that at length his senses were overpowered, his eyes swam in his head, his head gradually declined, and he fell into a deep sleep.

On waking, he found himself on the green knoll from whence he had first seen the old man of the glen. He rubbed his eyes—it was a bright sunny morning. The birds were hopping and twittering among the bushes, and the eagle was wheeling aloft, and breasting the pure mountain breeze. "Surely," thought Rip, "I have not slept here all night." He recalled the occurrences before he fell asleep.

190

200

210

220

8. A tight garment for the upper body.
9. A hat like a sugar loaf; cigar-shaped.

The strange man with the keg of liquor—the mountain ravine—the wild retreat among the rocks—the woe-begone party at nine-pins—the flagon—"Oh! that 230 wicked flagon!" thought Rip—"what excuse shall I make to Dame Van Winkle?"

He looked round for his gun, but in place of the clean, well-oiled fowling-piece, he found an old firelock lying by him, the barrel incrusted with rust, the lock falling off, and the stock worm-eaten. He now suspected that the grave roisterers of the mountain had put a trick upon him, and having dosed him with liquor, had robbed him of his gun. Wolf, too, had disappeared, but he might have strayed away after a squirrel or partridge. He whistled after him, and shouted his name, but all in vain; the echoes repeated his whistle and shout, but no dog was to be seen.

He determined to revisit the scene of the last evening's gambol, and if he met 240 with any of the party, to demand his dog and gun. As he rose to walk, he found himself stiff in the joints, and wanting in his usual activity. "These mountain beds do not agree with me," thought Rip, "and if this frolic should lay me up with a fit of the rheumatism, I shall have a blessed time with Dame Van Winkle." With some difficulty he got down into the glen; he found the gully up which he and his companion had ascended the preceding evening; but to his astonishment a mountain stream was now foaming down it, leaping from rock to rock, and filling the glen with babbling murmurs. He, however, made shift to scramble up its sides, working his toilsome way through thickets of birch, sassafras, and witch-hazel; and sometimes tripped up or entangled by the wild grape-vines that twisted their coils 250 and tendrils from tree to tree, and spread a kind of network in his path.

At length he reached to where the ravine had opened through the cliffs to the amphitheater; but no traces of such opening remained. The rocks presented a high impenetrable wall, over which the torrent came tumbling in a sheet of feathery foam, and fell into a broad deep basin, black from the shadows of the surrounding forest. Here, then, poor Rip was brought to a stand. He again called and whistled after his dog; he was only answered by the cawing of a flock of idle crows, sporting high in air about a dry tree that overhung a sunny precipice; and who, secure in their elevation, seemed to look down and scoff at the poor man's perplexities. What was to be done? The morning was passing away, and Rip felt 260 famished for want of his breakfast. He grieved to give up his dog and gun; he dreaded to meet his wife; but it would not do to starve among the mountains. He shook his head, shouldered the rusty firelock, and, with a heart full of trouble and anxiety, turned his steps homeward.

As he approached the village, he met a number of people, but none whom he knew, which somewhat surprised him, for he had thought himself acquainted with every one in the country round. Their dress, too, was of a different fashion from that to which he was accustomed. They all stared at him with equal marks of surprise, and whenever they cast eyes upon him, invariably stroked their chins. The constant recurrence of this gesture induced Rip, involuntarily, to do the same, 270 when, to his astonishment, he found his beard had grown a foot long.

He had now entered the skirts of the village. A troop of strange children ran at his heels, hooting after him, and pointing at his gray beard. The dogs, too, not one of which he recognized for an old acquaintance, barked at him as he passed. The very village was altered: it was larger and more populous. There were rows of houses which he had never seen before, and those which had been his familiar haunts had disappeared. Strange names were over the doors—strange faces at the windows—everything was strange. His mind now misgave him; he began to doubt whether both he and the world around him were not bewitched. Surely this was his native village, which he had left but a day before. There stood the Kaatskill 280 mountains—there ran the silver Hudson at a distance—there was every hill and dale precisely as it had always been—Rip was sorely perplexed—"That flagon last night," thought he, "has addled my poor head sadly!"

It was with some difficulty that he found the way to his own house, which he approached with silent awe, expecting every moment to hear the shrill voice of Dame Van Winkle. He found the house gone to decay—the roof fallen in, the windows shattered, and the doors off the hinges. A half-starved dog, that looked like Wolf, was skulking about it. Rip called him by name, but the cur snarled, showed his teeth, and passed on. This was an unkind cut indeed.—"My very dog," sighed poor Rip, "has forgotten me!" 290

He entered the house, which, to tell the truth, Dame Van Winkle had always kept in neat order. It was empty, forlorn, and apparently abandoned. This desolateness overcame all his connubial fears—he called loudly for his wife and children—the lonely chambers rang for a moment with his voice, and then all again was silence.

He now hurried forth, and hastened to his old resort, the village inn—but it too was gone. A large rickety wooden building stood in its place, with great gaping windows, some of them broken, and mended with old hats and petticoats, and over the door was painted, "The Union Hotel, by Jonathan Doolittle." Instead of the great tree that used to shelter the quiet little Dutch inn of yore, there now was 300 reared a tall naked pole, with something on the top that looked like a red nightcap, and from it was fluttering a flag, on which was a singular assemblage of stars and stripes—all this was strange and incomprehensible. He recognized on the sign, however, the ruby face of King George, under which he had smoked so many a peaceful pipe, but even this was singularly metamorphosed. The red coat was changed for one of blue and buff, a sword was held in the hand instead of a scepter, the head was decorated with a cocked hat, and underneath was painted in large characters, GENERAL WASHINGTON.

There was, as usual, a crowd of folk about the door, but none that Rip recollected. The very character of the people seemed changed. There was a busy, 310 bustling, disputatious tone about it, instead of the accustomed phlegm and drowsy tranquillity. He looked in vain for the sage Nicholas Vedder, with his broad face, double chin, and fair long pipe, uttering clouds of tobacco smoke, instead of idle speeches; or Van Bummel, the schoolmaster, doling forth the contents of an ancient newspaper. In place of these, a lean, bilious-looking fellow, with his pockets full of handbills, was haranguing vehemently about rights of citizens—election—members of Congress—liberty—Bunker's hill—heroes of seventy-six—and other words, that were a perfect Babylonish jargon to the bewildered Van Winkle.

The appearance of Rip, with his long, grizzled beard, his rusty fowling-piece, 320 his uncouth dress, and the army of women and children that had gathered at his heels, soon attracted the attention of the tavern politicians. They crowded round him, eying him from head to foot, with great curiosity. The orator bustled up to him, and drawing him partly aside, inquired, "on which side he voted?" Rip stared in vacant stupidity. Another short but busy little fellow pulled him by the arm, and rising on tiptoe, inquired in his ear, "whether he was Federal or Democrat." Rip was equally at a loss to comprehend the question; when a knowing, self-important old gentleman, in a sharp cocked hat, made his way through the crowd, putting them to the right and left with his elbows as he passed, and planting himself before Van Winkle, with one arm akimbo, the other resting on his cane, his keen eyes and sharp hat penetrating, as it were, into his very soul, demanded in an austere tone, "what brought him to the election with a gun on his shoulder, and a mob at his heels, and whether he meant to breed a riot in the village?" 330

"Alas! gentlemen," cried Rip, somewhat dismayed, "I am a poor, quiet man, a native of the place, and a loyal subject of the King, God bless him!"

Here a general shout burst from the bystanders—"a Tory! a Tory! a spy! a refugee! hustle him! away with him!"

It was with great difficulty that the self-important man in the cocked hat restored order; and having assumed a tenfold austerity of brow, demanded again of the unknown culprit, what he came there for, and whom he was seeking. The poor man humbly assured him that he meant no harm, but merely came there in search of some of his neighbors, who used to keep about the tavern. 340

"Well—who are they?—name them."

Rip bethought himself a moment, and inquired, "Where's Nicholas Vedder?"

There was a silence for a little while, when an old man replied, in a thin, piping voice, "Nicholas Vedder? why, he is dead and gone these eighteen years! There was a wooden tombstone in the churchyard that used to tell all about him, but that's rotten and gone too."

"Where's Brom Dutcher?"

"Oh, he went off to the army in the beginning of the war; some say he was killed at the storming of Stony-Point—others say he was drowned in the squall, at the foot of Anthony's Nose. I don't know—he never came back again." 350

"Where's Van Bummel, the schoolmaster?"

"He went off to the wars, too; was a great militia general, and is now in Congress."

Rip's heart died away at hearing of these sad changes in his home and friends, and finding himself thus alone in the world. Every answer puzzled him, too, by treating of such enormous lapses of time, and of matters which he could not understand: war—Congress—Stony-Point!—he had no courage to ask after any more friends, but cried out in despair, "Does nobody here know Rip Van Winkle?" 360

"Oh, Rip Van Winkle!" exclaimed two or three. "Oh, to be sure! that's Rip Van Winkle yonder, leaning against the tree."

Rip looked, and beheld a precise counterpart of himself as he went up the mountain; apparently as lazy, and certainly as ragged. The poor fellow was now completely confounded. He doubted his own identity, and whether he was himself or another man. In the midst of his bewilderment, the man in the cocked hat demanded who he was, and what was his name?

"God knows," exclaimed he, at his wit's end; "I'm not myself—I'm somebody else—that's me yonder—no—that's somebody else, got into my shoes—I was my- 370 self last night, but I fell asleep on the mountain, and they've changed my gun, and everything's changed, and I'm changed, and I can't tell what's my name, or who I am!"

The bystanders began now to look at each other, nod, wink significantly, and tap their fingers against their foreheads. There was a whisper, also, about securing the gun, and keeping the old fellow from doing mischief; at the very suggestion of which, the self-important man with the cocked hat retired with some precipitation. At this critical moment a fresh comely woman passed through the throng to get a peep at the gray-bearded man. She had a chubby child in her arms, which, frightened at his looks, began to cry. "Hush, Rip," cried she, "hush, you little fool; 380 the old man won't hurt you." The name of the child, the air of the mother, the tone of her voice, all awakened a train of recollections in his mind.

"What is your name, my good woman?" asked he.

"Judith Gardenier."

"And your father's name?"

"Ah, poor man, his name was Rip Van Winkle; it's twenty years since he went away from home with his gun, and never has been heard of since—his dog came home without him; but whether he shot himself, or was carried away by the Indians, nobody can tell. I was then but a little girl."

Rip had but one question more to ask; but he put it with a faltering voice: 390

"Where's your mother?"

Oh, she too had died but a short time since: she broke a blood-vessel in a fit of passion at a New England peddler.

There was a drop of comfort, at least, in this intelligence. The honest man could contain himself no longer. He caught his daughter and her child in his arms. "I am your father!" cried he—"young Rip Van Winkle once—old Rip Van Winkle now!—Does nobody know poor Rip Van Winkle?"

All stood amazed, until an old woman, tottering out from among the crowd, put her hand to her brow, and peering under it in his face for a moment, exclaimed, "Sure enough! it is Rip Van Winkle—it is himself. Welcome home again, 400 old neighbor. Why, where have you been these twenty long years?"

Rip's story was soon told, for the whole twenty years had been to him but as one night. The neighbors stared when they heard it; some were seen to wink at each other, and put their tongues in their cheeks; and the self-important man in the cocked hat, who, when the alarm was over, had returned to the field, screwed down the corners of his mouth, and shook his head—upon which there was a general shaking of the head throughout the assemblage.

It was determined, however, to take the opinion of old Peter Vanderdonk, who was seen slowly advancing up the road. He was a descendant of the historian of that name, who wrote one of the earliest accounts of the province. Peter was the 410 most ancient inhabitant of the village, and well versed in all the wonderful events and traditions of the neighborhood. He recollected Rip at once, and corroborated his story in the most satisfactory manner. He assured the company that it was a fact, handed down from his ancestor the historian, that the Kaatskill mountains had always been haunted by strange beings. That it was affirmed that the great Hendrick Hudson, the first discoverer of the river and country, kept a kind of vigil there every twenty years, with his crew of the "Half Moon," being permitted in this way to revisit the scenes of his enterprise, and keep a guardian eye upon the river and the great city called by his name. That his father had once seen them in their old Dutch dresses playing at nine-pins in a hollow of the mountain; and that he 420 himself had heard, one summer afternoon, the sound of their balls, like distant peals of thunder.

To make a long story short, the company broke up, and returned to the more important concerns of the election. Rip's daughter took him home to live with her; she had a snug, well-furnished house, and a stout cheery farmer for a husband, whom Rip recollected for one of the urchins that used to climb upon his back. As to Rip's son and heir, who was the ditto of himself, seen leaning against the tree, he was employed to work on the farm; but evinced a hereditary disposition to attend to anything else but his business.

Rip now resumed his old walks and habits; he soon found many of his for- 430 mer cronies, though all rather the worse for the wear and tear of time; and preferred making friends among the rising generation, with whom he soon grew into great favor.

Having nothing to do at home, and being arrived at that happy age when a man can do nothing with impunity, he took his place once more on the bench, at the inn door, and was reverenced as one of the patriarchs of the village, and a chronicle of the old times "before the war." It was some time before he could get into the regular track of gossip, or could be made to comprehend the strange events that had taken place during his torpor. How that there had been a revolutionary war—that the country had thrown off the yoke of old England—and that, 440 instead of being a subject of his Majesty George the Third, he was now a free citizen of the United States. Rip, in fact, was no politician; the changes of states and empires made but little impression on him; but there was one species of despotism under which he had long groaned, and that was—petticoat government. Happily that was at an end; he had got his neck out of the yoke of matrimony, and could go in and out whenever he pleased, without dreading the tyranny of Dame Van Winkle. Whenever her name was mentioned, however, he shook his head, shrugged his shoulders, and cast up his eyes; which might pass either for an expression of resignation to his fate, or joy at his deliverance.

He used to tell his story to every stranger that arrived at Mr. Doolittle's hotel. 450 He was observed, at first, to vary on some points every time he told it, which was doubtless owing to his having so recently awaked. It at last settled down precisely to the tale I have related, and not a man, woman, or child in the neighborhood but knew it by heart. Some always pretended to doubt the reality of it, and insisted that Rip had been out of his head, and that this was one point on which he always remained flighty. The old Dutch inhabitants, however, almost universally gave it full credit. Even to this day, they never hear a thunderstorm of a summer afternoon about the Kaatskill, but they say Hendrick Hudson and his crew are at their game of nine-pins; and it is a common wish of all henpecked husbands in the neighborhood, when life hangs heavy on their hands, that they might have a 460 quieting draught out of Rip Van Winkle's flagon.

NOTE.—The foregoing tale, one would suspect, had been suggested to Mr. Knickerbocker by a little German superstition about the Emperor Frederick *der Rothbart* and the Kypphauser mountain; the subjoined note, however, which he had appended to the tale, shows that it is an absolute fact, narrated with his usual fidelity.

"The story of Rip Van Winkle may seem incredible to many, but nevertheless I give it my full belief, for I know the vicinity of our old Dutch settlements to have been very subject to marvelous events and appearances. Indeed, I have heard many stranger stories than this, in the villages along the Hudson, all of which were   470 too well authenticated to admit of a doubt. I have even talked with Rip Van Winkle myself, who, when last I saw him, was a very venerable old man, and so perfectly rational and consistent on every other point that I think no conscientious person could refuse to take this into the bargain; nay, I have seen a certificate on the subject taken before a country justice, and signed with a cross, in the justice's own handwriting. The story, therefore, is beyond the possibility of doubt."

[1819]

Questions for Writing and Discussion
1. What is Irving's attitude or tone toward Diedrich Knickerbocker? Is it serious, ironic, admiring, satirical?
2. Characterize Rip Van Winkle. In what ways is he admirable, or is he a lazy good-for-nothing?
3. Characterize Dame Van Winkle. Is she presented negatively or sympathetically?
4. Analyze the fantastic and realistic elements in Rip's encounter with the bowlers and in his experiences upon waking up. What details make the experience seem fantastic? What details make it appear "real"?
5. How has life in general changed during Rip's twenty-year sleep? How do America's new values resemble those of Rip's now-deceased wife? Do these contrasting value systems provide the theme of the story?
6. Some critics maintain that the story is about loss of identity. How well do you think this theme works?
7. What clues are there in the story that it is all a "tall tale" concocted by Rip to explain his absence?

❧ NATHANIEL HAWTHORNE
(1804–1864)

My Kinsman, Major Molineux

Nathaniel Hawthorne is one of the major figures of American literature and, with Washington Irving (1783–1859) and Edgar Allan Poe (1809–1849), among the important early practitioners of the short story. Perhaps more than any other early author, he imbued the form with moral seriousness.

Born in Salem, Massachusetts, of Puritan stock, Hawthorne early developed a habit of solitude with nature and books, particularly the English classics. At Bowdoin College, he met fellow students Henry Wadsworth Longfellow (1807–1882) and a future president, Franklin Pierce.

His first publication was *Fanshawe* (1828), a gothic romance printed at his own expense. There followed a long, secret apprenticeship, during which he published anonymously or under a pseudonym. Success came with *Twice-Told Tales* (1837), a collection of stories and sketches, many of which had previously appeared in magazines and gift-books. He married Sophia Peabody in 1842. Since supporting a wife and children on an author's income was impossible, he worked in government customs offices to augment what he could earn by writing. His most famous novel, *The Scarlet Letter* (1850), began as a short story, but his publisher convinced him to expand it, and Hawthorne thereafter published few short pieces.

Hawthorne is classed with the American Romantics. Like many of them, he was suspicious of science and rationalism, but he was opposed to Transcendentalism and the idea of man's innate goodness. Hawthorne's subject was America's past, specifically the Puritan consciousness. He was a meticulous observer, but his realistic tendencies are tempered by a fondness for allegory and a deep moral sense. Frederick Lewis Pattee has summed up his contribution to the short story in this way: "he turned it from its German romantic extravagances and frivolity and horrors into sane and moral channels; he made of it the study of a single intense situation . . . and he made it respectable even in New England. . . ."

A FTER THE KINGS of Great Britain had assumed the right of appointing the colonial governors, the measures of the latter seldom met with the ready and general approbation which had been paid to those of their predecessors, under the original charters. The people looked with most jealous scrutiny to the exercise of power which did not emanate from themselves, and they usually rewarded their rulers with slender gratitude for the compliances by which, in softening their instructions from beyond the sea, they had incurred the reprehension of those who gave them. The annals of Massachusetts Bay will inform us, that of six governors in the space of about forty years from the surrender of the old charter, under James II., two were imprisoned by a popular insurrection; a third, as Hutchinson inclines to believe,[1] was driven from the province by the whizzing of a musket-ball; a fourth, in the opinion of the same historian, was hastened to his grave by continual bickerings with the House of Representatives; and the remaining two, as well as their successors, till the Revolution, were favored with few and brief intervals of peaceful sway. The inferior members of the court party, in times of high political excitement, led scarcely a more desirable life. These remarks may serve as a

10

1. Thomas Hutchinson, author of a history of Massachusetts.

preface to the following adventures, which chanced upon a summer night, not far
from a hundred years ago.[2] The reader, in order to avoid a long and dry detail of
colonial affairs, is requested to dispense with an account of the train of circumstances that had caused much temporary inflammation of the popular mind. 20

It was near nine o'clock of a moonlight evening, when a boat crossed the
ferry with a single passenger, who had obtained his conveyance at that unusual
hour by the promise of an extra fare. While he stood on the landing-place, searching in either pocket for the means of fulfilling his agreement, the ferryman lifted a
lantern, by the aid of which, and the newly risen moon, he took a very accurate
survey of the stranger's figure. He was a youth of barely eighteen years, evidently
country-bred, and now, as it should seem, upon his first visit to town. He was clad
in a coarse gray coat, well worn, but in excellent repair; his under garments[3] were
durably constructed of leather, and fitted tight to a pair of serviceable and well-
shaped limbs; his stockings of blue yarn were the incontrovertible work of a 30
mother or a sister; and on his head was a three-cornered hat, which in its better
days had perhaps sheltered the graver brow of the lad's father. Under his left arm
was a heavy cudgel formed of an oak sapling, and retaining a part of the hardened
root; and his equipment was completed by a wallet, not so abundantly stocked as
to incommode the vigorous shoulders on which it hung. Brown, curly hair, well-
shaped features, and bright, cheerful eyes were nature's gifts, and worth all that art
could have done for his adornment.

The youth, one of whose names was Robin, finally drew from his pocket the
half of a little province bill of five shillings, which, in the depreciation in that sort
of currency, did but satisfy the ferryman's demand, with the surplus of a sexangu- 40
lar piece of parchment, valued at three pence. He then walked forward into the
town, with as light a step as if his day's journey had not already exceeded thirty
miles, and with as eager an eye as if he were entering London city, instead of the
little metropolis of a New England colony. Before Robin had proceeded far, however, it occurred to him that he knew not whither to direct his steps; so he paused,
and looked up and down the narrow street, scrutinizing the small and mean
wooden buildings that were scattered on either side.

"This low hovel cannot be my kinsman's dwelling," thought he, "nor yonder
house, where the moonlight enters at the broken casement; and truly I see none
hereabouts that might be worthy of him. It would have been wise to inquire my 50
way of the ferryman, and doubtless he would have gone with me, and earned a
shilling from the Major for his pains. But the next man I meet will do as well."

He resumed his walk, and was glad to perceive that the street now became
wider, and the houses more respectable in their appearance. He soon discerned a
figure moving on moderately in advance, and hastened his steps to overtake it. As
Robin drew nigh, he saw that the passenger was a man in years, with a full periwig
of gray hair, a wide-skirted coat of dark cloth, and silk stockings rolled above his
knees. He carried a long and polished cane, which he struck down perpendicu-
larly before him at every step; and at regular intervals he uttered two successive
hems, of a peculiarly solemn and sepulchral intonation. Having made these obser- 60

2. i.e., approximately 1732.
3. The clothes under his coat; outergarments.

vations, Robin laid hold of the skirt of the old man's coat, just when the light from the open door and windows of a barber's shop fell upon both their figures.

"Good evening to you, honored sir," said he, making a low bow, and still retaining his hold of the skirt. "I pray you tell me whereabouts is the dwelling of my kinsman, Major Molineux."

The youth's question was uttered very loudly; and one of the barbers, whose razor was descending on a well-soaped chin, and another who was dressing a Ramillies wig,[4] left their occupations, and came to the door. The citizen, in the mean time, turned a long-favored countenance upon Robin, and answered him in a tone of excessive anger and annoyance. His two sepulchral hems, however, broke into the very centre of his rebuke, with most singular effect, like a thought of the cold grave obtruding among wrathful passions.

"Let go my garment, fellow! I tell you, I know not the man you speak of. What! I have authority, I have—hem, hem—authority; and if this be the respect you show for your betters, your feet shall be brought acquainted with the stocks by daylight, tomorrow morning!"

Robin released the old man's skirt, and hastened away, pursued by an ill-mannered roar of laughter from the barber's shop. He was at first considerably surprised by the result of his question, but, being a shrewd youth, soon thought himself able to account for the mystery.

"This is some country representative," was his conclusion, "who has never seen the inside of my kinsman's door, and lacks the breeding to answer a stranger civilly. The man is old, or verily—I might be tempted to turn back and smite him on the nose. Ah, Robin, Robin! even the barber's boys laugh at you for choosing such a guide! You will be wiser in time, friend Robin."

He now became entangled in a succession of crooked and narrow streets, which crossed each other, and meandered at no great distance from the waterside. The smell of tar was obvious to his nostrils, the masts of vessels pierced the moonlight above the tops of the buildings, and the numerous signs, which Robin paused to read, informed him that he was near the centre of business. But the streets were empty, the shops were closed, and lights were visible only in the second stories of a few dwelling-houses. At length, on the corner of a narrow lane, through which he was passing, he beheld the broad countenance of a British hero swinging before the door of an inn, whence proceeded the voices of many guests. The casement of one of the lower windows was thrown back, and a very thin curtain permitted Robin to distinguish a party at supper, round a well-furnished table. The fragrance of the good cheer steamed forth into the outer air, and the youth could not fail to recollect that the last remnant of his travelling stock of provision had yielded to his morning appetite, and that noon had found and left him dinnerless.

"Oh, that a parchment three-penny might give me a right to sit down at yonder table!" said Robin, with a sigh. "But the Major will make me welcome to the best of his victuals; so I will even step boldly in, and inquire my way to his dwelling."

He entered the tavern, and was guided by the murmur of voices and the

4. A wig with a long, braided tail.

fumes of tobacco to the public-room. It was a long and low apartment, with oaken walls, grown dark in the continual smoke, and a floor which was thickly sanded, but of no immaculate purity. A number of persons—the larger part of whom appeared to be mariners, or in some way connected with the sea—occupied the wooden benches, or leather-bottomed chairs, conversing on various matters, and occasionally lending their attention to some topic of general interest. Three or four little groups were draining as many bowls of punch, which the West India trade had long since made a familiar drink in the colony. Others, who had the appearance of men who lived by regular and laborious handicraft, preferred the insulated bliss of an unshared potation, and became more taciturn under its influence. Nearly all, in short, evinced a predilection for the Good Creature in some of its various shapes, for this is a vice to which, as Fast Day[5] sermons of a hundred years ago will testify, we have a long hereditary claim. The only guests to whom Robin's sympathies inclined him were two or three sheepish countrymen, who were using the inn somewhat after the fashion of a Turkish caravansary;[6] they had gotten themselves into the darkest corner of the room, and heedless of the Nicotian[7] atmosphere, were supping on the bread of their own ovens, and the bacon cured in their own chimney-smoke. But though Robin felt a sort of brotherhood with these strangers, his eyes were attracted from them to a person who stood near the door, holding whispered conversation with a group of ill-dressed associates. His features were separately striking almost to grotesqueness, and the whole face left a deep impression on the memory. The forehead bulged out into a double prominence, with a vale between; the nose came boldly forth in an irregular curve, and its bridge was of more than a finger's breadth; the eyebrows were deep and shaggy, and the eyes glowed beneath them like fire in a cave.

While Robin deliberated of whom to inquire respecting his kinsman's dwelling, he was accosted by the innkeeper, a little man in a stained white apron, who had come to pay his professional welcome to the stranger. Being in the second generation from a French Protestant,[8] he seemed to have inherited the courtesy of his parent nation; but no variety of circumstances was ever known to change his voice from the one shrill note in which he now addressed Robin.

"From the country, I presume, sir?" said he, with a profound bow. "Beg leave to congratulate you on your arrival, and trust you intend a long stay with us. Fine town here, sir, beautiful buildings, and much that may interest a stranger. May I hope for the honor of your commands in respect to supper?"

"The man sees a family likeness! the rogue has guessed that I am related to the Major!" thought Robin, who had hitherto experienced little superfluous civility. All eyes were now turned on the country lad, standing at the door, in his worn three-cornered hat, gray coat, leather breeches, and blue yarn stockings, leaning on an oaken cudgel, and bearing a wallet on his back.

Robin replied to the courteous innkeeper, with such an assumption of confidence as befitted the Major's relative. "My honest friend," he said, "I shall make it a point to patronize your house on some occasion, when"—here he could not help

5. A day of fasting and prayer observed throughout New England.
6. An unfurnished inn or courtyard where eastern caravans would stop for the night.
7. Tobacco smoke.
8. A descendant of French Huguenots who left France to escape persecution in the late seventeenth century.

lowering his voice—"when I may have more than a parchment three-pence in my pocket. My present business," continued he, speaking with lofty confidence, "is 150 merely to inquire my way to the dwelling of my kinsman, Major Molineux."

There was a sudden and general movement in the room, which Robin interpreted as expressing the eagerness of each individual to become his guide. But the innkeeper turned his eyes to a written paper on the wall, which he read, or seemed to read, with occasional recurrences to the young man's figure.

"What have we here?" said he, breaking his speech into little dry fragments. "'Left the house of the subscriber, bounden servant,[9] Hezekiah Mudge,—had on, when he went away, gray coat, leather breeches, master's third-best hat. One pound currency reward to whosoever shall lodge him in any jail of the province.' Better trudge, boy; better trudge!"   160

Robin had begun to draw his hand towards the lighter end of the oak cudgel, but a strange hostility in every countenance induced him to relinquish his purpose of breaking the courteous innkeeper's head. As he turned to leave the room, he encountered a sneering glance from the bold-featured personage whom he had before noticed; and no sooner was he beyond the door, than he heard a general laugh, in which the innkeeper's voice might be distinguished, like the dropping of small stones into a kettle.

"Now, is it not strange," thought Robin, with his usual shrewdness,—"is it not strange that the confession of an empty pocket should outweigh the name of my kinsman, Major Molineux? Oh, if I had one of those grinning rascals in the 170 woods, where I and my oak sapling grew up together, I would teach him that my arm is heavy though my purse be light!"

On turning the corner of the narrow lane, Robin found himself in a spacious street, with an unbroken line of lofty houses on each side, and a steepled building at the upper end, whence the ringing of a bell announced the hour of nine. The light of the moon, and the lamps from the numerous shop-windows, discovered people promenading on the pavement, and amongst them Robin hoped to recognize his hitherto inscrutable relative. The result of his former inquiries made him unwilling to hazard another, in a scene of such publicity, and he determined to walk slowly and silently up the street, thrusting his face close to that of every eld- 180 erly gentleman, in search of the Major's lineaments. In his progress, Robin encountered many gay and gallant figures. Embroidered garments of showy colors, enormous periwigs, gold-laced hats, and silver-hilted swords glided past him and dazzled his optics. Travelled youths, imitators of the European fine gentlemen of the period, trod jauntily along, half dancing to the fashionable tunes which they hummed, and making poor Robin ashamed of his quiet and natural gait. At length, after many pauses to examine the gorgeous display of goods in the shop-windows, and after suffering some rebukes for the impertinence of his scrutiny into people's faces, the Major's kinsman found himself near the steepled building, still unsuccessful in his search. As yet, however, he had seen only one side of the 190 thronged street; so Robin crossed, and continued the same sort of inquisition down the opposite pavement, with stronger hopes than the philosopher seeking an honest man, but with no better fortune. He had arrived about midway towards

9. The innkeeper implies that Robin is an indentured servant who has illegally left his master.

the lower end, from which his course began, when he overheard the approach of some one who struck down a cane on the flag-stones at every step, uttering, at regular intervals, two sepulchral hems.

"Mercy on us!" quoth Robin, recognizing the sound.

Turning a corner, which chanced to be close at his right hand, he hastened to pursue his researches in some other part of the town. His patience now was wearing low, and he seemed to feel more fatigue from his rambles since he crossed the ferry, than from his journey of several days on the other side. Hunger also pleaded loudly within him, and Robin began to balance the propriety of demanding, violently, and with lifted cudgel, the necessary guidance from the first solitary passenger whom he should meet. While a resolution to this effect was gaining strength, he entered a street of mean appearance, on either side of which a row of ill-built houses was straggling towards the harbor. The moonlight fell upon no passenger along the whole extent, but in the third domicile which Robin passed there was a half-opened door, and his keen glance detected a woman's garment within.

"My luck may be better here," said he to himself.

Accordingly, he approached the door, and beheld it shut closer as he did so; yet an open space remained, sufficing for the fair occupant to observe the stranger, without a corresponding display on her part. All that Robin could discern was a strip of scarlet petticoat, and the occasional sparkle of an eye, as if the moonbeams were trembling on some bright thing.

"Pretty mistress," for I may call her so with a good conscience, thought the shrewd youth, since I know nothing to the contrary,—"my sweet pretty mistress, will you be kind enough to tell me whereabouts I must seek the dwelling of my kinsman, Major Molineux?"

Robin's voice was plaintive and winning, and the female, seeing nothing to be shunned in the handsome country youth, thrust open the door, and came forth into the moonlight. She was a dainty little figure, with a white neck, round arms, and a slender waist, at the extremity of which her scarlet petticoat jutted out over a hoop, as if she were standing in a balloon. Moreover, her face was oval and pretty, her hair dark beneath the little cap, and her bright eyes possessed a sly freedom, which triumphed over those of Robin.

"Major Molineux dwells here," said this fair woman.

Now, her voice was the sweetest Robin had heard that night, the airy counterpart of a stream of melted silver; yet he could not help doubting whether that sweet voice spoke Gospel truth. He looked up and down the mean street, and then surveyed the house before which they stood. It was a small, dark edifice of two stories, the second of which projected over the lower floor, and the front apartment had the aspect of a shop for petty commodities.

"Now, truly, I am in luck," replied Robin, cunningly, "and so indeed is my kinsman, the Major, in having so pretty a housekeeper. But I prithee trouble him to step to the door; I will deliver him a message from his friends in the country, and then go back to my lodgings at the inn."

"Nay, the Major has been abed this hour or more," said the lady of the scarlet petticoat; "and it would be to little purpose to disturb him to-night, seeing his evening draught was of the strongest. But he is a kind-hearted man, and it would be as much as my life's worth to let a kinsman of his turn away from the door. You are the good old gentleman's very picture, and I could swear that was his rainy-weather hat. Also he has garments very much resembling those leather small-clothes. But come in, I pray, for I bid you hearty welcome in his name."

So saying, the fair and hospitable dame took our hero by the hand; and the touch was light, and the force was gentleness, and though Robin read in her eyes what he did not hear in her words, yet the slender-waisted woman in the scarlet petticoat proved stronger than the athletic country youth. She had drawn his half-willing footsteps nearly to the threshold, when the opening of a door in the neighborhood startled the Major's housekeeper, and, leaving the Major's kinsman, she 250 vanished speedily into her own domicile. A heavy yawn preceded the appearance of a man, who, like the Moonshine of Pyramus and Thisbe, carried a lantern,[10] needlessly aiding his sister luminary in the heavens. As he walked sleepily up the street, he turned his broad, dull face on Robin, and displayed a long staff, spiked at the end.

"Home, vagabond, home!" said the watchman, in accents that seemed to fall asleep as soon as they were uttered. "Home, or we'll set you in the stocks by peep of day!"

"This is the second hint of the kind," thought Robin. "I wish they would end my difficulties, by setting me there tonight."   260

Nevertheless, the youth felt an instinctive antipathy towards the guardian of midnight order, which at first prevented him from asking his usual question. But just when the man was about to vanish behind the corner, Robin resolved not to lose the opportunity, and shouted lustily after him,—

"I say, friend! will you guide me to the house of my kinsman, Major Molineux?"

The watchman made no reply, but turned the corner and was gone; yet Robin seemed to hear the sound of drowsy laughter stealing along the solitary street. At that moment, also, a pleasant titter saluted him from the open window above his head; he looked up, and caught the sparkle of a saucy eye; a round arm 270 beckoned to him, and next he heard light footsteps descending the staircase within. But Robin, being of the household of a New England clergyman, was a good youth, as well as a shrewd one; so he resisted temptation, and fled away.

He now roamed desperately, and at random, through the town, almost ready to believe that a spell was on him, like that by which a wizard of his country had once kept three pursuers wandering, a whole winter night, within twenty paces of the cottage which they sought. The streets lay before him, strange and desolate, and the lights were extinguished in almost every house. Twice, however, little parties of men, among whom Robin distinguished individuals in outlandish attire, came hurrying along; but, though on both occasions they paused to address him, 280 such intercourse did not at all enlighten his perplexity. They did but utter a few words in some language of which Robin knew nothing, and perceiving his inability to answer, bestowed a curse upon him in plain English and hastened away. Finally, the lad determined to knock at the door of every mansion that might ap-

10. In Shakespeare's *A Midsummer Night's Dream*, simple craftsmen perform the play, "Pyramus and Thisbe," in which one of the characters portrays the moon by carrying a lantern.

pear worthy to be occupied by his kinsman, trusting that perseverance would overcome the fatality that had hitherto thwarted him. Firm in this resolve, he was passing beneath the walls of a church, which formed the corner of two streets, when, as he turned into the shade of its steeple, he encountered a bulky stranger, muffled in a cloak. The man was proceeding with the speed of earnest business, but Robin planted himself full before him, holding the oak cudgel with both 290 hands across his body as a bar to further passage.

"Halt, honest man, and answer me a question," said he, very resolutely. "Tell me, this instant, whereabouts is the dwelling of my kinsman, Major Molineux!"

"Keep your tongue between your teeth, fool, and let me pass!" said a deep, gruff voice, which Robin partly remembered. "Let me pass, I say, or I'll strike you to the earth!"

"No, no, neighbor!" cried Robin, flourishing his cudgel, and then thrusting its larger end close to the man's muffled face. "No, no, I'm not the fool you take me for, nor do you pass till I have an answer to my question. Whereabouts is the dwelling of my kinsman, Major Molineux?" 300

The stranger, instead of attempting to force his passage, stepped back into the moonlight, unmuffled his face, and stared full into that of Robin.

"Watch here an hour, and Major Molineux will pass by," said he.

Robin gazed with dismay and astonishment on the unprecedented physiognomy of the speaker. The forehead with its double prominence, the broad hooked nose, the shaggy eyebrows, and fiery eyes were those which he had noticed at the inn, but the man's complexion had undergone a singular, or, more properly, a twofold change. One side of the face blazed an intense red, while the other was black as midnight, the division line being in the broad bridge of the nose; and a mouth which seemed to extend from ear to ear was black or red, in contrast to the 310 color of the cheek. The effect was as if two individual devils, a fiend of fire and a fiend of darkness, had united themselves to form this infernal visage. The stranger grinned in Robin's face, muffled his party-colored features, and was out of sight in a moment.

"Strange things we travellers see!" ejaculated Robin.

He seated himself, however, upon the steps of the church-door, resolving to wait the appointed time for his kinsman. A few moments were consumed in philosophical speculations upon the species of man who had just left him; but having settled this point shrewdly, rationally, and satisfactorily, he was compelled to look elsewhere for his amusement. And first he threw his eyes along the street. It was of 320 more respectable appearance than most of those into which he had wandered; and the moon, creating, like the imaginative power, a beautiful strangeness in familiar objects, gave something of romance to a scene that might not have possessed it in the light of day. The irregular and often quaint architecture of the houses, some of whose roofs were broken into numerous little peaks, while others ascended, steep and narrow, into a single point, and others again were square; the pure snow-white of some of their complexions, the aged darkness of others, and the thousand sparklings, reflected from bright substances in the walls of many; these matters engaged Robin's attention for a while, and then began to grow wearisome. Next he endeavored to define the forms of distant objects, starting away, with almost 330 ghostly indistinctness, just as his eye appeared to grasp them; and finally he took a minute survey of an edifice which stood on the opposite side of the street, directly in front of the church-door, where he was stationed. It was a large, square mansion, distinguished from its neighbors by a balcony, which rested on tall pillars, and by an elaborate Gothic window, communicating therewith.

"Perhaps this is the very house I have been seeking," thought Robin.

Then he strove to speed away the time, by listening to a murmur which swept continually along the street, yet was scarcely audible, except to an unaccustomed ear like his; it was a low, dull, dreamy sound, compounded of many noises, each of which was at too great a distance to be separately heard. Robin marvelled 340 at this snore of a sleeping town, and marvelled more whenever its continuity was broken by now and then a distant shout, apparently loud where it originated. But altogether it was a sleep-inspiring sound, and, to shake off its drowsy influence, Robin arose, and climbed a window-frame, that he might view the interior of the church. There the moonbeams came trembling in, and fell down upon the deserted pews, and extended along the quiet aisles. A fainter yet more awful radiance was hovering around the pulpit, and one solitary ray had dared to rest upon the open page of the great Bible. Had nature, in that deep hour, become a worshipper in the house which man had builded? Or was that heavenly light the visible sanctity of the place,—visible because no earthly and impure feet were within the 350 walls? The scene made Robin's heart shiver with a sensation of loneliness stronger than he had ever felt in the remotest depths of his native woods; so he turned away and sat down again before the door. There were graves around the church, and now an uneasy thought obtruded into Robin's breast. What if the object of his search, which had been so often and so strangely thwarted, were all the time mouldering in his shroud? What if his kinsman should glide through yonder gate, and nod and smile to him in dimly passing by?

"Oh that any breathing thing were here with me!" said Robin.

Recalling his thoughts from this uncomfortable track, he sent them over forest, hill, and stream, and attempted to imagine how that evening of ambiguity and 360 weariness had been spent by his father's household. He pictured them assembled at the door, beneath the tree, the great old tree, which had been spared for its huge twisted trunk and venerable shade, when a thousand leafy brethren fell. There, at the going down of the summer sun, it was his father's custom to perform domestic worship, that the neighbors might come and join with him like brothers of the family, and that the wayfaring man might pause to drink at that fountain, and keep his heart pure by freshening the memory of home. Robin distinguished the seat of every individual of the little audience; he saw the good man in the midst, holding the Scriptures in the golden light that fell from the western clouds; he beheld him close the book and all rise up to pray. He heard the old thanksgiv- 370 ings for daily mercies, the old supplications for their continuance, to which he had so often listened in weariness, but which were now among his dear remembrances. He perceived the slight inequality of his father's voice when he came to speak of the absent one; he noted how his mother turned her face to the broad and knotted trunk; how his elder brother scorned, because the beard was rough upon his upper lip, to permit his features to be moved; how the younger sister drew down a low hanging branch before her eyes; and how the little one of all, whose sports had hitherto broken the decorum of the scene, understood the prayer for her playmate, and burst into clamorous grief. Then he saw them go in at the door; and when Robin would have entered also, the latch tinkled into its place, and he was excluded from his home. 380

"Am I here, or there?" cried Robin, starting; for all at once, when his thoughts had become visible and audible in a dream, the long, wide, solitary street shone out before him.

He aroused himself, and endeavored to fix his attention steadily upon the large edifice which he had surveyed before. But still his mind kept vibrating between fancy and reality; by turns, the pillars of the balcony lengthened into the tall, bare stems of pines, dwindled down to human figures, settled again into their true shape and size, and then commenced a new succession of changes. For a single moment, when he deemed himself awake, he could have sworn that a visage— 390 one which he seemed to remember, yet could not absolutely name as his kinsman's—was looking towards him from the Gothic window. A deeper sleep wrestled with and nearly overcame him, but fled at the sound of footsteps along the opposite pavement. Robin rubbed his eyes, discerned a man passing at the foot of the balcony, and addressed him in a loud, peevish, and lamentable cry.

"Hallo, friend! must I wait here all night for my kinsman, Major Molineux?"

The sleeping echoes awoke, and answered the voice; and the passenger, barely able to discern a figure sitting in the oblique shade of the steeple, traversed the street to obtain a nearer view. He was himself a gentleman in his prime, of open, intelligent, cheerful, and altogether prepossessing countenance. Perceiving a 400 country youth, apparently homeless and without friends, he accosted him in a tone of real kindness, which had become strange to Robin's ears.

"Well, my good lad, why are you sitting here?" inquired he. "Can I be of service to you in any way?"

"I am afraid not, sir," replied Robin, despondingly; "yet I shall take it kindly, if you'll answer me a single question. I've been searching, half the night, for one Major Molineux; now, sir, is there really such a person in these parts, or am I dreaming?"

"Major Molineux! The name is not altogether strange to me," said the gentleman, smiling. "Have you any objection to telling me the nature of your business 410 with him?"

Then Robin briefly related that his father was a clergyman, settled on a small salary, at a long distance back in the country, and that he and Major Molineux were brothers' children. The Major, having inherited riches, and acquired civil and military rank, had visited his cousin, in great pomp, a year or two before; had manifested much interest in Robin and an elder brother, and, being childless himself, had thrown out hints respecting the future establishment of one of them in life. The elder brother was destined to succeed to the farm which his father cultivated in the interval of sacred duties; it was therefore determined that Robin should profit by his kinsman's generous intentions, especially as he seemed to be 420 rather the favorite, and was thought to possess other necessary endowments.

"For I have the name of being a shrewd youth," observed Robin, in this part of his story.

"I doubt not you deserve it," replied his new friend, good-naturedly; "but pray proceed."

"Well, sir, being nearly eighteen years old, and well grown, as you see," continued Robin, drawing himself up to his full height, "I thought it high time to begin the world. So my mother and sister put me in handsome trim, and my father gave me half the remnant of his last year's salary, and five days ago I started for this place, to pay the Major a visit. But, would you believe it, sir! I crossed the   430 ferry a little after dark, and, have yet found nobody that would show me the way to his dwelling; only, an hour or two since, I was told to wait here, and Major Molineux would pass by."

"Can you describe the man who told you this?" inquired the gentleman.

"Oh, he was a very ill-favored fellow, sir," replied Robin, "with two great bumps on his forehead, a hook nose, fiery eyes; and, what struck me as the strangest, his face was of two different colors. Do you happen to know such a man, sir?"

"Not intimately," answered the stranger, "but I chanced to meet him a little time previous to your stopping me. I believe you may trust his word, and that the   440 Major will very shortly pass through this street. In the mean time, as I have a singular curiosity to witness your meeting, I will sit down here upon the steps and bear you company."

He seated himself accordingly, and soon engaged his companion in animated discourse. It was but of brief continuance, however, for a noise of shouting, which had long been remotely audible, drew so much nearer that Robin inquired its cause.

"What may be the meaning of this uproar!" asked he. "Truly, if your town be always as noisy, I shall find little sleep while I am an inhabitant."

"Why, indeed, friend Robin, there do appear to be three or four riotous fel-   450 lows abroad to-night," replied the gentleman. "You must not expect all the stillness of your native woods here in our streets. But the watch will shortly be at the heels of these lads and"—

"Ay, and set them in the stocks by peep of day," interrupted Robin, recollecting his own encounter with the drowsy lantern-bearer. "But, dear sir, if I may trust my ears, an army of watchmen would never make head against such a multitude of rioters. There were at least a thousand voices went up to make that one shout."

"May not a man have several voices, Robin, as well as two complexions?" said his friend.

"Perhaps a man may; but Heaven forbid that a woman should!" responded   460 the shrewd youth, thinking of the seductive tones of the Major's housekeeper.

The sounds of a trumpet in some neighboring street now became so evident and continual, that Robin's curiosity was strongly excited. In addition to the shouts, he heard frequent bursts from many instruments of discord, and a wild and confused laughter filled up the intervals. Robin rose from the steps, and looked wistfully towards a point whither people seemed to be hastening.

"Surely some prodigious merry-making is going on," exclaimed he. "I have laughed very little since I left home, sir, and should be sorry to lose an opportunity. Shall we step round the corner by that darkish house, and take our share of the fun?"   470

"Sit down again, sit down, good Robin," replied the gentleman, laying his hand on the skirt of the gray coat. "You forget that we must wait here for your kinsman; and there is reason to believe that he will pass by, in the course of a very few moments."

The near approach of the uproar had now disturbed the neighborhood; windows flew open on all sides; and many heads, in the attire of the pillow, and confused by sleep suddenly broken, were protruded to the gaze of whoever had leisure to observe them. Eager voices hailed each other from house to house, all demanding the explanation, which not a soul could give. Half-dressed men hurried towards the unknown commotion, stumbling as they went over the stone 480 steps that thrust themselves into the narrow foot-walk. The shouts, the laughter, and the tuneless bray, the antipodes of music, came onwards with increasing din, till scattered individuals, and then denser bodies, began to appear round a corner at the distance of a hundred yards.

"Will you recognize your kinsman, if he passes in this crowd?" inquired the gentleman.

"Indeed, I can't warrant it, sir; but I'll take my stand here, and keep a bright lookout," answered Robin, descending to the outer edge of the pavement.

A mighty stream of people now emptied into the street, and came rolling slowly towards the church. A single horseman wheeled the corner in the midst of 490 them, and close behind him came a band of fearful wind-instruments, sending forth a fresher discord now that no intervening buildings kept it from the ear. Then a redder light disturbed the moonbeams, and a dense multitude of torches shone along the street, concealing, by their glare, whatever object they illuminated. The single horseman, clad in a military dress, and bearing a drawn sword, rode onward as the leader, and, by his fierce and variegated countenance, appeared like war personified; the red of one cheek was an emblem of fire and sword; the blackness of the other betokened the mourning that attends them. In his train were wild figures in the Indian dress, and many fantastic shapes without a model, giving the whole march a visionary air, as if a dream had broken forth 500 from some feverish brain, and were sweeping visibly through the midnight streets. A mass of people, inactive, except as applauding spectators, hemmed the procession in; and several women ran along the sidewalk, piercing the confusion of heavier sounds with their shrill voices of mirth or terror.

"The double-faced fellow has his eye upon me," muttered Robin, with an indefinite but an uncomfortable idea that he was himself to bear a part in the pageantry.

The leader turned himself in the saddle, and fixed his glance full upon the country youth, as the steed went slowly by. When Robin had freed his eyes from those fiery ones, the musicians were passing before him, and the torches were 510 close at hand; but the unsteady brightness of the latter formed a veil which he could not penetrate. The rattling of wheels over the stones sometimes found its way to his ear, and confused traces of a human form appeared at intervals, and then melted into the vivid light. A moment more, and the leader thundered a command to halt: the trumpets vomited a horrid breath, and then held their peace; the shouts and laughter of the people died away, and there remained only a universal hum, allied to silence. Right before Robin's eyes was an uncovered cart.

There the torches blazed the brightest, there the moon shone out like day, and there, in tar-and-feathery dignity, sat his kinsman, Major Molineux!

He was an elderly man, of large and majestic person, and strong, square fea- 520 tures, betokening a steady soul; but steady as it was, his enemies had found means to shake it. His face was pale as death, and far more ghastly; the broad forehead was contracted in his agony, so that his eyebrows formed one grizzled line; his eyes were red and wild, and the foam hung white upon his quivering lip. His whole frame was agitated by a quick and continual tremor, which his pride strove to quell, even in those circumstances of overwhelming humiliation. But perhaps the bitterest pang of all was when his eyes met those of Robin; for he evidently knew him on the instant, as the youth stood witnessing the foul disgrace of a head grown gray in honor. They stared at each other in silence, and Robin's knees shook, and his hair bristled, with a mixture of pity and terror. Soon, however, a 530 bewildering excitement began to seize upon his mind; the preceding adventures of the night, the unexpected appearance of the crowd, the torches, the confused din and the hush that followed, the spectre of his kinsman reviled by that great multi-tude,—all this, and, more than all, a perception of tremendous ridicule in the whole scene, affected him with a sort of mental inebriety. At that moment a voice of sluggish merriment saluted Robin's ears; he turned instinctively, and just behind the corner of the church stood the lantern-bearer, rubbing his eyes, and drowsily enjoying the lad's amazement. Then he heard a peal of laughter like the ringing of silvery bells; a woman twitched his arm, a saucy eye met his, and he saw the lady of the scarlet petticoat. A sharp, dry cachinnation appealed to his memory, and, 540 standing on tiptoe in the crowd, with his white apron over his head, he beheld the courteous little innkeeper. And lastly, there sailed over the heads of the multitude a great, broad laugh, broken in the midst by two sepulchral hems; thus "Haw, haw, haw,—hem, hem,—haw, haw, haw, haw!"

The sound proceeded from the balcony of the opposite edifice, and thither Robin turned his eyes. In front of the Gothic window stood the old citizen, wrapped in a wide gown, his gray periwig exchanged for a nightcap, which was thrust back from his forehead, and his silk stockings hanging about his legs. He supported himself on his polished cane in a fit of convulsive merriment, which manifested itself on his solemn old features like a funny inscription on a tomb- 550 stone. Then Robin seemed to hear the voices of the barbers, of the guests of the inn, and of all who had made sport of him that night. The contagion was spread-ing among the multitude, when all at once, it seized upon Robin, and he sent forth a shout of laughter that echoed through the street,—every man shook his sides, every man emptied his lungs, but Robin's shout was the loudest there. The cloud-spirits peeped from their silvery islands, as the congregated mirth went roaring up the sky! The Man in the Moon heard the far bellow. "Oho," quoth he, "the old earth is frolicsome to-night!"

When there was a momentary calm in that tempestuous sea of sound, the leader gave the sign, the procession resumed its march. On they went, like fiends 560 that throng in mockery around some dead potentate, mighty no more, but majes-tic still in his agony. On they went, in counterfeited pomp, in senseless uproar, in frenzied merriment, trampling all on an old man's heart. On swept the tumult, and left a silent street behind.

"Well, Robin, are you dreaming?" inquired the gentleman, laying his hand on the youth's shoulder.

Robin started, and withdrew his arm from the stone post to which he had instinctively clung, as the living stream rolled by him. His cheek was somewhat pale, and his eye not quite as lively as in the earlier part of the evening.   570

"Will you be kind enough to show me the way to the ferry?" said he, after a moment's pause.

"You have, then, adopted a new subject of inquiry?" observed his companion, with a smile.

"Why, yes, sir," replied Robin, rather dryly. "Thanks to you, and to my other friends, I have at last met my kinsman, and he will scarce desire to see my face again. I begin to grow weary of a town life, sir. Will you show me the way to the ferry?"

"No, my good friend Robin,—not tonight, at least," said the gentleman. "Some few days hence, if you wish it, I will speed you on your journey. Or, if you   580 prefer to remain with us, perhaps, as you are a shrewd youth, you may rise in the world without the help of your kinsman, Major Molineux."   [1832]

Questions for Discussion and Writing

1. Hawthorne repeatedly calls Robin "a shrewd young man." Is this phrase used seriously or ironically? How do you know?

2. In what ways can this story be compared with the fable of "The Country Mouse and the City Mouse"? Is the "moral" of the story the same?

3. Aspects of Robin's experiences in this story are nightmarish and "unreal." Since dreams are often thought to reveal something of the individual's psychology, what might we learn about Robin's subconscious through these nightmarish experiences?

4. Robin is obviously an innocent young man who learns something important from these experiences. What exactly do you think he learns in this story, and what in particular does he learn by witnessing the humiliation of his kinsman?

5. Why does Robin laugh at Major Molineux? Is he laughing at him, at the situation, at himself, or simply because everyone else is?

ᘔ CAROLINE M. KIRKLAND (MARY CLAVERS)
(1801–1864)

Henry Beckworth

Caroline Kirkland (née Stansbury), who often wrote under the pseudonym of Mrs. Mary Clavers, was a pioneer both in life and literature.

Her father was a New York bookseller and publisher; her aunt a headmistress of several girls' schools in New York state. Caroline was an apt pupil and in her teens taught at one of her Aunt's schools in New Hartford,

New York. There she married William Kirkland in 1828. The young couple moved to Geneva, New York, and founded a girls' school of their own, which failed. In 1835, Mr. Kirkland accepted the post of principal of the Detroit Female Seminary. The Kirklands speculated in land, and in 1837 the family moved to a homestead near Pickney, Michigan—at that time on the western frontier.

Mrs. Kirkland soon learned that the realities of homesteading were very different from the way such a life was portrayed in the romanticized accounts circulated at the time—often to lure settlers. The result was a series of stories and sketches from a woman's viewpoint about the realities and hardships of life in the bush. Unlike the idealized homesteaders of romantic fiction, her characters were always overworked and often ill; the hardy and free woodsmen of conventional fiction were portrayed by Kirkland as little better than vagabonds. These views were novel in themselves, but many of her sketches also record the day-to-day drudgeries of women's lives—truly an innovation at the time.

In 1843, the Kirklands lost all their money in a land swindle and were forced to return to New York to teach. Mrs. Kirkland continued to write, alternating in style between conventional sentiment and realism. She died unexpectedly of a stroke in 1864. Although Kirkland's work was highly praised by Edgar Allan Poe (1809–1849) and William Cullen Bryant (1794–1878), it fell into obscurity after her death and has remained there until recent times. Her two important collections of stories and sketches, *A New Home* (1839) and *Forest Life* (1842) are now recognized as important precursors to the Realistic and Local color movements.

> Sudden partings, such as press,
> The life from our young hearts; and choking sighs
> Which ne'er might be repeated, who could guess
> If ever more should meet those mutual eyes—
>
> —BYRON.

Henry Beckworth, the eldest son of a Massachusetts farmer, of small means and many mouths, was glad to accept a situation as clerk in the comprehensive "variety store" of his cousin, Ellis Irving, who was called a great merchant in the neighboring town of Langton. This cousin Ellis had fallen into the dangerous and not very usual predicament of having every body's good word; and it was not until he had failed in business, that any one discovered that he had a fault in the world.

While he was yet in his hey-dey, and before the world knew that he had been so good natured as to endorse for his wife's harum-scarum brother, his clerk, Henry Beckworth, had never dared to acknowledge, even in his dreams, that he 10 loved to very dizziness his sweet cousin Agnes Irving. But when mortification and apoplexy had done their work upon Mr. Irving, and his delicate wife had ascertained that the remnant of her days must pass in absolute poverty, dependent for food and raiment upon her daughter's needle, Henry found his wits and his tongue, and made so good use of both, that, ere long, his cousin Agnes did not deny that she liked him very well.

Now young ladies who have been at boarding school and learned to paint water-melons in water colors, and work Rebecca at the well[1] in chenille and gold thread, find real, thrifty, housewifely sewing, very slow and hard work, to earn even bread and salt by; but the dove-eyed Agnes had been the sole care and pride 20 of a genuine New England housewife, who could make hard gingerbread as well as soft, and who had plumed herself on being able to put every stitch into six fine shirts between Sunday evening and Saturday night. And so the fair child, though delicately bred, earned her mother's living and her own, with cheerful and ungrudging industry; and Henry sent all the surplus of his clerky gains to his father, who sometimes found the cry of "crowdie, crowdie, a' the day,"[2] rather difficult to pacify.

But by-and-bye, Mrs. Irving became so feeble that Agnes was obliged to nurse her instead of plying her skillful needle; and then matters went far astray, so that after a while the kind neighbors brought in almost all that was consumed in 30 that sad little household; Henry Beckworth being then out of employ, and unable for the time to find any way of aiding his cousin, save by his personal services in the sick room.

He grew almost mad under his distress, and the anxious, careful love which is the nursling of poverty, and at length seeing Mrs. Irving's health a little amended, he gave a long, sad, farewell kiss to his Agnes, and left her with an assurance that she should hear from him soon. He dared not tell her that he was quitting her to go to sea, in order that he might have immediate command of a trifling sum which he could devote to her service.

He made his way to the nearest sea-port, secured a berth before the mast in a 40 vessel about to sail for the East Indies; and then put into a letter all the love, and hope, and fear, and caution, and encouragement, and resolution, and devotedness, that one poor sheet could carry, giving the precious document into the care of a Langton man, who was returning "direct," as he said, to the spot where poor Henry had left his senses.

This said letter told Agnes, among other things, how and when to draw on Messers. —————————, for Henry's wages, which were left subject to her order— and the lover went to sea, with a heavy heart indeed, but with a comforting security that he had done all that poverty would let him, for the idol of his heart.

An East India voyage is very long, and most people experience many a 50 changing mood and many a wayward moment during its course; but Henry Beckworth's heart beat as if it would burst his blue jacket, when he found himself on shore again, and thought of what awaited him at Langton.

---

1. A scene from the story of Isaac, the Old Testament patriarch, popular as a subject for needlework in the nineteenth century.
2. Crowdie is a kind of cheese, i.e., the old man found it difficult to get enough to eat.

He called on Messrs. —————, to ascertain whether any thing remained of his pay and found that every dollar was untouched. At first this angered him a little; "for," as he justly argued, "if Agnes loved me as I love her—but never mind!" This I give as a fair specimen of his thoughts on his homeward journey. All his contemplations, however incoherent or wide of the mark, came invariably to one conclusion—that Agnes would surely be willing to marry him, poor as he was, rather than he should go to sea again.   60

It was evening, and a very dull, lead-colored evening, when the stage that contained our lover stopped at the only public-house in Langton. The True Blue Hotel, kept, as the oval sign which creaked by its side informed the grateful public, by Job Jephson, (at this moment J. Jephson, Esquire, of Tinkerville, in Michigan,) the very Job Jephson to whose kindly care Henry had committed his parting letter. The stage passed on, and Mr. Beckworth paced the tesselated floor of Jephson's bar-room, until the worthy proprietor and himself were left its sole occupants.

"Why, Henry, my boy, is that you? Do tell! Why your hat was slouched over your eyes so, that I did not know you! Why, man! where on *airth* have you sprung   70 from!"

Henry asked after every body, and then after Agnes Irving and her mother.

"Agnes Irving!"

"Dead!" said Henry, wildly enough.

"Dead! no, married to be sure! three months ago; and this very day a week ago, her mother was buried."

It is really surprising how instantaneously pride comes to one's aid on some occasions. The flashing thought of the loved one's death, had been anguish intolerable and inconcealable; the certainty of what was far worse only blanched Henry's cheek, and set his teeth firmly together while his lips questioned on, and the lo-   80 quacious host of the True Blue proceeded.

"Poor Agnes saw hard times after you went away. She had to give up the house you left her in, and take a room at Mr. Truesdell's. And then Mrs. Irving did nothing but pine after the comforts she had lost, for her mind was kind o' broke up by trouble. And Agnes tried to find some other place to board, because her mother took such an awful dislike to Mrs. Truesdell; but there wasn't nobody willing to take them in, because the old lady was so particular. And so, John Harrington—you know John?—made up to her again, though she'd refused him two or three times before; and said he loved her better than ever, and that he would take her mother home and do for her as if she was his own. Now, you see,   90 the neighbors had got pretty much tired of sending in things, because they thought Aggy ought n't to refuse such a good offer, and so after a while John got her. After all, the poor old lady did not seem to enjoy her new home, but pined away faster than ever, and said she knew Aggy had sold herself for her sake, but that was only a notion you know, for John was an excellent match for a poor———
———"

"Did you give my cousin the letter I handed you?" interrupted Henry.

"I'll just tell you all about that," responded Mr. Jephson, complacently drawing a chair for Henry, and inviting him to sit, as if for a long story. "I'll just tell you

how that was. When you and I parted that time, I thought I was all ready for a   100
start home; but there was a chance turned up to spekilate[3] a little, and arter that I
went down South to trade away some notions, so that when I got back to Langton
it was quite cold weather, and I took off my best coat and laid it away, for where's
the use of wearing good clothes under a great coat, you know? and there, to be
sure was your letter in the pocket of it. Well, before I found it again Agnes was
getting ready to be married; and, thinks I to myself, like enough it's a love-letter,
and might break off the match if she got it, gals are so foolish! so I just locked up
the letter and said nothing to nobody and"——————there lay Mr. Jephson on
his bar-room floor.

Henry turned from the place with some glimmering of an intention to seek   110
his lost love and tell her all, but one moment's lapse cured this madness; so he
only sat down and looked at Job, who was picking himself up and talking all the
while.

"Man alive! what do you put yourself into such a plaguy passion for? I done
it all for the best; and as to forgetting, who does not forget sometimes? Plague take
you! you've given my back such a wrench I sha'n't be able to go to trainin' tomorrow, and tore my pantaloons besides; and, arter all, you may likely thank me
for it as long as you live. There's as good fish in the sea as ever was caught—but I
swan![4] you're as white as the wall, and no mistake," and he caught the poor soul
as he was falling from his chair.   120

"Well, now, if this does n't beat cock-fighting!" muttered he, as he laid his insensible guest at full length on the floor and ran to the bar for some "camphire,"[5]
which he administered in all haste, "to take on so about a gal without a cent, but
he won't come to after all, and I shall have to bleed him:" saying which he pulled
off one sleeve of Henry's jacket and proceeded in due form to the operation.

"He won't bleed, I vow! Hang the fellow! if he dies, I shall be took up for
manslaughter. Why, Harry, I say, shaking him soundly, and dragging at his arm
with no gentle force. At last blood came slowly, and Beckworth became once more
conscious of misery, and Mr. Jephson's tongue set out as if fresh oiled by the relief
of his fears for his own safety.   130

"Now, Henry, don't make such a fool of yourself! You always used to be a fellow of some sconce.[6] What can't be cured must be endured." But as Henry's lips
resumed their color, and he raised himself from the floor, Mr. Jephson's habitual
prudence urged him farther and farther from the reach of the well arm. His fears
were groundless, however, for all that Henry now wanted was to be alone, that he
might weep like a woman.

"Promise me that you will never tell any one that I have been here this
night," said he at length; "this is all I ask. Since Agnes is another man's wife, God
forbid I should wish my name mentioned in her presence."

"Why, law! I'll promise that, to be sure; but you should n't make so much   140
out o' nothing: Aggy has got the best house in town, and every thing comfortable;

3. Speculate in a money-making venture.
4. Declare.
5. Camphor. Used to revive someone who has fainted.
6. Wit, sense.

and it a'n't no ways likely she would fret after *you*." And with this comforting assurance Henry prepared for departure.

"I say, Beckworth!" said Mr. Jephson as his guest left the room with his
valise; "I sha'n't charge you anything for the bleeding."   [1839]

Questions for Discussion and Writing

1. In what sense is this a love story?
2. In what ways does this story depart from the conventions of the typical love
   story?
3. What picture of life on the frontier does the story present?
4. Is this story tragic? comic? both? What is the predominant tone, if any?
5. Why might this story be considered an early instance of Realism? What is
   Realistic about it?

ᔥ EDGAR ALLAN POE
(1809–1849)

The Murders in the Rue Morgue

In his short and troubled life, Edgar Allan Poe was highly influential in shaping
the short story. He was its first major critic and theorist and one of its most
creative practitioners.

Born of itinerant actors, Poe was orphaned at age two and subsequently
raised (but not adopted) by a childless couple, Mr. and Mrs. John Allan—hence
his middle name. Relations between Poe and his godfather were often stormy.
The two men parted permanently when Poe deliberately had himself expelled
from West Point.

The rest of Poe's life was spent in poverty and in a vain quest to achieve
literary and financial stability as a magazine editor. He edited seven different
magazines, but always lost his position by quarreling with the owner or outraging readers with his caustic reviews and opinions. Poe's marriage to his thirteen-
year-old cousin, Virginia Clemm (1836), has caused much controversy, but the
marriage was in most respects successful until Virginia's death in 1847. Illness
and problems with drinking led to his untimely and still mysterious death in
Baltimore in 1849.

Poe's use of Gothic materials is one of his chief innovations. Instead of locating terror in exterior atmosphere and events, he makes his narrators the sources
of their own fears. Gothic horror becomes psychological terror. Poe was also
interested in the psychology of crime and detection. He became known for his
"tales of ratiocination," in which a detective uses logic to solve a mystery. His
best stories in these genres penetrate the human heart and mind and have made
him both a beloved popular writer and the object of intense scholarly study.

What song the Syrens sang, or what name Achilles assumed when he hid himself among women, although puzzling questions, are not beyond *all* conjecture.
—SIR THOMAS BROWNE

T HE MENTAL FEATURES discoursed of as the analytical, are, in themselves, but little susceptible of analysis. We appreciate them only in their effects. We know of them, among other things, that they are always to their possessor, when inordinately possessed, a source of the liveliest enjoyment. As the strong man exults in his physical ability, delighting in such exercises as call his muscles into action, so glories the analyst in that moral activity which *disentangles*. He derives pleasure from even the most trivial occupations bringing his talent into play. He is fond of enigmas, of conundrums, hieroglyphics; exhibiting in his solutions of each a degree of *acumen* which appears to the ordinary apprehension præternatural. His results, brought about by the very soul and essence of method, have, in truth, the whole air of intuition.

The faculty of re-solution is possibly much invigorated by mathematical study, and especially by that highest branch of it which, unjustly, and merely on account of its retrograde operations, has been called, as if *par excellence,* analysis. Yet to calculate is not in itself to analyze. A chess-player, for example, does the one, without effort at the other. It follows that the game of chess, in its effects upon mental character, is greatly misunderstood. I am not now writing a treatise, but simply prefacing a somewhat peculiar narrative by observations very much at random; I will, therefore, take occasion to assert that the higher powers of the reflective intellect are more decidedly and more usefully tasked by the unostentatious game of draughts[1] than by all the elaborate frivolity of chess. In this latter, where the pieces have different and *bizarre* motions, with various and variable values, what is only complex, is mistaken (a not unusual error) for what is profound. The *attention* is here called powerfully into play. If it flag for an instant, an oversight is committed, resulting in injury or defeat. The possible moves being not only manifold, but involute, the chances of such oversights are multiplied; and in nine cases out of ten, it is the more concentrative rather than the more acute player who conquers. In draughts, on the contrary, where the moves are *unique* and have but little variation, the probabilities of inadvertence are diminished, and the mere attention being left comparatively unemployed, what advantages are obtained by either party are obtained by superior *acumen*. To be less abstract, let us suppose a game of draughts where the pieces are reduced to four kings, and where, of course, no oversight is to be expected. It is obvious that here the victory can be decided (the players being at all equal) only by some *recherche*[2] movement, the result of some strong exertion of the intellect. Deprived of ordinary resources, the analyst throws himself into the spirit of his opponent, identifies himself therewith, and not unfrequently sees thus, at a glance, the sole methods (sometimes indeed absurdly simple ones) by which he may seduce into error or hurry into miscalculation.

1. Checkers.
2. Exquisite, i.e., clever or brilliant.

Whist[3] has long been known for its influence upon what is termed the calcu- 40
lating power; and men of the highest order of intellect have been known to take
an apparently unaccountable delight in it, while eschewing chess as frivolous.
Beyond doubt there is nothing of a similar nature so greatly tasking the faculty of
analysis. The best chess-player in Christendom *may* be little more than the best
player of chess; but proficiency in whist implies capacity for success in all these
more important undertakings where mind struggles with mind. When I say proficiency, I mean that perfection in the game which includes a comprehension of *all*
the sources whence legitimate advantage may be derived. These are not only manifold, but multiform, and lie frequently among recesses of thought altogether inaccessible to the ordinary understanding. To observe attentively is to remember 50
distinctly; and, so far, the concentrative chess-player will do very well at whist;
while the rules of Hoyle[4] (themselves based upon the mere mechanism of the
game) are sufficiently and generally comprehensible. Thus to have a retentive
memory, and proceed by "the book" are points commonly regarded as the sum
total of good playing. But it is in matters beyond the limits of mere rule that the
skill of the analyst is evinced. He makes, in silence, a host of observations and inferences. So, perhaps, do his companions; and the difference in the extent of the
information obtained, lies not so much in the validity of the inference as in the
quality of the observation. The necessary knowledge is that of *what* to observe.
Our player confines himself not at all; nor, because the game is the object, does he 60
reject deductions from things external to the game. He examines the countenance
of his partner, comparing it carefully with that of each of his opponents. He considers the mode of assorting the cards in each hand; often counting trump by
trump, and honor by honor, through the glances bestowed by their holders upon
each. He notes every variation of face as the play progresses, gathering a fund of
thought from the differences in the expression of certainty, of surprise, of triumph,
or chagrin. From the manner of gathering up a trick he judges whether the person
taking it, can make another in the suit. He recognizes what is played through
feint, by the manner with which it is thrown upon the table. A casual or inadver-
tent word; the accidental dropping or turning of a card, with the accompanying 70
anxiety or carelessness in regard to its concealment; the counting of the tricks,
with the order of their arrangement; embarrassment, hesitation, eagerness, or trep-
idation—all afford, to his apparently intuitive perception, indications of the true
state of affairs. The first two or three rounds having been played, he is in full possession of the contents of each hand, and thenceforward puts down his cards with
as absolute a precision of purpose as if the rest of the party had turned outward
the faces of their own.

The analytical power should not be confounded with simple ingenuity; for
while the analyst is necessarily ingenious, the ingenious man is often remarkably
incapable of analysis. The constructive or combining power, by which ingenuity is 80
usually manifested, and to which the phrenologists[5] (I believe erroneously) have
assigned a separate organ, supposing it a primitive faculty, has been so frequently

3. A card game resembling bridge.
4. Edmund Hoyle, author of a widely used book on the rules of indoor games, especially card games.
5. Pseudo-scientists who claimed that the contours of the skull were clues to mental ability and personality.

seen in those whose intellect bordered otherwise upon idiocy, as to have attracted general observation among writers on morals. Between ingenuity and the analytic ability there exists a difference far greater, indeed, than that between the fancy and the imagination, but of a character very strictly analogous. It will be found, in fact, that the ingenious are always fanciful, and the *truly* imaginative never otherwise than analytic.

The narrative which follows will appear to the reader somewhat in the light of a commentary upon the propositions just advanced.

Residing in Paris during the spring and part of the summer of 18——, I there became acquainted with a Monsieur C. Auguste Dupin. This young gentleman was of an excellent, indeed of an illustrious family, but, by a variety of untoward events, had been reduced to such poverty that the energy of his character succumbed beneath it, and he ceased to bestir himself in the world, or to care for the retrieval of his fortunes. By courtesy of his creditors, there still remained in his possession a small remnant of his patrimony; and, upon the income arising from this, he managed, by means of a rigorous economy, to procure the necessities of life, without troubling himself about its superfluities. Books, indeed, were his sole luxuries, and in Paris these are easily obtained.

Our first meeting was at an obscure library in the Rue Montmartre, where the accident of our both being in search of the same very rare and very remarkable volume, brought us into closer communion. We saw each other again and again. I was deeply interested in the little family history which he detailed to me with all that candor which a Frenchman indulges whenever mere self is the theme. I was astonished, too, at the vast extent of his reading; and, above all, I felt my soul enkindled within me by the wild fervor, and the vivid freshness of his imagination. Seeking in Paris the objects I then sought, I felt that the society of such a man would be to me a treasure beyond price; and this feeling I frankly confided to him. It was at length arranged that we should live together during my stay in the city; and as my worldly circumstances were somewhat less embarrassed than his own, I was permitted to be at the expense of renting, and furnishing in a style which suited the rather fantastic gloom of our common temper, a time-eaten and grotesque mansion, long deserted through superstitions into which we did not inquire, and tottering to its fall in a retired and desolate portion of the Faubourg St. Germain.

Had the routine of our life at this place been known to the world, we should have been regarded as madmen—although, perhaps, as madmen of a harmless nature. Our seclusion was perfect. We admitted no visitors. Indeed the locality of our retirement had been carefully kept a secret from my own former associates; and it had been many years since Dupin had ceased to know or be known in Paris. We existed within ourselves alone.

It was a freak of fancy in my friend (for what else shall I call it?) to be enamored of the night for her own sake; and into this *bizarrerie*, as into all his others, I quietly fell; giving myself up to his wild whims with a perfect *abandon*. The sable divinity would not herself dwell with us always; but we could counterfeit her presence. At the first dawn of the morning we closed all the massy shutters of our old building; lighted a couple of tapers which, strongly perfumed, threw out only the ghastliest and feeblest of rays. By the aid of these we then busied our souls in

dreams—reading, writing, or conversing, until warned by the clock of the advent 130
of the true Darkness. Then we sallied forth into the streets, arm in arm, continuing
the topics of the day, or roaming far and wide until a late hour, seeking, amid the
wild lights and shadows of the populous city, that infinity of mental excitement
which quiet observation can afford.

At such times I could not help remarking and admiring (although from his
rich ideality I had been prepared to expect it) a peculiar analytic ability in Dupin.
He seemed, too, to take an eager delight in its exercise—if not exactly in its display—and did not hesitate to confess the pleasure thus derived. He boasted to me,
with a low chuckling laugh, that most men, in respect to himself, wore windows
in their bosoms, and was wont to follow up such assertions by direct and very 140
startling proofs of his intimate knowledge of my own. His manner at these moments was frigid and abstract; his eyes were vacant in expression; while his voice,
usually a rich tenor, rose into a treble which would have sounded petulant but for
the deliberateness and entire distinctness of the enunciation. Observing him in
these moods, I often dwelt meditatively upon the old philosophy of the Bi-Part
Soul, and amused myself with the fancy of a double Dupin—the creative and the
resolvent.

Let it not be supposed, from what I have just said, that I am detailing any
mystery, or penning any romance. What I have described in the Frenchman was
merely the result of an excited, or perhaps of a diseased, intelligence. But of the 150
character of his remarks at the periods in question an example will best convey the
idea.

We were strolling one night down a long dirty street, in the vicinity of the
Palais Royal. Being both, apparently, occupied with thought, neither of us had
spoken a syllable for fifteen minutes at least. All at once Dupin broke forth with
these words:

"He is a very little fellow, that's true, and would do better for the *Théâtre des
Variétés*."

"There can be no doubt of that," I replied, unwittingly, and not at first observing (so much had I been absorbed in reflection) the extraordinary manner in 160
which the speaker had chimed in with my meditations. In an instant afterward I
recollected myself, and my astonishment was profound.

"Dupin," said I, gravely, "this is beyond my comprehension. I do not hesitate
to say that I am amazed, and can scarcely credit my senses. How was it possible
you should know I was thinking of ————?" Here I paused, to ascertain beyond a doubt whether he really knew of whom I thought.

"———— of Chantilly," said he, "why do you pause? You were remarking
to yourself that his diminutive figure unfitted him for tragedy."

This was precisely what had formed the subject of my reflections. Chantilly
was a *quondam*[6] cobbler of the Rue St. Denis, who, becoming stage-mad, had at- 170
tempted the *rôle* of Xerxes, in Crébillon's tragedy so called, and been notoriously
Pasquinaded[7] for his pains.

6. Former.
7. Satirized.

"Tell me, for Heaven's sake," I exclaimed, "the method—if method there is— by which you have been enabled to fathom my soul in this matter." In fact, I was even more startled than I would have been willing to express.

"It was the fruiterer," replied my friend, "who brought you to the conclusion that the mender of soles was not of sufficient height for Xerxes *et id genus omne.*"[8]

"The fruiterer!—you astonish me—I know no fruiterer whomsoever."

"The man who ran up against you as we entered the street—it may have been fifteen minutes ago."   180

I now remembered that, in fact, a fruiterer, carrying upon his head a large basket of apples, had nearly thrown me down, by accident, as we passed from the Rue C—— into the thoroughfare where we stood; but what this had to do with Chantilly I could not possibly understand.

There was not a particle of *charlatânerie*[9] about Dupin. "I will explain," he said, "and that you may comprehend all clearly, we will first retrace the course of your meditations, from the moment in which I spoke to you until that of the *rencontre*[10] with the fruiterer in question. The larger links of the chain run thus— Chantilly, Orion, Dr. Nichols, Epicurus, Stereotomy, the street stones, the fruiterer."   190

There are few persons who have not, at some period of their lives, amused themselves in retracing the steps by which particular conclusions of their own minds have been attained. The occupation is often full of interest; and he who attempts it for the first time is astonished by the apparently illimitable distance and incoherence between the starting-point and the goal. What, then, must have been my amazement, when I heard the Frenchman speak what he had just spoken, and when I could not help acknowledging that he had spoken the truth. He continued:

"We had been talking of horses, if I remember aright, just before leaving the Rue C——. This was the last subject we discussed. As we crossed into this   200 street, a fruiterer, with a large basket upon his head, brushing quickly past us, thrust you upon a pile of paving-stones collected at a spot where the causeway is undergoing repair. You stepped upon one of the loose fragments, slipped, slightly strained your ankle, appeared vexed or sulky, muttered a few words, turned to look at the pile, and then proceeded in silence. I was not particularly attentive to what you did; but observation has become with me, of late, a species of necessity.

"You kept your eyes upon the ground—glancing, with a petulant expression, at the holes and ruts in the pavement (so that I saw you were still thinking of the stones), until we reached the little alley called Lamartine, which has been paved, by way of experiment, with the overlapping and riveted blocks. Here your counte- 210 nance brightened up, and, perceiving your lips move, I could not doubt that you murmured the word 'stereotomy,' a term very affectedly applied to this species of pavement. I knew that you could not say to yourself 'stereotomy' without being brought to think of atomies, and thus of the theories of Epicurus; and since, when

8. "and it's all one of a kind."
9. Charlatan, imposter.
10. Encounter.

we discussed this subject not very long ago, I mentioned to you how singularly, yet with how little notice, the vague guesses of that noble Greek had met with confirmation in the late nebular cosmogony, I felt that you could not avoid casting your eyes upward to the great *nebula* in Orion, and I certainly expected that you would do so. You did look up; and I was now assured that I had correctly followed your steps. But in that bitter *tirade* upon Chantilly, which appeared in yes-   220
terday's '*Musée,*' the satirist, making some disgraceful allusions to the cobbler's change of name upon assuming the buskin,[11] quoted a Latin line about which we have often conversed. I mean the line

> Perdidit antiquum litera prima sonum.[12]

"I had told you that this was in reference to Orion, formerly written Urion; and, from certain pungencies connected with this explanation, I was aware that you could not have forgotten it. It was clear, therefore, that you would not fail to combine the two ideas of Orion and Chantilly. That you did combine them I saw by the character of the smile which passed over your lips. You thought of the poor cobbler's immolation. So far, you had been stooping in your gait; but now I saw   230
you draw yourself up to your full height. I was then sure that you reflected upon the diminutive figure of Chantilly. At this point I interrupted your meditations to remark that as, in fact, he *was* a very little fellow—that Chantilly—he would do better at the *Théâtre des Variétés*."

Not long after this, we were looking over an evening edition of the *Gazette des Tribunaux,* when the following paragraphs arrested our attention.

"EXTRAORDINARY MURDERS.—This morning, about three o'clock, the inhabitants of the Quartier St. Roch were roused from sleep by a succession of terrific shrieks, issuing, apparently, from the fourth story of a house in the Rue Morgue, known to be in the sole occupancy of one Madame L'Espanaye, and her daughter,   240
Mademoiselle Camille L'Espanaye. After some delay, occasioned by a fruitless attempt to procure admission in the usual manner, the gateway was broken in with a crowbar, and eight or ten of the neighbors entered, accompanied by two *gendarmes.*[13] By this time the cries had ceased; but, as the party rushed up the first flight of stairs, two or more rough voices, in angry contention, were distinguished, and seemed to proceed from the upper part of the house. As the second landing was reached, these sounds, also, had ceased, and every thing remained perfectly quiet. The party spread themselves, and hurried from room to room. Upon arriving at a large back chamber in the fourth story (the door of which, being found locked, with the key inside, was forced open), a spectacle presented itself which   250
struck every one present not less with horror than with astonishment.

"The apartment was in the wildest disorder—the furniture broken and thrown about in all directions. There was only one bedstead; and from this the

---

11. High boots worn by tragic actors in ancient times.
12. "The first letter destroys the antique sound."
13. Policemen.

bed had been removed, and thrown into the middle of the floor. On a chair lay a razor, besmeared with blood. On the hearth were two or three long and thick tresses of gray human hair, also dabbled with blood, and seeming to have been pulled out by the roots. Upon the floor were found four Napoleons, an ear-ring of topaz, three large silver spoons, three smaller of *métal d'Alger*,[14] and two bags, containing nearly four thousand francs in gold. The drawers of a *bureau*, which stood in one corner, were open, and had been, apparently, rifled, although many articles still remained in them. A small iron safe was discovered under the *bed* (not under the bedstead). It was open, with the key still in the door. It had no contents beyond a few old letters, and other papers of little consequence.

"Of Madame L'Espanaye no traces were here seen; but an unusual quantity of soot being observed in the fire-place, a search was made in the chimney, and (horrible to relate!) the corpse of the daughter, head downward, was dragged therefrom; it having been thus forced up the narrow aperture for a considerable distance. The body was quite warm. Upon examining it, many excoriations were perceived, no doubt occasioned by the violence with which it had been thrust up and disengaged. Upon the face were many severe scratches, and, upon the throat, dark bruises, and deep indentations of finger nails, as if the deceased had been throttled to death.

"After a thorough investigation of every portion of the house without farther discovery, the party made its way into a small paved yard in the rear of the building, where lay the corpse of the old lady, with her throat so entirely cut that, upon an attempt to raise her, the head fell off. The body, as well as the head, was fearfully mutilated—the former so much so as scarcely to retain any semblance of humanity.

"To this horrible mystery there is not as yet, we believe, the slightest clew."

The next day's paper had these additional particulars:

"*The Tragedy in the Rue Morgue.*—Many individuals have been examined in relation to this most extraordinary and frightful affair," [the word '*affaire*' has not yet, in France, that levity of import which it conveys with us] "but nothing whatever has transpired to throw light upon it. We give below all the material testimony elicited.

"*Pauline Dubourg,* laundress, deposes that she has known both the deceased for three years, having washed for them during that period. The old lady and her daughter seemed on good terms—very affectionate toward each other. They were excellent pay. Could not speak in regard to their mode or means of living. Believe that Madame L. told fortunes for a living. Was reputed to have money put by. Never met any person in the house when she called for the clothes or took them home. Was sure that they had no servant in employ. There appeared to be no furniture in any part of the building except in the fourth story.

"*Pierre Moreau,* tobacconist, deposes that he has been in the habit of selling small quantities of tobacco and snuff to Madame L'Espanaye for nearly four years. Was born in the neighborhood, and has always resided there. The deceased and her daughter had occupied the house in which the corpses were found, for more

14. An imitation silver alloy.

than six years. It was formerly occupied by a jeweller, who under-let the upper rooms to various persons. The house was the property of Madame L. She became dissatisfied with the abuse of the premises by her tenant, and moved into them 300 herself, refusing to let any portion. The old lady was childish. Witness had seen the daughter some five or six times during the six years. The two lived an exceedingly retired life—were reputed to have money. Had heard it said among the neighbors that Madame L. told fortunes—did not believe it. Had never seen any person enter the door except the old lady and her daughter, a porter once or twice, and a physician some eight or ten times.

"Many other persons, neighbors, gave evidence to the same effect. No one was spoken of as frequenting the house. It was not known whether there were any living connections of Madame L. and her daughter. The shutters of the front windows were seldom opened. Those in the rear were always closed, with the excep- 310 tion of the large back room, fourth story. The house was a good house—not very old.

"*Isidore Musèt, gendarme,* deposes that he was called to the house about three o'clock in the morning, and found some twenty or thirty persons at the gateway, endeavoring to gain admittance. Forced it open, at length, with a bayonet—not with a crowbar. Had but little difficulty in getting it open, on account of its being a double or folding gate, and bolted neither at bottom nor top. The shrieks were continued until the gate was forced—and then suddenly ceased. They seemed to be screams of some person (or persons) in great agony—were loud and drawn out, not short and quick. Witness led the way up stairs. Upon reaching the first 320 landing, heard two voices in loud and angry contention—the one a gruff voice, the other much shriller—a very strange voice. Could distinguish some words of the former, which was that of a Frenchman. Was positive that it was not a woman's voice. Could distinguish the words '*sacré*' and '*diable.*' The shrill voice was that of a foreigner. Could not be sure whether it was the voice of a man or of a woman. Could not make out what was said, but believed the language to be Spanish. The state of the room and of the bodies was described by this witness as we described them yesterday.

"*Henri Duval,* a neighbor, and by trade a silver-smith, deposes that he was one of the party who first entered the house. Corroborates the testimony of Musèt 330 in general. As soon as they forced an entrance, they reclosed the door, to keep out the crowd, which collected very fast, notwithstanding the lateness of the hour. The shrill voice, this witness thinks, was that of an Italian. Was certain it was not French. Could not be sure that it was a man's voice. It might have been a woman's. Was not acquainted with the Italian language. Could not distinguish the words, but was convinced by the intonation that the speaker was an Italian. Knew Madame L. and her daughter. Had conversed with both frequently. Was sure that the shrill voice was not that of either of the deceased.

"———— *Odenheimer, restaurateur.*—This witness volunteered his testimony. Not speaking French, was examined through an interpreter. Is a native of 340 Amsterdam. Was passing the house at the time of the shrieks. They lasted for several minutes—probably ten. They were long and loud—very awful and distressing. Was one of those who entered the building. Corroborated the previous evidence in every respect but one. Was sure that the shrill voice was that of a man—of a Frenchman. Could not distinguish the words uttered. They were loud and quick—unequal—spoken apparently in fear as well as in anger. The voice was harsh—not so much shrill as harsh. Could not call it a shrill voice. The gruff voice said repeatedly, 'sacré,' 'diable,' and once 'mon Dieu.'

"*Jules Mignaud,* banker, of the firm of Mignaud et Fils, Rue Deloraine. Is the elder Mignaud. Madame L'Espanaye had some property. Had opened an account 350 with his banking house in the spring of the year———(eight years previously). Made frequent deposits in small sums. Had checked for nothing until the third day before her death, when she took out in person the sum of 4000 francs. This sum was paid in gold, and a clerk sent home with the money.

"*Adolphe Le Bon,* clerk to Mignaud et Fils, deposes that on the day in question, about noon, he accompanied Madame L'Espanaye to her residence with the 4000 francs, put up in two bags. Upon the door being opened, Mademoiselle L. appeared and took from his hands one of the bags, while the old lady relieved him of the other. He then bowed and departed. Did not see any person in the street at the time. It is a by-street—very lonely. 360

"*William Bird,* tailor, deposes that he was one of the party who entered the house. Is an Englishman. Has lived in Paris two years. Was one of the first to ascend the stairs. Heard the voices in contention. The gruff voice was that of a Frenchman. Could make out several words, but cannot now remember all. Heard distinctly 'sacré' and 'mon Dieu.' There was a sound at the moment as if of several persons struggling—a scraping and scuffling sound. The shrill voice was very loud—louder than the gruff one. Is sure that it was not the voice of an Englishman. Appeared to be that of a German. Might have been a woman's voice. Does not understand German.

"Four of the above-named witnesses, being recalled, deposed that the door 370 of the chamber in which was found the body of Mademoiselle L. was locked on the inside when the party reached it. Every thing was perfectly silent—no groans or noises of any kind. Upon forcing the door no person was seen. The windows, both of the back and front room, were down and firmly fastened from within. A door between the two rooms was closed but not locked. The door leading from the front room into the passage was locked, with the key on the inside. A small room in the front of the house, on the fourth story, at the head of the passage, was open, the door being ajar. This room was crowded with old beds, boxes, and so forth. These were carefully removed and searched. There was not an inch of any portion of the house which was not carefully searched. Sweeps were sent up and 380 down the chimneys. The house was a four-story one, with garrets (*mansardes*). A trap-door on the roof was nailed down very securely—did not appear to have been opened for years. The time elapsing between the hearing of the voices in contention and the breaking open of the room door was variously stated by the witnesses. Some made it as short as three minutes—some as long as five. The door was opened with difficulty.

"*Alfonzo Garcio,* undertaker, deposes that he resides in the Rue Morgue. Is a native of Spain. Was one of the party who entered the house. Did not proceed up stairs. Is nervous, and was apprehensive of the consequences of agitation. Heard

the voices in contention. The gruff voice was that of a Frenchman. Could not dis- 390
tinguish what was said. The shrill voice was that of an Englishman—is sure of
this. Does not understand the English language, but judges by the intonation.

"*Alberto Montani,* confectioner, deposes that he was among the first to ascend
the stairs. Heard the voices in question. The gruff voice was that of a Frenchman.
Distinguished several words. The speaker appeared to be expostulating. Could not
make out the words of the shrill voice. Spoke quick and unevenly. Thinks it the
voice of a Russian. Corroborates the general testimony. Is an Italian. Never conversed with a native of Russia.

"Several witnesses, recalled, here testified that the chimneys of all the rooms
on the fourth story were too narrow to admit the passage of a human being. By 400
'sweeps' were meant cylindrical sweeping-brushes, such as are employed by those
who clean chimneys. These brushes were passed up and down every flue in the
house. There is no back passage by which any one could have descended while
the party proceeded up stairs. The body of Mademoiselle L'Espanaye was so firmly
wedged in the chimney that it could not be got down until four or five of the party
united their strength.

"*Paul Dumas,* physician, deposes that he was called to view the bodies about
daybreak. They were both then lying on the sacking of the bedstead in the chamber where Mademoiselle L. was found. The corpse of the young lady was much
bruised and excoriated. The fact that it had been thrust up the chimney would 410
sufficiently account for these appearances. The throat was greatly chafed. There
were several deep scratches just below the chin, together with a series of livid
spots which were evidently the impression of fingers. The face was fearfully discolored, and the eyeballs protruded. The tongue had been partially bitten through. A
large bruise was discovered upon the pit of the stomach, produced, apparently, by
the pressure of a knee. In the opinion of M. Dumas, Mademoiselle L'Espanaye had
been throttled to death by some person or persons unknown. The corpse of the
mother was horribly mutilated. All the bones of the right leg and arm were more
or less shattered. The left *tibia* much splintered, as well as all the ribs of the left
side. Whole body dreadfully bruised and discolored. It was not possible to say 420
how the injuries had been inflicted. A heavy club of wood, or a broad bar of
iron—a chair—any large, heavy, and obtuse weapon would have produced such
results, if wielded by the hands of a very powerful man. No woman could have inflicted the blows with any weapon. The head of the deceased, when seen by witness, was entirely separated from the body, and was also greatly shattered. The
throat had evidently been cut with some very sharp instrument—probably with a
razor.

"*Alexandre Etienne,* surgeon, was called with M. Dumas to view the bodies.
Corroborated the testimony, and the opinions of M. Dumas.

"Nothing further of importance was elicited, although several other persons 430
were examined. A murder so mysterious, and so perplexing in all its particulars,
was never before committed in Paris—if indeed a murder has been committed at
all. The police are entirely at fault—an unusual occurrence in affairs of this nature.
There is not, however, the shadow of a clew apparent."

The evening edition of the paper stated that the greatest excitement still continued in the Quartier St. Roch—that the premises in question had been carefully re-searched, and fresh examinations of witnesses instituted, but all to no purpose. A postscript, however, mentioned that Adolphe Le Bon had been arrested and imprisoned—although nothing appeared to criminate him beyond the facts already detailed.   440

Dupin seemed singularly interested in the progress of this affair—at least so I judged from his manner, for he made no comments. It was only after the announcement that Le Bon had been imprisoned, that he asked me my opinion respecting the murders.

I could merely agree with all Paris in considering them an insoluble mystery. I saw no means by which it would be possible to trace the murderer.

"We must not judge of the means," said Dupin, "by this shell of an examination. The Parisian police, so much extolled for *acumen,* are cunning, but no more. There is no method in their proceedings, beyond the method of the moment. They make a vast parade of measures; but, not unfrequently, these are so ill-adapted to   450 the objects proposed, as to put us in mind of Monsieur Jourdain's calling for his *robe-de-chambre—pour mieux entendre la musique.* The results attained by them are not unfrequently surprising, but, for the most part, are brought about by simple diligence and activity. When these qualities are unavailing, their schemes fail. Vidocq, for example, was a good guesser, and a persevering man. But, without educated thought, he erred continually by the very intensity of his investigations. He impaired his vision by holding the object too close. He might see, perhaps, one or two points with unusual clearness, but in so doing he, necessarily, lost sight of the matter as a whole. Thus there is such a thing as being too profound. Truth is not always in a well. In fact, as regards the more important knowledge, I do believe   460 that she is invariably superficial. The depth lies in the valleys where we seek her, and not upon the mountain-tops where she is found. The modes and sources of this kind of error are well typified in the contemplation of the heavenly bodies. To look at a star by glances—to view it in a side-long way, by turning toward it the exterior portions of the *retina* (more susceptible of feeble impressions of light than the interior), is to behold the star distinctly—is to have the best appreciation of its lustre—a lustre which grows dim just in proportion as we turn our vision *fully* upon it. A greater number of rays actually fall upon the eye in the latter case, but in the former, there is the more refined capacity for comprehension. By undue profundity we perplex and enfeeble thought; and it is possible to make even Venus   470 herself vanish from the firmament by a scrutiny too sustained, too concentrated, or too direct.

"As for these murders, let us enter into some examinations for ourselves, before we make up an opinion respecting them. An inquiry will afford us amusement," [I thought this an odd term, so applied, but said nothing] "and besides, Le Bon once rendered me a service for which I am not ungrateful. We will go and see the premises with our own eyes. I know G——, the Prefect of Police, and shall have no difficulty in obtaining the necessary permission."

The permission was obtained, and we proceeded at once to the Rue Morgue. This is one of those miserable thoroughfares which intervene between the Rue   480 Richelieu and the Rue St. Roch. It was late in the afternoon when we reached it, as this quarter is at a great distance from that in which we resided. The house was readily found; for there were still many persons gazing up at the closed shutters, with an objectless curiosity, from the opposite side of the way. It was an ordinary Parisian house, with a gateway, on one side of which was a glazed watch-box, with a sliding panel in the window, indicating a *loge de concierge*.[15] Before going in we walked up the street, turned down an alley, and then, again turning, passed in the rear of the building—Dupin, meanwhile, examining the whole neighborhood, as well as the house, with a minuteness of attention for which I could see no possible object.   490

Retracing our steps we came again to the front of the dwelling, rang, and, having shown our credentials, were admitted by the agents in charge. We went up stairs—into the chamber where the body of Mademoiselle L'Espanaye had been found, and where both the deceased still lay. The disorders of the room had, as usual, been suffered to exist. I saw nothing beyond what had been stated in the *Gazette des Tribunaux*. Dupin scrutinized every thing—not excepting the bodies of the victims. We then went into the other rooms, and into the yard; a *gendarme* accompanying us throughout. The examination occupied us until dark, when we took our departure. On our way home my companion stepped in for a moment at the office of one of the daily papers.   500

I have said that the whims of my friend were manifold, and that *Je les ménagais:*—for this phrase there is no English equivalent. It was his humor, now, to decline all conversation on the subject of the murder, until about noon the next day. He then asked me, suddenly, if I had observed any thing *peculiar* at the scene of the atrocity.

There was something in his manner of emphasizing the word *"peculiar,"* which caused me to shudder, without knowing why.

"No, nothing *peculiar,*" I said; "nothing more, at least, than we both saw stated in the paper."

"The *Gazette,*" he replied, "has not entered, I fear, into the unusual horror of 510 the thing. But dismiss the idle opinions of this print. It appears to me that this mystery is considered insoluble, for the very reason which should cause it to be regarded as easy of solution—I mean for the *outré* character of its features. The police are confounded by the seeming absence of motive—not for the murder itself—but for the atrocity of the murder. They are puzzled, too, by the seeming impossibility of reconciling the voices heard in contention, with the facts that no one was discovered upstairs but the assassinated Mademoiselle L'Espanaye, and that there were no means of egress without the notice of the party ascending. The wild disorder of the room; the corpse thrust, with the head downward, up the chimney; the frightful mutilation of the body of the old lady; these considerations, 520 with those just mentioned, and others which I need not mention, have sufficed to paralyze the powers, by putting completely at fault the boasted *acumen,* of the government agents. They have fallen into the gross but common error of confounding the unusual with the abstruse. But it is by these deviations from the plane of the ordinary, that reason feels its way, if at all, in its search for the true. In

---

15. A small room for the concierge, i.e., the female porter.

investigations such as we are now pursuing, it should not be so much asked 'what has occurred,' as 'what has occurred that has never occurred before.' In fact, the facility with which I shall arrive, or have arrived, at the solution of this mystery, is in the direct ratio of its apparent insolubility in the eyes of the police."

I stared at the speaker in mute astonishment. 530

"I am now awaiting," continued he, looking toward the door of our apartment—"I am now awaiting a person who, although perhaps not the perpetrator of these butcheries, must have been in some measure implicated in their perpetration. Of the worst portion of the crimes committed, it is probable that he is innocent. I hope that I am right in this supposition; for upon it I build my expectation of reading the entire riddle. I look for the man here—in this room—every moment. It is true that he may not arrive; but the probability is that he will. Should he come, it will be necessary to detain him. Here are pistols; and we both know how to use them when occasion demands their use."

I took the pistols, scarcely knowing what I did, or believing what I heard, 540 while Dupin went on, very much as if in a soliloquy. I have already spoken of his abstract manner at such times. His discourse was addressed to myself; but his voice, although by no means loud, had that intonation which is commonly employed in speaking to some one at a great distance. His eyes, vacant in expression, regarded only the wall.

"That the voices heard in contention," he said, "by the party upon the stairs, were not the voices of the women themselves, was fully proved by the evidence. This relieves us of all doubt upon the question whether the old lady could have first destroyed the daughter, and afterward have committed suicide. I speak of this point chiefly for the sake of method; for the strength of Madame L'Espanaye 550 would have been utterly unequal to the task of thrusting her daughter's corpse up the chimney as it was found; and the nature of the wounds upon her own person entirely precludes the idea of self-destruction. Murder, then, has been committed by some third party; and the voices of this third party were those heard in contention. Let me now advert—not to the whole testimony respecting these voices— but to what was *peculiar* in that testimony. Did you observe any thing peculiar about it?"

I remarked that, while all the witnesses agreed in supposing the gruff voice to be that of a Frenchman, there was much disagreement in regard to the shrill, or, as one individual termed it, the harsh voice. 560

"That was the evidence itself," said Dupin, "but it was not the peculiarity of the evidence. You have observed nothing distinctive. Yet there *was* something to be observed. The witnesses, as you remark, agreed about the gruff voice; they were here unanimous. But in regard to the shrill voice, the peculiarity is—not that they disagreed—but that, while an Italian, an Englishman, a Spaniard, a Hollander, and a Frenchman attempted to describe it, each one spoke of it as that *of a foreigner.* Each is sure that it was not the voice of one of his own countrymen. Each likens it—not to the voice of an individual of any nation with whose language he is conversant—but the converse. The Frenchman supposes it the voice of a Spaniard, and 'might have distinguished some words *had he been acquainted with the Spanish.*' 570 The Dutchman maintains it to have been that of a Frenchman; but we find it stated that '*not understanding French this witness was examined through an interpreter.*'

The Englishman thinks it the voice of a German, and *'does not understand German.'*
The Spaniard 'is sure' that it was that of an Englishman, but 'judges by the intonation' altogether, *'as he has no knowledge of the English.'* The Italian believes it the
voice of a Russian, but *'has never conversed with a native of Russia.'* A second
Frenchman differs, moreover, with the first, and is positive that the voice was that
of an Italian; but, *not being cognizant of that tongue,* is, like the Spaniard, 'convinced
by the intonation.' Now, how strangely unusual must that voice have really been,
about which such testimony as this *could* have been elicited!—in whose *tones,*   580
even, denizens of the five great divisions of Europe could recognize nothing familiar! You will say that it might have been the voice of an Asiatic—of an African.
Neither Asiatics nor Africans abound in Paris; but, without denying the inference,
I will now merely call your attention to three points. The voice is termed by one
witness 'harsh rather than shrill.' It is represented by two others to have been
'quick and *unequal.'* No words—no sounds resembling words—were by any witness mentioned as distinguishable.

      "I know not," continued Dupin, "what impression I may have made, so far,
upon your own understanding; but I do not hesitate to say that legitimate deductions even from this portion of the testimony—the portion respecting the gruff   590
and shrill voices—are in themselves sufficient to engender a suspicion which
should give direction to all farther progress in the investigation of the mystery. I
said 'legitimate deductions'; but my meaning is not thus fully expressed. I designed to imply that the deductions are the *sole* proper ones, and that the suspicion arises *inevitably* from them as the single result. What the suspicion is,
however, I will not say just yet. I merely wish you to bear in mind that, with myself, it was sufficiently forcible to give a definite form—a certain tendency—to my
inquiries in the chamber.

      "Let us now transport ourselves, in fancy, to this chamber. What shall we
first seek here? The means of egress employed by the murderers. It is not too   600
much to say that neither of us believe in præternatural events. Madame and
Mademoiselle L'Espanaye were not destroyed by spirits. The doers of the deed
were material and escaped materially. Then how? Fortunately there is but one
mode of reasoning upon the point, and that mode *must* lead us to a definite decision. Let us examine, each by each, the possible means of egress. It is clear that the
assassins were in the room where Mademoiselle L'Espanaye was found, or at least
in the room adjoining, when the party ascended the stairs. It is, then, only from
these two apartments that we have to seek issues. The police have laid bare the
floors, the ceiling, and the masonry of the walls, in every direction. No *secret* issues could have escaped their vigilance. But, not trusting to *their* eyes, I examined   610
with my own. There were, then, *no* secret issues. Both doors leading from the
rooms into the passage were securely locked, with the keys inside. Let us turn to
the chimneys. These, although of ordinary width for some eight or ten feet above
the hearths, will not admit, throughout their extent, the body of a large cat. The
impossibility of egress, by means already stated, being thus absolute, we are reduced to the windows. Through those of the front room no one could have escaped without notice from the crowd in the street. The murderers *must* have
passed, then, through those of the back room. Now, brought to this conclusion in
so unequivocal a manner as we are, it is not our part, as reasoners, to reject it on

account of apparent impossibilities. It is only left for us to prove that these appar- 620
ent 'impossibilities' are, in reality, not such.

"There are two windows in the chamber. One of them is unobstructed by
furniture, and is wholly visible. The lower portion of the other is hidden from
view by the head of the unwieldy bedstead which is thrust close up against it. The
former was found securely fastened from within. It resisted the utmost force of
those who endeavored to raise it. A large gimlet-hole had been pierced in its frame
to the left, and a very stout nail was found fitted therein, nearly to the head. Upon
examining the other window, a similar nail was seen similarly fitted in it; and a
vigorous attempt to raise this sash failed also. The police were now entirely satisfied that egress had not been in these directions. And, *therefore,* it was thought a 630
matter of supererogation to withdraw the nails and open the windows.

"My own examination was somewhat more particular, and was so for the
reason I have just given—because here it was, I knew, that all apparent impossibilities *must* be proved to be not such in reality.

"I proceeded to think thus—*a posteriori*.[16] The murderers *did* escape from
one of these windows. This being so, they could not have re-fastened the sashes
from the inside, as they were found fastened;—the consideration which put a
stop, through its obviousness, to the scrutiny of the police in this quarter. Yet the
sashes *were* fastened. They *must,* then, have the power of fastening themselves.
There was no escape from this conclusion. I stepped to the unobstructed case- 640
ment, withdrew the nail with some difficulty, and attempted to raise the sash. It
resisted all my efforts, as I had anticipated. A concealed spring must, I now knew,
exist; and this corroboration of my idea convinced me that my premises, at least,
were correct, however mysterious still appeared the circumstances attending the
nails. A careful search soon brought to light the hidden spring. I pressed it, and,
satisfied with the discovery, forbore to upraise the sash.

"I now replaced the nail and regarded it attentively. A person passing out
through this window might have reclosed it, and the spring would have caught—
but the nail could not have been replaced. The conclusion was plain, and again
narrowed in the field of my investigations. The assassins *must* have escaped 650
through the other window. Supposing, then, the springs upon each sash to be the
same, as was probable, there *must* be found a difference between the nails, or at
least between the modes of their fixture. Getting upon the sacking of the bedstead,
I looked over the head-board minutely at the second casement. Passing my hand
down behind the board, I readily discovered and pressed the spring, which was,
as I had supposed, identical in character with its neighbor. I now looked at the
nail. It was as stout as the other, and apparently fitted in the same manner—
driven in nearly up to the head.

"You will say that I was puzzled; but, if you think so, you must have misunderstood the nature of the inductions. To use a sporting phrase, I had not been 660
once 'at fault.' The scent had never for an instant been lost. There was no flaw in
any link of the chain. I had traced the secret to its ultimate result,—and that result
was *the nail.* It had, I say, in every respect, the appearance of its fellow in the other
window; but this fact was an absolute nullity (conclusive as it might seem to be)

16. Reasoning from experience, from effect to cause.

when compared with the consideration that here, at this point, terminated the clew. 'There *must* be something wrong,' I said, 'about the nail.' I touched it; and the head, with about a quarter of an inch of the shank, came off in my fingers. The rest of the shank was in the gimlet-hole, where it had been broken off. The fracture was an old one (for its edges were incrusted with rust), and had apparently been accomplished by the blow of a hammer, which had partially imbedded, in 670 the top of the bottom sash, the head portion of the nail. I now carefully replaced this head portion in the indentation whence I had taken it, and the resemblance to a perfect nail was complete—the fissure was invisible. Pressing the spring, I gently raised the sash for a few inches; the head went up with it, remaining firm in its bed. I closed the window, and the semblance of the whole nail was again perfect.

"This riddle, so far, was now unriddled. The assassin had escaped through the window which looked upon the bed. Dropping of its own accord upon his exit (or perhaps purposely closed), it had become fastened by the spring; and it was the retention of this spring which had been mistaken by the police for that of the nail,—farther inquiry being thus considered unnecessary.   680

"The next question is that of the mode of descent. Upon this point I had been satisfied in my walk with you around the building. About five feet and a half from the casement in question there runs a lightning-rod. From this rod it would have been impossible for any one to reach the window itself, to say nothing of entering it. I observed, however, that the shutters of the fourth story were of the peculiar kind called by Parisian carpenters *ferrades*—a kind rarely employed at the present day, but frequently seen upon very old mansions at Lyons and Bordeaux. They are in the form of an ordinary door (a single, not a folding door), except that the lower half is latticed or worked in open trellis—thus affording an excellent hold for the hands. In the present instance these shutters are fully three feet and a 690 half broad. When we saw them from the rear of the house, they were both about half open—that is to say, they stood off at right angles from the wall. It is probable that the police, as well as myself, examined the back of the tenement; but, if so, in looking at these *ferrades* in the line of their breadth (as they must have done), they did not perceive this great breadth itself, or, at all events, failed to take it into due consideration. In fact, having once satisfied themselves that no egress could have been made in this quarter, they would naturally bestow here a very cursory examination. It was clear to me, however, that the shutter belonging to the window at the head of the bed, would, if swung fully back to the wall, reach to within two feet of the lightning-rod. It was also evident that, by exertion of a very unusual de- 700 gree of activity and courage, an entrance into the window, from the rod, might have been thus effected. By reaching to the distance of two feet and a half (we now suppose the shutter open to its whole extent) a robber might have taken a firm grasp upon the trellis-work. Letting go, then, his hold upon the rod, placing his feet securely against the wall, and springing boldly from it, he might have swung the shutter so as to close it, and, if we imagine the window open at the time, might even have swung himself into the room.

"I wish you to bear especially in mind that I have spoken of a *very* unusual degree of activity as requisite to success in so hazardous and so difficult a feat. It is my design to show you first, that the thing might possibly have been accom- 710 plished:—but, secondly and *chiefly,* I wish to impress upon your understanding the *very extraordinary*—the almost præternatural character of that agility which could have accomplished it.

"You will say, no doubt, using the language of the law, that 'to make out my case, I should rather undervalue than insist upon a full estimation of the activity required in this matter. This may be the practice in law, but it is not the usage of reason. My ultimate object is only the truth. My immediate purpose is to lead you to place in juxtaposition, that *very unusual* activity of which I have just spoken, with that *very peculiar* shrill (or harsh) and *unequal* voice, about whose nationality no two persons could be found to agree, and in whose utterance no syllabification 720 could be detected."

At these words a vague and half-formed conception of the meaning of Dupin flitted over my mind. I seemed to be upon the verge of comprehension, without power to comprehend—as men, at times, find themselves upon the brink of re-membrance, without being able, in the end, to remember. My friend went on with his discourse.

"You will see," he said, "that I have shifted the question from the mode of egress to that of ingress. It was my design to convey the idea that both were ef-fected in the same manner, at the same point. Let us now revert to the interior of the room. Let us survey the appearances here. The drawers of the bureau, it is 730 said, had been rifled, although many articles of apparel still remained within them. The conclusion here is absurd. It is a mere guess—a very silly one—and no more. How are we to know that the articles found in the drawers were not all these drawers had originally contained? Madame L'Espanaye and her daughter lived an exceedingly retired life—saw no company—seldom went out—had little use for numerous changes of habiliment. Those found were at least of as good quality as any likely to be possessed by these ladies. If a thief had taken any, why did he not take the best—why did he not take all? In a word, why did he abandon four thousand francs in gold to encumber himself with a bundle of linen? The gold *was* abandoned. Nearly the whole sum mentioned by Monsieur Mignaud, the 740 banker, was discovered, in bags, upon the floor. I wish you therefore, to discard from your thoughts the blundering idea of *motive,* engendered in the brains of the police by that portion of the evidence which speaks of money delivered at the door of the house. Coincidences ten times as remarkable as this (the delivery of the money, and murder committed within three days upon the party receiving it), happen to all of us every hour of our lives, without attracting even momentary no-tice. Coincidences, in general, are great stumbling-blocks in the way of that class of thinkers who have been educated to know nothing of the theory of probabili-ties—that theory to which the most glorious objects of human research are in-debted for the most glorious of illustration. In the present instance, had the gold 750 been gone, the fact of its delivery three days before would have formed something more than a coincidence. It would have been corroborative of this idea of motive. But, under the real circumstances of the case, if we are to suppose gold the motive of this outrage, we must also imagine the perpetrator so vacillating an idiot as to have abandoned his gold and his motive together.

"Keeping now steadily in mind the points to which I have drawn your atten-tion—that peculiar voice, that unusual agility, and that startling absence of motive in a murder so singularly atrocious as this—let us glance at the butchery itself.

Here is a woman strangled to death by manual strength, and thrust up a chimney head downward. Ordinary assassins employ no much mode of murder as this. Least of all, do they thus dispose of the murdered. In the manner of thrusting the corpse up the chimney, you will admit that there was something *excessively outré*— something altogether irreconcilable with our common notions of human action, even when we suppose the actors the most depraved of men. Think, too, how great must have been that strength which could have thrust the body *up* such an aperture so forcibly that the united vigor of several persons was found barely sufficient to drag it *down!*

"Turn, now, to other indications of the employment of a vigor most marvellous. On the hearth were thick tresses—very thick tresses—of gray human hair. These had been torn out by the roots. You are aware of the great force necessary in tearing thus from the head even twenty or thirty hairs together. You saw the locks in question as well as myself. Their roots (a hideous sight!) were clotted with fragments of the flesh of the scalp—sure token of the prodigious power which had been exerted in uprooting perhaps half a million hairs at a time. The throat of the old lady was not merely cut, but the head absolutely severed from the body: the instrument was a mere razor. I wish you also to look at the *brutal* ferocity of these deeds. Of the bruises upon the body of Madame L'Espanaye I do not speak. Monsieur Dumas, and his worthy coadjutor Monsieur Etienne, have pronounced that they were inflicted by some obtuse instrument; and so far these gentlemen are very correct. The obtuse instrument was clearly the stone pavement in the yard, upon which the victim had fallen from the window which looked in upon the bed. This idea, however simple it may now seem, escaped the police for the same reason that the breadth of the shutters escaped them—because, by the affair of the nails, their perceptions had been hermetically sealed against the possibility of the windows having ever been opened at all.

"If now, in addition to all these things, you have properly reflected upon the odd disorder of the chamber, we have gone so far as to combine the ideas of an agility astounding, a strength superhuman, a ferocity brutal, a butchery without motive, a *grotesquerie* in horror absolutely alien from humanity, and a voice foreign in tone to the ears of men of many nations, and devoid of all distinct or intelligible syllabification. What result, then, has ensued? What impression have I made upon your fancy?"

I felt a creeping of the flesh as Dupin asked me the question. "A madman," I said, "has done this deed—some raving maniac, escaped from a neighboring *Maison de Santé.*"

"In some respects," he replied, "your idea is not irrelevant. But the voices of madmen, even in their wildest paroxysms, are never found to tally with that peculiar voice heard upon the stairs. Madmen are of some nation, and their language, however incoherent in its words, has always the coherence of syllabification. Besides, the hair of a madman is not such as I now hold in my hand. I disentangled this little tuft from the rigidly clutched fingers of Madame L'Espanaye. Tell me what you can make of it."

"Dupin!" I said, completely unnerved; "this hair is most unusual—this is no *human* hair."

"I have not asserted that it is," said he; "but, before we decide this point, I wish you to glance at the little sketch I have here traced upon this paper. It is a *facsimile* drawing of what has been described in one portion of the testimony as 'dark bruises and deep indentations of finger nails' upon the throat of Mademoiselle L'Espanaye, and in another (by Messrs. Dumas and Etienne) as a 'series of livid spots, evidently the impression of fingers.'   870

"You will perceive," continued my friend, spreading out the paper upon the table before us, "that this drawing gives the idea of a firm and fixed hold. There is no *slipping* apparent. Each finger has retained—possibly until the death of the victim—the fearful grasp by which it originally imbedded itself. Attempt, now, to place all your fingers, at the same time, in the respective impressions as you see them."

I made the attempt in vain.

"We are possibly not giving this matter a fair trial," he said. "The paper is spread out upon a plane surface; but the human throat is cylindrical. Here is a billet of wood, the circumference of which is about that of the throat. Wrap the   880 drawing around it, and try the experiment again."

I did so; but the difficulty was even more obvious than before. "This," I said, "is the mark of no human hand."

"Read now," replied Dupin, "this passage from Cuvier."

It was a minute anatomical and generally descriptive account of the large fulvous[17] Ourang-Outang of the East Indian Islands. The gigantic stature, the prodigious strength and activity, the wild ferocity, and the imitative propensities of these mammalia are sufficiently well known to all. I understood the full horrors of the murder at once.

"The description of the digits," said I, as I made an end of the reading, "is in   890 exact accordance with this drawing. I see that no animal but an Ourang-Outang, of the species here mentioned, could have impressed the indentations as you have traced them. This tuft of tawny hair, too, is identical in character with that of the beast of Cuvier. But I cannot possibly comprehend the particulars of this frightful mystery. Besides, there were *two* voices heard in contention, and one of them was unquestionably the voice of a Frenchman."

"True; and you will remember an expression attributed almost unanimously, by the evidence, to this voice,—the expression, '*mon Dieu!*' This, under the circumstances, has been justly characterized by one of the witnesses (Montani, the confectioner) as an expression of remonstrance or expostulation. Upon these two   900 words, therefore, I have mainly built my hopes of a full solution of the riddle. A Frenchman was cognizant of the murder. It is possible—indeed it is far more than probable—that he was innocent of all participation in the bloody transactions which took place. The Ourang-Outang may have escaped from him. He may have traced it to the chamber; but, under the agitating circumstances which ensued, he could never have recaptured it. It is still at large. I will not pursue these guesses—for I have no right to call them more—since the shades of reflection upon which they are based are scarcely of sufficient depth to be appreciable by my own intel-

17. Dull yellow or tawny.

lect, and since I could not pretend to make them intelligible to the understanding of another. We will call them guesses, then, and speak of them as such. If the Frenchman in question is indeed, as I suppose, innocent of this atrocity, this advertisement, which I left last night, upon our return home, at the office of *Le Monde* (a paper devoted to the shipping interest, and much sought by sailors), will bring him to our residence." 910

He handed me a paper, and I read thus:

"CAUGHT—*In the Bois de Boulogne, early in the morning of the* ———*inst.* (the morning of the murder), *a very large, tawny Ourang-Outang of the Bornese species. The owner (who is ascertained to be a sailor, belonging to a Maltese vessel) may have the animal again, upon identifying it satisfactorily, and paying a few charges arising from its capture and keeping. Call at No.* ——— *Rue* ———, *Faubourg St. Germain—au* 920 *troisième.*"[18]

"How was it possible," I asked, "that you should know the man to be a sailor, and belonging to a Maltese vessel?"

"I do *not* know it," said Dupin. "I am not *sure* of it. Here, however, is a small piece of ribbon, which from its form, and from its greasy appearance, has evidently been used in tying the hair in one in those long *queues*[19] of which sailors are so fond. Moreover, this knot is one which few besides sailors can tie, and is peculiar to the Maltese. I picked the ribbon up at the foot of the lightning-rod. It could not have belonged to either of the deceased. Now if, after all, I am wrong in 930 my induction from this ribbon, that the Frenchman was a sailor belonging to a Maltese vessel, still I can have done no harm in saying what I did in the advertisement. If I am in error, he will merely suppose that I have been misled by some circumstance into which he will not take the trouble to inquire. But if I am right, a great point is gained. Cognizant although innocent of the murder, the Frenchman will naturally hesitate about replying to the advertisement—about demanding that Ourang-Outang. He will reason thus:—'I am innocent; I am poor; my Ourang-Outang is of great value—to one in my circumstances a fortune of itself—why should I lose it through idle apprehensions of danger? Here it is, within my grasp. It was found in the Bois de Boulogne—at a vast distance from the scene of that 940 butchery. How can it ever be suspected that a brute beast should have done that deed? The police are at fault—they have failed to procure the slightest clew. Should they even trace the animal, it would be impossible to prove me cognizant of the murder, or to implicate me in guilt on account of that cognizance. Above all, *I am known*. The advertiser designates me as the possessor of the beast. I am not sure to what limit his knowledge may extend. Should I avoid claiming a property of so great value, which it is known that I possess, I will render the animal at least, liable to suspicion. It is not my policy to attract attention either to myself or to the beast. I will answer the advertisement, get the Ourang-Outang, and keep it close until this matter has blown over.'" 950

At this moment we heard a step upon the stairs.

18. On the third floor.
19. Pigtails.

"Be ready," said Dupin, "with your pistols, but neither use them nor show them until at a signal from myself."

The front door of the house had been left open, and the visitor had entered, without ringing, and advanced several steps upon the staircase. Now, however, he seemed to hesitate. Presently we heard him descending. Dupin was moving quickly to the door, when we again heard him coming up. He did not turn back a second time, but stepped up with decision, and rapped at the door of our chamber.

"Come in," said Dupin, in a cheerful and hearty tone.

A man entered. He was a sailor, evidently,—a tall, stout, and muscular-looking person, with a certain dare-devil expression of countenance, not altogether unprepossessing. His face, greatly sunburnt, was more than half hidden by whisker and *mustachio*. He had with him a huge oaken cudgel, but appeared to be otherwise unarmed. He bowed awkwardly, and bade us "good evening," in French accents, which, although somewhat Neufchatelish, were still sufficiently indicative of a Parisian origin.

"Sit down, my friend," said Dupin. "I suppose you have called about the Ourang-Outang. Upon my word, I almost envy you the possession of him; a remarkably fine, and no doubt a very valuable animal. How old do you suppose him to be?"

The sailor drew a long breath, with the air of a man relieved of some intolerable burden, and then replied, in an assured tone:

"I have no way of telling—but he can't be more than four or five years old. Have you got him here?"

"Oh, no; we had no conveniences for keeping him here. He is at a livery stable in the Rue Dubourg, just by. You can get him in the morning. Of course you are prepared to identify the property?"

"To be sure I am, sir."

"I shall be sorry to part with him," said Dupin.

"I don't mean that you should be at all this trouble for nothing, sir," said the man. "Couldn't expect it. Am very willing to pay reward for the finding of the animal—that is to say, any thing in reason."

"Well," replied my friend, "that is all very fair, to be sure. Let me think!— what should I have? Oh! I will tell you. My reward shall be this. You shall give me all the information in your power about these murders in the Rue Morgue."

Dupin said the last words in a very low tone, and very quietly. Just as quietly, too, he walked toward the door, locked it, and put the key in his pocket. He then drew a pistol from his bosom and placed it, without the least flurry, upon the table.

The sailor's face flushed up as if he were struggling with suffocation. He started to his feet and grasped his cudgel; but the next moment he fell back into his seat, trembling violently, and with the countenance of death itself. He spoke not a word. I pitied him from the bottom of my heart.

"My friend," said Dupin, in a kind tone, "you are alarming yourself unnecessarily—you are indeed. We mean you no harm whatever. I pledge you the honor of a gentleman, and of a Frenchman, that we intend you no injury. I perfectly well know that you are innocent of the atrocities in the Rue Morgue. It will not do, however, to deny that you are in some measure implicated in them. From what I have already said, you must know that I have had means of information about this matter—means of which you could never have dreamed. Now the thing stands thus. You have done nothing which you could have avoided—nothing, certainly, which renders you culpable. You were not even guilty of robbery, when you might have robbed with impunity. You have nothing to conceal. You have no reason for concealment. On the other hand, you are bound by every principle of honor to confess all you know. An innocent man is now imprisoned, charged with that crime of which you can point out the perpetrator." 1010

The sailor had recovered his presence of mind, in a great measure, while Dupin uttered these words; but his original boldness of bearing was all gone.

"So help me God!" said he, after a brief pause, "I *will* tell you all I know about this affair;—but I do not expect you to believe one half I say—I would be a fool indeed if I did. Still, I *am* innocent, and I will make a clean breast if I die for it."

What he stated was, in substance, this. He had lately made a voyage to the Indian Archipelago. A party, of which he formed one, landed at Borneo, and passed into the interior on an excursion of pleasure. Himself and a companion had captured the Ourang-Outang. This companion dying, the animal fell into his 1020 own exclusive possession. After great trouble, occasionally by the intractable ferocity of his captive during the home voyage, he at length succeeded in lodging it safely at his own residence in Paris, where, not to attract toward himself the unpleasant curiosity of his neighbors, he kept it carefully secluded, until such time as it should recover from a wound in the foot, received from a splinter on board ship. His ultimate design was to sell it.

Returning home from some sailors' frolic on the night, or rather in the morning, of the murder, he found the beast occupying his own bedroom, into which it had broken from a closet adjoining, where it had been, as was thought, securely confined. Razor in hand, and fully lathered, it was sitting before a looking-glass, 1030 attempting the operation of shaving, in which it had no doubt previously watched its master through the keyhole of the closet. Terrified at the sight of so dangerous a weapon in the possession of an animal so ferocious, and so well able to use it, the man, for some moments, was at a loss what to do. He had been accustomed, however, to quiet the creature, even in its fiercest moods, by the use of a whip, and to this he now resorted. Upon sight of it, the Ourang-Outang sprang at once through the door of the chamber, down the stairs, and thence, through a window, unfortunately open, into the street.

The Frenchman followed in despair; the ape, razor still in hand, occasionally stopping to look back and gesticulate at his pursuer, until the latter had nearly 1040 come up with it. It then again made off. In this manner the chase continued for a long time. The streets were profoundly quiet, as it was nearly three o'clock in the morning. In passing down an alley in the rear of the Rue Morgue, the fugitive's attention was arrested by a light gleaming from the open window of Madame L'Espanaye's chamber, in the fourth story of her house. Rushing to the building, it perceived the lightning-rod, clambered up with inconceivable agility, grasped the shutter, which was thrown fully back against the wall, and, by its means, swung itself directly upon the headboard of the bed. The whole feat did not occupy a minute. The shutter was kicked open again by the Ourang-Outang as it entered the room. 1050

The sailor, in the meantime, was both rejoiced and perplexed. He had strong hopes of now recapturing the brute, as it could scarcely escape from the trap into which it had ventured, except by the rod, where it might be intercepted as it came down. On the other hand, there was much cause for anxiety as to what it might do in the house. This latter reflection urged the man still to follow the fugitive. A lightning-rod is ascended without difficulty, especially by a sailor; but, when he had arrived as high as the window, which lay far to his left, his career was stopped; the most that he could accomplish was to reach over so as to obtain a glimpse of the interior of the room. At this glimpse he nearly fell from his hold through excess of horror. Now it was that those hideous shrieks arose upon the 1060 night, which had startled from slumber the inmates of the Rue Morgue. Madame L'Espanaye and her daughter, habited in their night clothes, had apparently been occupied in arranging some papers in the iron chest already mentioned, which had been wheeled into the middle of the room. It was open, and its contents lay beside it on the floor. The victims must have been sitting with their backs toward the window; and, from the time elapsing between the ingress of the beast and the screams, it seems probable that it was not immediately perceived. The flapping-to of the shutter would naturally have been attributed to the wind.

As the sailor looked in, the gigantic animal had seized Madame L'Espanaye by the hair (which was loose, as she had been combing it), and was flourishing the 1070 razor about her face, in imitation of the motions of a barber. The daughter lay prostrate and motionless; she had swooned. The screams and struggles of the old lady (during which the hair was torn from her head) had the effect of changing the probably pacific purposes of the Ourang-Outang into those of wrath. With one determined sweep of its muscular arm it nearly severed her head from her body. The sight of blood inflamed its anger into phrensy. Gnashing its teeth, and flashing fire from its eyes, it flew upon the body of the girl, and imbedded its fearful talons in her throat, retaining its grasp until she expired. Its wandering and wild glances fell at this moment upon the head of the bed, over which the face of its master, rigid with horror, was just discernible. The fury of the beast, who no doubt bore 1080 still in mind the dreaded whip, was instantly converted into fear. Conscious of having deserved punishment, it seemed desirous of concealing its bloody deeds, and skipped about the chamber in an agony of nervous agitation; throwing down and breaking the furniture as it moved, and dragging the bed from the bedstead. In conclusion, it seized first the corpse of the daughter, and thrust it up the chimney, as it was found; then that of the old lady, which it immediately hurled through the window headlong.

As the ape approached the casement with its mutilated burden, the sailor shrank aghast to the rod, and, rather gliding than clambering down it, hurried at once home—dreading the consequences of the butchery, and gladly abandoning, 1090 in his terror, all solicitude about the fate of the Ourang-Outang. The words heard by the party upon the staircase were the Frenchman's exclamations of horror and affright, commingled with the fiendish jabberings of the brute.

I have scarcely any thing to add. The Ourang-Outang must have escaped from the chamber, by the rod, just before the breaking of the door. It must have closed the window as it passed through it. It was subsequently caught by the owner himself, who obtained for it a very large sum at the *Jardin des Plantes*. Le Bon was instantly released, upon our narration of the circumstances (with some comments from Dupin) at the *bureau* of the Prefect of Police. This functionary, however well disposed to my friend, could not altogether conceal his chagrin at the turn which affairs had taken, and was fain to indulge in a sarcasm or two about the propriety of every person minding his own business. 1100

"Let him talk," said Dupin, who had not thought it necessary to reply. "Let him discourse; it will ease his conscience. I am satisfied with having defeated him in his own castle. Nevertheless, that he failed in the solution of this mystery, is by no means that matter for wonder which he supposes it; for, in truth, our friend the Prefect is somewhat too cunning to be profound. In his wisdom is no *stamen*. It is all head and no body, like the pictures of the Goddess Laverna—or, at best, all head and shoulders, like a codfish. But he is a good creature after all. I like him especially for one master stroke of cant, by which he has attained his reputation 1110 for ingenuity. I mean the way he has '*de nier ce qui est, et d'expliquer ce qui n'est pas*.'"[20]   [1841]

Questions for Discussion and Writing

1. Poe is usually credited with creating the major conventions of the detective story. List the conventions you find in this story. How many of them are still common in literature, film, and television?

2. What is the purpose of the discussion of reasoning? How does it contribute to or detract from the story?

3. How do the story's setting and atmosphere contribute to its effectiveness? Underline or highlight particularly effective passages.

4. From what point of view is the story told? How would the story change if told by Dupin himself or by an omniscient narrator?

5. Does this story have a theme? If so, what do you think it is?

---

20. "Of denying that which is and explaining that which is not."

Sidebar: EXPLORING SUB-GENRES

The Detective Story

Although elements of the detective story may be found in literature as old as the Bible's *Book of Daniel* (sixth century B.C.) and Virgil's *Aeneid* (first century B.C.), credit for inventing the form is almost universally assigned to Edgar Allan Poe. Even here, however, Poe may have been indebted to E. T. A. Hoffmann, specifically "Mademoiselle de Scudery" (1820), for his immediate inspiration, but beyond doubt it was Poe who gave the form its characteristic shape and codified its basic conventions.

Like the short story itself, the detective story is the result of social and technological changes set in motion by the Industrial Revolution. Most countries, including the United States, had no organized police force until the mass migration of people from the country created the need for officers to keep law and order in the rapidly growing and often violent cities. Paris (where Poe's Auguste Dupin solves his cases) was the first to establish a regular police force, the Sûreté, in 1810. In England, Sir Robert Peel

Illustration by Sidney Paget (1861–1908) of a scene in Sir Arthur Conan Doyle's novel The Hound of the Baskervilles *(1902). From* The Hound of the Baskervilles *by Sir Arthur Conan Doyle. Reprinted with permission of Garland Publishing.*

organized London's "Bobbies" in 1829. The dangers and violence of city life may be responsible, too, for a reversal of the popular attitude toward crime. In earlier literature, sympathy almost always lay on the side of the "criminal," whether Reynard the Fox or Robin Hood, but the detective story upholds law and order against the anarchic tendencies of crime and the criminal. Even today, the form is most popular in countries like England, France, and the United States where public sentiment is clearly on the side of the law.

However based in social reality the detective story may be, its particular form is shaped by conventions, nearly all of which have their origin in Poe's five detective stories. "The Murders in the Rue Morgue" exhibits many of these: the lone, eccentric amateur detective, the bungling or incompetent police, the commission of a crime whose clues create an intellectual puzzle, the arrest of an innocent party, and the solution to the crime in a novel and unexpected way. Equally important is Poe's creation of the narrator, the Watson-like figure who admiringly reports Dupin's successes and vainly tries to understand his "methods." These conventions are in many ways direct outgrowths of the Romantic spirit: Dupin may be seen as the lone individual and individualist in opposition to the methodical but inept police, the representatives of ordinary society. Moreover, Poe's interest in the logical and psychological aspects of interpreting clues and solving the puzzle mirrors the Romantics' interest in the workings of the mind. Crime itself pits the instinctual, anarchic urges of the individual against those of rationality and order in conventional bourgeois society.

After almost two centuries of crime literature in print, film, theater, and television, it seems almost incomprehensible that Poe's formulas lay unused for almost forty years after his stories were published. It may, in fact, have been the continued popularity of James Fenimore Cooper's Leatherstocking series that gave new impetus to the detective story. Cooper's heroes, whose woodcraft parallels the skills of the typical detective, may have inspired a generation of writers to combine popular Gothic elements with Poe's formulas to resuscitate the detective genre, but it was perhaps Englishman Wilkie Collins who was most responsible for reinventing the form in such novels as *The Woman in White* (1860) and *The Moonstone* (1868).

The short story of crime and detection did not become popular, however, until Conan Doyle adopted Poe's formulas, beginning with "A Study in Scarlet" in 1887. Conan Doyle streamlined Poe's psychological probings, infused more action and racy dialogue into his stories, set his mysteries amidst the daily life of late-Victorian England, and above all created in Holmes and Watson the ultimate eccentric detective and his ordinary "sidekick." For the next forty years, detective fiction used Conan Doyle's conventions in the so-called classic detective story as later practiced by Agatha Christie and countless others. The "classic" or "formal" detective story uses all of Poe's conventions along with a few additions: the setting is often some enclosed location, such as a hotel or English country house;

the characters are stereotypical representatives of a cross-section of polite society; the crime is almost inevitably murder.

Commentators on the "classic" detective story have noted that it works better in the settled societies of England and Europe than in the raucous democracies of North America. The classic detective story resembles the European novel of manners; in America the romance, in both its popular and literary forms, has been the characteristic mode. America's indigenous mysteries are of the "hard-boiled" school that came to prominence in the so-called pulp magazines such as *The Black Mask* that arose after World War I.

Of the scores who practiced the form, Dashiell Hammet and Raymond Chandler emerged as writers of lasting importance, not only for the ingenuity of their plots, but also for their literary accomplishments. Combining a naturalistic attention to surface detail with straightforward, no-nonsense prose, an ear for slang, and a gift for similes, the hard-boiled writers created a uniquely American hero: the fiercely independent private eye, with his suspicion of the wealthy, the powerful, and the intellectually pretentious; the lone hero with his own code of justice battling the corruption of gangsters, politicians, and entrenched interests. Quick with his fists and the gun, devastating to women, faithful to his own (not society's) moral code, the private eye dispenses rough justice in a dangerous and violent world.

The conventionality of the detective story makes it easy to parody, or in the case of Jorge Luis Borges, to manipulate for far different purposes. Borges counts on our knowledge of detective story conventions and violates our expectations at nearly every turn to create a world in which logic backfires and injustice triumphs. Somerset Maugham's "The Letter" and Susan Glaspell's "A Jury of Her Peers" also reverse our usual assumptions and expectations. They look at crime from new points of view, other than those of the police. These are not, of course, detective stories, but they use detective story conventions and situations to comment on society.

Like any highly conventional form, the detective story encourages ingenious plots and characters within the limits of its formal requirements. Authors have created a vast array of detectives, male and female, from almost every walk of life, and set these sleuths to work unraveling mysteries of great originality and complexity. The form provides challenges for writers, but why, especially when it is almost certain that the criminal will be caught, do readers and viewers continue to find the form attractive? Does the appeal lie in suspense, or in the pleasing expectation that justice will be done? How much does the appeal of the genre rely on the challenge of solving the puzzle of "whodunit"? What do the characteristics of the detective reveal about the kinds of men and women we admire? Critics are still debating whether the detective story is capable of the highest achievements of art. Meanwhile, cultural and literary critics and ordinary readers alike analyze the changing conventions of the genre for what the changes say about our cultural attitudes, values, and ideas.

❧ EDGAR ALLAN POE
(1809–1849)

The Tell-Tale Heart

TRUE!—NERVOUS—VERY, very dreadfully nervous I had been and am; but why *will* you say that I am mad? The disease had sharpened my senses—not destroyed—not dulled them. Above all was the sense of hearing acute. I heard all things in the heaven and in the earth. I heard many things in hell. How, then, am I mad? Hearken! and observe how healthily—how calmly I can tell you the whole story.

It is impossible to say how first the idea entered my brain; but once conceived, it haunted me day and night. Object there was none. Passion there was none. I loved the old man. He had never wronged me. He had never given me insult. For his gold I had no desire. I think it was his eye! yes, it was this! One of his 10 eyes resembled that of a vulture—a pale blue eye, with a film over it. Whenever it fell upon me, my blood ran cold; and so by degrees—very gradually—I made up my mind to take the life of the old man, and thus rid myself of the eye for ever.

Now this is the point. You fancy me mad. Madmen know nothing. But you should have seen *me*. You should have seen how wisely I proceeded—with what caution—with what foresight—with what dissimulation I went to work! I was never kinder to the old man than during the whole week before I killed him. And every night, about midnight, I turned the latch of his door and opened it—oh, so gently! And then, when I had made an opening sufficient for my head, I put in a dark lantern, all closed, closed, so that no light shone out, and then I thrust in my 20 head. Oh, you would have laughed to see how cunningly I thrust it in! I moved it slowly—very, very slowly, so that I might not disturb the old man's sleep. It took me an hour to place my whole head within the opening so far that I could see him as he lay upon his bed. Ha!—would a madman have been so wise as this? And then, when my head was well in the room, I undid the lantern cautiously—oh, so cautiously—cautiously (for the hinges creaked)—I undid it just so much that a single thin ray fell upon the vulture eye. And this I did for seven long nights— every night just at midnight—but I found the eye always closed; and so it was impossible to do the work; for it was not the old man who vexed me, but his Evil Eye.[1] And every morning, when the day broke, I went boldly into the chamber, 30 and spoke courageously to him, calling him by name in a hearty tone, and inquiring how he had passed the night. So you see he would have been a very profound old man, indeed, to suspect that every night, just at twelve, I looked in upon him while he slept.

Upon the eighth night I was more than usually cautious in opening the door. A watch's minute hand moves more quickly than did mine. Never before that night had I *felt* the extent of my own powers—of my sagacity. I could scarcely contain my feelings of triumph. To think that there I was, opening the door, little by little, and he not even to dream of my secret deeds or thoughts. I fairly chuckled at the idea; and perhaps he heard me; for he moved on the bed suddenly, as if star- 40

1. The ability to cause harm by a look.

tled. Now you may think that I drew back—but no. His room was as black as pitch with the thick darkness (for the shutters were close fastened, through fear of robbers), and so I knew that he could not see the opening of the door, and I kept pushing it on steadily, steadily.

I had my head in, and was about to open the lantern, when my thumb slipped upon the tin fastening, and the old man sprang up in the bed, crying out—"Who's there?"

I kept quite still and said nothing. For a whole hour I did not move a muscle, and in the meantime I did not hear him lie down. He was still sitting up in the bed listening;—just as I have done, night after night, hearkening to the death watches in the wall.[2]

Presently I heard a slight groan, and I knew it was the groan of mortal terror. It was not a groan of pain or of grief—oh, no!—it was the low stifled sound that arises from the bottom of the soul when overcharged with awe. I knew the sound well. Many a night, just at midnight, when all the world slept, it has welled up from my own bosom, deepening, with its dreadful echo, the terrors that distracted me. I say I knew it well. I knew what the old man felt, and pitied him, although I chuckled at heart. I knew that he had been lying awake ever since the first slight noise, when he had turned in the bed. His fears had been ever since growing upon him. He had been trying to fancy them causeless, but could not. He had been saying to himself—"It is nothing but the wind in the chimney—it is only a mouse crossing the floor," or "it is merely a cricket which has made a single chirp." Yes, he had been trying to comfort himself with these suppositions; but he had found all in vain. *All in vain;* because Death, in approaching him, had stalked with his black shadow before him, and enveloped the victim. And it was the mournful influence of the unperceived shadow that caused him to feel—although he neither saw nor heard—to *feel* the presence of my head within the room.

When I had waited a long time, very patiently, without hearing him lie down, I resolved to open a little—a very, very little crevice in the lantern. So I opened it—you cannot imagine how stealthily, stealthily—until, at length, a single dim ray, like the thread of the spider, shot from out the crevice and fell upon the vulture eye.

It was open—wide, wide open—and I grew furious as I gazed upon it. I saw it with perfect distinctness—all a dull blue, with a hideous veil over it that chilled the very marrow in my bones; but I could see nothing else of the old man's face or person: for I had directed the ray as if by instinct, precisely upon the damned spot.

And now have I not told you that what you mistake for madness is but overacuteness of the senses?—now, I say, there came to my ears a low, dull, quick sound, such as a watch makes when enveloped in cotton. I knew *that* sound well too. It was the beating of the old man's heart. It increased my fury, as the beating of a drum stimulates the soldier into courage.

But even yet I refrained and kept still. I scarcely breathed. I held the lantern motionless. I tried how steadily I could maintain the ray upon the eye. Meantime the hellish tattoo of the heart increased. It grew quicker and quicker, and louder

2. Insects that burrow into old wood and make a clicking noise to attract a mate.

and louder every instant. The old man's terror *must* have been extreme! It grew
louder, I say, louder every moment!—do you mark me well? I have told you that I
am nervous: so I am. And now at the dead hour of the night, amid the dreadful silence of that old house, so strange a noise as this excited me to uncontrollable terror. Yet, for some minutes longer I refrained and stood still. But the beating grew   90
louder, louder! I thought the heart must burst. And now a new anxiety seized
me—the sound would be heard by a neighbor! The old man's hour had come!
With a loud yell, I threw open the lantern and leaped into the room. He shrieked
once—once only. In an instant I dragged him to the floor, and pulled the heavy
bed over him. I then smiled gaily, to find the deed so far done. But, for many minutes, the heart beat on with a muffled sound. This, however, did not vex me; it
would not be heard through the wall. At length it ceased. The old man was dead. I
removed the bed and examined the corpse. Yes, he was stone, stone dead. I placed
my hand upon the heart and held it there many minutes. There was no pulsation.
He was stone dead. His eye would trouble me no more.   100

If still you think me mad, you will think so no longer when I describe the
wise precautions I took for the concealment of the body. The night waned, and I
worked hastily, but in silence. First of all I dismembered the corpse. I cut off the
head and the arms and the legs.

I then took up three planks from the flooring of the chamber, and deposited
all between the scantlings.[3] I then replaced the boards so cleverly, so cunningly,
that no human eye—not even *his*—could have detected any thing wrong. There
was nothing to wash out—no stain of any kind—no blood-spot whatever. I had
been too wary for that. A tub had caught all—ha! ha!

When I had made an end of these labors, it was four o'clock—still dark as   110
midnight. As the bell sounded the hour, there came a knocking at the street door.
I went down to open it with a light heart,—for what had I *now* to fear? There entered three men, who introduced themselves, with perfect suavity, as officers of the
police. A shriek had been heard by a neighbor during the night; suspicion of foul
play had been aroused; information had been lodged at the police office, and they
(the officers) had been deputed to search the premises.

I smiled,—for *what* had I to fear? I bade the gentlemen welcome. The shriek,
I said, was my own in a dream. The old man, I mentioned, was absent in the
country. I took my visitors all over the house. I bade them search—search *well*. I
led them, at length, to *his* chamber. I showed them his treasures, secure, undis-   120
turbed. In the enthusiasm of my confidence, I brought chairs into the room, and
desired them *here* to rest from their fatigues, while I myself, in the wild audacity of
my perfect triumph, placed my own seat upon the very spot beneath which reposed the corpse of the victim.

The officers were satisfied. My *manner* had convinced them. I was singularly
at ease. They sat, and while I answered cheerily, they chatted familiar things. But,
ere long, I felt myself getting pale and wished them gone. My head ached, and I
fancied a ringing in my ears: but still they sat and still they chatted. The ringing became
more distinct:—it continued and became more distinct: I talked more freely to get

---

3. Narrow boards that support the floor.

rid of the feeling: but it continued and gained definitiveness—until, at length, I 130
found that the noise was *not* within my ears.

No doubt I now grew *very* pale;—but I talked more fluently, and with a
heightened voice. Yet the sound increased—and what could I do? It was *a low,
dull, quick sound—much such a sound as a watch makes when enveloped in cotton.* I
gasped for breath—and yet the officers heard it not. I talked more quickly—more
vehemently; but the noise steadily increased. I arose and argued about trifles, in a
high key and with violent gesticulations, but the noise steadily increased. Why
would they not be gone? I paced the floor to and fro with heavy strides, as if excited to fury by the observation of the men—but the noise steadily increased. Oh
God! what *could* I do? I foamed—I raved—I swore! I swung the chair upon which 140
I had been sitting, and grated it upon the boards, but the noise arose over all and
continually increased. It grew louder—louder—*louder!* And still the men chatted
pleasantly, and smiled. Was it possible they heard not? Almighty God!—no, no!
They heard!—they suspected!—they *knew!*—they were making a mockery of my
horror!—this I thought, and this I think. But any thing was better than this agony!
Any thing was more tolerable than this derision! I could bear those hypocritical
smiles no longer! I felt that I must scream or die!—and now—again!—hark!
louder! louder! louder! *louder!*—

"Villians!" I shrieked, "dissemble no more! I admit the deed!—tear up the
planks!—here, here!—it is the beating of his hideous heart!"   [1843] 150

Questions for Discussion and Writing
1, Poe did not invent the horror story, but he was a master of the genre and
   helped establish its conventions. How would you characterize the horror
   story as you have encountered it in fiction, television, and film?
2. Characterize the narrator. What motivates him? Can he be dismissed as
   merely a madman, or is he more complex than this?
3. The narrator claims that his victim's eye is what drives him to murder. Why
   does the victim's eye obsess him? What might it symbolize?   160
4. What does the narrator hear? Does he imagine the sound or really hear it?
5. As a conventional horror story does this story—do these stories in general—
   have any significance beyond entertainment?

ꙮ NIKOLAI VASILIEVICH GOGOL
(1809–1852)

TRANSLATED BY CONSTANCE GARNETT

The Overcoat

A famous remark, "We all came out from under Gogol's 'Overcoat,'" has been
attributed to writers as different as Ivan Turgenev (1818–1883), Leo Tolstoy
(1828–1910), and Feodor Dostoyevsky (1821–1881). Often called "the father

of Russian Realism," Nikolai Gogol was a vital link between the eighteenth-century conventions of his predecessors and the Realistic movement of the nineteenth century. His work, however, is also characterized by fantasy and even surrealism.

Born at Sorochintsky in the province of Poltava to a family of Ukrainian Cossack aristocrats, Gogol took his first job in a government office, a position he hated but which served as a source for many of his best-known works. His first literary attempt was so poorly reviewed that he bought all the copies he could find and burned them. His next, a collection of stories set in his native Ukraine and called *Evenings in a Farm Near Dikanka* (1831), was well received; and his brilliant play, *The Inspector General* (1836), was so devastating a satire on government bureaucracy that he was wise to flee to Rome. *Dead Souls,* a novel about the crushing oppression of serfs, appeared in 1842.

Genius is often eccentric, and so it was with Gogol. At one point he walked sideways wherever he went, and he gradually came to believe that literary work was inimical to salvation. He declined into melancholy, destroyed some of his manuscripts, and died in 1852.

As a short story writer, Gogol is credited by Frank O'Connor with being the first to champion the cause of the "little man," specifically the lowly functionary whose quiet life can come to embody a pervasive frustration and sense of mean-inglessness. Interpretations of "The Overcoat" are as many and varied as those of Melville's "Bartleby the Scrivener," another tragicomic story of an underpaid clerk.

I N THE DEPARTMENT OF . . . but I had better not mention which department. There is nothing in the world more touchy than a department, a regiment, a government office, and, in fact, any sort of official body. Nowadays every private individual considers all society insulted in his person. I have been told that very lately a complaint was lodged by a police inspector of which town I don't remember, and that in this complaint he set forth clearly that the institutions of the State were in danger and that his sacred name was being taken in vain; and, in proof thereof, he appended to his complaint an enormously long volume of some romantic work in which a police inspector appeared on every tenth page, occasionally, indeed, in an intoxicated condition. And so, to avoid any unpleasantness, we had better call the department of which we are speaking "a certain department." 10

And so, in a *certain department* there was a *certain clerk;* a clerk of whom it cannot be said that he was very remarkable; he was short, somewhat pock-marked, with rather reddish hair and rather dim, bleary eyes, with a small bald patch on the top of his head, with wrinkles on both sides of his cheeks and the sort of complexion which is usually described as hemorrhoidal . . . nothing can be done about that, it is the Petersburg climate. As for his grade in the civil service (for among us a man's rank is what must be established first) he was what is called a perpetual titular councilor,[1] a class at which, as we all know, various writers who indulge in the praiseworthy habit of attacking those who cannot defend them- 20 selves jeer and jibe to their hearts' content. This clerk's surname was Bashmachkin. From the very name it is clear that it must have been derived from a shoe (*bashmak*); but when and under what circumstances it was derived from a shoe, it is impossible to say. Both his father and his grandfather and even his brother-in-law, and all the Bashmachkins without exception wore boots, which they simply resoled two or three times a year. His name was Akaky Akakievich. Perhaps it may strike the reader as a rather strange and contrived name, but I can assure him that it was not contrived at all, that the circumstances were such that it was quite out of the question to give him any other name. Akaky Akakievich was born toward nightfall, if my memory does not deceive me, on the twenty-third of March. His 30 mother, the wife of a government clerk, a very good woman, made arrangements in due course to christen the child. She was still lying in bed, facing the door, while on her right hand stood the godfather, an excellent man called Ivan Ivanovich Yeroshkin, one of the head clerks in the Senate, and the godmother, the wife of a police official and a woman of rare qualities, Arina Semeonovna Belobriushkova. Three names were offered to the happy mother for selection— Mokky, Sossy, or the name of the martyr Khozdazat. "No," thought the poor lady, "they are all such names!" To satisfy her, they opened the calendar[2] at another page, and the names which turned up were: Trifily, Dula, Varakhasy. "What an infliction!" said the mother. "What names they all are! I really never heard such 40 names. Varadat or Varukh would be bad enough, but Trifily and Varakhasy!" They turned over another page and the names were: Pavsikakhy and Vakhisy. "Well, I see," said the mother, "it is clear that it is his fate. Since that is how it is, he had better be named after his father; his father is Akaky; let the son be Akaky, too." This was how he came to be Akaky Akakievich. The baby was christened and cried and made sour faces during the ceremony, as though he foresaw that he would be a titular councilor. So that was how it all came to pass. We have reported it here so that the reader may see for himself that it happened quite inevitably and that to give him any other name was out of the question.

No one has been able to remember when and how long ago he entered the 50 department, nor who gave him the job. Regardless of how many directors and higher officials of all sorts came and went, he was always seen in the same place, in the same position, at the very same duty, precisely the same copying clerk, so that they used to declare that he must have been born a copying clerk, uniform, bald patch, and all. No respect at all was shown him in the department. The porters, far from getting up from their seats when he came in, took no more notice of him than if a simple fly had flown across the reception room. His superiors treated him with a sort of despotic aloofness. The head clerk's assistant used to throw papers under his nose without even saying "Copy this" or "Here is an interesting, nice little case" or some agreeable remark of the sort, as is usually done in 60 well-bred offices. And he would take it, gazing only at the paper without looking

---

1. The ninth grade (out of fourteen) in the Russian civil service; hence, near the bottom of the scale.
2. The Russian Orthodox calendar noted saints' days; by custom, children were to be named after saints.

to see who had put it there and whether he had the right to do so; he would take it and at once begin copying it. The young clerks jeered and made jokes at him to the best of their clerkly wit, and told before his face all sorts of stories of their own invention about him; they would say of his landlady, an old woman of seventy, that she beat him, would ask when the wedding was to take place, and would scatter bits of paper on his head, calling them snow. Akaky Akakievich never answered a word, however, but behaved as though there were no one there. It had no influence on his work; in the midst of all this teasing, he never made a single mistake in his copying. It was only when the jokes became too unbearable, when they jolted his arm, and prevented him from going on with his work, that he would say: "Leave me alone! Why do you insult me?" and there was something touching in the words and in the voice in which they were uttered. There was a note in it of something that aroused compassion, so that one young man, new to the office, who, following the example of the rest, had allowed himself to tease him, suddenly stopped as though cut to the heart, and from that time on, everything was, as it were, changed and appeared in a different light to him. Some unseen force seemed to repel him from the companions with whom he had become acquainted because he thought they were well-bred and decent men. And long afterward, during moments of the greatest gaiety, the figure of the humble little clerk with a bald patch on his head appeared before him with his heart-rending words: "Leave me alone! Why do you insult me?" and within those moving words he heard others: "I am your brother." And the poor young man hid his face in his hands, and many times afterward in his life he shuddered, seeing how much inhumanity there is in man, how much savage brutality lies hidden under refined, cultured politeness, and, my God! even in a man whom the world accepts as a gentleman and a man of honor. . . .

It would be hard to find a man who lived for his work as did Akaky Akakievich. To say that he was zealous in his work is not enough; no, he loved his work. In it, in that copying, he found an interesting and pleasant world of his own. There was a look of enjoyment on his face; certain letters were favorites with him, and when he came to them he was delighted; he chuckled to himself and winked and moved his lips, so that it seemed as though every letter his pen was forming could be read in his face. If rewards had been given according to the measure of zeal in the service, he might to his amazement have even found himself a civil councilor; but all he gained in the service, as the wits, his fellow clerks, expressed it, was a button in his buttonhole[3] and hemorrhoids where he sat. It cannot be said, however, that no notice had ever been taken of him. One director, being a good-natured man and anxious to reward him for his long service, sent him something a little more important than his ordinary copying; he was instructed to make some sort of report from a finished document for another office; the work consisted only of altering the headings and in places changing the first person into the third. This cost him so much effort that he was covered with perspiration: he mopped his brow and said at last, "No, I'd rather copy something."

From that time on they left him to his copying forever. It seemed as though

3. A clerk of many years' service would normally have been awarded a medal to wear in his buttonhole.

nothing in the world existed for him except his copying. He gave no thought at all to his clothes; his uniform was—well, not green but some sort of rusty, muddy color. His collar was very low and narrow, so that, although his neck was not particularly long, yet, standing out of the collar, it looked as immensely long as those of the dozens of plaster kittens with nodding heads which foreigners carry about on their heads and peddle in Russia. And there were always things sticking to his uniform, either bits of hay or threads; moreover, he had a special knack of passing under a window at the very moment when various garbage was being flung out into the street, and so was continually carrying off bits of melon rind and similar litter on his hat. He had never once in his life noticed what was being done and what was going on in the street, all those things at which, as we all know, his colleagues, the young clerks, always stare, utilizing their keen sight so well that they notice anyone on the other side of the street with a trouser strap hanging loose— an observation which always calls forth a sly grin. Whatever Akaky Akakievich looked at, he saw nothing but his clear, evenly written lines, and it was only perhaps when a horse suddenly appeared from nowhere and placed its head on his shoulder, and with its nostrils blew a real gale upon his cheek, that he would notice that he was not in the middle of his writing, but rather in the middle of the street.

On reaching home, he would sit down at once at the table, hurriedly eat his soup and a piece of beef with an onion; he did not notice the taste at all but ate it all with the flies and anything else that Providence happened to send him. When he felt that his stomach was beginning to be full, he would get up from the table, take out a bottle of ink and begin copying the papers he had brought home with him. When he had none to do, he would make a copy especially for his own pleasure, particularly if the document were remarkable not for the beauty of its style but because it was addressed to some new or distinguished person.

Even at those hours when the gray Petersburg sky is completely overcast and the whole population of clerks have dined and eaten their fill, each as best he can, according to the salary he receives and his personal tastes; when they are all resting after the scratching of pens and bustle of the office, their own necessary work and other people's, and all the tasks that an overzealous man voluntarily sets himself even beyond what is necessary; when the clerks are hastening to devote what is left of their time to pleasure; some more enterprising are flying to the theater, others to the street to spend their leisure staring at women's hats, some to spend the evening paying compliments to some attractive girl, the star of a little official circle, while some—and this is the most frequent of all—go simply to a fellow clerk's apartment on the third or fourth story, two little rooms with a hall or a kitchen, with some pretensions to style, with a lamp or some such article that has cost many sacrifices of dinners and excursions—at the time when all the clerks are scattered about the apartments of their friends, playing a stormy game of whist, sipping tea out of glasses, eating cheap biscuits, sucking in smoke from long pipes, telling, as the cards are dealt, some scandal that has floated down from higher circles, a pleasure which the Russian can never by any possibility deny himself, or, when there is nothing better to talk about, repeating the everlasting anecdote of the commanding officer who was told that the tail had been cut off the horse on

the Falconet monument[4]—in short, even when everyone was eagerly seeking entertainment, Akaky Akakievich did not indulge in any amusement. No one could say that they had ever seen him at an evening party. After working to his heart's content, he would go to bed, smiling at the thought of the next day and wondering what God would send him to copy. So flowed on the peaceful life of a man who knew how to be content with his fate on a salary of four hundred rubles, and so perhaps it would have flowed on to extreme old age, had it not been for the various disasters strewn along the road of life, not only of titular, but even of privy, actual court, and all other councilors, even those who neither give counsel to oth-   160
ers nor accept it themselves.

    There is in Petersburg a mighty foe of all who receive a salary of about four hundred rubles. That foe is none other than our northern frost, although it is said to be very good for the health. Between eight and nine in the morning, precisely at the hour when the streets are filled with clerks going to their departments, the frost begins indiscriminately giving such sharp and stinging nips at all their noses that the poor fellows don't know what to do with them. At that time, when even those in the higher grade have a pain in their brows and tears in their eyes from the frost, the poor titular councilors are sometimes almost defenseless. Their only protection lies in running as fast as they can through five or six streets in a   170
wretched, thin little overcoat and then warming their feet thoroughly in the porter's room, till all their faculties and talents for their various duties thaw out again after having been frozen on the way. Akaky Akakievich had for some time been feeling that his back and shoulders were particularly nipped by the cold, although he did try to run the regular distance as fast as he could. He wondered at last whether there were any defects in his overcoat. After examining it thoroughly in the privacy of his home, he discovered that in two or three places, on the back and the shoulders, it had become a regular sieve; the cloth was so worn that you could see through it and the lining was coming out. I must note that Akaky Akakievich's overcoat had also served as a butt for the jokes of the clerks. It had   180
even been deprived of the honorable name of overcoat and had been referred to as the "dressing gown."[5] It was indeed of rather a peculiar make. Its collar had been growing smaller year by year as it served to patch the other parts. The patches were not good specimens of the tailor's art, and they certainly looked clumsy and ugly. On seeing what was wrong, Akaky Akakievich decided that he would have to take the overcoat to Petrovich, a tailor who lived on the fourth floor up a back staircase, and, in spite of having only one eye and being pockmarked all over his face, was rather successful in repairing the trousers and coats of clerks and others—that is, when he was sober, be it understood, and had no other enterprise in his mind. Of this tailor I ought not, of course, say much, but since it is now the   190
rule that the character of every person in a novel must be completely described, well, there's nothing I can do but describe Petrovich too. At first he was called simply Grigory, and was a serf belonging to some gentleman or other. He began to be

4. A famous statue of Peter the First; the horse stands on its hind legs, with the tail serving as another support for the statue.
5. The Russian word refers to a woman's dressing gown.

called Petrovich[6] from the time that he got his freedom and began to drink rather heavily on every holiday, at first only on the main holidays, but afterward, on all church holidays indiscriminately, wherever there was a cross in the calendar.[7] In this he was true to the customs of his forefathers, and when he quarreled with his wife he used to call her a worldly woman and a German. Since we have now mentioned the wife, it will be necessary to say a few words about her, too, but unfortunately not much is known about her, except indeed that Petrovich had a wife and that she wore a cap and not a kerchief,[8] but apparently she could not boast of beauty; anyway, none but soldiers of the guard peered under her cap when they met her, and they twitched their mustaches and gave vent to a rather peculiar sound.

As he climbed the stairs leading to Petrovich's—which, to do them justice, were all soaked with water and slops and saturated through and through with that smell of ammonia which makes the eyes smart, and is, as we all know, inseparable from the backstairs of Petersburg houses—Akaky Akakievich was already wondering how much Petrovich would ask for the job, and inwardly resolving not to give more than two rubles. The door was open, because Petrovich's wife was frying some fish and had so filled the kitchen with smoke that you could not even see the cockroaches. Akaky Akakievich crossed the kitchen unnoticed by the good woman, and walked at last into a room where he saw Petrovich sitting on a big, wooden, unpainted table with his legs tucked under him like a Turkish pasha. The feet, as is usual with tailors when they sit at work, were bare; and the first object that caught Akaky Akakievich's eye was the big toe, with which he was already familiar, with a misshapen nail as thick and strong as the shell of a tortoise. Around Petrovich's neck hung a skein of silk and another of thread and on his knees was a rag of some sort. He had for the last three minutes been trying to thread his needle, but could not get the thread into the eye and so was very angry with the darkness and indeed with the thread itself, muttering in an undertone: "She won't go in, the savage! You wear me out, you bitch." Akaky Akakievich was unhappy that he had come just at the minute when Petrovich was in a bad humor; he liked to give him an order when he was a little "elevated," or, as his wife expressed it, "had fortified himself with vodka, the one-eyed devil." In such circumstances Petrovich was as a rule very ready to give way and agree, and invariably bowed and thanked him. Afterward, it is true, his wife would come wailing that her husband had been drunk and so had asked too little, but adding a single ten-kopek piece would settle that. But on this occasion Petrovich was apparently sober and consequently curt, unwilling to bargain, and the devil knows what price he would be ready to demand. Akaky Akakievich realized this, and was, as the saying is, beating a retreat, but things had gone too far, for Petrovich was screwing up his solitary eye very attentively at him and Akaky Akakievich involuntarily said: "Good day, Petrovich!"

6. As a serf, he would have been called only by his first name, Grigory; but on becoming free, he could use his second name, Petrovich—son of Peter.

7. A cross on the calendar indicated a saint's day.

8. i.e., was manly and assertive.

"I wish you a good day, sir," said Petrovich, and squinted at Akaky Akakievich's hands, trying to discover what sort of goods he had brought.

"Here I have come to you, Petrovich, do you see . . . !"

It must be noticed that Akaky Akakievich for the most part explained himself by apologies, vague phrases, and meaningless parts of speech which have absolutely no significance whatever. If the subject were a very difficult one, it was his 240 habit indeed to leave his sentences quite unfinished, so that very often after a sentence had begun with the words, "It really is, don't you know . . ." nothing at all would follow and he himself would be quite oblivious to the fact that he had not finished his thought, supposing he had said all that was necessary.

"What is it?" said Petrovich, and at the same time with his solitary eye he scrutinized his whole uniform from the collar to the sleeves, the back, the skirts, the buttonholes—with all of which he was very familiar since they were all his own work. Such scrutiny is habitual with tailors; it is the first thing they do on meeting one.

"It's like this, Petrovich . . . the overcoat, the cloth . . . you see everywhere 250 else it is quite strong; it's a little dusty and looks as though it were old, but it is new and it is only in one place just a little . . . on the back, and just a little worn on one shoulder and on this shoulder, too, a little . . . do you see? that's all, and it's not much work . . ."

Petrovich took the "dressing gown," first spread it out over the table, examined it for a long time, shook his head, and put his hand out to the window sill for a round snuffbox with a portrait on the lid of some general—which general I can't exactly say, for a finger had been thrust through the spot where a face should have been, and the hole had been pasted over with a square piece of paper. After taking a pinch of snuff, Petrovich held the "dressing gown" up in his hands and looked at 260 it against the light, and again he shook his head; then he turned it with the lining upward and once more shook his head; again he took off the lid with the general pasted up with paper and stuffed a pinch into his nose, shut the box, put it away, and at last said: "No, it can't be repaired; a wretched garment!" Akaky Akakievich's heart sank at those words.

"Why can't it, Petrovich?" he said, almost in the imploring voice of a child. "Why, the only thing is, it is a bit worn on the shoulders; why, you have got some little pieces . . ."

"Yes, the pieces will be found all right," said Petrovich, "but it can't be patched, the stuff is rotten; if you put a needle in it, it would give way." 270

"Let it give way, but you just put a patch on it."

"There is nothing to put a patch on. There is nothing for it to hold on to; there is a great strain on it; it is not worth calling cloth; it would fly away at a breath of wind."

"Well, then, strengthen it with something—I'm sure, really, this is . . .!"

"No," said Petrovich resolutely, "there is nothing that can be done, the thing is no good at all. You had far better, when the cold winter weather comes, make yourself leg wrappings out of it, for there is no warmth in stockings; the Germans invented them just to make money." (Petrovich enjoyed a dig at the Germans occasionally.) "And as for the overcoat, it is obvious that you will have to have a new 280 one."

At the word "new" there was a mist before Akaky Akakievich's eyes, and everything in the room seemed blurred. He could see nothing clearly but the general with the piece of paper over his face on the lid of Petrovich's snuffbox.

"A new one?" he said, still feeling as though he were in a dream; "why, I haven't the money for it."

"Yes, a new one," Petrovich repeated with barbarous composure.

"Well, and if I did have a new one, how much would it . . .?"

"You mean what will it cost?"

"Yes."   290

"Well, at least one hundred and fifty rubles," said Petrovich, and he compressed his lips meaningfully. He was very fond of making an effect; he was fond of suddenly disconcerting a man completely and then squinting sideways to see what sort of a face he made.

"A hundred and fifty rubles for an overcoat!" screamed poor Akaky Akakievich—it was perhaps the first time he had screamed in his life, for he was always distinguished by the softness of his voice.

"Yes," said Petrovich, "and even then it depends on the coat. If I were to put marten on the collar, and add a hood with silk linings, it would come to two hundred."   300

"Petrovich, please," said Akaky Akakievich in an imploring voice, not hearing and not trying to hear what Petrovich said, and missing all his effects, "repair it somehow, so that it will serve a little longer."

"No, that would be wasting work and spending money for nothing," said Petrovich, and after that Akaky Akakievich went away completely crushed, and when he had gone Petrovich remained standing for a long time with his lips pursed up meaningfully before he began his work again, feeling pleased that he had not demeaned himself or lowered the dignity of the tailor's art.

When he got into the street, Akaky Akakievich felt as though he was in a dream. "So that is how it is," he said to himself. "I really did not think it would be   310 this way . . ." and then after a pause he added, "So that's it! So that's how it is at last! and I really could never have supposed it would be this way. And there . . ." There followed another long silence, after which he said: "So that's it! well, it really is so utterly unexpected . . . who would have thought . . . what a circumstance . . ." Saying this, instead of going home he walked off in quite the opposite direction without suspecting what he was doing. On the way a clumsy chimney sweep brushed the whole of his sooty side against him and blackened his entire shoulder; a whole hatful of plaster scattered upon him from the top of a house that was being built. He noticed nothing of this, and only after he had jostled against a policeman who had set his halberd[9] down beside him and was shaking some snuff   320 out of his horn into his rough fist, he came to himself a little and then only because the policeman said: "Why are you poking yourself right in one's face, haven't you enough room on the street?" This made him look around and turn homeward; only there he began to collect his thoughts, to see his position in a clear and true light, and began talking to himself no longer incoherently but reasonably and openly as with a sensible friend with whom one can discuss the most intimate and

_____

9. Originally an ax-like weapon, but here probably a sign that the officer is a sergeant.

vital matters. "No," said Akaky Akakievich, "it is no use talking to Petrovich now; just now he really is . . . his wife must have been giving it to him. I had better go to him on Sunday morning; after Saturday night he will have a crossed eye and be sleepy, so he'll want a little drink and his wife won't give him a kopek. I'll slip ten 330 kopeks into his hand and then he will be more accommodating and maybe take the overcoat . . ."

So reasoning with himself, Akaky Akakievich cheered up and waited until the next Sunday; then, seeing from a distance Petrovich's wife leaving the house, he went straight in. Petrovich certainly had a crossed eye after Saturday. He could hardly hold his head up and was very drowsy; but, despite all that, as soon as he heard what Akaky Akakievich was speaking about, it seemed as though the devil had nudged him. "I can't," he said, "you must order a new one." Akaky Akakievich at once slipped a ten-kopek piece into his hand. "I thank you, sir, I will have just a drop to your health, but don't trouble yourself about the overcoat; it is no good for 340 anything. I'll make you a fine new coat; you can have faith in me for that."

Akaky Akakievich would have said more about repairs, but Petrovich, without listening, said: "A new one I'll make you without fail; you can rely on that; I'll do my best. It could even be like the fashion that is popular, with the collar to fasten with silver-plated hooks under a flap."

Then Akaky Akakievich saw that there was no escape from a new overcoat and he was utterly depressed. How indeed, for what, with what money could he get it? Of course he could to some extent rely on the bonus for the coming holiday, but that money had long ago been appropriated and its use determined beforehand. It was needed for new trousers and to pay the cobbler an old debt for 350 putting some new tops on some old boots, and he had to order three shirts from a seamstress as well as two items of undergarments which it is indecent to mention in print; in short, all that money absolutely must be spent, and even if the director were to be so gracious as to give him a holiday bonus of forty-five or even fifty, instead of forty rubles, there would be still left a mere trifle, which would be but a drop in the ocean compared to the fortune needed for an overcoat. Though, of course, he knew that Petrovich had a strange craze for suddenly demanding the devil knows what enormous price, so that at times his own wife could not help crying out: "Why, you are out of your wits, you idiot! Another time he'll undertake a job for nothing, and here the devil has bewitched him to ask more than he is 360 worth himself." Though, of course, he knew that Petrovich would undertake to make it for eighty rubles, still where would he get those eighty rubles? He might manage half of that sum; half of it could be found, perhaps even a little more; but where could he get the other half? . . . But, first of all, the reader ought to know where that first half was to be found. Akaky Akakievich had the habit every time he spent a ruble of putting aside two kopeks in a little box which he kept locked, with a slit in the lid for dropping in the money. At the end of every six months he would inspect the pile of coppers there and change them for small silver. He had done this for a long time, and in the course of many years the sum had mounted up to forty rubles and so he had half the money in his hands, but where was he to 370 get the other half; where was he to get another forty rubles? Akaky Akakievich thought and thought and decided at last that he would have to diminish his ordinary expenses, at least for a year; give up burning candles in the evening, and if he

had to do any work he must go into the landlady's room and work by her candle;
that as he walked along the streets he must walk as lightly and carefully as possible, almost on tiptoe, on the cobbles and flagstones, so that his soles might last a
little longer than usual; that he must send his linen to the wash less frequently,
and that, to preserve it from being worn, he must take it off every day when he
came home and sit in a thin cotton dressing gown, a very ancient garment which
Time itself had spared. To tell the truth, he found it at first rather difficult to get   380
used to these privations, but after a while it became a habit and went smoothly
enough—he even became quite accustomed to being hungry in the evening; on
the other hand, he had spiritual nourishment, for he carried ever in his thoughts
the idea of his future overcoat. His whole existence had in a sense become fuller,
as though he had married, as though some other person were present with him, as
though he were no longer alone but an agreeable companion had consented to
walk the path of life hand in hand with him, and that companion was none other
than the new overcoat with its thick padding and its strong, durable lining. He became, as it were, more alive, even more strong-willed, like a man who has set before himself a definite goal. Uncertainty, indecision, in fact all the hesitating and   390
vague characteristics, vanished from his face and his manners. At times there was a
gleam in his eyes; indeed, the most bold and audacious ideas flashed through his
mind. Why not really have marten on the collar? Meditation on the subject always
made him absent-minded. On one occasion when he was copying a document, he
very nearly made a mistake, so that he almost cried out "ough" aloud and crossed
himself. At least once every month he went to Petrovich to talk about the overcoat:
where it would be best to buy the cloth, and what color it should be, and what
price; and, though he returned home a little anxious, he was always pleased at the
thought that at last the time was at hand when everything would be bought and
the overcoat would be made. Things moved even faster than he had anticipated.   400
Contrary to all expectations, the director bestowed on Akaky Akakievich a bonus
of no less than sixty rubles. Whether it was that he had an inkling that Akaky
Akakievich needed a coat, or whether it happened by luck, owing to this he found
he had twenty rubles extra. This circumstance hastened the course of affairs.
Another two or three months of partial starvation and Akaky Akakievich had actually saved up nearly eighty rubles. His heart, as a rule very tranquil, began to
throb.

The very first day he set out with Petrovich for the shops. They bought some
very good cloth, and no wonder, since they had been thinking of it for more than
six months, and scarcely a month had passed without their going out to the shop   410
to compare prices; now Petrovich himself declared that there was no better cloth
to be had. For the lining they chose calico, but of such good quality, that in
Petrovich's words it was even better than silk, and actually as strong and handsome to look at. Marten they did not buy, because it was too expensive, but instead they chose cat fur, the best to be found in the shop—cat which in the
distance might almost be taken for marten. Petrovich was busy making the coat
for two weeks, because there was a great deal of quilting; otherwise it would have
been ready sooner. Petrovich charged twelve rubles for the work; less than that it
hardly could have been; everything was sewn with silk, with fine double seams,
and Petrovich went over every seam afterwards with his own teeth, imprinting   420

various patterns with them. It was . . . it is hard to say precisely on what day, but probably on the most triumphant day in the life of Akaky Akakievich, that Petrovich at last brought the overcoat. He brought it in the morning, just before it was time to set off for the department. The overcoat could not have arrived at a more opportune time, because severe frosts were just beginning and seemed threatening to become even harsher. Petrovich brought the coat himself as a good tailor should. There was an expression of importance on his face, such as Akaky Akakievich had never seen there before. He seemed fully conscious of having completed a work of no little importance and of having shown by his own exam- 430 ple the gulf that separates tailors who only put in linings and do repairs from those who make new coats. He took the coat out of the huge handkerchief in which he had brought it (the handkerchief had just come home from the wash); he then folded it up and put it in his pocket for future use. After taking out the overcoat, he looked at it with much pride and holding it in both hands, threw it very deftly over Akaky Akakievich's shoulders, then pulled it down and smoothed it out behind with his hands; then draped it about Akaky Akakievich somewhat jauntily. Akaky Akakievich, a practical man, wanted to try it with his arms in the sleeves. Petrovich helped him to put it on, and it looked splendid with his arms in the sleeves, too. In fact, it turned out that the overcoat was completely and entirely successful. Petrovich did not let slip the occasion for observing that it was only be- 440 cause he lived in a small street and had no signboard, and because he had known Akaky Akakievich so long, that he had done it so cheaply, and that on Nevsky Prospekt they would have asked him seventy-five rubles for the tailoring alone. Akaky Akakievich had no inclination to discuss this with Petrovich; besides he was frightened of the big sums that Petrovich was fond of flinging airily about in conversation. He paid him, thanked him, and went off, with his new overcoat on, to the department. Petrovich followed him out and stopped in the street, staring for a long time at the coat from a distance and then purposely turned off and, taking a short cut through a side street, came back into the street, and got another view of the coat from the other side, that is, from the front.   450

Meanwhile Akaky Akakievich walked along in a gay holiday mood. Every second he was conscious that he had a new overcoat on his shoulders, and several times he actually laughed from inward satisfaction. Indeed, it had two advantages: one that it was warm and the other that it was good. He did not notice how far he had walked at all and he suddenly found himself in the department; in the porter's room he took off the overcoat, looked it over, and entrusted it to the porter's special care. I cannot tell how it happened, but all at once everyone in the department learned that Akaky Akakievich had a new overcoat and that the "dressing gown" no longer existed. They all ran out at once into the cloakroom to look at Akaky Akakievich's new overcoat; they began welcoming him and congratulating him so 460 that at first he could do nothing but smile and then felt positively embarrassed. When, coming up to him, they all began saying that he must "sprinkle" the new overcoat and that he ought at least to buy them all a supper, Akaky Akakievich lost his head completely and did not know what to do, how to get out of it, nor what to answer. A few minutes later, flushing crimson, he even began assuring them with great simplicity that it was not a new overcoat at all, that it wasn't much, that it was an old overcoat. At last one of the clerks, indeed the assistant of the head clerk of the room, probably in order to show that he wasn't too proud to mingle with those beneath him, said: "So be it, I'll give a party instead of Akaky Akakievich and invite you all to tea with me this evening; as luck would have it, it 470 is my birthday." The clerks naturally congratulated the assistant head clerk and eagerly accepted the invitation. Akaky Akakievich was beginning to make excuses, but they all declared that it was uncivil of him, that it would be simply a shame and a disgrace and that he could not possibly refuse. So, he finally relented, and later felt pleased about it when he remembered that through this he would have the opportunity of going out in the evening, too, in his new overcoat. That whole day was for Akaky Akakievich the most triumphant and festive day in his life. He returned home in the happiest frame of mind, took off the overcoat, and hung it carefully on the wall, admiring the cloth and lining once more, and then pulled out his old "dressing gown," now completely falling apart, and put it next to his 480 new overcoat to compare the two. He glanced at it and laughed: the difference was enormous! And long afterwards he went on laughing at dinner, as the position in which the "dressing gown" was placed recurred to his mind. He dined in excellent spirits and after dinner wrote nothing, no papers at all, but just relaxed for a little while on his bed, till it got dark; then, without putting things off, he dressed, put on his overcoat, and went out into the street. Where precisely the clerk who had invited him lived we regret to say we cannot tell; our memory is beginning to fail sadly, and everything there in Petersburg, all the streets and houses, are so blurred and muddled in our head that it is a very difficult business to put anything in orderly fashion. Regardless of that, there is no doubt that the clerk lived in the better 490 part of the town and consequently a very long distance from Akaky Akakievich. At first Akaky Akakievich had to walk through deserted streets, scantily lighted, but as he approached his destination the streets became more lively, more full of people, and more brightly lighted; passers-by began to be more frequent, ladies began to appear, here and there beautifully dressed, and beaver collars were to be seen on the men. Cabmen with wooden, railed sledges, studded with brass-topped nails, were less frequently seen; on the other hand, jaunty drivers in raspberry-colored velvet caps, with lacquered sledges and bearskin rugs, appeared and carriages with decorated boxes dashed along the streets, their wheels crunching through the snow.   500

Akaky Akakievich looked at all this as a novelty; for several years he had not gone out into the streets in the evening. He stopped with curiosity before a lighted shop window to look at a picture in which a beautiful woman was represented in the act of taking off her shoe and displaying as she did so the whole of a very shapely leg, while behind her back a gentleman with whiskers and a handsome imperial on his chin was sticking his head in at the door. Akaky Akakievich shook his head and smiled and then went on his way. Why did he smile? Was it because he had come across something quite unfamiliar to him, though every man retains some instinctive feeling on the subject, or was it that he reflected, like many other clerks, as follows: "Well, those Frenchmen! It's beyond anything! If they go in for 510 anything of the sort, it really is . . . !" Though possibly he did not even think that; there is no creeping into a man's soul and finding out all that he thinks. At last he reached the house in which the assistant head clerk lived in fine style; there was a lamp burning on the stairs, and the apartment was on the second floor. As he

went into the hall Akaky Akakievich saw rows of galoshes. Among them in the
middle of the room stood a hissing samovar puffing clouds of steam. On the walls
hung coats and cloaks among which some actually had beaver collars or velvet
lapels. From the other side of the wall there came noise and talk, which suddenly
became clear and loud when the door opened and the footman came out with a
tray full of empty glasses, a jug of cream, and a basket of biscuits. It was evident   520
that the clerks had arrived long before and had already drunk their first glass of
tea. Akaky Akakievich, after hanging up his coat with his own hands, went into
the room, and at the same moment there flashed before his eyes a vision of candles, clerks, pipes, and card tables, together with the confused sounds of conversation rising up on all sides and the noise of moving chairs. He stopped very
awkwardly in the middle of the room, looking about and trying to think of what
to do, but he was noticed and received with a shout and they all went at once into
the hall and again took a look at his overcoat. Though Akaky Akakievich was
somewhat embarrassed, yet, being a simplehearted man, he could not help being
pleased at seeing how they all admired his coat. Then of course they all aban-   530
doned him and his coat, and turned their attention as usual to the tables set for
whist. All this—the noise, the talk, and the crowd of people—was strange and
wonderful to Akaky Akakievich. He simply did not know how to behave, what to
do with his arms and legs and his whole body; at last he sat down beside the players, looked at the cards, stared first at one and then at another of the faces, and in
a little while, feeling bored, began to yawn—especially since it was long past the
time at which he usually went to bed. He tried to say goodbye to his hosts, but
they would not let him go, saying that he absolutely must have a glass of champagne in honor of the new coat. An hour later supper was served, consisting of
salad, cold veal, pastry and pies from the bakery, and champagne. They made   540
Akaky Akakievich drink two glasses, after which he felt that things were much
more cheerful, though he could not forget that it was twelve o'clock, and that he
ought to have been home long ago. That his host might not take it into his head to
detain him, he slipped out of the room, hunted in the hall for his coat, which he
found, not without regret, lying on the floor, shook it, removed some fluff from it,
put it on, and went down the stairs into the street. It was still light in the streets.
Some little grocery shops, those perpetual clubs for servants and all sorts of people, were open; others which were closed showed, however, a long streak of light
at every crack of the door, proving that they were not yet deserted, and probably
maids and menservants were still finishing their conversation and discussion, driv-   550
ing their masters to utter perplexity as to their whereabouts. Akaky Akakievich
walked along in a cheerful state of mind; he was even on the point of running,
goodness knows why, after a lady of some sort who passed by like lightning with
every part of her frame in violent motion. He checked himself at once, however,
and again walked along very gently, feeling positively surprised at the inexplicable
impulse that had seized him. Soon the deserted streets, which are not particularly
cheerful by day and even less so in the evening, stretched before him. Now they
were still more dead and deserted; the light of street lamps was scantier, the oil evidently running low; then came wooden houses and fences; not a soul anywhere;
only the snow gleamed on the streets and the low-pitched slumbering hovels   560
looked black and gloomy with their closed shutters. He approached the spot

where the street was intersected by an endless square, which looked like a fearful desert with its houses scarcely visible on the far side.

In the distance, goodness knows where, there was a gleam of light from some sentry box which seemed to be at the end of the world. Akaky Akakievich's lightheartedness faded. He stepped into the square, not without uneasiness, as though his heart had a premonition of evil. He looked behind him and to both sides—it was as though the sea were all around him. "No, better not look," he thought, and walked on, shutting his eyes, and when he opened them to see whether the end of the square was near, he suddenly saw standing before him, al- 570 most under his very nose, some men with mustaches; just what they were like he could not even distinguish. There was a mist before his eyes, and a throbbing in his chest. "Why, that overcoat is mine!" said one of them in a voice like a clap of thunder, seizing him by the collar. Akaky Akakievich was on the point of shouting "Help" when another put a fist the size of a clerk's head against his lips, saying: "You just shout now." Akaky Akakievich felt only that they took the overcoat off, and gave him a kick with their knees, and he fell on his face in the snow and was conscious of nothing more. A few minutes later he recovered consciousness and got up on his feet, but there was no one there. He felt that it was cold on the ground and that he had no overcoat, and began screaming, but it seemed as 580 though his voice would not carry to the end of the square. Overwhelmed with despair and continuing to scream, he ran across the square straight to the sentry box beside which stood a policeman leaning on his halberd and, so it seemed, looking with curiosity to see who the devil the man was who was screaming and running toward him from the distance. As Akaky Akakievich reached him, he began breathlessly shouting that he was asleep and not looking after his duty not to see that a man was being robbed. The policeman answered that he had seen nothing, that he had only seen him stopped in the middle of the square by two men, and supposed that they were his friends, and that, instead of abusing him for nothing, he had better go the next day to the police inspector, who would certainly find out 590 who had taken the overcoat. Akaky Akakievich ran home in a terrible state: his hair, which was still comparatively abundant on his temples and the back of his head, was completely disheveled; his sides and chest and his trousers were all covered with snow. When his old landlady heard a fearful knock at the door, she jumped hurriedly out of bed and, with only one slipper on, ran to open it, modestly holding her chemise over her bosom; but when she opened it she stepped back, seeing in what a state Akaky Akakievich was. When he told her what had happened, she clasped her hands in horror and said that he must go straight to the district commissioner, because the local police inspector would deceive him, make promises, and lead him a dance; that it would be best of all to go to the district 600 commissioner, and that she knew him, because Anna, the Finnish girl who was once her cook, was now in service as a nurse at the commissioner's; and that she often saw him himself when he passed by their house, and that he used to be every Sunday at church too, saying his prayers and at the same time looking good-humoredly at everyone, and that therefore by every token he must be a kind-hearted man. After listening to this advice, Akaky Akakievich made his way very gloomily to his room, and how he spent that night I leave to the imagination of those who are in the least able to picture the position of others.

Early in the morning he set off to the police commissioner's but was told that
he was asleep. He came at ten o'clock, he was told again that he was asleep; he   610
came at eleven and was told that the commissioner was not at home; he came at
dinnertime, but the clerks in the anteroom would not let him in, and insisted on
knowing what was the matter and what business had brought him and exactly
what had happened; so that at last Akaky Akakievich for the first time in his life
tried to show the strength of his character and said curtly that he must see the
commissioner himself, that they dare not refuse to admit him, that he had come
from the department on government business, and that if he made complaint of
them they would see. The clerks dared say nothing to this, and one of them went
to summon the commissioner. The latter received his story of being robbed of his
overcoat in an extremely peculiar manner. Instead of attending to the main point,   620
he began asking Akaky Akakievich questions: why had he been coming home so
late? wasn't he going, or hadn't he been, to some bawdy house? so that Akaky
Akakievich was overwhelmed with confusion, and went away without knowing
whether or not the proper measures would be taken regarding his overcoat. He
was absent from the office all that day (the only time that it had happened in his
life). Next day he appeared with a pale face, wearing his old "dressing gown"
which had become a still more pitiful sight. The news of the theft of the
overcoat—though there were clerks who did not let even this chance slip of jeer-
ing at Akaky Akakievich—touched many of them. They decided on the spot to get
up a collection for him, but collected only a very trifling sum, because the clerks   630
had already spent a good deal contributing to the director's portrait and on the
purchase of a book, at the suggestion of the head of their department, who was a
friend of the author, and so the total realized was very insignificant. One of the
clerks, moved by compassion, ventured at any rate to assist Akaky Akakievich
with good advice, telling him not to go to the local police inspector, because,
though it might happen that the latter might succeed in finding his overcoat because he wanted to impress his superiors, it would remain in the possession of the
police unless he presented legal proofs that it belonged to him; he urged that by
far the best thing would be to appeal to a Person of Consequence; that the Person
of Consequence, by writing and getting into communication with the proper au-   640
thorities, could push the matter through more successfully. There was nothing else
to do. Akaky Akakievich made up his mind to go to the Person of Consequence.
What precisely was the nature of the functions of the Person of Consequence has
remained a matter of uncertainty. It must be noted that this Person of
Consequence had only lately become a person of consequence, and until recently
had been a person of no consequence. Though, indeed, his position even now was
not reckoned of consequence in comparison with others of still greater consequence. But there is always to be found a circle of persons to whom a person of
little consequence in the eyes of others is a person of consequence. It is true that
he did his utmost to increase the consequence of his position in various ways, for   650
instance by insisting that his subordinates should come out onto the stairs to meet
him when he arrived at his office; that no one should venture to approach him directly but all proceedings should follow the strictest chain of command; that a col-
legiate registrar should report the matter to the governmental secretary; and the
governmental secretary to the titular councilor or whomsoever it might be, and

that business should only reach him through this channel. Everyone in Holy Russia has a craze for imitation; everyone apes and mimics his superiors. I have actually been told that a titular councilor who was put in charge of a small separate office, immediately partitioned off a special room for himself, calling it the head office, and posted lackeys at the door with red collars and gold braid, who took hold of the handle of the door and opened it for everyone who went in, though the "head office" was so tiny that it was with difficulty that an ordinary writing desk could be put into it. The manners and habits of the Person of Consequence were dignified and majestic, but hardly subtle. The chief foundation of his system was strictness; "strictness, strictness, and—strictness!" he used to say, and at the last word he would look very significantly at the person he was addressing, though, indeed, he had no reason to do so, for the dozen clerks who made up the whole administrative mechanism of his office stood in appropriate awe of him; any clerk who saw him in the distance would leave his work and remain standing at attention till his superior had left the room. His conversation with his subordinates was usually marked by severity and almost confined to three phrases: "How dare you? Do you know to whom you are speaking? Do you understand who I am?" He was, however, at heart a good-natured man, pleasant and obliging with his colleagues; but his advancement to a high rank had completely turned his head. When he received it, he was perplexed, thrown off his balance, and quite at a loss as to how to behave. If he chanced to be with his equals, he was still quite a decent man, a very gentlemanly man, in fact, and in many ways even an intelligent man; but as soon as he was in company with men who were even one grade below him, there was simply no doing anything with him: he sat silent and his position excited compassion, the more so as he himself felt that he might have been spending his time to so much more advantage. At times there could be seen in his eyes an intense desire to join in some interesting conversation, but he was restrained by the doubt whether it would not be too much on his part, whether it would not be too great a familiarity and lowering of his dignity, and in consequence of these reflections he remained everlastingly in the same mute condition, only uttering from time to time monosyllabic sounds, and in this way he gained the reputation of being a terrible bore.

So this was the Person of Consequence to whom our friend Akaky Akakievich appealed, and he appealed to him at a most unpropitious moment, very unfortunate for himself, though fortunate, indeed, for the Person of Consequence. The latter happened to be in his study, talking in the very best of spirits with an old friend of his childhood who had only just arrived and whom he had not seen for several years. It was at this moment that he was informed that a man called Bashmachkin was asking to see him. He asked abruptly, "What sort of man is he?" and received the answer, "A government clerk." "Ah! he can wait. I haven't time now," said the Person of Consequence. Here I must observe that this was a complete lie on the part of the Person of Consequence; he had time; his friend and he had long ago said all they had to say to each other and their conversation had begun to be broken by very long pauses during which they merely slapped each other on the knee, saying, "So that's how things are, Ivan Abramovich!"—"So that's it, Stepan Varlamovich!" but, despite that, he told the clerk to wait in order to show his friend, who had left the civil service some years before and was living at home in the country, how long clerks had to wait for him. At last, after they had talked or rather been silent, to their heart's content and had smoked a cigar in very comfortable armchairs with sloping backs, he seemed suddenly to recollect, and said to the secretary, who was standing at the door with papers for his signature: "Oh, by the way, there is a clerk waiting, isn't there? tell him he can come in." When he saw Akaky Akakievich's meek appearance and old uniform, he turned to him at once and said: "What do you want?" in a firm and abrupt voice, which he had purposely rehearsed in his own room in solitude be- 710 fore the mirror for a week before receiving his present post and the grade of a general. Akaky Akakievich, who was overwhelmed with appropriate awe beforehand, was somewhat confused and, as far as his tongue would allow him, explained to the best of his powers, with even more frequent "ers" than usual, that he had had a perfectly new overcoat and now he had been robbed of it in the most inhuman way, and that now he had come to beg him by his intervention either to correspond with his honor, the head police commissioner, or anybody else, and find the overcoat. This mode of proceeding struck the general for some reason as too familiar. "What next, sir?" he went on abruptly. "Don't you know the way to proceed? To whom are you addressing yourself? Don't you know how things are 720 done? You ought first to have handed in a petition to the office; it would have gone to the head clerk of the room, and to the head clerk of the section; then it would have been handed to the secretary and the secretary would have brought it to me . . ."

"But, your Excellency," said Akaky Akakievich, trying to gather the drop of courage he possessed and feeling at the same time that he was perspiring all over, "I ventured, your Excellency, to trouble you because secretaries . . . er . . . are people you can't depend on . . ."

"What? what? what?" said the Person of Consequence, "where did you get hold of that attitude? where did you pick up such ideas? What insubordination is 730 spreading among young men against their superiors and their chiefs!" The Person of Consequence did not apparently observe that Akaky Akakievich was well over fifty, and therefore if he could have been called a young man it would only have been in comparison with a man of seventy. "Do you know to whom you are speaking? Do you understand who I am? Do you understand that, I ask you?" At this point he stamped, and raised his voice to such a powerful note that Akaky Akakievich was not the only one to be terrified. Akaky Akakievich was positively petrified; he staggered, trembling all over, and could not stand; if the porters had not run up to support him, he would have flopped on the floor; he was led out almost unconscious. The Person of Consequence, pleased that the effect had sur- 740 passed his expectations and enchanted at the idea that his words could even deprive a man of consciousness, stole a sideway glance at his friend to see how he was taking it, and perceived not without satisfaction that his friend was feeling very uncertain and even beginning to be a little terrified himself.

How he got downstairs, how he went out into the street—of all that Akaky Akakievich remembered nothing; he had no feeling in his arms or his legs. In all his life he had never been so severely reprimanded by a general, and this was by one of another department, too. He went out into the snowstorm that was whistling through the streets, with his mouth open, and as he went he stumbled

off the pavement; the wind, as its way is in Petersburg, blew upon him from all   750
points of the compass and from every side street. In an instant it had blown a
quinsy[10] into his throat, and when he got home he was not able to utter a word;
he went to bed with a swollen face and throat. That's how violent the effects of an
appropriate reprimand can be!

Next day he was in a high fever. Thanks to the gracious assistance of the
Petersburg climate, the disease made more rapid progress than could have been
expected, and when the doctor came, after feeling his pulse he could find nothing
to do but prescribe a poultice, and that simply so that the patient might not be left
without the benefit of medical assistance; however, two days later he informed
him that his end was at hand, after which he turned to Akaky Akakievich's land-   760
lady and said: "And you had better lose no time, my good woman, but order him
now a pine coffin, for an oak one will be too expensive for him." Whether Akaky
Akakievich heard these fateful words or not, whether they produced a shattering
effect upon him, and whether he regretted his pitiful life, no one can tell, for he
was constantly in delirium and fever. Apparitions, each stranger than the one before, were continually haunting him: first he saw Petrovich and was ordering him
to make an overcoat trimmed with some sort of traps for robbers, who were, he
believed, continually under the bed, and he was calling his landlady every minute
to pull out a thief who had even got under the quilt; then he kept asking why his
old "dressing gown" was hanging before him when he had a new overcoat; then he   770
thought he was standing before the general listening to the appropriate reprimand
and saying, "I am sorry, your Excellency"; then finally he became abusive, uttering
the most awful language, so that his old landlady positively crossed herself, having
never heard anything of the kind from him before, and the more horrified because
these dreadful words followed immediately upon the phrase "your Excellency."
Later on, his talk was merely a medley of nonsense, so that it was quite unintelligible; all that was evident was that his incoherent words and thoughts were concerned with nothing but the overcoat. At last poor Akaky Akakievich gave up the
ghost. No seal was put upon his room nor upon his things, because, in the first
place, he had no heirs and, in the second, the property left was very small, to wit,   780
a bundle of quills, a quire of white government paper, three pairs of socks, two or
three buttons that had come off his trousers, and the "dressing gown" with which
the reader is already familiar. Who came into all this wealth God only knows; even
I who tell the tale must admit that I have not bothered to inquire. And Petersburg
carried on without Akaky Akakievich, as though, indeed, he had never been in the
city. A creature had vanished and departed whose cause no one had championed,
who was dear to no one, of interest to no one, who never attracted the attention of
a naturalist, though the latter does not disdain to fix a common fly upon a pin and
look at him under the microscope—a creature who bore patiently the jeers of the
office and for no particular reason went to his grave, though even he at the very   790
end of his life was visited by an exalted guest in the form of an overcoat that for
one instant brought color into his poor, drab life—a creature on whom disease fell
as it falls upon the heads of the mighty ones of this world . . . !

Several days after his death, a messenger from the department was sent to

10. Tonsilitis.

his lodgings with instructions that he should go at once to the office, for his chief was asking for him; but the messenger was obliged to return without him, explaining that he could not come, and to the inquiry "Why?" he added, "Well, you see, the fact is he is dead; he was buried three days ago." This was how they learned at the office of the death of Akaky Akakievich, and the next day there was sitting in his seat a new clerk who was very much taller and who wrote not in the same straight handwriting but made his letters more slanting and crooked.

But who could have imagined that this was not all there was to tell about Akaky Akakievich, that he was destined for a few days to make his presence felt in the world after his death, as though to make up for his life having been unnoticed by anyone? But so it happened, and our little story unexpectedly finishes with a fantastic ending.

Rumors were suddenly floating about Petersburg that in the neighborhood of the Kalinkin Bridge and for a little distance beyond, a corpse[11] had begun appearing at night in the form of a clerk looking for a stolen overcoat, and stripping from the shoulders of all passers-by, regardless of grade and calling, overcoats of all descriptions—trimmed with cat fur or beaver or padded, lined with raccoon, fox, and bear—made, in fact of all sorts of skin which men have adapted for the covering of their own. One of the clerks of the department saw the corpse with his own eyes and at once recognized it as Akaky Akakievich; but it excited in him such terror that he ran away as fast as his legs could carry him and so could not get a very clear view of him, and only saw him hold up his finger threateningly in the distance.

From all sides complaints were continually coming that backs and shoulders, not of mere titular councilors, but even of upper court councilors, had been exposed to catching cold, as a result of being stripped of their overcoats. Orders were given to the police to catch the corpse regardless of trouble or expense, dead or alive, and to punish him severely, as an example to others, and, indeed, they very nearly succeeded in doing so. The policeman of one district in Kiryushkin Alley snatched a corpse by the collar on the spot of the crime in the very act of attempting to snatch a frieze overcoat from a retired musician, who used, in his day, to play the flute. Having caught him by the collar, he shouted until he had brought two other policemen whom he ordered to hold the corpse while he felt just a minute in his boot to get out a snuffbox in order to revive his nose which had six times in his life been frostbitten, but the snuff was probably so strong that not even a dead man could stand it. The policeman had hardly had time to put his finger over his right nostril and draw up some snuff in the left when the corpse sneezed violently right into the eyes of all three. While they were putting their fists up to wipe their eyes, the corpse completely vanished, so that they were not even sure whether he had actually been in their hands. From that time forward, the policemen had such a horror of the dead that they were even afraid to seize the living and confined themselves to shouting from the distance: "Hey, you! Move on!" and the clerk's body began to appear even on the other side of the Kalinkin Bridge, terrorizing all timid people.

We have, however, quite neglected the Person of Consequence, who may in

---

11. According to the translator, "corpse" is a better translation than "ghost," which is sometimes used here.

reality almost be said to be the cause of the fantastic ending of this perfectly true 840
story. To begin with, my duty requires me to do justice to the Person of
Consequence by recording that soon after poor Akaky Akakievich had gone away
crushed to powder, he felt something not unlike regret. Sympathy was a feeling
not unknown to him; his heart was open to many kindly impulses, although his
exalted grade very often prevented them from being shown. As soon as his friend
had gone out of his study, he even began brooding over poor Akaky Akakievich,
and from that time forward, he was almost every day haunted by the image of the
poor clerk who had been unable to survive the official reprimand. The thought of
the man so worried him that a week later he actually decided to send a clerk to
find out how he was and whether he really could help him in any way. And when 850
they brought him word that Akaky Akakievich had died suddenly in delirium and
fever, it made a great impression on him; his conscience reproached him and he
was depressed all day. Anxious to distract his mind and to forget the unpleasant
incident, he went to spend the evening with one of his friends, where he found respectable company, and what was best of all, almost everyone was of the same
grade so that he was able to be quite uninhibited. This had a wonderful effect on
his spirits. He let himself go, became affable and genial—in short, spent a very
agreeable evening. At supper he drank a couple of glasses of champagne—a proceeding which we all know is not a bad recipe for cheerfulness. The champagne
made him inclined to do something unusual, and he decided not to go home yet 860
but to visit a lady of his acquaintance, a certain Karolina Ivanovna—a lady apparently of German extraction, for whom he entertained extremely friendly feelings. It
must be noted that the Person of Consequence was a man no longer young. He
was an excellent husband, and the respectable father of a family. He had two sons,
one already serving in an office, and a nice-looking daughter of sixteen with a
rather turned-up, pretty little nose, who used to come every morning to kiss his
hand, saying: "Bon jour, Papa." His wife, who was still blooming and decidedly
good-looking, indeed, used first to give him her hand to kiss and then turning his
hand over would kiss it. But though the Person of Consequence was perfectly satisfied with the pleasant amenities of his domestic life, he thought it proper to have 870
a lady friend in another quarter of the town. This lady friend was not a bit better
looking nor younger than his wife, but these puzzling things exist in the world
and it is not our business to criticize them. And so the Person of Consequence
went downstairs, got into his sledge, and said to his coachman, "To Karolina
Ivanovna." While luxuriously wrapped in his warm fur coat he remained in that
agreeable frame of mind sweeter to a Russian than anything that could be invented, that is, when one thinks of nothing while thoughts come into the mind by
themselves, one pleasanter than the other, without your having to bother following them or looking for them. Full of satisfaction, he recalled all the amusing moments of the evening he had spent, all the phrases that had started the intimate 880
circle of friends laughing; many of them he repeated in an undertone and found
them as amusing as before, and so, very naturally, laughed very heartily at them
again. From time to time, however, he was disturbed by a gust of wind which,
blowing suddenly, God knows why or where from, cut him in the face, pelting
him with flakes of snow, puffing out his coat collar like a sail, or suddenly flinging
it with unnatural force over his head and giving him endless trouble to extricate

himself from it. All at once, the Person of Consequence felt that someone had clutched him very tightly by the collar. Turning around he saw a short man in a shabby old uniform, and not without horror recognized him as Akaky Akakievich. The clerk's face was white as snow and looked like that of a corpse, but the horror 890 of the Person of Consequence was beyond all bounds when he saw the mouth of the corpse distorted into speech, and breathing upon him the chill of the grave, it uttered the following words: "Ah, so here you are at last! At last I've . . . er . . . caught you by the collar. It's your overcoat I want; you refused to help me and abused me into the bargain! So now give me yours!" The poor Person of Consequence very nearly dropped dead. Resolute and determined as he was in his office and before subordinates in general, and though anyone looking at his manly air and figure would have said: "Oh, what a man of character!" yet in this situation he felt, like very many persons of heroic appearance, such terror that not without reason he began to be afraid he would have some sort of fit. He actually flung his 900 overcoat off his shoulders as far as he could and shouted to his coachman in an unnatural voice: "Drive home! Let's get out of here!" The coachman, hearing the tone which he had only heard in critical moments and then accompanied by something even more tangible, hunched his shoulders up to his ears in case of worse following, swung his whip, and flew on like an arrow. In a little over six minutes, the Person of Consequence was at the entrance of his own house. Pale, panic-stricken, and without his overcoat, he arrived home instead of at Karolina Ivanovna's, dragged himself to his own room, and spent the night in great distress, so that next morning his daughter said to him at breakfast, "You look very pale today, Papa"; but her papa remained mute and said not a word to anyone of what 910 had happened to him, where he had been, and where he had been going. The incident made a great impression upon him. Indeed, it happened far more rarely that he said to his subordinates, "How dare you? Do you understand who I am?" and he never uttered those words at all until he had first heard all the facts of the case.

What was even more remarkable is that from that time on the apparition of the dead clerk ceased entirely; apparently the general's overcoat had fitted him perfectly; anyway nothing more was heard of overcoats being snatched from anyone. Many restless and anxious people refused, however, to be pacified, and still maintained that in remote parts of the town the dead clerk when on appearing. 920 One policeman, in Kolomna, for instance, saw with his own eyes an apparition appear from behind a house; but, being by natural constitution somewhat frail—so much so that on one occasion an ordinary grown-up suckling pig, making a sudden dash out of some private building, knocked him off his feet to the great amusement of the cabmen standing around, whom he fined two kopeks each for snuff for such disrespect—he did not dare to stop it, and so followed it in the dark until the apparition suddenly looked around and, stopping, asked him: "What do you want?" displaying a huge fist such as you never see among the living. The policeman said: "Nothing," and turned back on the spot. This apparition, however, was considerably taller and adorned with immense mustaches, and, directing its 930 steps apparently toward Obukhov Bridge, vanished into the darkness of the night.

[1842]

Questions for Discussion and Writing

1. Underline or highlight the details about Akaky and his way of life that make him appear ridiculous, absurd, or petty.

2. Mark those passages that portray Akaky in a sympathetic, even admirable light.

3. Compare these two sets of characteristics. On balance, is Akaky a sympathetic character or an object of satire? Can his good qualities be separated from his weaknesses?

4. Note the passages that implicitly or explicitly comment on the Russian civil service, including the police. What comments or criticism might Gogol be making about civil servants and the Russian government?

5. How do you interpret Akaky's reappearance at the end of the story? Why is this episode included? What dimension does it add to the story?

6. Analyze carefully the implied narrator's character and tone. How does his presence affect the story as a whole?

Sidebar: EXPLORING CRITICAL ISSUES

Social Criticism and the Short Story

Writers have long considered it part of their business to criticize society and comment on its problems, injustices, and inhumanities. While the short story affords less space than the novel for a detailed portrayal of society, writers can create a "microcosm" of society through a representative character or characters, or they may use particularly telling details relating to setting, or assume a certain degree of background knowledge on the reader's part. Whatever means an author uses to portray society or convey ideas and attitudes about it, readers need to be alert to the possibility that at least one interpretation of a story involves social criticism.

It is not always easy to tell whether a short story should be read as social criticism. The opening sentences of Nikolai Gogol's "The Overcoat" seem to invite such a reading, since they discuss the sensitivity of government bureaus to criticism. A little later, we see Akaky's poverty (suggesting economic injustice), the cruelty of his fellow workers (society's insensitivity as expressed through individuals), the petty and repetitive nature of Akaky's work (bureaucracies as soul-destroying machines), the difficulties Akaky encounters in saving enough money for a new coat (the injustices of a money economy), and the opulent life of the Head of Department (the unequal distribution of wealth). When Akaky is robbed and then tries to obtain justice, we see the indifference of the police and indeed of the entire "system." Akaky's death may suggest how society exploits and destroys the poor, and his return as a ghost may prefigure Russia's revolution.

If we read "The Overcoat" as social criticism, we interpret Akaky as a sympathetic character and his antagonists as representing various segments of society. Such a reading resembles allegory in that it ascribes symbolic significance to the characters and their actions. Such an approach, however, may seem too schematic and simple, and it may be better to emphasize other aspects of the story—Akaky's character, for example or his obsession with material needs. You may see him as a grotesque or as a symbol of the meaningless life of modern man. Thus, a sociological interpretation is not the only one possible.

Fiction that obviously criticizes society poses a problem. Should such stories be judged by their diagnosis of a social problem, or should they be judged aesthetically—by how good or bad they are as stories? Is it possible to separate a story's literary qualities from its thematic ideas? (For example, is it possible to write a good story that supports a clearly immoral idea like genocide?) At what point does a story with a clear social message become overly contrived, even propagandistic? Does Gogol, for instance, exaggerate the sufferings of Akaky to make his point? Mary Wilkens Freeman's "The Revolt of Mother" effectively dramatizes female repression in a patriarchal world, but is Mother's revolt believable? The author herself claimed that no farmer's wife would place her own comfort above the economic needs of the farm. Is she right? If the story is not "realistic," does that weaken its point about male domination? Does it make it less effective as a story? Similarly, Kate Chopin can be accused of rigging the ending of "Désirée's Baby" in order to make a social statement about racism. Is the ending a clever surprise, a devastating irony, or a contrived moral?

Subtlety creates problems of its own. Sherwood Anderson does not

deal openly with homosexuality in "Hands." Anderson instead uses ambiguity of motive and self-knowledge. He plants questions in the reader's mind that have no easy answers: Is Wing Biddlebaum a homosexual and potential child-molester, or have his motives and actions been misinterpreted? Is he not homosexual at all but simply a kind and gentle man whose life has been destroyed by small town bigotry; or does he refuse to admit to himself that his hands desire more than simple human touch?

Katherine Mansfield's "Daughters of the Late Colonel" uses ambiguity and humor to delve into the stunting or infantalizing of women who are denied freedom and responsibility. But exactly what is Mansfield criticizing, the society that produces such women, or the women themselves, for allowing their father to bully them? Are Constantia and Josephine ridiculous or pathetic in their continued devotion to a man who has controlled them all their lives? Or are they symbols of a problem larger than the relations between fathers and daughters? Are they examples of those who fear to live, or are they representatives of female repression generally?

Contemporary critical theories have turned the tables on authors by scrutinizing them for their political and social attitudes. Marxism, for example, has added a new dimension to the debate about literature and social criticism. Early Marxist critics claimed that all worthwhile literature should reflect class struggle and support the working class in its fight for justice. Any work that failed in this endeavor was at best irrelevant, at worst reactionary or fascist. Modern Marxist critics are still looking for evidence of class struggle, but some have added a new twist: regarding the

Guillaume Van Kerckhoven (seated) and Léon Rom (with rifle), ivory and rubber trade agents. As officers in the colonial regime of Belgium's King Leopold, Van Kerckhoven and Rom exploited, terrorized, and slaughtered a large number of central Africans in the late nineteenth century. Joseph Conrad, who visited the Congo in 1890, may have modeled Kurst in "Heart of Darkness" in part on these men. (Left, Collections Royal Military Museum, Brussels; right, photo courtesy of Adam Hochschild)

author as a conscious or (more likely) unconscious upholder of the status quo. In this view, literature is a product of the ruling classes, who control the means of literary production; hence, even when authors attempt to criticize society, they can only go so far. The critic's job, then is to explore the gaps in the story—the places where the author consciously or unconsciously held back on criticism in order not to offend. A Marxist would interpret many of the ambiguities in "Hands" as evidence of just such gaps. A Marxist reading of Mansfield's story might note the Colonel's repression of his daughters and praise Mansfield for thus exposing the military's role in society generally. However, Marxists might criticize Mansfield for satirizing the daughters' inability to control their servant, for this suggests support of the bourgeoisie and the status quo. Such places in the story could be seen either as unconscious reactionary attitudes or as evidence that Mansfield feared alienating her readers.

Feminism emphasizes the social dimension of a story by examining its treatment of women and also turns its attention to the attitudes and values of the authors themselves. Gogol's story, in which only one woman appears, could be interpreted as exposing the sexist attitudes of its author through his negative treatment of Petrovich's wife. A feminist critic could also point to the negligible role played by women in this story as evidence of the "marginalizing" of women in Czarist Russia. "Désirée's Baby," from this point of view, dramatizes Armand's sexism as well as his racism. Shirley Jackson's "The Lottery" may be emphasizing the fact that society often uses women as scapegoats for its problems. Ernest Gaines, on the other hand, may be praised for depicting a strong, independent woman of color.

Social criticism is often a source of innovation in fiction. Latin American writers like Juan Bosch and Gabriel Garcia Marquez have often approached social issues indirectly and symbolically rather than directly. Thus, the violent scene at the end of "The Woman" suggests Latin America's almost masochistic revolutions, while the stifling atmosphere in "Monologue of Isabel Watching It Rain in Macondo" symbolizes the repressive political climate. Toni Cade Bambara conveys African American pride and assertiveness through the voice of an angry pre-adolescent. Angela Carter and Margaret Atwood reinvent the fairy tale to make feminist statements.

Stories that originate in non-Western cultures present special problems of interpretation—Ruth Prawer Jhabvala's "In the Mountains," for example. It would be easy to read the story and conclude that Indians are much like Europeans or Americans: families quarrel; mothers worry about their rebellious, unmarried daughters; the claims of the spirit compete with the desires of the flesh. The issues may be similar, but the societies are not identical, and to assume a comfortable familiarity would be to miss important differences. For one thing, Pritam's family is itself a locus of cultural tensions, suggested in part by the automobiles but also by more subtle indications, such as the mother's taste for Horlick's malted milk and Bobby's love of scotch, both of which evoke memories of British colonialism. The clash of Indian and European ways subtly suggested by the family's habits occurs within the conflict between Pritam and her mother, which has both social and religious implications. The mother stands for certain traditions—marriage, family, caste hierarchies, respectability—even if she is self-indulgent and physical, wrapped up (literally and figuratively) in her material comforts. Pritam is equally complex, on the one hand representing a western-style feminism in revolt against traditional female roles, and on the other hand an orthodox Hindu's devotion to matters of the mind and spirit. Pritam describes her cousin Sarla as an "animal." The disgraced Doctor Sahib believes in successive reincarnations and calls Pritam "a highly developed soul." Can we correctly interpret these points without knowing Indian society and Hindu religious thought?

It is not easy to discern Jhabvala's point in this story. The various cultural and familial clashes constitute a miniature portrait of some of modern India's dilemmas, but where does the author's sympathy lie? What or whom is she criticizing and why? The stories by Ama Ata Aidoo and Chinua Achebe present similar problems of cross-cultural understanding, as do Yasunari Kawabata's "Immortality" and Paule Barton's "Emilie Plead Choose One Egg."

The author and critic Frank O'Connor says that the short story commonly depicts loners at the edges of society. These loners and these edges can make us keenly aware of society with all its virtues and vices. The short story can reveal much of society—near, far, past, present, and future—and challenges us as readers to examine and understand the world in which we live and the dilemmas of our time.

❧ HARRIET BEECHER STOWE
(1811–1896)

Uncle Lot

Harriet Beecher Stowe has often been criticized as a sentimentalist and moralist, but she is also an indisputably important and influential figure. No novel has had more profound and wide-reaching impact than her anti-slavery *Uncle Tom's Cabin* (1852), yet she remains on the fringes of the literary elite.

Born in Litchfield, Connecticut, to a puritanical Congregational minister, she was a precocious child who at age thirteen was teaching in her sister Catherine's girls' school. In 1832, the family moved to Cincinnati, Ohio. There, Catherine founded another girls' school, where Harriet began her writing career with a geography textbook. In 1834, she won a $50 prize for "Uncle Lot." In 1836, she married Calvin Stowe, a professor at her father's seminary. In Cincinnati, she also became interested in slavery, although one visit to Kentucky was her only trip to the slave-holding South.

In 1850, Calvin Stowe accepted a position at Bowdoin College in Maine, and a year later, Harriet's commitment to abolition resulted in the publication of

Uncle Tom's Cabin as a serial novel in *The National Era*. It was an instant popular success in the North and throughout Europe; it was hated in the South.

Accused of exaggerating the evils of slavery, she compiled *A Key to Uncle Tom's Cabin: Presenting the Original Facts and Documents on Which the Story is Founded* (1853).

Although her reputation rests on *Uncle Tom's Cabin*, Stowe was also among the early local colorists. Some critics regard her collections of stories, *Oldtown Folks* (1869), *Poganuc People* (1878), and *Oldtime Fireside Stories* (1872) as her most successful works artistically. Undoubtedly Stowe could lapse into sentimentality, but the mid-nineteenth century was a sentimental age. It was also a time when literature was regarded as a vehicle for morality, and Stowe had no reservations about using literature in a just cause.

Literary critics and historians still debate Stowe's place in American literature. The fact that this controversial writer was a woman only complicates the question of the place she and her writing should occupy in American letters.

A ND SO I AM to write a story—but of what, and where? Shall it be radiant with the sky of Italy? or eloquent with the beau ideal of Greece? Shall it breathe odor and languor from the orient, or chivalry from the occident? or gayety from France? or vigor from England? No, no; these are all too old—too romance-like—too obviously picturesque for me. No; let me turn to my own land—my own New England; the land of bright fires and strong hearts; the land of *deeds*, and not of words; the land of fruits, and not of flowers; the land often spoken against, yet always respected; "the latchet of whose shoes the nations of the earth are not worthy to unloose."

Now, from this very heroic apostrophe, you may suppose that I have something very heroic to tell. By no means. It is merely a little introductory breeze of patriotism, such as occasionally brushes over every mind, bearing on its wings the remembrance of all we ever loved or cherished in the land of our early years; and if it should seem to be rodomontade to any people in other parts of the earth, let them only imagine it to be said about "Old Kentuck," old England, or any other corner of the world in which they happened to be born, and they will find it quite rational.

But, as touching our story, it is time to begin. Did you ever see the little village of Newbury, in New England? I dare say you never did; for it was just one of those out of the way places where nobody ever came unless they came on purpose: a green little hollow, wedged like a bird's nest between half a dozen high hills, that kept off the wind and kept out foreigners; so that the little place was as straitly *sui generis* as if there were not another in the world. The inhabitants were all of that respectable old standfast family who make it a point to be born, bred, married, die, and be buried all in the selfsame spot. There were just so many houses, and just so many people lived in them; and nobody ever seemed to be sick, or to die either, at least while I was there. The natives grew old till they could not grow any older, and then they stood still, and *lasted* from generation to gener-

ation. There was, too, an unchangeability about all the externals of Newbury. Here
was a red house, and there was a brown house, and across the way was a yellow   30
house; and there was a straggling rail fence or a tribe of mullein stalks between.
The minister lived here, and 'Squire Moses lived there, and Deacon Hart lived
under the hill, and Messrs. Nadab and Abihu Peters lived by the cross road, and
the old "widder" Smith lived by the meeting house, and Ebenezer Camp kept a
shoemaker's shop on one side, and Patience Mosely kept a milliner's shop in front;
and there was old Comfort Scran, who kept store for the whole town, and sold axe
heads, brass thimbles, licorice ball, fancy handkerchiefs, and every thing else you
can think of. Here, too, was the general post office, where you might see letters
marvellously folded, directed wrong side upward, stamped with a thimble, and
superscribed to some of the Dollys, or Pollys, or Peters, or Moseses aforenamed or   40
not named.

For the rest, as to manners, morals, arts, and sciences, the people in
Newbury always went to their parties at three o'clock in the afternoon, and came
home before dark; always stopped all work the minute the sun was down on
Saturday night; always went to meeting on Sunday; had a school house with all
the ordinary inconveniences; were in neighborly charity with each other; read
their Bibles, feared their God, and were content with such things as they had—the
best philosophy, after all. Such was the place into which Master James Benton
made an irruption in the year eighteen hundred and no matter what. Now, this
James is to be our hero, and he is just the hero for a sensation—at least, so you   50
would have thought, if you had been in Newbury the week after his arrival.
Master James was one of those whole-hearted, energetic Yankees, who rise in the
world as naturally as cork does in water. He possessed a great share of that characteristic national trait so happily denominated "cuteness,"[1] which signifies an ability
to do every thing without trying, and to know every thing without learning, and
to make more use of one's *ignorance* than other people do of their knowledge. This
quality in James was mingled with an elasticity of animal spirits, a buoyant cheerfulness of mind, which, though found in the New England character, perhaps, as
often as any where else, is not ordinarily regarded as one of its distinguishing
traits.   60

As to the personal appearance of our hero, we have not much to say of it—
not half so much as the girls in Newbury found it necessary to remark, the first
Sabbath that he shone out in the meeting house. There was a saucy frankness of
countenance, a knowing roguery of eye, a joviality and prankishness of demeanor,
that was wonderfully captivating, especially to the ladies.

It is true that Master James had an uncommonly comfortable opinion of
himself, a full faith that there was nothing in creation that he could not learn and
could not do; and this faith was maintained with an abounding and triumphant
joyfulness, that fairly carried your sympathies along with him, and made you feel
quite as much delighted with his qualifications and prospects as he felt himself.   70
There are two kinds of self-sufficiency; one is amusing, and the other is provoking.
His was the amusing kind. It seemed, in truth, to be only the buoyancy and over-

---

1. Acuteness, cleverness.

flow of a vivacious mind, delighted with every thing delightful, in himself or others. He was always ready to magnify his own praise, but quite as ready to exalt his
neighbor, if the channel of discourse ran that way: his own perfections being more
completely within his knowledge, he rejoiced in them more constantly; but, if
those of any one else came within the same range, he was quite as much astonished and edified as if they had been his own.

Master James, at the time of his transit to the town of Newbury, was only
eighteen years of age; so that it was difficult to say which predominated in him 80
most, the boy or the man. The belief that he could, and the determination that he
would, be something in the world had caused him to abandon his home, and,
with all his worldly effects tied in a blue cotton pocket handkerchief, to proceed to
seek his fortune in Newbury. And never did stranger in Yankee village rise to promotion with more unparalleled rapidity, or boast a greater plurality of employment. He figured as schoolmaster all the week, and as chorister on Sundays, and
taught singing and reading in the evenings, besides studying Latin and Greek with
the minister, nobody knew when; thus fitting for college, while he seemed to be
doing every thing else in the world besides.

James understood every art and craft of popularity, and made himself might- 90
ily at home in all the chimney corners of the region round about; knew the geography of every body's cider barrel and apple bin, helping himself and every one
else therefrom with all bountifulness; rejoicing in the good things of this life, devouring the old ladies' doughnuts and pumpkin pies with most flattering appetite,
and appearing equally to relish every body and thing that came in his way.

The degree and versatility of his acquirements were truly wonderful. He
knew all about arithmetic and history, and all about catching squirrels and planting corn; made poetry and hoe handles with equal celerity; wound yarn and took
out grease spots for old ladies, and made nosegays and knick-knacks for young
ones; caught trout Saturday afternoons, and discussed doctrines on Sundays, with 100
equal adroitness and effect. In short, Mr. James moved on through the place

"Victorious,
Happy and glorious,"

welcomed and privileged by every body in every place; and when he had told his
last ghost story, and fairly flourished himself out of doors at the close of a long
winter's evening, you might see the hard face of the good man of the house still
phosphorescent with his departing radiance, and hear him exclaim, in a paroxysm
of admiration, that "Jemeses talk re'ely did beat all; that he was sartainly most a
miraculous cre'tur!"

It was wonderfully contrary to the buoyant activity of Master James's mind to 110
keep a school. He had, moreover, so much of the boy and the rogue in his composition, that he could not be strict with the iniquities of the curly pates under his
charge; and when he saw how determinately every little heart was boiling over
with mischief and motion, he felt in his soul more disposed to join in and help
them to a frolic than to lay justice to the line, as was meet. This would have made
a sad case, had it not been that the activity of the master's mind communicated it-

self to his charge, just as the reaction of one brisk little spring will fill a manufactory with motion; so that there was more of an impulse towards study in the golden, good-natured day of James Benton than in the time of all that went before or came after him.

But when "school was out," James's spirits foamed over as naturally as a tumbler of soda water, and he could jump over benches and burst out of doors with as much rapture as the veriest little elf in his company. Then you might have seen him stepping homeward with a most felicitous expression of countenance, occasionally reaching his hand through the fence for a bunch of currants, or over it after a flower, or bursting into some back yard to help an old lady empty her wash tub, or stopping to pay his *devoirs* to Aunt This or Mistress That, for James well knew the importance of the "powers that be," and always kept the sunny side of the old ladies.

We shall not answer for James's general flirtations, which were sundry and manifold; for he had just the kindly heart that fell in love with every thing in feminine shape that came in his way, and if he had not been blessed with an equal facility in falling out again, we do not know what ever would have become of him. But at length he came into an abiding captivity, and it is quite time that he should; for, having devoted thus much space to the illustration of our hero, it is fit we should do something in behalf of our heroine; and, therefore, we must beg the reader's attention while we draw a diagram or two that will assist him in gaining a right idea of her.

Do you see yonder brown house, with its broad roof sloping almost to the ground on one side, and a great, unsupported, sun bonnet of a piazza shooting out over the front door? You must often have noticed it; you have seen its tall well sweep, relieved against the clear evening sky, or observed the feather beds and bolsters lounging out of its chamber windows on a still summer morning; you recollect its gate, that swung with a chain and a great stone; its pantry window, latticed with little brown slabs, and looking out upon a forest of bean poles. You remember the zephyrs that used to play among its pea brush, and shake the long tassels of its corn patch, and how vainly any zephyr might essay to perform similar flirtations with the considerate cabbages that were solemnly vegetating near by. Then there was the whole neighborhood of purple-leaved beets and feathery parsnips; there were the billows of gooseberry bushes rolled up by the fence, interspersed with rows of quince trees; and far off in one corner was one little patch, penuriously devoted to ornament, which flamed with marigolds, poppies, snappers, and four-o'clocks. Then there was a little box by itself with one rose geranium in it, which seemed to look around the garden as much like a stranger as a French dancing master in a Yankee meeting house.

That is the dwelling of Uncle Lot Griswold. Uncle Lot, as he was commonly called, had a character that a painter would sketch for its lights and contrasts rather than its symmetry. He was a chestnut burr, abounding with briers without and with substantial goodness within. He had the strong-grained practical sense, the calculating worldly wisdom of his class of people in New England; he had, too, a kindly heart; but all the strata of his character were crossed by a vein of surly petulance, that, half way between joke and earnest, colored every thing that he said and did.

If you asked a favor of Uncle Lot, he generally kept you arguing half an hour, to prove that you really needed it, and to tell you that he could not all the while be troubled with helping one body or another, all which time you might observe him regularly making his preparations to grant your request, and see, by an odd glimmer of his eye, that he was preparing to let you hear the "conclusion of the whole matter," which was, "Well, well—I guess—I'll go, on the *hull*—I 'spose I must, at least;" so off he would go and work while the day lasted, and then wind up with a   170
farewell exhortation "not to be a callin' on your neighbors when you could get along without." If any of Uncle Lot's neighbors were in any trouble, he was always at hand to tell them that "they shouldn't a' done so;" that "it was strange they couldn't had more sense;" and then to close his exhortations by laboring more diligently than any to bring them out of their difficulties, groaning in spirit, meanwhile, that folks would make people so much trouble.

"Uncle Lot, father wants to know if you will lend him your hoe to-day," says a little boy, making his way across a cornfield.

"Why don't your father use his own hoe?"

"Ours is broke."   180

"Broke! How came it broke?"

"I broke it yesterday, trying to hit a squirrel."

"What business had you to be hittin' squirrels with a hoe? say!"

"But father wants to borrow yours."

"Why don't you have that mended? It's a great pester to have every body usin' a body's things."

"Well, I can borrow one some where else, I suppose," says the suppliant. After the boy has stumbled across the ploughed ground, and is fairly over the fence, Uncle Lot calls,—

"Halloo, there, you little rascal! what are you goin' off without the hoe for?"   190

"I didn't know as you meant to lend it."

"I didn't say I wouldn't, did I? Here, come and take it—stay, I'll bring it; and do tell your father not to be a lettin' you hunt squirrels with his hoes next time."

Uncle Lot's household consisted of Aunt Sally, his wife, and an only son and daughter; the former, at the time our story begins, was at a neighboring literary institution. Aunt Sally was precisely as clever, as easy to be entreated, and kindly in externals, as her helpmate was the reverse. She was one of those respectable, pleasant old ladies whom you might often have met on the way to church on a Sunday, equipped with a great fan and a psalm book, and carrying some dried orange peel or a stalk of fennel, to give to the children if they were sleepy in meet-   200
ing. She was as cheerful and domestic as the tea kettle that sung by her kitchen fire, and slipped along among Uncle Lot's angles and peculiarities as if there never was any thing the matter in the world; and the same mantle of sunshine seemed to have fallen on Miss Grace, her only daughter.

Pretty in her person and pleasant in her ways, endowed with native self-possession and address, lively and chatty, having a mind and a will of her own, yet good-humored withal, Miss Grace was a universal favorite. It would have puzzled a city lady to understand how Grace, who never was out of Newbury in her life, knew the way to speak, and act, and behave, on all occasions, exactly as if she had been taught how. She was just one of those wild flowers which you may some-   210 times see waving its little head in the woods, and looking so civilized and garden-like, that you wonder if it really did come up and grow there by nature. She was an adept in all household concerns, and there was something amazingly pretty in her energetic way of bustling about, and "putting things to rights." Like most Yankee damsels, she had a longing after the tree of knowledge, and, having exhausted the literary fountains of a district school, she fell to reading whatsoever came in her way. True, she had but little to read; but what she perused she had her own thoughts upon, so that a person of information, in talking with her, would feel a constant wondering pleasure to find that she had so much more to say of this, that, and the other thing than he expected.   220

Uncle Lot, like every one else, felt the magical brightness of his daughter, and was delighted with her praises, as might be discerned by his often finding occasion to remark that "he didn't see why the boys need to be all the time a' comin' to see Grace, for she was nothing so extror'nary, after all." About all matters and things at home she generally had her own way, while Uncle Lot would scold and give up with a regular good grace that was quite creditable.

"Father," says Grace, "I want to have a party next week."

"You sha'n't go to havin' your parties, Grace. I always have to eat bits and ends a fortnight after you have one, and I won't have it so." And so Uncle Lot walked out, and Aunt Sally and Miss Grace proceeded to make the cake and pies 230 for the party.

When Uncle Lot came home, he saw a long array of pies and rows of cakes on the kitchen table.

"Grace—Grace—Grace, I say! What is all this here flummery for?"

"Why, it is *to eat,* father," said Grace, with a good-natured look of consciousness.

Uncle Lot tried his best to look sour; but his visage began to wax comical as he looked at his merry daughter; so he said nothing, but quietly sat down to his dinner.

"Father," said Grace, after dinner, "we shall want two more candlesticks next 240 week."

"Why, can't you have your party with what you've got?"

"No, father, we want two more."

"I can't afford it, Grace—there's no sort of use on't—and you sha'n't have any."

"O, father, now do," said Grace.

"I won't, neither," said Uncle Lot, as he sallied out of the house, and took the road to Comfort Scran's store.

In half an hour he returned again; and fumbling in his pocket, and drawing forth a candlestick, levelled it at Grace.   250

"There's your candlestick."

"But, Father, I said I wanted *two.*"

"Why, can't you make one do?"

"No, I can't; I must have two."

"Well, then, there's t'other; and here's a fol-de-rol for you to tie round your neck." So saying, he bolted for the door, and took himself off with all speed. It was much after this fashion that matters commonly went on in the brown house.

But having tarried long on the way, we must proceed with the main story.

James thought Miss Grace was a glorious girl; and as to what Miss Grace thought of Master James, perhaps it would not have been developed had she not been called to stand on the defensive for him with Uncle Lot. For, from the time that the whole village of Newbury began to be wholly given unto the praise of Master James, Uncle Lot set his face as a flint against him—from the laudable fear of following the multitude. He therefore made conscience of stoutly gainsaying every thing that was said in his behalf, which, as James was in high favor with Aunt Sally, he had frequent opportunities to do.

So when Miss Grace perceived that Uncle Lot did not like our hero as much as he ought to do, she, of course, was bound to like him well enough to make up for it. Certain it is that they were remarkably happy in finding opportunities of being acquainted; that James waited on her, as a matter of course, from singing school; that he volunteered making a new box for her geranium on an improved plan; and above all, that he was remarkably particular in his attentions to Aunt Sally—a stroke of policy which showed that James had a natural genius for this sort of matters. Even when emerging from the meeting house in full glory, with flute and psalm book under his arm, he would stop to ask her how she did; and if it was cold weather, he would carry her foot stove all the way home from meeting, discoursing upon the sermon, and other serious matters, as Aunt Sally observed, "in the pleasantest, prettiest way that ever ye see." This flute was one of the crying sins of James in the eyes of Uncle Lot. James was particularly fond of it, because he had learned to play on it by intuition; and on the decease of the old pitchpipe, which was slain by a fall from the gallery, he took the liberty to introduce the flute in its place. For this, and other sins, and for the good reasons above named, Uncle Lot's countenance was not towards James, neither could he be moved to him-ward by any manner of means.

To all Aunt Sally's good words and kind speeches, he had only to say that "he didn't like him; that he hated to see him a' manifesting and glorifying there in the front gallery Sundays, and a' acting every where as if he was master of all: he didn't like it, and he wouldn't." But our hero was no whit cast down or discomfited by the malcontent aspect of Uncle Lot. On the contrary, when report was made to him of divers of his hard speeches, he only shrugged his shoulders, with a very satisfied air, and remarked that "he knew a thing or two for all that."

"Why, James," said his companion and chief counsellor, "do you think Grace likes you?"

"I don't know," said our hero, with a comfortable appearance of certainty.

"But you can't get her, James, if Uncle Lot is cross about it."

"Fudge! I can make Uncle Lot like me if I have a mind to try."

"Well then, Jim, you'll have to give up that flute of yours, I tell you now."

"Fa, sol, la—I can make him like me and my flute too."

"Why, how will you do it?"

"O, I'll work it," said our hero.

"Well, Jim, I tell you now, you don't know Uncle Lot if you say so; for he is just the *settest* crittur in his way that ever you saw."

"I *do* know Uncle Lot, though, better than most folks; he is no more cross than I am; and as to his being *set,* you have nothing to do but make him think he is in his own way when he is in yours—that is all."

"Well," said the other, "but you see I don't believe it."

"And I'll bet you a gray squirrel that I'll go there this very evening, and get him to like me and my flute both," said James.

Accordingly the late sunshine of that afternoon shone full on the yellow buttons of James as he proceeded to the place of conflict. It was a bright, beautiful evening. A thunder storm had just cleared away, and the silver clouds lay rolled up in masses around the setting sun; the rain drops were sparkling and winking to each other over the ends of the leaves, and all the bluebirds and robins, breaking forth into song, made the little green valley as merry as a musical box.

James's soul was always overflowing with that kind of poetry which consists in feeling unspeakably happy; and it is not to be wondered at, considering where he was going, that he should feel in a double ecstasy on the present occasion. He stepped gayly along, occasionally springing over a fence to the right to see whether the rain had swollen the trout brook, or to the left to notice the ripening of Mr. Somebody's watermelons—for James always had an eye on all his neighbors' matters as well as his own.

In this way he proceeded till he arrived at the picket fence that marked the commencement of Uncle Lot's ground. Here he stopped to consider. Just then four or five sheep walked up, and began also to consider a loose picket, which was hanging just ready to drop off; and James began to look at the sheep. "Well, mister," said he, as he observed the leader judiciously drawing himself through the gap, "in with you—just what I wanted;" and having waited a moment to ascertain that all the company were likely to follow, he ran with all haste towards the house, and swinging open the gate, pressed all breathless to the door.

"Uncle Lot, there are four or five sheep in your garden!" Uncle Lot dropped his whetstone and scythe.

"I'll drive them out," said our hero; and with that, he ran down the garden alley, and made a furious descent on the enemy; bestirring himself, as Bunyan says, "lustily and with good courage," till every sheep had skipped out much quicker than it skipped in; and then, springing over the fence, he seized a great stone, and nailed on the picket so effectually that no sheep could possibly encourage the hope of getting in again. This was all the work of a minute, and he was back again; but so exceedingly out of breath that it was necessary for him to stop a moment and rest himself. Uncle Lot looked ungraciously satisfied.

"What under the canopy set you to scampering so?" said he; "I could a' driv out them critturs myself."

"If you are at all particular about driving them out *yourself,* I can let them in again," said James.

Uncle Lot looked at him with an odd sort of twinkle in the corner of his eye.

"'Spose I must ask you to walk in," said he.

"Much obliged," said James; "but I am in a great hurry." So saying, he started in very business-like fashion towards the gate.

"You'd better jest stop a minute."

"Can't stay a minute."

"I don't see what possesses you to be all the while in sich a hurry; a body   350
would think you had all creation on your shoulders."

"Just my situation, Uncle Lot," said James, swinging open the gate.

"Well, at any rate, have a drink of cider, can't ye?" said Uncle Lot, who was
now quite engaged to have his own way in the case.

James found it convenient to accept this invitation, and Uncle Lot was twice
as good-natured as if he had staid in the first of the matter.

Once fairly forced into the premises, James thought fit to forget his long
walk and excess of business, especially as about that moment Aunt Sally and Miss
Grace returned from an afternoon call. You may be sure that the last thing these
respectable ladies looked for was to find Uncle Lot and Master James *tête-à-tête,*   360
over a pitcher of cider; and when, as they entered, our hero looked up with something of a mischievous air, Miss Grace, in particular, was so puzzled that it took
her at least a quarter of an hour to untie her bonnet strings. But James staid, and
acted the agreeable to perfection. First, he must needs go down into the garden to
look at Uncle Lot's wonderful cabbages, and then he promenaded all around the
corn patch, stopping every few moments and looking up with an appearance of
great gratification, as if he had ever seen such corn in his life; and then he examined Uncle Lot's favorite apple tree with an expression of wonderful interest.

"I never!" he broke forth, having stationed himself against the fence opposite
to it; "what kind of an apple tree is that?"   370

"It's a bellflower, or somethin' another," said Uncle Lot.

"Why, where *did* you get it? I never saw such apples!" said our hero, with his
eyes still fixed on the tree.

Uncle Lot pulled up a stalk or two of weeds, and threw them over the fence,
just to show that he did not care any thing about the matter; and then he came up
and stood by James.

"Nothin' so remarkable, as I know on," said he.

Just then, Grace came to say that supper was ready. Once seated at table, it
was astonishing to see the perfect and smiling assurance with which our hero continued his addresses to Uncle Lot. It sometimes goes a great way towards making   380
people like us to take it for granted that they do already; and upon this principle
James proceeded. He talked, laughed, told stories, and joked with the most fearless assurance, occasionally seconding his words by looking Uncle Lot in the face,
with a countenance so full of good will as would have melted any snowdrift of
prejudices in the world.

James also had one natural accomplishment, more courtier-like than all the
diplomacy in Europe, and that was the gift of feeling a *real* interest for any body in
five minutes; so that, if he began to please in jest, he generally ended in earnest.
With great simplicity of mind, he had a natural tact for seeing into others, and
watched their motions with the same delight with which a child gazes at the   390
wheels and springs of a watch, to "see what it will do."

The rough exterior and latent kindness of Uncle Lot were quite a spirit-
stirring study; and when tea was over, as he and Grace happened to be standing
together in the front door, he broke forth,—

"I do really like your father, Grace!"

"Do you?" said Grace.

"Yes, I do. He has something *in him,* and I like him all the better for having to fish it out."

"Well, I hope you will make him like you," said Grace, unconsciously; and then she stopped, and looked a little ashamed.   400

James was too well bred to see this, or look as if Grace meant any more than she said—a kind of breeding not always attendant on more fashionable polish—so he only answered,—

"I think I shall, Grace, though I doubt whether I can get him to own it."

"He is the kindest man that ever was," said Grace; "and he always acts as if he was ashamed of it."

James turned a little away, and looked at the bright evening sky, which was glowing like a calm, golden sea; and over it was the silver new moon, with one lit-tle star to hold the candle for her. He shook some bright drops off from a rosebush near by, and watched to see them shine as they fell, while Grace stood very quietly   410
waiting for him to speak again.

"Grace," said he, at last, "I am going to college this fall."

"So you told me yesterday," said Grace.

James stooped down over Grace's geranium, and began to busy himself with pulling off all the dead leaves, remarking in the mean while,—

"And if I do get *him* to like me, Grace, will you like me too?"

"I like you now very well," said Grace.

"Come, Grace, you know what I mean," said James, looking steadfastly at the top of the apple tree.

"Well, I wish, then, you would understand what *I* mean, without my saying   420
any more about it," said Grace.

"O, to be sure I will!" said our hero, looking up with a very intelligent air; and so, as Aunt Sally would say, the matter was settled, with "no words about it."

Now shall we narrate how our hero, as he saw Uncle Lot approaching the door, had the impudence to take out his flute, and put the parts together, arrang-ing and adjusting the stops with great composure?

"Uncle Lot," said he, looking up, "this is the best flute that ever I saw."

"I hate them tooting critturs," said Uncle Lot, snappishly.

"I declare! I wonder how you can," said James, "for I do think they exceed————"   430

So saying, he put the flute to his mouth, and ran up and down a long flour-ish.

"There! what do you think of that?" said he, looking in Uncle Lot's face with much delight.

Uncle Lot turned and marched into the house, but soon faced to the right-about, and came out again, for James was fingering "Yankee Doodle"—that appro-priate national air for the descendants of the Puritans.

Uncle Lot's patriotism began to bestir itself; and now, if it had been any thing, as he said, but "that 'are flute"—as it was, he looked more than once at James's fingers.   440

"How under the sun *could* you learn to do that?" said he.

"O, it's easy enough," said James, proceeding with another tune; and, having played it through, he stopped a moment to examine the joints of his flute, and in the mean time addressed Uncle Lot: "You can't think how grand this is for pitching tunes—I always pitch the tunes on Sunday with it."

"Yes; but I don't think it's a right and fit instrument for the Lord's house," said Uncle Lot.

"Why not? It is only a kind of a long pitchpipe, you see," said James; "and, seeing the old one is broken, and this will answer, I don't see why it is not better than nothing."   450

"Why, yes, it may be better than nothing," said Uncle Lot; "but, as I always tell Grace and my wife, it ain't the right kind of instrument, after all; it ain't solemn."

"Solemn!" said James; "that is according as you work it: see here, now."

So saying, he struck up Old Hundred,[2] and proceeded through it with great perseverance.

"There, now!" said he.

"Well, well, I don't know but it is," said Uncle Lot; "but, as I said at first, I don't like the look of it in meetin'."

"But yet you really think it is better than nothing," said James, "for you see I   460 couldn't pitch my tunes without it."

"Maybe 'tis," said Uncle Lot; "but that isn't sayin' much."

This, however, was enough for Master James, who soon after departed, with his flute in his pocket, and Grace's last words in his heart; soliloquizing as he shut the gate, "There, now, I hope Aunt Sally won't go to praising me; for, just so sure as she does, I shall have it all to do over again."

James was right in his apprehension. Uncle Lot could be privately converted, but not brought to open confession; and when, the next morning, Aunt Sally remarked, in the kindness of her heart,—

"Well, I always knew you would come to like James," Uncle Lot only re-   470 sponded, "Who said I did like him?"

"But I'm sure you *seemed* to like him last night."

"Why, I couldn't turn him out o' doors, could I? I don't think nothin' of him but what I always did."

But it was to be remarked that Uncle Lot contented himself at this time with the mere general avowal, without running it into particulars, as was formerly his wont. It was evident that the ice had begun to melt, but it might have been a long time in dissolving, had not collateral incidents assisted.

It so happened that, about this time, George Griswold, the only son before referred to, returned to his native village, after having completed his theological   480 studies at a neighboring institution. It is interesting to mark the gradual development of mind and heart, from the time that the white-headed, bashful boy quits the country village for college, to the period when he returns, a formed and matured man, to notice how gradually the rust of early prejudices begins to cleave from him—how his opinions, like his handwriting, pass from the cramped and limited forms of a country school into that confirmed and characteristic style which is to mark the man for life. In George this change was remarkably striking. He was endowed by nature with uncommon acuteness of feeling and fondness for

2. A hymn tune, also known as the "Doxology."

reflection—qualities as likely as any to render a child backward and uninteresting in early life.

When he left Newbury for college, he was a taciturn and apparently phlegmatic boy, only evincing sensibility by blushing and looking particularly stupefied whenever any body spoke to him. Vacation after vacation passed, and he returned more and more an altered being; and he who once shrunk from the eye of the deacon, and was ready to sink if he met the minister, now moved about among the dignitaries of the place with all the composure of a superior being.

It was only to be regretted that, while the mind improved, the physical energies declined, and that every visit to his home found him paler, thinner, and less prepared in body for the sacred profession to which he had devoted himself. But now he was returned, a minister—a real minister, with a right to stand in the pulpit and preach; and what a joy and glory to Aunt Sally—and to Uncle Lot, if he were not ashamed to own it!

The first Sunday after he came, it was known far and near that George Griswold was to preach; and never was a more ready and expectant audience.

As the time for reading the first psalm approached, you might see the white-headed men turning their faces attentively towards the pulpit; the anxious and expectant old women, with their little black bonnets, bent forward to see him rise. There were the children looking, because every body else looked; there was Uncle Lot in the front pew, his face considerately adjusted; there was Aunt Sally, seeming as pleased as a mother could seem; and Miss Grace, lifting her sweet face to her brother, like a flower to the sun; there was our friend James in the front gallery, his joyous countenance a little touched with sobriety and expectation; in short, a more embarrassingly attentive audience never greeted the first effort of a young minister. Under these circumstances there was something touching in the fervent self-forgetfulness which characterized the first exercises of the morning—something which moved every one in the house.

The devout poetry of his prayer, rich with the Orientalism of Scripture, and eloquent with the expression of strong yet chastened emotion, breathed over his audience like music, hushing every one to silence, and beguiling every one to feeling. In the sermon, there was the strong intellectual nerve, the constant occurrence of argument and statement, which distinguishes a New England discourse; but it was touched with life by the intense, yet half-subdued, feeling with which he seemed to utter it. Like the rays of the sun, it enlightened and melted at the same moment.

The strong peculiarities of New England doctrine, involving, as they do, all the hidden machinery of mind, all the mystery of its divine relations and future progression, and all the tremendous uncertainties of its eternal good or ill, seemed to have dwelt in his mind, to have burned in his thoughts, to have wrestled with his powers, and they gave to his manner the fervency almost of another world; while the exceeding paleness of his countenance, and a tremulousness of voice that seemed to spring from bodily weakness, touched the strong workings of his mind with a pathetic interest, as if the being so early absorbed in another world could not be long for this.

When the services were over, the congregation dispersed with the air of people who had *felt* rather than *heard;* and all the criticism that followed was similar to that of old Deacon Hart—an upright, shrewd man—who, as he lingered a moment at the church door, turned and gazed with unwonted feeling at the young preacher.

"He's a blessed cre'tur!" said he, the tears actually making their way to his eyes; "I hain't been so near heaven this many a day. He's a blessed cre'tur of the Lord; that's my mind about him!"

As for our friend James, he was at first sobered, then deeply moved, and at last wholly absorbed by the discourse; and it was only when meeting was over that he began to think where he really was. 540

With all his versatile activity, James had a greater depth of mental capacity that he was himself aware of, and he began to feel a sort of electric affinity for the mind that had touched him in a way so new; and when he saw the mild minister standing at the foot of the pulpit stairs, he made directly towards him.

"I do want to hear more from you," said he, with a face full of earnestness; "may I walk home with you?"

"It is a long and warm walk," said George, smiling.

"O, I don't care for that, if it does not trouble *you*," said James; and leave being gained, you might have seen them slowly passing along under the trees, 550 James pouring forth all the floods of inquiry which the sudden impulse of his mind had brought out, and supplying his guide with more questions and problems for solution than he could have gone through with in a month.

"I cannot answer all your questions now," said he, as they stopped at Uncle Lot's gate.

"Well, then, when will you?" said James, eagerly. "Let me come home with you to-night?"

The minister smiled assent, and James departed so full of new thoughts, that he passed Grace without even seeing her. From that time a friendship commenced between the two, which was a beautiful illustration of the affinities of opposites. It 560 was like a friendship between morning and evening—all freshness and sunshine on one side, and all gentleness and peace on the other.

The young minister, worn by long-continued ill health, by the fervency of his own feelings, and the gravity of his own reasonings, found pleasure in the healthful buoyancy of a youthful, unexhausted mind, while James felt himself sobered and made better by the moonlight tranquillity of his friend. It is one mark of a superior mind to understand and be influenced by the superiority of others; and this was the case with James. The ascendency which his new friend acquired over him was unlimited, and did more in a month towards consolidating and developing his character than all the four years' course of a college. Our religious 570 habits are likely always to retain the impression of the first seal which stamped them, and in this case it was a peculiarly happy one. The calmness, the settled purpose, the mild devotion of his friend, formed a just alloy to the energetic and reckless buoyancy of James's character, and awakened in him a set of feelings without which the most vigorous mind must be incomplete.

The effect of the ministrations of the young pastor, in awakening attention to the subjects of his calling in the village, was marked, and of a kind which brought pleasure to his own heart. But, like all other excitement, it tends to exhaustion, and it was not long before he sensibly felt the decline of the powers of life. To the

best regulated mind there is something bitter in the relinquishment of projects for 580
which we have been long and laboriously preparing, and there is something far
more bitter in crossing the long-cherished expectations of friends. All this George
felt. He could not bear to look on his mother, hanging on his words and following
his steps with eyes of almost childish delight—on his singular father, whose whole
earthly ambition was bound up in his success, and think how soon the "candle of
their old age" must be put out. When he returned from a successful effort, it was
painful to see the old man, so evidently delighted, and so anxious to conceal his
triumph, as he would seat himself in his chair, and begin with, "George, that 'are
doctrine is rather of a puzzler; but you seem to think you've got the run on't. I
should re'ly like to know what business you have to think you know better than 590
other folks about it;" and, though he would cavil most courageously at all George's
explanations, yet you might perceive, through all, that he was inly uplifted to hear
how his boy could talk.

If George was engaged in argument with any one else, he would sit by, with
his head bowed down, looking out from under his shaggy eyebrows with a shamefaced satisfaction very unusual with him. Expressions of affection from the naturally gentle are not half so touching as those which are forced out from the
hard-favored and severe; and George was affected, even to pain, by the evident
pride and regard of his father.

"He never said so much to any body before," thought he, "and what will he 600
do if I die?"

In such thoughts as these Grace found her brother engaged one still autumn
morning, as he stood leaning against the garden fence.

"What are you solemnizing here for, this bright day, brother George?" said
she, as she bounded down the alley.

The young man turned and looked on her happy face with a sort of twilight
smile.

"How *happy* you are, Grace!" said he.

"To be sure I am; and you ought to be too, because you are better."

"I am happy, Grace—that is, I hope I shall be." 610

"You are sick, I know you are," said Grace; "you look worn out. O, I wish
your heart could *spring* once, as mine does."

"I am not well, dear Grace, and I fear I never shall be," said he, turning away,
and fixing his eyes on the fading trees opposite.

"O George! dear George, don't, don't say *that,* you'll break all our hearts,"
said Grace, with tears in her own eyes.

"Yes, but it is *true,* sister: I do not feel it on my own account so much as
——— However," he added, "it will all be the same in heaven."

It was but a week after this that a violent cold hastened the progress of debil-
ity into a confirmed malady. He sunk very fast. Aunt Sally, with the self-deceit of a 620
fond and cheerful heart, thought every day that "he *would* be better," and Uncle
Lot resisted conviction with all the obstinate pertinacity of his character, while the
sick man felt that he had not the heart to undeceive them.

James was now at the house every day, exhausting all his energy and invention in the case of his friend; and any one who had seen him in his hours of recklessness and glee, could scarcely recognize him as the being whose step was so

careful, whose eye so watchful, whose voice and touch were so gentle, as he moved around the sick bed. But the same quickness which makes a mind buoyant in gladness, often makes it gentlest and most sympathetic in sorrow.

It was now nearly morning in the sick room. George had been restless and feverish all night; but towards day he fell into a slight slumber, and James sat by his side, almost holding his breath lest he should waken him. It was yet dusk, but the sky was brightening with a solemn glow, and the stars were beginning to disappear; all, save the bright and morning one, which, standing alone in the east, looked tenderly through the casement, like the eye of our heavenly Father, watching over us when all earthly friendships are fading.

George awoke with a placid expression of countenance, and fixing his eyes on the brightening sky, murmured faintly,—

"The sweet, immortal morning sheds
Its blushes round the spheres."

A moment after, a shade passed over his face; he pressed his fingers over his eyes, and the tears dropped silently on his pillow.

"George! *dear* George!" said James, bending over him.

"It's my friends—it's my father—my mother," said he faintly.

"Jesus Christ will watch over them," said James, soothingly.

"O, yes, I know he will; for *he* loved his own which were in the world; he loved them unto the end. But I am dying—and before I have done any good."

"O, do not say so," said James; "think, think what you have done, if only for *me*. God bless you for it! God *will* bless you for it; it will follow you to heaven; it will bring me there. Yes, I will do as you have taught me. I will give my life, my soul, my whole strength to it; and then you will not have lived in vain."

George smiled, and looked upward; "his face was as that of an angel;" and James, in his warmth, continued,—

"It is not I alone who can say this; we all bless you; every one in this place blesses you; you will be had in everlasting remembrance by some hearts here, I know."

"Bless God!" said George.

"We do," said James. "I bless him that I ever knew you; we all bless him, and we love you, and shall forever."

The glow that had kindled over the pale face of the invalid again faded as he said,—

"But, James, I must, I ought to tell my father and mother; I ought to, and how can I?"

At that moment the door opened, and Uncle Lot made his appearance. He seemed struck with the paleness of George's face; and coming to the side of the bed, he felt his pulse, and laid his hand anxiously on his forehead, and clearing his voice several times, inquired "if he didn't feel a little better."

"No, father," said George; then taking his hand, he looked anxiously in his face, and seemed to hesitate a moment. "Father," he began, "you know that we ought to submit to God."

There was something in his expression at this moment which flashed the truth into the old man's mind. He dropped his son's hand with an exclamation of agony, and turning quickly, left the room.

"Father! father!" said Grace, trying to rouse him, as he stood with his arms 680 folded by the kitchen window.

"Get away, child!" said he, roughly.

"Father, mother says breakfast is ready."

"I don't want any breakfast," said he, turning short about. "Sally, what are you fixing in that 'ere porringer?"

"O, it's only a little tea for George; 'twill comfort him up, and make him feel better, poor fellow."

"You won't make him feel better—he's gone," said Uncle Lot, hoarsely.

"O, dear heart, no!" said Aunt Sally.

"Be still a' contradicting me; I won't be contradicted all the time by nobody. 690 The short of the case is, that George is goin' to *die* just as we've got him ready to be a minister and all; and I wish to pity I was in my grave myself, and so ———" said Uncle Lot, as he plunged out of the door, and shut it after him.

It is well for man that there is one Being who sees the suffering heart *as it is,* and not as it manifests itself through the repellances of outward infirmity, and who, perhaps, feels more for the stern and wayward than for those whose gentler feelings win for them human sympathy. With all his singularities, there was in the heart of Uncle Lot a depth of religious sincerity; but there are few characters where religion does any thing more than struggle with natural defect, and modify what would else be far worse. 700

In this hour of trial, all the native obstinacy and pertinacity of the old man's character rose, and while he felt the necessity of submission, it seemed impossible to submit; and thus, reproaching himself, struggling in vain to repress the murmurs of nature, repulsing from him all external sympathy, his mind was "tempest-tossed, and not comforted."

It was on the still afternoon of the following Sabbath that he was sent for, in haste, to the chamber of his son. He entered, and saw that the hour was come. The family were all there. Grace and James, side by side, bent over the dying one, and his mother sat afar off, with her face hid in her apron, "that she might not see the death of the child." The aged minister was there, and the Bible lay open before 710 him. The father walked to the side of the bed. He stood still, and gazed on the face now brightening with "life and immortality." The son lifted up his eyes; he saw his father, smiled, and put out his hand. "I am glad *you* are come," said he. "O George, to the pity, don't! *don't* smile on me so! I know what is coming; I have tried, and tried, and I *can't*, I *can't* have it so;" and his frame shook, and he sobbed audibly. The room was still as death; there was none that seemed able to comfort him. At last the son repeated, in a sweet, but interrupted voice, those words of man's best Friend: "Let not your heart be troubled; in my Father's house are many mansions."

"Yes, but I *can't help* being troubled; I suppose the Lord's will must be done, but it'll *kill* me." 720

"O father, don't, don't break my heart," said the son, much agitated. "I shall see you again in heaven, and you shall see me again; and then 'your heart shall rejoice, and your joy no man taketh from you.'"

"I never shall get to heaven if I feel as I do now," said the old man. "I *cannot* have it so."

The mild face of the sufferer was overcast. "I wish he saw all that *I* do," said he, in a low voice. Then looking towards the minister, he articulated, "Pray for us."

They knelt in prayer. It was soothing, as *real* prayer always must be; and when they rose, every one seemed more calm. But the sufferer was exhausted; his countenance changed; he looked on his friends; there was a faint whisper, "Peace I 730 leave with you"—and he was in heaven.

We need not dwell on what followed. The seed sown by the righteous often blossoms over their grave; and so was it with this good man. The words of peace which he spoke unto his friends while he was yet with them came into remembrance after he was gone; and though he was laid in the grave with many tears, yet it was with softened and submissive hearts.

"The Lord bless him," said Uncle Lot, as he and James were standing, last of all, over the grave. "I believe my heart is gone to heaven with him; and I think the Lord really *did* know what was best, after all."

Our friend James seemed now to become the support of the family; and the 740 bereaved old man unconsciously began to transfer to him the affections that had been left vacant.

"James," said he to him one day, "I suppose you know that you are about the same to me as a son."

"I hope so," said James, kindly.

"Well, well, you'll go to college next week, and none o' y'r keepin' school to get along. I've got enough to bring you safe out—that is, if you'll be *car'ful* and *stiddy.*"

James knew the heart too well to refuse a favor in which the poor old man's mind was comforting itself. He had the self-command to abstain from any extraor- 750 dinary expressions of gratitude, but took it kindly, as a matter of course.

"Dear Grace," said he to her, the last evening before he left home, "I am changed; we both are altered since we first knew each other; and now I am going to be gone a long time, but I am sure———"

He stopped to arrange his thoughts.

"Yes, you may be sure of all those things that you wish to say, and cannot," said Grace.

"Thank you," said James; then, looking thoughtfully, he added, "God help me. I believe I have mind enough to be what I mean to; but whatever I am or have shall be given to God and my fellow-men; and then, Grace, your brother in 760 heaven will rejoice over me."

"I believe he does *now*," said Grace. "God bless you, James; I don't know what would have become of us if you had not been here."

"Yes, you will live to be like him, and to do even more good," she added, her face brightening as she spoke, till James thought she really must be right.

It was five years after this that James was spoken of as an eloquent and successful minister in the state of C., and was settled in one of its most thriving villages. Late one autumn evening, a tall, bony, hard-favored man was observed making his way into the outskirts of the place.   770

"Halloa, there!" he called to a man over the other side of a fence; "what town is this 'ere?"

"It's Farmington, sir."

"Well, I want to know if you know any thing of a boy of mine that lives here?"

"A boy of yours? Who?"

"Why, I've got a boy here, that's livin' *on the town,* and I thought I'd jest look him up."

"I don't know any boy that is living on the town. What's his name?"

"Why," said the old man, pushing his hat off from his forehead, "I believe they call him James Benton."

"James Benton! Why, that is our minister's name!"

"O, wal, I believe he *is* the minister, come to think on't. He's a boy o' mine, though. Where does he live?"

"In that white house that you see set back from the road there, with all those trees round it."

At that instant a tall, manly-looking person approached from behind. Have we not seen that face before? It is a touch graver than of old, and its lines have a more thoughtful significance; but all the vivacity of James Benton sparkles in that quick smile as his eye falls on the old man.

"I *thought* you could not keep away from us long," said he, with the prompt cheerfulness of his boyhood, and laying hold of both of Uncle Lot's hard hands.

They approached the gate; a bright face glances past the window, and in a moment Grace is at the door.

"Father! *dear* father!"

"You'd *better* make believe be so glad," said Uncle Lot, his eyes glistening as he spoke.

"Come, come, father, I have authority in these days," said Grace, drawing him towards the house; "so no disrespectful speeches; away with your hat and coat, and sit down in this great chair."

"So, ho! Miss Grace," said Uncle Lot, "you are at your old tricks, ordering round as usual. Well, if I must, I must;" so down he sat.

"Father," said Grace, as he was leaving them, after a few days' stay, "it's Thanksgiving day next month, and you and mother must come and stay with us."

Accordingly, the following month found Aunt Sally and Uncle Lot by the minister's fireside, delighted witnesses of the Thanksgiving presents which a willing people were pouring in; and the next day they had once more the pleasure of seeing a son of theirs in the sacred desk, and hearing a sermon that every body said was "the best that he ever preached;" and it is to be remarked, that this was the standing commentary on all James's discourses, so that it was evident he was going on unto perfection.

"There's a great deal that's worth having in this 'ere life after all," said Uncle Lot, as he sat by the coals of the bright evening fire of that day; "that is, if we'd only take it when the Lord lays it in our way."

"Yes," said James; "and let us only take it as we should, and this life will be cheerfulness, and the next fulness of joy."   [1834]

Questions for Discussion and Writing

1. Analyze Stowe's handling of character, especially those of James Benton, Uncle Lot, and Grace. How individualized or how drawn as types are each of them?
2. What do the local color details convey about life in New England at the time? Do these details help to make the story "realistic," or do they idealize or romanticize the locale?
3. How do you respond to George's death scene? Do you find it realistic, sentimental, touching?
4. Does the story have any thematic idea, or is it simply a depiction of a way of life?

Sidebar: EXPLORING CRITICAL ISSUES

Popular versus Literary Short Stories

Many readers would assign the label "popular" to Harriet Beecher Stowe's "Uncle Lot," H. Rider Haggard's "Hunter Quatermain's Story," Arthur Conan Doyle's "The Blue Carbuncle," O. Henry's "The Gift of the Magi," Agatha Christie's "The Case of the Perfect Maid," and Raymond Chandler's "The Curtain." Others might view the stories by Irving, Poe, Elizabeth Gaskell, Saki, Wilbur Daniel Steele, and H. E. Bates similarly. In either case, "popular" would mean not on the same level as work by such literary figures as Henry James and James Joyce. What do these distinctions mean? What criteria—if any—distinguish so-called popular stories from so-called literary ones by, say, Gogol, Katherine Mansfield, or Angela Carter?

The word "popular" possesses at least two different meanings. One sense is similar to "best selling," which in turn implies "read and enjoyed by a wide audience." By this criterion, popular stories are simply those that sell many copies. Some writers, however, such as Ernest Hemingway and Margaret Atwood, have large sales but are not considered popular in any derogatory way. These authors do not have much in common with, say, Agatha Christie or H. Rider Haggard, except for the fact that their books have sold well. Also, it seems wrongheaded to say that if a book sells well, it cannot have any literary merit. The criterion of sales does not work very well.

The other sense in which we use the word "popular" is to mean "highly conventional, predictable." Popular stories in this sense include those easily classified by subgenre, such as westerns, ghost stories, or love stories. Each of these types of stories has stock characters and plots that follow set patterns with only minor variations. Readers seek out such stories because they know and enjoy the conventions. But, again, a work can be highly conventional without being considered popular, and vice versa. Popular stories do not necessarily fall into a subgenre. "Uncle Lot," for example, does not fall in the "love story" category. Joseph Conrad's "The Heart of Darkness" has the hallmarks of an adventure story, but few readers would call it "popular." Thus, looking at subgenres and their conventions does not lead to easy distinctions between the popular and the literary.

We seem to have backed ourselves into a corner. One way out, of course, is to deny that there are any objective differences between popular and literary. Some critics and scholars have taken exactly this line and have argued that what we call literary fiction is no more than individual taste or the taste of a powerful group (the aristocracy in the eighteenth century, for example, or the intelligentsia in the twentieth). In this view, the wealthy and well-educated subtly keep or increase their power by declaring themselves arbiters of sound aesthetic judgment and foisting their opinions off on the public. Thus, the distinction between popular and literary may be seen as false, and any attempt to separate the two by some measure of essence or quality is futile. This view solves the problem of definition and logic, but creates other problems, at least for a formal course on literature. If there is no distinction between popular and literary work, then what criteria do we use to decide what to read and study in the limited time available? Is not more to be gained from some pieces of literature than from others?

Keeping the distinction but trying to eliminate all evaluative connotations of the terms "literary" and "popular" is another approach. By this strategy, we would no longer equate "popular" with "second rate" but simply say that both categories are capable of excellence of a certain kind. This approach, however, still leaves the problem of trying to define the kinds of excellence particular to each category. Further, this approach seems counter-intuitive. Many readers feel a difference (or claim they do), even if they cannot define it, just as most of us know there is a difference between love and lust or patriotism and chauvinism. Wrestle as we may with the terminology, in practice we make distinctions and evaluations as best we can, looking at specific cases to see if we can isolate criteria that work more often than not.

One possible criterion is complexity of theme. Popular fiction, so this argument goes, oversimplifies subjects, ideas, and issues, whereas literary fiction portrays them as complicated and many-sided. Take, for instance, the question of love as treated by O. Henry in "The Gift of the Magi." Here, the love between Jim and Della is simple and pure, as evidenced by their willingness to sacrifice what each holds most dear. O. Henry presents love as self-sacrificing devotion. But many readers come away from this story asking, "Is this really all there is to love? Can it be this simple?" Such readers might well turn then to Chekhov's "The Lady With the Pet Dog." There they will find a murkier picture. Dmitry begins by rejecting the whole idea of love: for him, the "lower race" provides diversion, physical release, and transient pleasure, nothing more. Anna, for her part, is fleeing a disappointing marriage, perhaps in search of adventure. Somewhere along the line, they do fall in love, or think they do, but, hemmed in by laws and social conventions and restrained, too, by their own cowardice and inability to act, they are left at the end of the story contemplating an unhappy and uncertain future. Some readers will say that their cowardice

"'Will you buy my hair?' asked Della." *Lisbeth Zwerger's illustration for a
1982 edition of O. Henry's* The Gift of the Magi *(1906). From* The Gift of
the Magi *by O. Henry, illustrated by Lisbeth Zwerger. Copyright 1982
by Michael Neugebauer Verlag AG, Gossau Zurich, Switzerland. Used
by permission of North-South Books Inc., New York.*

proves they are not in love. Others will argue that love, contrary to the old
saying, does not conquer all. Still others will claim that Dmitry and Anna
have simply confused love and lust, or that their so-called love is merely a
desire for what they cannot have.

On the basis of these examples, is O. Henry to be classed as a popular
writer because he simplifies complex issues and leaves us with a warm
glow? Is Chekhov, by contrast, a literary author because he refuses to over-
simplify, knows that love and lust are difficult to distinguish, and denies
us a story-book happy ending? Perhaps so, but this distinction does not
necessarily diminish the power of each story.

Similar questions arise with respect to character. Popular fiction presents conventional characters who act more out of the requirements of the plot than from psychological probability. Characters in popular fiction, in other words, are shallow and simple, while characters in literary fiction are more complex, subtle, and life-like. This generalization holds up well when applied to, say, Quatermain in H. Rider Haggard's story on the one hand and McLindon in Faulkner's "Dry September" on the other. These two "men of action" are treated very differently by their authors. Haggard never looks beneath the surface of Quatermain. What you see is what you get. Faulkner, however, complicates McLindon by showing his behavior after the lynching—the brutal treatment of his wife and the other details that suggest guilt, frustration, perhaps even self-loathing. Haggard only wants us to admire a brave man of action; Faulkner wants us to understand the complex psychology of racism, hatred, and violence.

One could examine other elements of fiction—such as style, plot, structure, and point of view—and other specific stories, testing the idea that degree of complexity, depth, and nuance is the key difference between the literary and the popular. The problem remains, however, that no single criterion or set of criteria can show consistently or conclusively that there are real differences between the popular and the literary. Poe, for example, has been dismissed as a "vulgar" writer and hailed as a genius. F. Scott Fitzgerald wrote dozens of second-rate stories for popular magazines; yet a handful of his work rises above conventionality to the level of enduring art. Moreover, critics continue to wrestle with the work of writers who straddle the borderline between the two modes: Maugham, Bates, Steele, and Chandler, to cite a few examples. Each of these writers has been acclaimed a master by some critics and called a mere popularizer by others. In the end, readers must judge for themselves.

Distinguishing the popular from the artistic is a problem not only in the short story, but in such popular media as film and television. How much weight does one give a critic's opinion? How does one weigh the desire to escape and be entertained against the desire for substantial, thought-provoking "quality"? Are these two types of experiences with art ever one and the same, or always at odds? Distressingly, the questions that matter most will never be satisfactorily answered. The systematic study of literature does not claim to yield easy or permanent answers to difficult questions. It claims only that such questions are important and deserving of careful, disciplined thought.

❧ ELIZABETH CLEGHORN GASKELL
(1810–1865)

Lizzie Leigh

Elizabeth Gaskell has recently been rediscovered by feminist criticism as a writer who dealt seriously and frankly with social problems—particularly those of women. She was born Elizabeth Stevenson in London to staunchly Unitarian parents. Her father was a civil servant, essayist, and magazine editor. Her mother died a month after she was born, so she was adopted by her aunt and raised near Manchester.

Unitarians believed in educating women, with the result that Elizabeth received a solid grounding in Latin and modern languages at home and then studied at girls' schools until 1827. She met and married William Gaskell in 1832 and turned to writing as therapy after the death of her son in 1845. The result was *Mary Barton: A Tale of Manchester Life* (1848), which raised considerable controversy for depicting the exploitation of factory workers.

Impressed by *Mary Barton*, Charles Dickens invited Mrs. Gaskell to contribute to *Household Words,* and the result was a series of sketches that eventually became *Cranford* (1853), the novel some consider her masterpiece for its stylistic economy and vivid portraits of small town life. Gaskell again outraged readers with *Ruth* (1853), a novel dealing sympathetically with the "fallen woman."

Gaskell's life illustrates the difficulties faced by authors who were women. She said her life consisted of three important and sometimes conflicting elements: her Christian beliefs, her duties as wife and mother, and her activities as a social reformer. Although her husband was supportive, the demands of raising a family, serving as hostess for both of their professional activities, and coping with her own fame created considerable strain.

Her work also epitomizes the problems of writing short fiction in Victorian England. The novel, with its greater length, allowed for the depiction of a rich social tapestry, a leisurely unfolding of plot, and expansive prose style. But Gaskell preferred short pieces because they permitted experimentation, and required greater concision and focus. In them, as in her novels, she explored her central themes—the tensions between self-fulfillment and duty, female sexuality, the twin dangers of repression and expression, and the role of women in society.

CHAPTER 1

WHEN DEATH IS PRESENT in a household on a Christmas Day, the very contrast between the time as it now is, and the day as it has often been, gives a poignancy to sorrow,—a more utter blankness to the desolation. James Leigh died just as the far-away bells of Rochdale Church were ringing for morning service on Christmas Day, 1836. A few minutes before his death, he opened his already glazing eyes, and made a sign to his wife, by the faint motion of his lips, that he had yet something to say. She stooped close down, and caught the broken whisper, "I forgive her, Anne! May God forgive me."

"Oh my love, my dear! only get well, and I will never cease showing my

thanks for those words. May God in heaven bless thee for saying them. Thou'rt 10
not so restless, my lad! may be—Oh God!"

For even while she spoke, he died.

They had been two-and-twenty years man and wife; for nineteen of those
years their life had been as calm and happy, as the most perfect uprightness on the
one side, and the most complete confidence and loving submission on the other,
could make it. Milton's famous line might have been framed and hung up as the
rule of their married life, for he was truly the interpreter, who stood between God
and her; she would have considered herself wicked if she had ever dared even to
think him austere, though as certainly as he was an upright man, so surely was he
hard, stern, and inflexible. But for three years the moan and the murmur had 20
never been out of her heart; she had rebelled against her husband as against a
tyrant, with a hidden sullen rebellion, which tore up the old land-marks of wifely
duty and affection, and poisoned the fountains whence gentlest love and reverence
had once been for ever springing.

But those last blessed words replaced him on his throne in her heart, and
called out penitent anguish for all the bitter estrangement of later years. It was this
which made her refuse all the entreaties of her sons, that she would see the kind-
hearted neighbours, who called on their way from church, to sympathize and con-
dole. No! she would stay with the dead husband that had spoken tenderly at last,
if for three years he had kept silence; who knew but what, if she had only been 30
more gentle and less angrily reserved he might have relented earlier—and in time!

She sat rocking herself to and fro by the side of the bed, while the footsteps
below went in and out; she had been in sorrow too long to have any violent burst
of deep grief now; the furrows were well worn in her cheeks, and the tears flowed
quietly, if incessantly, all the day long. But when the winter's night drew on, and
the neighbours had gone away to their homes, she stole to the window, and gazed
out, long and wistfully, over the dark grey moors. She did not hear her son's voice,
as he spoke to her from the door, nor his footstep as he drew nearer. She started
when he touched her.

"Mother! come down to us. There's no one but Will and me. Dearest mother, 40
we do so want you." The poor lad's voice trembled, and he began to cry. It appeared to require an effort on Mrs Leigh's part to tear herself away from the window, but with a sigh she complied with his request.

The two boys (for though Will was nearly twenty-one, she still thought of
him as a lad) had done everything in their power to make the house-place comfortable for her. She herself, in the old days before her sorrow, had never made a
brighter fire or a cleaner hearth, ready for her husband's return home, than now
awaited her. The tea-things were all put out, and the kettle was boiling; and the
boys had calmed their grief down into a kind of sober cheerfulness. They paid her
every attention they could think of, but received little notice on her part; she did 50
not resist—she rather submitted to all their arrangements; but they did not seem
to touch her heart.

When tea was ended,—it was merely the form of tea that had been gone
through,—Will moved the things away to the dresser. His mother leant back languidly in her chair.

"Mother, shall Tom read you a chapter? He's a better scholar than I."

"Aye, lad!" said she, almost eagerly. "That's it. Read me the Prodigal Son. Aye, aye, lad. Thank thee."

Tom found the chapter, and read it in the high-pitched voice which is customary in village-schools. His mother bent forward, her lips parted, her eyes dilated; her whole body instinct with eager attention. Will sat with his head depressed, and hung down. He knew why that chapter had been chosen; and to him it recalled the family's disgrace. When the reading was ended, he still hung down his head in gloomy silence. But her face was brighter than it had been before for the day. Her eyes looked dreamy, as if she saw a vision; and by and by she pulled the Bible towards her, and putting her finger underneath each word, began to read them aloud in a low voice to herself; she read again the words of bitter sorrow and deep humiliation; but most of all she paused and brightened over the father's tender reception of the repentant prodigal.

So passed the Christmas evening in the Upclose Farm.

The snow had fallen heavily over the dark waving moorland, before the day of the funeral. The black storm-laden dome of heaven lay very still and close upon the white earth, as they carried the body forth out of the house which had known his presence so long as its ruling power. Two and two the mourners followed, making a black procession, in their winding march over the unbeaten snow, to Milne-Row Church—now lost in some hollow of the bleak moors, now slowly climbing the heaving ascents. There was no long tarrying after the funeral, for many of the neighbours who accompanied the body to the grave had far to go, and the great white flakes which came slowly down, were the boding fore-runners of a heavy storm. One old friend alone accompanied the widow and her sons to their home.

The Upclose Farm had belonged for generations to the Leighs; and yet its possession hardly raised them above the rank of labourers. There was the house and outbuildings, all of an old-fashioned kind, and about seven acres of barren unproductive land, which they had never possessed capital enough to improve; indeed they could hardly rely upon it for subsistence; and it had been customary to bring up the sons to some trade—such as a wheelwright's, or blacksmith's.

James Leigh had left a will, in the possession of the old man who accompanied them home. He read it aloud. James had bequeathed the farm to his faithful wife, Anne Leigh, for her life-time; and afterwards, to his son William. The hundred and odd pounds in the savings'-bank was to accumulate for Thomas.

After the reading was ended, Anne Leigh sat silent for a time; and then she asked to speak to Samuel Orme alone. The sons went into the back-kitchen, and thence strolled out into the fields regardless of the driving snow. The brothers were dearly fond of each other, although they were very different in character. Will, the elder, was like his father, stern, reserved, and scrupulously upright. Tom (who was ten years younger) was gentle and delicate as a girl, both in appearance and character. He had always clung to his mother, and dreaded his father. They did not speak as they walked, for they were only in the habit of talking about facts, and hardly knew the more sophisticated language applied to the description of feelings.

Meanwhile their mother had taken hold of Samuel Orme's arm with her trembling hand.

"Samuel, I must let[1] the farm—I must."

"Let the farm! What's come o'er the woman?"

"Oh, Samuel!" said she, her eyes swimming in tears, "I'm just fain to go and live in Manchester, I mun[2] let the farm."

Samuel looked, and pondered, but did not speak for some time. At last he said—

"If thou hast made up thy mind, there's no speaking again it; and thou must e'en go. Thou 'lt be sadly pottered wi' Manchester ways; but that's not my look out. Why, thou 'lt have to buy potatoes, a thing thou hast never done afore in all thy born life. Well! it's not my look out. It's rather for me than again me. Our Jenny is going to be married to Tom Higginbotham, and he was speaking of wanting a bit of land to begin upon. His father will be dying sometime, I reckon, and then he'll step into the Croft Farm. "But meanwhile—

"Then, thou 'lt let the farm," said she, still as eagerly as ever.

"Aye, aye, he'll take it fast enough, I've a notion. But I'll not drive a bargain with thee just now; it would not be right; we'll wait a bit."

"No; I cannot wait, settle it out at once."

"Well, well; I'll speak to Will about it. I see him out yonder. I'll step to him, and talk it over."

Accordingly he went and joined the two lads, and without more ado, began the subject to them.

"Will, thy mother is fain to go live in Manchester, and covets to let the farm. Now, I'm willing to take it for Tom Higginbotham; but I like to drive a keen bargain, and there would be no fun chaffering with thy mother just now. Let thee and me buckle to, my lad! and try and cheat each other; it will warm us this cold day."

"Let the farm!" said both the lads at once, with infinite surprise. "Go live in Manchester!"

When Samuel Orme found that the plan had never before been named to either Will or Tom, he would have nothing to do with it, he said, until they had spoken to their mother; likely she was "dazed" by her husband's death; he would wait a day or two, and not name it to any one; not to Tom Higginbotham himself, or may be he would set his heart upon it. The lads had better go in and talk it over with their mother. He bade them good day, and left them.

Will looked very gloomy, but he did not speak till they got near the house. Then he said,—

"Tom, go to th' shippon[3], and supper the cows. I want to speak to mother alone."

When he entered the house-place, she was sitting before the fire, looking into its embers. She did not hear him come in; for some time she had lost her quick perception of outward things.

"Mother! what's this about going to Manchester?" asked he.

1. Rent it to tenants.
2. Yorkshire dialect for "must."
3. Cattle shed.

"Oh, lad!" said she, turning round, and speaking in a beseeching tone, "I must go and seek our Lizzie. I cannot rest here for thinking on her. Many's the time I've left thy father sleeping in bed, and stole to th' window, and looked and looked my heart out towards Manchester, till I thought I must just set out and tramp over moor and moss straight away till I got there, and then lift up every downcast face till I came to our Lizzie. And often, when the south wind was blow- 150 ing soft among the hollows, I've fancied (it could but be fancy, thou knowest) I heard her crying upon me; and I've thought the voice came closer and closer, till at last it was sobbing out "Mother" close to the door; and I've stolen down, and undone the latch before now, and looked out into the still black night, thinking to see her,—and turned sick and sorrowful when I heard no living sound but the sough[4] of the wind dying away. Oh! speak not to me of stopping here, when she may be perishing for hunger, like the poor lad in the parable." And now she lifted up her voice and wept aloud.

Will was deeply grieved. He had been old enough to be told the family shame when, more than two years before, his father had had his letter to his 160 daughter returned by her mistress in Manchester, telling him that Lizzie had left her service some time—and why. He had sympathized with his father's stern anger; though he had thought him something hard, it is true, when he had forbidden his weeping, heart-broken wife to go and try to find her poor sinning child, and declared that henceforth they would have no daughter; that she should be as one dead, and her name never more be named at market or at meal time, in blessing or in prayer. He had held his peace, with compressed lips and contracted brow, when the neighbours had noticed to him how poor Lizzie's death[5] had aged both his father and his mother; and how they thought the bereaved couple would never hold up their heads again. He himself had felt as if that one event had made 170 him old before his time; and had envied Tom the tears he had shed over poor, pretty, innocent, dead Lizzie. He thought about her sometimes, till he ground his teeth together, and could have struck her down in her shame. His mother had never named her to him until now.

"Mother!" said he at last. "She may be dead. Most likely she is."

"No, Will; she is not dead," said Mrs Leigh. "God will not let her die till I've seen her once again. Thou dost not know how I've prayed and prayed just once again to see her sweet face, and tell her I've forgiven her, though she's broken my heart—she has, Will." She could not go on for a minute or two for the choking sobs. "Thou dost not know that, or thou wouldst not say she could be dead,—for 180 God is very merciful, Will; He is,—He is much more pitiful than man,—I could never ha' spoken to thy father as I did to Him,—and yet thy father forgave her at last. The last words he said were that he forgave her. Thou 'lt not be harder than thy father, Will? Do not try and hinder me going to seek her, for it's no use."

Will sat very still for a long time before he spoke. At last he said, "I'll not hinder you. I think she's dead, but that's no matter."

"She is not dead," said her mother, with low earnestness. Will took no notice of the interruption.

---

4. Murmuring.

5. Lizzie is not physically dead but as a "fallen woman" is dead to the family.

"We will all go to Manchester for a twelve-month, and let the farm to Tom Higginbotham. I'll get blacksmith's work; and Tom can have good schooling for a while, which he's always craving for. At the end of the year you'll come back, mother, and give over fretting for Lizzie, and think with me that she is dead,— and, to my mind, that would be more comfort than to think of her living"; he dropped his voice as he spoke these last words. She shook her head, but made no answer. He asked again,—

"Will you, mother, agree to this?"

"I'll agree to it a-this-ns," said she. "If I hear and see nought of her for a twelvemonth, me being in Manchester looking out, I'll just ha' broken my heart fairly before the year's ended, and then I shall know neither love nor sorrow for her any more, when I'm at rest in the grave—I'll agree to that, Will."

"Well, I suppose it must be so. I shall not tell Tom, mother, why we're flitting to Manchester. Best spare him."

"As thou wilt," said she, sadly, "so that we go, that's all."

Before the wild daffodils were in flower in the sheltered copses round Upclose Farm, the Leighs were settled in their Manchester home; if they could ever grow to consider that place as a home, where there was no garden, or out-building, no fresh breezy outlet, no far-stretching view, over moor and hollow,— no dumb animals to be tended, and, what more than all they missed, no old haunting memories, even though those remembrances told of sorrow, and the dead and gone.

Mrs Leigh heeded the loss of all these things less than her sons. She had more spirit in her countenance than she had had for months, because now she had hope; of a sad enough kind, to be sure, but still it was hope. She performed all her household duties, strange and complicated as they were, and bewildered as she was with all the town-necessities of her new manner of life; but when her house was "sided," and the boys come home from their work, in the evening, she would put on her things and steal out, unnoticed, as she thought, but not without many a heavy sigh from Will, after she had closed the house-door and departed. It was often past midnight before she came back, pale and weary, with almost a guilty look upon her face; but that face so full of disappointment and hope de- ferred, that Will had never the heart to say what he thought of the folly and hope-lessness of the search. Night after night it was renewed, till days grew to weeks and weeks to months. All this time Will did his duty towards her as well as he could, without having sympathy with her. He staid at home in the evenings for Tom's sake, and often wished he had Tom's pleasure in reading, for the time hung heavy on his hands, as he sat up for his mother.

I need not tell you how the mother spent the weary hours. And yet I will tell you something. She used to wander out, at first as if without a purpose, till she rallied her thoughts, and brought all her energies to bear on the one point; then she went with earnest patience along the least known ways to some new part of the town, looking wistfully with dumb entreaty into people's faces; sometimes catch-ing a glimpse of a figure which had a kind of momentary likeness to her child's, and following that figure with never wearying perseverance, till some light from shop or lamp showed the cold strange face which was not her daughter's. Once or twice a kind-hearted passer-by, struck by her look of yearning woe, turned back and offered help, or asked her what she wanted. When so spoken to, she answered only, "You don't know a poor girl they call Lizzie Leigh, do you?" and when they denied all knowledge, she shook her head, and went on again. I think they believed her to be crazy. But she never spoke first to any one. She sometimes took a few minutes' rest on the door-steps, and sometimes (very seldom) covered   240 her face and cried; but she could not afford to lose time and chances in this way; while her eyes were blinded with tears, the lost one might pass by unseen.

One evening, in the rich time of shortening autumn-days, Will saw an old man, who, without being absolutely drunk, could not guide himself rightly along the foot-path, and was mocked for his unsteadiness of gait by the idle boys of the neighbourhood. For his father's sake Will regarded old age with tenderness, even when most degraded and removed from the stern virtues which dignified that father; so he took the old man home, and seemed to believe his often-repeated assertions that he drank nothing but water. The stranger tried to stiffen himself up into steadiness as he drew nearer home, as if there were some one there, for whose   250 respect he cared even in his half-intoxicated state, or whose feelings he feared to grieve. His home was exquisitely clean and neat even in outside appearance; threshold, windows, and window-sill, were outward signs of some spirit of purity within. Will was rewarded for his attention by a bright glance of thanks, succeeded by a blush of shame, from a young woman of twenty or thereabouts. She did not speak, or second her father's hospitable invitations to him to be seated. She seemed unwilling that a stranger should witness her father's attempts at stately sobriety, and Will could not bear to stay and see her distress. But when the old man, with many a flabby shake of the hand, kept asking him to come again some other evening and see them, Will sought her down-cast eyes, and, though he   260 could not read their veiled meaning, he answered timidly, "If it's agreeable to everybody, I'll come—and thank ye." But there was no answer from the girl to whom this speech was in reality addressed; and Will left the house liking her all the better for never speaking.

He thought about her a great deal for the next day or two; he scolded himself for being so foolish as to think of her, and then fell to with fresh vigour, and thought of her more than ever. He tried to depreciate her; he told himself she was not pretty, and then made indignant answer that he liked her looks much better than any beauty of them all. He wished he was not so country looking, so red-faced, so broad-shouldered; while she was like a lady, with her smooth colourless   270 complexion, her bright dark hair and her spotless dress. Pretty, or not pretty, she drew his footsteps towards her; he could not resist the impulse that made him wish to see her once more, and find out some fault which should unloose his heart from her unconscious keeping. But there she was, pure and maidenly as before. He sat and looked, answering her father at cross-purposes, while she drew more and more into the shadow of the chimney-corner out of sight. Then the spirit that possessed him (it was not he himself, sure, that did so impudent a thing!) made him get up and carry the candle to a different place, under the pretence of giving her more light at her sewing, but, in reality, to be able to see her better; she could not stand this much longer, but jumped up, and said she must   280 put her little niece to bed; and surely, there never was, before or since, so troublesome a child of two years old; for, though Will staid an hour and a half longer, she never came down again. He won the father's heart, though, by his capacity as a listener, for some people are not at all particular, and, so that they themselves may talk on undisturbed, are not so unreasonable as to expect attention to what they say.

Will did gather this much, however, from the old man's talk. He had once been quite in a genteel line of business, but had failed for more money than any greengrocer he had heard of; at least, any who did not mix up fish and game with greengrocery proper. This grand failure seemed to have been the event of his life, 290 and one on which he dwelt with a strange kind of pride. It appeared as if at present he rested from his past exertions (in the bankrupt line), and depended on his daughter, who kept a small school for very young children. But all these particulars Will only remembered and understood, when he had left the house; at the time he heard them, he was thinking of Susan. After he had made good his footing at Mr Palmer's, he was not long, you may be sure, without finding some reason for returning again and again. He listened to her father, he talked to the little niece, but he looked at Susan, both while he listened and while he talked. Her father kept on insisting upon his former gentility, the details of which would have appeared very questionable to Will's mind, if the sweet, delicate, modest Susan had 300 not thrown an inexplicable air of refinement over all she came near. She never spoke much; she was generally diligently at work; but when she moved it was so noiselessly, and when she did speak, it was in so low and soft a voice, that silence, speech, motion and stillness, alike seemed to remove her high above Will's reach into some saintly and inaccessible air of glory—high above his reach, even as she knew him! And, if she were made acquainted with the dark secret behind, of his sister's shame, which was kept ever present to his mind by his mother's nightly search among the outcast and forsaken, would not Susan shrink away from him with loathing, as if he were tainted by the involuntary relationship? This was his dread; and thereupon followed a resolution that he would withdraw from her 310 sweet company before it was too late. So he resisted internal temptation, and staid at home, and suffered and sighed. He became angry with his mother for her untiring patience in seeking for one who, he could not help hoping, was dead rather than alive. He spoke sharply to her, and received only such sad deprecatory answers as made him reproach himself, and still more lose sight of peace of mind. This struggle could not last long without affecting his health; and Tom, his sole companion through the long evenings, noticed his increasing languor, his restless irritability, with perplexed anxiety, and at last resolved to call his mother's attention to his brother's haggard, care-worn looks. She listened with a startled recollection of Will's claims upon her love. She noticed his decreasing appetite, and 320 half-checked sighs.

"Will, lad! what's come o'er thee?" said she to him, as he sat listlessly gazing into the fire.

"There's nought the matter with me," said he, as if annoyed at her remark.

"Nay, lad, but there is." He did not speak again to contradict her; indeed she did not know if he had heard her, so unmoved did he look.

"Would'st like to go back to Upclose Farm?" asked she, sorrowfully.

"It's just blackberrying time," said Tom.

Will shook his head. She looked at him awhile, as if trying to read that expression of despondency and trace it back to its source.   330

"Will and Tom could go," said she; "I must stay here till I've found her, thou know'st," continued she, dropping her voice.

He turned quickly round, and with the authority he at all times exercised over Tom, bade him begone to bed.

When Tom had left the room he prepared to speak.

CHAPTER II

"MOTHER," then said Will, "why will you keep on thinking she's alive? If she were but dead, we need never name her name again. We've never heard nought on her since father wrote her that letter; we never knew whether she got it or not. She'd left her place before then. Many a one dies is—"

"Oh my lad! dunnot speak so to me, or my heart will break outright," said   340
his mother, with a sort of cry. Then she calmed herself, for she yearned to persuade him to her own belief. "Thou never asked, and thou 'rt too like thy father for me to tell without asking—but it were all to be near Lizzie's old place that I settled down on this side o' Manchester; and the very day at after we came, I went to her old missus, and asked to speak a word wi' her. I had a strong mind to cast it up to her, that she should ha' sent my poor lass away without telling on it to us first; but she were in black, and looked so sad I could na' find in my heart to threep it up.[6] But I did ask her a bit about our Lizzie. The master would have her turned away at a day's warning, (he's gone to t'other place; I hope he'll meet wi' more mercy there than he showed our Lizzie,—I do,—) and when the missus   350
asked her should she write to us, she says Lizzie shook her head; and when she speered at[7] her again, the poor lass went down on her knees, and begged her not, for she said it would break my heart, (as it has done, Will—God knows it has)," said the poor mother, choking with her struggle to keep down her hard overmastering grief, "and her father would curse her—Oh, God, teach me to be patient." She could not speak for a few minutes,—"and the lass threatened, and said she'd go drown herself in the canal, if the missus wrote home,—and so—

"Well! I'd got a trace of my child,—the missus thought she'd gone to th' workhouse to be nursed; and there I went,—and there, sure enough, she had been,—and they'd turned her out as soon as she were strong, and told her she   360
were young enough to work,—but whatten kind o'work would be open to her, lad, and her baby to keep?"

Will listened to his mother's tale with deep sympathy, not unmixed with the old bitter shame. But the opening of her heart had unlocked his, and after a while he spoke.

"Mother! I think I'd e'en better go home. Tom can stay wi' thee. I know I should stay too, but I cannot stay in peace so near—her—without craving to see her—Susan Palmer I mean."

6. To rebuke her.
7. Questioned.

"Has the old Mr Palmer thou telled me on a daughter?" asked Mrs Leigh.

"Aye, he has. And I love her above a bit. And it's because I love her I want to 370 leave Manchester. That's all."

Mrs Leigh tried to understand this speech for some time, but found it difficult of interpretation.

"Why should'st thou not tell her thou lov'st her? Thou 'rt a likely lad, and sure o' work. Thou 'lt have Upclose at my death; and as for that I could let thee have it now, and keep mysel by doing a bit of charring. It seems to me a very backwards sort o' way of winning her to think of leaving Manchester."

"Oh mother, she's so gentle and so good,—she's downright holy. She's never known a touch of sin; and can I ask her to marry me, knowing what we do about Lizzie, and fearing worse! I doubt if one like her could ever care for me; but if she 380 knew about my sister, it would put a gulf between us, and she'd shudder up at the thought of crossing it. You don't know how good she is, mother!"

"Will, Will! if she's so good as thou say'st, she'll have pity on such as my Lizzie. If she has no pity for such, she's a cruel Pharisee[8], and thou 'rt best without her."

But he only shook his head, and sighed; and for the time the conversation dropped.

But a new idea sprang up in Mrs Leigh's head. She thought that she would go and see Susan Palmer, and speak up for Will, and tell her the truth about Lizzie; and according to her pity for the poor sinner, would she be worthy or un- 390 worthy of him. She resolved to go the very next afternoon, but without telling any one of her plan. Accordingly she looked out the Sunday clothes she had never before had the heart to unpack since she came to Manchester, but which she now desired to appear in, in order to do credit to Will. She put on her old-fashioned black mode bonnet, trimmed with real lace; her scarlet cloth cloak, which she had had ever since she was married; and always spotlessly clean, she set forth on her unauthorized embassy. She knew the Palmers lived in Crown Street, though where she had heard it she could not tell; and modestly asking her way, she arrived in the street about a quarter to four o'clock. She stopped to inquire the exact number, and the woman whom she addressed told her that Susan Palmer's school 400 would not be loosed till four, and asked her to step in and wait until then at her house.

"For," said she, smiling, "them that wants Susan Palmer wants a kind friend of ours; so we, in a manner, call cousins. Sit down, missus, sit down. I'll wipe the chair, so that it shanna dirty your cloak. My mother used to wear them bright cloaks, and they're right gradely[9] things again a green field."

"Han ye known Susan Palmer long?" asked Mrs Leigh, pleased with the admiration of her cloak.

"Ever since they comed to live in our street. Our Sally goes to her school."

"Whatten sort of a lass is she, for I ha' never seen her?" 410

"Well,—as for looks, I cannot say. It's so long since I first knowed her, that I've clean forgotten what I thought of her then. My master says he never saw such

8. Hypocrite.
9. Excellent; handsome.

a smile for gladdening the heart. But may be it's not looks you're asking about. The best thing I can say of her looks is, that she's just one a stranger would stop in the street to ask help from if he needed it. All the little childer creeps as close as they can to her; she'll have as many as three or four hanging to her apron all at once."

"Is she cocket[10] at all?"

"Cocket, bless you! you never saw a creature less set up in all your life. Her father's cocket enough. No! she's not cocket any way. You've not heard much of Susan Palmer, I reckon, if you think she's cocket. She's just one to come quietly in, and do the very thing most wanted; little things, maybe, that any one could do, but that few would think on, for another. She'll bring her thimble wi' her, and mend up after the childer o' nights,—and she writes all Betty Harker's letters to her grandchild out at service,—and she's in nobody's way, and that's a great matter, I take it. Here's the childer running past! School is loosed. You'll find her now, missus, ready to hear and to help. But we none on us frab[11] her by going near her in school-time."

Poor Mrs Leigh's heart began to beat, and she could almost have turned round and gone home again. Her country breeding had made her shy of strangers, and this Susan Palmer appeared to her like a real born lady by all accounts. So she knocked with a timid feeling at the indicated door, and when it was opened, dropped a simple curtsey without speaking. Susan had her little niece in her arms, curled up with fond endearment against her breast, but she put her gently down to the ground, and instantly placed a chair in the best corner of the room for Mrs Leigh, when she told her who she was. "It's not Will as has asked me to come," said the mother, apologetically, "I'd a wish just to speak to you myself!"

Susan coloured up to her temples, and stooped to pick up the little toddling girl. In a minute or two Mrs Leigh began again.

"Will thinks you would na respect us if you knew all; but I think you could na help feeling for us in the sorrow God has put upon us; so I just put on my bon- net, and came off unknownst to the lads. Every one says you're very good, and that the Lord has keeped you from falling from his ways; but maybe you've never yet been tried and tempted as some is. I'm perhaps speaking too plain, but my heart's welly broken, and I can't be choice in my words as them who are happy can. Well now! I'll tell you the truth. Will dreads you to hear it, but I'll just tell it you. You mun know,"—but here the poor woman's words failed her, and she could do nothing but sit rocking herself backwards and forwards, with sad eyes, straight-gazing into Susan's face, as if they tried to tell the tale of agony which the quivering lips refused to utter. Those wretched stony eyes forced the tears down Susan's cheeks, and, as if this sympathy gave the mother strength, she went on in a low voice, "I had a daughter once, my heart's darling. Her father thought I made too much on her, and that she'd grow marred staying at home; so he said she mun go among strangers, and learn to rough it. She were young, and liked the thought of seeing a bit of the world; and her father heard on a place in Manchester. Well! I'll not weary you. That poor girl were led astray; and first thing we heard on it, was when a letter of her father's was sent back by her missus, saying she'd left her

10. Proud; stuck-up.
11. Bother.

place, or, to speak right, the master had turned her into the street soon as he had heard of her condition—and she not seventeen!"

She now cried aloud; and Susan wept too. The little child looked up into their faces, and, catching their sorrow, began to whimper and wail. Susan took it softly up, and hiding her face in its little neck, tried to restrain her tears, and think of comfort for the mother. At last she said:

"Where is she now?"

"Lass! I dunnot know," said Mrs Leigh, checking her sobs to communicate this addition to her distress. "Mrs Lomax told me she went"—

"Mrs Lomax—what Mrs Lomax?"

"Her as lives in Brabazon-street. She told me my poor wench went to the work-house fra there. I'll not speak again the dead; but if her father would but ha' letten me,—but he were one who had no notion—no, I'll not say that; best say nought. He forgave her on his death-bed. I dare say I did na go th' right way to work."

"Will you hold the child for me one instant?" said Susan.

"Ay, if it will come to me. Childer used to be fond on me till I got the sad look on my face that scares them, I think."

But the little girl clung to Susan; so she carried it upstairs with her. Mrs Leigh sat by herself—how long she did not know.

Susan came down with a bundle of far-worn baby-clothes.

"You must listen to me a bit, and not think too much about what I'm going to tell you. Nanny is not my niece, nor any kin to me that I know of. I used to go out working by the day. One night, as I came home, I thought some woman was following me; I turned to look. The woman, before I could see her face (for she turned it to one side), offered me something. I held out my arms by instinct: she dropped a bundle into them with a bursting sob that went straight to my heart. It was a baby. I looked round again; but the woman was gone. She had run away as quick as lightning. There was a little packet of clothes—very few—and as if they were made out of its mother's gowns, for they were large patterns to buy for a baby. I was always fond of babies; and I had not my wits about me, father says; for it was very cold, and when I'd seen as well as I could (for it was past ten) that there was no one in the street, I brought it in and warmed it. Father was very angry when he came, and said he'd take it to the workhouse the next morning, and flyted[12] me sadly about it. But when morning came I could not bear to part with it; it had slept in my arms all night; and I've heard what workhouse bringing up is. So I told father I'd give up going out working, and stay at home and keep school, if I might only keep the baby; and after awhile, he said if I earned enough for him to have his comforts, he'd let me; but he's never taken to her. Now, don't tremble so,—I've but a little more to tell,—and maybe I'm wrong in telling it; but I used to work next door to Mrs Lomax's, in Brabazon-street, and the servants were all thick together; and I heard about Bessy (they called her) being sent away. I don't know that ever I saw her; but the time would be about fitting to this child's age, and I've sometimes fancied it was her's. And now, will you look at the little clothes that came with her—bless her!"

12. Frightened.

But Mrs Leigh had fainted. The strange joy and shame, and gushing love for the little child had overpowered her; it was some time before Susan could bring her round. There she was all trembling, sick impatience to look at the little frocks. Among them was a slip of paper which Susan had forgotten to name, that had been pinned to the bundle. On it was scrawled in a round stiff hand,

"Call her Anne. She does not cry much, and takes a deal of notice. God bless you and forgive me."

The writing was no clue at all; the name "Anne," common though it was, seemed something to build upon. But Mrs Leigh recognized one of the frocks instantly, as being made out of part of a gown that she and her daughter had bought together in Rochdale.

She stood up, and stretched out her hands in the attitude of blessing over Susan's bent head.

"God bless you, and show you His mercy in your need, as you have shown it to this little child."

She took the little creature in her arms, and smoothed away her sad looks to a smile, and kissed it fondly, saying over and over again, "Nanny, Nanny, my little Nanny." At last the child was soothed, and looked in her face and smiled back again.

"It has her eyes," said she to Susan.

"I never saw her to the best of my knowledge. I think it must be her's by the frock. But where can she be?"

"God knows," said Mrs Leigh; "I dare not think she's dead. I'm sure she isn't."

"No! she's not dead. Every now and then a little packet is thrust in under our door, with may be two half-crowns in it; once it was half-a-sovereign. Altogether I've got seven-and-thirty shillings wrapped up for Nanny. I never touch it, but I've often thought the poor mother feels near to God when she brings this money. Father wanted to set the policeman to watch, but I said No, for I was afraid if she was watched she might not come, and it seemed such a holy thing to be checking her in, I could not find in my heart to do it."

"Oh, if we could but find her! I'd take her in my arms, and we'd just lie down and die together."

"Nay, don't speak so!" said Susan gently, "for all that's come and gone, she may turn right at last. Mary Magdalen[13] did, you know."

"Eh! but I were nearer right about thee than Will. He thought you would never look on him again if you knew about Lizzie. But thou 'rt not a Pharisee."

"I'm sorry he thought I could be so hard," said Susan in a low voice, and colouring up. Then Mrs Leigh was alarmed, and in her motherly anxiety, she began to fear lest she had injured Will in Susan's estimation.

"You see Will thinks so much of you—gold would not be good enough for you to walk on, in his eye. He said you'd never look at him as he was, let alone his being brother to my poor wench. He loves you so, it makes him think meanly on everything belonging to himself, as not fit to come near ye,—but he's a good lad, and a good son—thou 'lt be a happy woman if thou 'lt have him,—so don't let my words go against him; don't!"

13. One of Jesus' followers, often thought to be a reformed prostitute.

But Susan hung her head and made no answer. She had not known until now, that Will thought so earnestly and seriously about her; and even now she felt afraid that Mrs Leigh's words promised her too much happiness, and that they could not be true. At any rate the instinct of modesty made her shrink from saying 550 anything which might seem like a confession of her own feelings to a third person. Accordingly she turned the conversation on the child.

"I'm sure he could not help loving Nanny," said she. "There never was such a good little darling; don't you think she'd win his heart if he knew she was his niece, and perhaps bring him to think kindly on his sister?"

"I dunnot know," said Mrs Leigh, shaking her head. "He has a turn in his eye like his father, that makes me————. He's right down good though. But you see I've never been a good one at managing folk; one severe look turns me sick, and then I say just the wrong thing, I'm so fluttered. Now I should like nothing better than to take Nancy home with me, but Tom knows nothing but that his sister is 560 dead, and I've not the knack of speaking rightly to Will. I dare not do it, and that's the truth. But you mun not think badly of Will. He's so good hissel,[14] that he can't understand how any one can do wrong; and, above all, I'm sure he loves you dearly."

"I don't think I could part with Nancy," said Susan, anxious to stop this revelation of Will's attachment to herself. "He'll come round to her soon; he can't fail; and I'll keep a sharp look-out after the poor mother, and try and catch her the next time she comes with her little parcels of money."

"Aye, lass! we mun get hold of her; my Lizzie. I love thee dearly for thy kindness to her child; but, if thou can'st catch her for me, I'll pray for thee when I'm 570 too near my death to speak words; and while I live, I'll serve thee next to her,— she mun come first, thou know'st. God bless thee, lass. My heart is lighter by a deal than it was when I comed in. Them lads will be looking for me home, and I mun go, and leave this little sweet one," kissing it. "If I can take courage, I'll tell Will all that has come and gone between us two. He may come and see thee, mayn't he?"

"Father will be very glad to see him, I'm sure," replied Susan. The way in which this was spoken satisfied Mrs Leigh's anxious heart that she had done Will no harm by what she had said; and with many a kiss to the little one, and one more fervent tearful blessing on Susan, she went homewards.   580

CHAPTER III

THAT NIGHT Mrs Leigh stopped[15] at home; that only night for many months. Even Tom, the scholar, looked up from his books in amazement; but then he remembered that Will had not been well, and that his mother's attention having been called to the circumstance, it was only natural she should stay to watch him. And no watching could be more tender, or more complete. Her loving eyes seemed never averted from his face; his grave, sad, care-worn face. When Tom

14. Himself.
15. Remained; stayed.

went to bed the mother left her seat, and going up to Will where he sat looking at the fire, but not seeing it, she kissed his forehead, and said,

"Will! lad, I've been to see Susan Palmer!"

She felt the start under her hand which was placed on his shoulder, but he was silent for a minute or two. Then he said,

"What took you there, mother?"

"Why, my lad, it was likely I should wish to see one you cared for; I did not put myself forward. I put on my Sunday clothes, and tried to behave as yo'd ha liked me. At least I remember trying at first; but after, I forgot all."

She rather wished that he would question her as to what made her forget all. But he only said,

"How was she looking, mother?"

"Will, thou seest I never set eyes on her before; but she's a good gentle looking creature; and I love her dearly, as I've reason to."

Will looked up with momentary surprise; for his mother was too shy to be usually taken with strangers. But after all it was natural in this case, for who could look at Susan without loving her? So still he did not ask any questions, and his poor mother had to take courage, and try again to introduce the subject near to her heart. But how?

"Will!" said she (jerking it out, in sudden despair of her own powers to lead to what she wanted to say), "I told her all."

"Mother! you've ruined me," said he standing up, and standing opposite to her with a stern white look of affright on his face.

"No! my own dear lad; dunnot look so scared, I have not ruined you!" she exclaimed, placing her two hands on his shoulders and looking fondly into his face. "She's not one to harden her heart against a mother's sorrow. My own lad, she's too good for that. She's not one to judge and scorn the sinner. She's too deep read in her New Testament for that. Take courage, Will; and thou mayst, for I watched her well, though it is not for one woman to let out another's secret. Sit thee down, lad, for thou look'st very white."

He sat down. His mother drew a stool towards him, and sat at his feet.

"Did you tell her about Lizzie, then?" asked he, hoarse and low.

"I did, I told her all; and she fell a crying over my deep sorrow, and the poor wench's sin. And then a light comed into her face, trembling and quivering with some new glad thought; and what dost thou think it was, Will, lad? Nay, I'll not misdoubt but that thy heart will give thanks as mine did, afore God and His angels, for her great goodness. That little Nanny is not her niece, she's our Lizzie's own child, my little grandchild." She could no longer restrain her tears, and they fell hot and fast, but still she looked into his face.

"Did she know it was Lizzie's child? I do not comprehend," said he, flushing red.

"She knows now: she did not at first, but took the little helpless creature in, out of her own pitiful loving heart, guessing only that it was the child of shame and she's worked for it, and kept it, and tended it ever sin' it were a mere baby, and loves it fondly. Will! won't you love it?" asked she beseechingly.

He was silent for an instant; then he said, "Mother, I'll try. Give me time, for all these things startle me. To think of Susan having to do with such a child!"

"Aye, Will! and to think (as may be yet) of Susan having to do with the child's mother! For she is tender and pitiful, and speaks hopefully of my lost one, and will try and find her for me, when she comes, as she does sometimes, to thrust money under the door, for her baby. Think of that, Will. Here's Susan, good and pure as the angels in heaven, yet, like them, full of hope and mercy, and one who, like them, will rejoice over her as repents. Will, my lad, I'm not afeared of you now, and I must speak, and you must listen. I am your mother, and I dare to command you, because I know I am in the right and that God is on my side. If He should lead the poor wandering lassie to Susan's door, and she comes back crying and sorrowful, led by that good angel to us once more, thou shalt never say a cast-ing-up word to her about her sin, but be tender and helpful towards one 'who was lost and is found,' so may God's blessing rest on thee, and so mayst though lead Susan home as they wife."

She stood, no longer as the meek, imploring, gentle mother, but firm and dignified, as if the interpreter of God's will. Her manner was so unusual and solemn, that it overcame all Will's pride and stubbornness. He rose softly while she was speaking, and bent his head as if in reverence at her words, and the solemn injunction which they conveyed. When she had spoken, he said in so sub-dued a voice that she was almost surprised at the sound, "Mother, I will."

"I may be dead and gone,—but all the same,—thou wilt take home the wan-dering sinner, and heal up her sorrows, and lead her to her Father's house. My lad! I can speak no more; I'm turned very faint."

He placed her in a chair; he ran for water. She opened her eyes and smiled.

"God bless you, Will. Oh! I am so happy. It seems as if she were found; my heart is so filled with gladness."

That night Mr Palmer stayed out late and long. Susan was afraid that he was at his old haunts and habits,—getting tipsy at some public-house; and this thought oppressed her, even though she had so much to make her happy, in the consciousness that Will loved her. She sat up long, and then she went to bed, leav-ing all arranged as well as she could for her father's return. She looked at the little rosy sleeping girl who was her bed-fellow, with redoubled tenderness, and with many a prayerful thought. The little arms entwined her neck as she lay down, for Nanny was a light sleeper, and was conscious that she, who was loved with all the power of that sweet childish heart, was near her, and by her, although she was too sleepy to utter any of her half-formed words.

And by-and-bye she heard her father come home, stumbling uncertain, try-ing first the windows, and next the door-fastenings, with many a loud incoherent murmur. The little Innocent twined around her seemed all the sweeter and more lovely, when she thought sadly of her erring father. And presently he called aloud for a light; she had left matches and all arranged as usual on the dresser, but, fear-ful of some accident from fire, in his unusually intoxicated state, she now got up softly, and putting on a cloak, went down to his assistance.

Alas! the little arms that were unclosed from her soft neck belonged to a light, easily awakened sleeper. Nanny missed her darling Susy, and terrified at being left alone in the vast mysterious darkness, which had no bounds, and seemed infinite, she slipped out of bed, and tottered in her little night-gown to-wards the door. There was a light below, and there was Susy and safety! So she went onwards two steps towards the steep abrupt stairs; and then dazzled with sleepiness, she stood, she wavered, she fell! Down on her head on the stone floor she fell! Susan flew to her, and spoke all soft, entreating, loving words; but her white lids covered up the blue violets of eyes, and there was no murmur came out of the pale lips. The warm tears that rained down did not awaken her; she lay stiff, and weary with her short life, on Susan's knee. Susan went sick with terror. She carried her upstairs, and laid her tenderly in bed; she dressed herself most hastily, with her trembling fingers. Her father was asleep on the settle down stairs; and useless, and worse than useless if awake. But Susan flew out of the door, and down the quiet resounding street, towards the nearest doctor's house. Quickly she 690 went; but as quickly a shadow followed, as if impelled by some sudden terror. Susan rung wildly at the night-bell,—the shadow crouched near. The doctor looked out from an upstairs window.

"A little child has fallen down stairs at No. 9, Crown-street, and is very ill,— dying I'm afraid. Please, for God's sake, sir, come directly. No. 9, Crown-street."

"I'll be there directly," said he, and shut the window.

"For that God you have just spoken about,—for His sake,—tell me are you Susan Palmer? Is it my child that lies a-dying?" said the shadow, springing forwards, and clutching poor Susan's arm.

"It is a little child of two years old,—I do not know whose it is; I love it as 700 my own. Come with me, whoever you are; come with me."

The two sped along the silent street,—as silent as the night were they. They entered the house; Susan snatched up the light, and carried it upstairs. The other followed.

She stood with wild glaring eyes by the bedside, never looking at Susan, but hungrily gazing at the little white still child. She stooped down, and put her hand tight on her own heart, as if to still its beating, and bent her ear to the pale lips. Whatever the result was, she did not speak; but threw off the bed-clothes wherewith Susan had tenderly covered up the little creature, and felt its left side.

Then she threw up her arms with a cry of wild despair.   710

"She is dead! she is dead!"

She looked so fierce, so mad, so haggard, that for an instant Susan was terrified—the next, the holy God had put courage into her heart, and her pure arms were round that guilty wretched creature, and her tears were falling fast and warm upon her breast. But she was thrown off with violence.

"You killed her—you slighted her—you let her fall down those stairs! you killed her!"

Susan cleared off the thick mist before her, and gazing at the mother with her clear, sweet, angel-eyes, said mournfully—

"I would have laid down my own life for her."   720

"Oh, the murder is on my soul!" exclaimed the wild bereaved mother, with the fierce impetuosity of one who has none to love her and to be beloved, regard to whom might teach self-restraint.

"Hush!" said Susan, her finger on her lips. "Here is the doctor. God may suffer her to live."

The poor mother turned sharp round. The doctor mounted the stair. Ah! that mother was right; the little child was really dead and gone.

And when he confirmed her judgment, the mother fell down in a fit. Susan, with her deep grief, had to forget herself, and forget her darling (her charge for years), and question the doctor what she must do with the poor wretch, who lay 730 on the floor in such extreme of misery.

"She is the mother!" said she.

"Why did not she take better care of her child?" asked he, almost angrily.

But Susan only said, "The little child slept with me; and it was I that left her."

"I will go back and make up a composing draught[16]; and while I am away you must get her to bed."

Susan took out some of her own clothes, and softly undressed the stiff, powerless, form. There was no other bed in the house but the one in which her father slept. So she tenderly lifted the body of her darling; and was going to take it down 740 stairs, but the mother opened her eyes, and seeing what she was about, she said,

"I am not worthy to touch her, I am so wicked; I have spoken to you as I never should have spoken; but I think you are very good; may I have my own child to lie in my arms for a little while?"

Her voice was so strange a contrast to what it had been before she had gone into the fit that Susan hardly recognized it; it was now so unspeakably soft, so irresistibly pleading, the features too had lost their fierce expression, and were almost as placid as death. Susan could not speak, but she carried the little child, and laid it in its mother's arms; then as she looked at them, something overpowered her, and she knelt down, crying aloud,
                                                                          750
"Oh, my God, my God, have mercy on her, and forgive, and comfort her."

But the mother kept smiling, and stroking the little face, murmuring soft tender words, as if it were alive; she was going mad, Susan thought; but she prayed on, and on, and ever still she prayed with streaming eyes.

The doctor came with the draught. The mother took it, with docile unconsciousness of its nature as medicine. The doctor sat by her; and soon she fell asleep. Then he rose softly, and beckoning Susan to the door, he spoke to her there.

"You must take the corpse out of her arms. She will not awake. That draught will make her sleep for many hours. I will call before noon again. It is now day- 760 light. Good-bye."

Susan shut him out; and then gently extricating the dead child from its mother's arms, she could not resist making her own quiet moan over her darling. She tried to learn off its little placid face, dumb and pale before her.

Not all the scalding tears of care
  Shall wash away that vision fair;
Not all the thousand thoughts that rise,
  Not all the sights that dim her eyes,
    Shall e'er usurp the place
    Of that little angel-face.
                                                                          770

16. A sedative.

And then she remembered what remained to be done. She saw that all was right in the house; her father was still dead asleep on the settle, in spite of all the noise of the night. She went out through the quiet streets, deserted still although it was broad daylight, and to where the Leighs lived. Mrs Leigh, who kept her country hours, was opening her window shutters. Susan took her by the arm, and, without speaking, went into the house-place. There she knelt down before the astonished Mrs Leigh, and cried as she had never done before; but the miserable night had overpowered her, and she who had gone through so much calmly, now that the pressure seemed removed could not find the power to speak.

"My poor dear! What has made thy heart so sore as to come and cry a-this-   780 ons. Speak and tell me. Nay, cry on, poor wench, if thou canst not speak yet. It will ease the heart, and then thou canst tell me."

"Nanny is dead!" said Susan. "I left her to go to father, and she fell down stairs, and never breathed again. Oh, that's my sorrow! but I've more to tell. Her mother is come—is in our house! Come and see if it's your Lizzie." Mrs Leigh could not speak, but, trembling, put on her things, and went with Susan in dizzy haste back to Crown-street.

CHAPTER IV

As THEY ENTERED the house in Crown-street, they perceived that the door would not open freely on its hinges, and Susan instinctively looked behind to see the cause of the obstruction. She immediately recognized the appearance of a little   790 parcel, wrapped in a scrap of newspaper, and evidently containing money. She stooped and picked it up. "Look!" said she, sorrowfully, "the mother was bringing this for her child last night."

But Mrs Leigh did not answer. So near to the ascertaining if it were her lost child or no, she could not be arrested, but pressed onwards with trembling steps and a beating, fluttering heart. She entered the bed-room, dark and still. She took no heed of the little corpse, over which Susan paused, but she went straight to the bed, and withdrawing the curtain, saw Lizzie,—but not the former Lizzie, bright, gay, buoyant, and undimmed. This Lizzie was old before her time; her beauty was gone; deep lines of care, and alas! of want (or thus the mother imagined) were printed on the cheek, so round, and fair, and smooth, when last she gladdened her mother's eyes. Even in her sleep she bore the look of woe and despair which was the prevalent expression of her face by day; even in her sleep she had forgotten how to smile. But all these marks of the sin and sorrow she had passed through   800 only made her mother love her the more. She stood looking at her with greedy eyes, which seemed as though no gazing could satisfy their longing; and at last she stooped down and kissed the pale, worn hand that lay outside the bed-clothes. No touch disturbed the sleeper; the mother need not have laid the hand so gently down upon the counter-pane. There was no sign of life, save only now and then a deep sob-like sigh. Mrs Leigh sat down beside the bed, and, still holding back the curtain, looked on and on, as if she could never be satisfied.

Susan would fain have stayed by her darling one; but she had many calls upon her time and thoughts, and her will had now, as ever, to be given up to that of others. All seemed to devolve the burden of their cares on her. Her father, ill-humoured from his last night's intemperance, did not scruple to reproach her with being the cause of little Nanny's death; and when, after bearing his upbraiding meekly for some time, she could no longer restrain herself, but began to cry, he wounded her even more by his injudicious attempts at comfort: for he said it was as well the child was dead; it was none of theirs, and why should they be troubled with it? Susan wrung her hands at this, and came and stood before her father, and implored him to forbear. Then she had to take all requisite steps for the coroner's inquest; she had to arrange for the dismissal of her school; she had to summon a little neighbour, and send his willing feet on a message to William Leigh, who, she felt, ought to be informed of his mother's whereabouts, and of the whole state of affairs. She asked her messenger to tell him to come and speak to her,—that his mother was at her house. She was thankful that her father sauntered out to have a gossip at the nearest coach-stand, and to relate as many of the night's adventures as he knew; for as yet he was in ignorance of the watcher and the watched, who silently passed away the hours upstairs.

At dinner-time Will came. He looked red, glad, impatient, excited. Susan stood calm and white before him, her soft, loving eyes gazing straight into his.

"Will," said she, in a low, quiet voice, "your sister is upstairs."

"My sister!" said he, as if affrighted at the idea, and losing his glad look in one of gloom. Susan saw it, and her heart sank a little, but she went on as calm to all appearance as ever.

"She was little Nanny's mother, as perhaps you know. Poor little Nanny was killed last night by a fall down stairs." All the calmness was gone; all the suppressed feeling was displayed in spite of every effort. She sat down, and hid her face from him, and cried bitterly. He forgot everything but the wish, the longing to comfort her. He put his arm round her waist, and bent over her. But all he could say, was, "Oh, Susan, how can I comfort you! Don't take on so,—pray don't!" He never changed the words, but the tone varied every time he spoke. At last she seemed to regain her power over herself; and she wiped her eyes, and once more looked upon him with her own quiet, earnest, unfearing gaze.

"Your sister was near the house. She came in on hearing my words to the doctor. She is asleep now, and your mother is watching her. I wanted to tell you all myself. Would you like to see your mother?"

"No!" said he. "I would rather see none but thee. Mother told me thou knew'st all." His eyes were downcast in their shame.

But the holy and pure, did not lower or veil her eyes.

She said, "Yes, I know all—all but her sufferings. Think what they must have been!"

He made answer low and stern, "She deserved them all; every jot."

"In the eye of God, perhaps she does. He is the judge: we are not."

"Oh!" she said with a sudden burst, "Will Leigh! I have thought so well of you; don't go and make me think you cruel and hard. Goodness is not goodness unless there is mercy and tenderness with it. There is your mother who has been nearly heart-broken, now full of rejoicing over her child—think of your mother."

"I do think of her," said he. "I remember the promise I gave her last night. Thou shouldst give me time. I would do right in time. I never think it o'er in quiet. But I will do what is right and fitting, never fear. Thou hast spoken out very plain to me; and misdoubted me, Susan; I love thee so, that thy words cut me. If I did hang back a bit from making sudden promises, it was because not even for love of thee, would I say what I was not feeling; and at first I could not feel all at 860 once as thou wouldst have me. But I'm not cruel and hard; for if I had been, I should na' have grieved as I have done."

He made as if he were going away; and indeed he did feel he would rather think it over in quiet. But Susan, grieved at her incautious words, which had all the appearance of harshness, went a step or two nearer—paused—and then, all over blushes, said in a low soft whisper—

"Oh Will! I beg your pardon. I am very sorry—won't you forgive me?"

She who had always drawn back, and been so reserved, said this in the very softest manner; with eyes now uplifted beseechingly, now dropped to the ground. Her sweet confusion told more than words could do; and Will turned back, all 870 joyous in his certainty of being beloved, and took her in his arms and kissed her.

"My own Susan!" he said.

Meanwhile the mother watched her child in the room above.

It was late in the afternoon before she awoke; for the sleeping draught had been very powerful. The instant she awoke, her eyes were fixed on her mother's face with a gaze as unflinching as if she were fascinated. Mrs Leigh did not turn away; nor move. For it seemed as if motion would unlock the stony command over herself which, while so perfectly still, she was enabled to preserve. But by-and-bye Lizzie cried out in a piercing voice of agony—

"Mother, don't look at me! I have been so wicked!" and instantly she hid her 880 face, and grovelled among the bedclothes, and lay like one dead—so motionless was she.

Mrs Leigh knelt down by the bed, and spoke in the most soothing tones.

"Lizzie, dear, don't speak so. I'm thy mother, darling; don't be afeard of me. I never left off loving thee, Lizzie. I was always a-thinking of thee. Thy father forgave thee afore he died." (There was a little start here, but no sound was heard.) "Lizzie, lass, I'll do aught for thee; I'll live for thee; only don't be afeard of me. Whate'er thou art or hast been, we'll ne'er speak on 't. We'll leave th' oud times behind us, and go back to the Upclose Farm. I but left it to find thee, my lass; and God has led me to thee. Blessed be His name. And God is good too, Lizzie. Thou 890 hast not forgot thy Bible, I'll be bound, for thou wert always a scholar. I'm no reader, but I learnt off them texts to comfort me a bit, and I've said them many a time a day to myself. Lizzie, lass, don't hide thy head so, it's thy mother as is speaking to thee. Thy little child clung to me only yesterday; and if it's gone to be an angel, it will speak to God for thee. Nay, don't sob a that 'as; thou shalt have it again in Heaven; I know thou 'lt strive to get there, for thy little Nanny's sake— and listen! I'll tell thee God's promises to them that are penitent—only doan't be afeard."

Mrs Leigh folded her hands, and strove to speak very clearly, while she repeated every tender and merciful text she could remember. She could tell from the 900 breathing that her daughter was listening; but she was so dizzy and sick herself when she had ended, that she could not go on speaking. It was all she could do to keep from crying aloud.

At last she heard her daughter's voice.

"Where have they taken her to?" she asked.

"She is downstairs. So quiet, and peaceful, and happy she looks."

"Could she speak? Oh, if God—if I might but have heard her little voice! Mother, I used to dream of it. May I see her once again—Oh mother, if I strive very hard, and God is very merciful, and I go to heaven, I shall not know her—I shall not know my own again—she will shun me as a stranger and cling to Susan 910 Palmer and to you. Oh woe! Oh woe!" She shook with exceeding sorrow.

In her earnestness of speech she had uncovered her face, and tried to read Mrs Leigh's thoughts through her looks. And when she saw those aged eyes brimming full of tears, and marked the quivering lips, she threw her arms round the faithful mother's neck, and wept there as she had done in many a childish sorrow; but with a deeper, a more wretched grief.

Her mother hushed her on her breast; and lulled her as if she were a baby; and she grew still and quiet.

They sat thus for a long, long time. At last Susan Palmer came up with some tea and bread and butter for Mrs Leigh. She watched the mother feed her sick, un- 920 willing child, with every fond inducement to eat which she could devise; they neither of them took notice of Susan's presence. That night they lay in each other's arms; but Susan slept on the ground beside them.

They took the little corpse (the little unconscious sacrifice, whose early calling-home had reclaimed her poor wandering mother), to the hills, which in her life-time she had never seen. They dared not lay her by the stern grand-father in Milne-Row churchyard, but they bore her to a lone moorland graveyard, where long ago the quakers used to bury their dead. They laid her there on the sunny slope, where the earliest spring-flowers blow.

Will and Susan live at the Upclose Farm. Mrs. Leigh and Lizzie dwell in a 930 cottage so secluded that, until you drop into the very hollow where it is placed, you do not see it. Tom is a schoolmaster in Rochdale, and he and Will help to support their mother. I only know that, if the cottage be hidden in a green hollow of the hills, every sound of sorrow in the whole upland is heard there—every call of suffering or of sickness for help is listened to, by a sad, gentle-looking woman, who rarely smiles (and when she does, her smile is more sad than other people's tears), but who comes out of her seclusion whenever there's a shadow in any household. Many hearts bless Lizzie Leigh, but she—she prays always and ever for forgiveness—such forgiveness as may enable her to see her child once more. Mrs Leigh is quiet and happy. Lizzie is to her eyes something precious,—as the lost 940 piece of silver—found once more. Susan is the bright one who brings sunshine to all. Children grow around her and call her blessed. One is called Nanny. Her, Lizzy often takes to the sunny graveyard in the uplands, and while the little creature gathers the daisies, and makes chains, Lizzie sits by a little grave, and weeps bitterly.

[1850]

Questions for Discussion and Writing

1. What features make this story Romantic or Realistic?
2. What are society's attitudes toward sexuality, unwed mothers, illegitimate children, and drunkenness as revealed in this story?
3. Does the author share society's views? How do you know? Underline or highlight passages where the author seems to express views in support of or contrary to those of society as a whole.
4. What is the purpose of Anne's death? Why might the author have included this incident in the story?
5. Analyze the major characters, particularly Mrs. Leigh, Will, and Susan Palmer. Do they seem realistic? Why or why not? Are they intended as realistic characters?
6. Why might this story have offended its Victorian readers?
7. What aspects of this story might offend contemporary readers?
8. What is the theme of the story? How effectively is it conveyed?

Sidebar: EXPLORING SUBGENRES

The Love Story

The love story calls to mind the epitome of conventional plots: "boy meets girl, boy wins girl, boy loses girl, boy wins girl." To this follows the familiar ending, "and they lived happily ever after." This formula, with only slight variations, is the basis of countless stories in literature, film, and television. It is so familiar that we may not recognize it as literary formula. It may seem, in fact, like "real life"—or at least the way real life is supposed to be. Like many cultural artifacts, however, it has a history.

The feeling of love and the capacity to love have, of course, always existed, but the expression of love is strongly conditioned by cultural influences, including stories. Many of the great love stories of the ancient world—Dido and Aeneas, Pyramus and Thisbe, Hero and Leander—did not lead to happy endings but to tragedy. So, too, did many of the great love stories of the Middle Ages: Tristan and Iseult, Lancelot and Guinevere, Troilus and Criseyede. However, it was during the Middle Ages that the modern cult of romantic love began. The Medieval romances mentioned above were influenced by the code of Courtly Love, which held that love was an ennobling passion to be pursued outside of the social and economic confines of arranged marriages. Much of this code endured through the Renaissance and can be seen both in Shakespeare's tragedies of doomed lovers, such as *Romeo and Juliet* and *Antony and Cleopatra,* and in his romantic comedies such as *A Midsummer Night's Dream* and *Much Ado About Nothing.*

It is probably no accident that love stories with happy resolutions became popular in the late Middle Ages and Renaissance, for it was then that attitudes about love and marriage were changing among the aristocracy and upper middle classes. Previously, marriage had been regarded more as a social and economic institution than as the culmination of romantic love. Indeed, until well into the nineteenth century, the problem of lovers in novels (as well, as in life) was to find a compatible mate within the proper social and economic sphere—and, indeed, the question persists to this day.

From the Renaissance forward, however, love gradually emerged as *the* value, the goal, to be cherished and sought above all others. In eighteenth and nineteenth-century novels, the problem of finding a compatible mate is paramount for heroines, and for males is usually second only to discovering one's life's work. The trend is visible in the works of Jane

Bal à Bougival (1883) by French Impressionist painter Pierre Auguste Renoir (1841–1919). (Courtesy, Museum of Fine Arts, Boston)

Austen (1775–1817) and Charles Dickens (1812–1870), for example. If marriage had for centuries been treated as a social and economic concern, to be arranged by the families, it was now seen as a deeply personal matter to be determined by feelings of love. Part wish fulfillment, part vicarious pleasure, part lesson, the love story formula came to encapsulate the way love "is supposed to be."

Many of the attitudes toward love from the Middle Ages onward appear in the short story and its precursors. Boccaccio's "Fiametta's Story" emerged from the Courtly Love tradition in which love was treated (for literary purposes at least) as the topic of central interest. Federigo may be seen in that tradition—nobly pursuing a married woman and willing to sacrifice anything for her sake. Other basic conventions also appear: the beautiful woman, the devoted and worthy lover, the social obstacles to their union, the woman's uncertainty, the climactic incident that brings them together, and finally the happy ending. Part of the appeal of such stories is their affirmation of the beauty and power of love, the value of marriage and the family (usually more implied than shown), the vicarious thrill as we "identify with" the lovers and their situation, and of course the reassurance that virtues like chastity and devotion are rewarded. While many aspects of the love story have remained constant from Boccaccio's day to the present, the virtues considered particularly worthy have, of course, changed. Among heroines of the past, chastity and fidelity were the primary virtues. Now, with pre-and extra-marital sex being the staples of literature, film, and television, intelligence, strength of character, and independence are more highly valued.

The short story and the magazines that featured it came to prominence in the early nineteenth century, when social ideas about love and marriage were attaining their present form, especially among the rapidly growing middle classes. Not surprisingly, therefore, the love story has been one of the genre's most common and enduring subjects. Think, for example, of "Uncle Lot," "A Landscape Painter," "The Two Soldiers," and "The Gilded Six-Bits," to name just a few.

In many other stories, love forms a secondary theme or background event to the main concerns. In Elizabeth Gaskell's "Lizzie Leigh," for example, the main plot concerns Mrs. Leigh's concern for her fallen daughter—a situation that often served as a warning to young women of the consequences of premarital sex. Parallel to it is the subplot of Will's love for Susan Palmer, which is treated as a chaste and noble passion. O. Henry kept such conventions alive as an antidote to the "immorality" and "cynicism" of Realism.

Once the conventions of the love story were established, authors could use them in new ways. For example, Turgenev's "Yermolai and the Miller's Wife" is not at first glance a love story, yet much of the story's impact depends upon our seeing the tragic lost love of the Miller's Wife and measuring her simple humanity against the brutal indifference of her master and mistress. Knowing the historical context, we can conclude that one of Turgenev's purposes was to assert the humanity of the serfs. Turgenev reverses the conventions of the love story—the characters do not over-come obstacles and live happily ever after—to make a social statement.

Realist, Modernist, and even Post-Modernist authors came to view the conventional love story as hopelessly corny and dangerously escapist. Their impulse to upset these formulas gave rise to a new set of conven-tions—tougher, less sentimental, less optimistic. Henry James's "A Landscape Artist" reads like a conventional love story until its last page. Anton Chekhov's "The Lady With the Pet Dog" ends not in consummation and union but in frustration and separation; James Joyce's "Araby" reverses the reader's expectations of a romantic conclusion. Joyce Carol Oates's "Where Are You Going, Where Have You Been?" begins as a story of teenage rebellion and romance but ends with a sense of doom, vulnerabil-ity, and loss. Alice Munro's "The Progress of Love" and Lorrie Moore's "You're Ugly, Too" play off traditional love story conventions, presenting courtship and marriage as they appear to jaded, Post-modern eyes. Often one cannot fully appreciate the meaning and originality of such stories without perceiving how each deviates from or exploits the love story con-ventions of the past.

The persistent popularity of the love story in all its guises leads to im-portant questions. Does love deserve to be given as much value and prominence as it is given, in literature and life? Why do we persist in valu-ing love as a means of selecting a mate, when nearly half of all marriages based on it end in divorce. Do men and women inevitably want different things from a relationship, causing predictable stresses, strains, or implo-sions, and if so, how can these differences be accommodated? Have fic-tional treatments of love, sex, and marriage affected our perceptions and expectations of them?

Reading many stories and being alert to their conventions, whether the traditional, idealized romantic style or the more recent, cynical variety, allows us to explore these questions in greater depth than any one person can from experience. In addition to their entertainment value, these sto-ries can help us attain a better sense of how to negotiate the joys, sorrows, and intricacies of a powerful human emotion.

✐ IVAN SERGEYEVICH TURGENEV
(1818–1883)

TRANSLATED BY RICHARD FREEBORN

Yermolay and the Miller's Wife

Ivan Turgenev was a key figure in Europe's cosmopolitan literature in the last half of the nineteenth century. He is credited with helping to bring poetry and sensitivity to the short story.

Turgenev was born of a wealthy land-owning family. His mother, by turns overly loving and dictatorial, ran her son's life as she ran her estate—with an inflexible will and a taste for cruelty. It is said that she turned Turgenev against serfdom and shaped his strong, domineering female characters, as well as his weak and unimpressive men. When Turgenev was nine, the family moved to Moscow, where he attended school. He later studied at the Universities of Moscow and St. Petersburg, and then in Berlin, but he did not earn a degree. In Berlin, he was influenced by Russian westernizers—intellectuals who wanted Russia to adopt European manners and culture. In the 1840s, he fell under the spell of opera singer Pauline Viardot, who was already married. He loved her passionately for years without ever receiving the slightest encouragement from her.

Turgenev began writing a series of stories and sketches in 1847 focusing on Russia's rural life and peasantry. Collected in 1852 under the title *A Sportsman's Sketches,* they were immediately popular and highly influential. In the same year, Turgenev's laudatory obituary of Gogol so enraged the authorities that he was placed under house arrest for several months. Nevertheless, *A Sportsman's Sketches* has sometimes been compared with Harriet Beecher Stowe's *Uncle Tom's Cabin* (1852), as it is credited with encouraging the abolition of serfdom in 1861.

Unfavorable criticism of his novel *Fathers and Sons* (1862) led Turgenev to self-imposed exile from his native land, to which he did not return except for brief visits until 1880. In the 1870s, he settled on his French estate near Bougival, where he met Emile Zola (1840–1902), Guy de Maupassant (1850–1893), and Gustave Flaubert (1821–1880). His story "A King Lear of the Steppes" and the novella *The Torrents of Spring* (1870) date from this period.

Turgenev's impact on the short story has been profound. He was a master of the indirect method of characterization, whereby personality is revealed not through analysis or psychological probing but by the subtle manipulation of atmosphere and mood. The influence of this method can be seen in the stories of Maupassant, Joseph Conrad (1857–1924), Virginia Woolf (1882–1941), and H. E. Bates (1905–1974), among others.

IN THE EVENING the hunter Yermolay and I set off for "cover." But perhaps not all my readers know what "cover" means. Pray listen, gentlemen.

In the springtime, a quarter of an hour before sundown, you go into a wood with your gun but without your dog. You seek out a place for yourself somewhere close by a thicket, look around you, inspect the firing mechanism on your gun and exchange winks with your companion. A quarter of an hour passes. The sun sinks below the horizon, but it is still light in the wood; the air is fresh and translucent; there is the spirited chatter of birds; the young grass glows with a happy emerald brilliance. You wait. The interior of the wood gradually darkens; the crimson rays of an evening sunset slowly slide across the roots and trunks of the trees, rise higher and higher, moving from the lower, still almost bare, 10 branches to the motionless tips of the sleep-enfolded trees. Then the very tips grow faint; the pink sky becomes a dark blue. The woodland scent increases, accompanied by slight wafts of a warm dampness; the breeze that has flown into the wood around you begins to die down. The birds fall asleep—not all at once, but by types: first the finches fall silent, a few instants later the robins, after them the yellow buntings. The wood grows darker and darker. The trees fuse into large blackening masses; the first small stars emerge diffidently in the blue sky. The birds are all asleep. Only the redstarts and little woodpeckers continue to make an occasional sleepy whistling. . . . Then they are quiet as well. Once again the ring- 20 ing voice of the chiff-chaff resounds overhead; somewhere or other an oriole gives a sad cry and a nightingale offers the first trills of its song. Your heart is heavy with anticipation, and suddenly—but only hunters will know what I mean—suddenly the deep quiet is broken by a special kind of croaking and hissing, there is a measured beat of rapidly flapping wings—and a woodcock, beautifully inclining its long beak, flies out from behind a dark birch into your line of fire.

That is what is meant by "standing in cover."

In such a fashion Yermolay and I set off for "cover"; but forgive me, gentlemen: I must first of all acquaint you with Yermolay.

Imagine to yourself a man of about forty-five, tall and lean, with a long deli- 30 cate nose, a narrow forehead, little grey eyes, dishevelled hair and wide, scornful lips. This man used to go about winter and summer in a yellowish nankeen[1] coat of German cut, but belted with a sash; he wore wide blue trousers and a cap edged with astrakhan[2] which had been given him, on a jovial occasion, by a bankrupt landowner. Two bags were fixed to the sash, one in front, which had been artfully twisted into two halves for powder and bird-shot, and the other behind—for game; his cotton wadding Yermolay used to extract from his own, seemingly inexhaustible cap. With the money earned by him from selling his game he could easily have purchased a cartridge belt and pouch, but the thought of making such a purchase never even so much as entered his head and he continued to load his 40 gun in his customary fashion, arousing astonishment in onlookers by the skill with which he avoided the danger of overpouring or mixing the shot and the powder. His gun had a single barrel, with a flintlock, endowed, moreover, with the awful habit of "kicking" brutally, as a result of which Yermolay's right cheek was always more swollen than his left. How he managed to hit anything with this gun even a wiseacre might be at a loss to explain, but hit he did.

He also had a setter, a most remarkable creature named Valetka. Yermolay never fed him. "Likely I'd start feeding a dog," he would argue, "since a dog's a clever animal and'll find his food on his own." And so it was, in fact: although Valetka astonished even indifferent passers-by with his unusual thinness, he lived 50 and lived a long time; despite his miserable condition, he never even once got lost and displayed no desire to abandon his master. Once, when he was young, he disappeared for a day or two, carried away by love; but that foolishness soon took leave of him. Valetka's most remarkable characteristic was an incomprehensible indifference to everything under the sun. If I had not been talking about a dog, I

1. Strong cotton cloth.
2. Persian lamb's wool.

would have used the word "disillusionment." He usually sat with his short tail tucked underneath him, frowning, shuddering from time to time and never smiling. (It is well known that dogs are capable of smiling, and even of smiling very charmingly.) He was extremely ugly, and there was not a single idle house-serf who let pass an opportunity of laughing venomously at his appearance; but Valetka endured all these taunts, and even blows, with astonishing composure. He provided particular satisfaction for cooks, who immediately dropped whatever they were doing and dashed after him with shouts and swearing whenever, through a weakness common not only to dogs, he used to stick his famished muzzle through the half-open door of the enticingly warm and sweet-smelling kitchen. Out hunting, he distinguished himself by his tirelessness and possessed a good scent; but if he happened to catch up with a wounded hare, he at once gobbled the whole lot down with pleasure, right to the last little bone, in some cool, shady place under a leafy bush and at a respectful distance from Yermolay who swore at him in any and every dialect, known and unknown.

Yermolay belonged to one of my neighbours, a landowner of the old school. Landowners of the old school dislike "wildfowl" and stick to domestic poultry. It is only on unusual occasions, such as birthdays, name-days[3] and elections, that the cooks of old-time landowners embark on preparing long-beaked birds and, succumbing to a high state of excitement, as do all Russians when they have no clear idea of what they are doing, they invent such fancy accompaniments for the birds that guests for the most part study the dishes set in front of them with attentiveness and curiosity, but can in no wise resolve to taste them. Yermolay was under orders to supply the master's kitchen once a month with a couple of brace[4] of grouse and partridge, but he was otherwise permitted to live where and how he wanted. He had been rejected as a man unfit for any kind of real work—a "nogood," as we say in the Oryol region. Naturally, he was given no powder and shot, following precisely the same principles as he adopted in not feeding his dog. Yermolay was a man of the most unusual kind: free and easy as a bird, garrulous to a fair extent, to all appearances scatter-brained and awkward; he had a strong liking for drink, could never settle in one place, when on the move he ambled and swayed from side to side—and, ambling and swaying, he would polish off between thirty and forty miles a day. He had been involved in a most extraordinary variety of adventures, spending nights in marshes, up trees, on roofs, beneath bridges, more than once under lock and key in attics, cellars and barns, relieved of his gun, his dog, his most essential clothing, receiving forceful and prolonged beatings—and yet after a short time he would return home clothed, with his gun and with his dog. One could not call him a happy man, although he was almost always in a reasonably good humour; generally, he looked a trifle eccentric.

Yermolay enjoyed passing the time of day with any congenial character, especially over a drink, but never for very long: he would soon get up and be on his way. "And where are you off to, you devil? It's night outside." "I'm for Chaplino." "What's the good of you traipsin' off to Chaplino, more'n seven miles away?" "I'm for spending the night there with the peasant Sofron." "Spend the night here."

---

3. Christening day, when a child was given its Christian or first name(s).
4. A pair; two.

"No, that's impossible." And Yermolay would be off with his Valetka into the dark night, through bushes and ditches, and the peasant Sofron would most likely not let him into his yard—what's more, might bash him one on the neck "for being such a disturbance to honest folk."

Yet no one could compare with Yermolay in skill at catching fish in the springtime flood-water or in grabbing crayfish with his bare hands, in scenting out game, luring quail, training hawks, capturing nightingales with "woodsprite pipe" song or "cuckoo's fly by."[5] Of one thing he was incapable: training dogs. He lacked the patience for it.

He also had a wife. He would visit her once a week. She lived in a scrappy, partly collapsed little hut, managed somehow or other, never knew from one day to the next whether she would have enough to eat and, in general, endured a bitter fate. Yermolay, that carefree and good-natured fellow, treated her roughly and coarsely, assumed a threatening and severe air in his own home—and his poor wife had no idea of how to indulge him, shuddered at his glance, bought drink for him with her last copeck and dutifully covered him with her own sheepskin coat when he, collapsing majestically on the stove, fell into a Herculean sleep. I myself had occasion more than once to notice in him involuntary signs of a certain morose ferocity. I disliked the expression on his face when he used to kill a winged bird by biting into it. But Yermolay never remained at home longer than a day: and once outside his home territory he again turned into "Yermolka," as he was known by his nickname for a good sixty odd miles around and as he used to call himself on occasion. The meanest house-serf felt himself superior to this tramp—and perhaps precisely for this reason always treated him in a friendly fashion; while peasants at first took pleasure in driving him away and trapping him like a hare in the field, but later they let him go with a blessing and, once they were acquainted with this eccentric fellow, kept their hands off him, even giving him bread and striking up a conversation with him. . . . This was the fellow I chose as my hunting companion, and it was with him that I set off for "cover" in a large birch wood on the bank of the Ista.

Many Russian rivers, after the pattern of the Volga, have one hilly bank and the other of meadowland; the Ista also. This small river winds in an exceedingly capricious fashion, crawling like a snake, never flowing straight for five hundred yards at a time, and in certain places, from the top of a steep hill, one can see six or seven miles of dams, ponds, watermills and kitchen gardens surrounded by willows and flocks of geese. There is a multitude of fish in the Ista, especially bullyheads[6] (in hot weather peasants lift them out by hand from beneath the overhanging bushes). Little sandpipers whistle and flit to and fro along the stony banks which are dotted with outlets for cold, sparkling spring water; wild ducks swim out into the centre of ponds and look guardedly about them; herons stand up stiffly in the shade, in the inlets and below the river's steep sides.

We stood in cover for about an hour, shot a couple of brace of woodcock and, wishing to try our luck again before sunrise (one can go out for cover in the morning as well), decided to spend the night at the nearest mill. We made our

5. Whistling in imitation of a nightingale's song.
6. Bullheads; catfish.

way out of the wood and went down the hill. The river was rolling along, its surface dark-blue waves; the air thickened under the pressure of the night-time moisture. We knocked at the mill gates. Dogs began to yelp in the yard.

"Who's there?" called a husky and sleepy voice.

"Hunters. Let us in for the night."

There was no answer.

"We'll pay."   150

"I'll go and tell the master. . . . Aw, damn you dogs! Nothing awful's hap-
penin' to you!"

We heard the workman enter the hut; soon he returned to the gates.

"No, the master says, he won't give orders to let you in."

"Why won't he?"

"He's frightened. You're hunters—soon as you're in here you'll likely set fire
to the mill. Just look at them firing-pieces you got there!"

"What nonsense!"

"The year afore last this mill of ours burned down. Cattle-dealers spent the
night here and some way or another, you know, they set fire to it."   160

"Anyway, friend, we're not spending the night outside!"

"Spend it anyway you know. . . ." He went off with a clattering of boots.

Yermolay dispatched after him a variety of unpleasant expressions. "Let's go
into the village," he said, finally, with a sigh. But it was more than a mile to the
village.

"We'll spend the night here," I said. "It's warm outside, and the miller'll let us
have some straw if we pay him."

Yermolay tacitly agreed. We began knocking on the gates again.

"What d'you need now?" the workman's voice called again. "I've told you—
you can't come in."   170

We explained to him what we wanted. He went off to consult his master and
came back with him. The wicket-gate creaked. The miller appeared, a tall man
with a plump face, bull-necked, and large and round of stomach. He agreed to my
suggestion.

A hundred paces from the mill stood a structure with a roof, but open on all
four sides. Straw and hay were brought out to us there; the workman set up a
samovar[7] on the grass beside the river and, squatting on his haunches, began
blowing busily up the samovar's chimney. The charcoal flared up and brightly illumined his youthful face. The miller ran off to waken his wife and eventually proposed that I should spend the night in the hut; but I preferred to remain out in the   180
open air. The miller's wife brought us some milk, eggs, potatoes and bread. Soon
the samovar was bubbling and we set about having some tea. It was windless and
mists were rising from the river; corncrakes were crying in the vicinity; from the
direction of the mill-wheels came such faint noises as the drip-drip of water from
the paddles of the seepage of water through the cross-beams of the dam. We built
a small fire. While Yermolay baked potatoes in the ashes, I managed to doze off.

A light-voiced, suppressed whispering awoke me. I raised my head: before
the fire, on an upturned tub, the miller's wife was sitting and conversing with my

7. A Russian tea urn.

hunting companion. Earlier I had recognized, by her dress, movements and way of speaking, that she was a former house-serf—not from among the peasantry or the bourgeoisie; but it was only now that I could take a good look at her features. She appeared to be about thirty; her thin, pale face still contained traces of a remarkable beauty; I was particularly taken by her eyes, so large and melancholy. She leaned her elbows on her knees and placed her face in her hands. Yermolay sat with his back to me and was engaged in laying sticks on the fire.

"There's sickness again among the cattle in Zheltukhina," the miller's wife was saying. "Both of father Ivan's cows have died . . . Lord have mercy on us!"

"And what about your pigs?" asked Yermolay after a short silence.

"They're alive."

"You ought to give me a little porker, you ought."

The miller's wife said nothing and after a while gave a sigh.

"Who are you with?" she asked.

"With the squire—the Kostomarov squire."

Yermolay threw a few fir fronds on the fire; at once they broke into a universal crackling and thick white smoke poured straight into his face.

"Why didn't your husband let us into the hut?"

"He was frightened."

"There's a fat old pot-belly for you . . . Arina Timofeyevna, be a dear and bring me a wee glass of some of the good stuff!"

The miller's wife rose and disappeared into the gloom. Yermolay began singing softly:

> A-walking to my sweetheart
> Wore the shoes off my feet . . .

Arina returned with a small carafe and a glass. Yermolay straightened up, crossed himself and gulped down the drink at one go. "That's lovely!" he added.

The miller's wife again seated herself on the tub.

"So, Arina Timofeyevna, tell me, are you still feeling poorly?"

"I'm still poorly."

"How so?"

"The coughing at night hurts me so."

"It seems the master's gone to sleep," said Yermolay after a brief silence. "Don't you go to no doctor, Arina, or it'll get worse.

"I won't be going in any case."

"You come and be my guest."

Arina lowered her head.

"I'll drive my own—my wife, that's to say—I'll drive her away for that occasion," Yermolay continued. "Sure an' all I will!"

"You'd do better to wake up your master, Yermolay Petrovich. See, the potatoes are done."

"Let him go on snoozing," my faithful servant remarked with indifference. "He's run about so much it's right he should sleep."

I turned over in the hay. Yermolay rose and approached me.

"Come and eat, sir—the potatoes are ready."

I emerged from beneath my roofed structure and the miller's wife got up from her place on the tub, wishing to leave us. I started talking to her.

"Have you been at this mill long?"

"Two years come Whitsun."[8]

"And where is your husband from?"

Arina did not catch the drift of my question.

"Whereabouts is your husband from?" Yermolay repeated, raising his voice.   240

"From Belev. He's a townsman from Belev."

"And you're also from Belev?"

"No, I'm a serf . . . I was one, that is."

"Whose?"

"Mr Zverkov's. Now I'm free."

"What Zverkov?"

"Alexander Silych."

"Were you by any chance his wife's chambermaid?"

"How d'you know that? Yes, I was."

I looked now with renewed curiosity and sympathy at Arina.   250

"I know you master," I continued.

"You do?" she answered softly, and lowered her eyes.

It is fitting that I should tell the reader why I looked at Arina with such sympathy. During my period of residence in St Petersburg I happened to become acquainted with Mr. Zverkov. He occupied a fairly important position and passed as a capable and well-informed man. He had a wife, plump, emotional, given to floods of tears and bad temper—a vulgar and burdensome creature; there was also a runt of a son, a real little milord, spoiled and witless. Mr Zverkov's own appearance did little in his favour: out of a broad, almost square face, mousey little eyes peered cunningly and his nose protruded, large and sharp, with wide-open nos-   260 trils; grey close-cropped hair rose in bristles above his wrinkled forehead and his thin lips were ceaselessly quivering and shaping themselves into sickly smiles. Mr Zverkov's habitual stance was with his little legs set wide apart and his fat little hands thrust in his pockets. On one occasion it somehow came about that I shared a carriage with him on a trip out of town. We struck up a conversation. As a man of experience and business acumen, Mr Zverkov began to instruct me concerning "the path of truth."

"Permit me to remark to you," he squeaked eventually, "that all of you, you young people, judge and explain every single matter in a random fashion; you know little about your own country; Russia, my good sirs, is a closed book to you,   270 that's what! All you read are German books. For example, you've just been saying this and that to me on this question of—well, that's to say, on this question of house-serfs. . . . Fine, I don't dispute it, that's all very fine; but you don't know them, you don't know what sort of people they are."

Mr Zverkov loudly blew his nose and took a pinch of snuff.

"Permit me to tell, for example, one little tiny anecdote, which could be of interest to you." Mr Zverkov cleared his throat with a cough. "You certainly know

8. Six Sundays after Easter celebrating the Holy Ghost.

what kind of a wife I have; it would seem hard to find anyone kinder than her, you will yourself agree. Her chambermaids don't just have food and lodging, but a veritable paradise on earth is created before their very eyes. . . . But my wife has 280 laid down a rule for herself: that she will not employ married chambermaids. That sort of thing just will not do. Children come along and so on—well, a chambermaid in that case can't look after her mistress as she should, can't see to all her habits: she's not up to it, she's got something else on her mind. You must judge such things according to human nature.

"Well, sir, one day we were driving through our village, it'd be about—how can I say exactly?—about fifteen years ago. We saw that the elder had a little girl, a daughter, extremely pretty; there was even something, you know, deferential in her manner. My wife says to me: 'Coco . . . 'You understand me, that's what she— er—calls me '. . . we'll take this little girl to St Petersburg; I like her, Coco . . .' 290 'Take her with pleasure,' I say. The elder, naturally, falls at our feet; such happiness, you understand, has been too much for him to expect. . . . Well, of course, the girl burst into tears like an idiot. It really is awful for them to start with—I mean, leaving the house where they were born; but there's nothing to be surprised at in that. Soon, however, she had grown used to us. To start with she was put in the maids' room, where they taught her what to do, of course. And what d'you think? The girl made astonishing progress; my wife simply fawned on her, and finally, passing over others, promoted her to be one of her own chambermaids. Take note of that! And one has to do her justice: my wife never had such a chambermaid, absolutely never had one like her: helpful, modest, obedient—simply every- 300 thing one could ask for. As a result, I must admit, my wife even took to spoiling her a bit too much: dressed her superbly, gave her the same food as she had, gave her tea to drink—well, you just can't imagine how it was!

"So she spent about ten years in my wife's service. Suddenly, one fine morning, just think of it, Arine—Arina was her name—came unannounced into my study and flopped down at my feet. I will tell you frankly that I can't abide that sort of thing. A man should never forget his dignity, isn't that true? 'What's it you want?' 'Good master, Alexander Silych, I beg your indulgence.' 'In what?' 'Allow me to get married.' I confess to you I was astonished. 'Don't you know, you silly girl, that the mistress hasn't got another chambermaid?' 'I'll go on serving the mis- 310 tress as I have done.' 'Nonsense! Nonsense! the mistress does not employ married chambermaids.' 'Malanya can take my place.' 'I beg you to keep your ideas to yourself.' 'As you wish . . .'

"I confess I was simply stunned. I will let you know that I'm the sort of man who finds nothing so insulting—I dare say even strongly insulting—as ingratitude. There's no need for me to tell you—you already know what my wife is: an angel in the very flesh, inexplicably good-natured. The blackest scoundrel, it seems, would take pity on her. I sent Arina away. I thought she'd probably come to her senses; I'm not one, you know, who likes to believe in man's black ingratitude and evil nature. Then what d'you think? Six months later she again honours me 320 with a visit and makes the very same request. This time, I admit, I drove her away in real earnest and gave her due warning and promised to tell my wife. I was flabbergasted. . . . But imagine my astonishment when a short while later my wife came to me in tears and in such an excited state that I was even alarmed for her.

'What on earth's happened?' 'It's Arina . . .' You'll appreciate that I'm ashamed to say it out loud. 'It simply can't be! Who was it?' 'The lackey Petrushka.'

"I exploded. I'm that sort of man—I just don't like half-measures! Petrushka wasn't to blame. He could be punished, but he wasn't to blame, in my opinion. Arina . . . well, what, well, I mean, what need to say anything more? It goes without saying that I at once ordered her hair to be cut off, had her dressed in her shabbiest clothes and packed off to the country. My wife was deprived of an excellent chambermaid, but I had no choice: one just cannot tolerate bad behaviour in one's own house. Better that a rotten limb should be cut off at once. . . . Well, now you judge for yourself—well, I mean, you know my wife, she's, she's, she's,—she's an angel, when all's said and done! After all, she was attached to Arina—and Arina knew that and yet behaved shamelessly. . . . Eh? No, say what you like—eh? There's no point in discussing it! In any case, I had no choice. The ingratitude of this girl annoyed and hurt me personally—yes, me, myself—for a long time. I don't care what you say, but you'll not find any heart, any feeling, in these people! No matter how much you feed a wolf, it's still got its heart set on the forest. . . . Science to the fore! But I simply wanted to demonstrate to you. . . ."

And Mr Zverkov, without finishing, turned his head away and buried himself more snugly in his coat, manfully suppressing an unwanted agitation.

The reader no doubt understands now why I looked at Arina with sympathy.

"Have you been married long to the miller?" I asked her at last.

"Two years."

"Do you mean that your master actually allowed you?"

"Someone bought me off."[9]

"Who?"

"Savely Alekseyevich."

"Who's he?"

"My husband." (Yermolay smiled to himself.)

"But did my master talk to you about me?" Arina added after a short pause.

I had no idea how to answer her question.

"Arina!" the miller shouted from a distance. She rose and walked away.

"Is her husband a good man?" I asked Yermolay.

"Not bad."

"Do they have any children?"

"There was one, but it died."

"The miller must've liked her, didn't he? Did he give a lot of money to buy her off?"

"I don't know. She knows how to read and write. In their business that's worth . . . that's a good thing. Reckon he must've liked her."

"Have you known her long?"

"A good while. Formerly I used to go to her master's. Their estate's round about these parts."

"And did you know the lackey Petrushka?"

"Pyotr Vasilyevich? Sure I did."

"Where is he now?"

9. Bought her freedom from serfdom.

"Went off to be a soldier."

We fell silent

"It seems she's not well, is that so?" I asked Yermolay finally.

"Some health she has! . . . Tomorrow, you'll see, they'll be flying well from cover. It'd be a good idea for you to get some sleep now."

A flock of wild ducks raced whistling over our heads and we heard them alight on the river not far away. It was already quite dark and beginning to grow cold; in the wood a nightingale was resonantly pouring out its song. We burrowed down in the hay and went to sleep.   [1852]

370

Questions for Discussion and Writing

1. How does the opening description of "cover" relate to the rest of the story? Why or why not is this opening effective?
2. Mark the passages that illustrate cruelty of one kind or another. What do they contribute to the story?
3. What does the narrator reveal about himself?
4. How would you describe the narrator's stance or tone? With whom, if anyone, does he take sides? Mark passages that reveal the narrator's attitude.
5. How are the episodes in this story structured or organized? Is there any structural principle at work in the story, or is its arrangement casual?
6. If viewed as having an element of social commentary, what point(s) might the story be making?

☜ HERMAN MELVILLE
(1819–1891)

Bartleby, the Scrivener
A Story of Wall Street

Herman Melville's life of adventures and financial vicissitudes reads like one of his most imaginative fictions. Only in this century did he achieve the fame and stature that in life eluded him.

He was born to prosperous parents who traced their ancestry to European royalty and to patriots in the American Revolution: his grandfather was among the "Indians" of the Boston Tea Party. Herman was twelve when his father suffered serious financial losses. After various odd jobs, Melville went to sea, first to Liverpool and later to the South Seas. These journeys resulted in the novels *Typee* (1846), *Omoo* (1847), and *Redburn* (1849), which sold briskly as adventure tales. He married in 1847 and tried farming, but kept returning to the writing of novels. His own taste differed from the public's taste for simple action-adventure—he was interested in social criticism and philosophical speculations. When he turned to short story writing in 1853, at the rate of $5 a page, he faced even more strictures on theme and method than he had in his novels, which may account in part for his use of indirection and allegory.

With the failure of *The Confidence Man* (1857), Melville gave up writing. Money from his wife's family financed travel abroad, but ill health, the Civil War, and family tragedies plunged him into depression. In 1866, he was appointed a customs inspector in New York and remained in this position for nearly twenty years. Privately he wrote poetry and his famous short novel, *Billy Budd,* published posthumously in 1924.

Melville is now considered among America's greatest novelists, but his fame as a short story writer rests on only a few stories. "Bartleby," the best known of these, is one of the most enigmatic and haunting stories ever written and has occasioned a bewildering number of interpretations. Bartleby's simple refusal, "I prefer not to," seems to come straight from the rebellious American spirit, as well as from the frustrations and tragedies that were Melville's own life.

I AM A RATHER elderly man. The nature of my avocations, for the last thirty years, has brought me into more than ordinary contact with what would seem an interesting and somewhat singular set of men, of whom, as yet, nothing, that I know of, has ever been written—I mean, the law-copyists, or scriveners. I have known very many of them, professionally and privately, and, if I pleased, could relate divers histories, at which good-natured gentlemen might smile, and sentimental souls might weep. But I waive the biographies of all other scriveners, for a few passages in the life of Bartleby, who was a scrivener, the strangest I ever saw, or heard of. While, of other law-copyists, I might write the complete life, of Bartleby nothing of that sort can be done. I believe that no materials exist, for a full and   10 satisfactory biography of this man. It is an irreparable loss to literature. Bartleby was one of those beings of whom nothing is ascertainable, except from the original sources, and, in his case, those are very small. What my own astonished eyes saw of Bartleby, *that* is all I know of him, except, indeed, one vague report, which will appear in the sequel.

Ere introducing the scrivener, as he first appeared to me, it is fit I make some mention of myself, my *employés,* my business, my chambers, and general surroundings; because some such description is indispensable to an adequate understanding of the chief character about to be presented. Imprimis:[1] I am a man who, from his youth upwards, has been filled with a profound conviction that the easi-   20 est way of life is the best. Hence, though I belong to a profession proverbially energetic and nervous, even to turbulence, at times, yet nothing of that sort have I ever suffered to invade my peace. I am one of those unambitious lawyers who never address a jury, or in any way draw down public applause; but, in the cool tranquillity of a snug retreat, do a snug business among rich men's bonds, and mortgages, and title-deeds. All who know me, consider me an eminently *safe* man. The late John Jacob Astor,[2] a personage little given to poetic enthusiasm, had no hesitation in pronouncing my first grand point to be prudence; my next, method.

---

1. First of all.
2. Astor (1763–1848) made a fortune in the fur trade and then as a real estate speculator in New York City.

I do not speak it in vanity, but simply record the fact, that I was not unemployed in my profession by the late John Jacob Astor; a name which, I admit, I love to 30 repeat; for it hath a rounded and orbicular sound to it, and rings like unto bullion. I will freely add, that I was not insensible to the late John Jacob Astor's good opinion.

Some time prior to the period at which this little history begins, my avocations had been largely increased. The good old office, now extinct in the State of New York, of a Master in Chancery,[3] had been conferred upon me. It was not a very arduous office, but very pleasantly remunerative. I seldom lose my temper; much more seldom indulge in dangerous indignation at wrongs and outrages; but I must be permitted to be rash here and declare, that I consider the sudden and violent abrogation of the office of Master in Chancery, by the new Constitution, as a 40 ————premature act; inasmuch as I had counted upon a life-lease of the profits, whereas I only received those of a few short years. But this is by the way.

My chambers were up stairs, at No.————Wall Street. At one end, they looked upon the white wall of the interior of a spacious sky-light shaft, penetrating the building from top to bottom.

This view might have been considered rather tame than otherwise, deficient in what landscape painters call "life." But, if so, the view from the other end of my chambers offered, at least, a contrast, if nothing more. In that direction, my windows commanded an unobstructed view of a lofty brick wall, black by age and everlasting shade; which wall required no spy-glass to bring out its lurking beau- 50 ties, but, for the benefit of all near-sighted spectators, was pushed up to within ten feet of my window-panes. Owing to the great height of the surrounding buildings, and my chambers being on the second floor, the interval between this wall and mine not a little resembled a huge square cistern.

At the period just preceding the advent of Bartleby, I had two persons as copyists in my employment, and a promising lad as an office-boy. First, Turkey; second, Nippers; third, Ginger Nut. These may seem names, the like of which are not usually found in the Directory. In truth, they were nicknames, mutually conferred upon each other by my three clerks, and were deemed expressive of their respective persons or characters. Turkey was a short, pursy Englishman, of about 60 my own age—that is, somewhere not far from sixty. In the morning, one might say, his face was of a fine florid hue, but after twelve o'clock, meridian—his dinner hour—it blazed like a grate full of Christmas coals; and continued blazing—but, as it were, with a gradual wane—till six o'clock, P.M., or thereabouts; after which, I saw no more of the proprietor of the face, which, gaining its meridian with the sun, seemed to set with it, to rise, culminate, and decline the following day, with the like regularity and undiminished glory. There are many singular coincidences I have known in the course of my life, not the least among which was the fact, that, exactly when Turkey displayed his fullest beams from his red and radiant countenance, just then, too, at that critical moment, began the daily period when I con- 70 sidered his business capacities as seriously disturbed for the remainder of the twenty-four hours. Not that he was absolutely idle, or averse to business then; far from it. The difficulty was, he was apt to be altogether too energetic. There was a

3. Courts that settled cases more quickly than those tried by jury.

strange, inflamed, flurried, flighty recklessness of activity about him. He would be incautious in dipping his pen into his inkstand. All his blots upon my documents were dropped there after twelve o'clock, meridian. Indeed, not only would he be reckless, and sadly given to making blots in the afternoon, but, some days, he went further, and was rather noisy. At such times, too, his face flamed with augmented blazonry, as if cannel[4] coal had been heaped on anthracite. He made an unpleasant racket with his chair; spilled his sand-box;[5] in mending his pens, impatiently split them all to pieces, and threw them on the floor in a sudden passion; stood up, and leaned over his table, boxing his papers about in a most indecorous manner, very sad to behold in an elderly man like him. Nevertheless, as he was in many ways a most valuable person to me, and all the time before twelve o'clock, meridian, was the quickest, steadiest creature, too, accomplishing a great deal of work in a style not easily to be matched—for these reasons, I was willing to overlook his eccentricities, though, indeed, occasionally, I remonstrated with him. I did this very gently, however, because, though the civilest, nay, the blandest and most reverential of men in the morning, yet, in the afternoon, he was disposed, upon provocation, to be slightly rash with his tongue—in fact, insolent. Now, valuing his morning services as I did, and resolved not to lose them—yet, at the same time, made uncomfortable by his inflamed ways after twelve o'clock—and being a man of peace, unwilling by my admonitions to call forth unseemly retorts from him, I took upon me, one Saturday noon (he was always worse on Saturdays) to hint to him, very kindly, that, perhaps, now that he was growing old, it might be well to abridge his labors; in short, he need not come to my chambers after twelve o'clock, but, dinner over, had best go home to his lodgings, and rest himself till tea-time. But no; he insisted upon his afternoon devotions. His countenance became intolerably fervid, as he oratorically assured me—gesticulating with a long ruler at the other end of the room—that if his services in the morning were useful, how indispensable, then, in the afternoon?

"With submission, sir," said Turkey, on this occasion, "I consider myself your right-hand man. In the morning I but marshal and deploy my columns; but in the afternoon I put myself at their head, and gallantly charge the foe, thus"—and he made a violent thrust with the ruler.

"But the blots, Turkey," intimated I.

"True; but, with submission, sir, behold these hairs! I am getting old. Surely, sir, a blot or two of a warm afternoon is not to be severely urged against gray hairs. Old age—even if it blot the page—is honorable. With submission, sir, we *both* are getting old."

This appeal to my fellow-feeling was hardly to be resisted. At all events, I saw that go he would not. So, I made up my mind to let him stay, resolving, nevertheless, to see to it that, during the afternoon, he had to do with my less important papers.

Nippers, the second on my list, was a whiskered, sallow, and, upon the whole, rather piratical-looking young man, of about five-and-twenty. I always deemed him the victim of two evil powers—ambition and indigestion. The ambi-

---

4. A very hard, hot-burning coal.
5. Sand was used to hasten the drying of ink.

tion was evinced by a certain impatience of the duties of a mere copyist, an un-
warrantable usurpation of strictly professional affairs, such as the original drawing
up of legal documents. The indigestion seemed betokened in an occasional ner- 120
vous testiness and grinning irritability, causing the teeth to audibly grind together
over mistakes committed in copying; unnecessary maledictions, hissed, rather
than spoken, in the heat of business; and especially by a continual discontent with
the height of the table where he worked. Though of a very ingenious mechanical
turn, Nippers could never get this table to suit him. He put chips under it, blocks
of various sorts, bits of pasteboard, and at last went so far as to attempt an exquisite adjustment, by final pieces of folded blotting-paper. But no invention would
answer. If, for the sake of easing his back, he brought the table-lid at a sharp angle
well up towards his chin, and wrote there like a man using the steep roof of a
Dutch house for his desk, then he declared that it stopped the circulation in his 130
arms. If now he lowered the table to his waistbands, and stooped over it in writing, then there was a sore aching in his back. In short, the truth of the matter was,
Nippers knew not what he wanted. Or, if he wanted anything, it was to be rid of a
scrivener's table altogether. Among the manifestations of his diseased ambition was
a fondness he had for receiving visits from certain ambiguous-looking fellows in
seedy coats, whom he called his clients. Indeed, I was aware that not only was he,
at times, considerable of a ward-politician, but he occasionally did a little business
at the Justices' courts, and was not unknown on the steps of the Tombs.[6] I have
good reason to believe, however, that one individual who called upon him at my
chambers, and who, with a grand air, he insisted was his client, was no other than 140
a dun,[7] and the alleged titledeed, a bill. But, with all his failings, and the annoy-
ances he caused me, Nippers, like his compatriot Turkey, was a very useful man to
me; wrote a neat, swift hand; and, when he chose, was not deficient in a gentlemanly sort of deportment. Added to this, he always dressed in a gentlemanly sort
of way; and so, incidentally, reflected credit upon my chambers. Whereas, with respect to Turkey, I had much ado to keep him from being a reproach to me. His
clothes were apt to look oily, and smell of eating-houses. He wore his pantaloons
very loose and baggy in summer. His coats were execrable; his hat not to be handled. But while the hat was a thing of indifference to me, inasmuch as his natural
civility and deference, as a dependent Englishman, always led him to doff it the 150
moment he entered the room, yet his coat was another matter. Concerning his
coats, I reasoned with him; but with no effect. The truth was, I suppose, that a
man with so small an income could not afford to sport such a lustrous face and a
lustrous coat at one and the same time. As Nippers once observed, Turkey's money
went chiefly for red ink. One winter day, I presented Turkey with a highly respectable-looking coat of my own—a padded gray coat, of a most comfortable
warmth, and which buttoned straight up from the knee to the neck. I thought
Turkey would appreciate the favor, and abate his rashness and obstreperousness of
afternoons. But no; I verily believe that buttoning himself up in so downy and
blanket-like a coat had a pernicious effect upon him—upon the same principle 160
that too much oats are bad for horses. In fact, precisely as a rash, restive horse is

6. A jail in New York City.
7. A bill collector.

said to feel his oats, so Turkey felt his coat. It made him insolent. He was a man whom prosperity harmed.

Though, concerning the self-indulgent habits of Turkey, I had my own private surmises, yet, touching Nippers, I was well persuaded that, whatever might be his faults in other respects, he was, at least, a temperate young man. But, indeed, nature herself seemed to have been his vintner, and, at his birth, charged him so thoroughly with an irritable, brandy-like disposition, that all subsequent potations were needless. When I consider how, amid the stillness of my chambers, Nippers would sometimes impatiently rise from his seat, and stooping over his table, spread his arms wide apart, seize the whole desk, and move it, and jerk it, with a grim, grinding motion on the floor, as if the table were a perverse voluntary agent, intent on thwarting and vexing him, I plainly perceive that, for Nippers, brandy-and-water were altogether superfluous.

It was fortunate for me that, owing to its peculiar cause—indigestion—the irritability and consequent nervousness of Nippers were mainly observable in the morning, while in the afternoon he was comparatively mild. So that, Turkey's paroxysms only coming on about twelve o'clock, I never had to do with their eccentricities at one time. Their fits relieved each other, like guards. When Nippers's was on, Turkey's was off; and *vice versa*. This was a good natural arrangement, under the circumstances.

Ginger Nut, the third on my list, was a lad, some twelve years old. His father was a carman, ambitious of seeing his son on the bench instead of a cart, before he died. So he sent him to my office, as student at law, errand-boy, cleaner and sweeper, at the rate of one dollar a week. He had a little desk to himself, but he did not use it much. Upon inspection, the drawer exhibited a great array of the shells of various sorts of nuts. Indeed, to this quick-witted youth, the whole noble science of the law was contained in a nut-shell. Not the least among the employments of Ginger Nut, as well as one which he discharged with the most alacrity, was his duty as cake and apple purveyor for Turkey and Nippers. Copying law-papers being proverbially a dry, husky sort of business, my two scriveners were fain to moisten their mouths very often with Spitzenbergs,[8] to be had at the numerous stalls nigh the Custom House and Post Office. Also, they sent Ginger Nut very frequently for that peculiar cake—small, flat, round, and very spicy—after which he had been named by them. Of a cold morning, when business was but dull, Turkey would gobble up scores of these cakes, as if they were mere wafers—indeed, they sell them at the rate of six or eight for a penny—the scrape of his pen blending with the crunching of the crisp particles in his mouth. Of all the fiery afternoon blunders and flurried rashnesses of Turkey, was his once moistening a ginger-cake between his lips, and clapping it on to a mortgage, for a seal. I came within an ace of dismissing him then. But he mollified me by making an oriental bow, and saying—

"With submission, sir, it was generous of me to find you in stationery on my own account."

Now my original business—that of a conveyancer and title hunter, and

___

8. A kind of apple.

drawer-up of recondite documents of all sorts—was considerably increased by receiving the Master's office. There was now great work for scriveners. Not only
must I push the clerks already with me, but I must have additional help.

In answer to my advertisement, a motionless young man one morning
stood upon my office threshold, the door being open, for it was summer. I can see 210
that figure now—pallidly neat, pitiably respectable, incurably forlorn! It was
Bartleby.

After a few words touching his qualifications, I engaged him, glad to have
among my corps of copyists a man of so singularly sedate an aspect, which I
thought might operate beneficially upon the flighty temper of Turkey, and the fiery
one of Nippers.

I should have stated before that ground-glass folding-doors divided my
premises into two parts, one of which was occupied by my scriveners, the other
by myself. According to my humor, I threw open these doors, or closed them. I resolved to assign Bartleby a corner by the folding-doors, but on my side of them, so 220
as to have this quiet man within easy call, in case any trifling thing was to be
done. I placed his desk close up to a small side-window in that part of the room, a
window which originally had afforded a lateral view of certain grimy backyards
and bricks, but which, owing to subsequent erections, commanded at present no
view at all, though it gave some light. Within three feet of the panes was a wall,
and the light came down from far above, between two lofty buildings, as from a
very small opening in a dome. Still further to a satisfactory arrangement, I procured a high green folding screen, which might entirely isolate Bartleby from my
sight, though not remove him from my voice. And thus, in a manner, privacy and
society were conjoined.   230

At first, Bartleby did an extraordinary quantity of writing. As if long famish-
ing for something to copy, he seemed to gorge himself on my documents. There
was no pause for digestion. He ran a day and night line, copying by sunlight and
by candle-light. I should have been quite delighted with his application, had he
been cheerfully industrious. But he wrote on silently, palely, mechanically.

It is, of course, an indispensable part of a scrivener's business to verify the
accuracy of his copy, word by word. Where there are two or more scriveners in an
office, they assist each other in this examination, one reading from the copy, the
other holding the original. It is a very dull, wearisome, and lethargic affair. I can
readily imagine that, to some sanguine temperaments, it would be altogether intol- 240
erable. For example, I cannot credit that the mettlesome poet, Byron, would have
contentedly sat down with Bartleby to examine a law document of, say five hundred pages, closely written in a crimpy hand.

Now and then, in the haste of business, it had been my habit to assist in
comparing some brief document myself, calling Turkey or Nippers for this purpose. One object I had, in placing Bartleby so handy to me behind the screen,
was, to avail myself of his services on such trivial occasions. It was on the third
day, I think, of his being with me, and before any necessity had arisen for having
his own writing examined, that, being much hurried to complete a small affair I
had in hand, I abruptly called to Bartleby. In my haste and natural expectancy of 250
instant compliance, I sat with my head bent over the original on my desk, and my

right hand sideways, and somewhat nervously extended with the copy, so that, immediately upon emerging from his retreat, Bartleby might snatch it and proceed to business without the least delay.

In this very attitude did I sit when I called to him, rapidly stating what it was I wanted him to do—namely, to examine a small paper with me. Imagine my surprise, nay, my consternation, when, without moving from his privacy, Bartleby, in a singularly mild, firm voice, replied, "I would prefer not to."

I sat awhile in perfect silence, rallying my stunned faculties. Immediately it occurred to me that my ears had deceived me, or Bartleby had entirely misunder- 260 stood my meaning. I repeated my request in the clearest tone I could assume; but in quite as clear a one came the previous reply, "I would prefer not to."

"Prefer not to," echoed I, rising in high excitement, and crossing the room with a stride. "What do you mean? Are you moon-struck? I want you to help me compare this sheet here—take it," and I thrust it towards him.

"I would prefer not to," said he.

I looked at him steadfastly. His face was leanly composed; his gray eye dimly calm. Not a wrinkle of agitation rippled him. Had there been the least uneasiness, anger, impatience or impertinence in his manner; in other words, had there been anything ordinarily human about him, doubtless I should have violently dismissed 270 him from the premises. But as it was, I should have as soon thought of turning my pale plaster-of-paris bust of Cicero out of doors. I stood gazing at him awhile, as he went on with his own writing, and then reseated myself at my desk. This is very strange, thought I. What had one best do? But my business hurried me. I concluded to forget the matter for the present, reserving it for my future leisure. So, calling Nippers from the other room, the paper was speedily examined.

A few days after this, Bartleby concluded four lengthy documents, being quadruplicates of a week's testimony taken before me in my High Court of Chancery. It became necessary to examine them. It was an important suit, and great accuracy was imperative. Having all things arranged, I called Turkey, Nippers 280 and Ginger Nut, from the next room, meaning to place the four copies in the hands of my four clerks, while I should read from the original. Accordingly, Turkey, Nippers, and Ginger Nut had taken their seats in a row, each with his document in his hand, when I called to Bartleby to join this interesting group.

"Bartleby! quick, I am waiting."

I heard a slow scrape of his chair legs on the uncarpeted floor, and soon he appeared standing at the entrance of his hermitage.

"What is wanted?" said he, mildly.

"The copies, the copies," said I, hurriedly. "We are going to examine them. There"—and I held towards him the fourth quadruplicate.   290

"I would prefer not to," he said, and gently disappeared behind the screen.

For a few moments I was turned into a pillar of salt,[9] standing at the head of my seated column of clerks. Recovering myself, I advanced towards the screen, and demanded the reason for such extraordinary conduct.

9. Lot's wife was turned to a pillar of salt when she looked back at the destruction of Sodom and Gomorrah. Genesis 19:17–29.

"*Why* do you refuse?"

"I would prefer not to."

With any other man I should have flown outright into a dreadful passion, scorned all further words, and thrust him ignominiously from my presence. But there was something about Bartleby that not only strangely disarmed me, but, in a wonderful manner, touched and disconcerted me. I began to reason with him.   300

"These are your own copies we are about to examine. It is labor saving to you, because one examination will answer for your four papers. It is common usage. Every copyist is bound to help examine his copy. Is it not so? Will you not speak? Answer!"

"I prefer not to," he replied in a flute-like tone. It seemed to me that, while I had been addressing him, he carefully revolved every statement that I made; fully comprehended the meaning; could not gainsay the irresistible conclusion; but, at the same time, some paramount consideration prevailed with him to reply as he did.

"You are decided, then, not to comply with my request—a request made ac-   310
cording to common usage and common sense?"

He briefly gave me to understand, that on that point my judgment was sound. Yes: his decision was irreversible.

It is not seldom the case that, when a man is browbeaten in some unprecedented and violently unreasonable way, he begins to stagger in his own plainest faith. He begins, as it were, vaguely to surmise that, wonderful as it may be, all the justice and all the reason is on the other side. Accordingly, if any disinterested persons are present, he turns to them for some reinforcement for his own faltering mind.

"Turkey," said I, "what do you think of this? Am I not right?"   320

"With submission, sir," said Turkey, in his blandest tone, "I think that you are."

"Nippers," said I, "what do *you* think of it?"

"I think I should kick him out of the office."

(The reader of nice perceptions will here perceive that, it being morning, Turkey's answer is couched in polite and tranquil terms, but Nippers replies in ill-tempered ones. Or, to repeat a previous sentence, Nippers's ugly mood was on duty, and Turkey's off.)

"Ginger Nut," said I, willing to enlist the smallest suffrage in my behalf, "what do *you* think of it?"   330

"I think sir, he's a little *luny*," replied Ginger Nut, with a grin.

"You hear what they say," said I, turning towards the screen, "come forth and do your duty."

But he vouchsafed no reply. I pondered a moment in sore perplexity. But once more business hurried me. I determined again to postpone the consideration of this dilemma to my future leisure. With a little trouble we made out to examine the papers without Bartleby, though at every page or two Turkey deferentially dropped his opinion, that this proceeding was quite out of the common; while Nippers, twitching in his chair with a dyspeptic nervousness, ground out, between his set teeth, occasional hissing maledictions against the stubborn oaf behind the   340 screen. And for his (Nippers's) part, this was the first and the last time he would do another man's business without pay.

Meanwhile Bartleby sat in his hermitage, oblivious to everything but his own peculiar business there.

Some days passed, the scrivener being employed upon another lengthy work. His late remarkable conduct led me to regard his ways narrowly. I observed that he never went to dinner; indeed, that he never went anywhere. As yet I had never, of my personal knowledge, known him to be outside of my office. He was a perpetual sentry in the corner. At about eleven o'clock though, in the morning, I noticed that Ginger Nut would advance toward the opening in Bartleby's screen, as 350 if silently beckoned thither by a gesture invisible to me where I sat. The boy would then leave the office, jingling a few pence, and reappear with a handful of ginger-nuts, which he delivered in the hermitage, receiving two of the cakes for his trouble.

He lives, then, on ginger-nuts, thought I; never eats a dinner, properly speaking; he must be a vegetarian, then; but no; he never eats even vegetables, he eats nothing but ginger-nuts. My mind then ran on in reveries concerning the probable effects upon the human constitution of living entirely on ginger-nuts. Ginger-nuts are so called, because they contain ginger as one of their peculiar con- stituents, and the final flavoring one. Now, what was ginger? A hot, spicy thing. 360 Was Bartleby hot and spicy? Not at all. Ginger, then, had no effect upon Bartleby. Probably he preferred it should have none.

Nothing so aggravates an earnest person as a passive resistance. If the indi- vidual so resisted be of a not inhumane temper, and the resisting one perfectly harmless in his passivity, then, in the better moods of the former, he will endeavor charitably to construe to his imagination what proves impossible to be solved by his judgment. Even so, for the most part, I regarded Bartleby and his ways. Poor fellow! thought I, he means no mischief; it is plain he intends no insolence; his as- pect sufficiently evinces that his eccentricities are involuntary. He is useful to me. I can get along with him. If I turn him away, the chances are he will fall in with 370 some less indulgent employer, and then he will be rudely treated, and perhaps dri- ven forth miserably to starve. Yes, Here I can cheaply purchase a delicious self- approval. To befriend Bartleby; to humor him in his strange wilfulness, will cost me little or nothing, while I lay up in my soul what will eventually prove a sweet morsel for my conscience. But this mood was not invariable with me. The passive- ness of Bartleby sometimes irritated me. I felt strangely goaded on to encounter him in new opposition—to elicit some angry spark from him answerable to my own. But, indeed, I might as well have essayed to strike fire with my knuckles against a bit of Windsor soap.[10] But one afternoon the evil impulse in me mastered me, and the following little scene ensued: 380

"Bartleby," said I, "when those papers are all copied, I will compare them with you."

"I would prefer not to."

"How? Surely you do not mean to persist in that mulish vagary?"

No answer.

10. Brown hand soap.

I threw open the folding-doors near by, and, turning upon Turkey and Nippers, exclaimed:

"Bartleby a second time says, he won't examine his papers. What do you think of it, Turkey?"

It was afternoon, be it remembered. Turkey sat glowing like a brass boiler; his bald head steaming; his hands reeling among his blotted papers.

"Think of it?" roared Turkey. "I think I'll just step behind his screen, and black his eyes for him!"

So saying, Turkey rose to his feet and threw his arms into a pugilistic position. He was hurrying away to make good his promise, when I detained him, alarmed at the effect of incautiously rousing Turkey's combativeness after dinner.

"Sit down, Turkey," said I, "and hear what Nippers has to say. What do you think of it, Nippers? Would I not be justified in immediately dismissing Bartleby?"

"Excuse me, that is for you to decide, sir. I think his conduct quite unusual, and, indeed, unjust, as regards Turkey and myself. But it may only be a passing whim."

"Ah," exclaimed I, "you have strangely changed your mind, then—you speak very gently of him now."

"All beer," cried Turkey; "gentleness is effects of beer—Nippers and I dined together to-day. You see how gentle *I* am, sir. Shall I go and black his eyes?"

"You refer to Bartleby, I suppose. No, not to-day, Turkey," I replied; "pray, put up your fists."

I closed the doors, and again advanced towards Bartleby. I felt additional incentives tempting me to my fate. I burned to be rebelled against again. I remembered that Bartleby never left the office.

"Bartleby," said I, "Ginger Nut is away; just step around to the Post Office, won't you?" (it was but a three minutes' walk) "and see if there is anything for me."

"I would prefer not to."

"You *will* not?"

"I *prefer* not."

I staggered to my desk, and sat there in a deep study. My blind inveteracy returned. Was there any other thing in which I could procure myself to be ignominiously repulsed by this lean, penniless wight?—my hired clerk? What added thing is there, perfectly reasonable, that he will be sure to refuse to do?

"Bartleby!"

No answer.

"Bartleby," in a louder tone.

No answer.

"Bartleby," I roared.

Like a very ghost, agreeably to the laws of magical invocation, at the third summons, he appeared at the entrance of his hermitage.

"Go to the next room, and tell Nippers to come to me."

"I prefer not to," he respectfully and slowly said, and mildly disappeared.

"Very good, Bartleby," said I, in a quiet sort of serenely-severe self-possessed tone, intimating the unalterable purpose of some terrible retribution very close at hand. At the moment I half intended something of the kind. But upon the whole, as it was drawing towards my dinner-hour, I thought it best to put on my hat and walk home for the day, suffering much from perplexity and distress of mind.

Shall I acknowledge it? The conclusion of this whole business was, that it soon became a fixed fact of my chambers, that a pale young scrivener, by the name of Bartleby, had a desk there; that he copied for me at the usual rate of four cents a folio (one hundred words); but he was permanently exempt from examining the work done by him, that duty being transferred to Turkey and Nippers, out of compliment, doubtless, to their superior acuteness; moreover, said Bartleby was never, on any account, to be dispatched on the most trivial errand of any sort; and that even if entreated to take upon him such a matter, it was generally understood that he would "prefer not to"—in other words, that he would refuse point-blank.

As days passed on, I became considerably reconciled to Bartleby. His steadiness, his freedom from all dissipation, his incessant industry (except when he chose to throw himself into a standing revery behind his screen), his great stillness, his unalterableness of demeanor under all circumstances, made him a valuable acquisition. One prime thing was this—*he was always there*—first in the morning, continually through the day, and the last at night. I had a singular confidence in his honesty. I felt my most precious papers perfectly safe in his hands. Sometimes, to be sure, I could not, for the very soul of me, avoid falling into sudden spasmodic passions with him. For it was exceeding difficult to bear in mind all the time those strange peculiarities, privileges, and unheard-of exemptions, forming the tacit stipulations on Bartleby's part under which he remained in my office. Now and then, in the eagerness of dispatching pressing business, I would inadvertently summon Bartleby, in a short, rapid tone, to put his finger, say, on the incipient tie of a bit of red tape with which I was about compressing some papers. Of course, from behind the screen the usual answer, "I prefer not to," was sure to come; and then, how could a human creature, with the common infirmities of our nature, refrain from bitterly exclaiming upon such perverseness—such unreasonableness? However, every added repulse of this sort which I received only tended to lessen the probability of my repeating the inadvertence.

Here it must be said, that, according to the custom of most legal gentlemen occupying chambers in densely-populated law buildings, there were several keys to my door. One was kept by a woman residing in the attic, which person weekly scrubbed and daily swept and dusted my apartments. Another was kept by Turkey for convenience sake. The third I sometimes carried in my own pocket. The fourth I knew not who had.

Now, one Sunday morning I happened to go to Trinity Church, to hear a celebrated preacher, and finding myself rather early on the ground I thought I would walk round to my chambers for a while. Luckily I had my key with me; but upon applying it to the lock, I found it resisted by something inserted from the inside. Quite surprised, I called out; when to my consternation a key was turned from within; and thrusting his lean visage at me, and holding the door ajar, the apparition of Bartleby appeared, in his shirt-sleeves, and otherwise in a strangely tattered deshabille, saying quietly that he was sorry, but he was deeply engaged just then, and—preferred not admitting me at present. In a brief word or two, he moreover

added, that perhaps I had better walk round the block two or three times, and by
that time he would probably have concluded his affairs.   480

Now, the utterly unsurmised appearance of Bartleby, tenanting my law-
chambers of a Sunday morning, with his cadaverously gentlemanly *nonchalance,*
yet withal firm and self-possessed, had such a strange effect upon me, that incontinently I slunk away from my own door, and did as desired. But not without
sundry twinges of impotent rebellion against the mild effrontery of this unaccountable scrivener. Indeed, it was his wonderful mildness chiefly, which not only
disarmed me, but unmanned me, as it were. For I consider that one, for the time,
is a sort of unmanned when he tranquilly permits his hired clerk to dictate to him,
and order him away from his own premises. Furthermore, I was full of uneasiness
as to what Bartleby could possibly be doing in my office in his shirt-sleeves, and in   490
an otherwise dismantled condition of a Sunday morning. Was anything amiss
going on? Nay, that was out of the question. It was not to be thought of for a moment that Bartleby was an immoral person. But what could he be doing there?—
copying? Nay again, whatever might be his eccentricities, Bartleby was an
eminently decorous person. He would be the last man to sit down to his desk in
any state approaching to nudity. Besides, it was Sunday; and there was something
about Bartleby that forbade the supposition that he would by any secular occupation violate the proprieties of the day

Nevertheless, my mind was not pacified; and full of a restless curiosity, at
last I returned to the door. Without hindrance I inserted my key, opened it, and   500
entered. Bartleby was not to be seen. I looked round anxiously, peeped behind his
screen; but it was very plain that he was gone. Upon more closely examining the
place, I surmised that for an indefinite period Bartleby must have ate, dressed, and
slept in my office, and that too without plate, mirror, or bed. The cushioned seat
of a rickety old sofa in one corner bore the faint impress of a lean, reclining form.
Rolled away under his desk, I found a blanket; under the empty grate, a blacking
box and brush; on a chair, a tin basin, with soap and a ragged towel; in a newspaper a few crumbs of ginger-nuts and a morsel of cheese. Yes, thought I, it is evident enough that Bartleby has been making his home here, keeping bachelor's hall
all by himself. Immediately then the thought came sweeping across me, what mis-   510
erable friendlessness and loneliness are here revealed! His poverty is great; but his
solitude, how horrible! Think of it. Of a Sunday, Wall Street is deserted as Petra;[11]
and every night of every day it is an emptiness. This building, too, which of weekdays hums with industry and life, at nightfall echoes with sheer vacancy, and all
through Sunday is forlorn. And here Bartleby makes his home; sole spectator of a
solitude which he has seen all populous—a sort of innocent and transformed
Marius brooding among the ruins of Carthage![12]

For the first time in my life a feeling of overpowering stinging melancholy
seized me. Before, I had never experienced aught but a not unpleasing sadness.
The bond of a common humanity now drew me irresistibly to gloom. A fraternal   520
melancholy! For both I and Bartleby were sons of Adam. I remembered the bright

11. Abandoned ancient city between the Dead Sea and the Gulf of Aqaba.
12. Ancient city in North Africa, near present-day Tunis. Destroyed by Rome in 146 B.C.

silks and sparkling faces I had seen that day, in gala trim, swan-like sailing down
the Mississippi of Broadway; and I contrasted them with the pallid copyist, and
thought to myself, Ah, happiness courts the light, so we deem the world is gay;
but misery hides aloof, so we deem that misery there is none. These sad fancy-
ings—chimeras, doubtless, of a sick and silly brain—led on to other and more
special thoughts, concerning the eccentricities of Bartleby. Presentiments of
strange discoveries hovered round me. The scrivener's pale form appeared to me
laid out, among uncaring strangers, in its shivering winding-sheet.[13]

Suddenly I was attracted by Bartleby's closed desk, the key in open sight left   530
in the lock.

I mean no mischief, seek the gratification of no heartless curiosity, thought I;
besides, the desk is mine, and its contents, too, so I will make bold to look within.
Everything was methodically arranged, the papers smoothly placed. The pigeon-
holes were deep, and removing the files of documents, I groped into their recesses.
Presently I felt something there, and dragged it out. It was an old bandanna handkerchief, heavy and knotted. I opened it, and saw it was a saving's bank.

I now recalled all the quiet mysteries which I had noted in the man. I remembered that he never spoke but to answer; that, though at intervals he had
considerable time to himself, yet I had never seen him reading—no, not even a   540
newspaper; that for long periods he would stand looking out, at his pale window
behind the screen, upon the dead brick wall; I was quite sure he never visited any
refectory or eating-house; while his pale face clearly indicated that he never drank
beer like Turkey, or tea and coffee even, like other men; that he never went anywhere in particular that I could learn; never went out for a walk, unless, indeed,
that was the case at present; that he had declined telling who he was, or whence
he came, or whether he had any relatives in the world; that though so thin and
pale, he never complained of ill-health. And more than all, I remembered a certain
unconscious air of pallid—how shall I call it?—of pallid haughtiness, say, or rather
an austere reserve about him, which had positively awed me into my tame compli-   550
ance with his eccentricities, when I had feared to ask him to do the slightest inci-
dental thing for me, even though I might know, from his long-continued
motionlessness, that behind his screen he must be standing in one of those dead-
wall reveries of his.

Revolving all these things, and coupling them with the recently discovered
fact, that he made my office his constant abiding place and home, and not forget-
ful of his morbid moodiness; revolving all these things, a prudential feeling began
to steal over me. My first emotions had been those of pure melancholy and sincer-
est pity; but just in proportion as the forlornness of Bartleby grew and grew to my
imagination, did that same melancholy merge into fear, that pity into repulsion. So   560
true it is, and so terrible, too, that up to a certain point the thought or sight of
misery enlists our best affections; but, in certain special cases, beyond that point it
does not. They err who would assert that invariably this is owing to the inherent
selfishness of the human heart. It rather proceeds from a certain hopelessness of
remedying excessive and organic ill. To a sensitive being, pity is not seldom pain.
And when at last it is perceived that such pity cannot lead to effectual succor,

13. Burial shroud.

common sense bids the soul be rid of it. What I saw that morning persuaded me
that the scrivener was the victim of innate and incurable disorder. I might give
alms to his body; but his body did not pain him; it was his soul that suffered, and
his soul I could not reach.   570

I did not accomplish the purpose of going to Trinity Church that morning.
Somehow, the things I had seen disqualified me for the time from church-going. I
walked homeward, thinking what I would do with Bartleby. Finally, I resolved
upon this—I would put certain calm questions to him the next morning, touching
his history, etc., and if he declined to answer them openly and unreservedly (and I
supposed he would prefer not), then to give him a twenty dollar bill over and
above whatever I might owe him, and tell him his services were no longer required; but that if in any other way I could assist him, I would be happy to do so,
especially if he desired to return to his native place, wherever that might be, I
would willingly help to defray the expenses. Moreover, if, after reaching home, he   580
found himself at any time in want of aid, a letter from him would be sure of a
reply.

The next morning came.

"Bartleby," said I, gently calling to him behind his screen.

No reply.

"Bartleby," said I, in a still gentler tone, "come here; I am not going to ask
you to do anything you would prefer not to do—I simply wish to speak to you."

Upon this he noiselessly slid into view.

"Will you tell me, Bartleby, where you were born?"

"I would prefer not to."   590

"Will you tell me *anything* about yourself?"

"I would prefer not to."

"But what reasonable objection can you have to speak to me? I feel friendly
towards you."

He did not look at me while I spoke, but kept his glance fixed upon my bust
of Cicero, which, as I then sat, was directly behind me, some six inches above my
head.

"What is your answer, Bartleby?" said I, after waiting a considerable time for
a reply, during which his countenance remained immovable, only there was the
faintest conceivable tremor of the white attenuated mouth.   600

"At present I prefer to give no answer," he said, and retired into his
hermitage.

It was rather weak in me I confess, but his manner, on this occasion, nettled
me. Not only did there seem to lurk in it a certain calm disdain, but his perverseness seemed ungrateful, considering the undeniable good usage and indulgence he
had received from me.

Again I sat ruminating what I should do. Mortified as I was at his behavior,
and resolved as I had been to dismiss him when I entered my office, nevertheless I
strangely felt something superstitious knocking at my heart, and forbidding me to
carry out my purpose, and denouncing me for a villain if I dared to breathe one   610
bitter word against this forlornest of mankind. At last, familiarly drawing my chair
behind his screen, I sat down and said: "Bartleby, never mind, then, about revealing your history; but let me entreat you, as a friend, to comply as far as may be

with the usages of this office. Say now, you will help to examine papers to-morrow or next day: in short, say now, that in a day or two you will begin to be a little reasonable:—say so, Bartleby."

"At present I would prefer not to be a little reasonable," was his mildly cadaverous reply.

Just then the folding-doors opened, and Nippers approached. He seemed suffering from an unusually bad night's rest, induced by severer indigestion than common. He overheard those final words of Bartleby. 620

"*Prefer not,* eh?" gritted Nippers—"I'd *prefer* him, if I were you, sir," addressing me—"I'd *prefer* him; I'd give him preferences, the stubborn mule! What is it, sir, pray, that he *prefers* not to do now?"

Bartleby moved not a limb.

"Mr. Nippers," said I, "I'd prefer that you would withdraw for the present."

Somehow, of late, I had got into the way of involuntarily using this word "prefer" upon all sorts of not exactly suitable occasions. And I trembled to think that my contact with the scrivener had already and seriously affected me in a mental way. And what further and deeper aberration might it not yet produce? This 630 apprehension had not been without efficacy in determining me to summary measures.

As Nippers, looking very sour and sulky, was departing, Turkey blandly and deferentially approached.

"With submission, sir," said he, "yesterday I was thinking about Bartleby here, and I think that if he would but prefer to take a quart of good ale every day, it would do much towards mending him, and enabling him to assist in examining his papers."

"So you have got the word, too," said I, slightly excited.

"With submission, what word, sir?" asked Turkey, respectfully crowding 640 himself into the contracted space behind the screen, and by so doing, making me jostle the scrivener. "What word, sir?"

"I would prefer to be left alone here," said Bartleby, as if offended at being mobbed in his privacy.

"*That's* the word, Turkey," said I—"*that's* it."

"Oh, *prefer*? oh yes—queer word. I never use it myself. But, sir, as I was saying, if he would but prefer—"

"Turkey," interrupted I, "you will please withdraw."

"Oh certainly, sir, if you prefer that I should."

As he opened the folding-door to retire, Nippers at his desk caught a 650 glimpse of me, and asked whether I would prefer to have a certain paper copied on blue paper or white. He did not in the least roguishly accent the word "prefer." It was plain that it involuntarily rolled from his tongue. I thought to myself, surely I must get rid of a demented man, who already has in some degree turned the tongues, if not the heads of myself and clerks. But I thought it prudent not to break the dismission at once.

The next day I noticed that Bartleby did nothing but stand at his window in his dead-wall revery. Upon asking him why he did not write, he said that he had decided upon doing no more writing.

"Why, how now? what next?" exclaimed I, "do no more writing?" 660

"No more."

"And what is the reason?"

"Do you not see the reason for yourself?" he indifferently replied.

I looked steadfastly at him, and perceived that his eyes looked dull and glazed. Instantly it occurred to me, that his unexampled diligence in copying by his dim window for the first few weeks of his stay with me might have temporarily impaired his vision.

I was touched. I said something in condolence with him. I hinted that of course he did wisely in abstaining from writing for a while; and urged him to embrace that opportunity of taking wholesome exercise in the open air. This, however, he did not do. A few days after this, my other clerks being absent, and being in a great hurry to dispatch certain letters by the mail, I thought that, having nothing else earthly to do, Bartleby would surely be less inflexible than usual, and carry these letters to the post-office. But he blankly declined. So, much to my inconvenience, I went myself.

Still added days went by. Whether Bartleby's eyes improved or not, I could not say. To all appearance, I thought they did. But when I asked him if they did, he vouchsafed no answer. At all events, he would do no copying. At last, in reply to my urgings, he informed me that he had permanently given up copying.

"What!" exclaimed I; "suppose your eyes should get entirely well—better than ever before—would you not copy then?"

"I have given up copying," he answered, and slid aside.

He remained as ever, a fixture in my chamber. Nay—if that were possible— he became still more of a fixture than before. What was to be done? He would do nothing in the office; why should he stay there? In plain fact, he had now become a millstone to me, not only useless as a necklace, but afflictive to bear. Yet I was sorry for him. I speak less than truth when I say that, on his own account, he occasioned me uneasiness. If he would but have named a single relative or friend, I would instantly have written, and urged their taking the poor fellow away to some convenient retreat. But he seemed alone, absolutely alone in the universe. A bit of wreck in the mid-Atlantic. At length, necessities connected with my business tyrannized over all other considerations. Decently as I could, I told Bartleby that in six days' time he must unconditionally leave the office. I warned him to take measures, in the interval, for procuring some other abode. I offered to assist him in this endeavor, if he himself would but take the first step towards a removal. "And when you finally quit me, Bartleby," added I, "I shall see that you go not away entirely unprovided. Six days from this hour, remember."

At the expiration of that period, I peeped behind the screen, and lo! Bartleby was there.

I buttoned up my coat, balanced myself; advanced slowly towards him, touched his shoulder, and said, "The time has come; you must quit this place; I am sorry for you; here is money; but you must go."

"I would prefer not," he replied, with his back still towards me.

"You *must*."

He remained silent.

Now I had an unbounded confidence in this man's common honesty. He had frequently restored to me sixpences and shillings carelessly dropped upon the floor, for I am apt to be very reckless in such shirt-button affairs. The proceeding, then, which followed will not be deemed extraordinary.

"Bartleby," said I, "I owe you twelve dollars on account; here are thirty-two; 710 the odd twenty are yours—Will you take it?" and I handed the bills towards him.

But he made no motion.

"I will leave them here, then," putting them under a weight on the table. Then taking my hat and cane and going to the door, I tranquilly turned and added—"After you have removed your things from these offices, Bartleby, you will of course lock the door—since every one is now gone for the day but you—and if you please, slip your key underneath the mat, so that I may have it in the morning. I shall not see you again; so good-bye to you. If, hereafter, in your new place of abode, I can be of any service to you, do not fail to advise me by letter. Good-bye, Bartleby, and fare you well."   720

But he answered not a word; like the last column of some ruined temple, he remained standing mute and solitary in the middle of the otherwise deserted room.

As I walked home in a pensive mood, my vanity got the better of my pity. I could not but highly plume myself on my masterly management in getting rid of Bartleby. Masterly I call it, and such it must appear to any dispassionate thinker. The beauty of my procedure seemed to consist in its perfect quietness. There was no vulgar bullying, no bravado of any sort, no choleric hectoring, and striding to and fro across the apartment, jerking out vehement commands for Bartleby to bundle himself off with his beggarly traps. Nothing of the kind. Without loudly 730 bidding Bartleby depart—as an inferior genius might have done—I *assumed* the ground that depart he must; and upon that assumption built all I had to say. The more I thought over my procedure, the more I was charmed with it. Nevertheless, next morning, upon awakening, I had my doubts—I had somehow slept off the fumes of vanity. One of the coolest and wisest hours a man has, is just after he awakes in the morning. My procedure seemed as sagacious as ever—but only in theory. How it would prove in practice—there was the rub. It was truly a beautiful thought to have assumed Bartleby's departure; but, after all, that assumption was simply my own, and none of Bartleby's. The great point was, not whether I had assumed that he would quit me, but whether he would prefer so to do. He was more 740 a man of preferences than assumptions.

After breakfast, I walked down town, arguing the probabilities *pro* and *con*. One moment I thought it would prove a miserable failure, and Bartleby would be found all alive at my office as usual; the next moment it seemed certain that I should find his chair empty. And so I kept veering about. At the corner of Broadway and Canal Street, I saw quite an excited group of people standing in earnest conversation.

"I'll take odds he doesn't," said a voice as I passed.

"Doesn't go?—done!" said I, "put up your money."

I was instinctively putting my hand in my pocket to produce my own, when 750 I remembered that this was an election day. The words I had overheard bore no reference to Bartleby, but to the success or non-success of some candidate for the mayoralty. In my intent frame of mind, I had, as it were, imagined that all Broadway shared in my excitement, and were debating the same question with me. I passed on, very thankful that the uproar of the street screened my momentary absent-mindedness.

As I had intended, I was earlier than usual at my office door. I stood listening for a moment. All was still. He must be gone. I tried the knob. The door was locked. Yes, my procedure had worked to a charm; he indeed must be vanished. Yet a certain melancholy mixed with this: I was almost sorry for my brilliant success. I was fumbling under the door mat for the key, which Bartleby was to have left there for me, when accidentally my knee knocked against a panel, producing a summoning sound, and in response a voice came to me from within—"Not yet; I am occupied."

It was Bartleby.

I was thunderstruck. For an instant I stood like the man who, pipe in mouth, was killed one cloudless afternoon long ago in Virginia, by summer lightning; at his own warm open window he was killed, and remained leaning out there upon the dreamy afternoon, till some one touched him, when he fell.

"Not gone!" I murmured at last. But again obeying that wondrous ascendancy which the inscrutable scrivener had over me, and from which ascendancy, for all my chafing, I could not completely escape, I slowly went down stairs and out into the street, and while walking round the block, considered what I should next do in this unheard-of perplexity. Turn the man out by an actual thrusting I could not; to drive him away by calling him hard names would not do; calling in the police was an unpleasant idea; and yet, permit him to enjoy his cadaverous triumph over me—this, too, I could not think of. What was to be done? or, if nothing could be done, was there anything further that I could *assume* in the matter? Yes, as before I had prospectively assumed that Bartleby would depart, so now I might retrospectively assume that departed he was. In the legitimate carrying out of this assumption, I might enter my office in a great hurry, and pretending not to see Bartleby at all, walk straight against him as if he were air. Such a proceeding would in a singular degree have the appearance of a home-thrust. It was hardly possible that Bartleby could withstand such an application of the doctrine of assumptions. But upon second thoughts the success of the plan seemed rather dubious. I resolved to argue the matter over with him again.

"Bartleby," said I, entering the office, with a quietly severe expression, "I am seriously displeased. I am pained, Bartleby. I had thought better of you. I had imagined you of such a gentlemanly organization, that in any delicate dilemma a slight hint would suffice—in short, an assumption. But it appears I am deceived. Why," I added, unaffectedly starting, "you have not even touched that money yet," pointing to it, just where I had left it the evening previous.

He answered nothing.

"Will you, or will you not, quit me?" I now demanded in a sudden passion, advancing close to him.

"I would prefer *not* to quit you," he replied, gently emphasizing the *not*.

"What earthly right have you to stay here? Do you pay any rent? Do you pay my taxes? Or is this property yours?"

He answered nothing.

"Are you ready to go on and write now? Are your eyes recovered? Could you copy a small paper for me this morning? or help examine a few lines? or step round to the post-office? In a word, will you do anything at all, to give a coloring to your refusal to depart the premises?"

He silently retired into his hermitage.

I was now in such a state of nervous resentment that I thought it but prudent to check myself at present from further demonstrations. Bartleby and I were alone. I remembered the tragedy of the unfortunate Adams and the still more unfortunate Colt in the solitary office of the latter; and how poor Colt, being dreadfully incensed by Adams, and imprudently permitting himself to get wildly excited, was at unawares hurried into his fatal act—an act which certainly no man 810 could possibly deplore more than the actor himself. Often it had occurred to me in my ponderings upon the subject that had that altercation taken place in the public street, or at a private residence, it would not have terminated as it did. It was the circumstance of being alone in a solitary office, up stairs, of a building entirely unhallowed by humanizing domestic associations—an uncarpeted office, doubtless, of a dusty, haggard sort of appearance—that it must have been, which greatly helped to enhance the irritable desperation of the hapless Colt.

But when this old Adam of resentment rose in me and tempted me concerning Bartleby, I grappled him and threw him. How? Why, simply by recalling the divine injunction: "A new commandment give I unto you, that ye love one an- 820 other." Yes, this it was that saved me. Aside from higher considerations, charity often operates as a vastly wise and prudent principle—a great safeguard to its possessor. Men have committed murder for jealousy's sake, and anger's sake, and hatred's sake, and selfishness' sake, and spiritual pride's sake; but no man, that ever I heard of, ever committed a diabolical murder for sweet charity's sake. Mere self-interest, then, if no better motive can be enlisted, should, especially with high-tempered men, prompt all beings to charity and philanthropy. At any rate, upon the occasion in question, I strove to drown my exasperated feelings towards the scrivener by benevolently construing his conduct. Poor fellow, poor fellow! thought I, he don't mean anything; and besides, he has seen hard times, and ought 830 to be indulged.

I endeavored, also, immediately to occupy myself, and at the same time to comfort my despondency. I tried to fancy, that in the course of the morning, at such time as might prove agreeable to him, Bartleby, of his own free accord, would emerge from his hermitage and take up some decided line of march in the direction of the door. But no. Half-past twelve o'clock came; Turkey began to glow in the face, overturn his inkstand, and become generally obstreperous; Nippers abated down into quietude and courtesy; Ginger Nut munched his noon apple; and Bartleby remained standing at his window in one of his profoundest dead-wall reveries. Will it be credited? Ought I to acknowledge it? That afternoon I left the 840 office without saying one further word to him.

Some days now passed, during which, at leisure intervals I looked a little into "Edwards on the Will," and "Priestley on Necessity." Under the circumstances, those books induced a salutary feeling. Gradually I slid into the persuasion that these troubles of mine, touching the scrivener, had been all predestinated from eternity, and Bartleby was billeted upon me for some mysterious purpose of an all-wise Providence, which it was not for a mere mortal like me to fathom. Yes, Bartleby, stay there behind your screen, thought I; I shall persecute you no more;

you are harmless and noiseless as any of these old chairs; in short, I never feel so private as when I know you are here. At last I see it, I feel it; I penetrate to the pre- 850 destinated purpose of my life. I am content. Others may have loftier parts to enact; but my mission in this world, Bartleby, is to furnish you with office-room for such period as you may see fit to remain.

I believe that this wise and blessed frame of mind would have continued with me, had it not been for the unsolicited and uncharitable remarks obtruded upon me by my professional friends who visited the rooms. But thus it often is, that the constant friction of illiberal minds wears out at last the best resolves of the more generous. Though to be sure, when I reflected upon it, it was not strange that people entering my office should be struck by the peculiar aspect of the unac- countable Bartleby, and so be tempted to throw out some sinister observations 860 concerning him. Sometimes an attorney, having business with me, and calling at my office, and finding no one but the scrivener there, would undertake to obtain some sort of precise information from him touching my whereabouts; but without heeding his idle talk, Bartleby would remain standing immovable in the middle of the room. So after contemplating him in that position for a time, the attorney would depart, no wiser than he came.

Also, when a reference was going on, and the room full of lawyers and wit- nesses, and business driving fast, some deeply-occupied legal gentleman present, seeing Bartleby wholly unemployed, would request him to run round to his (the legal gentleman's) office and fetch some papers for him. Thereupon, Bartleby 870 would tranquilly decline, and yet remain idle as before. Then the lawyer would give a great stare, and turn to me. And what could I say? At last I was made aware that all through the circle of my professional acquaintance, a whisper of wonder was running round, having reference to the strange creature I kept at my office. This worried me very much. And as the idea came upon me of his possibly turn- ing out a long-lived man, and keep occupying my chambers, and denying my au- thority; and perplexing my visitors; and scandalizing my professional reputation; and casting a general gloom over the premises; keeping soul and body together to the last upon his savings (for doubtless he spent but half a dime a day), and in the end perhaps outlive me, and claim possession of my office by right of his perpet- 880 ual occupancy: as all these dark anticipations crowded upon me more and more, and my friends continually intruded their relentless remarks upon the apparition in my room; a great change was wrought in me. I resolved to gather all my facul- ties together, and forever rid me of this intolerable incubus.

Ere revolving any complicated project, however, adapted to this end, I first simply suggested to Bartleby the propriety of his permanent departure. In a calm and serious tone, I commended the idea to his careful and mature consideration. But, having taken three days to meditate upon it, he apprised me, that his original determination remained the same; in short, that he still preferred to abide with me.   890

What shall I do? I now said to myself, buttoning up my coat to the last but- ton. What shall I do? what ought I to do? what does conscience say I *should* do with this man, or, rather, ghost. Rid myself of him, I must; go, he shall. But how? You will not thrust him, the poor, pale, passive mortal—you will not thrust such a helpless creature out of your door? you will not dishonor yourself by such cruelty?

No, I will not, I cannot do that. Rather would I let him live and die here, and then mason up his remains in the wall. What, then, will you do? For all your coaxing, he will not budge. Bribes he leaves under your own paper-weight on your table; in short, it is quite plain that he prefers to cling to you.

Then something severe, something unusual must be done. What! surely you 900 will not have him collared by a constable, and commit his innocent pallor to the common jail? And upon what ground could you procure such a thing to be done?—a vagrant, is he? What! he a vagrant, a wanderer, who refuses to budge? It is because he will *not* be a vagrant, then, that you seek to count him *as* a vagrant. That is too absurd. No visible means of support: there I have him. Wrong again: for indubitably he *does* support himself, and that is the only unanswerable proof that any man can show of his possessing the means so to do. No more, then. Since he will not quit me, I must quit him. I will change my offices; I will move else-where, and give him fair notice, that if I find him on my new premises I will then proceed against him as a common trespasser.   910

Acting accordingly, next day I thus addressed him: "I find these chambers too far from the City Hall; the air is unwholesome. In a word, I propose to remove my offices next week, and shall no longer require your services. I tell you this now, in order that you may seek another place."

He made no reply, and nothing more was said.

On the appointed day I engaged carts and men, proceeded to my chambers, and, having but little furniture, everything was removed in a few hours. Throughout, the scrivener remained standing behind the screen, which I directed to be removed the last thing. It was withdrawn; and, being folded up like a huge folio, left him the motionless occupant of a naked room. I stood in the entry 920 watching him a moment, while something from within me upbraided me.

I re-entered, with my hand in my pocket—and—and my heart in my mouth.

"Good-bye, Bartleby; I am going—good-bye, and God some way bless you; and take that," slipping something in his hand. But it dropped upon the floor, and then—strange to say—I tore myself from him whom I had so longed to be rid of.

Established in my new quarters, for a day or two I kept the door locked, and started at every footfall in the passages. When I returned to my rooms, after any little absence, I would pause at the threshold for an instant, and attentively listen, ere applying my key. But these fears were needless. Bartleby never came nigh me.   930

I thought all was going well, when a perturbed-looking stranger visited me, inquiring whether I was the person who had recently occupied rooms at No.———Wall Street.

Full of forebodings, I replied that I was.

"Then, sir," said the stranger, who proved a lawyer, "you are responsible for the man you left there. He refuses to do any copying; he refuses to do anything; he says he prefers not to; and he refuses to quit the premises."

"I am very sorry, sir," said I, with assumed tranquillity, but an inward tremor, "but, really, the man you allude to is nothing to me—he is no relation or appren-tice of mine, that you should hold me responsible for him."   940

"In mercy's name, who is he?"

"I certainly cannot inform you. I know nothing about him. Formerly I employed him as a copyist; but he has done nothing for me now for some time past."

"I shall settle him, then—good morning, sir."

Several days passed, and I heard nothing more; and, though I often felt a charitable prompting to call at the place and see poor Bartleby, yet a certain squeamishness, of I know not what, withheld me.

All is over with him, by this time, thought I, at last, when, through another week, no further intelligence reached me. But, coming to my room the day after, I found several persons waiting at my door in a high state of nervous excitement.   950

"That's the man—here he comes," cried the foremost one, whom I recognized as the lawyer who had previously called upon me alone.

"You must take him away, sir, at once," cried a portly person among them, advancing upon me, and whom I knew to be the landlord of No.———Wall Street. "These gentlemen, my tenants, cannot stand it any longer; Mr. B———," pointing to the lawyer, "has turned him out of his room, and he now persists in haunting the building generally, sitting upon the banisters of the stairs by day, and sleeping in the entry by night. Everybody is concerned; clients are leaving the offices; some fears are entertained of a mob; something you must do, and that without delay."   960

Aghast at this torrent, I fell back before it, and would fain have locked myself in my new quarters. In vain I persisted that Bartleby was nothing to me—no more than to any one else. In vain—I was the last person known to have anything to do with him, and they held me to the terrible account. Fearful, then, of being exposed in the papers (as one person present obscurely threatened), I considered the matter, and, at length, said, that if the lawyer would give me a confidential interview with the scrivener, in his (the lawyer's) own room, I would, that afternoon, strive my best to rid them of the nuisance they complained of.

Going up stairs to my old haunt, there was Bartleby silently sitting upon the banister at the landing.   970

"What are you doing here, Bartleby?" said I.

"Sitting upon the banister," he mildly replied.

I motioned him into the lawyer's room, who then left us.

"Bartleby," said I, "are you aware that you are the cause of great tribulation to me, by persisting in occupying the entry after being dismissed from the office?"

No answer.

"Now one of two things must take place. Either you must do something, or something must be done to you. Now what sort of business would you like to engage in? Would you like to re-engage in copying for some one?"

"No; I would prefer not to make any change."   980

"Would you like a clerkship in a dry-goods store?"

"There is too much confinement about that. No, I would not like a clerkship; but I am not particular."

"Too much confinement," I cried, "why, you keep yourself confined all the time!"

"I would prefer not to take a clerkship," he rejoined, as if to settle that little item at once.

"How would a bar-tender's business suit you? There is no trying of the eye-sight in that."

"I would not like it at all; though, as I said before, I am not particular."   990

His unwonted wordiness inspirited me. I returned to the charge.

"Well, then, would you like to travel through the country collecting bills for the merchants? That would improve your health."

"No, I would prefer to be doing something else."

"How, then, would going as a companion to Europe, to entertain some young gentleman with your conversation—how would that suit you?"

"Not at all. It does not strike me that there is anything definite about that. I like to be stationary. But I am not particular."

"Stationary you shall be, then," I cried, now losing all patience, and, for the first time in all my exasperating connection with him, fairly flying into a passion. 1000 "If you do not go away from these premises before night, I shall feel bound—indeed, I *am* bound—to—to—to quit the premises myself!" I rather absurdly concluded, knowing not with what possible threat to try to frighten his immobility into compliance. Despairing of all further efforts, I was precipitately leaving him, when a final thought occurred to me—one which had not been wholly unindulged before.

"Bartleby," said I, in the kindest tone I could assume under such exciting circumstances, "will you go home with me now—not to my office, but my dwelling—and remain there till we can conclude upon some convenient arrangement for you at our leisure? Come, let us start now, right away."   1010

"No: at present I would prefer not to make any change at all."

I answered nothing; but, effectually dodging every one by the suddenness and rapidity of my flight, rushed from the building, ran up Wall Street towards Broadway, and, jumping into the first omnibus, was soon removed from pursuit. As soon as tranquillity returned, I distinctly perceived that I had now done all that I possibly could, both in respect to the demands of the landlord and his tenants, and with regard to my own desire and sense of duty, to benefit Bartleby, and shield him from rude persecution. I now strove to be entirely care-free and quiescent; and my conscience justified me in the attempt; though, indeed, it was not so successful as I could have wished. So fearful was I of being again hunted out by the 1020 incensed landlord and his exasperated tenants, that, surrendering my business to Nippers, for a few days, I drove about the upper part of the town and through the suburbs, in my rockaway; crossed over to Jersey City and Hoboken, and paid fugitive visits to Manhattanville and Astoria. In fact, I almost lived in my rockaway[14] for the time.

When again I entered my office, lo, a note from the landlord lay upon the desk. I opened it with trembling hands. It informed me that the writer had sent to the police, and had Bartleby removed to the Tombs as a vagrant. Moreover, since I knew more about him than any one else, he wished me to appear at that place, and make a suitable statement of the facts. These tidings had a conflicting effect 1030 upon me. At first I was indignant; but at last, almost approved. The landlord's energetic, summary disposition, had led him to adopt a procedure which I do not

14. Open, four-wheeled carriage.

think I would have decided upon myself; and yet, as a last resort, under such peculiar circumstances, it seemed the only plan.

As I afterwards learned, the poor scrivener, when told that he must be conducted to the Tombs, offered not the slightest obstacle, but, in his pale, unmoving way, silently acquiesced.

Some of the compassionate and curious by-standers joined the party; and headed by one of the constables arm-in-arm with Bartleby, the silent procession filed its way through all the noise, and heat, and joy of the roaring thoroughfares at noon. 1040

The same day I received the note, I went to the Tombs, or, to speak more properly, the Halls of Justice. Seeking the right officer, I stated the purpose of my call, and was informed that the individual I described was, indeed, within. I then assured the functionary that Bartleby was a perfectly honest man, and greatly to be compassionated, however unaccountably eccentric. I narrated all I knew, and closed by suggesting the idea of letting him remain in as indulgent confinement as possible, till something less harsh might be done—though, indeed, I hardly knew what. At all events, if nothing else could be decided upon, the alms-house must receive him. I then begged to have an interview. 1050

Being under no disgraceful charge, and quite serene and harmless in all his ways, they had permitted him freely to wander about the prison, and, especially, in the inclosed grass-platted yards thereof. And so I found him there, standing all alone in the quietest of the yards, his face towards a high wall, while all around, from the narrow slits of the jail windows, I thought I saw peering out upon him the eyes of murderers and thieves.

"Bartleby!"

"I know you," he said, without looking round—"and I want nothing to say to you."

"It was not I that brought you here, Bartleby," said I, keenly pained at his 1060 implied suspicion. "And to you, this should not be so vile a place. Nothing reproachful attaches to you by being here. And see, it is not so sad a place as one might think. Look, there is the sky, and here is the grass."

"I know where I am," he replied, but would say nothing more, and so I left him.

As I entered the corridor again, a broad meat-like man, in an apron, accosted me, and, jerking his thumb over his shoulder, said—"Is that your friend?"

"Yes."

"Does he want to starve? If he does, let him live on the prison fare, that's all."

"Who are you?" asked I, not knowing what to make of such an unofficially 1070 speaking person in such a place.

"I am the grub-man. Such gentlemen as have friends here, hire me to provide them with something good to eat."

"Is this so?" said I, turning to the turnkey.

He said it was.

"Well, then," said I, slipping some silver into the grub-man's hands (for so they called him), "I want you to give particular attention to my friend there; let him have the best dinner you can get. And you must be as polite to him as possible."

"Introduce me, will you?" said the grub-man, looking at me with an expres- 1080
sion which seemed to say he was all impatience for an opportunity to give a specimen of his breeding.

Thinking it would prove of benefit to the scrivener, I acquiesced; and, asking
the grub-man his name, went up with him to Bartleby.

"Bartleby, this is a friend; you will find him very useful to you."

"Your sarvant, sir, your sarvant," said the grub-man, making a low salutation
behind his apron. "Hope you find it pleasant here, sir; nice grounds—cool apartments—hope you'll stay with us some time—try to make it agreeable. What will
you have for dinner to-day?"

"I prefer not to dine to-day," said Bartleby, turning away. "It would disagree 1090
with me; I am unused to dinners." So saying, he slowly moved to the other side of
the inclosure, and took up a position fronting the dead-wall.

"How's this?" said the grub-man, addressing me with a stare of astonishment.
"He's odd, ain't he?"

"I think he is a little deranged," said I, sadly.

"Deranged? deranged is it? Well, now, upon my word, I thought that friend
of yourn was a gentleman forger; they are always pale and genteel-like, them forgers. I can't help pity 'em—can't help it, sir. Did you know Monroe Edwards?" he
added, touchingly, and paused. Then, laying his hand piteously on my shoulder,
sighed, "he died of consumption at Sing-Sing. So you weren't acquainted with 1100
Monroe?"

"No, I was never socially acquainted with any forgers. But I cannot stop
longer. Look to my friend yonder. You will not lose by it. I will see you again."

Some few days after this, I again obtained admission to the Tombs, and went
through the corridors in quest of Bartleby; but without finding him.

"I saw him coming from his cell not long ago," said a turnkey, "may be he's
gone to loiter in the yards."

So I went in that direction.

"Are you looking for the silent man?" said another turnkey, passing me.
"Yonder he lies—sleeping in the yard there. 'Tis not twenty minutes since I saw 1110
him lie down."

The yard was entirely quiet. It was not accessible to the common prisoners.
The surrounding walls, of amazing thickness, kept off all sounds behind them.
The Egyptian character of the masonry weighed upon me with its gloom. But a
soft imprisoned turf grew under foot. The heart of the eternal pyramids, it seemed,
wherein, by some strange magic, through the clefts, grass-seed, dropped by birds,
had sprung.

Strangely huddled at the base of the wall, his knees drawn up, and lying on
his side, his head touching the cold stones, I saw the wasted Bartleby. But nothing
stirred. I paused; then went close up to him; stooped over, and saw that his dim 1120
eyes were open; otherwise he seemed profoundly sleeping. Something prompted
me to touch him. I felt his hand, when a tingling shiver ran up my arm and down
my spine to my feet.

The round face of the grub-man peered upon me now. "His dinner is ready.
Won't he dine to-day, either? Or does he live without dining?"

"Lives without dining," said I, and closed the eyes.

"Eh!—He's asleep, ain't he?"

"With kings and counselors," murmured I.

There would seem little need for proceeding further in this history. Imagination will readily supply the meagre recital of poor Bartleby's interment. But, ere parting with the reader, let me say, that if this little narrative has sufficently interested him, to awaken curiosity as to who Bartleby was, and what manner of life he led prior to the present narrator's making his acquaintance, I can only reply, that in such curiosity I fully share, but am wholly unable to gratify it. Yet here I hardly know whether I should divulge one little item of rumor, which came to my ear a few months after the scrivener's decease. Upon what basis it rested, I could never ascertain; and hence, how true it is I cannot now tell. But, inasmuch as this vague report has not been without a certain suggestive interest to me, however sad, it may prove the same with some others; and so I will briefly mention it. The report was this: that Bartleby had been a subordinate clerk in the Dead Letter Office at Washington, from which he had been suddenly removed by a change in the administration. When I think over this rumor, hardly can I express the emotions which seize me. Dead letters! does it not sound like dead men? Conceive a man by nature and misfortune prone to a pallid hopelessness, can any business seem more fitted to heighten it than that of continually handling these dead letters, and assorting them for the flames? For by the cart-load they are annually burned. Sometimes from out the folded paper the pale clerk takes a ring—the finger it was meant for, perhaps, moulders in the grave; a bank-note sent in swiftest charity—he whom it would relieve, nor eats nor hungers any more; pardon for those who died despairing; hope for those who died unhoping; good tidings for those who died stifled by unrelieved calamities. On errands of life, these letters speed to death.

Ah, Bartleby! Ah, humanity!

[1853]

Questions for Discussion and Writing

1. Describe your reaction to this story, especially to Bartleby. Analyze your reactions by specific references to the story. What incidents in particular influence your reaction?

2. The character of the narrator is complex and controversial. Underline passages that portray him favorably and those that portray him unfavorably. Compare these sets of passages. What picture emerges from this combination of qualities?

3. In your view, does the narrator do too much for Bartleby or too little? What more, if anything, should he have done?

4. Melville subtitles the story "A Tale of Wall Street." What part do walls (real and metaphorical) play in the story? What, if anything, do they symbolize?

5. Is Bartleby admirable in refusing to do what he would prefer not to? Why or why not?

6. Analyze Turkey, Nippers, and Ginger. What is their role in the story?

❧ HENRY JAMES
(1843–1916)

A Landscape Painter

Henry James' accomplishments as a novelist have overshadowed his work in the short story, but it was his conscious artistry and attention to form that helped to make the short story artistically acceptable both in America and England.

James was one of four sons born into a wealthy and cultured New York family. His father was a philosopher and theologian who educated his sons to be "citizens of the world." Consequently Henry, Jr., spent his formative years in Europe, immersing himself in the work of French Realists. After 1868, he lived abroad, becoming friends with Gustave Flaubert (1821–1893), Emile Zola (1840–1902), Guy de Maupasant (1850–1893), and Ivan Turgenev (1818–1883).

James writes almost exclusively about artists and intellectuals, the monied upper classes, and the aristocracy. He explores the cultural conflicts between Americans and Europeans, the role of the artist in society, the destructive influences of greed and lust, and the redemptive powers of love, generosity of spirit, and empathy.

Stylistically, James is a master of subtlety, rhythm, and complexity. Indeed, many critics fault his later novels for their dense, elaborate, nuanced prose, which at times dissolves into abstraction. But James was striving after subtle effects. He was not so much interested in depicting exterior reality as in recording the impressions that external reality makes on the minds of his characters. In this respect, he can be compared to Impressionist painters. He also wanted to demonstrate the actual workings of the mind and heart. "A Landscape Painter" is an early story that illustrates many of James's methods and demonstrates both his leisurely pace and perfect control over his materials.

D O YOU REMEMBER how, a dozen years ago, a number of our friends were startled by the report of the rupture of young Locksley's engagement with Miss Leary? This event made some noise in its day. Both parties possessed certain claims to distinction: Locksley in his wealth, which was believed to be enormous, and the young lady in her beauty, which was in truth very great. I used to hear that her lover was fond of comparing her to the Venus of Milo; and, indeed, if you can imagine the mutilated goddess with her full complement of limbs, dressed out by Madame de Crinoline,[1] and engaged in small-talk beneath the drawing-room chandelier, you may obtain a vague notion of Miss Josephine Leary. Locksley, you remember, was rather a short man, dark, and not particularly good-looking; and   10
when he walked about with his betrothed it was half a matter of surprise that he should have ventured to propose to a young lady of such heroic proportions. Miss

---

1. i.e., in crinoline, a stiffened cloth used for petticoats.

Leary had the gray eyes and auburn hair which I have always attributed to the famous statue. The one defect in her face, in spite of an expression of great candour
and sweetness, was a certain lack of animation. What it was besides her beauty
that attracted Locksley I never discovered; perhaps, since his attachment was so
short-lived, it was her beauty alone. I say that his attachment was of brief duration, because the break was understood to have come from him. Both he and Miss
Leary very wisely held their tongues on the matter; but among their friends and
enemies it of course received a hundred explanations. That most popular with 20
Locksley's well-wishers was, that he had backed out (these events are discussed,
you know, in fashionable circles very much as an expected prize-fight which has
miscarried is canvassed in reunions of another kind) only on flagrant evidence of
the lady's—what, faithlessness?—on over-whelming proof of the most *mercenary*
spirit on the part of Miss Leary. You see, our friend was held capable of doing battle for an "idea." It must be owned that this was a novel charge; but, for myself,
having long known Mrs. Leary, the mother, who was a widow with four daughters,
to be an inveterate old screw,[2] it was not impossible for me to believe that her
first-born had also shown the cloven foot. I suppose that the young lady's family
had, on their own side, a very plausible version of their disappointment. It was, 30
however, soon made up to them by Josephine's marriage with a gentleman of expectations very nearly as brilliant as those of her old suitor. And what was *his*
compensation? That is precisely my story.

Locksley disappeared, as you will remember, from public view. The events
above alluded to happened in March. On calling at his lodgings in April I was told
he had gone to the country. But toward the last of May I met him. He told me that
he was on the look-out for a quiet, unfrequented place at the seaside, where he
might rusticate and sketch. He was looking very poorly. I suggested Newport, and
I remember he hardly had the energy to smile at the simple joke. We parted without my having been able to satisfy him, and for a very long time I quite lost sight 40
of him. He died seven years ago, at the age of thirty-five. For five years, accordingly, he managed to shield his life from the eyes of men. Through circumstances
which I need not go into, a good many of his personal belongings have become
mine. You will remember that he was a man of what are called cultivated tastes;
that is, he was fond of reading, wrote a little, and painted a good deal. He wrote
some rather amateurish verse, but he produced a number of remarkable paintings.
He left a mass of papers, on many subjects, few of which are calculated to be generally interesting. A few of them, however, I highly prize—that portion which constitutes his private diary. It extends from his twenty-fifth to his thirtieth year, at
which period it breaks off suddenly. If you will come to my house I will show you 50
such of his pictures and sketches as I possess, and, I trust, convert you to my
opinion that he had in him the stuff of a charming artist. Meanwhile I will place
before you the last hundred pages of his diary, as an answer to your inquiry regarding the ultimate view taken by the great Nemesis[3] of his treatment of Miss
Leary—his scorn of the magnificent Venus Victrix.[4] The recent passing away of the

2. Greedy or miserly.
3. Goddess of retribution.
4. Goddess of victory.

one person who had a voice paramount to mine in the disposal of Locksley's effects enables me to act without reserve.

Chowderville, June 9th.—I have been sitting some minutes, pen in hand, wondering whether on this new earth, beneath this new sky, I had better resume this occasional history of nothing at all. I think I will at all events make the experiment. If we fail, as Lady MacBeth remarks, we fail. I find my entries have been longest when I have had least to say. I doubt not, therefore, that, once I have had a sufficient dose of dulness, I shall sit scribbling from morning till night. If nothing happens—But my prophetic soul tells me that something *will* happen. I am determined that something shall—if it be nothing else than that I paint a picture.

When I came up to bed half-an-hour ago I was deadly sleepy. Now, after looking out of the window a little, my brain is immensely refreshed, and I feel as if I could write till morning. But, unfortunately, I have nothing to write about. And then, if I expect to rise early, I must turn in betimes. The whole village is asleep, godless metropolitan that I am! The lamps on the square, outside, flicker in the wind; there is nothing abroad but the blue darkness and the smell of the rising tide. I have spent the whole day on my legs, trudging from one side of the peninsula to the other. What a trump is old Mrs Monkhouse, to have thought of this place! I must write her a letter of passionate thanks. Never before have I seen such a pretty little coast—never before have I been so taken with wave and rock and cloud. I am filled with ecstasy at the life, light, and transparency of the air. I am enamoured of all the moods and tenses of the ocean; and as yet, I suppose, I have not seen half of them. I came in to supper hungry, weary, footsore, sunburnt, dirty—happier, in short, than I have been for a twelvemonth. And now, if you please, for the prodigies of the brush!

June 11th.—Another day afoot, and also afloat. I resolved this morning to leave this abominable little tavern; I can't stand my feather-bed another night. I determined to find some other prospect than the town-pump and the "drugstore." I questioned my host, after breakfast, as to the possibility of getting lodgings in any of the outlying farms and cottages. But my host either did not or would not know anything about the matter. So I resolved to wander forth and seek my fortune—to roam inquisitive through the neighbourhood and appeal to the indigenous sentiment of hospitality. But never have I seen a folk so devoid of this amiable quality. By dinner-time I had given up in despair. After dinner I strolled down to the harbour, which is close at hand. The brightness and breeziness of the water tempted me to hire a boat and resume my explorations. I procured an old tub, with a short stump of a mast, which, being planted quite in the centre, gave the craft much the appearance of an inverted mushroom. I made for what I took to be, and what is, an island, lying long and low, some four or five miles over against the town. I sailed for half-an-hour directly before the wind, and at last found myself aground on the shelving beach of a quiet little cove. Such a dear little cove—so bright, so still, so warm, so remote from Chowderville, which lay in the distance, white and semi-circular! I leaped ashore, and dropped my anchor. Before me rose a steep cliff, crowned with an old ruined fort or tower. I made my way up, and round to the landward entrance. The fort is a hollow old shell; looking upwards, from the beach, you see the harmless blue sky through the gaping loopholes. Its interior is choked with rocks and brambles and masses of fallen masonry. I scrambled up to the parapet, and obtained a noble sea-view. Beyond the broad bay I saw the miniature town and country mapped out before me; and on the other hand, I saw the infinite Atlantic—over which, by the by, all the pretty things are brought from Paris. I spent the whole afternoon in wandering hither and thither on the hills that encircle the little cove in which I had landed, heedless of the minutes and the miles, watching the sailing clouds and the flitting, gleaming sails, listening to the musical attrition of the tidal pebbles, passing the time anyhow. The only particular sensation I remember was that of being ten years 110 old again, together with a general impression of Saturday afternoon, of the liberty to go in wading or even swimming, and of the prospect of limping home in the dusk with a wondrous story of having almost caught a turtle. When I returned I found—but I know very well what I found, and I need hardly repeat it here for my mortification. Heaven knows I never was a practical character. What thought I about the tide? There lay the old tub, high and dry, with the rusty anchor protruding from the flat green stones and the shallow puddles left by the receding wave. Moving the boat an inch, much more a dozen yards, was quite beyond my strength. I slowly reascended the cliff, to see if from its summit any help was discernible. None was within sight, and I was about to go down again, in profound 120 dejection, when I saw a trim little sail-boat shoot out from behind a neighbouring bluff, and advance along the short. I quickened pace. On reaching the beach I found the new-comer standing out about a hundred yards. The man at the helm appeared to regard me with some interest. With a mute prayer that his disposition might not be hostile—he didn't look like a wild islander—I invited him by voice and gesture to make for a little point of rocks a short distance above us, where I proceeded to join him. I told him my story, and he readily took me aboard. He was a civil old gentleman, of the seafaring sort, who appeared to be cruising about in the evening-breeze for his pleasure. On landing I visited the proprietor of my old tub, related my misadventure, and offered to pay damages if the boat shall 130 turn out in the morning to have sustained any. Meanwhile, I suppose, it is held secure against the next tidal revolution, however violent.

But for my old gentleman. I have decidedly picked up an acquaintance, if not made a friend. I gave him a very good cigar, and before we reached home we had become thoroughly intimate. In exchange for my cigar he gave me his name; and there was that in his tone which seemed to imply that I had by no means the worst of the exchange. His name is Richard Quarterman, "though most people," he added, "call me Cap'n, for respect." He then proceeded to inquire my own titles and pretensions. I told him no lies, but I told him only half the truth; and if he chooses to indulge mentally in any romantic understatements, why, he is welcome, 140 and bless his simple heart! The fact is, I have simply broken with the past. I have decided, coolly and calmly, as I believe, that it is necessary to my success, or, at any rate, to my happiness, to abjure for a while my conventional self, and to assume a simple, natural character. How can a man be simple and natural who is known to have a large income? That is the supreme curse. It's bad enough to have it; to be known to have it, to be known only because you have it, is most damnable. I suppose I am too proud to be successfully rich. Let me see how poverty will serve my turn. I have taken a fresh start—I have determined to stand upon my merits. If they fail me I shall fall back upon my dollars, but with God's

help I will test them, and see what kind of stuff I am made of. To be young, strong 150
and poor—such in this blessed nineteenth century, is the great basis of solid success. I have resolved to take at least one brief draught from the founts of inspiration of my time. I replied to Captain Quarterman with such reservations as a brief
survey of these principles dictated. What a luxury to pass in a poor man's mind for
his brother! I begin to respect myself. Thus much the Captain knows: that I am an
educated man, with a taste for painting; that I have gone hither for the purpose of
studying and sketching coast-scenery; toning myself up with the sea air. I have
reason to believe, moreover, that he suspects me of limited means and of being a
very frugal mind. Amen! *Vogue la galère!*[5] But the point of my story is in his very
hospitable offer of lodgings—I had been telling him of my want of success in the 160
morning in the pursuit of the same. He is a queer mixture of the gentleman of the
old school and the hot-headed merchant-captain.

"Young man," said he, after taking several meditative puffs of his cigar, "I
don't see the point of your living in a tavern when there are folks about you with
more house-room than they know what to do with. A tavern is only half a house,
just as one of these new-fashioned screw-propellers is only half a ship. Suppose
you walk round and take a look at my place. I own quite a respectable tenement
over yonder to the left of the town. Do you see that old wharf with the tumble-
down warehouses, and the long row of elms behind it? I live right in the midst of
the elms. We have the sweetest little garden in the world, stretching down to the 170
water's edge. It's all as quiet as anything can be, short of a churchyard. The back
windows, you know, overlook the harbour; and you can see twenty miles up the
bay, and fifty miles out to sea. You can paint to yourself there the livelong day,
with no more fear of intrusion than if you were out yonder at the light-ship.
There's no one but myself and my daughter, who's a perfect lady, sir. She teaches
music in a young ladies' school. You see, money's an object, as they say. We have
never taken boarders yet, because none ever came in our track; but I guess we can
learn the ways. I suppose you've boarded before; you can put us up to a thing or
two."

There was something so kindly and honest in the old man's weather-beaten 180
face, something so friendly in his address, that I forthwith struck a bargain with
him, subject to his daughter's approval. I am to have her answer to-morrow. This
same daughter strikes me as rather a dark spot in the picture. Teacher in a young
ladies' school—probably the establishment of which Mrs. Monkhouse spoke to
me. I suppose she's over thirty. I think I know the species.

June 12th, A.M.—I have really nothing to do but to scribble. "Barkis is willing".[6] Captain Quarterman brought me word this morning that his daughter
makes no objection. I am to report this evening; but I shall send my slender baggage in an hour or two.

P.M.—Here I am, domiciled, almost domesticated. The house is less than a 190
mile from the inn, and reached by a very pleasant road, which skirts the harbour.
At about six o'clock I presented myself; Captain Quarterman had described the

5. Come what may.
6. In Dicken's novel *David Copperfield*, Barkis is a very obliging character whose motto is, "Barkis is willing."

place. A very civil old negress admitted me, and ushered me into the garden, where I found my friends watering their flowers. The old man was in his house-coat and slippers—he gave me a cordial welcome. There is something delightfully easy in his manners—and in Miss Quarterman's, too for that matter. She received me very nicely. The late Mrs. Quarterman was probably a superior being. As for the young lady's being thirty, she is about twenty-four. She wore a fresh white dress, with a blue ribbon on her neck, and a rosebud in her button-hole—or whatever corresponds to the button-hole on the feminine bosom. I thought I dis- 200 cerned in this costume, a vague intention of courtesy, of gaiety, of celebrating my arrival. I don't believe Miss Quarterman wears white muslin every day. She shook hands with me, and made me a pleasing little speech about their taking me in. "We have never had any inmates before," said she; "and we are consequently new to the business. I don't know what you expect. I hope you don't expect a great deal. You must ask for anything you want. If we can give it, we shall be very glad to do so; if we can't, I give you warning that we shall simply tell you so." Brava, Miss Quarterman! The best of it is, that she is decidedly beautiful—and in the grand manner; tall, and with roundness in her lines. What is the orthodox de-scription of a pretty girl?—white and red? Miss Quarterman is not a pretty girl, 210 she is a handsome woman. She leaves an impression of black and red; that is, she is a brunette with colour. She has a great deal of wavy black hair, which encircles her head like a dusky glory, a smoky halo. Her eyebrows, too, are black, but her eyes themselves are of a rich blue gray, the colour of those slate-cliffs which I saw yesterday, weltering under the tide. She has perfect teeth, and her smile is almost unnaturally brilliant. Her chin is surpassingly round. She has a capital movement, too, and looked uncommonly well as she strolled in the garden-path with a big spray of geranium lifted to her nose. She has very little to say, apparently, but when she speaks, it is to the point, and if the point suggests it, she doesn't hesitate to laugh very musically. Indeed, if she is not talkative, it is not from timidity. Is it 220 from indifference? Time will elucidate this, as well as other mysteries. I cling to the hypothesis that she is amiable. She is, moreover, intelligent; she is probably fond of keeping herself *to* herself, as the phrase is, and is even, possibly, very proud. She is, in short, a woman of character. There you are, Miss Quarterman, at as full length as I can paint you. After tea she gave us some music in the parlour. I con-fess that I was more taken with the picture of the dusky little room, lighted by the single candle on the piano, and by her stately way of sitting at the instrument, than by the quality of her playing, though that is evidently high.

June 18th.—I have now been here almost a week. I occupy two very pleasant rooms. My painting-room is a large and rather bare apartment, with a very good 230 north light. I have decked it out with a few old prints and sketches, and have al-ready grown very fond of it. When I had disposed my artistic odds and ends so as to make it look as much like a studio as possible, I called in my hosts. The Captain snuffed about, silently, for some moments, and then inquired hopefully if I had ever tried my hand at a ship. On learning that I had not yet got to ships, he relapsed into a prudent reserve. His daughter smiled and questioned, very gra-ciously, and called everything beautiful and delightful; which rather disappointed me, as I had taken her to be a woman of some originality. She is rather a puzzle. Or is she, indeed, a very commonplace person, and the fault in me, who am for-

ever taking women to mean a great deal more than their Maker intended? 240
Regarding Miss Quarterman I have collected a few facts. She is not twenty-four,
but twenty-seven years old. She has taught music ever since she was twenty, in a
large boarding-school just out of the town, where she originally obtained her education. Her salary in this establishment, which is, I believe, a tolerably flourishing
one, and the proceeds of a few additional lessons, constitute the chief revenues of
the household. But the Captain fortunately owns his house, and his needs and
habits are of the simplest kind. What does he or his daughter know of the great
worldly theory of necessities, the great worldly scale of pleasures? The young
lady's only luxuries are a subscription to the circulating library, and an occasional
walk on the beach, which, like one of Miss Brontë's heroines, she paces in com- 250
pany with an old Newfoundland dog. I am afraid she is sadly ignorant. She reads
nothing but novels. I am bound to believe, however, that she has derived from the
perusal of these works a certain second-hand acquaintance with life. "I read all the
novels I can get," she said yesterday; "but I only like the good ones. I do so like
The Missing Bride, which I have just finished." I must set her to work at some of
the masters. I should like some of those fretful daughters of gold, in New York, to
see how this woman lives. I wish, too, that half a dozen of *ces messieurs*[7] of the
clubs might take a peep at the present way of life of their humble servant. We
breakfast at eight o'clock. Immediately afterwards Miss Quarterman, in a shabby
old bonnet and shawl, starts off to school. If the weather is fine the Captain goes 260
a-fishing, and I am left quite to my own devices. Twice I have accompanied the
old man. The second time I was lucky enough to catch a big blue-fish, which we
had for dinner. The Captain is an excellent specimen of the pure navigator, with
his loose blue clothes, his ultra-divergent legs, his crisp white hair, his jolly thick-
skinned visage. He comes of a sea-faring English race. There is more or less of the
ship's cabin in the general aspect of this antiquated house. I have heard the winds
whistle about its walls, on two or three occasions, in true mid-ocean style. And
then the illusion is heightened, somehow or other, by the extraordinary intensity
of the light. My painting-room is a grand observatory of the clouds. I sit by the
half-hour watching them sail past my high uncurtained windows. At the back part 270
of the room something tells you that they belong to an ocean-sky; and there, in
truth, as you draw nearer, you behold the vast gray complement of sea. This quarter of the town is perfectly quiet. Human activity seems to have passed over it,
never again to return, and to have left a deposit of melancholy resignation. The
streets are clean, bright and airy; but this fact only deepens the impression of vanished uses. It seems to say that the protecting heavens look down on their decline
and can't help them. There is something ghostly in the perpetual stillness. We frequently hear the rattling of the yards and the issuing of orders on the barks and
schooners anchored out in the harbour.

    June 28th.—My experiment works far better than I had hoped. I am thor- 280
oughly at my ease; my peace of mind quite passeth understanding. I work diligently; I have none but pleasant thoughts. The past has almost lost its bitterness.
For a week, now, I have been out sketching daily. The Captain carries me to a certain point on the short of the bay, I disembark and strike across the uplands to a

---

7. Gentlemen.

spot where I have taken a kind of tryst with a particular effect of rock and shadow, which has been tolerably faithful to its appointment. Here I set up my easel, and paint till sunset. Then I retrace my steps and meet the boat. I am in every way much encouraged; the horizon of my work grows perceptibly wider. And then I am inexpressibly happy in the conviction that I am not wholly unfit for a life of (moderate) industry and (comparative) privation. I am quite in love with my 290 poverty, if I may call it so. And why should I not? At this rate I don't spend eight hundred a year.

July 12th.—We have been having a week of bad weather: constant rain, night and day. This is certainly at once the brightest and the blackest spot in New England. The skies can smile, assuredly, but they have also lachrymal moods. I have been painting rather languidly, and at a great disadvantage, at my window. . . . Through all pouring and pattering Miss Miriam—her name is Miriam, and it exactly fits her—sallies forth to her pupils. She envelops her beautiful head in a great woollen hood, her beautiful figure in a kind of feminine mackintosh; her feet she puts into heavy clogs, and over the whole she balances a cotton umbrella. When 300 she comes home, with the rain-drops glistening on her rich cheeks and her dark lashes, her cloak bespattered with mud and her hands red with the cool damp, she is a very honourable figure. I never fail to make her a very low bow, for which she repays me with a familiar, but not a vulgar, nod. The working-day side of her character is what especially pleases me in Miss Quarterman. This holy working-dress sits upon her with the fine effect of an antique drapery. Little use has she for whale-bones and furbelows.[8] What a poetry there is, after all, in red hands! I kiss yours, Mademoiselle. I do so because you are self-helpful; because you earn your living; because you are honest, simple, and ignorant (for a sensible woman, that is); because you speak and act to the point; because, in short, you are so unlike— 310 certain of your sisters.

July 16th.—On Monday it cleared up generously. When I went to my window, on rising, I found sky and sea looking, for their brightness and freshness, like a clever English water-colour. The ocean is of a deep purple blue; above it, the pure, bright sky looks pale, though it hangs over the island horizon a canopy of denser tissue. Here and there on the dark, breezy water gleams the white cap of a wave, or flaps the white cloak of a fishing-boat. I have been sketching sedulously; I have discovered, within a couple of miles' walk, a large, lonely pond, set in a really grand landscape of barren rocks and grassy slopes. At one extremity is a broad outlook on the open sea; at the other, buried in the foliage of an apple-orchard, 320 stands an old haunted-looking farm-house. To the west of the pond is a wide expanse of rock and grass, of sand and marsh. The sheep browse over it—poorly— as they might upon a Highland moor. Except a few stunted firs and cedars, there is not a tree in sight. When I want shade I have to look for it in the shelter of one of the large stones which hold up to the sun a shoulder coated with delicate gray, figured over with fine, pale, sea-green moss, or else in one of the long, shallow dells where a tangle of blackberry-bushes hedges about a pool that reflects the sky. I am giving my best attention to a plain brown hillside, and trying to make it look like something in nature; and as we have now had the same clear sky for several days,

8. Whalebone was used in women's corsets; furbelows were pleated borders on petticoats.

I have almost finished quite a satisfactory little study. I go forth immediately after 330
breakfast. Miss Quarterman supplies me with a little parcel of bread and cold
meat, which at the noonday hour, in my sunny solitude, within sight of the slumbering ocean, I voraciously convey to my lips with my discoloured fingers. At
seven o'clock I return to tea, at which repast we each tell the story of our day's
work. For poor Miss Quarterman it is always the same story: a wearisome round
of visits to the school, and to the houses of the mayor, the parson, the butcher, the
baker, whose young ladies, of course, all receive instruction on the piano. But she
doesn't complain, nor, indeed, does she look very weary. When she has put on a
fresh light dress for tea, and arranged her hair anew, and with these improvements
flits about with the quiet hither and thither of her gentle footstep, preparing our 340
evening meal, peeping into the teapot, cutting the solid loaf—or when, sitting
down on the low door-step, she reads out select scraps from the evening-paper—
or else when, tea being over, she folds her arms (an attitude which becomes her
mightily) and, still sitting on the door-step, gossips away the evening in comfortable idleness, while her father and I indulge in the fragrant pipe and watch the
lights shining out, one by one, in different quarters of the darkening bay: at these
moments she is as pretty, as cheerful, as careless as it becomes a sensible woman to
be. What a pride the Captain takes in his daughter, and she, in return, how perfect
is her devotion to the old man! He is proud of her grace, of her tact, or her good
sense, of her wit, such as it is. He believes her to be the most accomplished of 350
women. He waits upon her as if, instead of his old familiar Miriam, she were some
new arrival—say a daughter-in-law lately brought home. And à propos of daughters-in-law, if I were his own son he could not be kinder to me. They are certainly—nay, why should I not say it?—we are certainly a very happy little
household. Will it last for ever? I say we, because both father and daughter have
given me a hundred assurances—he direct, and she, if I don't flatter myself, after
the manner of her sex, indirect—that I am already a valued friend. It is natural
enough that they should like me, because I have tried to please them. The way to
the old man's heart is through a studied consideration of his daughter. He knows,
I imagine, that I admire Miss Quarterman, but if I should at any time fall below 360
the mark of ceremony, I should have an account to settle with him. All this is as it
should be. When people have to economise with the dollars and cents, they have
a right to be splendid in their feelings. I have done my best to be nice to the
stately Miriam without making love to her. That I haven't done that, however, is a
fact which I do not, in any degree, set down here to my credit; for I would defy
the most impertinent of men (whoever he is) to forget himself with this young
lady. Those animated eyes have a power to keep people in their place. I mention
the circumstance simply because in future years, when my charming friend shall
have become a distant shadow, it will be pleasant, in turning over these pages, to
find written testimony to a number of points which I shall be apt to charge solely 370
upon my imagination. I wonder whether Miss Quarterman, in days to come, referring to the tables of her memory for some trivial matter-of-fact, some prosaic date
or half-buried landmark, will also encounter this little secret of ours, as I may call
it—will decipher an old faint note to this effect, overlaid with the memoranda of
intervening years. Of course she will. Sentiment aside, she is a woman of a retentive faculty. Whether she forgives or not I know not; but she certainly doesn't for-

get. Doubtless, virtue is its own reward; but there is a double satisfaction in being polite to a person on whom it tells!

Another reason for my pleasant relations with the Captain is, that I afford him a chance to rub up his rusty worldly lore and trot out his little scraps of old-fashioned reading, some of which are very curious. It is a great treat for him to spin his threadbare yarns over again to a submissive listener. These warm July evenings, in the sweet-smelling garden, are just the proper setting for his traveller's tales. An odd enough understanding subsists between us on this point. Like many gentlemen of his calling, the Captain is harassed by an irresistible desire to romance, even on the least promising themes; and it is vastly amusing to observe how he will auscultate, as it were, his auditor's inmost mood, to ascertain whether it is in condition to be practised upon. Sometimes his artless fables don't "take" at all: they are very pretty, I conceive, in the deep and briny well of the Captain's fancy, but they won't bear being transplanted into the dry climate of my land-bred mind. At other times, the auditor being in a dreamy, sentimental, and altogether unprincipled mood, he will drink the old man's salt-water by the bucketful and feel none the worse for it. Which is the worse, willfully to tell, or willfully to believe, a pretty little falsehood which will not hurt any one? I suppose you can't believe willfully; you only pretend to believe. My part of the game, therefore, is certainly as bad as the Captain's. Perhaps I take kindly to his beautiful perversions of fact because I am myself engaged in one, because I am sailing under false colours of the deepest dye. I wonder whether my friends have any suspicion of the real state of the case. How should they? I take for granted that I play my little part pretty well. I am delighted to find it comes so easy. I do not mean that I find little difficulty in foregoing my old luxuries and pleasures—for to these, thank heaven, I was not so indissolubly wedded that one wholesome shock could not loosen my bonds—but that I manage more cleverly than I expected to stifle those innumerable tacit allusions which might serve effectually to belie my character.

Sunday, July 20th.—This has been a very pleasant day for me; although in it, of course, I have done no manner of work. I had this morning a delightful *tête-à-tête* with my hostess. She had sprained her ankle coming down stairs, and so, instead of going forth to Sunday-school and to meeting, she was obliged to remain at home on the sofa. The Captain, who is of a very punctilious piety, went off alone. When I came into the parlour, as the church-bells were ringing, Miss Quarterman asked me if I never went to a place of worship.

"Never when there is anything better to do at home," said I.

"What is better than going to church?" she asked, with charming simplicity.

She was reclining on the sofa, with her foot on a pillow and her Bible in her lap. She looked by no means afflicted at having to be absent from divine service; and, instead of answering her question, I took the liberty of telling her so.

"I *am* sorry to be absent," said she. "You know it's my only festival in the week."

"So you look upon it as a festival."

"Isn't it a pleasure to meet one's acquaintance? I confess I am never deeply interested in the sermon, and I very much dislike teaching the children; but I like wearing my best bonnet, and singing in the choir, and walking part of the way home with—"

"With whom?"

"With anyone who offers to walk with me."

"With Mr Prendergast, for instance," said I.

Mr Prendergast is a young lawyer in the village, who calls here once a week, and whose attentions to Miss Quarterman have been remarked.

"Yes," she answered. "Mr Prendergast will do as an instance."

"How he will miss you!"   430

"I suppose he will. We sing off the same book. What are you laughing at? He kindly permits me to hold the book, while he stands with his hands in his pocket. Last Sunday I quite lost patience. 'Mr Prendergast,' said I, 'do hold the book! Where are your manners?' He burst out laughing in the midst of the reading. He will certainly have to hold the book to-day."

"What a masterful soul he is! I suppose he will call after meeting."

"Perhaps he will. I hope so."

"I hope he won't," said I, frankly. "I am going to sit down here and talk to you, and I wish our conversation not to be interrupted."

"Have you anything particular to say?"   440

"Nothing so particular as Mr Prendergast, perhaps."

Miss Quarterman has a very pretty affectation of being more matter-of-fact than she really is.

"His rights, then," she remarked, "are paramount to yours."

"Ah, you admit that he has rights?"

"Not at all. I simply assert that you have none."

"I beg your pardon. I have claims which I mean to enforce. I have a claim upon your undivided attention when I pay you a morning-call."

"You have had all the attention I am capable of. Have I been so very rude?"

"Not so very rude, perhaps, but rather inconsiderate. You have been sighing   450
for the company of a third person, whom you can't expect me to care much about."

"Why not, pray? If I, a lady, can put up with Mr Prendergast's society, why shouldn't you, one of his own sex?"

"Because he is so outrageously conceited. You, as a lady, or at any rate as a woman, like conceited men."

"Ah, yes; I have no doubt that I, as a woman, have all kinds of weak tastes. That's a very old story."

"Admit, at any rate, that our friend is conceited."

"Admit it! Why, I have said so a hundred times. I have told him so."   460

"Indeed, it has come to that, then?"

"To what, pray?"

"To that critical point in the friendship of a lady and gentleman when they bring against each other all kinds of delightful accusations and rebukes. Take care, Miss Quarterman! A couple of intelligent New-Englanders, of opposite sexes, young, unmarried, are pretty far gone, when they begin to scan each other's faults. So you told Mr Prendergast that he is conceited? And I suppose you added that he was also dreadfully satirical and sceptical? What was his rejoinder? Let me see. Did he ever tell you that you were a wee bit affected?"

"No; he left that for you to say, in this very ingenious manner. Thank you, sir." 470

"He left it for me to deny, which is a great deal prettier. Do you think the manner ingenious?"

"I think the matter, considering the day and hour, very profane, Mr Locksley. Suppose you go away and let me peruse my Bible."

"Meanwhile what shall I do?"

"Go and read yours, if you have one."

"My Bible," I said, "is the female mind."

I was nevertheless compelled to retire, with the promise of a second audience in half-an-hour. Poor Miss Quarterman owes it to her conscience to read a 480 certain number of chapters. In what a terrible tradition she has been reared, and what an edifying spectacle is the piety of women! Women find a place for everything in their commodious little minds, just as they do in their wonderfully subdivided trunks when they go on a journey. I have no doubt that this young lady stows away her religion in a corner, just as she does her Sunday-bonnet—and, when the proper moment comes, draws it forth, and reflects, while she puts it on before the glass and blows away the strictly imaginary dust (for what worldly impurity can penetrate through half a dozen layers of cambric and tissue-paper?): "Dear me, what a comfort it is to have a nice, fresh holiday-creed!"—When I returned to the parlour Miriam was still sitting with her Bible in her lap. Somehow 490 or other I no longer felt in the mood for jesting; so I asked her, without chaffing, what she had been reading, and she answered me in the same tone. She inquired how I had spent my half-hour.

"In thinking good Sabbath thoughts," I said. "I have been walking in the garden." And then I spoke my mind. "I have been thanking heaven that it has led me, a poor friendless wanderer, into so peaceful an anchorage."

"Are you so very poor and friendless?"

"Did you ever hear of an art-student who was not poor? Upon my word, I have yet to sell my first picture. Then, as for being friendless, there are not five people in the world who really care for me." 500

"*Really* care? I am afraid you look too close. And then I think five good friends is a very large number. I think myself very well-off with half-a-one. But if you are friendless, it's probably your own fault."

"Perhaps it is," said I, sitting down in the rocking-chair; "and also, perhaps it isn't. Have you found me so very difficult to live with? Haven't you, on the contrary, found me rather sociable?"

She folded her arms, and quietly looked at me for a moment, before answering. I shouldn't wonder if I blushed a little.

"You want a lump of sugar, Mr Locksley; that's the long and short of it. I haven't given you one since you have been here. How you must have suffered! But 510 it's a pity you couldn't have waited a little longer, instead of beginning to put out your paws and bark. For an artist, you are very slap-dash. Men never know how to wait. 'Have I found you very difficult to live with? haven't I found you sociable?' Perhaps, after all, considering what I have in my mind, it is as well that you asked for your lump of sugar. I have found you very indulgent. You let us off easily, but you wouldn't like us a bit if you didn't pity us. Don't I go deep? Sociable? ah, well, no—decidedly not! You are entirely too particular. You are considerate of me, because you know that I know that you are so. There's the rub, you see: I know that you know that I know it! Don't interrupt me; I am going to be striking. I want you to understand why I don't consider you sociable. You call poor Mr Prendergast 520 conceited, but, really, I believe he has more humility than you. He envies my father and me—thinks us so cultivated. You don't envy any one, and yet I don't think you're a saint. You treat us kindly because you think virtue in a lowly station ought to be encouraged. Would you take the same amount of pains for a person you thought your equal, a person equally averse with yourself to being under an obligation? There are differences. Of course it's very delightful to fascinate people. Who wouldn't? There is no harm in it, as long as the fascinator doesn't set up for a public benefactor. If I were a man, a clever man like yourself, who had seen the world, who was not to be dazzled and encouraged, but to be listened to, counted with, would you be equally amiable? It will perhaps seem absurd to you, and it 530 will certainly seem egotistical, but I consider myself sociable, for all that I have only a couple of friends—my father and Miss Blankenberg. That is, I mingle with people without any *arrière-pensée*.[9] Of course the people I see are mainly women. Not that I wish you to do so: on the contrary, if the contrary is agreeable to you. But I don't believe you mingle in the same way with men. You may ask me what I know about it! Of course I know nothing; I simply guess. When I have done, indeed, I mean to beg your pardon for all I have said; but until then, give me a chance. You are incapable of exposing yourself to be bored, whereas I take it as my waterproof takes the rain. You have no idea what heroism I show in the exercise of my profession! Every day I have occasion to pocket my pride and to stifle my 540 sense of the ridiculous—of which of course you think I haven't a bit. It is for instance a constant vexation to me to be poor. It makes me frequently hate rich women; it makes me despise poor ones. I don't know whether you suffer acutely from the smallness of your own means; but if you do, I dare say you shun rich men. I don't, I like to bleed; to go into rich people's houses, and to be very polite to the ladies, especially if they are very much dressed, very ignorant and vulgar. All women are like me in this respect, and all men more or less like you. That is, after all, the text of my sermon. Compared with us it has always seemed to me that you are arrant cowards—that we alone are brave. To be sociable you must have a great deal of patience. You are too fine a gentleman. Go and teach school, 550 or open a corner-grocery, or sit in a law-office all day, waiting for clients: then you will be sociable. As yet you are only selfish. It *is* your own fault if people don't care for you; you don't care for them. That you should be indifferent to their good opinion is all very well; but you don't care for their indifference. You are amiable, you are very kind, and you are also very lazy. You consider that you are working now, don't you? Many persons would not call it work."

It was now certainly my turn to fold my arms.

"And now," added my companion, as I did so, "be so good as to excuse me."

"This was certainly worth waiting for," said I. "I don't know what answer to

9. Mental reservation or ulterior motive.

make. My head swims. Sugar, did you say? I don't know whether you have been giving me sugar or vitriol. So you advise me to open a corner-grocery, do you?"

"I advise you to do something that will make you a little less satirical. You had better marry, for instance."

"*Je ne demande pas mieux.*[10] Will you have me? I can't afford it."

"Marry a rich woman."

I shook my head.

"Why not?" asked Miss Quarterman. "Because people would accuse you of being mercenary? What of that? I mean to marry the first rich man who offers. Do you know that I am tired of living alone in this weary old way, teaching little girls their scales, and turning and patching my dresses? I mean to marry the first man who offers."

"Even if he is poor?"

"Even if he is poor and has a hump."

"I am your man, then. Would you take me if I were to offer?"

"Try and see."

"Must I get upon my knees?"

"No, you needn't even do that. Am I not on mine? It would be too fine an irony. Remain as you are, lounging back in your chair, with your thumbs in your waistcoat."

If I were writing a romance now, instead of transcribing facts, I would say that I knew not what might have happened at this juncture had not the door opened and admitted the Captain and Mr Prendergast. The latter was in the highest spirits.

"How are you, Miss Miriam? So you have been breaking your leg, eh? How are you, Mr Locksley? I wish I were a doctor now. Which is it, right or left?"

In this simple fashion he made himself agreeable to Miss Miriam. He stopped to dinner and talked without ceasing. Whether our hostess had talked herself out in her very animated address to myself an hour before, or whether she preferred to oppose no obstacle to Mr Prendergast's fluency, or whether she was indifferent to him, I know not; but she held her tongue with that easy grace, that charming tacit intimation of "We could if we would," of which she is so perfect a mistress. This very interesting woman has a number of pretty traits in common with her town-bred sisters; only, whereas in these they are laboriously acquired, in her they are richly natural. I am sure that, if I were to plant her in Madison Square to-morrow, she would, after one quick, all-compassing glance, assume the *nil admirari*[11] in a manner to drive the finest lady of them all to despair. Prendergast is a man of excellent intentions but no taste. Two or three times I looked at Miss Quarterman to see what impression his sallies were making upon her. They seemed to produce none whatever. But I know better, *moi.*[12] Not one of them escaped her. But I suppose she said to herself that her impressions on this point were no business of mine. Perhaps she was right. It is a disagreeable word to use

10. "I ask for nothing more."
11. "I wonder at nothing."
12. "But I know better, I do."

of a woman you admire; but I can't help fancying that she has been a little soured. By what? Who shall say? By some old love-affair, perhaps.

July 24th.—This evening the Captain and I took a half-hour's turn about the port. I asked him frankly, as a friend, whether Prendergast wants to marry his daughter.

"I guess he does," said the old man, "and yet I hope he don't. You know what he is: he's smart, promising, and already sufficiently well-off. But somehow he isn't for a man what my Miriam is for a female."

"That he isn't!" said I; "and honestly, Captain Quarterman, I don't know who is—" 610

"Unless it be yourself," said the Captain.

"Thank you. I know a great many ways in which Mr Prendergast is more worthy of her than I."

"And I know one in which you are more worthy of her than he—that is in being what we used to call one of the old sort."

"Miss Quarterman made him sufficiently welcome in her quiet way on Sunday," I rejoined.

"Oh, she respects him," said Quarterman. "As she's situated, she might marry him on that. You see, she's weary of hearing little girls drum on the piano. With her ear for music," added the Captain, "I wonder she has borne it so long." 620

"She is certainly meant for better things," said I.

"Well," answered the Captain, who has an honest habit of depreciating your agreement when it occurs to him that he has obtained it for sentiments which fall somewhat short of the stoical—"well," said he, with a very dry, edifying expression, "she's born to do her duty. We are all of us born for that."

"Sometimes our duty is rather dismal," said I.

"So it be; but what's the help for it? I don't want to die without seeing my daughter provided for. What she makes by teaching is a pretty slim subsistence. There was a time when I thought she was going to be fixed for life, but it all blew 630 over. There was a young fellow here, from down Boston way, who came about as near to it as you can come when you actually don't. He and Miriam were excellent friends. One day Miriam came up to me, and looked me in the face, and told me she had passed her word.

"'Who to?' says I, though of course I knew, and Miriam told me as much. 'When do you expect to marry?' I asked.

"'When Alfred'—his name was Alfred—'grows rich enough,' says she.

"'When will that be?'

"'It may not be for years,' said Poor Miriam.

"A whole year passed, and, so far as I could see, the young man hadn't accu- 640 mulated very much. He was for ever running to and fro between this place and Boston. I asked no questions, because I knew that my poor girl wished it so. But at last, one day, I began to think it was time to take an observation, and see whereabouts we stood.

"'Has Alfred made his little pile yet?' I asked.

"'I don't know, father,' said Miriam.

"'When are you to be married?'

"'Never!' said my poor little girl, and burst into tears. 'Please ask me no questions,' said she. 'Our engagement is over. Ask me no questions.'

"'Tell me one thing,' said I: 'Where is that d——d scoundrel who has bro-   650
ken my daughter's heart?'

"You should have seen the look she gave me.

"'Broken my heart, sir? You are very much mistaken. I don't know who you mean.'

"'I mean Alfred Bannister,' said I. That was his name.

"'I believe Mr Bannister is in China,' says Miriam, as grand as the Queen of Sheba. And there was an end of it. I never learnt the ins and outs of it. I have been told that Bannister is amassing considerable wealth in the China-trade."

August 7th.—I have made no entry for more than a fortnight. They tell me I have been very ill; and I find no difficulty in believing them. I suppose I took cold,   660
sitting out so late, sketching. At all events, I have had a mild intermittent fever. I have slept so much, however, that the time has seemed rather short. I have been tenderly nursed by this kind old mariner, his daughter, and his black domestic. God bless them, one and all! I say his daughter, because old Cynthia informs me that for half-an-hour one morning, at dawn, after a night during which I had been very feeble, Miss Quarterman relieved guard at my bedside, while I lay sleeping like a log. It is very jolly to see sky and ocean once again. I have got myself into my easy-chair, by the best window, with my shutters closed and the lattice open; and here I sit with my book on my knee, scratching away feebly enough. Now and then I peep from my cool, dark sick-chamber out into the world of light. High   670
noon at midsummer—what a spectacle! There are no clouds in the sky, no waves on the ocean, the sun has it all to himself. To look long at the garden makes the eyes water. And we—"Hobbs, Nobbs, Stokes and Nokes"—propose to paint that luminosity. *Allons donc!*[13]

The handsomest of women has just tapped, and come in with a plate of early peaches. The peaches are of a gorgeous colour and plumpness; but Miss Quarterman looks pale and thin. The hot weather doesn't agree with her, and besides she is overworked. Damn her drudgery! Of course I thanked her warmly for her attentions during my illness. She disclaims all gratitude, and refers me to her father and the dusky Cynthia.   680

"I allude more especially," I said, "to that little hour at the end of a weary night when you stole in, like a kind of moral Aurora, and drove away the shadows from my brain. That morning, you know, I began to get better."

"It was indeed a very little hour," said Miss Quarterman, colouring. "It was about ten minutes." And then she began to scold me for presuming to touch a pen during my convalescence. She laughs at me, indeed, for keeping a diary at all. "Of all things, a sentimental man is the most despicable!" she exclaimed.

I confess I was somewhat nettled—the thrust seemed gratuitous.

"Of all things a woman without sentiment is the most wanting in sweetness."

"Sentiment and sweetness are all very well when you have time for them,"   690
said Miss Quarterman. " I haven't. I am not rich enough. Good morning!"

13. "Nonsense!"

Speaking of another woman, I would say that she flounced out of the room. But such was the gait of Juno[14] when she moved stiffly over the grass from where Paris stood with Venus holding the apple, gathering up her divine vestment and leaving the others to guess at her face.

Juno has just come back to say that she forgot what she came for half-an-hour ago. What will I be pleased to like for dinner?

"I have just been writing in my diary that you flounced out of the room," said I.

"Have you, indeed? Now you can write that I have bounced in. There's a nice   700
cold chicken downstairs," etc. etc.

August 14th.—This afternoon I sent for a light vehicle, and treated Miss Quarterman to a drive. We went successively over the three beaches. What a spin we had coming home! I shall never forget that breezy trot over Weston's Beach. The tide was very low, and we had the whole glittering, weltering strand to ourselves. There was a heavy blow last night, which has not yet subsided, and the waves have been lashed into a magnificent fury. Trot, trot, trot, trot, we trundled over the hard sand. The sound of the horse's hoofs rang out sharp against the monotone of the thunderous surf, as we drew nearer and nearer to the long line of the cliffs. At our left, almost from the zenith of the pale evening-sky to the high   710
western horizon of the tumultuous dark-green sea, was suspended, so to speak, one of those gorgeous vertical sunsets that Turner[15] sometimes painted. It was a splendid confusion of purple and green and gold—the clouds flying and floating in the wind like the folds of a mighty banner borne by some triumphal fleet which had rounded the curve of the globe. As we reached the point where the cliffs begin I pulled up, and we remained for some time looking at their long, diminishing, crooked perspective, blue and dun as it receded, with the white surge playing at their feet.

August 17th.—This evening, as I lighted my bedroom-candle, I saw that the Captain had something to say to me. So I waited below until my host and his   720
daughter had performed their usual osculation, and the latter had given me that confiding hand-shake which I never fail to extract.

"Prendergast has got his discharge," said the old man, when he heard his daughter's door close.

"What do you mean?"

He pointed with his thumb to the room above, where we heard, through the thin partition, the movement of Miss Quarterman's light step.

"You mean that he has proposed to Miss Miriam?"

The Captain nodded.

"And has been refused?"   730

"Flat."

"Poor fellow!" said I, very honestly. "Did he tell you himself?"

"Yes, with tears in his eyes. He wanted me to speak for him. I told him it was no use. Then he began to say hard things of my poor girl."

---

14. Paris judged a "beauty contest" involving Juno (Hera), Minerva (Athena), and Venus (Aphrodite). He gave the prize, a golden apple, to Aphrodite.
15. J. M. W. Turner (1775–1851), English painter

"A pack of falsehoods. He says she has no heart. She has promised always to regard him as a friend; it's more than I will, hang him!"

"Poor fellow!" said I; and now, as I write, I can only repeat, considering what a hope was here disappointed, Poor fellow!

August 23rd.—I have been lounging about all day, thinking of it, dreaming of it, spooning over it, as they say. This is a decided waste of time. I think, accordingly, the best thing for me to do is sit down and lay the ghost by writing out my little story.

On Thursday evening Miss Quarterman happened to intimate that she had a holiday on the morrow, it being the birthday of the lady in whose establishment she teaches.

"There is to be a tea-party at four o'clock in the afternoon for the resident pupils and teachers," Miriam said. "Tea at four! what do you think of that? And then there is to be a speech-making by the smartest young lady. As my services are not required I propose to be absent. Suppose, father, you take us out in your boat. Will you come, Mr Locksley? We shall have a neat little picnic. Let us go over to old Fort Plunkett, across the bay. We will take our dinner with us, and send Cynthia to spend the day with her sister, and put the housekey in our pocket, and not come home till we please."

I entered into the project with passion, and it was accordingly carried into execution the next morning, when—about ten o'clock—we pushed off from our little wharf at the garden-foot. It was a perfect summer's day; I can say no more for it; and we made a quiet run over to the point of our destination. I shall never forget the wondrous stillness which brooded over earth and water as we weighed anchor in the lee of my old friend—or old enemy—the ruined fort. The deep, translucent water reposed at the base of the warm sunlit cliff like a great basin of glass, which I half expected to hear shiver and crack as our keel ploughed through it. And how colour and sound stood out in the transparent air! How audibly the little ripples on the beach whispered to the open sky. How our irreverent voices seemed to jar upon the privacy of the little cove! The delicate rocks doubled themselves without a flaw in the clear, dark water. The gleaming white beach lay fringed with its deep deposits of odorous sea-weed, which looked like masses of black lace. The steep, straggling sides of the cliffs lifted their rugged angles against the burning blue of the sky. I remember, when Miss Quarterman stepped ashore and stood upon the beach, relieved against the cool darkness of a recess in the cliff, while her father and I busied ourselves with gathering up our baskets and fastening the anchor—I remember, I say, what a picture she made. There is a certain purity in the air of this place which I have never seen surpassed—a lightness, a brilliancy, a crudity, which allows perfect liberty of self-assertion to each individual object in the landscape. The prospect is ever more or less like a picture which lacks its final process, its reduction to unity. Miss Quarterman's figure, as she stood there on the beach, was almost *criarde;*[16] but how it animated the whole scene! Her light muslin dress, gathered up over her white petticoat, her little black mantilla,[17] the blue veil which she had knotted about her neck, the little silken dome

16. Loud, overdressed.
17. Short cape.

which she poised over her head in one gloved hand, while the other retained her
crisp draperies, and which cast down upon her face a sharp circle of shade, where   780
her cheerful eyes shone darkly and her parted lips said things I lost—these are
some of the points I hastily noted.

"Young woman," I cried out, over the water, "I do wish you might know how
pretty you look!"

"How do you know I don't?" she answered. "I should think I might. You
don't look so badly yourself. But it's not I; it's the aerial perspective."

"Hang it—I am going to become profane!" I called out again.

"Swear ahead," said the Captain.

"I am going to say you are infernally handsome."

"Dear me! is that all?" cried Miss Quarterman, with a little light laugh which   790
must have made the tutelar sirens of the cove ready to die with jealousy down in
their submarine bowers.

By the time the Captain and I had landed our effects our companion had
tripped lightly up the forehead of the cliff—in one place it is very retreating—and
disappeared over its crown. She soon returned, with an intensely white pocket-
handkerchief added to her other provocations, which she waved to us, as we
trudged upward, carrying our baskets. When we stopped to take breath on the
summit and wipe our foreheads, we of course rebuked her for roaming about idly
with her parasol and gloves.

"Do you think I am going to take any trouble or do any work?" cried Miss   800
Miriam, in the greatest good-humour. "Is not this my holiday? I am not going to
raise a finger, nor soil these beautiful gloves, for which I paid so much at Mr
Dawson's at Chowderville. After you have found a shady place for your provisions,
I should like you to look for a spring. I am very thirsty."

"Find the spring yourself, miss," said her father. "Mr Locksley and I have a
spring in this basket. Take a pull, sir."

And the Captain drew forth a stout black bottle.

"Give me a cup, and I will look for some water," said Miriam. "Only I'm so
afraid of the snakes! If you hear a scream you may know it's a snake."

"Screaming snakes!" said I; "that's a new species."   810

What cheap fun it all sounds now! As we looked about us shade seemed
scarce, as it generally is in this region. But Miss Quarterman, like the very adroit
and practical young person she is, for all that she would have me believe the contrary, immediately discovered flowing water in the shelter of a pleasant little dell,
beneath a clump of firs. Hither, as one of the young gentlemen who imitate
Tennyson[18] would say, we brought our basket, he and I; while Miriam dipped the
cup, and held it dripping to our thirsty lips, and laid the cloth, and on the grass
disposed the platters round. I should have to be a poet, indeed, to describe half
the happiness and the silly sweetness and artless revelry of this interminable summer's day. We ate and drank and talked; we ate occasionally with our fingers, we   820
drank out of the necks of our bottles, and we talked with our mouths full, as befits

18. Alfred, Lord Tennyson, English poet (1809–1892).

(and excuses) those who talk perfect nonsense. We told stories without the least point. The Captain and I made atrocious puns. I believe, indeed, that Miss Quarterman herself made one little punkin, as I called it. If there had been any superfluous representative of humanity present to notice the fact, I should say that we made fools of ourselves. But as there was no one to criticise us we were brilliant enough. I am conscious myself of having said several witty things, which Miss Quarterman understood: *in vino veritas*.[19] The dear old Captain twanged the long bow indefatigably. The bright high sun dawdled above us, in the same place, and drowned the prospect with light and warmth. One of these days I mean to paint a picture which, in future ages, when my dear native land shall boast a national school of art, will hang in the Salon Carré of the great central museum (located, let us say, in Chicago) and recall to folks—or rather make them forget—Giorgione, Bordone, and Veronese: A Rural Festival; three persons feasting under some trees; scene, nowhere in particular; time and hour, problematical. Female figure, a rich *brune;* young man reclining on his elbow; old man drinking. An empty sky, with no end of expression. The whole stupendous in colour, drawing, feeling. Artist uncertain; supposed to be Robinson, 1900.

After dinner the Captain began to look out across the bay, and, noticing the uprising of a little breeze, expressed a wish to cruise about for an hour or two. He proposed to us to walk along the shore to a point a couple of miles northward, and there meet the boat. His daughter having agreed to this proposition, he set off with the lightened hamper, and in less than half-an-hour we saw him standing out from shore. Miss Quarterman and I did not begin our walk for a long, long time. We sat and talked beneath the trees. At our feet a wide cleft in the hills—almost a glen—stretched down to the silent beach; beyond lay the familiar ocean-line. But, as many philosophers have observed, there is an end to all things. At last we got up. My companion remarked that, as the air was freshening, she supposed she ought to put on her shawl. I helped her to fold it into the proper shape, and then I placed it on her shoulders; it being an old shawl of faded red (Canton crape, I believe they call it), which I have seen very often. And then she tied her veil once more about her neck, and gave me her hat to hold, while she effected a partial redistribution of her hair-pins. By way of being humorous, I spun her hat round on my stick; at which she was kind enough to smile, as with downcast face and uplifted elbows she fumbled among her braids. And then she shook out the creases of her dress and drew on her gloves; and finally she said "Well!"—that inevitable tribute to time and morality which follows upon even the mildest forms of dissipation. Very slowly it was that we wandered down the little glen. Slowly, too, we followed the course of the narrow and sinuous beach, as it keeps to the foot of the low cliffs. We encountered no sign of human life. Our conversation I need hardly repeat. I think I may trust it to the keeping of my memory; it was the sort of thing that comes back to one—after. If something ever happens which I think *may,* that apparently idle hour will seem, as one looks back, very symptomatic, and what we didn't say be perceived to have been more significant than what we did. There was

19. "In wine is truth."

something between us—there *is* something between us—and we listened to its impalpable presence—I liken it to the hum (very faint) of an unseen insect—in the
golden stillness of the afternoon. I must add that if she expects, foresees, if she
waits, she does so with a supreme serenity. If she is my fate (and she has the air of
it), she is conscious that it's *her* fate to be so.

September 1st.—I have been working steadily for a week. This is the first day   870
of autumn. Read aloud to Miss Quarterman a little Wordsworth.[20]

September 10th. Midnight.—Worked without interruption—until yesterday,
inclusive, that is. But with the day now closing—or opening—begins a new era.
My poor vapid old diary, at last you shall hold a *fact*.

For three days past we have been having damp, autumnal weather; dusk has
gathered early. This evening, after tea, the Captain went into town—on business,
as he said: I believe, to attend some Poorhouse or Hospital Board. Miriam and I
went into the parlour. The place seemed cold; she brought in the lamp from the
dining-room, and proposed we should have a little fire. I went into the kitchen,
procured half-a-dozen logs, and, while she drew the curtains and wheeled up the   880
table, I kindled a lively, crackling blaze. A fortnight ago she would not have allowed me to do this without a protest. She would not have offered to do it herself—not she!—but she would have said that I was not here to serve, but to be
served, and would at least have made a show of calling the negress. I should have
had my own way, but we have changed all that. Miriam went to her piano, and I
sat down to a book. I read not a word, but sat considering my fate and watching it
come nearer and nearer. For the first time since I have known her (my fate) she
had put on a dark, warm dress; I think it was of the material called alpaca. The
first time I saw her (I remember such things) she wore a white dress with a blue
neck-ribbon; now she wore a black dress with the same ribbon. That is, I remem-   890
ber wondering, as I sat there eyeing her, whether it *was* the same ribbon, or merely
another like it. My heart was in my throat; and yet I thought of a number of trivialities of the same kind. At last I spoke.

"Miss Quarterman," I said, "do you remember the first evening I passed beneath your roof, last June?"

"Perfectly," she replied, without stopping.

"You played the same piece."

"Yes; I played it very badly, too. I only half knew it. But it is a showy piece,
and I wished to produce an effect. I didn't know then how indifferent you are to
music."   900

"I paid no particular attention to the piece. I was intent upon the performer."

"So the performer supposed."

"What reason had you to suppose so?"

"I am sure I don't know. Did you ever know a woman to be able to give a
reason when she has guessed aright?"

"I think they generally contrive to make up a reason afterwards. Come, what
was yours?"

"Well, you stared so hard."

20. William Wordsworth (1770–1850), English poet.

"Fie! I don't believe it. That's unkind."

"You said you wished me to invent a reason. If I really had one, I don't re- 910 member it."

"You told me you remembered the occasion in question perfectly."

"I meant the circumstances. I remember what we had for tea; I remember what dress I wore. But I don't remember my feelings. They were naturally not very memorable."

"What did you say when your father proposed that I should come here?"

"I asked how much you would be willing to pay?"

"And then?"

"And then, if you looked respectable."

"And then?"   920

"That was all. I told my father to do as he pleased."

She continued to play, and leaning back in my chair I continued to look at her. There was a considerable pause.

"Miss Quarterman," said I, at last.

"Well, sir?"

"Excuse me for interrupting you so often. But"—and I got up and went to the piano—"but, you know, I thank heaven that it has brought you and me together."

She looked up at me and bowed her head with a little smile, as her hands still wandered over the keys.   930

"Heaven has certainly been very good to us," said she.

"How much longer are you going to play?" I asked.

"I'm sure I don't know. As long as you like."

"If you want to do as I like, you will stop immediately."

She let her hands rest on the keys a moment, and gave me a rapid, questioning look. Whether she found a sufficient answer in my face I know not; but she slowly rose, and, with a very pretty affectation of obedience, began to close the instrument. I helped her to do so.

"Perhaps you would like to be quite alone," she said. "I suppose your own room is too cold."   940

"Yes," I answered, "you have hit it exactly. I wish to be alone. I wish to monopolise this cheerful blaze. Hadn't you better go into the kitchen and sit with the cook? It takes you women to make such cruel speeches."

"When we women are cruel, Mr Locksley, it is the merest accident. We are not wilfully so. When we learn that we have been unkind we very humbly ask pardon, without even knowing what our crime has been." And she made me a very low curtsey.

"I will tell you what your crime has been," said I. "Come and sit by the fire. It's rather a long story."

"A long story? Then let me get my work."   950

"Confound your work! Excuse me, but you exasperate me. I want you to listen to me. Believe me, you will need all your attention."

She looked at me steadily a moment, and I returned her glance. During that moment I was reflecting whether I might put my arm round her waist and kiss her; but I decided that I might do nothing of the sort. She walked over and quietly seated herself in a low chair by the fire. Here she patiently folded her arms. I sat down before her.

"With you, Miss Quarterman," said I, "one must be very explicit. You are not in the habit of taking things for granted. You have a great deal of imagination, but you rarely exercise it on behalf of other people."   960

"Is that my crime?" asked my companion.

"It's not so much a crime as a vice, and perhaps not so much a vice as a virtue. Your crime is, that you are so stone-cold to a poor devil who loves you."

She burst into a rather shrill laugh. I wonder whether she thought I meant Prendergast.

"Who are you speaking for, Mr Locksley?" she asked.

"Are there so many? For myself."

"Honestly?"

"Do you think me capable of deceiving you?"

"What is that French phrase that you are for ever using? I think I may say   970
'Allons donc!'"

"Let us speak plain English, Miss Quarterman."

"'Stone-cold' is certainly very plain English. I don't see the relative importance of the two branches of your proposition. Which is the principal, and which the subordinate clause—that I am stone-cold, as you call it, or that you love me, as you call it?"

"As I call it? What would you have me call it? For pity's sake, Miss Quarterman, be serious, or I shall call it something else. Yes, I love you. Don't you believe it?"

"How can I help believing what you tell me?"   980

"Dearest, bravest of women," said I.

And I attempted to take her hand.

"No, no, Mr Locksley," said she—"not just yet, if you please."

"Actions speak louder than words," said I.

"There is no need of speaking loud. I hear you perfectly."

"I certainly shall not whisper," said I; "although it is the custom, I believe, for lovers to do so. Will you be my wife?"

I don't know whether *she* whispered or not, but before I left her she consented.

September 12th.—We are to be married in about three weeks.   990

September 19th.—I have been in New York a week, transacting business. I got back yesterday. I find everyone here talking about our engagement. Miriam tells me that it was talked about a month ago, and that there is a very general feeling of disappointment that I am so very poor.

"Really, if you don't mind it," I remarked, "I don't see why others should."

"I don't know whether you are poor or not," says Miriam, "but I know that I am rich."

"Indeed! I was not aware that you had a private fortune," etc. etc.

This little farce is repeated in some shape every day. I am very idle. I smoke a great deal, and lounge about all day, with my hands in my pockets. I am free   1000 from that ineffable weariness of ceaseless *buying* which I suffered from six months ago. That intercourse was conducted by means of little parcels, and I have resolved that this engagement, at all events, shall have no connection with the shops. I was cheated of my poetry once; I won't be a second time. Fortunately there is not much danger of this, for my mistress is positively lyrical. She takes an enthusiastic interest in her simple outfit—showing me triumphantly certain of her purchases, and making a great mystery about others, which she is pleased to denominate table-cloths and napkins. Last evening I found her sewing buttons on a table-cloth. I had heard a great deal of a certain pink silk dress, and this morning, accordingly, she marched up to me, arrayed in this garment, upon which all the art and taste and eyesight, and all the velvet and lace, of Chowderville have been lavished.

"There is only one objection to it," said Miriam, parading before the glass in my painting-room: "I am afraid it is above our station."

"By Jove! I will paint your portrait in it and make our fortune," said I. "All the other men who have handsome wives will bring them to be painted."

"You mean all the women who have handsome dresses," Miriam replied, with great humility.

Our wedding is fixed for next Thursday. I tell Miriam that it will be as little of a wedding, and as much of a marriage, as possible. Her father and her good friend Miss Blankenberg (the schoolmistress) alone are to be present. My secret oppresses me considerably; but I have resolved to keep it for the honeymoon, when it may leak out as occasion helps it. I am harassed with a dismal apprehension that if Miriam were to discover it now, the whole thing would have to be done over again. I have taken rooms at a romantic little watering-place called Cragthorpe, ten miles off. The hotel is already quite purged of cockneys,[21] and we shall be almost alone.

September 28th.—We have been here two days. The little transaction in the church went off smoothly. I am truly sorry for the Captain. We drove directly over here, and reached the place at dusk. It was a raw, black day. We have a couple of good rooms, close to the savage sea. I am nevertheless afraid I have made a mistake. It would perhaps have been wiser to go to New York. These things are not immaterial; we make our own heaven, but we scarcely make our own earth. I am writing at a little table by the window, looking out on the rocks, the gathering dusk, the rising fog. My wife has wandered down to the rocky platform in front of the house. I can see her from here, bareheaded, in that old crimson shawl, talking to one of the landlord's little boys. She has just given the infant a kiss, bless her tender heart! I remember her telling me once that she was very fond of little boys; and, indeed, I have noticed that they are seldom too dirty for her to take on her knee. I have been reading over these pages for the first time in—I don't know when. They are filled with *her*—even more in thought than in word. I believe I will show them to her when she comes in. I will give her the book to read, and sit by her, watching her face—watching the great secret dawn upon her.

21. Townsmen, tourists.

Later.—Somehow or other, I can write this quietly enough; but I hardly think I shall ever write any more. When Miriam came in I handed her this book.

"I want you to read it," said I.

She turned very pale, and laid it on the table, shaking her head.

"I know it," she said.

"What do you know?"

"That you have ever so much money. But believe me, Mr Locksley, I am none 1050
the worse for the knowledge. You intimated in one place in your book that I am fitted by nature for wealth and splendour. I verily believe I am. You pretend to hate your money; but you would not have had me without it. If you really love me—and I think you do—you will not let this make any difference. I am not such a fool as to attempt to talk now about what passed through me when you asked me to—to do *this*. But I remember what I said."

"What do you expect me to do?" I asked. "Shall I call you some horrible name and cast you off?"

"I expect you to show the same courage that I am showing. I never said I loved you. I never deceived you in that. I said I would be your wife. So I will, 1060
faithfully. I haven't so much heart as you think; and yet, too, I have a great deal more. I am incapable of more than one deception.—Mercy! didn't you see it? didn't you know it? see that I saw it? know that I knew it? It was diamond cut diamond. You cheated me and I mystified you. Now that you tell me your secret I can tell you mine. *Now* we are free, with the fortune that you know. Excuse me, but it sometimes comes over me! *Now* we can be good and honest and true. It was all a make-believe virtue before."

"So you read that thing?" I asked: actually—strange as it may seem—for something to say.

"Yes, while you were ill. It was lying with your pen in it, on the table. I read 1070
it because I suspected. Otherwise I wouldn't have done so."

"It was the act of a false woman," said I.

"A false woman? No, it was the act of any woman—placed as I was placed. You don't believe it?" And she began to smile. "Come, you may abuse me in your diary if you like—I shall never peep into it again!"   [1866]

Questions for Discussion and Writing
1. Early in the story, Locksley asks, "How can a man be simple (i.e., lead a simple life) and natural who is known to have a large income?" What light does the story shed on this question?
2. Is the "surprise" ending a surprise? Why or why not?
3. What do setting and atmosphere contribute to the story?
4. Who has been more deceitful, Locksley or Miss Quarterman? Is either of them justified in such deceit?
5. Was Miss Quarterman wise to tell Locksley she had read his diary?
6. What features of the story are anti-Romantic?
7. Is this a love story? Why or why not?

❧ GUSTAVE FLAUBERT
(1821–1880)

A Simple Soul[1]

In the shift of Western sensibility from Romanticism to Realism, Gustave Flaubert has traditionally been regarded as a central and seminal influence. Ironically, however, Flaubert admitted that by temperament he was highly Romantic, while Post-Modern critics have interpreted his work as challenging the very Realism that earlier critics believed he pioneered.

Flaubert's mother descended from an old Norman family; his father was a staff surgeon in the hospital of Rouen. From an early age he showed an interest in writing but went to Paris to study law in 1840. He took little interest in his studies, however, and continued to write, meeting Victor Hugo (1802–1885), Louise Colet (1810–1876), and other writers and artists. His studies were interrupted by illness that forced him to return to Rouen. When both his father and his beloved sister died in 1846, he settled with his mother at Croisset, near Rouen, and lived there the rest of his life. At about the same time, he entered an extended liaison with Louise Colet, which lasted until 1855.

His first attempt at a novel was so infused with Romantic sentiment that friends urged him to burn it and turn to a more down-to-earth subject. The result, four years in the writing, was *Madame Bovary,* which began serialization in October 1856 in the *Revue de Paris.* The government prosecuted Flaubert for indecency, but he was acquitted, and the book appeared with much publicity in 1857.

Although Flaubert's work was widely admired, the last years of his life were unhappy. The Franco-Prussian War of 1870–1871 and his mother's death in 1872, together with the passing of some of his closest friends, plunged Flaubert into melancholy.

"A Simple Soul," like *Madame Bovary,* is known for its scrupulously objective point of view as well as its stylistic beauty and exactness. Flaubert was a perfectionist and would often spend a week on a single page. But his precision and objectivity often lead to ambiguity: are we to despise or admire Felicite's "simplicity"? Is the story a satire on religious faith or a depiction of its highest values?

CHAPTER I

Félicité

FOR HALF A CENTURY the housewives of Pont-l'Evêque had envied Madame Aubain her servant Félicité.

For a hundred francs a year, she cooked and did the housework, washed,

1. The French word is *coeur,* which may be translated either as "heart" or "soul."

ironed, mended, harnessed the horse, fattened the poultry, made the butter, and remained faithful to her mistress—although the latter was by no means an agreeable person.

Madame Aubain had married a comely youth without any money, who died in the beginning of 1809, leaving her with two young children and a number of debts. She sold all her property excepting the farm of Toucques and the farm of Geffosses, the income of which barely amounted to 5,000 francs; then she left her house in Saint-Melaine, and moved into a less pretentious one which had belonged to her ancestors and stood back of the market-place. This house, with its slate-covered roof, was built between a passage-way and a narrow street that led to the river. The interior was so unevenly graded that it caused people to stumble. A narrow hall separated the kitchen from the parlour, where Madame Aubain sat all day in a straw armchair near the window. Eight mahogany chairs stood in a row against the white wainscoting. An old piano, standing beneath a barometer, was covered with a pyramid of old books and boxes. On either side of the yellow marble mantelpiece, in Louis XV style, stood a tapestry armchair. The clock represented a temple of Vesta;[2] and the whole room smelled musty, as it was on a lower level than the garden.

On the first floor was Madame's bedchamber, a large room papered in a flowered design and containing the portrait of Monsieur dressed in the costume of a dandy. It communicated with a smaller room, in which there were two little cribs, without any mattresses. Next, came the parlour (always closed), filled with furniture covered with sheets. Then a hall, which led to the study, where books and papers were piled on the shelves of a book-case that enclosed three quarters of the big black desk. Two panels were entirely hidden under pen-and-ink sketches, Gouache[3] landscapes and Audran[4] engravings, relics of better times and vanished luxury. On the second floor, a garret-window lighted Félicité's room, which looked out upon the meadows.

She arose at daybreak, in order to attend mass, and she worked without interruption until night; then, when dinner was over, the dishes cleared away, and the door securely locked, she would bury the log under the ashes and fall asleep in front of the hearth with a rosary in her hand. Nobody could bargain with greater obstinacy, and as for cleanliness, the lustre on her brass saucepans was the envy and despair of other servants. She was most economical, and when she ate she would gather up crumbs with the tip of her finger, so that nothing should be wasted of the loaf of bread weighing twelve pounds which was baked especially for her and lasted three weeks.

Summer and winter she wore a dimity[5] kerchief fastened in the back with a pin, a cap which concealed her hair, a red skirt, grey stockings, and an apron with a bib like those worn by hospital nurses.

Her face was thin and her voice shrill. When she was twenty-five, she looked

2. Roman goddess of the hearth.
3. A technique of opaque water-color painting.
4. A family of seventeenth- and eighteenth-century French engravers.
5. A sturdy cotton cloth with raised stripes or other decoration woven into the texture.

forty. After she had passed fifty, nobody could tell her age; erect and silent always, she resembled a wooden figure working automatically.

CHAPTER II

The Heroine

LIKE EVERY OTHER woman, she had had an affair of the heart. Her father, who was a mason, was killed by falling from a scaffolding. Then her mother died and her sisters went their different ways; a farmer took her in, and while she was quite small, let her keep cows in the fields. She was clad in miserable rags, beaten for the slightest offence, and finally dismissed for a theft of thirty sous which she did not commit. She took service on another farm where she tended the poultry; and as she was well thought of by her master, her fellow-workers soon grew jealous.

One evening in August (she was then eighteen years old), they persuaded her to accompany them to the fair at Colleville. She was immediately dazzled by the noise, the lights in the trees, the brightness of the dresses, the laces and gold crosses, and the crowd of people all hopping at the same time. She was standing modestly at a distance, when presently a young man of well-to-do appearance, who had been leaning on the pole of a wagon and smoking his pipe, approached her, and asked her for a dance. He treated her to cider and cake, bought her a silk shawl, and then, thinking she had guessed his purpose, offered to see her home. When they came to the end of a field he threw her down brutally. But she grew frightened and screamed, and he walked off.

One evening, on the road leading to Beaumont, she came upon a wagon loaded with hay, and when she overtook it, she recognised Théodore. He greeted her calmly, and asked her to forget what had happened between them, as it "was all the fault of the drink."

She did not know what to reply and wished to run away.

Presently he began to speak of the harvest and of the notables of the village; his father had left Colleville and bought the farm of Les Écots, so that now they would be neighbors. "Ah!" she exclaimed. He then added that his parents were looking around for a wife for him, but that he, himself, was not so anxious and preferred to wait for a girl who suited him. She hung her head. He then asked her whether she had ever thought of marrying. She replied, smilingly, that it was wrong of him to make fun of her. "Oh! no, I am in earnest," he said, and put his left arm around her waist while they sauntered along. The air was soft, the stars were bright, and the huge load of hay oscillated in front of them, drawn by four horses whose ponderous hoofs raised clouds of dust. Without a word from their driver they turned to the right. He kissed her again and she went home. The following week, Théodore obtained meetings.

They met in yards, behind walls or under isolated trees. She was not ignorant, as girls of well-to-do families are—for the animals had instructed her;—but her reason and her instinct of honour kept her from falling. Her resistance exasperated Théodore's love and so in order to satisfy it (or perchance ingenuously), he offered to marry her. She would not believe him at first, so he made solemn promises. But, in a short time he mentioned a difficulty; the previous year, his parents had purchased a substitute[6] for him; but any day he might be drafted and the prospect of serving in the army alarmed him greatly. To Félicité his cowardice appeared a proof of his love for her, and her devotion to him grew stronger. When she met him, he would torture her with his fears and his entreaties. As last, he 90 announced that he was going to the prefect himself for information, and would let her know everything on the following Sunday, between eleven o'clock and midnight.

When the time drew near, she ran to meet her lover.

But instead of Théodore, one of his friends was at the meeting-place.

He informed her that she would never see her sweetheart again; for, in order to escape the conscription, he had married a rich old woman, Madame Lehoussais, of Toucques.

The poor girl's sorrow was frightful. She threw herself on the ground, she cried and called on the Lord, and wandered around desolately until sunrise. Then 100 she went back to the farm, declared her intention of leaving, and at the end of the month, after she had received her wages, she packed all her belongings in a handkerchief and started for Pont-l'Evêque.

In front of the inn, she met a woman wearing widow's weeds[7], and upon questioning her, learned that she was looking for a cook. The girl did not know very much, but appeared so willing and so modest in her requirements, that Madame Aubain finally said:

"Very well, I will give you a trial."

And half an hour later Félicité was installed in her house.

At first she lived in a constant anxiety that was caused by "the style of the 110 household" and the memory of "Monsieur," that hovered over everything. Paul and Virginia, the one aged seven, and the other barely four, seemed made of some precious material; she carried them pig-a-back, and was greatly mortified when Madame Aubain forbade her to kiss them every other minute.

But in spite of all this, she was happy. The comfort of her new surroundings had obliterated her sadness.

Every Thursday, friends of Madame Aubain dropped in for a game of cards, and it was Félicité's duty to prepare the table and heat the foot-warmers. They arrived at exactly eight o'clock and departed before eleven.

Every Monday morning, the dealer in second-hand goods, who lived under 120 the alley-way, spread out his wares on the sidewalk. Then the city would be filled with a buzzing of voices in which the neighing of horses, the bleating of lambs, the grunting of pigs, could be distinguished, mingled with the sharp sound of wheels on the cobble-stones. About twelve o'clock, when the market was in full swing, there appeared at the front door a tall, middle-aged peasant, with a hooked nose and a cap on the back of his head; it was Robelin, the farmer of Geffosses. Shortly afterwards came Liébard, the farmer of Toucques, short, rotund, and ruddy, wearing a grey jacket and spurred boots.

---

6. One could avoid military service by hiring someone else to serve in his place.
7. Garments.

Both men brought their landlady either chickens or cheese. Félicité would invariably thwart their ruses and they held her in great respect.   130

At various times, Madame Aubain received a visit from the Marquis de Grémanville, one of her uncles, who was ruined and lived at Falaise on the remainder of his estates. He always came at dinner-time and brought an ugly poodle with him, whose paws soiled the furniture. In spite of his efforts to appear a man of breeding (he even went so far as to raise his hat every time he said "My deceased father"), his habits got the better of him, and he would fill his glass a little too often and relate broad[8] stories. Félicité would show him out very politely and say: "You have had enough for this time, Monsieur de Grémanville! Hoping to see you again!" and would close the door.

She opened it gladly for Monsieur Bourais, a retired lawyer. His bald head 140 and white cravat, the ruffling of his shirt, his flowing brown coat, the manner in which he took his snuff, his whole person, in fact, produced in her the kind of awe which we feel when we see extraordinary persons. As he managed Madame's estates, he spent hours with her in Monsieur's study; he was in constant fear of being compromised, had a great regard for the magistracy and some pretensions to learning.

In order to facilitate the children's studies, he presented them with an engraved geography which represented various scenes of the world: cannibals with feather head-dresses, a gorilla kidnapping a young girl, Arabs in the desert, a whale being harpooned, etc.   150

Paul explained the pictures to Félicité. And, in fact, this was her only literary education.

The children's studies were under the direction of a poor devil employed at the town-hall, who sharpened his pocketknife on his boots and was famous for his penmanship.

When the weather was fine, they went to Geffosses. The house was built in the centre of the sloping yard; and the sea looked like a grey spot in the distance. Félicité would take slices of cold meat from the lunch basket and they would sit down and eat in a room next to the dairy. This room was all that remained of a cottage that had been torn down. The dilapidated wall-paper trembled in the 160 drafts. Madame Aubain, overwhelmed by recollections, would hang her head, while the children were afraid to open their mouths. Then, "Why don't you go and play?" their mother would say; and they would scamper off.

Paul would go to the old barn, catch birds, throw stones into the pond, or pound the trunks of the trees with a stick till they resounded like drums. Virginia would feed the rabbits and run to pick the wild flowers in the fields and her flying legs would disclose her little embroidered pantalettes. One autumn evening, they struck out for home through the meadows. The new moon illumined part of the sky and a mist hovered like a veil over the sinuosities of the river. Oxen, lying in the pastures, gazed mildly at the passing persons. In the third field, however, sev- 170 eral of them got up and surrounded them. "Don't be afraid," cried Félicité; and murmuring a sort of lament she passed her hand over the back of the nearest ox;

---

8. Slightly racy or dirty stories.

he turned away and the others followed. But when they came to the next pasture, they heard frightful bellowing.

It was a bull which was hidden from them by the fog. He advanced towards the two women, and Madame Aubain prepared to flee for her life. "No, no! not so fast," warned Félicité. Still they hurried on, for they could hear the noisy breathing of the bull close behind them. His hoofs pounded the grass like hammers, and presently he began to gallop! Félicité turned around and threw patches of grass in his eyes. He hung his head, shook his horns, and bellowed with fury. Madame 180 Aubain and the children, huddled at the end of the field, were trying to jump over the ditch. Félicité continued to back before the bull, blinding him with dirt, while she shouted to them to make haste.

Madame Aubain finally slid into the ditch, after shoving first Virginia and then Paul into it, and though she stumbled several times she managed, by dint of courage, to climb the other side of it.

The bull had driven Félicité up against a fence; the foam from his muzzle flew in her face and in another minute he would have disembowelled her. She had just time to slip between two bars and the huge animal, thwarted, paused.

For years, this occurrence was a topic of conversation in Pont-l'Evêque. But 190 Félicité took no credit to herself, and probably never knew that she had been heroic.

Virginia occupied her thoughts solely, for the shock she had sustained gave her a nervous affection, and the physician, M. Poupart, prescribed the salt-water bathing at Trouville. In those days, Trouville was not greatly patronised. Madame Aubain gathered information, consulted Bourais, and made preparations as if they were going on an extended trip.

The baggage was sent the day before on Liébard's cart. On the following morning, he brought around two horses, one of which had a woman's saddle with a velveteen back to it, while on the crupper of the other was a rolled shawl that 200 was to be used for a seat. Madame Aubain mounted the second horse, behind Liébard. Félicité took charge of the little girl, and Paul rode M. Lechaptois' donkey, which had been lent for the occasion on the condition that they should be careful of it.

The road was so bad that it took two hours to cover the eight miles. The two horses sank knee-deep into the mud and stumbled into ditches; sometimes they had to jump over them. In certain places. Liébard's mare stopped abruptly. He waited patiently till she started again, and talked of the people whose estates bordered the road, adding his own moral reflections to the outline of their histories. Thus, when they were passing through Toucques, and came to some windows 210 draped with nasturtiums, he shrugged his shoulders and said: "There's a woman, Madame Lehoussais, who, instead of taking a young man—" Félicité could not catch what followed; the horses began to trot, the donkey to gallop, and they turned into a lane; then a gate swung open, two farm-hands appeared and they all dismounted at the very threshold of the farm-house.

Mother Liébard, when she caught sight of her mistress, was lavish with joyful demonstrations. She got up a lunch which comprised a leg of mutton, tripe, sausages, a chicken fricassée, sweet cider, a fruit tart, and some preserved prunes; then to all this the good woman added polite remarks about Madame, who ap-

peared to be in better health, Mademoiselle, who had grown to be "superb," and 220
Paul, who had become singularly sturdy; she spoke also of their deceased grandparents, whom the Liébards had known, for they had been in the service of the
family for several generations.

Like its owners, the farm had an ancient appearance. The beams of the ceiling were mouldy, the walls black with smoke, and the windows grey with dust.
The oak sideboard was filled with all sorts of utensils, plates, pitchers, tin bowls,
wolf-traps. The children laughed when they saw a huge syringe. There was not a
tree in the yard that did not have mushrooms growing around its foot, or a bunch
of mistletoe hanging in its branches. Several of the trees had been blown down,
but they had started to grow in the middle and all were laden with quantities of 230
apples. The thatched roofs, which were of unequal thickness, looked like brown
velvet and could resist the fiercest gales. But the wagon-shed was fast crumbling to
ruins. Madame Aubain said that she would attend to it, and then gave orders to
have the horses saddled.

It took another thirty minutes to reach Trouville. The little caravan dismounted in order to pass Les Écores, a cliff that overhangs the bay, and a few minutes later, at the end of the dock, they entered the yard of the Golden Lamb, an
inn kept by Mother David.

During the first few days, Virginia felt stronger, owing to the change of air
and the action of the sea-baths. She took them in her little chemise, as she had no 240
bathing suit, and afterwards her nurse dressed her in the cabin of a customs officer, which was used for that purpose by other bathers.

In the afternoon, they would take the donkey and go to the Roches-Noires,
near Hennequeville. The path led at first through undulating grounds, and thence
to a plateau, where pastures and tilled fields alternated. At the edge of the road,
mingling with the brambles, grew holly bushes, and here and there stood large
dead trees whose branches traced zigzags upon the blue sky.

Ordinarily, they rested in a field facing the ocean, with Deauville on their
left, and Havre on their right. The sea glittered brightly in the sun and was as
smooth as a mirror, and so calm that they could scarcely distinguish its murmur; 250
sparrows chirped joyfully and the immense canopy of heaven spread over it all.
Madame Aubain brought out her sewing, and Virginia amused herself by braiding
reeds; Félicité wove lavender blossoms, while Paul was bored and wished to go
home.

Sometimes they crossed the Toucques in a boat, and started to hunt for
seashells. The outgoing tide exposed starfish and sea-urchins, and the children
tried to catch the flakes of foam which the wind blew away. The sleepy waves lap-
ping the sand unfurled themselves along the shore that extended as far as the eye
could see, but where land began, it was limited by the downs which separated it
from the "Swamp," a large meadow shaped like a hippodrome. When they went 260
home that way, Trouville, on the slope of a hill below, grew larger and larger as
they advanced, and, with all its houses of unequal height, seemed to spread out
before them in a sort of giddy confusion.

When the heat was too oppressive, they remained in their rooms. The dazzling sunlight cast bars of light between the shutters. Not a sound in the village,
not a soul on the sidewalk. This silence intensified the tranquillity of everything.

In the distance, the hammers of some calkers pounded the hull of a ship, and the sultry breeze brought them an odour of tar.

The principal diversion consisted in watching the return of the fishing-smacks. As soon as they passed the beacons, they began to ply to windward. The 270 sails were lowered to one third of the masts, and with their foresails swelled up like balloons they glided over the waves and anchored in the middle of the harbour. Then they crept up alongside of the dock and the sailors threw the quivering fish over the side of the boat; a line of carts was waiting for them, and women with white caps sprang forward to receive the baskets and embrace their men-folk.

One day, one of them spoke to Félicité, who, after a little while, returned to the house gleefully. She had found one of her sisters, and presently Nastasie Barette, wife of Léroux, made her appearance, holding an infant in her arms, another child by the hand, while on her left was a little cabin-boy with his hands in his pockets and his cap on his ear. 280

At the end of fifteen minutes, Madame Aubain bade her go.

They always hung around the kitchen, or approached Félicité when she and the children were out walking. The husband, however, did not show himself.

Félicité developed a great fondness for them; she bought them a stove, some shirts, and a blanket; it was evident that they exploited her. Her foolishness annoyed Madame Aubain, who, moreover did not like the nephew's familiarity, for he called her son "thou";[9]—and, as Virginia began to cough and the season was over, she decided to return to Pont-l'Evêque.

Monsieur Bourais assisted her in the choice of a college. The one at Caën[10] was considered the best. So Paul was sent away and bravely said good-bye to them 290 all, for he was glad to go to live in a house where he would have boy companions.

Madame Aubain resigned herself to the separation from her son because it was unavoidable. Virginia brooded less and less over it. Félicité regretted the noise he made, but soon a new occupation diverted her mind; beginning from Christmas, she accompanied the little girl to her catechism lesson every day.

CHAPTER III

Death

AFTER SHE HAD MADE a curtsey at the threshold, she would walk up the aisle between the double lines of chairs, open Madame Aubain's pew, sit down and look around.

Girls and boys, the former on the right, the latter on the left-hand side of the church, filled the stalls of the choir; the priest stood beside the reading-desk; on 300 one stained window of the side-aisle the Holy Ghost hovered over the Virgin; on another one, Mary knelt before the Child Jesus, and behind the altar, a wooden group represented Saint Michael felling the dragon.

The priest first read a condensed lesson of sacred history. Félicité evoked Paradise, the Flood, the Tower of Babel, the blazing cities, the dying nations, the

9. I.e., "tu," the familiar form of "you" rather than the formal "vous."
10. City in Normandy on the Channel coast.

shattered idols; and out of this she developed a great respect for the Almighty and a great fear of His wrath. Then, when she listened to the Passion, she wept. Why had they crucified Him who loved little children, nourished the people, made the blind see, and who, out of humility, had wished to be born among the poor, in a stable? The sowings, the harvests, the wine-presses, all those familiar things which 310 the Scriptures mention, formed a part of her life; the word of God sanctified them; and she loved the lambs with increased tenderness for the sake of the Lamb, and the doves because of the Holy Ghost.

She found it hard, however, to think of the latter as a person,[11] for was it not a bird, a flame, and sometimes only a breath? Perhaps it is its light that at night hovers over swamps, its breath that propels the clouds, its voice that renders church-bells harmonious. And Félicité worshipped devoutly, while enjoying the coolness and the stillness of the church.

As for the dogma, she could not understand it and did not even try. The priest discoursed, the children recited, and she went to sleep, only to awaken with 320 a start when they were leaving the church and their wooden shoes clattered on the stone pavement.

In this way, she learned her catechism, her religious education having been neglected in her youth; and thenceforth she imitated all Virginia's religious practises, fasted when she did, and went to confession with her. At the Corpus-Christi Day[12] they both decorated an altar.

She worried in advance over Virginia's first communion. She fussed about the shoes, the rosary, the book, and the gloves. With what nervousness she helped the mother dress the child!

During the entire ceremony, she felt anguished. Monsieur Bourais hid part of 330 the choir from view, but directly in front of her, the flock of maidens, wearing white wreaths over their lowered veils, formed a snow-white field, and she recognised her darling by the slenderness of her neck and her devout attitude. The bell tinkled. All the heads bent and there was a silence. Then, at the peals of the organ the singers and the worshippers struck up the Agnus Dei; the boys' procession began; behind them came the girls. With clasped hands, they advanced step by step to the lighted altar, knelt at the first step, received one by one the Host,[13] and returned to their seats in the same order. When Virginia's turn came, Félicité leaned forward to watch her, and through that imagination which springs from true affection, she at once became the child, whose face and dress became hers, 340 whose heart beat in her bosom, and when Virginia opened her mouth and closed her lids, she did likewise and came very near fainting.

The following day, she presented herself early at the church so as to receive communion from the curé. She took it with the proper feeling, but did not experience the same delight as on the previous day.

Madame Aubain wished to make an accomplished girl of her daughter; and as Guyot could not teach English nor music, she decided to send her to the Ursulines at Honfleur.

---

11. i.e., as one of the three "persons" of the Holy Trinity.
12. Annual feast in the Roman Catholic Church celebrating the Holy Eucharist.
13. The bread of Holy Communion.

The child made no objection, but Félicité sighed and thought Madame was heartless. Then, she thought that perhaps her mistress was right, as these things 350 were beyond her sphere. Finally, one day, and old *fiacre* stopped in front of the door and a nun stepped out. Félicité put Virginia's luggage on top of the carriage, gave the coachman some instructions, and smuggled six jars of jam, a dozen pears, and a bunch of violets under the seat.

At the last minute, Virginia had a fit of sobbing; she embraced her mother again and again, while the latter kissed her on her forehead, and said: "Now, be brave, be brave!" The step was pulled up and the *fiacre* rumbled off.

Then Madame Aubain had a fainting spell, and that evening all her friends, including the two Lormeaus, Madame Lechaptois, the ladies Rochefeuille, Messieurs de Houppeville and Bourais, called on her and tendered their sympathy. 360

At first the separation proved very painful to her. But her daughter wrote her three times a week and the other days she, herself, wrote to Virginia. Then she walked in the garden, read a little, and in his way managed to fill out the emptiness of the hours.

Each morning, out of habit, Félicité entered Virginia's room and gazed at the walls. She missed combing her hair, lacing her shoes, tucking her in her bed, and the bright face and little hand when they used to go out for a walk. In order to occupy herself she tried to make lace. But her clumsy fingers broke the threads; she had no heart for anything, lost her sleep and "wasted away," as she put it.

In order to have some distraction, she asked leave to receive the visits of her 370 nephew Victor.

He would come on Sunday, after church, with ruddy cheeks and bared chest, bringing with him the scent of the country. She would set the table and they would sit down opposite each other, and eat their dinner; she ate as little as possible, herself, to avoid any extra expense, but would stuff him so with food that he would finally go to sleep. At the first stroke of vespers, she would wake him up, brush his trousers, tie his cravat, and walk to church with him, leaning on his arm with maternal pride.

His parents always told him to get something out of her, either a package of brown sugar, or soap, or brandy, and sometimes even money. He brought her his 380 clothes to mend, and she accepted the task gladly, because it meant another visit from him.

In August, his father took him on a coasting-vessel.

It was vacation time and the arrival of the children consoled Félicité. But Paul was capricious, and Virginia was growing too old to be thee-and-thou'd,[14] a fact which seemed to produce a sort of embarrassment in their relations.

Victor went successively to Morlaix, to Dunkirk, and to Brighton; whenever he returned from a trip he would bring her a present. The first time it was a box of shells; the second, a coffee-cup; the third, a big doll of ginger-bread. He was growing handsome, had a good figure, a tiny moustache, kind eyes, and a little leather 390 cap that sat jauntily on the back of his head. He amused his aunt by telling her stories mingled with nautical expressions.

14. i.e., addressed in the familiar form of the second person; see footnote 9, above.

One Monday, the 14th of July, 1819 (she never forgot the date), Victor announced that he had been engaged on a merchant-vessel and that in two days he would take the steamer at Honfleur and join his sailer, which was going to start from Havre very soon. Perhaps he might be away two years.

The prospect of his departure filled Félicité with despair, and in order to bid him farewell, on Wednesday night, after Madame's dinner, she put on her patterns[15] and trudged the four miles that separated Pont-l'Evêque from Honfleur. 400

When she reached the Calvary, instead of turning to the right, she turned to the left and lost herself in coal-yards; she had to retrace her steps; some people she spoke to advised her to hasten. She walked helplessly around the harbour filled with vessels, and knocked against hawsers. Presently the ground sloped abruptly, lights flittered to and fro, and she thought all at once that she had gone mad when she saw some horses in the sky.

Others, on the edge of the dock, neighed at the sight of the ocean. A derrick pulled them up in the air and dumped them into a boat, where passengers were bustling about among barrels of cider, baskets of cheese, and bags of meal; chickens cackled, the captain swore, and a cabin-boy rested on the railing, apparently 410 indifferent to his surroundings. Félicité, who did not recognise him, kept shouting: "Victor!" He suddenly raised his eyes, but while she was preparing to rush up to him, they withdrew the gangplank.

The packet,[16] towed by singing women, glided out of the harbour. Her hull squeaked and the heavy waves beat up against her sides. The sail had turned and nobody was visible;—and on the ocean, silvered by the light of the moon, the vessel formed a black spot that grew dimmer and dimmer, and finally disappeared.

When Félicité passed the Calvary again, she felt as if she must entrust that which was dearest to her to the Lord; and for a long while she prayed, with uplifted eyes and a face wet with tears. The city was sleeping; some customs officials 420 were taking the air; and the water kept pouring through the holes of the dam with a deafening roar. The town clock struck two.

The parlour of the convent would not open until morning, and surely a delay would annoy Madame; so, in spite of her desire to see the other child, she went home. The maids of the inn were just arising when she reached Pont-l'Evêque.

So the poor boy would be on the ocean for months! His previous trips had not alarmed her. One can come back from England and Brittany; but America, the colonies, the islands, were all lost in an uncertain region at the very end of the world. 430

From that time on, Félicité thought solely of her nephew. On warm days she feared he would suffer from thirst, and when it stormed, she was afraid he would be struck by lightning. When she harkened to the wind that rattled in the chimney and dislodged the tiles on the roof, she imagined that he was being buffeted by the same storm, perched on top of a shattered mast, with his whole body bent backward and covered with sea-foam; or,—these were recollections of the en-

15. Wooden-soled overshoes worn to keep ordinary shoes out of mud or water.
16. A boat carrying mail and/or goods and passengers.

graved geography—he was being devoured by savages, or captured in a forest by apes, or dying on some lonely coast. She never mentioned her anxieties, however.

Madame Aubain worried about her daughter.

The sisters thought that Virginia was affectionate but delicate. The slightest 440 emotion enervated her. She had to give up her piano lessons. Her mother insisted upon regular letters from the convent. One morning, when the postman failed to come, she grew impatient and began to pace to and fro, from her chair to the window. It was really extraordinary! No news since four days!

In order to console her mistress by her own example, Félicité said:

"Why, Madame, I haven't had any news since six months!"—

"From whom?"—

The servant replied gently:

"Why—from my nephew."

"Oh, yes, your nephew!" And shrugging her shoulders, Madame Aubain 450 continued to pace the floor as if to say: "I did not think of it.—Besides, I do not care, a cabin-boy, a pauper!—but my daughter—what a difference! just think of it!—

Félicité, although she had been reared roughly, was very indignant. Then she forgot about it.

It appeared quite natural to her that one should lose one's head about Virginia.

The two children were of equal importance; they were united in her heart and their fate was to be the same.

The chemist informed her that Victor's vessel had reached Havana. He had 460 read the information in a newspaper.

Félicité imagined that Havana was a place where people did nothing but smoke, and that Victor walked around among negroes in a cloud of tobacco. Could a person, in case of need, return by land? How far was it from Pont-l'Evêque? In order to learn these things she questioned Monsieur Bourais. He reached for his map and began some explanations concerning longitudes, and smiled with superiority at Félicité's bewilderment. At last, he took his pencil and pointed out an imperceptible black point in the scallops of an oval blotch, adding: "There it is." She bent over the map; the maze of coloured lines hurt her eyes without enlightening her; and when Bourais asked her what puzzled her, she re- 470 quested him to show her the house Victor lived in. Bourais threw up his hands, sneezed, and then laughed uproariously; such ignorance delighted his soul; but Félicité failed to understand the cause of his mirth, she whose intelligence was so limited that she perhaps expected to see even the picture of her nephew!

It was two weeks later that Liébard came into the kitchen at market-time, and handed her a letter from her brother-in-law. As neither of them could read, she called upon her mistress.

Madame Aubain, who was counting the stitches of her knitting, laid her work down beside her, opened the letter, started, and in a low tone and with a searching look said: "They tell you of a—misfortune. Your nephew—."   480

He had died. The letter told nothing more.

Félicité dropped on a chair, leaned her head against the back, and closed her lids; presently they grew pink. Then, with drooping head, inert hands, and staring eyes she repeated at intervals:

"Poor little chap! poor little chap!"

Liébard watched her and sighed. Madame Aubain was trembling.

She proposed to the girl to go see her sister in Trouville.

With a single motion, Félicité replied that it was not necessary.

There was a silence. Old Liébard thought it about time for him to take leave.
Then Félicité uttered:

"They have no sympathy, they do not care!"

Her head fell forward again, and from time to time, mechanically, she toyed with the long knitting needles on the work-table.

Some women passed through the yard with a basket of wet clothes.

When she saw them through the window, she suddenly remembered her own wash; as she had soaked it the day before, she must go and rinse it now. So she arose and left the room.

Her tub and her board were on the bank of the Toucques. She threw a heap of clothes on the ground, rolled up her sleeves, and grasped her bat; and her loud pounding could be heard in the neighboring gardens. The meadows were empty, the breeze wrinkled the stream, at the bottom of which were long grasses that looked like the hair of corpses floating in the water. She restrained her sorrow and was very brave until night; but, when she had gone to her own room, she gave way to it, burying her face in the pillow and pressing her two fists against her temples.

A long while afterward, she learned through Victor's captain, the circumstances which surrounded his death. At the hospital they had bled him too much, treating him for yellow fever. Four doctors held him at one time. He died almost instantly, and the chief surgeon had said:

"Here goes another one!"

His parents had always treated him barbarously; she preferred not to see them again, and they made no advances, either from forgetfulness or out of innate hardness.

Virginia was growing weaker.

A cough, continual fever, oppressive breathing, and spots on her cheeks indicated some serious trouble. Monsieur Poupart had advised a sojourn in Provence. Madame Aubain decided that they would go, and she would have had her daughter come home at once, had it not been for the climate of Pont-l'Evêque.

She made an arrangement with a livery-stable man who drove her over to the convent every Tuesday. In the garden there was a terrace, from which the view extends to the Seine. Virginia walked in it, leaning on her mother's arm and treading the dead vine leaves. Sometimes the sun, shining through the clouds, made her blink her lids, when she gazed at the sails in the distance, and let her eyes roam over the horizon from the chateau of Tancarville to the lighthouses of Havre. Then they rested in the arbour. Her mother had brought a little cask of fine Malaga wine, and Virginia, laughing at the idea of becoming intoxicated, would drink a few drops of it, but never more.

Her strength returned. Autumn passed. Félicité began to reassure Madame

Aubain. But, one evening, when she returned home after an errand, she met M. Boupart's coach in front of the door; M. Boupart himself was standing in the 530 vestibule and Madame Aubain was tying the strings of her bonnet. "Give me my foot-warmer, my purse, and my gloves; and be quick about it," she said.

Virginia had congestion of the lungs; perhaps it was desperate.

"Not yet," said the physician, and both got into the carriage, while the snow fell in thick flakes. It was almost night and very cold.

Félicité rushed to the church to light a candle. Then she ran after the coach which she overtook after an hour's chase, sprang up behind and held onto the straps. But suddenly a thought crossed her mind: "The yard had been left open; supposing that burglars got in!" And down she jumped.

The next morning, at daybreak, she called at the doctor's. He had been 540 home, but had left again. Then she waited at the inn, thinking that strangers might bring her a letter. At last, at daylight she took the diligence[17] for Lisieux.

The convent was at the end of a steep and narrow street. When she arrived about at the middle of it, she heard strange noises, a funeral knell. "It must be for some one else," thought she; and she pulled the knocker violently.

After several minutes had elapsed, she heard footsteps, the door was half opened and a nun appeared. The good sister, with an air of compunction, told her that "she had just passed away." And at the same time the tolling of Saint-Léonard's increased.

Félicité reached the second floor. Already at the threshold, she caught sight 550 of Virginia lying on her back, with clasped hands, her mouth open, and her head thrown back, beneath a black crucifix inclined toward her, and stiff curtains which were less white than her face. Madame Aubain lay at the foot of the couch, clasping it with her arms and uttering groans of agony. The Mother Superior was standing on the right side of the bed. The three candles on the bureau made red blurs, and the windows were dimmed by the fog outside. The nuns carried Madame Aubain from the room.

For two nights, Félicité never left the corpse. She would repeat the same prayers, sprinkle holy water over the sheets, get up, come back to the bed, and contemplate the body. At the end of the first vigil, she noticed that the face had 560 taken on a yellow tinge, the lips grew blue, the nose grew pinched, the eyes were sunken. She kissed them several times and would not have been greatly astonished had Virginia opened them; to souls like these the supernatural is always quite simple. She washed her, wrapped her in a shroud, put her into the casket, laid a wreath of flowers on her head, and arranged her curls. They were blond and of an extraordinary length for her age. Félicité cut off a big lock and put half of it into her bosom, resolving never to part with it.

The body was taken to Pont-l'Evêque, according to Madame Aubain's wishes; she followed the hearse in a closed carriage.

After the ceremony it took three quarters of an hour to reach the cemetery. 570 Paul, sobbing, headed the procession; Monsieur Bourais followed, and then came the principal inhabitants of the town, the women covered with black capes, and Félicité. The memory of her nephew, and the thought that she had not been able

17. Stage-coach.

to render him these honours, made her doubly unhappy, and she felt as if he were being buried with Virginia.

Madame Aubain's grief was uncontrollable. At first she rebelled against God, thinking that he was unjust to have taken away her child—she who had never done anything wrong, and whose conscience was so pure! But no! she ought to have taken her South. Other doctors would have saved her. She accused herself, prayed to be able to join her child, and cried in the midst of her dreams. Of the latter, one more especially haunted her. Her husband, dressed like a sailor, had come back from a long voyage, and with tears in his eyes told her that he had received the order to take Virginia away. Then they both consulted about a hiding-place.

Once she came in from the garden, all upset. A moment before (and she showed the place), the father and daughter had appeared to her, one after the other; they did nothing but look at her.

During several months she remained inert in her room. Félicité scolded her gently; she must keep up for her son and also for the other one, for "her memory."

"Her memory!" replied Madame Aubain, as if she were just awakening, "Oh! yes, yes, you do not forget her!" This was an allusion to the cemetery where she had been expressly forbidden to go.

But Félicité went there every day. At four o'clock exactly, she would go through the town, climb the hill, open the gate and arrive at Virginia's tomb. It was a small column of pink marble with a flat stone at its base, and it was surrounded by a little plot enclosed by chains. The flower-beds were bright with blossoms. Félicité watered their leaves, renewed the gravel, and knelt on the ground in order to till the earth properly. When Madame Aubain was able to visit the cemetery she felt very much relieved and consoled.

Years passed, all alike and marked by no other events than the return of the great church holidays: Easter, Assumption, All Saints' Day. Household happenings constituted the only data to which in later years they often referred. Thus, in 1825, workmen painted the vestibule; in 1827, a portion of the roof almost killed a man by falling into the yard. In the summer of 1828, it was Madame's turn to offer the hallowed bread; at that time, Bourais disappeared mysteriously; and the old acquaintances, Guyot, Liébard, Madame Lechaptois, Robelin, old Grémanville, paralysed since a long time, passed away one by one. One night, the driver of the mail in Pont-l'Evêque announced the Revolution of July.[18] A few days afterward a new sub-prefect was nominated, the Baron de Larsonnière, ex-consul in America, who, besides his wife, had his sister-in-law and her three grown daughters with him. They were often seen on their lawn, dressed in loose blouses, and they had a parrot and a negro servant. Madame Aubain received a call, which she returned promptly. As soon as she caught sight of them, Félicité would run and notify her mistress. But only one thing was capable of arousing her: a letter from her son.

He could not follow any profession as he was absorbed in drinking. His mother paid his debts and he made fresh ones; and the sighs that she heaved while she knitted at the window reached the ears of Félicité who was spinning in the kitchen.

18. The Revolution of July 1830.

They walked in the garden together, always speaking of Virginia, and asking each other if such and such a thing would have pleased her, and what she would probably have said on this or that occasion. 620

All her little belongings were put away in a closet of the room which held the two little beds. But Madame Aubain looked them over as little as possible. One summer day, however, she resigned herself to the task and when she opened the closet the moths flew out.

Virginia's frocks were hung under a shelf where there were three dolls, some hoops, a doll-house, and a basin which she had used. Félicité and Madame Aubain also took out the skirts, the handkerchiefs, and the stockings and spread them on the beds, before putting them away again. The sun fell on the piteous things, disclosing their spots and the creases formed by the motions of the body. 630 The atmosphere was warm and blue, and a blackbird trilled in the garden; everything seemed to live in happiness. They found a little hat of soft brown plush, but it was entirely moth-eaten. Félicité asked for it. Their eyes met and filled with tears; at last the mistress opened her arms and the servant threw herself against her breast and they hugged each other and giving vent to their grief in a kiss which equalized them for a moment.

It was the first time that this had ever happened, for Madame Aubain was not of an expansive nature. Félicité was as grateful for it as if it had been some favour, and thenceforth loved her with animal-like devotion and a religious veneration. 640

Her kind-heartedness developed. When she heard the drums of a marching regiment passing through the street, she would stand in the doorway with a jug of cider and give the soldiers a drink. She nursed cholera victims. She protected Polish refugees, and one of them even declared that he wished to marry her. But they quarrelled, for one morning when she returned from the Angelus she found him in the kitchen coolly eating a dish which he had prepared for himself during her absence.

After the Polish refugees, came Colmiche, an old man who was credited with having committed frightful misdeeds in '93. He lived near the river in the ruins of a pig-sty. The urchins peeped at him through the cracks in the walls and threw 650 stones that fell on his miserable bed, where he lay gasping with catarrh,[19] with long hair, inflamed eyelids, and a tumour as big as his head on one arm.

She got him some linen, tried to clean his hovel and dreamed of installing him in the bake-house without his being in Madame's way. When the cancer broke, she dressed it every day; sometimes she brought him some cake and placed him in the sun on a bundle of hay; and the poor old creature, trembling and drooling, would thank her in his broken voice, and put out his hands whenever she left him. Finally he died; and she had a mass said for the repose of his soul.

That day a great joy came to her; at dinner-time, Madame de Larsonnière's servant called with the parrot, the cage, and the perch and chain and lock. A note 660 from the baroness told Madame Aubain that as her husband had been promoted to a prefecture, they were leaving that night, and she begged her to accept the bird as a remembrance and a token of her esteem.

19. A runny nose.

Since a long time the parrot had been on Félicité's mind, because he came from America, which reminded her of Victor, and she had approached the negro on the subject.

Once even, she had said:

"How glad Madame would be to have him!"

The man had repeated this remark to his mistress who, not being able to keep the bird, took this means of getting rid of it.   670

CHAPTER IV

The Bird

HE WAS CALLED Loulou. His body was green, his head blue, the tips of his wings were pink and his breast was golden.

But he had the tiresome tricks of biting his perch, pulling his feathers out, scattering refuse and spilling the water of his bath. Madame Aubain grew tired of him and gave him to Félicité for good.

She undertook his education, and soon he was able to repeat: "Pretty boy! Your servant, sir! I salute you, Marie!" His perch was placed near the door and several persons were astonished that he did not answer to the name of "Jacquot," for every parrot is called Jacquot. They called him a goose and a log, and these taunts were like so many dagger thrusts to Félicité. Strange stubbornness of the bird   680 which would not talk when people watched him!

Nevertheless, he sought society; for on Sunday when the ladies Rochefeuille, Monsieur de Houppeville, and the new habitués, Onfroy, the chemist, Monsieur Varin and Captain Mathieu, dropped in for their game of cards, he struck the window-panes with his wings and made such a racket that it was impossible to talk.

Bourais' face must have appeared very funny to Loulou. As soon as he saw him he would begin to roar. His voice reechoed in the yard, and the neighbours would come to the windows and begin to laugh, too; and in order that the parrot might not see him, Monsieur Bourais edged along the wall, pushed his hat over his eyes to hide his profile, and entered by the garden door, and the looks he gave   690 the bird lacked affection. Loulou, having thrust his head into the butcher-boy's basket, received a slap, and from that time he always tried to nip his enemy. Fabu threatened to wring his neck, although he was not cruelly inclined, notwithstanding his big whiskers and tattooings. On the contrary, he rather liked the bird and, out of deviltry, tried to teach him oaths. Félicité, whom his manner alarmed, put Loulou in the kitchen, took off his chain and let him walk all over the house.

When he went downstairs, he rested his beak on the steps, lifted his right foot and then his left one; but his mistress feared that such feats would give him vertigo. He became ill and was unable to eat. There was a small growth under his tongue like those chickens are sometimes afflicted with. Félicité pulled it off with   700 her nails and cured him. One day, Paul was imprudent enough to blow the smoke of his cigar in his face; another time, Madame Lormeau was teasing him with the tip of her umbrella and he swallowed the tip. Finally he got lost.

She had put him on the grass to cool him and went away only for a second; when she returned, she found no parrot! She hunted among the bushes, on the

bank of the river, and on the roofs, without paying any attention to Madame
Aubain who screamed at her: "Take care! you must be insane!" Then she searched
every garden in Pont-l'Evêque and stopped the passers-by to inquire of them:
"Haven't you perhaps seen my parrot?" To those who had never seen the parrot,
she described him minutely. Suddenly she thought she saw something green flut- 710
tering behind the mills at the foot of the hill. But when she was at the top of the
hill she could not see it. A hod-carrier told her that he had just seen the bird in
Saint-Melaine, in Mother Simon's store. She rushed to the place. The people did
not know what she was talking about. At last she came home, exhausted, with her
slippers worn to shreds, and despair in her heart. She sat down on the bench near
Madame and was telling her of her search when presently a light weight dropped
on her shoulder—Loulou! What the deuce had he been doing? Perhaps he had
just taken a little walk around the town!

She did not easily forget her scare, in fact, she never got over it. In consequence of a cold, she caught a sore throat; and some time afterward she had an 720
earache. Three years later she was stone deaf, and spoke in a very loud voice even
in church. Although her sins might have been proclaimed throughout the diocese
without any shame to herself, or ill effects to the community, the curé thought it
advisable to receive her confession in the vestry-room.

Imaginary buzzings also added to her bewilderment. Her mistress often said
to her: "My goodness, how stupid you are!" and she would answer: "Yes,
Madame," and look for something.

The narrow circle of her ideas grew more restricted than it already was; the
bellowing of the oxen, the chime of the bells no longer reached her intelligence.
All things moved silently, like ghosts. Only one noise penetrated her ears: the par- 730
rot's voice.

As if to divert her mind, he reproduced for her the tick-tack of the spit in
the kitchen, the shrill cry of the fish-vendors, the saw of the carpenter who had a
shop opposite, and when the door-bell rang, he would imitate Madame Aubain:
"Félicité! go to the front door."

They held conversations together, Loulou repeating the three phrases of his
repertory over and over, Félicité replying by words that had no greater meaning,
but in which she poured out her feelings. In her isolation, the parrot was almost a
son, a lover. He climbed upon her fingers, pecked at her lips, clung to her shawl,
and when she rocked her head to and fro like a nurse, the big wings of her cap 740
and the wings of the bird flapped in unison. When clouds gathered on the horizon
and the thunder rumbled, Loulou would scream, perhaps because he remembered
the storms in his native forests. The dripping of the rain would excite him to
frenzy; he flapped around, struck the ceiling with his wings, upset everything, and
would finally fly into the garden to play. Then he would come back into the room,
light on one of the andirons, and hop around in order to get dry.

One morning during the terrible winter of 1837, when she had put him in
front of the fire-place on account of the cold, she found him dead in his cage,
hanging to the wire bars with his head down. He had probably died of congestion.
But she believed that he had been poisoned, and although she had no proofs 750
whatever, her suspicion rested on Fabu.

She wept so sorely that her mistress said: "Why don't you have him stuffed?"

She asked the advice of the chemist, who had always been kind to the bird.

He wrote to Havre for her. A certain man named Fellacher consented to do the work. But, as the diligence driver often lost parcels entrusted to him, Félicité resolved to take her pet to Honfleur herself.

Leafless apple-trees lined the edges of the road. The ditches were covered with ice. The dogs on the neighbouring farms barked; and Félicite, with her hands beneath her cape, her little black sabots[20] and her basket, trotted along nimbly in the middle of the sidewalk. She crossed the forest, passed by the Haut-Chêne and   760 reached Saint-Gatien.

Behind her, in a cloud of dust and impelled by the steep incline, a mail-coach drawn by galloping horses advanced like a whirlwind. When he saw a woman in the middle of the road, who did not get out of the way, the driver stood up in his seat and shouted to her and so did the postilion, while the four horses, which he could not hold back, accelerated their pace; the two leaders were almost upon her; with a jerk of the reins he threw them to one side, but, furious at the incident, he lifted his big whip and lashed her from her head to her feet with such violence that she fell to the ground unconscious.

Her first thought, when she recovered her senses, was to open the basket.   770 Loulou was unharmed. She felt a sting on her right cheek; when she took her hand away it was red, for the blood was flowing.

She sat down on a pile of stones, and sopped her cheek with her handkerchief; then she ate a crust of bread she had put in her basket, and consoled herself by looking at the bird.

Arriving at the top of Ecquemanville, she saw the lights of Honfleur shining in the distance like so many stars; further on, the ocean spread out in a confused mass. Then a weakness came over her; the misery of her childhood, the disappointment of her first love, the departure of her nephew, the death of Virginia; all these things came back to her at once, and, rising like a swelling tide in her throat,   780 almost choked her.

Then she wished to speak to the captain of the vessel, and without stating what she was sending, she gave him some instructions.

Fellacher kept the parrot a long time. He always promised that it would be ready for the following week; after six months he announced the shipment of a case, and that was the end of it. Really, it seemed as if Loulou would never come back to his home. "They have stolen him," thought Félicité.

Finally he arrived, sitting bolt upright on a branch which could be screwed into a mahogany pedestal, with his foot in the air, his head on one side, and in his beak a nut which the naturalist, from love of the sumptuous, had gilded. She put   790 him in her room.

This place, to which only a chosen few were admitted, looked like a chapel and a second-hand shop, so filled was it with devotional and heterogeneous things. The door could not be opened easily on account of the presence of a large wardrobe. Opposite the window that looked out into the garden, a bull's-eye[21] opened on the yard; a table was placed by the cot and held a wash-basin, two

20. Shoes made from a single piece of wood.
21. A window made of blown glass and hence with a protuberance.

combs, and a piece of blue soap in a broken saucer. On the walls were rosaries, medals, a number of Holy Virgins, and a holy-water basin made out of a cocoanut; on the bureau, which was covered with a napkin like an altar, stood the box of shells that Victor had given her; also a watering-can and a balloon, writing-books, the engraved geography and a pair of shoes; on the nail which held the mirror, hung Virginia's little plush hat! Félicité carried this sort of respect so far that she even kept one of Monsieur's old coats. All the things which Madame Aubain discarded, Félicité begged for her own room. Thus, she had artificial flowers on the edge of the bureau, and the picture of the Comte d'Artois in the recess of the window. By means of a board, Loulou was set on a portion of the chimney which advanced into the room. Every morning when she awoke, she saw him in the dim light of dawn and recalled bygone days and the smallest details of insignificant actions, without any sense of bitterness or grief.

As she was unable to communicate with people, she lived in a sort of somnambulistic torpor. The processions of Corpus-Christi Day seemed to wake her up. She visited the neighbours to beg for candlesticks and mats so as to adorn the temporary altars in the street.

In church, she always gazed at the Holy Ghost, and noticed that there was something about it that resembled a parrot. The likeness appeared even more striking on a coloured picture by Espinal, representing the baptism of our Savior. With his scarlet wings and emerald body, it was really the image of Loulou. Having bought the picture, she hung it near the one of the Comte d'Artois so that she could take them in at one glance.

They associated in her mind, the parrot becoming sanctified through the neighbourhood of the Holy Ghost, and the latter becoming more lifelike in her eyes, and more comprehensible. In all probability the Father had never chosen as messenger a dove, as the latter has no voice, but rather one of Loulou's ancestors. And Félicité said her prayers in front of the coloured picture, though from time to time she turned slightly toward the bird.

She desired very much to enter in the ranks of the "Daughters of the Virgin." But Madame Aubain dissuaded her from it.

A most important event occurred: Paul's marriage.

After being first a notary's clerk, then in business, then in the customs, and a tax collector, and having even applied for a position in the administration of woods and forests, he had at last, when he was thirty-six years old, by a divine inspiration, found his vocation: registrature! and he displayed such a high ability that an inspector had offered him his daughter and his influence.

Paul, who had become quite settled, brought his bride to visit his mother.

But she looked down upon the customs of Pont-l'Evêque, put on airs, and hurt Félicité's feelings. Madame Aubain felt relieved when she left.

The following week they learned of Monsieur Bourais's death in an inn. There were rumours of suicide, which were confirmed; doubts concerning his integrity arose. Madame Aubain looked over her accounts and soon discovered his numerous embezzlements; sales of wood which had been concealed from her, false receipts, etc. Furthermore, he had an illegitimate child, and entertained a friendship for "a person in Dozulé."

These base actions affected her very much. In March, 1853, she developed a pain in her chest; her tongue looked as if it were coated with smoke, and the leeches they applied did not relieve her oppression; and on the ninth evening she died, being just seventy-two years old.

People thought that she was younger, because her hair, which she wore in bands framing her pale face, was brown. Few friends regretted her loss, for her manner was so haughty that she did not attract them. Félicité mourned for her as servants seldom mourn for their masters. The fact that Madame should die before 850 herself perplexed her mind and seemed contrary to the order of things, and absolutely monstrous and inadmissible. Ten days later (the time to journey from Besançon), the heirs arrived. Her daughter-in-law ransacked the drawers, kept some of the furniture, and sold the rest; then they went back to their own home.

Madame's armchair, foot-warmer, work-table, the eight chairs, everything was gone! The places occupied by the pictures formed yellow squares on the walls. They had taken the two little beds, and the wardrobe had been emptied of Virginia's belongings! Félicité went upstairs, overcome with grief.

The following day a sign was posted on the door; the chemist screamed in her ear that the house was for sale.   860

For a moment she tottered, and had to sit down.

What hurt her most was to give up her room—so nice for poor Loulou! She looked at him in despair and implored the Holy Ghost, and it was this way that she contracted the idolatrous habit of saying her prayers kneeling in front of the bird. Sometimes the sun fell through the window on his glass eye, and lighted a great spark in it which sent Félicité into ecstasy.

Her mistress had left her an income of three hundred and eighty francs. The garden supplied her with vegetables. As for clothes, she had enough to last her till the end of her days, and she economised on the light by going to bed at dusk.

She rarely went out, in order to avoid passing in front of the second-hand 870 dealer's shop where there was some of the old furniture. Since her fainting spell, she dragged her leg, and as her strength was failing rapidly, old Mother Simon, who had lost her money in the grocery business, came every morning to chop the wood and pump the water.

Her eyesight grew dim. She did not open the shutters after that. Many years passed. But the house did not sell or rent. Fearing that she would be put out, Félicité did not ask for repairs. The laths of the roof were rotting away, and during one whole winter her bolster was wet. After Easter she spit blood.

Then Mother Simon went for a doctor. Félicité wished to know what her complaint was. But, being too deaf to hear, she caught only one word: 880 "Pneumonia." She was familiar with it and gently answered—"Ah! Like Madame," thinking it quite natural that she should follow her mistress.

The time for the altars in the street drew near.[22]

The first one was always erected at the foot of the hill, the second in front of the post-office, and the third in the middle of the street. This position occasioned some rivalry among the women and they finally decided upon Madame Aubain's yard.

Félicité's fever grew worse. She was sorry that she could not do anything for

22. Altars for the Corpus Christi celebration; see note 12, above.

the altar. If she could, at least, have contributed something toward it! Then she thought of the parrot. Her neighbours objected that it would not be proper. But 890 the curé gave his consent and she was so grateful for it that she begged him to accept after her death, her only treasure, Loulou. From Tuesday until Saturday, the day before the event, she coughed more frequently. In the evening her face was contracted, her lips stuck to her gums and she began to vomit; and on the following day, she felt so low that she called for a priest.

Three neighbours surrounded her when the dominie administered the Extreme Unction.[23] Afterwards she said that she wished to speak to Fabu.

He arrived in his Sunday clothes, very ill at ease among the funereal surroundings.

"Forgive me," she said, making an effort to extend her arm, "I believed it was 900 you who killed him!"

What did such accusations mean? Suspect a man like him of murder! And Fabu became excited and was about to make trouble.

"Don't you see she is not in her right mind?"

From time to time Félicité spoke to shadows. The women left her and Mother Simon sat down to breakfast.

A little later, she took Loulou and holding him up to Félicité:

"Say good-bye to him, now!" she commanded.

Although he was not a corpse, he was eaten up by worms; one of his wings was broken and the wadding was coming out of his body. But Félicité was blind 910 now, and she took him and laid him against her cheek. Then Mother Simon removed him in order to set him on the altar.

CHAPTER V

The Vision

THE GRASS EXHALED an odour of summer; flies buzzed in the air, the sun shone on the river and warmed the slated roof. Old Mother Simon had returned to Félicité and was peaceably falling asleep.

The ringing of bells woke her; the people were coming out of church. Félicité's delirium subsided. By thinking of the procession, she was able to see it as if she had taken part in it. All the school-children, the singers and the firemen walked on the sidewalks, while in the middle of the street came first the custodian of the church with his halberd, then the beadle with a large cross, the teacher in 920 charge of the boys and a sister escorting the little girls; three of the smallest ones, with curly heads, threw rose leaves into the air; the deacon with outstretched arms conducted the music; and two incense-bearers turned with each step they took toward the Holy Sacrament, which was carried by M. le Curé, attired in his handsome chasuble and walking under a canopy of red velvet supported by four men. A crowd of people followed, jammed between the walls of the houses hung with white sheets; at last the procession arrived at the foot of the hill.

A cold sweat broke out on Félicité's forehead. Mother Simon wiped it away

23. In the Roman Catholic Church, the last rites for the dying.

with a cloth, saying inwardly that some day she would have to go through the
same thing herself.   930

The murmur of the crowd grew louder, was very distinct for a moment and
then died away. A volley of musketry shook the window-panes. It was the postil-
ions saluting the Sacrament.

Félicité rolled her eyes and said as loudly as she could:

"Is he all right?" meaning the parrot.

Her death agony began. A rattle that grew more and more rapid shook her
body. Froth appeared at the corners of her mouth, and her whole frame trembled.
In a little while could be heard the music of the bass horns, the clear voices of the
children and the men's deeper notes. At intervals all was still, and their shoes
sounded like a herd of cattle passing over the grass.   940

The clergy appeared in the yard. Mother Simon climbed on a chair to reach
the bull's-eye, and in this manner could see the altar. It was covered with a lace
cloth and draped with green wreaths. In the middle stood a little frame containing
relics; at the corners were two little orange-trees, and all along the edge were silver
candlesticks, porcelain vases containing sun-flowers, lilies, peonies, and tufts of
hydrangeas. This mound of bright colours descended diagonally from the first
floor to the carpet that covered the sidewalk. Rare objects arrested one's eye. A
golden sugar-bowl was crowned with violets, earrings set with Alençon stones
were displayed on green moss, and two Chinese screens with their bright landscapes were near by. Loulou, hidden beneath roses, showed nothing but his blue   950
head which looked like a piece of lapis-lazuli.

The singers, the canopy-bearers and the children lined up against the sides
of the yard. Slowly the priest ascended the steps and placed his shining sun on the
lace cloth. Everybody knelt. There was deep silence; and the censers slipping on
their chains were swung high in the air. A blue vapour arose in Félicité's room. She
opened her nostrils and inhaled it with a mystic sensuousness; then she closed her
lids. Her lips smiled. The beats of her heart grew fainter and fainter, and vaguer,
like a fountain giving out, like an echo dying away;—and when she exhaled her
last breath, she thought she saw in the half-opened heavens a gigantic parrot
hovering above her head.   [1877]   960

Questions for Discussion and Writing

1. Félicité's name means "happiness." Is it ironic or an apt description of her
   life? Explain.

2. Underline those passages where the narrator seems sympathetic toward
   Félicité, and circle those that seem to ridicule or criticize her. On balance,
   which attitude prevails?

3. Most of Félicité's life is spent serving others. Is her desire to serve admirable
   or not? Is she merely a servile person, without an identity of her own? Does
   she ever achieve communication or genuine contact with any of the people
   she serves? If so, when? If not, why not?

4. Some critics see this story as depicting religious faith at its simplest and most
   sincere, while others believe that Flaubert was satirizing religion. In your
   view, which reading is better? Explain.

5. Analyze the other characters' treatment of Félicité. Are there consistent elements in the way others treat her? Is it possible that a theme of the story involves the ways others behave toward Félicité?

6. How does Flaubert use the setting in this story? Analyze in particular the way in which the house and its contents relate to Félicité and her life.

✒ GUY DE MAUPASSANT
(1850–1893)

TRANSLATED BY M. WALTER DUNNE

Bellflower

Guy De Maupassant showed generations of short story writers how realism and naturalism could be applied in stories of swift pace and scrupulous economy. His influence on the short story has been enormous.

Maupassant was the son of a stockbroker in Paris. After attending the Rouen Lycée, Maupassant entered government service, but he was more interested in rowing and in literary gatherings at the home of his mother's friend, Gustave Flaubert. It was here that he also met Turgenev. For seven years, Maupassant apprenticed himself to Flaubert, who reportedly once said to him, "You must make me see, with a single word, in what way one cab-horse is totally unlike fifty others that go before and after it."

After experimenting with poetry, Maupassant turned to the short story. His first effort, "Boule de suif" ("Ball of Fat" 1880), was a sensation: he had begun his career with a masterpiece. For the next five years, he was at the height of his powers, producing stories and novels whose pessimism sometimes shocked conventional readers and whose skill commanded both respect and enormous monetary reward. By 1886, however, his health was declining, the result of syphilis contracted years before. He continued to produce both stories and novels, some richly humorous, some scandalously risqué, but he eventually succumbed to disease, misanthropy, and madness.

Some say that Maupassant destroyed European Naturalism by exhausting its possibilities and leaving his literary descendants with nothing to say in that vein. Others accuse him of cynicism and an implacable hatred of people, whom he sees as merely cunning and instinctual. But Maupassant himself claimed that he simply presented the world as he found it and made no value judgments about what he saw. His critics often forget that he can be tender and lyrical as well as brutal and objective.

HOW STRANGE ARE those old recollections which haunt us, without our being able to get rid of them!

This one is so very old that I cannot understand how it has clung so vividly and tenaciously to my memory. Since then I have seen so many sinister things, either affecting or terrible, that I am astonished at not being able to pass a single day without the face of Mother Bellflower recurring to my mind's eye, just as I knew her formerly long, long ago, when I was ten or twelve years old.

She was an old seamstress who came to my parents' house once a week, every Thursday, to mend the linen. My parents lived in one of those country houses called châteaux, which are merely old houses with pointed roofs, to which are attached three or four adjacent farms.

The village, a large village, almost a small market town, was a few hundred yards off, and nestled round the church, a red brick church, which had become black with age.

Well, every Thursday Mother Bellflower came between half past six and seven in the morning, and went immediately into the linen-room and began to work. She was a tall, thin, bearded or rather hairy woman, for she had a beard all over her face, a surprising, an unexpected beard, growing in improbable tufts, in curly bunches which looked as if they had been sown by a madman over that great face, the face of a gendarme[1] in petticoats. She had them on her nose, under her nose, round her nose, on her chin, on her cheeks; and her eyebrows, which were extraordinarily thick and long, and quite gray, bushy and bristling, looked exactly like a pair of mustaches stuck on there by mistake.

She limped, but not like lame people generally do, but like a ship pitching. When she planted her great, bony, vibrant body on her sound leg, she seemed to be preparing to mount some enormous wave, and then suddenly she dipped as if to disappear into an abyss, and buried herself in the ground. Her walk reminded one of a ship in a storm, and her head, which was always covered with an enormous white cap, whose ribbons fluttered down her back, seemed to traverse the horizon from North to South and from South to North, at each limp.

I adored Mother Bellflower. As soon as I was up I used to go into the linen-room, where I found her installed at work, with a foot-warmer under her feet. As soon as I arrived, she made me take the foot-warmer and sit upon it, so that I might not catch cold in that large, chilly room under the roof.

"That draws the blood away from your head," she would say to me.

She told me stories, while mending the linen with her long, crooked, nimble fingers; behind her magnifying spectacles, for age had impaired her sight, her eyes appeared enormous to me, strangely profound, double.

As far as I can remember from the things she told me and by which my childish heart was moved, she had the large heart of a poor woman. She told me what had happened in the village, how a cow had escaped from the cowhouse and had been found the next morning in front of Prosper Malet's mill, looking at the sails[2] turning, or about a hen's egg which had been found in the church belfry without anyone being able to understand what creature had been there to lay it, or the queer story of Jean Pila's dog, who had gone ten leagues to bring back his master's breeches which a tramp had stolen while they were hanging up to dry out of doors, after he had been caught in the rain. She told me these simple adventures

1. Policeman.
2. Canvas attached to the arms of a windmill to catch the wind.

in such a manner that in my mind they assumed the proportions of never-to-be-forgotten dramas, of grand and mysterious poems; and the ingenious stories invented by the poets, which my mother told me in the evening, had none of the flavor, none of the fullness or of the vigor of the peasant woman's narratives.

Well, one Thursday when I had spent all the morning in listening to Mother Clochette, I wanted to go upstairs to her again during the day, after picking hazelnuts with the manservant in the wood behind the farm. I remember it all as clearly as what happened only yesterday.

On opening the door of the linen room, I saw the old seamstress lying on the floor by the side of her chair, her face turned down and her arms stretched out, but still holding her needle in one hand and one of my shirts in the other. One of her legs in a blue stocking, the longer one no doubt, was extended under her chair and her spectacles glistened by the wall, where they had rolled away from her.

I ran away uttering shrill cries. They all came running, and in a few minutes I was told that Mother Clochette was dead.

I cannot describe the profound, poignant, terrible emotion which stirred my childish heart. I went slowly down into the drawing-room and hid myself in a dark corner, in the depths of a great, old armchair, where I knelt and wept. I remained there for a long time no doubt, for night came on. Suddenly some one came in with a lamp—without seeing me, however—and I heard my father and mother talking with the medical man, whose voice I recognized.

He had been sent for immediately, and he was explaining the cause of the accident, of which I understood nothing, however. Then he sat down and had a glass of liqueur and a biscuit.

He went on talking, and what he then said will remain engraved on my mind until I die! I think I can give the exact words which he used.

"Ah!" said he, "the poor woman! she broke her leg the day of my arrival here. I had not even the time to wash my hands after getting off the diligence[3] before I was sent for in all haste, for it was a bad case, very bad.

"She was seventeen, and a pretty girl, very pretty! Would anyone believe it? I have never told her story before, in fact no one but myself and one other person, who is no longer living in this part of the country, ever knew it. Now that she is dead, I may be less discreet.

"A young assistant teacher had just come to live in the village; he was good-looking and had the bearing of a soldier. All the girls ran after him, but he was disdainful. Besides that, he was very much afraid of his superior, the schoolmaster, old Grabu, who occasionally got out of bed the wrong foot first.

"Old Grabu already employed pretty Hortense, who has just died here, and who was afterward nicknamed Clochette. The assistant master singled out the pretty young girl, who was no doubt flattered at being chosen by this disdainful conqueror; at any rate, she fell in love with him, and he succeeded in persuading her to give him a first meeting in the hayloft behind the school, at night after she had done her day's sewing.

"She pretended to go home, but instead of going downstairs when she left

___

3. Stage-coach.

the Grabus', she went upstairs and hid among the hay, to wait for her lover. He soon joined her, and he was beginning to say pretty things to her, when the door of the hayloft opened and the schoolmaster appeared, and asked: "What are you doing up there, Sigisbert?" Feeling sure that he would be caught, the young schoolmaster lost his presence of mind and replied stupidly: 'I came up here to rest a little among the bundles of hay, Monsieur Grabu.'

"The loft was very large and absolutely dark. Sigisbert pushed the frightened girl to the further end and said: 'Go there and hide yourself. I shall lose my situation, so get away and hide yourself.' 100

"When the schoolmaster heard the whispering, he continued: 'Why, you are not by yourself.'

" 'Yes I am, Monsieur Grabu!'

" 'But you are not, for you are talking.'

" 'I swear I am, Monsieur Grabu.'

" 'I will soon find out,' the old man replied, and double-locking the door, he went down to get a light.

"Then the young man, who was a coward such as one sometimes meets, lost his head, and he repeated, having grown furious all of a sudden: 'Hide yourself, so that he may not find you. You will deprive me of my bread for my whole life; you 110 will ruin my whole career! Do hide yourself!'

"They could hear the key turning in the lock again, and Hortense ran to the window which looked out onto the street, opened it quickly, and then in a low and determined voice said: 'You will come and pick me up when he is gone,' and she jumped out.

"Old Grabu found nobody, and went down again in great surprise. A quarter of an hour later, Monsieur Sigisbert came to me and related his adventure. The girl had remained at the foot of the wall unable to get up, as she had fallen from the second story, and I went with him to fetch her. It was raining in torrents, and I brought the unfortunate girl home with me, for the right leg was broken in three 120 places, and the bones had come out through the flesh. She did not complain, and merely said, with admiral resignation: 'I am punished, well punished!'

"I sent for assistance and for the workgirl's friends and told them a made-up story of a runaway carriage which had knocked her down and lamed her, outside my door. They believed me, and the gendarmes for a whole month tried in vain to find the author of this accident.

"That is all! Now I say that this woman was a heroine, and had the fiber of those who accomplish the grandest deeds in history.

"That was her only love affair, and she died a virgin. She was a martyr, a noble soul, a sublimely devoted woman! And if I did not absolutely admire her, I 130 should not have told you this story, which I would never tell anyone during her life: you understand why."

The doctor ceased; mamma cried and papa said some words which I did not catch; then they left the room, and I remained on my knees in the armchair and sobbed, while I heard a strange noise of heavy footsteps and something knocking against the side of the staircase.

They were carrying away Clochette's body.   [1880]

Questions for Discussion and Writing

1. In what sense is this a love story? Whose love does it concern, Clochette's or the narrator's?
2. Is the doctor right to call Hortense "a martyr, a noble soul, a sublimely devoted woman"? Why or why not?
3. Why does the story of Clochette, the Bellflower, stick in the narrator's mind?
4. How might a feminist critic respond to the story? From a feminist viewpoint, is Hortense a heroine or a fool?

Two Little Soldiers

EVERY SUNDAY, the moment they were dismissed, the two little soldiers made off. Once outside the barracks, they struck out to the right through Courbevoie, walking with long rapid strides, as though they were on a march.

When they were beyond the last of the houses, they slackened pace along the bare, dusty roadway which goes toward Bézons.

They were both small and thin, and looked quite lost in their coats, which were too big and too long. Their sleeves hung down over their hands, and they found their enormous red breeches, which compelled them to waddle, very much in the way. Under their stiff, high helmets their faces had little character—two poor, sallow Breton faces, simple with an almost animal simplicity, and with gentle and quiet blue eyes.

They never conversed during these walks, but went straight on, each with the same thoughts in his head. This thought atoned for the lack of conversation; it was this that just inside the little wood near Les Champioux they had found a place which reminded them of their own country, where they could feel happy again.

When they arrived under the trees where the roads from Colombes and from Chatou cross, they would take off their heavy helmets and wipe their foreheads. They always halted on the Bézons bridge to look at the Seine, and would remain there two or three minutes, bent double, leaning on the parapet.

Sometimes they would gaze out over the great basin of Argenteuil, where the skiffs might be seen scudding, with their white, careening sails, recalling perhaps the look of the Breton waters, the harbor of Vanne, near which they lived, and the fishing-boats standing out across the Morbihan to the open sea.

Just beyond the Seine they bought their provisions from a sausage merchant, a baker, and a wine-seller. A piece of blood-pudding, four sous' worth of bread, and a liter of "petit bleu" constituted the provisions, which they carried off in their handkerchiefs. After they had left Bézons they traveled slowly and began to talk.

In front of them a barren plain studded with clumps of trees led to the wood, to the little wood which had seemed to them to resemble the one at Kermarivan. Grainfields and hayfields bordered the narrow path, which lost itself in the young greenness of the crops, and Jean Kerderen would always say to Luc le Ganidec:

"It looks like it does near Plounivon."

"Yes; exactly."

Side by side they strolled, their souls filled with vague memories of their own country, with awakened images as naïve as the pictures on the colored broadsheets which you would buy for a penny. They kept on recognizing, as it were, now a corner of a field, a hedge, a bit of moorland, now a crossroad, now a granite cross. Then, too, they would always stop beside a certain landmark, a great stone, because it looked something like the cromlech[1] at Locneuven.

Every Sunday morning on arriving at the first clump of trees Luc le Ganidec would cut a switch, a hazel switch, and begin gently to peel off the bark, thinking meanwhile of the folk at home. Jean Kerderen carried the provisions.

From time to time Luc would mention a name, or recall some deed of their childhood in a few brief words, which caused long thoughts. And their own country, their dear, distant country, recaptured them little by little, seizing on their imaginations, and sending to them from afar her shapes, her sounds, her well-known prospects, her odors—odors of the green lands where the salt sea-air was blowing.

No longer conscious of the exhalations of the Parisian stables, on which the earth of the *banlieue* fattens, they scented the perfume of the flowering broom, which the salt breeze of the open sea plucks and bears away. And the sails of the boats from the river banks seemed like the white wings of the coasting vessels seen beyond the great plain which extended from their homes to the very margin of the sea.

They walked with short steps, Luc le Ganidec and Jean Kerderen, content and sad, haunted by a sweet melancholy, by the lingering, ever-present sorrow of a caged animal who remembers his liberty.

By the time that Luc had stripped the slender wand of its bark they reached the corner of the wood where every Sunday they took breakfast. They found the two bricks which they kept hidden in the thicket, and kindled a little fire of twigs, over which to roast the blood-pudding at the end of a bayonet.

When they had breakfasted, eaten their bread to the last crumb, and drunk their wine to the last drop, they remained seated side by side upon the grass, saying nothing, their eyes on the distance, their eyelids drooping, their fingers crossed as at mass, their red legs stretched out beside the poppies of the field. And the leather of their helmets and brass of their buttons glittered in the ardent sun, making the larks, which sang and hovered above their heads, cease in mid-song.

Toward noon they began to turn their eyes from time to time in the direction of the village of Bézons, because the girl with the cow was coming. She passed by them every Sunday on her way to milk and change the pasture of her cow—the only cow in this district which ever went out of the stable to grass. It was pastured in a narrow field along the edge of the wood a little farther on.

They soon perceived the girl, the only human being within vision, and were gladdened by the brilliant reflections thrown off by the tin milk-pail under the rays of the sun. They never talked about her. They were simply glad to see her, without understanding why.

She was a big strong wench with red hair, burned by the heat of sunny days, a sturdy product of the environs of Paris.

1. Prehistoric burial chamber of upright stones capped by a large stone.

Once, finding them seated in the same place, she said:

"Good morning. You two are always here, aren't you?"

Luc le Ganidec, the bolder, stammered:

"Yes, we come to rest."

That was all. But the next Sunday she laughed on seeing them, laughed with a protecting benevolence and a feminine keenness which knew well enough that they were bashful. And she asked:

"What are you doing there? Are you trying to see the grass grow?"

Luc was cheered up by this, and smiled likewise. "Maybe we are."

"That's pretty slow work," said she.   90

He answered, still laughing: "Well, yes, it is."

She went on. But coming back with a milk-pail full of milk, she stopped again before them, and said:

"Would you like a little? It will taste like home."

With the instinctive feeling that they were of the same peasant race as she, being herself perhaps also far away from home, she had divined and touched the spot.

They were both touched. Then with some difficulty, she managed to make a little milk run into the neck of the glass bottle in which they carried their wine. And Luc drank first, with little swallows, stopping every minute to see whether he   100
had drunk more than his half. Then he handed the bottle to Jean.

She stood upright before them, her hands on her hips, her pail on the ground at her feet, glad at the pleasure which she had given.

Then she departed, shouting: "*Allons,* adieu! Till next Sunday!"

And as long as they could see her at all, they followed with their eyes her tall silhouette, which faded, growing smaller and smaller, seeming to sink into the verdure of the fields.

When they were leaving the barracks the week after, Jean said to Luc:

"Oughtn't we to buy her something good?"

They were in great embarrassment before the problem of the choice of a del-   110
icacy for the girl with the cow. Luc was of the opinion that a little tripe would be the best, but Jean preferred some *berlingots*[2] because he was fond of sweets. His choice fairly made him enthusiastic, and they bought at a grocer's two sous' worth of white and red candies.

They ate their breakfast more rapidly than usual, being nervous with expectation.

Jean saw her first. "There she is!" he cried. Luc added: "Yes, there she is."

While yet some distance off she laughed at seeing them. Then she cried:

"Is everything going as you like it?"

And in unison they asked: 120

"Are you getting on all right?"

Then she conversed, talked to them of simple things in which they felt an interest—of the weather, of the crops, and of her master.

2. Caramel candies.

They were afraid to offer her the candies, which were slowly melting away in Jean's pocket.

At last Luc grew bold, and murmured:

"We have brought you something."

She demanded, "What is it? Tell me!"

Then Jean, blushing up to his ears, managed to get at the little paper cornu-
copia, and held it out.   130

She began to eat the little bonbons, rolling them from one cheek to the other where they made little round lumps. The two soldiers, seated before her, gazed at her with emotion and delight.

Then she went to milk her cow, and once more gave them some milk on coming back.

They thought of her all the week; several times they even spoke of her. The next Sunday she sat down with them for a little longer talk; and all three, seated side by side, their eyes lost in the distance, clasping their knees with their hands, told the small doings, the minute details of life in the villages where they had been born, while over there the cow, seeing that the milkmaid had stopped on her way, 140 stretched out toward her its heavy head with its dripping nostrils, and gave a long low to call her.

Soon the girl contented to eat a bit of bread with them and drink a mouthful of wine. She often brought them plums in her pocket, for the season of plums had come. Her presence sharpened the wits of the two little Breton soldiers, and they chattered like two birds.

But, one Tuesday, Luc le Ganidec asked for leave—a thing which had never happened before—and he did not return until ten o'clock at night. Jean racked his brains uneasily for a reason for his comrade's going out in this way.

The next Thursday Luc, having borrowed ten sous from his bedfellow, again 150 asked and obtained permission to leave the barracks for several hours. When he set off with Jean on their Sunday walk his manner was very queer, quite restless, and quite changed. Kerderen did not understand, but he vaguely suspected something without divining what it could be.

They did not say a word to one another until they reached their usual halting-
place, where, from their constant sitting in the same spot the grass was quite worn away. They ate their breakfast slowly. Neither of them felt hungry.

Before long the girl appeared. As on every Sunday, they watched her coming. When she was quite near, Luc rose and made two steps forward. She put her milk-
pail on the ground and kissed him. She kissed him passionately, throwing her 160 arms about his neck, without noticing Jean, without remembering that he was there, without even seeing him.

And he sat there desperate, poor Jean, so desperate that he did not under-
stand, his soul quite overwhelmed, his heart bursting, but not yet understanding himself. Then the girl seated herself beside Luc, and they began to chatter.

Jean did not look at them. He now divined why his comrade had gone out twice during the week, and he felt within him a burning grief, a kind of wound, that sense of rending which is caused by treason.

Luc and the girl went off together to change the position of the cow. Jean fol-

lowed them with his eyes. He saw them departing side by side. The red breeches 170
of his comrade made a bright spot on the road. It was Luc who picked up the mallet and hammered down the stake to which they tied the beast.

The girl stooped to milk her, while he stroked the cow's sharp spine with a
careless hand. Then they left the milk-pail on the grass, and went deep into the
wood.

Jean saw nothing but the wall of leaves where they had entered; and he felt
himself so troubled that if he had tried to rise he would certainly have fallen. He
sat motionless, stupefied by astonishment and suffering, with an agony which was
simple but deep. He wanted to cry, to run away, to hide himself, never to see anybody any more.   180

Soon he saw them issuing from the thicket. They returned slowly, holding
each other's hands as in the villages do those who are promised. It was Luc who
carried the pail.

They kissed one another once again before they separated, and the girl went
off after having thrown Jean a friendly "Good evening" and a smile which was full
of meaning. To-day she no longer thought of offering him any milk.

The two little soldiers sat side by side, motionless as usual, silent and calm,
their placid faces betraying nothing of all which troubled their hearts. The sun fell
on them. Sometimes the cow lowed, looking at them from afar.

At their usual hour they rose to go back. Luc cut a switch. Jean carried the 190
empty bottle to return it to the wine-seller at Bézons. Then they sallied out upon
the bridge, and, as they did every Sunday, stopped several minutes in the middle
to watch the water flowing.

Jean leaned, leaned more and more, over the iron railing, as though he saw
in the current something which attracted him. Luc said: "Are you trying to drink?"
Just as he uttered the last word Jean's head overbalanced his body, his legs described a circle in the air, and the little blue and red soldier fell in a heap, struck
the water, and disappeared.

Luc, his tongue paralyzed with anguish, tried in vain to shout. Farther down
he saw something stir; then the head of his comrade rose to the surface of the river 200
and sank immediately. Farther still he again perceived a hand, a single hand,
which issued from the stream and then disappeared. That was all.

The bargemen who dragged the river did not find the body that day.

Luc set out alone for the barracks going at a run, his soul filled with despair.
He told of the accident, with tears in his eyes, and a husky voice, blowing his nose
again and again: "He leaned over—he—he leaned over—so far—so far that his
head turned a somersault; and—and—so he fell—he fell—"

Choked with emotion, he could say no more. If he had only known! [1880]

Questions for Discussion and Writing

1. Many love stories involve a triangle such as this one. What conventional features of the love triangle do you find in this story?
2. How does this story's point of view affect its impact on us as readers?

Consider, for example, how different the story would be if told from the point of view of any one of the main characters.

3. Maupassant emphasizes that Jean and Luc are "little" soldiers. Would the story be different if both men were physically large?

4. Does Jean fall into the water or does he commit suicide? Explain your conclusion.

5. Is the ending appropriate? If not, why not? If so, at what level is it appropriate? At the realistic level? The psychological?

6. Evaluate the friendship between Jean and Luc. How does their friendship affect the love affair?

⚘ RUBÉN DARÍO
(1867–1916)

TRANSLATED BY JILL GIBIAN

The Ruby

Rubén Darío was one of the first Latin American writers to gain international recognition and was also a leading figure in the Modernist movement in Latin America.

Born Felix Rubén García Sarmiento in Metapa, Nicaragua (now named Ciudad Darío in his honor), his early education was largely self-directed, as he read voluminously in European literature. As a teenager, he made his first trip outside the country, and it seemed to set the stage for the rest of his life. Darío began his professional career as a journalist in Central America, but in 1886 moved to Chile, where he was impressed by the sophistication and cosmopolitanism of Valparaiso and Santiago. Six years later, he went to Spain as a member of Nicaragua's delegation to the four hundredth anniversary of Columbus's "discovery" of the New World. The next year he was chosen consul for Colombia to Buenos Aires, and later that year he made his first visit to Paris.

The effects of his wide reading and travels are noticeable in his first collection of stories and poems, *Azul* (*Blue*, 1888; revised 1890). Darío's innovations lay in his synthesis of Romanticism and the French *avant garde* movements, Symbolism and Parnassism (a movement in French poetry stressing form and "art for art's sake"). Most of his short stories were written before 1899. Unlike some Modernists, Darío took a deep interest in social issues, so that behind the apparently glittering surface of his work there often lies a political or metaphysical issue. "The Ruby" combines the Modernist's delight in inventive language with a fantasy of aesthetic and mythical implications.

Darío's life after 1899 was devoted mainly to journalism, diplomacy, and poetry, through which he influenced the second generation of Latin America Modernists. He died prematurely of the effects of alcohol and narcotics.

"**A**H! SO IT'S TRUE! So that Parisian scholar has succeeded in extracting from the depths of his retorts, from his matrasses, the purple crystal with which the walls of my palace are inlaid."

And upon saying that, the little gnome scurried back and forth, from one place to another, with short hops, through the deep cave that served as his dwelling, causing his long beard and the bell on his pointed blue cap to shake.

It *was* true, a friend of the centenarian Chevreul—a would-be Althotas—the chemist Frémy,[1] had just discovered the method of making rubies and sapphires.

Excited and deeply moved, the gnome, who was erudite and had a rather lively temperament, continued his monologue.   10

"Oh, sages of the Middle Ages! Oh, Albertus Magnus, Averroes, Raimundus Lullus![2] All of you failed to see the shining wonder of the Philosopher's Stone,[3] and lo and behold, without studying the Aristotelian formulas, without knowing the cabala and necromancy,[4] here comes a man of the nineteenth century to invent in broad daylight what we produce in our subterranean world. The magic formula! For twenty days fuse a mixture of silica and lead aluminate; colored with potassium dichromate or with cobalt oxide. Words that truly resemble a diabolical language."

Laughter.

Then he stood still.   20

The corpus delecti[5] was there, in the center of the grotto, on a large golden rock: a small ruby, round, gently sparkling, resembling a pomegranate seed in the sunlight.

The gnome blew a horn which he carried at his waist, and the echo resounded throughout the vast cavern. Within a few moments, an uproar, a mad rush, a clamor. All the gnomes had arrived.

The cave was spacious, and in it there was a strange white glow. It was the splendor of the carbuncles that sparkled in the stone roof, inlaid, sunken, bunched together, in a multitude of groups; with a soft light illuminating everything.   30

In that radiance, one could see the marvelous abode in all its splendor. On the walls, on top of pieces of silver and gold, among veins of lapis lazuli, a great array of precious stones created fanciful designs similar to the arabesques of a mosque. Rainbows emerged from the crystals of the diamonds, clear and pure like drops of water; near the hanging stalactites of chalcedony, the emeralds radiated their resplendent green; and the sapphires, in bouquets that dangled from the walls, resembled large trembling blue flowers. Rows of gilded topazes and amethysts encircled the area; and from the pavement thickly set with opals, from on top of the polished chrysoprase and the agate, a thin stream of water gushed

---

1. Edmond Frémy (1814–1894), a French chemist, developed a method of making artificial rubies identical to natural ones in both color and other physical characteristics.
2. Albertus Magnus (1206–1280), medieval philosopher also reputed to be a magician; Averroes (1126–1198), Arab scholar and physician; Raimundus Lullus (ca. 1235–1316), Spanish mystic and poet.
3. Alchemists sought to discover a substance that would change base metals into gold or silver.
4. Necromancy is foretelling the future by communicating with the dead.
5. Evidence of a crime.

forth from time to time and fell with musical sweetness, in harmonious drops like 40
the notes of a metal flute blown very softly.

There was Puck,[6] that rascal Puck who had meddled in the matter. He had
brought the corpus delecti, the false ruby, the one that lay there upon the golden
rock like a sacrilege amongst all that sparkling wonder.

When the gnomes got together, some with their hammers and small hatchets
in their hands, others dressed up in their bright red pointed hoods embroidered
with jewels, all of them curious, Puck said: "You have asked me to bring you the
latest example of human counterfeiting and I have satisfied your desires."

The gnomes, seated with their legs crossed Turkish style, pulled on their
mustaches, gave thanks to Puck by slowly bowing their heads, while those closest 50
to him examined with amazement his pretty wings, similar to those of a dragonfly.

He continued: "Oh Earth! Oh, Woman! From the time I saw Titania[7] I've
been nothing but a slave of the one; an almost mystical admirer of the other."

And then, as if he were speaking in a blissful dream state: "Those rubies! In
the great city of Paris, while flying invisibly, I saw them everywhere. They sparkled
on the necklaces of courtesans, on the bizarre ornaments of the parvenus, on the
rings of Italian princes, and on the bracelets of the prima donnas."

And with a mischievous smile he continued: "I stole into a certain very fashionable crimson colored boudoir. . . . There was a beautiful woman asleep. From
her neck I plucked the medallion and from the medallion the ruby. There you 60
have it."

Everyone burst out laughing. What a jingling of bells!

"Wow, that Puck sure is a devil!"

And then they gave their opinions about that fake, man-made, or what's
worse, sage-made stone!

"Glass!"

"Witchcraft!"

"Poison and cabala!"

"Chemistry!"

"It pretends to imitate a section of the rainbow!" 70

"The rubicund treasure from the depths of the globe!"

"Made from the solidified rays of the setting sun."

The oldest gnome, walking with gnarled legs and a long snow-white beard,
looked like a patriarch with his face covered with wrinkles. "Gentlemen!" he said.
"You don't know what you're saying."

Everyone listened.

"I, I am older than all of you, since I'm now barely fit to hammer the facets
of the diamonds; I, who witnessed the building of these deep fortresses; I, who
chiseled the bones of the earth, who molded the gold, who one day gave a punch
to a stone wall, and fell into a lake where I raped a nymph; I, the elder, I shall tell 80
you how the ruby was made. Listen."

6. The mischievous fairy in Shakespeare's *A Midsummer Night's Dream*.
7. Queen of the fairies in *A Midsummer Night's Dream*.

Puck smiled, inquisitively. All the gnomes surrounded the ancient fellow whose gray hairs appeared pale in the brilliance of the jewels and whose hands cast moving shadows on the walls covered with precious stones, like a canvas covered with honey where grains of rice were flung.

"One day, our squadrons that were in charge of the diamond mines went on strike, a strike that shook the whole earth, and we fled through the craters of the volcanoes.

"The world was happy, everything was full of vigor and youth; and the roses, and the fresh green leaves, and the birds in whose beaks the seeds enter and the chirping bursts out, and the whole countryside greeted the sun and the fragrant springtime.

"The hills in bloom were full of harmony produced by the warbling of birds and the buzzing of bees; it was a great and sacred wedding orchestrated by light: on the trees the sap glistened profoundly, and among the animals everything was stirring either in the form of bleating or chanting, and in the gnomes there was laughter and happiness.

"I had gone out through an extinct crater. Before my eyes there was an enormous field. With one leap I put myself on a large tree, an old evergreen oak. Then I climbed down the trunk, and I found myself near a stream, a small clear river where the waters babbled crystalline jokes to one another. I was thirsty. I tried to drink there. . . . Now, listen more closely."

"Arms, backs, naked breasts, white lilies, roses, small ivory rolls topped with cherries; echoes of golden festive laughter: and there amongst the foam, amongst the choppy waters, beneath the green branches. . . ."

"Nymphs?"

"No, women. I knew which of the caves was mine. By banging on the ground, I made the black sand open up and arrived at my palace. You poor little young gnomes, you have much to learn!

"I scurried along beneath the shoots of some new ferns, over some stones which had been polished by the foamy murmuring current; and she, the beautiful one, the woman, I seized her by the waist, with this arm which was once so muscular; she shouted, I banged on the ground; we descended. Above, all was fear and wonderment; below, the arrogant and victorious gnome.

"One day I was hammering a chunk of an immense diamond which shone like a star and which broke into small particles with the stroke of my mallet.

"The floor of my workshop resembled the remains of a shattered sun. The beloved woman was resting on one side, a human rose amongst sapphire flower pots, a golden empress on a bed of rock crystal, completely naked and magnificent like a goddess.

"But in the midst of my palace, my queen, my beloved, my beauty, was deceiving me. When a man is truly in love, his passion penetrates everything, and he is capable of transcending the earth.

"She was in love with a man, and from her prison, she would transmit her sighs to him. They would pass through the pores of the terrestrial crust and reach him; and he, equally in love with her, would kiss the roses of a certain garden; and she, his beloved, I noticed, would experience—sudden convulsions in which she extended her lips, pink and fresh like the petals of a centifolia rose. How could they feel each other's presence? With all my magical powers, I do not know.

"I had just finished my work: a huge pile of diamonds all made in one day; the earth opened up its granite crevices like thirsty lips, awaiting the brilliant breaking up of the rich crystal. At the end of the task, tired, I broke one last rock with my hammer and fell asleep.

"I awoke a little while later, upon hearing something like a moan.

"From her bed, from her quarters which were richer and more dazzling than those of all the queens in the Orient, my beloved, my abducted woman, had fled in desperation. Oh! And trying to escape through the hole opened by my granite mallet, naked and beautiful, she destroyed her body, once as white and smooth as orange blossoms, marble and roses, on the edges of the broken diamonds. With her wounded sides dripping blood, her groans were so touching they brought me to tears. Oh what grief!

"I got up, took her in my arms, and gave her my most ardent kisses; but the blood continued to flow inundating the room, and the huge diamond mass became tinged with scarlet.

"As I kissed her, I seemed to detect a perfume escaping from her burning lips: her soul; her body remained inert.

"When our grand patriarch, the godlike centenarian from the bowels of the earth, passed through, he found that multitude of red diamonds. . . .

A pause.

"Do you understand?"

The gnomes, very gravely rose.

They examined more closely the false stone, the work of the sage.

"Look, it doesn't have facets."

"It has a dull gleam."

"Impostor!"

"It's round like the shell of a scarab."

And in turn, one by one, they went to pull out of the walls pieces of the arabesque, rubies as large as an orange, red and sparkling like a blood-tinged diamond; and they said:

"This is ours, oh Mother Earth!"

It was an orgy of brilliance and color.

And laughing, they began to throw into the air giant luminous stones.

Suddenly, with all the dignity of a gnome:

"Well then, we condemn it."

Everyone understood. They took the false ruby, broke it into many pieces and flung the fragments—with terrible disdain—into a pit below which led into a very ancient carbonized jungle.

Then, with joined hands they began dancing a wild sonorous dance on their rubies, on their opals, within the confines of those gleaming walls.

And they celebrated with laughter seeing themselves enlarged in the form of their shadows. By this time Puck was flying outside, in the buzzing of the new dawn, on his way to a flowering meadow. And he murmured—with his usual blushing smile,

"Earth. . . . Woman. . . . Because you, oh Mother Earth! You are great and fertile, your breast is inexhaustible and sacred; and from your dark womb flows the sap of the sturdy trees, and the gold and the diamond-like water, and the chaste lily. Everything that is pure and strong and that may not be falsified! And you, Woman, you are spirit and flesh, all love!"   [1888]

Questions for Discussion and Writing

1. What are gnomes, and how (at least in this story) do they resemble and differ from human beings?
2. The story presents three rubies—the natural, the artificial, and the mythical. Which one, if any, is the true ruby? Why?
3. Compare the old gnome's story of the origin of the ruby with other myths you know. What features does it share with them?
4. How does Puck's speech about Nature and Woman relate to the story as a whole?
5. What ideas does the story suggest about the nature of Art?
6. Darío is considered a Modernist writer. Does the label fit? Why or why not?

H. RIDER HAGGARD
(1856–1925)

Hunter Quatermain's Story

Sir Henry Rider Haggard's thirty-four novels, particularly *King Solomon's Mines* (1885) and *She* (1886), occupy a unique and important place in the popular imagination and have influenced every popular medium—from Hollywood films and Saturday morning cartoons to computer games. Perhaps more than any other writer of his time, Haggard shaped the popular idea of what an exciting story should be.

Haggard was the eighth child of the squire of Bradenham Hall, Norfolk. Henry and his father never got along: the father resented the child's physical weakness; the child could not understand the father's lack of imagination. His mother's influence was crucial, extending even to his interest in Egypt, which he would later exploit in his fiction. After grammar school, Haggard was sent to London to prepare for the Foreign Service, but he fell in love and was sent to Africa, where he served ably for six years and acquired many of the experiences he would later use in his fiction.

Returning to England, Haggard attempted farming in Norfolk, but the agricultural depression of the 1880s drove him to try writing as a way of supporting himself and his wife. Three enormously popular novels resulted, and Haggard suddenly found himself a wealthy celebrity. Haggard's later work never equaled his early successes, and he gradually turned from fiction writing to public service and to investigations of agricultural practice and policy. He was knighted in 1912.

Haggard's strengths are his dramatic plots marked by marvelous events, colorful writing, and authentic descriptions of landscape, natives, and wildlife. In these regards, his work has inspired imitators such as Joseph Conrad (1857–1924). His writing coincided with the height of the British Empire and hence with his audience's desire for fiction about Britain's exotic colonies and peoples. His characters, however, are little more than types, his plots and adventures frequently outlandish, and his attitudes toward Africans and other non-British people unenlightened or racist.

S IR HENRY CURTIS, as everybody acquainted with him knows, is one of the most hospitable men on earth. It was in the course of the enjoyment of his hospitality at his place in Yorkshire the other day that I heard the hunting story which I am now about to transcribe. Many of those who read it will no doubt have heard some of the strange rumours that are flying about to the effect that Sir Henry Curtis and his friend Captain Good, R.N.,[1] recently found a vast treasure of diamonds out in the heart of Africa, supposed to have been hidden by the Egyptians, or King Solomon, or some other antique person. I first saw the matter alluded to in a paragraph in one of the society papers the day before I started for Yorkshire to pay my visit to Curtis, and arrived, needless to say, burning with curiosity; for 10 there is something very fascinating to the mind in the idea of hidden treasure. When I reached the Hall, I at once asked Curtis about it, and he did not deny the truth of the story; but on my pressing him to tell it he would not, nor would Captain Good, who was also staying in the house.

"You would not believe me if I did," Sir Henry said, with one of the hearty laughs which seem to come right out of his great lungs. "You must wait till Hunter Quatermain comes; he will arrive here from Africa tonight, and I am not going to say a word about the matter, or Good either, until he turns up. Quatermain was with us all through; he has known about the business for years and years, and if it had not been for him we should no have been here to-day. I am going to meet him 20 presently."

I could not get a word more out of him, nor could anybody else, though we were all dying of curiosity, especially some of the ladies. I shall never forget how they looked in the drawing-room before dinner when Captain Good produced a great rough diamond, weighing fifty carats or more, and told them that he had many larger than that. If ever I saw curiosity and envy printed on fair faces, I saw them then.

It was just at this moment that the door was opened, and Mr. Allan Quatermain announced, whereupon Good put the diamond into his pocket, and sprang at a little man who limped shyly into the room, convoyed by Sir Henry 30 Curtis himself.

---

1. Royal Navy.

"Here he is, Good, safe and sound," said Sir Henry, gleefully. "Ladies and gentlemen, let me introduce you to one of the oldest hunters and the very best shot in Africa, who has killed more elephants and lions than any other man alive."

Everybody turned and stared politely at the curious-looking little lame man, and though his size was insignificant, he was quite worth staring at. He had short grizzled hair, which stood about an inch above his head like the bristles of a brush, gentle brown eyes, that seemed to notice everything, and a withered face, tanned to the colour of mahogany from exposure to the weather. He spoke, too, when he returned Good's enthusiastic greeting, with a curious little accent, which 40 made his speech noticeable.

It so happened that I sat next to Mr. Allan Quatermain at dinner, and, of course, did my best to draw him; but he was not to be drawn. He admitted that he had recently been a long journey into the interior of Africa with Sir Henry Curtis and Captain Good, and that they had found treasure, and then politely turned the subject and began to ask me questions about England, where he had never been before—that is, since he came to years of discretion. Of course, I did not find this very interesting, and so cast about for some means to bring the conversation round again.

Now, we were dining in an oak-panelled vestibule, and on the wall opposite 50 to me were fixed two gigantic elephant tusks, and under them a pair of buffalo horns, very rough and knotted, showing that they came off an old bull, and having the tip of one horn split and chipped. I noticed that Hunter Quatermain's eyes kept glancing at these trophies, and took an occasion to ask him if he knew anything about them.

"I ought to," he answered, with a little laugh; "the elephant to which those tusks belonged tore one of our party right in two about eighteen months ago, and as for the buffalo horns, they were nearly my death, and were the end of a servant of mine to whom I was much attached. I gave them to Sir Henry when he left Natal some months ago;" and Mr. Quatermain sighed and turned to answer a 60 question from the lady whom he had taken down to dinner, and who, needless to say, was also employed in trying to pump him about the diamonds.

Indeed, all round the table there was a simmer of scarcely suppressed excitement, which, when the servants had left the room, could no longer be restrained.

"Now, Mr. Quatermain," said the lady next him, "we have been kept in an agony of suspense by Sir Henry and Captain Good, who have persistently refused to tell us a word of this story about the hidden treasure till you came, and we simply can bear it no longer; so, please, begin at once."

"Yes," said everybody, "go on, please."

Hunter Quatermain glanced round the table apprehensively; he did not 70 seem to appreciate finding himself the object of so much curiosity.

"Ladies and gentlemen," he said at last, with a shake of his grizzled head, "I am very sorry to disappoint you, but I cannot do it. It is this way. At the request of Sir Henry and Captain Good I have written down a true and plain account of King Solomon's Mines and how we found them, so you will soon all be able to learn all about that wonderful adventure for yourselves; but until then I will say nothing about it, not from any wish to disappoint your curiosity, or to make myself important, but simply because the whole story partakes so much of the marvellous, that

I am afraid to tell it in a piecemeal, hasty fashion, for fear I should be set down as one of those common fellows of whom there are so many in my profession, who are not ashamed to narrate things they have not seen, and even to tell wonderful stories about wild animals they have never killed. And I think that my companions in adventure, Sir Henry Curtis and Captain Good, will bear me out in what I say."

"Yes, Quatermain, I think you are quite right," said Sir Henry. "Precisely the same considerations have forced Good and myself to hold our tongues. We did not wish to be bracketed with—well, with other famous travellers."

There was a murmur of disappointment at these announcements.

"I believe you are all hoaxing us," said the young lady next Mr. Quatermain, rather sharply.

"Believe me," answered the old hunter, with a quaint courtesy and a little bow of his grizzled head; "though I have lived all my life in the wilderness, and amongst savages, I have neither the heart, nor the want of manners, to wish to deceive one so lovely."

Whereat the young lady, who was pretty, looked appeased.

"This is very dreadful," I broke in. "We ask for bread and you give us a stone, Mr. Quatermain. The least that you can do is to tell us the story of the tusks opposite and the buffalo horns underneath. We won't let you off with less."

"I am but a poor story-teller," put in the old hunter, "but if you will forgive my want of skill, I shall be happy to tell you, not the story of the tusks, for it is part of the history of our journey to King Solomon's Mines, but that of the buffalo horns beneath them, which is now ten years old."

"Bravo, Quatermain!" said Sir Henry. "We shall all be delighted. Fire away! Fill up your glass first."

The little man did as he was bid, took a sip of claret, and began:—"About ten years ago I was hunting up in the far interior of Africa, at a place called Gatgarra, not a great way from the Chobe River. I had with me four native servants, namely, a driver and voorlooper, or leader who were natives of Matabeleland, a Hottentot called Hans, who had once been the slave of a Transvaal Boer, and a Zulu hunter, who for five years had accompanied me upon my trips, and whose name was Mashune. Now near Gatgarra I found a fine piece of healthy, park-like country, where the grass was very good, considering the time of year; and here I made a little camp or head-quarter settlement, from whence I went expeditions on all sides in search of game, especially elephant. My luck, however, was bad; I got but little ivory. I was therefore very glad when some natives brought me news that a large herd of elephants were feeding in a valley about thirty miles away. At first I thought of trekking down to the valley, waggon and all, but gave up the idea on hearing that it was infested with the deadly 'tsetse' fly, which is certain death to all animals, except men, donkeys, and wild game. So I reluctantly determined to leave the waggon in the charge of the Matabele leader and driver, and to start on a trip into the thorn country, accompanied only by the Hottentot Hans, and Mashune.

"Accordingly on the following morning we started, and on the evening of the next day reached the spot where the elephants were reported to be. But here again we were met by ill luck. That the elephants had been there was evident enough, for their spoor was plentiful, and so were other traces of their presence in the shape of mimosa trees torn out of the ground, and placed topsy-turvy on their flat crowns, in order to enable the great beasts to feed on their sweet roots; but the elephants themselves were conspicuous by their absence. They had elected to move on. This being so, there was only one thing to do, and that was to move after 130 them, which we did, and a pretty hunt they led us. For a fortnight[2] or more we dodged about after those elephants, coming up with them on two occasions, and a splendid herd they were—only, however, to lose them again. At length we came up with them a third time, and I managed to shoot one bull, and then they started off again, where it was useless to try and follow them. After this I gave it up in disgust, and we made the best of our way back to camp, not in the sweetest of tempers, carrying the tusks of the elephant I had shot.

"It was on the afternoon of the fifth day of our tramp that we reached the little koppie overlooking the spot where the waggon stood, and I confess that I climbed it with a pleasurable sense of home-coming, for his waggon is the hunter's 140 home, as much as his house is that of a civilized person. I reached the top of the koppie, and looked in the direction where the friendly white tent of the waggon should be, but there was no waggon, only a black burnt plain stretching away as far as the eye could reach. I rubbed my eyes, looked again, and made out on the spot of the camp, not my waggon, but some charred beams of wood. Half wild with grief and anxiety, followed by Hans and Mashune, I ran at full speed down the slope of the koppie, and across the space of plain below to the spring of water, where my camp had been. I was soon there, only to find that my worst suspicions were confirmed.

"The waggon and all its contents, including my spare guns and ammunition, 150 had been destroyed by a grass fire.

"Now before I started, I had left orders with the driver to burn off the grass round the camp, in order to guard against accidents of this nature, and here was the reward of my folly: a very proper illustration of the necessity, especially where natives are concerned, of doing a thing one's self if one wants it done at all. Evidently the lazy rascals had not burnt round the waggon; most probably, indeed, they had themselves carelessly fired the tall and resinous tambouki grass near by; the wind had driven the flames on to the waggon tent, and there was quickly an end of the matter. As for the driver and leader, I know not what became of them: probably fearing my anger, they bolted, taking the oxen with them. I have never 160 seen them from that hour to this.

"I sat down on the black veldt by the spring, and gazed at the charred axles and disselboom of my waggon, and I can assure you, ladies and gentlemen, I felt inclined to weep. As for Mashune and Hans they cursed away vigorously, one in Zulu and the other in Dutch. Ours was a pretty position. We were nearly 300 miles away from Bamangwato, the capital of Khama's country, which was the nearest spot where we could get any help, and our ammunition, spare guns, clothing, food, and everything else, were all totally destroyed. I had just what I stood in, which was a flannel shirt, a pair of 'veldt-schoons,' or shoes of raw hide, my eight-bore rifle, and a few cartridges. Hans and Mashune had also each a Martini rifle 170

2. Literally, fourteen nights; i.e., two weeks.

and some cartridges, not many. And it was with this equipment that we had to undertake a journey of 300 miles through a desolate and almost uninhabited region. I can assure you that I have rarely been in a worse position, and I have been in some queer ones. However, these things are the natural incidents of a hunter's life, and the only thing to do was to make the best of them.

"Accordingly, after passing a comfortless night by the remains of my waggon, we started next morning on our long journey towards civilization. Now if I were to set to work to tell you all the troubles and incidents of that dreadful journey I should keep you listening here till midnight; so I will, with your permission, pass on to the particular adventure of which the pair of buffalo horns opposite are the   180
melancholy memento.

"We had been travelling for about a month, living and getting along as best we could, when one evening we camped some forty miles from Bamangwato. By this time we were indeed in a melancholy plight, footsore, half starved, and utterly worn out; and, in addition, I was suffering from a sharp attack of fever, which half blinded me and made me as weak as a babe. Our ammunition, too, was exhausted; I had only one cartridge left for my eight-bore rifle, and Hans and Mashune, who were armed with Martini Henrys, had three between them. It was about an hour from sundown when we halted and lit a fire—for luckily we had still a few matches. It was a charming spot to camp, I remember. Just off the game   190
track we were following was a little hollow, fringed about with flat-crowned mimosa trees, and at the bottom of the hollow, a spring of clear water welled up out of the earth, and formed a pool, round the edges of which grew an abundance of watercresses of an exactly similar kind to those which were handed round the table just now. Now we had no food of any kind left, having that morning devoured the last remains of a little oribe antelope, which I had shot two days previously. Accordingly Hans, who was a better shot than Mashune, took two of the three remaining Martini cartridges, and started out to see if he could not kill a buck for supper. I was too weak to go myself.

"Meanwhile Mashune employed himself in dragging together some dead   200
boughs from the mimosa trees to make a sort of 'skerm,' or shelter for us to sleep in, about forty yards from the edge of the pool of water. We had been greatly troubled with lions in the course of our long tramp, and only on the previous night had very nearly been attacked by them, which made me nervous, especially in my weak state. Just as we had finished the skerm, or rather something which did duty for one, Mashune and I heard a shot apparently fired about a mile away.

"'Hark to it!' sung out Mashune in Zulu, more, I fancy, by way of keeping his spirits up than for any other reason—for he was a sort of black Mark Tapley, and very cheerful under difficulties. 'Hark to the wonderful sound with which the "Maboona" (the Boers) shook our fathers to the ground at the battle of the Blood   210
River. We are hungry now, my father; our stomachs are small and withered up like dried ox's paunch, but they will soon be full of good meat. Hans is a Hottentot,[3] and an "umfagozan," that is, a low fellow, but he shoots straight—ah! he certainly shoots straight. Be of a good heart, my father, there will soon be meat upon the fire, and we shall rise up men.'

_____

3. Native of the Cape of Good Hope region of South Africa.

"And so he went on talking nonsense till I told him to stop, because he made my head ache with his empty words.

"Shortly after we heard the shot the sun sank in his red splendour, and there fell upon earth and sky the great hush of the African wilderness. The lions were not up as yet, they would probably wait for the moon, and the birds and beasts were all at rest. I cannot describe the intensity of the quiet of the night: to me in my weak state, and fretting as I was over the non-return of the Hottentot Hans, it seemed almost ominous—as though Nature were brooding over some tragedy which was being enacted in her sight.

"It was quiet—quiet as death, and lonely as the grave.

"'Mashune,' I said at last, 'where is Hans? my heart is heavy for him.'

"'Nay, my father, I know not; mayhap he is weary, and sleeps, or mayhap he has lost his way.'

"'Mashune, art thou a boy to talk folly to me?' I answered. 'Tell me, in all the years thou hast hunted by my side, didst thou ever know a Hottentot to lose his path or to sleep upon the way to camp?'

"'Nay, Macumazahn' (that, ladies, is my native name, and means the man who 'gets up by night,' or who 'is always awake'), 'I know not where he is.'

"But though we talked thus, we neither of us liked to hint at what was in both our minds, namely, that misfortune had overtaken the poor Hottentot.

"'Mashune,' I said at last, 'go down to the water and bring me of those green herbs that grow there. I am hungered, and must eat something.'

"'Nay, my father; surely the ghosts are there; they come out of the water at night, and sit upon the banks to dry themselves. An Isanusi[4] told it me.'

"Mashune was, I think, one of the bravest men I ever knew in daytime, but he had a more than civilized dread of the supernatural.

"'Must I go myself, thou fool? I said, sternly.

"'Nay, Macumazahn, if thy heart yearns for strange things like a sick woman, I go, even if the ghosts devour me.'

"And accordingly he went, and soon returned with a large bundle of watercresses, of which I ate greedily.

"'Art thou not hungry?' I asked the great Zulu presently, as he sat eyeing me eating.

"'Never was I hungrier, my father.'

"'Then eat,' and I pointed to the watercresses.

"'Nay, Macumazahn, I cannot eat those herbs.'

"'If thou dost not eat thou wilt starve: eat. Mashune.'

"He stared at the watercresses doubtfully for a while, and at last seized a handful and crammed them into his mouth, crying out as he did so, 'Oh, why was I born that I should live to feed on green weeds like an ox? Surely if my mother could have known it she would have killed me when I was born!' and so he went on lamenting between each fistful of watercresses till all were finished, when he declared that he was full indeed of stuff, but it lay very cold on his stomach, 'like snow upon a mountain.' At any other time I should have laughed, for it must be admitted he had a ludicrous way of putting things. Zulus do not like green food.

4. Witch-finder (Haggard's note).

"Just after Mashune had finished his watercress, we heard the loud 'woof! woof!' of a lion, who was evidently promenading much nearer to our little skerm than was pleasant. Indeed, on looking into the darkness and listening intently, I could hear his snoring breath, and catch the light of his great yellow eyes. We shouted loudly, and Mashune threw some sticks on the fire to frighten him, which apparently had the desired effect, for we saw no more of him for a while.

"Just after we had this fright from the lion, the moon rose in her fullest splendour, throwing a robe of silver light over all the earth. I have rarely seen a more beautiful moonrise. I remember that sitting in the skerm I could with ease read faint pencil notes in my pocketbook. As soon as the moon was up game 270 began to trek down to the water just below us. I could, from where I sat, see all sorts of them passing along a little ridge that ran to our right, on their way to the drinking place. Indeed, one buck—a large eland—came within twenty yards of the skerm, and stood at gaze, staring at it suspiciously, his beautiful head and twisted horns standing out clearly against the sky. I had, I recollect, every mind to have a pull at him on the chance of providing ourselves with a good supply of beef; but remembering that we had but two cartridges left, and the extreme uncertainty of a shot by moonlight, I at length decided to refrain. The eland presently moved on to the water, and a minute or two afterwards there arose a great sound of splashing, followed by the quick fall of galloping hoofs.   280

" 'What's that, Mashune?' I asked.

" 'That dam lion; buck smell him,' replied the Zulu in English, of which he had a very superficial knowledge.

"Scarcely were the words out of his mouth before we heard a sort of whine over the other side of the pool, which was instantly answered by a loud coughing roar close to us.

" 'By Jove!' I said, 'there are two of them. They have lost the buck; we must look out they don't catch us.' And again we made up the fire, and shouted, with the result that the lions moved off.

" 'Mashune,' I said, 'do you watch till the moon gets over that tree, when it 290 will be the middle of the night. Then wake me. Watch well, now, or the lions will be picking those worthless bones of yours before you are three hours older. I must rest a little, or I shall die.'

" 'Koos!' (chief), answered the Zulu. 'Sleep, my father, sleep in peace; my eyes shall be open as the stars; and like the stars shall watch over you.'

"Although I was so weak, I could not at once follow his advice. To begin with, my head ached with fever, and I was torn with anxiety as to the fate of the Hottentot Hans; and, indeed, as to our own fate, left with sore feet, empty stomachs, and two cartridges, to find our way to Bamangwato, forty miles off. Then the mere sensation of knowing that there are one or more hungry lions prowling 300 round you somewhere in the dark is disquieting, however well one may be used to it, and, by keeping the attention on the stretch, tends to prevent one from sleeping. In addition to all these troubles, too, I was, I remember, seized with a dreadful longing for a pipe of tobacco, whereas, under the circumstances, I might as well have longed for the moon.

"At last, however, I fell into an uneasy sleep as full of bad dreams as a prickly pear is of points, one of which, I recollect, was that I was setting my naked foot

upon a cobra which rose upon its tail and hissed my name, 'Macumazahn,' into
my ear. Indeed, the cobra hissed with such persistency that at last I roused myself.

"'*Macumazahn, nanzia, nanzia!*' (there, there!) whispered Mashune's voice ₃₁₀
into my drowsy ears. Raising myself, I opened my eyes, and I saw Mashune kneeling by my side and pointing towards the water. Following the line of his outstretched hand, my eyes fell upon a sight that made me jump, old hunter as I was
even in those days. About twenty paces from the little skerm was a large ant-heap,
and on the summit of the ant-heap, her four feet rather close together, so as to find
standing space, stood the massive form of a big lioness. Her head was towards the
skerm, and in the bright moonlight I saw her lower it and lick her paws.

"Mashune thrust the Martini rifle into my hands, whispering that it was
loaded. I lifted it and covered the lioness, but found that even in that light I could
not make out the foresight of the Martini. As it would be madness to fire without ₃₂₀
doing so, for the result would probably be that I should wound the lioness, if, indeed, I did not miss altogether, I lowered the rifle; and, hastily tearing a fragment
of paper from one of the leaves of my pocketbook, which I had been consulting
just before I went to sleep, I proceeded to fix it on to the front sight. But all this
took a little time, and before the paper was satisfactorily arranged, Mashune again
gripped me by the arm, and pointed to a dark heap under the shade of a small mimosa tree which grew not more than ten paces from the skerm.

"'Well, what is it?' I whispered; 'I can see nothing.'

"'It is another lion,' he answered.

"'Nonsense! thy heart is dead with fear, thou seest double;' and I bent for- ₃₃₀
ward over the edge of the surrounding fence, and stared at the heap.

"Even as I said the words, the dark mass rose and stalked out into the moonlight. It was a magnificent, black-maned lion, one of the largest I had ever seen.
When he had gone two or three steps he caught sight of me, halted, and stood
there gazing straight towards us;—he was so close that I could see the firelight reflected in his wicked, greenish eyes.

"'Shoot, shoot!' said Mashune. 'The devil is coming—he is going to spring!'

"I raised the rifle, and got the bit of paper on the foresight, straight on to a
little patch of white hair just where the throat is set into the chest and shoulders.
As I did so, the lion glanced back over his shoulder, as, according to my experi- ₃₄₀
ence, a lion nearly always does before he springs. Then he dropped his body a little, and I saw his big paws spread out upon the ground as he put his weight on
them to gather purchase. In haste I pressed the trigger of the Martini, and not an
instant too soon; for, as I did so, he was in the act of springing. The report of the
rifle rang out sharp and clear on the intense silence of the night, and in another
second the great brute had landed on his head within four feet of us, and rolling
over and over towards us, was sending the bushes which composed our little
fence flying with convulsive strokes of his great paws. We sprang out of the other
side of the 'skerm,' and he rolled on to it and into it and then right through the
fire. Next he raised himself and sat upon his haunches like a great dog, and began ₃₅₀
to roar. Heavens! how he roared! I never heard anything like it before or since. He
kept filling his lungs with air, and the emitting it in the most heart-shaking volumes of sound. Suddenly, in the middle of one of the loudest roars, he rolled over

on to his side and lay still, and I knew that he was dead. A lion generally dies upon his side.

"With a sigh of relief I looked up towards his mate upon the ant-heap. She was standing there apparently petrified with astonishment, looking over her shoulder, and lashing her tail; but to our intense joy, when the dying beast ceased roaring, she turned, and, with one enormous bound, vanished into the night.

"Then we advanced cautiously towards the prostrate brute, Mashune dron- ing an improvised Zulu song as he went, about how Macumazahn, the hunter of hunters, whose eyes are open by night as well as by day, put his hand down the lion's stomach when it came to devour him and pulled out his heart by the roots, &c., &c., by way of expressing his satisfaction, in his hyperbolical Zulu way, at the turn events had taken.

"There was no need for caution; the lion was as dead as though he had al- ready been stuffed with straw. The Martini bullet had entered within an inch of the white spot I had aimed at, and travelled right through him, passing out at the right buttock, near the root of the tail. The Martini has wonderful driving power, though the shock it gives to the system is, comparatively speaking, slight, owing to the smallness of the hole it makes. But fortunately the lion is an easy beast to kill.

"I passed the rest of that night in a profound slumber, my head reposing upon the deceased lion's flank, a position that had, I thought, a beautiful touch of irony about it, though the smell of his singed hair was disagreeable. When I woke again the faint primrose lights of dawn were flushing in the eastern sky. For a mo- ment I could not understand the chill sense of anxiety that lay like a lump of ice at my heart, till the feel and smell of the skin of the dead lion beneath my head re- called the circumstances in which we were placed. I rose, and eagerly looked round to see if I could discover any signs of Hans, who, if he had escaped acci- dent, would surely return to us at dawn, but there were none. Then hope grew faint, and I felt that it was not well with the poor fellow. Setting Mashune to build up the fire I hastily removed the hide from the flank of the lion, which was indeed a splendid beast, and cutting off some lumps of flesh, we toasted and ate them greedily. Lions' flesh, strange as it may seem, is very good eating, and tasted more like veal than anything else.

"By the time that we had finished our much-needed meal the sun was get- ting up, and after a drink of water and a wash at the pool, we started to try and find Hans leaving the dead lion to the tender mercies of the hyaenas. Both Mashune and myself were, by constant practice, pretty good hands at tracking, and we had not much difficulty in following the Hottentot's spoor, faint as it was. We had gone on in this way for half-an-hour or so, and were, perhaps, a mile or more from the site of our camping-place, when we discovered the spoor of a soli- tary bull buffalo mixed up with the spoor of Hans, and were able from various in- dications, to make out that he had been tracking the buffalo. At length we reached a little glade in which there grew a stunted old mimosa thorn, with a peculiar and overhanging formation of root, under which a porcupine, or an ant-bear, or some such animal, had hollowed out a wide-lipped hole. About ten or fifteen paces from this thorn-tree there was a thick patch of bush.

"'See, Macumazahn! see!' said Mashune, excitedly, as we drew near the thorn; 'the buffalo has charged him. Look, here he stood to fire at him; see how firmly he planted his feet upon the earth; there is the mark of his crooked toe (Hans had one bent toe). Look! here the bull came like a boulder down the hill, his hoofs turning up the earth like a hoe. Hans had hit him: he bled as he came; there are the blood spots. It is all written down there, my father—there upon the earth.'

"'Yes,' I said; 'yes; but *where is Hans?*'

"Even as I said it Mashune clutched my arm, and pointed to the stunted thorn just by us. Even now, gentlemen, it makes me feel sick when I think of what I saw.

"For fixed in a stout fork of the tree some eight feet from the ground was Hans himself, or rather his dead body, evidently tossed there by the furious buffalo. One leg was twisted round the fork, probably in a dying convulsion. In the side, just beneath the ribs, was a great hole, from which the entrails protruded. But this was not all. The other leg hung down to within five feet of the ground. The skin and most of the flesh were gone from it. For a moment we stood aghast, and gazed at this horrifying sight. Then I understood what had happened. The buffalo, with that devilish cruelty which distinguishes the animal, had, after his enemy was dead, stood underneath his body, and licked the flesh off the pendant leg with his file-like tongue. I had heard of such a thing before, but had always treated the stories as hunters' yarns; but I had no doubt about it now. Poor Hans' skeleton foot and ankle were an ample proof.

"We stood aghast under the tree, and stared and stared at this awful sight, when suddenly our cogitations were interrupted in a painful manner. The thick bush about fifteen paces off burst asunder with a crashing sound, and uttering a series of ferocious pig-like grunts, the bull buffalo himself came charging out straight at us. Even as he came I saw the blood mark on his side where poor Hans' bullet had struck him, and also, as is often the case with particularly savage buffaloes, that his flanks had recently been terribly torn in an encounter with a lion.

"On he came, his head well up (a buffalo does not generally lower his head till he does so to strike); those great black horns—as I look at them before me, gentlemen, I seem to see them come charging at me as I did ten years ago, silhouetted against the green bush behind;—on, on!

"With a shout Mashune bolted off sideways towards the bush. I had instinctively lifted my eight-bore, which I had in my hand. It would have been useless to fire at the buffalo's head, for the dense horns must have turned the bullet; but as Mashune bolted, the bull slewed a little, with the momentary idea of following him, and as this gave me a ghost of a chance, I let drive my only cartridge at his shoulder. The bullet struck the shoulder-blade and smashed it up, and then travelled on under the skin into his flank; but it did not stop him, though for a second he staggered.

"Throwing myself on to the ground with the energy of despair, I rolled under the shelter of the projecting root of the thorn, crushing myself as far into the mouth of the ant-bear hole as I could. In a single instant the buffalo was after me. Kneeling down on his uninjured knee—for one leg, that of which I had broken the shoulder, was swinging helplessly to and fro—he set to work to try and hook me out of the hole with his crooked horn. At first he struck at me furiously, and it was one of the blows against the base of the tree which splintered the tip of the horn in the way that you see. Then he grew more cunning, and pushing his head as far under the root as possible, made long semicircular sweeps at me, grunting 450 furiously, and blowing saliva and hot steamy breath all over me. I was just out of reach of the horn, though every stroke, by widening the hole and making more room for his head, brought it closer to me, but every now and again I received heavy blows in the ribs from his muzzle. Feeling that I was being knocked silly, I made an effort and seizing his rough tongue, which was hanging from his jaws, I twisted it with all my force. The great brute bellowed with pain and fury, and jerked himself backwards so strongly, that he dragged me some inches further from the mouth of the hole, and again made a sweep at me, catching me this time round the shoulder-joint in the hook of his horn.

"I felt that it was all up now, and began to holloa. 460

"'He has got me!' I shouted in mortal terror. 'Gwasa, Mashune, gwasa!' ('Stab, Mashune, stab!')

"One hoist of the great head, and out of the hole I came like a periwinkle out of his shell. But even as I did so, I caught sight of Mashune's stalwart form advancing with his 'bangwan,' or broad stabbing assegai, raised above his head. In another quarter of a second I had fallen from the horn, and heard the blow of the spear, followed by the indescribable sound of steel shearing its way through flesh. I had fallen on my back, and, looking up, I saw that the gallant Mashune had driven the assegai a foot or more into the carcass of the buffalo, and was turning to fly. 470

"Alas! it was too late. Bellowing madly, and spouting blood from mouth and nostrils, the devilish brute was on him, and had thrown him up like a feather, and then gored him twice as he lay. I struggled up with some wild idea of affording help, but before I had gone a step the buffalo gave one long sighing bellow, and rolled over dead by the side of his victim.

"Mashune was still living, but a single glance at him told me that his hour had come. The buffalo's horn had driven a great hole in his right lung, and inflicted other injuries.

"I knelt down beside him in the uttermost distress, and took his hand.

"'Is he dead, Macumazahn?' he whispered. 'My eyes are blind; I cannot see.' 480

"'Yes, he is dead.'

"'Did the black devil hurt thee, Macumazahn?'

"'No, my poor fellow, I am not much hurt.'

"'Ow! I am glad.'

"Then came a long silence, broken only by the sound of the air whistling through the hole in his lung as he breathed.

"'Macumazahn, art thou there? I cannot feel thee.'

"'I am here, Mashune.'

"'I die, Macumazahn—the world flies round and round. I go—I go out into the dark! Surely, my father, at times in days to come—thou wilt think of Mashune 490 who stood by thy side—when thou killest elephants, as we used—as we used—'

"They were his last words, his brave spirit passed with them. I dragged his body to the hole under the tree, and pushed it in, placing his broad assegai by him, according to the custom of his people, that he might not go defenceless on his long journey; and then, ladies—I am not ashamed to confess—I stood alone there before it, and wept like a woman."   [1889]

Questions for Discussion and Writing

1. What function is served by the frame narrator's discussion of diamonds and King Solomon's mines?
2. What attitudes toward women do you find expressed or implied in the story?
3. How would you characterize Quatermain's attitude toward Mashune? Is he racist? Paternalistic? A genuine friend?
4. What details in the frame narrative lend credence to Quatermain's character as a reputable narrator?
5. What details in Quatermain's own narrative lend verisimilitude and authenticity to the story?
6. Do you find any of the events in the story too far-fetched to be believed? Explain.
7. What conventional elements of the adventure story as you have encountered it do you find in this story? Are any missing? Is Quatermain a conventional adventure hero? Why or why not?
8. Is there a theme to this story, or is it just an adventure yarn told for entertainment? Explain.

Sidebar: EXPLORING SUB-GENRES

The Adventure Story

Stories of adventure are among the oldest in oral and written literature, and they remain the most widespread and popular narrative form we have. The exploits of heroes or heroines as they battle the forces of nature, the army of an enemy, or even the opposition of the gods provide suspense, excitement, and wonder. Whether the adventure is told orally, written on the page, or dramatized on stage or in film, it fills us with "pity and fear," in the words of Aristotle.

Although adventure stories seem to embody an almost infinite variety of possibilities, the basic conventions of the form are relatively few and quite straightforward. Adventure stories feature a central hero or heroine who seeks or accidentally encounters an antagonist. The conflict between the two puts the protagonist in physical or spiritual danger, from which he or she must escape. If the outcome for the protagonist is happy, we call the outcome comic; if unsuccessful, tragic. Because the basic structure of the adventure story is so simple and widespread, it makes an excellent vehicle for expressing cultural values. The qualities held up for admiration in a protagonist are a good indication of the value system of the society that produces or admires the story.

Many stories in this anthology might be considered adventure stories: Hoffman's "The Sandman," Irving's "Rip Van Winkle," and even Hawthorne's "My Kinsman, Major Molineux" and Darío's "The Ruby" contain aspects of adventure. H. Rider Haggard's "Hunter Quatermain's Story," however, is unambiguously an adventure story. The chief purpose of the story is to portray exciting episodes in a heroic life and through them to convey certain ideas and values. Haggard's story represents one type that was extremely popular in late nineteenth century England and America— the story of "the great white hunter."

St. George and the Dragon (1506) by Raphael (1483–1520), Italian painter of the High Renaissance. St. George (303 AD?) was a Christian martyr and patron saint of England. (Andrew W. Mellon Collection, © 1997 Board of Trustees, National Gallery of Art Washington D.C.)

Quatermain at first seems an unlikely hero, being small, somewhat lame, no longer young—in short, not physically impressive. The story he tells is a fairly typical adventure, through which Quatermain emerges as a hero—a man we can admire for his bravery, resourcefulness, loyalty, leadership, marksmanship, and endurance. But other aspects of his character and of the story itself may disturb us. The indiscriminate killing of lions and elephants may offend present-day environmental consciences, and his casually superior attitude toward his servants is blatantly racist. The author's depiction of the character Mashune is more complicated. On the one hand, he is presented as an admirable character: loyal, brave, wise (though perhaps a bit comic in his reluctance to eat watercress). But even his good qualities seem indebted to the stereotype of the "noble savage." His speech and manner toward Quatermain, whom he calls "my father," may strike us as overly respectful, even obsequious. Is Mashune a truly admirable character or merely a "good native," appreciated by Quatermain and his audience for the wrong reasons? His and the frame narrator's treatment of women is equally suspect from our present-day perspective. Are Quatermain and his host simply respectful of women, or is their attitude condescending and sexist? However we answer these questions, the very fact that we raise them as we do indicates the difference between Haggard's cultural assumptions and our own.

Ambrose Bierce's "Chickamauga" comes out of a different adventure tradition—the war story. By the time Bierce was writing (1891), the Civil War had already assumed epic proportions in America's collective imagination. Bierce's young protagonist is filled with Romantic notions of the glories of war—an idea that Bierce mocks in the opening paragraph. At first his adventure is childish and innocent, almost amusing; but before it is finished it has turned first threatening, then nightmarish, hellish. By reversing the usual conventions of the war adventure story (as well as by careful management of the point of view), Bierce has produced a powerful anti-war story, compelling in its naked violence and bloody horror.

One way to read Joseph Conrad's "Heart of Darkness" is as a response to the attitudes and values represented by Haggard's glorification of colonialism and conquest. Instead of the confident Quatermain, Conrad gives us the self-conscious and ambiguous Marlowe. Instead of a conquering hero, he creates the crazed and degenerate Kurtz. All the conventions of the adventure story are here—the dangers of nature, the mystery and menace of the "savage" natives, the ever-present threats of disease and isolation, the "great white hunter." Many critics claim that Conrad turns these conventions back on themselves, using them to question and criticize the colonial exploitation in Africa. Other critics counter that Conrad's imperialism and racism are all too clear, whatever his conscious intentions may have been. Conrad's story has provoked an astonishing array of criticism and interpretation, but at its core it is a typical adventure story narrated by a participant lucky or heroic enough to have survived the experience.

Horacio Quiroga in "The Wilderness" uses the conventions of the adventure story to make a point about the relationship between man and nature. The conventional hero of adventure, like Quatermain, is the master of nature. It may threaten to overwhelm him, but in the end he conquers it—as the mounted trophies on the dining room wall testify. Quiroga's protagonist does not live though his ordeal, although he strives heroically, and has many of the skills and tools necessary to survive. This story suggests that no matter how resourceful man is, nature will always conquer.

Ernest Hemingway's "The Short Happy Life of Francis Macomber" uses an African safari as the setting for a characteristically ironic and complex treatment of the adventure story. The safari is, after all, something of a parody of genuine adventure. Traveling with a guide and all the comforts of home, Francis Macomber and his wife are essentially tourists in search of excitement. Even in this relatively tame situation, nature provides a real test of Macomber's courage—and he fails. As a result, his wife inflicts the ultimate humiliation by sleeping with the "great white hunter," Wilson. The next day, Macomber reasserts his masculinity by killing three buffalo. Threatened by her husband's new-found confidence, or acting on her own, Mrs. Macomber shoots him as a wounded buffalo charges. The story leaves unanswered the questions of whether Macomber would have survived the buffalo's charge and whether Mrs. Macomber deliberately kills her husband. In any case, Hemingway has used the conventions and trappings of the adventure story to make his own comment on the nature of courage, the meaning of manhood, and the relations of men and women.

Today, television and film provide the most popular and widely disseminated versions of the adventure story. In the form of such films as *Raiders of the Lost Ark* and the *Die Hard* series, adventure is alive and well in Hollywood. "Superhero" comic books, children's cartoons, and video games all contain adventure story conventions. What kinds of qualities do the heroes and heroines of these stories project? What cultural attitudes and values do they convey? Why, in an age when physical prowess is no longer much needed, do we continue to find tales of prowess entertaining? Why is the action-adventure hero almost always male? Why are women in these stories almost always in need of rescue? Like the adventure stories that preceded them, these incarnations of the form carry with them interesting insights into the culture that produces and enjoys them.

❧ AMBROSE BIERCE
(1842–1914)

Chickamauga

"Bitter Bierce," as he came to be known, is one of the most interesting, elusive, and enigmatic figures in the annals of the short story. He is known both for *The Devil's Dictionary* (1906, 1911), a cynical, satirical "dictionary" of epigrams and witticisms, and as the author of highly individual short stories that influenced

Stephen Crane, Ernest Hemingway, and such postmodern authors as Jorge Luis Borges and Carlos Fuentes.

Bierce was born the tenth of thirteen children in Horse Cave Creek, Meigs County, Ohio. In 1846, the family moved to Indiana, where Bierce attended local schools and as a teenager worked on an anti-slavery paper, *The Northern Indianan*. In 1859, he was sent to the Kentucky Military Institute. He enlisted in the army when the Civil War broke out and served with distinction at Shiloh and Chickamauga, and in Sherman's March to the Sea. He witnessed first hand the "rewards" of heroism when he carried a wounded comrade from the field, only to watch him die of his wounds. He himself might have died in 1864 had his brother not been on hand to nurse him.

After the war, Bierce knocked around in odd jobs before turning to journalism. While writing for various papers, he trained himself to write fiction. His first story, "The Haunted Valley," appeared in the July 1871 issue of the *Overland Monthly*.

The years from 1877 to 1899 were Bierce's most productive, in spite of illness and the break-up of his marriage in 1888. His fiction reflects his irascible personality, for it swims against the Realist/Naturalist currents of the day. Bierce hated the idea that people are so shaped by environment or heredity that they are not responsible for their decisions. His cynicism can be cheap and adolescent, but when used effectively produces taut, economical, and moving stories with a nightmarish quality. His most effective stories grew out of his war experiences and are Postmodern in showing how attempts to understand the world result in disillusionment or futility.

CHICKAMAUGA[1]

ONE SUNNY AUTUMN afternoon a child strayed away from its rude home in a small field and entered a forest unobserved. It was happy in a new sense of freedom from control, happy in the opportunity of exploration and adventure; for this child's spirit, in bodies of its ancestors, had for thousands of years been trained to memorable feats of discovery and conquest—victories in battles whose critical moments were centuries, whose victors' camps were cities of hewn stone. From the cradle of its race it had conquered its way through two continents and passing a great sea had penetrated a third, there to be born to war and dominion as a heritage.

The child was a boy aged about six years, the son of a poor planter. In his younger manhood the father had been a soldier, had fought against naked savages and followed the flag of his country into the capital of a civilized race to the far South. In the peaceful life of a planter the warrior-fire survived; once kindled, it is never extinguished. The man loved military books and pictures and the boy had understood enough to make himself a wooden sword, though even the eye of his

1. The Battle of Chickamauga (September 19–20, 1863) was one of the bloodiest of the American Civil War.

father would hardly have known it for what it was. This weapon he now bore bravely, as became the son of an heroic race, and pausing now and again in the sunny space of the forest assumed, with some exaggeration, the postures of aggression and defense that he had been taught by the engraver's art. Made reckless by the ease with which he overcame invisible foes attempting to stay his advance, he committed the common enough military error of pushing the pursuit to a dangerous extreme, until he found himself upon the margin of a wide but shallow brook, whose rapid waters barred his direct advance against the flying foe that had crossed with illogical ease. But the intrepid victor was not to be baffled; the spirit of the race which had passed the great sea burned unconquerable in that small breast and would not be denied. Finding a place where some bowlders in the bed of the stream lay but a step or a leap apart, he made his way across and fell again upon the rear-guard of his imaginary foe, putting all to the sword.

Now that the battle had been won, prudence required that he withdraw to his base of operations. Alas; like many a mightier conqueror, and like one, the mightiest, he could not

curb the lust for war,
Nor learn that tempted Fate will leave the loftiest star.

Advancing from the bank of the creek he suddenly found himself confronted with a new and more formidable enemy: in the path that he was following, sat, bolt upright, with ears erect and paws suspended before it, a rabbit! With a startled cry the child turned and fled, he knew not in what direction, calling with inarticulate cries for his mother, weeping, stumbling, his tender skin cruelly torn by brambles, his little heart beating hard with terror—breathless, blind with tears—lost in the forest! Then, for more than an hour, he wandered with erring feet through the tangled undergrowth, till at last, overcome by fatigue, he lay down in a narrow space between two rocks, within a few yards of the stream and still grasping his toy sword, no longer a weapon but a companion, sobbed himself to sleep. The wood birds sang merrily above his head; the squirrels, whisking their bravery of tail, ran barking from tree to tree, unconscious of the pity of it, and somewhere far away was a strange, muffled thunder, as if the partridges were drumming in celebration of nature's victory over the son of her immemorial enslavers. And back at the little plantation, where white men and black were hastily searching the fields and hedges in alarm, a mother's heart was breaking for her missing child.

Hours passed, and then the little sleeper rose to his feet. The chill of the evening was in his limbs, the fear of the gloom in his heart. But he had rested, and no longer wept. With some blind instinct which impelled to action he struggled through the undergrowth about him and came to a more open ground—on his right the brook, to the left a gentle acclivity studded with infrequent trees; over all, the gathering gloom of twilight. A thin, ghostly mist rose along the water. It frightened and repelled him; instead of recrossing, in the direction whence he had come, he turned his back upon it, and went forward toward the dark inclosing wood. Suddenly he saw before him a strange moving object which he took to be

some large animal—a dog, a pig—he could not name it; perhaps it was a bear. He 60
had seen pictures of bears, but knew of nothing to their discredit and had vaguely
wished to meet one. But something in form or movement of this object—something in the awkwardness of its approach—told him that it was not a bear, and curiosity was stayed by fear. He stood still and as it came slowly on gained courage
every moment, for he saw that at least it had not the long, menacing ears of the
rabbit. Possibly his impressionable mind was half conscious of something familiar
in its shambling, awkward gait. Before it had approached near enough to resolve
his doubts he saw that it was followed by another and another. To right and to left
were many more; the whole open space about him was alive with them—all mov-
ing toward the brook.   70

They were men. They crept upon their hands and knees. They used their
hands only, dragging their legs. They used their knees only, their arms hanging
idle at their sides. They strove to rise to their feet, but fell prone in the attempt.
They did nothing naturally, and nothing alike, save only to advance foot by foot in
the same direction. Singly, in pairs and in little groups, they came on through the
gloom, some halting now and again while others crept slowly past them, then resuming their movement. They came by dozens and by hundreds; as far on either
hand as one could see in the deepening gloom they extended and the black wood
behind them appeared to be inexhaustible. The very ground seemed in motion toward the creek. Occasionally one who had paused did not again go on, but lay 80
motionless. He was dead. Some, pausing, made strange gestures with their hands,
erected their arms and lowered them again, clasped their heads; spread their
palms upward, as men are sometimes seen to do in public prayer.

Not all this did the child note; it is what would have been noted by an elder
observer; he saw little but that these were men, yet crept like babes. Being men,
they were not terrible, though unfamiliarly clad. He moved among them freely,
going from one to another and peering into their faces with childish curiosity. All
their faces were singularly white and many were streaked and gouted with red.
Something in this—something too, perhaps, in their grotesque attitudes and
movements—reminded him of the painted clown whom he had seen last summer 90
in the circus, and he laughed as he watched them. But on and ever on they crept,
these maimed and bleeding men, as heedless as he of the dramatic contrast between his laughter and their own ghastly gravity. To him it was a merry spectacle.
He had seen his father's negroes creep upon their hands and knees for his amusement—had ridden them so, "making believe" they were his horses. He now approached one of these crawling figures from behind and with an agile movement
mounted it astride. The man sank upon his breast, recovered, flung the small boy
fiercely to the ground as an unbroken colt might have done, then turned upon
him a face that lacked a lower jaw—from the upper teeth to the throat was a great
red gap fringed with hanging shreds of flesh and splinters of bone. The unnatural 100
prominence of nose, the absence of chin, the fierce eyes, gave this man the appearance of a great bird of prey crimsoned in throat and breast by the blood of its
quarry. The man rose to his knees, the child to his feet. The man shook his fist at
the child; the child, terrified at last, ran to a tree near by, got upon the farther side
of it and took a more serious view of the situation. And so the clumsy multitude
dragged itself slowly and painfully along in hideous pantomime—moved forward

down the slope like a swarm of great black beetles, with never a sound of going—
in silence profound, absolute.

Instead of darkening, the haunted landscape began to brighten. Through the
belt of trees beyond the brook shone a strange red light, the trunks and branches   110
of the trees making a black lacework against it. It struck the creeping figures and
gave them monstrous shadows, which caricatured their movements on the lit
grass. It fell upon their faces, touching their whiteness with a ruddy tinge, accen-
tuating the stains with which so many of them were freaked and maculated. It
sparkled on buttons and bits of metal in their clothing. Instinctively the child
turned toward the growing splendor and moved down the slope with his horrible
companions; in a few moments had passed the foremost of the throng—not much
of a feat, considering his advantages. He placed himself in the lead, his wooden
sword still in hand, and solemnly directed the march, conforming his pace to
theirs and occasionally turning as if to see that his forces did not straggle. Surely   120
such a leader never before had such a following.

Scattered about upon the ground now slowly narrowing by the encroach-
ment of this awful march to water, were certain articles to which, in the leader's
mind, were coupled no significant associations: an occasional blanket, tightly
rolled lengthwise, doubled and the ends bound together with a string; a heavy
knapsack here, and there a broken rifle—such things, in short, as are found in the
rear of retreating troops, the "spoor" of men flying from their hunters. Everywhere
near the creek, which here had a margin of lowland, the earth was trodden into
mud by the feet of men and horses. An observer of better experience in the use of
his eyes would have noticed that these footprints pointed in both directions; the   130
ground had been twice passed over—in advance and in retreat. A few hours before, these desperate, stricken men, with their more fortunate and now distant
comrades, had penetrated the forest in thousands. Their successive battalions,
breaking into swarms and re-forming in lines, had passed the child on every
side—had almost trodden on him as he slept. The rustle and murmur of their
march had not awakened him. Almost within a stone's throw of where he lay they
had fought a battle; but all unheard by him were the roar of the musketry, the
shock of the cannon, "the thunder of the captains and the shouting." He had slept
through it all, grasping his little wooden sword with perhaps a tighter clutch in
unconscious sympathy with his martial environment, but as heedless of the   140
grandeur of the struggle as the dead who had died to make the glory.

The fire beyond the belt of woods on the farther side of the creek, reflected
to earth from the canopy of its own smoke, was now suffusing the whole landscape. It transformed the sinuous line of mist to the vapor of gold. The water
gleamed with dashes of red, and red, too, were many of the stones protruding
above the surface. But that was blood; the less desperately wounded had stained
them in crossing. On them, too, the child now crossed with eager steps; he was
going to the fire. As he stood upon the farther bank he turned about to look at the
companions of his march. The advance was arriving at the creek. The stronger had
already drawn themselves to the brink and plunged their faces into the flood.   150
Three or four who lay without motion appeared to have no heads. At this the
child's eyes expanded with wonder; even his hospitable understanding could not
accept a phenomenon implying such vitality as that. After slaking their thirst these

men had not had the strength to back away from the water, nor to keep their heads above it. They were drowned. In rear of these, the open spaces of the forest showed the leader as many formless figures of his grim command as at first; but not nearly so many were in motion. He waved his cap for their encouragement and smilingly pointed with his weapon in the direction of the guiding light—a pillar of fire to this strange exodus.

Confident of the fidelity of his forces, he now entered the belt of woods, 160 passed through it easily in the red illumination, climbed a fence, ran across a field, turning now and again to coquet with his responsive shadow, and so approached the blazing ruin of a dwelling. Desolation everywhere! In all the wide glare not a living thing was visible. He cared nothing for that; the spectacle pleased, and he danced with glee in imitation of the wavering flames. He ran about, collecting fuel, but every object that he found was too heavy for him to cast in from the distance to which the heat limited his approach. In despair he flung in his sword—a surrender to the superior forces of nature. His military career was at an end.

Shifting his position, his eyes fell upon some outbuildings which had an oddly familiar appearance, as if he had dreamed of them. He stood considering 170 them with wonder, when suddenly the entire plantation, with its inclosing forest, seemed to turn as if upon a pivot. His little world swung half around; the points of the compass were reversed. He recognized the blazing building as his own home!

For a moment he stood stupefied by the power of the revelation, then ran with stumbling feet, making a half-circuit of the ruin. There, conspicuous in the light of the conflagration, lay the dead body of a woman—the white face turned upward, the hands thrown out and clutched full of grass, the clothing deranged, the long dark hair in tangles and full of clotted blood. The greater part of the forehead was torn away, and from the jagged hole the brain protruded, overflowing the temple, a frothy mass of gray, crowned with clusters of crimson bubbles—the 180 work of a shell.

The child moved his little hands, making wild, uncertain gestures. He uttered a series of inarticulate and indescribable cries—something between the chattering of an ape and the gobbling of a turkey—a startling, soulless, unholy sound, the language of a devil. The child was a deaf mute.

Then he stood motionless, with quivering lips, looking down upon the wreck.   [1891]

Questions for Discussing and Writing

1. In what ways does this story resemble a fairy tale? How might the use of fairy tale conventions be related to Bierce's purpose in the story?

2. Compare the child's ideas about war with the way war is depicted in the story. What thematic idea emerges from the contrast?

3. Has Bierce tricked his readers by withholding the information that the child is a deaf mute until the very end? Would the story be possible without this device?

4. Locate a historical account of the Battle of Chickamauga and compare Bierce's story to it. Does the historical account affect you differently from Bierce's story? In what ways? Is one account more true than the other?

5. Most critics interpret this as an anti-war story. Can it be "deconstructed" as a pro-war story? Why or why not?

❧ MARY E. WILKENS FREEMAN
(1852–1930)

The Revolt of "Mother"

Although she wrote more than thirty books, Mary E. Wilkens Freeman is best known for her first two collections of short stories. Variously classed as a local colorist, realist, and feminist, she ultimately transcends simplistic labeling.

Mary Wilkens was born in Randolph, Massachusetts, where her father was a carpenter until the family moved to Brattleboro, Vermont, when she was fifteen. There her father established a dry goods store, and she attended high school and two female seminaries. The next decade was an extremely difficult one for her, as first her father's business failed, and then both her parents died.

Having written some juvenile stories and poems, she turned to short story writing, publishing her first story in 1882. Subsequent stories brought her to the attention of William Dean Howells (1837–1920), editor of *Harper's New Monthly Magazine,* the outstanding short story outlet of its day. Howells championed her as a realist and published "The Revolt of 'Mother'" in Harper's in September 1890. Most of her early stories were gathered into *A Humble Romance* (1887) and *A New England Nun* (1891).

Freeman tried various other genres, including the novel and ghost stories, but never equaled the success of her first efforts. Her stories resemble local color but are less interested in setting and dialect than in character. New England was then a region in economic and cultural decline. Many young men sought their fortunes elsewhere, leaving the women behind to cope with poverty and the stern heritage of New England's Puritanism. It is these characters that Freeman so effectively portrays. "The Revolt of 'Mother'" effectively combines local color, realism, and feminism in a story that has delighted readers for generations.

"Father!"

"What is it?"

"What are them men diggin' over there in the field for?"

There was a sudden dropping and enlarging of the lower part of the old man's face, as if some heavy weight had settled therein; he shut his mouth tight, and went on harnessing the great bay mare. He hustled the collar on to her neck with a jerk.

"Father!"

The old man slapped the saddle upon the mare's back.

"Look here, father, I want to know what them men are diggin' over in the   10
field for, an' I'm goin' to know."

"I wish you'd go into the house, mother, an' 'tend to your own affairs," the
old man said then. He ran his words together, and his speech was almost as inarticulate as a growl.

But the woman understood; it was her most native tongue. "I ain't goin' into
the house till you tell me what them men are doin' over there in the field," said
she.

Then she stood waiting. She was a small woman, short and straight-waisted
like a child in her brown cotton gown. Her forehead was mild and benevolent between the smooth curves of gray hair; there were meek downward lines about her   20
nose and mouth; but her eyes, fixed upon the old man, looked as if the meekness
had been the result of her own will, never of the will of another.

They were in the barn, standing before the wide open doors. The spring air,
full of the smell of growing grass and unseen blossoms, came in their faces. The
deep yard in front was littered with farm wagons and piles of wood; on the edges,
close to the fence and the house, the grass was a vivid green, and there were some
dandelions.

The old man glanced doggedly at his wife as he tightened the last buckles on
the harness. She looked as immovable to him as one of the rocks in his pasture-
land, bound to the earth with generations of blackberry vines. He slapped the   30
reins over the horse, and started forth from the barn.

"Father!" said she.

The old man pulled up. "What is it?"

"I want to know what them men are diggin' over there in that field for."

"They're diggin' a cellar, I s'pose, if you've got to know."

"A cellar for what?"

"A barn."

"A barn? You ain't goin' to build a barn over there where we was goin' to
have a house, father?"

The old man said not another word. He hurried the horse into the farm   40
wagon, and clattered out of the yard, jouncing as sturdily on his seat as a boy.

The woman stood a moment looking after him, then she went out of the
barn across a corner of the yard to the house. The house, standing at right angles
with the great barn and a long reach of sheds and out-buildings, was infinitesimal
compared with them. It was scarcely as commodious for people as the little boxes
under the barn eaves were for doves.

A pretty girl's face, pink and delicate as a flower, was looking out of one of
the house windows. She was watching three men who were digging over in the
field which bounded the yard near the road line. She turned quietly when the
woman entered.   50

"What are they digging for, mother?" said she. "Did he tell you?"

"They're diggin' for—a cellar for a new barn."

"Oh, mother, he ain't going to build another barn?"

"That's what he says."

A boy stood before the kitchen glass combing his hair. He combed slowly and painstakingly, arranging his brown hair in a smooth hillock over his forehead. He did not seem to pay any attention to the conversation.

"Sammy, did you know father was going to build a new barn?" asked the girl.

The boy combed assiduously.   60

"Sammy!"

He turned, and showed a face like his father's under his smooth crest of hair. "Yes, I s'pose I did," he said, reluctantly.

"How long have you known it?" asked his mother.

" 'Bout three months, I guess."

"Why didn't you tell of it?"

"Didn't think 'twould do no good."

"I don't see what father wants another barn for," said the girl, in her sweet, slow voice. She turned again to the window, and stared out at the digging men in the field. Her tender, sweet face was full of a gentle distress. Her forehead was as   70 bald and innocent as a baby's, with the light hair strained back from it in a row of curl-papers. She was quite large, but her soft curves did not look as if they covered muscles.

Her mother looked sternly at the boy. "Is he goin' to buy more cows?" said she.

The boy did not reply; he was tying his shoes.

"Sammy, I want you to tell me if he's goin' to buy more cows."

"I s'pose he is."

"How many?"

"Four, I guess."   80

His mother said nothing more. She went into the pantry, and there was a clatter of dishes. The boy got his cap from a nail behind the door, took an old arithmetic from the shelf, and started for school. He was lightly built, but clumsy. He went out of the yard with a curious spring in the hips, that made his loose homemade jacket tilt up in the rear.

The girl went to the sink, and began to wash the dishes that were piled up there. Her mother came promptly out of the pantry, and shoved her aside. "You wipe 'em," said she; "I'll wash. There's a good many this mornin'."

The mother plunged her hands vigorously into the water, the girl wiped the plates slowly and dreamily. "Mother," said she, "don't you think it's too bad father's   90 going to build that new barn, much as we need a decent house to live in?"

Her mother scrubbed a dish fiercely. "You ain't found out yet we're women-folks, Nanny Penn," said she. "You ain't seen enough of men-folks yet to. One of these days you'll find it out, an' then you'll know that we know only what men-folks think we do, so far as any use of it goes, an' how we'd ought to reckon men-folks in with Providence, an' not complain of what they do any more than we do of the weather."

"I don't care; I don't believe George is anything like that, anyhow," said Nanny. Her delicate face flushed pink, her lips pouted softly, as if she were going to cry.   100

"You wait an' see. I guess George Eastman ain't no better than other men.

You hadn't ought to judge father, though. He can't help it, 'cause he don't look at things jest the way we do. An' we've been pretty comfortable here, after all. The roof don't leak—ain't never but once—that's one thing. Father's kept it shingled right up."

"I do wish we had a parlor."

"I guess it won't hurt George Eastman any to come to see you in a nice clean kitchen. I guess a good many girls don't have as good a place as this. Nobody's ever heard me complain."

"I ain't complained either, mother."   110

"Well, I don't think you'd better, a good father an' a good home as you've got. S'pose your father made you go out an' work for your liven'? Lots of girls have to that ain't no stronger an' better able to than you be."

Sarah Penn washed the frying-pan with a conclusive air. She scrubbed the outside of it as faithfully as the inside. She was a masterly keeper of her box of a house. Her one living-room never seemed to have in it any of the dust which the friction of life with inanimate matter produces. She swept, and there seemed to be no dirt to go before the broom; she cleaned, and one could see no difference. She was like an artist so perfect that he has apparently no art. To-day she got out a mixing bowl and a board, and rolled some pies, and there was no more flour upon 120 her than her daughter who was doing finer work. Nanny was to be married in the fall, and she was sewing on some white cambric and embroidery. She sewed industriously while her mother cooked, her soft milk-white hands and wrists showed whiter than her delicate work.

"We must have the stove moved out in the shed before long," said Mrs. Penn. "Talk about not havin' things, it's been a real blessin' to be able to put a stove up in that shed in hot weather. Father did one good thing when he fixed that stove-pipe out there."

Sarah Penn's face as she rolled her pies had that expression of meek vigor which might have characterized one of the New Testament saints. She was making 130 mince-pies. Her husband, Adoniram Penn, liked them better than any other kind. She baked twice a week. Adoniram often liked a piece of pie between meals. She hurried this morning. It had been later than usual when she began, and she wanted to have a pie baked for dinner. However deep a resentment she might be forced to hold against her husband, she would never fail in sedulous attention to his wants.

Nobility of character manifests itself at loop-holes when it is not provided with large doors. Sarah Penn's showed itself to-day in flaky dishes of pastry. So she made the pies faithfully, while across the table she could see, when she glanced up from her work, the sight that rankled in her patient and steadfast soul—the dig- 140 ging of the cellar of the new barn in the place where Adoniram forty years ago had promised her their new house should stand.

The pies were done for dinner. Adoniram and Sammy were home a few minutes after twelve o'clock. The dinner was eaten with serious haste. There was never much conversation at the table in the Penn family. Adoniram asked a blessing, and they ate promptly, then rose up and went about their work.

Sammy went back to school, taking soft sly lopes out of the yard like a rabbit. He wanted a game of marbles before school, and feared his father would give

him some chores to do. Adoniram hastened to the door and called after him, but
he was out of sight.   150

"I don't see what you let him go for, mother," said he. "I wanted him to help
me unload that wood."

Adoniram went to work out in the yard unloading wood from the wagon.
Sarah put away the dinner dishes, while Nanny took down her curl-papers and
changed her dress. She was going down to the store to buy some more embroidery
and thread.

When Nanny was gone, Mrs. Penn went to the door. "Father!" she called.

"Well, what is it!"

"I want to see you jest a minute, father."

"I can't leave this wood nohow. I've got to git it unloaded an' go for a load of   160
gravel afore two o'clock. Sammy had ought to helped me. You hadn't ought to let
him go to school so early."

"I want to see you jest a minute."

"I tell ye I can't, nohow, mother."

"Father, you come here." Sarah Penn stood in the door like a queen; she held
her head as if it bore a crown; there was the patience which makes authority royal
in her voice. Adoniram went.

Mrs. Penn led the way into the kitchen, and pointed to a chair. "Sit down, father," said she; "I've got somethin' I want to say to you."

He sat down heavily; his face was quite stolid, but he looked at her with   170
restive eyes. "Well, what is it, mother?"

"I want to know what you're buildin' that new barn for, father?"

"I ain't got nothin' to say about it."

"It can't be you think you need another barn?"

"I tell ye I ain't got nothin' to say about it, mother; an' I ain't goin' to say
nothin'."

"Be you goin' to buy more cows?"

Adoniram did not reply; he shut his mouth tight.

"I know you be, as well as I want to. Now, father, look here"—Sarah Penn
had not sat down; she stood before her husband in the humble fashion of a   180
Scripture woman—"I'm goin' to talk real plain to you; I never have sence I married you, but I'm goin' to now. I ain't never complained, an' I ain't goin' to complain now, but I'm goin' to talk plain. You see this room here, father; you look at it
well. You see there ain't no carpet on the floor, an' you see the paper is all dirty, an'
droppin' off the walls. We ain't had no new paper on it for ten year, an' then I put
it on myself, an' it didn't cost but ninepence a roll. You see this room, father; it's all
the one I've had to work in an' eat in an' sit in sence we was married. There ain't
another woman in the whole town whose husband ain't got half the means you
have but what's got better. It's all the room Nanny's got to have her company in;
an' there ain't one of her mates but what's got better, an' their fathers not so able as   190
hers is. It's all the room she'll have to be married in. What would you have
thought, father, if we had had our weddin' in a room no better than this? I was
married in my mother's parlor, with a carpet on the floor, an' stuffed furniture, an'
a mahogany card-table. An' this is all the room my daughter will have to be married in. Look here, father!"

Sarah Penn went across the room as though it were a tragic stage. She flung open a door and disclosed a tiny bedroom, only large enough for a bed and bureau, with a path between. "There, father," said she—"there's all the room I've had to sleep in for forty year. All my children were born there—the two that died, an' the two that's livin'. I was sick with a fever there." 200

She stepped to another door and opened it. It led into the small, ill-lighted pantry. "Here," said she, "is all the buttery I've got—every place I've got for my dishes, to set away my victuals in, an' to keep my milk-pans in. Father, I've been takin' care of the milk of six cows in the place, an' now you're goin' to build a new barn, an' keep more cows, an' give me more to do in it."

She threw open another door. A narrow crooked flight of stairs wound upward from it. "There, father," said she, "I want you to look at the stairs that go up to them two unfinished chambers that are all the places our son an' daughter have had to sleep in all their lives. There ain't a prettier girl in town nor a more ladylike one than Nanny, an' that's the place she has to sleep in. It ain't so good as your 210 horse's stall; it ain't so warm an' tight."

Sarah Penn went back and stood before her husband. "Now, father," said she, "I want to know if you think you're doin' right an' accordin' to what you profess. Here, when we was married, forty year ago, you promised me faithful that we should have a new house built in that lot over in the field before the year was out. You said you had money enough, an' you wouldn't ask me to live in no such place as this. It is forty year now, an' you've been makin' more money, an' I've been savin' of it for you ever since, an' you ain't built no house yet. You've built sheds an' cow-houses an' one new barn, an' now you're goin' to build another. Father, I want to know if you think it's right. You're lodgin' your dumb beasts better than 220 you are your own flesh an' blood. I want to know if you think it's right."

"I ain't got nothin' to say."

"You can't say nothin' without ownin' it ain't right, father. An' there's another thing—I ain't complained; I've got along forty year, an' I s'pose I should forty more, if it wa'n't for that—if we don't have another house. Nanny she can't live with us after she's married. She'll have to go somewheres else to live away from us, an' it don't seem as if I could have it so, noways, father. She wa'n't ever strong. She's got considerable color, but there wa'n't ever any backbone to her. I've always took the heft of everything off her, an' she ain't fit to keep house an' do everything herself. She'll be all worn out inside of a year. Think of her doin' all the washin' an' 230 ironin' an' bakin' with them soft white hands an' arms, an' sweepin'! I can't have it so, noways, father."

Mrs. Penn's face was burning; her mild eyes gleamed. She had pleaded her little cause like a Webster; she had ranged from severity to pathos; but her opponent employed that obstinate silence which makes eloquence futile with mocking echoes. Adoniram arose clumsily.

"Father, ain't you got nothin' to say?" said Mrs. Penn.

"I've got to go off after that load of gravel. I can't stan' here talkin' all day."

"Father, won't you think it over, an' have a house built there instead of a barn?" 240

"I ain't got nothin' to say."

Adoniram shuffled out. Mrs. Penn went into her bedroom. When she came out, her eyes were red. She had a roll of unbleached cotton cloth. She spread it out on the kitchen table, and began cutting out some shirts for her husband. The men over in the field had a team to help them this afternoon; she could hear their halloos. She had a scanty pattern for the shirts; she had to plan and piece the sleeves.

Nanny came home with her embroidery, and sat down with her needlework. She had taken down her curl-papers, and there was a soft roll of fair hair like an aureole over her forehead; her face was as delicately fine and clear as porcelain. Suddenly she looked up, and the tender red flamed all over her face and neck. 250 "Mother," said she.

"What say?"

"I've been thinking—I don't see how we're goin' to have any—wedding in this room. I'd be ashamed to have his folks come if we didn't have anybody else."

"Mebbe we can have some new paper before then; I can put it on. I guess you won't have no call to be ashamed of your belongin's."

"We might have the wedding in the new barn," said Nanny, with gentle pettishness. "Why, mother, what makes you look so?"

Mrs. Penn had started, and was staring at her with a curious expression. She turned again to her work, and spread out a pattern carefully on the cloth. 260 "Nothin'," said she.

Presently Adoniram clattered out of the yard in his two-wheeled dump cart, standing as proudly upright as a Roman charioteer. Mrs. Penn opened the door and stood there a minute looking out; the halloos of the men sounded louder.

It seemed to her all through the spring months that she heard nothing but the halloos and the noises of saws and hammers. The new barn grew fast. It was a fine edifice for this little village. Men came on pleasant Sundays, in their meeting suits and clean shirt bosoms, and stood around it admiringly. Mrs. Penn did not speak of it, and Adoniram did not mention it to her, although sometimes, upon a return from inspecting it, he bore himself with injured dignity. 270

"It's a strange thing how your mother feels about the new barn," he said, confidentially, to Sammy one day.

Sammy only grunted after an odd fashion for a boy; he had learned it from his father.

The barn was all completed ready for use by the third week in July. Adoniram had planned to move his stock in on Wednesday; on Tuesday he received a letter which changed his plans. He came in with it early in the morning. "Sammy's been to the post-office," said he, "an' I've got a letter from Hiram." Hiram was Mrs. Penn's brother, who lived in Vermont.

"Well," said Mrs. Penn, "what does he say about the folks?" 280

"I guess they're all right. He says he thinks if I come up country right off there's a chance to buy jest the kind of a horse I want." He stared reflectively out of the window at the new barn.

Mrs. Penn was making pies. She went on clapping the rolling-pin into the crust, although she was very pale, and her heart beat loudly.

"I dun' know but what I'd better go," said Adoniram. "I hate to go off jest now, right in the midst of hayin', but the ten-acre lot's cut, an' I guess Rufus an' the others can git along without me three or four days. I can't get a horse round here to suit me, nohow, an' I've got to have another for all that wood-haulin' in the fall.

I told Hiram to watch out, an' if he got wind of a good horse to let me know. I 290
guess I'd better go."

"I'll get out your clean shirt an' collar," said Mrs. Penn calmly.

She laid out Adoniram's Sunday suit and his clean clothes on the bed in the
little bedroom. She got his shaving-water and razor ready. At last she buttoned on
his collar and fastened his black cravat.

Adoniram never wore his collar and cravat except on extra occasions. He
held his head high, with a rasped dignity. When he was all ready, with his coat and
hat brushed, and a lunch of pie and cheese in a paper bag, he hesitated on the
threshold of the door. He looked at his wife, and his manner was defiantly apologetic. "If them cows come to-day, Sammy can drive 'em into the new barn," said 300
he; "an' when they bring the hay up, they can pitch it in there."

"Well," replied Mrs. Penn.

Adoniram set his shaven face ahead and started. When he had cleared the
door-step, he turned and looked back with a kind of nervous solemnity. "I shall be
back by Saturday if nothin' happens," said he.

"Do be careful, father," returned his wife.

She stood in the door with Nanny at her elbow and watched him out of
sight. Her eyes had a strange, doubtful expression in them; her peaceful forehead
was contracted. She went in, and about her baking again. Nanny sat sewing. Her
wedding-day was drawing nearer, and she was getting pale and thin with her 310
steady sewing. Her mother kept glancing at her.

"Have you got that pain in your side this mornin'?" she asked.

"A little."

Mrs. Penn's face, as she worked, changed, her perplexed forehead smoothed,
her eyes were steady, her lips firmly set. She formed a maxim for herself, although
incoherently with her unlettered thoughts. "Unsolicited opportunities are the
guide-posts of the Lord to the new roads of life," she repeated in effect, and she
made up her mind to her course of action.

"S'posin' I *had* wrote to Hiram," she muttered once, when she was in the
pantry—"s'posin' I had wrote, an' asked him if he knew of any horse? But I didn't, 320
an' father's goin' wa'n't none of my doin'. It looks like a providence." Her voice
rang out quite loud at the last.

"What you talkin' about, mother?" called Nanny.

"Nothin'."

Mrs. Penn hurried her baking; at eleven o'clock it was all done. The load of
hay from the west field came slowly down the cart track, and drew up at the new
barn. Mrs. Penn ran out. "Stop!" she screamed—"stop!"

The men stopped and looked; Sammy upreared from the top of the load,
and stared at his mother.

"Stop!" she cried out again. "Don't you put the hay in that barn; put it in the 330
old one."

"Why, he said to put it in here," returned one of the hay-makers, wonderingly. He was a young man, a neighbor's son, whom Adoniram hired by the year to
help on the farm.

"Don't you put the hay in the new barn; there's room enough in the old one,
ain't there?" said Mrs. Penn.

"Room enough," returned the hired man, in his thick, rustic tones. "Didn't need the new barn, nohow, far as room's concerned. Well, I s'pose he changed his mind." He took hold of the horses' bridles.

Mrs. Penn went back to the house. Soon the kitchen windows were dark- 340
ened, and a fragrance like warm honey came into the room.

Nanny laid down her work. "I thought father wanted them to put the hay into the new barn?" she said, wonderingly.

"It's all right," replied her mother.

Sammy slid down from the load of hay, and came in to see if dinner was ready.

"I ain't goin' to get a regular dinner to-day, as long as father's gone," said his mother. "I've let the fire go out. You can have some bread an' milk an' pie. I thought we could get along." She set out some bowls of milk, some bread and a pie on the kitchen table. "You'd better eat your dinner now," said she. "You might 350
jest as well get through with it. I want you to help me afterward."

Nanny and Sammy stared at each other. There was something strange in their mother's manner. Mrs. Penn did not eat anything herself. She went into the pantry, and they heard her moving dishes while they ate. Presently she came out with a pile of plates. She got the clothes-basket out of the shed, and packed them in it. Nanny and Sammy watched. She brought out cups and saucers, and put them in with the plates.

"What you goin' to do, mother?" inquired Nanny, in a timid voice. A sense of something unusual made her tremble, as if it were a ghost. Sammy rolled his eyes over his pie.   360

"You'll see what I'm goin' to do," replied Mrs. Penn. "If you're through, Nanny, I want you to go up-stairs an' pack up your things; an' I want you, Sammy, to help me take down the bed in the bedroom."

"Oh, mother, what for?" gasped Nanny.

"You'll see."

During the next few hours a feat was performed by this simple, pious New England mother which was equal in its way to Wolfe's storming of the Heights of Abraham.[1] It took no more genius and audacity of bravery for Wolfe to cheer his wondering soldiers up those steep precipices, under the sleeping eyes of the enemy, than for Sarah Penn, at the head of her children, to move all their little 370
household goods into the new barn while her husband was away.

Nanny and Sammy followed their mother's instructions without a murmur; indeed, they were overawed. There is a certain uncanny and superhuman quality about all such purely original undertakings as their mother's was to them. Nanny went back and forth with her light loads, and Sammy tugged with sober energy.

At five o'clock in the afternoon the little house in which the Penns had lived for forty years had emptied itself into the barn.

Every builder builds somewhat for unknown purposes, and is in a measure a prophet. The architect of Adoniram Penn's barn, while he designed it for the comfort of four-footed animals, had planned better than he knew for the comfort of 380

---

1. General James Wolfe (1727–1759) defeated the French in Quebec in a daring raid on September 13, 1759, thus securing Canada for the British.

humans. Sarah Penn saw at a glance its possibilities. These great box-stalls, with quilts hung before them, would make better bedrooms than the one she had occupied for forty years, and there was a tight carriage-room. The harness-room, with its chimney and shelves, would make a kitchen of her dreams. The great middle space would make a parlor, by-and-by, fit for a palace. Up-stairs there was as much room as down. With partitions and windows, what a house would there be! Sarah looked at the row of stanchions before the allotted space for cows, and reflected that she would have her front entry there.

At six o'clock the stove was up in the harness-room, the kettle was boiling, and the table set for tea. It looked almost as home-like as the abandoned house 390 across the yard had ever done. The young hired man milked, and Sarah directed him calmly to bring the milk to the new barn. He came gaping, dropping little blots of foam from the brimming pails on the grass. Before the next morning he had spread the story of Adoniram Penn's wife moving into the new barn all over the little village. Men assembled in the store and talked it over, women with shawls over their heads scuttled into each other's houses before their work was done. Any deviation from the ordinary course of life in this quiet town was enough to stop all progress in it. Everybody paused to look at the staid, independent figure on the side track. There was a difference of opinion with regard to her. Some held her to be insane; some, of a lawless and rebellious spirit.   400

Friday the minister went to see her. It was in the forenoon, and she was at the barn door shelling pease for dinner. She looked up and returned his salutation with dignity, then she went on with her work. She did not invite him in. The saintly expression of her face remained fixed, but there was an angry flush over it.

The minister stood awkwardly before her, and talked. She handled the pease as if they were bullets. At last she looked up, and her eyes showed the spirit that her meek front had covered for a lifetime.

"There ain't no use talkin', Mr. Hersey," said she. "I've thought it all over an' over, an' I believe I'm doin' what's right. I've made it the subject of prayer, an' it's betwixt me an' the Lord an' Adoniram. There ain't no call for nobody else to worry 410 about it."

"Well, of course, if you have brought it to the Lord in prayer, and feel satisfied that you are doing right, Mrs. Penn," said the minister, helplessly. His thin gray-bearded face was pathetic. He was a sickly man; his youthful confidence had cooled; he had to scourge himself up to some of his pastoral duties as relentlessly as a Catholic ascetic, and then he was prostrated by the smart.

"I think it's right jest as much as I think it was right for our forefathers to come over from the old country 'cause they didn't have what belonged to 'em," said Mrs. Penn. She arose. The barn threshold might have been Plymouth Rock from her bearing. "I don't doubt you mean well, Mr. Hersey," said she, "but there 420 are things people hadn't ought to interfere with. I've been a member of the church for over forty year. I've got my own mind an' my own feet, an' I'm goin' to think my own thoughts an' go my own ways, an' nobody but the Lord is goin' to dictate to me unless I've a mind to have him. Won't you come in an' set down? How is Mis' Hersey?"

"She is well, I thank you," replied the minister. He added some more perplexed apologetic remarks; then he retreated.

He could expound the intricacies of every character study in the Scriptures, he was competent to grasp the Pilgrim Fathers and all historical innovators, but Sarah Penn was beyond him. He could deal with primal cases, but parallel ones worsted him. But, after all, although it was aside from his province, he wondered more how Adoniram Penn would deal with his wife than how the Lord would. Everybody shared the wonder. When Adoniram's four new cows arrived, Sarah ordered three to be put in the old barn, the other in the house shed where the cooking-stove had stood. That added to the excitement. It was whispered that all four cows were domiciled in the house.

Towards sunset on Saturday, when Adoniram was expected home, there was a knot of men in the road near the new barn. The hired man had milked, but he still hung around the premises. Sarah Penn had supper all ready. There were brown-bread and baked beans and a custard pie; it was the supper Adoniram loved on a Saturday night. She had a clean calico, and she bore herself imperturbably. Nanny and Sammy kept close at her heels. Their eyes were large, and Nanny was full of nervous tremors. Still there was to them more pleasant excitement than anything else. An inborn confidence in their mother over their father asserted itself.

Sammy looked out of the harness-room window. "There he is," he announced, in an awed whisper. He and Nanny peeped around the casing. Mrs. Penn kept on about her work. The children watched Adoniram leave the new horse standing in the drive while he went to the house door. It was fastened. Then he went around to the shed. That door was seldom locked, even when the family was away. The thought how her father would be confronted by the cow flashed upon Nanny. There was a hysterical sob in her throat. Adoniram emerged from the shed and stood looking about in a dazed fashion. His lips moved; he was saying something, but they could not hear what it was. The hired man was peeping around a corner of the old barn, but nobody saw him.

Adoniram took the new horse by the bridle and led him across the yard to the new barn. Nanny and Sammy slunk close to their mother. The barn doors rolled back, and there stood Adoniram, with the long mild face of the great Canadian farm horse looking over his shoulder.

Nanny kept behind her mother, but Sammy stepped suddenly forward, and stood in front of her.

Adoniram stared at the group. "What on airth you all down here for?" said he. "What's the matter over to the house?"

"We've come here to live, father," said Sammy. His shrill voice quavered out bravely.

"What"—Adoniram sniffed—"what is it smells like cookin'?" said he. He stepped forward and looked in the open door of the harness-room. Then he turned to his wife. His old bristling face was pale and frightened. "What on airth does this mean, mother?" he gasped.

"You come in here, father," said Sarah. She led the way into the harness-room and shut the door. "Now, father," said she, "you needn't be scared. I ain't crazy. There ain't nothin' to be upset over. But we've come here to live, an' we're goin' to live here. We've got jest as good a right here as new horses an' cows. The house wa'n't fit for us to live in any longer, an' I made up my mind I wa'n't goin' to stay there. I've done my duty by you forty year, an' I'm goin' to do it now; but I'm goin' to live here. You've got to put in some windows and partitions; an' you'll have to buy some furniture."

"Why, mother!" the old man gasped.

"You'd better take your coat off an' get washed—there's the wash-basin—an' then we'll have supper."   480

"Why, mother!"

Sammy went past the window, leading the new horse to the old barn. The old man saw him, and shook his head speechlessly. He tried to take off his coat, but his arms seemed to lack the power. His wife helped him. She poured some water into the tin basin, and put in a piece of soap. She got the comb and brush, and smoothed his thin gray hair after he had washed. Then she put the beans, hot bread, and tea on the table. Sammy came in, and the family drew up. Adoniram sat looking dazedly at his plate, and they waited.

"Ain't you goin' to ask a blessin', father?" said Sarah.

And the old man bent his head and mumbled.   490

All through the meal he stopped eating at intervals, and stared furtively at his wife; but he ate well. The home food tasted good to him, and his old frame was too sturdily healthy to be affected by his mind. But after supper he went out, and sat down on the step of the smaller door at the right of the barn, through which he had meant his Jerseys to pass in stately file, but which Sarah designed for her front house door, and he leaned his head on his hands.

After the supper dishes were cleared away and the milk-pans washed, Sarah went out to him. The twilight was deepening. There was a clear green glow in the sky. Before them stretched the smooth level of field; in the distance was a cluster of hay-stacks like the huts of a village; the air was very cool and calm and sweet. 500 The landscape might have been an ideal one of peace.

Sarah bent over and touched her husband on one of his thin, sinewy shoulders. "Father!"

The old man's shoulders heaved: he was weeping.

"Why, don't do so, father," said Sarah.

"I'll—put up the—partitions, an'—everything you—want, mother."

Sarah put her apron up to her face; she was overcome by her own triumph.

Adoniram was like a fortress whose walls had no active resistance, and went down the instant the right besieging tools were used. "Why, mother," he said, hoarsely, "I hadn't no idee you was so set on't as all this comes to."   [1891] 510

Questions for Discussion and Writing

1. Does the Penn family have difficulty communicating, or do its members communicate in ways other than the verbal? Explain.
2. Why does Mother defend Father when talking to Nanny Penn? Why would she defend him when she is in fact angry with him?
3. What other forces besides Father are arrayed against her?

4. What part does social pressure play in the story? Does society ultimately side with Father or with Mother? How do you know?

5. What makes Father's meek capitulation to Mother at the end psychologically probable or improbable? Explain how Freeman avoids or fails to avoid the "hard man with a soft heart" stereotype.

6. What does this story tell us about people in New England?

✒ MARK TWAIN (SAMUEL LANGHORNE CLEMENS)
(1835–1910)

Luck[1]

The life and literary career of Mark Twain embodies the years when America itself grew from struggling nation and cultural backwater to an important force in the world, including the world of literature.

Clemens was born on the frontier, in Florida, Missouri, and received only a rudimentary formal education. From 1853–1857, he traveled around the East and Midwest, sending observations to his brother, Orion, who published them in his newspapers. He was on the verge of seeking his fortune in South America when Horace Bixby accepted him as an apprentice steamboat pilot. In 1859, after eighteen months in training, he earned his license, leaving only when the Civil War brought navigation on the Mississippi to a halt.

In 1861, Clemens joined Orion in Nevada, where he tried prospecting, newspaper reporting, and humor writing; in 1863, he adopted the pen name Mark Twain, a riverboat term meaning "two fathoms deep" or safe water. Twain's breakthrough occurred when he turned a tall tale he had heard in California into "The Celebrated Jumping Frog of Calaveras County." Its publication in the *New York Saturday Press* in November of 1865 caused a sensation. During the next four years, he extended his reputation by publishing travel sketches in various newspapers, culminating in *The Innocents Abroad* (1869). The following year he married Olivia Langdon, daughter of a wealthy and genteel Eastern family. They enjoyed a close and affectionate relationship until "Livy's" death in 1904.

Twain's happiest and most productive period was 1874–1891, when he lived lavishly in the East, doted on his daughters, and enjoyed the fame brought by *Tom Sawyer, Life on the Mississippi* (both 1876), and *Huckleberry Finn* (1884). Even so, Twain's vision was darkening. It is sometimes claimed that his increasing pessimism resulted from failed investments and deaths in his family, but he had been debunking American institutions since *The Guilded Age* (1873), and his own frontier experiences of violence, greed, and bigotry had early soured

---

1. This is not a fancy sketch. I got it from a clergyman who was an instructor at Woolwich forty years ago, and who vouched for its truth. M.T.

his natural optimism and romanticism. With the rest of the country, he was shifting from Romanticism to Realism. American literature had been marked by sentimentality, excessive gentility, stereotyped characters, and relentless optimism. Mark Twain and his contemporaries gradually rejected these conventions and in the process helped the culture of America to mature.

IT WAS AT A BANQUET in London in honor of one of the two or three conspicuously illustrious English military names of this generation. For reasons which will presently appear, I will withhold his real name and titles and call him Lieutenant-General Lord Arthur Scorseby, Y.C., K.C.B.,[2] etc., etc., etc. What a fascination there is in a renowned name! There sat the man, in actual flesh, whom I had heard of so many thousands of times since that day, thirty years before, when his name shot suddenly to the zenith from a Crimean[3] battlefield, to remain forever celebrated. It was food and drink to me to look, and look, and look at that demi-god; scanning, searching, noting: the quietness, the reserve, the noble gravity of his countenance; the simple honesty that expressed itself all over him; the   10
sweet unconsciousness of his greatness—unconsciousness of the hundreds of admiring eyes fastened upon him, unconsciousness of the deep, loving, sincere worship welling out of the breasts of those people and flowing toward him.

The clergyman at my left was an old acquaintance of mine—clergyman now, but had spent the first half of his life in the camp and field and as an instructor in the military school at Woolwich. Just at the moment I have been talking about a veiled and singular light glimmered in his eyes and he leaned down and muttered confidentially to me—indicating the hero of the banquet with a gesture:

"Privately—he's an absolute fool."

This verdict was a great surprise to me. If its subject had been Napoleon, or   20
Socrates, or Solomon, my astonishment could not have been greater. Two things I was well aware of: that the Reverend was a man of strict veracity and that his judgment of men was good. Therefore I knew, beyond doubt or question, that the world was mistaken about this hero: he *was* a fool. So I meant to find out, at a convenient moment, how the Reverend, all solitary and alone, had discovered the secret.

Some days later the opportunity came, and this is what the Reverend told me:

About forty years ago I was an instructor in the military academy at Woolwich. I was present in one of the sections when young Scoresby underwent his preliminary examination. I was touched to the quick with pity, for the rest of   30
the class answered up brightly and handsomely, while he—why, dear me, he didn't know *anything,* so to speak. He was evidently good, and sweet, and lovable, and guileless; and so it was exceedingly painful to see him stand there, as serene as a graven image, and deliver himself of answers which were veritably miraculous for stupidity and ignorance. All the compassion in me was aroused in his behalf. I

2. Y.C. is unknown, perhaps a joke by Twain or a mistake for VC, Victoria Cross; K.C.B: Knight
    Commander of the Bath.
3. The Crimean War (1854–1856) pitted Britain, France, and Turkey against Russia.

said to myself, when he comes to be examined again he will be flung over, of course; so it will be simply a harmless act of charity to ease his fall as much as I can. I took him aside and found that he knew a little of Cæsar's history;[4] and as he didn't know anything else, I went to work and drilled him like a galley-slave on a certain line of stock questions concerning Cæsar which I knew would be used. If you'll believe me, he went through with flying colors on examination day! He went through on that purely superficial "cram," and got compliments too, while others, who knew a thousand times more than he, got plucked. By some strangely lucky accident—an accident not likely to happen twice in a century—he was asked no question outside of the narrow limits of his drill.

It was stupefying. Well, all through his course I stood by him, with something of the sentiment which a mother feels for a crippled child; and he always saved himself—just by miracle, apparently.

Now, of course, the thing that would expose him and kill him at last was mathematics. I resolved to make his death as easy as I could; so I drilled him and crammed him, and crammed him and drilled him, just on the line of questions which the examiners would be most likely to use, and then launched him on his fate. Well, sir, try to conceive of the result: to my consternation, he took the first prize! And with it he got a perfect ovation in the way of compliments.

Sleep? There was no more sleep for me for a week. My conscience tortured me day and night. What I had done I had done purely through charity, and only to ease the poor youth's fall. I never had dreamed of any such preposterous results as the thing that had happened. I felt as guilty and miserable as Frankenstein. Here was a wooden-head whom I had put in the way of glittering promotions and prodigious responsibilities, and but one thing could happen: he and his responsibilities would all go to ruin together at the first opportunity.

The Crimean War had just broken out. Of course there had to be a war, I said to myself. We couldn't have peace and give this donkey a chance to die before he is found out. I waited for the earthquake. It came. And it made me reel when it did come. He was actually gazetted to a captaincy in a marching regiment! Better men grow old and gray in the service before they climb to a sublimity like that. And who could ever have foreseen that they would go and put such a load of responsibility on such green and inadequate shoulders? I could just barely have stood it if they had made him a cornet; but a captain—think of it! I thought my hair would turn white.

Consider what I did—I who so loved repose and inaction. I said to myself, I am responsible to the country for this, and I must go along with him and protect the country against him as far as I can. So I took my poor little capital that I had saved up through years of work and grinding economy, and went with a sigh and bought a cornetcy in his regiment, and away we went to the field.

And there—oh, dear, it was awful. Blunders?—why, he never did anything *but* blunder. But, you see, nobody was in the fellow's secret. Everybody had him focused wrong, and necessarily misinterpreted his performance every time. Consequently they took his idiotic blunders for inspirations of genius. They did, honestly! His mildest blunders were enough to make a man in his right mind cry;

4. Julius Caesar's *Commentaries* is a common text in introductory Latin.

and they did make me cry—and rage and rave, too, privately. And the thing that kept me always in a sweat of apprehension was the fact that every fresh blunder he made increased the luster of his reputation! I kept saying to myself, he'll get so high that when discovery does finally come it will be like the sun falling out of the sky.

He went right along up, from grade to grade, over the dead bodies of his superiors, until at last, in the hottest moment of the battle of ——— down went our colonel, and my heart jumped into my mouth, for Scoresby was next in rank! Now for it, said I; we'll all land in Sheol in ten minutes, sure.

The battle was awfully hot; the allies were steadily giving way all over the 90 field. Our regiment occupied a position that was vital; a blunder now must be destruction. At this crucial moment, what does this immortal fool do but detach the regiment from its place and order a charge over a neighboring hill where there wasn't a suggestion of an enemy! "There you go!" I said to myself; "this *is* the end at last."

And away we did go, and were over the shoulder of the hill before the insane movement could be discovered and stopped. And what did we find? An entire and unsuspected Russian army in reserve! And what happened? We were eaten up? That is necessarily what would have happened in ninety-nine cases out of a hundred. But no; those Russians argued that no single regiment would come browsing 100 around there at such a time. It must be the entire English army, and that the sly Russian game was detected and blocked; so they turned tail, and away they went, pell-mell, over the hill and down into the field, in wild confusion, and we after them; they themselves broke the solid Russian center in the field, and tore through, and in no time there was the most tremendous rout you ever saw, and the defeat of the allies was turned into a sweeping and splendid victory! Marshal Canrobert looked on, dizzy with astonishment, admiration, and delight; and sent right off for Scoresby, and hugged him, and decorated him on the field in presence of all the armies!

And what was Scoresby's blunder that time? Merely the mistaking his right 110 hand for his left—that was all. An order had come to him to fall back and support our right; and, instead, he fell *forward* and went over the hill to the left. But the name he won that day as a marvelous military genius filled the world with his glory, and that glory will never fade while history books last.

He is just as good and sweet and lovable and unpretending as a man can be, but he doesn't know enough to come in when it rains. Now that is absolutely true. He is the supremest ass in the universe; and until half an hour ago nobody knew it but himself and me. He has been pursued, day by day and year by year, by a most phenomenal and astonishing luckiness. He has been a shining soldier in all our wars for a generation; he has littered his whole military life with blunders, and yet 120 has never committed one that didn't make him a knight or a baronet or a lord or something. Look at his breast; why, he is just clothed in domestic and foreign decorations. Well, sir, every one of them is the record of some shouting stupidity or other; and, taken together, they are proof that the very best thing in all this world that can befall a man is to be born lucky. I say again, as I said at the banquet, Scoresby's an absolute fool.   [1891]

Questions for Discussion and Writing

1. In his own footnote, Twain asserts that he received this story from a reliable source. Does this assertion make you believe that the story is true? Why or why not?

2. Does it matter whether the story is true? Why or why not?

3. Twain and other Realists enjoyed debunking American myths. What myth or idea does this story debunk?

4. Compare Scoresby to heroes and heroines from fairy tales and films like "Forrest Gump." What is the appeal of such unlikely success stories? Do we want to believe that sheer luck can lead to success? Do we suspect that success is largely a matter of luck? Explain.

5. If this story is a fairy tale or fantasy, how can it be considered Realistic?

SIR ARTHUR CONAN DOYLE
(1859–1930)

The Adventure of the Blue Carbuncle

Sir Arthur Conan Doyle is one of those rare authors whose tragedy is his own enormous success, today remembered only for what he regarded as a second-rate achievement.

Doyle was born in Edinburgh, Scotland, and educated at Jesuit schools, but he hated the rigid discipline and harsh conditions and so renounced Christianity, turning instead to science and philosophy and resolving to accept only what could be proven and demonstrated. In medical school at the University of Edinburgh he met Joseph Bell, an eccentric teacher whose powers of observation and deduction later inspired the creation of the character Sherlock Holmes.

In 1881, Doyle set up practice but while awaiting the patients who never came, he turned to writing and from 1879–1886 published a number of Gothic, mystery, and detective stories. Sherlock Holmes first appeared in the serialized version of *A Study in Scarlet* (1887), with no particular success, but the American editor J. M. Stoddart asked Doyle to write another Holmes novel, and the result was the hugely popular *The Sign of Four* (1890). Six new stories followed in the *Strand Magazine,* but already Doyle was tiring of his hero. When *The Strand* asked for more Holmes, he demanded the unheard-of price of £1,000 for twelve stories and was astonished when the magazine agreed. He tried killing off his hero in "The Final Problem," but the public outcry was so great he was forced to resurrect him. Although he continued writing Holmes stories until the last few years of his life, he was convinced that only his historical fiction was significant.

The enormous popularity of the Holmes stories—in literature, on the stage, on film and television—has received considerable attention. Some argue that the eccentric detective, with his genius and his weaknesses, is the secret of the stories' success. Others credit the humanity of Dr. Watson, the cleverness of the plotting, and Holmes's occasional defeats. For whatever reasons, Sherlock Holmes is a cultural phenomenon, a reassuring figure who combats the powers of evil and darkness.

I HAD CALLED UPON my friend Sherlock Holmes upon the second morning after Christmas, with the intention of wishing him the compliments of the season. He was lounging upon the sofa in a purple dressing-gown, a pipe-rack within his reach upon the right, and a pile of crumpled morning papers, evidently newly studied, near at hand. Beside the couch was a wooden chair, and on the angle of the back hung a very seedy and disreputable hard-felt hat, much the worse for wear, and cracked in several places. A lens and a forceps lying upon the seat of the chair suggested that the hat had been suspended in this manner for the purpose of examination.

"You are engaged," said I; "perhaps I interrupt you."   10

"Not at all. I am glad to have a friend with whom I can discuss my results. The matter is a perfectly trivial one"—he jerked his thumb in the direction of the old hat—"but there are points in connection with it which are not entirely devoid of interest and even of instruction."

I seated myself in his armchair and warmed my hands before his crackling fire, for a sharp frost had set in, and the windows were thick with the ice crystals. "I suppose," I remarked, "that, homely as it looks, this thing has some deadly story linked on to it—that it is the clue which will guide you in the solution of some mystery and the punishment of some crime."

"No, no. No crime," said Sherlock Holmes, laughing. "Only one of those   20 whimsical little incidents which will happen when you have four million human beings all jostling each other within the space of a few square miles. Amid the action and reaction of so dense a swarm of humanity, every possible combination of events may be expected to take place, and many a little problem will be presented which may be striking and bizarre without being criminal. We have already had experience of such."

"So much so," I remarked, "that of the last six cases which I have added to my notes, three have been entirely free of any legal crime."

"Precisely. You allude to my attempt to recover the Irene Adler papers, to the singular case of Miss Mary Sutherland, and to the adventure of the man with the   30 twisted lip.[1] Well, I have no doubt that this small matter will fall into the same innocent category. You know Peterson, the commissionaire?"[2]

"Yes."

"It is to him that this trophy belongs."

"It is his hat."

"No, no; he found it. Its owner is unknown. I beg that you will look upon it

---

1. Irene Adler from "A Scandal in Bohemia"; Mary Sutherland from "A Case of Identity"; and "The Man With the Twisted Lip."
2. A messenger or light porter.

not as a battered billycock[3] but as an intellectual problem. And, first, as to how it came here. It arrived upon Christmas morning, in company with a good fat goose, which is, I have no doubt, roasting at this moment in front of Peterson's fire. The facts are these: about four o'clock on Christmas morning, Peterson, who, as you know, is a very honest fellow, was returning from some small jollification and was making his way homeward down Tottenham Court Road. In front of him he saw, in the gaslight, a tallish man, walking with a slight stagger, and carrying a white goose slung over his shoulder. As he reached the corner of Goodge Street, a row broke out between this stranger and a little knot of roughs. One of the latter knocked off the man's hat, on which he raised his stick to defend himself and, swinging it over his head, smashed the shop window behind him. Peterson had rushed forward to protect the stranger from his assailants; but the man, shocked at having broken the window, and seeing an official-looking person in uniform[4] rushing towards him, dropped his goose, took to his heels, and vanished amid the labyrinth of small streets which lie at the back of Tottenham Court Road. The roughs had also fled at the appearance of Peterson, so that he was left in possession of the field of battle, and also of the spoils of victory in the shape of this battered hat and a most unimpeachable Christmas goose."

"Which surely he restored to their owner?"

"My dear fellow, there lies the problem. It is true that 'For Mrs. Henry Baker' was printed upon a small card which was tied to the bird's left leg, and it is also true that the initials 'H. B.' are legible upon the lining of this hat; but as there are some thousands of Bakers, and some hundreds of Henry Bakers in this city of ours, it is not easy to restore lost property to any one of them."

"What, then, did Peterson do?"

"He brought round both hat and goose to me on Christmas morning, knowing that even the smallest problems are of interest to me. The goose we retained until this morning, when there were signs that, in spite of the slight frost, it would be well that it should be eaten without unnecessary delay. Its finder has carried it off, therefore, to fulfill the ultimate destiny of a goose, while I continue to retain the hat of the unknown gentleman who lost his Christmas dinner."

"Did he not advertise?"

"No."

"Then, what clue could you have as to his identity?"

"Only as much as we can deduce."

"From his hat?"

"Precisely."

"But you are joking. What can you gather from this old battered felt?"

"Here is my lens. You know my methods. What can you gather yourself as to the individuality of the man who has worn this article?"

I took the tattered object in my hands and turned it over rather ruefully. It was a very ordinary black hat of the usual round shape, hard and much the worse for wear. The lining had been of red silk, but was a good deal discoloured. There was no maker's name; but, as Holmes had remarked, the initials "H. B." were

---

3. A kind of bowler hat.
4. As a commissionaire, Peterson would have worn an official-looking uniform.

scrawled upon one side. It was pierced in the brim for a hat-securer, but the elastic was missing. For the rest, it was cracked, exceedingly dusty, and spotted in several places, although there seemed to have been some attempt to hide the discoloured patches by smearing them with ink.

"I can see nothing," said I, handing it back to my friend.

"On the contrary, Watson, you can see everything. You fail, however, to reason from what you see. You are too timid in drawing your inferences."

"Then, pray tell me what it is that you can infer from this hat?"

He picked it up and gazed at it in the peculiar introspective fashion which was characteristic of him. "It is perhaps less suggestive than it might have been," he remarked, "and yet there are a few inferences which are very distinct, and a few others which represent at least a strong balance of probability. That the man was highly intellectual is of course obvious upon the face of it, and also that he was fairly well-to-do within the last three years, although he has now fallen upon evil days. He had foresight, but has less now than formerly, pointing to a moral retrogression, which, when taken with the decline of his fortunes, seems to indicate some evil influence, probably drink, at work upon him. This may account also for the obvious fact that his wife has ceased to love him." 90

"My dear Holmes!"

"He has, however, retained some degree of self-respect," he continued, disregarding my remonstrance. "He is a man who leads a sedentary life, goes out little, is out of training entirely, is middle-aged, has grizzled hair which he has had cut within the last few days, and which he anoints with lime-cream. These are the more patent facts which are to be deduced from his hat. Also, by the way, that it is extremely improbable that he has gas laid on in his house." 100

"You are certainly joking, Holmes."

"Not in the least. It is possible that even now, when I give you these results, you are unable to see how they are attained?"

"I have no doubt that I am very stupid, but I must confess that I am unable to follow you. For example, how did you deduce that this man was intellectual?" 110

For answer Holmes clapped the hat upon his head. It came right over the forehead and settled upon the bridge of his nose. "It is a question of cubic capacity," said he; "a man with so large a brain must have something in it."

"The decline of his fortunes, then?"

"This hat is three years old. These flat brims curled at the edge came in then. It is a hat of the very best quality. Look at the band of ribbed silk and the excellent lining. If this man could afford to buy so expensive a hat three years ago, and has had no hat since, then he has assuredly gone down in the world."

"Well, that is clear enough, certainly. But how about the foresight and the moral retrogression?" 120

Sherlock Holmes laughed. "Here is the foresight," said he, putting his finger upon the little disc and loop of the hat-securer. "They are never sold upon hats. If this man ordered one, it is a sign of a certain amount of foresight, since he went out of his way to take this precaution against the wind. But since we see that he has broken the elastic and has not troubled to replace it, it is obvious that he has less foresight now than formerly, which is a distinct proof of a weakening nature. On the other hand, he has endeavoured to conceal some of these stains upon the felt by daubing them with ink, which is a sign that he has not entirely lost his self-respect."

"Your reasoning is certainly plausible."

"The further points, that he is middle-aged, that his hair is grizzled, that it has been recently cut, and that he uses lime-cream, are all to be gathered from a close examination of the lower part of the lining. The lens discloses a large number of hair-ends, clean cut by the scissors of the barber. They all appear to be adhesive, and there is a distinct odour of lime-cream. This dust, you will observe, is not the gritty, gray dust of the street but the fluffy brown dust of the house, showing that it has been hung up indoors most of the time; while the marks of moisture upon the inside are proof positive that the wearer perspired very freely, and could therefore, hardly be in the best of training."

"But his wife—you said that she had ceased to love him."

"This hat has not been brushed for weeks. When I see you, my dear Watson, with a week's accumulation of dust upon your hat, and when your wife allows you to go out in such a state, I shall fear that you also have been unfortunate enough to lose your wife's affection."

"But he might be a bachelor."

"Nay, he was bringing home the goose as a peace-offering to his wife. Remember the card upon the bird's leg."

"You have an answer to everything. But how on earth do you deduce that the gas is not laid on in his house?"

"One tallow[5] stain, or even two, might come by chance; but when I see no less than five, I think that there can be little doubt that the individual must be brought into frequent contact with burning tallow—walks upstairs at night probably with his hat in one hand and a guttering candle in the other. Anyhow, he never got tallow-stains from a gas-jet. Are you satisfied?"

"Well, it is very ingenious," said I, laughing; "but since, as you said just now, there has been no crime committed, and no harm done save the loss of a goose, all this seems to be rather a waste of energy."

Sherlock Holmes had opened his mouth to reply, when the door flew open, and Peterson, the commissionaire, rushed into the apartment with flushed cheeks and the face of a man who is dazed with astonishment.

"The goose, Mr. Holmes! The goose, sir!" he gasped.

"Eh? What of it then? Has it returned to life and flapped off through the kitchen window?" Holmes twisted himself round upon the sofa to get a fairer view of the man's excited face.

"See here, sir! See what my wife found in its crop!" He held out his hand and displayed upon the centre of the palm a brilliantly scintillating blue stone, rather smaller than a bean in size, but of such purity and radiance that it twinkled like an electric point in the dark hollow of his hand.

Sherlock Holmes sat up with a whistle. "By Jove, Peterson!" said he, "this is treasure trove indeed. I suppose you know what you have got?"

"A diamond, sir? A precious stone. It cuts into glass as though it were putty."

5. Animal fat used in making candles.

"It's more than a precious stone. It is *the* precious stone."

"Not the Countess of Morcar's blue carbuncle!" I ejaculated.

"Precisely so. I ought to know its size and shape, seeing that I have read the advertisement about it in *The Times* every day lately. It is absolutely unique, and its value can only be conjectured, but the reward offered of £1000 is certainly not within a twentieth part of the market price."

"A thousand pounds! Great Lord of mercy!" The commissionaire plumped down into a chair and stared from one to the other of us.

"That is the reward, and I have reason to know that there are sentimental considerations in the background which would induce the Countess to part with half her fortune if she could but recover the gem."

"It was lost, if I remember aright, at the Hotel Cosmopolitan," I remarked.

"Precisely so, on December 22d, just five days ago. John Horner, a plumber, was accused of having abstracted it from the lady's jewel-case. The evidence against him was so strong that the case has been referred to the Assizes.[6] I have some account of the matter here, I believe." He rummaged amid his newspapers, glancing over the dates, until at last he smoothed one out, doubled it over, and read the following paragraph:

> "Hotel Cosmopolitan Jewel Robbery. John Horner, 26, plumber, was brought up upon the charge of having upon the 22d inst., abstracted from the jewel-case of the Countess of Morcar the valuable gem known as the blue carbuncle. James Ryder, upper-attendant at the hotel, gave his evidence to the effect that he had shown Horner up to the dressing-room of the Countess of Morcar upon the day of the robbery in order that he might solder the second bar of the grate, which was loose. He had remained with Horner some little time, but had finally been called away. On returning, he found that Horner had disappeared, that the bureau had been forced open, and that the small morocco casket in which, as it afterwards transpired, the Countess was accustomed to keep her jewel, was lying empty upon the dressing-table. Ryder instantly gave the alarm, and Horner was arrested the same evening; but the stone could not be found either upon his person or in his rooms. Catherine Cusack, maid to the Countess, deposed to having heard Ryder's cry of dismay on discovering the robbery, and to having rushed into the room, where she found matters as described by the last witness. Inspector Bradstreet, B division, gave evidence as to the arrest of Horner, who struggled frantically, and protested his innocence in the strongest terms. Evidence of a previous conviction for robbery having been given against the prisoner, the magistrate refused to deal summarily with the offence, but referred it to the Assizes. Horner, who had shown signs of intense emotion during the proceedings, fainted away at the conclusion and was carried out of court.

"Hum! So much for the police-court," said Holmes thoughtfully, tossing aside the paper. "The question for us now to solve is the sequence of events leading from a rifled jewel-case at one end to the crop of a goose in Tottenham Court Road at the other. You see, Watson, our little deductions have suddenly assumed a much more important and less innocent aspect. Here is the stone; the stone came from the goose, and the goose came from Mr. Henry Baker, the gentleman with the

6. County courts for civil and criminal law.

bad hat and all the other characteristics with which I have bored you. So now we must set ourselves very seriously to finding this gentleman and ascertaining what part he has played in this little mystery. To do this, we must try the simplest means first, and these lie undoubtedly in an advertisement in all the evening papers. If this fail, I shall have recourse to other methods." 220

"What will you say?"

"Give me a pencil and that slip of paper. Now, then:

"Found at the corner of Goodge Street, a goose and a black felt hat. Mr. Henry Baker can have the same by applying at 6:30 this evening at 221B, Baker Street.

That is clear and concise."

"Very. But will he see it?"

"Well, he is sure to keep an eye on the papers, since, to a poor man, the loss was a heavy one. He was clearly so scared by his mischance in breaking the win- 230 dow and by the approach of Peterson that he thought of nothing but flight, but since then he must have bitterly regretted the impulse which caused him to drop his bird. Then, again, the introduction of his name will cause him to see it, for everyone who knows him will direct his attention to it. Here you are, Peterson, run down to the advertising agency and have this put in the evening papers."

"In which, sir?"

"Oh, in the *Globe, Star, Pall Mall, St. James's, Evening News Standard, Echo,* and any others that occur to you."

"Very well, sir. And this stone?"

"Ah, yes. I shall keep the stone. Thank you. And, I say, Peterson, just buy a 240 goose on your way back and leave it here with me, for we must have one to give to this gentleman in place of the one which your family is now devouring."

When the commissionaire had gone, Holmes took up the stone and held it against the light. "It's a bonny thing," said he. "Just see how it glints and sparkles. Of course it is a nucleus and focus of crime. Every good stone is. They are the devil's pet baits. In the larger and older jewels every facet may stand for a bloody deed. This stone is not yet twenty years old. It was found in the banks of the Amoy River in southern China and is remarkable in having every characteristic of the carbuncle, save that it is blue in shade instead of ruby red. In spite of its youth, it has already a sinister history. There have been two murders, a vitriol- 250 throwing,[7] a suicide, and several robberies brought about for the sake of this forty-grain weight of crystallized charcoal. Who would think that so pretty a toy would be a purveyor to the gallows and the prison? I'll lock it up in my strong box now and drop a line to the Countess to say that we have it."

"Do you think that this man Horner is innocent?"

"I cannot tell."

"Well, then, do you imagine that this other one, Henry Baker, had anything to do with the matter?"

"It is, I think, much more likely that Henry Baker is an absolutely innocent man, who had no idea that the bird which he was carrying was of considerably 260

---

7. Acid—sometimes used in robberies to render the victim helpless or in acts of revenge.

more value than if it were made of solid gold. That, however, I shall determine by a very simple test if we have an answer to our advertisement."

"And you can do nothing until then?"

"Nothing."

"In that case I shall continue my professional round. But I shall come back in the evening at the hour you have mentioned, for I should like to see the solution of so tangled a business."

"Very glad to see you. I dine at seven. There is a woodcock, I believe. By the way, in view of recent occurrences, perhaps I ought to ask Mrs. Hudson to examine its crop."

I had been delayed at a case, and it was a little after half-past six when I found myself in Baker Street once more. As I approached the house I saw a tall man in a Scotch bonnet[8] with a coat which was buttoned up to his chin waiting outside in the bright semicircle which was thrown from the fanlight. Just as I arrived the door was opened and we were shown up together to Holmes's room.

"Mr. Henry Baker, I believe," said he, rising from his armchair and greeting his visitor with the easy air of geniality in which he could so readily assume. "Pray take this chair by the fire, Mr. Baker. It is a cold night, and I observe that your circulation is more adapted for summer than for winter. Ah, Watson, you have just come at the right time. Is that your hat, Mr. Baker?"

"Yes, sir, that is undoubtedly my hat."

He was a large man with rounded shoulders, a massive head, and a broad, intelligent face, sloping down to a pointed beard of grizzled brown. A touch of red in nose and cheeks, with a slight tremor of his extended hand, recalled Holmes's surmise as to his habits. His rusty black frock-coat was buttoned right up in front, with the collar turned up, and his lank wrists protruded from his sleeves without a sign of cuff or shirt. He spoke in a slow staccato fashion, choosing his words with care, and gave the impression generally of a man of learning and letters who had had ill-usage at the hands of fortune.

"We have retained these things for some days," said Holmes, "because we expected to see an advertisement from you giving your address. I am at a loss to know now why you did not advertise."

Our visitor gave a rather shamefaced laugh. "Shillings have not been so plentiful with me as they once were," he remarked. "I had no doubt that the gang of roughs who assaulted me had carried off both my hat and the bird. I did not care to spend more money in a hopeless attempt at recovering them."

"Very naturally. By the way, about the bird, we were compelled to eat it."

"To eat it!" Our visitor half rose from his chair in his excitement.

"Yes, it would have been of no use to anyone had we not done so. But I presume that this other goose upon the sideboard, which is about the same weight and perfectly fresh, will answer your purpose equally well?"

"Oh, certainly, certainly," answered Mr. Baker with a sigh of relief.

"Of course, we still have the feathers, legs, crop, and so on of your own bird, so if you wish—"

8. A cloth cap.

The man burst into a hearty laugh. "They might be useful to me as relics of   310
my adventure," said he, "but beyond that I can hardly see what use the *disjecta*
membra[9] of my late acquaintance are going to be to me. No, sir, I think that, with
your permission, I will confine my attentions to the excellent bird which I perceive upon the sideboard."

Sherlock Holmes glanced sharply across at me with a slight shrug of his
shoulders.

"There is your hat, then, and there your bird," said he. "By the way, would it
bore you to tell me where you got the other one from? I am somewhat of a fowl
fancier, and I have seldom seen a better grown goose."

"Certainly, sir," said Baker, who had risen and tucked his newly gained prop-   320
erty under his arm. "There are a few of us who frequent the Alpha Inn, near the
Museum—we are to be found in the Museum itself during the day, you understand. This year our good host, Windigate by name, instituted a goose club, by
which, on consideration of some few pence every week, we were each to receive a
bird at Christmas. My pence were duly paid, and the rest is familiar to you. I am
much indebted to you, sir, for a Scotch bonnet is fitted neither to my years nor my
gravity." With a comical pomposity of manner he bowed solemnly to both of us
and strode off upon his way.

"So much for Mr. Henry Baker," said Holmes when he had closed the door
behind him. "It is quite certain that he knows nothing whatever about the matter.   330
Are you hungry, Watson?"

"Not particularly."

"Then I suggest that we turn our dinner into a supper[10] and follow up this
clue while it is still hot."

"By all means."

It was a bitter night, so we drew on our ulsters[11] and wrapped cravats about
our throats. Outside, the stars were shining coldly in a cloudless sky, and the
breath of the passers-by blew out into smoke like so many pistol shots. Our footfalls rang out crisply and loudly as we swung through the doctors' quarter,
Wimpole Street, Harley Street, and so through Wigmore Street into Oxford Street.   340
In a quarter of an hour we were in Bloomsbury at the Alpha Inn, which is a small
public-house at the corner of one of the streets which runs down into Holborn.
Holmes pushed open the door of the private bar and ordered two glasses of beer
from the ruddy-faced, white-aproned landlord.

"Your beer should be excellent if it is as good as your geese," said he.

"My geese!" The man seemed surprised.

"Yes. I was speaking only half an hour ago to Mr. Henry Baker, who was a
member of your goose club."

"Ah! yes, I see. But you see, sir, them's not *our* geese."

"Indeed! Whose, then?"   350

"Well, I got the two dozen from a salesman in Covent Garden."

"Indeed? I know some of them. Which was it?"

9. Scattered remains.
10. A very late evening meal.
11. Long, loose overcoats with belts at the waist.

"Breckinridge is his name."

"Ah! I don't know him. Well, here's your good health, landlord, and prosperity to your house. Good-night."

"Now for Mr. Breckinridge," he continued, buttoning up his coat as we came out into the frosty air. "Remember, Watson, that though we have so homely a thing as a goose at one end of this chain, we have at the other a man who will certainly get seven years' penal servitude unless we can establish his innocence. It is possible that our inquiry may but confirm his guilt; but, in any case, we have a line of investigation which has been missed by the police, and which a singular chance has placed in our hands. Let us follow it out to the bitter end. Faces to the south, then, and quick march!"

We passed across Holborn, down Endell Street, and so through a zigzag of slums to Covent Garden Market. One of the largest stalls bore the name of Breckinridge upon it, and the proprietor, a horsy-looking man, with a sharp face and trim side-whiskers, was helping a boy to put up the shutters.

"Good-evening. It's a cold night," said Holmes.

The salesman nodded and shot a questioning glance at my companion.

"Sold out of geese, I see," continued Holmes, pointing at the bare slabs of marble.

"Let you have five hundred to-morrow morning."

"That's no good."

"Well, there are some on the stall with the gas-flare."

"Ah, but I was recommended to you."

"Who by?"

"The landlord of the Alpha."

"Oh, yes; I sent him a couple of dozen."

"Fine birds they were, too. Now where did you get them from?"

To my surprise the question provoked a burst of anger from the salesman.

"Now, then, mister," said he, with his head cocked and his arms akimbo, "what are you driving at? Let's have it straight, now."

"It is straight enough. I should like to know who sold you the geese which you supplied to the Alpha."

"Well, then, I shan't tell you. So now!"

"Oh, it is a matter of no importance; but I don't know why you should be so warm over such a trifle."

"Warm! You'd be as warm, maybe, if you were as pestered as I am. When I pay good money for a good article there should be an end of the business; but it's 'Where are the geese?' and 'Who did you sell the geese to?' and 'What will you take for the geese?' One would think they were the only geese in the world, to hear the fuss that is made over them."

"Well, I have no connection with any other people who have been making inquiries," said Holmes carelessly. "If you won't tell us the bet is off, that is all. But I'm always ready to back my opinion on a matter of fowls, and I have a fiver on it that the bird I ate is country bred."

"Well, then, you've lost your fiver, for it's town bred," snapped the salesman.

"It's nothing of the kind."

"I say it is."

"I don't believe it."   400

"D'you think you know more about fowls than I, who have handled them ever since I was a nipper? I tell you, all those birds that went to the Alpha were town bred."

"You'll never persuade me to believe that."

"Will you bet, then?"

"It's merely taking your money, for I know that I am right. But I'll have a sovereign on with you, just to teach you not to be obstinate."

The salesman chuckled grimly. "Bring me the books, Bill," said he.

The small boy brought round a small thin volume and a great greasy-backed one, laying them out together beneath the hanging lamp.   410

"Now then, Mr. Cocksure," said the salesman, "I thought that I was out of geese, but before I finish you'll find that there is still one left in my shop. You see this little book?"

"Well?"

"That's the list of the folk from whom I buy. D'you see? Well, then, here on this page are the country folk, and the numbers after their names are where their accounts are in the big ledger. Now, then! You see this other page in red ink? Well, that is a list of my town suppliers. Now, look at that third name. Just read it out to me."

"Mrs. Oakshott, 117, Brixton Road—249," read Holmes.   420

"Quite so. Now turn that up in the ledger."

Holmes turned to the page indicated. "Here you are, 'Mrs. Oakshott, 117, Brixton Road, egg and poultry supplier.'"

"Now, then, what's the last entry?"

"'December 22d. Twenty-four geese at 7s 6d.'"

"Quite so. There you are. And underneath?"

"'Sold to Mr. Windigate of the Alpha, at 12s.'"

"What have you to say now?"

Sherlock Holmes looked deeply chagrined. He drew a sovereign from his pocket and threw it down upon the slab, turning away with the air of a man   430 whose disgust is too deep for words. A few yards off he stopped under a lamppost and laughed in the hearty, noiseless fashion which was peculiar to him.

"When you see a man with whiskers of that cut and the 'Pink un'[12] protruding out of his pocket, you can always draw him by a bet," said he. "I daresay that if I had put £100 down in front of him, that man would not have given me such complete information as was drawn from him by the idea that he was doing me on a wager. Well, Watson, we are, I fancy, nearing the end of our quest, and the only point which remains to be determined is whether we should go on to this Mrs. Oakshott to-night, or whether we should reserve it for to-morrow. It is clear from what that surly fellow said that there are others besides ourselves who are anxious   440 about the matter, and I should—"

His remarks were suddenly cut short by a loud hubbub which broke out from the stall which we had just left. Turning round we saw a little rat-faced fellow

12. *The Sporting News*, consulted by those who bet on horse races.

standing in the centre of the circle of yellow light which was thrown by the swinging lamp, while Breckinridge, the salesman, framed in the door of his stall, was
shaking his fists fiercely at the cringing figure.

"I've had enough of you and your geese," he shouted. "I wish you were all at
the devil together. If you come pestering me any more with your silly talk I'll set
the dog at you. You bring Mrs. Oakshott here and I'll answer her, but what have
you to do with it? Did I buy the geese off you?"   450

"No; but one of them was mine all the same," whined the little man.

"Well, then, ask Mrs. Oakshott for it."

"She told me to ask you."

"Well, you can ask the King of Proosia, for all I care. I've had enough of it.
Get out of this!" He rushed fiercely forward, and the inquirer flitted away into the
darkness.

"Ha! this may save us a visit to Brixton Road," whispered Holmes. "Come
with me, and we will see what is to be made of this fellow." Striding through the
scattered knots of people who lounged round the flaring stalls, my companion
speedily overtook the little man and touched him upon the shoulder. He sprang   460
round, and I could see in the gas-light that every vestige of colour had been driven
from his face.

"Who are you, then? What do you want?" he asked in a quavering voice.

"You will excuse me," said Holmes blandly, "but I could not help overhearing
the questions which you put to the salesman just now. I think that I could be of
assistance to you."

"You? Who are you? How could you know anything of the matter?"

"My name is Sherlock Holmes. It is my business to know what other people
don't know."

"But you can know nothing of this?"   470

"Excuse me, I know everything of it. You are endeavouring to trace some
geese which were sold by Mrs. Oakshott, of Brixton Road, to a salesman named
Breckinridge, by him in turn to Mr. Windigate, of the Alpha, and by him to his
club, of which Mr. Henry Baker is a member."

"Oh, sir, you are the very man whom I have longed to meet," cried the little
fellow with outstretched hands and quivering fingers. "I can hardly explain to you
how interested I am in this matter."

Sherlock Holmes hailed a four-wheeler which was passing. "In that case we
had better discuss it in a cosy room rather than in this wind-swept market-place,"
said he. "But pray tell me, before we go farther, who it is that I have the pleasure of 480
assisting."

The man hesitated for an instant. "My name is John Robinson," he answered
with a sidelong glance.

"No, no; the real name," said Holmes sweetly. "It is always awkward doing
business with an alias."

A flush sprang to the white cheeks of the stranger. "Well, then," said he, "my
real name is James Ryder."

"Precisely so. Head attendant at the Hotel Cosmopolitan. Pray step into the
cab, and I shall soon be able to tell you everything which you would wish to
know."   490

The little man stood glancing from one to the other of us with half-frightened, half-hopeful eyes, as one who is not sure whether he is on the verge of a windfall or of a catastrophe. Then he stepped into the cab, and in half an hour we were back in the sitting-room at Baker Street. Nothing had been said during our drive, but the high, thin breathing of our new companion, and the claspings and unclaspings of his hands, spoke of the nervous tension within him.

"Here we are!" said Holmes cheerily as we filed into the room. "The fire looks very seasonable in this weather, You look cold, Mr. Ryder. Pray take the basket-chair. I will just put on my slippers before we settle this little matter of yours. Now, then! You want to know what became of those geese?"

"Yes, sir."

"Or rather, I fancy, of that goose. It was one bird, I imagine, in which you were interested—white, with a black bar across the tail."

Ryder quivered with emotion. "Oh, sir," he cried, "can you tell me where it went to?"

"It came here."

"Here?"

"Yes, and a most remarkable bird it proved. I don't wonder that you should take an interest in it. It laid an egg after it was dead—the bonniest, brightest little blue egg that ever was seen. I have it here in my museum."

Our visitor staggered to his feet and clutched the mantelpiece with his right hand. Holmes unlocked his strong-box and held up the blue carbuncle, which shone out like a star, with a cold, brilliant, many-pointed radiance. Ryder stood glaring with a drawn face, uncertain whether to claim or to disown it.

"The game's up, Ryder," said Holmes quietly. "Hold up, man, or you'll be into the fire! Give him an arm back into his chair, Watson. He's not got blood enough to go in for felony with impunity. Give him a dash of brandy. So! Now he looks a little more human. What a shrimp it is, to be sure!"

For a moment he had staggered and nearly fallen, but the brandy brought a tinge of colour into his cheeks, and he sat staring with frightened eyes at his accuser.

"I have almost every link in my hands, and all the proofs which I could possibly need, so there is little which you need tell me. Still, that little may as well be cleared up to make the case complete. You had heard, Ryder, of this blue stone of the Countess of Morcar's?"

"It was Catherine Cusack who told me of it," said he in a crackling voice.

"I see—her ladyship's waiting-maid. Well, the temptation of sudden wealth so easily acquired was too much for you, as it has been for better men before you; but you were not very scrupulous in the means you used. It seems to me, Ryder, that there is the making of a very pretty villain in you. You knew that this man Horner, the plumber, had been concerned in some such matter before, and that suspicion would rest the more readily upon him. What did you do, then? You made some small job in my lady's room—you and your confederate Cusack—and you managed that he should be the man sent for. Then, when he had left, you rifled the jewel-case, raised the alarm, and had this unfortunate man arrested. You then—"

Ryder threw himself down suddenly upon the rug and clutched at my companion's knees. "For God's sake, have mercy!" he shrieked. "Think of my father! of my mother! It would break their hearts. I never went wrong before! I never will again. I swear it. I'll swear it on a Bible. Oh, don't bring it into court! For Christ's sake, don't!" 540

"Get back into your chair!" said Holmes sternly. "It is very well to cringe and crawl now, but you thought little enough of this poor Horner in the dock for a crime of which he knew nothing."

"I will fly, Mr. Holmes. I will leave the country, sir. Then the charge against him will break down."

"Hum! We will talk about that. And now let us hear a true account of the next act. How came the stone into the goose, and how came the goose into the open market? Tell us the truth, for there lies your only hope of safety."

Ryder passed his tongue over his parched lips. "I will tell you it just as it 550 happened, sir," said he. "When Horner had been arrested, it seemed to me that it would be best for me to get away with the stone at once, for I did not know at what moment the police might not take it into their heads to search me and my room. There was no place about the hotel where it would be safe. I went out, as if on some commission, and I made for my sister's house. She had married a man named Oakshott, and lived in Brixton Road, where she fattened fowls for the market. All the way there every man I met seemed to me to be a policeman or a detective; and, for all that it was a cold night, the sweat was pouring down my face before I came to the Brixton Road. My sister asked me what was the matter, and why I was so pale; but I told her that I had been upset by the jewel robbery at the 560 hotel. Then I went into the back yard and smoked a pipe, and wondered what it would be best to do.

"I had a friend once called Maudsley, who went to the bad, and has just been serving his time in Pentonville. One day he had met me, and fell into talk about the ways of thieves, and how they could get rid of what they stole. I knew that he would be true to me, for I knew one or two things about him; so I made up my mind to go right on to Kilburn, where he lived, and take him into my confidence. He would show me how to turn the stone into money. But how to get to him in safety? I thought of the agonies I had gone through in coming from the hotel. I might at any moment be seized and searched, and there would be the stone in my 570 waistcoat pocket. I was leaning against the wall at the time and looking at the geese which were waddling about round my feet, and suddenly an idea came into my head which showed me how I could beat the best detective that ever lived.

"My sister had told me some weeks before that I might have the pick of her geese for a Christmas present, and I knew that she was always as good as her word. I would take my goose now, and in it I would carry my stone to Kilburn. There was a little shed in the yard, and behind this I drove one of the birds—a fine big one, white, with a barred tail. I caught it, and, prying its bill open, I thrust the stone down its throat as far as my finger could reach. The bird gave a gulp, and I felt the stone pass along its gullet and down into its crop. But the creature 580 flapped and struggled, and out came my sister to know what was the matter. As I turned to speak to her the brute broke loose and fluttered off among the others.

"'Whatever were you doing with that bird, Jem?' says she.

"'Well,' said I, 'you said you'd give me one for Christmas, and I was feeling which was the fattest.'

"'Oh,' says she, 'we've set yours aside for you—Jem's bird, we call it. It's the big white one over yonder. There's twenty-six of them, which makes one for you, and one for us, and two dozen for the market.'

"'Thank you, Maggie,' says I; 'but if it is all the same to you, I'd rather have that one I was handling just now.'

"'The other is a good three pound heavier,' said she, 'and we fattened it expressly for you.'

"'Never mind. I'll have the other, and I'll take it now,' said I.

"'Oh, just as you like,' said she, a little huffed. 'Which is it you want, then?'

"'That white one with the barred tail, right in the middle of the flock.'

"'Oh, very well. Kill it and take it with you.'

"Well, I did what she said, Mr. Holmes, and I carried the bird all the way to Kilburn. I told my pal what I had done, for he was a man that it was easy to tell a thing like that to. He laughed until he choked, and we got a knife and opened the goose. My heart turned to water, for there was no sign of the stone, and I knew that some terrible mistake had occurred. I left the bird, rushed back to my sister's, and hurried into the back yard. There was not a bird to be seen there.

"'Where are they all, Maggie?' I cried.

"'Gone to the dealer's, Jem.'

"'Which dealer's?'

"'Breckinridge, of Covent Garden.'

"'But was there another bird with a barred tail?' I asked, 'the same as the one I chose?'

"'Yes, Jem; there were two barred-tailed ones, and I could never tell them apart.'

"Well, then, of course I saw it all, and I ran off as hard as my feet would carry me to this man Breckinridge; but he had sold the lot at once, and not one word would he tell me as to where they had gone. You heard him yourselves tonight. Well, he has always answered me like that. My sister thinks that I am going mad. Sometimes I think that I am myself. And now—and now I am myself a branded thief, without ever having touched the wealth for which I sold my character. God help me! God help me!" He burst into convulsive sobbing, with his face buried in his hands.

There was a long silence, broken only by his heavy breathing, and by the measured tapping of Sherlock Holmes's finger-tips upon the edge of the table. Then my friend rose and threw open the door.

"Get out!" said he.

"What, sir! Oh, Heaven bless you!"

"No more words. Get out!"

And no more words were needed. There was a rush, a clatter upon the stairs, the bang of a door, and the crisp rattle of running footfalls from the street.

"After all, Watson," said Holmes, reaching up his hand for his clay pipe, "I am not retained by the police to supply their deficiencies. If Horner were in danger it would be another thing; but this fellow will not appear against him, and the case must collapse. I suppose that I am commuting a felony, but it is just possible ₆₃₀ that I am saving a soul. This fellow will not go wrong again; he is too terribly frightened. Send him to jail now, and you make him a jail-bird for life. Besides, it is the season of forgiveness. Chance has put in our way a most singular and whimsical problem, and its solution is its own reward. If you will have the goodness to touch the bell, Doctor, we will begin another investigation, in which, also a bird will be the chief feature."   [1892]

Questions for Discussion and Writing

1. Examine carefully Holmes's inferences from the hat and goose. Discuss alternative theories that fit the facts.
2. What is the purpose of this reasoning over the hat? What would be lost, if anything, if this portion of the story were eliminated?
3. How plausible are Holmes's insights? Which are the most plausible? Which seem contrived? Explain.
4. What part does coincidence or luck play in Holmes's solution of the mystery?
5. Why or why not is Holmes justified in not turning James Ryder over to the police? Defend or attack the way in which he places himself above the law.
6. How do you regard Dr. Watson? Is he simply a foil for Holmes, or does he have sufficient character and personality of his own to be plausible? Discuss the specific traits of his character.
7. What conventions of the detective story, as you have encountered them in literature, television, or film, do you see in this story? What differences do you see between this story and contemporary detective stories?

⮞ KATE CHOPIN
(1851–1904)

Désirée's Baby

Kate Chopin was influenced by the work of the local colorists Sarah Orne Jewett and Mary E. Wilkins Freeman, by the poet Walt Whitman, and by the French realist Guy de Maupassant. Her vivid stories of Louisiana and her explorations—daring for her time—of such subjects as marriage, divorce, and women's sexuality are unique, however. Some of her work was considered indelicate or scandalous when first published, especially her novel *The Awakening* (1899); her work was then largely forgotten and went out of print. Only with the reissue of *The Awakening* in 1964 did Kate Chopin's writing belatedly begin to receive the recognition and praise it deserves.

She was born Kate O'Flaherty in St. Louis, Missouri. Her father died when she was four, leaving her in the care of her mother and grandmother, both Louisiana Creoles. In 1870, she married Oscar Chopin and moved to New Orleans; they later moved to his large cotton plantation on the Red River in Louisiana. Together they had six children. When her husband died suddenly in

1883, she managed the plantation, which brought her into daily contact with French-Acadian, Creole, and mulatto workers. She gathered from them much of the material that was later to appear in her fiction.

In 1884, she sold the plantation and returned to St. Louis. Encouraged by those who received her colorful letters and inspired by her wide reading in French literature and modern science, she began writing stories. By 1899 she was contributing to *America, Vogue,* and the *Atlantic Monthly.* Unfortunately, hostile reactions to *The Awakening* discouraged her, and she wrote very little thereafter. She died in 1904 from a cerebral hemorrhage.

Both her life and writings mark Chopin as one who questioned the confining role society thrust upon women in the late nineteenth century. Although some of her stories end conventionally in happy marriages, the difficulty that some of her female characters experience in trying to adapt to society's roles creates the tension out of which her feminist ideas emerge.

Although the exact nature of her feminism will continue to be debated, her stories and novels certainly questioned ideas about women's roles in society, just as the lyrical techniques of her fiction challenged the conventions of dramatic plot and incident. However one reads her work, there is no escaping the individuality of her voice and vision, both of which transcend the limiting category of local color.

A s the day was pleasant, Madame Valmondé drove over to L'Abri to see Désirée and the baby.

It made her laugh to think of Désirée with a baby. Why, it seemed but yesterday that Désirée was little more than a baby herself; when Monsieur in riding through the gateway of Valmondé had found her lying asleep in the shadow of the big stone pillar.

The little one awoke in his arms and began to cry for "Dada." That was as much as she could do or say. Some people thought she might have strayed there of her own accord, for she was of the toddling age. The prevailing belief was that she had been purposely left by a party of Texans, whose canvas-covered wagon, late in the day, had crossed the ferry that Coton Maïs kept, just below the plantation. In time Madame Valmondé abandoned every speculation but the one that Désirée had been sent to her by a beneficent Providence to be the child of her affection, seeing that she was without child of the flesh. For the girl grew to be beautiful and gentle, affectionate and sincere,—the idol of Valmondé.

It was no wonder, when she stood one day against the stone pillar in whose shadow she had lain asleep, eighteen years before, that Armand Aubigny riding by and seeing her there, had fallen in love with her. That was the way all the Aubignys fell in love, as if struck by a pistol shot. The wonder was that he had not loved her before; for he had known her since his father brought him home from Paris, a boy of eight, after his mother died there. The passion that awoke in him that day, when he saw her at the gate, swept along like an avalanche, or like a prairie fire, or like anything that drives headlong over all obstacles.

Monsieur Valmondé grew practical and wanted things well considered: that is, the girl's obscure origin. Armand looked into her eyes and did not care. He was reminded that she was nameless. What did it matter about a name when he could give her one of the oldest and proudest in Louisiana? He ordered the *corbeille*[1] from Paris, and contained himself with what patience he could until it arrived; then they were married.

Madame Valmondé had not seen Désirée and the baby for four weeks. When she reached L'Abri she shuddered at the first sight of it, as she always did. It was a sad looking place, which for many years had not known the gentle presence of a mistress, old Monsieur Aubigny having married and buried his wife in France, and she having loved her own land too well ever to leave it. The roof came down steep and black like a cowl,[2] reaching out beyond the wide galleries that encircled the yellow stuccoed house. Big, solemn oaks grew close to it, and their thick-leaved, far-reaching branches shadowed it like a pall. Young Aubigny's rule was a strict one, too, and under it his negroes had forgotten how to be gay, as they had been during the old master's easy-going and indulgent lifetime.

The young mother was recovering slowly, and lay full length, in her soft white muslins and laces, upon a couch. The baby was beside her, upon her arm, where he had fallen asleep, at her breast. The yellow nurse woman sat beside a window fanning herself.

Madame Valmondé bent her portly figure over Désirée and kissed her, holding her an instant tenderly in her arms. Then she turned to the child.

"This is not the baby!" she exclaimed, in startled tones. French was the language spoken at Valmondé in those days.

"I knew you would be astonished," laughed Désirée, "at the way he has grown. The little *cochon de lait!*[3] Look at his legs, mamma, and his hands and finger-nails,—real finger-nails. Zandrine had to cut them this morning. Isn't it true, Zandrine?"

The woman bowed her turbaned head majestically, "Mais si,[4] Madame."

"And the way he cries," went on Désirée, "is deafening. Armand heard him the other day as far away as La Blanche's cabin."

Madame Valmondé had never removed her eyes from the child. She lifted it and walked with it over to the window that was lightest. She scanned the baby narrowly, then looked as searchingly at Zandrine, whose face was turned to gaze across the fields.

"Yes, the child has grown, has changed;" said Madame Valmondé, slowly, as she replaced it beside its mother. "What does Armand say?"

Désirée's face became suffused with a glow that was happiness itself.

"Oh, Armand is the proudest father in the parish, I believe, chiefly because it is a boy, to bear his name; though he says not,—that he would have loved a girl as well. But I know it isn't true. I know he says that to please me. And mamma," she added, drawing Madame Valmondé's head down to her, and speaking in a whisper,

---

1. Wedding gifts given by the groom.
2. A hooded garment.
3. Suckling pig.
4. "But yes."

"he hasn't punished one of them—not one of them—since baby is born. Even Négrillon, who pretended to have burnt his leg that he might rest from work—he only laughed, and said Négrillon was a great scamp. Oh, mamma, I'm so happy; it frightens me."

What Désirée said was true. Marriage, and later the birth of his son, had softened Armand Aubigny's imperious and exacting nature greatly. This was what made the gentle Désirée so happy, for she loved him desperately. When he frowned she trembled, but loved him. When he smiled, she asked no greater blessing of God. But Armand's dark, handsome face had not often been disfigured by frowns since the day he fell in love with her.

When the baby was about three months old, Désirée awoke one day to the conviction that there was something in the air menacing her peace. It was at first too subtle to grasp. It had only been a disquieting suggestion; an air of mystery among the blacks; unexpected visits from far-off neighbors who could hardly account for their coming. Then a strange, an awful change in her husband's manner, which she dared not ask him to explain. When he spoke to her, it was with averted eyes, from which the old love-light seemed to have gone out. He absented himself from home; and when there, avoided her presence and that of her child, without excuse. And the very spirit of Satan seemed suddenly to take hold of him in his dealings with the slaves. Désirée was miserable enough to die.

She sat in her room, one hot afternoon, in her *peignoir*,[5] listlessly drawing through her fingers the strands of her long, silky brown hair that hung about her shoulders. The baby, half naked, lay asleep upon her own great mahogany bed, that was like a sumptuous throne, with its satin-lined half-canopy. One of La Blanche's little quadroon[6] boys—half naked too—stood fanning the child slowly with a fan of peacock feathers. Désirée's eyes had been fixed absently and sadly upon the baby, while she was striving to penetrate the threatening mist that she felt closing about her. She looked from her child to the boy who stood beside him, and back again; over and over. "Ah!" It was a cry that she could not help; which she was not conscious of having uttered. The blood turned like ice in her veins, and a clammy moisture gathered upon her face.

She tried to speak to the little quadroon boy; but no sound would come, at first. When he heard his name uttered, he looked up, and his mistress was pointing to the door. He laid aside the great, soft fan, and obediently stole away, over the polished floor, on his bare tiptoes.

She stayed motionless, with gaze riveted upon her child, and her face the picture of fright.

Presently her husband entered the room, and without noticing her, went to a table and began to search among some papers which covered it.

"Armand," she called to him, in a voice which must have stabbed him, if he was human. But he did not notice. "Armand," she said again. Then she rose and tottered towards him. "Armand," she panted once more, clutching his arm, "look at our child. What does it mean? tell me."

---

5. Dressing gown.
6. One-quarter Negro blood; hence a Negro by the law of the day.

He coldly but gently loosened her fingers from about his arm and thrust the
hand away from him. "Tell me what it means!" she cried despairingly.   110

"It means," he answered lightly, "that the child is not white; it means that
you are not white."

A quick conception of all that this accusation meant for her nerved her with
unwonted courage to deny it. "It is a lie; it is not true, I am white! Look at my hair,
it is brown; and my eyes are gray, Armand, you know they are gray. And my skin
is fair," seizing his wrist. "Look at my hand; whiter than yours, Armand," she
laughed hysterically.

"As white as La Blanche's," he returned cruelly; and went away leaving her
alone with their child.

When she could hold a pen in her hand, she sent a despairing letter to   120
Madame Valmondé.

"My mother, they tell me I am not white. Armand has told me I am not
white. For God's sake tell them it is not true. You must know it is not true. I shall
die. I must die. I cannot be so unhappy, and live."

The answer that came was as brief:

"My own Désirée: Come home to Valmondé; back to your mother who loves
you. Come with your child."

When the letter reached Désirée she went with it to her husband's study, and
laid it open upon the desk before which he sat. She was like a stone image: silent,
white, motionless after she placed it there.   130

In silence he ran his cold eyes over the written words. He said nothing.
"Shall I go, Armand?" she asked in tones sharp with agonized suspense.

"Yes, go."

"Do you want me to go?"

"Yes, I want you to go."

He thought Almighty God had dealt cruelly and unjustly with him; and felt,
somehow, that he was paying Him back in kind when he stabbed thus into his
wife's soul. Moreover he no longer loved her, because of the unconscious injury
she had brought upon his home and his name.

She turned away like one stunned by a blow, and walked slowly towards the   140
door, hoping he would call her back.

"Good-by, Armand," she moaned.

He did not answer her. That was his last blow at fate.

Désirée went in search of her child. Zandrine was pacing the sombre gallery
with it. She took the little one from the nurse's arms with no word of explanation,
and descending the steps, walked away, under the live-oak branches.

It was an October afternoon; the sun was just sinking. Out in the still fields
the negroes were picking cotton.

Désirée had not changed the thin white garment nor the slippers which she
wore. Her hair was uncovered and the sun's rays brought a golden gleam from its 150
brown meshes. She did not take the broad, beaten road which led to the far-off
plantation of Valmondé. She walked across a deserted field, where the stubble
bruised her tender feet, so delicately shod, and tore her thin gown to shreds.

She disappeared among the reeds and willows that grew thick along the
banks of the deep, sluggish bayou; and she did not come back again.

Some weeks later there was a curious scene enacted at L'Abri. In the centre of the smoothly swept back yard was a great bonfire. Armand Aubigny sat in the wide hallway that commanded a view of the spectacle; and it was he who dealt out to a half dozen negroes the material which kept this fire ablaze.

A graceful cradle of willow, with all its dainty furbishings, was laid upon the 160 pyre, which had already been fed with the richness of a priceless *layette*.[7] Then there were silk gowns, and velvet and satin ones added to these; laces, too, and embroideries; bonnets and gloves; for the *corbeille* had been of rare quality.

The last thing to go was a tiny bundle of letters; innocent little scribblings that Désirée had sent to him during the days of their espousal. There was the remnant of one back in the drawer from which he took them. But it was not Désirée's; it was part of an old letter from his mother to his father. He read it. She was thanking God for the blessing of her husband's love:—

"But, above all," she wrote, "night and day, I thank the good God for having so arranged our lives that our dear Armand will never know that his mother, who 170 adores him, belongs to the race that is cursed with the brand of slavery."   [1893]

Questions for Discussion and Writing

1. This story uses a number of common conventions—the foundling child, love at first sight, the incriminating letter. Evaluate Chopin's use of these conventional devices.
2. Analyze the color images in the story, especially those that directly or indirectly refer to race. What functions do these images have in the story?
3. Judging from the story, what were the racial ideas and prejudices in Louisiana at the time it takes place?
4. Many observers today claim that our ideas about race are "socially constructed"; that is, that the notion of various human races is not scientifically but rather socially based. How might this story relate to the idea of race as a social convention rather than as a scientific fact?

☞ STEPHEN CRANE
(1871–1900)

The Open Boat
A Tale intended to be after the fact. Being the Experience of four Men from the Sunk Steamer "Commodore."

Stephen Crane's accomplishments and influence are great, especially considering the brevity of his life. Born into a cultured, though not literary, family, he was the fourteenth child of a strict Methodist minister who died when the boy was only nine, leaving the family in economic difficulty. After attending school in New Jersey, Crane spent three years at various colleges, excelling in athletics

---

7. The baby's clothes, furniture, toys, etc.

rather than academics and leaving without a degree. Influenced by Flaubert's *Madame Bovary,* he wrote the first draft of *Maggie: A Girl of the Streets* while still in college. When no publisher would touch *Maggie* because of its "sordid" content, he borrowed money to have it published at his own expense in 1893. Its sales were low, but it captured the attention of some well-known writers, such as William Dean Howells. *The Red Badge of Courage,* Crane's great Civil War novel, was serialized the following year.

By 1896, he was already famous and was chosen by a newspaper to cover a gun-running ship bound for the Cuban revolution. The ship sank en route, and the resulting experience produced "The Open Boat." Crane met and fell in love with Cora Taylor, proprietor of a bar and brothel in Florida. Together they went to Europe, reported on the Greco-Turkish war in 1897, and from there traveled to England, living in unaffordable luxury, but making the acquaintance of Joseph Conrad, Henry James, and other writers. Crane left to report on the Spanish-American War in Cuba in 1898. Returning to England, he was greeted by a swarm of creditors and tried but failed to write himself out of debt. He died of tuberculosis before his twenty-ninth birthday.

Crane helped move American literature from Romanticism to Realism and Naturalism. While he often portrays man as a part of nature, driven by forces he cannot control, he balances pessimism with humor and insight into the possibilities of social connections and justice. In style and thought he looks backward to Mark Twain and forward to Ernest Hemingway. He shook the foundations of the American novel, wrought technical innovations in the short story, and left the American literary language more plain and yet more poetical than he had found it.

I

NONE OF THEM knew the color of the sky. Their eyes glanced level, and were fastened upon the waves that swept toward them. These waves were of the hue of slate, save for the tops, which were of foaming white, and all of the men knew the colors of the sea. The horizon narrowed and widened, and dipped and rose, and at all times its edge was jagged with waves that seemed thrust up in points like rocks.

Many a man ought to have a bath-tub larger than the boat which here rode upon the sea. These waves were most wrongfully and barbarously abrupt and tall, and each froth-top was a problem in small boat navigation.

The cook squatted in the bottom and looked with both eyes at the six inches 10 of gunwale which separated him from the ocean. His sleeves were rolled over his fat forearms, and the two flaps of his unbuttoned vest dangled as he bent to bail out the boat. Often he said: "Gawd! That was a narrow clip." As he remarked it he invariably gazed eastward over the broken sea.

The oiler, steering with one of the two oars in the boat, sometimes raised himself suddenly to keep clear of water that swirled in over the stern. It was a thin little oar and it seemed often ready to snap.

The correspondent, pulling at the other oar, watched the waves and wondered why he was there.

The injured captain, lying in the bow, was at this time buried in that profound dejection and indifference which comes, temporarily at least, to even the bravest and most enduring when, willy nilly, the firm fails, the army loses, the ship goes down. The mind of the master of a vessel is rooted deep in the timbers of her, though he command for a day or a decade, and this captain had on him the stern impression of a scene in the grays of dawn of seven turned faces, and later a stump of a top-mast with a white ball on it that slashed to and fro at the waves, went low and lower, and down. Thereafter there was something strange in his voice. Although steady, it was deep with mourning, and of a quality beyond oration or tears.

"Keep 'er a little more south, Billie," said he.

"'A little more south,' sir," said the oiler in the stern.

A seat in this boat was not unlike a seat upon a bucking broncho, and, by the same token, a broncho is not much smaller. The craft pranced and reared, and plunged like an animal. As each wave came, and she rose for it, she seemed like a horse making at a fence outrageously high. The manner of her scramble over these walls of water is a mystic thing, and, moreover, at the top of them were ordinarily these problems in white water, the foam racing down from the summit of each wave, requiring a new leap, and a leap from the air. Then, after scornfully bumping a crest, she would slide, and race, and splash down a long incline, and arrive bobbing and nodding in front of the next menace.

A singular disadvantage of the sea lies in the fact that after successfully surmounting one wave you discover that there is another behind it just as important and just as nervously anxious to do something effective in the way of swamping boats. In a ten-foot dingey one can get an idea of the resources of the sea in the line of waves that is not probable to the average experience which is never at sea in a dingey. As each slaty wall of water approached, it shut all else from the view of the men in the boat, and it was not difficult to imagine that this particular wave was the final outburst of the ocean, the last effort of the grim water. There was a terrible grace in the move of the waves, and they came in silence, save for the snarling of the crests.

In the wan light, the faces of the men must have been gray. Their eyes must have glinted in strange ways as they gazed steadily astern. Viewed from a balcony, the whole thing would doubtless have been weirdly picturesque. But the men in the boat had no time to see it, and if they had had leisure there were other things to occupy their minds. The sun swung steadily up the sky, and they knew it was broad day because the color of the sea changed from slate to emerald-green, streaked with amber lights, and the foam was like tumbling snow. The process of the breaking day was unknown to them. They were aware only of this effect upon the color of the waves that rolled toward them.

In disjointed sentences the cook and the correspondent argued as to the difference between a life-saving station and a house of refuge. The cook had said: "There's a house of refuge just north of the Mosquito Inlet Light, and as soon as they see us, they'll come off in their boat and pick us up."

"As soon as who see us?" said the correspondent.

"The crew," said the cook.

"Houses of refuge don't have crews," said the correspondent. "As I understand them, they are only places where clothes and grub are stored for the benefit
of shipwrecked people. They don't carry crews."

"Oh, yes, they do," said the cook.

"No, they don't," said the correspondent.   70

"Well, we're not there yet, anyhow," said the oiler, in the stern.

"Well," said the cook, "perhaps it's not a house of refuge that I'm thinking of
as being near Mosquito Inlet Light. Perhaps it's a life-saving station."

"We're not there yet," said the oiler, in the stern.

II

As THE BOAT bounced from the top of each wave, the wind tore through the
hair of the hatless men, and as the craft plopped her stern down again the spray
slashed past them. The crest of each of these waves was a hill, from the top of
which the men surveyed, for a moment, a broad tumultuous expanse, shining and
wind-riven. It was probably splendid. It was probably glorious, this play of the
free sea, wild with lights of emerald and white and amber.   80

"Bully good thing it's an on-shore wind," said the cook. "If not, where would
we be? Wouldn't have a show."

"That's right," said the correspondent.

The busy oiler nodded his assent.

Then the captain, in the bow, chuckled in a way that expressed humor, contempt, tragedy, all in one. "Do you think we've got much of a show now, boys?"
said he.

Whereupon the three were silent, save for a trifle of hemming and hawing.
To express any particular optimism at this time they felt to be childish and stupid,
but they all doubtless possessed this sense of the situation in their mind. A young 90
man thinks doggedly at such times. On the other hand, the ethics of their condition was decidedly against any open suggestion of hopelessness. So they were
silent.

"Oh, well," said the captain, soothing his children, "we'll get ashore all
right."

But there was that in his tone which made them think, so the oiler quoth:
"Yes! If this wind holds!"

The cook was bailing: "Yes! If we don't catch hell in the surf."

Canton flannel gulls flew near and far. Sometimes they sat down on the sea,
near patches of brown seaweed that rolled over the waves with a movement like 100
carpets on a line in a gale. The birds sat comfortably in groups, and they were envied by some in the dingey, for the wrath of the sea was no more to them than it
was to a covey of prairie chickens a thousand miles inland. Often they came very
close and stared at the men with black bead-like eyes. At these times they were
uncanny and sinister in their unblinking scrutiny, and the men hooted angrily at
them, telling them to be gone. One came, and evidently decided to alight on the
top of the captain's head. The bird flew parallel to the boat and did not circle, but

made short sidelong jumps in the air in chicken-fashion. His black eyes were wistfully fixed upon the captain's head. "Ugly brute," said the oiler to the bird. "You
look as if you were made with a jack-knife." The cook and the correspondent 110
swore darkly at the creature. The captain naturally wished to knock it away with
the end of the heavy painter; but he did not dare do it, because anything resembling an emphatic gesture would have capsized this freighted boat, and so with his
open hand, the captain gently and carefully waved the gull away. After it had been
discouraged from the pursuit the captain breathed easier on account of his hair,
and others breathed easier because the bird struck their minds at this time as
being somehow gruesome and ominous.

In the meantime the oiler and the correspondent rowed. And also they
rowed.

They sat together in the same seat, and each rowed an oar. Then the oiler 120
took both oars; then the correspondent took both oars; then the oiler; then the
correspondent. They rowed and they rowed. The very ticklish part of the business
was when the time came for the reclining one in the stern to take his turn at the
oars. By the very last star of truth, it is easier to steal eggs from under a hen than it
was to change seats in the dingey. First the man in the stern slid his hand along
the thwart and moved with care, as if he were of Sèvres. Then the man in the rowing seat slid his hand along the other thwart. It was all done with the most extraordinary care. As the two sidled past each other, the whole party kept watchful
eyes on the coming wave, and the captain cried: "Look out now! Steady there!"

The brown mats of seaweed that appeared from time to time were like is- 130
lands, bits of earth. They were travelling, apparently, neither one way nor the
other. They were, to all intents, stationary. They informed the men in the boat that
it was making progress slowly toward the land.

The captain, rearing cautiously in the bow, after the dingey soared on a great
swell, said that he had seen the lighthouse at Mosquito Inlet. Presently the cook
remarked that he had seen it. The correspondent was at the oars then, and for
some reason he too wished to look at the lighthouse, but his back was toward the
far shore and the waves were important, and for some time he could not seize an
opportunity to turn his head. But at last there came a wave more gentle than the
others, and when at the crest of it he swiftly scoured the western horizon.   140

"See it?" said the captain.

"No," said the correspondent slowly. "I didn't see anything."

"Look again," said the captain. He pointed. "It's exactly in that direction."

At the top of another wave, the correspondent did as he was bid, and this
time his eyes chanced on a small still thing on the edge of the swaying horizon. It
was precisely like the point of a pin. It took an anxious eye to find a lighthouse so
tiny.

"Think we'll make it, captain?"

"If this wind holds and the boat don't swamp, we can't do much else," said
the captain.   150

The little boat, lifted by each towering sea, and splashed viciously by the
crests, made progress that in the absence of seaweed was not apparent to those in
her. She seemed just a wee thing wallowing, miraculously top up, at the mercy of

five oceans. Occasionally, a great spread of water, like white flames, swarmed into her.

"Bail her, cook," said the captain serenely.

"All right, captain," said the cheerful cook.

III

IT WOULD BE DIFFICULT to describe the subtle brotherhood of men that was here established on the seas. No one said that it was so. No one mentioned it. But it dwelt in the boat, and each man felt it warm him. They were a captain, an oiler, 160 a cook, and a correspondent, and they were friends, friends in a more curiously iron-bound degree than may be common. The hurt captain, lying against the water-jar in the bow, spoke always in a low voice and calmly, but he could never command a more ready and swiftly obedient crew than the motley three of the dingey. It was more than a mere recognition of what was best for the common safety. There was surely in it a quality that was personal and heartfelt. And after this devotion to the commander of the boat there was this comradeship that the correspondent, for instance, who had been taught to be cynical of men, knew even at the time was the best experience of his life. But no one said that it was so. No one mentioned it. 170

"I wish we had a sail," remarked the captain. "We might try my overcoat on the end of an oar and give you two boys a chance to rest." So the cook and the correspondent held the mast and spread wide the overcoat. The oiler steered, and the little boat made good way with her new rig. Sometimes the oiler had to scull sharply to keep a sea from breaking into the boat, but otherwise sailing was a success.

Meanwhile the lighthouse had been growing slowly larger. It had now almost assumed color, and appeared like a little gray shadow on the sky. The man at the oars could not be prevented from turning his head rather often to try for a glimpse of this little gray shadow. 180

At last, from the top of each wave the men in the tossing boat could see land. Even as the lighthouse was an upright shadow on the sky, this land seemed but a long black shadow on the sea. It certainly was thinner than paper. "We must be about opposite New Smyrna," said the cook, who had coasted this shore often in schooners. "Captain, by the way, I believe they abandoned that life-saving station there about a year ago."

"Did they?" said the captain.

The wind slowly died away. The cook and the correspondent were not now obliged to slave in order to hold high the oar. But the waves continued their old impetuous swooping at the dingey, and the little craft, no longer under way, strug- 190 gled woundily over them. The oiler or the correspondent took the oars again.

Shipwrecks are apropos of nothing. If men could only train for them and have them occur when the men had reached pink condition, there would be less drowning at sea. Of the four in the dingey none had slept any time worth mentioning for two days and two nights previous to embarking in the dingey, and in the excitement of clambering about the deck of a foundering ship they had also forgotten to eat heartily.

For these reasons, and for others, neither the oiler nor the correspondent was fond of rowing at this time. The correspondent wondered ingenuously how in the name of all that was sane could there be people who thought it amusing to row a boat. It was not an amusement; it was a diabolical punishment, and even a genius of mental aberrations could never conclude that it was anything but a horror to the muscles and a crime against the back. He mentioned to the boat in general how the amusement of rowing struck him, and the weary-faced oiler smiled in full sympathy. Previously to the foundering, by the way, the oiler had worked double-watch in the engine-room of the ship.

"Take her easy, now, boys," said the captain. "Don't spend yourselves. If we have to run a surf you'll need all your strength, because we'll sure have to swim for it. Take your time."

Slowly the land arose from the sea. From a black line it became a line of black and a line of white, trees and sand. Finally, the captain said that he could make out a house on the shore. "That's the house of refuge, sure," said the cook. "They'll see us before long, and come out after us."

The distant lighthouse reared high. "The keeper ought to be able to make us out now, if he's looking through a glass," said the captain. "He'll notify the life-saving people."

"None of those other boats could have got ashore to give word of the wreck," said the oiler, in a low voice. "Else the life-boat would be out hunting us."

Slowly and beautifully the land loomed out of the sea. The wind came again. It had veered from the north-east to the south-east. Finally, a new sound struck the ears of the men in the boat. It was the low thunder of the surf on the shore. "We'll never be able to make the lighthouse now," said the captain. "Swing her head a little more north, Billie."

"'A little more north,' sir," said the oiler.

Whereupon the little boat turned her nose once more down the wind, and all but the oarsman watched the shore grow. Under the influence of this expansion doubt and direful apprehension was leaving the minds of the men. The management of the boat was still most absorbing, but it could not prevent a quiet cheerfulness. In an hour, perhaps, they would be ashore.

Their backbones had become thoroughly used to balancing in the boat, and they now rode this wild colt of a dingey like circus men. The correspondent thought that he had been drenched to the skin, but happening to feel in the top pocket of his coat, he found therein eight cigars. Four of them were soaked with sea-water; four were perfectly scatheless. After a search, somebody produced three dry matches, and thereupon the four waifs rode in their little boat, and with an assurance of an impending rescue shining in their eyes, puffed at the big cigars and judged well and ill of all men. Everybody took a drink of water.

IV

"Cook," remarked the captain, "there don't seem to be any signs of life about your house of refuge."

"No," replied the cook. "Funny they don't see us!"

A broad stretch of lowly coast lay before the eyes of the men. It was of low dunes topped with dark vegetation. The roar of the surf was plain, and sometimes they could see the white lip of a wave as it spun up the beach. A tiny house was blocked out black upon the sky. Southward, the slim lighthouse lifted its little gray length.

Tide, wind, and waves were swinging the dingey northward. "Funny they don't see us," said the men.

The surf's roar was here dulled, but its tone was, nevertheless, thunderous and mighty. As the boat swam over the great rollers, the men sat listening to this roar. "We'll swamp sure," said everybody. 250

It is fair to say here that there was not a life-saving station within twenty miles in either direction, but the men did not know this fact, and in consequence they made dark and opprobrious remarks concerning the eyesight of the nation's life-savers. Four scowling men sat in the dingey and surpassed records in the invention of epithets.

"Funny they don't see us."

The light-heartedness of a former time had completely faded. To their sharpened minds it was easy to conjure pictures of all kinds of incompetency and blindness and, indeed, cowardice. There was the shore of the populous land, and it was bitter and bitter to them that from it came no sign. 260

"Well," said the captain, ultimately, "I suppose we'll have to make a try for ourselves. If we stay out here too long, we'll none of us have strength left to swim after the boat swamps."

And so the oiler, who was at the oars, turned the boat straight for the shore. There was a sudden tightening of muscles. There was some thinking.

"If we don't all get ashore—" said the captain. "If we don't all get ashore, I suppose you fellows know where to send news of my finish?"

They then briefly exchanged some addresses and admonitions. As for the reflections of the men, there was a great deal of rage in them. Perchance they might be formulated thus: "If I am going to be drowned—if I am going to be drowned— 270 if I am going to be drowned, why, in the name of the seven mad gods who rule the sea, was I allowed to come thus far and contemplate sand and trees? Was I brought here merely to have my nose dragged away as I was about to nibble the sacred cheese of life? It is preposterous. If this old ninny-woman, Fate, cannot do better than this, she should be deprived of the management of men's fortunes. She is an old hen who knows not her intention. If she has decided to drown me, why did she not do it in the beginning and save me all this trouble? The whole affair is absurd. . . . But no, she cannot mean to drown me. She dare not drown me. She cannot drown me. Not after all this work." Afterward the man might have had an impulse to shake his fist at the clouds: "Just you drown me, now, and then hear 280 what I call you!"

The billows that came at this time were more formidable. They seemed always just about to break and roll over the little boat in a turmoil of foam. There was a preparatory and long growl in the speech of them. No mind unused to the sea would have concluded that the dingey could ascend these sheer heights in time. The shore was still afar. The oiler was a wily surfman. "Boys," he said swiftly, "she won't live three minutes more, and we're too far out to swim. Shall I take her to sea again, captain?"

"Yes! go ahead!" said the captain.

This oiler, by a series of quick miracles, and fast and steady oarsmanship, 290 turned the boat in the middle of the surf and took her safely to sea again.

There was a considerable silence as the boat bumped over the furrowed sea to deeper water. Then somebody in gloom spoke. "Well, anyhow, they must have seen us from the shore by now."

The gulls went in slanting flight up the wind toward the gray desolate east. A squall, marked by dingy clouds, and clouds brick-red, like smoke from a burning building, appeared from the south-east.

"What do you think of those life-saving people? Ain't they peaches?"

"Funny they haven't seen us."

"Maybe they think we're out here for sport! Maybe they think we're fishin'. 300 Maybe they think we're damned fools."

It was a long afternoon. A changed tide tried to force them southward, but wind and wave said northward. Far ahead, where coastline, sea, and sky formed their mighty angle, there were little dots which seemed to indicate a city on the shore.

"St. Augustine?"

The captain shook his head. "Too near Mosquito Inlet."

And the oiler rowed, and then the correspondent rowed. Then the oiler rowed. It was a weary business. The human back can become the seat of more aches and pains than are registered in books for the composite anatomy of a regi- 310 ment. It is a limited area, but it can become the theater of innumerable muscular conflicts, tangles, wrenches, knots, and other comforts.

"Did you ever like to row, Billie?" asked the correspondent.

"No," said the oiler. "Hang it!"

When one exchanged the rowing-seat for a place in the bottom of the boat, he suffered a bodily depression that caused him to be careless of everything save an obligation to wiggle one finger. There was cold sea-water swashing to and fro in the boat, and he lay in it. His head, pillowed on a thwart, was within an inch of the swirl of a wave crest, and sometimes a particularly obstreperous sea came in-board and drenched him once more. But these matters did not annoy him. It is al- 320 most certain that if the boat had capsized he would have tumbled comfortably out upon the ocean as if he felt sure that it was a great soft mattress.

"Look! There's a man on the shore!"

"Where?"

"There! See 'im? See 'im?"

"Yes, sure! He's walking along."

"Now he's stopped. Look! He's facing us!"

"He's waving at us!"

"So he is! By thunder!"

"Ah, now we're all right! Now we're all right! There'll be a boat out here for 330 us in half an hour."

"He's going on. He's running. He's going up to that house there."

The remote beach seemed lower than the sea, and it required a searching glance to discern the little black figure. The captain saw a floating stick and they rowed to it. A bath-towel was by some weird chance in the boat, and tying this on the stick, the captain waved it. The oarsman did not dare turn his head, so he was obliged to ask questions.

"What's he doing now?"

"He's standing still again. He's looking. I think. . . . There he goes again. Toward the house. . . . Now he's stopped again."   340

"Is he waving at us?"

"No, not now! he was, though."

"Look! There comes another man!"

"He's running."

"Look at him go, would you."

"Why, he's on a bicycle. Now he's met the other man. They're both waving at us. Look!"

"There comes something up the beach."

"What the devil is that thing?"

"Why, it looks like a boat."   350

"Why, certainly it's a boat."

"No, it's on wheels."

"Yes, so it is. Well, that must be the life-boat. They drag them along shore on a wagon."

"That's the life-boat, sure."

"No, by—, it's—it's an omnibus."

"I tell you it's a life-boat."

"It is not! It's an omnibus. I can see it plain. See? One of these big hotel omnibuses."

"By thunder, you're right. It's an omnibus, sure as fate. What do you suppose   360 they are doing with an omnibus? Maybe they are going around collecting the life-crew, hey?"

"That's it, likely. Look! There's a fellow waving a little black flag. He's standing on the steps of the omnibus. There come those other two fellows. Now they're all talking together. Look at the fellow with the flag. Maybe he ain't waving it."

"That ain't a flag, is it? That's his coat. Why, certainly, that's his coat."

"So it is. It's his coat. He's taken it off and is waving it around his head. But would you look at him swing it."

"Oh, say, there isn't any life-saving station there. That's just a winter resort hotel omnibus that has brought over some of the boarders to see us drown."   370

"What's that idiot with the coat mean? What's he signaling, anyhow?"

"It looks as if he were trying to tell us to go north. There must be a life-saving station up there."

"No! He thinks we're fishing. Just giving us a merry hand. See? Ah, there, Willie."

"Well, I wish I could make something out of those signals. What do you suppose he means?"

"He don't mean anything. He's just playing."

"Well, if he'd just signal us to try the surf again, or to go to sea and wait, or go north, or go south, or go to hell—there would be some reason in it. But look at him. He just stands there and keeps his coat revolving like a wheel. The ass!" 380

"There come more people."

"Now there's quite a mob. Look! Isn't that a boat."

"Where? Oh, I see where you mean. No, that's no boat."

"That fellow is still waving his coat."

"He must think we like to see him do that. Why don't he quit it? It don't mean anything."

"I don't know. I think he is trying to make us go north. It must be that there's a life-saving station there somewhere."

"Say, he ain't tired yet. Look at 'im wave." 390

"Wonder how long he can keep that up. He's been revolving his coat ever since he caught sight of us. He's an idiot. Why aren't they getting men to bring a boat out? A fishing boat—one of those big yawls—could come out here all right. Why don't he do something?"

"Oh, it's all right, now."

"They'll have a boat out here for us in less than no time, now that they've seen us."

A faint yellow tone came into the sky over the low land. The shadows on the sea slowly deepened. The wind bore coldness with it, and the men began to shiver. 400

"Holy smoke!" said one, allowing his voice to express his impious mood, "if we keep on monkeying out here! If we've got to flounder out here all night!"

"Oh, we'll never have to stay here all night! Don't you worry. They've seen us now, and it won't be long before they'll come chasing out after us."

The shore grew dusky. The man waving a coat blended gradually into this gloom, and it swallowed in the same manner the omnibus and the group of people. The spray, when it dashed uproariously over the side, made the voyagers shrink and swear like men who were being branded.

"I'd like to catch the chump who waved the coat. I feel like soaking him one, just for luck." 410

"Why? What did he do?"

"Oh, nothing, but then he seemed so damned cheerful."

In the meantime the oiler rowed, and then the correspondent rowed, and then the oilier rowed. Gray-faced and bowed forward, they mechanically, turn by turn, plied the leaden oars. The form of the lighthouse had vanished from the southern horizon, but finally a pale star appeared, just lifting from the sea. The streaked saffron in the west passed before the all-merging darkness, and the sea to the east was black. The land had vanished, and was expressed only by the low and drear thunder of the surf.

"If I am going to be drowned—if I am going to be drowned—if I am going to 420 be drowned, why, in the name of the seven mad gods who rule the sea, was I allowed to come thus far and contemplate sand and trees? Was I brought here merely to have my nose dragged away as I was about to nibble the sacred cheese of life?"

The patient captain, dropped over the water-jar, was sometimes obliged to speak to the oarsman.

"Keep her head up! Keep her head up!"

"'Keep her head up,' sir." The voices were weary and low.

This was surely a quiet evening. All save the oarsman lay heavily and listlessly in the boat's bottom. As for him, his eyes were just capable of noting the tall 430 black waves that swept forward in a most sinister silence, save for an occasional subdued growl of a crest.

The cook's head was on a thwart, and he looked without interest at the water under his nose. He was deep in other scenes. Finally he spoke. "Billie," he murmured, dreamfully, "what kind of pie do you like best?"

V

"Pie," said the oiler and the correspondent, agitatedly. "Don't talk about those things, blast you!"

"Well," said the cook, "I was just thinking about ham sandwiches, and—"

A night on the sea in an open boat is a long night. As darkness settled finally, the shine of the light, lifting from the sea in the south, changed to full gold. On 440 the northern horizon a new light appeared, a small bluish gleam on the edge of the waters. These two lights were the furniture of the world. Otherwise there was nothing but waves.

Two men huddled in the stern, and distances were so magnificent in the dingey that the rower was enabled to keep his feet partly warmed by thrusting them under his companions. Their legs indeed extended far under the rowing-seat until they touched the feet of the captain forward. Sometimes, despite the efforts of the tired oarsman, a wave came piling into the boat, an icy wave of the night, and the chilling water soaked them anew. They would twist their bodies for a moment and groan, and sleep the dead sleep once more, while the water in the boat 450 gurgled about them as the craft rocked.

The plan of the oiler and the correspondent was for one to row until he lost the ability, and then arouse the other from his sea-water couch in the bottom of the boat.

The oiler plied the oars until his head drooped forward, and the overpowering sleep blinded him. And he rowed yet afterward. Then he touched a man in the bottom of the boat, and called his name. "Will you spell me for a little while?" he said, meekly.

"Sure, Billie," said the correspondent, awakening and dragging himself to a sitting position. They exchanged places carefully, and the oiler, cuddling down in 460 the sea-water at the cook's side, seemed to go to sleep instantly.

The particular violence of the sea had ceased. The waves came without snarling. The obligation of the man at the oars was to keep the boat headed so that the tilt of the rollers would not capsize her, and to preserve her from filling when the crests rushed past. The black waves were silent and hard to be seen in the darkness. Often one was almost upon the boat before the oarsman was aware.

In a low voice the correspondent addressed the captain. He was not sure that the captain was awake, although this iron man seemed to be always awake. "Captain, shall I keep her making for that light north, sir?"

The same steady voice answered him. "Yes. Keep it about two points off the 470 port bow."

The cook had tied a life-belt around himself in order to get even the warmth which this clumsy cork contrivance could donate, and he seemed almost stove-like when a rower, whose teeth invariably chattered wildly as soon as he ceased his labor, dropped down to sleep.

The correspondent, as he rowed, looked down at the two men sleeping underfoot. The cook's arm was around the oiler's shoulders, and, with their frag-mentary clothing and haggard faces, they were the babes of the sea, a grotesque rendering of the old babes in the wood.

Later he must have grown stupid at his work, for suddenly there was a 480 growling of water, and a crest came with a roar and a swash into the boat, and it was a wonder that it did not set the cook afloat in his life-belt. The cook contin-ued to sleep, but the oiler sat up, blinking his eyes and shaking with the new cold.

"Oh, I'm awfully sorry, Billie," said the correspondent, contritely.

"That's all right, old boy," said the oiler, and lay down again and was asleep.

Presently it seemed that even the captain dozed, and the correspondent thought that he was the one man afloat on all the oceans. The wind had a voice as it came over the waves, and it was sadder than the end.

There was a long, loud swishing astern of the boat, and a gleaming trail of phosphorescence, like blue flame, was furrowed on the black waters. It might 490 have been made by a monstrous knife.

Then there came a stillness, while the correspondent breathed with the open mouth and looked at the sea.

Suddenly there was another swish and another long flash of bluish light, and this time it was alongside the boat, and might almost have been reached with an oar. The correspondent saw an enormous fin speed like a shadow through the water, hurling the crystalline spray and leaving the long glowing trail.

The correspondent looked over his shoulder at the captain. His face was hid-den, and he seemed to be asleep. He looked at the babes of the sea. They certainly were asleep. So, being bereft of sympathy, he leaned a little way to one side and 500 swore softly into the sea.

But the thing did not then leave the vicinity of the boat. Ahead or astern, on one side or the other, at intervals long or short, fled the long sparkling streak, and there was to be heard the whiroo of the dark fin. The speed and power of the thing was greatly to be admired. It cut the water like a gigantic and keen projectile.

The presence of this biding thing did not affect the man with the same hor-ror that it would if he had been a picnicker. He simply looked at the sea dully and swore in an undertone.

Nevertheless, it is true that he did not wish to be alone. He wished one of his 510 companions to awaken by chance and keep him company with it. But the captain hung motionless over the water-jar, and the oiler and the cook in the bottom of the boat were plunged in slumber.

VI

"If I am going to be drowned—if I am going to be drowned—if I am going to be drowned, why, in the name of the seven mad gods who rule the sea, was I allowed to come thus far and contemplate sand and trees?"

During this dismal night, it may be remarked that a man would conclude that it was really the intention of the seven mad gods to drown him, despite the abominable injustice of it. For it was certainly an abominable injustice to drown a man who had worked so hard, so hard. The man felt it would be a crime most un-   520
natural. Other people had drowned at sea since galleys swarmed with painted sails, but still—

When it occurs to a man that nature does not regard him as important, and that she feels she would not maim the universe by disposing of him, he at first wishes to throw bricks at the temple, and he hates deeply the fact that there are no bricks and no temples. Any visible expression of nature would surely be pelleted with his jeers.

Then, if there be no tangible thing to hoot he feels, perhaps, the desire to confront a personification and indulge in pleas, bowed to one knee, and with hands supplicant, saying: "Yes, but I love myself."   530

A high cold star on a winter's night is the word he feels that she says to him. Thereafter he knows the pathos of his situation.

The men in the dingey had not discussed these matters, but each had, no doubt, reflected upon them in silence and according to his mind. There was seldom any expression upon their faces save the general one of complete weariness. Speech was devoted to the business of the boat.

To chime the notes of his emotion, a verse mysteriously entered the correspondent's head. He had even forgotten that he had forgotten this verse, but it suddenly was in his mind.

A soldier of the Legion lay dying in Algiers,   540
There was lack of woman's nursing, there was dearth of woman's tears;
But a comrade stood beside him, and he took that comrade's hand,
And he said: "I shall never see my own, my native land."

In his childhood, the correspondent had been made acquainted with the fact that a soldier of the Legion lay dying in Algiers, but he had never regarded the fact as important. Myriads of his school-fellows had informed him of the soldier's plight, but the dinning had naturally ended by making him perfectly indifferent. He had never considered it his affair that a soldier of the Legion lay dying in Algiers, nor had it appeared to him as a matter for sorrow. It was less to him than the breaking of a pencil's point.   550

Now, however, it quaintly came to him as a human, living thing. It was no longer merely a picture of a few throes in the breast of a poet, meanwhile drinking tea and warming his feet at the grate; it was an actuality—stern, mournful, and fine.

The correspondent plainly saw the soldier. He lay on the sand with his feet out straight and still. While his pale left hand was upon his chest in an attempt to thwart the going of his life, the blood came between his fingers. In the far Algerian distance, a city of low square forms was set against a sky that was faint with the last sunset hues. The correspondent, plying the oars and dreaming of the slow and slower movements of the lips of the soldier, was moved by a profound and per- 560 fectly impersonal comprehension. He was sorry for the soldier of the Legion who lay dying in Algiers.

The thing which had followed the boat and waited had evidently grown bored at the delay. There was no longer to be heard the slash of the cut water, and there was no longer the flame of the long trail. The light in the north still glimmered, but it was apparently no nearer to the boat. Sometimes the boom of the surf rang in the correspondent's ears, and he turned the craft seaward then and rowed harder. Southward, someone had evidently built a watch-fire on the beach. It was too low and too far to be seen, but it made a shimmering, roseate reflection upon the bluff back of it, and this could be discerned from the boat. The wind 570 came stronger, and sometimes a wave suddenly raged out like a mountain-cat, and there was to be seen the sheen and sparkle of a broken crest.

The captain, in the bow, moved on his water-jar and sat erect. "Pretty long night," he observed to the correspondent. He looked at the shore. "Those life-saving people take their time."

"Did you see that shark playing around?"

"Yes, I saw him. He was a big fellow, all right."

"Wish I had known you were awake."

Later the correspondent spoke into the bottom of the boat.

"Billie!" There was a slow and gradual disentanglement. "Billie, will you spell 580 me?"

"Sure," said the oiler.

As soon as the correspondent touched the cold comfortable seater in the bottom of the boat, and had huddled close to the cook's life-belt he was deep in sleep, despite the fact that his teeth played all the popular airs. This sleep was so good to him that it was but a moment before he heard a voice call his name in a tone that demonstrated the last stages of exhaustion. "Will you spell me?"

"Sure, Billie."

The light in the north had mysteriously vanished, but the correspondent took his course from the wide-awake captain. 590

Later in the night they took the boat farther out to sea, and the captain directed the cook to take one oar at the stern and keep the boat facing the seas. He was to call out if he should hear the thunder of the surf. This plan enabled the oiler and the correspondent to get respite together. "We'll give those boys a chance to get into shape again," said the captain. They curled down and, after a few preliminary chatterings and trembles, slept once more the dead sleep. Neither knew they had bequeathed to the cook the company of another shark, or perhaps the same shark.

As the boat caroused on the waves, spray occasionally bumped over the side and gave them a fresh soaking, but this had no power to break their repose. The 600 ominous slash of the wind and the water affected them as it would have affected mummies.

"Boys," said the cook, with the notes of every reluctance in his voice, "she's drifted in pretty close. I guess one of you had better take her to sea again." The correspondent, aroused, heard the crash of the toppled crests.

As he was rowing, the captain gave him some whiskey-and-water, and this steadied the chills out of him. "If I ever get ashore and anybody shows me even a photograph of an oar—"

At last there was a short conversation.

"Billie . . . Billie, will you spell me?"   610

"Sure," said the oiler.

VII

WHEN THE CORRESPONDENT again opened his eyes, the sea and the sky were each of the gray hue of the dawning. Later, carmine and gold was painted upon the waters. The morning appeared finally, in its splendor, with a sky of pure blue, and the sunlight flamed on the tips of the waves.

On the distant dunes were set many little black cottages, and a tall white windmill reared above them. No man, nor dog, nor bicycle appeared on the beach. The cottages might have formed a deserted village.

The voyagers scanned the shore. A conference was held in the boat. "Well," said the captain, "if no help is coming, we might better try a run through the surf 620 right away. If we stay out here much longer we will be too weak to do anything for ourselves at all." The others silently acquiesced in this reasoning. The boat was headed for the beach. The correspondent wondered if none ever ascended the tall wind-tower, and if then they never looked seaward. This tower was a giant, standing with its back to the plight of the ants. It represented in a degree, to the correspondent, the serenity of nature amid the struggles of the individual—nature in the wind, and nature in the vision of men. She did not seem cruel to him then, nor beneficent, nor treacherous, nor wise. But she was indifferent, flatly indifferent. It is, perhaps, plausible that a man in this situation, impressed with the unconcern of the universe, should see the innumerable flaws of his life, and have 630 them taste wickedly in his mind and wish for another chance. A distinction between right and wrong seems absurdly clear to him, then, in this new ignorance of the grave-edge, and he understands that if he were given another opportunity he would mend his conduct and his words, and be better and brighter during an introduction or at a tea.

"Now, boys," said the captain, "she is going to swamp sure. All we can do is to work her in as far as possible, and then when she swamps, pile out and scramble for the beach. Keep cool now, and don't jump until she swamps sure."

The oiler took the oars. Over his shoulders he scanned the surf. "Captain," he said, "I think I'd better bring her about, and keep her head-on to the seas and 640 back her in."

"All right, Billie," said the captain. "Back her in." The oiler swung the boat then and, seated in the stern, the cook and the correspondent were obliged to look over their shoulders to contemplate the lonely and indifferent shore.

The monstrous in-shore rollers heaved the boat high until the men were again enabled to see the white sheets of water scudding up the slanted beach. "We won't get in very close," said the captain. Each time a man could wrest his attention from the rollers, he turned his glance toward the shore, and in the expression of the eyes during this contemplation there was a singular quality. The correspondent, observing the others, knew that they were not afraid, but the full meaning of their glances was shrouded. 650

As for himself, he was too tired to grapple fundamentally with the fact. He tried to coerce his mind into thinking of it, but the mind was dominated at this time by the muscles, and the muscles said they did not care. It merely occurred to him that if he should drown it would be a shame.

There were no hurried words, no pallor, no plain agitation. The men simply looked at the shore. "Now, remember to get well clear of the boat when you jump," said the captain.

Seaward the crest of a roller suddenly fell with a thunderous crash, and the long white comber came roaring down upon the boat. 660

"Steady now," said the captain. The men were silent. They turned their eyes from the shore to the comber and waited. The boat slid up the incline, leaped at the furious top, bounced over it, and swung down the long back of the waves. Some water had been shipped and the cook bailed it out.

But the next crest crashed also. The tumbling, boiling flood of white water caught the boat and whirled it almost perpendicular. Water swarmed in from all sides. The correspondent had his hands on the gunwale at this time, and when the water entered at that place he swiftly withdrew his fingers, as if he objected to wetting them.

The little boat, drunken with this weight of water, reeled and snuggled deeper into the sea. 670

"Bail her out, cook! Bail her out," said the captain.

"All right, captain," said the cook.

"Now, boys, the next one will do for us, sure," said the oiler. "Mind to jump clear of the boat."

The third wave moved forward, huge, furious, implacable. It fairly swallowed the dingey, and almost simultaneously the men tumbled into the sea. A piece of life-belt had lain in the bottom of the boat, and as the correspondent went overboard he held this to his chest with his left hand.

The January water was icy, and he reflected immediately that it was colder than he had expected to find it off the coast of Florida. This appeared to his dazed mind as a fact important enough to be noted at the time. The coldness of the water was sad; it was tragic. This fact was somehow so mixed and confused with his opinion of his own situation that it seemed almost a proper reason for tears. The water was cold. 680

When he came to the surface he was conscious of little but the noisy water. Afterward he saw his companions in the sea. The oiler was ahead in the race. He was swimming strongly and rapidly. Off to the correspondent's left, the cook's

great white and corked back bulged out of the water, and in the rear the captain
was hanging with his one good hand to the keel of the overturned dingey.   690

There is a certain immovable quality to a shore, and the correspondent wondered at it amid the confusion of the sea.

It seemed also very attractive, but the correspondent knew that it was a long
journey, and he paddled leisurely. The piece of life-preserver lay under him, and
sometimes he whirled down the incline of a wave as if he were on a hand-sled.

But finally he arrived at a place in the sea where travel was beset with difficulty. He did not pause swimming to inquire what manner of current had caught
him, but there his progress ceased. The shore was set before him like a bit of
scenery on a stage, and he looked at it and understood with his eyes each detail
of it.   700

As the cook passed, much farther to the left, the captain was calling to him,
"Turn over on your back, cook! Turn over on your back and use the oar."

"All right, sir." The cook turned on his back, and, paddling with an oar, went
ahead as if he were a canoe.

Presently the boat also passed to the left of the correspondent with the captain clinging with one hand to the keel. He would have appeared like a man raising himself to look over a board fence, if it were not for the extraordinary
gymnastics of the boat. The correspondent marvelled that the captain could still
hold to it.

They passed on, nearer to shore—the oiler, the cook, the captain—and fol-   710
lowing them went the water-jar, bouncing gaily over the seas.

The correspondent remained in the grip of this strange new enemy—a current. The shore, with its white slope of sand and its green bluff, topped with little
silent cottages, was spread like a picture before him. It was very near to him then,
but he was impressed as one who in a gallery looks at a scene from Brittany or
Algiers.

He thought: "I am going to drown? Can it be possible? Can it be possible?
Can it be possible?" Perhaps an individual must consider his own death to be the
final phenomenon of nature.

But later a wave perhaps whirled him out of this small deadly current, for he   720
found suddenly that he could again make progress toward the shore. Later still, he
was aware that the captain, clinging with one hand to the keel of the dingey, had
his face turned away from the shore and toward him, and was calling his name.
"Come to the boat! Come to the boat!"

In his struggle to reach the captain and the boat, he reflected that when one
gets properly wearied, drowning must really be a comfortable arrangement, a cessation of hostilities accompanied by a large degree of relief, and he was glad of it,
for the main thing in his mind for some moments had been horror of the temporary agony. He did not wish to be hurt.

Presently he saw a man running along the shore. He was undressing with   730
most remarkable speed. Coat, trousers, shirt, everything flew magically off him.

"Come to the boat," called the captain.

"All right, captain." As the correspondent paddled, he saw the captain let
himself down to bottom and leave the boat. Then the correspondent performed

his one little marvel of the voyage. A large wave caught him and flung him with ease and supreme speed completely over the boat and far beyond it. It struck him even then as an event in gymnastics, and a true miracle of the sea. An overturned boat in the surf is not a plaything to a swimming man.

The correspondent arrived in water that reached only to his waist but his condition did not enable him to stand for more than a moment. Each wave knocked him into a heap, and the under-tow pulled at him.

Then he saw the man who had been running and undressing, and undressing and running, come bounding into the water. He dragged ashore the cook, and then waded toward the captain, but the captain waved him away, and sent him to the correspondent. He was naked, naked as a tree in winter, but a halo was about his head, and he shone like a saint. He gave a strong pull, and a long drag, and a bully heave at the correspondent's hand. The correspondent schooled in the minor formulae, said: "Thanks, old man." But suddenly the man cried: "What's that?" He pointed a swift finger. The correspondent said: "Go."

In the shallows, face downward, lay the oiler. His forehead touched sand that was periodically, between each wave, clear of the sea.

The correspondent did not know all that transpired afterward. When he achieved safe ground he fell, striking the sand with each particular part of his body. It was as if he had dropped from a roof but the thud was grateful to him.

It seems that instantly the beach was populated with men, with blankets, clothes, and flasks, and women with coffee-pots and all the remedies sacred to their minds. The welcome of the land to the men from the sea was warm and generous, but a still and dripping shape was carried slowly up the beach, and the land's welcome for it could only be the different and sinister hospitality of the grave.

When it came night, the white waves paced to and fro in the moonlight, and the wind brought the sound of the great sea's voice to the men on shore, and they felt that they could then be interpreters.   [1897]

Questions for Discussion and Writing

1. How is nature depicted in this story? Underline or highlight specific passages to prepare your answer.
2. What sort of society is formed by the four men in the boat? What functions does this social fabric serve?
3. Crane often adopts a tone of ironic understatement, as in lines 32–40. Highlight or underline other such passages and analyze their effect on the story. Do they emphasize or mitigate the sense of tragedy?
4. Consider "The Open Boat" as an adventure story. How does it resemble a conventional adventure story, and how does it differ?
5. What does the story say about the possibilities of communication?
6. What does the story say about the relationship between man and the universe?
7. In what ways could the three survivors of the ordeal be the interpreters of the sea?

✂ ANTON CHEKHOV
(1860–1904)

TRANSLATED BY CONSTANCE GARNETT

Easter Eve[1]

Anton Chekhov is a seminal figure in the Modernist movement. His plays are classics of the modern theater, and his short stories significantly altered the direction and emphasis of the genre.

Chekhov's grandfather was a serf who bought his freedom. His father was a grocer in the village of Tagonrog, until he went bankrupt and moved the family to Moscow in 1876. Anton stayed behind to finish high school, supporting himself by tutoring. In 1879 he joined his family in Moscow, entered medical school, and soon became the family's chief financial support by writing humorous sketches for newspapers. His first important story, "The Steppe," appeared in a Moscow literary journal in 1888. As Chekhov's reputation grew, he was criticized for avoiding social, political, and philosophical ideas in his fiction, and perhaps in response he embarked on a six-thousand mile overland journey to Sakhalin, site of a notorious penal colony. The journey did not make him a political writer, but it deepened his sympathy with the sufferings of ordinary people.

Chekhov seldom practiced medicine, but the detachment and objectivity of clinical work encouraged acute, impartial observation—a skill he brought to both fiction and drama. Conscious of the trivialities that constitute everyday life, he avoided melodrama and focused on ordinary but telling details as a way to explore his characters' lives. He was known in Europe by the 1890s, but his influence grew when Constance Garnett's translations began appearing after World War I. His example reinforced the work of innovators like Joyce and Mansfield, who later experimented with similar ways of freeing the short story from dependence upon plot and dramatic incident.

"Easter Eve" shows Chekhov's mastery of atmosphere and suggestion, while "The Lady With the Dog" uses understatement and the accumulation of detail to build a memorable tale of frustrated love. Readers accustomed to dramatic plots sometimes complain that "nothing happens" in a Chekhov story. In fact, a great deal happens just beneath the surface for the reader attuned to nuances and imaginative enough to grasp the pain (or the humor) behind apparently trivial details.

---

1. In the Russian Orthodox faith, Easter is preceded by a strict fast during Lent, culminating in an all-night vigil on Easter Eve.

I WAS STANDING on the bank of the River Goltva, waiting for the ferry-boat from the other side. At ordinary times the Goltva is a humble stream of moderate size, silent and pensive, gently glimmering from behind thick reeds; but now a regular lake lay stretched out before me. The waters of spring, running riot, had overflowed both banks and flooded both sides of the river for a long distance, submerging vegetable gardens, hayfields and marshes, so that it was no unusual thing to meet poplars and bushes sticking out above the surface of the water and looking in the darkness like grim solitary crags.

The weather seemed to me magnificent. It was dark, yet I could see the trees, the water and the people. . . . The world was lighted by the stars which were scat- 10 tered thickly all over the sky. I don't remember ever seeing so many stars. Literally one could not have put a finger in between them. There were some as big as a goose's egg, others tiny as hempseed. . . . They had come out for the festival procession, every one of them, little and big, washed, renewed and joyful, and every one of them was softly twinkling its beams. The sky was reflected in the water; the stars were bathing in its dark depths and trembling with the quivering eddies. The air was warm and still. . . . Here and there, far away on the further bank in the impenetrable darkness, several bright red lights were gleaming. . . .

A couple of paces from me I saw the dark silhouette of a peasant in a high hat, with a thick knotted stick in his hand.   20

"How long the ferry-boat is in coming!" I said.

"It is time it was here," the silhouette answered.

"You are waiting for the ferry-boat, too?"

"No, I am not," yawned the peasant—"I am waiting for the illumination. I should have gone, but, to tell you the truth, I haven't the five kopecks for the ferry."

"I'll give you the five kopecks."

"No; I humbly thank you. . . . With that five kopecks put up a candle for me over there in the monastery. . . . That will be more interesting, and I will stand here. What can it mean, no ferry-boat, as though it had sunk in the water!"   30

The peasant went up to the water's edge, took the rope in his hands, and shouted: "Ieronim! Ireon—im!"

As though in answer to his shout, the slow peal of a great bell floated across from the further bank. The note was deep and low, as from the thickest string of a double bass; it seemed as though the darkness itself had hoarsely uttered it. At once there was the sound of a cannon shot. It rolled away in the darkness and ended somewhere in the far distance behind me. The peasant took off his hat and crossed himself.

"Christ is risen," he said.

Before the vibrations of the first peal of the bell had time to die away in the 40 air a second sounded, after it at once a third, and the darkness was filled with an unbroken quivering clamor. Near the red lights fresh lights flashed, and all began moving together and twinkling restlessly.

"Ieron—im!" we heard a hollow prolonged shout.

"They are shouting from the other bank," said the peasant, "so there is no ferry there either. Our Ieronim has gone to sleep."

The lights and the velvety chimes of the bell drew one towards them. . . . I was already beginning to lose patience and grow anxious, but behold at last, staring into the dark distance, I saw the outline of something very much like a gibbet.[2] It was the long-expected ferry. It moved towards us with such deliberation 50 that if it had not been that its lines grew gradually more definite, one might have supposed that it was standing still or moving to the other bank.

"Make haste! Ieronim!" shouted my peasant. "The gentleman's tired of waiting!"

The ferry crawled to the bank, gave a lurch and stopped with a creak. A tall man in a monk's cassock and a conical cap stood on it, holding the rope.

"Why have you been so long?" I asked, jumping upon the ferry.

"Forgive me, for Christ's sake," Ieronim answered gently. "Is there no one else?"

"No one. . . ."   60

Ieronim took hold of the rope in both hands, bent himself to the figure of a mark of interrogation, and gasped. The ferry-boat creaked and gave a lurch. The outline of the peasant in the high hat began slowly retreating from me—so the ferry was moving off. Ieronim soon drew himself up and began working with one hand only. We were silent, gazing towards the bank to which we were floating. There the illumination for which the peasant was waiting had begun. At the water's edge barrels of tar were flaring like huge camp fires. Their reflections, crimson as the rising moon, crept to meet us in long broad streaks. The burning barrels lighted up their own smoke and the long shadows of men flitting about the fire; but further to one side and behind them from where the velvety chime floated 70 there was still the same unbroken black gloom. All at once, cleaving the darkness, a rocket zigzagged in a golden ribbon up the sky; it described an arc and, as though broken to pieces against the sky, was scattered crackling into sparks. There was a roar from the bank like a far-away hurrah.

"How beautiful!" I said.

"Beautiful beyond words!" sighed Ieronim. "Such a night, sir! Another time one would pay no attention to the fireworks, but to-day one rejoices in every vanity. Where do you come from?"

I told him where I came from.

"To be sure . . . a joyful day to-day. . . ." Ieronim went on in a weak sighing 80 tenor like the voice of a convalescent. "The sky is rejoicing and the earth, and what is under the earth. All the creatures are keeping holiday. Only tell me, kind sir, why, even in the time of great rejoicing, a man cannot forget his sorrows?"

I fancied that this unexpected question was to draw me into one of those endless religious conversations which bored and idle monks are so fond of. I was not disposed to talk much, and so I only asked:

"What sorrows have you, father?"

"As a rule only the same as all men, kind sir, but to-day a special sorrow has happened in the monastery: at mass, during the reading of the Bible, the monk and deacon Nikolay died."   90

"Well, it's God's will!" I said, falling into the monastic tone. "We must all die.

2. Gallows.

To my mind, you ought to rejoice indeed. . . . They say if anyone dies at Easter he goes straight to the kingdom of heaven."

"That's true."

We sank into silence. The figure of the peasant in the high hat melted into the lines of the bank. The tar barrels were flaring up more and more.

"The Holy Scripture points clearly to the vanity of sorrow, and so does reflection," said Ieronim, breaking the silence; "but why does the heart grieve and refuse to listen to reason? Why does one want to weep bitterly?"

Ieronim shrugged his shoulders, turned to me and said quickly: 100

"If I died, or anyone else, it would not be worth notice, perhaps; but, you see, Nikolay is dead! No one else but Nikolay! Indeed, it's hard to believe that he is no more! I stand here on my ferry-boat and every minute I keep fancying that he will lift up his voice from the bank. He always used to come to the bank and call to me that I might not be afraid on the ferry. He used to get up from his bed at night on purpose for that. He was a kind soul. My God! how kindly and gracious! Many a mother is not so good to her child as Nikolay was to me! Lord, save his soul!"

Ieronim took hold of the rope, but turned to me again at once.

"And such a lofty intelligence, your honour," he said in a vibrating voice.   110
"Such a sweet and harmonious tongue! Just as they will sing immediately at early matins: 'Oh lovely! oh sweet is Thy Voice!' Besides all other human qualities, he had, too, an extraordinary gift!"

"What gift?" I asked.

The monk scrutinized me, and as though he had convinced himself that he could trust me with a secret, he laughed good-humouredly.

"He had a gift for writing hymns of praise," he said. "It was a marvel, sir; you couldn't call it anything else! You will be amazed if I tell you about it. Our Father Archimandrite comes from Moscow, the Father Sub-Prior studied at the Kazan academy, we have wise monks and elders, but, would you believe it, no one   120
could write them; while Nikolay, a simple monk, a deacon, had not studied anywhere, and had not even any outer appearance of it, but he wrote them! A marvel! a real marvel!" Ieronim clasped his hands and, completely forgetting the rope, went on eagerly:

"The Father Sub-Prior has great difficulty in composing sermons; when he wrote the history of the monastery he worried all the brotherhood and drove a dozen times to town, while Nikolay wrote canticles! Hymns of praise! That's a very different thing from a sermon or a history!"

"Is it difficult to write them?" I asked.

"There's great difficulty!" Ieronim wagged his head. "You can do nothing by   130
wisdom and holiness if God has not given you the gift. The monks who don't understand argue that you only need to know the life of the saint for whom you are writing the hymn, and to make it harmonize with the other hymns of praise. But that's a mistake, sir. Of course, anyone who writes canticles must know the life of the saint to perfection, to the least trivial detail. To be sure, one must make them harmonize with the other canticles and know where to begin and what to write about. To give you an instance, the first response begins everywhere with 'the chosen' or 'the elect.'. . . The first line must always begin with the 'angel.' In the canticle

of praise to Jesus the Most Sweet, if you are interested in the subject, it begins like
this: 'Of angels Creator and Lord of all powers!' In the canticle to the Holy Mother   140
of God: 'Of angels the foremost sent down from on high,' to Nikolay, the Wonder-
worker—'an angel is semblance, though in substance a man,' and so on.
Everywhere you begin with the angel. Of course, it would be impossible without
making them harmonize, but the lives of the saints and conformity with the others
is not what matters; what matters is the beauty and sweetness of it. Everything must
be harmonious, brief and complete. There must be in every line softness, gracious-
ness and tenderness; not one word should be harsh or rough or unsuitable. It must
be written so that the worshipper may rejoice at heart and weep, while his mind is
stirred and he is thrown into a tremor. In the canticle to the Holy Mother are the
words: 'Rejoice, O Thou too high for human thought to reach! 'Rejoice, O Thou too   150
deep for angels' eyes to fathom!' In another place in the same canticle: 'Rejoice, O
tree that bearest the fair fruit of light that is the food of the faithful! Rejoice, O tree
of gracious spreading shade, under which there is shelter for multitudes!'"

Ieronim hid his face in his hands, as though frightened at something or overcome with shame, and shook his head.

"Tree that bearest the fair fruit of light ... tree of gracious spreading
shade, . . ." he muttered. "To think that a man should find words like those! Such
a power is a gift from God! For brevity he packs many thoughts into one phrase, and
how smooth and complete it all is! 'Light-radiating torch to all that be . . .' comes
in the canticle to Jesus the Most Sweet. 'Light-radiating!' There is no such word in   160
conversation or in books, but you see he invented it, he found it in his mind!
Apart from the smoothness and grandeur of language, sir, every line must be beau-
tified in every way; there must be flowers and lightning and wind and sun and all
the objects of the visible world. And every exclamation ought to be put so as to be
smooth and easy for the ear. 'Rejoice, thou flower of heavenly growth!' comes in
the hymn to Nikolay the Wonder-worker. It's not simply 'heavenly flower,' but
'flower of heavenly growth.' It's smoother so and sweet to the ear. That was just as
Nikolay wrote it! exactly like that! I can't tell you how he used to write!"

"Well, in that case it is a pity he is dead," I said; "but let us get on, father, or
we shall be late."   170

Ieronim started and ran to the rope; they were beginning to peal all the bells.
Probably the procession was already going on near the monastery, for all the dark
space behind the tar barrels was now dotted with moving lights.

"Did Nikolay print his hymns?" I asked Ieronim.

"How could he print them?" he sighed. "And, indeed, it would be strange to
print them. What would be the object? No one in the monastery takes any interest
in them. They don't like them. They knew Nikolay wrote them, but they let it pass
unnoticed. No one esteems new writings nowadays, sir!"

"Were they prejudiced against him?"

"Yes, indeed. If Nikolay had been an elder perhaps the brethren would have   180
been interested, but he wasn't forty, you know. There were some who laughed and
even thought his writing a sin."

"What did he write them for?"

"Chiefly for his own comfort. Of all the brotherhood, I was the only one who
read his hymns. I used to go to him in secret, that no one else might know of it,

and he was glad that I took an interest in them. He would embrace me, stroke my head, speak to me in caressing words as to a little child. He would shut his cell, make me sit down beside him, and begin to read. . . ."

Ieronim left the rope and came up to me.

"We were dear friends in a way," he whispered, looking at me with shining eyes. "Where he went I would go. If I were not there he would miss me. And he cared more for me than for anyone, and all because I used to weep over his hymns. It makes me sad to remember. Now I feel just like an orphan or a widow. You know, in our monastery they are all good people, kind and pious, but . . . there is no one with softness and refinement, they are just like peasants. They all speak loudly, and tramp heavily when they walk; they are noisy, they clear their throats, but Nikolay always talked softly, caressingly, and if he noticed that anyone was asleep or praying he would slip by like a fly or a gnat. His face was tender, compassionate. . . ."

Ieronim heaved a deep sigh and took hold of the rope again. We were by now approaching the bank. We floated straight out of the darkness and stillness of the river into an enchanted realm, full of stifling smoke, crackling lights and up-roar. By now one could distinctly see people moving near the tar barrels. The flickering of the lights gave a strange, almost fantastic, expression to their figures and red faces. From time to time one caught among the heads and faces a glimpse of a horse's head motionless as though cast in copper.

"They'll begin singing the Easter hymn directly, . . ." said Ieronim, "and Nikolay is gone; there is no one to appreciate it. . . . There was nothing written dearer to him than that hymn. He used to take in every word! You'll be there, sir, so notice what is sung; it takes your breath away!"

"Won't you be in church, then?"

"I can't; . . . I have to work the ferry. . . ."

"But won't they relieve you?"

"I don't know. . . . I ought to have been relieved at eight; but, as you see, they don't come! . . . And I must own I should have liked to be in the church. . . ."

"Are you a monk?"

"Yes . . . that is, I am a lay brother."

The ferry ran into the bank and stopped. I thrust a five kopeck piece into Ieronim's hand for taking me across, and jumped on land. Immediately a cart with a boy and a sleeping woman in it drove creaking onto the ferry. Ieronim, with a faint glow from the lights on his figure, pressed on the rope, bent down to it, and started the ferry back. . . .

I took a few steps through mud, but a little farther walked on a soft freshly trodden path. This path led to the dark monastery gates, that looked like a cavern through a cloud of smoke, through a disorderly crowd of people, unharnessed horses, carts and chaises. All this crowd was rattling, snorting, laughing, and the crimson light and wavering shadows from the smoke flickered over it all. . . . A perfect chaos! And in this hubbub the people yet found room to load a little can-non and to sell cakes. There was no less commotion on the other side of the wall in the monastery precincts, but there was more regard for decorum and order. Here there was a smell of juniper and incense. They talked loudly, but there was no sound of laughter or snorting. Near the tombstones and crosses people pressed close to one another with Easter cakes and bundles in their arms. Apparently many had come from a long distance for their cakes to be blessed and now were exhausted. Young lay brothers, making a metallic sound with their boots, ran busily along the iron slabs that paved the way from the monastery gates to the church door. They were busy and shouting on the belfry, too.

"What a restless night!" I thought. "How nice!"

One was tempted to see the same unrest and sleeplessness in all nature, from the night darkness to the iron slabs, the crosses on the tombs and the trees under 240 which the people were moving to and fro. But nowhere was the excitement and restlessness so marked as in the church. An unceasing struggle was going on in the entrance between the inflowing stream and the outflowing stream. Some were going in, others going out and soon coming back again to stand still for a little and begin moving again. People were scurrying from place to place, lounging about as though they were looking for something. The stream flowed from the entrance all round the church, disturbing even the front rows, where persons of weight and dignity were standing. There could be no thought of concentrated prayer. There were no prayers at all, but a sort of continuous, childishly irresponsible joy, seek- ing a pretext to break out and vent itself in some movement, even in senseless 250 jostling and shoving.

The same unaccustomed movement is striking in the Easter service itself. The altar gates are flung wide open, thick clouds of incense float in the air near the candelabra; wherever one looks there are lights, the gleam and splutter of can- dles. . . . There is no reading; restless and light-hearted singing goes on to the end without ceasing. After each hymn the clergy change their vestments and come out to burn incense, which is repeated every ten minutes.

I had no sooner taken a place, when a wave rushed from in front and forced me back. A tall thick-set deacon walked before me with a long red candle; the grey-headed archimandrite in his golden mitre hurried after him with the censer. 260 When they had vanished from sight the crowd squeezed me back to my former position. But ten minutes had not passed before a new wave burst on me, and again the deacon appeared. This time he was followed by the Father Sub-Prior, the man who, as Ieronim had told me, was writing the history of the monastery.

As I mingled with the crowd and caught the infection of the universal joyful excitement, I felt unbearably sore on Ieronim's account. Why did they not send someone to relieve him? Why could not someone of less feeling and less suscepti- bility go on the ferry? "Lift up thine eyes, O Sion, and look around," they sang in the choir, "for thy children have come to thee as to a beacon of divine light from north and south, and from east and from the sea. . . ." 270

I looked at the faces; they all had a lively expression of triumph, but not one was listening to what was being sung and taking it in, and not one was "holding his breath." Why was not Ieronim released? I could fancy Ieronim standing meekly somewhere by the wall, bending forward and hungrily drinking in the beauty of the holy phrase. All this that glided by the ears of people standing by me he would have eagerly drunk in with his delicately sensitive soul, and would have been spell-bound to ecstasy, to holding his breath, and there would not have been a man happier than he in all the church. Now he was plying to and fro over the dark river and grieving for his dead friend and brother.

The wave surged back. A stout smiling monk, playing with his rosary and 280
looking round behind him, squeezed sideways by me, making way for a lady in a
hat and velvet cloak. A monastery servant hurried after the lady, holding a chair
over our heads.

I came out of the church. I wanted to have a look at the dead Nikolay, the
unknown canticle writer. I walked about the monastery wall, where there was a
row of cells, peeped into several windows, and, seeing nothing, came back again. I
do not regret now that I did not see Nikolay; God knows, perhaps if I had seen
him I should have lost the picture my imagination paints for me now. I imagine
that lovable poetical figure, solitary and not understood, who went out at nights to
call to Ieronim over the water, and filled his hymns with flowers, stars and sun- 290
beams, as a pale timid man with soft, mild, melancholy features. His eyes must
have shone, not only with intelligence, but with kindly tenderness and that hardly
restrained childlike enthusiasm which I could hear in Ieronim's voice when he
quoted to me passages from the hymns.

When we came out of church after mass it was no longer night. The morning was beginning. The stars had gone out and the sky was a morose greyish blue.
The iron slabs, the tombstones and the buds on the trees were covered with dew.
There was a sharp freshness in the air. Outside the precincts I did not find the
same animated scene as I had beheld in the night. Horses and men looked exhausted, drowsy, scarcely moved, while nothing was left of the tar barrels but 300
heaps of black ash. When anyone is exhausted and sleepy he fancies that nature,
too, is in the same condition. It seemed to me that the trees and the young grass
were asleep. It seemed as though even the bells were not pealing so loudly and
gaily as at night. The restlessness was over, and of the excitement nothing was left
but a pleasant weariness, a longing for sleep and warmth.

Now I could see both banks of the river; a faint mist hovered over it in shifting masses. There was a harsh cold breath from the water. When I jumped on to
the ferry, a chaise and some two dozen men and women were standing on it already. The rope, wet and as I fancied drowsy, stretched far away across the broad
river and in places disappeared in the white mist. 310

"Christ is risen! Is there no one else?" asked a soft voice.

I recognized the voice of Ieronim. There was no darkness now to hinder me
from seeing the monk. He was a tall narrow-shouldered man of five-and-thirty,
with large rounded features, with half-closed listless-looking eyes and an unkempt
wedge-shaped beard. He had an extraordinarily sad and exhausted look.

"They have not relieved you yet?" I asked in surprise.

"Me?" he answered, turning to me his chilled and dewy face with a smile.
"There is no one to take my place now till morning. They'll all be going to the
Father Archimandrite's to break the fast directly."

With the help of a little peasant in a hat of reddish fur that looked like the 320
little wooden tubs in which honey is sold, he threw his weight on the rope; they
gasped simultaneously, and the ferry started.

We floated across, disturbing on the way the lazily rising mist. Everyone was
silent. Ieronim worked mechanically with one hand. He slowly passed his mild
lustreless eyes over us; then his glance rested on the rosy face of a young merchant's wife with black eyebrows, who was standing on the ferry beside me silently

shrinking from the mist that wrapped her about. He did not take his eyes off her face all the way.

There was little that was masculine in that prolonged gaze. It seemed to me that Ieronim was looking in the woman's face for the soft and tender features of his   330
dead friend.   [1887]

Questions on *Easter Eve* for Discussion and Writing
1. Is Chekhov able to achieve unity in this story? If so, what devices give the story its unity? If not, why does the story fail to achieve unity?
2. What are the tensions or conflicts within the story, and how are they revealed?
3. Analyze the contrasts between light and dark, quiet and noise, action and reflection. How do these relate to the occasion of Easter Eve?
4. How do you respond to Ieronim as a character? Do you find him tragic, touching, sentimental, pathetic, admirable? Explain.
5. Does this story have a theme, or does it simply sketch a situation without commenting on or interpreting it? How successful is the story?
6. Compare this story with other stories of this period. Why might Chekhov's first readers have found this story puzzling or difficult?

The Lady with the Dog

I

IT WAS SAID that a new person had appeared on the sea-front: a lady with a little dog. Dmitri Dmitritch Gurov, who had by then been a fortnight at Yalta, and so was fairly at home there, had begun to take an interest in new arrivals. Sitting in Verney's pavilion, he saw, walking on the sea-front, a fair-haired young lady of medium height, wearing a *béret;* a white Pomeranian dog was running behind her.

And afterwards he met her in the public gardens and in the square several times a day. She was walking alone, always wearing the same *béret,* and always with the same white dog; no one knew who she was, and every one called her simply "the lady with the dog."

"If she is here alone without a husband or friends, it wouldn't be amiss to   10
make her acquaintance," Gurov reflected.

He was under forty, but he had a daughter already twelve years old, and two sons at school. He had been married young, when he was a student in his second year, and by now his wife seemed half as old again as he. She was a tall, erect woman with dark eyebrows, staid and dignified, and, as she said of herself, intellectual. She read a great deal, used phonetic spelling, called her husband, not Dmitri, but Dimitri,[1] and he secretly considered her unintelligent, narrow, inelegant, was afraid of her, and did not like to be at home. He had begun being un-

---
1. All signs of advanced thinking of the time.

faithful to her long ago—had been unfaithful to her often, and, probably on that account, almost always spoke ill of women, and when they were talked about in his presence, used to call them "the lower race."

It seemed to him that he had been so schooled by bitter experience that he might call them what he liked, and yet he could not get on for two days together without "the lower race." In the society of men he was bored and not himself, with them he was cold and uncommunicative; but when he was in the company of women he felt free, and knew what to say to them and how to behave; and he was at ease with them even when he was silent. In his appearance, in his character, in his whole nature, there was something attractive and elusive which allured women and disposed them in his favour; he knew that, and some force seemed to draw him, too, to them.

Experience often repeated, truly bitter experience, had taught him long ago that with decent people, especially Moscow people—always slow to move and irresolute—every intimacy, which at first so agreeably diversifies life and appears a light and charming adventure, inevitably grows into a regular problem of extreme intricacy, and in the long run the situation becomes unbearable. But at every fresh meeting with an interesting woman this experience seemed to slip out of his memory, and he was eager for life, and everything seemed simple and amusing.

One evening he was dining in the gardens, and the lady in the *béret* came up slowly to take the next table. Her expression, her gait, her dress, and the way she did her hair told him that she was a lady, that she was married, that she was in Yalta for the first time alone, and that she was dull there. . . . The stories told of the immorality in such places as Yalta are to a great extent untrue; he despised them, and knew that such stories were for the most part made up by persons who would themselves have been glad to sin if they had been able; but when the lady sat down at the next table three paces from him, he remembered these tales of easy conquests, of trips to the mountains, and the tempting thought of a swift, fleeting love affair, a romance with an unknown woman, whose name he did not know, suddenly took possession of him.

He beckoned coaxingly to the Pomeranian, and when the dog came up to him he shook his finger at it. The Pomeranian growled: Gurov shook his finger at it again.

The lady looked at him and at once dropped her eyes.

"He doesn't bite," she said, and blushed.

"May I give him a bone?" he asked; and when she nodded he asked courteously, "Have you been long in Yalta?"

"Five days."

"And I have already dragged out a fortnight here."

There was a brief silence.

"Time goes fast, and yet it is so dull here!" she said, not looking at him.

"That's only the fashion to say it is dull here. A provincial will live in Belyov or Zhidra and not be dull, and when he comes here it's 'Oh, the dullness! Oh, the dust!' One would think he came from Grenada."[2]

She laughed. Then both continued eating in silence, like strangers, but after

2. An island in the British West Indies—i.e., an exotic place.

dinner they walked side by side; and there sprang up between them the light jesting conversation of people who are free and satisfied, to whom it does not matter
where they go or what they talk about. They walked and talked of the strange light
on the sea: the water was of a soft warm lilac hue, and there was a golden streak
from the moon upon it. They talked of how sultry it was after a hot day. Gurov
told her that he came from Moscow, that he had taken his degree in Arts, but had
a post in a bank; that he had trained as an opera-singer, but had given it up, that 70
he owned two houses in Moscow. . . . And from her he learnt that she had grown
up in Petersburg, but had lived in S——since her marriage two years before, that
she was staying another month in Yalta, and that her husband, who needed a holiday too, might perhaps come and fetch her. She was not sure whether her husband had a post in a Crown Department or under the Provincial Council—and
was amused by her own ignorance. And Gurov learnt, too, that she was called
Anna Sergeyevna.

Afterwards he thought about her in his room at the hotel—thought she
would certainly meet him next day; it would be sure to happen. As he got into bed
he thought how lately she had been a girl at school, doing lessons like his own 80
daughter; he recalled the diffidence, the angularity, that was still manifest in her
laugh and her manner of talking with a stranger. This must have been the first
time in her life she had been alone in surroundings in which she was followed,
looked at, and spoken to merely from a secret motive which she could hardly fail
to guess. He recalled her slender, delicate neck, her lovely grey eyes.

"There's something pathetic about her, anyway," he thought, and fell asleep.

II

A WEEK HAD PASSED since they had made acquaintance. It was a holiday. It
was sultry indoors, while in the street the wind whirled the dust round and round,
and blew people's hats off. It was a thirsty day, and Gurov often went into the
pavilion, and pressed Anna Sergeyevna to have syrup and water or an ice. One did 90
not know what to do with oneself.

In the evening when the wind had dropped a little, they went out on the
groyne[3] to see the steamer come in. There were a great many people walking
about the harbour; they had gathered to welcome some one, bringing bouquets.
And two peculiarities of a well-dressed Yalta crowd were very conspicuous: the
elderly ladies were dressed like young ones, and there were great numbers of
generals.

Owing to the roughness of the sea, the steamer arrived late, after the sun had
set, and it was a long time turning about before it reached the groyne. Anna
Sergeyevna looked through her lorgnette at the steamer and the passengers as 100
though looking for acquaintances, and when she turned to Gurov her eyes were
shining. She talked a great deal and asked disconnected questions, forgetting next
moment what she had asked; then she dropped her lorgnette in the crush.

The festive crowd began to disperse; it was too dark to see people's faces.
The wind had completely dropped, but Gurov and Anna Sergeyevna still stood as

3. A low wall projecting into the sea to prevent erosion.

though waiting to see some one else come from the steamer. Anna Sergeyevna was silent now, and sniffed the flowers without looking at Gurov.

"The weather is better this evening," he said. "Where shall we go now? Shall we drive somewhere?"

She made no answer.

Then he looked at her intently, and all at once put his arm round her and kissed her on the lips, and breathed in the moisture and the fragrance of the flowers; and he immediately looked round him, anxiously wondering whether any one had seen them.

"Let us go to your hotel," he said softly. And both walked quickly.

The room was close and smelt of the scent she had bought at the Japanese shop. Gurov looked at her and thought: "What different people one meets in the world!" From the past he preserved memories of careless, good-natured women, who loved cheerfully and were grateful to him for the happiness he gave them, however brief it might be; and of women like his wife who loved without any genuine feeling, with superfluous phrases, affectedly, hysterically, with an expression that suggested that it was not love nor passion, but something more significant; and of two or three others, very beautiful, cold women, on whose faces he had caught a glimpse of a rapacious expression—an obstinate desire to snatch from life more than it could give, and these were capricious, unreflecting, domineering, unintelligent women not in their first youth, and when Gurov grew cold to them their beauty excited his hatred, and the lace on their linen seemed to him like scales.

But in this case there was still the diffidence, the angularity of inexperienced youth, an awkward feeling; and there was a sense of consternation as though some one had suddenly knocked at the door. The attitude of Anna Sergeyevna—"the lady with the dog"—to what had happened was somehow peculiar, very grave, as though it were her fall—so it seemed, and it was strange and inappropriate. Her face dropped and faded, and on both sides of it her long hair hung down mournfully; she mused in a dejected attitude like "the woman who was a sinner" in an old-fashioned picture.

"It's wrong," she said. "You will be the first to despise me now."

There was a water-melon on the table. Gurov cut himself a slice and began eating it without haste. There followed at least half an hour of silence.

Anna Sergeyevna was touching; there was about her the purity of a good, simple woman who had seen little of life. The solitary candle burning on the table threw a faint light on her face, yet it was clear that she was very unhappy.

"How could I despise you?" asked Gurov. "You don't know what you are saying."

"God forgive me," she said, and her eyes filled with tears. "It's awful."

"You seem to feel you need to be forgiven."

"Forgiven? No. I am a bad, low woman; I despise myself and don't attempt to justify myself. It's not my husband but myself I have deceived. And not only just now; I have been deceiving myself for a long time. My husband may be a good, honest man, but he is a flunkey! I don't know what he does there, what his work is, but I know he is a flunkey! I was twenty when I was married to him. I have been tormented by curiosity; I wanted something better. 'There must be a different sort of life,' I said to myself. I wanted to live! To live, to live! . . . I was fired by curiosity . . . you don't understand it, but, I swear to God, I could not control myself; something happened to me: I could not be restrained. I told my husband I was ill, and came here. . . . And here I have been walking about as though I were dazed, like a mad creature; . . . and now I have become a vulgar, contemptible woman whom any one may despise."

Gurov felt bored already, listening to her. He was irritated by the naïve tone, by this remorse, so unexpected and inopportune; but for the tears in her eyes, he   160 might have thought she was jesting or playing a part.

"I don't understand," he said softly. "What is it you want?"

She hid her face on his breast and pressed close to him.

"Believe me, believe me, I beseech you . . ." she said. "I love a pure, honest life, and sin is loathsome to me. I don't know what I am doing. Simple people say: 'The Evil One has beguiled me.' And I may say of myself now that the Evil One has beguiled me."

"Hush, hush! . . ." he muttered.

He looked at her fixed, scared eyes, kissed her, talked softly and affection- ately, and by degrees she was comforted, and her gaiety returned; they both began   170 laughing.

Afterwards when they went out there was not a soul on the sea-front. The town with its cypresses had quite a deathlike air, but the sea still broke noisily on the shore; a single barge was rocking on the waves, and a lantern was blinking sleepily on it.

They found a cab and drove to Oreanda.

"I found out your surname in the hall just now: it was written on the board—Von Diderits," said Gurov. "Is your husband a German?"

"No; I believe his grandfather was a German, but he is an Orthodox Russian himself."   180

At Oreanda they sat on a seat not far from the church, looked down at the sea, and were silent. Yalta was hardly visible through the morning mist; white clouds stood motionless on the mountain-tops. The leaves did not stir on the trees, grasshoppers chirruped, and the monotonous hollow sound of the sea rising up from below, spoke of the peace, of the eternal sleep awaiting us. So it must have sounded when there was no Yalta, no Oreanda here; so it sounds now, and it will sound as indifferently and monotonously when we are all no more. And in this constancy, in this complete indifference to the life and death of each of us, there lies hid, perhaps, a pledge of our eternal salvation, of the unceasing move- ment of life upon earth, of unceasing progress toward perfection. Sitting beside a   190 young woman who in the dawn seemed so lovely, soothed and spellbound in these magical surroundings—the sea, mountains, clouds, the open sky—Gurov thought how in reality everything is beautiful in this world when one reflects: everything except what we think or do ourselves when we forget our human dig- nity and the higher aims of our existence.

A man walked up to them—probably a keeper—looked at them and walked away. And this detail seemed mysterious and beautiful, too. They saw a steamer come from Theodosia, with its lights out in the glow of dawn.

"There is dew on the grass," said Anna Sergeyevna, after a silence.

"Yes. It's time to go home."   200
They went back to the town.

Then they met every day at twelve o'clock on the sea-front, lunched and dined together, went for walks, admired the sea. She complained that she slept badly, that her heart throbbed violently; asked the same questions, troubled now by jealousy and now by the fear that he did not respect her sufficiently. And often in the square or gardens, when there was no one near them, he suddenly drew her to him and kissed her passionately. Complete idleness, these kisses in broad daylight while he looked round in dread of some one's seeing them, the heat, the smell of the sea, and the continual passing to and fro before him of idle, well-dressed, well-fed people, made a new man of him; he told Anna Sergeyevna how 210 beautiful she was, how fascinating. He was impatiently passionate, he would not move a step away from her, while she was often pensive and continually urged him to confess that he did not respect her, did not love her in the least, and thought of her as nothing but a common woman. Rather late almost every evening they drove somewhere out of town, to Oreanda or to the waterfall; and the expedition was always a success, the scenery invariably impressed them as grand and beautiful.

They were expecting her husband to come, but a letter came from him, saying that there was something wrong with his eyes, and he entreated his wife to come home as quickly as possible. Anna Sergeyevna made haste to go.   220

"It's a good thing I am going away," she said to Gurov. "It's the finger of destiny!"

She went by coach and he went with her. They were driving the whole day. When she had got into a compartment of the express, and when the second bell had rung, she said:

"Let me look at you once more. . . look at you once again. That's right."

She did not shed tears, but was so sad that she seemed ill, and her face was quivering.

"I shall remember you . . . think of you," she said. "God be with you; be happy. Don't remember evil against me. We are parting forever—it must be so, for 230 we ought never to have met. Well, God be with you."

The train moved off rapidly, its lights soon vanished from sight, and a minute later there was no sound of it, as though everything had conspired together to end as quickly as possible that sweet delirium, that madness. Left alone on the platform, and gazing into the dark distance, Gurov listened to the chirrup of the grasshoppers and the hum of the telegraph wires, feeling as though he had only just waked up. And he thought, musing, that there had been another episode or adventure in his life, and it, too, was at an end, and nothing was left of it but a memory. . . . He was moved, sad, and conscious of a slight remorse. This young woman whom he would never meet again had not been happy with him; he was 240 genuinely warm and affectionate with her, but yet in his manner, his tone, and his caresses there had been a shade of light irony, the coarse condescension of a happy man who was, besides, almost twice her age. All the time she had called him kind, exceptional, lofty; obviously he had seemed to her different from what he really was, so he had unintentionally deceived her. . . .

Here at the station was already a scent of autumn; it was a cold evening.

"It's time for me to go north," thought Gurov as he left the platform. "High time!"

III

AT HOME IN MOSCOW everything was in its winter routine; the stoves were heated, and in the morning it was still dark when the children were having break- 250 fast and getting ready for school, and the nurse would light the lamp for a short time. The frosts had begun already. When the first snow has fallen, on the first day of sledge-driving it is pleasant to see the white earth, the white roofs, to draw soft, delicious breath, and the season brings back the days of one's youth. The old limes and birches, white with hoar-frost, have a good-natured expression; they are nearer to one's heart than cypresses and palms, and near them one doesn't want to be thinking of the sea and the mountains.

Gurov was Moscow born; he arrived in Moscow on a fine frosty day, and when he put on his fur coat and warm gloves, and walked along Petrovka, and when on Saturday evening he heard the ringing of the bells, his recent trip and the 260 places he had seen lost all charm for him. Little by little he became absorbed in Moscow life, greedily read three newspapers a day, and declared he did not read the Moscow papers on principle! He already felt a longing to go to restaurants, clubs, dinner-parties, anniversary celebrations, and he felt flattered at entertaining distinguished lawyers and artists, and at playing cards with a professor at the doctors' club. He could already eat a whole plateful of salt fish and cabbage. . . .

In another month, he fancied, the image of Anna Sergeyevna would be shrouded in a mist in his memory, and only from time to time would visit him in his dreams with a touching smile as others did. But more than a month passed, real winter had come, and everything was still clear in his memory as though he 270 had parted with Anna Sergeyevna only the day before. And his memories glowed more and more vividly. When in the evening stillness he heard from his study the voices of his children, preparing their lessons, or when he listened to a song or the organ at the restaurant, or the storm howled in the chimney, suddenly everything would rise up in his memory: what had happened on the groyne, and the early morning with the mist on the mountains, and the steamer coming from Theodosia, and the kisses. He would pace a long time about his room, remembering it all and smiling; then his memories passed into dreams, and in his fancy the past was mingled with what was to come. Anna Sergeyevna did not visit him in dreams, but followed him about everywhere like a shadow and haunted him. 280 When he shut his eyes he saw her as though she were living before him, and she seemed to him lovelier, younger, tenderer than she was; and he imagined himself finer than he had been in Yalta. In the evenings she peeped out at him from the bookcase, from the fireplace, from the corner—he heard her breathing, the caressing rustle of her dress. In the street he watched the women, looking for some one like her.

He was tormented by an intense desire to confide his memories to some one. But in his home it was impossible to talk of his love, and he had no one outside; he could not talk to his tenants nor to any one at the bank. And what had he to

talk of? Had he been in love, then? Had there been anything beautiful, poetical, or 290
edifying or simply interesting in his relations with Anna Sergeyevna? And there
was nothing for him but to talk vaguely of love, of woman, and no one guessed
what it meant; only his wife twitched her black eyebrows, and said: "The part of a
lady-killer does not suit you at all, Dimitri."

One evening, coming out of the doctors' club with an official with whom he
had been playing cards, he could not resist saying:

"If only you knew what a fascinating woman I made the acquaintance of in
Yalta!"

The official got into his sledge and was driving away, but turned suddenly
and shouted: 300

"Dmitri Dmitritch!"

"What?"

"You were right this evening: the sturgeon was a bit too strong!"

Those words, so ordinary, for some reason moved Gurov to indignation, and
struck him as degrading and unclean. What savage manners, what people! What
senseless nights, what uninteresting, uneventful days! The rage for card-playing,
the gluttony, the drunkenness, the continual talk always about the same thing.
Useless pursuits and conversations always about the same things absorb the better
part of one's time, the better part of one's strength, and in the end there is left a life
grovelling and curtailed, worthless and trivial, and there is no escaping or getting 310
away from it—just as though one were in a madhouse or a prison.

Gurov did not sleep all night, and was filled with indignation. And he had a
headache all next day. And the next night he slept badly; he sat up in bed, thinking, or paced up and down his room. He was sick of his children, sick of the bank;
he had no desire to go anywhere or to talk of anything.

In the holidays in December he prepared for a journey, and told his wife he
was going to Petersburg to do something in the interests of a young friend—and
he set off for S——. What for? He did not very well know himself. He wanted to
see Anna Sergeyevna and to talk with her—to arrange a meeting, if possible.

He reached S——in the morning, and took the best room at the hotel, in 320
which the floor was covered with grey army cloth, and on the table was an inkstand, grey with dust and adorned with a figure on horseback, with its hat in its
hand and its head broken off. The hotel porter gave him the necessary information; Von Diderits lived in a house of his own in Old Gontcharny Street—it was
not far from the hotel: he was rich and lived in good style, and had his own
horses; every one in the town knew him. The porter pronounced the name
"Dridirits."

Gurov went without haste to Old Gontcharny Street and found the house.
Just opposite the house stretched a long grey fence adorned with nails.

"One would run away from a fence like that," thought Gurov, looking from 330
the fence to the windows of the house and back again.

He considered: to-day was a holiday, and the husband would probably be at
home. And in any case it would be tactless to go into the house and upset her. If
he were to send her a note it might fall into her husband's hands, and then it
might ruin everything. The best thing was to trust to chance. And he kept walking

up and down the street by the fence, waiting for the chance. He saw a beggar go in at the gate and dogs fly at him; then an hour later he heard a piano, and the sounds were faint and indistinct. Probably it was Anna Sergeyevna playing. The front door suddenly opened, and an old woman came out, followed by the familiar white Pomeranian. Gurov was on the point of calling to the dog, but his heart began beating violently, and in his excitement he could not remember the dog's name.

He walked up and down, and loathed the grey fence more and more, and by now he thought irritably that Anna Sergeyevna had forgotten him, and was perhaps already amusing herself with some one else, and that that was very natural in a young woman who had nothing to look at from morning till night but that confounded fence. He went back to his hotel room and sat for a long while on the sofa, not knowing what to do, then he had dinner and a long nap.

"How stupid and worrying it is!" he thought when he woke and looked at the dark windows: it was already evening. "Here I've had a good sleep for some reason. What shall I do in the night?"

He sat on the bed, which was covered by a cheap grey blanket, such as one sees in hospitals, and he taunted himself in his vexation:

"So much for the lady with the dog . . . so much for the adventure. . . . You're in a nice fix. . . ."

That morning at the station a poster in large letters had caught his eye. "The Geisha" was to be performed for the first time. He thought of this and went to the theatre.

"It's quite possible she may go to the first performance," he thought.

The theatre was full. As in all provincial theatres, there was a fog above the chandelier, the gallery was noisy and restless; in the front row the local dandies were standing up before the beginning of the performance, with their hands behind them; in the Governor's box the Governor's daughter, wearing a boa, was sitting in the front seat, while the Governor himself lurked modestly behind the curtain with only his hands visible; the orchestra was a long time tuning up; the stage curtain swayed. All the time the audience were coming in and taking their seats Gurov looked at them eagerly.

Anna Sergeyevna, too, came in. She sat down in the third row, and when Gurov looked at her his heart contracted, and he understood clearly that for him there was in the whole world no creature so near, so precious, and so important to him; she, this little woman, in no way remarkable, lost in a provincial crowd, with a vulgar lorgnette in her hand, filled his whole life now, was his sorrow and his joy, the one happiness that he now desired for himself, and to the sounds of the inferior orchestra, of the wretched provincial violins, he thought how lovely she was. He thought and dreamed.

A young man with small side-whiskers, tall and stooping, came in with Anna Sergeyevna and sat down beside her; he bent his head at every step and seemed to be continually bowing. Most likely this was the husband whom at Yalta, in a rush of bitter feeling, she had called a flunkey. And there really was in his long figure, his side-whiskers, and the small bald patch on his head, something of the flunkey's obsequiousness; his smile was sugary, and in his buttonhole there was some badge of distinction like the number on a waiter.

During the first interval the husband went away to smoke; she remained alone in her stall. Gurov, who was sitting in the stalls, too, went up to her and said in a trembling voice, with a forced smile:

"Good-evening."

She glanced at him and turned pale, then glanced again with horror, unable to believe her eyes, and tightly gripped the fan and the lorgnette in her hands, evidently struggling with herself not to faint. Both were silent. She was sitting, he was standing, frightened by her confusion and not venturing to sit down beside her. The violins and the flute began tuning up. He felt suddenly frightened; it seemed as though all the people in the boxes were looking at them. She got up and went quickly to the door; he followed her, and both walked senselessly along passages, and up and down stairs, and figures in legal, scholastic, and civil service uniforms, all wearing badges, flitted before their eyes. They caught glimpses of ladies, of fur coats hanging on pegs; the draughts blew on them, bringing a smell of stale tobacco. And Gurov, whose heart was beating violently, thought:

"Oh, heavens! Why are these people here and this orchestra! . . .

And at that instant he recalled how when he had seen Anna Sergeyevna off at the station he had thought that everything was over and they would never meet again. But how far they were still from the end!

On the narrow, gloomy staircase over which was written "To the Amphitheatre," she stopped.

"How you have frightened me!" she said, breathing hard, still pale and overwhelmed. "Oh, how you have frightened me! I am half dead. Why have you come? Why?"

"But do understand, Anna, do understand . . ." he said hastily in a low voice. "I entreat you to understand. . . ."

She looked at him with dread, with entreaty, with love; she looked at him intently, to keep his features more distinctly in her memory.

"I am so unhappy," she went on, not heeding him. "I have thought of nothing but you all the time; I live only in the thought of you. And I wanted to forget, to forget you; but why, oh, why, have you come?"

On the landing above them two schoolboys were smoking and looking down, but that was nothing to Gurov; he drew Anna Sergeyevna to him, and began kissing her face, her cheeks, and her hands.

"What are you doing, what are you doing!" she cried in horror, pushing him away. "We are mad. Go away to-day; go away at once. . . . I beseech you by all that is sacred, I implore you. . . . There are people coming this way!"

Some one was coming up the stairs.

"You must go away," Anna Sergeyevna went on in a whisper. "Do you hear, Dmitri Dmitritch? I will come and see you in Moscow. I have never been happy; I am miserable now, and I never, never shall be happy, never! Don't make me suffer still more! I swear I'll come to Moscow. But now let us part. My precious, good, dear one, we must part!"

She pressed his hand and began rapidly going downstairs, looking round at him, and from her eyes he could see that she really was unhappy. Gurov stood for a little while, listened, then, when all sound had died away, he found his coat and left the theatre.

IV

AND ANNA SERGEYEVNA BEGAN coming to see him in Moscow. Once in two or three months she left S——, telling her husband that she was going to consult a doctor about an internal complaint—and her husband believed her, and did not believe her. In Moscow she stayed at the Slaviansky Bazaar hotel, and at once sent a man in a red cap to Gurov. Gurov went to see her, and no one in Moscow knew of it.

Once he was going to see her in this way on a winter morning (the messenger had come the evening before when he was out). With him walked his daughter, whom he wanted to take to school; it was on the way. Snow was falling in big wet flakes.

"It's three degrees above freezing-point, and yet it is snowing," said Gurov to his daughter. "The thaw is only on the surface of the earth; there is quite a different temperature at a greater height in the atmosphere."

"And why are there no thunderstorms in the winter, father?"

He explained that, too. He talked, thinking all the while that he was going to see *her*, and no living soul knew of it, and probably never would know. He had two lives: one, open, seen and known by all who cared to know, full of relative truth and of relative falsehood, exactly like the lives of his friends and acquaintances; and another life running its course in secret. And through some strange, perhaps accidental, conjunction of circumstances, everything that was essential, of interest and of value to him, everything in which he was sincere and did not deceive himself, everything that made the kernel of his life, was hidden from other people; and all that was false in him, the sheath in which he hid himself to conceal the truth—such, for instance, as his work in the bank, his discussions at the club, his "lower race," his presence with his wife at anniversary festivities—all that was open. And he judged of others by himself, not believing in what he saw, and always believing that every man had his real, most interesting life under the cover of secrecy and under the cover of night. All personal life rested on secrecy, and possibly it was partly on that account that civilised man was so nervously anxious that personal privacy should be respected.

After leaving his daughter at school, Gurov went on to the Slaviansky Bazaar. He took off his fur coat below, went upstairs, and softly knocked at the door. Anna Sergeyevna, wearing his favourite grey dress, exhausted by the journey and the suspense, had been expecting him since the evening before. She was pale; she looked at him, and did not smile, and he had hardly come in when she fell on his breast. Their kiss was slow and prolonged, as though they had not met for two years.

"Well, how are you getting on there?" he asked. "What news?"

"Wait; I'll tell you directly. . . . I can't talk."

She could not speak; she was crying. She turned away from him, and pressed her handkerchief to her eyes.

"Let her have her cry out. I'll sit down and wait," he thought, and he sat down in an arm-chair.

Then he rang and asked for tea to be brought him, and while he drank his tea she remained standing at the window with her back to him. She was crying from emotion, from the miserable consciousness that their life was so hard for them; they could only meet in secret, hiding themselves from people, like thieves! Was not their life shattered?

"Come, do stop!" he said.

It was evident to him that this love of theirs would not soon be over, that he could not see the end of it. Anna Sergeyevna grew more and more attached to 480 him. She adored him, and it was unthinkable to say to her that it was bound to have an end some day; besides, she would not have believed it!

He went up to her and took her by the shoulders to say something affectionate and cheering, and at that moment he saw himself in the looking-glass.

His hair was already beginning to turn grey. And it seemed strange to him that he had grown so much older, so much plainer during the last few years. The shoulders on which his hands rested were warm and quivering. He felt compassion for this life, still so warm and lovely, but probably already not far from beginning to fade and wither like his own. Why did she love him so much? He always seemed to women different from what he was, and they loved in him not himself, 490 but the man created by their imagination, whom they had been eagerly seeking all their lives; and afterwards, when they noticed their mistake, they loved him all the same. And not one of them had been happy with him. Time passed, he had made their acquaintance, got on with them, parted, but he had never once loved; it was anything you like, but not love.

And only now when his head was grey he had fallen properly, really in love—for the first time in his life.

Anna Sergeyevna and he loved each other like people very close and akin, like husband and wife, like tender friends; it seemed to them that fate itself had meant them for one another, and they could not understand why he had a wife 500 and she a husband; and it was as though they were a pair of birds of passage, caught and forced to live in different cages. They forgave each other for what they were ashamed of in their past, they forgave everything in the present, and felt that this love of theirs had changed them both.

In moments of depression in the past he had comforted himself with any arguments that came into his mind, but now he no longer cared for arguments; he felt profound compassion, he wanted to be sincere and tender. . . .

"Don't cry, my darling," he said. "You've had your cry; that's enough. . . . Let us talk now, let us think of some plan."

Then they spent a long while taking counsel together, talked of how to avoid 510 the necessity for secrecy, for deception, for living in different towns and not seeing each other for long at a time. How could they be free from this intolerable bondage?

"How? How?" he asked, clutching his head. "How?"

And it seemed as though in a little while the solution would be found, and then a new and splendid life would begin; and it was clear to both of them that they had still a long, long road before them, and that the most complicated and difficult part of it was only just beginning. [1899]

Questions on *The Lady with the Dog* for Discussion and Writing

1. In what ways is this a conventional love story?
2. In what ways does the story depart from the conventions of a typical love story?
3. What effect does Chekhov achieve by not providing a conclusion—happy or sad—to the story?
4. There are numerous references to time, eternity, nature, God, and religion. Underline or circle as many of these as you can find. What relevance, if any, do they have to the story as a whole?
5. Analyze Gurov and Anna. Why are they attracted to one another? What does each hope to get from the affair?
6. How do you respond to this story? Do you find it satisfying, frustrating, interesting, boring, fascinating, tedious . . . ? Analyze your reactions and relate them to specific passages or incidents in the story.

⮞ JOSEPH CONRAD
(1857–1924)

Heart of Darkness

Joseph Conrad's life and accomplishments are as startling and romantic as the stories of his boyhood idol, the English writer Captain Marryat. Conrad was born Jozef Teodore Konrad Nalecz Korzeniowski to a Polish Ukrainian family opposed to Russia's domination of Poland. Both his parents were deported and died in exile, so Joseph was raised by his uncle Thaddeus Dobrowski. As a youth, he devoured tales of adventure at sea and after a European tour in 1873–1874 signed up with a French ship at Marseilles. In 1878, he joined a British merchant ship, and for sixteen years sailed the Pacific, learning English and absorbing materials that would later reappear in his fiction. English was his third language, after Polish and French. During a brief hiatus in his British employ, he piloted a Belgian boat up the Congo River in Africa, coming down with fever, dysentery, and gout in the process.

Conrad left the sea in 1894 and in the next year published his first novel, *Almayer's Folly*. In 1896, he married but could never write quickly enough to support his family comfortably. Many of his short stories were written under magazine deadlines, most of which he failed to meet. The short story was not Conrad's first love, but the money from magazines like *Blackwood's* (where "Heart of Darkness" first appeared in 1899) was essential.

Some of Conrad's work can be read as adventure fiction, but he is seldom interested in action for its own sake, and his protagonists are not conventional heroes. He has been called an Impressionist writer because he depicts external stimuli as received and interpreted by the individual mind. This technique, along with his pessimism, use of symbolism, and interest in psychology, links him with the early Modernists.

Conrad saw himself as a critic of colonialism. "Heart of Darkness" (and other accounts of atrocities and genocide committed in the Congo by agents in the Belgium rubber trade) helped spearhead a reform movement. Some recent commentators have, however, given new attention to the whole issue of imperialism in Conrad's work. There is no doubt, however, that "Heart of Darkness" is haunting, disquieting, and profound in its exploration of the human psyche. It is widely regarded as one of the great stories of all time.

I

THE *NELLIE*, a cruising yawl, swung to her anchor without a flutter of the sails, and was at rest. The flood had made, the wind was nearly calm, and being bound down the river, the only thing for it was to come to and wait for the turn of the tide.

The sea-reach of the Thames stretched before us like the beginning of an interminable waterway. In the offing the sea and the sky were welded together without a joint, and in the luminous space the tanned sails of the barges drifting up with the tide seemed to stand still in red clusters of canvas sharply peaked, with gleams of varnished sprits. A haze rested on the low shores that ran out to sea in vanishing flatness. The air was dark above Gravesend,[1] and farther back still seemed condensed into a mournful gloom, brooding motionless over the biggest, and the greatest, town on earth. 10

The director of Companies was our captain and our host. We four affectionately watched his back as he stood in the bows looking to seaward. On the whole river there was nothing that looked half so nautical. He resembled a pilot, which to a seaman is trustworthiness personified. It was difficult to realize his work was not out there in the luminous estuary, but behind him, within the brooding gloom.

Between us there was, as I have already said somewhere, the bond of the sea. Besides holding our hearts together through long periods of separation, it had the effect of making us tolerant of each other's yarns—and even convictions. The Lawyer—the best of old fellows—had, because of his many years and many virtues, the only cushion on deck, and was lying on the only rug. The Accountant had brought out already a box of dominoes, and was toying architecturally with the bones.[2] Marlow sat cross-legged right aft, leaning against the mizzen-mast. He had sunken cheeks, a yellow complexion, a straight back, an ascetic aspect, and, with his arms dropped, the palms of hands outwards, resembled an idol. The Director, satisfied the anchor had good hold, made his way aft and sat down amongst us. We exchanged a few words lazily. Afterwards there was silence on 20

---

1. A town near the mouth of the Thames in England.
2. Slang term for dominoes.

board the yacht. For some reason or other we did not begin that game of domi- 30
noes. We felt meditative, and fit for nothing but placid staring. The day was ending in a serenity of still and exquisite brilliance. The water shone pacifically; the
sky, without a speck, was a benign immensity of unstained light; the very mist on
the Essex marshes was like a gauzy and radiant fabric, hung from the wooded rises
inland, and draping the low shores in diaphanous folds. Only the gloom to the
west, brooding over the upper reaches, became more somber every minute, as if
angered by the approach of the sun.

　　And at last, in its curved and imperceptible fall, the sun sank low, and from
glowing white changed to a dull red without rays and without heat, as if about to
go out suddenly, stricken to death by the touch of that gloom brooding over a 40
crowd of men.

　　Forthwith a change came over the waters, and the serenity became less brilliant but more profound. The old river in its broad reach rested unruffled at the
decline of day, after ages of good service done to the race that peopled its banks,
spread out in the tranquil dignity of a waterway leading to the uttermost ends of
the earth. We looked at the venerable stream not in the vivid flush of a short day
that comes and departs for ever, but in the august light of abiding memories. And
indeed nothing is easier for a man who has, as the phrase goes, "followed the sea"
with reverence and affection, than to evoke the great spirit of the past upon the
lower reaches of the Thames. The tidal current runs to and fro in its unceasing 50
service, crowded with memories of men and ships it had borne to the rest of home
or to the battles of the sea. It had known and served all the men of whom the nation is proud, from Sir Francis Drake to Sir John Franklin, knights all, titled and
untitled—the great knights-errant of the sea. It had borne all the ships whose
names are like jewels flashing in the night of time, from the *Golden Hind* returning
with her round flanks full of treasure, to be visited by the Queen's Highness and
thus pass out of the gigantic tale, to the *Erebus* and *Terror*,[3] bound on other conquests—and that never returned. It had known the ships and the men. They had
sailed from Deptford, from Greenwich, from Erith—the adventurers and the settlers; kings' ships and the ships of men on 'Change; captains, admirals, the dark 60
"interlopers" of the Eastern trade, and the commissioned "generals" of East India
fleets. Hunters for gold or pursuers of fame, they all had gone out on that stream,
bearing the sword, and often the torch, messengers of the might within the land,
bearers of a spark from the sacred fire. What greatness had not floated on the ebb
of that river into the mystery of an unknown earth! . . . The dreams of men, the
seed of commonwealths, the germs of empires.

　　The sun set; the dusk fell on the stream, and lights began to appear along
the shore. The Chapman lighthouse, a three-legged thing erect on a mud-flat,
shone strongly. Lights of ships moved in the fairway—a great stir of lights going
up and going down. And farther west on the upper reaches the place of the mon- 70
strous town was still marked ominously on the sky, a brooding gloom in sunshine,
a lurid glare under the stars.

---

3. The *Golden Hind* was Sir Francis Drake's ship in which he sailed around the world, 1577–1580; *Erebus*
　and *Terror* were commanded by Sir John Franklin in 1845 on an expedition to discover a northwest
　passage.

"And this also," said Marlow suddenly, "has been one of the dark places of the earth."

He was the only man of us who still "followed the sea." The worst that could be said of him was that he did not represent his class. He was a seaman, but he was a wanderer too, while most seamen lead, if one may so express it, a sedentary life. Their minds are of the stay-at-home order, and their home is always with them—the ship; and so is their country—the sea. One ship is very much like another, and the sea is always the same. In the immutability of their surroundings the foreign shores, the foreign faces, the changing immensity of life, glide past, veiled not by a sense of mystery but by a slightly disdainful ignorance; for there is nothing mysterious to a seaman unless it be the sea itself, which is the mistress of his existence and as inscrutable as Destiny. For the rest, after his hours of work, a casual stroll or a casual spree on shore suffices to unfold for him the secret of a whole continent, and generally he finds the secret not worth knowing. The yarns of seamen have a direct simplicity, the whole meaning of which lies within the shell of a cracked nut. But Marlow was not typical (if his propensity to spin yarns be excepted), and to him the meaning of an episode was not inside like a kernel but outside, enveloping the tale which brought it out only as a glow brings out a haze, in the likeness of one of these misty halos that sometimes are made visible by the spectral illumination of moonshine.

His remark did not seem at all surprising. It was just like Marlow. It was accepted in silence. No one took the trouble to grunt even; and presently he said, very slow—

"I was thinking of very old times, when the Romans first came here, nineteen hundred years ago—the other day. . . . Light came out of this river since—you say Knights? Yes; but it is like a running blaze on a plain, like a flash of lightning in the clouds. We live in the flicker—may it last as long as the old earth keeps rolling! But darkness was here yesterday. Imagine the feelings of a commander of a fine—what d'ye call 'em?—trireme in the Mediterranean, ordered suddenly to the north; run overland across the Gauls in a hurry; put in charge of one of these craft the legionaries,—a wonderful lot of handy men they must have been too—used to build, apparently by the hundred, in a month or two, if we may believe what we read. Imagine him here—the very end of the world, a sea the color of lead, a sky the color of smoke, a kind of ship about as rigid as a concertina—and going up this river with stores, or orders, or what you like. Sandbanks, marshes, forests, savages,—precious little to eat fit for a civilized man, nothing but Thames water to drink. No Falernian wine here, no going ashore. Here and there a military camp lost in a wilderness, like a needle in a bundle of hay—cold, fog, tempests, disease, exile, and death,—death skulking in the air, in the water, in the bush. They must have been dying like flies here. Oh yes—he did it. Did it very well, too, no doubt, and without thinking much about it either, except afterwards to brag of what he had gone through in his time, perhaps. They were men enough to face the darkness. And perhaps he was cheered by keeping his eye on a chance of promotion to the fleet at Ravenna by-and-by, if he had good friends in Rome and survived the awful climate. Or think of a decent young citizen in a toga—perhaps too much dice, you know—coming out here in the train of some prefect, or tax-gatherer, or trader even, to mend his fortunes. Land in a swamp, march through the woods,

and in some inland post feel the savagery, the utter savagery, had closed round 120
him,—all that mysterious life of the wilderness that stirs in the forest, in the jungles, in the hearts of wild men. There's no initiation either into such mysteries. He
has to live in the midst of the incomprehensible, which is also detestable. And it
has a fascination, too, that goes to work upon him. The fascination of the abomination—you know. Imagine the growing regrets, the longing to escape, the powerless disgust, the surrender, the hate."

He paused.

"Mind," he began again, lifting one arm from the elbow, the palm of the
hand outwards, so that, with his legs folded before him, he had the pose of a
Buddha preaching in European clothes and without a lotus-flower—"Mind, none 130
of us would feel exactly like this. What saves us is efficiency—the devotion to efficiency. But these chaps were not much account, really. They were no colonists;
their administration was merely a squeeze, and nothing more, I suspect. They
were conquerors, and for that you want only brute force—nothing to boast of,
when you have it, since your strength is just an accident arising from the weakness
of others. They grabbed what they could get for the sake of what was to be got. It
was just robbery with violence, aggravated murder on a great scale, and men going
at it blind—as is very proper for those who tackle a darkness. The conquest of the
earth, which mostly means the taking it away from those who have a different
complexion or slightly flatter noses than ourselves, is not a pretty thing when you 140
look into it too much. What redeems it is the idea only. An idea at the back of it;
not a sentimental pretense but an idea; and an unselfish belief in the idea—something you can set up, and bow down before, and offer a sacrifice to. . . ."

He broke off. Flames glided in the river, small green flames, red flames,
white flames,[4] pursuing, overtaking, joining, crossing each other—then separating
slowly or hastily. The traffic of the great city went on in the deepening night upon
the sleepless river. We looked on, waiting patiently—there was nothing else to do
till the end of the flood; but it was only after a long silence, when he said, in a hesitating voice, "I suppose you fellows remember I did once turn fresh-water sailor
for a bit," that we knew we were fated, before the ebb began to run, to hear about 150
one of Marlow's inconclusive experiences.

"I don't want to bother you much with what happened to me personally," he
began, showing in this remark the weakness of many tellers of tales who seem so
often unaware of what their audience would best like to hear: "yet to understand
the effect of it on me you ought to know how I got out there, what I saw, how I
went up that river to the place where I first met the poor chap. It was the farthest
point of navigation and the culminating point of my experience. It seemed somehow to throw a kind of light on everything about me—and into my thoughts. It
was somber enough too—and pitiful—not extraordinary in any way—not very
clear either. No, not very clear. And yet it seemed to throw a kind of light.   160

"I had then, as you remember, just returned to London after a lot of Indian
Ocean, Pacific, China Seas—a regular dose of the East—six years or so, and I was
loafing about, hindering you fellows in your work and invading your homes, just
as though I had got a heavenly mission to civilize you. It was very fine for a time,

4. Each color of light designated a particular kind of boat.

but after a bit I did get tired of resting. Then I began to look for a ship—I should
think the hardest work on earth. But the ships wouldn't even look at me. And I
got tired of that game too.

"Now when I was a little chap I had a passion for maps. I would look for
hours at South America, or Africa, or Australia, and lose myself in all the glories of
exploration. At that time there were many blank spaces on the earth, and when I   170
saw one that looked particularly inviting on a map (but they all look that) I would
put my finger on it and say, When I grow up I will go there. The North Pole was
one of these places, I remember. Well, I haven't been there yet, and shall not try
now. The glamour's off. Other places were scattered about the Equator, and in
every sort of latitude all over the two hemispheres. I have been in some of them,
. . . well, we won't talk about that. But there was one yet—the biggest, the most
blank, so to speak—that I had a hankering after.

"True, by this time it was not a blank space any more. It had got filled since
my boyhood with rivers and lakes and names. It had ceased to be a blank space of
delightful mystery—a white patch for a boy to dream gloriously over. It had be-   180
come a place of darkness. But there was in it one river especially, a mighty big
river, that you could see on the map, resembling an immense snake uncoiled, with
its head in the sea, its body at rest curving afar over a vast country, and its tail lost
in the depths of the land. And as I looked at the map of it in a shop-window, it
fascinated me as a snake would a bird—a silly little bird. Then I remembered there
was a big concern, a Company for trade on that river. Dash it all! I thought to myself, they can't trade without using some kind of craft on that lot of fresh water—
steamboats! Why shouldn't I try to get charge of one. I went on along Fleet Street,
but could not shake off the idea. The snake had charmed me.

"You understand it was a Continental concern, that Trading society; but I   190
have a lot of relations living on the Continent, because it's cheap and not so nasty
as it looks, they say.

"I am sorry to own I began to worry[5] them. This was already a fresh departure for me. I was not used to get things that way, you know. I always went my
own road and on my own legs where I had a mind to go. I wouldn't have believed
it of myself; but, then—you see—I felt somehow I must get there by hook or by
crook. So I worried them. The men said 'My dear fellow,' and did nothing. Then—
would you believe it?—I tried the women. I, Charlie Marlow, set the women to
work—to get a job. Heavens! Well, you see, the notion drove me. I had an aunt, a
dear enthusiastic soul. She wrote: 'It will be delightful. I am ready to do anything,   200
anything for you. It is a glorious idea. I know the wife of a very high personage in
the Administration, and also a man who has lots of influence with,' &c., &c. She
was determined to make no end of fuss to get me appointed skipper of a river
steamboat, if such was my fancy.

"I got my appointment—of course; and I got it very quick. It appears the
Company had received news that one of their captains had been killed in a scuffle
with the natives. This was my chance, and it made me the more anxious to go. It
was only months and months afterwards, when I made the attempt to recover
what was left of the body, that I heard the original quarrel arose from a misunder-

5. Pester.

standing about some hens. Yes, two black hens. Fresleven—that was the fellow's 210
name, a Dane—thought himself wronged somehow in the bargain, so he went
ashore and started to hammer the chief of the village with a stick. Oh, it didn't
surprise me in the least to hear this, and at the same time to be told that Fresleven
was the gentlest, quietest creature that ever walked on two legs. No doubt he was;
but he had been a couple of years already out there engaged in the noble cause,
you know, and he probably felt the need at last of asserting his self-respect in some
way. Therefore he whacked the old nigger mercilessly, while a big crowd of his
people watched him, thunderstruck, till some man,—I was told the chief's son,—
in desperation at hearing the old chap yell, made a tentative jab with a spear at the
white man—and of course it went quite easy between the shoulder-blades. Then 220
the whole population cleared into the forest, expecting all kinds of calamities to
happen, while, on the other hand, the steamer Fresleven commanded left also in a
bad panic, in charge of the engineer, I believe. Afterwards nobody seemed to trouble much about Fresleven's remains, till I got out and stepped into his shoes. I
couldn't let it rest, though; but when an opportunity offered at last to meet my
predecessor, the grass growing through his ribs was tall enough to hide his bones.
They were all there. The supernatural being had not been touched after he fell.
And the village was deserted, the huts gaped black, rotting, all askew within the
fallen enclosures. A calamity had come to it, sure enough. The people had vanished. Mad terror had scattered them, men, women, and children, through the 230
bush, and they had never returned. What became of the hens I don't know either.
I should think the cause of progress got them, anyhow. However, through this glorious affair I got my appointment, before I had fairly begun to hope for it.

"I flew around like mad to get ready, and before forty-eight hours I was
crossing the Channel to show myself to my employers, and sign the contract. In a
very few hours I arrived in a city that always makes me think of a whited sepul-
cher.[6] Prejudice no doubt. I had no difficulty in finding the Company's offices. It
was the biggest thing in the town, and everybody I met was full of it. They were
going to run an over-sea empire, and make no end of coin by trade.

"A narrow and deserted street in deep shadow, high houses, innumerable 240
windows with venetian blinds, a dead silence, grass sprouting between the stones,
imposing carriage archways right and left, immense double doors standing pon-
derously ajar. I slipped through one of these cracks, went up a swept and ungar-
nished staircase, as arid as a desert, and opened the first door I came to. Two
women, one fat and the other slim, sat on straw-bottomed chairs, knitting black
wool. The slim one got up and walked straight at me—still knitting with downcast
eyes—and only just as I began to think of getting out of her way, as you would for
a somnambulist, stood still, and looked up. Her dress was as plain as an umbrella-
cover, and she turned round without a word and preceded me into a waiting-
room. I gave my name, and looked about. Deal table in the middle, plain chairs all 250
round the walls, on one end a large shining map, marked with all the colors of a
rainbow. There was a vast amount of red—good to see at any time, because one
knows that some real work is done in there, a deuce of a lot of blue, a little green,

6. Matthew 23: 27–28: Jesus used the term to describe hypocrites who appear beautiful on the outside but
   are rotten inside.

smears of orange, and, on the East Coast, a purple patch, to show where the jolly pioneers of progress drink the jolly lager-beer.[7] However, I wasn't going into any of these. I was going into the yellow. Dead in the center. And the river was there—fascinating—deadly—like a snake. Ough! A door opened, a white-haired secretarial head, but wearing a compassionate expression, appeared, and a skinny forefinger beckoned me into the sanctuary. Its light was dim, and a heavy writing-desk squatted in the middle. From behind that structure came out an impression 260 of pale plumpness in a frock-coat. The great man himself. He was five feet six, I should judge, and had his grip on the handle-end of ever so many millions. He shook hands, I fancy, murmured vaguely, was satisfied with my French. *Bon voyage.*

"In about forty-five seconds I found myself again in the waiting-room with the compassionate secretary, who, full of desolation and sympathy, made me sign some document. I believe I undertook amongst other things not to disclose any trade secrets. Well, I am not going to.

"I began to feel slightly uneasy. You know I am not used to such ceremonies, and there was something ominous in the atmosphere. It was just as though I had 270 been let into some conspiracy—I don't know—something not quite right; and I was glad to get out. In the other room the two women knitted black wool fever-ishly. People were arriving, and the younger one was walking back and forth intro-ducing them. The old one sat on her chair. Her flat cloth slippers were propped up on a foot-warmer, and a cat reposed on her lap. She wore a starched white af-fair on her head, had a wart on one cheek, and silver-rimmed spectacles hung on the tip of her nose. She glanced at me above the glasses. The swift and indifferent placidity of that look troubled me. Two youths with foolish and cheery counte-nances were being piloted over, and she threw at them the same quick glance of unconcerned wisdom. She seemed to know all about them and about me too. An 280 eerie feeling came over me. She seemed uncanny and fateful. Often far away there I thought of these two, guarding the door of Darkness, knitting black wool as for a warm pall, one introducing, introducing continuously to the unknown, the other scrutinizing the cheery and foolish faces with unconcerned old eyes. *Ave!* Old knitter of black wool. *Morituri te salutant.*[8] Not many of those she looked at ever saw her again—not half, by a long way.

"There was yet a visit to the doctor. 'A simple formality,' assured me the sec-retary, with an air of taking an immense part in all my sorrows. Accordingly a young chap wearing his hat over the left eyebrow, some clerk I suppose,—there must have been clerks in the business, though the house was as still as a house in 290 a city of the dead,—came from somewhere up-stairs, and led me forth. He was shabby and careless, with ink-stains on the sleeves of his jacket, and his cravat was large and billowy, under a chin shaped like the toe of an old boot. It was a little too early for the doctor, so I proposed a drink, and thereupon he developed a vein

7. Victorian maps were color-coded to show which countries controlled which colonies: red, blue, green, orange, purple, yellow were for British, French, Portuguese, Italian, German, and Belgian possessions respectively. Marlow was sailing to the Belgian Congo, present-day Democratic Republic of Congo.
8. The full phrase is "Ave Caesar, morituri te salutamus": "Hail, Caesar, they who are about to die salute you"—the gladiators' salute to the emperor before the games.

of joviality. As we sat over our vermouths he glorified the Company's business, and by-and-by I expressed casually my surprise at him not going out there. He became very cool and collected all at once. 'I am not such a fool as I look, quoth Plato to his disciples,' he said sententiously, emptied his glass with great resolution, and we rose.

"The old doctor felt my pulse, evidently thinking of something else the   300
while. 'Good, good for there,' he mumbled, and then with a certain eagerness asked me whether I would let him measure my head. Rather surprised, I said Yes, when he produced a thing like calipers and got the dimensions back and front and every way, taking notes carefully. He was an unshaven little man in a threadbare coat like a gabardine, with his feet in slippers, and I thought him a harmless fool. 'I always ask leave, in the interests of science, to measure the crania of those going out there,' he said. 'And when they come back too?' I asked. 'Oh, I never see them,' he remarked; 'and, moreover, the changes take place inside, you know.' He smiled, as if at some quiet joke. 'So you are going out there. Famous. Interesting too.' He gave me a searching glance, and made another note. 'Ever any madness in   310
your family?' he asked, in a matter-of-fact tone. I felt very annoyed. 'Is that question in the interests of science too?' 'It would be,' he said, without taking notice of my irritation, 'interesting for science to watch the mental changes of individuals, on the spot, but . . .' 'Are you an alienist?'[9] I interrupted. 'Every doctor should be— a little,' answered that original, imperturbably. 'I have a little theory which you Messieurs who go out there must help me to prove. This is my share in the advantages my country shall reap from the possession of such a magnificent dependency. The mere wealth I leave to others. Pardon my questions, but you are the first Englishman coming under my observation. . . .' I hastened to assure him I was not in the least typical. 'If I were,' said I, 'I wouldn't be talking like this with you.'   320
'What you say is rather profound, and probably erroneous,' he said, with a laugh. 'Avoid irritation more than exposure to the sun. Adieu. How do you English say, eh? Good-by. Ah! Good-by. Adieu. In the tropics one must before everything keep calm.' . . . He lifted a warning forefinger. . . .'Du calme, du calme. Adieu.'[10]

"One thing more remained to do—say good-by to my excellent aunt. I found her triumphant. I had a cup of tea—the last decent cup of tea for many days—and in a room that most soothingly looked just as you would expect a lady's drawing-room to look, we had a long quiet chat by the fireside. In the course of these confidences it became quite plain to me I had been represented to the wife of the high dignitary, and goodness knows to how many more people besides, as an excep-   330
tional and gifted creature—a piece of good fortune for the Company—a man you don't get hold of every day. Good heavens! and I was going to take charge of a two-penny-halfpenny river-steamboat with a penny whistle attached! It appeared, however, I was also one of the Workers, with a capital—you know. Something like an emissary of light, something like a lower sort of apostle. There had been a lot of such rot let loose in print and talk just about that time, and the excellent woman, living right in the rush of all that humbug, got carried off her feet. She talked about 'weaning those ignorant millions from their horrid ways,' till, upon my

9. One who treats mental illness.
10. "Keep calm, keep calm. Good-bye."

word, she made me quite uncomfortable.[11] I ventured to hint that the Company
was run for profit.   340

"'You forget, dear Charlie, that the laborer is worthy of his hire,' she said,
brightly. It's queer how out of touch with truth women are. They live in a world of
their own, and there had never been anything like it, and never can be. It is too
beautiful altogether, and if they were to set it up it would go to pieces before the
first sunset. Some confounded fact we men have been living contentedly with ever
since the day of creation would start up and knock the whole thing over.

"After this I got embraced, told to wear flannel, be sure to write often, and so
on—and I left. In the street—I don't know why—a queer feeling came to me that
I was an imposter. Odd thing that I, who used to clear out for any part of the
world at twenty-four hours' notice, with less thought than most men give to the 350
crossing of a street, had a moment—I won't say of hesitation, but of startled pause,
before this commonplace affair. The best way I can explain it to you is by saying
that, for a second or two, I felt as though, instead of going to the center of a continent, I were about to set off for the center of the earth.

"I left in a French steamer, and she called in every blamed port they have out
there, for, as far as I could see, the sole purpose of landing soldiers and custom-
house officers. I watched the coast. Watching a coast as it slips by the ship is like
thinking about an enigma. There it is before you—smiling, frowning, inviting,
grand, mean, insipid, or savage, and always mute with an air of whispering, Come
and find out. This one was almost featureless, as if still in the making, with an as- 360
pect of monotonous grimness. The edge of a colossal jungle, so dark-green as to
be almost black, fringed with white surf, ran straight, like a ruled line, far, far
away along a blue sea whose glitter was blurred by a creeping mist. The sun was
fierce, the land seemed to glisten and drip with steam. Here and there grayish-
whitish specks showed up, clustered inside the white surf, with a flag flying above
them perhaps. Settlements some centuries old, and still no bigger than pin-heads
on the untouched expanse of their background. We pounded along, stopped,
landed soldiers; went on, landed custom-house clerks to levy toll in what looked
like a God-forsaken wilderness, with a tin shed and a flag-pole lost in it; landed
more soldiers—to take care of the custom-house clerks, presumably. Some, I 370
heard, got drowned in the surf; but whether they did or not, nobody seemed particularly to care. They were just flung out there, and on we went. Every day the
coast looked the same, as though we had not moved; but we passed various
places—trading places—with names like Gran' Bassam Little Popo; names that
seemed to belong to some sordid farce acted in front of a sinister backcloth. The
idleness of a passenger, my isolation amongst all these men with whom I had no
point of contact, the oily and languid sea, the uniform somberness of the coast,
seemed to keep me away from the truth of things, within the toil of a mournful
and senseless delusion. The voice of the surf heard now and then was a positive
pleasure, like the speech of a brother. It was something natural, that had its rea- 380
son, that had a meaning. Now and then a boat from the shore gave one a momen-

---

11. Marlow refers here to what Rudyard Kipling called "The white man's burden," the idea that "civilized"
Europeans were morally obliged to "raise" the "savages" of Africa and other "uncivilized" countries. The
extent to which Marlow (and Conrad) believed in this idea is hotly debated by critics.

tary contact with reality. It was paddled by black fellows. You could see from afar the white of their eyeballs glistening. They shouted, sang; their bodies streamed with perspiration; they had faces like grotesque masks—these chaps; but they had bone, muscle, a wild vitality, an intense energy of movement, that was as natural and true as the surf along their coast. They wanted no excuse for being there. They were a great comfort to look at. For a time I would feel I belonged still to a world of straightforward facts; but the feeling would not last long. Something would turn up to scare it away. Once, I remember, we came upon a man-of-war anchored off the coast. There wasn't even a shed there, and she was shelling the   390 bush. It appears the French had one of their wars going on thereabouts. Her ensign dropped limp like a rag; the muzzles of the long six-inch guns stuck out all over the low hull; the greasy, slimy swell swung her up lazily and let her down, swaying her thin masts. In the empty immensity of earth, sky, and water, there she was, incomprehensible, firing into a continent. Pop, would go one of the six-inch guns; a small flame would dart and vanish, a little white smoke would disappear, a tiny projectile would give a feeble screech—and nothing happened. Nothing could happen. There was a touch of insanity in the proceeding, a sense of lugubrious drollery in the sight; and it was not dissipated by somebody on board assuring me earnestly there was a camp of natives—he called them enemies!—hidden out of   400 sight somewhere.

"We gave her her letters (I heard the men in that lonely ship were dying of fever at the rate of three a day) and went on. We called at some more places with farcical names, where the merry dance of death and trade goes on in a still and earthy atmosphere as of an overheated catacomb; all along the formless coast bordered by dangerous surf, as if Nature herself had tried to ward off intruders; in and out of rivers, streams of death in life, whose banks were rotting into mud, whose waters, thickened into slime, invaded the contorted mangroves, that seemed to writhe at us in the extremity of an impotent despair. Nowhere did we stop long enough to get a particularized impression, but the general sense of vague   410 and oppressive wonder grew upon me. It was like a weary pilgrimage amongst hints for nightmares.

"It was upward of thirty days before I saw the mouth of the big river. We anchored off the seat of the government. But my work would not begin till some two hundred miles farther on. So as soon as I could I made a start for a place thirty miles higher up.

"I had my passage on a little sea-going steamer. Her captain was a Swede, and knowing me for a seaman, invited me on the bridge. He was a young man, lean, fair, and morose, with lanky hair and a shuffling gait. As we left the miserable little wharf, he tossed his head contemptuously at the shore. 'Been living there?' he   420 asked. I said, 'Yes.' 'Fine lot these government chaps—are they not?' he went on, speaking English with great precision and considerable bitterness. 'It is funny what some people will do for a few francs a month. I wonder what becomes of that kind when it goes up country?' I said to him I expected to see that soon. 'So-o-o!' he exclaimed. He shuffled athwart, keeping one eye ahead vigilantly. 'Don't be too sure,' he continued. 'The other day I took up a man who hanged himself on the road. He was a Swede, too.' 'Hanged himself! Why, in God's name?' I cried. He kept on looking out watchfully. 'Who knows? The sun too much for him, or the country perhaps.'

"At last we opened a reach. A rocky cliff appeared, mounds of turned-up 430 earth by the shore, houses on a hill, others, with iron roofs, amongst a waste of excavations, or hanging to the declivity. A continuous noise of the rapids above hovered over this scene of inhabited devastation. A lot of people, mostly black and naked, moved about like ants. A jetty projected into the river. A blinding sunlight drowned all this at times in a sudden recrudescence of glare. 'There's your Company's station,' said the Swede, pointing to three wooden barrack-like structures on the rocky slope. 'I will send your things up. Four boxes did you say? So. Farewell.'

"I came upon a boiler wallowing in the grass, then found a path leading up the hill. It turned aside for the bowlders, and also for an undersized railway-truck 440 lying there on its back with its wheels in the air. One was off. The thing looked as dead as the carcass of some animal. I came upon more pieces of decaying machinery, a stack of rusty nails. To the left a clump of trees made a shady spot, where dark things seemed to stir feebly. I blinked, the path was steep. A horn tooted to the right, and I saw the black people run. A heavy and dull detonation shook the ground, a puff of smoke came out of the cliff, and that was all. No change appeared on the face of the rock. They were building a railway. The cliff was not in the way or anything; but this objectless blasting was all the work going on.

"A slight clinking behind me made me turn my head. Six black men advanced in a file, toiling up the path. They walked erect and slow, balancing small 450 baskets full of earth on their heads, and the clink kept time with their footsteps. Black rags were wound round their loins, and the short ends behind waggled to and fro like tails. I could see every rib, the joints of their limbs were like knots in a rope; each had an iron collar on his neck, and all were connected together with a chain whose bights[12] swung between them, rhythmically clinking. Another report from the cliff made me think suddenly of that ship of war I had seen firing into a continent. It was the same kind of ominous voice; but these men could by no stretch of imagination be called enemies. They were called criminals, and the outraged law, like the bursting shells, had come to them, an insoluble mystery from the sea. All their meager breasts panted together, the violently dilated nostrils 460 quivered, the eyes stared stonily uphill. They passed me within six inches, without a glance, with that complete, deathlike indifference of unhappy savages. Behind this raw matter one of the reclaimed, the product of the new forces at work, strolled despondently, carrying a rifle by its middle. He had a uniform jacket with one button off, and seeing a white man on the path, hoisted his weapon to his shoulder with alacrity. This was simple prudence, white men being so much alike at a distance that he could not tell who I might be. He was speedily reassured, and with a large, white, rascally grin, and a glance at his charge, seemed to take me into partnership in his exalted trust. After all, I also was a part of the great cause of these high and just proceedings.   470

"Instead of going up, I turned and descended to the left. My idea was to let

12. Bends (of chain).

that chain-gang get out of sight before I climbed the hill. You know I am not particularly tender; I've had to strike and to fend off. I've had to resist and to attack
sometimes—that's only one way of resisting—without counting the exact cost, according to the demands of such sort of life as I had blundered into. I've seen the
devil of violence, and the devil of greed, and the devil of hot desire; but, by all the
stars! these were strong, lusty, red-eyed devils, that swayed and drove men—men,
I tell you. But as I stood on this hillside, I foresaw that in the blinding sunshine of
that land I would become acquainted with a flabby, pretending, weak-eyed devil
of a rapacious and pitiless folly. How insidious he could be, too, I was only to find   480
out several months later and a thousand miles farther. For a moment I stood appalled, as though by a warning. Finally I descended the hill, obliquely, towards the
trees I had seen.

"I avoided a vast artificial hole somebody had been digging on the slope, the
purpose of which I found it impossible to divine. It wasn't a quarry or a sandpit,
anyhow. It was just a hole. It might have been connected with the philanthropic
desire of giving the criminals something to do. I don't know. Then I nearly fell into
a very narrow ravine, almost no more than a scar in the hillside. I discovered that
a lot of imported drainage-pipes for the settlement had been tumbled in there.
There wasn't one that was not broken. It was a wanton smash-up. At last I got   490
under the trees. My purpose was to stroll into the shade for a moment; but no
sooner within than it seemed to me I had stepped into a gloomy circle of some
Inferno. The rapids were near, and an uninterrupted, uniform, headlong, rushing
noise filled the mournful stillness of the grove, where not a breath stirred, not a
leaf moved, with a mysterious sound—as though the tearing pace of the launched
earth had suddenly become audible.

"Black shapes crouched, lay, sat between the trees, leaning against the
trunks, clinging to the earth, half coming out, half effaced within the dim light, in
all the attitudes of pain, abandonment, and despair. Another mine on the cliff
went off, followed by a slight shudder of the soil under my feet. The work was   500
going on. The work! And this was the place where some of the helpers had withdrawn to die.

"They were dying slowly—it was very clear. They were not enemies, they
were not criminals, they were nothing earthly now,—nothing but black shadows
of disease and starvation, lying confusedly in the greenish gloom. Brought from all
the recesses of the coast in all the legality of time contracts, lost in uncongenial
surroundings, fed on unfamiliar food, they sickened, became inefficient, and were
then allowed to crawl away and rest. These moribund shapes were free as air—
and nearly as thin. I began to distinguish the gleam of the eyes under the trees.
Then, glancing down, I saw a face near my hand. The black bones reclined at full   510
length with one shoulder against the tree, and slowly the eyelids rose and the
sunken eyes looked up at me, enormous and vacant, a kind of blind, white flicker
in the depths of the orbs, which died out slowly. The man seemed young—almost
a boy—but you know with them it's hard to tell. I found nothing else to do but to
offer him one of my good Swede's ship's biscuits I had in my pocket. The fingers
closed slowly on it and held—there was no other movement and no other glance.
He had tied a bit of white worsted round his neck—Why? Where did he get it?
Was it a badge—an ornament—a charm—a propitiatory act? Was there any idea at

all connected with it? It looked startling round his black neck, this bit of white thread from beyond the seas. 520

"Near the same tree two more bundles of acute angles sat with their legs drawn up. One, with his chin propped on his knees, stared at nothing, in an intolerable and appalling manner: his brother phantom rested its forehead, as if overcome with a great weariness; and all about others scattered in every pose of contorted collapse, as in some picture of a massacre or a pestilence. While I stood horror-struck, one of these creatures rose to his hands and knees, and went off on all-fours towards the river to drink. He lapped out of his hand, then sat up in the sunlight, crossing his shins in front of him, and after a time let his woolly head fall on his breastbone.

"I didn't want any more loitering in the shade, and I made haste towards the 530 station. When near the buildings I met a white man, in such an unexpected elegance of get-up that in the first moment I took him for a sort of vision. I saw a high starched collar, white cuffs, a light alpaca jacket, snowy trousers, a clean necktie, and varnished boots. No hat. Hair parted, brushed, oiled, under a green-lined parasol held in a big white hand. He was amazing, and had a penholder behind his ear.

"I shook hands with this miracle, and I learned he was the Company's chief accountant, and that all the bookkeeping was done at this station. He had come out for a moment, he said, 'to get a breath of fresh air.' The expression sounded wonderfully odd, with its suggestion of sedentary desk-life. I wouldn't have men- 540 tioned the fellow to you at all, only it was from his lips that I first heard the name of the man who is so indissolubly connected with the memories of that time. Moreover, I respected the fellow. Yes; I respected his collars, his vast cuffs, his brushed hair. His appearance was certainly that of a hairdresser's dummy; but in the great demoralization of the land he kept up his appearance. That's backbone. His starched collars and got-up shirtfronts were achievements of character. He had been out nearly three years; and, later on, I could not help asking him how he managed to sport such linen. He had just the faintest blush, and said modestly, 'I've been teaching one of the native women about the station. It was difficult. She had a distaste for the work.' Thus this man had verily accomplished something. 550 And he was devoted to his books, which were in apple-pie order.

"Everything else in the station was in a muddle,—heads, things, buildings. Strings of dusty niggers with splay feet arrived and departed; a stream of manufactured goods, rubbishy cottons, beads, and brass-wire sent into the depths of darkness, and in the return came a precious trickle of ivory.

"I had to wait in the station for ten days—an eternity. I lived in a hut in the yard, but to be out of the chaos I would sometimes get into the accountant's office. It was built of horizontal planks, and so badly put together that, as he bent over his desk, he was barred from neck to heels with narrow strips of sunlight. There was no need to open the big shutter to see. It was hot there too; big flies buzzed 560 fiendishly, and did not sting, but stabbed. I sat generally on the floor, while, of faultless appearance (and even slightly scented), perching on a high stool, he wrote, he wrote. Sometimes he stood up for exercise. When a truckle-bed with a sick man (some invalided agent from up-country) was put in there, he exhibited a gentle annoyance. 'The groans of this sick person,' he said, 'distract my attention.

And without that it is extremely difficult to guard against clerical errors in this climate.'

"One day he remarked, without lifting his head, 'In the interior you will no doubt meet Mr. Kurtz.' On my asking who Mr. Kurtz was, he said he was a first-class agent; and seeing my disappointment at this information, he added slowly, 570 laying down his pen, 'He is a very remarkable person.' Further questions elicited from him that Mr. Kurtz was at present in charge of a trading post, a very important one, in the true ivory-country, at 'the very bottom of there. Sends in as much ivory as all the others put together. . . .' He began to write again. The sick man was too ill to groan. The flies buzzed in a great peace.

"Suddenly there was a growing murmur of voices and a great tramping of feet. A caravan had come in. A violent babble of uncouth sounds burst out on the other side of the planks. All the carriers were speaking together, and in the midst of the uproar the lamentable voice of the chief agent was heard 'giving it up' tear-fully for the twentieth time that day. . . . He rose slowly. 'What a frightful row,' he 580 said. He crossed the room gently to look at the sick man, and returning, said to me, 'He does not hear.' 'What! Dead?' I asked, startled. 'No, not yet,' he answered, with great composure. Then, alluding with a toss of the head to the tumult in the station-yard, 'When one has got to make correct entries, one comes to hate those savages—hate them to the death.' He remained thoughtful for a moment. 'When you see Mr. Kurtz,' he went on, 'tell him from me that everything here'—he glanced at the desk—'is very satisfactory. I don't like to write to him—with those messengers of ours you never know who may get hold of your letter—at that Central Station.' He stared at me for a moment with his mild, bulging eyes. 'Oh, he will go far, very far,' he began again. 'He will be a somebody in the 590 Administration before long. They, above—the Council in Europe, you know—mean him to be.'

"He turned to his work. The noise outside had ceased, and presently in going out I stopped at the door. In the steady buzz of flies the homeward-bound agent was lying flushed and insensible; the other, bent over his books, was making correct entries of perfectly correct transactions; and fifty feet below the doorstep I could see the still tree-tops of the grove of death.

"Next day I left that station at last, with a caravan of sixty men, for a two-hundred-mile tramp.

"No use telling you much about that. Paths, paths, everywhere; a stamped-in 600 network of paths spreading over the empty land, through long grass, through burnt grass, through thickets, down and up chilly ravines, up and down stony hills ablaze with heat; and a solitude, nobody, not a hut. The population had cleared out a long time ago. Well, if a lot of mysterious niggers armed with all kinds of fearful weapons suddenly took to traveling on the road between Deal and Gravesend, catching the yokels right and left to carry heavy loads for them, I fancy every farm and cottage thereabouts would get empty very soon. Only here the dwellings were gone too. Still I passed through several abandoned villages. There's something pathetically childish in the ruins of grass walls. Day after day, with the stamp and shuffle of sixty pair of bare feet behind me, each pair under a 60-lb. 610 load. Camp, cook, sleep, strike camp, march. Now and then a carrier dead in har-ness, at rest in the long grass near the path, with an empty water-gourd and his long staff lying by his side. A great silence around and above. Perhaps on some quiet night the tremor of far-off drums, sinking, swelling, a tremor vast, faint; a sound weird, appealing, suggestive, and wild—and perhaps with as profound a meaning as the sound of bells in a Christian country. Once a white man in an un- buttoned uniform, camping on the path with an armed escort of lank Zanzibaris, very hospitable and festive—not to say drunk. Was looking after the upkeep of the road, he declared. Can't say I saw any road or any upkeep, unless the body of a middle-aged negro, with a bullet-hole in the forehead, upon which I absolutely 620 stumbled three miles farther on, may be considered as a permanent improvement. I had a white companion too, not a bad chap, but rather too fleshy and with the exasperating habit of fainting on the hot hillsides, miles away from the least bit of shade and water. Annoying, you know, to hold your own coat like a parasol over a man's head while he is coming-to. I couldn't help asking him once what he meant by coming there at all. 'To make money, of course. What do you think?' he said, scornfully. Then he got fever, and had to be carried in a hammock slung under a pole. As he weighed sixteen stone[13] I had no end of rows with the carriers. They jibbed, ran away, sneaked off with their loads in the night—quite a mutiny. So, one evening, I made a speech in English with gestures, not one of which was lost 630 to the sixty pairs of eyes before me, and the next morning I started the hammock off in front all right. An hour afterwards I came upon the whole concern wrecked in a bush—man, hammock, groans, blankets, horrors. The heavy pole had skinned his poor nose. He was very anxious for me to kill somebody, but there wasn't the shadow of a carrier near. I remembered the old doctor,—'It would be interesting for science to watch the mental changes of individuals, on the spot.' I felt I was becoming scientifically interesting. However, all that is to no purpose. On the fifteenth day I came in sight of the big river again, and hobbled into the Central Station. It was on a back water surrounded by scrub and forest, with a pretty border of smelly mud on one side, and on the three others inclosed by a 640 crazy fence of rushes. A neglected gap was all the gate it had, and the first glance at the place was enough to let you see the flabby devil was running that show. White men with long staves in their hands appeared languidly from amongst the buildings, strolling up to take a look at me, and then retired out of sight some- where. One of them, a stout, excitable chap with black mustaches, informed me with great volubility and many digressions, as soon as I told him who I was, that my steamer was at the bottom of the river. I was thunderstruck. What, how, why? Oh, it was 'all right.' The 'manager himself' was there. All quite correct. 'Everybody had behaved splendidly! splendidly!'—'you must,' he said in agitation, 'go and see the general manager at once. He is waiting!' 650

"I did not see the real significance of that wreck at once. I fancy I see it now, but I am not sure—not at all. Certainly the affair was too stupid—when I think of it—to be altogether natural. Still. . . . But at the moment it presented itself simply as a confounded nuisance. The steamer was sunk. They had started two days be- fore in a sudden hurry up the river with the manager on board, in charge of some volunteer skipper, and before they had been out three hours they tore the bottom out of her on stones, and she sank near the south bank. I asked myself what I was

13. A stone is 14 pounds; hence 224 pounds.

to do there, now my boat was lost. As a matter of fact, I had plenty to do in fishing my command out of the river. I had to set about it the very next day. That, and the repairs when I brought the pieces to the station, took some months.   660

"My first interview with the manager was curious. He did not ask me to sit down after my twenty-mile walk that morning. He was commonplace in complexion, in feature, in manners, and in voice. He was of middle size and or ordinary build. His eyes, of the usual blue, were perhaps remarkably cold, and he certainly could make his glance fall on one as trenchant and heavy as an ax. But even at these times the rest of his person seemed to disclaim the intention. Otherwise there was only an indefinable, faint expression of his lips, something stealthy—a smile—not a smile—I remember it, but I can't explain. It was unconscious, this smile was, though just after he had said something it got intensified for an instant. It came at the end of his speeches like a seal applied on the words to make the   670 meaning of the commonest phrase appear absolutely inscrutable. He was a common trader, from his youth up employed in these parts—nothing more. He was obeyed, yet he inspired neither love nor fear, nor even respect. He inspired uneasiness. That was it! Uneasiness. Not a definite mistrust—just uneasiness—nothing more. You have no idea how effective such a . . . a . . . faculty can be. He had no genius for organizing, for initiative, or for order even. That was evident in such things as the deplorable state of the station. He had no learning, and no intelligence. His position had come to him—why? Perhaps because he was never ill . . . He had served three terms of three years out there . . . Because triumphant health in the general rout of constitutions is a kind of power in itself. When he went   680 home on leave he rioted on a large scale—pompously. Jack ashore—with a difference—in externals only. This one could gather from his casual talk. He originated nothing, he could keep the routine going—that's all. But he was great. He was great by this little thing that it was impossible to tell what could control such a man. He never gave that secret away. Perhaps there was nothing within him. Such a suspicion made one pause—for out there there were no external checks. Once when various tropical diseases had laid low almost every 'agent' in the station, he was heard to say, 'Men who come out here should have no entrails.' He sealed the utterance with that smile of his, as though it had been a door opening into a darkness he had in his keeping. You fancied you had seen things—but the seal was on.   690 When annoyed at meal-times by the constant quarrels of the white men about precedence, he ordered an immense round table to be made, for which a special house had to be built. This was the station's mess-room. Where he sat was the first place—the rest were nowhere. One felt this to be his unalterable conviction. He was neither civil nor uncivil. He was quiet. He allowed his 'boy'—an overfed young negro from the coast—to treat the white men, under his very eyes, with provoking insolence.

"He began to speak as soon as he saw me. I had been very long on the road. He could not wait. Had to start without me. The up-river stations had to be relieved. There had been so many delays already that he did not know who was   700 dead and who was alive, and how they got on—and so on, and so on. He paid no attention to my explanations, and, playing with a stick of sealing-wax, repeated several times that the situation was 'very grave, very grave.' There were rumors that a very important station was in jeopardy, and its chief, Mr. Kurtz, was ill.

Hoped it was not true. Mr. Kurtz was . . . I felt weary and irritable. Hang Kurtz, I thought. I interrupted him by saying I had heard of Mr. Kurtz on the coast. 'Ah! So they talk of him down there,' he murmured to himself. Then he began again, assuring me Mr. Kurtz was the best agent he had, an exceptional man, of the greatest importance to the Company; therefore I could understand his anxiety. He was, he said, 'very, very uneasy.' Certainly he fidgeted on his chair a good deal, exclaimed, 710 'Ah, Mr. Kurtz!' broke the stick of sealing-wax and seemed dumbfounded by the accident. Next thing he wanted to know 'how long it would take to' . . . I interrupted him again. Being hungry, you know, and kept on my feet too, I was getting savage. 'How could I tell,' I said. 'I hadn't even seen the wreck yet—some months, no doubt! All this talk seemed to me so futile. 'Some months,' he said. 'Well, let us say three months before we can make a start. Yes. That ought to do the affair.' I flung out of his hut (he lived all alone in a clay hut with a sort of veranda) muttering to myself my opinion of him. He was a chattering idiot. Afterwards I took it back when it was borne in upon me startlingly with what extreme nicety he had estimated the time requisite for the 'affair.' 720

"I went to work the next day, turning, so to speak, my back on that station. In that way only it seemed to me I could keep my hold on the redeeming facts of life. Still, one must look about sometimes; and then I saw this station, these men strolling aimlessly about in the sunshine of the yard. I asked myself sometimes what it all meant. They wandered here and there with their absurd long staves in their hands, like a lot of faithless pilgrims bewitched inside a rotten fence. The word 'ivory' rang in the air, was whispered, was sighed. You would think they were praying to it. A taint of imbecile rapacity blew through it all, like a whiff from some corpse. By Jove! I've never seen anything so unreal in my life. And outside, the silent wilderness surrounding this cleared speck on the earth struck me as 730 something great and invincible, like evil or truth, waiting patiently for the passing away of this fantastic invasion.

"Oh, these months! well, never mind. Various things happened. One evening a grass shed full of calico, cotton prints, beads, and I don't know what else, burst into a blaze so suddenly that you would have thought the earth had opened to let an avenging fire consume all that trash. I was smoking my pipe quietly by my dismantled steamer, and saw them all cutting capers in the light, with their arms lifted high, when the stout man with mustaches came tearing down to the river, a tin pail in his hand, assured me that everybody was 'behaving splendidly, splendidly,' dipped about a quart of water and tore back again. I noticed there was a 740 hole in the bottom of his pail.

"I strolled up. There was no hurry. You see the thing had gone off like a box of matches. It had been hopeless from the very first. The flame had leaped high, driven everybody back, lighted up everything—and collapsed. The shed was already a heap of embers glowing fiercely. A nigger was being beaten near by. They said he had caused the fire in some way; be that as it may, he was screeching most horribly. I saw him, later on, for several days, sitting in a bit of shade looking very sick and trying to recover himself: afterwards he arose and went out—and the wilderness without a sound took him into its bosom again. As I approached the glow from the dark I found myself at the back of two men, talk- 750 ing. I heard the name of Kurtz pronounced, then the words, 'take advantage of this unfortunate accident.' One of the men was the manager. I wished him a good evening. 'Did you ever see anything like it—eh? it is incredible,' he said and walked off. The other man remained. He was a first-class agent, young, gentlemanly, a bit reserved, with a forked little beard and a hooked nose. He was stand-offish with the other agents, and they on their side said he was the manager's spy upon them. As to me, I had hardly ever spoken to him before. We got into talk, and by-and-by we strolled away from the hissing ruins. Then he asked me to his room, which was in the main building of the station. He struck a match, and I perceived that this young aristocrat had only a silver-mounted dressing-case but   760 also a whole candle all to himself. Just at that time the manager was the only man supposed to have any right to candles. Native mats covered the clay walls; a collection of spears, assegais, shields, knives was hung up in trophies. The business intrusted to this fellow was the making of bricks—so I had been informed; but there wasn't a fragment of a brick anywhere in the station, and he had been there more than a year—waiting. It seems he could not make bricks without something, I don't know what—straw maybe. Anyways, it could not be found there, and as it was not likely to be sent from Europe, it did not appear clear to me what he was waiting for. An act of special creation perhaps. However, they were all waiting—all the sixteen or twenty pilgrims of them—for something; and upon my word it did   770 not seem an uncongenial occupation, from they way they took it, though the only thing that ever came to them was disease—as far as I could see. They beguiled the time by backbiting and intriguing against each other in a foolish kind of way. There was an air of plotting about that station, but nothing came of it, of course. It was as unreal as everything else—as the philanthropic pretense of the whole concern, as their talk, as their government, as their show of work. The only real feeling was a desire to get appointed to a trading-post where ivory was to be had, so that they could earn percentages. They intrigued and slandered and hated each other only on that account,—but as to effectually lifting a little finger—oh, no. By heavens! there is something after all in the world allowing one man to steal a horse   780 while another must not look at a halter. Steal a horse straight out. Very well. He has done it. Perhaps he can ride. But there is a way of looking at a halter that would provoke the most charitable of saints into a kick.

"I had no idea why he wanted to be sociable, but as we chatted in there it suddenly occurred to me the fellow was trying to get at something—in fact, pumping me. He alluded constantly to Europe, to the people I was supposed to know there—putting leading questions as to my acquaintances in the sepulchral city, and so on. His little eyes glittered like mica discs—with curiosity,—though he tried to keep up a bit of superciliousness. At first I was astonished, but very soon I became awfully curious to see what he would find out from me. I couldn't possi-   790 bly imagine what I had in me to make it worth his while. It was very pretty to see how he baffled himself, for in truth my body was full of chills, and my head had nothing in it but that wretched steamboat business. It was evident he took me for a perfectly shameless prevaricator. At last he got angry, and, to conceal a movement of furious annoyance, he yawned. I rose. Then I noticed a small sketch in oils, on a panel, representing a woman, draped and blindfolded, carrying a lighted torch. The background was somber—almost black. The movement of the woman was stately, and the effect of the torchlight on the face was sinister.

"It arrested me, and he stood by civilly, holding an empty half-pint champagne bottle (medical comforts) with the candle stuck in it. To my question he
said Mr. Kurtz had painted this—in this very station more than a year ago—while
waiting for means to go to his trading-post. 'Tell me, pray,' said I, 'who is this Mr.
Kurtz?'

" 'The chief of the Inner Station,' he answered in a short tone, looking away.
'Much obliged,' I said, laughing. 'And you are the brickmaker of the Central
Station. Everyone knows that.' He was silent for a while. 'He is a prodigy,' he said
at last. 'He is an emissary of pity, and science, and progress, and devil knows what
else. We want,' he began to declaim suddenly, 'for the guidance of the cause intrusted to us by Europe, so to speak, higher intelligence, wide sympathies, a singleness of purpose.' 'Who says that?' I asked. 'Lots of them,' he replied. 'Some even
write that; and so *he* comes here, a special being, as you ought to know.' 'Why
ought I to know?' I interrupted, really surprised. He paid no attention. 'Yes. To-day
he is chief of the best station, next year he will be assistant-manager, two years
more and . . . but I dare say you know what he will be in two years' time. You are
the new gang—the gang of virtue. The same people who sent him specially also
recommended you. Oh, don't say no. I've my own eyes to trust.' Light dawned
upon me. My dear aunt's influential acquaintances were producing an unexpected
effect upon that young man. I nearly burst into a laugh. 'Do you read the
Company's confidential correspondence?' I asked. He hadn't a word to say. It was
great fun. 'When Mr. Kurtz,' I continued severely, 'is General Manager, you won't
have the opportunity.'

"He blew the candle out suddenly, and we went outside. The moon had
risen. Black figures strolled about listlessly, pouring water on the glow, whence
proceeded a sound of hissing; steam ascended in the moonlight, the beaten nigger
groaned somewhere. 'What a row the brute makes!' said the indefatigable man
with the mustaches, appearing near us. 'Serve him right. Transgression—punishment—bang! Pitiless, pitiless. That's the only way. This will prevent all conflagration for the future. I was just telling the manager . . .' He noticed my companion,
and became crestfallen all at once. 'Not in bed yet,' he said, with a kind of servile
heartiness; 'it's so natural. Ha! Danger-agitation.' He vanished. I went on to the
river-side, and the other followed me. I heard a scathing murmur at my ear. 'Heap
of muffs—go to.' The pilgrims could be seen in knots gesticulating, discussing.
Several had still their staves in their hands. I verily believe they took these sticks to
bed with them. Beyond the fence the forest stood up spectrally in the moonlight,
and through the dim stir, through the faint sounds of that lamentable courtyard,
the silence of the land when home to one's very heart,—its mystery, its greatness,
the amazing reality of its concealed life. The hurt nigger moaned feebly somewhere near by, and then fetched a deep sigh that made me mend my pace away
from there. I felt a hand introducing itself under my arm. 'My dear sir,' said the fellow, 'I don't want to be misunderstood, and especially by you, who will see Mr.
Kurtz long before I can have that pleasure. I wouldn't like him to get a false idea of
my disposition. . . .'

"I let him run on, this papier-maché Mephistopheles, and it seemed to me
that if I tried I could poke my forefinger through him, and would find nothing inside but a little loose dirt, maybe. He, don't you see, had been planning to be as-

sistant-manager by-and-by under the present man, and I could see that the coming of that Kurtz had upset them both not a little. He talked precipitately, and I did not try to stop him. I had my shoulders against the wreck of my steamer, hauled up on the slope like a carcass of some big river animal. The smell of mud, of primeval mud, by Jove! was in my nostrils, the high stillness of primeval forest 850 was before my eyes; there were shiny patches on the black creek. The moon had spread over everything a thin layer of silver—over the rank grass, over the mud, upon the wall of matted vegetation standing higher than the wall of a temple, over the great river I could see through a somber gap glittering, glittering, as it flowed broadly by without a murmur. All this was great, expectant, mute, while the man jabbered about himself. I wondered whether the stillness on the face of the immensity looking at us two were meant as an appeal or as a menace. What were we who had strayed in here? Could we handle that dumb thing, or would it handle us? I felt how big, how confoundedly big, was that thing that couldn't talk, and perhaps was deaf as well. What was in there? I could see a little ivory coming out 860 from there, and I had heard Mr. Kurtz was in there. I had heard enough about it too—God knows! Yet somehow it didn't bring any image with it—no more than if I had been told an angel or a fiend was in there. I believed it in the same way one of you might believe there are inhabitants in the planet Mars. I knew once a Scotch sailmaker who was certain, dead sure, there were people in Mars. If you asked him for some idea how they looked and behaved, he would get shy and mutter something about 'walking on all-fours.' If you as much as smiled, he would—though a man of sixty—offer to fight you. I would not have gone so far as to fight for Kurtz, but I went for him near enough to a lie. You know I hate, detest, and can't bear a lie, not because I am straighter than the rest of us, but simply be- 870 cause it appalls me. There is a taint of death, a flavor of mortality in lies,—which is exactly what I hate and detest in the world—what I want to forget. It makes me miserable and sick, like biting something rotten would do. Temperament, I suppose. Well, I went near enough to it by letting the young fool there believe anything he liked to imagine as to my influence in Europe. I became in an instant as much of a pretense as the rest of the bewitched pilgrims. This simply because I had a notion it somehow would be of help to that Kurtz whom at the time I did not see—you understand. He was just a word for me. I did not see the man in the name any more than you do. Do you see him? Do you see the story? Do you see anything? It seems to me I am trying to tell you a dream—making a vain attempt, 880 because no relation of a dream can convey the dream-sensation, that commingling of absurdity, surprise, and bewilderment in a tremor of struggling revolt, that notion of being captured by the incredible which is of the very essence of dreams. . . ."

He was silent for a while.

". . . No, it is impossible; it is impossible to convey the life-sensation of any given epoch of one's existence,—that which makes its truth, its meaning—its subtle and penetrating essence. It is impossible. We live, as we dream—alone. . . ."

He paused again as if reflecting, then added—

"Of course in this you fellows see more than I could then. You see me, 890 whom you know. . . ."

It had become so pitch dark that we listeners could hardly see one another.

For a long time already he, sitting apart, had been no more to us than a voice. There was not a word from anybody. The others might have been asleep, but I was awake. I listened, I listened on the watch for the sentence, for the word, that would give me the clew to the faint uneasiness inspired by this narrative that seemed to shape itself without human lips in the heavy night-air of the river.

"... Yes—I let him run on," Marlow began again, "and think what he pleased about the powers that were behind me. I did! And there was nothing behind me! There was nothing but that wretched, old, mangled steamboat I was 900 leaning against, while he talked fluently about 'the necessity for every man to get on.' 'And when one comes out here, you conceive, it is not to gaze at the moon.' Mr. Kurtz was a 'universal genius,' but even a genius would find it easier to work with 'adequate tools—intelligent men.' He did not make bricks—why, there was a physical impossibility in the way—as I was well aware; and if he did secretarial work for the manager, it was because 'no sensible man rejects wantonly the confidence of his superiors.' Did I see it? I saw it. What more did I want? What I really wanted was rivets, by heaven! Rivets. To get on with the work—to stop the hole. Rivets I wanted. There were cases of them down at the coast—cases—piled up—burst—split! You kicked a loose rivet at every second step in that station yard on 910 the hillside. Rivets had rolled into the grove of death. You could fill your pockets with rivets for the trouble of stooping down—and there wasn't one rivet to be found where it was wanted. We had plates that would do, but nothing to fasten them with. And every week the messenger, a lone negro, letter-bag on shoulder and staff in hand, left our station for the coast. And several times a week a coast caravan came in with trade goods,—ghastly glazed calico that made you shudder only to look at it, glass beads value about a penny a quart, confounded spotted cotton handkerchiefs. And no rivets. Three carriers could have brought all that was wanted to set that steamboat afloat.

"He was becoming confidential now, but I fancy my unresponsive attitude 920 must have exasperated him at last, for he judged it necessary to inform me he feared neither God nor devil, let alone any mere man. I said I could see that very well, but what I wanted was a certain quantity of rivets—and rivets were what really Mr. Kurtz wanted, if he had only known it. Now letters went to the coast every week. . . . 'My dear sir,' he cried, 'I write from dictation.' I demanded rivets. There was a way—for an intelligent man. He changed his manner; became very cold, and suddenly began to talk about a hippopotamus; wondered whether sleeping on board the steamer (I stuck to my salvage night and day) I wasn't disturbed. There was an old hippo that had the bad habit of getting out on the bank and roaming at night over the station grounds. The pilgrims use to turn out in a body 930 and empty every rifle they could lay hands on at him. Some even had sat up o' nights for him. All this energy was wasted, though. 'That animal has a charmed life,' he said; 'but you can say this only of brutes in this country. No man—you apprehend me?—no man here bears a charmed life.' He stood there for a moment in the moonlight with his delicate hooked nose set a little askew, and his mica eyes glittering without a wink, then, with a curt Good night, he strode off. I could see he was disturbed and considerably puzzled, which made me feel more hopeful than I had been for days. It was a great comfort to turn from that chap to my influential friend, the battered, twisted, ruined, tin-pot steamboat. I clambered on

board. She rang under my feet like an empty Huntley & Palmer biscuit-tin kicked   940
along a gutter; she was nothing so solid in make, and rather less pretty in shape,
but I had expended enough hard work on her to make me love her. No influential
friend would have served me better. She had given me a chance to come out a
bit—to find out what I could do. No, I don't like work. I had rather laze about
and think of all the fine things that can be done. I don't like work—no man
does—but I like what is in the work,—the chance to find yourself. Your own reality—for yourself, not for others—what no other man can ever know. They can
only see the mere show, and never can tell what it really means.

"I was not surprised to see somebody sitting aft, on the deck, with his legs
dangling over the mud. You see I rather chummed with the few mechanics there   950
were in that station, whom the other pilgrims naturally despised—on account of
their imperfect manners, I suppose. This was the foreman—a boiler-maker by
trade—a good worker. He was a lank, bony, yellow-faced man, with big intense
eyes. His aspect was worried, and his head was as bald as the palm of my hand;
but his hair in falling seemed to have stuck to his chin, and had prospered in the
new locality, for his beard hung down to his waist. He was a widower with six
young children (he had left them in charge of a sister of his to come out there),
and the passion of his life was pigeon-flying. He was an enthusiast and a connoisseur. He would rave about pigeons. After work hours he used sometimes to come
over from his hut for a talk about his children and his pigeons; at work, when he   960
had to crawl in the mud under the bottom of the steamboat, he would tie up that
beard of his in a kind of white serviette he brought for the purpose. It had loops to
go over his ears. In the evening he could be seen squatted on the bank rinsing that
wrapper in the creek with great care, then spreading it solemnly on a bush to dry.

"I slapped him on the back and shouted 'We shall have rivets!' He scrambled
to his feet exclaiming 'No! Rivets!' as though he couldn't believe his ears. Then in a
low voice, 'You . . . eh?' I don't know why we behaved like lunatics. I put my finger to the side of my nose and nodded mysteriously. 'Good for you!' he cried,
snapped his fingers above his head, lifting one foot. I tried a jig. We capered on
the iron deck. A frightful clatter came out of that hulk, and the virgin forest on the   970
other bank of the creek sent it back in a thundering roll upon the sleeping station.
It must have made some of the pilgrims sit up in their hovels. A dark figure obscured the lighted doorway of the manager's hut, vanished, then, a second or so
after, the doorway itself vanished too. We stopped, and the silence driven away by
the stamping of our feet flowed back again from the recesses of the land. The great
wall of vegetation, an exuberant and entangled mass of trunks branches, leaves,
boughs, festoons, motionless in the moonlight, was like a rioting invasion of
soundless life, a rolling wave of plants piled up, crested, ready to topple over the
creek, to sweep every little man of us out of his little existence. And it moved not.
A deadened burst of mighty splashes and snorts reached us from afar, as though   980
an ichthyosaurus had been taking a bath of glitter in that great river. 'After all,'
said the boiler-maker in a reasonable tone, 'why shouldn't we get the rivets?' Why
not, indeed! I did not know of any reason why we shouldn't. 'They'll come in
three weeks,' I said, confidently.

"But they didn't. Instead of rivets there came an invasion, an infliction, a visitation. It came in sections during the next three weeks, each section headed by a

donkey carrying a white man in new clothes and tan shoes, bowing from that elevation right and left to the impressed pilgrims. A quarrelsome band of footsore
sulky niggers trod on the heels of the donkey; a lot of tents, camp-stools, tin
boxes, white cases, brown bales would be shot down in the courtyard, and the air   990
of mystery would deepen a little over the muddle of the station. Five such install-
ments came, with their absurd air of disorderly flight with the loot of innumerable
outfit shops and provision stores, that, one would think, they were lugging, after a
raid, into the wilderness for equitable division. It was an inextricable mess of
things decent in themselves but that human folly made look like the spoils of
thieving.

"This devoted band called itself the Eldorado Exploring Expedition, and I
believe they were sworn to secrecy. Their talk, however, was the talk of sordid
buccaneers: it was reckless without hardihood, greedy without audacity, and cruel
without courage; there was not an atom of foresight or of serious intention in the   1000
whole batch of them, and they did not seem aware these things are wanted for the
work of the world. To tear treasure out of the bowels of the land was their desire,
with no more moral purpose at the back of it than there is in burglars breaking
into a safe. Who paid the expenses of the noble enterprise I don't know; but the
uncle of our manager was leader of that lot.

"In exterior he resembled a butcher in a poor neighborhood, and his eyes
had a look of sleepy cunning. He carried his fat paunch with ostentation on his
short legs, and during the time his gang infested the station spoke to no one but
his nephew. You could see these two roaming about all day long with their heads
close together in an everlasting confab.   1010

"I had given up worrying myself about the rivets. One's capacity for that
kind of folly is more limited than you would suppose. I said Hang!—and let
things slide. I had plenty of time for meditation, and now and then I would give
some thought to Kurtz. I wasn't very interested in him. No. Still, I was curious to
see whether this man, who had come out equipped with moral ideas of some sort,
would climb to the top after all, and how he would set about his work when
there."

II

"ONE EVENING AS I was lying flat on the deck of my steamboat, I heard voices
approaching—and there were the nephew and the uncle strolling along the bank.
I laid my head on my arm again, and had nearly lost myself in a doze, when some-   1020
body said in my ear, as it were: 'I am as harmless as a little child, but I don't like to
be dictated to. Am I the manager—or am I not? I was ordered to send him there.
It's incredible.'. . . I became aware that the two were standing on the shore alongside the forepart of the steamboat, just below my head. I did not move; it did not
occur to me to move: I was sleepy. 'It is unpleasant,' grunted the uncle. 'He asked
the Administration to be sent there,' said the other, 'with the idea of showing what
he could do; and I was instructed accordingly. Look at the influence that man
must have. Is it not frightful?' They both agreed it was frightful, then made several
bizarre remarks: 'Make rain and fine weather—one man—the Council—by the

nose'—bits of absurd sentences that got the better of my drowsiness, so that I had   1030
pretty near the whole of my wits about me when the uncle said, 'The climate may
do away with this difficulty for you. Is he alone there?' 'Yes,' answered the manager; 'he sent his assistant down the river with a note to me in these terms: "Clear
this poor devil out of the country, and don't bother sending more of that sort. I
had rather be alone than have the kind of men you can dispose of with me." It was
more than a year ago. Can you imagine such impudence!' 'Anything since then?'
asked the other, hoarsely. 'Ivory,' jerked the nephew; "lots of it—prime sort—
lots—most annoying, from him. 'And with that?' questioned the heavy rumble.
'Invoice,' was the reply fired out, so to speak. Then silence. They had been talking
about Kurtz.   1040

"I was broad awake by this time, but, lying perfectly at ease, remained still,
having no inducement to change my position. 'How did that ivory come all this
way?' growled the elder man, who seemed very vexed. The other explained that it
had come with a fleet of canoes in charge of an English half-caste clerk Kurtz had
with him; that Kurtz had apparently intended to return himself, the station being
by that time bare of goods and stores, but after coming three hundred miles, had
suddenly decided to go back, which he started to do alone in a small dug-out with
four paddlers, leaving the half-caste to continue down the river with the ivory. The
two fellows there seemed astounded at anybody attempting such a thing. They
were at a loss for an adequate motive. As to me, I seemed to see Kurtz for the first   1050
time. It was a distinct glimpse: the dug-out, four paddling savages, and the lone
white man turning his back suddenly on the headquarters, on relief, on thoughts
of home—perhaps; setting his face towards the depths of the wilderness, towards
his empty and desolate station. I did not know the motive. Perhaps he was just
simply a fine fellow who stuck to his work for its own sake. His name, you understand, had not been pronounced once. He was 'that man.' The half-caste, who, as
far as I could see, had conducted a difficult trip with great prudence and pluck,
was invariably alluded to as 'that scoundrel.' The 'scoundrel' had reported that the
'man' had been very ill—had recovered imperfectly. . . . The two below me moved
away then a few paces, and strolled back and forth at some little distance. I heard: 1060
'Military post—doctor—two hundred miles—quite alone now—unavoidable de-
lays—nine months—no news—strange rumors.' They approached again, just as
the manager was saying, 'No one, as far as I know, unless a species of wandering
trader—a pestilential fellow, snapping ivory from the natives.' Who was it they
were talking about now? I gathered in snatches that this was some man supposed
to be in Kurtz's district, and of whom the manager did not approve. 'We will not
be free from unfair competition till one of these fellows is hanged for an example,'
he said. 'Certainly,' grunted the other; 'get him hanged! Why not? Anything—anything can be done in this country. That's what I say; nobody here, you understand,
here, can endanger your position. And why? You stand the climate—you outlast   1070
them all. The danger is in Europe; but there before I left I took care to—' They
moved off and whispered, then their voices rose again. 'The extraordinary series of
delays is not my fault. I did my possible." The fat man sighed, 'Very sad.' 'And the
pestiferous absurdity of his talk,' continued the other; 'he bothered me enough
when he was here. "Each station should be like a beacon on the road towards better things, a center for trade of course, but also for humanizing, improving, in-

structing." Conceive you—that ass! And he wants to be manager! No, it's—' Here he got choked by excessive indignation, and I lifted my head the least bit. I was surprised to see how near they were—right under me. I could have spat upon their hats. They were looking on the ground, absorbed in thought. The manager was switching his leg with a slender twig: his sagacious relative lifted his head. 'You have been well since you came out this time?' he asked. The other gave a start. 'Who? I? Oh! Like a charm—like a charm. But the rest—oh, my goodness! All sick. They die so quick, too, that I haven't the time to send them out of the country—it's incredible!' 'H'm. Just so,' grunted the uncle. 'Ah! my boy, trust to this—I say, trust to this.' I saw him extend his short flipper of an arm for a gesture that took in the forest, the creek, the mud, the river,—seemed to beckon with a dishonoring flourish before the sunlit face of the land a treacherous appeal to the lurking death, to the hidden evil, to the profound darkness of its heart. It was so startling that I leaped to my feet and looked back at the edge of the forest, as though I had expected an answer of some sort to that black display of confidence. You know the foolish notions that come to one sometimes. The high stillness confronted these two figures with its ominous patience, waiting for the passing away of a fantastic invasion.

"They swore aloud together—out of sheer fright, I believe—then pretending not to know anything of my existence, turned back to the station. The sun was low; and leaning forward side by side, they seemed to be tugging painfully uphill their two ridiculous shadows of unequal length, that trailed behind them slowly over the tall grass without bending a single blade.

"In a few days the Eldorado Expedition went into the patient wilderness, that closed upon it as the sea closes over a diver. Long afterwards the news came that all the donkeys were dead. I know nothing as to the fate of the less valuable animals. They, no doubt, like the rest of us, found what they deserved. I did not inquire. I was then rather excited at the prospect of meeting Kurtz very soon. When I say very soon I mean it comparatively. It was just two months from the day we left the creek when we came to the bank below Kurtz's station.

"Going up that river was like traveling back to the earliest beginnings of the world, when vegetation rioted on the earth and the big trees were kings. An empty stream, a great silence, and impenetrable forest. The air was warm, thick, heavy, sluggish. There was no joy in the brilliance of sunshine. The long stretches of the waterway ran on, deserted, into the gloom of over-shadowed distances. On silvery sandbanks hippos and alligators sunned themselves side by side. The broadening waters flowed through a mob of wooded islands; you lost your way on that river as you would in a desert, and butted all day long against shoals, trying to find the channel, till you thought yourself bewitched and cut off for ever from everything you had known once—somewhere—far away—in another existence perhaps. There were moments when one's past came back to one, as it will sometimes when you have not a moment to spare to yourself; but it came in the shape of an unrestful and noisy dream, remembered with wonder amongst the overwhelming realities of this strange world of plants, and water, and silence. And this stillness of life did not in the least resemble a peace. It was the stillness of an implacable force brooding over an inscrutable intention. It looked at you with a vengeful aspect. I got used to it afterwards; I did not see it any more; I had no time. I had to keep

guessing at the channel; I had to discern, mostly by inspiration, the signs of hidden banks; I watched for sunken stones; I was learning to clap my teeth smartly before my heart flew out, when I shaved by a fluke some infernal sly old snag that would have ripped the life out of the tin-pot steamboat and drowned all the pilgrims; I had to keep a look-out for the signs of dead wood we could cut up in the night for next day's steaming. When you have to attend to things of that sort, to the mere incidents of the surface, the reality—the reality, I tell you—fades. The   1130
inner truth is hidden—luckily, luckily. But I felt it all the same; I felt often its mysterious stillness watching me at my monkey tricks, just as it watches you fellows performing on your respective tight-ropes for—what is it? half-a-crown a tumble—"

"Try to be civil, Marlow," growled a voice, and I knew there was at least one listener awake besides myself.

"I beg your pardon. I forgot the heartache which makes up the rest of the price. And indeed what does the price matter, if the trick be well done? You do your tricks very well. And I didn't do badly either, since I managed not to sink that steamboat on my first trip. It's a wonder to me yet. Imagine a blindfolded man   1140
set to drive a van over a bad road. I sweated and shivered over that business considerably, I can tell you. After all, for a seaman, to scrape the bottom of the thing that's supposed to float all the time under his care is the unpardonable sin. No one may know of it, but you never forget the thump—eh? A blow on the very heart. You remember it, you dream of it, you wake up at night and think of it—years after—and go hot and cold all over. I don't pretend to say that steamboat floated all the time. More than once she had to wade for a bit, with twenty cannibals splashing around and pushing. We had enlisted some of these chaps on the way for a crew. Fine fellows—cannibals—in their place. They were men one could work with, and I am grateful to them. And, after all, they did not eat each other   1150
before my face: they had brought along a provision of hippo-meat which went rotten, and made the mystery of the wilderness stink in my nostrils. Phoo! I can sniff it now. I had the manager on board and three or four pilgrims with their staves— all complete. Sometimes we came upon a station close by the bank, clinging to the skirts of the unknown, and the white men rushing out of a tumble-down hovel, with great gestures of joy and surprise and welcome, seemed very strange,—had the appearance of being held there captive by a spell. The word ivory would ring in the air for a while—and on we went again into the silence, along empty reaches, round the still bends, between the high walls of our winding way, reverberating in hollow claps the ponderous beat of the stern-wheel. Trees, trees, mil-   1160
lions of trees, massive, immense, running up high; and at their foot, hugging the bank against the stream, crept the little begrimed steamboat, like a sluggish beetle crawling on the floor of a lofty portico. It made you feel very small, very lost, and yet it was not altogether depressing that feeling. After all, if you were small, the grimy beetle crawled on—which was just what you wanted it to do. Where the pilgrims imagined it crawled to I don't know. To some place where they expected to get something, I bet! For me it crawled toward Kurtz—exclusively; but when the steam-pipes started leaking we crawled very slow. The reaches opened before us and closed behind, as if the forest had stepped leisurely across the water to bar the way for our return. We penetrated deeper and deeper into the heart of dark-   1170

ness. It was very quiet there. At night sometimes the roll of drums behind the curtain of trees would run up the river and remain sustained faintly, as if hovering in the air high over our heads, till the first break of day. Whether it meant war, peace, or prayer we could not tell. The dawns were heralded by the descent of a chill stillness; the woodcutters slept, their fires burned low; the snapping of a twig would make you start. We were wanderers in a prehistoric earth, on an earth that wore the aspect of an unknown planet. We could have fancied ourselves the first of men taking possession of an accursed inheritance, to be subdued at the cost of profound anguish and of excessive toil. But suddenly, as we struggled round a bend, there would be a glimpse of rush walls, of peaked grass-roofs, a burst of 1180 yells, a whirl of black limbs, a mass of hands clapping, of feet stamping, of bodies swaying, of eyes rolling, under the droop of heavy and motionless foliage. The steamer toiled along slowly on the edge of a black and incomprehensible frenzy. The prehistoric man was cursing us, praying to us, welcoming us—who could tell? We were cut off from the comprehension of our surroundings; we glided past like phantoms, wondering and secretly appalled, as sane men would be before an enthusiastic outbreak in a madhouse. We could not understand, because we were too far and could not remember, because we were traveling in the night of first ages, of those ages that are gone, leaving hardly a sign—and no memories.

"The earth seemed unearthly. We are accustomed to look upon the shackled 1190 form of a conquered monster, but there—there you could look at a thing monstrous and free. It was unearthly, and the men were—No, they were not inhuman. Well, you know, that was the worst of it—this suspicion of their not being inhuman. It would come slowly to one. They howled, and leaped, and spun, and made horrid faces; but what thrilled you was just the thought of their humanity—like yours—the thought of your remote kinship with this wild and passionate uproar. Ugly. Yes, it was ugly enough; but if you were man enough you would admit to yourself that there was in you just the faintest trace of a response to the terrible frankness of that noise, a dim suspicion of there being a meaning in which you—you so remote from the night of first ages—could comprehend. And why not? The 1200 mind of a man is capable of anything—because everything is in it, all the past as well as all the future. What was there after all? Joy, fear, sorrow, devotion, valor, rage—who can tell?—but truth—truth stripped of its cloak of time. Let the fool gape and shudder—the man knows, and can look on without a wink. But he must at least be as much of a man as these on the shore. He must meet that truth with his own true stuff—with his own inborn strength. Principles? Principles won't do. Acquisitions, clothes, pretty rags—rags that would fly off at the first good shake. No; you want a deliberate belief. An appeal to me in this fiendish row—is there? Very well; I hear; I admit, but I have a voice, too, and for good or evil mine is the speech that cannot be silenced. Of course, a fool, what with sheer fright and fine 1210 sentiments, is always safe. Who's that grunting? You wonder I didn't go ashore for a howl and a dance? Well, no—I didn't. Fine sentiments, you say? Fine sentiments, be hanged! I had no time. I had to mess about with white-lead and strips of woolen blanket helping to put bandages on those leaky steam-pipes—I tell you. I had to watch the steering, and circumvent those snags, and get the tin-pot along by hook or by crook. There was surface-truth enough in these things to save a wiser man. And between whiles I had to look after the savage who was fireman.

He was an improved specimen; he could fire up a vertical boiler. He was there
below me, and, upon my word, to look at him was as edifying as seeing a dog in a
parody of breeches and a feather hat, walking on his hindlegs. A few months of   1220
training had done for that really fine chap. He squinted at the steam-gauge and at
the water-gauge with an evident effort of intrepidity—and he had filed teeth too,
the poor devil, and the wool of his pate shaved into queer patterns, and three ornamental scars on each of his cheeks. He ought to have been clapping his hands
and stamping his feet on the bank, instead of which he was hard at work, a thrall
to strange witchcraft, full of improving knowledge. He was useful because he had
been instructed; and what he knew was this—that should the water in that transparent thing disappear, the evil spirit inside the boiler would get angry through
the greatness of his thirst, and take a terrible vengeance. So he sweated and fired
up and watched the glass fearfully (with an impromptu charm, made of rags, tied   1230
to his arm, and a piece of polished bone, as big as a watch, stuck flatways through
his lower lip), while the wooded banks slipped past us slowly, the short noise was
left behind the interminable miles of silence—and we crept on, towards Kurtz. But
the snags were thick, the water was treacherous and shallow, the boiler seemed indeed to have a sulky devil in it, and thus neither that fireman nor I had any time
to peer into our creepy thoughts.

"Some fifty miles below the Inner Station we came upon a hut of reeds, an
inclined and melancholy pole, with the unrecognizable tatters of what had been a
flag of some sort flying from it, and a neatly stacked wood-pile. This was unexpected. We came to the bank, and on the stack of firewood found a flat piece of   1240
board with some faded pencil-writing on it. When deciphered it said: 'Wood for
you. Hurry up. Approach cautiously.' There was a signature, but it was illegible—
not Kurtz—a much longer word. Hurry up. Where? Up the river? 'Approach cautiously.' We had not done so. But the warning could not have been meant for the
place where it could be only found after approach. Something was wrong above.
But what—and how much? That was the question. We commented adversely
upon the imbecility of that telegraphic style. The bush around said nothing, and
would not let us look very far, either. A torn curtain of red twill hung in the doorway of the hut, and flapped sadly in our faces. The dwelling was dismantled; but
we could see a white man had lived there not very long ago. There remained a   1250
rude table—a plank on two posts; a heap of rubbish reposed in a dark corner, and
by the door I picked up a book. It had lost its covers, and the pages had been
thumbed into a state of extremely dirty softness; but the back had been lovingly
stitched afresh with white cotton thread, which looked clean yet. It was an extraordinary find. Its title was, 'An Inquiry into some Points of Seamanship,' by a man
Tower, Towson—some such name—Master in his Majesty's Navy. The matter
looked dreary reading enough, with illustrative diagrams and repulsive tables of
figures, and the copy was sixty years old. I handled this amazing antiquity with
the greatest possible tenderness, lest it should dissolve in my hands. Within,
Towson or Towser was inquiring earnestly into the breaking strain of ships' chains   1260
and tackle, and other such matters. Not a very enthralling book; but at the first
glance you could see there a singleness of intention, an honest concern for the
right way of going to work, which made these humble pages, thought out so many
years ago, luminous with another than a professional light. The simple old sailor,

with his talk of chains and purchases, made me forget the jungle and the pilgrims in a delicious sensation of having come upon something unmistakably real. Such a book being there was wonderful enough; but still more astounding were the notes penciled in the margin, and plainly referring to the text. I couldn't believe my eyes! They were in cipher! Yes, it looked like cipher. Fancy a man lugging with him a book of that description into this nowhere and studying it—and making 1270 notes—in cipher at that! It was an extravagant mystery.

"I had been dimly aware for some time of a worrying noise, and when I lifted my eyes I saw the wood-pile was gone, and the manager, aided by all the pilgrims, was shouting at me from the river-side. I slipped the book into my pocket. I assure you to leave off reading was like tearing myself away from the shelter of an old and solid friendship.

"I started the lame engine ahead. 'It must be this miserable trader—this intruder,' exclaimed the manager, looking back malevolently at the place we had left. 'He must be English,' I said. 'It will not save him from getting into trouble if he is not careful,' muttered the manager darkly. I observed with assumed innocence that 1280 no man was safe from trouble in this world.

"The current was more rapid now, the steamer seemed at her last gasp, the stern-wheel flopped languidly, and I caught myself listening on tiptoe for the next beat of the float, for in sober truth I expected the wretched thing to give up every moment. It was like watching the last flickers of life. But still we crawled. Sometimes I would pick out a tree a little way ahead to measure our progress towards Kurtz by, but I lost it invariably before we got abreast. To keep the eyes so long on one thing was too much for human patience. The manager displayed a beautiful resignation. I fretted and fumed and took to arguing with myself whether or no I would talk openly with Kurtz; but before I could come to any conclusion it 1290 occurred to me that my speech or my silence, indeed any action of mine, would be a mere futility. What did it matter what anyone knew or ignored? What did it matter who was manager? One gets sometimes such a flash of insight. The essentials of this affair lay deep under the surface, beyond my reach, and beyond my power of meddling.

"Towards the evening of the second day we judged ourselves about eight miles from Kurtz's station. I wanted to push on; but the manager looked grave, and told me the navigation up there was so dangerous that it would be advisable, the sun being very low already, to wait where we were till next morning. Moreover, he pointed out that if the warning to approach cautiously were to be 1300 followed, we must approach in daylight—not at dusk, or in the dark. This was sensible enough. Eight miles meant nearly three hours' steaming for us, and I could also see suspicious ripples at the upper end of the reach. Nevertheless, I was annoyed beyond expression at the delay, and most unreasonably too, since one night more could not matter much after so many months. As we had plenty of wood, and caution was the word, I brought up in the middle of the stream. The reach was narrow, straight, with high sides like a railway cutting. The dusk came gliding into it long before the sun had set. The current ran smooth and swift, but a dumb immobility sat on the banks. The living trees, lashed together by the creepers and every living bush of the undergrowth, might have been changed into 1310 stone, even to the slenderest twig, to the lightest leaf. It was not sleep—it seemed unnatural, like a state of trance. Not the faintest sound of any kind could be heard. You looked on amazed, and began to suspect yourself of being deaf—then the night came suddenly, and struck you blind as well. About three in the morning some large fish leaped, and the loud splash made me jump as though a gun had been fired. When the sun rose there was a white fog, very warm and clammy, and more blinding than the night. It did not shift or drive; it was just there, standing all round you like something solid. At eight or nine, perhaps, it lifted as a shutter lifts. We had a glimpse of the towering multitude of trees, of the immense matted jungle, with the blazing little ball of the sun hanging over it—all perfectly still—   1320 and then the white shutter came down again, smoothly, as if sliding in greased grooves. I ordered the chain, which we had begun to heave in, to be paid out again. Before it stopped running with a muffled rattle, a cry, a very loud cry, as of infinite desolation, soared slowly in the opaque air. It ceased. A complaining clamor, modulated in savage discords, filled our ears. The sheer unexpectedness of it made my hair stir under my cap. I don't know how it struck the others: to me it seemed as though the mist itself had screamed, so suddenly, and apparently from all sides at once, did this tumultuous and mournful uproar arise. It culminated in a hurried outbreak of almost intolerably excessive shrieking, which stopped short, leaving us stiffened in a variety of silly attitudes, and obstinately listening to the   1330 nearly as appalling and excessive silence. 'Good God! What is the meaning—?' stammered at my elbow one of the pilgrims,—a little fat man, with sandy hair and red whiskers, who wore side-spring boots, and pink pyjamas tucked into his socks. Two others remained open-mouthed a whole minute, then dashed into the little cabin, to rush out incontinently and stand darting scared glances, with Winchesters at 'ready' in their hands. What we could see was just the steamer we were on, her outlines blurred as though she had been on the point of dissolving, and a misty strip of water, perhaps two feet broad, around her—and that was all. The rest of the world was nowhere, as far as our eyes and ears were concerned. Just nowhere. Gone, disappeared; swept off without leaving a whisper or a shadow   1340 behind.

"I went forward, and ordering the chain to be hauled in short, so as to be ready to trip the anchor and move the steamboat at once if necessary. 'Will they attack?' whispered an awed voice. 'We will be butchered in this fog,' murmured another. The faces twitched with the strain, the hands trembled slightly, the eyes forgot to wink. It was very curious to see the contrast of expressions of the white men and of the black fellows of our crew, who were as much strangers to that part of the river as we, though their homes were only eight hundred miles away. The whites, of course greatly discomposed, had besides a curious look of being painfully shocked by such an outrageous row. The others had an alert, naturally   1350 interested expression; but their faces were essentially quiet, even those of the one or two who grinned as they hauled at the chain. Several exchanged short, grunting phrases, which seemed to settle the matter to their satisfaction. Their headman, a young, broad-chested black, severely draped in dark-blue fringed cloths, with fierce nostrils and his hair all done up artfully in oily ringlets, stood near me. 'Aha!' I said, just for good fellowship's sake. 'Catch 'im,' he snapped, with a bloodshot widening of his eyes and a flash of sharp teeth—'catch 'im. Give 'im to us.' 'To you, eh?' I asked; 'what would you do with them?' 'Eat 'im!' he said curtly, and, leaning his elbow on the rail, looked out into the fog in a dignified and profoundly pensive attitude. I would no doubt have been properly horrified, had it not oc- 1360 curred to me that he and his chaps must be very hungry: that they must have been growing increasingly hungry for at least this month past. They had been engaged for six months (I don't think a single one of them had any clear idea of time, as we at the end of countless ages have. They still belonged to the beginnings of time— had no inherited experience to teach them as it were), and of course, as long as there was a piece of paper written over in accordance with some farcical law or other made down the river, it didn't enter anybody's head to trouble how they would live. Certainly they had brought with them some rotten hippo-meat, which couldn't have lasted very long, anyway, even if the pilgrims hadn't, in the midst of a shocking hullabaloo, thrown a considerable quantity of it overboard. It looked 1370 like a high-handed proceeding; but it was really a case of legitimate self-defense. You can't breathe dead hippo waking, sleeping, and eating, and at the same time keep your precarious grip on existence. Besides that, they had given them every week three pieces of brass wire, each about nine inches long; and the theory was they were to buy their provisions with that currency in river-side villages. You can see how *that* worked. There were either no villages, or the people were hostile, or the director, who like the rest of us fed out of tins, with an occasional old he-goat thrown in, didn't want to stop the steamer for some more or less recondite reason. So, unless they swallowed the wire itself, or made loops of it to snare the fishes with, I don't see what good their extravagant salary could be to them. I must say it 1380 was paid with a regularity worthy of a large and honorable trading company. For the rest, the only thing to eat—though it didn't look eatable in the least—I saw in their possession was a few lumps of some stuff like half-cooked dough, of a dirty lavender color,[14] they kept wrapped in leaves, and now and then swallowed a piece of, but so small that it seemed done for more for the looks of the thing than for any serious purpose of sustenance. Why in the name of all the gnawing devils of hunger they didn't go for us—they were thirty to five—and have a good tuck in for once, amazes me now when I think of it. They were big powerful men, with not much capacity to weigh the consequences, with courage, with strength, even yet, though their skins were no longer glossy and their muscles no longer hard. 1390 And I saw that something restraining, one of those human secrets that baffle probability, had come into play there. I looked at them with a swift quickening of interest—not because it occurred to me I might be eaten by them before very long, though I own to you that just then I perceived—in a new light, as it were—how unwholesome the pilgrims looked, and I hoped, yes, I positively hoped, that my aspect was not so—what shall I say?—so—unappetizing: a touch of fantastic vanity which fitted well with the dream-sensation that pervaded all my days at that time. Perhaps I had a little fever too. One can't live with one's finger everlastingly on one's pulse. I had often 'a little fever,' or a little touch of other things—the playful paw-strokes of the wilderness, the preliminary trifling before the more serious 1400 onslaught which came in due course. Yes; I looked at them as you would on any human being, with a curiosity of their impulses, motives, capacities, weaknesses, when brought to the test of an inexorable physical necessity. Restraint! What pos-

14. An accurate description of cassava dough, which is nutritious and keeps a long time.

sible restraint? Was it superstition, disgust, patience, fear—or some kind of primitive honor? No fear can stand up to hunger, no patience can wear it out, disgust
simply does not exist where hunger is; and as to superstition, beliefs, and what
you may call principles, they are less than chaff in a breeze. Don't you know the
devilry of lingering starvation, its exasperating torment, its black thoughts, its
somber and brooding ferocity? Well, I do. It takes a man all his inborn strength to
fight hunger properly. It's really easier to face bereavement, dishonor, and the 1410
perdition of one's soul—than this kind of prolonged hunger. Sad, but true. And
these chaps too had no earthly reason for any kind of scruple. Restraint! I would
just as soon have expected restraint from a hyena prowling amongst the corpses of
a battlefield. But there was the fact facing me—the fact dazzling, to be seen, like
the foam on the depths of the sea, like a ripple on a unfathomable enigma, a mystery greater—when I thought of it—than the curious, inexplicable note of desperate grief in this savage clamor that had swept by us on the river-bank, behind the
blind whiteness of the fog.

"Two pilgrims were quarreling in hurried whispers as to which bank. 'Left.'
'No, no; how can you? Right, right, of course.' 'It is very serious,' said the man- 1420
ager's voice behind me; 'I would be desolated if anything should happen to Mr.
Kurtz before we came up.' I looked at him, and had not the slightest doubt he was
sincere. He was just the kind of man who would wish to preserve appearances.
That was his restraint. But when he muttered something about going on at once, I
did not even take the trouble to answer him. I knew, and he knew, that it was impossible. Were we to let go our hold of the bottom, we would be absolutely in the
air—in space. We wouldn't be able to tell where we were going to—whether up or
down stream, or across—till we fetched against one bank or the other,—and then
we wouldn't know at first which it was. Of course I made no move. I had no mind
for a smash-up. You couldn't imagine a more deadly place for a shipwreck. 1430
Whether drowned at once or not, we were sure to perish speedily in one way or
another. 'I authorize you to take all the risks,' he said, after a short silence. 'I refuse
to take any,' I said shortly; which was just the answer he expected, though its tone
might have surprised him. 'Well, I must defer to your judgment. You are captain,'
he said, with marked civility. I turned my shoulder to him in sign of my appreciation, and looked into the fog. How long would it last? It was the most hopeless
look-out. The approach to this Kurtz grubbing for ivory in the wretched bush was
beset by as many dangers as though he had been an enchanted princess sleeping
in a fabulous castle. 'Will they attack, do you think?' asked the manager, in a confidential tone. 1440

"I did not think they would attack, for several obvious reasons. The thick fog
was one. If they left the bank in their canoes they would get lost in it, as we would
be if we attempted to move. Still, I had also judged the jungle of both banks quite
impenetrable—and yet eyes were in it, eyes that had seen us. The river-side
bushes were certainly thick; but the undergrowth behind was evidently penetra-
ble. However, during the short lift I had seen no canoes anywhere in the reach—
certainly not abreast of the steamer. But what made the idea of attack
inconceivable to me was the nature of the noise—of the cries we had heard. They
had not the fierce character boding of immediate hostile intention. Unexpected,
wild, and violent as they had been, they had given me an irresistible impression of 1450

sorrow. The glimpse of the steamboat had for some reason filled those savages with unrestrained grief. The danger, if any, I expounded, was from our proximity to a great human passion let loose. Even extreme grief may ultimately vent itself in violence—but more generally takes the form of apathy. . . .

"You should have seen the pilgrims stare! They had no heart to grin, or even to revile me; but I believe they thought me gone mad—with fright, maybe. I delivered a regular lecture. My dear boys, it was no good bothering. Keep a look-out? Well, you may guess I watched the fog for the signs of lifting as a cat watches a mouse; but for anything else our eyes were of no more use to us than if we had been buried miles deep in a heap of cotton-wool. It felt like it too—choking, warm, stifling. Besides, all I said, though it sounded extravagant, was absolutely true to fact. What we afterwards alluded to as an attack was really an attempt at repulse. The action was very far from being aggressive—it was not even defensive, in the usual sense: it was undertaken under the stress of desperation, and in its essence was purely protective.

"It developed itself, I should say, two hours after the fog lifted, and its commencement was at a spot, roughly speaking, about a mile and a half below Kurtz's station. We had just floundered and flopped round a bend, when I saw an islet, a mere grassy hummock of bright green, in the middle of the stream. It was the only thing of the kind; but as we opened the reach more, I perceived it was the head of a long sandbank, or rather a chain of shallow patches stretching down the middle of the river. They were discolored, just awash, and the whole lot was seen just under the water, exactly as a man's backbone is seen running down the middle of his back under the skin. Now, as far as I did see, I could go to the right or to the left of this. I didn't know either channel, of course. The banks looked pretty well alike, the depth appeared the same; but as I had been informed the station was on the west side, I naturally headed for the western passage.

"No sooner had we fairly entered it than I became aware it was much narrower than I had supposed. To the left of us there was the long uninterrupted shoal, and to the right a high, steep bank heavily overgrown with bushes. Above the bush the trees stood in serried ranks. The twigs overhung the current thickly, and from distance to distance a large limb of some tree projected rigidly over the stream. It was then well on in the afternoon, the face of the forest was gloomy, and a broad strip of shadow had already fallen on the water. In this shadow we steamed up—very slowly, as you may imagine. I sheered her well inshore—the water being deepest near the bank, as the sounding-pole informed me.

"One of my hungry and forbearing friends was sounding in the bows just below me. This steamboat was exactly like a decked scow. On the deck there were two little teak-wood houses, with doors and windows. The boiler was in the fore-end, and the machinery right astern. Over the whole there was a light roof, supported on stanchions. The funnel projected through that roof, and in front of the funnel a small cabin built of light planks served for a pilot-house. It contained a couch, two campstools, a loaded Martini-Henry leaning in one corner, a tiny table, and the steering-wheel. It had a wide door in front and a broad shutter at each side. All these were always thrown open, of course. I spent my days perched up there on the extreme fore-end of that roof, before the door. At night I slept, or tried to, on the couch. An athletic black belonging to some coast tribe, and edu-

cated by my poor predecessor, was the helmsman. He sported a pair of brass earrings, wore a blue cloth wrapper from the waist to the ankles, and thought all the
world of himself. He was the most unstable kind of fool I had ever seen. He   1500
steered with no end of a swagger while you were by; but if he lost sight of you, he
became instantly the prey of an abject funk, and would let that cripple of a steamboat get the upper hand of him in a minute.

    "I was looking down at the sounding-pole, and feeling much annoyed to see
at each try a little more of it stick out of that river, when I saw my poleman give
up the business suddenly, and stretch himself flat on the deck, without even taking the trouble to haul his pole in. He kept hold on it though, and it trailed in the
water. At the same time the fireman, whom I could also see below me, sat down
abruptly before his furnace and ducked his head. I was amazed. Then I had to
look at the river mighty quick, because there was a snag in the fairway. Sticks, lit-   1510
tle sticks, were flying about—thick: they were whizzing before my nose, dropping
below me, striking behind me against my pilot-house. All this time the river, the
shore, the woods, were very quiet—perfectly quiet. I could only hear the heavy
splashing thump of the stern-wheel and the patter of these things. We cleared the
snag clumsily. Arrows, by Jove! We were being shot at! I stepped in quickly to
close the shutter on the land side. That fool-helmsman, his hands on the spokes,
was lifting his knees high, stamping his feet, champing his mouth, like a reined-in
horse. Confound him! And we were staggering within ten feet of the bank. I had
to lean right out to swing the heavy shutter, and I saw a face amongst the leaves on
the level with my own, looking at me very fierce and steady; and then suddenly, as   1520
though a veil had been removed from my eyes, I made out, deep in the tangled
gloom, naked breasts, arms, legs, glaring eyes,—the bush was swarming with
human limbs in movement, glistening, of bronze color. The twigs shook, swayed,
and rustled, the arrows flew out of them, and then the shutter came to. 'Steer her
straight,' I said to the helmsman. He held his head rigid, face forward; but his eyes
rolled, he kept lifting and setting down his feet gently, his mouth foamed a little.
'Keep quiet!' I said in a fury. I might just as well have ordered a tree not to sway in
the wind. I darted out. Below me there was a great scuffle of feet on the iron deck;
confused exclamations; a voice screamed, 'Can you turn back?' I caught sight of a
V-shaped ripple on the water ahead. What? Another snag! A fusillade burst out   1530
under my feet. The pilgrims had opened their little Winchesters, and were simply
squirting lead into that bush. A deuce of a lot of smoke came up and drove slowly
forward. I swore at it. Now I couldn't see the ripple or the snag either. I stood in
the doorway, peering, and the arrows came in swarms. They might have been poisoned, but they looked as though they wouldn't kill a cat. The bush began to
howl. Our wood-cutters raised a warlike whoop; the report of a rifle just at my
back deafened me. I glanced over my shoulder, and the pilot-house was yet full of
noise and smoke when I made a dash at the wheel. The fool-nigger had dropped
everything, to throw the shutter open and let off that Martini-Henry. He stood before the wide opening, glaring, and I yelled at him to come back, while I straight-   1540
ened the sudden twist out of that steamboat. There was no room to turn even if I
had wanted to, the snag was somewhere very near ahead in that confounded
smoke, there was no time to lose, so I just crowded her into the bank—right into
the bank, where I knew the water was deep.

"We tore slowly along the overhanging bushes in a whirl of broken twigs and flying leaves. The fusillade below stopped short, as I had foreseen it would when the squirts got empty. I threw my head back to a glinting whizz that traversed the pilot-house, in at one shutter-hole and out at the other. Looking past that mad helmsman, who was shaking the empty rifle and yelling at the shore, I saw vague forms of men running bent double, leaping, gliding, distinct, incomplete, evanes- 1550 cent. Something big appeared in the air before the shutter, the rifle went overboard, and the man stepped back swiftly, looked at me over his shoulder in an extraordinary, profound, familiar manner, and fell upon my feet. The side of his head hit the wheel twice, and the end of what appeared a long cane clattered round and knocked over a little camp-stool. It looked as though after wrenching that thing from somebody ashore he had lost his balance in the effort. The thin smoke had blown away, we were clear of the snag, and looking ahead I could see that in another hundred yards or so I would be free to sheer off, away from the bank; but my feet felt so very warm and wet that I had to look down. The man had rolled on his back and stared straight up at me; both his hands clutched that 1560 cane. It was the shaft of a spear that, either thrown or lunged through the opening, had caught him in the side just below the ribs; the blade had gone in out of sight, after making a frightful gash; my shoes were full; a pool of blood lay very still, gleaming dark-red under the wheel; his eyes shone with an amazing luster. The fusillade burst out again. He looked at me anxiously, gripping the spear like something precious, with an air of being afraid I would try to take it away from him. I had to make an effort to free my eyes from his gaze and attend to the steering. With one hand I felt above my head for the line of the steam-whistle, and jerked out screech after screech hurriedly. The tumult of angry and warlike yells was checked instantly, and then from the depths of the woods went out such a 1570 tremulous and prolonged wail of mournful fear and utter despair as may be imagined to follow the flight of the last hope from the earth. There was a great commotion in the bush; the shower of arrows stopped, a few dropping shots rang out sharply—then silence, in which the languid beat of the stern-wheel came plainly to my ears. I put the helm hard a-starboard at the moment when the pilgrim in pink pyjamas, very hot and agitated, appeared in the doorway. 'The manager sends me—' he began in an official tone, and stopped short. 'Good God!' he said, glaring at the wounded man.

"We two whites stood over him, and his lustrous and inquiring glance enveloped us both. I declare it looked as though he would presently put to us some 1580 question in an understandable language; but he died without uttering a sound, without moving a limb, without twitching a muscle. Only in the very last moment, as though in response to some sign we could not see, to some whisper we could not hear, he frowned heavily, and that frown gave to his black death-mask an inconceivably somber, brooding, and menacing expression. The luster of inquiring glance faded swiftly into vacant glassiness. 'Can you steer?' I asked the agent eagerly. He looked very dubious; but I made a grab at his arm, and he understood at once I meant him to steer whether or no. To tell you the truth, I was morbidly anxious to change my shoes and socks. 'He is dead,' murmured the fellow, immensely impressed. 'No doubt about it,' said I, tugging like mad at the 1590 shoe-laces. 'And, by the way, I suppose Mr. Kurtz is dead as well by this time.'

"For the moment that was the dominant thought. There was a sense of extreme disappointment, as though I had found out I had been striving after something altogether without a substance. I couldn't have been more disgusted if I had traveled all this way for the sole purpose of talking with Mr. Kurtz. Talking with . . . I flung one shoe overboard, and became aware that was exactly what I had been looking forward to—a talk with Kurtz. I made the strange discovery that I had never imagined him as doing, you know, but as discoursing. I didn't say to myself, 'Now I will never see him,' or 'Now I will never shake him by the hand,' but, 'Now I will never hear him.' The man presented himself as a voice. Not of course that I did not connect him with some sort of action. Hadn't I been told in all the tones of jealousy and admiration that he had collected, bartered, swindled, or stolen more ivory than all the other agents together? That was not the point. The point was in his being a gifted creature, and that of all his gifts the one that stood out preeminently, that carried with it a sense of real presence, was his ability to talk, his words—the gift of expression, the bewildering, the illuminating, the most exalted and the most contemptible, the pulsating stream of light, or the deceitful flow from the heart of an impenetrable darkness.

"The other shoe went flying unto the devil-god of that river. I thought, By Jove! it's all over. We are too late; he has vanished—the gift has vanished, by means of some spear, arrow, or club. I will never hear that chap speak after all,—and my sorrow had a startling extravagance of emotion, even such as I had noticed in the howling sorrow of these savages in the bush. I couldn't have felt more of lonely desolation somehow, had I been robbed of a belief or had missed my destiny in life. . . . Why do you sigh in this beastly way, somebody? Absurd? Well, absurd. Good Lord! mustn't a man ever—Here, give me some tobacco."

There was a pause of profound stillness, then a match flared, and Marlow's lean face appeared, worn, hollow, with downward folds and dropped eyelids, with an aspect of concentrated attention; and as he took vigorous draws at his pipe, it seemed to retreat and advance out of the night in the regular flicker of the tiny flame. The match went out.

"Absurd!" he cried. "This is the worst of trying to tell. . . . Here you all are, each moored with two good addresses, like a hulk with two anchors, a butcher round one corner, a policeman round another, excellent appetites, and temperature normal—you hear—normal from year's end to year's end. And you say, Absurd! Absurd be—exploded! Absurd! My dear boys, what can you expect from a man who out of sheer nervousness had just flung overboard a pair of new shoes. Now I think of it, it is amazing I did not shed tears. I am, upon the whole, proud of my fortitude. I was cut to the quick at the idea of having lost the inestimable privilege of listening to the gifted Kurtz. Of course I was wrong. The privilege was waiting for me. Oh yes, I heard more than enough. And I was right, too. A voice. He was very little more than a voice. And I heard—him—it—this voice—other voices—all of them were so little more than voices—and the memory of that time itself lingers around me, impalpable, like a dying vibration of one immense jabber, silly, atrocious, sordid, savage, or simply mean, without any kind of sense. Voices, voices—even the girl herself—now—"

He was silent for a long time.

"I laid the ghost of his gifts at last with a lie," he began suddenly. "Girl!

What? Did I mention a girl? Oh, she is out of it—completely. They—the women I mean—are out of it—should be out of it. We must help them to stay in that beau- 1640 tiful world of their own, lest ours gets worse. Oh, she had to be out of it. You should have heard the disinterred body of Mr. Kurtz saying, 'My Intended.' You would have perceived directly then how completely she was out of it. And the lofty frontal bone of Mr. Kurtz! They say the hair goes on growing sometimes,[15] but this—ah—specimen, was impressively bald. The wilderness had patted him on the head, and, behold, it was like a ball—an ivory ball; it had caressed him, and—lo!—he had withered; it had taken him, loved him, embraced him, got into his veins, consumed his flesh, and sealed his soul to its own by the inconceivable ceremonies of some devilish initiation. He was its spoiled and pampered favorite. Ivory? I should think so. Heaps of it, stacks of it. The old mud shanty was burst- 1650 ing with it. You would think there was not a single tusk left either above or below the ground in the whole country. 'Mostly fossil,' the manager had remarked disparagingly. It was no more fossil than I am; but they call it fossil when it is dug up. It appears these niggers do bury the tusks sometimes—but evidently they couldn't bury this parcel deep enough to save the gifted Mr. Kurtz from his fate. We filled the steamboat with it, and had to pile a lot on the deck. Thus he could see and enjoy as long as he could see, because the appreciation of this favor had remained with him to the last. You should have heard him say, 'My ivory.' Oh yes, I heard him. 'My Intended, my ivory, my station, my river, my—' everything belonged to him. It made me hold my breath in expectation of hearing the wilder- 1660 ness burst in to a prodigious peal of laughter that would shake the fixed stars in their places. Everything belonged to him—but that was a trifle. The thing was to know what he belonged to, how many powers of darkness claimed him for their own. That was the reflection that made you creepy all over. It was impossible—it was not good for one either—trying to imagine. He had taken a high seat amongst the devils of the land—I mean literally. You can't understand. How could you?— with solid pavement under your feet, surrounded by kind neighbors ready to cheer you or to fall on you, stepping delicately between the butcher and the policeman, in the holy terror of scandal and gallows and lunatic asylums—how can you imagine what particular region of the first ages a man's untrammeled feet may 1670 take him into by the way of solitude—utter solitude without a policeman—by the way of silence—utter silence, where no warning voice of a kind neighbor can be heard whispering of public opinion? These little things make all the great difference. When they are gone you must fall back upon your own innate strength, upon your own capacity for faithfulness. Of course you may be too much of a fool to go wrong—too dull even to know you are being assaulted by the powers of darkness. I take it, no fool ever made a bargain for this soul with the devil: the fool is too much of a fool, or the devil too much of a devil—I don't know which. Or you may be such a thunderingly exalted creature as to be altogether deaf and blind to anything but heavenly sights and sounds. Then the earth for you is only a 1680 standing place—and whether to be like this is your loss or your gain I won't pretend to say. But most of us are neither one nor the other. The earth for us is a place to live in, where we must put up with sights, with sounds, with smells too,

15. A reference to the idea that hair continues to grow after death.

by Jove!—breathe dead hippo, so to speak, and not be contaminated. And there, don't you see? your strength comes in, the faith in your ability for the digging of unostentatious holes to bury the stuff in—your power of devotion, not to yourself, but to an obscure, back-breaking business. And that's difficult enough. Mind, I am not trying to excuse or even explain—I am trying to account to myself for— for—Mr. Kurtz—for the shade of Mr. Kurtz. This initiated wraith from the back of Nowhere honored me with its amazing confidence before it vanished altogether. 1690 This was because it could speak English to me. The original Kurtz had been educated partly in England, and—as he was good enough to say himself—his sympathies were in the right place. His mother was half-English, his father was half-French. All Europe contributed to the making of Kurtz; and by-and-by I learned that, most appropriately, the International Society for the Suppression of Savage Customs[16] had entrusted him with the making of a report, for its future guidance. And he had written it too. I've seen it. I've read it. It was eloquent, vibrating with eloquence, but too high-strung, I think. Seventeen pages of close writing he had found time for! But this must have been before his—let us say— nerves, went wrong, and caused him to preside at certain midnight dances ending 1700 with unspeakable rites, which—as far as I reluctantly gathered from what I heard at various times—were offered up to him—do you understand?—to Mr. Kurtz himself. But it was a beautiful piece of writing. The opening paragraph, however, in the light of later information, strikes me now as ominous. He began with the argument that we whites, from the point of development we had arrived at, 'must necessarily appear to them [savages] in the nature of supernatural beings—we approach them with the might as of a deity,' and so on, and so on. 'By the simple exercise of our will we can exert a power for good practically unbounded,' &c., &c. From that point he soared and took me with him. The peroration was magnificent, though difficult to remember, you know. It gave me the notion of an exotic 1710 Immensity ruled by an august Benevolence. It made me tingle with enthusiasm. This was the unbounded power of eloquence—of words—of burning noble words. There were no practical hints to interrupt the magic current of phrases, unless a kind of note at the foot of the last page, scrawled evidently much later, in an unsteady hand, may be regarded as the exposition of a method. It was very simple, and at the end of that moving appeal to every altruistic sentiment it blazed at you, luminous and terrifying, like a flash of lightning in a serene sky: 'Exterminate all the brutes!' The curious part was that he had apparently forgotten all about that valuable postscriptum, because, later on, when he in a sense came to himself, he repeatedly entreated me to take good care of 'my pamphlet' (he 1720 called it), as it was sure to have in the future a good influence upon his career. I had full information about all these things, and, besides, as it turned out, I was to have the care of his memory. I've done enough for it to give me the indisputable right to lay it, if I choose, for an everlasting rest in the dust-bin of progress, amongst all the sweepings and, figuratively speaking, all the dead cats of civilization. But then, you see, I can't choose. He wouldn't be forgotten. Whatever he was, he was not common. He had the power to charm or frighten rudimentary

16. Perhaps a reference to the International Society for the Suppression of Savage Customs, headed by King Leopold of Belgium.

souls into an aggravated witch-dance in his honor; he could also fill the small
souls of the pilgrims with bitter misgivings: he had one devoted friend at least,
and he had conquered one soul in the world that was neither rudimentary nor   1730
tainted with self-seeking. No; I can't forget him, though I am not prepared to affirm the fellow was exactly worth the life we lost in getting to him. I missed my
late helmsman awfully,—I missed him even while his body was still lying in the
pilot-house. Perhaps you will think it passing strange this regret for a savage who
was no more account than a grain of sand in a black Sahara. Well, don't you see,
he had done something, he had steered; for months I had him at my back—a
help—an instrument. It was a kind of partnership. He steered for me—I had to
look after him, I worried about his deficiencies, and thus a subtle bond had been
created, of which I only became aware when it was suddenly broken. And the intimate profundity of that look he gave me when he received his hurt remains to   1740
this day in my memory—like a claim of distant kinship affirmed in a supreme
moment.

"Poor fool! If he had only left that shutter alone. He had no restraint, no restraint—just like Kurtz—a tree swayed in the wind. As soon as I had put on a dry
pair of slippers, I dragged him out, after first jerking the spear out of his side,
which operation I confess I performed with my eyes shut tight. His heels leaped
together over the little door-step; his shoulders were pressed to my breast; I
hugged him from behind desperately. Oh! he was heavy, heavy; heavier than any
man on earth, I should imagine. Then without more ado I tipped him overboard.
The current snatched him as though he had been a wisp of grass, and I saw the   1750
body roll over twice before I lost sight of it for ever. All the pilgrims and the manager were then congregated on the awning-deck about the pilot-house, chattering
at each other like a flock of excited magpies, and there was a scandalized murmur
at my heartless promptitude. What they wanted to keep that body hanging about
for I can't guess. Embalm it, maybe. But I had also heard another, and a very ominous, murmur on the deck below. My friends the wood-cutters were likewise
scandalized, and with a better show of reason—though I admit that the reason itself was quite inadmissible. Oh, quite! I had made up my mind that if my late
helmsman was to be eaten, the fishes alone should have him. He had been a very
second-rate helmsman while alive, but now he was dead he might have become a   1760
first-class temptation, and possibly cause some startling trouble. Besides, I was
anxious to take the wheel, the man in pink pyjamas showing himself a hopeless
duffer at the business.

"This I did directly the simple funeral was over. We were going half-speed,
keeping right in the middle of the stream, and I listened to the talk about me.
They had given up Kurtz, they had given up the station; Kurtz was dead, and the
station had been burnt—and so on—and so on. The red-haired pilgrim was beside himself with the thought that at least this poor Kurtz had been properly re-
venged. 'Say! We must have made a glorious slaughter of them in the bush. Eh?
What do you think? Say?' He positively danced, the bloodthirsty little gingery beg-   1770
gar. And he had nearly fainted when he saw the wounded man! I could not help
saying, 'You made a glorious lot of smoke, anyhow.' I had seen, from the way the
tops of the bushes rustled and flew, that almost all the shots had gone too high.
You can't hit anything unless you take aim and fire from the shoulder; but these

chaps fired from the hip with their eyes shut. The retreat, I maintained—and I was right—was caused by the screeching of the steam-whistle. Upon this they forgot Kurtz, and began to howl at me with indignant protests.

"The manager stood by the wheel murmuring confidentially about the necessity of getting well away down the river before dark at all events, when I saw in the distance a clearing on the river-side and the outlines of some sort of building. 'What's this?' I asked. He clapped his hands in wonder. 'The station!' he cried. I edged in at once, still going half-speed.

"Through my glasses I saw the slope of a hill interspersed with rare trees and perfectly free from undergrowth. A long decaying building on the summit was half buried in the high grass; the large holes in the peaked roof gaped back from afar; the jungle and the woods made a background. There was no inclosure or fence of any kind; but there had been one apparently, for near the house half-a-dozen slim posts remained in a row, roughly trimmed, and with their upper ends ornamented with round curved balls. The rails, or whatever there had been between, had disappeared. Of course the forest surrounded all that. The river-bank was clear, and on the water-side I saw a white man under a hat like a cart-wheel beckoning persistently with his whole arm. Examining the edge of the forest above and below, I was almost certain I could see movements—human forms gliding here and there. I steamed past prudently, then stopped the engines and let her drift down. The man on the shore began to shout, urging us to land. 'We have been attacked,' screamed the manager. 'I know—I know. It's all right,' yelled back the other, as cheerful as you please. 'Come along. It's all right. I am glad.'

"His aspect reminded me of something I had seen—something funny I had seen somewhere. As I maneuvered to get alongside, I was asking myself, 'What does this fellow look like?' Suddenly I got it. He looked like a harlequin. His clothes had been made of some stuff that was brown holland probably, but it was covered with patches all over, with bright patches, blue, red, and yellow,—patches on the back, patches on front, patches on elbows, on knees; colored binding round his jacket, scarlet edging at the bottom of his trousers; and the sunshine made him look extremely gay and wonderfully neat withal, because you could see how beautifully all this patching had been done. A beardless, boyish face, very fair, no features to speak of, nose peeling, little blue eyes, smiles and frowns chasing each other over that open countenance like sunshine and shadow on a wind-swept plain. 'Look out, captain!' he cried; 'there's a snag lodged in here last night.' What! Another snag? I confess I swore shamefully. I had nearly holed my cripple, to finish off that charming trip. The harlequin on the bank turned his little pug nose up to me. 'You English?' he asked, all smiles. 'Are you?' I shouted from the wheel. The smiles vanished, and he shook his head as if sorry for my disappointment. Then he brightened up. 'Never mind!' he cried encouragingly. 'Are we in time?' I asked. 'He is up there,' he replied, with a toss of the head up the hill, and becoming gloomy all of a sudden. His face was like the autumn sky, overcast one moment and bright the next.

'When the manager, escorted by the pilgrims, all of them armed to the teeth, had gone to the house, this chap came on board. 'I say, I don't like this. These natives are in the bush,' I said. He assured me earnestly it was all right. 'They are simple people,' he added; 'well, I am glad you came. It took me all my time to keep them off.' 'But you said it was all right,' I cried. 'Oh, they meant no harm,' he said; and as I stared he corrected himself, 'Not exactly.' Then vivaciously, 'My faith, your pilot-house wants a clean up!' In the next breath he advised me to keep enough steam on the boiler to blow the whistle in case of any trouble. 'One good screech will do more for you than all your rifles. They are simple people,' he repeated. He rattled away at such a rate he quite overwhelmed me. He seemed to be trying to make up for lots of silence, and actually hinted, laughing, that such was the case. 'Don't you talk with Mr. Kurtz?' I said. 'You don't talk with that man— you listen to him,' he exclaimed with severe exaltation. 'But now—' He waved his 1830 arm, and in the twinkling of an eye was in the uttermost depths of despondency. In a moment he came up again with a jump, possessed himself of both my hands, shook them continuously, while he gabbed: 'Brother sailor . . . honor . . . pleasure . . . delight . . . introduce myself . . . Russian . . . son of an archpriest . . . Government of Tambov . . . What? Tobacco! English tobacco; the excellent English tobacco! Now, that's brotherly. Smoke? Where's a sailor that does not smoke?'

"The pipe soothed him, and gradually I made out he had run away from school, had gone to sea in a Russian ship; ran away again; served some time in English ships; was now reconciled with the arch-priest. He made a point of that. 'But when one is young one must see things, gather experience, ideas; enlarge the 1840 mind.' 'Here!' I interrupted. 'You can never tell! Here I have met Mr. Kurtz,' he said, youthfully solemn and reproachful. I held my tongue after that. It appears he had persuaded a Dutch trading-house on the coast to fit him out with stores and goods, and had started for the interior with a light heart, and no more idea of what would happen to him than a baby. He had been wandering about that river for nearly two years alone, cut off from everybody and everything. 'I am not so young as I look. I am twenty-five,' he said. 'At first old Van Shuyten would tell me to go to the devil,' he narrated with keen enjoyment; 'but I stuck to him, and talked and talked, till at last he got afraid I would talk the hind-leg off his favorite dog, so he gave me some cheap things and a few guns, and told me he hoped he 1850 would never see my face again. Good old Dutchman, Van Shuyten. I've sent him one small lot of ivory a year ago, so that he can't call me a little thief when I get back. I hope he got it. And for the rest I don't care. I had some wood stacked for you. That was my old house. Did you see?

"I gave him Towson's book. He made as though he would kiss me, but restrained himself. 'The only book I had left, and I thought I had lost it,' he said, looking at it ecstatically. 'So many accidents happen to a man going about alone, you know. Canoes get upset sometimes—and sometimes you've got to clear out so quick when the people get angry.' He thumbed the pages. 'You made notes in Russian?' I asked. He nodded. 'I thought they were written in cipher,' I said. He 1860 laughed, then became serious. 'I had lots of trouble to keep these people off,' he said. 'Did they want to kill you?' I asked. 'Oh no!' he cried, and checked himself. 'Why did they attack us?' I pursued. He hesitated, then said shamefacedly, 'They don't want him to go.' 'Don't they?' I said, curiously. He nodded a nod full of mystery and wisdom. 'I tell you,' he cried, 'this man has enlarged my mind.' He opened his arms wide, staring at me with his little blue eyes that were perfectly round."

III

"I LOOKED AT HIM, lost in astonishment. There he was before me, in motley,[17] as though he had absconded from a troupe of mimes, enthusiastic, fabulous. His very existence was improbable, inexplicable, and altogether bewildering. He was an insoluble problem. It was inconceivable how he had existed, how he had suc- ceeded in getting so far, how he had managed to remain—why he did not in- stantly disappear. 'I went a little farther,' he said, 'then still a little farther—till I had gone so far that I don't know how I'll ever get back. Never mind. Plenty time. I can manage. You take Kurtz away quick—quick—I tell you.' The glamour of youth enveloped his particolored rags, his destitution, his loneliness, the essential desolation of his futile wanderings. For months—for years—his life hadn't been worth a day's purchase; and there he was gallantly, thoughtlessly alive, to all ap- pearance indestructible solely by the virtue of his few years and of his unreflecting audacity. I was seduced into something like admiration—like envy. Glamour urged him on, glamour kept him unscathed. He surely wanted nothing from the wilder- ness but space to breathe in and to push on through. His need was to exist, and to move onwards at the greatest possible risk, and with a maximum of privation. If the absolutely pure, uncalculating, unpractical spirit of adventure had ever ruled a human being, it ruled this be-patched youth. I almost envied him the possession of this modest and clear flame. It seemed to have consumed all thought of self so completely, that, even while he was talking to you, you forgot that it was he—the man before your eyes—who had gone through these things. I did not envy him his devotion to Kurtz, though. He had not meditated over it. It came to him, and he accepted it with a sort of eager fatalism. I must say that to me it appeared about the most dangerous thing in every way he had come upon so far.

"They had come together unavoidably, like two ships becalmed near each other, and lay rubbing sides at last. I suppose Kurtz wanted an audience, because on a certain occasion, when encamped in the forest, they had talked all night, or more probably Kurtz had talked. 'We talked of everything,' he said, quite trans- ported at the recollection. 'I forgot there was such a thing as sleep. The night did not seem to last an hour. Everything! Everything! . . . Of love too.' 'Ah, he talked to you of love!' I said, much amused. 'It isn't what you think,' he cried, almost pas- sionately. 'It was in general. He made me see things—things.'

"He threw his arms up. We were on deck at the time, and the headman of my wood-cutters, lounging near by, turned upon him his heavy and glittering eyes. I looked around, and I don't know why, but I assure you that never, never before, did this land, this river, this jungle, the very arch of this blazing sky, ap- pear to me so hopeless and so dark, so impenetrable to human thought, so pitiless to human weakness. 'And, ever since, you have been with him, of course?' I said.

"On the contrary. It appears their intercourse had been very much broken by various causes. He had, as he informed me proudly, managed to nurse Kurtz through two illnesses (he alluded to it as you would to some risky feat), but as a rule Kurtz wandered alone, far in the depths of the forest. 'Very often coming to this station, I had to wait days and days before he would turn up,' he said. 'Ah, it

---

17. The many-colored clothes of a harlequin or jester.

was worth waiting for!—sometimes.' 'What was he doing? exploring or what?' I 1910
asked. 'Oh yes, of course'; he had discovered lots of villages, a lake too—he did
not know exactly in what direction, it was dangerous to inquire too much—but
mostly his expeditions had been for ivory. 'But he had no goods to trade with by
that time,' I objected. 'There's a good lot of cartridges left even yet,' he answered,
looking away. 'To speak plainly, he raided the country,' I said. He nodded. 'Not
alone, surely!' He muttered something about the villages round that lake. 'Kurtz
got the tribe to follow him, did he?' I suggested. He fidgeted a little. 'They adored
him,' he said. The tone of these words was so extraordinary that I looked at him
searchingly. It was curious to see his mingled eagerness and reluctance to speak of
Kurtz. The man filled his life, occupied his thoughts, swayed his emotions. 'What 1920
can you expect?' he burst out; 'he came to them with thunder and lightning, you
know—and they had never seen anything like it—and very terrible. He could be
very terrible. You can't judge Mr. Kurtz as you would an ordinary man. No, no,
no! Now—just to give you an idea—I don't mind telling you, he wanted to shoot
me too one day—but I don't judge him.' 'Shoot you!' I cried. 'What for?' 'Well, I
had a small lot of ivory the chief of that village near my house gave me. You see I
used to shoot game for them. Well, he wanted it, and wouldn't hear reason. He declared he would shoot me unless I gave him the ivory and then cleared out of the
country, because he could do so, and had a fancy for it, and there was nothing on
earth to prevent him killing whom he jolly well pleased. And it was true too. I 1930
gave him the ivory. What did I care! But I didn't clear out. No, no. I couldn't leave
him. I had to be careful, of course, till we got friendly again for a time. He had his
second illness then. Afterwards I had to keep out of the way; but I don't mind. He
was living for the most part in those villages on the lake. When he came down to
the river, sometimes he would take me, and sometimes it was better for me to be
careful. This man suffered too much. He hated all this, and somehow he couldn't
get away. When I had a chance I begged him to try and leave while there was time;
I offered to go back with him. And he would say yes, and then he would remain;
go off on another ivory hunt; disappear for weeks; forget himself amongst these
people—forget himself—you know.' 'Why! he's mad,' I said. He protested indig- 1940
nantly. Mr. Kurtz couldn't be mad. If I had heard him talk, only two days ago, I
wouldn't dare hint at such a thing. . . . I had taken up my binoculars while we
talked and was looking at the shore, sweeping the limit of the forest at each side
and at the back of the house. The consciousness of there being people in that
bush, so silent, so quiet—as silent and quiet as the ruined house on the hill—
made me uneasy. There was no sign on the face of nature of this amazing tale that
was not so much told as suggested to me in desolate exclamations, completed by
shrugs, in interrupted phrases, in hints ending in deep sighs. The woods were unmoved, like a mask—heavy, like the closed door of a prison—they looked with
their air of hidden knowledge, of patient expectation, of unapproachable silence. 1950
The Russian was explaining to me that it was only lately that Mr. Kurtz had come
down to the river, bringing along with him all the fighting men of that lake tribe.
He had been absent for several months—getting himself adored, I suppose—and
had come down unexpectedly, with the intention to all appearance of making a
raid either across the river or down stream. Evidently the appetite for more ivory
had got the better of the—what shall I say?—less material aspirations. However he

had got much worse suddenly. 'I heard he was lying helpless, and so I came up—
took my chance,' said the Russian. 'Oh, he is bad, very bad.' I directed my glass to
the house. There were no signs of life, but there was the ruined roof, the long mud
wall peeping above the grass, with three little square window-holes, no two of the   1960
same size; all this brought within reach of my hand, as it were. And then I made a
brusque movement, and one of the remaining posts of that vanished fence leaped
up in the field of my glass. You remember I told you I had been struck at the distance by certain attempts at ornamentation, rather remarkable in the ruinous aspect of the place. Now I had suddenly a nearer view, and its first result was to
make me throw my head back as if before a blow. Then I went carefully from post
to post with my glass, and I saw my mistake. These round knobs were not ornamental but symbolic; they were expressive and puzzling, striking and disturbing—
food for thought and also for the vultures if there had been any looking down
from the sky; but at all events for such ants as were industrious enough to ascend   1970
the pole. They would have been even more impressive, those heads on the stakes,
if their faces had not been turned to the house. Only one, the first I had made out,
was facing my way. I was not so shocked as you may think. The start back I had
given was really nothing but a movement of surprise. I had expected to see a knob
of wood there, you know. I returned deliberately to the first I had seen—and there
it was, black, dried, sunken, with closed eyelids—a head that seemed to sleep at
the top of that pole, and, with the shrunken dry lips showing a narrow white line
of the teeth, was smiling too, smiling continuously at some endless and jocose
dream of that eternal slumber.

"I am not disclosing any trade secrets. In fact the manager said afterwards   1980
that Mr. Kurtz's methods had ruined the district. I have no opinion on that point,
but I want you clearly to understand that there was nothing exactly profitable in
these heads being there. They only showed that Mr. Kurtz lacked restraint in the
gratification of his various lusts, that there was something wanting in him—some
small matter which, when the pressing need arose, could not be found under his
magnificent eloquence. Whether he knew of this deficiency himself I can't say. I
think the knowledge came to him at last—only at the very last. But the wilderness
had found him out early, and had taken on him a terrible vengeance for the fantastic invasion. I think it had whispered to him things about himself which he did
not know, things of which he had no conception till he took counsel with this   1990
great solitude—and the whisper had proved irresistibly fascinating. It echoed
loudly within him because he was hollow at the core. . . . I put down the glass,
and the head that had appeared near enough to be spoken to seemed at once to
have leaped away from me into inaccessible distance.

"The admirer of Mr. Kurtz was a bit crestfallen. In a hurried, indistinct voice
he began to assure me he had not dared to take these—say, symbols—down. He
was not afraid of the natives; they would not stir till Mr. Kurtz gave the word. His
ascendancy was extraordinary. The camps of these people surrounded the place,
and the chiefs came every day to see him. They would crawl. . . . 'I don't want to
know anything of the ceremonies used when approaching Mr. Kurtz,' I shouted.   2000
Curious, this feeling that came over me that such details would be more intolerable than those heads drying on the stakes under Mr. Kurtz's windows. After all,
that was only a savage sight, while I seemed at one bound to have been trans-

ported into some lightless region of subtle horrors, where pure, uncomplicated savagery was a positive relief, being something that had a right to exist—obviously—in the sunshine. The young man looked at me with surprise. I suppose it did not occur to him that Mr. Kurtz was no idol of mine. He forgot I hadn't heard any of these splendid monologues on, what was it? on love, justice, conduct of life—or what not. If it had come to crawling before Mr. Kurtz, he crawled as much as the veriest savage of them all. I had no idea of the conditions, he said: these heads were the heads of rebels. I shocked him excessively by laughing. Rebels! What would be the next definition I was to hear? There had been enemies, criminals, workers—and these were rebels. Those rebellious heads looked very subdued to me on their sticks. 'You don't know how such a life tries a man like Kurtz,' cried Kurtz's last disciple. 'Well, and you?' I said. 'I! I! I am a simple man. I have no great thoughts. I want nothing from anybody. How can you compare me to . . . ?' His feelings were too much for speech, and suddenly he broke down. 'I don't understand,' he groaned. 'I've been doing my best to keep him alive, and that's enough. I had no hand in all this. I have no abilities. There hasn't been a drop of medicine or a mouthful of invalid food for months here. He was shamefully abandoned. A man like this, with such ideas. Shamefully! Shamefully! I—I—haven't slept for the last ten nights. . . .'

"His voice lost itself in the calm of the evening. The long shadows of the forest had slipped down hill while we talked, had gone far beyond the ruined hovel, beyond the symbolic row of stakes. All this was in the gloom, while we down there were yet in the sunshine, and the stretch of the river abreast of the clearing glittered in a still and dazzling splendor, with a murky and over-shadowed bend above and below. Not a living soul was seen on the shore. The bushes did not rustle.

"Suddenly round the corner of the house a group of men appeared, as though they had come up from the ground. They waded waist-deep in the grass, in a compact body, bearing an improvised stretcher in their midst. Instantly, in the emptiness of the landscape, a cry arose whose shrillness pierced the still air like a sharp arrow flying straight to the very heart of the land; and, as if by enchantment, streams of human beings—of naked human beings—with spears in their hands, with bows, with shields, with wild glances and savage movements, were poured into the clearing by the dark-faced and pensive forest. The bushes shook, the grass swayed for a time, and then everything stood still in attentive immobility.

" 'Now, if he does not say the right thing to them we are all done for,' said the Russian at my elbow. The knot of men with the stretcher had stopped too, halfway to the steamer, as if petrified. I saw the man on the stretcher sit up, lank and with an uplifted arm, above the shoulders of the bearers. 'Let us hope that the man who can talk so well of love in general will find some particular reason to spare us this time,' I said. I resented bitterly the absurd danger of our situation, as if to be at the mercy of that atrocious phantom had been a dishonoring necessity. I could not hear a sound, but through my glasses I saw the thin arm extended commandingly, the lower jaw moving, the eyes of that apparition shining darkly far in its bony head that nodded with grotesque jerks. Kurtz—Kurtz—that means short in German—don't it? Well, the name was as true as everything else in his life—and death. He looked at least seven feet long. His covering had fallen off, and his body emerged from it pitiful and appalling as from a winding-sheet. I would see the cage of his ribs all astir, the bones of his arm waving. It was as though an animated image of death carved out of old ivory had been shaking its hand with menaces at a motionless crowd of men made of dark and glittering bronze. I saw him open his mouth wide—it gave him a weirdly voracious aspect, as though he had wanted to swallow all the air, all the earth, all the men before him. A deep voice reached me faintly. He must have been shouting. He fell back suddenly. The stretcher shook as the bearers staggered forward again, and almost at the same time I noticed that the crowd of savages was vanishing without any perceptible movement of retreat, as if the forest that had ejected these beings so suddenly had drawn them in again as the breath is drawn in a long aspiration.

"Some of the pilgrims behind the stretcher carried his arms—two shot-guns, a heavy rifle, and a light revolver-carbine —the thunderbolts of that pitiful Jupiter.[18] The manager bent over him murmuring as he walked beside his head. They laid him down in one of the little cabins—just a room for a bed-place and a camp-stool or two, you know. We had brought his belated correspondence, and a lot of torn envelopes and open letters littered his bed. His hand roamed feebly amongst these papers. I was struck by the fire of his eyes and the composed languor of his expression. It was not so much the exhaustion of disease. He did not seem in pain. This shadow looked satiated and calm, as though for the moment it had had its fill of all the emotions.

"He rustled one of the letters, and looking straight in my face said, 'I am glad.' Somebody had been writing to him about me. These special recommendations were turning up again. The volume of tone he emitted without effort, almost without the trouble of moving his lips, amazed me. A voice! a voice! It was grave, profound, vibrating, while the man did not seem capable of a whisper. However, he had enough strength in him—factitious no doubt—to very nearly make an end of us, as you shall hear directly.

"The manager appeared silently in the doorway; I stepped out at once and he drew the curtain after me. The Russian, eyed curiously by the pilgrims, was staring at the shore. I followed the direction of his glance.

"Dark human shapes could be made out in the distance, flitting indistinctly against the gloomy border of the forest, and near the river two bronze figures, leaning on tall spears, stood in the sunlight under fantastic head-dresses of spotted skins, warlike and still in statuesque repose. And from right to left along the lighted shore moved a wild and gorgeous apparition of a woman.

"She walked with measured steps, draped in striped and fringed cloths, treading the earth proudly, with a slight jingle and flash of barbarous ornaments. She carried her head high; her hair was done in the shape of a helmet; she had brass leggings to the knee, brass wire gauntlets to the elbow, a crimson spot on her tawny cheek, innumerable necklaces of glass beads on her neck; bizarre things, charms, gifts of witch-men, that hung about her, glittered and trembled at every step. She must have had the value of several elephant tusks upon her. She was savage and superb, wild-eyed and magnificent; there was something ominous and stately in her deliberate progress. And in the hush that had fallen suddenly upon

18. Chief god of the Romans.

the whole sorrowful land, the immense wilderness, the colossal body of the fe-
cund and mysterious life seemed to look at her, pensive, as though it had been
looking at the image of its own tenebrous and passionate soul.

"She came abreast of the steamer, stood still, and faced us. Her long shadow
fell to the water's edge. Her face had a tragic and fierce aspect of wild sorrow and 2100
of dumb pain mingled with the fear of some struggling, half-shaped resolve. She
stood looking at us without a stir and like the wilderness itself, with an air of
brooding over an inscrutable purpose. A whole minute passed, and then she made
a step forward. There was a low jingle, a glint of yellow metal, a sway of fringed
draperies, and she stopped as if her heart had failed her. The young fellow by my
side growled. The pilgrims murmured at my back. She looked at us all as if her life
had depended upon the unswerving steadiness of her glance. Suddenly she
opened her bared arms and threw them up rigid above her head, as though in an
uncontrollable desire to touch the sky, and at the same time the swift shadows
darted out on the earth, swept around on the river, gathering the steamer into a 2110
shadowy embrace. A formidable silence hung over the scene.

"She turned away slowly, walked on, following the bank, and passed into the
bushes to the left. Once only her eyes gleamed back at us in the dusk of the thickets before she disappeared.

"'If she had offered to come aboard I really think I would have tried to shoot
her,' said the man of patches, nervously. 'I had been risking my life every day for
the last fortnight to keep her out of the house. She got in one day and kicked up a
row about those miserable rags I picked up in the storeroom to mend my clothes
with. I wasn't decent. At least it must have been that, for she talked like a fury to
Kurtz for an hour, pointing at me now and then. I don't understand the dialect of 2120
this tribe. Luckily for me, I fancy Kurtz felt too ill that day to care, or there would
have been mischief. I don't understand. . . . No —it's too much for me. Ah, well,
it's all over now.'

"At this moment I heard Kurtz's deep voice behind the curtain, 'Save me!—
save the ivory, you mean. Don't tell me. Save *me*! Why, I've had to save you. You
are interrupting my plans now. Sick! Sick! Not so sick as you would like to believe. Never mind. I'll carry my ideas out yet—I will return. I'll show you what can
be done. You with your little peddling notions—you are interfering with me. I will
return. I . . .'

"The manager came out. He did me the honor to take me under the arm and 2130
lead me aside. 'He is very low, very low,' he said. He considered it necessary to
sigh, but neglected to be consistently sorrowful. 'We have done all we could for
him—haven't we? But there is no disguising the fact, Mr. Kurtz has done more
harm than good to the Company. He did not see the time was not ripe for vigorous action. Cautiously, cautiously—that's my principle. We must be cautious yet.
The district is closed to us for a time. Deplorable! Upon the whole, the trade will
suffer. I don't deny there is a remarkable quantity of ivory—mostly fossil. We must
save it, at all events—but look how precarious the position is—and why? Because
the method is unsound.' 'Do you,' said I, looking at the shore, 'call it "unsound
method"?' 'Without doubt,' he exclaimed, hotly. 'Don't you?' . . . 'No method at 2140
all,' I murmured after a while. 'Exactly,' he exulted. 'I anticipated this. Shows a
complete want of judgment. It is my duty to point it out in the proper quarter.'

'Oh,' said I, 'that fellow—what's his name?—the brickmaker, will make a readable report for you.' He appeared confounded for a moment. It seemed to me I had never breathed an atmosphere so vile, and I turned mentally to Kurtz for relief— positively for relief. 'Nevertheless I think Mr. Kurtz is a remarkable man,' I said with emphasis. He started, dropped on me a cold heavy glance, said very quietly, 'He *was*,' and turned his back on me. My hour of favor was over; I found myself lumped along with Kurtz as a partisan of methods for which the time was not ripe: I was unsound! Ah! but it was something to have at least a choice of night- 2150 mares.

"I had turned to the wilderness really, not to Mr. Kurtz, who, I was ready to admit, was as good as buried. And for a moment it seemed to me as if I also were buried in a vast grave full of unspeakable secrets. I felt an intolerable weight op- pressing my breast, the smell of the damp earth, the unseen presence of victorious corruption, the darkness of an impenetrable night. . . . The Russian tapped me on the shoulder. I heard him mumbling and stammering something about 'brother seaman—couldn't conceal—knowledge of matters that would affect Mr. Kurtz's reputation.' I waited. For him evidently Mr. Kurtz was not in his grave; I suspect that for him Mr. Kurtz was one of the immortals. 'Well!' said I at last, 'speak out. 2160 As it happens, I am Mr. Kurtz's friend—in a way.'

"He stated with a good deal of formality that had we not been 'of the same profession,' he would have kept the matter to himself without regard to conse- quences. 'He suspected there was an active ill-will towards him on the part of these white men that—' 'You are right,' I said, remembering a certain conversation I had overheard. 'The manager thinks you ought to be hanged.' He showed a con- cern at this intelligence which amused me at first. 'I had better get out of the way quietly,' he said, earnestly. 'I can do no more for Kurtz now, and they would soon find some excuse. What's to stop them? There's a military post three hundred miles from here.' 'Well, upon my word,' said I, 'perhaps you had better go if you 2170 have any friends amongst the savages near by.' 'Plenty,' he said. 'They are simple people—and I want nothing, you know.' He stood biting his lip, then: 'I don't want any harm to happen to these whites here, but of course I was thinking of Mr. Kurtz's reputation—but you are a brother seaman and—' 'All right,' said I, after a time. 'Mr. Kurtz's reputation is safe with me.' I did not know how truly I spoke.

"He informed me, lowering his voice, that it was Kurtz who had ordered the attack to be made on the steamer. 'He hated sometimes the idea of being taken away—and then again. . . . But I don't understand these matters. I am a simple man. He thought it would scare you away—that you would give it up, thinking him dead. I could not stop him. Oh, I had an awful time of it this last month.' 2180 'Very well,' I said. 'He is all right now.' 'Ye-e-es,' he muttered, not very convinced apparently. 'Thanks,' said I; 'I shall keep my eyes open.' 'But quiet—eh?' he urged, anxiously. 'It would be awful for his reputation if anybody here—' I promised a complete discretion with great gravity. 'I have a canoe and three black fellows waiting not very far. I am off. Could you give me a few Martini-Henry cartridges?' I could, and did, with proper secrecy. He helped himself, with a wink at me, to a handful of my tobacco. 'Between sailors—you know—good English tobacco.' At the door of the pilot-house he turned round—'I say, haven't you a pair of shoes you could spare?' He raised one leg. 'Look.' The soles were tied with knotted

strings sandal-wise under his bare feet. I rooted out an old pair, at which he 2190
looked with admiration before tucking it under his left arm. One of his pockets
(bright red) was bulging with cartridges, from the other (dark blue) peeped
'Towson's Inquiry,' &c., &c. He seemed to think himself excellently well equipped
for a renewed encounter with the wilderness. 'Ah! I'll never, never meet such a
man again. You ought to have heard him recite poetry—his own too it was, he
told me. Poetry!' He rolled his eyes at the recollection of these delights. 'Oh, he enlarged my mind!' 'Good-by,' said I. He shook hands and vanished in the night.
Sometimes I ask myself whether I had every really seen him—whether it was possible to meet such a phenomenon! . . .

"When I woke up shortly after midnight his warning came to mind with its 2200
hint of danger that seemed, in the starred darkness, real enough to make me get up
for the purpose of having a look round. On the hill a big fire burned, illuminating
fitfully a crooked corner of the station-house. One of the agents with a picket of a
few of our blacks, armed for the purpose, was keeping guard over the ivory; but
deep within the forest, red gleams that wavered, that seemed to sink and rise from
the ground amongst confused columnar shapes of intense blackness, showed the
exact position of the camp where Mr. Kurtz's adorers were keeping their uneasy
vigil. The monotonous beating of a big drum filled the air with muffled shocks and
a lingering vibration. A steady droning sound of many men chanting each to himself some weird incantation came out from the black, flat wall of the woods as the 2210
humming of bees comes out of a hive, and had a strange narcotic effect upon my
half-awake senses. I believe I dozed off leaning over the rail, till an abrupt burst of
yells, an overwhelming outbreak of a pent-up and mysterious frenzy, woke me up
in a bewildered wonder. It was cut short all at once, and the low droning went on
with an effect of audible and soothing silence. I glanced casually into the little
cabin. A light was burning within, but Mr. Kurtz was not there.

"I think I would have raised an outcry if I had believed my eyes. But I didn't
believe them at first—the thing seemed so impossible. The fact is I was completely
unnerved by a sheer blank fright, pure abstract terror, unconnected with any distinct shape of physical danger. What made this emotion so overpowering was— 2220
how shall I define it?—the moral shock I received, as if something altogether
monstrous, intolerable to thought and odious to the soul, had been thrust upon
me unexpectedly. This lasted of course the merest fraction of a second, and then
the usual sense of commonplace, deadly danger, the possibility of a sudden onslaught and massacre, or something of the kind, which I saw impending, was positively welcome and composing. It pacified me, in fact, so much, that I did not
raise an alarm.

"There was an agent buttoned up inside an ulster and sleeping on a chair on
deck within three feet of me. The yells had not awakened him; he snored very
slightly; I left him to his slumbers and leaped shore. I did not betray Mr. Kurtz—it 2230
was ordered I should never betray him—it was written I should be loyal to the
nightmare of my choice. I was anxious to deal with this shadow by myself
alone,—and to this day I don't know why I was so jealous of sharing with anyone
the peculiar blackness of that experience.

"As soon as I got on the bank I saw a trail—a broad trail through the grass. I
remember the exultation with which I said to myself, 'He can't walk—he is crawl-

ing on all-fours—I've got him.' The grass was wet with dew. I strode rapidly with clenched fists. I fancy I had some vague notion of falling upon him and giving him a drubbing. I don't know. I had some imbecile thoughts. The knitting old woman with the cat obtruded herself upon my memory as a most improper person to be 2240 sitting at the other end of such an affair. I saw a row of pilgrims squirting lead in the air out of Winchesters held to the hip. I thought I would never get back to the steamer, and imagined myself living alone and unarmed in the woods to an advanced age. Such silly things—you know. And I remember I confounded the beat of the drum with the beating of my heart, and was pleased at its calm regularity.

"I kept to the track though—then stopped to listen. The night was very clear: a dark blue space, sparkling with dew and starlight, in which black things stood very still. I thought I could see a kind of motion ahead of me. I was strangely cocksure of everything that night. I actually left the track and ran in a wide semicircle (I verily believe chuckling to myself) so as to get in front of that 2250 stir, of that motion I had seen—if indeed I had seen anything. I was circumventing Kurtz as though it had been a boyish game.

"I came upon him, and, if he had not heard me coming, I would have fallen over him too, but he got up in time. He rose, unsteady, long, pale, indistinct, like a vapor exhaled by the earth, and swayed slightly, misty and silent before me; while at my back the fires loomed between the trees, and the murmur of many voices issued from the forest. I had cut him off cleverly; but when actually confronting him I seemed to come to my senses, I saw the danger in its right proportion. It was by no means over yet. Suppose he began to shout? Though he could hardly stand, there was still plenty of vigor in his voice. 'Go away—hide yourself,' he said, in 2260 that profound tone. It was very awful. I glanced back. We were within thirty yards from the nearest fire. A black figure stood up, strode on long black legs, waving long black arms, across the glow. It had horns—antelope horns, I think—on its head. Some sorcerer, some witch-man, no doubt; it looked fiend-like enough. 'Do you know what you are doing?' I whispered. 'Perfectly,' he answered, raising his voice for that single word: it sounded to me far off and yet loud, like a hail through a speaking-trumpet. If he makes a row we are lost, I thought to myself. This clearly was not a case for fisticuffs, even apart from the very natural aversion I had to beat that Shadow—this wandering and tormented thing. 'You will be lost.' I said—'utterly lost.' One gets sometimes such a flash of inspiration, you know. I 2270 did say the right thing, though indeed he could not have been more irretrievably lost than he was at this very moment, when the foundations of our intimacy were being laid—to endure—to endure—even to the end—even beyond.

"'I had immense plans,' he muttered irresolutely. 'Yes,' said I; 'but if you try to shout I'll smash your head with—' there was not a stick or a stone near. 'I will throttle you for good,' I corrected myself. 'I was on the threshold of great things,' he pleaded, in a voice of longing, with a wistfulness of tone that made my blood run cold. 'And now for this stupid scoundrel—' 'Your success in Europe is assured in any case,' I affirmed, steadily. I did not want to have the throttling of him, you understand—and indeed it would have been very little use for any practical pur- 2280 pose. I tried to break the spell—the heavy, mute spell of the wilderness—that seemed to draw him to its pitiless breast by the awakening of forgotten and brutal instincts, by the memory of gratified and monstrous passions. This alone, I was convinced, had driven him out to the edge of the forest, to the bush, towards the gleam of fires, the throb of drums, the drone of weird incantations; this alone had beguiled his unlawful soul beyond the bounds of permitted aspirations. And, don't you see, the terror of the position was not in being knocked on the head—though I had a very lively sense of that danger too—but in this, that I had to deal with a being to whom I could not appeal in the name of anything high or low. I had, even like the niggers, to invoke him—himself—his own exalted and incredible degradation. There was nothing either above or below him, and I knew it. He had kicked himself loose of the earth. Confound the man! he had kicked the very earth to pieces. He was alone, and I before him did not know whether I stood on the ground or floated in the air. I've been telling you what we said—repeating the phrases we pronounced,—but what's the good? They were common everyday words,—the familiar, vague sounds exchanged on every waking day of life. But what of that? They had behind them, to my mind, the terrific suggestiveness of words heard in dreams, of phrases spoken in nightmares. Soul! If anybody had ever struggled with a soul, I am the man. And I wasn't arguing with a lunatic either. Believe me or not, his intelligence was perfectly clear—concentrated, it is true, upon himself with horrible intensity, yet clear; and therein was my only chance—barring, of course, the killing him there and then, which wasn't so good, on account of unavoidable noise. But his soul was mad. Being alone in the wilderness, it had looked within itself, and, by heavens! I tell you, it had gone mad. I had—for my sins, I suppose—to go through the ordeal of looking into it myself. No eloquence could have been so withering to one's belief in mankind as his final burst of sincerity. He struggled with himself, too. I saw it,—I heard it. I saw the inconceivable mystery of a soul that knew no restraint, no faith, and no fear, yet struggling blindly with itself. I kept my head pretty well; but when I had him at last stretched on the couch, I wiped my forehead, while my legs shook under me as though I had carried half a ton on my back down that hill. And yet I had only supported him, his bony arm clasped around my neck—and he was not much heavier than a child.

"When next day we left at noon, the crowd, of whose presence behind the curtain of trees I had been acutely conscious all the time, flowed out of the woods again, filled the clearing, covered the slope with a mass of naked, breathing, quivering, bronze bodies. I steamed up a bit, then swung down-stream, and two thousand eyes followed the evolutions of the splashing, thumping, fierce river-demon beating the water with its terrible tail and breathing black smoke into the air. In front of the first rank, along the river, three men, plastered with bright red earth from head to foot, strutted to and fro restlessly. When we came abreast again, they faced the river, stamped their feet, nodded their horned heads, swayed their scarlet bodies; they shook towards the fierce river-demon a bunch of black feathers, a mangy skin with a pendent tail—something that looked like a dried gourd; they shouted periodically together strings of amazing words that resembled no sounds of human language; and the deep murmurs of the crowd, interrupted suddenly, were like the response of some satanic litany.

"We had carried Kurtz into the pilot-house: there was more air there. Lying on the couch, he stared through the open shutter. There was an eddy in the mass of human bodies, and the woman with helmeted head and tawny cheeks rushed out to the very brink of the stream. She put out her hands, shouted something, and all that wild mob took up the shout in a roaring chorus of articulated, rapid, breathless utterance.

"'Do you understand this?' I asked.

"He kept on looking out past me with fiery, longing eyes, with a mingled expression of wistfulness and hate. He made no answer, but I saw a smile, a smile of indefinable meaning, appear on his colorless lips that a moment after twitched convulsively. 'Do I not?' he said slowly, gasping, as if the words had been torn out of him by a supernatural power.

"I pulled the string of the whistle, and I did this because I saw the pilgrims 2340 on deck getting out their rifles with an air of anticipating a jolly lark. At the sudden screech there was a movement of abject terror through that wedged mass of bodies. 'Don't! don't! you frighten them away,' cried someone on deck disconsolately. I pulled the string time after time. They broke and ran, they leaped, they crouched, they swerved, they dodged the flying terror of the sound. The three red chaps had fallen flat, face down on the shore, as though they had been shot dead. Only the barbarous and superb woman did not so much as flinch, and stretched tragically her bare arms after us over the somber and glittering river.

"And then that imbecile crowd down on the deck started their little fun, and I could see nothing more for smoke. 2350

"The brown current ran swiftly out of the heart of darkness, bearing us down towards the sea with twice the speed of our upward progress; and Kurtz's life was running swiftly too, ebbing, ebbing out of his heart into the sea of inexorable time. The manager was very placid, he had no vital anxieties now, he took us both in with a comprehensive and satisfied glance: the 'affair' had come off as well as could be wished. I saw the time approaching when I would be left alone of the party of 'unsound method.' The pilgrims looked upon me with disfavor. I was, so to speak, numbered with the dead. It is strange how I accepted this unforeseen partnership, this choice of nightmares forced upon me in the tenebrous land invaded by these mean and greedy phantoms. 2360

"Kurtz discoursed. A voice! a voice! It rang deep to the very last. It survived his strength to hide in the magnificent folds of eloquence the barren darkness of his heart. Oh, he struggled! he struggled! The wastes of his weary brain were haunted by shadowy images now—images of wealth and fame revolving obsequiously round his unextinguishable gift of noble and lofty expression. My Intended, my station, my career, my ideas—these were the subjects for the occasional utterances of elevated sentiments. The shade of the original Kurtz frequented the bedside of the hollow sham, whose fate it was to be buried presently in the mold of primeval earth. But both the diabolic love and the unearthly hate of the mysteries it had penetrated fought for the possession of that soul satiated with 2370 primitive emotions, avid of lying fame, of sham distinction, of all the appearances of success and power.

"Sometimes he was contemptibly childish. He desired to have kings meet him at railway-stations on his return from some ghastly Nowhere, where he intended to accomplish great things. 'You show them you have in you something that is really profitable, and then there will be no limits to the recognition of your ability,' he would say. 'Of course you must take care of the motives—right motives—always.' The long reaches that were like one and the same reach, monotonous bends that were exactly alike, slipped past the steamer with their multitude of secular trees looking patiently after this grimy fragment of another world, the forerunner of change, of conquest, of trade, of massacres, of blessings. I looked ahead—piloting. 'Close the shutter,' said Kurtz suddenly one day; 'I can't bear to look at this.' I did so. There was a silence. 'Oh, but I will wring your heart yet!' he cried at the invisible wilderness. 2380

"We broke down—as I had expected—and had to lie up for repairs at the head of an island. This delay was the first thing that shook Kurtz's confidence. One morning he gave me a packet of papers and a photograph,—the lot tied together with a shoestring. 'Keep this for me,' he said. 'This noxious fool' (meaning the manager) 'is capable of prying into my boxes when I am not looking.' In the afternoon I saw him. He was lying on his back with closed eyes, and I withdrew quietly, but I heard him mutter, 'Live rightly, die, die . . .' I listened. There was nothing more. Was he rehearsing some speech in his sleep, or was it a fragment of a phrase from some newspaper article? He had been writing for the papers and meant to do so again, 'for the furthering of my ideas. It's a duty.' 2390

"His was an impenetrable darkness. I looked at him as you peer down at a man who is lying at the bottom of a precipice where the sun never shines. But I had not much time to give him, because I was helping the engine-driver to take to pieces the leaky cylinders, to straighten a bent connecting-rod, and in other such matters. I lived in an infernal mess of rust, filings, nuts, bolts, spanners, hammers, ratchet-drills—things I abominate, because I don't get on with them. I tended the little forge we fortunately had aboard; I toiled wearily in a wretched scrap-heap—unless I had the shakes too bad to stand. 2400

"One evening coming in with a candle I was startled to hear him say a little tremulously, 'I am lying here in the dark waiting for death.' The light was within a foot of his eyes. I forced myself to murmur. 'Oh, nonsense!' and stood over him as if transfixed.

"Anything approaching the change that came over his features I have never seen before, and hope never to see again. Oh, I wasn't touched. I was fascinated. It was as though a veil had been rent. I saw on that ivory face the expression of somber pride, of ruthless power, of craven terror—of an intense and hopeless despair. Did he live his life again in every detail of desire, temptation, and surrender during that supreme moment of complete knowledge? He cried in a whisper at some image, at some vision,—he cried out twice, a cry that was no more than a breath— 2410

" 'The horror! The horror!'

"I blew the candle out and left the cabin. The pilgrims were dining in the mess-room, and I took my place opposite the manager, who lifted his eyes to give me a questioning glance, which I successfully ignored. He leaned back, serene, with that peculiar smile of his sealing the unexpressed depths of his meanness. A continuous shower of small flies streamed upon the lamp, upon the cloth, upon our hands and faces. Suddenly the manager's boy put his insolent black head in the doorway, and said in a tone of scathing contempt— 2420

" 'Mistah Kurtz—he dead.'

"All the pilgrims rushed out to see. I remained, and went on with my dinner.

I believe I was considered brutally callous. However, I did not eat much. There was a lamp in there—light, don't you know—and outside it was so beastly, beastly dark. I went no more near the remarkable man who had pronounced a judgment upon the adventures of his soul on this earth. The voice was gone. What else had been there? But I am of course aware that next day the pilgrims buried something in a muddy hole.   2430

"And then they very nearly buried me.

"However, as you see, I did not go to join Kurtz there and then. I did not. I remained to dream the nightmare out to the end, and to show my loyalty to Kurtz once more. Destiny. My destiny! Droll thing life is—that mysterious arrangement of merciless logic for a futile purpose. The most you can hope from it is some knowledge of yourself—that comes too late—a crop of unextinguishable regrets. I have wrestled with death. It is the most unexciting contest you can imagine. It takes place in an impalpable grayness, with nothing underfoot, with nothing around, without spectators, without clamor, without glory, without the great de- sire of victory, without the great fear of defeat, in a sickly atmosphere of tepid   2440 skepticism, without much belief in your own right, and still less in that of your adversary. If such is the form of ultimate wisdom, then life is a greater riddle than some of us think it to be. I was within a hair's-breadth of the last opportunity for pronouncement, and I found with humiliation that probably I would have nothing to say. This is the reason why I affirm that Kurtz was a remarkable man. He had something to say. He said it. Since I had peeped over the edge myself, I under- stand better the meaning of his stare, that could not see the flame of the candle, but was wide enough to embrace the whole universe, piercing enough to penetrate all the hearts that beat in the darkness. He had summed up—he had judged. 'The horror!' He was a remarkable man. After all, this was the expression of some sort   2450 of belief; it had candor, it had conviction, it had a vibrating note of revolt in its whisper, it had the appalling face of a glimpsed truth—the strange commingling of desire and hate. And it is not my own extremity I remember best—a vision of grayness without form filled with physical pain, and a careless contempt for the evanescence of all things—even of this pain itself. No! It is his extremity that I seem to have lived through. True, he had made that last stride, he had stepped over the edge, while I had been permitted to draw back my hesitating foot. And perhaps in this is the whole difference; perhaps all the wisdom, and all truth, and all sincerity, are just compressed into the inappreciable moment of time in which we step over the threshold of the invisible. Perhaps! I like to think my summing-   2460 up would not have been a world of careless contempt. Better his cry—much bet- ter. It was an affirmation, a moral victory paid for by innumerable defeats, by abominable terrors, by abominable satisfactions. But it was a victory! That is why I have remained loyal to Kurtz to the last, and even beyond, when a long time after I heard once more, not his own voice, but the echo of his magnificent eloquence thrown to me from a soul as translucently pure as a cliff of crystal.

"No, they did not bury me, though there is a period of time which I re- member mistily, with a shuddering wonder, like a passage through some incon- ceivable world that had no hope in it and no desire. I found myself back in the sepulchral city resenting the sight of people hurrying through the streets to filch a   2470

little money from each other, to devour their infamous cookery, to gulp their unwholesome beer, to dream their insignificant and silly dreams. They trespassed
upon my thoughts. They were intruders whose knowledge of life was to me an ir-
ritating pretense, because I felt so sure they could not possibly know the things I
knew. Their bearing, which was simply the bearing of commonplace individuals
going about their business in the assurance of perfect safety, was offensive to me
like the outrageous flauntings of folly in the face of a danger it is unable to comprehend. I had no particular desire to enlighten them, but I had some difficulty
in restraining myself from laughing in their faces, so full of stupid importance. I
dare say I was not very well at that time. I tottered about the streets—there were   2480
various affairs to settle—grinning bitterly at perfectly respectable persons. I admit
my behavior was inexcusable, but then my temperature was seldom normal in
these days. My dear aunt's endeavors to 'nurse up my strength' seemed altogether
beside the mark. It was not my strength that wanted nursing, it was my imagination that wanted soothing. I kept the bundle of papers given me by Kurtz, not
knowing exactly what to do with it. His mother had died lately, watched over, as
I was told, by his Intended. A clean-shaved man, with an official manner and
wearing gold-rimmed spectacles, called on me one day and made inquiries, at
first circuitous, afterwards suavely pressing, about what he was pleased to denominate certain 'documents.' I was not surprised, because I had had two rows   2490
with the manager on the subject out there. I had refused to give up the smallest
scrap out of that package, and I took the same attitude with the spectacled man.
He became darkly menacing at last, and with much heat argued that the
Company had the right to every bit of information about its 'territories.' And, said
he, 'Mr. Kurtz's knowledge of unexplored regions must have been necessarily extensive and peculiar—owing to his great abilities and to the deplorable circumstances in which he had been placed: therefore'—I assured him Mr. Kurtz's
knowledge, however extensive, did not bear upon the problems of commerce or
administration. He invoked then the name of science. 'It would be an incalcula-
ble loss if,' &c., &c. I offered him the report on the 'Suppression of Savage   2500
Customs,' with the postscriptum torn off. He took it up eagerly, but ended by
sniffing at it with an air of contempt. 'This is not what we had a right to expect,'
he remarked. 'Expect nothing else,' I said. 'There are only private letters.' He
withdrew upon some threat of legal proceedings, and I saw him no more; but another fellow, calling himself Kurtz's cousin, appeared two days later, and was anxious to hear all the details about his dear relative's last moments. Incidentally he
gave me to understand that Kurtz had been essentially a great musician. 'There
was the making of an immense success,' said the man, who was an organist, I believe, with lank gray hair flowing over a greasy coat-collar. I had no reason to
doubt his statement; and to this day I am unable to say what was Kurtz's profes-   2510
sion, whether he ever had any—which was the greatest of his talents. I had taken
him for a painter who wrote for the papers, or else for a journalist who could
print—but even the cousin (who took snuff during the interview) could not tell
me what he had been—exactly. He was a universal genius—on that point I
agreed with the old chap, who thereupon blew his nose noisily into a large cotton
handkerchief and withdrew in senile agitation, bearing off some family letters and

memoranda without importance. Ultimately a journalist anxious to know something of the fate of his 'dear colleague' turned up. This visitor informed me Kurtz's proper sphere ought to have been politics 'on the popular side.' He had furry straight eyebrows, bristly hair cropped short, an eye-glass on a broad ribbon, and, becoming expansive, confessed his opinion that Kurtz really couldn't write a bit—'but heavens! how that man could talk! He electrified large meetings. He had faith—don't you see?—he had the faith. He could get himself to believe anything—anything. He would have been a splendid leader of an extreme party.' 'What party?' I asked. 'Any party,' answered the other. 'He was an—an—extremist.' Did I not think so? I assented. Did I know, he asked, with a sudden flash of curiosity, 'what it was that had induced him to go out there?' 'Yes,' said I, and forthwith handed him the famous Report for publication, if he thought fit. He glanced through it hurriedly, mumbling all the time, judged 'it would do,' and took himself off with this plunder.

"Thus I was left at last with a slim packet of letters and the girl's portrait. She struck me as beautiful—I mean she had a beautiful expression. I know that the sunlight can be made to lie too, yet one felt that no manipulation of light and pose could have conveyed the delicate shade of truthfulness upon those features. She seemed ready to listen without mental reservation, without suspicion, without a thought for herself. I concluded I would go and give her back her portrait and those letters myself. Curiosity? Yes; and also some other feeling perhaps. All that had been Kurtz's had passed out of my hands: his soul, his body, his station, his plans, his ivory, his career. There remained only his memory and his Intended—and I wanted to give that up too to the past, in a way,—to surrender personally all that remained of him with me to that oblivion which is the last word of our common fate. I don't defend myself. I had no clear perception of what it was I really wanted. Perhaps it was an impulse of unconscious loyalty, or the fulfillment of one of these ironic necessities that lurk in the facts of human existence. I don't know. I can't tell. But I went.

"I thought his memory was like the other memories of the dead that accumulate in every man's life—a vague impress on the brain of shadows that had fallen on it in their swift and final passage; but before the high and ponderous door, between the tall houses of a street as still and decorous as a well-kept alley in a cemetery, I had a vision of him on the stretcher, opening his mouth voraciously, as if to devour all the earth with all its mankind. He lived then before me; he lived as much as he had ever lived—a shadow insatiable of splendid appearances, of frightful realities; a shadow darker than the shadow of the night, and draped nobly in the folds of a gorgeous eloquence. The vision seemed to enter the house with me—the stretcher, the phantom-bearers, the wild crowd of obedient worshipers, the gloom of the forests, the glitter of the reach between the murky bends, the beat of the drum, regular and muffled like the beating of a heart—the heart of a conquering darkness. It was a moment of triumph for the wilderness, an invading and vengeful rush which, it seemed to me, I would have to keep back alone for the salvation of another soul. And the memory of what I had heard him say afar there, with the horned shapes stirring at my back, in the glow of fires, within the patient woods, those broken phrases came back to me, were heard again in their ominous and terrifying simplicity. I remembered his abject pleading, his abject threats, the colossal scale of his vile desires, the meanness, the torment, the tempestuous anguish of his soul. And later on I seemed to see his collected languid manner, when he said one day, 'This lot of ivory now is really mine. The Company did not pay for it. I collected it myself at a very great personal risk. I am afraid they will try to claim it as theirs though. H'm. It is a difficult case. What do you think I ought to do—resist? Eh? I want no more than justice.' . . . He wanted no more than justice—no more than justice. I rang the bell before a mahogany door on the first floor, and while I waited he seemed to stare at me out of the glassy panel—stare with that wide and immense stare embracing, condemning, loathing all the universe. I seemed to hear the whispered cry, 'The horror! The horror!'

"The dusk was falling. I had to wait in a lofty drawing-room with three long windows from floor to ceiling that were like three luminous and bedraped columns. The bent gilt legs and backs of the furniture shone in indistinct curves. The tall marble fireplace had a cold and monumental whiteness. A grand piano stood massively in a corner, with dark gleams on the flat surfaces like a somber and polished sarcophagus. A high door opened—closed. I rose.

"She came forward, all in black, with a pale head, floating towards me in the dusk. She was in mourning. It was more than a year since his death, more than a year since the news came; she seemed as though she would remember and mourn for ever. She took both my hands in hers and murmured, 'I had heard you were coming.' I noticed she was not very young—I mean not girlish. She had a mature capacity for fidelity, for belief, for suffering. The room seemed to have grown darker, as if all the sad light of the cloudy evening had taken refuge on her forehead. This fair hair, this pale visage, this pure brow, seemed surrounded by an ashy halo from which the dark eyes looked out at me. Their glance was guileless, profound, confident, and trustful. She carried her sorrowful head as though she were proud of that sorrow, as though she would say, I—I alone know how to mourn for him as he deserves. But while we were shaking hands, such a look of awful desolation came upon her face that I perceived she was one of those creatures that are not the playthings of Time. For her he had died only yesterday. And, by Jove! The impression was so powerful that for me too he seemed to have died only yesterday—nay, this very minute. I saw her and him in the same instant of time—his death and her sorrow—I saw her sorrow in the very moment of his death. Do you understand? I saw them together—I heard them together. She had said, with a deep catch of the breath, 'I have survived;' while my strained ears seemed to hear distinctly, mingled with her tone of despairing regret, the summing-up whisper of his eternal condemnation. I asked myself what I was doing there, with a sensation of panic in my heart as though I had blundered into a place of cruel and absurd mysteries not fit for a human being to behold. She motioned me to a chair. We sat down, I laid the packet gently on the little table, and she put her hand over it . . . 'You knew him well,' she murmured, after a moment of mourning silence.

"'Intimacy grows quick out there,' I said. 'I knew him as well as it is possible for one man to know another.'

"'And you admired him,' she said. 'It was impossible to know him and not to admire him. Was it?'

"'He was a remarkable man,' I said, unsteadily. Then before the appealing fixity of her gaze, that seemed to watch for more words on my lips, I went on, 'It was impossible not to—'

"'Love him,' she finished eagerly, silencing me into an appalled dumbness. 'How true! how true! But when you think that no one knew him so well as I! I had all his noble confidence. I knew him best.'

"'You knew him best,' I repeated. And perhaps she did. But with every word spoken the room was growing darker, and only her forehead, smooth and white, remained illumined by the unextinguishable light of belief and love.

"'You were his friend,' she went on. 'His friend,' she repeated, a little louder. 'You must have been, if he had given you this, and sent you to me. I feel I can speak to you—and oh! I must speak. I want you—you who have heard his last words—to know I have been worthy of him. . . . It is not pride. . . . Yes! I am proud to know I understood him better than anyone on earth—he told me so himself. And since his mother died I have had no one—no one—to—to—'

"I listened. The darkness deepened. I was not even sure whether he had given me the right bundle. I rather suspect he wanted me to take care of another batch of his papers which, after his death, I saw the manager examining under the lamp. And the girl talked, easing her pain in the certitude of my sympathy; she talked as thirsty men drink. I had heard that her engagement with Kurtz had been disapproved by her people. He wasn't rich enough or something. And indeed I don't know whether he had not been a pauper all his life. He had given me some reason to infer that it was his impatience of comparative poverty that drove him out there.

"'. . .Who was not his friend who had heard him speak once?' she was saying. 'He drew men towards him by what was best in them.' She looked at me with intensity. 'It is the gift of the great,' she went on, and the sound of her low voice seemed to have the accompaniment of all the other sounds, full of mystery, desolation, and sorrow, I had ever heard—the ripple of the river, the soughing of the trees swayed by the wind, the murmurs of wild crows, the faint ring of incomprehensible words cried from afar, the whisper of a voice speaking from beyond the threshold of an eternal darkness. 'But you have heard him! You know!' she cried.

"'Yes, I know,' I said with something like despair in my heart, but bowing my head before the faith that was in her, before that great and saving illusion that shone with an unearthly glow in the darkness, in the triumphant darkness from which I could not have defended her—from which I could not even defend myself.

"'What a loss to me—to us!'—she corrected herself with beautiful generosity; then added in a murmur, 'To the world.' By the last gleams of twilight I could see the glitter of her eyes, full of tears—of tears that would not fall.

"'I have been very happy—very fortunate—very proud,' she went on. 'Too fortunate. Too happy for a little while. And now I am unhappy—for life.'

"She stood up; her fair hair seemed to catch all the remaining light in a glimmer of gold. I rose too.

"'And of all this,' she went on, mournfully, 'of all his promise, and of all his greatness, of his generous mind, of his noble heart, nothing remains—nothing but a memory. You and I—'

"'We shall always remember him,' I said, hastily.

"'No!' she cried. 'It is impossible that all this should be lost—that such a life should be sacrificed to leave nothing—but sorrow. You know what vast plans he had. I knew of them too—I could not perhaps understand,—but others knew of them. Something must remain. His words, at least, have not died.' 2660

"'His words will remain,' I said.

"'And his example,' she whispered to herself. 'Men looked up to him,—his goodness shone in every act. His example—'

"'True,' I said; 'his example too. Yes, his example. I forgot that.'

"'But I do not. I cannot—I cannot believe—not yet. I cannot believe that I shall never see him again, that nobody will see him again, never, never, never.'

"She put out her arms as if after a retreating figure, stretching them back and with clasped pale hands across the fading and narrow sheen of the window. Never see him! I saw him clearly enough then. I shall see this eloquent phantom as long as I live, and I shall see her too, a tragic and familiar Shade, resembling in this gesture another one, tragic also, and bedecked with powerless charms, stretching bare brown arms over the glitter of the infernal stream, the stream of darkness. She said suddenly very low, 'He died as he lived.' 2670

"'His end,' said I, with dull anger stirring in me, 'was in every way worthy of his life.'

"'And I was not with him,' she murmured. My anger subsided before a feeling of infinite pity.

"'Everything that could be done—' I mumbled. 2680

"'Ah, but I believed in him more than anyone on earth—more than his own mother, more than—himself. He needed me! Me! I would have treasured every sigh, every word, every sign, every glance.'

"I felt like a chill grip on my chest. 'Don't ,' I said, in a muffled voice.

"'Forgive me. I—I—have mourned so long in silence—in silence. . . . You were with him—to the last? I think of his loneliness. Nobody near to understand him as I would have understood. Perhaps no one to hear. . . .'

"'To the very end,' I said, shakily. 'I heard his very last words. . . .' I stopped in a fright.

"'Repeat them,' she murmured in a heart-broken tone. 'I want—I want— something—something—to—to live with.' 2690

"I was on the point of crying at her, 'Don't you hear them?' The dusk was repeating them in a persistent whisper all around us, in a whisper that seemed to swell menacingly like the first whisper of a rising wind. 'The horror! The horror!'

"'His last word—to live with,' she insisted. 'Don't you understand I loved him—I loved him—I loved him!'

"I pulled myself together and spoke slowly.

"'The last word he pronounced was—your name.'

"I heard a light sigh, and then my heart stood still, stopped dead short by an exulting and terrible cry, by the cry of inconceivable triumph and of unspeakable pain. 'I knew it—I was sure!'. . . She knew. She was sure. I heard her weeping; she had hidden her face in her hands. It seemed to me that the house would collapse before I could escape, that the heavens would fall upon my head. But nothing happened. The heavens do not fall for such a trifle. Would they have fallen, I won- 2700 der, if I had rendered Kurtz that justice which was his due? Hadn't he said he wanted only justice? But I couldn't. I could not tell her. It would have been too dark—too dark altogether. . . ."

Marlow ceased, and sat apart, indistinct and silent, in the pose of a meditating Buddha. Nobody moved for a time. "We have lost the first of the ebb," said the Director, suddenly. I raised my head. The offing was barred by a black bank of 2710 clouds, and the tranquil waterway leading to the uttermost ends of the earth flowed somber under an overcast sky—seemed to lead into the heart of an immense darkness.   [1899]

Questions for Discussion and Writing

1. Characterize the narrator, Marlow. How does his character affect the story he tells?
2. What is the function of the framing device? How would the story be different without it?
3. In what various ways is the term "darkness" used in the story?
4. Analyze the motives of the various characters or groups of characters. Why does each go to Africa? What does each hope to obtain?
5. What does Kurtz mean at the end when he cries, "The horror! The Horror!"
6. Why does Marlow lie to Kurtz's intended? Is he justified? Why or why not?
7. How does "Heart of Darkness" differ from a conventional adventure story? How do Marlow and Kurtz differ from typical adventure story heroes?

∾ O. HENRY (WILLIAM SIDNEY PORTER)
(1862–1910)

The Gift of the Magi

The stories of O. Henry are less well-known today than they were during his lifetime. In the early years of this century, O. Henry was an enormously popular author whose "trick ending" stories epitomized the form for many readers. He was regarded as America's premier short story writer.

Porter was born in North Carolina, but after high school drifted west and ended up in Texas, where he worked for a while on a cattle ranch. For two years (1894–1895) he was the owner of and sole writer for a paper called *The Rolling Stone*. When it failed, he moved to Austin, where he met his wife and worked as a bank teller. In 1895, he was dismissed for irregularities in his accounts and fled to Honduras to escape prosecution, but when his wife fell ill in 1897, he returned to Texas, was convicted, and spent three years in the Federal prison at Columbus, Ohio. To support his daughter, Porter began writing stories and publishing under the name of O. Henry.

Released in 1902, Porter went to New York City and continued writing so successfully that he was hired by the *Sunday World* at $100 per story—a high price at that time. No matter how much money he earned, however, he always spent more; debt may have been the motivation his creativity needed.

O. Henry loved to side with the underdog and society's outcasts—petty criminals, prostitutes, bums, the working poor. He became the poet laureate of New York City, creating his own *Arabian Nights* stories for the city he called "Baghdad-on-the-subway." A small handful of his stories are kept alive in anthologies, but critics fault him for lacking depth and seriousness, as well as for reducing the short story to a simple, plot-dominated formula. His faults, however, must be balanced against his skill in manipulating his formula, creating memorable characters, and capturing the vitality and tragicomedy of the American city.

ONE DOLLAR AND EIGHTY-SEVEN CENTS. That was all. And sixty cents of it was in pennies. Pennies saved one and two at a time by bulldozing the grocer and the vegetable man and the butcher until one's cheeks burned with the silent imputation of parsimony that such close dealing implied. Three times Della counted it. One dollar and eighty-seven cents. And the next day would be Christmas.

There was clearly nothing to do but flop down on the shabby little couch and howl. So Della did it. Which instigates the moral reflection that life is made up of sobs, sniffles, and smiles, with sniffles predominating.

While the mistress of the home is gradually subsiding from the first stage to the second, take a look at the home. A furnished flat at $8 per week. It did not exactly beggar description, but it certainly had the word on the lookout for the mendicancy squad.

In the vestibule below was a letter-box into which no letter would go, and an electric button from which no mortal finger could coax a ring. Also appertaining thereunto was a card bearing the name "Mr. James Dillingham Young."

The "Dillingham" had been flung to the breeze during a former period of prosperity when its possessor was being paid $30 per week. Now, when the income was shrunk to $20, the letters of "Dillingham" looked blurred, as though they were thinking seriously of contracting to a modest and unassuming D. But whenever Mr. James Dillingham Young came home and reached his flat above he was called "Jim" and greatly hugged by Mrs. James Dillingham Young, already introduced to you as Della. Which is all very good.

Della finished her cry and attended to her cheeks with the powder rag. She stood by the window and looked out dully at a gray cat walking a gray fence in a gray backyard. Tomorrow would be Christmas Day and she had only $1.87 with which to buy Jim a present. She had been saving every penny she could for months, with this result. Twenty dollars a week doesn't go far. Expenses had been greater than she had calculated. They always are. Only $1.87 to buy a present for Jim. Her Jim. Many a happy hour she had spent planning for something nice for

him. Something fine and rare and sterling—something just a little bit near to 30
being worthy of the honor of being owned by Jim.

There was a pier-glass between the windows of the room. Perhaps you have
seen a pier-glass in an $8 flat. A very thin and very agile person may, by observing
his reflection in a rapid sequence of longitudinal strips, obtain a fairly accurate
conception of his looks. Della, being slender, had mastered the art.

Suddenly she whirled from the window and stood before the glass. Her eyes
were shining brilliantly, but her face had lost its color within twenty seconds.
Rapidly she pulled down her hair and let it fall to its full length.

Now, there were two possessions of the James Dillingham Youngs in which
they both took a mighty pride. One was Jim's gold watch that had been his father's 40
and his grandfather's. The other was Della's hair. Had the Queen of Sheba lived in
the flat across the airshaft, Della would have let her hair hang out the window
some day to dry just to depreciate Her Majesty's jewels and gifts. Had King
Solomon[1] been the janitor, with all his treasures piled up in the basement, Jim
would have pulled out his watch every time he passed, just to see him pluck at his
beard from envy.

So now Della's beautiful hair fell about her rippling and shining like a cascade of brown waters. It reached below her knee and made itself almost a garment
for her. And then she did it up again nervously and quickly. Once she faltered for
a minute and stood still while a tear or two splashed on the worn red carpet. 50

On went her old brown jacket; on went her old brown hat. With a whirl of
skirts and with the brilliant sparkle still in her eyes, she fluttered out the door and
down the stairs to the street.

Where she stopped the sign read: "Mme. Sofronie. Hair Goods of All Kinds."
One flight up Della ran, and collected herself, panting. Madame, large, too white,
chilly, hardly looked the "Sofronie."

"Will you buy my hair?" asked Della.

"I buy hair," said Madame. "Take yer hat off and let's have a sight at the looks
of it."

Down rippled the brown cascade. 60

"Twenty dollars," said Madame, lifting the mass with a practised hand.

"Give it to me quick," said Della.

Oh, and the next two hours tripped by on rosy wings. Forget the hashed
metaphor. She was ransacking the stores for Jim's present.

She found it at last. It surely had been made for Jim and no one else. There
was no other like it in any of the stores, and she had turned all of them inside out.
It was a platinum fob chain simple and chaste in design, properly proclaiming its
value by substance alone and not by meretricious ornamentation—as all good
things should do. It was even worthy of The Watch. As soon as she saw it she
knew that it must be Jim's. It was like him. Quietness and value—the description 70
applied to both. Twenty-one dollars they took from her for it, and she hurried
home with the 87 cents. With that chain on his watch Jim might be properly anxious about the time in any company. Grand as the watch was, he sometimes

1. Solomon, King of Israel ca. 962–922 B.C., was noted for his wealth and wisdom; the Queen of Sheba
(present-day Yemen) visited him, bringing lavish gifts, to test his wisdom. I Kings 10: 1–13.

looked at it on the sly on account of the old leather strap that he used in place of a chain.

When Della reached home her intoxication gave way a little to prudence and reason. She got out her curling irons and lighted the gas and went to work repairing the ravages made by generosity added to love. Which is always a tremendous task, dear friends—a mammoth task.

Within forty minutes her head was covered with tiny, close-lying curls that   80
made her look wonderfully like a truant schoolboy. She looked at her reflection in the mirror long, carefully, and critically.

"If Jim doesn't kill me," she said to herself, "before he takes a second look at me, he'll say I look like a Coney Island Chorus girl. But what could I do—oh! what could I do with a dollar and eighty-seven cents?"

At 7 o'clock the coffee was made and the frying-pan was on the back of the stove hot and ready to cook the chops.

Jim was never late. Della doubled the fob chain in her hand and sat on the corner of the table near the door that he always entered. Then she heard his step on the stair away down on the first flight, and she turned white for just a moment.   90
She had a habit of saying little silent prayers about the simplest everyday things, and now she whispered: "Please God, make him think I am still pretty."

The door opened and Jim stepped in and closed it. He looked thin and very serious. Poor fellow, he was only twenty-two—and to be burdened with a family! He needed a new overcoat and he was without gloves.

Jim stepped inside the door, as immovable as a setter at the scent of quail. His eyes were fixed upon Della, and there was an expression in them that she could not read, and it terrified her. It was not anger, nor surprise, nor disapproval, nor horror, nor any of the sentiments that she had been prepared for. He simply started at her fixedly with that peculiar expression on his face.   100

Della wriggled off the table, and went for him.

"Jim, darling," she cried, "don't look at me that way. I had my hair cut off and sold it because I couldn't have lived through Christmas without giving you a present. It'll grow out again—you won't mind, will you? I just had to do it. My hair grows awfully fast. Say 'Merry Christmas!' Jim, and let's be happy. You don't know what a nice—what a beautiful, nice gift I've got for you."

"You've cut off your hair?" asked Jim, laboriously, as if he had not arrived at that patent fact yet even after the hardest mental labor.

"Cut it off and sold it," said Della. "Don't you like me just as well, anyhow? I'm me without my hair, ain't I?"   110

Jim looked about the room curiously.

"You say your hair is gone?" he said, with an air almost of idiocy.

"You needn't look for it," said Della. "It's sold, I tell you—sold and gone, too. It's Christmas Eve, boy. Be good to me, for it went for you. Maybe the hairs of my head were numbered," she went on with a sudden serious sweetness, "but nobody could ever count my love for you. Shall I put the chops on, Jim?"

Out of his trance Jim seemed quickly to wake. He enfolded his Della. For ten seconds let us regard with discreet scrutiny some inconsequential object in the other direction. Eight dollars a week or a million a year—what is the difference? A mathematician or a wit would give you the wrong answer. The magi brought valu-   120 able gifts, but that was not among them. This dark assertion will be illuminated later on.

Jim drew a package from his overcoat pocket and threw it upon the table.

"Don't make any mistake, Dell," he said, "about me. I don't think there's anything in the way of a haircut or a shave or a shampoo that could make me like my girl any less. But if you'll unwrap that package you may see why you had me going a while at first."

White fingers and nimble tore at the string and paper. And then an ecstatic scream of joy; and then alas! a quick feminine change to hysterical tears and wails, necessitating the employment of all the comforting powers of the lord of the flat.   130

For there lay The Combs—the set of combs, side and back, that Della had worshipped for long in a Broadway window. Beautiful combs, pure tortoise shell, with jeweled rims—just the shade to wear in the beautiful vanished hair. They were expensive combs, she knew, and her heart had simply craved and yearned over them without the least hope of possession. And now, they were hers, but the tresses that should have adorned the coveted adornments were gone.

But she hugged them to her bosom, and at length she was able to look up with dim eyes and a smile and say: "My hair grows so fast, Jim!"

And then Della leaped up like a little singed cat and cried, "Oh, oh!"

Jim had not yet seen his beautiful present. She held it out to him eagerly   140 upon her open palm. The dull precious metal seemed to flash with a reflection of her bright and ardent spirit.

"Isn't it a dandy, Jim? I hunted all over town to find it. You'll have to look at the time a hundred times a day now. Give me your watch. I want to see how it looks on it."

Instead of obeying, Jim tumbled down on the couch and put his hands under the back of his head and smiled.

"Dell," said he, "let's put our Christmas presents away and keep 'em a while. They're too nice to use just at present. I sold the watch to get the money to buy your combs. And now suppose you put the chops on."   150

The magi, as you know, were wise men—wonderfully wise men—who brought gifts to the Babe in the manger. They invented the art of giving Christmas presents. Being wise, their gifts were no doubt wise ones, possibly bearing the privilege of exchange in case of duplication. And here I have lamely related to you the uneventful chronicle of two foolish children in a flat who most unwisely sacrificed for each other the greatest treasures of their house. But in a last word to the wise of these days let it be said that of all who give gifts these two were the wisest. Of all who give and receive gifts, such as they are wisest. Everywhere they are wisest. They are the magi.   [1906]

Questions for Discussion and Writing

1. Note the places where the narrator addresses the reader directly or comments on the characters or action, for example, in the last paragraph of the story. What is the effect of these comments? How do they attempt to shape our response to the story? How do you react to them?

2. Do Jim and Della take excessive pride in their watch and hair respectively? Are they punished for their pride? Explain your reaction.
3. Do you admire Della and Jim for their self-sacrifice, or are they simply young and foolish? Explain.
4. Do you find the ending of the story happy, tragic, or sentimental? Explain.

ᗒ SAKI (H. H. MUNRO)
(1870–1916)

Sredni Vashtar

"Saki" was the pen-name adopted by Hector Hugh Munro, who in the early years of this century produced dozens of clever, satirical stories for an audience that wanted light, entertaining fiction. Saki was never an avant-garde writer, but like many other popular writers, he was too good not to transcend the conventions and formulas his audience demanded.

His early life resembles that of Rudyard Kipling (1865–1936). Born in Burma, where his father was an English army officer, he lost his mother at age two, and was sent to live with aunts in Devonshire. It was a big house, with lots of servants, but his aunts were strict and petty; he was glad to escape to boarding school and then to grammar school, which he left in 1887. After three years of travel, two years of intense reading, and two years as a military policeman in Burma, he returned to England and took up journalism. From 1900 on, he supported himself as a writer of satirical sketches, stories, and novels, interspersed with periods as a war correspondent and parliamentary commentator. He took the name "Saki" from the cupbearer of the gods in *The Rubiyat of Omar Khayyám*. When World War I broke out, he joined the army and was later killed in action in France.

Saki's output was large and varied. In one type of story, he satirizes the silly social conventions and maneuvering for precedence among the minor aristocracy and upper middle classes. In other stories, he deals with the bizarre or the uncanny. Beneath the surface cleverness there often lies a serious thematic or psychological purpose. However bizarre "Sredni Vashtar" seems, it moves with cool, detached precision toward a solution that is both logical and frightening, as well as laden with psychological insight.

CONRADIN WAS TEN years old, and the doctor had pronounced his professional opinion that the boy would not live another five years. The doctor was silky and effete, and counted for little, but his opinion was endorsed by Mrs. De Ropp, who counted for nearly everything. Mrs. De Ropp was Conradin's cousin and guardian, and in his eyes she represented those three-fifths of the world that are necessary and disagreeable and real; the other two-fifths, in perpetual antagonism to the foregoing, were summed up in himself and his imagination. One of these days Conradin supposed he would succumb to the mastering pressure of wearisome necessary things—such as illnesses and coddling restrictions and drawn-out dullness. Without his imagination, which was rampant under the spur of loneliness, he would have succumbed long ago.   10

Mrs. De Ropp would never, in her honestest moments, have confessed to herself that she disliked Conradin, though she might have been dimly aware that thwarting him "for his good" was a duty which she did not find particularly irksome. Conradin hated her with a desperate sincerity which he was perfectly able to mask. Such few pleasures as he could contrive for himself gained an added relish from the likelihood that they would be displeasing to his guardian, and from the realm of his imagination she was locked out—an unclean thing, which should find no entrance.

In the dull, cheerless garden, overlooked by so many windows that were   20 ready to open with a message not to do this or that, or a reminder that medicines were due, he found little attraction. The few fruit-trees that it contained were set jealously apart from his plucking, as though they were rare specimens of their kind blooming in an arid waste; it would probably have been difficult to find a market-gardener who would have offered ten shillings for their entire yearly produce. In a forgotten corner, however, almost hidden behind a dismal shrubbery, was a disused tool-shed of respectable proportions, and within its walls Conradin found a haven, something that took on the varying aspects of a playroom and a cathedral. He had peopled it with a legion of familiar phantoms, evoked partly from fragments of history and partly from his own brain, but it also boasted two   30 inmates of flesh and blood. In one corner lived a ragged-plumaged Houdan[1] hen, on which the boy lavished an affection that had scarcely another outlet. Further back in the gloom stood a large hutch, divided into two compartments, one of which was fronted with close iron bars. This was the abode of a large polecat-ferret, which a friendly butcher-boy had once smuggled, cage and all, into its present quarters, in exchange for a long-secreted hoard of small silver. Conradin was dreadfully afraid of the lithe, sharp-fanged beast, but it was his most treasured possession. Its very presence in the tool-shed was a secret and fearful joy, to be kept scrupulously from the knowledge of the Woman, as he privately dubbed his cousin. And one day, out of Heaven knows what material, he spun the beast a   40 wonderful name, and from that moment it grew into a god and a religion. The Woman indulged in religion once a week at a church near by, and took Conradin with her, but to him the church service was an alien rite in the House of Rimmon.[2] Every Thursday, in the dim and musty silence of the tool-shed, he worshipped with mystic and elaborate ceremonial before the wooden hutch where dwelt Sredni Vashtar, the great ferret. Red flowers in their season and scarlet berries in the winter-time were offered at his shrine, for he was a god who laid some special stress on the fierce impatient side of things, as opposed to the Woman's religion, which, as far as Conradin could observe, went to great lengths in the contrary direction. And on great festivals powdered nutmeg was strewn in front of his hutch,   50

1. Black and white chickens known for laying many eggs.
2. Assyrian god of Thunder.

an important feature of the offering being that the nutmeg had to be stolen. These festivals were of irregular occurrence, and were chiefly appointed to celebrate some passing event. On one occasion, when Mrs. De Ropp suffered from acute toothache for three days, Conradin kept up the festival during the entire three days, and almost succeeded in persuading himself that Sredni Vashtar was personally responsible for the toothache. If the malady had lasted for another day the supply of nutmeg would have given out.

The Houdan hen was never drawn into the cult of Sredni Vashtar. Conradin had long ago settled that she was an Anabaptist.[3] He did not pretend to have the remotest knowledge as to what an Anabaptist was, but he privately hoped that it 60 was dashing and not very respectable. Mrs. De Ropp was the ground plan on which he based and detested all respectability.

After a while Conradin's absorption in the tool-shed began to attract the notice of his guardian. "It is not good for him to be pottering down there in all weathers," she promptly decided, and at breakfast one morning she announced that the Houdan hen had been sold and taken away overnight. With her short-sighted eyes she peered at Conradin, waiting for an outbreak of rage and sorrow, which she was ready to rebuke with a flow of excellent precepts and reasoning. But Conradin said nothing: there was nothing to be said. Something perhaps in his white set face gave her a momentary qualm, for at tea that afternoon there was 70 toast on the table, a delicacy which she usually banned on the ground that it was bad for him; also because the making of it "gave trouble," a deadly offence in the middle-class feminine eye.

"I thought you liked toast," she exclaimed, with an injured air, observing that he did not touch it.

"Sometimes," said Conradin.

In the shed that evening there was an innovation in the worship of the hutch-god. Conradin had been wont to chant his praises, tonight he asked a boon.

"Do one thing for me, Sredni Vashtar."

The thing was not specified. As Sredni Vashtar was a god he must be sup- 80 posed to know. And choking back a sob as he looked at that other empty corner, Conradin went back to the world he so hated.

And every night, in the welcome darkness of his bedroom and every evening in the dusk of the tool-shed, Conradin's bitter litany went up: "Do one thing for me, Sredni Vashtar."

Mrs. De Ropp noticed that the visits to the shed did not cease, and one day she made a further journey on inspection.

"What are you keeping in that locked hutch?" she asked.

"I believe it's guinea-pigs. I'll have them all cleared away."

Conradin shut his lips tight, but the Woman ransacked his bedroom till she 90 found the carefully hidden key, and forthwith marched down to the shed to complete her discovery. It was a cold afternoon, and Conradin had been bidden to keep to the house. From the furthest window of the dining-room the door of the shed could just be seen beyond the corner of the shrubbery, and there Conradin stationed himself. He saw the Woman enter, and then he imagined her opening

3. Sixteenth-century Protestants, opposed to infant baptism.

the door of the sacred hutch and peering down with her short-sighted eyes into the thick straw bed where his god lay hidden. Perhaps she would prod at the straw in her clumsy impatience. And Conradin fervently breathed his prayer for the last time. But he knew as he prayed that he did not believe. He knew that the Woman would come out presently with that pursed smile he loathed so well on   100 her face, and that in an hour or two the gardener would carry away his wonderful god, a god no longer, but a simple brown ferret in a hutch. And he knew that the Woman would triumph always as she triumphed now, and that he would grow ever more sickly under her pestering and domineering and superior wisdom, till one day nothing would matter much more with him, and the doctor would be proved right. And in the sting and misery of his defeat, he began to chant loudly and defiantly the hymn of his threatened idol:

> Sredni Vashtar went forth,
> His thoughts were red thoughts and his teeth were white.
> His enemies called for peace, but he brought them death.   110
> Sredni Vashtar the Beautiful.

And then of a sudden he stopped his chanting and drew closer to the window-pane. The door of the shed still stood ajar as it had been left, and the minutes were slipping by. They were long minutes, but they slipped by nevertheless. He watched the starlings running and flying in little parties across the lawn; he counted them over and over again, with one eye always on that swinging door. A sour-faced maid came in to lay the table for tea, and still Conradin stood and waited and watched. Hope had crept by inches into his heart, and now a look of triumph began to blaze in his eyes that had only known the wistful patience of defeat. Under his breath, with a furtive exultation, he began once again the pæan of   120 victory and devastation. And presently his eyes were rewarded: out through that doorway came a long, low, yellow-and-brown beast, with eyes a-blink at the waning daylight, and dark wet stains around the fur of jaws and throat. Conradin dropped on his knees. The great polecat-ferret made its way down to a small brook at the foot of the garden, drank for a moment, then crossed a little plank bridge and was lost to sight in the bushes. Such was the passing of Sredni Vashtar.

"Tea is ready," said the sour-faced maid; "where is the mistress?"

"She went down to the shed some time ago," said Conradin. And while the maid went to summon her mistress to tea, Conradin fished a toasting-fork[4] out of the sideboard drawer and proceeded to toast himself a piece of bread. And during   130 the toasting of it and the buttering of it with much butter and the slow enjoyment of eating it, Conradin listened to the noises and silences which fell in quick spasms beyond the dining-room door. The loud foolish screaming of the maid, the answering chorus of wondering ejaculations from the kitchen region, the scuttering footsteps and hurried embassies for outside help, and then, after a lull, the scared sobbings and the shuffling tread of those who bore a heavy burden into the house.

---

4. Used for toasting bread at an open fire.

"Whoever will break it to the poor child? I couldn't for the life of me!" exclaimed a shrill voice. And while they debated the matter among themselves, Conradin made himself another piece of toast.   [1912] 140

Questions for Discussion and Writing

1. Is this a horror story, a fantasy, a fable, an allegory, a realistic, or a humorous story? Defend your answer in detail.
2. What psychological points does the story make?
3. Do you read this story realistically or as a fable, allegory, or fantasy? Why?
4. How would the story differ if Conradin's victim were a male? Explain.

❧ JAMES JOYCE
(1882–1941)

Araby

James Joyce is a towering figure in twentieth-century literature and the Modernist movement. His fame rests mainly on four books: *Dubliners* (1914), *Portrait of the Artist as a Young Man* (1917), *Ulysses* (1922), and *Finnegan's Wake* (1939). Each of these is a masterpiece of its kind, and together they reshaped the form and structure of fiction.

Joyce's father was a tax collector when his eldest son was born in 1882. In 1888, the family's finances were such that Joyce could attend a Jesuit boarding school, but in 1892, the family's fortunes began their long decline. Joyce then attended the Christian Brothers School in Dublin, where he won many honors. In 1899, he entered University College.

Joyce's iconoclasm manifested itself early. At university, he renounced Catholicism, declared his support for controversial writers such as the dramatist Henrik Ibsen (1828–1906) and the poet W. B. Yeats (1865–1939), and turned away from the Irish Nationalist movements that were popular among his classmates.

After graduation, Joyce left for the continent, ostensibly to study medicine. He seldom returned, but on one occasion fell in love with a hotel maid from Galway, Nora Barnacle. They eloped in 1904 but did not marry until 1931.

His books appeared slowly and almost always encountered difficulties throughout the publication process. *Dubliners* was twice accepted by publishers but then rejected for being obscene and possibly libelous. *Portrait* was called morbid and pornographic and might not have been published but for the efforts of the American poet Ezra Pound. *Ulysses* had to be privately issued in Paris and required an obscenity trial in the United States before it could be published. Nevertheless, by 1920 he was the international symbol of Modernism to whom writers visiting Paris made devoted pilgrimage.

Joyce's passion was language, with which he experimented daringly throughout his life. *Dubliners* also innovates in style and point of view and introduces
the technique of momentary revelation or epiphany, which for many writers
changed the whole theory of the short story. "Araby" is a seminal story in a
book that has become a landmark in the history of the genre.

NORTH RICHMOND STREET, being blind, was a quiet street except at the hour
when the Christian Brothers' School set the boys free. An uninhabited house
of two storeys stood at the blind end, detached from its neighbours in a square
ground. The other houses of the street, conscious of decent lives within them,
gazed at one another with brown imperturbable faces.

The former tenant of our house, a priest, had died in the back drawing-
room. Air, musty from having been long enclosed, hung in all the rooms, and the
waste room behind the kitchen was littered with old useless papers. Among these
I found a few paper-covered books, the pages of which were curled and damp: *The
Abbot,* by Walter Scott, *The Devout Communicant* and *The Memoirs of Vidocq.* I liked 10
the last best because its leaves were yellow. The wild garden behind the house
contained a central apple-tree and a few straggling bushes under one of which I
found the late tenant's rusty bicycle-pump. He had been a very charitable priest; in
his will he had left all his money to institutions and the furniture of his house to
his sister.

When the short days of winter came dusk fell before we had well eaten our
dinners. When we met in the street the houses had grown sombre. The space of
sky above us was the colour of ever-changing violet and towards it the lamps of
the street lifted their feeble lanterns. The cold air stung us and we played till our
bodies glowed. Our shouts echoed in the silent street. The career of our play 20
brought us through the dark muddy lanes behind the houses where we ran the
gauntlet of the rough tribes from the cottages, to the back doors of the dark dripping gardens where odours arose from the ashpits, to the dark odorous stables
where a coachman smoothed and combed the horse or shook music from the
buckled harness. When we returned to the street light from the kitchen windows
had filled the areas. If my uncle was seen turning the corner we hid in the shadow
until we had seen him safely housed. Or if Mangan's sister came out on the
doorstep to call her brother in to his tea we watched her from our shadow peer up
and down the street. We waited to see whether she would remain or go in and, if
she remained, we left our shadow and walked up to Mangan's steps resignedly. She 30
was waiting for us, her figure defined by the light from the half-opened door. Her
brother always teased her before he obeyed and I stood by the railings looking at
her. Her dress swung as she moved her body and the soft rope of her hair tossed
from side to side.

Every morning I lay on the floor in the front parlour watching her door. The
blind was pulled down to within an inch of the sash so that I could not be seen.
When she came out on the doorstep my heart leaped. I ran to the hall, seized my
books and followed her. I kept her brown figure always in my eye and, when we

came near the point at which our ways diverged, I quickened my pace and passed
her. This happened morning after morning. I had never spoken to her, except for   40
a few casual words, and yet her name was like a summons to all my foolish blood.

Her image accompanied me even in places the most hostile to romance. On
Saturday evenings when my aunt went marketing I had to go to carry some of the
parcels. We walked through the flaring streets, jostled by drunken men and bar-
gaining women, amid the curses of labourers, the shrill litanies of shop-boys who
stood on guard by the barrels of pigs' cheeks, the nasal chanting of street-singers,
who sang a *come-all-you* about O'Donovan Rossa, or a ballad about the troubles in
our native land.[1] These noises converged in a single sensation of life for me: I
imagined that I bore my chalice safely through a throng of foes. Her name sprang
to my lips at moments in strange prayers and praises which I myself did not un-   50
derstand. My eyes were often full of tears (I could not tell why) and at times a
flood from my heart seemed to pour itself out into my bosom. I thought little of
the future. I did not know whether I would ever speak to her or not or, if I spoke
to her, how I could tell her of my confused adoration. But my body was like a
harp and her words and gestures were like fingers running upon the wires.

One evening I went into the back drawing-room in which the priest had
died. It was a dark rainy evening and there was no sound in the house. Through
one of the broken panes I heard the rain impinge upon the earth, the fine incessant needles of water playing in the sodden beds. Some distant lamp or lighted
window gleamed below me. I was thankful that I could see so little. All my senses   60
seemed to desire to veil themselves and, feeling that I was about to slip from them,
I pressed the palms of my hands together until they trembled, murmuring:
"*O love! O love!*" many times.

At last she spoke to me. When she addressed the first words to me I was so
confused that I did not know what to answer. She asked me was I going to *Araby.*
I forgot whether I answered yes or no. It would be a splendid bazaar, she said she
would love to go.

"And why can't you?" I asked.

While she spoke she turned a silver bracelet round and round her wrist. She
could not go, she said, because there would be a retreat that week in her convent.[2]   70
Her brother and two other boys were fighting for their caps and I was alone at the
railings. She held one of the spikes, bowing her head towards me. The light from
the lamp opposite our door caught the white curve of her neck, lit up her hair that
rested there and, falling, lit up the hand upon the railing. It fell over one side of
her dress and caught the white border of a petticoat, just visible as she stood at
ease.

"It's well for you," she said.

"If I go," I said, "I will bring you something."

What innumerable follies laid waste my waking and sleeping thoughts after
that evening! I wished to annihilate the tedious intervening days. I chafed against   80

1. A political song beginning "Come all you gallant Irishmen." O'Donovan Rossa was Jeremiah O'Donovan,
   an Irish leader who advocated violent revolution against the British.
2. i.e., convent school, run by nuns.

the work of school. At night in my bedroom and by day in the classroom her image came between me and the page I strove to read. The syllables of the word *Araby* were called to me through the silence in which my soul luxuriated and cast an Eastern enchantment over me. I asked for leave to go to the bazaar on Saturday night. My aunt was surprised and hoped it was not some Freemason affair. I answered few questions in class. I watched my master's[3] face pass from amiability to sternness; he hoped I was not beginning to idle. I could not call my wandering thoughts together. I had hardly any patience with the serious work of life which, now that it stood between me and my desire, seemed to me child's play, ugly monotonous child's play.   90

On Saturday morning I reminded my uncle that I wished to go to the bazaar in the evening. He was fussing at the hallstand, looking for the hat-brush, and answered me curtly:

"Yes, boy, I know."

As he was in the hall I could not go into the front parlour and lie at the window. I left the house in bad humour and walked slowly towards the school. The air was pitilessly raw and already my heart misgave me.

When I came home to dinner my uncle had not yet been home. Still it was early. I sat staring at the clock for some time and, when its ticking began to irritate me, I left the room. I mounted the staircase and gained the upper part of the   100 house. The high cold empty gloomy rooms liberated me and I went from room to room singing. From the front window I saw my companions playing below in the street. Their cries reached me weakened and indistinct and, leaning my forehead against the cool glass, I looked over at the dark house where she lived. I may have stood there for an hour, seeing nothing but the brown-clad figure cast by my imagination, touched discreetly by the lamplight at the curved neck, at the hand upon the railings and at the border below the dress.

When I came downstairs again I found Mrs. Mercer sitting at the fire. She was an old garrulous woman, a pawnbroker's widow, who collected used stamps for some pious purpose. I had to endure the gossip of the tea-table. The meal was   110 prolonged beyond an hour and still my uncle did not come. Mrs. Mercer stood up to go: she was sorry she couldn't wait any longer, but it was after eight o'clock and she did not like to be out late, as the night air was bad for her. When she had gone I began to walk up and down the room, clenching my fists. My aunt said:

"I'm afraid you may put off your bazaar for this night of Our Lord."

At nine o'clock I heard my uncle's latchkey in the halldoor. I heard him talking to himself and heard the hallstand rocking when it had received the weight of his overcoat. I could interpret these signs. When he was midway through his dinner I asked him to give me the money to go to the bazaar. He had forgotten.

"The people are in bed and after their first sleep now," he said.   120

I did not smile. My aunt said to him energetically:

"Can't you give him the money and let him go? You've kept him late enough as it is."

My uncle said he was very sorry he had forgotten. He said he believed in the

---

3. Schoolmaster, teacher.

old saying: "All work and no play makes Jack a dull boy." He asked me where I
was going and, when I had told him a second time he asked me did I know *The
Arab's Farewell to his Steed.*[4] when I left the kitchen he was about to recite the
opening lines of the piece to my aunt.

I held a florin[5] tightly in my hand as I strode down Buckingham Street towards the station. The sight of the streets thronged with buyers and glaring with   130
gas recalled to me the purpose of my journey. I took my seat in a third-class carriage of a deserted train. After an intolerable delay the train moved out of the station slowly. It crept onward among ruinous houses and over the twinkling river. At
Westland Row Station a crowd of people pressed to the carriage doors; but the
porters moved them back, saying that it was a special train for the bazaar. I remained alone in the bare carriage. In a few minutes the train drew up beside an
improvised wooden platform. I passed out on to the road and saw by the lighted
dial of a clock that it was ten minutes to ten. In front of me was a large building
which displayed the magical name.

I could not find any sixpenny entrance and, fearing that the bazaar would be   140
closed, I passed in quickly through a turnstile, handing a shilling to a weary-looking man. I found myself in a big hall girdled at half its height by a gallery. Nearly
all the stalls were closed and the greater part of the hall was in darkness. I recognised a silence like that which pervades a church after a service. I walked into the
centre of the bazaar timidly. A few people were gathered about the stalls which
were still open. Before a curtain, over which the words *Café Chantant* were written
in coloured lamps, two men were counting money on a salver. I listened to the fall
of the coins.

Remembering with difficulty why I had come I went over to one of the stalls
and examined porcelain vases and flowered tea-sets. At the door of the stall a   150
young lady was talking and laughing with two young gentlemen. I remarked their
English accents and listened vaguely to their conversation.

"O, I never said such a thing!"

"O, but you did!"

"O, but I didn't!"

"Didn't she say that?"

"Yes. I heard her."

"O, there's a . . . fib!"

Observing me the young lady came over and asked me did I wish to buy
anything. The tone of her voice was not encouraging; she seemed to have spoken   160
to me out of a sense of duty. I looked humbly at the great jars that stood like eastern guards at either side of the dark entrance to the stall and murmured:

"No, thank you."

The young lady changed the position of one of the vases and went back to
the two young men. They began to talk of the same subject. Once or twice the
young lady glanced at me over her shoulder.

I lingered before her stall, though I knew my stay was useless, to make my

---

4. A poem by Caroline Norton (1808–1877).
5. A silver coin worth two shillings.

interest in her wares seem the more real. Then I turned away slowly and walked   170
down the middle of the bazaar. I allowed the two pennies to fall against the sixpence in my pocket. I heard a voice call from one end of the gallery that the light
was out. The upper part of the hall was now completely dark.

Gazing up into the darkness I saw myself as a creature driven and derided by
vanity; and my eyes burned with anguish and anger.   [1914]

Questions for Discussion and Writing

1. How would you describe the atmosphere of the story? How does it contribute to the overall effect of the story?
2. How does the setting contribute to the effect of the story?
3. Who is the narrator of the story, and what is his attitude toward the boy?
4. What does the name of the bazaar convey to the boy? Why is it "magical"?
5. How would you characterize the boy's love for Mangan's sister? What kind of
   love is it?
6. At the end of the story, the boy sees himself "as a creature driven and derided
   by vanity." What does this mean? (You might want to consult a dictionary for
   various meanings of the words "vain" and "vanity" before answering.) Is it an
   accurate description?
7. Does this story have a plot? If so, summarize it briefly. If not, then how is the
   story organized and unified?

⌖ D.H. LAWRENCE
(1885–1930)

The Prussian Officer

D.H. Lawrence is at once an heroic and exasperating figure. His uncompromising integrity frequently brought him into conflict with the civil authorities and
censors. Many regard him as a hero for his defiance and integrity. On the other
hand, his lapses into self-pity, his views on women, and his heavy-handed moralizing can be disturbing.

Lawrence was among the very few British writers to emerge from the working classes. His father was a coal miner at Eastwood, near Nottingham. Being
weak and sickly, Lawrence was encouraged to pursue an education by his
mother. Scholarships enabled him to attend Nottingham High School and later
to train for a teacher's certificate. He taught from 1908 to 1911, when tuberculosis forced him to resign.

The rest of Lawrence's life was a remarkable mixture of travel, writing, fighting with authorities, forming friendships and feuding with other literary figures,
and searching vainly for health. In 1912, Lawrence risked social ostracism by
fleeing to Germany with the wife of a former professor. They married in 1914
and returned to England, only to be suspected of spying for Germany. Ford

Madox Ford, editor of *The English Review,* was among the first to spot Lawrence's talent and publish his stories, including "The Prussian Officer" in 1914. *The Rainbow* (1915) was declared obscene and seized by the police. After the war, Lawrence and Frieda left England and lived in Europe, Australia, Mexico, and the Southwestern United States.

Lawrence remains a highly controversial figure for his obsession with sex, his attitude toward women, and a style marked by repetition and bombast. His notions about the need for passion and connection with the natural world strike some as profound, others as cranky. Few would deny, however, that Lawrence's psychological probing of character, his vivid natural descriptions, and his caustic social criticism make him an important figure in Modernism.

Many critics contend that Lawrence is at his best in the short story, where limits on length control his tendency toward verbosity and pomposity. "The Prussian Officer" is widely regarded as important for its technical innovations, psychological insight, and use of natural symbolism. He is one of the great innovators of our century.

I

THEY HAD MARCHED more than thirty kilometres since dawn, along the white, hot road where occasional thickets of trees threw a moment of shade, then out into the glare again. On either hand, the valley, wide and shallow, glittered with heat; dark green patches of rye, pale young corn, fallow and meadow and black pine woods spread in a dull, hot diagram under a glistening sky. But right in front of the mountains ranged across, pale blue and very still, snow gleaming gently out of the deep atmosphere. And towards the mountains, on and on, the regiment marched between the rye fields and the meadows between the scraggy fruit trees set regularly on either side the high road. The burnished, dark green rye threw off a suffocating heat, the mountains drew gradually nearer and more dis- 10 tinct. While the feet of the soldiers grew hotter, sweat ran through their hair under their helmets, and their knapsacks could burn no more in contact with their shoulders, but seemed instead to give off a cold, prickly sensation.

He walked on and on in silence, staring at the mountains ahead, that rose sheer out of the land, and stood fold behind fold, half earth, half heaven, the heaven, the barrier with slits of soft snow, in the pale bluish peaks.

He could now walk almost without pain. At the start, he had determined not to limp. It had made him sick to take the first steps, and during the first mile or so, he had compressed his breath, and the cold drops of sweat had stood on his forehead. But he had walked it off. What were they after all but bruises! He had 20 looked at them, as he was getting up: deep bruises on the backs of his thighs. And since he had made his first step in the morning, he had been conscious of them, till now he had a tight, hot place in his chest, with suppressing the pain, and holding himself in. There seemed no air when he breathed. But he walked almost lightly.

The Captain's hand had trembled at taking his coffee at dawn: his orderly saw it again. And he saw the fine figure of the Captain wheeling on horseback at the farm-house ahead, a handsome figure in pale blue uniform with facings of scarlet, and the metal gleaming on the black helmet and the sword-scabbard, and dark streaks of sweat coming on the silky bay horse. The orderly felt he was con- 30 nected with that figure moving so suddenly on horseback: he followed it like a shadow, mute and inevitable and damned by it. And the officer was always aware of the tramp of the company behind, the march of his orderly among the men.

The Captain was a tall man of about forty, grey at the temples. He had a handsome, finely knit figure, and was one of the best horsemen in the West. His orderly, having to rub him down, admired the amazing riding-muscles of his loins.

For the rest, the orderly scarcely noticed the officer any more than he noticed himself. It was rarely he saw his master's face: he did not look at it. The Captain had reddish brown, stiff hair, that he wore short upon his skull. His moustache was also cut short and bristly over a full brutal mouth. His face was 40 rather rugged, the cheeks thin. Perhaps the man was the more handsome for the deep lines in his face, the irritable tension of his brow, which gave him the look of a man who fights with life. His fair eyebrows stood bushy over light blue eyes that were always flashing with cold fire.

He was a Prussian aristocrat, haughty and overbearing. But his mother had been a Polish Countess. Having made too many gambling debts when he was young, he had ruined his prospects in the Army, and remained an infantry captain. He had never married: his position did not allow of it, and no woman had ever moved him to it. His time he spent riding—occasionally he rode one of his own horses at the races—and at the officers' club. Now and then he took himself a mis- 50 tress. But after such an event, he returned to duty with his brow still more tense, his eyes still more hostile and irritable. With the men, however, he was merely impersonal, though a devil when roused; so that, on the whole, they feared him, but had no great aversion from him. They accepted him as the inevitable.

To his orderly he was at first cold and just and indifferent: he did not fuss over trifles. So that his servant knew practically nothing about him, except just what orders he would give, and how he wanted them obeyed. That was quite simple. Then the change gradually came.

The orderly was a youth of about twenty-two, of medium height, and well built. He had strong, heavy limbs, was swarthy, with a soft, black, young mous- 60 tache. There was something altogether warm and young about him. He had firmly marked eyebrows over dark, expressionless eyes, that seemed never to have thought, only to have received life direct through his senses, and acted straight from instinct.

Gradually the officer had become aware of his servant's young, vigorous, unconscious presence about him. He could not get away from the sense of the youth's person, while he was in attendance. It was like a warm flame upon the older man's tense, rigid body, that had become almost unliving, fixed. There was something so free and self-contained about him, and something in the young fellow's movement, that made the officer aware of him. And this irritated the 70 Prussian. He did not choose to be touched into life by his servant. He might easily have changed his man,[1] but he did not. He now very rarely looked direct at his orderly, but kept his face averted, as if to avoid seeing him. And yet as the young sol-

---

1. Might easily have chosen another orderly.

dier moved unthinking about the apartment, the elder watched him, and would notice the movement of his strong young shoulders under the blue cloth, the bend of his neck. And it irritated him. To see the soldier's young, brown, shapely peasant's hand grasp the loaf or the wine-bottle sent a flash of hate or of anger through the elder man's blood. It was not that the youth was clumsy: it was rather the blind, instinctive sureness of movement of an unhampered young animal that irritated the officer to such a degree.

Once, when a bottle of wine had gone over, and the red gushed out on to the tablecloth, the officer had started up with an oath, and his eyes, bluey like fire, had held those of the confused youth for a moment. It was a shock for the young soldier. He felt something sink deeper, deeper into his soul, where nothing had ever gone before. It left him rather blank and wondering. Some of his natural completeness in himself was gone, a little uneasiness took its place. And from that time an undiscovered feeling had held between the two men.

Henceforward the orderly was afraid of really meeting his master. His subconsciousness remembered those steely blue eyes and the harsh brows, and did not intend to meet them again. So he always stared past his master, and avoided him. Also, in a little anxiety, he waited for the three months to have gone, when his time would be up. He began to feel a constraint in the Captain's presence, and the soldier even more than the officer wanted to be left alone, in his neutrality as servant.

He had served the Captain for more than a year, and knew his duty. This he performed easily, as if it were natural to him. The officer and his commands he took for granted, as he took the sun and the rain, and he served as a matter of course. It did not implicate him personally.

But now if he were going to be forced into a personal interchange with his master he would be like a wild thing caught, he felt he must get away.

But the influence of the young soldier's being had penetrated through the officer's stiffened discipline, and perturbed the man in him. He, however, was a gentleman, with long, fine hands and cultivated movements, and was not going to allow such a thing as the stirring of his innate self. He was a man of passionate temper, who had always kept himself suppressed. Occasionally there had been a duel, an outburst before the soldiers. He knew himself to be always on the point of breaking out. But he kept himself hard to the idea of the Service. Whereas the young soldier seemed to live out his warm, full nature, to give it off in his very movements, which had a certain zest, such as wild animals have in free movement. And this irritated the officer more and more.

In spite of himself, the Captain could not regain his neutrality of feeling towards his orderly. Nor could he leave the man alone. In spite of himself, he watched him, gave him sharp orders, tried to take up as much of his time as possible. Sometimes he flew into a rage with the young soldier, and bullied him. Then the orderly shut himself off, as it were out of earshot, and waited, with sullen, flushed face, for the end of the noise. The words never pierced to his intelligence, he made himself, protectively, impervious to the feelings of his master.

He had a scar on his left thumb, a deep seam going across the knuckle. The officer had long suffered from it, and wanted to do something to it. Still it was there, ugly and brutal on the young, brown hand. At last the Captain's reserve gave

way. One day, as the orderly was smoothing out the tablecloth, the officer pinned
down his thumb with a pencil, asking:

"How did you come by that?"

The young man winced and drew back at attention.

"A wood axe, Herr Hauptmann," he answered.

The officer waited for further explanation. None came. The orderly went
about his duties. The elder man was sullenly angry. His servant avoided him. And
the next day he had to use all his will-power to avoid seeing the scarred thumb.
He wanted to get hold of it and— A hot flame ran in his blood.

He knew his servant would soon be free, and would be glad. As yet, the sol-   130
dier had held himself off from the elder man. The Captain grew madly irritable.
He could not rest when the soldier was away, and when he was present, he glared
at him with tormented eyes. He hated those fine, black brows over the unmean-
ing, dark eyes, he was infuriated by the free movement of the handsome limbs,
which no military discipline could make stiff. And he became harsh and cruelly
bullying, using contempt and satire. The young soldier only grew more mute and
expressionless.

"What cattle were you bred by, that you can't keep straight eyes? Look me in
the eyes when I speak to you."

And the soldier turned his dark eyes to the other's face, but there was no   140
sight in them: he stared with the slightest possible cast, holding back his sight,
perceiving the blue of his master's eyes, but receiving no look from them. And
the elder man went pale, and his reddish eyebrows twitched. He gave his order,
barrenly.

Once he flung a heavy military glove into the young soldier's face. Then he
had the satisfaction of seeing the black eyes flare up into his own, like a blaze
when straw is thrown on a fire. And he had laughed with a little tremor and a
sneer.

But there were only two months more. The youth instinctively tried to keep
himself intact: he tried to serve the officer as if the latter were an abstract authority   150
and not a man. All his instinct was to avoid personal contact, even definite hate.
But in spite of himself the hate grew, responsive to the officer's passion. However,
he put it in the background. When he had left the Army he could dare acknowledge it. By nature he was active, and had many friends. He thought what amazing
good fellows they were. But, without knowing it, he was alone. Now this solitari-
ness was intensified. It would carry him through his term. But the officer seemed
to be going irritably insane, and the youth was deeply frightened.

The soldier had a sweetheart, a girl from the mountains, independent and
primitive. The two walked together, rather silently. He went with her, not to talk,
but to have his arm round her, and for the physical contact. This eased him, made   160
it easier for him to ignore the Captain; for he could rest with her held fast against
his chest. And she, in some unspoken fashion, was there for him. They loved each
other.

The Captain perceived it, and was mad with irritation. He kept the young
man engaged all the evenings long, and took pleasure in the dark look that came
on his face. Occasionally, the eyes of the two men met, those of the younger sullen
and dark, doggedly unalterable, those of the elder sneering with restless contempt.

The officer tried hard not to admit the passion that had got hold of him. He would not know that his feeling for his orderly was anything but that of a man incensed by his stupid, perverse servant. So, keeping quite justified and conventional in his consciousness, he let the other thing run on. His nerves, however, were suffering. At last he slung the end of a belt in his servant's face. When he saw the youth start back, the pain-tears in his eyes and the blood on his mouth, he had felt at once a thrill of deep pleasure and of shame.

But this, he acknowledged to himself, was a thing he had never done before. The fellow was too exasperating. His own nerves must be going to pieces. He went away for some days with a woman.

It was a mockery of pleasure. He simply did not want the woman. But he stayed on for his time. At the end of it, he came back in an agony of irritation, torment, and misery. He rode all the evening, then came straight in to supper. His orderly was out. The officer sat with his long, fine hands lying on the table, perfectly still, and all his blood seemed to be corroding.

At last his servant entered. He watched the strong, easy young figure, the fine eyebrows, the thick black hair. In a week's time the youth had got back his old well-being. The hands of the officer twitched and seemed to be full of mad flame. The young man stood at attention, unmoving, shut off.

The meal went in silence. But the orderly seemed eager. He made a clatter with the dishes.

"Are you in a hurry?" asked the officer, watching the intent, warm face of his servant. The other did not reply.

"Will you answer my question?"said the Captain.

"Yes, sir," replied the orderly, standing with his pile of deep Army plates. The Captain waited, looked at him, then asked again:

"Are you in a hurry?"

"Yes, sir," came the answer, that sent a flash through the listener.

"For what?"

"I was going out, sir."

"I want you this evening."

There was a moment's hesitation. The officer had a curious stiffness of countenance.

"Yes, sir," replied the servant, in his throat.

"I want you to-morrow evening also—in fact you may consider your evenings occupied, unless I give you leave."

The mouth with the young moustache set close.

"Yes, sir," answered the orderly, loosening his lips for a moment. He again turned to the door.

"And why have you a piece of pencil in your ear?"

The orderly hesitated, then continued on his way without answering. He set the plates in a pile outside the door, took the stump of pencil from his ear, and put it in his pocket. He had been copying a verse for his sweetheart's birthday card. He returned to finish clearing the table. The officer's eyes were dancing, he had a little, eager smile.

"Why have you a piece of pencil in your ear?" he asked.

The orderly took his hands full of dishes. His master was standing near the great green stove, a little smile on his face, his chin thrust forward. When the young soldier saw him his heart suddenly ran hot. He felt blind. Instead of answering, he turned dazedly to the door. As he was crouching to set down the dishes, he was pitched forward by a kick from behind. The pots went in a stream down the stairs, he clung to the pillar of the banisters. And as he was rising he was kicked heavily again and again, so that he clung sickly to the post for some mo- 220 ments. His master had gone swiftly into the room and closed the door. The maid-servant downstairs looked up the staircase and made a mocking face at the crockery disaster.

The officer's heart was plunging. He poured himself a glass of wine, part of which he spilled on the floor, and gulped the remainder, leaning against the cool, green stove. He heard his man collecting the dishes from the stairs. Pale, as if intoxicated, he waited. The servant entered again. The Captain's heart gave a pang, as of pleasure, seeing the young fellow bewildered and uncertain on his feet, with pain.

"Schöner!" he said.   230

The soldier was a little slower in coming to attention.

"Yes, sir!"

The youth stood before him, with pathetic young moustache, and fine eyebrows very distinct on his forehead of dark marble.

"I asked you a question."

"Yes, sir."

The officer's tone bit like acid.

"Why had you a pencil in your ear?"

Again the servant's heart ran hot, and he could not breathe. With dark, strained eyes, he looked at the officer, as if fascinated. And he stood there sturdily 240 planted, unconscious. The withering smile came into the Captain's eyes, and he lifted his foot.

"I—I forgot it—sir," panted the soldier, his dark eyes fixed on the other man's dancing blue ones.

"What was it doing there?"

He saw the young man's breast heaving as he made an effort for words.

"I had been writing."

"Writing what?"

Again the soldier looked him up and down. The officer could hear him panting. The smile came into the blue eyes. The soldier worked his dry throat, but 250 could not speak. Suddenly the smile lit like a flame on the officer's face, and a kick came heavily against the orderly's thigh. The youth moved a pace sideways. His face went dead, with two black, staring eyes.

"Well?" said the officer.

The orderly's mouth had gone dry, and his tongue rubbed in it as on dry brown-paper. He worked his throat. The officer raised his foot. The servant went stiff.

"Some poetry, sir," came the crackling, unrecognizable sound of his voice.

"Poetry, what poetry?" asked the Captain, with a sickly smile.

Again there was the working in the throat. The Captain's heart had suddenly 260 gone down heavily, and he stood sick and tired.

"For my girl, sir," he heard the dry, inhuman sound.

"Oh!" he said, turning away. "Clear the table."

"Click!" went the soldier's throat; then again, "click!" and then the half-articulate:

"Yes, sir."

The young soldier was gone, looking old, and walking heavily.

The officer, left alone, held himself rigid, to prevent himself from thinking. His instinct warned him that he must not think. Deep inside him was the intense gratification of his passion, still working powerfully. Then there was a counter-action, a horrible breaking down of something inside him, a whole agony of reaction. He stood there for an hour motionless, a chaos of sensations, but rigid with a will to keep blank his consciousness, to prevent his mind grasping. And he held himself so until the worst of the stress had passed, when he began to drink, drank himself to an intoxication, till he slept obliterated. When he woke in the morning he was shaken to the base of his nature. But he had fought off the realization of what he had done. He had prevented his mind from taking it in, had suppressed it along with his instincts, and the conscious man had nothing to do with it. He felt only as after a bout of intoxication, weak, but the affair itself all dim and not to be recovered. Of the drunkenness of his passion he successfully refused remembrance. And when his orderly appeared with coffee, the officer assumed the same self he had had the morning before. He refused the event of the past night—denied it had ever been—and was successful in his denial. He had not done any such thing—not he himself. Whatever there might be lay at the door of a stupid, insubordinate servant.

The orderly had gone about in a stupor all the evening. He drank some beer because he was parched, but not much, the alcohol made his feeling come back, and he could not bear it. He was dulled, as if nine-tenths of the ordinary man in him were inert. He crawled about disfigured. Still, when he thought of the kicks, he went sick, and when he thought of the threat of more kicking, in the room afterwards, his heart went hot and faint, and he panted, remembering the one that had come. He had been forced to say, "For my girl." He was much too done even to want to cry. His mouth hung slightly open, like an idiot's. He felt vacant, and wasted. So, he wandered at his work, painfully, and very slowly and clumsily, fumbling blindly with the brushes, and finding it difficult, when he sat down, to summon the energy to move again. His limbs, his jaw, were slack and nerveless. But he was very tired. He got to bed at last, and slept inert, relaxed, in a sleep that was rather stupor than slumber, a dead night of stupefaction shot through with gleams of anguish.

In the morning were the manœuvres. But he woke even before the bugle sounded. The painful ache in his chest, the dryness of his throat, the awful steady feeling of misery made his eyes come awake and dreary at once. He knew, without thinking, what had happened. And he knew that the day had come again, when he must go on with his round. The last bit of darkness was being pushed out of the room. He would have to move his inert body and go on. He was so young, and had known so little trouble, that he was bewildered. He only wished it would stay night, so that he could lie still, covered up by the darkness. And yet nothing would prevent the day from coming, nothing would save him from having to get

up and saddle the Captain's horse, and make the Captain's coffee. It was there, in- 310
evitable. And then, he thought, it was impossible. Yet they would not leave him
free. He must go and take the coffee to the Captain. He was too stunned to understand it. He only knew it was inevitable—inevitable, however long he lay inert.

At last, after heaving at himself, for he seemed to be a mass of inertia, he got
up. But he had to force every one of his movements from behind, with his will. He
felt lost, and dazed, and helpless. Then he clutched hold of the bed, the pain was
so keen. And looking at his thighs he saw the darker bruises on his swarthy flesh,
and he knew that if he pressed one of his fingers on one of the bruises, he should
faint. But he did not want to faint—he did not want anybody to know. No one
should ever know. It was between him and the Captain. There were only the two
people in the world now—himself and the Captain.   320

Slowly, economically, he got dressed and forced himself to walk. Everything
was obscure, except just what he had his hands on. But he managed to get
through his work. The very pain revived his dull senses. The worst remained yet.
He took the tray and went up to the Captain's room. The officer, pale and heavy,
sat at the table. The orderly, as he saluted, felt himself put out of existence. He
stood still for a moment submitting to his own nullification—then he gathered
himself, seemed to regain himself, and then the Captain began to grow vague, unreal, and the younger soldier's heart beat up. He clung to this situation—that the
Captain did not exist—so that he himself might live. But when he saw his officer's
hand tremble as he took the coffee, he felt everything falling shattered. And he 330
went away, feeling as if he himself were coming to pieces, disintegrated. And when
the Captain was there on horseback, giving orders, while he himself stood, with
rifle and knapsack, sick with pain, he felt as if he must shut his eyes—as if he
must shut his eyes on everything. It was only the long agony of marching with a
parched throat that filled him with one single, sleep-heavy intention: to save himself.

II

He was getting used even to his parched throat. That the snowy peaks were
radiant among the sky, that the whity-green glacier-river twisted through its pale
shoals, in the valley below, seemed almost supernatural. But he was going mad
with fever and thirst. He plodded on uncomplaining. He did not want to speak, 340
not to anybody. There were two gulls, like flakes of water and snow, over the river.
The scent of green rye soaked in sunshine came like a sickness. And the march
continued, monotonously, almost like a bad sleep.

At the next farm-house, which stood low and broad near the high road, tubs
of water had been put out. The soldiers clustered round to drink. They took off
their helmets, and the steam mounted from their wet hair. The Captain sat on
horseback, watching. He needed to see his orderly. His helmet threw a dark
shadow over his light, fierce eyes, but his moustache and mouth and chin were
distinct in the sunshine. The orderly must move under the presence of the figure
of the horseman. It was not that he was afraid, or cowed. It was as if he was dis- 350
embowelled, made empty, like an empty shell. He felt himself as nothing, a
shadow creeping under the sunshine. And, thirsty as he was, he could scarcely

drink, feeling the Captain near him. He would not take off his helmet to wipe his wet hair. He wanted to stay in shadow, not to be forced into consciousness. Starting, he saw the light heel of the officer prick the belly of the horse; the Captain cantered away, and he himself could relapse into vacancy.

Nothing, however, could give him back his living place in the hot, bright morning. He felt like a gap among it all. Whereas the Captain was prouder, over-riding. A hot flash went through the young servant's body. The Captain was firmer and prouder with life, he himself was empty as a shadow. Again the flash went   360 through him, dazing him out. But his heart ran a little firmer.

The company turned up the hill, to make a loop for the return. Below, from among the trees, the farm-bell clanged. He saw the labourers, mowing bare-foot at the thick grass, leave off their work and go downhill, their scythes hanging over their shoulders, like long, bright claws curving down behind them. They seemed like dream-people, as if they had no relation to himself. He felt as in a blackish dream; as if all the other things were there and had form, but he himself was only a consciousness, a gap that could think and perceive.

The soldiers were tramping silently up the glaring hill-side. Gradually his head began to revolve, slowly, rhythmically. Sometimes it was dark before his eyes,   370 as if he saw this world through a smoked glass, frail shadows and unreal. It gave him a pain in his head to walk.

The air was too scented, it gave no breath. All the lush green-stuff seemed to be issuing its sap, till the air was deathly, sickly with the smell of greenness. There was the perfume of clover, like pure honey and bees. Then there grew a faint acrid tang—they were near the beeches; and then a queer clattering noise, and a suffocating, hideous smell; they were passing a flock of sheep, a shepherd in a black smock, holding his crook. Why should the sheep huddle together under this fierce sun? He felt that the shepherd would not see him, though he could see the shepherd.   380

At last there was the halt. They stacked rifles in a conical stack, put down their kit in a scattered circle around it, and dispersed a little, sitting on a small knoll high on the hill-side. The chatter began. The soldiers were steaming with heat, but were lively. He sat still, seeing the blue mountains rising upon the land, twenty kilometres away. There was a blue fold in the ranges, then out of that, at the foot, the broad, pale bed of the river, stretches of whity-green water between pinkish-grey shoals among the dark pine woods. There it was, spread out a long way off. And it seemed to come downhill, the river. There was a raft being steered, a mile away. It was a strange country. Nearer, a red-roofed, broad farm with white base and square dots of windows crouched beside the wall of beech foliage on the   390 wood's edge. There were long strips of rye and clover and pale green corn. And just at his feet, below the knoll, was a darkish bog, where globe flowers stood breathless still on their slim stalks. And some of the pale gold bubbles were burst, and a broken fragment hung in the air. He thought he was going to sleep.

Suddenly something moved into this coloured mirage before his eyes. The Captain, a small, light-blue and scarlet figure, was trotting evenly between the strips of corn, along the level brow of the hill. And the man making flag-signals was coming on. Proud and sure moved the horseman's figure, the quick, bright thing, in which was concentrated all the light of this morning, which for the rest

lay a fragile, shining shadow. Submissive, apathetic, the young soldier sat and 400
stared. But as the horse slowed to a walk, coming up the last steep path, the great
flash flared over the body and soul of the orderly. He sat waiting. The back of his
head felt as if it were weighted with a heavy piece of fire. He did not want to eat.
His hands trembled slightly as he moved them. Meanwhile the officer on horseback was approaching slowly and proudly. The tension grew in the orderly's soul.
Then again, seeing the Captain ease himself on the saddle, the flash blazed
through him.

The Captain looked at the patch of light blue and scarlet, and dark heads,
scattered closely on the hill-side. It pleased him. The command pleased him. And
he was feeling proud. His orderly was among them in common subjection. The of- 410
ficer rose a little on his stirrups to look. The young soldier sat with averted, dumb
face. The Captain relaxed on his seat. His slim-legged, beautiful horse, brown as a
beech nut, walked proudly uphill. The Captain passed into the zone of the company's atmosphere: a hot smell of men, of sweat, of leather. He knew it very well.
After a word with the lieutenant, he went a few paces higher, and sat there, a dominant figure, his sweat-marked horse swishing its tail, while he looked down on
his men, on his orderly, a nonentity among the crowd.

The young soldier's heart was like fire in his chest, and he breathed with difficulty. The officer, looking downhill, saw three of the young soldiers, two pails of
water between them, staggering across a sunny green field. A table had been set up 420
under a tree, and there the slim lieutenant stood, importantly busy. Then the
Captain summoned himself to an act of courage. He called his orderly.

The flame leapt into the young soldier's throat as he heard the command,
and he rose blindly, stifled. He saluted, standing below the officer. He did not look
up. But there was the flicker in the Captain's voice.

"Go to the inn and fetch me . . ." the officer gave his commands. "Quick!" he
added.

At the last word, the heart of the servant leapt with a flash, and he felt the
strength come over his body. But he turned in mechanical obedience, and set off at
a heavy run downhill, looking almost like a bear, his trousers bagging over his 430
military boots. And the officer watched this blind, plunging run all the way.

But it was only the outside of the orderly's body that was obeying so humbly
and mechanically. Inside had gradually accumulated a core into which all the energy of that young life was compact and concentrated. He executed his commission, and plodded quickly back uphill. There was a pain in his head as he walked
that made him twist his features unknowingly. But hard there in the centre of his
chest was himself, himself, firm, and not to be plucked to pieces.

The Captain had gone up into the wood. The orderly plodded through the
hot, powerfully smelling zone of the company's atmosphere. He had a curious
mass of energy inside him now. The Captain was less real than himself. He ap- 440
proached the green entrance to the wood. There, in the half-shade, he saw the
horse standing, the sunshine and the flickering shadow of leaves dancing over his
brown body. There was a clearing where timber had lately been felled. Here, in the
gold-green shade beside the brilliant cup of sunshine, stood two figures, blue and
pink, the bits of pink showing out plainly. The Captain was talking to his lieutenant.

The orderly stood on the edge of the bright clearing, where great trunks of trees, stripped and glistening, lay stretched like naked, brown-skinned bodies. Chips of wood littered the trampled floor, like splashed light, and the bases of the felled trees stood here and there, with their raw, level tops. Beyond was the bril- 458 liant, sunlit green of a beech.

"Then I will ride forward," the orderly heard his Captain say. The lieutenant saluted and strode away. He himself went forward. A hot flash passed through his belly, as he tramped towards his officer.

The Captain watched the rather heavy figure of the young soldier stumble forward, and his veins, too, ran hot. This was to be man to man between them. He yielded before the solid, stumbling figure with bent head. The orderly stooped and put the food on a level-sawn tree-base. The Captain watched the glistening, sun-inflamed, naked hands. He wanted to speak to the young soldier, but could not. The servant propped a bottle against his thigh, pressed open the 460 cork, and poured out the beer into the mug. He kept his head bent. The captain accepted the mug.

"Hot!" he said, as if amiably.

The flame sprang out of the orderly's heart, nearly suffocating him.

"Yes, sir," he replied, between shut teeth.

And he heard the sound of the Captain's drinking, and he clenched his fists, such a strong torment came into his wrists. Then came the faint clang of the closing of the pot-lid. He looked up. The Captain was watching him. He glanced swiftly away. Then he saw the officer stoop and take a piece of bread from the tree-base. Again the flash of flame went through the young solider, seeing the stiff body 470 stoop beneath him, and his hands jerked. He looked away. He could feel the officer was nervous. The bread fell as it was being broken. The officer ate the other piece. The two men stood tense and still, the master laboriously chewing his bread, the servant staring with averted face, his fist clenched.

Then the young soldier started. The officer had pressed open the lid of the mug again. The orderly watched the lid of the mug, and the white hand that clenched the handle, as if he were fascinated. It was raised. The youth followed it with his eyes. And then he saw the thin, strong throat of the elder man moving up and down as he drank, the strong jaw working. And the instinct which had been jerking at the young man's wrists suddenly jerked free. He jumped, feeling as if it 480 were rent in two by a strong flame.

The spur of the officer caught in a tree-root, he went down backwards with a crash, the middle of his back thudding sickeningly against a sharp-edged tree-base, the pot flying away. And in a second the orderly, with serious, earnest young face, and under-lip between his teeth, had got his knee in the officer's chest and was pressing the chin backward over the farther edge of the tree-stump, pressing, with all his heart behind in a passion of relief, the tension of his wrists exquisite with relief. And with the base of his palms he shoved at the chin, with all his might. And it was pleasant, too, to have that chin, that hard jaw already slightly rough with beard, in his hands. He did not relax one hair's breadth, but, all the 490 force of all his blood exulting in his thrust, he shoved back the head of the other man, till there was a little "cluck" and a crunching sensation. Then he felt as if his head went to vapour. Heavy convulsions shook the body of the officer, frightening and horrifying the young soldier. Yet it pleased him, too, to repress them. It pleased him to keep his hands pressing back the chin, to feel the chest of the other man yield in expiration to the weight of his strong, young knees, to feel the hard twitchings of the prostrate body jerking his own whole frame, which was pressed down on it.

But it went still. He could look into the nostrils of the other man, the eyes he could scarcely see. How curiously the mouth was pushed out, exaggerating the 500 full lips, and the moustache bristling up from them. Then, with a start, he noticed the nostrils gradually filled with blood. The red brimmed, hesitated, ran over, and went in a thin trickle down the face to the eyes.

It shocked and distressed him. Slowly, he got up. The body twitched and sprawled there, inert. He stood and looked at it in silence. It was a pity *it* was broken. It represented more than the thing which had kicked and bullied him. He was afraid to look at the eyes. They were hideous now, only the whites showing, and the blood running to them. The face of the orderly was drawn with horror at the sight. Well, it was so. In his heart he was satisfied. He had hated the face of the Captain. It was extinguished now. There was a heavy relief in the orderly's soul. 510 That was as it should be. But he could not bear to see the long, military body lying broken over the tree-base, the fine fingers crisped. He wanted to hide it away.

Quickly, busily, he gathered it up and pushed it under the felled tree-trunks, which rested their beautiful, smooth length either end on logs. The face was horrible with blood. He covered it with the helmet. Then he pushed the limbs straight and decent, and brushed the dead leaves off the fine cloth of the uniform. So, it lay quite still in the shadow under there. A little strip of sunshine ran along the breast, from a chink between the logs. The orderly sat by it for a few moments. Here his own life also ended.

Then, through his daze, he heard the lieutenant, in a loud voice, explaining 520 to the men outside the wood, that they were to suppose the bridge on the river below was held by the enemy. Now they were to march to the attack in such and such a manner. The lieutenant had no gift of expression. The orderly, listening from habit, got muddled. And when the lieutenant began it all again he ceased to hear.

He knew he must go. He stood up. It surprised him that the leaves were glittering in the sun, and the chips of wood reflecting white from the ground. For him a change had come over the world. But for the rest it had not—all seemed the same. Only he had left it. And he could not go back. It was his duty to return with the beer-pot and the bottle. He could not. He had left all that. The lieutenant was 530 still hoarsely explaining. He must go, or they would overtake him. And he could not bear contact with any one now.

He drew his fingers over his eyes, trying to find out where he was. Then he turned away. He saw the horse standing in the path. He went up to it and mounted. It hurt him to sit in the saddle. The pain of keeping his seat occupied him as they cantered through the wood. He would not have minded anything, but he could not get away from the sense of being divided from the others. The path led out of the trees. On the edge of the wood he pulled up and stood watching. There in the spacious sunshine of the valley soldiers were moving in a little

swarm. Every now and then, a man harrowing on a strip of fallow shouted to his 540
oxen, at the turn. The village and the white-towered church was small in the sunshine. And he no longer belonged to it—he sat there, beyond, like a man outside
in the dark. He had gone out from everyday life into the unknown and he could
not, he even did not want to go back.

Turning from the sun-blazing valley, he rode deep into the wood. Tree-
trunks, like people standing grey and still, took no notice as he went. A doe, herself a moving bit of sunshine and shadow, went running through the flecked
shade. There were bright green rents in the foliage. Then it was all pine wood,
dark and cool. And he was sick with pain, he had an intolerable great pulse in his
head, and he was sick. He had never been ill in his life. He felt lost, quite dazed 550
with all this.

Trying to get down from the horse, he fell, astonished at the pain and his
lack of balance. The horse shifted uneasily. He jerked its bridle and sent it canter-
ing jerkily away. It was his last connection with the rest of things.

But he only wanted to lie down and not be disturbed. Stumbling through
the trees, he came on a quiet place where beeches and pine trees grew on a slope.
Immediately he had lain down and closed his eyes, his consciousness went racing
on without him. A big pulse of sickness beat in him as if it throbbed through the
whole earth. He was burning with dry heat. But he was too busy, too tearingly active in the incoherent race of delirium to observe.   560

III

HE CAME TO with a start. His mouth was dry and hard, his heart beat heavily,
but he had not the energy to get up. His heart beat heavily. Where was he?—the
barracks—at home? There was something knocking. And, making an effort, he
looked around—trees, and litter of greenery, and reddish, bright, still pieces of
sunshine on the floor. He did not believe he was himself, he did not believe what
he saw. Something was knocking. He made a struggle towards consciousness, but
relapsed. Then he struggled again. And gradually his surroundings fell into relationship with himself. He knew, and a great pang of fear went through his heart.
Somebody was knocking. He could see the heavy, black rags of a fir tree overhead.
Then everything went black. Yet he did not believe he had closed his eyes. He had 570
not. Out of the blackness sight slowly emerged again. And someone was knocking. Quickly, he saw the blood-disfigured face of his Captain, which he hated. And
he held himself still with horror. Yet, deep inside him, he knew that it was so, the
Captain should be dead. But the physical delirium got hold of him. Someone was
knocking. He lay perfectly still, as if dead, with fear. And he went unconscious.

When he opened his eyes again he started, seeing something creeping swiftly
up a tree-trunk. It was a little bird. And the bird was whistling overhead. Tap-tap-
tap—it was the small, quick bird rapping the tree-trunk with its beak, as if its
head were a little round hammer. He watched it curiously. It shifted sharply, in its
creeping fashion. Then, like a mouse, it slid down the bare trunk. Its swift creep- 580
ing sent a flash of revulsion through him. He raised his head. It felt a great weight.

Then, the little bird ran out of the shadow across a still patch of sunshine, its little head bobbing swiftly, its white legs twinkling brightly for a moment. How neat it was in its build, so compact, with pieces of white on its wings. There were several of them. They were so pretty—but they crept like swift, erratic mice, running here and there among the beech-mast.

He lay down again exhausted, and his consciousness lapsed. He had a horror of the little creeping birds. All his blood seemed to be darting and creeping in his head. And yet he could not move.

He came to with a further ache of exhaustion. There was the pain in his 590 head, and the horrible sickness, and his inability to move. He had never been ill in his life. He did not know where he was or what he was. Probably he had got sun-stroke. Or what else?—he had silenced the Captain for ever—some time ago—oh, a long time ago. There had been blood on his face, and his eyes had turned up-wards. It was all right, somehow. It was peace. But now he had got beyond him-self. He had never been here before. Was it life, or not life? He was by himself. They were in a big, bright place, those others, and he was outside. The town, all the country, a big bright place of light: and he was outside, here, in the darkened open beyond, where each thing existed alone. But they would all have to come out there sometime, those others. Little, and left behind him, they all were. There had 600 been father and mother and sweetheart. What did they all matter? This was the open land.

He sat up. Something scuffled. It was a little brown squirrel running in lovely undulating bounds over the floor, its red tail completing the undulation of its body—and then, as it sat up, furling and unfurling. He watched it, pleased. It ran on again, friskily, enjoying itself. It flew wildly at another squirrel, and they were chasing each other, and making little scolding, chattering noises. The soldier wanted to speak to them. But only a hoarse sound came out of his throat. The squirrels burst away—they flew up the trees. And then he saw the one peeping round at him, half-way up a tree trunk. A start of fear went through him, though 610 in so far as he was conscious, he was amused. It still stayed, its little keen face staring at him half way up the tree-trunk, its little ears pricked up, its clawey little hands clinging to the bark, its white breast reared. He started from it in panic.

Struggling to his feet, he lurched away. He went on walking, walking, look-ing for something—for a drink. His brain felt hot and inflamed for want of water. He stumbled on. Then he did not know anything. He went unconscious as he walked. Yet he stumbled on, his mouth open.

When, to his dumb wonder, he opened his eyes on the world again, he no longer tried to remember what it was. There was thick, golden light behind golden-green glitterings, and tall, grey-purple shafts, and darknesses further off, 620 surrounding him, growing deeper. He was conscious of a sense of arrival. He was amid the reality, on the real, dark bottom. But there was the thirst burning in his brain. He felt lighter, not so heavy. He supposed it was newness. The air was mut-tering with thunder. He thought he was walking wonderfully swiftly and was com-ing straight to relief—or was it to water?

Suddenly he stood still with fear. There was a tremendous flare of gold, im-mense—just a few dark trunks like bars between him and it. All the young level wheat was burnished gold glaring on its silky green. A woman, full-skirted, a black cloth on her head for head-dress, was passing like a block of shadow through the glistening, green corn, into the full glare. There was a farm, too, pale blue in shadow, and the timber black. And there was a church spire, nearly fused away in the gold. The woman moved on, away from him. He had no language with which to speak to her. She was the bright, solid unreality. She would make a noise of words that would confuse him, and her eyes would look at him without seeing him. She was crossing there to the other side. He stood against a tree.

When at last he turned, looking down the long, bare grove whose flat bed was already filling dark, he saw the mountains in a wonder-light, not far away, and radiant. Behind the soft, grey ridge of the nearest range the further mountains stood golden and pale grey, the snow all radiant like pure, soft gold. So still, gleaming in the sky, fashioned pure out of the ore of the sky, they shone in their silence. He stood and looked at them, his face illuminated. And like the golden, lustrous gleaming of the snow he felt his own thirst bright in him. He stood and gazed, leaning against a tree. And then everything slid away into space.

During the night the lightning fluttered perpetually, making the whole sky white. He must have walked again. The world hung livid round him for moments, fields a level sheen of grey-green light, trees in dark bulk, and the range of clouds black across a white sky. Then the darkness fell like a shutter, and the night was whole. A faint flutter of a half-revealed world, that could not quite leap out of the darkness!—Then there again stood a sweep of pallor for the land, dark shapes looming, a range of clouds hanging overhead. The world was a ghostly shadow, thrown for a moment upon the pure darkness, which returned ever whole and complete.

And the mere delirium of sickness and fever went on inside him—his brain opening and shutting like the night—then sometimes convulsions of terror from something with great eyes that stared round a tree—then the long agony of the march, and the sun decomposing his blood—then the pang of hate for the Captain, followed by a pang of tenderness and ease. But everything was distorted, born of an ache and resolving into an ache.

In the morning he came definitely awake. Then his brain flamed with the sole horror of thirstiness! The sun was on his face, the dew was steaming from his wet clothes. Like one possessed, he got up. There, straight in front of him, blue and cool and tender, the mountains ranged across the pale edge of the morning sky. He wanted them—he wanted them alone—he wanted to leave himself and be identified with them. They did not move, they were still and soft, with white, gentle markings of snow. He stood still, mad with suffering, his hands crisping and clutching. Then he was twisting in a paroxysm on the grass.

He lay still, in a kind of dream of anguish. His thirst seemed to have separated itself from him, and to stand apart, a single demand. Then the pain he felt was another single self. Then there was the clog of his body, another separate thing. He was divided among all kinds of separate beings. There was some strange, agonized connection between them, but they were drawing further apart. Then they would all split. The sun, drilling down on him, was drilling through the bond. Then they would all fall, fall through the everlasting lapse of space. Then again, his consciousness reasserted itself. He roused on to his elbow and stared at the gleaming mountains. There they ranked, all still and wonderful between earth and heaven. He started till his eyes went black, and the mountains, as they stood in their beauty, so clean and cool, seemed to have it, that which was lost in him.

IV

WHEN THE SOLDIERS found him, three hours later, he was lying with his face over his arm, his black hair giving off heat under the sun. But he was still alive. Seeing the open, black mouth the young soldiers dropped him in horror.   680

He died in the hospital at night, without having seen again.

The doctors saw the bruises on his legs, behind, and were silent.

The bodies of the two men lay together, side by side, in the mortuary, the one white and slender, but laid rigidly at rest, the other looking as if every moment it must rouse into life again, so young and unused, from a slumber.   [1914]

Questions for Discussion and Writing

1. Analyze the descriptive passages at the beginning and end of the story. How do these relate to the action of the story? What purpose do they serve?
2. Examine the structure of the story. Note that it begins "in the middle" and then moves backward and forward in time. What advantages does Lawrence gain by this structure? What are the disadvantages?
3. Why is the Captain angry with the Soldier?
4. How would a Marxist critic interpret this story? What might it be saying about class and economic struggle?
5. Freudian critics argue that the Captain is a latent homosexual. Do you agree with such a reading? Why or why not?
6. Why does the Soldier kill the Captain?
7. This story is often read allegorically—that is, with each character representing an idea, impulse, personality type, or psychological state. Attempt such a reading yourself.

Sidebar: EXPLORING CRITICAL ISSUES

Psychoanalysis and the Short Story

Stories have always been about characters and what makes them tick, and so in a general sense, literature has always had a psychological element, but it was not until the turn of this century that systematic, scientific psychology developed in the theories of Sigmund Freud (1856–1939). Freud admitted that much of what he knew about the workings of the human mind he learned from literature, but even without this connection the link between the two fields seems natural. Unfortunately, it is also uneasy and problematic.

One problem is that psychoanalysis may be applied to literature in a number of ways. Psychoanalytic theories may be used to investigate the literary work itself, the psychological makeup of the author, characters within the work, and the effects a work has upon its audience. Obviously, psychoanalytical criticism is not just one activity. Second, there is no universally agreed upon psychological theory. Freud's theories are the most popular among literary critics, but Freudians disagree among themselves about what principles to apply and how to apply them. Moreover, there are also other competing theories that can be used in place of Freud's—behaviorism, for example.

Even if we agree on a Freudian approach, however, application reveals its own difficulties. A fundamental problem is Freud's premise that creative works are similar to dreams (products of the unconscious and not literally but symbolically "true") and hence can be interpreted using psychoanalytical techniques. Certainly there are similarities between works of the imagination and dreams, but dreams come uncensored and unbidden; there is no craftsmanship at work in the structure and content of a dream, as there is with a literary work. Psychoanalytic critics would argue, however, that literature may affect us as dreams do, providing escape from re-

Sigmund Freud (1856–1939), Austrian founder of psychoanalysis. (Corbis/Bettman)

ality and opportunities to fulfill repressed and unconscious desires or to express anxieties.

Second, there is also a fundamental problem in trying to psychoanalyze a literary character, because a fictional creation is not a real person. Psychoanalysis was developed for real patients lying on real couches, not for imaginary creations made up of words on a page. Since fictional characters, especially in short stories, are seldom fully developed, there is much we do not and cannot know about them. How can an imaginary and incomplete character be psychoanalyzed? Another problem is whether it is fair to use this method to analyze characters in the works of authors who never heard of Freud. Can the works of nineteenth-century authors, who operated on very different psychological premises from those of modern psychology, be analyzed using systems their authors knew nothing about? Doesn't this distort their work in some fundamental way?

Finally, there is the problem of terminology. Freud's influence on our century has been so profound that many of his ideas and terms have entered into daily conversation without our being fully aware of it. Words and phrases like "unconscious motivation," "Oedipus complex," "repression," "Freudian slip," and "sibling rivalry" are used loosely in casual conversation, often by people who have no idea of their origin. The glib use of psychological terminology in everyday speech does not, however, give us license to use this jargon sloppily in literary analysis. A psychoanalytical approach to a work of literature must be grounded in the reading of at least some psychological theory.

For the interests of this discussion, however, let us review the basic tenets of Freudian psychology. Basic to Freud's understanding of the mind is the notion that most of its activities are unconscious. At the lowest and most basic level is the irrational and unconscious *id,* the source of our biological drives—for food, sex, elimination, anger, etc.—and our instincts for pleasure. Many of these basic urges, especially the quest for sexual gratification and power, are antisocial, even anarchic. At the highest level of the mind is the *superego,* what has traditionally been thought of as conscience and the rational understanding of society's norms and values. Between the *id* and the *superego* lies the *ego,* which negotiates between the demands of the *id* for pleasure and the demands of the *superego* for socially acceptable and moral conduct. As noted above, most of our motivations are unconscious; that is, we do not really understand why we act as we do, because our real motives (as opposed to those we might admit to ourselves) lie buried in the unconscious.

One of the earliest manifestations of the above system, Freud argued, is the Oedipus Complex, so called because in Sophocles' play *Oedipus Rex,* the protagonist kills his father and marries his mother without knowing who they really are. Freud argues that all boys want to bond with their mother and exclude their father, but since this is not possible, the desire is repressed. Moreover, the child fears that the father, sensing this rivalry, wants to castrate him. Eventually the boy acknowledges defeat, acknowledges the prior claims and superior force of the father, and displaces his love for his mother by attaching his desires to another woman. The equivalent (reversed) pattern in females is called the Electra Complex.

These ideas regarding children's sexuality are among his most well known and controversial, but they are of course not his only contribution to psychological theory. A number of his ideas have become widely accepted (if not always fully understood) ways to describe the workings of the mind. A few of the more important of these may be briefly defined, as follows:

Repression: the way in which the mind hides or buries its desires and anxieties in the subconscious.

Sublimation: redirecting immoral or anti-social impulses to a constructive or socially acceptable end: e.g., using athletics to vent aggression or expressing unconscious desires through creativity.

Displacement: exchanging an unacceptable or dangerous object of emotion for a safe one: e.g., from father to lover.

Denial: refusing to accept reality.

Isolation: experiencing something without receiving the expected response: e.g., not receiving praise for a good deed or punishment for a bad one.

Intellectualization: dealing with an anxiety or a frightening emotion (the desire to murder, for example) by talking about it.

Sibling rivalry: the natural antagonism between brothers and sisters for affection and approval from the parents and for domination over the other children in the family.

In spite of their limitations, psychoanalytic approaches to literature have enriched literary analysis. Nevertheless, one cannot simply lay a psychoanalytical grid over a story and produce an interesting reading. Like any method, psychoanalysis requires imagination and tact. Without pretending that the following analyses are ideal applications of the method, let us examine some works that seem to lend themselves to a psychological approach.

Fairy tales were initially thought of as interesting relics of the folk imagination or as amusing stories for children, but recent criticism has seen in them far more than either of these approaches would admit. The Tale of "The Blue Beard," for example, can be read on one level as a cautionary tale against disobedience or undue curiosity (especially on the part of young women) and as a warning against greed. But neither of these interpretations accounts for the disturbing elements of the story—its violence and the bizarre ways in which the characters behave. At the rational level, it is difficult to understand the youngest daughter's motivation for marrying Blue Beard, when she is put off by his appearance and suspicious of the fate of his former wives. Yet marry him she does, apparently because of his wealth, or is sibling rivalry at work here?

Perhaps one way to approach this story psychoanalytically is to see it as an illustration of the operation of the id—that part of the subconscious that propels us toward sexual license and anti-social mayhem. Blue Beard, in spite of a veneer of respectability, indulges both of these lusts in a succession of wives whom he first beds and then murders. The key, long a sexual symbol, functions symbolically here; the magic blood that cannot be wiped off is the sign of her disobedience and a manifestation of Blue Beard's powers. For her part, the behavior of the young bride suggests the fascination with the horrible that we all feel on occasion—the pull of the id. It may not be going too far to connect this attraction/repulsion with the so-called death wish—the subconscious desire to escape the difficulties of life through annihilation. The climactic scene brings these elements together as Blue Beard threatens to kill her with a sword (an obvious phallic symbol). Her rescue may be seen as the socially necessary triumph of the superego (society and its rules) intervening in time to save her.

Freud left no doubt that his theories could be applied to literature, for he did so himself. One famous instance is his analysis of Hoffman's "The Sandman" in his essay on "The Uncanny" (in volume 17 of the complete works). As noted above, the Oedipus complex is central to Freud's thought. Freud sees in "The Sandman" a classic case of Oedipal fixation and fear of castration. The evil Dr. Coppelius becomes associated in Nathanael's mind with the Sand Man, both of whom are father (authority) figures. Thus, when Nathanael is caught spying by Dr. Coppelius, who threatens to put out his eyes with hot coals, Freud sees this as the boy's fear of castration (blinding in Freud's view is symbolic castration). Fortunately, the "good father" overcomes the "bad father" for the moment, but not long afterward, he dies. The Oedipal dilemma is thus temporarily resolved, but it reappears when Nathanael falls in love with Clara, and the Sand Man (this time in the guise of Coppola, the barometer-seller) visits Nathanael and plunges him into despondency, thus separating him from Clara. With Olympia, the automaton, Freud again notes that there are two fathers, and again Coppelius intervenes (claiming, significantly, to have made her eyes) and carries off Olympia. Finally, when Nathanael has reunited with Clara, Coppelius returns and Nathanael commits suicide. Freud remarks that the story makes sense only when we realize that Nathanael's fear of losing his eyes and his loathing for Coppelius are related to the Oedipal triangle and his fear of castration.

D. H. Lawrence's "The Prussian Officer" was written when Freud's theories were becoming known in England. Lawrence almost certainly knew at least something of Freud. Seen from a Freudian perspective, the Prussian Officer is a classic case of repression: jealousy and a refusal to acknowledge his own homosexual tendencies produce in the Officer a cruelly misdirected sadism toward the object of his desire, the young orderly—a classic case of displacement.

There is another way to apply Freudian theory to this story. Lawrence's animal imagery in reference to the orderly clearly identifies him with the instinctual as opposed to the rational or intellectual. The two men may thus be seen as representing the classic dualism of human nature: the rational/intellectual superego vs. the instinctual id. But Lawrence treats the theme differently from the way earlier writers would do, because for him the instinctual is not "bestial" but that part of us that is in touch with healthy natural urges. The bullying of the Officer is symptomatic of the operation of the superego; but given no appropriate outlet for instinctual urges (the Officer cannot marry but indulges in brief, unsatisfactory affairs with a succession of mistresses), the superego bullies the id until the id takes its revenge—with great pleasure in doing so. That the two men may represent aspects of a single self is emphasized by the story's end in which the two men lie side by side in the mortuary.

Conrad Aiken's "Silent Snow, Secret Snow" was written under Freud's direct influence. Since Aiken himself wrote a Freudian study of American literature, he obviously knew Freud's ideas and was adept at using them. Aiken tells us that the idea for the story came when he was living in the English town of Rye, where every morning as he lay in bed he could hear the heavy tread of the postman coming down the hill. The rest, he says, is pure imagination. What imagination has produced, however, can be seen as a classic study of a descent into madness, as young Paul retreats further and further from reality into a world of his own making. In fact, Peter A. Martin has reported in the *Journal of the American Psychoanalytic Association* (January 1960) that the story accurately details the course of a recognized psychological condition caused by hostile impulses toward the outside world, as a result of which the patient believes he sees layers of snow between him and reality.

The problem with this approach is that it reduces fiction to a psychological case study and apparently closes off other interpretations. Clinical case studies are not all that interesting from a literary point of view. The challenge to a Freudian/psychoanalytical approach to this story is not to allow it to dictate *the* meaning. Can the snow be interpreted symbolically? Do we have to accept a diagnosis of mental illness, or could Paul simply be discovering what many artists discover—the attractions of the world of imagination?

In Joyce Carol Oates's "Where Are You Going? Where Have You Been?" we return to the Blue Beard theme. The questions posed by the title are those parents often ask their children and thus suggest the parental authority that is otherwise mostly absent from the story. There is a significant difference, however, in that the ironically named Arnold Friend at first seems very attractive, both physically and personally, in part, of course, because he is also a rebel. As the story progresses, though, he becomes increasingly threatening, as does Blue Beard, and what once appeared as exciting teenage rebellion becomes actual menace. He seems like a figure in a nightmare. The ringing telephone holds the potential of rescue, but will it come in time? Or has Connie's curiosity about the forbidden gone beyond what she can control, and will it lead to her destruction? Like "The Blue Beard," Oates's story can be read as a cautionary tale whose moral is that "bad boys" cannot be trusted, but more importantly the story points to the attraction and the threat of evil, of the demon lover. For Arnold Friend appears to possess uncanny knowledge of Connie's name and address, her family's whereabouts, even her sister's dress. Here again, the romance of danger may be linked with the death wish and the tug of the id in opposition to the superego as represented by the parents and Connie's own fears.

Like any system of interpretation, psychoanalytic criticism has the advantage of opening up the story and taking us beneath its surfaces. Such analysis also helps to explain the peculiar power of stories and why certain motifs keep appearing. Margaret Atwood's "Bluebeard's Egg" is another manifestation of the Blue Beard theme, only in this case the Blue Beard figure is the opposite of the threatening, menacing id. Or is he? Applying Freud's ideas—or those of any other psychological theories—may stimulate thought and the critical imagination to see beneath the surface to ideas and themes that lie beneath.

❧ SUSAN GLASPELL
(1882–1948)

A Jury of Her Peers

Susan Glaspell spent most of her writing life as a journalist and playwright, but with "A Jury of Her Peers" she carved for herself a permanent place in the canon of American short stories.

She was born in Davenport, Iowa, where she attended public school and graduated from high school in 1894. After earning a degree from Drake University in Des Moines in 1899, she spent a year as a political reporter but then returned home to write full time. In 1902, she entered the University of Chicago for graduate study and was influenced there by the "Chicago Renaissance." By 1909, she had published her first novel and was contributing stories to *Harper's* magazine, among others.

In 1913, Glaspell returned to Davenport and fell in love with a married man, George Cram Cook—an eccentric disciple of Henry David Thoreau's (1817–1862). They married after his divorce and moved to Provincetown, New Jersey. The following year they attempted to found an ideal community in conjunction with the Provincetown Players, a theatrical group. Over the next decade, Glaspell wrote ten plays that were performed by the Provincetown Players. Her masterpiece, *Trifles* (1916), became "A Jury of Her Peers" the following year.

Cook's search for an ideal community took them to Greece in 1922, where he died two years later. Glaspell returned to America, formed a liaison with novelist Norman Matson, and continued to write until the end of her life.

Glaspell's work often depicts conflicts between men and women. In "A Jury of Her Peers," she deals with questions of perception, the value of women's work, and the issue of justice.

WHEN MARTHA HALE opened the storm-door and got a cut of the north wind, she ran back for her big woolen scarf. As she hurriedly wound that round her head her eye made a scandalized sweep of her kitchen. It was no ordinary thing that called her away—it was probably farther from ordinary than anything that had ever happened in Dickson County. But what her eye took in was that her kitchen was in no shape for leaving: her bread all ready for mixing, half the flour sifted and half unsifted.

She hated to see things half done; but she had been at that when the team from town stopped to get Mr. Hale, and then the sheriff came running in to say his wife wished Mrs. Hale would come too—adding, with a grin, that he guessed she 10 was getting scarey and wanted another woman along. So she had dropped everything right where it was.

"Martha!" now came her husband's impatient voice. "Don't keep folks waiting out here in the cold."

She again opened the storm-door, and this time joined the three men and the one woman waiting for her in the big two-seated buggy.

After she had the robes tucked around her she took another look at the woman who sat beside her on the back seat. She had met Mrs. Peters the year before at the county fair, and the thing she remembered about her was that she didn't seem like a sheriff's wife. She was small and thin and didn't have a strong 20 voice. Mrs. Gorman, sheriff's wife before Gorman went out and Peters came in, had a voice that somehow seemed to be backing up the law with every word. But if Mrs. Peters didn't look like a sheriff's wife, Peters made it up in looking like a sheriff. He was to a dot the kind of man who could get himself elected sheriff—a heavy man with a big voice, who was particularly genial with the law-abiding, as if to make it plain that he knew the difference between criminals and non-criminals. And right there it came into Mrs. Hale's mind, with a stab, that this man who was so pleasant and lively with all of them was going to the Wrights' now as a sheriff.

"The country's not very pleasant this time of year," Mr. Peters at last ventured, as if she felt they ought to be talking as well as the men.   30

Mrs. Hale scarcely finished her reply, for they had gone up a little hill and could see the Wright place now, and seeing it did not make her feel like talking. It looked very lonesome this cold March morning. It had always been a lonesome-looking place. It was down in a hollow, and the poplar trees around it were lonesome-looking trees. The men were looking at it and talking about what had happened. The county attorney was bending to one side of the buggy, and kept looking steadily at the place as they drew up to it.

"I'm glad you came with me," Mrs. Peters said nervously, as the two women were about to follow the men in through the kitchen door.

Even after she had her foot on the door-step, her hand on the knob, Martha 40

Hale had a moment of feeling she could not cross that threshold. And the reason it seemed she couldn't cross it now was simply because she hadn't crossed it before. Time and time again it had been in her mind, "I ought to go over and see Minnie Foster"—she still thought of her as Minnie Foster, though for twenty years she had been Mrs. Wright. And then there was always something to do and Minnie Foster would go from her mind. But *now* she could come.

The men went over to the stove. The women stood close together by the door. Young Henderson, the country attorney, turned around and said, "Come up to the fire, ladies."

Mrs. Peters took a step forward, then stopped. "I'm not—cold," she said.   50

And so the two women stood by the door, at first not even so much as looking around the kitchen.

The men talked for a minute about what a good thing it was the sheriff had sent his deputy out that morning to make a fire for them, and then Sheriff Peters stepped back from the stove, unbuttoned his outer coat, and leaned his hands on the kitchen table in a way that seemed to mark the beginning of official business. "Now, Mr. Hale," he said in a sort of semi-official voice, "before we move things about, you tell Mr. Henderson just what it was you saw when you came here yesterday morning."

The county attorney was looking around the kitchen.   60

"By the way," he said, "has anything been moved?" He turned to the sheriff. "Are things just as you left them yesterday?"

Peters looked from cupboard to sink; from that to a small worn rocker a little to one side of the kitchen table.

"It's just the same."

"Somebody should have been left here yesterday," said the county attorney.

"Oh—yesterday," returned the sheriff, with a little gesture as of yesterday having been more than he could bear to think of. "When I had to send Frank to Morris Center for that man who went crazy—let me tell you, I had my hands full *yesterday.* I knew you could get back from Omaha by to-day, George, and as long   70 as I went over everything here myself—"

"Well, Mr. Hale," said the county attorney, in a way of letting what was past and gone go, "tell just what happened when you came here yesterday morning."

Mrs. Hale, still leaning against the door, had that sinking feeling of the mother whose child is about to speak a piece. Lewis often wandered along and got things mixed up in a story. She hoped he would tell this straight and plain, and not say unnecessary things that would just make things harder for Minnie Foster. He didn't begin at once, and she noticed that he looked queer—as if standing in that kitchen and having to tell what he had seen there yesterday morning made him almost sick.   80

"Yes, Mr. Hale?" the county attorney reminded.

"Harry and I had started to town with a load of potatoes," Mrs. Hale's husband began.

Harry was Mrs. Hale's oldest boy. He wasn't with them now, for the very good reason that those potatoes never got to town yesterday and he was taking them this morning, so he hadn't been home when the sheriff stopped to say he wanted Mr. Hale to come over to the Wright place and tell the county attorney his story there, where he could point it all out. With all Mrs. Hale's other emotions came the fear that maybe Harry wasn't dressed warm enough—they hadn't any of them realized how that north wind did bite.

"We come along this road," Hale was going on, with a motion of his hand to the road over which they had just come, "and as we got in sight of the house I says to Harry, 'I'm goin' to see if I can't get John Wright to take a telephone.' You see," he explained to Henderson, "unless I can get somebody to go in with me they won't come out this branch road except for a price I can't pay. I'd spoke to Wright about it once before; but he put me off, saying folks talked too much anyway, and all he asked was peace and quiet—guess you know about how much he talked himself. But I thought maybe if I went to the house and talked about it before his wife, and said all the women-folks liked the telephones, and that in this lonesome stretch of road it would be a good thing—well, I said to Harry that that was what I was going to say—though I said at the same time that I didn't know as what his wife wanted made much difference to John—"

Now, there he was!—saying things he didn't need to say. Mrs. Hale tried to catch her husband's eye, but fortunately the county attorney interrupted with:

"Let's talk about that a little later, Mr. Hale. I do want to talk about that, but I'm anxious now to get along to just what happened when you got here."

When he began this time, it was very deliberately and careful:

"I didn't see or hear anything. I knocked at the door. And still it was all quiet inside. I knew they must be up—it was past eight o'clock. So I knocked again, louder, and I thought I heard somebody say 'Come in.' I wasn't sure—I'm not sure yet. But I opened the door—this door," jerking a hand toward the door by which the two women stood, "and there, in that rocker"—pointing to it—"sat Mrs. Wright."

Every one in the kitchen looked at the rocker. It came into Mrs. Hale's mind that the rocker didn't look in the least like Minnie Foster—the Minnie Foster of twenty years before. It was a dingy red, with wooden rungs up the back and the middle rung was gone, and the chair sagged to one side.

"How did she—look?" the county attorney was inquiring.

"Well," said Hale, "she looked—queer."

"How do you mean—queer?"

As he asked it he took out a note-book and pencil. Mrs. Hale did not like the sight of that pencil. She kept her eye fixed on her husband, as if to keep him from saying unnecessary things that would go into that note-book and make trouble.

Hale did speak guardedly, as if the pencil had affected him too.

"Well, as if she didn't know what she was going to do next. And kind of—done up."

"How did she seem to feel about your coming?"

"Why, I don't think she minded—one way or other. She didn't pay much attention. I said, 'Ho' do, Mrs. Wright? It's cold, ain't it?' And she said, 'Is it?'—and went on pleatin' at her apron.

"Well, I was surprised. She didn't ask me to come up to the stove, or to sit down, but just set there, not even lookin' at me. And so I said: 'I want to see John.'

"And then she—laughed. I guess you would call it a laugh.

"I thought of Harry and the team outside, so I said, a little sharp, 'Can I see John?' 'No,' says she—kind of dull like. 'Ain't he home?' says I. Then she looked at me. 'Yes,' says she, 'he's home.' 'Then why can't I see him?' I asked her, out of patience with her now. 'Cause he's dead' says she, just as quiet and dull—and fell to pleatin' her apron. 'Dead?' says I, like you do when you can't take in what you've heard.

"She just nodded her head, not getting a bit excited, but rockin' back and   140
forth.

" 'Why—where is he?' says I, not knowing *what* to say.

"She just pointed upstairs—like this"—pointing to the room above.

"I got up, with the idea of going up there myself. By this time I—didn't know what to do. I walked from there to here; then I says: 'Why, what did he die of?'

" 'He died of a rope around his neck,' says she; and just went on pleatin' at her apron."

Hale stopped speaking, and stood staring at the rocker, as if he were still seeing the woman who had sat there the morning before. Nobody spoke; it was as if   150
every one were seeing the woman who had sat there the morning before.

"And what did you do then?" the county attorney at last broke the silence.

"I went out and called Harry. I thought I might—need help. I got Harry in, and we went upstairs." His voice fell almost to a whisper. "There he was—lying over the—"

"I think I'd rather have you go into that upstairs," the county attorney interrupted, "where you can point it all out. Just go on now with the rest of the story."

"Well, my first thought was to get that rope off. It looked—"

He stopped, his face twitching.

"But Harry, he went up to him, and he said, 'No, he's dead all right, and we'd   160
better not touch anything.' So we went downstairs.

"She was still sitting that same way. 'Has anybody been notified?' I asked. 'No,' says she, unconcerned.

" 'Who did this, Mrs. Wright?' said Harry. He said it business-like, and she stopped pleatin' at her apron. 'I don't know' she says. 'You don't *know?*' says Harry. 'Weren't you sleepin' in the bed with him?' 'Yes,' says she, 'but I was on the inside.' 'Somebody slipped a rope around his neck and strangled him, and you didn't wake up?' says Harry. 'I didn't wake up,' she said after him.

'We may have looked as if we didn't see how that could be, for after a minute she said, 'I sleep sound.'   170

"Harry was going to ask her more questions, but I said maybe that weren't our business; maybe we ought to let her tell her story first to the coroner or the sheriff. So Harry went fast as he could over to High Road—the Rivers' place, where there's a telephone."

"And what did she do when she knew you had gone for the coroner?" The attorney got his pencil in his hand all ready for writing.

"She moved from that chair to this one over here"—Hale pointed to a small chair in the corner—"and just sat there with her hands held together and looking down. I got a feeling that I ought to make some conversation, so I said I had come in to see if John wanted to put in a telephone; and at that she started to laugh, and then she stopped and looked at me—scared." 180

At the sound of a moving pencil the man who was telling the story looked up.

"I dunno—maybe it wasn't scared," he hastened; "I wouldn't like to say it was. Soon Harry got back and then Dr. Lloyd came, and you, Mr. Peters, an so I guess that's all I know that you don't."

He said that last with relief, and moved a little, as if relaxing. Every one moved a little. The county attorney walked toward the stair door.

"I guess we'll go upstairs first—then out to the barn and around there."

He paused and looked around the kitchen. 190

"You're convinced there was nothing important here?" he asked the sheriff. "Nothing that would—point to any motive?"

The sheriff too looked all around, as if to re-convince himself.

"Nothing here but kitchen things," he said, with a little laugh for the insignificance of kitchen things.

The county attorney was looking at the cupboard—a peculiar, ungainly structure, half closet and half cupboard, the upper part of it being built in the wall, and the lower part just the old-fashioned kitchen cupboard. As if its queerness attracted him, he got a chair and opened the upper part and looked in. After a moment he drew his hand away sticky. 200

"Here's a nice mess," he said resentfully.

The two women had drawn nearer, and now the sheriff's wife spoke.

"Oh—her fruit," she said, looking to Mrs. Hale for sympathetic understanding. She turned back to the county attorney and explained: "She worried about that when it turned so cold last night. She said the fire would go out and her jars might burst."

Mrs. Peters' husband broke into a laugh.

"Well, can you beat the women! Held for murder, and worrying about her preserves!"

The young attorney set his lips. 210

"I guess before we're through with her she may have something more serious than preserves to worry about."

"Oh, well," said Mrs. Hale's husband, with good-natured superiority, "women are used to worrying over trifles."

The two women moved a little closer together. Neither of them spoke. The county attorney seemed suddenly to remember his manners—and think of his future.

"And yet," said he, with the gallantry of a young politician, "for all their worries, what would we do without the ladies?"

The women did not speak, did not unbend. He went to the sink and began 220 washing his hands. He turned to wipe them on the roller towel—whirled it for a cleaner place.

"Dirty towels! Not much of a housekeeper, would you say, ladies?" He kicked his foot against some dirty pans under the sink.

"There's a great deal of work to be done on a farm," said Mrs. Hale stiffly.

"To be sure. And yet"—with a little bow to her—"I know there are some Dickson County farm-houses that do not have such roller towels." He gave it a pull to expose its full length again.

"Those towels get dirty awful quick. Men's hands aren't always as clean as they might be."   230

"Ah, loyal to your sex, I see," he laughed. He stopped and gave her a keen look. "But you and Mrs. Wright were neighbors. I suppose you were friends, too."

Martha Hale shook her head.

"I've seen little enough of her of late years. I've not been in this house—it's more than a year."

"And why was that? You didn't like her?"

"I liked her well enough," she replied with spirit. "Farmer's wives have their hands full, Mr. Henderson. And then"—She looked around the kitchen.

"Yes" he encouraged.

"It never seemed a very cheerful place," said she, more to herself than to him. 240

"No," he agreed; "I don't think any one would call it cheerful. I shouldn't say she had the home-making instinct."

"Well, I don't know as Wright had, either," she muttered.

"You mean they didn't get on very well?" he was quick to ask.

"No; I don't mean anything," she answered, with decision. As she turned a little away from him, she added: "But I don't think a place would be any the cheer-fuler for John Wright's bein' in it."

"I'd like to talk to you about that a little later, Mrs. Hale," he said. "I'm anx-ious to get the lay of things upstairs now."

He moved toward the stair door, followed by the two men.   250

"I suppose anything Mrs. Peters does'll be all right?" the sheriff inquired. "She was to take in some clothes for her, you know—and a few little things. We left in such a hurry yesterday."

The county attorney looked at the two women whom they were leaving alone there among the kitchen things.

"Yes—Mrs. Peters," he said, his glance resting on the woman who was not Mrs. Peters, the big farmer woman who stood behind the sheriff's wife. "Of course Mrs. Peters is one of us," he said, in a manner of entrusting responsibility. "And keep your eye out, Mrs. Peters, for anything that might be of use. No telling; you women might come upon a clue to the motive—and that's the thing we need."   260

Mr. Hale rubbed his face after the fashion of a show man getting ready for a pleasantry.

"But would the women know a clue if they did come upon it?" he said; and, having delivered himself of this, he followed the others through the stair door.

The women stood motionless and silent, listening to the footsteps, first upon the stairs, then in the room above them.

Then, as if releasing herself from something strange, Mrs. Hale began to arrange the dirty pans under the sink, which the county attorney's disdainful push of the foot had deranged.

"I'd hate to have men comin' into my kitchen," she said testily—"snoopin' 270 round and criticizin'."

"Of course it's no more than their duty," said the sheriff's wife, in her manner of timid acquiescence.

"Duty's all right," replied Mrs. Hale bluffly; "but I guess that deputy sheriff that come out to make the fire might have got a little of this on." She gave the roller towel a pull. "Wish I'd thought of that sooner! Seems mean to talk about her for not having things slicked up, when she had to come away in such a hurry."

She looked around the kitchen. Certainly it was not "slicked up." Her eye was held by a bucket of sugar on a low shelf. The cover was off the wooden bucket, and beside it was a paper bag—half full. 280

Mrs. Hale moved toward it.

"She was putting this in there," she said to herself—slowly.

She thought of the flour in her kitchen at home—half sifted, half not sifted. She had been interrupted and had left things half done. What had interrupted Minnie Foster? Why had that work been left half done? She made a move as if to finish it,—unfinished things always bothered her,—and then she glanced around and saw that Mrs. Peters was watching her—and she didn't want Mrs. Peters to get that feeling she had got of work begun and then—for some reason—not finished.

"It's a shame about her fruit," she said, and walked toward the cupboard that the county attorney had opened, and got on the chair, murmuring: "I wonder if it's 290 all gone."

It was a sorry enough looking sight, but "Here's one that's all right," she said at last. She held it toward the light. "This is cherries, too." She looked again. "I declare I believe that's the only one."

With a sigh, she got down from the chair, went to the sink, and wiped off the bottle.

She'll feel awful bad, after all her hard work in the hot weather. I remember the afternoon I put up my cherries last summer."

She set the bottle on the table, and, with another sigh, started to sit down in the rocker. But she did not sit down. Something kept her from sitting down in that 300 chair. She straightened—stepped back, and, half turned away, stood looking at it, seeing the woman who sat there "pleatin' at her apron."

The thin voice of the sheriff's wife broke in upon her: "I must be getting those things from the front room closet." She opened the door into the other room, started in, stepped back. "You coming with me, Mrs. Hale?" she asked nervously. "You—you could help me get them."

They were soon back—the dark coldness of that shut-up room was not a thing to linger in.

"My!" said Mrs. Peters, dropping the things on the table and hurrying to the stove. 310

Mrs. Hale stood examining the clothes the woman who was being detained in town had said she wanted.

"Wright was close!" she exclaimed, holding up a shabby black skirt that bore the marks of much making over. "I think maybe that's why she kept so much to herself. I s'pose she felt she couldn't do her part; and then, you don't enjoy things when you feel shabby. She used to wear pretty clothes and be lively—when she was Minnie Foster, one of the town girls, singing in the choir. But that—oh, that was twenty years ago."

With a carefulness in which there was something tender, she folded the shabby clothes and piled them at one corner of the table. She looked at Mrs. 320 Peters, and there was something in the other woman's look that irritated her.

"She don't care," she said to herself. "Much difference it makes to her whether Minnie Foster had pretty clothes when she was a girl."

Then she looked again, and she wasn't so sure; in fact, she hadn't at any time been perfectly sure about Mrs. Peters. She had that shrinking manner, and yet her eyes looked as if they could see a long way into things.

"This all you was to take in?" asked Mrs. Hale.

"No," said the sheriff's wife; "she said she wanted an apron. Funny thing to want," she ventured in her nervous little way, "for there's not much to get you dirty in jail, goodness knows. But I suppose just to make her feel more natural. If you're 330 used to wearing an apron—. She said they were in the bottom drawer of this cupboard. Yes—here they are. And then her little shawl that always hung on the stair door."

She took the small gray shawl from behind the door leading upstairs, and stood a minute looking at it.

Suddenly Mrs. Hale took a quick step toward the other woman.

"Mrs. Peters!"

"Yes, Mrs. Hale?"

"Do you think she—did it?"

A frightened look blurred the other things in Mrs. Peters' eyes.   340

"Oh, I don't know," she said, in a voice that seemed to shrink away from the subject.

"Well, I don't think she did," affirmed Mrs. Hale stoutly. "Asking for an apron, and her little shawl. Worryin' about her fruit."

"Mr. Peters says—" Footsteps were heard in the room above; she stopped, looked up, then went on in a lowered voice: "Mr. Peters says—it looks bad for her. Mr. Henderson is awful sarcastic in a speech, and he's going to make fun of her saying she didn't—wake up."

For a moment Mrs. Hale had no answer. Then, "Well, I guess John Wright didn't wake up—when they was slippin' that rope under his neck," she muttered. 350

"No, it's *strange*," breathed Mrs. Peters. "They think it was such a—funny way to kill a man."

She began to laugh; at sound of the laugh, abruptly stopped.

"That's just what Mr. Hale said," said Mrs. Hale, in a resolutely natural voice. "There was a gun in the house. He says that's what he can't understand."

"Mr. Henderson said, coming out, that what was needed for the case was a motive. Something to show anger—or sudden feeling."

"Well, I don't see any signs of anger around here," said Mrs. Hale. "I don't—She stopped. It was as if her mind tripped on something. Her eye was caught by a dish-towel in the middle of the kitchen table. Slowly she moved toward the table. 360 One half of it was wiped clean, the other half messy. Her eyes made a slow, almost unwilling turn to the bucket of sugar and the half empty bag beside it. Things begun—and not finished.

After a moment she stepped back, and said, in that manner of releasing herself:

"Wonder how they're finding things upstairs? I hope she had it a little more red up there. You know,"—she paused, and feeling gathered,—"it seems kind of *sneaking*; locking her up in town and coming out here to get her own house to turn against her!"

"But, Mrs. Hale," said the sheriff's wife, "the law is the law."   370

"I s'pose 'tis," answered Mrs. Hale shortly.

She turned to the stove, saying something about that fire not being much to brag of. She worked with it a minute, and when she straightened up she said aggressively:

"The law is the law—and a bad stove is a bad stove. How'd you like to cook on this?—pointing with the poker to the broken lining. She opened the oven door and started to express her opinion of the oven; but she was swept into her own thoughts, thinking of what it would mean, year after year, to have that stove to wrestle with. The thought of Minnie Foster trying to bake in that oven—and the thought of her never going over to see Minnie Foster—.   380

She was startled by hearing Mrs. Peters say: "A person gets discouraged—and loses heart."

The sheriff's wife had looked from the stove to the sink—to the pail of water which had been carried in from outside. The two women stood there silent, above them the footsteps of the men who were looking for evidence against the woman who had worked in that kitchen. That look of seeing into things, of seeing through a thing to something else, was in the eyes of the sheriff's wife now. When Mrs. Hale next spoke to her, it was gently:

"Better loosen up your things, Mrs. Peters. We'll not feel them when we go out."   390

Mrs. Peters went to the back of the room to hang up the fur tippet[1] she was wearing. A moment later she exclaimed, "Why, she was piecing a quilt," and held up a large sewing basket piled high with quilt pieces.

Mrs. Hale spread some of the blocks on the table.

"It's log-cabin pattern," she said, putting several of them together. "Pretty, isn't it?"

They were so engaged with the quilt that they did not hear the footsteps on the stairs. Just as the stair door opened Mrs. Hale was saying:

"Do you suppose she was going to quilt it or just knot it?"[2]

The sheriff threw up his hands.   400

"They wonder whether she was going to quilt it or just knot it!"

There was a laugh for the ways of women, a warming of hands over the stove, and then the county attorney said briskly:

"Well, let's go right out to the barn and get that cleared up."

1. A cape.
2. These are two ways of joining the three layers of a quilt. Quilting means sewing them together with small stitches and is the more time-consuming and artistic method; knotting means joining the three layers by a series of loops of yarn tied on the underside.

"I don't see as there's anything so strange," Mrs. Hale said resentfully, after the outside door had closed on the three men—"our taking up our time with little things while we're waiting for them to get the evidence. I don't see as it's anything to laugh about."

"Of course they've got awful important things on their minds," said the sheriff's wife apologetically.   410

They returned to an inspection of the blocks for the quilt. Mrs. Hale was looking at the fine, even sewing, and preoccupied with thoughts of the woman who had done that sewing, when she heard the sheriff's wife say, in a queer tone:

"Why, look at this one."

She turned to take the block held out to her.

"The sewing," said Mrs. Peters, in a troubled way. "All the rest of them have been so nice and even—but—this one. Why, it looks as if she didn't know what she was about!"

Their eyes met—something flashed to life, passed between them; then, as if with an effort, they seemed to pull away from each other. A moment Mrs. Hale sat 420
there, her hands folded over that sewing which was so unlike all the rest of the sewing. Then she had pulled a knot and drawn the threads.

"Oh, what are you doing, Mrs. Hale?" asked the sheriff's wife, startled.

"Just pulling out a stitch or two that's not sewed very good," said Mrs. Hale mildly.

"I don't think we ought to touch things," Mrs. Peters said, a little helplessly.

"I'd just finish up this end," answered Mrs. Hale, still in that mild, matter-of-fact fashion.

She threaded a needle and started to replace bad sewing with good. For a little while she sewed in silence. Then, in that thin, timid voice, she heard: 430

"Mrs. Hale!"

"Yes, Mrs. Peters?"

"What do you suppose she was so—nervous about?"

"Oh, I don't know," said Mrs. Hale, as if dismissing a thing not important enough to spend much time on. "I don't know as she was—nervous. I sew awful queer sometimes when I'm just tired."

She cut a thread, and out of the corner of her eye looked up at Mrs. Peters. The small lean face of the sheriff's wife seemed to have tightened up. Her eyes had that look of peering into something. But the next moment she moved, and said in her thin, indecisive way: 440

"Well, I must get those clothes wrapped. They may be through sooner than we think. I wonder where I could find a piece of paper—and string."

"In that cupboard, maybe," suggested Mrs. Hale, after a glance around.

One piece of the crazy sewing remained unripped. Mrs. Peters' back turned, Martha Hale now scrutinized that piece, compared it with the dainty, accurate sewing of the other blocks. The difference was startling. Holding this block made her feel queer, as if the distracted thoughts of the woman who had perhaps turned to it to try and quiet herself were communicating themselves to her.

Mrs. Peters' voice roused her.   450

"Here's a bird-cage," she said. "Did she have a bird, Mrs. Hale?"

"Why, I don't know whether she did or not." She turned to look at the cage Mrs. Peters was holding up. "I've not been here in so long." She sighed. "There was a man round last year selling canaries cheap—but I don't know as she took one. Maybe she did. She used to sing real pretty herself."

Mrs. Peters looked around the kitchen.

"Seems kind of funny to think of a bird here." She half laughed—an attempt to put up a barrier. "But she must have had one—or why would she have a cage? I wonder what happened to it."

"I suppose maybe the cat got it," suggested Mrs. Hale, resuming her sewing. 460

"No; she didn't have a cat. She's got that feeling some people have about cats—being afraid of them. When they brought her to our house yesterday, my cat got in the room, and she was real upset and asked me to take it out."

"My sister Bessie was like that," laughed Mrs. Hale.

The sheriff's wife did not reply. The silence made Mrs. Hale turn round. Mrs. Peters was examining the bird-cage.

"Look at this door," she said slowly. "It's broke. One hinge has been pulled apart."

Mrs. Hale came nearer.

"Looks as if some one must have been—rough with it." 470

Again their eyes met—startled, questioning, apprehensive. For a moment neither spoke nor stirred. Then Mrs. Hale, turning away, said brusquely:

"If they're going to find any evidence, I wish they'd be about it. I don't like this place."

"But I'm awful glad you came with me, Mrs. Hale." Mrs. Peters put the bird-cage on the table and sat down. "It would be lonesome for me—sitting here alone."

"Yes, it would, wouldn't it?" agreed Mrs. Hale, a certain determined natural-ness in her voice. She picked up the sewing, but now it dropped in her lap, and she murmured in a different voice: "But I tell you what I *do* wish, Mrs. Peters. I 480 wish I had come over sometimes when she was here. I wish—I had."

"But of course you were awful busy, Mrs. Hale. Your house—and your children."

"I could've come," retorted Mrs. Hale shortly. "I stayed away because it weren't cheerful—and that's why I ought to have come. I"—she looked around— "I've never liked this place. Maybe because it's down in a hollow and you don't see the road. I don't know what it is, but it's a lonesome place, and always was. I wish I had come over to see Minnie Foster sometimes. I can see now—" She did not put it into words.

"Well, you mustn't reproach yourself," counseled Mrs. Peters. "Somehow, we 490 just don't see how it is with other folks till—something comes up."

"Not having children makes less work," mused Mrs. Hale, after a silence, "but it makes a quiet house—and Wright out to work all day—and no company when he did come in. Did you know John Wright, Mrs. Peters?"

"Not to know him. I've seen him in town. They say he was a good man."

"Yes—good," conceded John Wright's neighbor grimly. "He didn't drink, and kept his word as well as most, I guess, and paid his debts. But he was a hard man, Mrs. Peters. Just to pass the time of day with him." She stopped, shivered a little. "Like a raw wind that gets to the bone." Her eye fell upon the cage on the table before her, and she added, almost bitterly: "I should think she would've wanted a 500 bird!"

Suddenly she leaned forward, looking intently at the cage. "But what do you s'pose went wrong with it?"

"I don't know," returned Mrs. Peters; "unless it got sick and died."

But after she said it she reached over and swung the broken door. Both women watched it as if somehow held by it.

"You didn't know—her?" Mrs. Hale asked, a gentler note in her voice.

"Not till they brought her yesterday," said the sheriff's wife.

"She—come to think of it, she was kind of like a bird herself. Real sweet and pretty, but kind of timid and—fluttery. How—she—did—change."   510

That held her for a long time. Finally, as if struck with a happy thought and relieved to get back to everyday things, she exclaimed:

"Tell you what, Mrs. Peters, why don't you take the quilt in with you? It might take up her mind."

"Why, I think that's a real nice idea, Mrs. Hale," agreed the sheriff's wife, as if she too were glad to come into the atmosphere of a simple kindness. "There couldn't possibly be any objection to that, could there? Now, just what will I take? I wonder if her patches are in here—and her things."

They turned to the sewing basket.

"Here's some red," said Mrs. Hale, bringing out a roll of cloth. Underneath 520 that was a box. "Here, maybe her scissors are in here—and her things." She held it up. "What a pretty box! I'll warrant that was something she had a long time ago— when she was a girl."

She held it in her hand a moment; then, with a little sigh, opened it.

Instantly her hand went to her nose.

"Why—!"

Mrs. Peters drew nearer—then turned away.

"There's something wrapped up in this piece of silk, " faltered Mrs. Hale.

"This isn't her scissors," said Mrs. Peters in a shrinking voice.

Her hand not steady, Mrs. Hale raised the piece of silk. "Oh, Mrs. Peters!" 530 she cried. "It's—"

Mrs. Peters bent closer.

"It's the bird," she whispered.

"But, Mrs. Peters!" cried Mrs. Hale. "*Look* at it! Its neck—look at its neck! It's all—other side *to.*"

She held the box away from her.

The sheriff's wife again bent closer.

"Somebody wrung its neck," said she, in a voice that was slow and deep.

And then again the eyes of the two women met—this time clung together in a look of dawning comprehension, of growing horror. Mrs. Peters looked from the 540 dead bird to the broken door of the cage. Again their eyes met. And just then there was a sound at the outside door.

Mrs. Hale slipped the box under the quilt pieces in the basket, and sank into the chair before it. Mrs. Peters stood holding to the table. The county attorney and the sheriff came in from outside.

"Well, ladies," said the county attorney, as one turning from serious things to little pleasantries, "have you decided whether she was going to quilt it or knot it?"

"We think," began the sheriff's wife in a flurried voice, "that she was going to—knot it."

He was too preoccupied to notice the change that came in her voice on that last. 550

"Well, that's very interesting, I'm sure," he said tolerantly. He caught sight of the bird-cage. "Has the bird flown?"

"We think the cat got it," said Mrs. Hale in a voice curiously even.

He was walking up and down, as if thinking something out.

"Is there a cat?" he asked absently.

Mrs. Hale shot a look up at the sheriff's wife.

"Well, not *now*," said Mrs. Peters. "They're superstitious, you know; they leave."

She sank into her chair. 560

The county attorney did not heed her. "No sign at all of any one having come in from the outside," he said to Peters, in the manner of continuing an interrupted conversation. "Their own rope. Now let's go upstairs again and go over it, piece by piece. It would have to have been some one who knew just the—"

The stair door closed behind them and their voices were lost.

The two women sat motionless, not looking at each other, but as if peering into something and at the same time holding back. When they spoke now it was as if they were afraid of what they were saying, but as if they could not help saying it.

"She liked that bird," said Martha Hale, low and slowly. "She was going to bury it in that pretty box." 570

"When I was a girl," said Mrs. Peters, under her breath, "my kitten—there was a boy took a hatchet, and before my eyes—before I could get there—" She covered her face an instant. "If they hadn't held me back I would have"—she caught herself, looked upstairs where footsteps were heard, and finished weakly—"hurt him."

Then they sat without speaking or moving.

"I wonder how it would seem," Mrs. Hale at least began, as if feeling her way over strange ground—"never to have had any children around?" Her eyes made a slow sweep of the kitchen, as if seeing what that kitchen had meant through all the years. "No, Wright wouldn't like the bird, she said after that—"a thing that sang. She used to sing. He killed that too." Her voice tightened. 580

Mrs. Peters moved uneasily.

"Of course we don't know who killed the bird."

"I knew John Wright," was Mrs. Hale's answer.

"It was an awful thing was done in this house that night, Mrs. Hale," said the sheriff's wife. "Killing a man while he slept—slipping a thing round his neck that choked the life out of him."

Mrs. Hale's hand went out to the bird-cage.

"His neck. Choked the life out of him"

"We don't *know* who killed him," whispered Mrs. Peters wildly. "We don't 590 know."

Mrs. Hale had not moved. "If there had been years and years of—nothing, then a bird to sing to you, it would be awful—still—after the bird was still."

It was as if something within her not herself had spoken, and it found in Mrs. Peters something she did not know as herself.

"I know what stillness is, " she said, in a queer, monotonous voice, "When we homesteaded in Dakota, and my first baby died—after he was two years old— and me with no other then—"

Mrs. Hale stirred.

"How soon do you suppose they'll be through looking for evidence?"   600

"I know what stillness is," repeated Mrs. Peters, in just the same way. Then she too pulled back. "The law has got to punish crime, Mrs. Hale," she said in her tight little way.

"I wish you'd seen Minnie Foster," was the answer, "when she wore a white dress with blue ribbons, and stood up there in the choir and sang."

The picture of that girl, the fact that she had lived neighbor to that girl for twenty years, and had let her die for lack of life, was suddenly more than she could bear.

"Oh, I *wish* I'd come over here once in a while!" she cried. "That was a crime! That was a crime! Who's going to punish that?"   610

"We mustn't take on," said Mrs. Peters, with a frightened look toward the stairs.

"I might 'a' *known* she needed help! I tell you, It's *queer,* Mrs. Peters. We live close together, and we live far apart. We all go through the same things—it's all just a different kind of the same thing! If it weren't—why do you and I *understand?* Why do we *know*—what we know this minute?"

She dashed her hand across her eyes. Then, seeing the jar of fruit on the table, she reached out for it and choked out:

"If I was you I wouldn't *tell* her her fruit was gone! Tell her it *ain't.* Tell her it's all right—all of it. Here—take this in to prove it to her! She—she may never know whether it was broke or not."   620

She turned away.

Mrs. Peters reached out for the bottle of fruit as if she were glad to take it— as if touching a familiar thing, having something to do, could keep her from something else. She got up, looked about for something to wrap the fruit in, took a petticoat from the pile of clothes she had brought from the front room, and nervously started winding that round the bottle.

"My!" she began, in a high, false voice, "it's a good thing the men couldn't hear us! Getting all stirred up over a little thing like a —dead canary." She hurried over that. "As if that could have anything to do with—with—My, wouldn't they *laugh?*"   630

Footsteps were heard on the stairs.

"Maybe they would," muttered Mrs. Hale—"maybe they wouldn't."

"No, Peters," said the county attorney incisively; "it's all perfectly clear, except the reason for doing it. But you know juries when it comes to women. If there was some definite thing—something to show. Something to make a story about. A thing that would connect up with this clumsy way of doing it."

In a covert way Mrs. Hale looked at Mrs. Peters. Mrs. Peters was looking at her. Quickly they looked away from each other. The outer door opened and Mr. Hale came in.

"I've got the team round now," he said. "Pretty cold out there." 640

"I'm going to stay here awhile by myself," the county attorney suddenly announced. "You can send Frank out for me, can't you?" he asked the sheriff. "I want to go over everything. I'm not satisfied we can't do better."

Again, for one brief moment, the two women's eyes found one another.

The sheriff came up to the table.

"Did you want to see what Mrs. Peters was going to take in?"

The county attorney picked up the apron. He laughed.

"Oh, I guess they're not very dangerous things the ladies have picked out."

Mrs. Hale's hand was on the sewing basket in which the box was concealed. She felt that she ought to take her hand off the basket. She did not seem able to. 650 He picked up one of the quilt blocks which she had piled on to cover the box. Her eyes felt like fire. She had a feeling that if he took up the basket she would snatch it from him.

But he did not take it up. With another little laugh, he turned away, saying:

"No; Mrs. Peters doesn't need supervising. For that matter, a sheriff's wife is married to the law. Ever think of it that way, Mrs. Peters?"

Mrs. Peters was standing beside the table. Mrs. Hale shot a look up at her; but she could not see her face. Mrs. Peters had turned away. When she spoke, her voice was muffled.

"Not—just that way," she said. 660

"Married to the law!" chuckled Mrs. Peters' husband. He moved toward the door into the front room, and said to the county attorney:

"I just want you to come in here a minute, George. We ought to take a look at these windows."

"Oh—windows," said the county attorney scoffingly.

"We'll be right out, Mr. Hale," said the sheriff to the farmer, who was still waiting by the door.

Hale went to look after the horses. The sheriff followed the county attorney into the other room. Again—for one moment—the two women were alone in that kitchen. 670

Martha Hale sprang up, her hands tight together, looking at that other woman, with whom it rested. At first she could not see her eyes, for the sheriff's wife had not turned back, since she turned away at that suggestion of being married to the law. But now Mrs. Hale made her turn back. Her eyes made her turn back. Slowly, unwillingly, Mrs. Peters turned her head until her eyes met the eyes of the other woman. There was a moment when they held each other in a steady, burning look in which there was no evasion nor flinching. Then Martha Hale's eyes pointed the way to the basket in which was hidden the thing that would make certain the conviction of the other woman—that woman who was not there and yet who had been there with them all through the hour. 680

For a moment Mrs. Peters did not move. And then she did it. With a rush forward, she threw back the quilt pieces, got the box, tried to put it in her hand-bag. It was too big. Desperately she opened it, started to take the bird out. But there she broke—she could not touch the bird. She stood helpless, foolish.

There was the sound of a knob turning in the inner door. Martha Hale snatched the box from the sheriff's wife, and got it in the pocket of her big coat just as the sheriff and the county attorney came back into the kitchen.

"Well, Henry," said the county attorney facetiously, "at least we found out that she was not going to quilt it. She was going to—what is it you call it, ladies?"

Mrs. Hale's hand was against the pocket of her coat.   690

"We call it—knot it, Mr. Henderson."   [1917]

Questions for Discussion and Writing

1. In what ways is this story a local color story? In what ways is it a detective story?
2. Mrs. Hale keeps thinking of Minnie Foster. What are the differences between Minnie Foster and Mrs. Wright? Why are the differences important?
3. What do the women discover about the nature of the Wrights' marriage?
4. What is the men's attitude toward women and "women's things"?
5. What does the phrase, "married to the law" mean in the context of the story?
6. How does Glaspell depict males? Is her depiction fair? Explain.
7. Why did Mrs. Wright kill her husband?
8. Are the women justified in not telling the sheriff what they have learned? Why or why not?

✒ SHERWOOD ANDERSON
(1876–1941)

Hands

Sherwood Anderson led a restless, varied life. Consciously seeking to capture the American experience, he experimented in a variety of genres. It was in the short story that he made his most lasting and original contribution.

He was born in Camden, Ohio, to a hard-working but unsuccessful father and a mother whose practicality and determination kept the family going. Anderson later credited her with sparking his desire to see beneath the surface of people's lives. Anderson helped support the family and dropped out of high school after less than a year. When his mother died in 1895, he moved to Chicago and worked as a laborer, then joined the Army—too late to fight in the Spanish-American War.

Leaving the army, he returned to high school, graduating in two semesters. He returned to Chicago and worked first for *Women's Home Companion* and then as an advertising copywriter. He married for the first time in 1904, and in 1907 returned to Ohio, where he established and successfully ran The Anderson Manufacturing Company. Five years later he suffered a mental breakdown, walked out of his factory, and was found much later in an incoherent state. After recovering, he returned to advertising and began submitting short stories to magazines. His first collection, *Winesburg, Ohio* (1919), brought critical acclaim; by 1925, some critics were hailing him as America's most important novelist.

Anderson's importance to the American Modernist movement can hardly be overestimated. Rebelling against what he called "the tyranny of plot," he explored the lives of people he saw all around him—"grotesques" driven by an obsession, a ruling passion, or a determining event in their lives. His plain but poetic style and his insistence on probing his characters' psychology influenced subsequent writers as diverse as Ernest Hemingway (1899–1961), William Faulkner (1897–1962), and Flannery O'Connor (1925–1964). Many of his best stories are haunting depictions of ordinary people trapped by circumstances beyond their control or portraits of young people encountering the complexities of life for the first time.

U PON THE HALF DECAYED veranda of a small frame house that stood near the edge of a ravine near the town of Winesburg, Ohio, a fat little old man walked nervously up and down. Across a long field that had been seeded for clover but that had produced only a dense crop of yellow mustard weeds, he could see the public highway along which went a wagon filled with berry pickers returning from the fields. The berry pickers, youths and maidens, laughed and shouted boisterously. A boy clad in a blue shirt leaped from the wagon and attempted to drag after him one of the maidens, who screamed and protested shrilly. The feet of the boy in the road kicked up a cloud of dust that floated across the face of the departing sun. Over the long field came a thin girlish voice. "Oh, you 10 Wing Biddlebaum, comb your hair, it's falling into your eyes," commanded the voice to the man, who was bald and whose nervous little hands fiddled about the bare white forehead as though arranging a mass of tangled locks.

Wing Biddlebaum, forever frightened and beset by a ghostly band of doubts, did not think of himself as in any way a part of the life of the town where he had lived for twenty years. Among all the people of Winesburg but one had come close to him. With George Willard, son of Tom Willard, the proprietor of the New Willard House, he had formed something like a friendship. George Willard was the reporter on the *Winesburg Eagle* and sometimes in the evenings he walked out along the highway to Wing Biddlebaum's house. Now as the old man walked up 20 and down on the veranda, his hands moving nervously about, he was hoping that George Willard would come and spend the evening with him. After the wagon containing the berry pickers had passed, he went across the field through the tall mustard weeds and climbing a rail fence peered anxiously along the road to the town. For a moment he stood thus, rubbing his hands together and looking up and down the road, and then, fear overcoming him, ran back to walk again upon the porch of his own house.

In the presence of George Willard, Wing Biddlebaum, who for twenty years had been the town mystery, lost something of his timidity, and his shadowy personality, submerged in a sea of doubts, came forth to look at the world. With the young reporter at his side, he ventured in the light of day into Main Street or strode up and down on the rickety front porch of his own house, talking excitedly. The voice that had been low and trembling became shrill and loud. The bent figure straightened. With a kind of wriggle, like a fish returned to the brook by the fisherman, Biddlebaum the silent began to talk, striving to put into words the ideas that had been accumulated by his mind during long years of silence.

Wing Biddlebaum talked much with his hands. The slender expressive fingers, forever active, forever striving to conceal themselves in his pockets or behind his back, came forth and became the piston rods of his machinery of expression.

The story of Wing Biddlebaum is a story of hands. Their restless activity, like unto the beating of the wings of an imprisoned bird, had given him his name. Some obscure poet of the town had thought of it. The hands alarmed their owner. He wanted to keep them hidden away and looked with amazement at the quiet inexpressive hands of other men who worked beside him in the fields, or passed, driving sleepy teams on country roads.

When he talked to George Willard, Wing Biddlebaum closed his fists and beat with them upon a table or on the walls of his house. The action made him more comfortable. If the desire to talk came to him when the two were walking in the fields, he sought out a stump or the top board of a fence and with his hands pounding busily talked with renewed ease.

The story of Wing Biddlebaum's hands is worth a book in itself. Sympathetically set forth it would tap many strange, beautiful qualities in obscure men. It is a job for a poet. In Winesburg the hands had attracted attention merely because of their activity. With them Wing Biddlebaum had picked as high as a hundred and forty quarts of strawberries in a day. They became his distinguishing feature, the source of his fame. Also they made more grotesque an already grotesque and elusive individuality. Winesburg was proud of the hands of Wing Biddlebaum in the same spirit in which it was proud of Banker White's new stone house and Wesly Moyer's bay stallion, Tony Tip, that had won the two-fifteen trot at the fall races in Cleveland.

As for George Willard, he had many times wanted to ask about the hands. At times an almost overwhelming curiosity had taken hold of him. He felt that there must be a reason for their strange activity and their inclination to keep hidden away and only a growing respect for Wing Biddlebaum kept him from blurting out the questions that were often in his mind.

Once he had been on the point of asking. The two were walking in the fields on a summer afternoon and had stopped to sit upon a grassy bank. All afternoon Wing Biddlebaum had talked as one inspired. By a fence he had stopped and beating like a giant woodpecker upon the top board had shouted at George Willard, condemning his tendency to be too much influenced by the people about him. "You are destroying yourself," he cried. "You have the inclination to be alone and to dream and you are afraid of dreams. You want to be like others in town here. You hear them talk and you try to imitate them."

On the grassy bank Wing Biddlebaum had tried again to drive his point home. His voice became soft and reminiscent, and with a sigh of contentment he launched into a long rambling talk, speaking as one lost in a dream.

Out of the dream Wing Biddlebaum made a picture for George Willard. In the picture men lived again in a kind of pastoral golden age. Across a green open country came clean-limbed young men, some afoot, some mounted upon horses. In crowds the young men came to gather about the feet of an old man who sat be- 80 neath a tree in a tiny garden who talked to them.

Wing Biddlebaum became wholly inspired. For once he forgot the hands. Slowly they stole forth and lay upon George Willard's shoulders. Something new and bold came into the voice that talked. "You must try to forget all you have learned," said the old man. "You must begin to dream. From this time on you must shut your ears to the roaring of the voices."

Pausing in his speech, Wing Biddlebaum looked long and earnestly at George Willard. His eyes glowed. Again he raised the hands to caress the boy and then a look of horror swept over his face.

With a convulsive movement of his body, Wing Biddlebaum sprang to his 90 feet and thrust his hands deep into his trousers pockets. Tears came to his eyes. "I must be getting along home. I can talk no more with you," he said nervously.

Without looking back, the old man had hurried down the hillside and across a meadow, leaving George Willard perplexed and frightened upon the grassy slope. With a shiver of dread the boy arose and went along the road toward town. "I'll not ask him about his hands," he thought, touched by the memory of the terror he had seen in the man's eyes. "There's something wrong, but I don't want to know what it is. His hands have something to do with his fear of me and of everyone."

And George Willard was right. Let us look briefly into the story of the hands. 100 Perhaps our talking of them will arouse the poet who will tell the hidden wonder story of the influence for which the hands were but fluttering pennants of promise.

In his youth Wing Biddlebaum had been a school teacher in a town in Pennsylvania. He was not then known as Wing Biddlebaum, but went by the less euphonic name of Adolph Myers. As Adolph Myers he was much loved by the boys of his school.

Adolph Myers was meant by nature to be a teacher of youth. He was one of those rare, little-understood men who rule by a power so gentle that it passes as a lovable weakness. In their feeling for the boys under their charge such men are not 110 unlike the finer sort of women in their love of men.

And yet that is but crudely stated. It needs the poet there. With the boys of his school, Adolph Myers had walked in the evening or had sat talking until dusk upon the school-house steps lost in a kind of dream. Here and there went his hands, caressing the shoulders of the boys, playing about the tousled heads. As he talked his voice became soft and musical. There was a caress in that also. In a way the voice and the hands, the stroking of the shoulders and the touching of the hair were a part of the schoolmaster's effort to carry a dream into the young minds. By the caress that was in his fingers he expressed himself. He was one of these men in whom the force that creates life is diffused, not centralized. Under the caress of his hands doubt and disbelief went out of the minds of the boys and they began also to dream.

And then the tragedy. A half-witted boy of the school became enamored of the young master. In his bed at night he imagined unspeakable things and in the morning went forth to tell his dreams as facts. Strange, hideous accusations fell from his loose-hung lips. Through the Pennsylvania town went a shiver. Hidden, shadowy doubts that had been in men's minds concerning Adolph Myers were galvanized into beliefs.

The tragedy did not linger. Trembling lads were jerked out of bed and questioned. "He put his arms about me," said one. "His fingers were always playing in my hair," said another.

One afternoon a man of the town, Henry Bradford, who kept a saloon, came to the schoolhouse door. Calling Adolph Myers into the school yard he began to beat him with his fists. As his hard knuckles beat down into the frightened face of the schoolmaster, his wrath became more and more terrible. Screaming with dismay, the children ran here and there like disturbed insects. "I'll teach you to put your hands on my boy, you beast," roared the saloon keeper, who tired of beating the master, had begun to kick him about the yard.

Adolph Myers was driven from the Pennsylvania town in the night. With lanterns in their hands a dozen men came to the door of the house where he lived alone and commanded that he dress and come forth. It was raining and one of the men had a rope in his hands. They had intended to hang the schoolmaster, but something in his figure, so small, white, and pitiful, touched their hearts and they let him escape. As he ran away into the darkness they repented of their weakness and ran after him, swearing and throwing sticks and great balls of soft mud at the figure that screamed and ran faster and faster into the darkness.

For twenty years Adolph Myers had lived alone in Winesburg. He was but forty but looked sixty-five. The name of Biddlebaum he got from a box of goods seen at a freight station as he hurried through an eastern Ohio town. He had an aunt in Winesburg, a black-toothed old woman who raised chickens, and with her he lived until she died. He had been ill for a year after the experience in Pennsylvania, and after his recovery worked as a day laborer in the fields, going timidly about and striving to conceal his hands. Although he did not understand what had happened he felt that the hands must be to blame. Again and again the fathers of the boys talked of the hands. "Keep your hands to yourself," the saloon keeper had roared, dancing with fury in the schoolhouse yard.

Upon the veranda of his house by the ravine, Wing Biddlebaum continued to walk up and down until the sun had disappeared and the road beyond the field was lost in the grey shadows. Going into his house he cut slices of bread and spread honey upon them. When the rumble of the evening train that took away the express cars loaded with the day's harvest of berries had passed and restored the silence of the summer night, he went again to walk upon the veranda. In the darkness he could not see the hands and they became quiet. Although he still hungered for the presence of the boy, who was the medium through which he ex-

pressed his love of man, the hunger became again a part of his loneliness and his waiting. Lighting a lamp, Wing Biddlebaum washed the few dishes soiled by his simple meal and, setting up a folding cot by the screen door that led to the porch, prepared to undress for the night. A few stray white bread crumbs lay on the cleanly washed floor by the table; putting the lamp upon a low stool he began to pick up the crumbs, carrying them to his mouth one by one with unbelievable ra- 170
pidity. In the dense blotch of light beneath the table, the kneeling figure looked like a priest engaged in some service of his church. The nervous expressive fingers, flashing in and out of the light, might well have been mistaken for the fingers of the devotee going swiftly through decade after decade of his rosary.   [1919]

Questions for Discussion and Writing

1. What are the conventional images or stereotypes about life in a small town? Which of these are reflected in this story? How are they confirmed or contradicted by the story?

2. Is "Wing" an appropriate or ironic nickname for the protagonist?

3. Wing Biddlebaum encourages George Willard to "dream" and "shut [his] ears to the roaring voices." Why does he offer this advice? What does he mean by it? Has he been able to follow this advice in his own life?

4. Why was Adolph Myers (Wing Biddlebaum) driven from his job and home in Pennsylvania? Was he guilty of anything? If so, what?

5. Is this story a psychological study of its protagonist? If so, what does it reveal about him? Is the story a sociological study of small town life? If so, what does it say about life in Winesburg, Ohio?

6. Anderson criticized what he called "the tyranny of plot" in short stories. Does this story achieve unity without plot? What devices does Anderson use to tell his story without using plot?

✎ VIRGINIA WOOLF

(1882–1941)

Kew Gardens[1]

When Virginia Woolf committed suicide by drowning in 1941, she left a rich literary legacy and a host of unanswered questions that have become more contentious as her reputation has grown. Once almost neglected, she is now at the center of crucial debates about Modernism, feminism, and elitism.

She was born into the extraordinary Stephen family. Her father, Leslie Stephen, was a well-known man of letters; her uncle a publisher; her sister Vanessa married the critic Clive Bell and became important as a painter in London's art scene. Virginia developed slowly, impeded by bouts of mental

---

1. A large park in west London containing ornamental and botanical gardens.

illness that began in 1895—some say because of her mother's untimely death, others because of sexual abuse as a child.

When Leslie Stephen died in 1904, his four children moved to the Bloomsbury section of London and there became the center of a group of important avant garde artists, writers, and intellectuals who became famous—or infamous—as the Bloomsbury circle. The group never stood for a single ideology, except for perhaps philosopher G. E. Moore's idea that the purposes of life were "the pleasures of human intercourse and the enjoyment of beautiful objects," but its influence on British literature and the arts has been profound and long-lasting.

Woolf's works show a restless, inquiring, constantly experimenting creativity, from the stream of consciousness technique of *To the Lighthouse* (1927) to the androgynous fantasy of *Orlando* (1928) and the impressionism of *The Waves* (1931). Her essays on Modernism and feminism have become classics, while her stories experimented with techniques ranging from prose poems to psychological "moments of being" and well-plotted traditional tales. These were not merely attempts to refine technique or to try something new for the sake of novelty: Woolf was interested in learning how to present interior reality. Realism, she argued, had exhausted the possibilities for recreating exterior reality and had overlooked the subjective, inner dimension in which people really live. Together with James Joyce (1882–1941), D. H. Lawrence (1885–1930), Katherine Mansfield (1888–1923), and the other Modernists, Woolf reshaped twentieth-century literature, searching for new aesthetic principles and opening realms of the unconscious and subconscious as new areas to explore.

F ROM THE OVAL-SHAPED flower-bed there rose perhaps a hundred stalks spreading into heart-shaped or tongue-shaped leaves half way up and unfurling at the tip red or blue or yellow petals marked with spots of colour raised upon the surface; and from the red, blue or yellow gloom of the throat emerged a straight bar, rough with gold dust and slightly clubbed at the end. The petals were voluminous enough to be stirred by the summer breeze, and when they moved, the red, blue and yellow lights passed one over the other, staining an inch of the brown earth beneath with a spot of the most intricate colour. The light fell either upon the smooth grey back of a pebble, or the shell of a snail with its brown circular veins, or, falling into a raindrop, it expanded with such intensity of red, blue and 10 yellow the thin walls of water that one expected them to burst and disappear. Instead, the drop was left in a second silver grey once more, and the light now settled upon the flesh of a leaf, revealing the branching thread of fibre beneath the surface, and again it moved on and spread its illumination in the vast green spaces beneath the dome of the heart-shaped and tongue-shaped leaves. Then the breeze stirred rather more briskly overhead and the colour was flashed into the air above, into the eyes of the men and women who walk in Kew Gardens in July.

The figures of these men and women straggled past the flower-bed with a curiously irregular movement not unlike that of the white and blue butterflies who

crossed the turf in zig-zag flights from bed to bed. The man was about six inches 20
in front of the woman, strolling carelessly, while she bore on with greater purpose,
only turning her head now and then to see that the children were not too far behind. The man kept this distance in front of the woman purposely, though perhaps unconsciously, for he wanted to go on with his thoughts.

"Fifteen years ago I came here with Lily," he thought. "We sat somewhere
over there by a lake, and I begged her to marry me all through the hot afternoon.
How the dragon-fly kept circling round us: how clearly I see the dragon-fly and
her shoe with the square silver buckle at the toe. All the time I spoke I saw her
shoe and when it moved impatiently I knew without looking up what she was
going to say: the whole of her seemed to be in her shoe. And my love, my desire, 30
were in the dragon-fly; for some reason I thought that if it settled there, on that
leaf, the broad one with the red flower in the middle of it, if the dragon-fly settled
on the leaf she would say "Yes" at once. But the dragon-fly went round and round:
it never settled anywhere—of course not, happily not, or I shouldn't be walking
here with Eleanor and the children—Tell me, Eleanor, d'you ever think of the
past?"

"Why do you ask, Simon?"

"Because I've been thinking of the past. I've been thinking of Lily, the woman
I might have married . . . Well, why are you silent? Do you mind my thinking of
the past?"   40

"Why should I mind, Simon? Doesn't one always think of the past, in a garden with men and women lying under the trees? Aren't they one's past, all that remains of it, those men and women, those ghosts lying under the trees, . . . one's
happiness, one's reality?"

"For me, a square silver shoe-buckle and a dragon-fly—"

"For me, a kiss. Imagine six little girls sitting before their easels twenty years
ago, down by the side of a lake, painting the water-lilies, the first red water-lilies
I'd ever seen. And suddenly a kiss, there on the back of my neck. And my hand
shook all the afternoon so that I couldn't paint. I took out my watch and marked
the hour when I would allow myself to think of the kiss for five minutes only—it 50
was so precious—the kiss of an old grey-haired woman with a wart on her nose,
the mother of all my kisses all my life. Come Caroline, come Hubert."

They walked on past the flower-bed, now walking four abreast, and soon diminished in size among the trees and looked half transparent as the sunlight and
shade swam over their backs in large trembling irregular patches.

In the oval flower-bed the snail, whose shell had been stained red, blue and
yellow for the space of two minutes or so, now appeared to be moving very
slightly in its shell, and next began to labour over the crumbs of loose earth which
broke away and rolled down as it passed over them. It appeared to have a definite
goal in front of it, differing in this respect from the singular high-stepping angular 60
green insect who attempted to cross in front of it, and waited for a second with its
antennae trembling as if in deliberation, and then stepped off as rapidly and
strangely in the opposite direction. Brown cliffs with deep green lakes in the hollows, flat blade-like trees that waved from root to tip, round boulders of grey
stone, vast crumpled surfaces of a thin crackling texture—all these objects lay
across the snail's progress between one stalk and another to his goal. Before he de-

cided whether to circumvent the arched tent of a dead leaf or to breast it there came past the bed the feet of other human beings.

This time they were both men. The younger of the two wore an expression of perhaps unnatural calm; he raised his eyes and fixed them very steadily in front of him while his companion spoke, and directly his companion had done speaking he looked on the ground again and sometimes opened his lips only after a long pause and sometimes did not open them at all. The elder man had a curiously uneven and shaky method of walking, jerking his hand forward and throwing up his head abruptly, rather in the manner of an impatient carriage horse tired of waiting outside a house; but in the man these gestures were irresolute and pointless. He talked almost incessantly; he smiled to himself and again began to talk, as if the smile had been an answer. He was talking about spirits—the spirits of the dead, who, according to him, were even now telling him all sorts of odd things about their experiences in Heaven.

"Heaven was known to the ancients as Thessaly, William, and now, with this war, the spirit matter is rolling between the hills like thunder." He paused, seemed to listen, smiled, jerked his head and continued:—

"You have a small electric battery and a piece of rubber to insulate the wire—isolate?—insulate?—well, we'll skip the details, no good going into details that wouldn't be understood—and in short the little machine stands in any convenient position by the head of the bed, we will say, on a neat mahogany stand. All arrangements being properly fixed by workmen under my direction, the widow applies her ear and summons the spirit by sign as agreed. Women! Widows! Women in black—"

Here he seemed to have caught sight of a woman's dress in the distance, which in the shade looked a purple black. He took off his hat, placed his hand upon his heart, and hurried towards her muttering and gesticulating feverishly. But William caught him by the sleeve and touched a flower with the tip of his walking-stick in order to divert the old man's attention. After looking at it for a moment in some confusion the old man bent his ear to it and seemed to answer a voice speaking from it, for he began talking about the forests of Uruguay which he had visited hundreds of years ago in company with the most beautiful young woman in Europe. He could be heard murmuring about forests of Uruguay blanketed with the wax petals of tropical roses, nightingales, sea beaches, mermaids and women drowned at sea, as he suffered himself to be moved on by William, upon whose face the look of stoical patience grew slowly deeper and deeper.

Following his steps so closely as to be slightly puzzled by his gestures came two elderly women of the lower middle class, one stout and ponderous, the other rosy-cheeked and nimble. Like most people of their station they were frankly fascinated by any signs of eccentricity betokening a disordered brain, especially in the well-to-do; but they were too far off to be certain whether the gestures were merely eccentric or genuinely mad. After they had scrutinised the old man's back in silence for a moment and given each other a queer, sly look, they went on energetically piecing together their very complicated dialogue:

"Nell, Bert, Lot, Cess, Phil, Pa, he says, I says, she says, I says, I says, I says—"
"My Bert, Sis, Bill, Grandad, the old man, sugar,

Sugar, flour, kippers, greens
Sugar, sugar, sugar."

The ponderous woman looked through the pattern of falling words at the flowers standing cool, firm and upright in the earth, with a curious expression. She saw them as a sleeper waking from a heavy sleep sees a brass candlestick reflecting the light in an unfamiliar way, and closes his eyes and opens them, and seeing the brass candlestick again, finally starts broad awake and stares at the candlestick with all his powers. So the heavy woman came to a standstill opposite the oval-shaped flower-bed, and ceased even to pretend to listen to what the other woman was saying. She stood there letting the words fall over her, swaying the top part of her body slowly backwards and forwards, looking at the flowers. Then she suggested that they should find a seat and have their tea.

The snail had now considered every possible method of reaching his goal without going round the dead leaf or climbing over it. Let alone the effort needed for climbing a leaf, he was doubtful whether the thin texture which vibrated with such an alarming crackle when touched even by the tip of his horns would bear his weight; and this determined him finally to creep beneath it, for there was a point where the leaf curved high enough from the ground to admit him. He had just inserted his head in the opening and was taking stock of the high brown roof and was getting used to the cool brown light when two other people came past outside on the turf. This time they were both young, a young man and a young woman. They were both in the prime of youth, or even in that season which precedes the prime of youth, the season before the smooth pink folds of the flower have burst their gummy case, when the wings of the butterfly, though fully grown, are motionless in the sun.

"Lucky it isn't Friday," he observed.

"Why? D'you believe in luck?"

"They make you pay sixpence on Friday."

"What's sixpence anyway? Isn't it worth sixpence?"

"What's 'it'—what do you mean by 'it'?"

"O anything—I mean—you know what I mean."

Long pauses came between each of these remarks: they were uttered in toneless and monotonous voices. The couple stood still on the edge of the flower-bed, and together pressed the end of her parasol deep down into the soft earth. The action and the fact that this hand rested on the top of hers expressed their feelings in a strange way, as these short insignificant words also expressed something, words with short wings for their heavy body of meaning, inadequate to carry them far and thus alighting awkwardly upon the very common objects that surrounded them and were to their inexperienced touch so massive: but who knows (so they thought as they pressed the parasol into the earth) what precipices aren't concealed in them, or what slopes of ice don't shine in the sun on the other side? Who knows? Who has ever seen this before? Even when she wondered what sort of tea they gave you at Kew, he felt that something loomed up behind her words, and stood vast and solid behind them; and the mist very slowly rose and uncovered—O Heavens,—what were those shapes?—little white tables, and waitresses who looked first at her and then at him; and there was a bill that he would pay

with a real two shilling piece, and it was real, all real, he assured himself, fingering
the coin in his pocket, real to everyone except to him and to her; even to him it   160
began to seem real and then—but it was too exciting to stand and think any
longer, and he pulled the parasol out of the earth with a jerk and was impatient to
find the place where one had tea with other people, like other people.

"Come along, Trissie; it's time we had our tea."

"Wherever *does* one have one's tea?" she asked with the oddest thrill of excitement in her voice, looking vaguely round and letting herself be drawn on
down the grass path, trailing her parasol, turning her head this way and that way,
forgetting her tea, wishing to go down there and then down there, remembering
orchids and cranes among wild flowers, a Chinese pagoda and a crimson-crested
bird; but he bore her on.   170

Thus one couple after another with much the same irregular and aimless
movement passed the flower-bed and were enveloped in layer after layer of green-
blue vapour, in which at first their bodies had substance and a dash of colour, but
later both substance and colour dissolved in the green-blue atmosphere. How hot
it was! So hot that even the thrush chose to hop, like a mechanical bird, in the
shadow of the flowers, with long pauses between one movement and the next; instead of rambling vaguely the white butterflies danced once above another, making with their white shifting flakes the outline of a shattered marble column above
the tallest flowers; the glass roofs of the palm house shone as if a whole market full
of shiny green umbrellas had opened in the sun; and in the drone of the aeroplane 180
the voice of the summer sky murmured its fierce soul. Yellow and black, pink and
snow white, shapes of all these colours, men, women and children, were spotted
for a second upon the horizon, and then, seeing the breadth of yellow that lay
upon the grass, they wavered and sought shade beneath the trees, dissolving like
drops of water in the yellow and green atmosphere, staining it faintly with red and
blue. It seemed as if all gross and heavy bodies had sunk down in the heat motionless and lay huddled upon the ground, but their voices went wavering from
them as if they were flames lolling from the thick waxen bodies of candles. Voices,
yes, voices, wordless voices, breaking the silence suddenly with such depth of
contentment, such passion of desire, or, in the voices of children, such freshness   190
of surprise; breaking the silence? But there was no silence; all the time the motor
omnibuses were turning their wheels and changing their gear; like a vast nest of
Chinese boxes all of wrought steel turning ceaselessly one within another the city
murmured; on the top of which the voices cried aloud and the petals of myriads of
flowers flashed their colours into the air.   [1919]

Questions for Discussion and Writing

1. This story seems to be all setting and atmosphere. Does anything of significance happen? If so, what?

2. What is the function of the snail? Why does the narrator give the snail
   human qualities such as thinking and doubting?

3. What do the four pairs of humans contribute to the story? Are they simply
   random passersby, or do they appear to have been included for a reason?
   Explain.

4. How is time handled in this story? Does time move or stand still? How is the passing of time suggested or implied?

5. Analyze carefully the last paragraph of the story. How does it relate to what has gone before?

⛯ KATHERINE MANSFIELD
(1888–1923)

The Daughters of the Late Colonel

Katherine Mansfield is inevitably linked with Virginia Woolf (1882–1941) and D. H. Lawrence (1885–1930) as a contributor to British Modernism. She is among the few writers to build a major reputation solely on the basis of short stories.

Although usually regarded as British, Katherine Mansfield Beauchamp was born in Wellington, New Zealand, to upper-middle-class parents. She attended university in England (1903–1906) and on her return to New Zealand became bored with provincial life and begged to return to England. She did so, with an allowance of £100 a year ($500). Always sexually adventuresome, Katherine found herself pregnant to a man too young to marry—so she married a musician named George Bowden, then left him the next day. She went to Germany to have the baby but miscarried. While there, she observed the wealthy German patrons and satirized them in stories published in her first collection, *In a German Pension* (1911). In 1909, she contracted gonorrhea and from 1910 until her death was often an invalid.

In 1912, she met John Middleton Murry, with whom she edited the avant garde journals *Blue Review* and *Rhythm,* while publishing stories in these and other magazines. She married Murry in 1918. She was close friends for a time with D. H. Lawrence and may have contracted tuberculosis from him in 1916. The last years of her life were spent in a futile search for a congenial climate and good health.

Considering her illnesses and the time she spent traveling, editing, and writing reviews, her output of short stories is impressive. No two are alike. She experimented constantly with subject matter, style, theme, setting, handling of interior thought processes, and point of view. With James Joyce (1882–1941), Sherwood Anderson (1876–1941), and others she helped create the plotless story that focuses on a moment of revelation or epiphany. "Daughters of the Late Colonel" shows both her technical mastery (including an exquisite balancing of tone) and acute psychological insight. "Miss Brill" is a masterpiece of characterization, delicately balancing sympathy and irony.

I

T HE WEEK AFTER was one of the busiest weeks of their lives. Even when they went to bed it was only their bodies that lay down and rested; their minds went on, thinking things out, talking things over, wondering, deciding, trying to remember where . . .

Constantia lay like a statue, her hands by her sides, her feet just overlapping each other, the sheet up to her chin. She stared at the ceiling.

"Do you think father would mind if we gave his top-hat to the porter?"

"The porter?" snapped Josephine. "Why ever the porter? What a very extra-ordinary idea!"

"Because," said Constantia slowly, "he must often have to go to funerals. And   10 I noticed at—at the cemetery that he only had a bowler." She paused. "I thought then how very much he'd appreciate a top-hat. We ought to give him a present, too. He was always very nice to father."

"But," cried Josephine, flouncing on her pillow and staring across the dark at Constantia, "father's head!" And suddenly, for one awful moment, she nearly gig-gled. Not, of course, that she felt in the least like giggling. It must have been habit. Years ago, when they had stayed awake at night talking, their beds had simply heaved. And now the porter's head, disappearing, popped out, like a candle, under father's hat . . . The giggle mounted, mounted; she clenched her hands; she fought it down; she frowned fiercely at the dark and said "Remember" terribly   20 sternly.

"We can decide to-morrow," she sighed.

Constantia had noticed nothing; she sighed.

"Do you think we ought to have our dressing-gowns dyed as well?"

"Black?" almost shrieked Josephine.

"Well, what else?" said Constantia. "I was thinking—it doesn't seem quite sincere, in a way, to wear black out of doors and when we're fully dressed, and then when we're at home—"

"But nobody sees us," said Josephine. She gave the bedclothes such a twitch that both her feet became uncovered, and she had to creep up the pillows to get   30 them well under again.

"Kate does," said Constantia. "And the postman very well might."

Josephine thought of her dark-red slippers, which matched her dressing-gown, and of Constantia's favourite indefinite green ones which went with hers. Black! Two black dressing-gowns and two pairs of black woolly slippers, creeping off to the bathroom like black cats.

"I don't think it's absolutely necessary," said she.

Silence. Then Constantia said, "We shall have to post the papers with the no-tice in them tomorrow to catch the Ceylon mail[1]. . . . How many letters have we had up till now?"   40

"Twenty-three."

Josephine had replied to them all, and twenty-three times when she came to

---

1. The Colonel served in the British colony of Ceylon; they are sending the English newspapers with his obituary to Ceylon so that friends there will receive the news of his death.

"We miss our dear father so much" she had broken down and had to use her handkerchief, and on some of them even to soak up a very light-blue tear with an edge of blotting-paper. Strange! She couldn't have put it on—but twenty-three times. Even now, though, when she said over to herself sadly. "We miss our dear father *so* much" she could have cried if she'd wanted to.

"Have you got enough stamps?" came from Constantia.

"Oh, how can I tell?" said Josephine crossly.

"What's the good of asking me that now?" 50

"I was just wondering," said Constantia mildly.

Silence again. There came a little rustle, a scurry, a hop.

"A mouse," said Constantia.

"It can't be a mouse because there aren't any crumbs," said Josephine.

"But it doesn't know there aren't," said Constantia.

A spasm of pity squeezed her heart. Poor little thing! She wished she'd left a tiny piece of biscuit on the dressing-table. It was awful to think of it not finding anything. What would it do?

"I can't think how they manage to live at all," she said slowly.

"Who?" demanded Josephine.

And Constantia said more loudly than she meant to, "Mice." 60

Josephine was furious. "Oh, what nonsense, Con!" she said. "What have mice got to do with it? You're asleep."

"I don't think I am," said Constantia. She shut her eyes to make sure. She was.

Josephine arched her spine, pulled up her knees, folded her arms so that her fists came under her ears, and pressed her cheek hard against the pillow.

II

Another thing which complicated matters was they had Nurse Andrews staying on with them that week. It was their own fault; they had asked her. It was Josephine's idea. On the morning—well, on the last morning, when the doctor 70 had gone, Josephine had said to Constantia, "Don't you think it would be rather nice if we asked Nurse Andrews to stay on for a week as our guest?"

"Very nice," said Constantia.

"I thought," went on Josephine quickly, "I should just say this afternoon, after I've paid her, 'My sister and I would be very pleased, after all you've done for us, Nurse Andrews, if you would stay on for a week as our guest.' I'd have to put that in about being our guest in case—"

"Oh, but she could hardly expect to be paid!" cried Constantia.

"One never knows," said Josephine sagely.

Nurse Andrews had, of course, jumped at the idea. But it was a bother. It 80 meant they had to have regular sit-down meals at the proper times, whereas if they'd been alone they could just have asked Kate if she wouldn't have minded bringing them a tray wherever they were. And meal-times now that the strain was over were rather a trial.

Nurse Andrews was simply fearful about butter. Really they couldn't help feeling that about butter, at least, she took advantage of their kindness. And she had that maddening habit of asking for just an inch more bread to finish what she had on her plate, and then, at the last mouthful, absent-mindedly—of course it wasn't absent-mindedly—taking another helping. Josephine got very red when this happened, and she fastened her small, bead-like eyes on the tablecloth as if she saw a minute strange insect creeping through the web of it. But Constantia's long, pale face lengthened and set, and she gazed away—away—far over the desert, to where that line of camels unwound like a thread of wool. . . .

"When I was with Lady Tukes," said Nurse Andrews, "she had such a dainty little contrayvance for the buttah. It was a silvah Cupid balanced on the—on the bordah of a glass dish, holding a tayny fork. And when you wanted some buttah you simply pressed his foot and he bent down and speared you a piece. It was quite a gayme."

Josephine could hardly bear that. But "I think those things are very extravagant" was all she said.

"But whey?" asked Nurse Andrews, beaming through her eyeglasses. "No one, surely, would take more buttah than one wanted—would one?"

"Ring, Con," cried Josephine. She couldn't trust herself to reply.

And proud young Kate, the enchanted princess, came in to see what the old tabbies[2] wanted now. She snatched away their plates of mock something or other and slapped down a white, terrified blancamange.[3]

"Jam, please, Kate," said Josephine kindly.

Kate knelt and burst open the sideboard, lifted the lid of the jam-pot, saw it was empty, put it on the table, and stalked off.

"I'm afraid," said Nurse Andrews a moment later, "there isn't any."

"Oh, what a bother!" said Josephine. She bit her lip. "What had we better do?"

Constantia looked dubious. "We can't disturb Kate again," she said softly.

Nurse Andrews waited, smiling at them both. Her eyes wandered, spying at everything behind her eye-glasses. Constantia in despair went back to her camels. Josephine frowned heavily—concentrated. If it hadn't been for this idiotic woman she and Con would, of course, have eaten their blancamange without. Suddenly the idea came.

"I know," she said. "Marmalade. There's some marmalade in the sideboard. Get it, Con."

"I hope," laughed Nurse Andrews, and her laugh was like a spoon tinkling against a medicine-glass—"I hope it's not very bittah marmalayde."

III

But, after all, it was not long now, and then she'd be gone for good. And there was no getting over the fact that she had been very kind to father. She had nursed him day and night at the end. Indeed, both Constantia and Josephine felt privately she had rather overdone the not leaving him at the very last. For when they had gone in to say good-bye Nurse Andrews had sat beside his bed the whole

2. Tabby cats; i.e., "old biddies."
3. A dessert similar to vanilla pudding.

time, holding his wrist and pretending to look at her watch. It couldn't have been necessary. It was so tactless, too. Supposing father had wanted to say something—something private to them. Not that he had. Oh, far from it! He lay there, purple, 130 a dark, angry purple in the face, and never even looked at them when they came in. Then, as they were standing there, wondering what to do, he had suddenly opened one eye. Oh, what a difference it would have made, what a difference to their memory of him, how much easier to tell people about it, if he had only opened both! But no—one eye only. It glared at them a moment and then . . . went out.

IV

It had made it very awkward for them when Mr. Farolles, of St. John's,[4] called the same afternoon.

"The end was quite peaceful, I trust?" were the first words he said as he glided towards them through the dark drawing-room. 140

"Quite," said Josephine faintly. They both hung their heads. Both of them felt certain that eye wasn't at all a peaceful eye.

"Won't you sit down?" said Josephine.

"Thank you, Miss Pinner," said Mr. Farolles gratefully. He folded his coat-tails and began to lower himself into father's arm-chair, but just as he touched it he almost sprang up and slid into the next chair instead.

He coughed. Josephine clasped her hands; Constantia looked vague.

"I want you to feel, Miss Pinner," said Mr. Farolles, "and you, Miss Constantia, that I'm trying to be helpful. I want to be helpful to you both, if you will let me. These are the times," said Mr. Farolles, very simply and earnestly, 150 "when God means us to be helpful to one another."

"Thank you very much, Mr. Farolles," said Josephine and Constantia.

"Not at all," said Mr. Farolles gently. He drew his kid gloves through his fingers and leaned forward. "And if either of you would like a little Communion, either or both of you, here *and* now, you have only to tell me. A little Communion is often very help—a great comfort," he added tenderly.

But the idea of a little Communion terrified them. What! In the drawing-room by themselves—with no—no altar or anything! The piano would be much too high, thought Constantia, and Mr. Farolles could not possibly lean over it with the chalice. And Kate would be sure to come bursting in and interrupt them, 160 thought Josephine. And supposing the bell rang in the middle? It might be somebody important—about their mourning. Would they get up reverently and go out, or would they have to wait . . . in torture?

"Perhaps you will send round a note by your good Kate if you would care for it later," said Mr. Farolles.

"Oh yes, thank you very much!" they both said.

Mr. Farolles got up and took his black straw hat from the round table.

"And about the funeral," he said softly. "I may arrange that—as your dear father's old friend and yours, Miss Pinner—and Miss Constantia?"

---

4. Clergymen are often referred to as "Mister" rather than "Reverend" or "Father."

Josephine and Constantia got up too.   170

"I should like it to be quite simple," said Josephine firmly, "and not too expensive. At the same time, I should like—"

"A good one that will last," thought dreamy Constantia, as if Josephine were
buying a nightgown. But of course Josephine didn't say that. "One suitable to our
father's position." She was very nervous.

"I'll run round to our good friend Mr. Knight," said Mr. Farolles soothingly.
"I will ask him to come and see you. I am sure you will find him very helpful indeed."

V

Well, at any rate, all that part of it was over, though neither of them could
possibly believe that father was never coming back. Josephine had had a moment   180
of absolute terror at the cemetery, while the coffin was lowered, to think that she
and Constantia had done this thing without asking his permission. What would
father say when he found out? For he was bound to find out sooner or later. He always did. "Buried. You two girls had me *buried!*" She heard his stick thumping.
Oh, what would they say? What possible excuse could they make? It sounded
such an appallingly heartless thing to do. Such a wicked advantage to take of a
person because he happened to be helpless at the moment. The other people
seemed to treat it all as a matter of course. They were strangers; they couldn't be
expected to understand that father was the very last person for such a thing to
happen to. No, the entire blame for it all would fall on her and Constantia. And   190
the expense, she thought, stepping into the tight-buttoned cab. When she had to
show him the bills. What would he say then?

She heard him absolutely roaring, "And do you expect me to pay for this
gimcrack excursion of yours?"

"Oh," groaned poor Josephine aloud, "we shouldn't have done it, Con!"

And Constantia, pale as a lemon in all that blackness, said in a frightened
whisper, "Done what, Jug?"

"Let them bu-bury father like that," said Josephine, breaking down and crying into her new, queer-smelling mourning handkerchief.

"But what else could we have done?" asked Constantia wonderingly, "We   200
couldn't have kept him, Jug—we couldn't have kept him unburied. At any rate,
not in a flat that size."

Josephine blew her nose; the cab was dreadfully stuffy.

"I don't know," she said forlornly. "It is all so dreadful. I feel we ought to
have tried to, just for a time at least. To make perfectly sure. One thing's certain"—
and her tears sprang out again—"father will never forgive us for this—never!"

VI

Father would never forgive them. That was what they felt more than ever
when, two mornings later, they went into his room to go through his things. They
had discussed it quite calmly. It was even down on Josephine's list of things to be

done. *Go through father's things and settle about them.* But that was a very different 210
matter from saying after breakfast:

"Well, are you ready, Con?"

"Yes, Jug—when you are."

"Then I think we'd better get it over."

It was dark in the hall. It had been a rule for years never to disturb father in
the morning, whatever happened. And now they were going to open the door
without knocking even . . . Constantia's eyes were enormous at the idea; Josephine
felt weak in the knees.

"You—you go first," she gasped, pushing Constantia.

But Constantia said, as she always had said on those occasions, "No, Jug, 220
that's not fair. You're eldest."

Josephine was just going to say—what at other times she wouldn't have
owned to for the world—what she kept for her very last weapon, "But you're
tallest," when they noticed that the kitchen door was open, and there stood
Kate. . . .

"Very stiff," said Josephine, grasping the door-handle and doing her best to
turn it. As if anything ever deceived Kate!

It couldn't be helped. That girl was . . . Then the door was shut behind them,
but—but they weren't in father's room at all. They might have suddenly walked
through the wall by mistake into a different flat altogether. Was the door just be- 230
hind them? They were too frightened to look. Josephine knew that if it was it was
holding itself tight shut; Constantia felt that, like the doors in dreams, it hadn't any
handle at all. It was the coldness which made it so awful. Or the whiteness—
which? Everything was covered. The blinds were down, a cloth hung over the mirror, a sheet hid the bed; a huge fan of white paper filled the fireplace. Constantia
timidly put out her hand; she almost expected a snowflake to fall. Josephine felt a
queer tingling in her nose, as if her nose was freezing. Then a cab klop-klopped
over the cobbles below, and the quiet seemed to shake into little pieces.

"I had better pull up a blind," said Josephine bravely.

"Yes, it might be a good idea," whispered Constantia.   240

They only gave the blind a touch, but it flew up and the cord flew after,
rolling round the blindstick, and the little tassel tapped as if trying to get free. That
was too much for Constantia.

"Don't you think—don't you think we might put it off for another day?" she
whispered.

"Why?" snapped Josephine, feeling, as usual, much better now that she
knew for certain that Constantia was terrified. "It's got to be done. But I do wish
you wouldn't whisper, Con."

"I didn't know I was whispering," whispered Constantia.

"And why do you keep on staring at the bed?" said Josephine, raising her 250
voice almost defiantly. "There's nothing *on* the bed."

"Oh, Jug, don't say so!" said poor Connie. "At any rate, not so loudly."

Josephine felt herself that she had gone too far. She took a wide swerve over
to the chest of drawers, put out her hand, but quickly drew it back again.

"Connie!" she gasped, and she wheeled round and leaned with her back
against the chest of drawers.

"Oh, Jug—what?"

Josephine could only glare. She had the most extraordinary feeling that she had just escaped something simply awful. But how could she explain to Constantia that father was in the chest of drawers? He was in the top drawer with his handkerchiefs and neckties, or in the next with his shirts and pyjamas, or in the lowest of all with his suits. He was watching there, hidden away—just behind the door-handle—ready to spring. 260

She pulled a funny old-fashioned face at Constantia, just as she used to in the old days when she was going to cry.

"I can't open," she nearly wailed.

"No, don't, Jug," whispered Constantia earnestly. "It's much better not to. Don't let's open anything. At any rate, not for a long time."

"But—but it seems so weak," said Josephine, breaking down.

"But why not be weak for once, Jud?" argued Constantia, whispering quite 270 fiercely. "If it is weak." And her pale stare flew from the locked writing-table—so safe—to the huge glittering wardrobe, and she began to breathe in a queer, panting way. "Why shouldn't we be weak for once in our lives, Jug? It's quite excusable. Let's be weak—be weak, Jug. It's much nicer to be weak than to be strong."

And then she did one of those amazingly bold things that she'd done about twice before in their lives; she marched over to the wardrobe, turned the key, and took it out of the lock. Took it out of the lock and held it up to Josephine, showing Josephine by her extraordinary smile that she knew what she'd done, she'd risked deliberately father being in there among his overcoats.

If the huge wardrobe had lurched forward, had crashed down on Constantia, 280 Josephine wouldn't have been surprised. On the contrary, she would have thought it the only suitable thing to happen. But nothing happened. Only the room seemed quieter than ever, and bigger flakes of cold air fell on Josephine's shoulders and knees. She began to shiver.

"Come, Jug," said Constantia, still with that awful callous smile, and Josephine followed just as she had that last time, when Constantia had pushed Benny into the round pond.

VII

But the strain told on them when they were back in the dining-room. They sat down, very shaky, and looked at each other.

"I don't feel I can settle to anything," said Josephine," until I've had some- 290 thing. Do you think we could ask Kate for two cups of hot water?"

"I really don't see why we shouldn't," said Constantia carefully. She was quite normal again. "I won't ring. I'll go to the kitchen door and ask her."

"Yes, do," said Josephine, sinking down into a chair. "Tell her, just two cups, Con, nothing else—on a tray."

"She needn't even put the jug on, need she?" said Constantia, as though Kate might very well complain if the jug had been there.

"Oh no, certainly not! The jug's not at all necessary. She can pour it direct out of the kettle," cried Josephine, feeling that would be a labour-saving indeed.

Their cold lips quivered at the greenish brims. Josephine curved her small [300] red hands round the cup; Constantia sat up and blew on the wavy stream, making it flutter from one side to the other.

"Speaking of Benny," said Josephine.

And though Benny hadn't been mentioned Constantia immediately looked as though he had.

"He'll expect us to send him something of father's, of course. But it's so difficult to know what to send to Ceylon."

"You mean things get unstuck so on the voyage," murmured Constantia.

"No, lost," said Josephine sharply. "You know there's no post. Only runners."

Both paused to watch a black man in white linen drawers running through [310] the pale fields for dear life, with a large brown-paper parcel in his hands. Josephine's black man was tiny; he scurried along glistening like an ant. But there was something blind and tireless about Constantia's tall, thin fellow, which made him, she decided, a very unpleasant person indeed . . . On the veranda, dressed all in white and wearing a cork helmet, stood Benny. His right hand shook up and down, as father's did when he was impatient. And behind him, not in the least interested, sat Hilda, the unknown sister-in-law. She swung in a cane rocker and flicked over the leaves of the *Tatler*.[5]

"I think his watch would be the most suitable present," said Josephine.

Constantia looked up; she seemed surprised. [320]

"Oh, would you trust a gold watch to a native?"

"But of course I'd disguise it," said Josephine. "No one would know it was a watch." She liked the idea of having to make a parcel such a curious shape that no one could possibly guess what it was. She even thought for a moment of hiding the watch in a narrow cardboard corset-box that she'd kept by her for a long time, waiting for it to come in for something. It was such beautiful firm cardboard. But, no, it wouldn't be appropriate for this occasion. It had lettering on it: *Medium Women's 28. Extra Firm Busks*. It would be almost too much of a surprise for Benny to open that and find father's watch inside.

"And of course it isn't as though it would be going—ticking, I mean," said [330] Constantia, who was still thinking of the native love of jewellery. "At least," she added, "it would be very strange if after all that time it was."

VIII

Josephine made no reply. She had flown off on one of her tangents. She had suddenly thought of Cyril. Wasn't it more usual for the only grandson to have the watch? And then dear Cyril was so appreciative, and a gold watch meant so much to a young man. Benny, in all probability, had quite got out of the habit of watches; men so seldom wore waistcoats[6] in those hot climates. Whereas Cyril in London wore them from year's end to year's end. And it would be so nice for her and Constantia, when he came to tea, to know it was there. "I see you've got on grandfather's watch, Cyril." It would be somehow so satisfactory. [340]

5. A newspaper specializing in society news and gossip.
6. Vests.

Dear boy! What a blow his sweet, sympathetic little note had been! Of course they quite understood; but it was most unfortunate.

"It would have been such a point, having him," said Josephine.

"And he would have enjoyed it so," said Constantia, not thinking what she was saying.

However, as soon as he got back he was coming to tea with his aunties. Cyril to tea was one of their rare treats.

"Now, Cyril, you mustn't be frightened of our cakes. Your Auntie Con and I bought them at Buszard's this morning. We know what a man's appetite is. So don't be ashamed of making a good tea." 350

Josephine cut recklessly into the rich dark cake that stood for her winter gloves or the soling and heeling of Constantia's only respectable shoes. But Cyril was most unmanlike in appetite.

"I say, Aunt Josephine, I simply can't. I've only just had lunch, you know."

"Oh, Cyril, that can't be true! It's after four," cried Josephine. Constantia sat with her knife poised over the chocolate-roll.

"It is, all the same," said Cyril. "I had to meet a man at Victoria, and he kept me hanging about till . . . there was only time to get lunch and to come on here. And he gave me—phew"—Cyril put his hand to his forehead—"a terrific blow-out," he said. 360

It was disappointing—to-day of all days. But still he couldn't be expected to know.

"But you'll have a meringue, won't you, Cyril?" said Aunt Josephine. "These meringues were bought specially for you. Your dear father was so fond of them. We were sure you are, too."

"I *am*, Aunt Josephine," cried Cyril ardently. "Do you mind if I take half to begin with?"

"Not at all, dear boy; but we mustn't let you off with that."

"Is your dear father still so fond of meringues?" asked Auntie Con gently. She winced faintly as she broke through the shell of hers. 370

"Well, I don't quite know, Auntie Con," said Cyril breezily.

At that they both looked up.

"Don't know?" almost snapped Josephine. "Don't know a thing like that about your own father, Cyril?"

"Surely," said Auntie Con softly.

Cyril tried to laugh it off. "Oh, well," he said, "it's such a long time since—" He faltered. He stopped. Their faces were too much for him.

"Even *so*," said Josephine.

And Auntie Con looked.

Cyril put down his teacup. "Wait a bit," he cried. "Wait a bit, Aunt 380 Josephine. What am I thinking of?"

He looked up. They were beginning to brighten. Cyril slapped his knee.

"Of course," he said, "it was meringues. How could I have forgotten? Yes, Aunt Josephine, you're perfectly right. Father's most frightfully keen on meringues."

They didn't only beam. Aunt Josephine went scarlet with pleasure; Auntie Con gave a deep, deep sigh.

"And now, Cyril, you must come and see father," said Josephine. "He knows you were coming today."

"Right," said Cyril, very firmly and heartily. He got up from his chair; sud- 390 denly he glanced at the clock.

"I say, Auntie Con, isn't your clock a bit slow? I've got to meet a man at—at Paddington just after five. I'm afraid I shan't be able to stay very long with grandfather."

"Oh, he won't expect you to stay *very* long!" said Aunt Josephine.

Constantia was still gazing at the clock. She couldn't make up her mind if it was fast or slow. It was one or the other, she felt almost certain of that. At any rate, it had been.

Cyril still lingered. "Aren't you coming along, Auntie Con?"

"Of course," said Josephine, "we shall all go. Come on, Con."   400

IX

They knocked at the door, and Cyril followed his aunts into grandfather's hot, sweetish room.

"Come on," said Grandfather Pinner. "Don't hang about. What is it? What've you been up to?"

He was sitting in front of a roaring fire, clasping his stick. He had a thick rug over his knees. On his lap there lay a beautiful pale yellow silk handkerchief.

"It's Cyril, father," said Josephine shyly. And she took Cyril's hand and led him forward.

"Good afternoon, grandfather," said Cyril, trying to take his hand out of Aunt Josephine's. Grandfather Pinner shot his eyes at Cyril in the way he was fa- 410 mous for. Where was Auntie Con? She stood on the other side of Aunt Josephine; her long arms hung down in front of her; her hands were clasped. She never took her eyes off grandfather.

"Well," said Grandfather Pinner, beginning to thump, "what have you got to tell me?"

What had he, what had he got to tell him? Cyril felt himself smiling like a perfect imbecile. The room was stifling, too.

But Aunt Josephine came to his rescue. She cried brightly, "Cyril says his father is still very fond of meringues, father dear."

"Eh?" said Grandfather Pinner, curving his hand like a purple meringue-shell 420 over one ear.

Josephine repeated, "Cyril says his father is still very fond of meringues."

"Can't hear," said old Colonel Pinner. And he waved Josephine away with his stick, then pointed with his stick to Cyril. "Tell me what she's trying to say," he said.

(My God!) "Must I?" said Cyril, blushing and staring at Aunt Josephine.

"Do, dear," she smiled. "It will please him so much."

"Come on, out with it!" cried Colonel Pinner testily, beginning to thump again.

And Cyril leaned forward and yelled, "Father's still very fond of meringues." 430

At that Grandfather Pinner jumped as though he had been shot.

"Don't shout!" he cried. "What's the matter with the boy? *Meringues!* What about 'em?"

"Oh, Aunt Josephine, must we go on?" groaned Cyril desperately.

"It's quite all right, dear boy," said Aunt Josephine, as though he and she were at the dentist's together. "He'll understand in a minute." And she whispered to Cyril, "He's getting a bit deaf, you know." Then she leaned forward and really bawled at Grandfather Pinner, "Cyril only wanted to tell you, father dear, that *his* father is still very fond of meringues."

Colonel Pinner heard that time, heard and brooded, looking Cyril up and   440
down.

"What an esstrordinary thing!" said old Grandfather Pinner. "What an esstrordinary thing to come all this way here to tell me!"

And Cyril felt it *was*.

"Yes, I shall send Cyril the watch," said Josephine.

"That would be very nice," said Constantia. "I seem to remember last time he came there was some little trouble about the time."

X

They were interrupted by Kate bursting through the door in her usual fashion, as though she had discovered some secret panel in the wall.

"Fried or boiled?" asked the bold voice.   450

Fried or boiled? Josephine and Constantia were quite bewildered for the moment. They could hardly take it in.

"Fried or boiled what, Kate?" asked Josephine, trying to begin to concentrate.

Kate gave a loud sniff. "Fish."

"Well, why didn't you say so immediately?" Josephine reproached her gently. "How could you expect us to understand, Kate? There are a great many things in this world, you know, which are fried or boiled." And after such a display of courage she said quite brightly to Constantia, "Which do you prefer, Con?"

"I think it might be nice to have it fried," said Constantia. "On the other   460
hand, of course boiled fish is very nice. I think I prefer both equally well . . . Unless you . . . In that case—"

"I shall fry it," said Kate, and she bounced back, leaving their door open and slamming the door of her kitchen.

Josephine gazed at Constantia; she raised her pale eyebrows until they rippled away into her pale hair. She got up. She said in a very lofty, imposing way, "Do you mind following me into the drawing-room, Constantia? I've something of great importance to discuss with you."

For it was always to the drawing-room they retired when they wanted to talk over Kate.   470

Josephine closed the door meaningly. "Sit down, Constantia," she said, still very grand. She might have been receiving Constantia for the first time. And Con looked round vaguely for a chair, as though she felt indeed quite a stranger.

"Now the question is," said Josephine, bending forward, "whether we shall keep her or not."

"That is the question," agreed Constantia.

"And this time," said Josephine firmly, "we must come to a definite decision."

Constantia looked for a moment as though she might begin going over all the other times, but she pulled herself together and said, "Yes, Jug."

"You see, Con," explained Josephine, "everything is so changed now." 480
Constantia looked up quickly. "I mean," went on Josephine, "we're not dependent on Kate as we were." And she blushed faintly. "There's not father to cook for."

"That is perfectly true," agreed Constantia. "Father certainly doesn't want any cooking now, whatever else—"

Josephine broke in sharply, "You're not sleepy, are you, Con?"

"Sleepy, Jug?" Constantia was wide-eyed.

"Well, concentrate more," said Josephine sharply, and she returned to the subject. "What it comes to is, if we did"—and this she barely breathed, glancing at the door—"give Kate notice"—she raised her voice again—"we could manage our own food." 490

"Why not?" cried Constantia. She couldn't help smiling. The idea was so exciting. She clasped her hands. What should we live on, Jug?"

"Oh, eggs in various forms!" said Jug, lofty again. "And, besides, there are all the cooked foods."

"But I've always heard," said Constantia, "they are considered so very expensive."

"Not if one buys them in moderation," and Josephine. But she tore herself away from this fascinating bypath and dragged Constantia after her. "What we've got to decide now, however, is whether we really do trust Kate or not."

Constantia leaned back. Her flat little laugh flew from her lips. 500

"Isn't it curious, Jug," said she, "that just on this one subject I've never been able to quite make up my mind?"

XI

She never had. The whole difficulty was to prove anything. How did one prove things, how could one? Suppose Kate had stood in front of her and deliberately made a face. Mightn't she very well have been in pain? Wasn't it impossible, at any rate, to ask Kate if she was making a face at her? If Kate answered "No"— and of course she would say "No"—what a position! How undignified! Then again Constantia suspected, she was almost certain that Kate went to her chest of drawers when she and Josephine were out, not to take things but to spy. Many times she had come back to find her amethyst cross in the most unlikely places, under 510 her lace ties or on top of her evening Bertha. More than once she had laid a trap for Kate. She had arranged things in a special order and then called Josephine to witness.

"You see, Jug?"

"Quite, Con."

"Now we shall be able to tell."

But, oh dear, when she did go to look, she was as far off from a proof as

ever! If anything was displaced, it might so very well have happened as she closed
the drawer; a jolt might have done it so easily.

"You come, Jug, and decide. I really can't. It's too difficult."   520

But after a pause and a long glare Josephine would sigh, "Now you've put
the doubt into my mind, Con, I'm sure I can't tell myself."

"Well, we can't postpone it again," said Josephine. "If we postpone it this
time—"

XII

But at that moment in the street below a barrel-organ struck up. Josephine
and Constantia sprang to their feet together.

"Run, Con," said Josephine. "Run quickly. There's sixpence on the—"

Then they remembered. It didn't matter. They would never have to stop the
organ-grinder again. Never again would she and Constantia be told to make that
monkey take his noise somewhere else. Never would sound that loud, strange bel-   530
low when father thought they were not hurrying enough. The organ-grinder might
play there all day and the stick would not thump.

It never will thump again,
It never will thump again,

played the barrel-organ.

What was Constantia thinking? She had such a strange smile; she looked different. She couldn't be going to cry.

"Jug, Jug," said Constantia softly, pressing her hands together. "Do you know
what day it is? It's Saturday. It's a week to-day, a whole week."

A week since father died,   540
A week since father died,

cried the barrel-organ. And Josephine, too, forgot to be practical and sensible; she
smiled faintly, strangely. On the Indian carpet there fell a square of sunlight, pale
red; it came and went and came—and stayed, deepened—until it shone almost
golden.

"The sun's out," said Josephine, as though it really mattered.

A perfect fountain of bubbling notes shook from the barrel-organ, round,
bright notes, carelessly scattered.

Constantia lifted her big, cold hands as if to catch them, and then her hands
fell again. She walked over to the mantelpiece to her favourite Buddha. And the   550
stone and gilt image, whose smile always gave her such a queer feeling, almost a
pain and yet a pleasant pain, seemed to-day to be more than smiling. He knew
something; he had a secret. "I know something that you don't know," said her
Buddha. Oh, what was it, what could it be? And yet she had always felt there was
. . . something.

The sunlight pressed through the windows, thieved its way in, flashed its light over the furniture and the photographs. Josephine watched it. When it came to mother's photograph, the enlargement over the piano, it lingered as though puzzled to find so little remained of mother, except the earrings shaped like tiny pagodas and a black feather boa. Why did the photographs of dead people always 560 fade so? wondered Josephine. As soon as a person was dead their photograph died too. But, of course, this one of mother was very old. It was thirty-five years old. Josephine remembered standing on a chair and pointing out that feather boa to Constantia and telling her that it was a snake that had killed their mother in Ceylon. . . . Would everything have been different if mother hadn't died? She didn't see why. Aunt Florence had lived with them until they had left school, and they had moved three times and had their yearly holiday and . . . and there'd been changes of servants, of course.

Some little sparrows, young sparrows they sounded, chirped on the window-ledge. *Yeep—eyeep—yeep.* But Josephine felt they were not sparrows, not 570 on the window-ledge. It was inside her, that queer little crying noise. *Yeep— eyeep—yeep.* Ah, what was it crying, so weak and forlorn?

If mother had lived, might they have married? But there had been nobody for them to marry. There had been father's Anglo-Indian friends before he quarrelled with them. But after that she and Constantia never met a single man except clergymen. How did one meet men? Or even if they'd met them, how could they have got to know men well enough to be more than strangers? One read of people having adventures, being followed, and so on. But nobody had ever followed Constantia and her. Oh yes, there had been one year at Eastbourne a mysterious man at their boarding-house who had put a note on the jug of hot water outside 580 their bedroom door! But by the time Connie had found it the steam had made the writing too faint to read; they couldn't even make out to which of them it was addressed. And he had left next day. And that was all. The rest had been looking after father, and at the same time keeping out of father's way. But now? But now? The thieving sun touched Josephine gently. She lifted her face. She was drawn over to the window by gentle beams. . . .

Until the barrel-organ stopped playing Constantia stayed before the Buddha, wondering, but not as usual, not vaguely. This time her wonder was like longing. She remembered the times she had come in here, crept out of bed in her nightgown when the moon was full, and lain on the floor with her arms outstretched, 590 as though she was crucified. Why? The big, pale moon had made her do it. The horrible dancing figures on the carved screen had leered at her and she hadn't minded. She remembered too how, whenever they were at the seaside, she had gone off by herself and got as close to the sea as she could, and sung something, something she had made up, while she gazed all over that restless water. There had been this other life, running out, bringing things home in bags, getting things on approval, discussing them with Jug, and taking them back to get more things on approval, and arranging father's trays and trying not to annoy father. But it all seemed to have happened in a kind of tunnel. It wasn't real. It was only when she came out of the tunnel into the moonlight or by the sea or into a thunderstorm 600 that she really felt herself. What did it mean? What was it she was always wanting? What did it all lead to? Now? Now?

She turned away from the Buddha with one of her vague gestures. She went over to where Josephine was standing. She wanted to say something to Josephine, something frightfully important, about—about the future and what . . .

"Don't you think perhaps—" she began.

But Josephine interrupted her. "I was wondering if now—" she murmured. They stopped; they waited for each other.

"Go on, Con," said Josephine.

"No, no, Jug; after you," said Constantia.   610

"No, say what you were going to say. You began," said Josephine.

"I . . . I'd rather hear what you were going to say first," said Constantia.

"Don't be absurd, Con."

"Really, Jug."

"Connie!"

"Oh, *Jug!*"

A pause. Then Constantia said faintly, "I can't say what I was going to say, Jug, because I've forgotten what it was . . . that I was going to say."

Josephine was silent for a moment. She stared at a big cloud where the sun had been. Then she replied shortly, "I've forgotten too."   [1922] 620

Questions for Discussion and Writing

1. From the various clues given, reconstruct the lives of Constantia and Josephine.

2. Analyze the characters of Josephine and Constantia carefully and specify the differences you find, if any.

3. What sort of man was the Colonel?

4. What is Mansfield's attitude toward the sisters? Underline or circle those passages that convey the author's attitude.

5. Analyze the relationship between the two sisters and Kate, the maid. What do the passages involving Kate say about the two sisters?

6. Is this a story about two individual women, or is it about the position of women generally? Are Josephine and Constantia typical in any way, or are they isolated cases? Explain.

7. Mansfield has often been called a highly poetic or "lyrical" writer. Specify the poetic devices you see in the story.

Miss Brill

ALTHOUGH IT WAS so brilliantly fine—the blue sky powdered with gold and great spots of light like white wine splashed over the Jardins Publiques—Miss Brill was glad that she had decided on her fur. The air was motionless, but when you opened your mouth there was just a faint chill, like a chill from a glass of iced water before you sip, and now and again a leaf came drifting—from nowhere, from the sky. Miss Brill put up her hand and touched her fur. Dear little thing! It was nice to feel it again. She had taken it out of its box that afternoon, shaken out

the mothpowder, given it a good brush, and rubbed the life back into the dim little eyes. "What has been happening to me?" said the sad little eyes. Oh, how sweet
it was to see them snap at her again from the red eiderdown!... But the nose, 10
which was of some black composition, wasn't at all firm. It must have had a
knock, somehow. Never mind—a little dab of black sealing-wax when the time
came—when it was absolutely necessary. . . . Little rogue! Yes, she really felt like
that about it. Little rogue biting its tail just by her left ear. She could have taken it
off and laid it on her lap and stroked it. She felt a tingling in her hands and arms,
but that came from walking, she supposed. And when she breathed, something
light and sad—no, not sad, exactly—something gentle seemed to move in her
bosom.

There were a number of people out this afternoon, far more than last
Sunday. And the band sounded louder and gayer. That was because the Season 20
had begun. For although the band played all the year round on Sundays, out of
season it was never the same. It was like some one playing with only the family to
listen; it didn't care how it played if there weren't any strangers present. Wasn't the
conductor wearing a new coat, too? She was sure it was new. He scraped with his
foot and flapped his arms like a rooster about to crow, and the bandsmen sitting in
the green rotunda blew out their cheeks and glared at the music. Now there came
a little "flutey" bit—very pretty!—a little chain of bright drops. She was sure it
would be repeated. It was; she lifted her head and smiled.

Only two people shared her "special" seat: a fine old man in a velvet coat, his
hands clasped over a huge carved walking-stick, and a big old woman, sitting up- 30
right, with a roll of knitting on her embroidered apron. They did not speak. This
was disappointing, for Miss Brill always looked forward to the conversation. She
had become really quite expert, she thought, at listening as though she didn't listen, at sitting in other people's lives just for a minute while they talked round her.

She glanced, sideways, at the old couple. Perhaps they would go soon. Last
Sunday, too, hadn't been as interesting as usual. An Englishman and his wife, he
wearing a dreadful Panama hat and she button boots. And she'd gone on the
whole time about how she ought to wear spectacles; she knew she needed them;
but that it was no good getting any: they'd be sure to break and they'd never keep
on. And he'd been so patient. He'd suggested everything—gold rims, the kind that 40
curved round your ears, little pads inside the bridge. No, nothing would please
her. "They'll always be sliding down my nose!" Miss Brill had wanted to shake her.

The old people sat on the bench, still as statues. Never mind, there was always the crowd to watch. To and fro, in front of the flower-beds and the band rotunda, the couples and groups paraded, stopped to talk, to greet, to buy a handful
of flowers from the old beggar who had his tray fixed to the railings. Little children ran among them, swooping and laughing; little boys with big white silk bows
under their chins, little girls, little French dolls, dressed up in velvet and lace. And
sometimes a tiny staggerer came suddenly rocking into the open from under the
trees, stopped, stared, as suddenly sat down "flop," until its small high-stepping 50
mother, like a young hen, rushed scolding to its rescue. Other people sat on the
benches and green chairs, but they were nearly always the same, Sunday after
Sunday, and—Miss Brill had often noticed—there was something funny about

nearly all of them. They were odd, silent, nearly all old, and from way they stared they looked as though they'd just come from dark little rooms or even—even cupboards!

Behind the rotunda the slender trees with yellow leaves down drooping, and through them just a line of sea, and beyond the blue sky with gold-veined clouds.

Tum-tum-tum tiddle-um! tiddle-um! tum tiddley-um tum ta! blew the band.

Two young girls in red came by and two young soldiers in blue met them, 60 and they laughed and paired and went off arm-in-arm. Two peasant women with funny straw hats passed, gravely, leading beautiful smoke-coloured donkeys. A cold, pale nun hurried by. A beautiful woman came along and dropped her bunch of violets, and a little boy ran after to hand them to her, and she took them and threw them away as if they'd been poisoned. Dear me! Miss Brill didn't know whether to admire that or not! And now an ermine toque and a gentleman in grey met just in front of her. He was tall, stiff, dignified, and she was wearing the ermine toque she'd bought when her hair was yellow. Now everything, her hair, her face, even her eyes, was the same colour as the shabby ermine, and her hand, in its cleaned glove, lifted to dab her lips, was a tiny yellowish paw. On, she was so 70 pleased to see him—delighted! She rather thought they were going to meet that afternoon. She described where she'd been—everywhere, here, there, along by the sea. The day was so charming—didn't he agree? And wouldn't he, perhaps . . . But he shook his head, lighted a cigarette, slowly breathed a great deep puff into her face, and, even while she was still talking and laughing, flicked the match away and walked on. The ermine toque was alone; she smiled more brightly than ever. But even the band seemed to know what she was feeling and played more softly, played tenderly, and the drum beat, "The Brute! The Brute!" over and over. What would she do? What was going to happen now? But as Miss Brill wondered, the ermine toque turned, raised her hand as though she'd seen some one else, 80 much nicer, just over there, and pattered away. And the band changed again and played more quickly, more gaily than ever, and the old couple on Miss Brill's seat got up and marched away, and such a funny old man with long whiskers hobbled along in time to the music and was nearly knocked over by four girls walking abreast.

Oh, how fascinating it was! How she enjoyed it! How she loved sitting here, watching it all! It was like a play. It was exactly like a play. Who could believe the sky at the back wasn't painted! But it wasn't till a little brown dog trotted on solemn and then slowly trotted off, like a little "theatre" dog, a little dog that had been drugged, that Miss Brill discovered what it was that made it so exciting. They 90 were all on the stage. They weren't only the audience, not only looking on; they were acting. Even she had a part and came every Sunday. No doubt somebody would have noticed if she hadn't been there; she was part of the performance after all. How strange she'd never thought of it like that before! And yet it explained why she made such a point of starting from home at just the same time each week—so as not to be late for the performance—and it also explained why she had quite a queer, shy feeling at telling her English pupils how she spent her Sunday afternoons. No wonder! Miss Brill nearly laughed out loud. She was on the stage. She thought of the old invalid gentleman to whom she read the newspaper four after-

noons a week while he slept in the garden. She had got quite used to the frail head 100
on the cotton pillow, the hollowed eyes, the open mouth and the high pinched
nose. If he'd been dead she mightn't have noticed for weeks; she wouldn't have
minded. But suddenly he knew he was having the paper read to him by an actress!
"An actress!" The old head lifted; two points of light quivered in the old eyes.

"An actress—are ye?" And Miss Brill smoothed the newspaper as though it
were the manuscript of her part and said gently: "Yes, I have been an actress for a
long time."

The band had been having a rest. Now they started again. And what they
played was warm, sunny, yet there was just a faint chill—a something, what was
it?—not sadness—no, not sadness—a something that made you want to sing. The 110
tune lifted, lifted, the light shone; and it seemed to Miss Brill that in another moment all of them, all the whole company, would begin singing. The young ones,
the laughing ones who were moving together, they would begin, and the men's
voices, very resolute and brave, would join them. And then she too, she too, and
the others on the benches—they would come in with a kind of accompaniment—
something low, that scarcely rose or fell, something so beautiful—moving. . . . And
Miss Brill's eyes filled with tears and she looked smiling at all the other members
of the company. Yes, we understand, we understand, she thought—though what
they understood she didn't know.

Just at that moment a boy and a girl came and sat down where the old cou- 120
ple had been. They were beautifully dressed; they were in love. The hero and
heroine, of course, just arrived from his father's yacht. And still soundlessly
singing, still with that trembling smile, Miss Brill prepared to listen.

"No, not now," said the girl. "Not here, I can't."

"But why? Because of that stupid old thing at the end there?" asked the boy.
"Why does she come here at all—who wants her? Why doesn't she keep her silly
old mug at home?"

"It's her fu-fur which is so funny," giggled the girl. "It's exactly like a fried
whiting."

"Ah, be off with you!" said the boy in an angry whisper. Then: "Tell me, ma 130
petite chère—"

"No, not here," said the girl. "Not *yet*."

On her way home she usually bought a slice of honey-cake at the baker's. It
was her Sunday treat. Sometimes there was an almond in her slice, sometimes not.
It made a great difference. If there was an almond it was like carrying home a tiny
present—a surprise—something that might very well not have been there. She
hurried on the almond Sundays and struck the match for the kettle in quite a
dashing way.

But to-day she passed the baker's by, climbed the stairs, went into the little 140
dark room—her room like a cupboard—and sat down on the red eiderdown. She
sat there for a long time. The box that the fur came out of was on the bed. She un-
clasped the necklet quickly; quickly, without looking, laid it inside. But when she
put the lid on she thought she heard something crying.   [1920]

Questions for Discussion and Writing

1. What devices does Mansfield use to convey Miss Brill's character?
2. What part does music play in the story?
3. Evaluate Miss Brill's idea that everyone is acting in a play. How does this idea function in the story?
4. How do you interpret Miss Brill's pleasure in eavesdropping on other people's lives? Is her interest malicious or just normal curiosity? Explain.
5. What does Miss Brill learn about herself in the course of the story?
6. How do you interpret the last sentence?
7. Overall, how do you regard Miss Brill? Is she a sympathetic character, or is she being satirized? How do you know?

ᴥ WILBUR DANIEL STEELE
(1886–1970)

Footfalls

The meteoric rise and fall of the reputation of Wilbur Daniel Steele illustrates how rapidly literary fashion and taste can change. For twenty-five years, Steele's stories, novels, and stage adaptations were constantly in the public eye; today, his books are out of print, and his name is nearly forgotten. Nevertheless, his best stories retain their appeal, and his methods and themes illustrate an important phase in the short story.

Steele was born in Greensboro, North Carolina. He grew up in Denver, Colorado, where his father was a university professor. Wilbur received a B.A. in history and economics from the University of Denver, went on to study art at the Boston Museum School, then spent two years at the Académie Julien in Paris. He returned to the United States in 1910, determined to write, and scored his first significant success with "White Horse Winter" in the *Atlantic Monthly* for April 1912.

Steele's colorful settings, vivid characters, dramatic plots (often involving the supernatural or mental illness) soon earned him favorable comparisons with Rudyard Kipling (1865–1936). Each year from 1919 to 1921, a story by Steele was selected for inclusion in the annual *Best Short Stories* volumes, and in 1922 the O. Henry Committee presented him with a special prize for consistent excellence in short story writing. His reputation reached its zenith in 1929 when he was named by a leading magazine, along with Robert Frost (1874–1963), Sherwood Anderson (1876–1941), Thornton Wilder (1897–1975), and Thomas Wolfe (1900–1938), as one of "America's favorite authors."

Eventually, however, the critical reaction set in, and his stories were dismissed as "machine made"—i.e., formulaic, repetitive in their effects and devices, and conventional in theme. He enjoyed a large popular following in magazines and as a playwright until the end of the 1930s, but thereafter his work slipped into obscurity. Modernist methods and the changing world view made Steele's turn-of-the-century style obsolete. However, "Footfalls" and a handful of other stories are worth reconsidering for their dramatic intensity and genuine power of atmosphere and characterization.

THIS IS NOT AN EASY STORY; not a road for tender or for casual feet. Better the meadows. Let me warn you, it is as hard as that old man's soul and as sunless as his eyes. It has its inception in catastrophe, and its end in an act of almost incredible violence; between them it tells barely how a man, being blind, can become also deaf and dumb.

He lived in one of those old Puritan sea towns where the strain has come down austere and moribund, so that his act would not be quite unbelievable. Except, that the town is no longer Puritan and Yankee. It has been betrayed; it has become an outpost of the Portuguese islands.

This man, this blind cobbler himself, was a Portuguese, from St. Michael, in 10 the Western Islands, and his name was Boaz Negro.

He was happy. An unquenchable exuberance lived in him. When he arose in the morning he made vast, as it were uncontrollable, gestures with his stout arms. He came into his shop singing. His voice, strong and deep as the chest from which it emanated, rolled out through the doorway and along the street, and the fishermen, done with their morning work and lounging and smoking along the wharfs said, "Boaz is to work already." Then they came up to sit in the shop.

In that town a cobbler's shop is a club. One sees the interior always dimly thronged. They sit on the benches watching the artisan at his work for hours, and they talk about everything in the world. A cobbler is known by the company he 20 keeps.

Boaz Negro kept young company. He would have nothing to do with the old. On his own head the gray hairs set thickly.

He had a grown son. But the benches in his shop were for the lusty and valiant young, men who could spend the night drinking and then at three o'clock in the morning turn out in the rain and dark to pull at the weirs, sing songs, buffet one another among the slippery fish in the boat's bottom, and make loud jokes about the fundamental things, love and birth and death. Hearkening to their boasts and strong prophecies, his breast heaved and his heart beat faster. He was a large, full-blooded fellow, fashioned for exploits; the flame in his darkness burned 30 higher even to hear of them.

It is scarcely conceivable how Boaz Negro could have come through this much of his life still possessed of that unquenchable and priceless exuberance; how he would sing in the dawn; how, simply listening to the recital of deeds in gale or brawl, he could easily forget himself a blind man, tied to a shop and a last;[1] easily make of himself a lusty young fellow breasting the sunlit and adventurous tide of life.

He had had a wife, whom he had loved. Fate, which had scourged him with the initial scourge of blindness, had seen fit to take his Angelina away. He had had

---

1. Wooden model of a foot on which a shoe is made.

four sons. Three, one after another, had been removed, leaving only Manuel, the 40
youngest. Recovering slowly, with infinite agony, from each of these recurrent
blows, his unquenchable exuberance had lived. And there was another thing quite
as extraordinary. He had never done anything but work, and that sort of thing may
kill the flame where an abrupt catastrophe fails. Work in the dark. Work, work,
work! And accompanied by privation; an almost miserly scale of personal economy. Yes, indeed, he had "skinned his fingers," especially in the earlier years.
When it tells most.

How he had worked! Not alone in the daytime, but also, sometimes, when
orders were heavy, far into the night. It was strange for one, passing along that deserted street at midnight, to hear issuing from the black shop of Boaz Negro the 50
rhythmical tap-tap-tap of hammer on wooden peg.

Nor was that sound all: no man in town could get far past that shop in his
nocturnal wandering unobserved. No more than a dozen footfalls, and from the
darkness Boaz's voice rolled forth, fraternal, stentorian, "Good night, Antone!"
"Good night to you, Caleb Snow!"

To Boaz Negro it was still broad day.

Now, because of this, he was what might be called a substantial man. He
owned his place, his shop, opening on the sidewalk, and behind it the dwelling
house with trellised galleries upstairs and down.

And there was always something for his son, a "piece for the pocket," a dol- 60
lar, five, even a ten-dollar bill if he had "got to have it." Manuel was "a good boy."
Boaz not only said this; he felt that he was assured of it in his understanding, to
the infinite peace of his heart.

It was curious that he should be ignorant only of the one nearest to him. Not
because he was physically blind. Be certain he knew more of other men and of
other men's sons than they or their neighbors did. More, that is to say, of their
hearts, their understandings, their idiosyncrasies, and their ultimate weight in the
balance pan of eternity.

His simple explanation of Manuel was that Manuel "wasn't too stout." To
others he said this, and to himself. Manuel was not indeed too robust. How 70
should he be vigorous when he never did anything to make him so? He never
worked. Why should he work, when existence was provided for, and when there
was always that "piece for the pocket"? Even a ten-dollar bill on a Saturday night!
No. Manuel "wasn't too stout."

In the shop they let it go at that. The missteps and frailties of everyone else
in the world were canvassed there with the most shameless publicity. But Boaz
Negro was a blind man, and in a sense their host. Those reckless, strong young
fellows respected and loved him. It was allowed to stand at that. Manuel was "a
good boy." Which did not prevent them, by the way, from joining later in the general condemnation of that father's laxity—"the ruination of the boy!" 80

"He should have put him to work, that's what."

"He should have said to Manuel, 'Look here, if you want a dollar, go earn it
first.' "

As a matter of fact, only one man ever gave Boaz the advice direct. That was
Campbell Wood. And Wood never sat in that shop.

In every small town there is one young man who is spoken of as "rising." As often as not he is not a native, but "from away."

In this town Campbell Wood was that man. He had come from another part of the state to take a place in the bank. He lived in the upper story of Boaz Negro's house, the ground floor now doing for Boaz and the meager remnant of his family. The old woman who came in to tidy up for the cobbler looked after Wood's rooms as well.

Dealing with Wood, one had first of all the sense of his incorruptibility. A little ruthless perhaps, as if one could imagine him, in defense of his integrity, cutting off his friend, cutting off his own hand, cutting off the very stream flowing out from the wellsprings of human kindness. An exaggeration, perhaps.

He was by long odds the most eligible young man in town, good-looking in a spare, ruddy, sandy-haired Scottish fashion, important, incorruptible, "rising." But he took good care of his heart. Precisely that; like a sharp-eyed duenna to his own heart. One felt that here was the man, if ever was the man, who held his destiny in his own hand. Failing, of course, some quite gratuitous and unforeseeable catastrophe.

Not that he was not human, or even incapable of laughter or passion. He was, in a way, immensely accessible. He never clapped one on the shoulder; on the other hand, he never failed to speak. Not even to Boaz.

Returning from the bank in the afternoon, he had always a word for the cobbler. Passing out again to supper at his boarding place, he had another, about the weather, the prospects of rain. And if Boaz was at work in the dark when he returned from an evening at the Board of Trade, there was a "Good night, Mr. Negro!"

On Boaz's part, his attitude toward his lodger was curious and paradoxical. He did not pretend to anything less than reverence for the young man's position; precisely on account of that position he was conscious toward Wood of a vague distrust. This was because he was an uneducated fellow.

To the uneducated the idea of large finance is as uncomfortable as the idea of the law. It must be said for Boaz that, responsive to Wood's unfailing civility, he fought against the sensation of dim and somehow shameful distrust.

Nevertheless his whole parental soul was in arms that evening when, returning from the bank and finding the shop empty of loungers, Wood paused a moment to propose the bit of advice already referred to.

"Haven't you ever thought of having Manuel learn the trade?"

A suspicion, a kind of premonition, lighted the fires of defense.

"Shoemaking," said Boaz, "is good enough for a blind man."

"Oh, I don't know. At least it's better than doing nothing at all."

Boaz's hammer was still. He sat silent, monumental. Outwardly. For once his unfailing response had failed him, "Manuel ain't too stout, you know." Perhaps it had become suddenly inadequate.

He hated Wood; he despised Wood; more than ever before, a hundredfold more, quite abruptly, he distrusted Wood.

How could a man say such things as Wood had said? And where Manuel himself might hear!

Where Manuel had heard! Boaz's other emotions—hatred and contempt and distrust—were overshadowed. Sitting in darkness, no sound had come to his ears, no footfall, no infinitesimal creaking of a floor plank. Yet by some sixth uncanny sense of the blind he was aware that Manuel was standing in the dusk of the entry joining the shop to the house.

Boaz made a Herculean effort. The voice came out of his throat, harsh, bitter, and loud enough to have carried ten times the distance to his son's ears.

"Manuel is a good boy!"

"Yes—h'm—yes—I suppose so."   140

Wood shifted his weight. He seemed uncomfortable.

"Well, I'll be running along, I—ugh! Heavens!"

Something was happening. Boaz heard exclamations, breathings, the rustle of sleeve cloth in large, frantic, and futile graspings—all without understanding. Immediately there was an impact on the floor, and with it the unmistakable clink of metal. Boaz even heard that the metal was minted, and that the coins were gold. He understood. A coin sack, gripped not quite carefully enough for a moment under the other's overcoat, had shifted, slipped, escaped, and fallen.

And Manuel had heard!

It was a dreadful moment for Boaz, dreadful in its native sense, as full of   150
dread. Why? It was a moment of horrid revelation, ruthless clarification. His son, his link with the departed Angelina, that "good boy"—Manuel, standing in the shadow of the entry, visible alone to the blind, had heard the clink of falling gold, and—and Boaz wished that he had not!

There, amazing, disconcerting, destroying, stood the sudden fact.

Sitting as impassive and monumental as ever, his strong, bleached hands at rest on his work, round drops of sweat came out on Boaz's forehead. He scarcely took the sense of what Wood was saying. Only fragments.

"Government money, understand—for the breakwater workings—huge—too many people know, here, everywhere—don't trust the safe—tin safe—'Noah's   160
Ark'—give you my word—heavens, no!"

It boiled down to this—the money, more money than was good for that antiquated "Noah's Ark" at the bank—and whose contemplated sojourn there overnight was public to too many minds—in short, Wood was not only incorruptible, he was canny. To what one of those minds, now, would it occur that he should take away that money bodily, under casual cover of his coat, to his own lodgings behind the cobbler shop of Boaz Negro? For this one, this important, night!

He was sorry the coin sack had slipped, because he did not like to have the responsibility of secret sharer cast upon anyone, even upon Boaz, even by acci-   170
dent. On the other hand, how tremendously fortunate that it had been Boaz and not another. So far as that went, Wood had no more anxiety now than before. One incorruptible knows another.

"I'd trust you, Mr. Negro" (that was one of the fragments which came and stuck in the cobbler's brain), "as far as I would myself. As long as it's only you. I'm just going up here and throw it under the bed. Oh yes, certainly."

Boaz ate no supper. For the first time in his life food was dry in his gullet. Even under those other successive crushing blows of Fate the full and generous

habit of his functionings had carried on unabated; he had always eaten what
was set before him. Tonight, over his untouched plate, he watched Manuel 180
with his sightless eyes, keeping track of his every mouthful, word, intonation,
breath. What profit he expected to extract from this catlike surveillance it is impossible to say.

When they arose from the supper table Boaz made another Herculean effort.
"Manuel, you're a good boy!"

The formula had a quality of appeal, of despair, and of command.

"Manuel, you should be short of money, maybe. Look, what's this? A tenner?
Well, there's a piece for the pocket; go and enjoy yourself."

He would have been frightened had Manuel, upsetting tradition, declined
the offering. With the morbid contrariness of the human imagination, the boy's 190
avid grasping gave him no comfort.

He went out into the shop, where it was already dark, drew to him his last,
his tools, mallets, cutters, pegs, leather. And having prepared to work, he remained idle. He found himself listening.

It has been observed that the large phenomena of sunlight and darkness
were nothing to Boaz Negro. A busy night was broad day. Yet there was a difference; he knew it with the blind man's eyes, the ears.

Day was a vast confusion, or rather a wide fabric, of sounds; great and little
sounds all woven together, voices, footfalls, wheels, far-off whistles and foghorns,
flies buzzing in the sun. Night was another thing. Still there were voices and foot- 200
falls, but rare, emerging from the large, pure body of silence as definite, surprising,
and yet familiar entities.

Tonight there was an easterly wind coming off the water and carrying the
sound of waves. So far as other fugitive sounds were concerned it was the same as
silence. The wind made little difference to the ears. It nullified, from one direction
at least, the other two visual processes of the blind, the sense of touch and the
sense of smell. It blew away from the shop, toward the living house.

As has been said, Boaz found himself listening, scrutinizing with an extraordinary attention this immense background of sound. He heard footfalls. The story
of that night was written, for him, in footfalls.   210

He heard them moving about the house, the lower floor, prowling here,
there, halting for long spaces, advancing, retreating softly on the planks. About
this aimless, interminable perambulation there was something to twist the nerves,
something led and at the same time driven, like a succession of frail and indecisive
charges.

Boaz lifted himself from his chair. All his impulse called to make a stir, join
battle, cast in the breach the reinforcement of his presence, authority, good will.
He sank back again; his hands fell down. The curious impotence of the spectator
held him.

He heard footfalls, too, on the upper floor, a little fainter, borne to the inner 220
rather than the outer ear, along the solid causeway of partitions and floor, the legs
of his chair, the bony framework of his body. Very faint indeed. Sinking back easily into the background of the wind. They, too, came and went, this room, that, to
the passage, the stairhead, and away. About them too there was the same quality of
being led and at the same time of being driven.

Time went by. In his darkness it seemed to Boaz that hours must have
passed. He heard voices. Together with the footfalls, that abrupt, brief, and (in
view of Wood's position) astounding interchange of sentences made up his history
of the night. Wood must have opened the door at the head of the stair; by the
sound of his voice he would be standing there, peering below perhaps; perhaps 230
listening.

"What's wrong down there?" he called. "Why don't you go to bed?"

After a moment came Manuel's voice, "Ain't sleepy."

"Neither am I. Look here, do you like to play cards?"

"What kind? Euchre? I like euchre all right. Or pitch."

"Well, what would you say to coming up and having a game of pitch then,
Manuel? If you can't sleep?"

"That'd be all right."

The lower footfalls ascended to joint the footfalls on the upper floor. There
was the sound of a door closing.   240

Boaz sat still. In the gloom he might have been taken for a piece of furniture,
of machinery, an extraordinary lay figure, perhaps, for the trying on of the boots
he made. He seemed scarcely to breathe, only the sweat starting from his brow
giving him an aspect of life.

He ought to have run, and leaped up that inner stair and pounded with his
fists on that door. He seemed unable to move. At rare intervals feet passed on the
sidewalk outside, just at his elbow, so to say, and yet somehow, tonight, immeasur-
ably far away. Beyond the orbit of the moon. He heard Rugg, the policeman, noting the silence of the shop, muttering, "Boaz is to bed tonight," as he passed.

The wind increased. It poured against the shop with its deep, continuous 250
sound of a river. Submerged in its body, Boaz caught the note of the town bell
striking midnight.

Once more, after a long time, he heard footfalls. He heard them coming
around the corner of the shop from the house, footfalls half swallowed by the
wind, passing discreetly, without haste, retreating, merging step by step with the
huge, incessant background of the wind.

Boaz's muscles tightened all over him. He had the impulse to start up, to
fling open the door, shout into the night, "What are you doing? Stop there! Say!
What are you doing and where are you going?"

And as before, the curious impotence of the spectator held him motionless. 260
He had not stirred in his chair. And those footfalls, upon which hinged, as it were,
that momentous decade of his life, were gone.

There was nothing to listen for now. Yet he continued to listen. Once or
twice, half arousing himself, he drew toward him his unfinished work. And then
relapsed into immobility.

As has been said, the wind, making little difference to the ears, made all the
difference in the world with the sense of feeling and the sense of smell. From the
one important direction of the house. That is how it could come about that Boaz
Negro could sit, waiting and listening to nothing, in the shop and remain ignorant
of disaster until the alarm had gone away and come back again, pounding, shout- 270
ing, clanging.

"Fire!" he heard them bawling in the street. "Fire! Fire!"
Only slowly did he understand that the fire was in his own house.

There is nothing stiller in the world than the skeleton of a house in the dawn after a fire. It is as if everything living, positive, violent, had been completely drained in the one flaming act of violence, leaving nothing but negation till the end of time. It is worse than a tomb. A monstrous stillness! Even the footfalls of the searchers cannot disturb it, for they are separate and superficial. In its presence they are almost frivolous.

Half an hour after dawn the searchers found the body, if what was left from that consuming ordeal might be called a body. The discovery came as a shock. It seemed incredible that the occupant of that house, no cripple or invalid, but an able man in the prime of youth, should not have awakened and made good his escape. It was the upper floor which had caught; the stairs had stood to the last. It was beyond calculation. Even if he had been asleep!

And he had not been asleep. This second and infinitely more appalling discovery began to be known. Slowly. By a hint, a breath of rumor here; there an allusion, half taken back. The man whose incinerated body still lay curled in its bed of cinders had been dressed at the moment of disaster; even to the watch, the cuff buttons, the studs, the very scarf pin. Fully clothed to the last detail, precisely as those who had dealings at the bank might have seen Campbell Wood any weekday morning for the past eight months. A man does not sleep with his clothes on. The skull of the man had been broken, as if with a blunt instrument of iron. On the charred lacework of the floor lay the leg of an old andiron with which Boaz Negro and his Angelina had set up housekeeping in that new house.

It needed only Mr. Asa Whitelaw, coming up the street from that gaping "Noah's Ark" at the bank, to round out the scandalous circle of circumstance.

"Where is Manuel?"

Boaz Negro still sat in his shop, impassive, monumental, his thick, hairy arms resting on the arms of his chair. The tools and materials of his work remained scattered about him, as his irresolute gathering of the night before had left them. Into his eyes no change could come. He had lost his house, the visible monument of all those years of "skinning his fingers." It would seem that he had lost his son. And he had lost something incalculably precious—that hitherto unquenchable exuberance of the man.

"Where is Manuel?"

When he spoke his voice was unaccented and stale, like the voice of a man already dead.

"Yes, where is Manuel?"

He had answered them with their own question.

"When did you last see him?"

Neither he nor they seemed to take note of that profound irony.

"At supper."

"Tell us, Boaz, you knew about this money?"

The cobbler nodded his head.

"And did Manuel?"

He might have taken sanctuary in a legal doubt. How did he know what Manuel knew? Precisely! As before, he nodded his head.

"After supper, Boaz, you were in the shop? But you heard something?"

"Yes." 320

He went on to tell them what he had heard, the footfalls, below and above, the extraordinary conversation which had broken for a moment the silence of the inner hall. The account was bare, the phrases monosyllabic. He reported only what had been registered on the sensitive tympanums of his ears, to the last whisper of footfalls stealing past the dark wall of the shop. Of all the formless tangle of thoughts, suspicions, interpretations and the special and personal knowledge given to the blind which moved in his brain, he said nothing.

He shut his lips there. He felt himself on the defensive. Just as he distrusted the higher ramifications of finance (his house had gone down uninsured), so before the rites and processes of that inscrutable creature, the law, he felt himself 330 menaced by the invisible and the unknown, helpless, oppressed; in an abject sense, skeptical.

"Keep clear of the law!" they had told him in his youth. The monster his imagination had summoned then still stood beside him in his age.

Having exhausted his monosyllabic and superficial evidence, they could move him no farther. He became deaf and dumb. He sat before them, an image cast in some immensely heavy stuff, inanimate. His lack of visible emotion impressed them. Remembering his exuberance, it was only the stranger to see him unmoving and unmoved. Only once did they catch sight of something beyond. As they were preparing to leave he opened his mouth. What he said was like a swan 340 song to the years of his exuberant happiness. Even now there was no color of expression in his words, which sounded mechanical.

"Now I have lost everything. My house. My last son. Even my honor. You would not think I would like to live. But I go to live. I go to work. That *cachorra*,[2] one day he shall come back again, in the dark night, to have a look. I shall go to show you all. That *cachorra!*"

(And from that time on, it was noted, he never referred to the fugitive by any other name than *cachorra,* which is a gender of dog. "That *cachorra!*" As if he had forfeited the relationship not only of the family, but of the very genus, the very race! "That *cachorra!*") 350

He pronounced this resolution without passion. When they assured him that the culprit would come back again indeed, much sooner than he expected, "with a rope around his neck," he shook his head slowly.

"No, you shall not catch that *cachorra* now. But one day . . ."

There was something about its very colorlessness which made it sound oracular. It was at least prophetic. They searched, laid their traps, proceeded with all their placards, descriptions, rewards, clues, trails. But on Manuel Negro they never laid their hands.

Months passed and became years. Boaz Negro did not rebuild his house. He might have done so, out of his earnings, for upon himself he spent scarcely any- 360 thing, reverting to his old habit of an almost miserly economy. Yet perhaps it

2. Bitch.

would have been harder after all. For his earning were less and less. In that town a cobbler who sits in an empty shop is apt to want for trade. Folk take their boots to mend where they take their bodies to rest and their minds to be edified.

No longer did the walls of Boaz's shop resound to the boastful recollections of young men. Boaz had changed. He had become not only different, but opposite. A metaphor will do best. The spirit of Boaz Negro had been a meadowed hillside giving upon the open sea, the sun, the warm, wild winds from beyond the blue horizon. And covered with flowers, always hungry and thirsty for the sun and the fabulous wind and bright showers of rain. It had become an entrenched camp, lying silent, sullen, verdureless, under a gray sky. He stood solitary against the world. His approaches were closed. He was blind, and he was also deaf and dumb.

Against that, what can young fellows do who wish for nothing but to rest themselves and talk about their friends and enemies? They had come and they had tried. They had raised their voices even higher than before. Their boasts had grown louder, more presumptuous, more preposterous, until, before the cold separation of that unmoving and as if contemptuous presence in the cobbler's chair, they burst of their own air, like toy balloons. And they went and left Boaz alone.

There was another thing which served, if not to keep them away, at least not to entice them back. That was the aspect of the place. It was not cheerful. It invited no one. In its way that fire-bitten ruin grew to be almost as great a scandal as the act itself had been. It was plainly an eyesore. A valuable property, on the town's main thoroughfare—and an eyesore! The neighboring owners protested.

Their protestations might as well have gone against a stone wall. That man was deaf and dumb. He had become, in a way, a kind of vegetable, for the quality of a vegetable is that, while it is endowed with life, it remains fixed in one spot. For years Boaz was scarcely seen to move out of that shop which was left him, a small, square, blistered promontory on the shores of ruin.

He must indeed have carried out some rudimentary sort of a domestic program under the debris at the rear (he certainly did not sleep or eat in the shop). One or two lower rooms were left fairly intact. The outward aspect of the place was formless; it grew to be no more than a mound in time; the charred timbers, one or two still standing, lean and naked against the sky, lost their blackness and faded to a silvery gray. It would have seemed strange, had they not grown accustomed to the thought, to imagine that blind man, like a mole, or some slow slug, turning himself mysteriously in the bowels of that gray mound—that time-silvered "eyesore."

When they saw him, however, he was in the shop. They opened the door to take in their work (when other cobblers turned them off), and they saw him seated in his chair in the half-darkness, his whole person, legs, torso, neck, head, as motionless as the vegetable of which we have spoken—only his hands and his bare arms endowed with visible life. The gloom had bleached the skin to the color of damp ivory, and against the background of his immobility they moved with a certain amazing monstrousness, interminably. No, they were never still. One wondered what they could be at. Surely he could not have had enough work now to keep those insatiable hands so monstrously in motion. Even far into the night. Tap-tap-tap! Blows continuous and powerful. On what? On nothing? On the bare iron last? And for what purpose? To what conceivable end?

Well, one could imagine those arms, growing paler, also growing thicker and
more formidable with that unceasing labor; the muscles feeding themselves om- 410
nivorously on their own waste, the cords toughening, the bone tissues revitalizing
themselves without end. One could imagine the whole aspiration of that mute and
motionless man pouring itself out into those pallid arms, and the arms taking it up
with a kind of blind greed. Storing it up. Against a day!

"That *cachorra!* One day . . ."

What were the thoughts of the man? What moved within that motionless
cranium covered with long hair? Who can say? Behind everything, of course,
stood that bitterness against the world—the blind world—blinder than he would
ever be. And against "that *cachorra.*" But this was no longer a thought; it was the
man.   420

Just as all muscular aspiration flowed into his arms, so all the energies of his
senses turned to his ears. The man had become, you might say, two arms and two
ears. Can you imagine a man listening, intently, through the waking hours of nine
years?

Listening to footfalls. Marking with a special emphasis of concentration the
beginning, rise, full passage, falling away, and dying of all the footfalls. By day, by
night, winter and summer and winter again. Unraveling the skein of footfalls passing up and down the street!

For three years he wondered when they would come. For the next three
years he wondered if they would ever come. It was during the last three that a 430
doubt began to trouble him. It gnawed at his huge moral strength. Like a hidden
seepage of water, it undermined (in anticipation) his terrible resolution. It was a
sign perhaps of age, a slipping away of the reckless infallibility of youth.

Supposing, after all, that his ears should fail him? Supposing they were capable of being tricked, without his being able to know it? Supposing that that *cachorra* should come and go, and he, Boaz, living in some vast delusion, some
unrealized distortion of memory, should let him pass unknown? Supposing precisely this thing had already happened!

Or the other way around. What if he should hear the footfalls coming, even
into the very shop itself? What if he should be as sure of them as of his own soul? 440
What, then, if he should strike? And what, then, if it were not that *cachorra* after
all? How many tens and hundreds of millions of people were there in the world?
Was it possible for them all to have footfalls distinct and different?

Then they would take him and hang him. And that *cachorra* might then
come and go at his own will, undisturbed.

As he sat there sometimes the sweat rolled down his nose, cold as rain.

Supposing!

Sometimes, quite suddenly, in broad day, in the blooming silence of the
night, he would start. Not outwardly. But beneath the pale integument of his skin
all his muscles tightened and his nerves sang. His breathing stopped. It seemed al- 450
most as if his heart stopped.

Was that it? Were those the feet, there, emerging faintly from the distance?
Yes, there was something about them. Yes! Memory was in travail. Yes, yes, yes!
No! How could he be sure? Ice ran down into his empty eyes. The footfalls were

already passing. They were gone, swallowed up already by time and space. Had that been that *cachorra?*

Nothing in his life had been so hard to meet as this insidious drain of distrust in his own powers; this sense of a traitor within the walls. His iron-gray hair had turned white. It was always this now, from the beginning of the day to the end of the night; how was he to know? How was he to be inevitably, unshakably sure?   460

Curiously, after all this purgatory of doubts, he did know them. For a moment at least, when he had heard them, he was unshakably sure.

It was on an evening of the winter holidays, the Portuguese festival of Menin' Jesus.[3] Christ was born again in a hundred mangers on a hundred tiny altars; there was cake and wine; songs went shouting by to the accompaniment of mandolins and tramping feet. The wind blew cold under a clear sky. In all the houses there were lights; even in Boaz Negro's shop a lamp was lit just now, for a man had been in for a pair of boots which Boaz had patched. The man had gone out again. Boaz was thinking of blowing out the light. It meant nothing to him.

He leaned forward, judging the position of the lamp chimney by the heat on   470 his face, and puffed out his cheeks to blow. Then his cheeks collapsed suddenly, and he sat back again.

It was not odd that he had failed to hear the footfalls until they were actually within the door. A crowd of merrymakers was passing just then; their songs and tramping almost shook the shop.

Boaz sat back. Beneath his passive exterior his nerves thrummed; his muscles had grown as hard as wood. Yes! Yes! But no! He had heard nothing; no more than a single step, a single foot pressure on the planks within the door. Dear God! He could not tell!

Going through the pain of an enormous effort, he opened his lips.   480
"What can I do for you?"

"Well, I—I don't know. To tell the truth—"

The voice was unfamiliar, but it might be assumed. Boaz held himself. His face remained blank, interrogating, slightly helpless.

"I am a little deaf," he said. "Come nearer."

The footfalls came halfway across the intervening floor, and there appeared to hesitate. The voice, too, had a note of uncertainty.

"I was just looking around. I have a pair of—well, you mend shoes?"

Boaz nodded his head. It was not in response to the words, for they meant nothing. What he had heard were the footfalls on the floor.   490

Now he was sure. As has been said, for a moment at least after he had heard them he was unshakably sure. The congestion of his muscles had passed. He was at peace.

The voice became audible once more. Before the massive preoccupation of the blind man it became still less certain of itself.

"Well, I haven't got the shoes with me. I was—just looking around."

It was amazing to Boaz, this miraculous sensation of peace.

"Wait!" Then, bending his head as if listening to the winter wind, "It's cold

3. Festival of the Infant Jesus.

tonight. You've left the door open. But wait!" Leaning down, his hand fell on a rope's end hanging by the chair. The gesture was one continuous, undeviating movement of the hand. No hesitation. No groping. How many hundreds, how many thousands of times had his hand schooled itself in that gesture!

A single strong pull. With a little bang the front door had swung to and latched itself. Not only the front door. The other door, leading to the rear, had closed too and latched itself with a little bang. And leaning forward from his chair, Boaz blew out the light.

There was not a sound in the shop. Outside, feet continued to go by, ringing on the frozen road; voices were lifted; the wind hustled about the corners of the wooden shell with a continuous, shrill note of whistling. All of this outside, as on another planet. Within the blackness of the shop the complete silence persisted.

Boaz listened. Sitting on the edge of his chair, half couching, his head, with its long, unkempt white hair, bent slightly to one side, he concentrated upon this chambered silence the full powers of his senses. He hardly breathed. The other person in that room could not be breathing at all, it seemed.

No, there was not a breath, not the stirring of a sole on wood, not the infinitesimal rustle of any fabric. It was as if in this utter stoppage of sound, even the blood had ceased to flow in the veins and arteries of that man, who was like a rat caught in a trap.

It was appalling even to Boaz; even to the cat. Listening became more than a labor. He began to have to fight against a growing impulse to shout out loud, to leap, sprawl forward without aim in that unstirred darkness—do something. Sweat rolled down from behind his ears, into his shirt collar. He gripped the chair arms. To keep quiet he sank his teeth into his lower lip. He would not! He would not!

And of a sudden he heard before him, in the center of the room, an outburst of breath, an outrush from lungs in the extremity of pain, thick, laborious, fearful. A coughing up of dammed air.

Pushing himself from the arms of the chair, Boaz leaped.

His fingers, passing swiftly through the air, closed on something. It was a sheaf of hair, bristly and thick. It was a man's beard.

On the road outside, up and down the street for a hundred yards, merry-making people turned to look at one another. With an abrupt cessation of laughter, of speech. Inquiringly. Even with an unconscious dilation of the pupils of their eyes.

"What was that?"

There had been a scream. There could be no doubt of that. A single, long-drawn note. Immensely high-pitched. Not as if it were human.

"God's sake! What was that? Where'd it come from?"

Those nearest said it came from the cobbler shop of Boaz Negro.

They went and tried the door. It was closed; even locked, as if for the night. There was no light behind the window shade. But Boaz would not have a light. They beat on the door. No answer.

But from where, then, had that prolonged, as if animal, note come?

They ran about, penetrating into the side lanes, interrogating, prying. Coming back at last, inevitably, to the neighborhood of Boaz Negro's shop.

The body lay on the floor at Boaz's feet, where it had tumbled down slowly after a moment from the spasmodic embrace of his arms; those ivory-colored arms which had beaten so long upon the bare iron surface of a last. Blows continuous and powerful! It seemed incredible. They were so weak now. They could not have lifted the hammer now.   550

But that beard! That bristly, thick, square beard of a stranger!

His hands remembered it. Standing with his shoulders fallen forward and his weak arms hanging down, Boaz began to shiver. The whole thing was incredible. What was on the floor there, upheld in the vast gulf of darkness, he could not see. Neither could he hear it; smell it. Nor (if he did not move his foot) could he feel it. What he did not hear, smell, or touch did not exist. It was not there. Incredible!

But that beard! All the accumulated doubtings of those years fell down upon him. After all, the thing he had been so fearful of in his weak imaginings had happened. He had killed a stranger. He, Boaz Negro, had murdered an innocent man!

And all on account of that beard. His deep panic made him lightheaded. He 560 began to confuse cause and effect. If it were not for that beard, it would have been that *cachorra.*

On this basis he began to reason with a crazy directness. And to act. He went and pried open the door into the entry. From a shelf he took down his razor. A big, heavy-heeled blade, made long ago for a beard which turned the jaw black again an hour after shaving. And the old, brown, polished strop. His hands began to hurry. And the mug, half full of soap. And water. It would have to be cold water. But after all, he thought (lightheadedly), at this time of night . . .

Outside, they were at the shop again. The crowd's habit is to forget a thing quickly, once it is out of sight and hearing. But there had been something about 570 that solitary cry which continued to bother them, even in memory. Where had it been? Where had it come from? And those who had stood nearest the cobbler shop were heard again. They were certain now, dead certain. They could swear!

In the end they broke down the door.

If Boaz heard them he gave no sign. An absorption as complete as it was monstrous wrapped him. Kneeling in the glare of the lantern they had brought, as impervious as his own shadow sprawling behind him, he continued to shave the dead man on the floor.

No one touched him. Their minds and imaginations were arrested by the gigantic proportions of the act. The unfathomable presumption of the act. As throw- 580 ing murder in their faces to the tune of a jig in a barbershop. It is a fact that none of them so much as thought of touching him. No less than all of them, together with all other men, shorn of their imaginations—that is to say, the expressionless and imperturbable creature of the Law—would be sufficient to touch that ghastly man.

On the other hand, they could not leave him alone. They could not go away. They watched. They saw the damp, lather-soaked beard of that victimized stranger falling away, stroke by stroke of the flashing, heavy razor. The dead denuded by the blind!

It was seen that Boaz was about to speak. It was something important he was 590 to utter; something, one would say, fatal. The words would not come all at once. They swelled his cheeks out. His razor was arrested. Lifting his face, he encircled the watchers with a gaze at once of imploration and of command. As if he could see them. As if he could read his answer in the expressions of their faces.

"Tell me one thing now. Is it that *cachorra?*"

For the first time those men in the room made sounds. They shuffled their feet. It was as if an uncontrollable impulse to ejaculation, laughter, derision, forbidden by the presence of death, had gone down into their boot soles.

"Manuel?" one of them said. "You mean *Manuel?*"

Boaz laid the razor down on the floor beside its work. He got up from his knees slowly, as if his joints hurt. He sat down in his chair, rested his hands on the arms, and once more encircled the company with his sightless gaze.

"Not Manuel. Manuel was a good boy. But tell me now, is it that *cachorra?*"

Here was something out of their calculations; something for them, mentally, to chew on. Mystification is a good thing sometimes. It gives the brain a fillip, stirs memory, put the gears of imagination in mesh. One man, an old, tobacco-chewing fellow, began to stare harder at the face on the floor. Something moved in his intellect.

"No, but look here now, by God—"

He had even stopped chewing. But he was forestalled by another.

"Say now, if it don't look like that fellow Wood, himself. The bank fellow— that was burned—remember? Himself."

"That *cachorra* was not burned. Not that Wood. You damned fool!"

Boaz spoke from his chair. They hardly knew his voice, emerging from its long silence; it was so didactic and arid.

"That *cachorra* was not burned. It was my boy that was burned. It was that *cachorra* called my boy upstairs. That *cachorra* killed my boy. That *cachorra* put his clothes on my boy, and he set my house on fire. I knew that all the time. Because when I heard those feet come out of my house and go away, I knew they were the feet of that *cachorra* from the bank. I did not know where he was going to. Something said to me, 'You better ask him where he is going to.' But then I said, 'You are foolish.' He had the money from the bank. I did not know. And then my house was on fire. No, it was not my boy that went away; it was that *cachorra* all the time. You damned fools! Did you think I was waiting for my own boy?

"Now I show you all," he said at the end. "And now I can get hanged."

No one ever touched Boaz Negro for that murder. For murder it was in the eye and letter of the Law. But the Law in a small town is sometimes a curious creature; it is sometimes blind only in one eye.

Their minds and imaginations in that town were arrested by the romantic proportions of the act. Simply, no one took it up. I believe the man, Wood, was understood to have died of heart failure.

When they asked Boaz why he had not told what he knew as to the identity of that fugitive in the night, he seemed to find it hard to say exactly. How could a man of no education define for them his own but half-defined misgivings about the Law, his sense of oppression, constraint, and awe, of being on the defensive, even, in an abject way, his skepticism? About his wanting, come what might, to "keep clear of the Law"?

He did say this, "You would have laughed at me."

And this, "If I told folks it was Wood went away, then I say he would not 640 dare come back again."

That was the last. Very shortly he began to refuse to talk about the thing at all. The act was completed. Like the creature of fable, it had consumed itself. Out of that old man's consciousness it had departed. Amazingly. Like a dream dreamed out.

Slowly at first, in a makeshift, piece-at-a-time, poor man's way, Boaz commenced to rebuild his house. That "eyesore" vanished.

And slowly at first, like the miracle of a green shoot pressing out from the dead earth, that priceless and unquenchable exuberance of the man was seen returning. Unquenchable, after all. [1920] 650

Questions for Discussion and Writing

1. Carefully analyze the plot of this story. Do its events, especially the ending, seem to you probable or improbable? Are the events connected by probability and logic, or are they contrived? Explain your reasons.
2. Analyze the author's style. Is it appropriately dramatic and intense, or is it overwrought and melodramatic? Why?
3. Why, in the context of 1920s Modernism, would this story seem out of date and old fashioned?

☞ HORACIO QUIROGA
(1878–1937)

The Wilderness

One of Horacio Quiroga's best collections of stories is *Stories of Love, Madness, and Death* (1917), a title that could well describe the author's turbulent and at times quixotic life. He is sometimes called the Poe of the Spanish American short story.

Quiroga was born in Salto, Uruguay, near the border with Argentina. When Horacio was only three months old, his father was killed in a hunting accident. His mother moved the family to Montevideo and married again, but eventually this man, despairing over the effects of a stroke, shot himself to death. At twenty-three, Quiroga killed a friend in a hand gun accident.

In 1901, Quiroga published his first volume of stories, *Coral Reefs*, strongly influenced by Edgar Allan Poe (1809–1849), and in 1904 *Another's Crime*, a more Modernist work. In 1903, he accompanied a fellow writer on an archeological expedition to the Misiones region of northern Argentina. The area deeply impressed Quiroga, and in 1904 he bought land with the idea of raising cotton. The venture failed, and from 1906 to 1911, he taught at a normal school in Buenos Aires. He married one of his pupils, but when they moved to his ranch, the harsh and lonely life, complicated by a tumultuous marriage, drove Ana Maria to suicide in 1915.

From 1917 on, Quiroga worked as a bureaucrat with the Uruguayan consulate in Buenos Aires, continuing to seek refuge in the Misiones district when the job and city life became too tedious. By the early 1930s, ill health was wearing him down. Shortly after being diagnosed with prostate cancer, he died of a self-inflicted dose of cyanide.

Quiroga's taut and economical writing influenced his successors to regard the short story as a serious art form. Landscape, especially the jungle and its creatures, figures prominently in his work, often suggesting the nature of everyday life or the condition of the world. As a pioneer of the short story Quiroga enjoys a secure position in the history of Latin American fiction.

THE CANOE GLIDED along the edge of the woods, or what might seem to be woods in all that darkness. More by instinct than from any clue, Subercasaux felt its nearness, for the gloom was a single impervious block, starting at the rower's hands and extending up to the zenith. The man knew his river well enough so as to not be unaware of where he was, but on such a night, and under threat of rain, landing his craft in the midst of piercing *tacuara* canes and patches of rotten reeds was very different from going ashore in his own little port. And Subercasaux was not alone in his canoe.

The atmosphere was sultry to the point of asphyxiation. In no direction his face might turn could he find a little air to breathe. And at that moment, clearly 10 and distinctly, some raindrops pattered in the canoe.

Subercasaux raised his eyes, looking vainly into the sky for a tremor of brightness or the fissure of a lightning bolt. All afternoon, and now as well, one could not hear a single thunderclap.

"Rain for the whole night," he thought. And turning to his companions, who kept silent at the stern:

"Put on your rain-capes," he said briefly. "And hold on tight."

In fact, the canoe was now bending branches as it moved along, and two or three times the portside oar had skidded on a submerged limb. But even at the price of breaking an oar, Subercasaux stayed in contact with the foliage, since if he 20 got five meters offshore he could go back and forth all night in front of his port, without managing to see it.

Skimming the water at the very edge of the woods, the rower advanced a while longer. The drops were falling more densely now, but also at greater intervals. They would cease abruptly, as if they had fallen from who-knows-where, and then begin again, large, warm, and separate, only to break off once more in the same darkness and the same atmospheric depression.

"Hold on tight," repeated Subercasaux to his two companions. "We've made it home."

For he had just caught a glimpse of the mouth of his port. With two vigor- 30 ous strokes of the oars he propelled the canoe onto the clay bank, and as he fastened the craft to its post his two silent companions jumped to the ground, which in spite of the darkness was easy to see, since it was covered with myriads of shiny little worms that made its surface undulate with their red and green fires.

As far as the top of the bluff—which the three travelers climbed in the rain, at last compact and uniform—the soaking clay shone phosphorescently. But then they were shut in again by the darkness, and in its midst had to search for the sulky[1] they'd left resting on its shafts.

The saying "You can't even see your hands in front of your eyes" is made to order. And on such nights the momentary flash of a match is of no use but to deepen the dizzying darkness right afterward, to the point of making you lose your balance.

They found the sulky, nevertheless, but not the horse. And leaving his two companions on guard next to one of the wheels—where they stood motionless under their drooping capes, noisily spattered by rain—Subercasaux went off among the painful thorns to the end of the trail, where he found his horse, tangled up in its reins, of course.

He hadn't taken more than twenty minutes to look for the animal and bring it in, but when he sought his bearings in the vicinity of the sulky—saying: "Are you there, kids?" and hearing: "Yes, daddy"—Subercasaux became fully aware, for the first time that night, that the two companions he had abandoned to the night and the rain were his two children, aged five and six, who didn't stand as high as the hub of the sulky wheel, and who were huddled together, dripping water from their rain-capes, and calmly waiting for their father to return.

Finally they were on their way home, chattering and happy. When moments of worry or danger had passed, Subercasaux's voice was very different from the one he used to speak to his youngsters when he had to address them as grown-ups. Now it had lowered by two tones, and no one there would have thought, upon hearing the tenderness of their voices, that the man then laughing with the children was none other than the one with the curt and harsh accent of a half an hour before. And now the real talkers were Subercasaux and his daughter, since the little boy—the baby of the family—had fallen asleep on his father's knees.

II

Subercasaux usually got up at daybreak; and though he did it noiselessly, he was well aware that in the next room his boy, as much of an early riser as he was, had been lying with his eyes open for quite a while, waiting to hear his father before he got out of bed. And then the unchanging ritual of morning greetings would begin, passing from one bedroom to the other:

"Good morning, daddy!"
"Good morning, my dear little boy!"
"Good morning, darling little daddy!"
"Good morning, spotless little lamb!"
"Good morning, little mouse with no tail!"
"My little raccoon!"
"Little daddy armadillo!"
"Little cat-face!"
"Little snake-tail!"

---

1. Light, two-wheeled carriage for one person.

And in this colorful style it would go on for a good while longer—till, once they were dressed, they would go have coffee under the palms, while the little lady kept on sleeping like a stone, till the sun in her face awakened her.

With his two young children—in their temper and training handiwork of his own—Subercasaux considered himself the happiest father on earth. But this he had achieved at the cost of greater grief than usually experienced by married men.

Abruptly, as things happen that are inconceivable for their appalling unfairness, Subercasaux had lost his wife. He was suddenly left alone, with two little children who hardly knew him, and in the same house, built by him and fixed up by her, where every nail and every brushmark on the wall was a sharp reminder of shared happiness.

The next day he found out, when he chanced to open the wardrobe, what it is to all of a sudden see your already buried wife's underthings; and on a hanger, the dress that she never had time to try out.

He went through the urgent and fateful need, if you want to go on living, to destroy every last trace of the past, when with his eyes set and dry he burned the letters he had written to his wife, and she had saved since their courtship with more devotion than her big-city clothes. And that same afternoon he found out, at last, what it's like to be finally worn out from sobbing, and hold back in your arms a young child who's struggling to get loose so he can go play with the cook's little boy.

Hard, that was terribly hard . . . But now he was laughing with his two kids, who along with him formed a single person, given the uncommon way in which Subercasaux brought up his children.

The youngsters, for example, had no fear of the dark, nor of being alone, nor of anything that contributes to the terror of babies raised at their mother's skirts. More than once night descended when Subercasaux still wasn't back from the river, and the children lit the wind-lantern to wait for him, unworrying. Or they would wake up alone in the middle of a furious storm that kept them blinded behind the windowpanes, only to go back to sleep again at once, secure and confident of their daddy's return.

They feared nothing, except what their father warned them they should fear; and at the top of the list, naturally, were snakes. Free as they were, exuding health and stopping to look at everything with eyes as big as those of happy puppies, they wouldn't have known what to do for a moment without their father's company. But if, when he left, he let them know he was going to be gone for such and such a time, the kids were content to stay and play together. Similarly, if on their long joint trips through the woods or on the river Subercasaux had to go off for some minutes or hours, they would quickly improvise a game, and wait for him unfailingly in the same place, in this way repaying, with blind and cheerful obedience, the confidence their father placed in them.

They went horseback-riding on their own, and this from the time the boy was four years old. Like all free creatures, they were perfectly aware of their limits, and never went beyond them. Sometimes, alone, they would get as far as the Yabebirí, to the pink sandstone cliff above the river.

"Make sure of the terrain and sit down afterward," their father had told them.

The cliff rises straight up to a height of twenty meters from deep and shaded waters which cool the crevices at its base. There on top, tiny as they were, Subercasaux's youngsters would approach the edge, testing the stones with their feet; and, once secure, sit down and let their sandals frolic over the abyss.

Naturally, Subercasaux had achieved all this in successive stages, each one of them charged with its own anxieties.

"Some day a kid'll get killed on me," he said to himself. "And for the rest of 130 my days I'll be asking myself if I was right to bring them up this way."

Yes, he was right. And among the few consolations of a father left alone with motherless children, the greatest is being able to raise them in accordance with a single course of conduct.

Subercasaux was therefore happy, and the children felt warmly bound to that big man who would play with them for hours on end, teach them to read on the floor with large heavy letters made of red lead, and sew up the rips in their pants with his huge toughened hands.

From sewing gunnysacks in the Chaco,[2] when he was a cotton planter there, Subercasaux had retained both the custom of sewing and his pleasure in it. He 140 sewed his own clothes, those of his children, the holsters for his revolver, and the sails of his canoe—all with cobbler's thread, and knotting every stitch. So it was that his shirts could tear at any point except where he had tied his waxen thread.

When it came to games, the children both recognized their father as a master, especially in his way of running on all fours—so outlandish that it made them shout with laughter right away.

Since in addition to his regular activities Subercasaux was a restless experimenter, whose interests took a new tack every three months, his children, constantly at his side, were acquainted with a lot of things not usually known to children of that age. They had seen—and sometimes helped in—the dissection of 150 animals, the making of creolina,[3] the extraction of latex from trees to seal their raincoats; they had seen their father's shirts dyed all sorts of colors, the construction of eight-ton outworks for the study of cements, the making of superphosphates, orange wine, yerba[4] dryers of the Mayfarth type, and the suspension of a car-cable from the woods to the bungalow, hung at ten meters above the ground, along which the youngsters would then go flying down to the house in little cable-cars.

Around that time Subercasaux had been attracted to a vein or deposit of white clay left exposed by the last great retreat of the Yabebirí. From the study of this clay he had gone on to the others of the region, which he fired in his pottery- 160 ovens—constructed, of course, by him. And if he had to get data on cooking, vitrification,[5] and the like, using specimens of no particular form, he preferred to experiment with pots, masks, and imaginary animals, in all of which his children helped him with great success.

At night, and on stormy afternoons when it was really dark, the factory moved into high gear. Subercasaux would light the oven early, and the experi-

2. A region of south central South America. It includes parts of Argentina, Paraguay, and Bolivia.
3. A preservative.
4. An herb.
5. Glassmaking.

menters, shrunk by the cold and rubbing their hands, would sit down in its warmth to model clay.

But the smaller of his ovens easily generated 1,000°C in two hours, and at this point, every time they opened the door to feed it, a veritable bolt of fire that burned their lashes came out of the white-glowing hearth. So the ceramics-makers would retreat to a far end of the workshop, till the icy wind that came whistling in between the shafts of *tacuara*[6] in the walls would drive them back, workbench and all, to get cooked with their backs to the oven.

Except for the youngsters' naked legs, which now took the blasts of heat, everything went along well. Subercasaux had a weakness for prehistoric pots; the little girl preferred to model fancy hats; and the boy, without fail, made snakes.

Sometimes, however, the monotonous snore of the oven didn't cheer them up enough, and then they turned to the gramophone, and the same old records in use since Subercasaux's marriage, which the kids had abused with all sorts of nee- dles, nails, thorns, and bits of *tacuara* that they themselves would sharpen. By turns, each of them would take charge of attending the machine, which amounted to automatically changing records without even lifting their eyes from the clay, and resuming their work right away. When all the records had been played, it was an- other's turn to repeat exactly the same operation. They didn't even listen to the music anymore, since they knew it perfectly by heart; but the noise entertained them.

At ten o'clock the ceramics-makers considered their task concluded, and rose to proceed for the first time to the critical inspection of their works of art, since till all of them had finished not the slightest commentary was allowed. And then it was quite a sight to see the jubilation over the ornamental fantasies of the little lady, and the enthusiasm aroused by the boy's relentless collection of snakes. After which Subercasaux would put out the fire in the oven, and all holding hands they would run through the icy night to their house.

III

Three days after the nocturnal canoe-trip we've told about, Subercasaux was left without a servant girl; and this incident, trifling and inconsequential anywhere else, altered the life of the three exiles in the extreme.

In the first moments of his bereavement Subercasaux had been able to count on the help of a fine woman to raise his children, the same cook who wept and found the house too lonely at the death of her mistress.

The next month she left, and Subercasaux went through all sorts of grief to replace her with three or four sullen girls pulled out of the back country, and who'd only stay a few days, because they found their boss's character too harsh.

Subercasaux, as a matter of fact, was partly guilty, and he admitted it. He spoke with the girls just barely enough to make himself understood, and what he said had an excessively masculine logic and precision. When they swept the din- ing room, for example, he cautioned them to also sweep around every leg of the table. And this, expressed so sparingly, exasperated and fatigued the girls.

6. A cane, similar to bamboo.

For the space of three months he couldn't even get a girl to wash the dishes for him. And in those three months Subercasaux learned a bit more than how to bathe his children. 210

He learned, not how to cook, because he already knew that, but how to scour pots and pans with the very sand of his patio, squatting in the icy wind, which made his hands turn blue. He learned to interrupt his work again and again to run and take the milk off the fire or open the smoking oven; and he also learned to bring in three buckets of water (not a one less) from the well at night, to wash his kitchenware.

This problem of the three inescapable buckets was the substance of one of his nightmares, and it took him a month to realize that he couldn't do without them. In the first days he had naturally put off cleaning pots and dishes, which he 220 piled up side by side on the floor, so as to wash them all at once. But after wasting a whole morning on his haunches scraping burned cooking vessels (they all got burned), he opted for cook-eat-and-scrub, a three-step process the delights of which aren't known to husbands either.

He really had no time left for anything, especially during the short days of winter. Subercasaux had entrusted the children with keeping the two bedrooms in order, a job they did passably well. But he himself didn't feel he had spirit enough to sweep the patio: a scientific, radial, circular, and exclusively feminine task, which—though he knew it was basic to well-being in huts in the wilderness— transcended his patience. 230

In that loose, undisturbed sand, turned into a plant-laboratory by the climate of alternating rains and burning sun, the sand-fleas spread so much that you could see them crawling over the shoeless feet of the children. Subercasaux, though he always wore *stormboots,* paid a heavy tribute to the fleas. Almost always lame, he would have to spend a whole hour after the midday meal with his boy's feet in his hands, blinded by sun in the patio or on the veranda and splattered by rain. When he finished with the youngster it was his own turn; and when he stood up at last, with bended back, the boy would call him again because three new fleas had bored deep into the skin of his feet.

Luckily, the girl seemed to be immune; there was no way her little toenails 240 could tempt the fleas, seven out of ten of which fell by right to the boy and only three to his father. But those three were too many for a man whose feet were the key to the rustic life he led.

Sand-fleas, in general, are more harmless than snakes, botflies, and even the little *barigüis.* They walk high on their legs across the skin, and all of a sudden pierce it swiftly, going down to the raw flesh, where they make a little pouch that they fill with eggs. Neither the extraction of the flea nor of its nest is usually troublesome, nor do its bites go bad more than might be expected. But for every hundred clean fleas there's one that carries an infection, and with that you have to be careful. 250

Subercasaux had such an infection in one of his toes—the insignificant little toe of his right foot—and couldn't manage to subdue it. From a little pink hole it had grown to a swollen and terribly painful split along the edge of his toenail. Iodine, bichloride, hydrogen peroxide, formaldehyde—there was nothing he had failed to try. He wore his shoes, however, but didn't leave the house; and his endless labors in the woods were now reduced, on rainy afternoons, to slow and silent walks around the patio, when as the sun went down the sky would clear, and the woods, outlined against the light like a shadow pantomime, would come nearer and nearer in the superbly pure air till it touched your very eyes.

Subercasaux realized that in other living conditions he could have con-   260 quered the infection, which only called for a little rest. The afflicted man slept badly, shaken by chills and sharp pains late at night. At daybreak he would finally fall into a very heavy sleep, and at that moment would have given anything to stay in bed till even as late as eight o'clock. But the little boy was as much of an early bird in winter as in summer, and Subercasaux would get up shaking with fever to light the Primus stove and prepare the coffee. Then there was the midday meal, and the scrubbing of pots. And for diversion, at noon, the endless saga of his youngster's fleas.

"Things can't go on this way," Subercasaux finally said to himself. "At all costs I have to get a maid."   270

But how? During his married years this terrible concern with servant girls had been one of his regular anxieties. The girls would come and go, as we've said, without saying why, and this when there was a lady of the house. Subercasaux would abandon all his tasks and stay on his horse for three days, galloping along the trails from Apariciocué to San Ignacio, after any useless girl who might want to wash the diapers. At last, some day at noon, he would emerge from the woods with a halo of horseflies around his head, and his horse's neck ragged and bloody—but triumphant. The girl would arrive the next day, astraddle behind her father, with a bundle; and exactly a month later would leave with the same bundle, on foot. And Subercasaux would again put aside his hoe or machete to go get   280 his horse, already waiting and sweating motionless in the sun.

Those were bad experiences, that had left him with a bitter taste, and now had to start up again. But which way would he go?

During his nights of sleeplessness Subercasaux had already heard the distant rumbling of the woods, battered by rain. Spring is usually dry in Misiones,[7] and winter very rainy. But when the pattern is reversed—something always to be expected of the climate in Misiones—the clouds disgorge a meter of rain in three months, of the meter and a half supposed to fall in all the year.

They were already almost hemmed in. The Horqueta, which cuts across the road to the shore of the Paraná, had no bridges at all at that time and was passable   290 only at the wagon ford, where the water fell in foamy rapids over round and shifting stones, trod by horses quaking with fear. And this under normal conditions; for when the stream had to take on the rain of a seven-day storm, the ford was submerged under two fathoms of racing water, strung out in deep bands which suddenly broke up and coiled into whirlpools. And the settlers from the Yabebirí, detained on their horses before the flooded grassland, watched dead deer go by, revolving as they floated on. It was like this for ten or fifteen days.

The Horqueta could still be crossed when Subercasaux decided to go out;

---

7. A province of northern Argentina, between Paraguay and Brazil.

but in his state he didn't dare cover such a distance on horseback. And after all, what was he likely to find in the direction of Cazador Creek?

Then he remembered a young fellow he'd employed at one time, bright and hard-working as few are, who had told him laughing—the very day he arrived, as he scrubbed a frying pan in the dirt—that he'd stay for a month, because his boss needed him, but not one day more, because that was no work for a man. The fellow lived at the mouth of the Yabebirí, across from Toro Island, and that meant a strenuous trip; for if the Yabebirí plays its game of dropping and rising up again, the eight-hour stretch of rowing will crush the fingers of anyone who's not already used to it.

Subercasaux made his decision, however. And despite the threatening weather went down to the river with his children, with the cheerful air of one who finally sees the open sky. The youngsters repeatedly kissed their father's hand, as they usually did when they were full of joy. Despite his feet and all the rest, Subercasaux kept up all his courage for his children—but for them it was something very different to take a hike with their daddy through the woods aswarm with surprises, and then run barefoot along the shore, over the warm and springy mud of the Yabebirí.

There what they expected awaited them: the canoe full of water, which had to be bailed out with the usual scoop and the gourds for keeping bugs that the children always slung over their shoulders when they went into the woods.

Subercasaux was so hopeful that he wasn't disturbed enough by the dubious look of the muddied waters—of a river where you can usually see the bottom as far as two meters down.

"The rains," he thought, "still aren't coming down hard with the southeaster . . . It'll be a day or two before it rises."

They kept on working. Standing in the water on both sides of the canoe, they bailed away as best they could. Subercasaux, at the start, hadn't dared to take off his boots, which kept sticking in the deep mud, so badly that it caused him great pains to pull out his foot. Finally he took them off, and with his feet free and sunk like wedges in the stinking mud, he finished bailing out the canoe, turned it over, and cleaned off the bottom, all in two hours of feverish activity.

Ready at last, they left. For an hour the canoe glided along more rapidly than the rower would have liked. He was rowing badly, braced by a single foot, his naked heel scarred by the edge of the supportbeam. And even so he was moving fast, because the Yabebirí was racing now. Finally, the sticks swollen with bubbles starting to fringe the backwaters, and the moustache of straw caught up against a big root, led Subercasaux to realize what was going to happen if he waited another second to veer the prow toward his port.

Servant girl, young man . . . a rest at last! . . . , and more hopes gone. So he rowed without losing a stroke. The four hours he spent, tortured by worry and fatigue, going back up a river he'd gone down in an hour, in air so rarefied that his lungs gasped in vain—only he could thoroughly appreciate. When he got to his port the warm and frothy water had already risen two meters above the beach. And down the channel came dead branches, half submerged, their tips bobbing up and sinking in the sway.

The travelers reached the bungalow when it was already close to dark, though barely four o'clock, and just as the sky, with a single flash from its zenith to the river, at last disgorged its huge supply of water. They had supper at once and went to bed exhausted, under the clamor on the metal roof, which was hammered all night by the deluge with unrelenting violence.

IV

At daybreak, a chill to the bone awoke the master of the house. Till then he 350 had slept like a block of lead. Contrary to what was usual since he'd had the infected toe, his foot hardly hurt at all, despite the exertions of the day before. He took the raincoat tossed on the bedstead and pulled it on top of him, and tried to go back to sleep.

Impossible. The cold went straight through him. The frost inside spread outward to all his pores, now turned into needles of bristling ice, a sensation he got from the slightest rub against his clothes. Curled up in a ball, assailed all up and down his spinal cord by intense and rhythmic waves of cold, the ailing man watched the hours go by with no success at getting warm. Luckily, the children were still asleep.   360

"In the state I'm in you don't do dumb things like yesterday's," he kept telling himself. "These are the consequences . . ."

As a distant dream, a pricelessly rare bliss he once possessed, he fancied he could spend all day in bed, warm and rested at last, while at the table he heard the noise of the cups of *café con leche* that the servant—that first great servant woman—was setting before the children . . .

Stay in bed till ten, at least! . . . In four hours the fever would pass, and even his lower back wouldn't hurt so much . . . What did he need, after all, to get well? A little rest, nothing more. He'd said that himself ten times . . .

The day was moving on, and the sick man thought he heard the happy noise 370 of the cups, amid the heavy throbbing of his leaden temples. What a delight to hear that noise! . . . He would rest a little, finally . . .

"Daddy!"

"My dear boy . . ."

"Good morning, sweet little daddy! You're not up yet? It's late, daddy,"

"Yes, my love, I was just getting up . . ."

And Subercasaux got dressed in a hurry, reproaching himself for his laziness, which had made him forget his children's coffee.

The rain had finally stopped, but without the slightest breath of wind being left to sweep away the prevailing humidity. And at noon it started again—a warm, 380 tranquil, monotonous rain, which dissolved the valley of the Horqueta, the sown fields and the grasslands, in a misty and extremely dreary film of water.

After lunch the kids entertained themselves by renewing their stock of paper boats, which they had used up the afternoon before. They made hundreds of them, fitting them inside each other like ice-cream cones, ready to be tossed into the wake of the canoe, when they went out on the river again. Subercasaux took advantage of the chance to go to bed for a while, where he at once resumed his curled-up posture, lying motionless with his knees against his chest.

Again, on his temple, he could feel the enormous weight that held it to the pillow, so firmly that the pillow seemed to form an integral part of his head. How good he felt that way! Oh, to stay one, ten, a hundred days without moving! The monotonous drumming of the water on the metal roof lulled him toward sleep, and in its murmur he could hear distinctly, so well as to extract a smile, the tinkling of the cutlery being handled swiftly by the servant in the kitchen. What a servant he had! . . . And he heard the noise of the dishes, dozens of plates, cups, and pots that the servants—there were ten of them now!—scraped and scrubbed with dizzying speed. What a joy to be nice and warm at last, in bed, without a single, not a single worry! . . . When, at what previous time had he dreamed of being sick, with an awful problem? . . . How foolish he'd been! . . . And how nice it is like this, listening to the noise of hundreds of spotless cups . . .

"Daddy!"
"Darling girl . . ."
"I'm getting hungry, daddy!"
"Yes, sweetheart, right away . . ."
And the sick man went out in the rain to fix coffee for his children.

Without being quite sure what he had done that afternoon, Subercasaux watched the night come on with intense delight. He did remember that the delivery-boy hadn't brought milk that afternoon, and that he'd looked at his wound a long while, without noting anything special about it.

He fell into bed without even undressing, and in no time the fever laid him low again. The boy that hadn't come with the milk . . . Crazy! . . . Now he was fine, perfectly fine, resting.

With only a few days more of rest, even a few hours more, he'd get well. Right! Right! . . . There's justice in spite of everything . . . And also a little compensation . . . for someone who'd loved his children as he had . . . But he'd get up healthy. A man can get sick sometimes . . . and need to rest a little. And what a rest he was having now, to the lull of the rain on the metal roof! . . . But hadn't a month gone by already? . . . He ought to get up.

The sick man opened his eyes. He saw nothing but darkness, pierced by flashing specks that shrank and expanded by turns, approaching his eyes moving swiftly to and fro.

"I must have a very high fever," said the sick man to himself.

And he lit the wind-lantern on the night-table. The humid wick sputtered on for some time while Subercasaux kept his eyes on the roof. From far away, very far away, came the memory of a night like this when he was very, very sick . . . How silly can you get? . . . He was healthy, because when a man who's only tired is lucky enough to hear from his bed the furious clinking of the kitchen service, it's because the mother is watching over her children . . .

He woke up again. From the corner of his eye he saw the lighted lantern, and after a hard effort to focus his attention, recovered his self-awareness.

In his right arm, from his elbow to the tips of his fingers, he now felt intense pain. He tried to bring up his arm but couldn't do it. He pushed away the raincoat, and saw his livid hand, traced in streaks of violet; frozen, dead. Without closing his eyes, he thought awhile about what that meant, along with his chills and having rubbed the open vessels of his wound against the foul mud of the Yabebirí, and then he came to the clear, absolute and conclusive understanding that his whole being was dying too, that he was passing into death.

A great silence fell within him, as if the rain, the noise, and the very rhythm of things had abruptly fallen back toward the infinite. And as though he were already detached from himself, he saw far off in a landscape a bungalow totally cut 440 off from all human aid, where two small children, with no milk and all alone, were left abandoned by God and men, in a most iniquitous and dreadful state of helplessness.

His little children . . .

With a supreme effort he sought to wrest himself out of that torment which made him grapple, hour after hour and day after day, with the fate of his beloved children. In vain he would think: Life has higher forces that escape us . . . God provides . . .

"But they won't have anything to eat!" his heart would cry out tumultuously. And he would be dead, lying right where he was and witnessing that unprece- 450 dented horror . . .

But, in spite of the livid daylight reflected from the wall, darkness began to engulf him again, with its dizzying white dots, which receded and came back again to pulsate in his very eyes . . . Yes! Of course! He'd had a dream! It shouldn't be allowed to dream such things . . . Now he was going to get up, rested.

"Daddy! . . . Daddy . . . My dear little daddy! . . ."

"My son . . ."

"Aren't you going to get up today, daddy? It's very late. We're really hungry, daddy!"

"My little boy . . . I'm not going to get up just yet . . . You kids get up and 460 eat some crackers . . . There's still two left in the can . . . And come back afterward."

"Can we come in now, daddy?"

"No sweetheart . . . Later I'll make the coffee . . . I'll be calling you."

He still got to hear the laughing and chatter of his children as they got up, and then a *crescendo* reverberation, a dizzy jingling that radiated from the core of his brain and went on to throb in rhythmic waves against his dreadfully aching skull. And that was all he heard.

He opened his eyes again, and as he did so felt his head falling toward the left, so freely that it surprised him. He no longer felt any reverberation at all. Only 470 a growing but painless trouble with judging the distance of objects . . . And his mouth held wide-open to breathe.

"Kids . . . Come here right away . . ."

In no time the children appeared at the half-opened door, but viewing the lighted lantern and their father's countenance, came forward silently with their eyes opened wide.

The ailing man was still brave enough to smile, and as he made that awful face the children opened their eyes still wider.

"Kids," said Subercasaux when he had them at his side. "Pay attention,

sweethearts, because you're big now and can understand everything . . . I'm going   480
to die, kids . . . But don't be distressed . . . Soon you'll be grown-ups, and you'll be
good and honest . . . And then you'll remember your daddy . . . Be sure you understand, my dear children . . . In a while I'll die, and you won't have a father anymore . . . You'll be alone in the house . . . But don't be alarmed or afraid . . . And
now good-bye, my children . . . You're going to give me a kiss now . . . One kiss
each . . . But quickly, kids . . . A kiss . . . for your daddy . . ."

   The children left without touching the half-opened door, and went to linger
in their room, looking out on the drizzle in the patio. They didn't stir from there.
The girl alone, glimpsing the import of what had just come to pass, would pout   490
from time to time with her arm at her face, while the boy distractedly scratched
the window frame, uncomprehending.
   Neither one nor the other dared to make any noise.
   But at the same time there wasn't the slightest noise from the next room,
where for three hours their father, with his shoes and clothes on under his raincoat, had been lying dead in the light of the lantern.   [1923]

Questions for Discussion and Writing
1. Who or what is Subercasaux's antagonist?
2. What skills does Subercasaux possess? Why are these not sufficient to enable
   him to survive?
3. As the story moves to its inevitable conclusion, how does Quiroga maintain
   suspense?
4. Does this story depict man as pathetic or heroic? Cite specifics to support
   your answer.
5. Compare this story to Crane's "The Open Boat." Which is more effective?
   Why?

❧ AGATHA CHRISTIE
(1891–1976)

The Case of the Perfect Maid

Agatha Christie may well be the most popular writer ever. Her publishers say
that over two billion of her books have been sold worldwide, and there is no
reason to doubt the claim.

   She was born Agatha Miller in Torquay, a seaside resort in southern England.
Her father, a wealthy American, never sent her to school, but at an early age she
taught herself to read. Given free rein of her father's library, she read whatever
captured her interest and let her imagination run free. As a young woman, she
went to Paris to study music but abandoned it because she was too shy to perform in public.

   In 1914, she married Archibald Christie. While he fought in World War I,
she worked in a hospital pharmacy, learning a great deal about poisons and

drugs. Encouraged by her sister to write, she created a prissy Belgian detective named Hercule Poirot in *The Mysterious Affair at Styles,* published in 1920.

Before she retired in 1973, Christie published sixty-six novels and dozens of short stories. Her play, *The Mousetrap* (1952), has been running continuously in London for over forty years. Miss Marple, the heroine of "The Case of the Perfect Maid," seems an unlikely detective until she employs her sharp powers of observation, keen mind, and absolute skepticism about people to the solution of a puzzle. She solves many cases by comparing people in the case to those she has known in her village and by paying close attention to gossip that the police, of course, consider trivial.

Christie's virtues as a writer are those of many popular novelists. She writes in a clear and plain style, using little description and abundant dialogue. Her characters are not deep but are sketched with enough detail to stimulate the reader's imagination. Her plots are masterpieces of the "classic" or "well made" detective genre. Her novels and stories continue to be read all over the world, and many have been turned into films or television series.

"OH, IF YOU PLEASE, Madam, could I speak to you a moment?"

It might be thought that this request was in the nature of an absurdity, since Edna, Miss Marple's little maid, was actually speaking to her mistress at the moment.

Recognizing the idiom, however, Miss Marple said promptly, "Certainly, Edna, come in and shut the door. What is it?"

Obediently shutting the door, Edna advanced into the room, pleated the corner of her apron between her fingers, and swallowed once or twice.

"Yes, Edna?" said Miss Marple encouragingly.

"Oh, please, Ma'am, It's my cousin, Gladdie."   10

"Dear me," said Miss Marple, her mind leaping into the worst—and, alas, the most usual conclusion. "Not—not in trouble?"

Edna hastened to reassure her. "Oh, no, ma'am, nothing of that kind. Gladdie's not that kind of girl. It's just that she's upset. You see, she's lost her place."

"Dear me, I am sorry to hear that. She was at Old Hall, wasn't she, with the Miss—Misses—Skinner?"

"Yes, ma'am, that's right, ma'am. And Gladdie's very upset about it—very upset indeed."

"Gladys has changed places rather often before, though, hasn't she?"   20

"Oh, yes, ma'am. She always one for a change. Gladdie is. She never seems to get really settled, if you know what I mean. But she's always been the one to give the notice, you see!"

"And this time it's the other way round?" asked Miss Marple dryly.

"Yes, ma'am, and it's upset Gladdie something awful."

Miss Marple looked slightly surprised. Her recollection of Gladys, who had occasionally come to drink tea in the kitchen on her "days out," was a stout, giggling girl of unshakably equable temperament.

Edna went on. "You see, ma'am, it's the way it happened—the way Miss Skinner looked."

"How," inquired Miss Marple patiently, "did Miss Skinner look?"

This time Edna got well away with her news bulletin.

"Oh, ma'am, it was ever such a shock to Gladdie. You see, one of Miss Emily's brooches was missing, and such a hue and cry for it as never was, and of course nobody likes a thing like that to happen; it's upsetting, ma'am, if you know what I mean. And Gladdie's helped search everywhere, and there was Miss Lavinia saying she was going to the police about it, and then it turned up again, pushed right to the back of a drawer in the dressing-table, and very thankful Gladdie was.

"And the very next day as ever was a plate got broken, and Miss Lavinia she bounced out right away and told Gladdie to take a month's notice. And what Gladdie feels is it couldn't have been the plate and that Miss Lavinia was just making an excuse of that, and that it must be because of the brooch and they think as she took it and put it back when the police was mentioned, and Gladdie wouldn't do such a thing, not never she wouldn't, and what she feels is as it will get round and tell against her and it's a very serious thing for a girl, as you know, ma'am."

Miss Marple nodded. Though having no particular liking for the bouncing, self-opinioned Gladys, she was quite sure of the girl's intrinsic honesty and could well imagine that the affair must have upset her.

Edna said wistfully, "I suppose, ma'am, there isn't anything you could do about it? Gladdie's in ever such a taking."

"Tell her not to be silly," said Miss Marple crisply. "If she didn't take the brooch—which I'm sure she didn't—then she has no cause to be upset."

"It'll get about," said Edna dismally.

Miss Marple said, "I—er—am going up that way this afternoon. I'll have a word with the Misses Skinner." "Oh, thank you, madam," said Edna.

Old Hall was a big Victorian house surrounded by woods and park land. Since it had been proved unlettable and unsalable as it was, an enterprising speculator had divided it into four flats with a central hot water system, and the use of "the grounds" to be held in common by the tenants. The experiment had been satisfactory. A rich and eccentric old lady and her maid occupied one flat. The old lady had a passion for birds and entertained a feathered gathering to meals every day. A retired Indian judge and his wife rented a second. A very young couple, recently married, occupied the third, and the fourth had been taken only two months ago by two maiden ladies of the name of Skinner. The four sets of tenants were only on the most distant terms with each other, since none of them had anything in common. The landlord had been heard to say that this was an excellent thing. What he dreaded were friendships followed by estrangements and subsequent complaints to him.

Miss Marple was acquainted with all the tenants, though she knew none of them well. The elder Miss Skinner, Miss Lavinia, was what might be termed the working member of the firm. Miss Emily, the younger, spent most of her time in bed suffering from various complaints which, in the opinion of St. Mary Mead, were largely imaginary. Only Miss Lavinia believed devoutly in her sister's martyr-dom and patience under affliction, and willingly ran errands and trotted up and down to the village for things that "my sister had suddenly fancied."

It was the view of St. Mary Mead that if Miss Emily suffered half as much as she said she did, she would have sent for Doctor Haydock long ago. But Miss Emily, when this was hinted to her, shut her eyes in a superior way and murmured that her case was not a simple one—the best specialists in London had been baf- 80
fled by it—and that a wonderful new man had put her on a most revolutionary course of treatment and that she really hoped her health would improve under it. No humdrum G.P. could possibly understand her case.

"And it's my opinion," said the outspoken Miss Hartnell, "that she's very wise not to send for him. Dear Doctor Haydock, in that breezy manner of his, would tell her that there was nothing the matter with her and to get up and not make a fuss! Do her a lot of good!"

Failing such arbitrary treatment, however, Miss Emily continued to lie on sofas, to surround herself with strange little pill boxes, and to reject nearly every-thing that had been cooked for her and ask for something else—usually some- 90
thing difficult and inconvenient to get.

The door was opened to Miss Marple by "Gladdie," looking more depressed than Miss Marple had ever thought possible. In the sitting-room (a quarter of the late drawing-room, which had been partitioned into a dining-room, drawing-room, bathroom, and housemaid's cupboard), Miss Lavinia rose to greet Miss Marple.

Lavinia Skinner was a tall, gaunt, bony female of fifty. She had a gruff voice and an abrupt manner.

"Nice to see you," she said. "Emily's lying down—feeling low today, poor 100
dear. Hope she'll see you, it would cheer her up, but there are times when she doesn't feel up to seeing anybody. Poor dear, she's wonderfully patient."

Miss Marple responded politely. Servants were the main topic of conversa-tion in St. Mary Mead, so it was not difficult to lead the conversation in that direc-tion. Miss Marple said she had heard that that nice girl, Gladys Holmes, was leaving.

Miss Lavinia nodded. "Wednesday week. Broke things, you know. Can't have that."

Miss Marple sighed and said we all had to put up with things nowadays. It was so difficult to get girls to come to the country. Did Miss Skinner really think it 110
was wise to part with Gladys?

"Know it's difficult to get servants," admitted Miss Lavinia. "The Devereuxs haven't got anybody—but then, I don't wonder—always quarreling, jazz on all night—meals any time—that girl knows nothing of housekeeping, I pity her hus-band! Then the Larkins have just lost their maid. Of course, what with the judge's Indian temper and his wanting chota hazri,[1] as he calls it, at six in the morning and Mrs. Larkin always fussing, I don't wonder at that, either. Mrs. Carmichael's

---

1. Early, light breakfast.

Janet is a fixture, of course—though in my opinion she's the most disagreeable woman, and absolutely bullies the old lady."

"Then don't you think you might reconsider your decision about Gladys? She really is a nice girl. I know all her family; very honest and superior."

Miss Lavinia shook her head.

"I've got my reasons," she said importantly.

Miss Marple murmured, "You missed a brooch, I understand—"

"Now, who has been talking? I suppose the girl has. Quite frankly, I'm almost certain she took it. And then got frightened and put it back—but, of course, one can't say anything unless one is sure." She changed the subject. "Do come and see Miss Emily, Miss Marple. I'm sure it would do her good."

Miss Marple followed meekly to where Miss Lavinia knocked on a door, was bidden enter, and ushered her guest into the best room in the flat, most of the light of which was excluded by half-drawn blinds. Miss Emily was lying in bed, apparently enjoying the half-gloom and her own indefinite sufferings.

The dim light showed her to be a thin, indecisive-looking creature, with a good deal of grayish-yellow hair untidily wound around her head and erupting into curls, the whole thing looking like a bird's nest of which no self-respecting bird could be proud. There was a smell in the room of Eau de Cologne, stale biscuits, and camphor.

With half-closed eyes and in a thin, weak voice, Emily Skinner explained that this was "one of her bad days."

"The worst of ill health is," said Miss Emily in a melancholy tone, "that one knows what a burden one is to everyone around one.

"Lavinia is very good to me. Lavvie dear, I do so hate giving trouble but if my hot-water bottle could only be filled in the way I like it—too full it weighs on me so—on the other hand, if it is not sufficiently filled, it gets cold immediately!"

"I'm sorry, dear. Give it to me. I will empty a little out."

"Perhaps, if you're doing that, it might be refilled. There are no rusks in the house, I suppose—no, no, it doesn't matter. I can do without. Some weak tea and a slice of lemon—no lemons? No, really, I couldn't drink tea without lemon. I think the milk was slightly turned this morning. It has put me right against milk in my tea. It doesn't matter. I can do without my tea. Only I do feel so weak. Oysters, they say, are nourishing. I wonder if I could fancy a few? No, no, too much bother to get hold of them so late in the day. I can fast until tomorrow."

Lavinia left the room murmuring something incoherent about bicycling down to the village.

Miss Emily smiled feebly at her guest and remarked that she did hate giving anyone any trouble.

Miss Marple told Edna that evening that she was afraid her embassy had met with no success.

She was rather troubled to find that rumors as to Gladys's dishonesty were already going around the village.

In the post office, Miss Wetherby tackled her, "My dear Jane, they gave her a written reference saying she was willing and sober and respectable, but saying nothing about honesty. That seems to me most significant! I hear there was some trouble about a brooch. I think there must be something in it, you know, because one doesn't let a servant go nowadays unless it's something rather grave. They'll find it most difficult to get anyone else. Girls simply will not go to Old Hall. They're nervous coming home on their days out. You'll see, the Skinners won't find anyone else, and then, perhaps that dreadful hypochondriac sister will have to get up and do something!"

Great was the chagrin of the village when it was made known that the Misses 170 Skinner had engaged, from an agency, a new maid who, by all accounts, was a perfect paragon.

"A three years' reference recommending her most warmly, she prefers the country, and actually asks less wages than Gladys. I really feel we have been most fortunate."

"Well, really," said Miss Marple, to whom these details were imparted by Miss Lavinia in the fishmonger's shop. "It does seem too good to be true."

It then became the opinion of St. Mary Mead that the paragon would cry off at the last minute and fail to arrive.

None of these prognostications came true, however, and the village was able 180 to observe the domestic treasure, by name, Mary Higgins, driving through the village in Reed's taxi to Old Hall. It had to be admitted that her appearance was good. A most respectable-looking woman, very neatly dressed.

When Miss Marple next visited Old Hall, on the occasion of recruiting stall-holders for the vicarage fete, Mary Higgins opened the door. She was certainly a most superior-looking maid, at a guess forty years of age, with neat black hair, rosy cheeks, a plump figure discreetly arrayed in black with a white apron and cap—"quite the good, old-fashioned type of servant," as Miss Marple explained afterward, and with the proper, inaudible, respectful voice, so different from the loud but adenoidal accents of Gladys.   190

Miss Lavinia was looking far less harassed than usual and, although she regretted that she could not take a stall owing to her preoccupation with her sister, she nevertheless tendered a handsome monetary contribution, and promised to produce a consignment of penwipers and babies' socks.

Miss Marple commented on her air of well-being.

"I really feel I owe a great deal to Mary. I am so thankful I had the resolution to get rid of that other girl. Mary is really invaluable. Cooks nicely and waits beautifully and keeps our little flat scrupulously clean—mattresses turned over every day. And she is really wonderful with Emily!"

Miss Marple hastily inquired after Emily.   200

"Oh, poor dear, she has been very much under the weather lately. She can't help it, of course, but it really makes things a little difficult sometimes. Wanting certain things cooked and then, when they come, saying she can't eat now—and then wanting them again half an hour later and everything spoiled and having to be done again. It makes, of course, a lot of work—but fortunately Mary does not seem to mind at all. She's used to waiting on invalids, she says, and understands them. It is such a comfort."

"Dear me," said Miss Marple. "You are fortunate."

"Yes, indeed. I really feel Mary has been sent to us as an answer to prayer."

"She sounds to me," said Miss Marple, "almost too good to be true. I 210 should—well, I should be a little careful if I were you."

Lavinia Skinner failed to perceive the point of this remark. She said, "Oh! I assure you I do all I can to make her comfortable. I don't know what I should do if she left."

"I don't expect she'll leave until she's ready to leave," said Miss Marple and stared very hard at her hostess.

Miss Lavinia said, "If one has no domestic worries, it takes such a load off one's mind, doesn't it? How is your little Edna shaping?"

"She's doing quite nicely. Not much ahead, of course. Not like your Mary. Still I do know all about Edna because she's a village girl." 220

As she went out into the hall she heard the invalid's voice fretfully raised. "This compress has been allowed to get quite dry—Doctor Allerton particularly said moisture continually renewed. There, there, leave it. I want a cup of tea and a boiled egg—boiled only three minutes and a half, remember, and send Miss Lavinia to me."

The efficient Mary emerged from the bedroom and, saying to Lavinia, "Miss Emily is asking for you, madam," proceeded to open the door for Miss Marple, helping her into her coat and handing her her umbrella in the most irreproachable fashion.

Miss Marple took the umbrella, dropped it, tried to pick it up, and dropped 230 her bag, which flew open. Mary politely retrieved various odds and ends—a handkerchief, an engagement book, an old-fashioned leather purse, two shillings, three pennies, and a striped piece of peppermint rock.

Miss Marple received the last with some signs of confusion.

"Oh, dear, that must have been Mrs. Clement's little boy. He was sucking it, I remember, and he took my bag to play with. He must have put it inside. It's terribly sticky, isn't it?"

"Shall I take it, madam?"

"Oh, would you? Thank you so much."

Mary stooped to retrieve the last item, a small mirror upon recovering which 240 Miss Marple exclaimed fervently, "How lucky, now, that that isn't broken."

She thereupon departed, Mary standing politely by the door holding a piece of striped rock with a completely expressionless face.

For ten days longer St. Mary Mead had to endure hearing of the excellencies of Miss Lavinia's and Miss Emily's treasure.

On the eleventh day, the village awoke to its big thrill.

Mary, the paragon, was missing! Her bed had not been slept in, and the front door was found ajar. She had slipped out quietly during the night.

And not Mary alone was missing! Two brooches and five rings of Miss 250 Lavinia's; three rings, a pendant, a bracelet and four brooches of Miss Emily's were missing, also!

It was the beginning of a chapter of catastrophe.

Young Mrs. Devereux had lost her diamonds which she kept in an unlocked drawer and also some valuable furs given to her as a wedding present. The judge and his wife also had had jewelry taken and a certain amount of money. Mrs. Carmichael was the greatest sufferer. Not only had she some very valuable jewels but she also kept in the flat a large sum of money which had gone. It had been

Janet's evening out, and her mistress was in the habit of walking round the gardens at dusk calling to the birds and scattering crumbs. It seemed clear that Mary, the 260 perfect maid, had had keys to fit all the flats!

There was, it must be confessed, a certain amount of ill-natured pleasure in St. Mary Mead. Miss Lavinia had boasted so much of her marvelous Mary.

"And all the time, my dear, just a common thief!"

Interesting revelation followed. Not only had Mary disappeared into the blue, but the agency who had provided her and vouched for her credentials was alarmed to find that the Mary Higgins who had applied to them and whose references they had taken up had, to all intents and purposes, never existed. It was the name of a bona fide servant who had lived with the bona fide sister of a dean, but the real Mary Higgins was existing peacefully in a place in Cornwall.   270

"Damned clever, the whole thing," Inspector Slack was forced to admit. "And, if you ask me, that woman works in with a gang. There was a case of much the same kind in Northumberland a year ago. Stuff was never traced, and they never caught her. However, we'll do better than that in Much Benham!"

Inspector Slack was always a confident man.

Nevertheless, weeks passed, and Mary Higgins remained triumphantly at large. In vain Inspector Slack redoubled that energy that so belied his name.

Miss Lavinia remained tearful. Miss Emily was so upset, and felt so alarmed by her condition that she actually sent for Doctor Haydock.

The whole of the village was terribly anxious to know what he thought of 280 Miss Emily's claims to ill health, but naturally could not ask him. Satisfactory data came to hand on the subject, however, through Mr. Meek, the chemist's assistant, who was walking out with Clara, Mrs. Price-Ridley's maid. It was then known that Doctor Haydock had prescribed a mixture of asafetida and valerian[2] which, according to Mr. Meek, was the stock remedy for malingerers in the army!

Soon afterward it was learned that Miss Emily, not relishing the medical attention she had had, was declaring that in the state of her health she felt it her duty to be near the specialist in London who understood her case. It was, she said, only fair to Lavinia.

The flat was put up for subletting.   290

It was a few days after that that Miss Marple, rather pink and flustered, called at the police station in Much Benham and asked for Inspector Slack.

Inspector Slack did not like Miss Marple. But he was aware that the chief constable, Colonel Melchett, did not share that opinion. Rather grudgingly, therefore, he received her.

"Good afternoon, Miss Marple, what can I do for you?"

"Oh, dear," said Miss Marple, "I'm afraid you're in a hurry."

"Lots of work on," said Inspector Slack, "but I can spare a few moments."

"Oh, dear," said Miss Marple. "I hope I shall be able to put what I say properly. So difficult, you know, to explain oneself, don't you think? No, perhaps you 300 don't. But you see, not having been educated in the modern style—just a governess, you know, who taught one the dates of the kings of England and general

2. Both are antispasmodics, though valerian is also a stimulant.

knowledge—Doctor Brewer—three kinds of diseases of wheat—blight, mildew—
now what was the third—was it smut?"

"Do you want to talk about smut?" asked Inspector Slack and then blushed.

"Oh, no, no." Miss Marple hastily disclaimed any wish to talk about smut.
"Just an illustration, you know. And how needles are made, and all that.
Discursive, you know, but not teaching one to keep to the point. Which is what I
want to do. It's about Miss Skinner's maid, Gladys, you know."

"Mary Higgins," said Inspector Slack.   310

"Oh, yes, the second maid. But it's Gladys Holmes I mean—rather an impertinent girl and far too pleased with herself but really strictly honest, and it's so important that that should be recognized."

"No charge against her so far as I know," said the Inspector.

"No, I know there isn't a charge—but that makes it worse. Because, you see,
people go on thinking things. Oh, dear—I knew I should explain badly. What I really mean is that the important thing is to find Mary Higgins."

"Certainly," said Inspector Slack. "Have you any ideas on the subject?"

"Well, as a matter of fact, I have," said Miss Marple. "May I ask you a question? Are fingerprints of no use to you?"   320

"Ah," said Inspector Slack, "that's where she was a bit too artful for us. Did
most of her work in rubber gloves or housemaid's gloves, it seems. And she'd been
careful—wiped off everything in her bedroom and on the sink. Couldn't find a
single fingerprint in the place!"

"If you did have her fingerprints, would it help?"

"It might, madam. They may be known at the Yard.[3] This isn't her first job,
I'd say!"

Miss Marple nodded brightly. She opened her bag and extracted a small
cardboard box. Inside it, wedged in cotton wool, was a small mirror.

"From my handbag," said Miss Marple. "The maid's prints are on it. I think   330
they should be satisfactory—she touched an extremely sticky substance a moment
previously."

Inspector Slack stared. "Did you get her fingerprints on purpose?"

"Of course."

"You suspected her then?"

"Well, you know it did strike me that she was a little too good to be true. I
practically told Miss Lavinia so. But she simply wouldn't take the hint! I'm afraid,
you know, Inspector, that I don't believe in paragons. Most of us have our faults—
and domestic service shows them up very quickly!"

"Well," said Inspector Slack, recovering his balance, "I'm obliged to you, I'm   340
sure. We'll send these up to the Yard and see what they have to say."

He stopped. Miss Marple had put her head a little on one side and was regarding him with a good deal of meaning.

"You wouldn't consider, I suppose, Inspector, looking a little nearer home?"

"What do you mean, Miss Marple?"

"It's very difficult to explain, but when you come across a peculiar thing you

---

3. Scotland Yard is the popular name for the London Metropolitan Police Force. Its Criminal Investigation
   Division (CID) is famous for its forensic techniques and often assists local police forces.

notice it. Although, often, peculiar things may be the merest trifles. I've felt that all along, you know; I mean about Gladys and the brooch. She's an honest girl; she didn't take that brooch. Then why did Miss Skinner think she did? Miss Skinner's not a fool; far from it! Why was she so anxious to let a girl go who was a good servant when servants are hard to get? It was peculiar, you know. So I wondered. I wondered a good deal. And I noticed another peculiar thing! Miss Emily's a hypochondriac, but she's the first hypochondriac who hasn't sent for some doctor or other at once. Hypochondriacs love doctors. Miss Emily didn't!"

"What are you suggesting, Miss Marple?"

"Well, I'm suggesting, you know, that Miss Lavinia and Miss Emily are peculiar people. Miss Emily spends nearly all her time in a dark room. And if that hair of hers isn't a wig I—I'll eat my own back switch! And what I say is this—it's perfectly possible for a thin, pale, gray-haired, whining woman to be the same as a black-haired, rosy-cheeked, plump woman. And nobody that I can find ever saw Miss Emily and Mary Higgins at one and the same time.

"Plenty of time to get impressions of all the keys, plenty of time to find out all about the other tenants, and then—get rid of the local girl. Miss Emily takes a brisk walk across country one night and arrives at the station as Mary Higgins next day. And then, at the right moment, Mary Higgins disappears, and off goes the hue and cry after her. I'll tell you where you'll find her, Inspector. On Miss Emily Skinner's sofa! Get her fingerprints if you don't believe me, but you'll find I'm right! A couple of clever thieves, that's what the Skinners are—and no doubt in league with a clever post and rails or fence or whatever you call it. But they won't get away with it this time! I'm not going to have one of our village girl's character for honesty taken away like that! Gladys Holmes is as honest as the day, and everybody's going to know it! Good afternoon!"

Miss Marple had stalked out before Inspector Slack had recovered.

"Whew!" he muttered. "I wonder if she's right?"

He soon found out that Miss Marple was right again.

Colonel Melchett congratulated Slack on his efficiency, and Miss Marple had Gladys come to tea with Edna and spoke to her seriously on settling down in a good situation when she got one.   [1925]

Questions for Discussion and Writing

1. Miss Marple is one of Agatha Christie's most famous detectives. What qualities make her a successful detective? How does she make good use of her age and sex? What are her methods?

2. What conventions of the mystery story are observed? Discuss any of the conventions that are not observed?

3. Does this mystery play fair with readers; that is, are all the necessary clues provided so that readers can solve the mystery for themselves? Discuss the seemingly trivial clues that later proved crucial.

4. Why is Miss Marple able to solve the mystery when the police cannot?

5. How are women depicted in this story? Do you approve of this depiction? Why or why not?

❧ W. SOMERSET MAUGHAM
(1874–1965)

The Letter

Somerset Maugham made no innovations in the short story and by his own assessment was only "in the very front row of the second-raters," yet for their readability, craftsmanship, and humanity, his stories continue to appeal to a wide spectrum of readers.

Like many authors, Maugham had a lonely childhood. He was orphaned at eight, raised by elderly relatives, and unhappy at school because of shyness and a stammer. He trained in medicine but was determined to write and struggled for more than a decade. When success finally came in 1907, it was in the theater; later he became a respected and best-selling novelist and short story writer. *Of Human Bondage* (1915) sold over five million copies and is still considered by some critics as a classic in the Realistic mode.

Maugham met Gerald Haxton in 1914 while driving an ambulance in the war, and Gerald remained his secretary and companion for most of his life. Together they traveled the world before settling at Cap Ferrat on the French Riviera, where until World War II, Maugham wrote in the morning, rested in the afternoon, and entertained celebrities in the evening. During the war, he became a spokesman for England in America.

Maugham's desire to entertain may be his fatal flaw—at least to those who demand something innovative in fiction. He was influenced by Anton Chekhov (1860–1904) and Guy de Maupassant (1850–1893) and shares with the latter a pessimistic view of human nature, which he explores in stories with strong, clear plots, vivid characters, and colorful settings. But while many critics damn him with faint praise, others see him as an accomplished artist whose achievements have been undervalued by the Modernist aesthetic.

"The Letter" is based on a real incident and illustrates Maugham's ability to create taut drama and reveal the passions that lie just beneath the civilized surface.

OUTSIDE ON THE QUAY the sun beat fiercely. A stream of motors, lorries and buses, private cars and hirelings, sped up and down the crowded thoroughfare, and every chauffeur blew his horn; rickshaws threaded their nimble path amid the throng, and the panting coolies found breath to yell at one another; coolies, carrying heavy bales, sidled along with their quick jog-trot and shouted to the passer-by to make way; itinerant vendors proclaimed their wares. Singapore is the meeting-place of a hundred peoples; and men of all colours, black Tamils, yellow Chinks, brown Malays, Armenians, Jews and Bengalis, called to one another in raucous tones. But inside the office of Messrs. Ripley, Joyce & Naylor it was pleasantly cool; it was dark after the dusty glitter of the street and agreeably quiet after its unceasing din. Mr. Joyce sat in his private room, at the table, with an elec- 10 tric fan turned full on him. He was leaning back, his elbows on the arms of the chair, with the tips of the outstretched fingers of one hand resting neatly against the tips of the outstretched fingers of the other. His gaze rested on the battered volumes of the Law Reports which stood on a long shelf in front of him. On the top of a cupboard were square boxes of japanned tin[1] on which were painted the names of various clients.

There was a knock at the door.

"Come in."

A Chinese clerk, very neat in his white ducks, opened it "Mr. Crosbie is here, sir."

He spoke beautiful English, accenting each word with precision, and Mr. Joyce had often wondered at the extent of his vocabulary. Ong Chi Seng was a Cantonese, and he had studied law at Gray's Inn. He was spending a year or two with Messrs. Ripley, Joyce & Naylor in order to prepare himself for practice on his own account. He was industrious, obliging, and of exemplary character.

"Show him in," said Mr. Joyce.

He rose to shake hands with his visitor and asked him to sit down. The light fell on him as he did so. The face of Mr. Joyce remained in shadow. He was by nature a silent man, and now he looked at Robert Crosbie for quite a minute without speaking. Crosbie was a big fellow well over six feet high, with broad shoulders, and muscular. He was a rubber-planter, hard with the constant exercise of walking over the estate and with the tennis which was his relaxation when the day's work was over. He was deeply sunburned. His hairy hands, his feet in clumsy boots, were enormous, and Mr. Joyce found himself thinking that a blow of that great fist would easily kill the fragile Tamil. But there was no fierceness in his blue eyes; they were confiding and gentle; and his face, with its big, undistinguished features, was open, frank and honest. But at this moment it bore a look of deep distress. It was drawn and haggard.

"You look as though you hadn't had much sleep the last night or two," said Mr. Joyce.

"I haven't."

Mr. Joyce noticed now the old felt hat, with its broad double brim, which Crosbie had placed on the table; and then his eyes travelled to the khaki shorts he wore, showing his red hairy thighs, the tennis shirt open at the neck, without a tie, and the dirty khaki jacket with the ends of the sleeves turned up. He looked as though he had just come in from a long tramp among the rubber trees. Mr. Joyce gave a slight frown.

"Oh, I'm all right." "You must pull yourself together, you know. You must keep your head."

"Have you seen your wife to-day?"

"No, I'm to see her this afternoon. You know, it is a dammed shame that they should have arrested her."

"I think they had to do that," Mr. Joyce answered in his level, soft tone.

"I should have thought they'd have let her out on bail."

"It's a very serious charge."

---

1. Highly glossed, as if varnished.

"It is damnable. She did what any decent woman would do in her place. Only, nine women out of ten wouldn't have the pluck. Leslie's the best woman in the world. She wouldn't hurt a fly. Why, hang it all, man, I've been married to her for twelve years, do you think I don't know her? God, if I'd got hold of the man I'd have wrung his neck. I'd have killed him without a moment's hesitation. So would you."

"My dear fellow, everybody's on your side. No one has a good word to say for Hammond. We're going to get her off. I don't suppose either the assessors or the judge will go into court without having already made up their minds to bring in a verdict of not guilty."

"The whole thing's a farce," said Crosbie violently. "She ought never to have been arrested in the first place, and then it's terrible, after all the poor girl's gone through, to subject her to the ordeal of a trial. There's not a soul I've met since I've been in Singapore, man or woman, who hasn't told me that Leslie was absolutely justified. I think it's awful to keep her in prison all these weeks."

"The law is the law. After all, she confesses that she killed the man. It is terrible, and I'm dreadfully sorry both for you and for her."

"I don't matter a hang," interrupted Crosbie.

"But the fact remains that murder has been committed, and in a civilized community a trial is inevitable."

"Is it murder to exterminate noxious vermin? She shot him as she would have shot a mad dog."

Mr. Joyce leaned back again in his chair and once more placed the tips of his ten fingers together. The little construction he formed looked like the skeleton of a roof. He was silent for a moment.

"I should be wanting in my duty as your legal adviser," he said at last, in an even voice, looking at his client with his cool, brown eyes, "if I did not tell you that there is one point which causes me just a little anxiety. If your wife had only shot Hammond once, the whole thing would be absolutely plain sailing. Unfortunately she fired six times."

"Her explanation is perfectly simple. In the circumstances any one would have done the same."

"I daresay," said Mr. Joyce, "and of course I think the explanation is very reasonable. But it's no good closing our eyes to the facts. It's always a good plan to put yourself in another man's place, and I can't deny that if I were prosecuting for the Crown that's the point on which I should centre my enquiry."

"My dear fellow, that's perfectly idiotic."

Mr. Joyce shot a sharp glance at Robert Crosbie. The shadow of a smile hovered over his shapely lips. Crosbie was a good fellow, but he could hardly be described as intelligent.

"I daresay it's of no importance," answered the lawyer, "I just thought it was a point worth mentioning. You haven't got very long to wait now, and when it's all over I recommend you to go off somewhere with your wife on a trip and forget all about it. Even though we are almost dead certain to get an acquittal, a trial of that sort is anxious work and you'll both want a rest."

For the first time Crosbie smiled, and his smile strangely changed his face. You forgot the uncouthness and saw only the goodness of his soul.

"I think I shall want it more than Leslie. She's borne up wonderfully. By God, there's a plucky little woman for you."

"Yes, I've been very much struck by her self-control," said the lawyer. "I should never have guessed that she was capable of such determination." 110

His duties as her counsel had made it necessary for him to have a good many interviews with Mrs. Crosbie since her arrest. Though things had been made as easy as could be for her, the fact remained that she was in jail, awaiting her trial for murder, and it would not have been surprising if her nerves had failed her. She appeared to bear her ordeal with composure. She read a great deal, took such exercise as was possible, and by favour of the authorities worked at the pillow lace which had always formed the entertainment of her long hours of leisure. When Mr. Joyce saw her she was neatly dressed in cool, fresh, simple frocks, her hair was carefully arranged, and her nails were manicured. Her manner was collected. She was able even to jest upon the little inconveniences of her position. There was 120 something casual about the way in which she spoke of the tragedy, which suggested to Mr. Joyce that only her good breeding prevented her from finding something a trifle ludicrous in a situation which was eminently serious. It surprised him, for he had never thought that she had a sense of humour.

He had known her off and on for a good many years. When she paid visits to Singapore she generally came to dine with his wife and himself, and once or twice she had passed a week-end with them at their bungalow by the sea. His wife had spent a fortnight with her on the estate and had met Geoffrey Hammond several times. The two couples had been on friendly, if not on intimate, terms, and it was on this account that Robert Crosbie had rushed over to Singapore immedi- 130 ately after the catastrophe and begged Mr. Joyce to take charge personally of his unhappy wife's defence.

The story she told him the first time he saw her, she had never varied in the smallest detail. She told it as coolly then, a few hours after the tragedy, as she told it now. She told it connectedly, in a level, even voice, and her only sign of confusion was when a slight colour came into her cheeks as she described one or two of its incidents. She was the last woman to whom one would have expected such a thing to happen. She was in the early thirties, a fragile creature, neither short nor tall, and graceful rather than pretty. Her wrists and ankles were very delicate, but she was extremely thin and you could see the bones of her hands through the 140 white skin, and the veins were large and blue. Her face was colourless, slightly sallow, and her lips were pale. You did not notice the colour of her eyes. She had a great deal of light brown hair and it had a slight natural wave; it was the sort of hair that with a little touching-up would have been very pretty, but you could not imagine that Mrs. Crosbie would think of resorting to any such device. She was a quiet, pleasant, unassuming woman. Her manner was engaging and if she was not very popular it was because she suffered from a certain shyness. This was comprehensible enough, for the planter's life is lonely, and in her own house, with people she knew, she was in her quiet way charming. Mrs. Joyce after her fortnight's stay had told her husband that Leslie was a very agreeable hostess. There was more in 150 her, she said, than people thought; and when you came to know her you were surprised how much she had read and how entertaining she could be.

She was the last woman in the world to commit murder.

Mr. Joyce dismissed Robert Crosbie with such reassuring words as he could find and, once more alone in his office, turned over the pages of the brief. But it was a mechanical action, for all its details were familiar to him. The case was the sensation of the day, and it was discussed in all the clubs, at all the dinner tables, up and down the Peninsula from Singapore to Penang. The facts that Mrs. Crosbie gave were simple. Her husband had gone to Singapore on business and she was alone for the night. She dined by herself, late, at a quarter to nine, and after dinner 160 sat in the sitting-room working at her lace. It opened on to the verandah. There was no one in the bungalow, for the servants had retired to their own quarters at the back of the compound. She was surprised to hear a step on the gravel path in the garden, a booted step which suggested a white man rather than a native, for she had not heard a motor drive up and she could not imagine who could be coming to see her at that time of night. Someone ascended the few stairs that led up to the bungalow, walked across the verandah, and appeared at the door of the room in which she sat. At the first moment she did not recognize the visitor. She sat with a shaded lamp and he stood with his back to the darkness.

"May I come in?" he said. 170

She did not even recognize the voice.

"Who is it?" she asked.

She worked with spectacles, and she took them off as she spoke.

"Geoff Hammond."

"Of course. Come in and have a drink."

She rose and shook hands with him cordially. She was a little surprised to see him, for though he was a neighbour neither she nor Robert had been lately on very intimate terms with him, and she had not seen him for some weeks. He was the manager of a rubber estate nearly eight miles from theirs and she wondered why he had chosen this late hour to come and see them. 180

"Robert's away," she said. "He had to go to Singapore for the night."

Perhaps he thought his visit called for some explanation, for he said:

"I'm sorry. I felt rather lonely to-night, so I thought I'd just come along and see how you were getting on."

"How on earth did you come? I never heard a car."

"I left it down the road. I thought you might both be in bed and asleep."

This was natural enough. The planter gets up at dawn in order to take the roll-call of the workers, and soon after dinner he is glad to go to bed. Hammond's car was in point of fact found next day a quarter of a mile from the bungalow.

Since Robert was away there was no whisky and soda in the room. Leslie did 190 not call the boy, since he was probably asleep, but fetched it herself. Her guest mixed himself a drink and filled his pipe.

Geoff. Hammond had a host of friends in the colony. He was at this time in the late thirties, but he had come out as a lad. He had been one of the first to volunteer on the outbreak of war, and had done very well. A wound in the knee caused him to be invalided out of the army after two years, but he returned to the Federated Malay States with a D.S.O. and an M.C.[2] He was one of the best billiard players in the colony. He had been a beautiful dancer and a fine tennis player, but,

2. Distinguished Service Order and Military Cross.

though able no longer to dance, and his tennis, with a stiff knee, was not so good as it had been, he had the gift of popularity and was universally liked. He was a tall, good-looking fellow, with attractive blue eyes and a fine head of black, curling hair. Old stagers said his only fault was that he was too fond of the girls, and after the catastrophe they shook their heads and vowed that they had always known this would get him into trouble.

He began now to talk to Leslie about the local affairs, the forthcoming races in Singapore, the price of rubber, and his chances of killing a tiger which had been lately seen in the neighbourhood. She was anxious to finish by a certain date the piece of lace on which she was working, for she wanted to send it home for her mother's birthday, and so put on her spectacles again and drew towards her chair the little table on which stood the pillow.

"I wish you wouldn't wear those great horn-spectacles," he said. "I don't know why a pretty woman should do her best to look plain."

She was a trifle taken aback at this remark. He had never used that tone with her before. She thought the best thing was to make light of it.

"I have no pretensions to being a raving beauty, you know, and, if you ask me point blank, I'm bound to tell you that I don't care two pins if you think me plain or not."

"I don't think you're plain. I think you're awfully pretty."

"Sweet of you," she answered ironically. "But in that case I can only think you half-witted."

He chuckled. But he rose from his chair and sat down in another by her side.

"You're not going to have the face to deny that you have the prettiest hands in the world," he said.

He made a gesture as though to take one of them. She gave him a little tap.

"Don't be an idiot. Sit down where you were before and talk sensibly, or else I shall send you home."

He did not move.

"Don't you know that I'm awfully in love with you?" he said.

She remained quite cool.

"I don't. I don't believe it for a minute, and even if it were true I don't want you to say it."

She was the more surprised at what he was saying, since during the seven years she had known him he had never paid her any particular attention. When he came back from the war they had seen a good deal of one another, and once when he was ill Robert had gone over and brought him back to their bungalow in his car. He had stayed with them then for a fortnight. But their interests were dissimilar and the acquaintance had never ripened into friendship. For the last two or three years they had seen little of him. Now and then he came over to play tennis, now and then they met him at some planter's who was giving a party, but it often happened that they did not set eyes on him for a month at a time.

Now he took another whisky and soda. Leslie wondered if he had been drinking before. There was something odd about him, and it made her a trifle uneasy. She watched him help himself with disapproval.

"I wouldn't drink any more if I were you," she said, good-humouredly still.

He emptied his glass and put it down.

"Do you think I'm talking to you like this because I'm drunk?" he asked abruptly.

"That is the most obvious explanation, isn't it?"

"Well, it's a lie. I've loved you ever since I first knew you. I've held my tongue as long as I could, and now it's got to come out. I love you, I love you, I love you."

She rose and carefully put aside the pillow.

"Good-night," she said.

"I'm not going now."

At last she began to lose her temper.

"But, you poor fool, don't you know that I've never loved any one but Robert, and even if I didn't love Robert you're the last man I should care for."

"What do I care? Robert's away."

"If you don't go away this minute I shall call the boys and have you thrown out."

"They're out of earshot."

She was very angry now. She made a movement as though to go on to the verandah from which the house-boy would certainly hear her, but he seized her arm.

"Let me go," she cried furiously.

"Not much. I've got you now."

She opened her mouth and called "Boy, boy," but with a quick gesture he put his hand over it. Then before she knew what he was about he had taken her in his arms and was kissing her passionately. She struggled, turning her lips away from his burning mouth.

"No, no, no," she cried. "Leave me alone. I won't."

She grew confused about what happened then. All that had been said before she remembered accurately, but now his words assailed her ears through a mist of horror and fear. He seemed to plead for her love. He broke into violent protestations of passion. And all the time he held her in his tempestuous embrace. She was helpless, for he was a strong, powerful man, and her arms were pinioned to her sides; her struggles were unavailing and she felt herself growing weaker; she was afraid she would faint, and his hot breath on her face made her feel desperately sick. He kissed her mouth, her eyes, her cheeks, her hair. The pressure of his arms was killing her. He lifted her off her feet. She tried to kick him, but he only held her more closely. He was carrying her now. He wasn't speaking any more, but she knew that his face was pale and his eyes hot with desire. He was taking her into the bedroom. He was no longer a civilized man, but a savage. And as he ran he stumbled against a table which was in the way. His stiff knee made him a little awkward on his feet, and with the burden of the woman in his arms he fell. In a moment she had snatched herself away from him. She ran round the sofa. He was up in a flash and flung himself towards her. There was a revolver on the desk. She was not a nervous woman, but Robert was to be away for the night and she had meant to take it into her room when she went to bed. That was why it happened to be there. She was frantic with terror now. She did not know what she was doing. She heard a report. She saw Hammond stagger. He gave a cry. He said something, she didn't know what. He lurched out of the room on to the verandah.

She was in a frenzy now, she was beside herself, she followed him out, yes, that was it, she must have followed him out, though she remembered nothing of it, she followed firing automatically shot after shot till the six chambers were empty. Hammond fell down on the floor of the verandah. He crumpled up into a bloody heap.

When the boys, startled by the reports, rushed up, they found her standing over Hammond with the revolver still in her hand, and Hammond lifeless. She looked at them for a moment without speaking. They stood in a frightened, huddled bunch. She let the revolver fall from her hand and without a word turned and went into the sitting-room. They watched her go into her bedroom and turn the key in the lock. They dared not touch the dead body, but looked at it with terrified eyes, talking excitedly to one another in undertones. Then the head-boy collected himself; he had been with them for many years, he was Chinese and a level-headed fellow. Robert had gone into Singapore on his motor-cycle and the car stood in the garage. He told the seis[3] to get it out; they must go at once to the Assistant District Officer and tell him what had happened. He picked up the revolver and put it in his pocket. The A.D.O., a man called Withers, lived on the outskirts of the nearest town, which was about thirty-five miles away. It took them an hour and a half to reach him. Every one was asleep, and they had to rouse the boys. Presently Withers came out and they told him their errand. The head-boy showed him the revolver in proof of what he said. The A.D.O. went into his room to dress, sent for his car, and in a little while was following them back along the deserted road. The dawn was just breaking as he reached the Crosbies' bungalow. He ran up the steps of the verandah, and stopped short as he saw Hammond's body lying where he fell. He touched the face. It was quite cold.

"Where's mem?"[4] he asked the house-boy.

The Chinese pointed to the bedroom. Withers went to the door and knocked. There was no answer. He knocked again.

"Mrs. Crosbie," he called.

"Who is it?"

"Withers."

There was another pause. Then the door was unlocked and slowly opened. Leslie stood before him. She had not been to bed and wore the tea-gown in which she had dined. She stood and looked silently at the A.D.O.

"Your house-boy fetched me," he said. "Hammond. What have you done?"

"He tried to rape me and I shot him."

"My God! I say, you'd better come out here. You must tell me exactly what happened."

"Not now. I can't. You must give me time. Send for my husband."

Withers was a young man, and he did not know exactly what to do in an emergency which was so out of the run of his duties. Leslie refused to say anything till at last Robert arrived. Then she told the two men the story, from which since then, though she had repeated it over and over again, she had never in the slightest degree diverged.

3. Servants.
4. Memsahib, form of address for a white woman of high rank.

The point to which Mr. Joyce recurred was the shooting. As a lawyer he was bothered that Leslie had fired not once but six times, and the examination of the dead man showed that four of the shots had been fired close to the body. One might almost have thought that when the man fell she stood over him and emp- 340 tied the contents of the revolver into him. She confessed that her memory, so accurate for all that had preceded, failed her here. Her mind was blank. It pointed to an uncontrollable fury; but uncontrollable fury was the last thing you would have expected from this quiet and demure woman. Mr. Joyce had known her a good many years, and had always thought her an unemotional person; during the weeks that had passed since the tragedy her composure had been amazing.

Mr. Joyce shrugged his shoulders.

"The fact is, I suppose," he reflected, "that you can never tell what hidden possibilities of savagery there are in the most respectable of women."

There was a knock at the door.   350

"Come in."

The Chinese clerk entered and closed the door behind him. He closed it gently, with deliberation, but decidedly, and advanced to the table at which Mr. Joyce was sitting.

"May I trouble you, sir, for a few words' private conversation?" he said.

The elaborate accuracy with which the clerk expressed himself always faintly amused Mr. Joyce, and now he smiled.

"It's no trouble, Chi Seng," he replied.

"The matter on which I desire to speak to you, sir, is delicate and confidential."   360

"Fire away."

Mr. Joyce met his clerk's shrewd eyes. As usual Ong Chi Seng was dressed in the height of local fashion. He wore very shiny patent-leather shoes and gay silk socks. In his black tie was a pearl and ruby pin, and on the fourth finger of his left hand a diamond ring. From the pocket of his neat white coat protruded a gold fountain pen and a gold pencil. He wore a gold wrist-watch, and on the bridge of his nose invisible pince-nez. He gave a little cough.

"The matter has to do with the case R. v. Crosbie, sir."

"Yes?"

"A circumstance has come to my knowledge, sir, which seems to me to put a 370 different complexion on it."

"What circumstance?"

"It has come to my knowledge, sir, that there is a letter in existence from the defendant to the unfortunate victim of the tragedy."

"I shouldn't be at all surprised. In the course of the last seven years I have no doubt that Mrs. Crosbie often had occasion to write to Mr. Hammond."

Mr. Joyce had a high opinion of his clerk's intelligence and his words were designed to conceal his thoughts.

"That is very probable, sir. Mrs. Crosbie must have communicated with the deceased frequently, to invite him to dine with her for example, or to propose a 380 tennis game. That was my first thought when the matter was brought to my notice. This letter, however, was written on the day of the late Mr. Hammond's death."

Mr. Joyce did not flicker an eyelash. He continued to look at Ong Chi Seng with the smile of faint amusement with which he generally talked to him.

"Who has told you this?"

"The circumstances were brought to my knowledge, sir, by a friend of mine."

Mr. Joyce knew better than to insist.

"You will no doubt recall, sir, that Mrs. Crosbie has stated that until the fatal night she had had no communication with the deceased for several weeks." 390

"Have you got the letter?"

"No, sir."

"What are its contents?"

"My fliend gave me a copy. Would you like to peruse it, sir?"

"I should."

Ong Chi Seng took from an inside pocket a bulky wallet. It was filled with papers, Singapore dollar notes and cigarette cards. From the confusion he presently extracted a half sheet of thin note-paper and placed it before Mr. Joyce. The letter read as follows:

R. will be away for the night. I absolutely must see you. I shall expect you at eleven. I 400
am desperate and if you don't come I won't answer for the consequences. Don't drive
up.—L.

It was written in the flowing hand which the Chinese were taught at the foreign schools. The writing, so lacking in character, was oddly incongruous with the ominous words.

"What makes you think that this note was written by Mrs. Crosbie?"

"I have every confidence in the veracity of my informant, sir," replied Ong Chi Seng. "And the matter can very easily be put to the proof. Mrs. Crosbie will no doubt be able to tell you at once whether she wrote such a letter or not." 410

Since the beginning of the conversation Mr. Joyce had not taken his eyes off the respectful countenance of his clerk. He wondered now if he discerned in it a faint expression of mockery.

"It is inconceivable that Mrs. Crosbie should have written such a letter," said Mr. Joyce.

"If that is your opinion, sir, the matter is of course ended. My fliend spoke to me on the subject only because he thought, as I was in your office, you might like to know of the existence of this letter before a communication was made to the Deputy Public Prosecutor."

"Who has the original?" asked Mr. Joyce sharply. 420

Ong Chi Seng made no sign that he perceived in this question and its manner a change of attitude.

"You will remember, sir, no doubt, that after the death of Mr. Hammond it was discovered that he had relations with a Chinese woman. The letter is at present in her possession."

That was one of the things which had turned public opinion most vehemently against Hammond. It came to be known that for several months he had a Chinese woman living in his house.

For a moment neither of them spoke. Indeed everything had been said and each understood the other perfectly. 430

"I'm obliged to you, Chi Seng. I will give the matter my consideration."

"Very good, sir. Do you wish me to make a communication to that effect to my friend?"

"I daresay it would be as well if you kept in touch with him," Mr. Joyce answered with gravity.

"Yes, sir."

The clerk noiselessly left the room, shutting the door again with deliberation, and left Mr. Joyce to his reflections. He stared at the copy, in its neat, impersonal writing, of Leslie's letter. Vague suspicions troubled him. They were so disconcerting that he made an effort to put them out of his mind. There must be a simple explanation of the letter, and Leslie without doubt could give it at once, but, by heaven, an explanation was needed. He rose from his chair, put the letter in his pocket, and took his topee.[5] When he went out Ong Chi Seng was busily writing at his desk.

"I'm going out for a few minutes, Chi Seng," he said.

"Mr. George Reed is coming by appointment at twelve o'clock, sir. Where shall I say you've gone?"

Mr. Joyce gave him a thin smile.

"You can say that you haven't the least idea."

But he knew perfectly well that Ong Chi Seng was aware that he was going to the jail. Though the crime had been committed in Belanda and the trial was to take place at Belanda Bharu, since there was in the jail there no convenience for the detention of a white woman Mrs. Crosbie had been brought to Singapore.

When she was led into the room in which he waited she held out her thin, distinguished hand, and gave him a pleasant smile. She was as ever neatly and simply dressed and her abundant, pale hair was arranged with care.

"I wasn't expecting to see you this morning," she said graciously.

She might have been in her own house, and Mr. Joyce almost expected to hear her call the boy and tell him to bring the visitor a gin pahit.

"How are you?" he asked.

"I'm in the best of health, thank you." A flicker of amusement flashed across her eyes. "This is a wonderful place for a rest cure."

The attendant withdrew and they were left alone.

"Do sit down," said Leslie.

He took a chair. He did not quite know how to begin. She was so cool that it seemed almost impossible to say to her the thing he had come to say. Though she was not pretty there was something agreeable in her appearance. She had elegance, but it was the elegance of good breeding in which there was nothing of the artifice of society. You had only to look at her to know what sort of people she had and what kind of surroundings she had lived in. Her fragility gave her a singular refinement. It was impossible to associate her with the vaguest idea of grossness.

"I'm looking forward to seeing Robert this afternoon," she said, in her good-humored, easy voice. (It was a pleasure to hear her speak, her voice and her accent were so distinctive of her class.) "Poor dear, it's been a great trial to his nerves. I'm thankful it'll all be over in a few days."

5. Pith helmet.

"It's only five days now."

"I know. Each morning when I awake I say to myself, 'one less.' " She smiled then. "Just as I used to do at school and the holidays were coming."

"By the way, am I right in thinking that you had no communication whatever with Hammond for several weeks before the catastrophe?"   480

"I'm quite positive of that. The last time we met was at a tennis-party at the MacFarrens.' I don't think I said more than two words to him. They have two courts, you know, and we didn't happen to be in the same sets."

"And you haven't written to him?"

"Oh, no."

"Are you quite sure of that?"

"Oh, quite," she answered, with a little smile. "There was nothing I should write to him for except to ask him to dine or to play tennis, and I hadn't done either for months."

"At one time you'd been on fairly intimate terms with him. How did it hap- 490 pen that you had stopped asking him to anything?"

Mrs. Crosbie shrugged her thin shoulders.

"One gets tired of people. We hadn't anything very much in common. Of course, when he was ill Robert and I did everything we could for him, but the last year or two he'd been quite well, and he was very popular. He had a good many calls on his time, and there didn't seem to be any need to shower invitations upon him."

"Are you quite certain that was all?"

Mrs. Crosbie hesitated for a moment.

"Well, I may just as well tell you. It had come to our ears that he was living 500 with a Chinese woman, and Robert said he wouldn't have him in the house. I had seen her myself."

Mr. Joyce was sitting in a straight-backed arm-chair, resting his chin on his hand, and his eyes were fixed on Leslie. Was it his fancy that as she made this remark her black pupils were filled on a sudden, for the fraction of a second, with a dull red light? The effect was startling. Mr. Joyce shifted in his chair. He placed the tips of his ten fingers together. He spoke very slowly, choosing his words.

"I think I should tell you that there is in existence a letter in your handwriting to Geoff Hammond."

He watched her closely. She made no movement, nor did her face change 510 colour, but she took a noticeable time to reply.

"In the past I've often sent him little notes to ask him to something or other, or to get me something when I knew he was going to Singapore."

"This letter asks him to come and see you because Robert was going to Singapore."

"That's impossible. I never did anything of the kind."

"You'd better read it for yourself."

He took it out of his pocket and handed it to her. She gave it a glance and with a smile of scorn handed it back to him.

"That's not my handwriting."   520

"I know, it's said to be an exact copy of the original."

She read the words now, and as she read a horrible change came over her.

Her colourless face grew dreadful to look at. It turned green. The flesh seemed on a sudden to fall away and her skin was tightly stretched over the bones. Her lips receded, showing her teeth, so that she had the appearance of making a grimace. She stared at Mr. Joyce with eyes that started from their sockets. He was looking now at a gibbering death's head.

"What does it mean?" she whispered.

Her mouth was so dry that she could utter no more than a hoarse sound. It was no longer a human voice.

"That is for you to say," he answered.

"I didn't write it. I swear I didn't write it."

"Be very careful what you say. If the original is in your handwriting it would be useless to deny it."

"It would be a forgery."

"It would be difficult to prove that. It would be easy to prove that it was genuine."

A shiver passed through her lean body. But great beads of sweat stood on her forehead. She took a handkerchief from her bag and wiped the palms of her hands. She glanced at the letter again and gave Mr. Joyce a sidelong look.

"It's not dated. If I had written it and forgotten all about it, it might have been written years ago. If you'll give me time, I'll try and remember the circumstances."

"I noticed there was no date. If this letter were in the hands of the prosecution they would cross-examine the boys. They would soon find out whether someone took a letter to Hammond on the day of his death."

Mrs. Crosbie clasped her hands violently and swayed in her chair so that he thought she would faint.

"I swear to you that I didn't write that letter."

Mr. Joyce was silent for a little while. He took his eyes from her distraught face, and looked down on the floor. He was reflecting.

"In these circumstances we need not go into the matter further," he said slowly, at last breaking the silence. "If the possessor of this letter sees fit to place it in the hands of the prosecution you will be prepared."

His words suggested that he had nothing more to say to her, but he made no movement of departure. He waited. To himself he seemed to wait a very long time. He did not look at Leslie, but he was conscious that she sat very still. She made no sound. At last it was he who spoke.

"If you have nothing more to say to me I think I'll be getting back to my office."

"What would anyone who read the letter be inclined to think that it meant?" she asked then.

"He'd know that you had told a deliberate lie," answered Mr. Joyce sharply.

"When?"

"You have stated definitely that you had had no communication with Hammond for at least three months."

"The whole thing has been a terrible shock to me. The events of that dreadful night have been a nightmare. It's not very strange if one detail has escaped my memory."

"It would be very unfortunate when your memory has reproduced so exactly 570
every particular of your interview with Hammond, that you should have forgotten
so important a point as that he came to see you in the bungalow on the night of
his death at your express desire."

"I hadn't forgotten. After what happened I was afraid to mention it. I thought
you'd none of you believe my story if I admitted that he'd come at my invitation. I
daresay it was stupid of me; but I lost my head, and after I'd said once that I'd had
no communication with Hammond I was obliged to stick to it."

By now Leslie had recovered her admirable composure, and she met Mr.
Joyce's appraising glance with candour. Her gentleness was very disarming.

"You will be required to explain, then, *why* you asked Hammond to come 580
and see you when Robert was away for the night."

She turned her eyes full on the lawyer. He had been mistaken in thinking
them insignificant, they were rather fine eyes, and unless he was mistaken they
were bright now with tears. Her voice had a little break in it.

"It was a surprise I was preparing for Robert. His birthday is next month. I
knew he wanted a new gun and you know I'm dreadfully stupid about sporting
things. I wanted to talk to Geoff about it. I thought I'd get him to order it for me."

"Perhaps the terms of the letter are not very clear to your recollection. Will
you have another look at it?"

"No, I don't want to," she said quickly.   590

"Does it seem to you the sort of letter a woman would write to a somewhat
distant acquaintance because she wanted to consult him about buying a gun?"

"I daresay it's rather extravagant and emotional. I do express myself like that,
you know. I'm quite prepared to admit it's very silly." She smiled. "And after all,
Geoff Hammond wasn't quite a distant acquaintance. When he was ill I'd nursed
him like a mother. I asked him to come when Robert was away, because Robert
wouldn't have him in the house."

Mr. Joyce was tired of sitting so long in the same position. He rose and
walked once or twice up and down the room, choosing the words he proposed to
say; then he leaned over the back of the chair in which he had been sitting. He 600
spoke slowly in a tone of deep gravity.

"Mrs. Crosbie, I want to talk to you very, very seriously. This case was comparatively plain sailing. There was only one point which seemed to me to require
explanation: as far as I could judge, you had fired no less than four shots into
Hammond when he was lying on the ground. It was hard to accept the possibility
that a delicate, frightened, and habitually self-controlled woman, of gentle nurture
and refined instincts, should have surrendered to an absolutely uncontrolled
frenzy. But of course it was admissible. Although Geoffrey Hammond was much
liked and on the whole thought highly of, I was prepared to prove that he was the
sort of man who might be guilty of the crime which in justification of your act you 610
accused him of. The fact, which was discovered after his death, that he had been
living with a Chinese woman gave us something very definite to go upon. That
robbed him of any sympathy which might have been felt for him. We made up our
minds to make use of the odium which such a connection cast upon him in the
minds of all respectable people. I told your husband this morning that I was cer-

tain of an acquittal, and I wasn't just telling him that to give him heart. I do not believe the assessors would have left the court."

They looked into one another's eyes. Mrs. Crosbie was strangely still. She was like a little bird paralyzed by the fascination of a snake. He went on in the same quiet tones.

"But this letter has thrown an entirely different complexion on the case. I am your legal adviser, I shall represent you in Court. I take your story as you tell it me, and I shall conduct your defence according to its terms. It may be that I believe your statements, and it may be that I doubt them. The duty of counsel is to persuade the Court that the evidence placed before it is not such as to justify it in bringing in a verdict of guilty, and any private opinion he may have of the guilt or innocence of his client is entirely beside the point."

He was astonished to see in Leslie's eyes the flicker of a smile. Piqued, he went on somewhat dryly.

"You're not going to deny that Hammond came to your house at your urgent, and I may even say, hysterical, invitation?"

Mrs. Crosbie, hesitating for an instant, seemed to consider.

"They can prove that the letter was taken to his bungalow by one of the house-boys. He rode over on his bicycle."

"You mustn't expect other people to be stupider than you. The letter will put them on the track of suspicions which have entered nobody's head. I will not tell you what I personally thought when I saw the copy. I do not wish you to tell me anything but what is needed to save your neck."

Mrs. Crosbie gave a shrill cry. She sprang to her feet, white with terror.

"You don't think they'd hang me?"

"If they came to the conclusion that you hadn't killed Hammond in self-defence, it would be the duty of the assessors to bring in a verdict of guilty. The charge is murder. It would be the duty of the judge to sentence you to death."

"But what can they prove?" she gasped.

"I don't know what they can prove. You know. I don't want to know. But if their suspicions are aroused, if they begin to make enquiries, if the natives are questioned—what is it that can be discovered?"

She crumpled up suddenly. She fell on the floor before he could catch her. She had fainted. He looked round the room for water, but there was none there, and he did not want to be disturbed. He stretched her out on the floor and kneeling beside her waited for her to recover. When she opened her eyes he was disconcerted by the ghastly fear that he saw in them.

"Keep quite still," he said. "You'll be better in a moment."

"You won't let them hang me," she whispered.

She began to cry, hysterically, while in undertones he sought to quieten her.

"For goodness' sake, pull yourself together," he said.

"Give me a minute."

Her courage was amazing. He could see the effort she made to regain her self-control, and soon she was once more calm.

"Let me get up now."

He gave her his hand and helped her to her feet. Taking her arm, he led her to the chair. She sat down wearily.

"Don't talk to me for a minute or two," she said.

"Very well."

When at last she spoke it was to say something which he did not expect. She gave a little sigh.

"I'm afraid I've made rather a mess of things," she said.

He did not answer, and once more there was a silence.

"Isn't it possible to get hold of the letter?" she said at last.   670

"I do not think anything would have been said to me about it if the person in whose possession it is was not prepared to sell it."

"Who's got it?"

"The Chinese woman who was living in Hammond's house."

A spot of colour flickered for an instant on Leslie's cheekbones.

"Does she want an awful lot for it?"

"I imagine that she has a very shrewd idea of its value. I doubt if it would be possible to get hold of it except for a very large sum."

"Are you going to let me be hanged?"

"Do you think it's so simple as all that to secure possession of an unwelcome   680
piece of evidence? It's no different from suborning a witness. You have no right to make any such suggestion to me."

"Then what is going to happen to me?"

"Justice must take its course."

She grew very pale. A little shudder passed through her body.

"I put myself in your hands. Of course I have no right to ask you to do anything that isn't proper."

Mr. Joyce had not bargained for the little break in her voice which her habitual self-restraint made quite intolerably moving. She looked at him with humble eyes and he thought that if he rejected their appeal they would haunt him for the   690
rest of his life. After all, nothing could bring poor Hammond back to life again. He wondered what really was the explanation of that letter. It was not fair to conclude from it that she had killed Hammond without provocation. He had lived in the East a long time and his sense of professional honour was not perhaps so acute as it had been twenty years before. He stared at the floor. He made up his mind to do something which he knew was unjustifiable, but it stuck in his throat and he felt dully resentful towards Leslie. It embarrassed him a little to speak.

"I don't know exactly what your husband's circumstances are?"

Flushing a rosy red, she shot a swift glance at him.

"He has a good many tin shares and a small share in two or three rubber es-   700
tates. I suppose he could raise money."

"He would have to be told what it was for."

She was silent for a moment. She seemed to think.

"He's in love with me still. He would make any sacrifice to save me. Is there any need for him to see the letter?"

Mr. Joyce frowned a little, and, quick to notice, she went on.

"Robert is an old friend of yours. I'm not asking you to do anything for me,

I'm asking you to save a rather simple, kind man who never did you any harm from all the pain that's possible."

Mr. Joyce did not reply. He rose to go and Mrs. Crosbie, with the grace that was natural to her, held out her hand. She was shaken by the scene, and her look was haggard, but she made a brave attempt to speed him with courtesy.

"It's so good of you to take all this trouble for me. I can't begin to tell you how grateful I am."

Mr. Joyce returned to his office. He sat in his own room, quite still, attempting to do no work, and pondered. His imagination brought him many strange ideas. He shuddered a little. At last there was the discreet knock on the door which he was expecting. Ong Chi Seng came in.

"I was just going out to have my tiffin, sir," he said.

"All right."

"I didn't know if there was anything you wanted before I went, sir."

"I don't think so. Did you make another appointment for Mr. Reed?"

"Yes, sir. He will come at three o'clock."

"Good."

Ong Chi Seng turned away, walked to the door, and put his long slim fingers on the handle. Then, as though on an afterthought, he turned back.

"Is there anything you wish me to say to my fliend, sir?"

Although Ong Chi Seng spoke English so admirably he had still a difficulty with the letter r, and he pronounced it "fliend."

"What friend?"

"About the letter Mrs. Crosbie wrote to Hammond deceased, sir."

"Oh! I'd forgotten about that. I mentioned it to Mrs. Crosbie and she denies having written anything of the sort. It's evidently a forgery."

Mr. Joyce took the copy from his pocket and handed it to Ong Chi Seng. Ong Chi Seng ignored the gesture.

"In that case, sir, I suppose there would be no objection if my fliend delivered the letter to the Deputy Public Prosecutor."

"None. But I don't quite see what good that would do your friend."

"My fliend, sir, thought it was his duty in the interests of justice."

"I am the last man in the world to interfere with any one who wishes to do his duty, Chi Seng."

The eyes of the lawyer and of the Chinese clerk met. Not the shadow of a smile hovered on the lips of either, but they understood each other perfectly.

"I quite understand, sir," said Ong Chi Seng, "but from my study of the case R. v. Crosbie I am of opinion that the production of such a letter would be damaging to our client."

"I have always had a very high opinion of your legal acumen, Chi Seng."

"It has occurred to me, sir, that if I could persuade my fliend to induce the Chinese woman who has the letter to deliver it into our hands it would save a great deal of trouble."

Mr. Joyce idly drew faces on his blotting-paper.

"I suppose your friend is a business man. In what circumstances do you think he would be induced to part with the letter?"

"He has not got the letter. The Chinese woman has the letter. He is only a relation of the Chinese woman. She is an ignorant woman; she did not know the value of the letter till my fliend told her."

"What value did he put on it?"

"Ten thousand dollars, sir."

"Good God! Where on earth do you suppose Mrs. Crosbie can get ten thousand dollars! I tell you the letter's a forgery."   760

He looked up at Ong Chi Seng as he spoke. The clerk was unmoved by the outburst. He stood at the side of the desk, civil, cool and observant.

"Mr. Crosbie owns an eighth share of the Betong Rubber Estate and a sixth share of the Selantan River Rubber Estate. I have a fliend who will lend him the money on the security of his properties."

"You have a large circle of acquaintance, Chi Seng."

"Yes, sir."

"Well, you can tell them to go to hell. I would never advise Mr. Crosbie to give a penny more than five thousand for a letter that can be very easily explained."   770

"The Chinese woman does not want to sell the letter, sir. My fliend took a long time to persuade her. It is useless to offer her less than the sum mentioned."

Mr. Joyce looked at Ong Chi Seng for at least three minutes. The clerk bore the searching scrutiny without embarrassment. He stood in a respectful attitude with downcast eyes. Mr. Joyce knew his man. Clever fellow, Chi Seng, he thought, I wonder how much he's going to get out of it.

"Ten thousand dollars is a very large sum."

"Mr. Crosbie will certainly pay it rather than see his wife hanged, sir."

Again Mr. Joyce paused. What more did Chi Seng know than he had said? He must be pretty sure of his ground if he was obviously so unwilling to bargain. 780 That sum had been fixed because whoever it was that was managing the affair knew it was the largest amount that Robert Crosbie could raise.

"Where is the Chinese woman now?" asked Mr. Joyce.

"She is staying at the house of my fliend, sir."

"Will she come here?"

"I think it more better if you go to her, sir. I can take you to the house tonight and she will give you the letter. She is a very ignorant woman, sir, and she does not understand cheques."

"I wasn't thinking of giving her a cheque. I will bring banknotes with me."

"It would only be waste of valuable time to bring less than ten thousand dol- 790 lars, sir."

"I quite understand."

"I will go and tell my fliend after I have had my tiffin, sir."

"Very good. You'd better meet me outside the club at ten o'clock to-night."

"With pleasure, sir," said Ong Chi Seng.

He gave Mr. Joyce a little bow and left the room. Mr. Joyce went out to have luncheon too. He went to the club and here, as he had expected, he saw Robert Crosbie. He was sitting at a crowded table, and as he passed him, looking for a place, Mr. Joyce touched him on the shoulder.

"I'd like a word or two with you before you go," he said.   800

"Right you are. Let me know when you're ready."

Mr. Joyce had made up his mind how to tackle him. He played a rubber of bridge after luncheon in order to allow time for the club to empty itself. He did not want on this particular matter to see Crosbie in his office. Presently Crosbie came into the card-room and looked on till the game was finished. The other players went on their various affairs, and the two were left alone.

"A rather unfortunate thing has happened, old man," said Mr. Joyce, in a tone which he sought to render as casual as possible. "It appears that your wife sent a letter to Hammond asking him to come to the bungalow on the night he was killed."

"But that's impossible," cried Crosbie. "She's always stated that she had had no communication with Hammond. I know from my own knowledge that she hadn't set eyes on him for a couple of months."

"The fact remains that the letter exists. It's in the possession of the Chinese woman Hammond was living with. Your wife meant to give you a present on your birthday, and she wanted Hammond to help her to get it. In the emotional excitement that she suffered from after the tragedy, she forgot all about it, and having once denied having any communication with Hammond, she was afraid to say that she had made a mistake. It was of course very unfortunate, but I daresay it was not unnatural."

Crosbie did not speak. His large, red face bore an expression of complete bewilderment and Mr. Joyce was at once relieved and exasperated by his lack of comprehension. He was a stupid man, and Mr. Joyce had no patience with stupidity. But his distress since the catastrophe had touched a soft spot in the lawyer's heart; and Mrs. Crosbie had struck the right note when she asked him to help her, not for her sake, but for her husband's.

"I need not tell you that it would be very awkward if this letter found its way into the hands of the prosecution. Your wife has lied, and she would be asked to explain the lie. It alters things a little if Hammond did not intrude, an unwanted guest, but came to your house by invitation. It would be easy to arouse in the accusers a certain indecision of mind."

Mr. Joyce hesitated. He was face to face now with his decision. If it had been a time for humour, he could have smiled at the reflection that he was taking so grave a step, and that the man for whom he was taking it had not the smallest conception of its gravity. If he gave the matter a thought, he probably imagined that what Mr. Joyce was doing was what any lawyer did in the ordinary run of business.

"My dear Robert, you are not only my client, but my friend. I think we must get hold of that letter. It'll cost a good deal of money. Except for that I should have preferred to say nothing to you about it."

"How much?"

"Ten thousand dollars."

"That's a devil of a lot. With the slump and one thing and another it'll take just about all I've got."

"Can you get it at once?"

"I suppose so. Old Charlie Meadows will let me have it on my tin shares and on those two estates I'm interested in."

"Then will you?"

"Is it absolutely necessary?"

"If you want your wife to be acquitted." 850

Crosbie grew very red. His mouth sagged strangely.

"But . . ." He could not find words, his face now was purple. "But I don't understand. She can explain. You don't mean to say they'd find her guilty? They couldn't hang her for putting a noxious vermin out of the way."

"Of course they wouldn't hang her. They might only find her guilty of manslaughter. She'd probably get off with two or three years."

Crosbie started to his feet and his red face was distraught with horror.

"Three years."

Then something seemed to dawn in that slow intelligence of his. His mind was darkness across which shot suddenly a flash of lightning, and though the suc- 860 ceeding darkness was as profound, there remained the memory of something not seen but perhaps just descried. Mr. Joyce saw that Crosbie's big red hands, coarse and hard with all the odd jobs he had set them to, trembled.

"What was the present she wanted to make me?"

"She says she wanted to give you a new gun."

Once more that great red face flushed a deeper red.

"When have you got to have the money ready?"

There was something odd in his voice now. It sounded as though he spoke with invisible hands clutching at his throat.

"At ten o'clock to-night. I thought you could bring it to my office at about 870 six."

"Is the woman coming to you?"

"No, I'm going to her."

"I'll bring the money. I'll come with you."

Mr. Joyce looked at him sharply.

"Do you think there's any need for you to do that? I think it would be better if you left me to deal with this matter by myself."

"It's my money, isn't it? I'm going to come."

Mr. Joyce shrugged his shoulders. They rose and shook hands. Mr. Joyce looked at him curiously. 880

At ten o'clock they met in the empty club.

"Everything all right?" asked Mr. Joyce.

"Yes. I've got the money in my pocket."

"Let's go then."

They walked down the steps. Mr. Joyce's car was waiting for them in the square, silent at that hour, and as they came to it Ong Chi Seng stepped out of the shadow of a house. He took his seat beside the driver and gave him a direction. They drove past the Hotel de l'Europe and turned up by the Sailors' Home to get into Victoria Street. Here the Chinese shops were open still, idlers lounged about, and in the roadway rickshaws and motor-cars and gharries[6] gave a busy air to the 890 scene. Suddenly their car stopped and Chi Seng turned around.

"I think it more better if we walk here, sir," he said.

6. Horse-drawn cabs.

They got out and he went on. They followed a step or two behind. Then he asked them to stop.

"You wait here, sir. I go in and speak to my fliend."

He went into a shop, open to the street, where three or four Chinese were standing behind the counter. It was one of those strange shops where nothing was on view and you wondered what it was they sold there. They saw him address a stout man in a duck suit with a large gold chain across his breast and the man shot a quick glance out into the night. He gave Chi Seng a key and Chi Seng came out. 900 He beckoned to the two men waiting and slid into a doorway at the side of the shop. They followed him and found themselves at the foot of a flight of stairs.

"If you wait a minute I will light a match," he said, always resourceful. "You come upstairs, please."

He held a Japanese match in front of them, but it scarcely dispelled the darkness and they groped their way up behind him. On the first floor he unlocked a door and going in lit a gas-jet.

"Come in, please," he said.

It was a small square room, with one window, and the only furniture consisted of two low Chinese beds covered with matting. In one corner was a large 910 chest, with an elaborate lock and on this stood a shabby tray with an opium pipe on it and a lamp. There was in the room the faint, acrid scent of the drug. They sat down and Ong Chi Seng offered them cigarettes. In a moment the door was opened by the fat Chinaman whom they had seen behind the counter. He bade them good evening in very good English and sat down by the side of his fellow-countryman.

"The Chinese woman is just coming," said Chi Seng.

A boy from the shop brought in a tray with a tea-pot and cups and the Chinaman offered them a cup of tea. Crosbie refused. The Chinese talked to one another in undertones, but Crosbie and Mr. Joyce were silent. At last there was the 920 sound of a voice outside; some one was calling in a low tone; and the Chinaman went to the door. He opened it, spoke a few words, and ushered a woman in. Mr. Joyce looked at her. He had heard much about her since Hammond's death, but he had never seen her. She was a stoutish person, not very young, with a broad, phlegmatic face. She was powdered and rouged and her eyebrows were a thin black line, but she gave you the impression of a woman of character. She wore a pale blue jacket and a white skirt, her costume was not quite European nor quite Chinese, but on her feet were little Chinese silk slippers. She wore heavy gold chains round her neck, gold bangles on her wrists, gold ear-rings and elaborate gold pins in her black hair. She walked in slowly, with the air of a woman sure of 930 herself, but with a certain heaviness of tread, and sat down on the bed beside Ong Chi Seng. He said something to her and nodding she gave an incurious glance at the two white men.

"Has she got the letter?" asked Mr. Joyce.

"Yes, sir."

Crosbie said nothing, but produced a roll of five-hundred-dollar notes. He counted out twenty and handed them to Chi Seng.

"Will you see if that is correct?"

The clerk counted them and gave them to the fat Chinaman.

"Quite correct, sir." 940

The Chinaman counted them once more and put them in his pocket. He spoke again to the woman and she drew from her bosom a letter. She gave it to Chi Seng who cast his eyes over it.

"This is the right document, sir," he said, and was about to give it to Mr. Joyce when Crosbie took it from him.

"Let me look at it," he said.

Mr. Joyce watched him read and then held out his hand for it.

"You'd better let me have it."

Crosbie folded it up deliberately and put it in his pocket.

"No, I'm going to keep it myself. It's cost me enough money." 950

Mr. Joyce made no rejoinder. The three Chinese watched the little passage, but what they thought about it, or whether they thought, it was impossible to tell from their impassive countenances. Mr. Joyce rose to his feet.

"Do you want me any more to-night, sir?" said Ong Chi Seng.

"No." He knew the clerk wished to stay behind in order to get his agreed share of the money, and he turned to Crosbie. "Are you ready?"

Crosbie did not answer, but stood up. The Chinaman went to the door and opened it for them. Chi Seng found a bit of candle and lit it in order to light them down, and the two Chinese accompanied them to the street. They left the woman sitting quietly on the bed smoking a cigarette. When they reached the street the 960 Chinese left them and went once more upstairs.

"What are you going to do with that letter?" asked Mr. Joyce.

"Keep it."

They walked to where the car was waiting for them and here Mr. Joyce offered his friend a lift. Crosbie shook his head.

"I'm going to walk." He hesitated a little and shuffled his feet. "I went to Singapore on the night of Hammond's death partly to buy a new gun that a man I knew wanted to dispose of. Good-night."

He disappeared quickly into the darkness.

Mr. Joyce was quite right about the trial. The assessors went into court fully 970 determined to acquit Mrs. Crosbie. She gave evidence on her own behalf. She told her story simply and with straightforwardness. The D.P.P. was a kindly man and it was plain that he took no great pleasure in his task. He asked the necessary questions in a deprecating manner. His speech for the prosecution might really have been a speech for the defence, and the assessors took less than five minutes to consider their popular verdict. It was impossible to prevent the great outburst of applause with which it was received by the crowd that packed the court-house. The judge congratulated Mrs. Crosbie and she was a free woman.

No one had expressed a more violent disapprobation of Hammond's behaviour than Mrs. Joyce; she was a woman loyal to her friends and she had insisted 980 on the Crosbies staying with her after the trial, for she in common with every one else had no doubt of the result, till they could make arrangements to go away. It was out of the question for poor, dear, brave Leslie to return to the bungalow at which the horrible catastrophe had taken place. The trial was over by half-past twelve and when they reached the Joyces' house a grand luncheon was awaiting them. Cocktails were ready, Mrs. Joyce's million-dollar cocktail was celebrated through all the Malay States, and Mrs. Joyce drank Leslie's health. She was a talkative, vivacious woman, and now she was in the highest spirits. It was fortunate, for the rest of them were silent. She did not wonder, her husband never had much to say, and the other two were naturally exhausted from the long strain to which they had been subjected. During luncheon she carried on a bright and spirited monologue. Then coffee was served.

"Now, children," she said in her gay, bustling fashion, "you must have a rest and after tea I shall take you both for a drive to the sea."

Mr. Joyce, who lunched at home only by exception, had of course to go back to his office.

"I'm afraid I can't do that, Mrs. Joyce," said Crosbie. "I've got to get back to the estate at once."

"Not to-day?" she cried.

"Yes, now. I've neglected it for too long and I have urgent business. But I shall be very grateful if you will keep Leslie until we have decided what to do."

Mrs. Joyce was about to expostulate, but her husband prevented her.

"If he must go, he must, and there's an end of it."

There was something in the lawyer's tone which made her look at him quickly. She held her tongue and there was a moment's silence. Then Crosbie spoke again.

"If you'll forgive me, I'll start at once so that I can get there before dark." He rose from the table. "Will you come and see me off, Leslie?"

"Of course."

They went out of the dining-room together.

"I think that's rather inconsiderate of him," said Mrs. Joyce. "He must know that Leslie wants to be with him just now."

"I'm sure he wouldn't go if it wasn't absolutely necessary."

"Well, I'll just see that Leslie's room is ready for her. She wants a complete rest, of course, and then amusement."

Mrs. Joyce left the room and Joyce sat down again. In a short time he heard Crosbie start the engine of his motor-cycle and then noisily scrunch over the gravel of the garden path. He got up and went into the drawing-room. Mrs. Crosbie was standing in the middle of it, looking into space, and in her hand was an open letter. He recognized it. She gave him a glance as he came in and he saw that she was deathly pale.

"He knows," she whispered.

Mr. Joyce went up to her and took the letter from her hand. He lit a match and set the paper afire. She watched it burn. When he could hold it no longer he dropped it on the tiled floor and they both looked at the paper curl and blacken. Then he trod it into ashes with his foot.

"What does he know?"

She gave him a long, long stare and into her eyes came a strange look. Was it contempt or despair? Mr. Joyce could not tell.

"He knows that Geoff was my lover."

Mr. Joyce made no movement and uttered no sound.

"He'd been my lover for years. He became my lover almost immediately after he came back from the war. We knew how careful we must be. When we became lovers I pretended I was tired of him, and he seldom came to the house when Robert was there. I used to drive out to a place we knew and he met me, two or three times a week, and when Robert went to Singapore he used to come to the bungalow late, when the boys had gone for the night. We saw one another constantly, all the time, and not a soul had the smallest suspicion of it. And then lately, a year ago, he began to change. I didn't know what was the matter. I couldn't believe that he didn't care for me any more. He always denied it. I was frantic. I 1040 made him scenes. Sometimes I thought he hated me. Oh, if you knew what agonies I endured. I passed through hell. I knew he didn't want me any more and I wouldn't let him go. Misery! Misery! I loved him. I'd given him everything. He was all my life. And then I heard he was living with a Chinese woman. I couldn't believe it. I wouldn't believe it. At last I saw her, I saw her with my own eyes, walking in the village, with her gold bracelets and her necklaces, an old, fat, Chinese woman. She was older than I was. Horrible! They all knew in the kampong that she was his mistress. And when I passed her, she looked at me and I knew that she knew I was his mistress too. I sent for him. I told him I must see him. You've read the letter. I was mad to write it. I didn't know what I was doing. I didn't care. 1050 I hadn't seen him for ten days. It was a lifetime. And when last we'd parted he took me in his arms and kissed me and told me not to worry. And he went straight from my arms to hers."

She had been speaking in a low voice, vehemently, and now she stopped and wrung her hands.

"That damned letter. We'd always been so careful. He always tore up any word I wrote to him the moment he'd read it. How was I to know he'd leave that one? He came and I told him I knew about the Chinawoman. He denied it. He said it was only scandal. I was beside myself. I don't know what I said to him. Oh, I hated him then. I tore him limb from limb. I said everything I could to wound him. 1060 I insulted him. I could have spat in his face. And at last he turned on me. He told me he was sick and tired of me and never wanted to see me again. He said I bored him to death. And then he acknowledged that it was true about the Chinawoman. He said he'd known her for years, before the war, and she was the only woman who really meant anything to him, and the rest was just pastime. And he said he was glad I knew, and now at last I'd leave him alone. And then I don't know what happened, I was beside myself, I saw red. I seized the revolver and I fired. He gave a cry and I saw I'd hit him. He staggered and rushed for the verandah. I ran after him and fired again. He fell, and then I stood over him and I fired and fired till the revolver went click, click, and I knew there were no more cartridges." 1070

At last she stopped, panting. Her face was no longer human, it was distorted with cruelty, and rage and pain. You would never have thought that this quiet, refined woman was capable of such a fiendish passion. Mr. Joyce took a step backwards. He was absolutely aghast at the sight of her. It was not a face, it was a gibbering, hideous mask. Then they heard a voice calling from another room, a loud, friendly, cheerful voice. It was Mrs. Joyce.

"Come along, Leslie darling, your room's ready. You must be dropping with sleep."

Mrs. Crosbie's features gradually composed themselves. Those passions, so clearly delineated, were smoothed away as with your hand you would smooth a 1080 crumpled paper, and in a minute the face was cool and calm and unlined. She was a trifle pale, but her lips broke into a pleasant, affable smile. She was once more the well-bred and even distinguished woman.

"I'm coming, Dorothy dear. I'm sorry to give you so much trouble." [1926]

Questions for Discussion and Writing

1. Is this a detective story? If so, in what ways? If not, why not?
2. Is the ending a surprise or a logical conclusion to what has gone before? What are the relevant clues? Are they sufficient to foresee the ending?
3. What social criticisms and comments does the story make?
4. What is the narrator's attitude toward Mrs. Crosbie? Does it suggest a prejudice against women? Explain.
5. What is the narrator's attitude toward the Chinese? Does it suggest racism? Explain.

☜ F. SCOTT FITZGERALD
(1896–1940)

Babylon Revisited

Francis Scott Key Fitzgerald lived a life as fabulous and tragic as that of his doomed heroes. In only forty-four years, he made and squandered several fortunes, rose to the heights of literary creativity, and descended to the depths of a for-hire hack. Especially as a short story writer, he walked the thin line between commercialism and art, producing stories that are sometimes merely conventional but that occasionally transcend the magazine formulas and show true genius.

He was born in St. Paul, Minnesota, to prosperous parents. Even as a young man, he imitated rich and beautiful people, first at an Eastern prep school and then at Princeton University. He joined the army during World War I, writing and revising his first novel, *This Side of Paradise,* on weekends. When Scribner's accepted it in 1919, he was able to marry socialite Zelda Sayre. They flourished in the 1920s, a prosperous era in American history, when postwar confidence and optimism combined with a rising standard of living from industrialization. Known as the Jazz Age or the Roaring Twenties, this era was the heyday of American magazines, especially the *Saturday Evening Post.* The *Post* and Fitzgerald became almost synonymous, as he contributed dozens of stories to its pages for fees as high as $4,000 (today, $36,000) each. While Fitzgerald's writing for the *Post* has sometimes led critics to brand him as a popularizer, his most fertile period was 1925–1933, when he was most closely associated with that magazine. Short stories were a way for him to try out themes and techniques that later appeared in his novels, *The Great Gatsby* (1925) and *Tender is the Night* (1934).

"Babylon Revisited" is probably Fitzgerald's most famous story and is certainly one of his most effective. Written after the stock market crash of 1929, when the vogue of success stories had fallen into disfavor, it questions the very values those stories had extolled: fabulous wealth, marriage to a beautiful woman, and life in the "fast lane." Behind the story also lies the ghost of Puritanism. Charlie Wales's difficulties seem quintessentially American, and just as Fitzgerald had chronicled the excesses of the Jazz Age, he also documented the dissipation of that era and the fundamental moral and spiritual conflicts that have long been a part of the American experience.

I

"AND WHERE'S MR. CAMPBELL?" Charlie asked.

"Gone to Switzerland. Mr. Campbell's a pretty sick man, Mr. Wales."

"I'm sorry to hear that. And George Hardt?" Charlie inquired.

"Back in America, gone to work."

"And where is the Snow Bird?"

"He was in here last week. Anyway, his friend, Mr. Schaeffer, is in Paris."

Two familiar names from the long list of a year and a half ago. Charlie scribbled an address in his notebook and tore out the page.

"If you see Mr. Schaeffer, give him this," he said. "It's my brother-in-law's address. I haven't settled on a hotel yet."   10

He was not really disappointed to find Paris was so empty. But the stillness in the Ritz bar was strange and portentous. It was not an American bar any more— he felt polite in it, and not as if he owned it. It had gone back into France. He felt the stillness from the moment he got out of the taxi and saw the doorman, usually in a frenzy of activity at this hour, gossiping with a *chasseur*[1] by the servants' entrance.

Passing through the corridor, he heard only a single, bored voice in the once-clamorous women's room. When he turned into the bar he traveled the twenty feet of green carpet with his eyes fixed straight ahead by old habit; and then, with his foot firmly on the rail, he turned and surveyed the room, encountering only a single pair of eyes that fluttered up from a newspaper in the corner.   20 Charlie asked for the head barman, Paul, who in the latter days of the bull market had come to work in his own custom-built car—disembarking, however, with due nicety at the nearest corner. But Paul was at his country house today and Alix giving him information.

"No, no more," Charlie said, "I'm going slow these days."

Alix congratulated him: "You were going pretty strong a couple of years ago."

"I'll stick to it all right," Charlie assured him. "I've stuck to it for over a year and a half now."

"How do you find conditions in America?"

"I haven't been to America for months. I'm in business in Prague, represent- 30 ing a couple of concerns there. They don't know about me down there."

1. Porter.

Alix smiled.

"Remember the night of George Hardt's bachelor dinner here?" said Charlie. "By the way, what's become of Claude Fessenden?"

Alix lowered his voice confidentially: "He's in Paris, but he doesn't come here any more. Paul doesn't allow it. He ran up a bill of thirty thousand francs, charging all his drinks and his lunches, and usually his dinner, for more than a year. And when Paul finally told him he had to pay, he gave him a bad check."

Alix shook his head sadly.

"I don't understand it, such a dandy fellow. Now he's all bloated up—" He 40 made a plump apple of his hands.

Charlie watched a group of strident queens installing themselves in a corner.

"Nothing affects them," he thought. "Stocks rise and fall, people loaf or work, but they go on forever." The place oppressed him. He called for the dice and shook with Alix for the drink.

"Here for long, Mr. Wales?"

"I'm here for four or five days to see my little girl."

"Oh-h! You have a little girl?"

Outside, the fire-red, gas-blue, ghost-green signs shone smokily through the tranquil rain. It was late afternoon and the streets were in movement; the bistros 50 gleamed. At the corner of the Boulevard des Capucines he took a taxi. The Place de la Concorde moved by in pink majesty; they crossed the logical Seine, and Charlie felt the sudden provincial quality of the Left Bank.

Charlie directed his taxi to the Avenue de l'Opéra, which was out of his way. But he wanted to see the blue hour spread over the magnificent façade, and imagine that the cab horns, playing endlessly the first few bars of *Le Plus que Lent*, were the trumpets of the Second Empire.[2] They were closing the iron grill in front of Brentano's Bookstore, and people were already at dinner behind the trim little bourgeois hedge of Duval's. He had never eaten at a really cheap restaurant in Paris. Five-course dinner, four francs fifty, eighteen cents, wine included. For some 60 odd reason he wished that he had.

As they rolled on to the Left Bank, and he felt its sudden provincialism, he thought, "I spoiled this city for myself. I didn't realize it, but the days came along one after another, and then two years were gone, and everything was gone, and I was gone."

He was thirty-five, and good to look at. The Irish mobility of his face was sobered by a deep wrinkle between his eyes. As he rang his brother-in-law's bell in the Rue Palatine, the wrinkle deepened till it pulled down his brows; he felt a cramping sensation in his belly. From behind the maid who opened the door darted a lovely little girl of nine who shrieked "Daddy!" and flew up, struggling 70 like a fish, into his arms. She pulled his head around by one ear and set her cheek against his.

"My old pie," he said.

"Oh, daddy, daddy, daddy, daddy, dads, dads, dads!"

She drew him into the salon, where the family waited, a boy and a girl his

2. Second Empire 1852–1870, under Napoleon III.

daughter's age, his sister-in-law and her husband. He greeted Marion with his voice pitched carefully to avoid either feigned enthusiasm or dislike, but her response was more frankly tepid, though she minimized her expression of unalterable distrust by directing her regard toward his child. The two men clasped hands in a friendly way and Lincoln Peters rested his for a moment on Charlie's shoulder.   80

The room was warm and comfortably American. The three children moved intimately about, playing through the yellow oblongs that led to other rooms; the cheer of six o'clock spoke in the eager smacks of the fire and the sounds of French activity in the kitchen. But Charlie did not relax; his heart sat up rigidly in his body and he drew confidence from his daughter, who from time to time came close to him, holding in his arms the doll he had brought.

"Really extremely well," he declared in answer to Lincoln's question. "There's a lot of business there that isn't moving at all, but we're doing even better than ever. In fact, damn well. I'm bringing my sister over from America next month to keep house for me. My income last year was bigger than it was when I had money.   90 You see, the Czechs—"

His boasting was for a specific purpose; but after a moment, seeing a faint restiveness in Lincoln's eye, he changed the subject:

"Those are fine children of yours, well brought up, good manners."

"We think Honoria's a great little girl too."

Marion Peters came back from the kitchen. She was a tall woman with worried eyes, who had once possessed a fresh American loveliness. Charlie had never been sensitive to it and was always surprised when people spoke of how pretty she had been. From the first there had been an instinctive antipathy between them.

"Well, how do you find Honoria?" she asked.   100

"Wonderful. I was astonished how much she's grown in ten months. All the children are looking well."

"We haven't had a doctor for a year. How do you like being back in Paris?"

"It seems very funny to see so few Americans around."

"I'm delighted," Marion said vehemently. "Now at least you can go into a store without their assuming you're a millionaire. We've suffered like everybody, but on the whole it's a good deal pleasanter."

"But it was nice while it lasted," Charlie said. "We were a sort of royalty, almost infallible, with a sort of magic around us. In the bar this afternoon"—he stumbled, seeing his mistake—"there wasn't a man I knew."   110

She looked at him keenly. "I should think you'd have had enough of bars."

"I only stayed a minute. I take one drink every afternoon, and no more."

"Don't you want a cocktail before dinner?" Lincoln asked.

"I take only one drink every afternoon, and I've had that."

"I hope you keep to it," said Marion.

Her dislike was evident in the coldness with which she spoke, but Charlie only smiled; he had larger plans. Her very aggressiveness gave him an advantage, and he knew enough to wait. He wanted them to initiate the discussion of what they knew had brought him to Paris.

At dinner he couldn't decide whether Honoria was most like him or her   120 mother. Fortunate if she didn't combine the traits of both that had brought them to disaster. A great wave of protectiveness went over him. He thought he knew what to do for her. He believed in character; he wanted to jump back a whole generation and trust in character again as the eternally valuable element. Everything else wore out.

He left soon after dinner, but not to go home. He was curious to see Paris by night with clearer and more judicious eyes than those of other days. He bought a *strapontin*[3] for the Casino and watched Josephine Baker[4] go through her chocolate arabesques.

After an hour he left and strolled toward Montmartre, up the Rue Pigalle into 130 the Place Blanche. The rain had stopped and there were a few people in evening clothes disembarking from taxis in front of cabarets, and *cocottes*[5] prowling singly or in pairs, and many Negroes. He passed a lighted door from which issued music, and stopped with the sense of familiarity; it was Bricktop's, where he had parted with so many hours and so much money. A few doors farther on he found another ancient rendezvous and incautiously put his head inside. Immediately an eager orchestra burst into sound, a pair of professional dancers leaped to their feet and a maitre d'hôtel swooped toward him, crying, "Crowd just arriving, sir!" But he withdrew quickly.

"You have to be damn drunk," he thought. 140

Zelli's was closed, the bleak and sinister cheap hotels surrounding it were dark; up in the Rue Blanche there was more light and a local, colloquial French crowd. The Poet's Cave had disappeared, but the two great mouths of the Café of Heaven and the Café of Hell still yawned—even devoured, as he watched, the meager contents of a tourist bus—a German, a Japanese, and an American couple who glanced at him with frightened eyes.

So much for the effort and ingenuity of Montmartre. All the catering to vice and waste was on an utterly childish scale, and he suddenly realized the meaning of the word "dissipate"—to dissipate into thin air; to make nothing out of something. In the little hours of the night every move from place to place was an enor- 150 mous human jump, an increase of paying for the privilege of slower and slower motion.

He remembered thousand-franc notes given to an orchestra for playing a single number, hundred-franc notes tossed to a doorman for calling a cab.

But it hadn't been given for nothing.

It had been given, even the most wildly squandered sum, as an offering to destiny that he might not remember the things most worth remembering, the things that now he would always remember—his child taken from his control, his wife escaped to a grave in Vermont.

In the glare of a *brasserie*[6] a woman spoke to him. He bought her some eggs 160 and coffee, and then, eluding her encouraging stare, gave her a twenty-franc note and took a taxi to his hotel.

3. Folding chair.
4. African-American dancer (1906–1975), very popular in Paris in the 1920s and 1930s.
5. Prostitutes.
6. Bar and grill.

II

He woke upon a fine fall day—football weather. The depression of yesterday was gone and he liked the people on the streets. At noon he sat opposite Honoria at Le Grand Vatel, the only restaurant he could think of not reminiscent of champagne dinners and long luncheons that began at two and ended in a blurred and vague twilight.

"Now, how about vegetables? Oughtn't you to have some vegetables?"

"Well, yes."

"Here's *épinards* and *chou-fleur* and carrots and *haricots*."[7]   170

"I'd like *chou-fleur.*"

"Wouldn't you like to have two vegetables?"

"I usually only have one at lunch."

The waiter was pretending to be inordinately fond of children. *"Qu'elle est mignonne la petite! Elle parle exactement comme une française."*[8]

"How about dessert? Shall we wait and see?"

The waiter disappeared. Honoria looked at her father expectantly.

"What are we going to do?"

"First, we're going to that toy store in the Rue Saint-Honoré and buy you anything you like. And then we're going to the vaudeville at the Empire."   180

She hesitated. "I like it about the vaudeville, but not the toy store."

"Why not?"

"Well, you brought me this doll." She had it with her. "And I've got lots of things. And we're not rich any more, are we?"

"We never were. But today you are to have anything you want."

"All right," she agreed resignedly.

When there had been her mother and a French nurse he had been inclined to be strict; now he extended himself, reached out for a new tolerance; he must be both parents to her and not shut any of her out of communication.

"I want to get to know you," he said gravely. "First let me introduce myself. 190 My name is Charles J. Wales, of Prague."

"Oh, daddy!" her voice cracked with laughter.

"And who are you, please?" he persisted, and she accepted a role immediately: "Honoria Wales, Rue Palatine, Paris."

"Married or single?"

"No, not married. Single."

He indicated the doll. "But I see you have a child, madame."

Unwilling to disinherit it, she took it to her heart and thought quickly: "Yes, I've been married, but I'm not married now. My husband is dead."

He went on quickly, "And the child's name?"   200

"Simone. That's after my best friend at school."

"I'm very pleased that you're doing so well at school."

"I'm third this month," she boasted. "Elsie"—that was her cousin—"is only about eighteenth, and Richard is about at the bottom."

---

7. Spinach, cauliflower, green beans.
8. "The little one is so sweet. She speaks exactly like a little French girl."

"You like Richard and Elsie, don't you?"

"Oh, yes. I like Richard quite well and I like her all right."

Cautiously and casually he asked: "And Aunt Marion and Uncle Lincoln— which do you like best?"

"Oh, Uncle Lincoln, I guess."

He was increasingly aware of her presence. As they came in, a murmur of "... adorable" followed them, and now the people at the next table bent all their silences upon her, staring as if she were something no more conscious than a flower.

"Why don't I live with you?" she asked suddenly. "Because mamma's dead?"

"You must stay here and learn more French. It would have been hard for daddy to take care of you so well."

"I don't really need much taking care of any more. I do everything for myself."

Going out of the restaurant, a man and a woman unexpectedly hailed him. "Well, the old Wales!"

"Hello there, Lorraine. . . . Dunc."

Sudden ghosts out of the past: Duncan Schaeffer, a friend from college. Lorraine Quarrles, a lovely, pale blonde of thirty; one of a crowd who had helped him make months into days in the lavish times of three years ago.

"My husband couldn't come this year," she said, in answer to his question. "We're poor as hell. So he gave me two hundred a month and told me I could do my worst on that. . . . This your little girl?"

"What about coming back and sitting down?" Duncan asked.

"Can't do it." He was glad for an excuse. As always, he felt Lorraine's passionate, provocative attraction, but his own rhythm was different now.

"Well, how about dinner?" she asked.

"I'm not free. Give me your address and let me call you."

"Charlie, I believe you're sober," she said judicially. "I honestly believe he's sober, Dunc. Pinch him and see if he's sober."

Charlie indicated Honoria with his head. They both laughed.

"What's your address?" said Duncan skeptically.

He hesitated, unwilling to give the name of his hotel.

"I'm not settled yet. I'd better call you. We're going to see the vaudeville at the Empire."

"There! That's what I want to do," Lorraine said. "I want to see some clowns and acrobats and jugglers. That's just what we'll do, Dunc."

"We've got to do an errand first," said Charlie. "Perhaps we'll see you there."

"All right, you snob. . . . Good-by, beautiful little girl."

"Good-by."

Honoria bobbed politely.

Somehow, an unwelcome encounter. They liked him because he was functioning, because he was serious; they wanted to see him, because he was stronger than they were now, because they wanted to draw a certain sustenance from his strength.

At the Empire, Honoria proudly refused to sit upon her father's folded coat. She was already an individual with a code of her own, and Charlie was more and more absorbed by the desire of putting a little of himself into her before she crystallized utterly. It was hopeless to try to know her in so short a time.

Between the acts they came upon Duncan and Lorraine in the lobby where the band was playing.

"Have a drink?"

"All right, but not up at the bar. We'll take a table."

"The perfect father."

Listening abstractedly to Lorraine, Charlie watched Honoria's eyes leave their table, and he followed them wistfully about the room, wondering what they saw. He met her glance and she smiled.

"I liked that lemonade," she said.

What had she said? What had he expected? Going home in a taxi afterward, he pulled her over until her head rested against his chest.

"Darling, do you ever think about your mother?"

"Yes, sometimes," she answered vaguely.

"I don't want you to forget her. Have you got a picture of her?"

"Yes, I think so. Anyhow, Aunt Marion has. Why don't you want me to forget her?"

"She loved you very much."

"I loved her too."

They were silent for a moment.

"Daddy, I want to come and live with you," she said suddenly.

His heart leaped; he had wanted it to come like this.

"Aren't you perfectly happy?"

"Yes, but I love you better than anybody. And you love me better than anybody, don't you, now that mummy's dead?"

"Of course I do. But you won't always like me best, honey. You'll grow up and meet somebody your own age and go marry him and forget you ever had a daddy."

"Yes, that's true," she agreed tranquilly.

He didn't go in. He was coming back at nine o'clock and he wanted to keep himself fresh and new for the thing he must say then.

"When you're safe inside, just show yourself in that window."

"All right. Good-by, dads, dads, dads, dads."

He waited in the dark street until she appeared, all warm and glowing, in the window above and kissed her fingers out into the night.

III

They were waiting. Marion sat behind the coffee service in a dignified black dinner dress that just faintly suggested mourning. Lincoln was walking up and down with the animation of one who had already been talking. They were as anxious as he was to get into the question. He opened it almost immediately:

"I suppose you know what I want to see you about—why I really came to Paris."

Marion played with the black stars on her necklace and frowned.

"I'm awfully anxious to have a home," he continued. "And I'm awfully anxious to have Honoria in it. I appreciate your taking in Honoria for her mother's sake, but things have changed now"—he hesitated and then continued more forcibly—"changed radically with me, and I want to ask you to reconsider the matter. It would be silly for me to deny that about three years ago I was acting badly—"   300

Marion looked up at him with hard eyes.

"—but all that's over. As I told you, I haven't had more than a drink a day for over a year, and I take that drink deliberately, so that the idea of alcohol won't get too big in my imagination. You see the idea?"

"No," said Marion succinctly.

"It's a sort of stunt I set myself. It keeps the matter in proportion."

"I get you," said Lincoln. "You don't want to admit it's got any attraction for you."

"Something like that. Sometimes I forget and don't take it. But I try to take it. Anyhow, I couldn't afford to drink in my position. The people I represent are more   310 than satisfied with what I've done, and I'm bringing my sister over from Burlington to keep house for me, and I want awfully to have Honoria too. You know that even when her mother and I weren't getting along well we never let anything that happened touch Honoria. I know she's fond of me and I know I'm able to take care of her and—well, there you are. How do you feel about it?"

He knew that now he would have to take a beating. It would last an hour or two hours, and it would be difficult, but if he modulated his inevitable resentment to the chastened attitude of the reformed sinner, he might win his point in the end.

Keep your temper, he told himself. You don't want to be justified. You want   320 Honoria.

Lincoln spoke first: "We've been talking it over ever since we got your letter last month. We're happy to have Honoria here. She's a dear little thing, and we're glad to be able to help her, but of course that isn't the question—"

Marion interrupted suddenly. "How long are you going to stay sober, Charlie?" she asked.

"Permanently, I hope."

"How can anybody count on that?"

"You know I never did drink heavily until I gave up business and came over here with nothing to do. Then Helen and I began to run around with—"   330

"Please leave Helen out of it. I can't bear to hear you talk about her like that."

He stared at her grimly; he had never been certain how fond of each other the sisters were in life.

"My drinking only lasted about a year and a half—from the time we came over until I—collapsed."

"It was time enough."

"It was time enough," he agreed.

"My duty is entirely to Helen," she said. "I try to think what she would have wanted me to do. Frankly, from the night you did that terrible thing you haven't   340 really existed for me. I can't help that. She was my sister."

"Yes."

"When she was dying she asked me to look out for Honoria. If you hadn't been in a sanitarium then, it might have helped matters."

He had no answer.

"I'll never in my life be able to forget the morning when Helen knocked at my door, soaked to the skin and shivering, and said you'd locked her out."

Charlie gripped the sides of the chair. This was more difficult than he expected; he wanted to launch out into a long expostulation and explanation, but he only said: "The night I locked her out—" and she interrupted, "I don't feel up to 350 going over that again."

After a moment's silence Lincoln said: "We're getting off the subject. You want Marion to set aside her legal guardianship and give you Honoria. I think the main point for her is whether she has confidence in you or not."

"I don't blame Marion," Charlie said slowly, "but I think she can have entire confidence in me. I had a good record up to three years ago. Of course, it's within human possibilities I might go wrong any time. But if we wait much longer I'll lose Honoria's childhood and my chance for a home." He shook his head. "I'll simply lose her, don't you see?"

"Yes, I see," said Lincoln.   360

"Why didn't you think of all this before?" Marion asked.

"I suppose I did, from time to time, but Helen and I were getting along badly. When I consented to the guardianship, I was flat on my back in a sanitarium and the market had cleaned me out. I knew I'd acted badly, and I thought if it would bring any peace to Helen, I'd agree to anything. But now it's different. I'm functioning, I'm behaving damn well, so far as—"

"Please don't swear at me," Marion said.

He looked at her, startled. With each remark the force of her dislike became more and more apparent. She had built up all her fear of life into one wall and faced it toward him. This trivial reproof was possibly the result of some trouble 370 with the cook several hours before. Charlie became increasingly alarmed at leaving Honoria in this atmosphere of hostility against himself; sooner or later it would come out, in a word here, a shake of the head there, and some of that distrust would be irrevocably implanted in Honoria. But he pulled his temper down out of his face and shut it up inside him; he had won a point, for Lincoln realized the absurdity of Marion's remark and asked her lightly since when she had objected to the word "damn."

"Another thing," Charlie said: "I'm able to give her certain advantages now. I'm going to take a French governess to Prague with me. I've got a lease on a new apartment—"   380

He stopped, realizing that he was blundering. They couldn't be expected to accept with equanimity the fact that his income was again twice as large as their own.

"I suppose you can give her more luxuries than we can," said Marion. "When you were throwing away money we were living along watching every ten francs. . . . I suppose you'll start doing it again."

"Oh, no," he said. "I've learned. I worked hard for ten years, you know— until I got lucky in the market, like so many people. Terribly lucky. It won't happen again."

There was a long silence. All of them felt their nerves straining, and for the 390
first time in a year Charlie wanted a drink. He was sure now that Lincoln Peters
wanted him to have his child.

Marion shuddered suddenly; part of her saw that Charlie's feet were planted
on the earth now, and her own maternal feeling recognized the naturalness of his
desire; but she had lived for a long time with a prejudice—a prejudice founded on
a curious disbelief in her sister's happiness, which, in the shock of one terrible
night, had turned to hatred for him. It had all happened at a point in her life
where the discouragement of ill health and adverse circumstances made it necessary for her to believe in tangible villainy and a tangible villain.

"I can't help what I think!" she cried out suddenly. "How much you were re- 400
sponsible for Helen's death, I don't know. It's something you'll have to square with
your own conscience."

An electric current of agony surged through him; for a moment he was almost on his feet, an unuttered sound echoing in his throat. He hung on to himself
for a moment, another moment.

"Hold on there," said Lincoln uncomfortably. "I never thought you were responsible for that."

"Helen died of heart trouble," Charlie said dully.

"Yes, heart trouble." Marion spoke as if the phrase had another meaning for
her. Then, in the flatness that followed her outburst, she saw him plainly and she 410
knew he had somehow arrived at control over the situation. Glancing at her husband, she found no help from him, and as abruptly as if it were a matter of no importance, she threw up the sponge.

"Do what you like!" she cried, springing up from her chair. "She's your child.
I'm not the person to stand in your way. I think if it were my child I'd rather see
her—" She managed to check herself. "You two decide it. I can't stand this. I'm
sick. I'm going to bed."

She hurried from the room; after a moment Lincoln said:

"This has been a hard day for her. You know how strongly she feels—" His
voice was almost apologetic: "When a woman gets an idea in her head."   420

"Of course."

"It's going to be all right. I think she sees now that you—can provide for the
child, and so we can't very well stand in your way or Honoria's way."

"Thank you, Lincoln."

"I'd better go along and see how she is."

"I'm going."

He was still trembling when he reached the street, but a walk down the Rue
Bonaparte to the *quais*[9] set him up, and as he crossed the Seine, fresh and new by
the *quai* lamps, he felt exultant. But back in his room he couldn't sleep. The image
of Helen haunted him. Helen whom he had loved so until they had senselessly 430
begun to abuse each other's love, tear it into shreds. On that terrible February
night that Marion remembered so vividly, a slow quarrel had gone on for hours.
There was a scene at the Florida, and then he attempted to take her home, and
then she kissed young Webb at a table; after that there was what she had hysteri-

---

9. Docks.

cally said. When he arrived home alone he turned the key in the lock in wild anger. How could he know she would arrive an hour later alone, that there would be a snow storm in which she wandered about in slippers, too confused to find a taxi? Then the aftermath, her escaping pneumonia by a miracle, and all the attendant horror. They were "reconciled," but that was the beginning of the end, and Marion, who had seen with her own eyes and who imagined it to be one of many scenes from her sister's martyrdom, never forgot. 440

Going over it again brought Helen nearer, and in the white, soft light that steals upon half sleep near morning he found himself talking to her again. She said that he was perfectly right about Honoria and that she wanted Honoria to be with him. She said she was glad he was being good and doing better. She said a lot of other things—very friendly things—but she was in a swing in a white dress, and swinging faster and faster all the time, so that at the end he could not hear clearly all that she said.

IV

He woke up feeling happy. The door of the world was open again. He made plans, vistas, futures for Honoria and himself, but suddenly he grew sad, remembering all the plans he and Helen had made. She had not planned to die. The present was the thing—work to do and someone to love. But not to love too much, for he knew the injury that a father can do to a daughter or a mother to a son by attaching them too closely: afterward, out in the world, the child would seek in the marriage partner the same blind tenderness and, failing probably to find it, turn against love and life. 450

It was another bright, crisp day. He called Lincoln Peters at the bank where he worked and asked if he could count on taking Honoria when he left for Prague. Lincoln agreed that there was no reason for delay. One thing—the legal guardianship. Marion wanted to retain that awhile longer. She was upset by the whole matter, and it would oil things if she felt that the situation was still in her control for another year. Charlie agreed, wanting only the tangible, visible child. 460

Then the question of a governess. Charlie sat in a gloomy agency and talked to a cross Béarnaise and to a buxom Breton peasant, neither of whom he could have endured. There were others whom he would see tomorrow.

He lunched with Lincoln Peters at Griffons, trying to keep down his exultation.

"There's nothing quite like your own child," Lincoln said. "But you understand how Marion feels too."

"She's forgotten how hard I worked for seven years there," Charlie said. "She just remembers one night." 470

"There's another thing," Lincoln hesitated. "While you and Helen were tearing around Europe throwing money away, we were just getting along. I didn't touch any of the prosperity because I never got ahead enough to carry anything but my insurance. I think Marion felt there was some kind of injustice in it—you not even working toward the end, and getting richer and richer."

"It went just as quick as it came," said Charlie.

"Yes, a lot of it stayed in the hands of *chasseurs* and saxaphone players and

maitres d'hôtel—well, the big party's over now. I just said that to explain Marion's
feeling about those crazy years. If you drop in about six o'clock tonight before   480
Marion's too tired, we'll settle the details on the spot."

Back at his hotel, Charlie found a *pneumatique*[10] that had been redirected
from the Ritz bar, where Charlie had left his address for the purpose of a certain
man.

> Dear Charlie:
> You were so strange when we saw you the other day that I wondered if I
> did something to offend you. If so, I'm not conscious of it. In fact, I have
> thought about you too much for the last year, and it's always been in the back
> of my mind that I might see you if I came over here. We *did* have such good
> times that crazy spring, like the night you and I stole the butcher's tricycle, and   490
> the time we tried to call on the president and you had the old derby rim and
> the wire cane. Everybody seems so old lately, but I don't feel old a bit. Couldn't
> we get together some time today for old time's sake? I've got a vile hangover for
> the moment, but will be feeling better this afternoon and will look for you
> about five in the sweatshop at the Ritz.
>
> > Always devotedly,
> > Lorraine

His first feeling was one of awe that he had actually, in his mature years,
stolen a tricycle and pedaled Lorraine all over the Étoile[11] between the small hours
and dawn. In retrospect it was a nightmare. Locking out Helen didn't fit in with   500
any other act of his life, but the tricycle incident did—it was one of many. How
many weeks or months of dissipation to arrive at that condition of utter irrespon-
sibility?

He tried to picture how Lorraine had appeared to him then—very attractive;
Helen was unhappy about it, though she said nothing. Yesterday, in the restaurant,
Lorraine had seemed trite, blurred, worn away. He emphatically did not want to
see her, and he was glad Alix had not given away his hotel address. It was a relief
to think, instead, of Honoria, to think of Sundays spent with her and of saying
good morning to her and knowing she was there in his house at night, drawing
her breath in the darkness.   510

At five he took a taxi and bought presents for all the Peterses—a piquant
cloth doll, a box of Roman soldiers, flowers for Marion, big linen handkerchiefs
for Lincoln.

He saw, when he arrived in the apartment, that Marion had accepted the inevitable. She greeted him now as though he were a recalcitrant member of the
family, rather than a menacing outsider. Honoria had been told she was going;
Charlie was glad to see that her tact made her conceal her excessive happiness.
Only on his lap did she whisper her delight and the question "When?" before she
slipped away with the other children.

He and Marion were alone for a minute in the room, and on an impulse he   520
spoke out boldly:

10. A message sent by pneumatic tube.
11. A district in Paris.

"Family quarrels are bitter things. They don't go according to any rules. They're not like aches or wounds; they're more like splits in the skin that won't heal because there's not enough material. I wish you and I could be on better terms."

"Some things are hard to forget," she answered. "It's a question of confidence." There was no answer to this and presently she asked, "When do you propose to take her?"

"As soon as I can get a governess. I hoped the day after tomorrow."

"That's impossible. I've got to get her things in shape. Not before Saturday."   530

He yielded. Coming back into the room, Lincoln offered him a drink.

"I'll take my daily whisky," he said.

It was warm here, it was a home, people together by a fire. The children felt very safe and important; the mother and father were serious, watchful. They had things to do for the children more important than his visit here. A spoonful of medicine was, after all, more important than the strained relations between Marion and himself. They were not dull people, but they were very much in the grip of life and circumstances. He wondered if he couldn't do something to get Lincoln out of his rut at the bank.

A long peal at the doorbell; the *bonne à tout faire*[12] passed through and went   540 down the corridor. The door opened upon another long ring, and then voices, and the three in the salon looked up expectantly; Richard moved to bring the corridor within his range of vision, and Marion rose. Then the maid came back along the corridor, closely followed by the voices, which developed under the light into Duncan Schaeffer and Lorraine Quarrles.

They were gay, they were hilarious, they were roaring with laughter. For a moment Charlie was astounded; unable to understand how they ferreted out the Peterses' address.

"Ah-h-h!" Duncan wagged his finger roguishly at Charlie, "Ah-h-h!"

They both slid down another cascade of laughter. Anxious and at a loss,   550 Charlie shook hands with them quickly and presented them to Lincoln and Marion. Marion nodded, scarcely speaking. She had drawn back a step toward the fire; her little girl stood beside her, and Marion put an arm about her shoulder.

With growing annoyance at the intrusion, Charlie waited for them to explain themselves. After some concentration Duncan said:

"We came to invite you out to dinner. Lorraine and I insist that all this shishi, cagy business 'bout your address got to stop."

Charlie came closer to them, as if to force them backward down the corridor.

"Sorry, but I can't. Tell me where you'll be and I'll phone you in half an hour."   560

This made no impression. Lorraine sat down suddenly on the side of a chair, and focusing her eyes on Richard, cried, "Oh, what a nice little boy! Come here, little boy." Richard glanced at his mother, but did not move. With a perceptible shrug of her shoulder, Lorraine turned back to Charlie:

12. Maid of all work.

"Come and dine. Sure your cousins won' mine. See you so sel'om. Or solemn."

"I can't," said Charlie sharply. "You two have dinner and I'll phone you."

Her voice became suddenly unpleasant. "All right, we'll go. But I remember once when you hammered on my door at four A.M. I was enough of a good sport to give you a drink. Come on, Dunc."

Still in slow motion, with blurred, angry faces, with uncertain feet, they retired along the corridor.

"Good night," Charlie said.

"Good night!" responded Lorraine emphatically.

When he went back into the salon Marion had not moved, only now her son was standing in the circle of her other arm. Lincoln was still swinging Honoria back and forth like a pendulum from side to side.

"What an outrage!" Charlie broke out. "What an absolute outrage!"

Neither of them answered. Charlie dropped into an armchair, picked up his drink, set it down again and said:

"People I haven't seen for two years having the colossal nerve—"

He broke off. Marion had made the sound "Oh!" in one swift, furious breath, turned her body from him with a jerk and left the room.

Lincoln set down Honoria carefully.

"You children go in and start your soup," he said, and when they obeyed, he said to Charlie:

"Marion's not well and she can't stand shocks. That kind of people make her really physically sick."

"I didn't tell them to come here. They wormed your name out of somebody. They deliberately—"

"Well, it's too bad. It doesn't help matters. Excuse me a minute."

Left alone, Charlie sat tense in his chair. In the next room he could hear the children eating, talking in monosyllables, already oblivious to the scene between their elders. He heard a murmur of conversation from a farther room and then the ticking bell of a telephone receiver picked up, and in a panic he moved to the other side of the room and out of earshot.

In a minute Lincoln came back. "Look here, Charlie. I think we'd better call off dinner for tonight. Marion's in bad shape."

"Is she angry with me?"

"Sort of," he said, almost roughly. "She's not strong and—"

"You mean she's changed her mind about Honoria?"

"She's pretty bitter right now. I don't know. You phone me at the bank tomorrow."

"I wish you'd explain to her I never dreamed these people would come here. I'm just as sore as you are."

"I couldn't explain anything to her now."

Charlie got up. He took his coat and hat and started down the corridor. Then he opened the door of the dining room and said in a strange voice, "Good night, children."

Honoria rose and ran around the table to hug him.

"Good night, sweetheart," he said vaguely, and then trying to make his voice more tender, trying to conciliate something. "Good night, dear children."

V

Charlie went directly to the Ritz bar with the furious idea of finding Lorraine and Duncan, but they were not there, and he realized that in any case there was nothing he could do. He had not touched his drink at the Peterses, and now he ordered a whisky-and-soda. Paul came over to say hello.

"It's a great change," he said sadly. "We do about half the business we did. So many fellows I hear about back in the States lost everything, maybe not in the first crash, but then in the second. Your friend George Hardt lost every cent, I hear. Are you back in the States?"   620

"No, I'm in business in Prague."

"I heard that you lost a lot in the crash."

"I did," and he added grimly, "but I lost everything I wanted in the boom."

"Selling short."

"Something like that."

Again the memory of those days swept over him like a nightmare—the people they had met traveling; then people who couldn't add a row of figures or speak a coherent sentence. The little man Helen had consented to dance with at the ship's party, who had insulted her ten feet from the table; the women and girls carried screaming with drink or drugs out of public places—   630

The men who locked their wives out in the snow, because the snow of twenty-nine wasn't real snow. If you didn't want it to be snow, you just paid some money.

He went to the phone and called the Peterses' apartment; Lincoln answered.

"I called up because this thing is on my mind. Has Marion said anything definite?"

"Marion's sick," Lincoln answered shortly. "I know this thing isn't altogether your fault, but I can't have her go to pieces about it. I'm afraid we'll have to let it slide six months; I can't take the chance of working her up to this state again."

"I see."   640

"I'm sorry, Charlie."

He went back to his table. His whisky glass was empty, but he shook his head when Alix looked at it questioningly. There wasn't much he could do now except send Honoria some things; he would send her a lot of things tomorrow. He thought rather angrily that this was just money—he had given so many people money. . . .

"No, no more," he said to another waiter. "What do I owe you?"

He would come back some day; they couldn't make him pay forever. But he wanted his child, and nothing was much good now, beside that fact. He wasn't young any more, with a lot of nice thoughts and dreams to have by himself. He   650 was absolutely sure Helen wouldn't have wanted him to be so alone.   [1930]

Questions for Discussion and Writing

1. Why is the setting in Paris so important?
2. Who or what is Charlie's antagonist? With whom or what is he in conflict?
3. Analyze Marion's character. Is she right to be suspicious of Charlie? Is she right to blame him for Helen's death? Is she simply jealous of his success? Is she the villain of the story?
4. Is Charlie's reformation genuine? Give reasons to support your answer.
5. What does the story suggest about life in the "Roaring Twenties"? What does it say about the relationship between past and present? About "family values"?
6. Fitzgerald was a popular and well-paid writer who has also been highly praised by critics. Judging by this story, does he deserve his reputation? What, if anything, lifts him above the typical popular author?

❧ KATHERINE ANNE PORTER

(1890–1980)

Flowering Judas

Katherine Anne Porter's life and work in many ways resemble those of Katherine Mansfield (1888–1923). Both were social and literary pioneers whose short stories found new ways of illuminating character and society.

She was born Callie Russell Porter in Indian Creek, Texas, the fourth of five children. Her mother died when Callie was two, and the family moved in with her paternal grandmother—a domineering woman who treated her grown son as a child and hence shaped Callie's attitudes profoundly. Her schooling was erratic, and at one point Porter aspired to be a dancer, then an actress. At sixteen, she eloped but left her husband in 1914 to try acting in Chicago. Shortly thereafter, she nearly died of either influenza or tuberculosis and experienced a "rebirth" of ambition and creativity while convalescing. She tried journalism in New York and Denver, then lived for a short time in Mexico and several years in Europe.

Much of Porter's life was spent in travel and in stormy marriages and love affairs. A woman of great beauty and charm, she surprised her fourth husband on their wedding day by revealing that she was almost thirty years his senior. She was most productive during the 1930s, but even then she was a slow writer, often working on a story for years before being satisfied. She supported herself by teaching and lecturing until her novel, *Ship of Fools* (1962), a moral and political allegory, made her independently wealthy. Porter's work was influenced by Katherine Mansfield (1888–1923) and in turn influenced Eudora Welty (b. 1990) and Flannery O'Connor (1925–1964), both, like her, writers from the South. Porter's stories are notable for their intense emotion, social conscience, and complexity of character and situations.

BRAGGIONI SITS HEAPED upon the edge of a straight-backed chair much too small for him, and sings to Laura in a furry, mournful voice. Laura has begun to find reasons for avoiding her own house until the latest possible moment, for Braggioni is there almost every night. No matter how late she is, he will be sitting there with a surly, waiting expression, pulling at his kinky yellow hair, thumbing the strings of his guitar, snarling a tune under his breath. Lupe the Indian maid meets Laura at the door, and says with a flicker of a glance towards the upper room, "He waits."

Laura wishes to lie down, she is tired of her hairpins and the feel of her long tight sleeves, but she says to him, "Have you a new song for me this evening?" If 10
he says yes, she asks him to sing it. If he says no, she remembers his favorite one, and asks him to sing it again. Lupe brings her a cup of chocolate and a plate of rice, and Laura eats at the small table under the lamp, first inviting Braggioni, whose answer is always the same: "I have eaten, and besides, chocolate thickens the voice."

Laura says, "Sing, then," and Braggioni heaves himself into song. He scratches the guitar familiarly as though it were a pet animal, and sings passionately off key, taking the high notes in a prolonged painful squeal. Laura, who haunts the markets listening to the ballad singers, and stops every day to hear the blind boy playing his reed-flute in Sixteenth of September Street, listens to 20
Braggioni with pitiless courtesy, because she dares not smile at his miserable performance. Nobody dares to smile at him. Braggioni is cruel to everyone, with a kind of specialized insolence, but he is so vain of his talents, and so sensitive to slights, it would require a cruelty and vanity greater than his own to lay a finger on the vast cureless wound of his self-esteem. It would require courage, too, for it is dangerous to offend him, and nobody has this courage.

Braggioni loves himself with such tenderness and amplitude and eternal charity that his followers—for he is a leader of men, a skilled revolutionist, and his skin has been punctured in honorable warfare—warm themselves in the reflected glow, and say to each other: "He has a real nobility, a love of humanity raised 30
above mere personal affections." The excess of this self-love has flowed out, inconveniently for her, over Laura, who, with so many others, owes her comfortable situation and her salary to him. When he is in a very good humor, he tells her, "I am tempted to forgive you for being a *gringa. Gringita!*"[1] and Laura, burning, imagines herself leaning forward suddenly, and with a sound back-handed slap wiping the suety smile from his face. If he notices her eyes at these moments he gives no sign.

She knows what Braggioni would offer her, and she must resist tenaciously without appearing to resist, and if she could avoid it she would not admit even to herself the slow drift of his intention. During these long evenings which have spoiled a long month for her, she sits in her deep chair with an open book on her 40
knees, resting her eyes on the consoling rigidity of the printed page when the sight and sound of Braggioni singing threaten to identify themselves with all her remembered afflictions and to add their weight to her uneasy premonitions of the future. The gluttonous bulk of Braggioni has become a symbol of her many disillusions, for a revolutionist should be lean, animated by heroic faith, a vessel of ab-

---

1. Feminine, diminutive form of *gringo*, meaning foreigner, especially American.

stract virtues. This is nonsense, she knows it now and is ashamed of it. Revolution must have leaders, and leadership is a career for energetic men. She is, her comrades tell her, full of romantic error, for what she defines as cynicism in them is merely "a developed sense of reality." She is almost too willing to say, "I am wrong, I suppose I don't really understand the principles," and afterward she makes a secret truce with herself, determined not to surrender her will to such expedient logic. But she cannot help feeling that she has been betrayed irreparably by the disunion between her way of living and her feeling of what life should be, and at times she is almost contented to rest in this sense of grievance as a private store of consolation. Sometimes she wishes to run away, but she stays. Now she longs to fly out of this room, down the narrow stairs, and into the street where the houses lean together like conspirators under a single mottled lamp, and leave Braggioni singing to himself.

Instead she looks at Braggioni, frankly and clearly, like a good child who understands the rules of behavior. Her knees cling together under sound blue serge, and her round white collar is not purposely nun-like. She wears the uniform of an idea, and has renounced vanities. She was born Roman Catholic, and in spite of her fear of being seen by someone who might make a scandal of it[2], she slips now and again into some crumbling little church, kneels on the chilly stone, and says a Hail Mary on the gold rosary she bought in Tehuantepec. It is no good and she ends by examining the altar with its tinsel flowers and ragged brocades, and feels tender about the battered doll-shape of some male saint whose white, lace-trimmed drawers hang limply around his ankles below the hieratic dignity of his velvet robe. She has encased herself in a set of principles derived from her early training, leaving no detail of gesture or of personal taste untouched, and for this reason she will not wear lace made on machines. This is her private heresy, for in her special group the machine is sacred, and will be the salvation of the workers. She loves fine lace, and there is a tiny edge of fluted cobweb on this collar, which is one of twenty precisely alike, folded in blue tissue paper in the upper drawer of her clothes chest.

Braggioni catches her glance solidly as if he had been waiting for it, leans forward, balancing his paunch between his spread knees, and sings with tremendous emphasis, weighing his words. He has, the song relates, no father and no mother, nor even a friend to console him; lonely as a wave of the sea he comes and goes, lonely as a wave. His mouth opens round and yearns sideways, his balloon cheeks grow oily with the labor of song. He bulges marvelously in his expensive garments. Over his lavender collar, crushed upon a purple necktie, held by a diamond hoop: over his ammunition belt of tooled leather worked in silver, buckled cruelly around his gasping middle; over the tops of his glossy yellow shoes Braggioni swells with ominous ripeness, his mauve silk hose stretched taut, his ankles bound with the stout leather thongs of his shoes.

When he stretches his eyelids at Laura she notes again that his eyes are the true tawny yellow cat's eyes. He is rich, not in money, he tells her, but in power, and this power brings with it the blameless ownership of things, and the right to indulge his love of small luxuries. "I have a taste for the elegant refinements," he

---

2. Marxist-inspired revolutionaries were usually atheist and anti-clerical.

said once, flourishing a yellow silk handkerchief before her nose. "Smell that? It is
Jockey Club, imported from New York." Nonetheless he is wounded by life. He
will say so presently. "It is true everything turns to dust in the hand, to gall on the
tongue." He sighs and his leather belt creaks like a saddle girth. "I am disappointed in everything as it comes. Everything." He shakes his head. "You, poor
thing, you will be disappointed too. You are born for it. We are more alike than
you realize in some things. Wait and see. Some day you will remember what I
have told you, you will know that Braggioni was your friend."

Laura feels a slow chill, a purely physical sense of danger, a warning in her
blood that violence, mutilation, a shocking death, wait for her with lessening pa-   100
tience. She has translated this fear into something homely, immediate, and sometimes hesitates before crossing the street. "My personal fate is nothing, except as
the testimony of a mental attitude," she reminds herself, quoting from some forgotten philosophic primer, and is sensible enough to add, "Anyhow, I shall not be
killed by an automobile if I can help it."

"It may be true I am as corrupt, in another way, as Braggioni," she thinks in
spite of herself, "as callous, as incomplete," and if this is so, any kind of death
seems preferable. Still she sits quietly, she does not run. Where could she go?
Uninvited she has promised herself to this place; she can no longer imagine herself
as living in another country, and there is no pleasure in remembering her life be-   110
fore she came here.

Precisely what is the nature of this devotion, its true motives, and what are
its obligations? Laura cannot say. She spends part of her days in Xochimilco, near
by, teaching Indian children to say in English, "The cat is on the mat." When she
appears in the classroom they crowd about her with smiles on their wise, innocent, clay-colored faces, crying, "Good morning, my titcher!" in immaculate
voices, and they make of her desk a fresh garden of flowers every day.

During her leisure she goes to union meetings and listens to busy important
voices quarreling over tactics, methods, internal politics. She visits the prisoners of
her own political faith in their cells, where they entertain themselves with count-   120
ing cockroaches, repenting of their indiscretions, composing their memoirs, writing out manifestos and plans for their comrades who are still walking about free,
hands in pockets, sniffing fresh air. Laura brings them food and cigarettes and a
little money, and she brings messages disguised in equivocal phrases from the men
outside who dare not set foot in the prison for fear of disappearing into the cells
kept empty for them. If the prisoners confuse night and day, and complain, "Dear
little Laura, time doesn't pass in this infernal hole, and I won't know when it is
time to sleep unless I have a reminder," she brings them their favorite narcotics,
and says in a tone that does not wound them with pity, "Tonight will really be
night for you," and though her Spanish amuses them, they find her comforting,   130
useful. If they lose patience and all faith, and curse the slowness of their friends in
coming to their rescue with money and influence, they trust her not to repeat
everything, and if she inquires, "Where do you think we can find money, or influence?" they are certain to answer, "Well, there is Braggioni, why doesn't he do
something?"

She smuggles letters from headquarters to men hiding from firing squads in
back streets in mildewed houses, where they sit in tumbled beds and talk bitterly

as if all Mexico were at their heels, when Laura knows positively they might appear at the band concert in the Alameda on Sunday morning, and no one would notice them. But Braggioni says, "Let them sweat a little. The next time they may be careful. It is very restful to have them out of the way for a while." She is not afraid to knock on any door in any street after midnight, and enter in the darkness, and say to one of these men who is really in danger: "They will be looking for you—seriously—tomorrow morning after six. Here is some money from Vicente. Go to Vera Cruz and wait."

She borrows money from the Roumanian agitator to give to his bitter enemy the Polish agitator. The favor of Braggioni is their disputed territory, and Braggioni holds the balance nicely, for he can use them both. The Polish agitator talks love to her over café tables, hoping to exploit what he believes is her secret sentimental preference for him, and he gives her misinformation which he begs her to repeat as the solemn truth to certain persons. The Roumanian is more adroit. He is generous with his money in all good causes, and lies to her with an air of ingenuous candor, as if he were her good friend and confidant. She never repeats anything they may say. Braggioni never asks questions. He has other ways to discover all that he wishes to know about them.

Nobody touches her, but all praise her gray eyes, and the soft, round under lip which promises gayety, yet is always grave, nearly always firmly closed: and they cannot understand why she is in Mexico. She walks back and forth on her errands, with puzzled eyebrows, carrying her little folder of drawings and music and school papers. No dancer dances more beautifully than Laura walks, and she inspires some amusing, unexpected ardors, which cause little gossip, because nothing comes of them. A young captain who had been a soldier in Zapata's[3] army attempted, during a horseback ride near Cuernavaca, to express his desire for her with the noble simplicity befitting a rude folk-hero: but gently, because he was gentle. This gentleness was his defeat, for when he alighted, and removed her foot from the stirrup, and essayed to draw her down into his arms, her horse, ordinarily a tame one, shied fiercely, reared and plunged away. The young hero's horse careered blindly after his stable-mate, and the hero did not return to the hotel until rather late that evening. At breakfast he came to her table in full charro[4] dress, gray buckskin jacket and trousers with strings of silver buttons down the leg, and he was in a humorous, careless mood. "May I sit with you?" and "You are a wonderful rider. I was terrified that you might be thrown and dragged. I should never have forgiven myself. But I cannot admire you enough for your riding!"

"I learned to ride in Arizona," said Laura.

"If you will ride with me again this morning, I promise you a horse that will not shy with you," he said. But Laura remembered that she must return to Mexico City at noon.

Next morning the children made a celebration and spent their playtime writing on the blackboard, "We lov ar ticher," and with tinted chalks they drew wreaths of flowers around the words. The young hero wrote her a letter: "I am a very foolish, wasteful, impulsive man. I should have first said I love you, and then

3. Emiliano Zapata (1877?–1919), leader in the Mexican revolution, 1910–1917.
4. Cowboy.

you would not have run away. But you shall see me again." Laura thought, "I must send him a box of colored crayons," but she was trying to forgive herself for having spurred her horse at the wrong moment.

A brown, shock-haired youth came and stood in her patio one night and sang like a lost soul for two hours, but Laura could think of nothing to do about it. The moonlight spread a wash of gauzy silver over the clear spaces of the garden, and the shadows were cobalt blue. The scarlet blossoms of the Judas trees[5] were dull purple, and the names of the colors repeated themselves automatically in her mind, while she watched not the boy, but his shadow, fallen like a dark garment across the fountain rim, trailing in the water. Lupe came silently and whispered expert counsel in her ear: "If you will throw him one little flower, he will sing another song or two and go away! Laura threw the flower, and he sang a last song and went away with the flower tucked in the band of his hat. Lupe said, "He is one of the organizers of the Typographers Union, and before that he sold corridos[6] in the Merced market, and before that, he came from Guanajuato, where I was born. I would not trust any man, but I trust least those from Guanajuato."

She did not tell Laura that he would be back again the next night, and the next, nor that he would follow her at a certain fixed distance around the Merced market, though the Zócolo, up Francisco I. Madero Avenue, and so along the Paseo de la Reforma to Chapultepec Park, and into the Philospher's Footpath, still with that flower withering in his hat, and an indivisible attention in his eyes.

Now Laura is accustomed to him, it means nothing except that he is nineteen years old and is observing a convention with all propriety, as though it were founded on a law of nature, which in the end it might well prove to be. He is beginning to write poems which he prints on a wooden press, and he leaves them stuck like handbills in her door. She is pleasantly disturbed by the abstract, unhurried watchfulness of his black eyes which will in time turn easily towards another object. She tells herself that throwing the flower was a mistake, for she is twenty-two years old and knows better; but she refuses to regret it, and persuades herself that her negation of all external events as they occur is a sign that she is gradually perfecting herself in the stoicism she strives to cultivate against that disaster she fears, though she cannot name it.

She is not at home in the world. Every day she teaches children who remain strangers to her, though she loves their tender round hands and their charming opportunist savagery. She knocks at unfamiliar doors not knowing whether a friend or a stranger shall answer, and even if a known face emerges from the sour gloom of that unknown interior, still it is the face of a stranger. No matter what this stranger says to her, nor what her message to him, the very cells of that flesh reject knowledge and kinship in one monotonous word. No. No. No. She draws her strength from this one holy talismanic word which does not suffer her to be led into evil. Denying everything, she may walk anywhere in safety, she looks at everything without amazement.

No, repeats this firm unchanging voice of her blood; and she looks at

5. Also known as the redbud tree, for its flowers. Tradition says that Judas Iscariot hanged himself on this tree.
6. Bullfight tickets.

Braggioni without amazement. He is a great man, he wishes to impress this simple girl who covers her great round breasts with thick dark cloth, and who hides long, invaluably beautiful legs under a heavy skirt. She is almost thin except for the incomprehensible fullness of her breasts, like a nursing mother's, and Braggioni, who considers himself a judge of women, speculates again on the puzzle of her notorious virginity, and takes the liberty of speech which she permits without a 230 sign of modesty, indeed, without any sort of sign, which is disconcerting.

"You think you are so cold, *gringita!* Wait and see. You will surprise yourself some day! May I be there to advise you!" He stretches his eyelids at her, and his ill-humored cat's eyes waver in a separate glance for the two points of light marking the opposite ends of a smoothly drawn path between the swollen curve of her breasts. He is not put off by that blue serge, nor by her resolutely fixed gaze. There is all the time in the world. His cheeks are bellying with the wind of song. "O girl with the dark eyes," he sings, and reconsiders. "But yours are not dark. I can change all that. O girl with the green eyes, you have stolen my heart away!" then his mind wanders to the song, and Laura feels the weight of his attention being 240 shifted elsewhere. Singing thus, he seems harmless, he is quite harmless, there is nothing to do but sit patiently and say "No," when the moment comes. She draws a full breath, and her mind wanders also, but not far. She dares not wander too far.

Not for nothing has Braggioni taken pains to be a good revolutionist and a professional lover of humanity. He will never die of it. He has the malice, the cleverness, the wickedness, the sharpness of wit, the hardness of heart, stipulated for loving the world profitably. *He will never die of it.* He will live to see himself kicked out from his feeding trough by other hungry world-saviors. Traditionally he must sing in spite of his life which drives him to bloodshed, he tells Laura, for his father 250 was a Tuscany peasant who drifted to Yucatan and married a Maya woman: a woman of race, an aristocrat. They gave him the love and knowledge of music, thus: and under the tip of his thumbnail, the strings of the instrument complain like exposed nerves.

Once he was called Delgadito by all the girls and married women who ran after him; he was so scrawny all his bones showed under his thin cotton clothing, and he could squeeze his emptiness to the very backbone with his two hands. He was a poet and the revolution was only a dream then; too many women loved him and sapped away his youth, and he could never find enough to eat anywhere, anywhere! Now he is a leader of men, crafty men who whisper in his ear, hungry men 260 who wait for hours outside his office for a word with him, emaciated men with wild faces who waylay him at the street gate with a timid, "Comrade, let me tell you . . ." and they blow the foul breath from their empty stomachs in his face.

He is always sympathetic. He gives them handfuls of small coins from his own pocket, he promises them work, there will be demonstrations, they must join the unions and attend the meetings, above all they must be on the watch for spies. They are closer to him than his own brothers, without them he can do nothing—until tomorrow, comrade!

Until tomorrow. "They are stupid, they are lazy, they are treacherous, they would cut my throat for nothing," he says to Laura. He has good food and abun- 270 dant drink, he hires an automobile and drives in the Paseo on Sunday morning, and enjoys plenty of sleep in a soft bed beside a wife who dares not disturb him; and he sits pampering his bones in easy billows of fat, singing to Laura, who knows and thinks these things about him. When he was fifteen, he tried to drown himself because he loved a girl, his first love, and she laughed at him. "A thousand women have paid for that," and his tight little mouth turns down at the corners. Now he perfumes his hair with Jockey Club, and confides to Laura: "One woman is really as good as another for me, in the dark. I prefer them all."

His wife organizes unions among the girls in the cigarette factories, and walks in picket lines, and even speaks at meetings in the evening. But she cannot 280 be brought to acknowledge the benefits of true liberty. "I tell her I must have my freedom, net. She does not understand my point of view." Laura has heard this many times. Braggioni scratches the guitar and meditates. "She is an instinctively virtuous woman, pure gold, no doubt of that. If she were not, I should lock her up, and she knows it."

His wife, who works so hard for the good of the factory girls, employs part of her leisure lying on the floor weeping because there are so many women in the world, and only one husband for her, and she never knows where nor when to look for him. He told her: "Unless you can learn to cry when I am not here, I must go away for good." That day he went away and took a room at the Hotel 290 Madrid.

It is this month of separation for the sake of higher principles that has been spoiled not only for Mrs. Braggioni, whose sense of reality is beyond criticism, but for Laura, who feels herself bogged in a nightmare. Tonight Laura envies Mrs. Braggioni, who is alone, and free to weep as much as she pleases about a concrete wrong. Laura has just come from a visit to the prison, and she is waiting for to-morrow with a bitter anxiety as if tomorrow may not come, but time may be caught immovably in this hour, with herself transfixed, Braggioni singing on for-ever, and Eugenio's body not yet discovered by the guard.

Braggioni says: "Are you going to sleep?" Almost before she can shake her 300 head, he begins telling her about the May-day disturbances coming on in Morelia, for the Catholics hold a festival in honor of the Blessed Virgin, and the Socialists celebrate their martyrs on that day. "There will be two independent processions, starting from either end of town, and they will march until they meet, and the rest depends . . ." He asks her to oil and load his pistols. Standing up, he unbuckles his ammunition belt, and spreads it laden across her knees. Laura sits with the shells slipping through the cleaning cloth dipped in oil, and he says again he can-not understand why she works so hard for the revolutionary idea unless she loves some man who is in it. "Are you not in love with someone?" "No," says Laura. "And no one is in love with you?" "No." "Then it is your own fault. No woman 310 need go begging. Why, what is the matter with you? The legless beggar woman in the Alameda has a perfectly faithful lover. Did you know that?"

Laura peers down the pistol barrel and says nothing, but a long, slow faint-ness rises and subsides in her; Braggioni curves his swollen fingers around the throat of the guitar and softly smothers the music out of it, and when she hears him again he seems to have forgotten her, and is speaking in the hypnotic voice he uses when talking in small rooms to a listening, close-gathered crowd. Some day this world, now seemingly so composed and eternal, to the edges of every sea shall be merely a tangle of gaping trenches, of crashing walls and broken bodies. Everything must be torn from its accustomed place where it has rotted for centuries, hurled skyward and distributed, cast down again clean as rain, without separate identity. Nothing shall survive that the stiffened hands of poverty have created for the rich and no one shall be left alive except the elect spirits destined to procreate a new world cleansed of cruelty and injustice, ruled by benevolent anarchy: "Pistols are good, I love them, cannon are even better, but in the end I pin my faith to good dynamite," he concludes, and strokes the pistol lying in her hands. "Once I dreamed of destroying this city, in case it offered resistance to General Ortíz[7], but it fell into his hands like an overripe pear."

He is made restless by his own words, rises and stands waiting. Laura holds up the belt to him: "Put that on, and go kill somebody in Morelia, and you will be happier," she says softly. The presence of death in the room makes her bold. "Today, I found Eugenio going into a stupor. He refused to allow me to call the prison doctor. He had taken all the tablets I brought him yesterday. He said he took them because he was bored."

"He is a fool, and his death is his own business," says Braggioni, fastening his belt carefully.

"I told him if he had waited only a little while longer, you would have got him set free," says Laura. "He said he did not want to wait."

"He is a fool and we are well rid of him," says Braggioni, reaching for his hat.

He goes away. Laura knows his mood has changed, she will not see him any more for a while. He will send word when he needs her to go on errands into strange streets, to speak to the strange faces that will appear, like clay masks with the power of human speech, to mutter their thanks to Braggioni for his help. Now she is free, and she thinks, I must run while there is time. But she does not go.

Braggioni enters his own house where for a month his wife has spent many hours every night weeping and tangling her hair upon her pillow. She is weeping now, and she weeps more at the sight of him, the cause of all her sorrows. He looks about the room. Nothing is changed, the smells are good and familiar, he is well acquainted with the woman who comes toward him with no reproach except grief on her face. He says to her tenderly: "You are so good, please don't cry any more, you dear good creature." She says, "Are you tired, my angel? Sit here and I will wash your feet." She brings a bowl of water, and kneeling, unlaces his shoes, and when from her knees she raises her sad eyes under her blackened lids, he is sorry for everything, and bursts into tears. "Ah, yes, I am hungry, I am tired, let us eat something together," he says, between sobs. His wife leans her head on his arm and says, "Forgive me!" and this time he is refreshed by the solemn, endless rain of her tears.

Laura takes off her serge dress and puts on a white linen nightgown and goes to bed. She turns her head a little to one side, and lying still, reminds herself that it is time to sleep. Numbers tick in her brain like little clocks, soundless doors close of themselves around her. If you would sleep, you must not remember anything, the children will say tomorrow, good morning, my teacher, the poor prisoners who come every day bringing flowers to their jailor. 1—2—3—4—5—it is

7. Pascual Ortíz Rubio (1877–1963), president of Mexico, 1930–1932.

monstrous to confuse love with revolution, night with day, life with death—ah, Eugenio!

The tolling of the midnight bell is a signal, but what does it mean? Get up, Laura, and follow me: come out of your sleep, out of your bed, out of this strange house. What are you doing in this house? Without a word, without fear she rose and reached for Eugenio's hand, but he eluded her with a sharp, sly smile and drifted away. This is not all, you shall see—Murderer, he said, follow me. I will 370 show you a new country, but it is far away and we must hurry. No, said Laura, not unless you take my hand, no; and she clung first to the stair rail, and then to the topmost branch of the Judas tree that bent down slowly and set her upon the earth, and then to the rocky ledge of a cliff, then to the jagged wave of a sea that was not water but a desert of crumbling stone. Where are you taking me, she asked in wonder but without fear. To death, and it is a long way off, and we must hurry, said Eugenio. No, said Laura, not unless you take my hand. Then eat these flowers, poor prisoner, said Eugenio in a voice of pity, take and eat: and from the Judas tree he stripped the warm bleeding flowers, and held them to her lips. She saw that his hand was fleshless, a cluster of small white petrified branches, and his 380 eye sockets were without light, but she ate the flowers greedily for they satisfied both hunger and thirst. Murderer! said Eugenio, and Cannibal! This is my body and my blood. Laura cried No! And at the sound of her own voice, she awoke trembling, and was afraid to sleep again.   [1930]

Questions for Discussion and Writing

1. Analyze the imagery used to describe Braggioni and his playing and singing. How does this imagery define his character?
2. What does Braggioni want from Laura? What does he expect to gain from revolution?
3. What has Laura experienced and learned while in Mexico? Explain how these experiences have affected her positively or negatively.
4. Do Laura's actions yield good or evil results? Underline or highlight specific passages.
5. What are the conflicts in the story? Are they resolved?
6. What is the meaning of Laura's dream at the end of the story?

ᴈᵂ WILLIAM FAULKNER
(1897–1962)

Dry September

William Faulkner is one of the giants of twentieth-century American literature. His work, while closely associated with the South, has great breadth. Like Hemingway's, Faulkner's mythic stature and image often obscure the reality, but separating the two is difficult if not impossible.

He was born William Cuthbert Faulkner in New Albany, Mississippi but spent most of his life in Oxford, Mississippi, a university town. When World War I broke out, he joined the Canadian Air Force, but war ended while he was still in training. After the war, he tried university study briefly, worked in the post office, wrote for a newspaper in New Orleans, lived in Paris with the other expatriates, and finally returned to Oxford in 1926 to write full time. Although he early on received many rejections, he remained confident that his talent would, in time, be recognized.

His early publications—a work of poetry *The Marble Faun* (1924) and a novel *Soldier's Pay* (1926)—were largely conventional, but his wide reading eventually brought him to James Joyce and T. S. Eliot, two high priests of Modernism. In 1929, Faulkner published *Sartoris,* a novel in which he creates and introduces his real material—a fictional county in Mississippi called Yoknapatawpha, a place much like the one in which he had grown up and now lived. *The Sound and the Fury* (1929) announced that a major new Modernist talent had arrived. Employing shifting time sequences, multiple points of view, stream of consciousness, and a complex web of unifying images and symbols, the novel explores sensational events like incest, attempted rape, and suicide to tell the tragic story of the Compson family.

Faulkner's short stories form an important part of the Yoknapatawpha saga. In them, he uses the same style and techniques as in his novels: sentences spun out in heaped-up words and images, polysyllabic diction, stream of consciousness passages, shifting points of view, and unsequential narratives. "Dry September" is more conventionally written and plotted, but, like all of Faulkner's best work, it imbues its heroes and victims—outwardly simple characters—with dignity and events with a feeling of Greek tragedy.

I

THROUGH THE BLOODY September twilight, aftermath of sixty-two rainless days, it had gone like a fire in dry grass—the rumor, the story, whatever it was. Something about Miss Minnie Cooper and a Negro. Attacked, insulted, frightened: none of them, gathered in the barber shop on that Saturday evening where the ceiling fan stirred, without freshening it, the vitiated air, sending back upon them, in recurrent surges of stale pomade and lotion, their own stale breath and odors, knew exactly what had happened.

"Except it wasn't Will Mayes," a barber said. He was a man of middle age; a thin, sand-colored man with a mild face, who was shaving a client. "I know Will Mayes. He's a good nigger. And I know Miss Minnie Cooper, too."   10

"What do you know about her?" a second barber said.

"Who is she?" the client said. "A young girl?"

"No," the barber said. "She's about forty, I reckon. She aint married. That's why I dont believe—"

"Believe, hell!" a hulking youth in a sweat-stained silk shirt said. "Wont you take a white woman's word before a nigger's?"

"I dont believe Will Mayes did it," the barber said. "I know Will Mayes."

"Maybe you know who did it, then. Maybe you already got him out of town, you damn niggerlover."

"I dont believe anybody did anything. I dont believe anything happened. I 20 leave it to you fellows if them ladies that get old without getting married dont have notions that a man cant—"

"Then you are a hell of a white man," the client said. He moved under the cloth. The youth had sprung to his feet.

"You dont?" he said. "Do you accuse a white woman of lying?"

The barber held the razor poised above the half-risen client. He did not look around.

"It's this durn weather," another said. "It's enough to make a man do anything. Even to her."

Nobody laughed. The barber said in his mild, stubborn tone: "I aint accus- 30 ing nobody of nothing. I just know and you fellows know how a woman that never—"

"You damn niggerlover!" the youth said.

"Shut up, Butch," another said. "We'll get the facts in plenty of time to act."

"Who is? Who's getting them?" the youth said. "Facts, hell! I—"

"You're a fine white man," the client said. "Aint you?" In his frothy beard he looked like a desert rat in the moving pictures. "You tell them, Jack," he said to the youth. "If there aint any white men in this town, you can count on me, even if I aint only a drummer[1] and a stranger."

"That's right, boys," the barber said. "Find out the truth first. I know Will 40 Mayes."

"Well, by God!" the youth shouted. "To think that a white man in this town—"

"Shut up, Butch," the second speaker said. "We got plenty of time."

The client sat up. He looked at the speaker. "Do you claim that anything excuses a nigger attacking a white woman? Do you mean to tell me you are a white man and you'll stand for it? You better go back North where you came from. The South dont want your kind here."

"North what?" the second said. "I was born and raised in this town."

"Well, by God!" the youth said. He looked about with a strained, baffled 50 gaze, as if he was trying to remember what it was he wanted to say or to do. He drew his sleeve across his sweating face. "Damn if I'm going to let a white woman—"

"You tell them, Jack," the drummer said. "By God, if they—"

The screen door crashed open. A man stood in the floor, his feet apart and his heavy-set body poised easily. His white shirt was open at the throat; he wore a felt hat. His hot, bold glance swept the group. His name was McLendon. He had commanded troops at the front in France and had been decorated for valor.

"Well," he said, "are you going to sit there and let a black son rape a white woman on the streets of Jefferson?"
                                                                              60

Butch sprang up again. The silk of his shirt clung flat to his heavy shoulders.

1. Traveling salesman.

At each armpit was a dark halfmoon. "That's what I been telling them! That's what I—"

"Did it really happen?" a third said. "This aint the first man scare she ever had, like Hawkshaw says. Wasn't there something about a man on the kitchen roof, watching her undress, about a year ago?"

"What?" the client said. "What's that?" The barber had been slowly forcing him back into the chair; he arrested himself reclining, his head lifted, the barber still pressing him down.

McLendon whirled on the third speaker. "Happen? What the hell difference does it make? Are you going to let the black sons get away with it until one really does it?"

"That's what I'm telling them!" Butch shouted. He cursed, long and steady, pointless.

"Here, here," a fourth said. "Not so loud. Dont talk so loud."

"Sure," McLendon said; "no talking necessary at all. I've done my talking. Who's with me?" He poised on the balls of his feet, roving his gaze.

The barber held the drummer's face down, the razor poised. "Find out the facts first, boys. I know Willy Mayes. It wasn't him. Let's get the sheriff and do this thing right."

McLendon whirled upon him his furious, rigid face. The barber did not look away. They looked like men of different races. The other barbers had ceased also above their prone clients. "You mean to tell me," McLendon said, "that you'd take a nigger's word before a white woman's? Why, you damn niggerloving—"

The third speaker rose and grasped McLendon's arm; he too had been a soldier. "Now, now. Let's figure this thing out. Who knows anything about what really happened?"

"Figure out hell!" McLendon jerked his arm free. "All that're with me get up from there. The ones that aint—" He roved his gaze, dragging his sleeve across his face.

Three men rose. The drummer in the chair sat up. "Here," he said, jerking at the cloth about his neck; "get this rag off me. I'm with him. I dont live here, but by God, if our mothers and wives and sisters—" He smeared the cloth over his face and flung it to the floor. McLendon stood in the floor and cursed the others. Another rose and moved toward him. The remainder sat uncomfortable, not looking at one another, then one by one they rose and joined him.

The barber picked the cloth from the floor. He began to fold it neatly. "Boys, dont do that. Will Mayes never done it. I know."

"Come on," McLendon said. He whirled. From his hip pocket protruded the butt of a heavy automatic pistol. They went out. The screen door crashed behind them reverberant in the dead air.

The barber wiped the razor carefully and swiftly, and put it away, and ran to the rear, and took his hat from the wall. "I'll be back as soon as I can," he said to the other barbers. "I cant let—" He went out, running. The two other barbers followed him to the door and caught it on the rebound, leaning out and looking up the street after him. The air was flat and dead. It had a metallic taste at the base of the tongue.

"What can he do?" the first said. The second one was saying "Jees Christ,

Jees Christ" under his breath. "I'd just as lief be Will Mayes as Hawk, if he gets
McLendon riled."   110
    "Jees Christ, Jees Christ," the second whispered.
    "You reckon he really done it to her?" the first said.

II

    She was thirty-eight or thirty-nine. She lived in a small frame house with
her invalid mother and a thin, sallow, unflagging aunt, where each morning between ten and eleven she would appear on the porch in a lace-trimmed boudoir
cap, to sit swinging in the porch swing until noon. After dinner she lay down for
a while, until the afternoon began to cool. Then, in one of the three or four new
voile dresses which she had each summer, she would go downtown to spend the
afternoon in the stores with the other ladies, where they would handle the goods
and haggle over the prices in cold, immediate voices, without any intention of 120
buying.
    She was of comfortable people—not the best in Jefferson, but good people
enough—and she was still on the slender side of ordinary looking, with a bright,
faintly haggard manner and dress. When she was young she had had a slender,
nervous body and a sort of hard vivacity which had enabled her for a time to ride
upon the crest of the town's social life as exemplified by the high school party and
church social period of her contemporaries while still children enough to be un-
classconscious.
    She was the last to realize that she was losing ground; that those among
whom she had been a little brighter and louder flame than any other were begin- 130
ning to learn the pleasure of snobbery—male—and retaliation—female. That was
when her face began to wear that bright, haggard look. She still carried it to parties on shadowy porticoes and summer lawns, like a mask or a flag, with that baf-
flement of furious repudiation of truth in her eyes. One evening at a party she
heard a boy and two girls, all school-mates, talking. She never accepted another
invitation.
    She watched the girls with whom she had grown up as they married and got
homes and children, but no man ever called on her steadily until the children of
the other girls had been calling her "aunty" for several years, while their mothers
told them in bright voices about how popular Aunt Minnie had been as a girl. 140
Then the town began to see her driving on Sunday afternoons with the cashier in
the bank. He was a widower of about forty—a high-colored man, smelling always
faintly of the barber shop or of whisky. He owned the first automobile in town, a
red runabout; Minnie had the first motoring bonnet and veil the town ever saw.
Then the town began to say: "Poor Minnie." "But she is old enough to take care of
herself," others said. That was when she began to ask her old schoolmates that
their children call her "cousin" instead of "aunty."
    It was twelve years now since she had been relegated into adultery by public
opinion, and eight years since the cashier had gone to a Memphis bank, returning
for one day each Christmas, which he spent at an annual bachelors' party at a 150
hunting club on the river. From behind their curtains the neighbors would see the
party pass, and during the over-the-way Christmas day visiting they would tell her

about him, about how well he looked, and how they heard that he was prospering in the city, watching with bright, secret eyes her haggard, bright face. Usually by that hour there would be the scent of whisky on her breath. It was supplied her by a youth, a clerk at the soda fountain: "Sure; I buy it for the old gal. I reckon she's entitled to a little fun."

Her mother kept to her room altogether now; the gaunt aunt ran the house. Against that background Minnie's bright dresses, her idle and empty days, had a quality of furious unreality. She went out in the evenings only with women now, neighbors, to the moving pictures. Each afternoon she dressed in one of the new dresses and went downtown alone, where her young "cousins" were already strolling in the late afternoons with their delicate, silken heads and thin, awkward arms and conscious hips, clinging to one another or shrieking and giggling with paired boys in the soda fountain when she passed and went on along the serried store fronts, in the doors of which the sitting and lounging men did not even follow her with their eyes any more.

III

The barber went swiftly up the street where the sparse lights, insect-swirled, glared in rigid and violent suspension in the lifeless air. The day had died in a pall of dust; above the darkened square, shrouded by the spent dust, the sky was as clear as the inside of a brass bell. Below the east was a rumor of the twice-waxed moon.

When he overtook them McLendon and three others were getting into a car parked in an alley. McLendon stooped his thick head, peering out beneath the top. "Changed your mind, did you?" he said. "Damn good thing; by God, tomorrow when this town hears about how you talked tonight—"

"Now, now," the other ex-soldier said. "Hawkshaw's all right. Come on, Hawk; jump in."

"Will Mayes never done it, boys," the barber said. "If anybody done it. Why, you all know well as I do there aint any town where they got better niggers than us. And you know how a lady will kind of think things about men when there aint any reason to, and Miss Minnie anyway—"

"Sure, sure," the soldier said. "We're just going to talk to him a little; that's all."

"Talk hell!" Butch said. "When we're through with the—"

"Shut up, for God's sake!" the soldier said. "Do you want everybody in town—"

"Tell them, by God!" McLendon said. "Tell every one of the sons that'll let a white woman—"

"Let's go; let's go; here's the other car." The second car slid squealing out of a cloud of dust at the alley mouth. McLendon started his car and took the lead. Dust lay like fog in the street. The street lights hung nimbused as in water. They drove on out of town.

A rutted lane turned at right angles. Dust hung above it too, and above all the land. The dark bulk of the ice plant, where the Negro Mayes was night watchman, rose against the sky. "Better stop here, hadn't we?" the soldier said.

McLendon did not reply. He hurled the car up and slammed to a stop, the head-lights glaring on the blank wall.

"Listen here, boys," the barber said; "if he's here, dont that prove he never done it? Dont it? If it was him, he would run. Dont you see he would?" The sec-ond car came up and stopped. McLendon got down; Butch sprang down beside him. "Listen, boys," the barber said.

"Cut the lights off!" McLendon said. The breathless dark rushed down. There was no sound in it save their lungs as they sought air in the parched dust in which for two months they had lived; then the diminishing crunch of McLendon's and Butch's feet, and a moment later McLendon's voice:

"Will! . . . Will!"

Below the east the wan hemorrhage of the moon increased. It heaved above the ridge, silvering the air, the dust, so that they seemed to breathe, live, in a bowl of molten lead. There was no sound of nightbird nor insect, no sound save their breathing and a faint ticking of contracting metal about the cars. Where their bod-ies touched one another they seemed to sweat dryly, for no more moisture came. "Christ!" a voice said; "let's get out of here."

But they didn't move until vague noises began to grow out of the darkness ahead; then they got out and waited tensely in the breathless dark. There was an-other sound: a blow, a hissing expulsion of breath and McLendon cursing in un-dertone. They stood a moment longer, then they ran forward. They ran in a stumbling clump, as though they were fleeing something. "Kill him, kill the son," a voice whispered. McLendon flung them back.

"Not here," he said. "Get him into the car." "Kill him, kill the black son!" the voice murmured. They dragged the Negro to the car. The barber had waited be-side the car. He could feel himself sweating and he knew he was going to be sick at the stomach.

"What is it, captains?" the Negro said. "I aint done nothing. 'Fore God, Mr. John." Someone produced handcuffs. They worked busily about the Negro as though he were a post, quiet, intent, getting in one another's way. He submitted to the handcuffs, looking swiftly and constantly from dim face to dim face. "Who's here, captains?" he said, leaning to peer into the faces until they could feel his breath and smell his sweaty reek. He spoke a name or two. "What you all say I done, Mr. John?"

McLendon jerked the car door open. "Get in!" he said.

The Negro did not move. "What you all going to do with me, Mr John? I aint done nothing. White folks, captains, I aint done nothing: I swear 'fore God." He called another name.

"Get in!" McLendon said. He struck the Negro. The others expelled their breath in a dry hissing and struck him with random blows and he whirled and cursed them, and swept his manacled hands across their faces and slashed the bar-ber upon the mouth, and the barber struck him also. "Get him in there," McLendon said. They pushed at him. He ceased struggling and got in and sat qui-etly as the others took their places. He sat between the barber and the soldier, drawing his limbs in so as not to touch them, his eyes going swiftly and constantly from face to face. Butch clung to the running board. The car moved on. The bar-ber nursed his mouth with his handkerchief.

"What's the matter, Hawk?" the soldier said.

"Nothing," the barber said. They regained the highroad and turned away from town. The second car dropped back out of the dust. They went on, gaining speed; the final fringe of houses dropped behind.

"Goddamn, he stinks!" the soldier said.

"We'll fix that," the drummer in front beside McLendon said. On the running board Butch cursed into the hot rush of air. The barber leaned suddenly forward and touched McLendon's arm.   250

"Let me out, John," he said.

"Jump out, niggerlover," McLendon said without turning his head. He drove swiftly. Behind them the sourceless lights of the second car glared in the dust. Presently McLendon turned into a narrow road. It was rutted with disuse. It led back to an abandoned brick kiln—a series of reddish mounds and weed- and vine-choked vats without bottom. It had been used for pasture once, until one day the owner missed one of his mules. Although he prodded carefully in the vats with a long pole, he could not even find the bottom of them.

"John," the barber said.   260

"Jump out, then," McLendon said, hurling the car along the ruts. Beside the barber the Negro spoke:

"Mr. Henry."

The barber sat forward. The narrow tunnel of the road rushed up and past. Their motion was like an extinct furnace blast: cooler, but utterly dead. The car bounded from rut to rut.

"Mr. Henry," the Negro said.

The barber began to tug furiously at the door. "Look out, there!" the soldier said, but the barber had already kicked the door open and swung onto the running board. The soldier leaned across the Negro and grasped at him, but he had   270 already jumped. The car went on without checking speed.

The impetus hurled him crashing through dust-sheathed weeds, into the ditch. Dust puffed about him, and in a thin, vicious crackling of sapless stems he lay choking and retching until the second car passed and died away. Then he rose and limped on until he reached the highroad and turned toward town, brushing at his clothes with his hands. The moon was higher, riding high and clear of the dust at last, and after a while the town began to glare beneath the dust. He went on, limping. Presently he heard cars and the glow of them grew in the dust behind him and he left the road and crouched again in the weeds until they passed. McLendon's car came last now. There were four people in it and Butch was not on   280 the running board.

They went on; the dust swallowed them; the glare and the sound died away. The dust of them hung for a while, but soon the eternal dust absorbed it again. The barber climbed back onto the road and limped on toward town.

IV

As she dressed for supper on that Saturday evening, her own flesh felt like fever. Her hands trembled among the hooks and eyes, and her eyes had a feverish look, and her hair swirled crisp and crackling under the comb. While she was still

dressing the friends called for her and sat while she donned her sheerest underthings and stockings and a new voile dress. "Do you feel strong enough to go out?"
they said, their eyes bright too, with a dark glitter. "When you have had time to   290
get over the shock, you must tell us what happened. What he said and did; everything."

In the leafed darkness, as they walked toward the square, she began to
breathe deeply, something like a swimmer preparing to dive, until she ceased
trembling, the four of them walking slowly because of the terrible heat and out of
solicitude for her. But as they neared the square she began to tremble again, walking with her head up, her hands clenched at her sides, their voices about her murmurous, also with that feverish, glittering quality of their eyes.

They entered the square, she in the center of the group, fragile in her fresh
dress. She was trembling worse. She walked slower and slower, as children eat ice   300
cream, her head up and her eyes bright in the haggard banner of her face, passing
the hotel and the coatless drummers in chairs along the curb looking around at
her: "That's the one: see? The one in pink in the middle." "Is that her? What did
they do with the nigger? Did they—?" "Sure. He's all right." "All right, is he?"
"Sure. He went on a little trip." Then the drug store, where even the young men
lounging in the doorway tipped their hats and followed with their eyes the motion
of her hips and legs when she passed.

They went on, passing the lifted hats of the gentlemen, the suddenly ceased
voices, deferent, protective. "Do you see?" the friends said. Their voices sounded
like long, hovering sighs of hissing exultation. "There's not a Negro on the square.   310
Not one."

They reached the picture show. It was like a miniature fairyland with its
lighted lobby and colored lithographs of life caught in its terrible and beautiful
mutations. Her lips began to tingle. In the dark, when the picture began, it would
be all right; she could hold back the laughing so it would not waste away so fast
and so soon. So she hurried on before the turning faces, the undertones of low astonishment, and they took their accustomed places where she could see the aisle
against the silver glare and the young men and girls coming in two and two
against it.

The lights flicked away; the screen glowed silver, and soon life began to un-   320
fold, beautiful and passionate and sad, while still the young men and girls entered,
scented and sibilant in the half dark, their paired backs in silhouette delicate and
sleek, their slim, quick bodies awkward, divinely young, while beyond them the
silver dream accumulated, inevitably on and on. She began to laugh. In trying to
suppress it, it made more noise than ever; heads began to turn. Still laughing, her
friends raised her and led her out, and she stood at the curb, laughing on a high,
sustained note, until the taxi came up and they helped her in.

They removed the pink voile and the sheer underthings and the stockings,
and put her to bed, and cracked ice for her temples, and sent for the doctor. He
was hard to locate, so they ministered to her with hushed ejaculations, renewing   330
the ice and fanning her. While the ice was fresh and cold she stopped laughing
and lay still for a time, moaning only a little. But soon the laughing welled again
and her voice rose screaming.

"Shhhhhhhhhhh! Shhhhhhhhhhhhhhh!" they said, freshening the icepack, smoothing her hair, examining it for gray; "poor girl!" Then to one another: "Do you suppose anything really happened?" their eyes darkly aglitter, secret and passionate. "Shhhhhhhhhh! Poor girl! Poor Minnie!"

V

It was midnight when McLendon drove up to his neat new house. It was trim and fresh as a birdcage and almost as small, with its clean, green-and-white paint. He locked the car and mounted the porch and entered. His wife rose from a 340 chair beside the reading lamp. McLendon stopped in the floor and stared at her until she looked down.

"Look at that clock," he said, lifting his arm, pointing. She stood before him, her face lowered, a magazine in her hands. Her face was pale, strained, and weary-looking. "Haven't I told you about sitting up like this, waiting to see when I come in?"

"John," she said. She laid the magazine down. Poised on the balls of his feet, he glared at her with his hot eyes, his sweating face.

"Didn't I tell you?" He went toward her. She looked up then. He caught her shoulder. She stood passive, looking at him.   350

"Don't, John. I couldn't sleep . . . The heat; something. Please, John. You're hurting me."

"Didn't I tell you?" He released her and half struck, half flung her across the chair, and she lay there and watched him quietly as he left the room.

He went on through the house, ripping off his shirt, and on the dark, screened porch at the rear he stood and mopped his head and shoulders with the shirt and flung it away. He took the pistol from his hip and laid it on the table beside the bed, and sat on the bed and removed his shoes, and rose and slipped his trousers off. He was sweating again already, and he stooped and hunted furiously for the shirt. At last he found it and wiped his body again, and, with his body 360 pressed against the dusty screen, he stood panting. There was no movement, no sound, not even an insect. The dark world seemed to lie stricken beneath the cold moon and the lidless stars.   [1931]

Questions for Discussion and Writing

1. Much of what happens in this story is only suggested. What effect does Faulkner achieve by not dramatizing or describing these events?
2. What do the details of setting and atmosphere contribute to the story? Do they help to explain what happens in the story?
3. Why does Minnie laugh at the movie theater?
4. What comments does the story make about hysteria and mob rule? What psychological bases are suggested for these reactions?
5. Is the barber courageous or cowardly in his actions? What does the story reveal about courage and cowardice?
6. Why does McLendon bully his wife when he returns?

⍩ CONRAD AIKEN
(1889–1973)

Silent Snow, Secret Snow

Conrad Aiken, a masterful and prolific poet, critic, short story writer, remains relatively little known. His father was a prosperous physician in Savannah, Georgia, and theirs seemed an ordinary family until one morning when Conrad was eleven. He awoke to hear his parents quarreling violently and then heard two pistol shots. He found both his parents dead. Calmly, he told the servants to keep the younger children in their rooms and walked to the police station to report the murder/suicide. He spent the rest of his childhood with relatives in Bedford, Massachusetts.

Aiken entered Harvard University with the same class as T. S. Eliot (1888–1965), journalist Walter Lippmann (1889–1974), humorist Robert Benchley (1889–1945), and critic Van Wyck Brooks (1886–1963). At Harvard, he read widely in contemporary poetry and psychology, but Edgar Allan Poe (1809–1849) remained the single most important influence on his writing and thinking. His first published story, "The Dark City" published in *Dial* in April 1922, was the beginning of a productive period that included the Pulitzer Prize and the Shelley Award for *Selected Poems* in 1929. Altogether he published thirty volumes of poetry, five novels, several collections of stories, and a large volume of critical essays and studies.

Aiken's stories are noted for their psychological ideas and Modernist techniques in the tradition of Anton Chekhov (1860–1904) and Katherine Mansfield (1888–1923). Often a story line will consist almost entirely of interior incidents that show the developing of an individual mind. The idea for "Silent Snow, Secret Snow" came, Aiken said, when he was living in Rye, England, and every morning he would hear the postman's footsteps as they came down the hill toward his house. The rest he imagined.

JUST WHY IT SHOULD have happened, or why it should have happened just when it did, he could not, of course, possibly have said; nor perhaps could it even have occurred to him to ask. The thing was above all a secret, something to be preciously concealed from Mother and Father; and to that very fact it owed an enormous part of its deliciousness. It was like a peculiarly beautiful trinket to be carried unmentioned in one's trouserpocket—a rare stamp, an old coin, a few tiny gold links found trodden out of shape on the path in the park, a pebble of carnelian,[1] a sea shell distinguishable from all others by an unusual spot or stripe— and, as if it were any one of these, he carried around with him everywhere a warm

---

1. A semi-precious stone, sometimes used in jewelry.

and persistent and increasingly beautiful sense of possession. Nor was it only a sense of possession—it was also a sense of protection. It was as if, in some delightful way, his secret gave him a fortress, a wall behind which he could retreat into heavenly seclusion. This was almost the first thing he had noticed about it—apart from the oddness of the thing itself—and it was this that now again, for the fiftieth time, occurred to him, as he sat in the little schoolroom. It was the half hour for geography. Miss Buell was revolving with one finger, slowly, a huge terrestrial globe which had been placed on her desk. The green and yellow continents passed and repassed, questions were asked and answered, and now the little girl in front of him, Deirdre, who had a funny little constellation of freckles on the back of her neck, exactly like the Big Dipper, was standing up and telling Miss Buell that the equator was the line that ran around the middle:

Miss Buell's face, which was old and grayish and kindly, with gray stiff curls beside the cheeks, and eyes that swam very brightly, like little minnows, behind thick glasses, wrinkled itself into a complication of amusements.

"Ah! I see. The earth is wearing a belt, or a sash. Or someone drew a line round it!"

"Oh, no—not that—I mean—"

In the general laughter, he did not share, or only a very little. He was thinking about the Arctic and Antarctic regions, which of course, on the globe, were white. Miss Buell was now telling them about the tropics, the jungles, the steamy heat of equatorial swamps, where the birds and butterflies, and even the snakes, were like living jewels. As he listened to these things, he was already, with a pleasant sense of half-effort, putting his secret between himself and the words. Was it really an effort at all? For effort implied something voluntary, and perhaps even something one did not especially want; whereas this was distinctly pleasant, and came almost of its own accord. All he needed to do was to think of that morning, the first one, and then of all the others—

But it was all so absurdly simple! It had amounted to so little. It was nothing, just an idea—and just why it should have become so wonderful, so permanent, was a mystery—a very pleasant one, to be sure, but also, in an amusing way, foolish. However, without ceasing to listen to Miss Buell, who had now moved up to the north temperate zone, he deliberately invited his memory of the first morning. It was only a moment or two after he had waked up—or perhaps the moment itself. But was there, to be exact, an exact moment? Was one awake all at once? Or was it gradual? Anyway, it was after he had stretched a lazy hand up towards the headrail, and yawned, and then relaxed again among his warm covers, all the more grateful on a December morning, that the thing had happened. Suddenly, for no reason, he had thought of the postman, he remembered the postman. Perhaps there was nothing so odd in that. After all, he heard the postman almost every morning in his life—his heavy boots could be heard clumping round the corner at the top of the little cobbled hill-street, and then, progressively nearer, progressively louder, the double knock at each door, the crossings and recrossings of the street, till finally the clumsy steps came stumbling across to the very door, and the tremendous knock came which shook the house itself.

(Miss Buell was saying "Vast wheat-growing areas in North America and Siberia.")

Deirdre had for the moment placed her left hand across the back of her neck.)

But on this particular morning, the first morning, as he lay there with his eyes closed, he had for some reason *waited* for the postman. He wanted to hear him come round the corner. And that was precisely the joke—he never did. He never came. He never had come—*round the corner*—again. For when at last the steps *were* heard, they had already, he was quite sure, come a little down the hill, to the first house; and even so, the steps were curiously different—they were softer, they had a new secrecy about them, they were muffled and indistinct; and while the rhythm of them was the same, it now said a new thing—it said peace, it said remoteness, it said cold, it said sleep. And he had understood the situation at once—nothing could have seemed simpler—there had been snow in the night, such as all winter he had been longing for; and it was this which had rendered the postman's first footsteps inaudible, and the later ones faint. Of course! How lovely! And even now it must be snowing—it was going to be a snowy day—the long white ragged lines were drifting and sifting across the street, across the faces of the old houses, whispering and hushing, making little triangles of white in the corners between cobblestones, seething a little when the wind blew them over the ground to a drifted corner; and so it would be all day, getting deeper and deeper and silenter and silenter.

(Miss Buell was saying "Land of perpetual snow.")

All this time, of course (while he lay in bed), he had kept his eyes closed, listening to the nearer progress of the postman, the muffled footsteps thumping and slipping on the snow-sheathed cobbles; and all the other sounds—the double knocks, a frosty far-off voice or two, a bell ringing thinly and softly as if under a sheet of ice—had the same slightly abstracted quality, as if removed by one degree from actuality—as if everything in the world had been insulated by snow. But when at last, pleased, he opened his eyes, and turned them towards the window, to see for himself this long-desired and now so clearly imagined miracle—what he saw instead was brilliant sunlight on a roof; and when, astonished, he jumped out of bed and stared down into the street, expecting to see the cobbles obliterated by the snow, he saw nothing but the bare bright cobbles themselves.

Queer, the effect this extraordinary surprise had had upon him—all the following morning he had kept with him a sense of snow falling about him, a secret screen of new snow between himself and the world. If he had not dreamed such a thing—and how could he have dreamed it while awake?—how else could one explain it? In any case, the delusion had been so vivid as to affect his entire behavior. He could not now remember whether it was on the first or the second morning— or was it even the third?—that his mother had drawn attention to some oddness in his manner.

"But my darling"—she had said at the breakfast table—"what has come over you? You don't seem to be listening. . . ."

And how often that very thing had happened since!

(Miss Buell was now asking if anyone knew the difference between the North Pole and the Magnetic Pole. Deirdre was holding up her flickering brown hand, and he could see the four white dimples that marked the knuckles.)

Perhaps it hadn't been either the second or third morning—or even the fourth or fifth. How could he be sure? How could he be sure just when the delicious *progress* had become clear? Just when it had really *begun?* The intervals weren't very precise. . . . All he now knew was, that at some point or other—perhaps the second day, perhaps the sixth—he had noticed that the presence of the snow was a little more insistent, the sound of it clearer; and, conversely, the sound of the postman's footsteps more indistinct. Not only could he not hear the steps come round the corner, he could not even hear them at the first house. It was below the first house that he heard them; and then, a few days later, it was below the second house that he heard them; and a few days later again, below the third. Gradually, gradually, the snow was becoming heavier, the sound of its seething louder, the cobblestones more and more muffled. When he found, each morning, on going to the window, after the ritual of listening, that the roofs and cobbles were as bare as ever, it made no difference. This was, after all, only what he had expected. It was even what pleased him, what rewarded him: the thing was his own, belonged to no one else. No one else knew about it, not even his mother and father. There, outside, were the bare cobbles; and here, inside, was the snow. Snow growing heavier each day, muffling the world, hiding the ugly, and deadening increasingly—above all—the steps of the postman.

"But my darling"—she had said at the luncheon table—"what has come over you? You don't seem to listen when people speak to you. That's the third time I've asked you to pass your plate. . . ."

How was one to explain this to Mother? or to Father? There was, of course, nothing to be done about it, nothing. All one could do was to laugh embarrassedly, pretend to be a little ashamed, apologize, and take a sudden and somewhat disingenuous interest in what was being done or said. The cat had stayed out all night. He had a curious swelling on his left cheek—perhaps somebody had kicked him, or a stone had struck him. Mrs. Kempton was or was not coming to tea. The house was going to be house cleaned, or "turned out," on Wednesday instead of Friday. A new lamp was provided for his evening work—perhaps it was eyestrain which accounted for this new and so peculiar vagueness of his—Mother was looking at him with amusement as she said this, but with something else as well. A new lamp? A new lamp. Yes Mother, No Mother, Yes Mother. School is going very well. The geometry is very easy. The history is very dull. The geography is very interesting—particularly when it takes one to the North Pole. Why the North Pole? Oh, well, it would be fun to be an explorer. Another Peary or Scott or Shackleton.[2] And then abruptly he found his interest in the talk at an end, stared at the pudding on his plate, listened, waited, and began once more—ah, how heavenly, too, the first beginnings—to hear or feel—for could he actually hear it?—the silent snow, the secret snow.

(Miss Buell was telling them about the search for the Northwest Passage, about Hendrik Hudson, the Half Moon.)

This had been, indeed, the only distressing feature of the new experience: the fact that it so increasingly had brought him into a kind of mute misunderstanding, or even conflict, with his father and mother. It was as if he were trying to lead a double life. On the one hand he had to be Paul Hasleman, and keep up the

---

2. Robert Peary, Robert Scott, and Ernest Shackleton were all famous polar explorers.

appearance of being that person—dress, wash, and answer intelligently when spoken to—; on the other, he had to explore this new world which had been opened   150
to him. Nor could there be the slightest doubt—not the slightest—that the new
world was the profounder and more wonderful of the two. It was irresistible. It
was miraculous. Its beauty was simply beyond anything—beyond speech as beyond thought—utterly incommunicable. But how then, between the two worlds,
of which he was thus constantly aware, was he to keep a balance? One must get
up, one must go to breakfast, one must talk with Mother, go to school, do one's
lessons—and, in all this, try not to appear too much of a fool. But if all the while
one was also trying to extract the full deliciousness of another and quite separate
existence, one which could not easily (if at all) be spoken of—how was one to
manage? How was one to explain? Would it be safe to explain? Would it be ab-   160
surd? Would it merely mean that he would get into some obscure kind of trouble?

These thoughts came and went, came and went, as softly and secretly as the
snow; they were not precisely a disturbance, perhaps they were even a pleasure;
he liked to have them; their presence was something almost palpable, something
he could stroke with his hand, without closing his eyes, and without ceasing to
see Miss Buell and the schoolroom and the globe and the freckles on Deirdre's
neck; nevertheless he did in a sense cease to see, or to see the obvious external
world, and substituted for this vision the vision of snow, the sound of snow, and
the slow, almost soundless, approach of the postman. Yesterday, it had been only
at the sixth house that the postman had become audible; the snow was much   170
deeper now, it was falling more swiftly and heavily, the sound of its seething was
more distinct, more soothing, more persistent. And this morning, it had been—as
nearly as he could figure—just above the seventh house—perhaps only a step or
two above: at most, he had heard two or three footsteps before the knock
sounded. . . . And with each such narrowing of the sphere, each nearer approach
of the limit at which the postman was first audible, it was odd how sharply was
increased the amount of illusion which had to be carried into the ordinary business of daily life. Each day it was harder to get out of bed, to go to the window, to
look out at the—as always—perfectly empty and snowless street. Each day it was
more difficult to go through the perfunctory motions of greeting Mother and   180
Father at breakfast, to reply to their questions, to put his books together and go to
school. And at school, how extraordinarily hard to conduct with success simultaneously the public life and the life that was secret. There were times when he
longed—positively ached—to tell everyone about it—to burst out with it—only to
be checked almost at once by a far-off feeling as of some faint absurdity which was
inherent in it—but *was* it absurd?—and more importantly by a sense of mysterious power in his very secrecy. Yes; it must be kept secret. That, more and more,
became clear. At whatever cost to himself, whatever pain to others—

(Miss Buell looked straight at him, smiling, and said, "Perhaps we'll ask Paul.
I'm sure Paul will come out of his day-dream long enough to be able to tell us.   190
Won't you, Paul?" He rose slowly from his chair, resting one hand on the brightly
varnished desk, and deliberately stared through the snow towards the blackboard.
It was an effort, but it was amusing to make it. "Yes," he said slowly, "it was what
we now call the Hudson River. This he thought to be the Northwest Passage. He

was disappointed." He sat down again, and as he did so Deirdre half turned in her chair and gave him a shy smile, of approval and admiration.)

At whatever pain to others.

This part of it was very puzzling, very puzzling. Mother was very nice, and so was Father. Yes, that was all true enough. He wanted to be nice to them, to tell them everything—and yet, was it really wrong of him to want to have a secret place of his own?

At bedtime, the night before, Mother had said, "If this goes on, my lad, we'll have to see a doctor, we will! We can't have our boy—" But what was it she had said? "Live in another world"? "Live so far away"? The word "far" had been in it, he was sure, and then Mother had taken up a magazine again and laughed a little, but with an expression which wasn't mirthful. He had felt sorry for her. . . .

The bell rang for dismissal. The sound came to him through long curved parallels of falling snow. He saw Deirdre rise, and had himself risen almost as soon—but not quite as soon—as she.

2

On the walk homeward, which was timeless, it pleased him to see through the accompaniment, or counterpoint, of snow, the items of mere externality on his way. There were many kinds of bricks in the sidewalks, and laid in many kinds of pattern. The garden walls too were various, some of wooden palings, some of plaster, some of stone. Twigs of bushes leaned over the walls; the little hard green winter-buds of lilac, on gray stems, sheathed and fat; other branches very thin and fine and black and desiccated. Dirty sparrows huddled in the bushes, as dull in color as dead fruit left in leafless trees. A single starling creaked on a weather vane. In the gutter, beside a drain, was a scrap of torn and dirty newspaper, caught in a little delta of filth: the word ECZEMA appeared in large capitals, and below it was a letter from Mrs. Amelia D. Cravath, 2100 Pine Street, Fort Worth, Texas, to the effect that after being a sufferer for years she had been cured by Caley's Ointment. In the little delta, beside the fan-shaped and deeply runneled continent of brown mud, were lost twigs, descended from their parent trees, dead matches, a rusty horse-chestnut burr, a small concentration of sparkling gravel on the lip of the sewer, a fragment of eggshell, a streak of yellow sawdust which had been wet and was now dry and congealed, a brown pebble, and a broken feather. Further on was a cement sidewalk, ruled into geometrical parallelograms, with a brass inlay at one end commemorating the contractors who had laid it, and, halfway across, an irregular and random series of dog-tracks, immortalized in synthetic stone. He knew these well, and always stepped on them; to cover the little hollows with his own foot had always been a queer pleasure; today he did it once more, but perfunctorily and detachedly, all the while thinking of something else. That was a dog, a long time ago, who had made a mistake and walked on the cement while it was still wet. He had probably wagged his tail, but that hadn't been recorded. Now, Paul Hasleman, aged twelve, on his way home from school, crossed the same river, which in the meantime had frozen into rock. Homeward through the snow, the snow falling in bright sunshine. Homeward?

Then came the gateway with the two posts surmounted by egg-shaped stones which had been cunningly balanced on their ends, as if by Columbus, and mortared in the very act of balance: a source of perpetual wonder. On the brick 240 wall just beyond, the letter H had been stenciled, presumably for some purpose. H? H.

The green hydrant, with a little green-painted chain attached to the brass screwcap.

The elm tree, with the great gray wound in the bark, kidney-shaped, into which he always put his hand—to feel the cold but living wood. The injury, he had been sure, was due to the gnawings of a tethered horse. But now it deserved only a passing palm, a merely tolerant eye. There were more important things. Miracles. Beyond the thoughts of trees, mere elms. Beyond the thoughts of side-walks, mere stone, mere brick, mere cement. Beyond the thoughts even of his own 250 shoes, which trod these sidewalks obediently, bearing a burden—far above—of elaborate mystery. He watched them. They were not very well polished; he had ne-glected them, for a very good reason: they were one of the many parts of the in-creasing difficulty of the daily return to daily life, the morning struggle. To get up, having at last opened one's eyes, to go to the window, and discover no snow, to wash, to dress, to descend the curving stairs to breakfast—

At whatever pain to others, nevertheless, one must persevere in severance, since the incommunicability of the experience demanded it. It was desirable of course to be kind to Mother and Father, especially as they seemed to be worried, but it was also desirable to be resolute. If they should decide—as appeared 260 likely—to consult the doctor, Doctor Howells, and have Paul inspected, his heart listened to through a kind of dictaphone, his lungs, his stomach—well, that was all right. He would go through with it. He would give them answer for question, too—perhaps such answers as they hadn't expected? No. That would never do. For the secret world must, at all costs, be preserved.

The bird-house in the apple-tree was empty—it was the wrong time of year for wrens. The little round black door had lost its pleasure. The wrens were enjoy-ing other houses, other nests, remoter trees. But this too was a notion which he only vaguely and grazingly entertained—as if, for the moment, he merely touched an edge of it; there was something further on, which was already assuming a 270 sharper importance; something which already teased at the corners of his eyes, teasing also at the corner of his mind. It was funny to think that he so wanted this, so awaited it—and yet found himself enjoying this momentary dalliance with the bird-house, as if for a quite deliberate postponement and enhancement of the ap-proaching pleasure. He was aware of his delay, of his smiling and detached and now almost uncomprehending gaze at the little bird-house; he knew what he was going to look at next: it was his own little cobbled hill-street, his own house, the little river at the bottom of the hill, the grocer's shop with the cardboard man in the window—and now, thinking of all this, he turned his head, still smiling, and looking quickly right and left through the snow-laden sunlight.   280

And the mist of snow, as he had foreseen, was still on it—a ghost of snow falling in the bright sunlight, softly and steadily floating and turning and pausing, soundlessly meeting the snow that covered, as with a transparent mirage, the bare bright cobbles. He loved it—he stood still and loved it. Its beauty was paralyzing—beyond all words, all experience, all dream. No fairy-story he had ever read could be compared with it—none had ever given him this extraordinary combination of ethereal loveliness with a something else, unnameable, which was just faintly and deliciously terrifying. What was this thing? As he thought of it, he looked upward towards his own bedroom window, which was open—and it was as if he looked straight into the room and saw himself lying half awake in his bed. 290 There he was—at this very instant he was still perhaps actually there—more truly there than standing here at the edge of the cobbled hill-street, with one hand lifted to shade his eyes against the snow-sun. Had he indeed ever left his room, in all this time? since that very first morning? Was the whole progress still being enacted there, was it still the same morning, and himself not yet wholly awake? And even now, had the postman not yet come round the corner? . . .

This idea amused him, and automatically, as he thought of it, he turned his head and looked toward the top of the hill. There was, of course, nothing there— nothing and no one. The street was empty and quiet. And all the more because of its emptiness it occurred to him to count the houses—a thing which, oddly 300 enough, he hadn't before thought of doing. Of course, he had known there weren't many—many, that is, on his own side of the street, which were the ones that figured in the postman's progress—but nevertheless it came to him as something of a shock to find that there were precisely *six*, above his own house—his own house was the seventh.

Six!

Astonished, he looked at his own house—looked at the door, on which was the number thirteen—and then realized that the whole thing was exactly and logically and absurdly what he ought to have known. Just the same, the realization gave him abruptly, and even a little frighteningly, a sense of hurry. He was being 310 hurried—he was being rushed. For—he knit his brows—he couldn't be mistaken—it was just above the *seventh* house, his *own* house, that the postman had first been audible this very morning. But in that case—in that case—did it mean that tomorrow he would hear nothing? The knock he had heard must have been the knock of their own door. Did it mean—and this was an idea which gave him a really extraordinary feeling of surprise—that he would never hear the postman again?—that tomorrow morning the postman would already have passed the house, in a snow by then so deep as to render his footsteps completely inaudible? That he would have made his approach down the snow-filled street so soundlessly, so secretly, that he, Paul Hasleman, there lying in bed, would not have waked in 320 time, or, waking, would have heard nothing?

But how could that be? Unless even the knocker should be muffled in the snow—frozen tight, perhaps? . . . But in that case—

A vague feeling of disappointment came over him; a vague sadness, as if he felt himself deprived of something which he had long looked forward to, something much prized. After all this, all this beautiful progress, the slow delicious advance of the postman through the silent and secret snow, the knock creeping closer each day, and the footsteps nearer, the audible compass of the world thus daily narrowed, narrowed, narrowed, as the snow soothingly and beautifully encroached and deepened, after all this, was he to be defrauded of the one thing he 330 had so wanted—to be about to count, as it were, the last two or three solemn footsteps, as they finally approached his own door? Was it all going to happen, at the end, so suddenly? or indeed, had it already happened? with no slow and subtle gradations of menace, in which he could luxuriate?

He gazed upward again, towards his own window which flashed in the sun: and this time almost with a feeling that it would be better if he *were* still in bed, in that room; for in that case this must still be the first morning, and there would be six more mornings to come—or, for that matter, seven or eight or nine—how could he be sure?—or even more.

3

After supper, the inquisition began. He stood before the doctor, under the 340 lamp, and submitted silently to the usual thumpings and tappings.

"Now will you please say 'Ah!'?"

"Ah!"

"Now again please, if you don't mind."

"Ah."

"Say it slowly and hold it if you can—"

"Ah-h-h-h-h—"

"Good."

How silly all this was. As if it had anything to do with his throat! Or his heart or lungs!   350

Relaxing his mouth, of which the corners, after all this absurd stretching, felt uncomfortable, he avoided the doctor's eyes, and stared towards the fireplace, past his mother's feet (in gray slippers) which projected from the green chair, and his father's feet (in brown slippers) which stood neatly side by side on the hearth rug.

"Hm. There is certainly nothing wrong there . . ."

He felt the doctor's eyes fixed upon him, and, as if merely to be polite, returned the look, but with a feeling of justifiable evasiveness.

"Now, young man, tell me,—do you feel all right?"

"Yes, sir, quite all right."

"No headaches? No dizziness?"   360

"No, I don't think so."

"Let me see. Let's get a book, if you don't mind—yes, thank you, that will do splendidly—and now, Paul, if you'll just read it, holding it as you would normally hold it—"

He took the book and read:

"And another praise have I to tell for this the city our mother, the gift of a great god, a glory of the land most high; the might of horses, the might of young horses, the might of the sea. . . . For thou, son of Cronus, our lord Poseidon, hast throned herein this pride, since in these roads first thou didst show forth the curb that cures the rage of steeds. And the shapely oar, apt to men's hands, hath a wonderous speed 370 on the brine, following the hundred-footed Nereids. . . . O land that art praised above all lands, now is it for thee to make those bright praises seen in deeds."

He stopped, tentatively, and lowered the heavy book.

"No—as I thought—there is certainly no superficial sign of eyestrain."

Silence thronged the room, and he was aware of the focused scrutiny of the three people who confronted him. . . .

"We could have his eyes examined—but I believe it is something else."

"What could it be?" This was his father's voice.

"It's only this curious absent-minded—" This was his mother's voice.

In the presence of the doctor, they both seemed irritatingly apologetic.   380

"I believe it is something else. Now, Paul—I would like very much to ask you a question or two. You will answer them, won't you—you know I'm an old, old friend of yours, eh? That's right! . . . ."

His back was thumped twice by the doctor's fat fist—then the doctor was grinning at him with false amiability, while with one finger-nail he was scratching the top button of his waistcoat. Beyond the doctor's shoulder was the fire, the fingers of flame making light prestidigitation against the sooty fireback, the soft sound of their random flutter the only sound.

"I would like to know—is there anything that worries you?"

The doctor was again smiling, his eyelids low against the little black pupils, 390 in each of which was a tiny white bead of light. Why answer him? Why answer him at all? "At whatever pain to others"—but it was all a nuisance, this necessity for resistance, this necessity for attention: it was as if one had been stood up on a brilliantly lighted stage, under a great round blaze of spotlight; as if one were merely a trained seal, or a performing dog, or a fish, dipped out of an aquarium and held up by the tail. It would serve them right if he were merely to bark or growl. And meanwhile, to miss these last few precious hours, these hours of which every minute was more beautiful than the last, more menacing—? He still looked, as if from a great distance, at the beads of light in the doctor's eyes, at the fixed false smile, and then, beyond, once more at his mother's slippers, his father's slip- 400 pers, the soft flutter of the fire. Even here, even amongst these hostile presences, and in this arranged light, he could see the snow, he could hear it—it was in the corners of the room, where the shadow was deepest, under the sofa, behind the half-opened door which led to the dining room. It was gentler here, softer, its seethe the quietest of whispers, as if, in deference to a drawing room, it had quite deliberately put on its "manners"; it kept itself out of sight, obliterated itself, but distinctly with an air of saying, "Ah, but just wait! Wait till we are alone together! Then I will begin to tell you something new! Something white! something cold! something sleepy! something of cease, and peace, and the long bright curve of space! Tell them to go away. Banish them. Refuse to speak. Leave them, go upstairs 410 to your room, turn out the light and get into bed—I will go with you, I will be waiting for you, I will tell you a better story than Little Kay of the Skates, or The Snow Ghost—I will surround your bed, I will close the windows, pile a deep drift against the door, so that none will ever again be able to enter. Speak to them! . . ."
It seemed as if the little hissing voice came from a slow white spiral of falling flakes in the corner by the front window—but he could not be sure. He felt himself smiling, then, and said to the doctor, but without looking at him, looking beyond him still—

"Oh, no, I think not—"

"But are you sure, my boy?"   420

His father's voice came softly and coldly then—the familiar voice of silken warning. . . .

"You needn't answer at once, Paul—remember we're trying to help you— think it over and be quite sure, won't you?"

He felt himself smiling again, at the notion of being quite sure. What a joke! As if he weren't so sure that reassurance was no longer necessary, and all this cross-examination a ridiculous farce, a grotesque parody! What could they know about it? These gross intelligences, these humdrum minds so bound to the usual, the ordinary? Impossible to tell them about it! Why, even now, even now, with the proof so abundant, so formidable, so imminent, so appallingly present here in this   430 very room, could they believe it?—could even his mother believe it? No—it was only too plain that if anything were said about it, the merest hint given, they would be incredulous—they would laugh—they would say "Absurd!"—think things about him which weren't true. . . .

"Why no, I'm not worried—why should I be?"

He looked then straight at the doctor's low-lidded eyes, looked from one of them to the other, from one bead of light to the other, and gave a little laugh.

The doctor seemed to be disconcerted by this. He drew back in his chair, resting a fat white hand on either knee. The smile faded slowly from his face.

"Well, Paul!" he said, and paused gravely, "I'm afraid you don't take this   440 quite seriously enough. I think you perhaps don't quite realize—don't quite real- ize—" He took a deep quick breath, and turned, as if helpless, at a loss for words, to the others. But Mother and Father were both silent—no help was forthcoming.

"You must surely know, be aware, that you have not been quite yourself, of late? Don't you know that? . . ."

It was amusing to watch the doctor's renewed attempt at a smile, a queer dis- organized look, as of confidential embarrassment.

"I feel all right, sir," he said, and again gave the little laugh.

"And we're trying to help you." The doctor's tone sharpened.

"Yes, sir, I know. But why? I'm all right. I'm just *thinking*, that's all."   450

His mother made a quick movement forward, resting a hand on the back of the doctor's chair.

"Thinking?" she said. "But my dear, about what?"

This was a direct challenge—and would have to be directly met. But before he met it, he looked again into the corner by the door, as if for reassurance. He smiled again at what he saw, at what he heard. The little spiral was still there, still softly whirling, like the ghost of a white kitten chasing the ghost of a white tail, and making as it did so the faintest of whispers. It was all right! If only he could remain firm, everything was going to be all right.

"Oh, about anything, about nothing.—*you* know the way you do!"   460

"You mean—day-dreaming?"

"Oh, no—thinking!"

"But thinking about *what*?"

"Anything."

He laughed a third time—but this time, happening to glance upward to- wards his mother's face, he was appalled at the effect his laughter seemed to have upon her. Her mouth had opened in an expression of horror. . . . This was too bad! Unfortunate! He had known it would cause pain, of course—but he hadn't expected it to be quite so bad as this. Perhaps—perhaps if he just gave them a tiny gleaming hint—?

"About the snow," he said.

"What on earth!" This was his father's voice. The brown slippers came a step nearer on the hearth-rug.

"But my dear, what do you mean!" This was his mother's voice.

The doctor merely stared.

"Just *snow*, that's all. I like to think about it."

"Tell us about it, my boy."

"But that's all it is. There's nothing to tell. *You* know what snow is."

This he said almost angrily, for he felt that they were trying to corner him. He turned sideways so as no longer to face the doctor, and the better to see the inch of blackness between the window-sill and the lowered curtains,—the cold inch of beckoning and delicious night. At once he felt better, more assured.

"Mother—can I go to bed, now, please? I've got a headache."

"But I thought you said—"

"It's just come. It's all these questions—! Can I, Mother?"

"You can go as soon as the doctor has finished."

"Don't you think this thing ought to be gone into thoroughly, and *now*?" This was Father's voice. The brown slippers again came a step nearer, the voice was the well-known "punishment" voice, resonant and cruel.

"Oh, what's the use, Norman—"

Quite suddenly, everyone was silent. And without precisely facing them, nevertheless he was aware that all three of them were watching him with an extraordinary intensity—staring hard at him—as if he had done something monstrous, or was himself some kind of monster. He could hear the soft irregular flutter of the flames; the cluck-click-cluck-click of the clock; far and faint, two sudden spurts of laughter from the kitchen, as quickly cut off as begun; a murmur of water in the pipes; and then, the silence seemed to deepen, to spread out, to become world-long and worldwide, to become timeless and shapeless, and to center inevitably and rightly, with a slow and sleepy but enormous concentration of all power, on the beginning of a new sound. What this new sound was going to be, he knew perfectly well. It might begin with a hiss, but it would end with a roar—there was no time to lose—he must escape. It mustn't happen here—

Without another word, he turned and ran up the stairs.

4

Not a moment too soon. The darkness was coming in long white waves. A prolonged sibilance filled the night—a great seamless seethe of wild influence went abruptly across it—a cold low humming shook the windows. He shut the door and flung off his clothes in the dark. The bare black floor was like a little raft tossed in waves in snow, almost overwhelmed, washed under whitely, up again,

smothered in curled billows of feather. The snow was laughing: it spoke from all
sides at once: it pressed closer to him as he ran and jumped exulting into his bed.   510

"Listen to us!" it said. "Listen! We have come to tell you the story we told
you about. You remember? Lie down. Shut your eyes, now—you will no longer
see much—in this white darkness who could see, or want to see? We will take the
place of everything. . . . Listen—"

A beautiful varying dance of snow began at the front of the room, came forward and then retreated, flattened out towards the floor, then rose fountain-like to
the ceiling, swayed, recruited itself from a new stream of flakes which poured
laughing in through the humming window, advanced again, lifted long white
arms. It said peace, it said remoteness, it said cold—it said—

But then a gash of horrible light fell brutally across the room from the open-   520
ing door—the snow drew back hissing—something alien had come into the
room—something hostile. This thing rushed at him, clutched at him, shook
him—and he was not merely horrified, he was filled with such a loathing as he
had never known. What was this? this cruel disturbance? this act of anger and
hate? It was as if he had to reach up a hand toward another world for any understanding of it—an effort of which he was only barely capable. But of that other
world he still remembered just enough to know the exorcising words. They tore
themselves from his other life suddenly—

"Mother! Mother! Go away! I hate you!"

And with that effort, everything was solved, everything became all right: the   530
seamless hiss advanced once more, the long white wavering lines rose and fell like
enormous whispering sea-waves, the whisper becoming louder, the laughter more
numerous.

"Listen!" it said. "We'll tell you the last, the most beautiful and secret story—
shut your eyes—it is a very small story—a story that gets smaller and smaller—it
comes inward instead of opening like a flower—it is a flower becoming a seed—a
little cold seed—do you hear? We are leaning closer to you—"

The hiss was now becoming a roar—the whole world was a vast moving
screen of snow—but even now it said peace, it said remoteness, it said cold, it said
sleep.   [1932]   540

___

Questions for Discussion and Writing

1. What is this story about? A descent into madness? Going through a phase?
   Something else? Explain your answer.
2. How does Paul see the exterior world of everyday reality? How does he appear to react to or regard that world?
3. Is Paul retreating from reality or exercising the powers of his imagination? Is
   he an artist in the making?
4. What does the snow symbolize?
5. What do the footsteps of the postman suggest?

ペ JUAN BOSCH
(b. 1909)

TRANSLATED BY GUSTAVO PELLÓN

The Woman

Juan Bosch has lived a double career as an influential writer and political activist. He was born in the Dominican Republic, where from an early age he witnessed the exploitation of the peasants by wealthy tobacco growers. He also grew up resenting the United States' intervention in Latin America's affairs during its occupation of the Dominican Republic from 1916 to 1924. Beginning with his first collection of stories, *Camino Real* (1933), he championed the cause of Dominican nationalism and the dignity of the peasants. His political ideas and activities earned the disfavor of the repressive regime of Rafael Trujillo, who imprisoned him in 1933.

In 1937, Bosch and his family left their native land and for the next twenty-four years lived in exile. He was imprisoned again in 1958 by the Cuban dictator, Fulgencio Batista. When Trujillo was assassinated in 1961, he returned to the Dominican Republic and was elected his country's president in 1963. A military coup forced him from office and again from the country. Two years later, civil war provided the excuse for the United States again to invade. Joaquin Balaguer, helped in part by American support, defeated Bosch in an election.

Bosch's early stories are part of the *criollismo* movement. *Criollismo* reacted against the European influences of Modernism and attempted to redefine Latin American literature by focusing on native settings, themes, and characters. In many ways it resembles the political and proletarian literatures of Europe and the United States during the 1920s and 1930s. Bosch's later stories, however, are often experimental, using fantasy and the marvelous to explore both the inner lives of his characters and the political and social situations in which they find themselves.

"The Woman" is among Bosch's earliest works. Its symbolic treatment of the road and its poetic language have led to numerous readings—feminist, Marxist, and nationalistic. Though much of its style is lost in translation, it retains an intensity that imbues its actions with emotional and symbolic significance.

THE ROAD IS DEAD. Nobody nor anything will bring it back to life. Long, infinitely long, not even its gray skin betrays any sign of life. The sun killed it; the steel sun, glowing red-hot—a red that turned to white. Later the white steel became transparent, and there it remains, on the road's back.

Many centuries must have passed since its death. Men with pickaxes and shovels dug it up. They sang and dug; there were some, however, who neither sang nor dug. All that took very long. You could tell they came from far away; they sweated and stank. In the afternoon, the white steel would turn red; then a very small bonfire would flare up behind the pupils of the men who were digging up the road.   10

Death crossed the savannas, and the hills and the winds covered her with dust. Later the dust also died and it came to rest on the gray skin.

Along the sides there are thorny bushes. Often the eye grows sick from so much vastness. But the plains are bare. Scrubland in the distance. Perhaps birds of prey crown the cactus. And the cactus are out there, farther off, stuffed into the white steel.

There are huts too, almost all of them low and made of mud. Some are painted white and cannot be seen under the sun. Only the coarse roof stands out, dry, eager to be burned day after day. Gray hairs emanated from those roofs down which water never rolls.   20

The dead road, totally dead, lies there, dug up, gray. The woman first looked like a black dot, then like a stone that someone might have left on the long mummy. There she lay, without a breeze to stir her rags. The sun did not burn her; only the screams of her child made her feel pain. The child was bronzed, tiny, with his eyes full of light, and he grasped at his mother trying to pull her with his little hands. Soon the road would burn the tiny body, at least the knees, of that naked and screaming child.

The house was nearby, but could not be seen.

As he advanced, what seemed like a stone thrown in the middle of the great dead road grew. It continued to grow, and Quico said to himself: "A calf, no doubt, 30 run over by a car."

He looked around: the plain, the savanna. A distant hill covered with brush, as if that hill were only a little mound of sand piled up by the winds. The bed of a river; the dry jaws of the earth which held water a thousand years ago. The golden plain cracked and split under the heavy transparent steel. The cactus, crowned with birds of prey.

Now closer, Quico saw that it was a person. He distinctly heard the screams of the child.

Her husband had beaten her. He chased her through the only room of the hut, which was hot like an oven, pulling her by the hair and pounding her head 40 with his fists.

"You slut! You slut! I'm going to kill you like a lousy bitch!"

"But nobody came by, Chepe; nobody came by!" she tried to explain.

"No, eh? Now you're going to see!" And he beat her again.

The child clutched at his father's legs. He saw the woman bleeding through the nose. The blood didn't frighten him, no, it only made him want to cry and scream a lot. Mommy would die for sure if she kept on bleeding.

It was all because the woman didn't sell the goat's milk, as he had ordered her to do. When he returned from the hills, four days later, he didn't find the money. She said the milk had gone sour; the truth was that she had drunk it, pre- 50 ferring not to have a few coins rather than let the child suffer from hunger for so long.

Later he told her to leave with her son: "I'll kill you if you come back to this house!"

The woman lay sprawled on the earth floor, bleeding a lot, hearing nothing. Chepe, in a frenzy, dragged her to the road. And there she lay, half dead, on the back of the great mummy.

Quico had water for two more days of travel, but used almost all of it to sprinkle the woman's forehead. He took her to the hut, by having her lean on his arm, and he considered ripping his striped shirt to wipe off her blood. Chepe 60 came in through the backyard.

"I told you I didn't want to see you here again, damn you!"

It seems that he had not seen the stranger. That white transparent steel had surely turned him into a beast. His hair was bleached stiff and his corneas were red.

Quico shouted at him, but he, half-crazed, once more threatened his victim. He was about to hit her. That was when the fight broke out between the two men.

The child, tiny, so tiny, began to shout again; now he wrapped himself in his mother's skirt.

The fight was like a silent song. They didn't say a word. Only the screams of 70 the child and the violent steps could be heard.

The woman saw how Quico was choking Chepe: his fingers hooked onto her husband's throat. The latter's eyes began to close; his mouth was opening, and the blood was rushing to his face.

She didn't know what happened, but nearby, next to the door there was a rock; a rock like a hunk of lava, rough, almost black, heavy. She felt a brutal force growing within her. She raised it. The blow sounded dull. Quico first let go of the other's throat, bent his knees, then opening his arms wide, he fell backward, without complaining, without a struggle.

The earth of the floor absorbed that blood which was so red, so abundant. 80 Chepe could see the light shimmering on it.

The woman's hands twitched over her face, all her hair loose and her eyes straining to pop out. She ran. She felt weak in all her joints. She wanted to see if someone was coming; but on the big dead road, totally dead, there was only the sun which killed her. In the distance, beyond the plain, the hill of sand which the winds piled up. And the cactus, stuffed into the steel.   [1933]

Questions for Discussion and Writing

1. This story unites lyrical description with intense dramatic action. How does the author unify these conflicting forces?
2. Analyze the images of heat and the sun. What function do these images serve in the story?
3. Why is the road described as dead? Since roads are obviously dead, what purpose does such description serve?
4. Why does the woman defend her husband?
5. What social or political implications does this story have? How are these communicated?

☞ LANGSTON HUGHES
(1902–1967)

Cora Unashamed

Langston Hughes' accomplishments as a poet, playwright, novelist, short story writer, essayist, and music critic place him in the forefront of the black artists and intellectuals who emerged during the Harlem Renaissance. Hughes was born in Joplin, Missouri, to a father whose bitterness over the difficulties of finding steady work led him to settle in Mexico. Hughes' mother refused to join her husband and spent much of her time in a fruitless search for jobs. As a result, Langston spent much of his youth with relatives. In spite of these difficulties, he graduated from high school and entered Columbia University.

Hughes did not find either New York's weather or the racial climate at Columbia congenial. The time he spent in Harlem, however, yielded valuable insight into black American culture and introduced him to other writers, especially Arna Bontemps (1902–1973), with whom he formed a life-long friendship. He eventually graduated from Lincoln University in Pennsylvania. Hughes then worked as a cook, launderer, table clearer, and seaman on voyages to Europe and Africa, storing up impressions and ideas that later emerged in his writing. Like many other writers of the time, he leaned to the left politically.

For many critics, however, Hughes was not radical enough. In spite of pioneering work to free African-American literature from the Plantation School and an insistence on writing for black audiences, he has been criticized for being too accommodating to white society and for perpetuating black stereotypes through his most famous creation, Jesse B. Semple—the chief character in a series of satirical sketches. Semple struggles with the ordinary problems of life but keeps a common sense perspective as he offers shrewdly satirical comments on American ways and values. Hughes' accomplishments will no doubt survive his critics. He wrote, as he said, for ordinary people confronting the problems of life, including racism.

MELTON WAS ONE of those miserable in-between little places, not large enough to be a town, nor small enough to be a village—that is, a village in the rural, charming sense of the word. Melton had no charm about it. It was merely a nondescript collection of houses and buildings in a region of farms—one of those sad American places with sidewalks, but no paved streets; electric lights, but no sewage; a station, but no trains that stopped, save a jerky local, morning and evening. And it was 150 miles from any city at all—even Sioux City.

Cora Jenkins was one of the least of the citizens of Melton. She was what the people referred to when they wanted to be polite, as a Negress, and when they wanted to be rude, as a nigger—sometimes adding the word "wench" for no good   10 reason, for Cora was usually an inoffensive soul, except that she sometimes cussed.

She had been in Melton for forty years. Born there. Would die there probably. She worked for the Studevants, who treated her like a dog. She stood it. Had to stand it; or work for poorer white folks who would treat her worse; or go jobless. Cora was like a tree—once rooted, she stood, in spite of storms and strife, wind, and rocks, in the earth.

She was the Studevants' maid of all work—washing, ironing, cooking, scrubbing, taking care of kids, nursing old folks, making fires, carrying water.

Cora, bake three cakes for Mary's birthday tomorrow night. You Cora, give Rover a bath in that tar soap I bought. Cora, take Ma some jello, and don't let her have even a taste of that raisin pie. She'll keep us up all night if you do. Cora, iron my stockings. Cora, come here . . . Cora, put . . . Cora . . . Cora. . . Cora! Cora!

And Cora would answer, "Yes, m'am."

The Studevants thought they owned her, and they were perfectly right: they did. There was something about the teeth in the trap of economic circumstance that kept her in their power practically all her life—in the Studevant kitchen, cooking; in the Studevant parlor, sweeping; in the Studevant backyard, hanging clothes.

You want to know how that could be? How a trap could close so tightly? Here is the outline:

Cora was the oldest of a family of eight children—the Jenkins niggers. The only Negroes in Melton, thank God! Where they came from originally—that is, the old folks—God knows. The kids were born there. The old folks are still there now: Pa drives a junk wagon. The old woman ails around the house, ails and quarrels. Seven kids are gone. Only Cora remains. Cora simply couldn't go, with nobody else to help take care of Ma. And before that she couldn't go, with nobody to see that her brothers and sisters got through school (she the oldest, and Ma ailing). And before that—well, somebody had to help Ma look after one baby behind another that kept on coming.

As a child Cora had no playtime. She always had a little brother, or a little sister in her arms. Bad, crying, bratty babies, hungry and mean. In the eighth grade she quit school and went to work with the Studevants.

After that, she ate better. Half day's work at first, helping Ma at home the rest of the time. Then full days, bringing home her pay to feed her father's children. The old man was rather a drunkard. What little money he made from closet-cleaning, ash-hauling, and junk-dealing he spent mostly on the stuff that makes you forget you have eight kids.

He passed the evenings telling long, comical lies to the white riff-raff of the town, and drinking licker. When his horse died, Cora's money went for a new one to haul her Pa and his rickety wagon around. When the mortgage money came due, Cora's wages kept the man from taking the roof from over their heads. When Pa got in jail, Cora borrowed ten dollars from Mrs. Studevant and got him out.

Cora stinted, and Cora saved, and wore the Studevants' old clothes, and ate the Studevants' leftover food, and brought her pay home. Brothers and sisters grew up. The boys, lonesome, went away, as far as they could from Melton. One by one, the girls left too, mostly in disgrace. "Ruinin' ma name," Pa Jenkins said, "Ruinin' ma good name! They can't go out berryin' but what they come back in disgrace." There was something about the cream-and-tan Jenkins girls that at- tracted the white farm hands.   60

Even Cora, the humble, had a lover once. He came to town on a freight train (long ago now), and worked at the livery-stable. (That was before autos got to be so common.) Everybody said he was an I. W. W.[1] Cora didn't care. He was the first man and the last she ever remembered wanting. She had never known a colored lover. There weren't any around. That was not her fault.

This white boy, Joe, he always smelt like the horses. He was some kind of foreigner. Had an accent, and yellow hair, big hands, and grey eyes.

It was summer. A few blocks beyond the Studevants' house, meadows and orchards and sweet fields stretched away to the far horizon. At night, stars in the velvet sky. Moon sometimes. Crickets and katydids and lightning bugs. The scent   70 of grass. Cora waiting. That boy, Joe, a cigarette spark far off, whistling in the dark. Love didn't take long—Cora with the scent of Studevants' supper about her, and a cheap perfume. Joe, big and strong and careless as the horses he took care of, smelling like the stable.

Ma would quarrel because Cora came home late, or because none of the kids had written for three or four weeks, or because Pa was drunk again. Thus the summer passed, a dream of big hands and grey eyes.

Cora didn't go anywhere to have her child. Nor tried to hide it. When the baby grew big within her, she didn't feel that it was a disgrace. The Studevants told her to go home and stay there. Joe left town. Pa cussed. Ma cried. One April   80 morning the kid was born. She had grey eyes, and Cora called her Josephine, after Joe.

Cora was humble and shameless before the fact of the child. There were no Negroes in Melton to gossip, and she didn't care what the white people said. They were in another world. Of course, she hadn't expected to marry Joe, or keep him. He was of that other world, too. But the child was hers—a living bridge between two worlds. Let people talk.

Cora went back to work at the Studevants'—coming home at night to nurse her kid, and quarrel with Ma. About that time, Mrs. Art Studevant had a child, too, and Cora nursed it. The Studevants' little girl was named Jessie. As the two   90 children began to walk and talk, Cora sometimes brought Josephine to play with Jessie—until the Studevants objected, saying she could get her work done better if she left her child at home.

"Yes, m'am," said Cora.

But in a little while they didn't need to tell Cora to leave her child at home, for Josephine died of whooping-cough. One rosy afternoon, Cora saw the little body go down into the ground in a white casket that cost four weeks' wages.

Since Ma was ailing, Pa, smelling of licker, stood with her at the grave. The two of them alone. Cora was not humble before the fact of death. As she turned away from the hole, tears came—but at the same time a stream of curses so violent   100 that they made the grave-tenders look up in startled horror.

---

1. Industrial Workers of the World. Labor unions were often suspected of dangerous left-wing tendencies.

She cussed out God for taking away the life that she herself had given. She screamed, "My baby! God damn it! My baby! I bear her and you take her away!" She looked at the sky where the sun was setting and yelled in defiance. Pa was amazed and scared. He pulled her up on his rickety wagon and drove off, clattering down the road between green fields and sweet meadows that stretched away to the far horizon. All through the ugly town Cora wept and cursed, using all the bad words she had learned from Pa in his drunkenness.

The next week she went back to the Studevants. She was gentle and humble in the face of life—she loved their baby. In the afternoons on the back porch, she 110 would pick little Jessie up and rock her to sleep, burying her dark face in the milky smell of the white child's hair.

II

The years passed. Pa and Ma Jenkins only dried up a little. Old Man Studevant died. The old lady had two strokes. Mrs. Art Studevant and her husband began to look their age, greying hair and sagging stomachs. The children were grown, or nearly so. Kenneth took over the management of the hardware store that Grandpa had left. Jack went off to college. Mary was a teacher. Only Jessie remained a child—her last year in high-school. Jessie, nineteen now, and rather slow in her studies, graduating at last. In the Fall she would go to Normal.

Cora hated to think about her going away. In her heart she had adopted 120 Jessie. In that big and careless household it was always Cora who stood like a calm and sheltering tree for Jessie to run to in her troubles. As a child, when Mrs. Art spanked her, as soon as she could, the tears still streaming, Jessie would find her way to the kitchen and Cora. At each school term's end, when Jessie had usually failed in some of her subjects (she quite often failed, being a dull child), it was Cora who saw the report-card first with the bad marks on it. Then Cora would devise some way of breaking the news gently to the old folks.

Her mother was always a little ashamed of stupid Jessie, for Mrs. Art was the civic and social leader of Melton, president of the Woman's Club three years straight, and one of the pillars of her church. Mary, the elder, the teacher, would 130 follow with dignity in her footsteps, but Jessie! That child! Spankings in her youth, and scoldings now, did nothing to Jessie's inner being. She remained a plump, dull, freckled girl, placid and strange. Everybody found fault with her but Cora.

In the kitchen Jessie bloomed. She laughed. She talked. She was sometimes even witty. And she learned to cook wonderfully. With Cora, everything seemed so simple—not hard and involved like algebra, or Latin grammar, or the civic problems of Mama's club, or the sermons at church. Nowhere in Melton, nor with anyone, did Jessie feel so comfortable as with Cora in the kitchen. She knew her mother looked down on her as a stupid girl. And with her father there was no 140 bond. He was always too busy buying and selling to bother with the kids. And often he was off in the city. Old doddering Grandma made Jessie sleepy and sick. Cousin Nora (Mother's cousin) was as stiff and prim as a minister's daughter. And Jessie's older brothers and sister went their ways, seeing Jessie hardly at all, except at the big table at mealtimes.

Like all the unpleasant things in the house, Jessie was left to Cora. And Cora was happy. To have a child to raise, a child the same age as her Josephine would have been, gave her a purpose in life, a warmth inside herself. It was Cora who nursed and mothered and petted and loved the dull little Jessie through the years. And now Jessie was a young woman, graduating (late) from high-school.   150

But something had happened to Jessie. Cora knew it before Mrs. Art did. Jessie was not too stupid to have a boy-friend. She told Cora about it like a mother. She was afraid to tell Mrs. Art. Afraid! Afraid! Afraid!

Cora said, "I'll tell her." So, humble and unashamed about her life, one afternoon she marched into Mrs. Art's sun-porch and announced quite simply, "Jessie's going to have a baby."

Cora smiled, but Mrs. Art stiffened like a bolt. Her mouth went dry. She rose like a soldier. Sat down. Rose again. Walked straight toward the door, turned around, and whispered, "What?"

"Yes, m'am, a baby. She told me. A little child. Its father is Willie Matsoulos,   160 whose folks runs the ice-cream stand on Main. She told me. They want to get married, but Willie ain't here now. He don't know yet about the child."

Cora would have gone on humbly and shamelessly talking about the little unborn had not Mrs. Art fallen into uncontrollable hysterics. Cousin Nora came running from the library, her glasses on a chain. Old Lady Studevant's wheel-chair rolled up, doddering and shaking with excitement. Jessie came, when called, red and sweating, but had to go out, for when her mother looked up from the couch and saw her she yelled louder than ever. There was a rush for camphor bottles and water and ice. Crying and praying followed all over the house. Scandalization! Oh, my Lord! Jessie was in trouble.   170

"She ain't in trouble neither," Cora insisted. "No trouble having a baby you want. I had one."

"Shut up, Cora!"

"Yes, ma'm. . . . But I had one."

"Hush, I tell you."

"Yes, m'am."

III

Then it was that Cora began to be shut out. Jessie was confined to her room. That afternoon, when Miss Mary came home from school, the four white women got together behind closed doors in Mrs. Art's bedroom. For once Cora cooked supper in the kitchen without being bothered by an interfering voice. Mr.   180 Studevant was away in Des Moines. Somehow Cora wished he was home. Big and gruff as he was, he had more sense than the women. He'd probably make a shot-gun wedding out of it. But left to Mrs. Art, Jessie would never marry the Greek boy at all. This Cora knew. No man had been found yet good enough for sister Mary to mate with. Mrs. Art had ambitions which didn't include the likes of Greek ice-cream makers' sons.

Jessie was crying when Cora brought her supper up. The black woman sat down on the bed and lifted the white girl's head in her dark hands. "Don't you mind, honey," Cora said. "Just sit tight, and when the boy comes back I'll tell him

how things are. If he loves you he'll want you. And there ain't no reason why you 190
can't marry, neither—you both white. Even if he is a foreigner, he's a right nice
boy."

"He loves me," Jessie said. "I know he does. He said so."

But before the boy came back (or Mr. Studevant either) Mrs. Art and Jessie
went to Kansas City. "For an Easter shopping trip," the weekly paper said.

Then Spring came in full bloom, and the fields and orchards at the edge of
Melton stretched green and beautiful to the far horizon. Cora remembered her
own Spring, twenty years ago, and a great sympathy and pain welled up in her
heart for Jessie, who was the same age that Josephine would have been, had she
lived. Sitting on the kitchen porch shelling peas, Cora thought back over her own 200
life—years and years of working for the Studevants; years and years of going home
to nobody but Ma and Pa; little Josephine dead; only Jessie to keep her heart
warm. And she knew that Jessie was the dearest thing she had in the world. All
the time the girl was gone now, she worried.

After ten days, Mrs. Art and her daughter came back. But Jessie was thinner
and paler than she'd ever been in her life. There was no light in her eyes at all.
Mrs. Art looked a little scared as they got off the train.

"She had an awful attack of indigestion in Kansas City," she told the neighbors and club women. "That's why I stayed away so long, waiting for her to be
able to travel. Poor Jessie! She looks healthy, but she's never been a strong child. 210
She's one of the worries of my life." Mrs. Art talked a lot, explained a lot, about
how Jessie had eaten the wrong things in Kansas City.

At home, Jessie went to bed. She wouldn't eat. When Cora brought her food
up, she whispered, "The baby's gone."

Cora's face went dark. She bit her lips to keep from cursing. She put her
arms about Jessie's neck. The girl cried. Her food went untouched.

A week passed. They tried to *make* Jessie eat then. But the food wouldn't stay
in her stomach. Her eyes grew yellow, her tongue white, her heart acted crazy.
They called in old Doctor Brown, but within a month (as quick as that) Jessie
died. 220

She never saw the Greek boy any more. Indeed, his father had lost his license, "due to several complaints by the mothers of children, backed by the
Woman's Club," that he was selling tainted ice-cream. Mrs. Art Studevant had
started a campaign to rid the town of objectionable tradespeople and questionable
characters. Greeks were bound to be one or the other. For a while they even
closed up Pa Jenkins' favorite bootlegger. Mrs. Studevant thought this would
please Cora, but Cora only said, "Pa's been drinkin' so long he just as well keep
on." She refused further to remark on her employer's campaign of purity. In the
midst of this clean-up Jessie died.

On the day of the funeral, the house was stacked with flowers. (They held 230
the funeral, not at the church, but at home, on account of old Grandma
Studevant's infirmities.) All the family dressed in deep mourning. Mrs. Art was
prostrate. As the hour for the services approached, she revived, however, and ate
an omelette, "to help me go through the afternoon."

"And Cora," she said, "cook me a little piece of ham with it. I feel so weak."

"Yes, m'am."

The senior class from the high-school came in a body. The Woman's Club came with their badges. The Reverend Doctor McElroy had on his highest collar and longest coat. The choir sat behind the coffin, with a special soloist to sing "He Feedeth His Flocks Like a Shepherd." It was a beautiful Spring afternoon, and a 240 beautiful funeral.

Except that Cora was there. Of course, her presence created no comment (she was the family servant), but it was what she did, and how she did it, that has remained the talk of Melton to this day—for Cora was not humble in the face of death.

When the Reverend Doctor McElroy had finished his eulogy, and the senior class had read their memorials, and the songs had been sung, and they were about to allow the relatives and friends to pass around for one last look at Jessie Studevant, Cora got up from her seat by the dining-room door. She said, "Honey, I want to say something." She spoke as if she were addressing Jessie. She ap- 250 proached the coffin and held out her brown hands over the white girl's body. Her face moved in agitation. People sat stone-still and there was a long pause. Suddenly she screamed. "They killed you! And for nothin'. . . . They killed your child. . . . They took you away from here in the Springtime of your life, and now you'se gone, gone, gone!"

Folks were paralyzed in their seats.

Cora went on: "They preaches you a pretty sermon and they don't say nothin'. They sings you a song, and they don't say nothin'. But Cora's here, honey, and she's gone tell 'em what they done to you. She's gonna tell 'em why they took you to Kansas City."   260

A loud scream rent the air. Mrs. Art fell back in her chair, stiff as a board. Cousin Nora and sister Mary sat like stones. The men of the family rushed forward to grab Cora. They stumbled over wreaths and garlands. Before they could reach her, Cora pointed her long fingers at the women in black and said, "They killed you, honey. They killed you and your child. I told 'em you loved it, but they didn't care. They killed it before it was . . ."

· A strong hand went around Cora's waist. Another grabbed her arm. The Studevant males half pulled, half pushed her through the aisles of folding chairs, through the crowded dining-room, out into the empty kitchen, through the screen door into the backyard. She struggled against them all the way, accusing their 270 women. At the door she sobbed, great tears coming for the love of Jessie.

She sat down on a wash-bench in the backyard, crying. In the parlor she could hear the choir singing weakly. In a few moments she gathered herself to-gether, and went back into the house. Slowly, she picked up her few belongings from the kitchen and pantry, her aprons and her umbrella, and went off down the alley, home to Ma. Cora never came back to work for the Studevants.

Now she and Ma live from the little garden they raise, and from the junk Pa collects—when they can take by main force a part of his meager earnings before he buys his licker.

Anyhow, on the edge of Melton, the Jenkins niggers, Pa and Ma and Cora, 280 somehow manage to get along.   [1933]

Questions for Discussion and Writing

1. Does Hughes reinforce stereotypes by his depiction of Cora's family? Underline passages to support your conclusion.
2. What aspects of this story would have seemed innovative or even radical in 1933?
3. Does Hughes pile too many sufferings on Cora? Does he, in other words, make her pathetic rather than heroic? Explain.
4. What hypocrisies does the story expose?

❧ ERNEST HEMINGWAY
(1899–1961)

The Short Happy Life of Francis Macomber

No American writer in this century has lived a more romantic life than Ernest Hemingway. His image as a man's man, of both action and imagination, probably inspired more imitators than any writer since Byron. Yet the real man behind the myth of "Papa" Hemingway was much different from the legend he created.

Hemingway was born in the conventional suburb of Oak Park, Illinois. His father inspired the boy's interest in sports and the out of doors; his mother was deeply involved in the arts. After high school he worked as a reporter for the *Kansas City Star,* but when war erupted in Europe in 1914, he volunteered for ambulance duty with the Red Cross in 1918 and was wounded. While convalescing, he began writing short stories. In 1921, he returned to Europe where he wrote dispatches for the *Toronto Star* and mingled with expatriates like James Joyce (1882–1941) and F. Scott Fitzgerald (1896–1940).

Contrary to his later image as a leisured man of the world, Hemingway was a hard worker and conscious artist who set about to create a new kind of prose: simple to the point of starkness, yet suggestive enough to reveal the inner lives of his characters, often by the description of the scene around them. His early short stories were repeatedly rejected by editors who did not understand his elliptical style of narration in which, as he explained in a famous metaphor of an iceberg, only one-eighth is above the surface; the other seven-eighths lie below.

As part of the "Lost Generation"—the disillusioned youth who survived World War I—Hemingway searched for new values in a world stripped of certainty. The result was the famous Hemingway "code": the ability to display grace under pressure and to acknowledge frankly the tragic brevity of human life. Ironically, as he grew older Hemingway sank into confusion and despondency over his loss of health, his waning literary powers, and his four failed marriages. Like his father, he committed suicide, leaving behind a still-potent legend and a body of work that continues to influence writers today.

IT WAS NOW lunch time and they were all sitting under the double green fly of the dining tent pretending that nothing had happened.

"Will you have lime juice or lemon squash?" Macomber asked.

"I'll have a gimlet," Robert Wilson told him.

"I'll have a gimlet, too. I need something," Macomber's wife said.

"I suppose it's the thing to do," Macomber agreed. "Tell him to make three gimlets."

The mess boy had started them already, lifting the bottles out of the canvas cooling bags that sweated wet in the wind that blew through the trees that shaded the tents.   10

"What had I ought to give them?" Macomber asked.

"A quid[1] would be plenty," Wilson told him. "You don't want to spoil them."

"Will the headman distribute it?"

"Absolutely."

Francis Macomber had, half an hour before, been carried to his tent from the edge of the camp in triumph on the arms and shoulders of the cook, the personal boys, the skinner and the porters. The gun-bearers had taken no part in the demonstration. When the native boys put him down at the door of his tent, he had shaken all their hands, received their congratulations, and then gone into the tent and sat on the bed until his wife came in. She did not speak to him when she 20 came in and he left the tent at once to wash his face and hands in the portable wash basin outside and go over to the dining tent to sit in a comfortable canvas chair in the breeze and the shade.

"You've got your lion," Robert Wilson said to him, "and a damned fine one too."

Mrs. Macomber looked at Wilson quickly. She was an extremely handsome and well-kept woman of the beauty and social position which had, five years before, commanded five thousand dollars as the price of endorsing, with photographs, a beauty product which she had never used. She had been married to Francis Macomber for eleven years.   30

"He is a good lion, isn't he?" Macomber said. His wife looked at him now. She looked at both these men as though she had never seen them before.

One, Wilson, the white hunter, she knew she had never truly seen before. He was about middle height with sandy hair, a stubby mustache, a very red face and extremely cold blue eyes with faint white wrinkles at the corners that grooved merrily when he smiled. He smiled at her now and she looked away from his face at the way his shoulders sloped in the loose tunic he wore with the four big cartridges held in loops where the left breast pocket should have been, at his big

1. One pound in English money.

brown hands, his old slacks, his very dirty boots and back to his red face again. She noticed where the baked red of his face stopped in a white line that marked the circle left by his Stetson hat that hung now from one of the pegs of the tent pole.

"Well, here's to the lion," Robert Wilson said. He smiled at her again and, not smiling, she looked curiously at her husband.

Francis Macomber was very tall, very well built if you did not mind that length of bone, dark, his hair cropped like an oarsman, rather thin-lipped, and was considered handsome. He was dressed in the same sort of safari clothes that Wilson wore except that his were new, he was thirty-five years old, kept himself very fit, was good at court games, had a number of big-game fishing records, and had just shown himself, very publicly, to be a coward.

"Here's to the lion," he said. "I can't ever thank you for what you did."

Margaret, his wife, looked away from him and back to Wilson.

"Let's not talk about the lion," she said.

Wilson looked over at her without smiling and now she smiled at him.

"It's been a very strange day," she said. "Hadn't you ought to put your hat on even under the canvas at noon? You told me that, you know."

"Might put it on," said Wilson.

"You know you have a very red face, Mr. Wilson," she told him and smiled again.

"Drink," said Wilson.

"I don't think so," she said. "Francis drinks a great deal, but his face is never red."

"It's red today," Macomber tried a joke.

"No," said Margaret. "It's mine that's red today. But Mr. Wilson's is always red."

"Must be racial," said Wilson. "I say, you wouldn't like to drop my beauty as a topic, would you?"

"I've just started on it."

"Let's chuck it," said Wilson.

"Conversation is going to be so difficult," Margaret said.

"Don't be silly, Margot," her husband said.

"No difficulty," Wilson said. "Got a damn fine lion."

Margot looked at them both and they both saw that she was going to cry. Wilson had seen it coming for a long time and he dreaded it. Macomber was past dreading it.

"I wish it hadn't happened. Oh, I wish it hadn't happened," she said and started for her tent. She made no noise of crying but they could see that her shoulders were shaking under the rose-colored, sun-proofed shirt she wore.

"Women upset," said Wilson to the tall man. "Amounts to nothing. Strain on the nerves and one thing'n another."

"No," said Macomber. "I suppose that I rate that for the rest of my life now."

"Nonsense. Let's have a spot of the giant killer," said Wilson. "Forget the whole thing. Nothing to it anyway."

"We might try," said Macomber. "I won't forget what you did for me though."

"Nothing," said Wilson. "All nonsense."

So they sat there in the shade where the camp was pitched under some wide-topped acacia trees with a boulder-strewn cliff behind them, and a stretch of grass that ran to the bank of a boulder-filled stream in front with forest beyond it, and drank their just-cool lime drinks and avoided one another's eyes while the boys set the table for lunch. Wilson could tell that the boys all knew about it now and when he saw Macomber's personal boy looking curiously at his master while he was putting dishes on the table he snapped at him in Swahili. The boy turned away with his face blank.

"What were you telling him?" Macomber asked.

"Nothing. Told him to look alive or I'd see he got about fifteen of the best."

"What's that? Lashes?"

"It's quite illegal," Wilson said. "You're supposed to fine them."

"Do you still have them whipped?"

"Oh, yes. They could raise a row if they chose to complain. But they don't. They prefer it to the fines."

"How strange!" said Macomber.

"Not strange, really," Wilson said. "Which would you rather do? Take a good birching or lose your pay?"

Then he felt embarrassed at asking it and before Macomber could answer he went on, "We all take a beating every day, you know, one way or another."

This was no better. "Good God," he thought. "I am a diplomat, aren't I?"

"Yes, we take a beating," said Macomber, still not looking at him. "I'm awfully sorry about that lion business. It doesn't have to go any further, does it? I mean no one will hear about it, will they?"

"You mean will I tell it at the Mathaiga Club?" Wilson looked at him now coldly. He had not expected this. So he's a bloody four-letter man as well as a bloody coward, he thought. I rather liked him too until today. But how is one to know about an American?

"No," said Wilson. "I'm a professional hunter. We never talk about our clients. You can be quite easy on that. It's supposed to be bad form to ask us not to talk though."

He decided now that to break would be much easier. He would eat, then, by himself and could read a book with his meals. They would eat by themselves. He would see them through the safari on a very formal basis—what was it the French called it? Distinguished consideration—and it would be a damn sight easier than having to go through this emotional trash. He'd insult him and make a good clean break. Then he could read a book with his meals and he'd still be drinking their whisky. That was the phrase for it when a safari went bad. You ran into another white hunter and you asked, "How is everything going?" and he answered, "Oh, I'm still drinking their whisky," and you knew everything had gone to pot.

"I'm sorry," Macomber said and looked at him with his American face that would stay adolescent until it became middle-aged, and Wilson noted his crew-cropped hair, fine eyes only faintly shifty, good nose, thin lips and handsome jaw. "I'm sorry I didn't realize that. There are lots of things I don't know."

So what could he do, Wilson thought. He was all ready to break it off quickly and neatly and here the beggar was apologizing after he had just insulted him. He made one more attempt. "Don't worry about me talking," he said. "I have a living to make. You know in Africa no woman ever misses her lion and no white man ever bolts."

"I bolted like a rabbit," Macomber said.

Now what in hell were you going to do about a man who talked like that, Wilson wondered.

Wilson looked at Macomber with his flat, blue, machine-gunner's eyes and the other smiled back at him. He had a pleasant smile if you did not notice how his eyes showed when he was hurt.   140

"Maybe I can fix it up on buffalo," he said. "We're after them next, aren't we?"

"In the morning if you like," Wilson told him. Perhaps he had been wrong. This was certainly the way to take it. You most certainly could not tell a damned thing about an American. He was all for Macomber again. If you could forget the morning. But, of course, you couldn't. The morning had been about as bad as they come.

"Here comes the Memsahib," he said. She was walking over from her tent looking refreshed and cheerful and quite lovely. She had a very perfect oval face, so perfect that you expected her to be stupid. But she wasn't stupid, Wilson   150 thought, no, not stupid.

"How is the beautiful red-faced Mr. Wilson? Are you feeling better, Francis, my pearl?"

"Oh, much," said Macomber.

"I've dropped the whole thing," she said, sitting down at the table. "What importance is there to whether Francis is any good at killing lions? That's not his trade. That's Mr. Wilson's trade. Mr. Wilson is really very impressive killing anything. You do kill anything, don't you?"

"Oh, anything," said Wilson. "Simply anything." They are, he thought, the hardest in the world; the hardest, the cruelest, the most predatory and the most at-   160 tractive and their men have softened or gone to pieces nervously as they have hardened. Or is it that they pick men they can handle? They can't know that much at the age they marry, he thought. He was grateful that he had gone through his education on American women before now because this was a very attractive one.

"We're going after buff in the morning," he told her.

"I'm coming," she said.

"No, you're not."

"Oh, yes, I am. Mayn't I, Francis?"

"Why not stay in camp?"

"Not for anything," she said. "I wouldn't miss something like today for any-   170 thing."

When she left, Wilson was thinking, when she went off to cry, she seemed a hell of a fine woman. She seemed to understand, to realize, to be hurt for him and for herself and to know how things really stood. She is away for twenty minutes and now she is back, simply enamelled in that American female cruelty. They are the damnedest women. Really the damnedest.

"We'll put on another show for you tomorrow," Francis Macomber said.

"You're not coming," Wilson said.

"You're very mistaken," she told him. "And I want *so* to see you perform
again. You were lovely this morning. That is if blowing things' heads off is lovely." 180

"Here's the lunch," said Wilson. "You're very merry, aren't you?"

"Why not? I didn't come out here to be dull."

"Well, it hasn't been dull," Wilson said. He could see the boulders in the
river and the high bank beyond with the trees and he remembered the morning.

"Oh, no," she said. "It's been charming. And tomorrow. You don't know how
I look forward to tomorrow."

"That's eland he's offering you," Wilson said.

"They're the big cowy things that jump like hares, aren't they?"

"I suppose that describes them," Wilson said.

"It's very good meat," Macomber said.   190

"Didn't you shoot it, Francis?" she asked.

"Yes."

"They're not dangerous, are they?"

"Only if they fall on you," Wilson told her.

"I'm so glad."

"Why not let up on the bitchery just a little, Margot," Macomber said, cutting the eland steak and putting some mashed potato, gravy and carrot on the
down-turned fork that tined through the piece of meat.

"I suppose I could," she said, "since you put it so prettily."

"Tonight we'll have champagne for the lion," Wilson said. "It's a bit too hot at 200
noon."

"Oh, the lion," Margot said. "I'd forgotten the lion!"

So, Robert Wilson thought to himself, she *is* giving him a ride, isn't she? Or
do you suppose that's her idea of putting up a good show? How should a woman
act when she discovers her husband is a bloody coward? She's damn cruel but
they're all cruel. They govern, of course, and to govern one has to be cruel sometimes. Still, I've seen enough of their damn terrorism.

"Have some more eland," he said to her politely.

That afternoon, late, Wilson and Macomber went out in the motor car with
the native driver and the two gun-bearers. Mrs. Macomber stayed in the camp. It 210
was too hot to go out, she said, and she was going with them in the early morning. As they drove off Wilson saw her standing under the big tree, looking pretty
rather than beautiful in her faintly rosy khaki, her dark hair drawn back off her
forehead and gathered in a knot low on her neck, her face as fresh, he thought, as
though she were in England. She waved to them as the car went off through the
swale of high grass and curved around through the trees into the small hills of orchard bush.

In the orchard bush they found a herd of impala, and leaving the car they
stalked one old ram with long, wide-spread horns and Macomber killed it with a
very creditable shot that knocked the buck down at a good two hundred yards 220
and sent the herd off bounding wildly and leaping over one another's backs in
long, leg-drawn-up leaps as unbelievable and as floating as those one makes sometimes in dreams.

"That was a good shot," Wilson said. "They're a small target."

"Is it a worthwhile head?" Macomber asked.

"It's excellent," Wilson told him. "You shoot like that and you'll have no trouble."

"Do you think we'll find buffalo tomorrow?"

"There's a good chance of it. They feed out early in the morning and with luck we may catch them in the open." 230

"I'd like to clear away that lion business," Macomber said. "It's not very pleasant to have your wife see you do something like that."

I should think it would be even more unpleasant to do it, Wilson thought, wife or no wife, or to talk about it having done it. But he said, "I wouldn't think about that any more. Anyone could be upset by his first lion. That's all over."

But that night after dinner and a whisky and soda by the fire before going to bed, as Francis Macomber lay on his cot with his mosquito bar over him and listened to the night noises, it was not all over. It was neither all over nor was it beginning. It was there exactly as it happened with some parts of it indelibly emphasized and he was miserably ashamed at it. But more than shame he felt cold, 240 hollow fear in him. The fear was still there like a cold slimy hollow in all the emptiness where once his confidence had been and it made him feel sick. It was still there with him now.

It had started the night before when he had wakened and heard the lion roaring somewhere up along the river. It was a deep sound and at the end there were sort of coughing grunts that made him seem just outside the tent, and when Francis Macomber woke in the night to hear it he was afraid. He could hear his wife breathing quietly, asleep. There was no one to tell he was afraid, nor to be afraid with him, and, lying alone, he did not know the Somali proverb that says a brave man is always frightened three times by a lion; when he first sees his track, 250 when he first hears him roar and when he first confronts him. Then while they were eating breakfast by lantern light out in the dining tent, before the sun was up, the lion roared again and Francis thought he was just at the edge of camp.

"Sounds like an old-timer," Robert Wilson said, looking up from his kippers and coffee. "Listen to him cough."

"Is he very close?"

"A mile or so up the stream."

"Will we see him?"

"We'll have a look."

"Does his roaring carry that far? It sounds as though he were right in camp." 260

"Carries a hell of a long way," said Robert Wilson. "It's strange the way it carries. Hope he's a shootable cat. The boys said there was a very big one about here."

"If I get a shot, where should I hit him," Macomber asked, "to stop him?"

"In the shoulders," Wilson said. "In the neck if you can make it. Shoot for bone. Break him down."

"I hope I can place it properly," Macomber said.

"You shoot very well," Wilson told him. "Take your time. Make sure of him. The first one in is the one that counts."

"What range will it be?"

"Can't tell. Lion has something to say about that. Won't shoot unless it's close 270 enough so you can make sure."

"At under a hundred yards?" Macomber asked.

Wilson looked at him quickly.

"Hundred's about right. Might have to take him a bit under. Shouldn't chance a shot at much over that. A hundred's a decent range. You can hit him wherever you want at that. Here comes the Memsahib."

"Good morning," she said. "Are we going after that lion?"

"As soon as you deal with your breakfast," Wilson said. "How are you feeling?"

"Marvellous," she said. "I'm very excited."   280

"I'll just go and see that everything is ready," Wilson went off. As he left the lion roared again.

"Noisy beggar," Wilson said. "We'll put a stop to that."

"What's the matter, Francis?" his wife asked him.

"Nothing," Macomber said.

"Yes, there is," she said. "What are you upset about?"

"Nothing," he said.

"Tell me," she looked at him. "Don't you feel well?"

"It's that damned roaring," he said. "It's been going on all night, you know."

"Why didn't you wake me," she said. "I'd love to have heard it."   290

"I've got to kill the damned thing," Macomber said, miserably.

"Well, that's what you're out here for, isn't it?"

"Yes. But I'm nervous. Hearing the thing roar gets on my nerves."

"Well then, as Wilson said, kill him and stop his roaring."

"Yes, darling," said Francis Macomber. "It sounds easy, doesn't it?"

"You're not afraid, are you?"

"Of course not. But I'm nervous from hearing him roar all night."

"You'll kill him marvellously," she said. "I know you will. I'm awfully anxious to see it."

"Finish your breakfast and we'll be starting."   300

"It's not light yet," she said. "This is a ridiculous hour."

Just then the lion roared in a deep-chested moaning, suddenly guttural, ascending vibration that seemed to shake the air and ended in a sigh and a heavy, deep-chested grunt.

"He sounds almost here," Macomber's wife said.

"My God," said Macomber. "I hate that damned noise."

"It's very impressive."

"Impressive. It's frightful."

Robert Wilson came up then carrying his short, ugly, shockingly big-bored .505 Gibbs and grinning.   310

"Come on," he said. "Your gun-bearer has your Springfield and the big gun. Everything's in the car. Have you solids?"[2]

"Yes."

"I'm ready," Mrs. Macomber said.

"Must make him stop that racket," Wilson said. "You get in front. The Memsahib can sit back here with me."

They climbed into the motor car and, in the gray first daylight, moved off up

2. Bullets with solid, not hollow, slugs.

the river through the trees. Macomber opened the breech of his rifle and saw he had metal-cased bullets, shut the bolt and put the rifle on safety. He saw his hand was trembling. He felt in his pocket for more cartridges and moved his fingers over the cartridges in the loops of his tunic front. He turned back to where Wilson sat in the rear seat of the doorless, box-bodied motor car beside his wife, them both grinning with excitement, and Wilson leaned forward and whispered,

"See the birds dropping. Means the old boy has left his kill."

On the far bank of the stream Macomber could see, above the trees, vultures circling and plummeting down.

"Chances are he'll come to drink along here," Wilson whispered. "Before he goes to lay up. Keep an eye out."

They were driving slowly along the high bank of the stream which here cut deeply to its boulder-filled bed, and they wound in and out through big trees as they drove. Macomber was watching the opposite bank when he felt Wilson take hold of his arm. The car stopped.

"There he is," he heard the whisper. "Ahead and to the right. Get out and take him. He's a marvellous lion."

Macomber saw the lion now. He was standing almost broadside, his great head up and turned toward them. The early morning breeze that blew toward them was just stirring his dark mane, and the lion looked huge, silhouetted on the rise of bank in the gray morning light, his shoulders heavy, his barrel of a body bulking smoothly.

"How far is he?" asked Macomber, raising his rifle.

"About seventy-five. Get out and take him."

"Why not shoot from where I am?"

"You don't shoot them from cars," he heard Wilson saying in his ear. "Get out. He's not going to stay there all day."

Macomber stepped out of the curved opening at the side of the front seat, onto the step and down onto the ground. The lion still stood looking majestically and coolly toward this object that his eyes only showed in silhouette, bulking like some super-rhino. There was no man smell carried toward him and he watched the object, moving his great head a little from side to side. Then watching the object, not afraid, but hesitating before going down the bank to drink with such a thing opposite him, he saw a man figure detach itself from it and he turned his heavy head and swung away toward the cover of the trees as he heard a cracking crash and felt the slam of a .30-06 220-grain solid bullet that bit his flank and ripped in sudden hot scalding nausea through his stomach. He trotted, heavy, big-footed, swinging wounded full-bellied, through the trees toward the tall grass and cover, and the crash came again to go past him ripping the air apart. Then it crashed again and he felt the blow as it hit his lower ribs and ripped on through, blood sudden hot and frothy in his mouth, and he galloped toward the high grass where he could crouch and not be seen and make them bring the crashing thing close enough so he could make a rush and get the man that held it.

Macomber had not thought how the lion felt as he got out of the car. He only knew his hands were shaking and as he walked away from the car it was almost impossible for him to make his legs move. They were stiff in the thighs, but he could feel the muscles fluttering. He raised the rifle, sighted on the junction of the lion's head and shoulders and pulled the trigger. Nothing happened though he pulled until he thought his finger would break. Then he knew he had the safety on and as he lowered the rifle to move the safety over he moved another frozen pace forward, and the lion seeing his silhouette now clear of the car, turned and started off at a trot, and, as Macomber fired, he heard a whunk that meant that the bullet was home; but the lion kept on going. Macomber shot again and everyone saw the bullet throw a spout of dirt beyond the trotting lion. He shot again, remembering to lower his aim, and they all heard the bullet hit, and the lion went into a gallop and was in the tall grass before he had the bolt pushed forward.

Macomber stood there feeling sick at his stomach, his hands that held the Springfield still cocked, shaking, and his wife and Robert Wilson were standing by him. Beside him too were the two gun-bearers chattering in Wakamba.

"I hit him," Macomber said. "I hit him twice."

"You gut-shot him and you hit him somewhere forward," Wilson said without enthusiasm. The gun-bearers looked very grave. They were silent now.

"You may have killed him," Wilson went on. "We'll have to wait a while before we go in to find out."

"What do you mean?"

"Let him get sick before we follow him up."

"Oh," said Macomber.

"He's a hell of a fine lion," Wilson said cheerfully. "He's gotten into a bad place though."

"Why is it bad?"

"Can't see him until you're on him."

"Oh," said Macomber.

"Come on," said Wilson. "The Memsahib can stay here in the car. We'll go to have a look at the blood spoor."

"Stay here, Margot," Macomber said to his wife. His mouth was very dry and it was hard for him to talk.

"Why?" she asked.

"Wilson says to."

"We're going to have a look," Wilson said. "You stay here. You can see even better from here."

"All right."

Wilson spoke in Swahili to the driver. He nodded and said, "Yes, Bwana."

Then they went down the steep bank and across the stream, climbing over and around the boulders and up the other bank, pulling up by some projecting roots, and along it until they found where the lion had been trotting when Macomber first shot. There was dark blood on the short grass that the gun-bearers pointed out with grass stems, and that ran away behind the river bank trees.

"What do we do?" asked Macomber.

"Not much choice," said Wilson. "We can't bring the car over. Bank's too steep. We'll let him stiffen up a bit and then you and I'll go in and have a look for him."

"Can't we set the grass on fire?" Macomber asked.

"Too green."

"Can't we send beaters?"

Wilson looked at him appraisingly. "Of course we can," he said. "But it's just a touch murderous. You see we know the lion's wounded. You can drive an unwounded lion—he'll move on ahead of a noise—but a wounded lion's going to charge. You can't see him until you're right on him. He'll make himself perfectly flat in cover you wouldn't think would hide a hare. You can't very well send boys in there to that sort of a show. Somebody bound to get mauled."

"What about the gun-bearers?"

"Oh, they'll go with us. It's their *shauri*. You see, they signed on for it. They don't look too happy though, do they?"

"I don't want to go in there," said Macomber. It was out before he knew he'd said it.

"Neither do I," said Wilson very cheerily. "Really no choice though." Then, as an afterthought, he glanced at Macomber and saw suddenly how he was trembling and the pitiful look on his face.

"You don't have to go in, of course," he said. "That's what I'm hired for, you know. That's why I'm so expensive."

"You mean you'd go in by yourself? Why not leave him there?"

Robert Wilson, whose entire occupation had been with the lion and the problem he presented, and who had not been thinking about Macomber except to note that he was rather windy, suddenly felt as though he had opened the wrong door in a hotel and seen something shameful.

"What do you mean?"

"Why not just leave him?"

"You mean pretend to ourselves he hasn't been hit?"

"No. Just drop it."

"It isn't done."

"Why not?"

"For one thing, he's certain to be suffering. For another, some one else might run onto him."

"I see."

"But you don't have to have anything to do with it."

"I'd like to," Macomber said. "I'm just scared, you know."

"I'll go ahead when we go in," Wilson said, "with Kongoni tracking. You keep behind me and a little to one side. Chances are we'll hear him growl. If we see him we'll both shoot. Don't worry about anything. I'll keep you backed up. As a matter of fact, you know, perhaps you'd better not go. It might be much better. Why don't you go over and join the Memsahib while I just get it over with?"

"No, I want to go."

"All right," said Wilson. "But don't go in if you don't want to. This is my *shauri* now, you know."

"I want to go," said Macomber.

They sat under a tree and smoked.

"Want to go back and speak to the Memsahib while we're waiting?" Wilson asked.

"No."

"I'll just step back and tell her to be patient."

"Good," said Macomber. He sat there, sweating under his arms, his mouth dry, his stomach hollow feeling, wanting to find courage to tell Wilson to go on   460 and finish off the lion without him. He could not know that Wilson was furious because he had not noticed the state he was in earlier and sent him back to his wife. While he sat there Wilson came up. "I have your big gun," he said. "Take it. We've given him time, I think. Come on."

Macomber took the big gun and Wilson said:

"Keep behind me and about five yards to the right and do exactly as I tell you." Then he spoke in Swahili to the two gun-bearers, who looked the picture of gloom.

"Let's go," he said.

"Could I have a drink of water?" Macomber asked. Wilson spoke to the older   470 gun-bearer, who wore a canteen on his belt, and the man unbuckled it, unscrewed the top and handed it to Macomber, who took it noticing how heavy it seemed and how hairy and shoddy the felt covering was in his hand. He raised it to drink and looked ahead at the high grass with the flat-topped trees behind it. A breeze was blowing toward them and the grass rippled gently in the wind. He looked at the gun-bearer and he could see the gun-bearer was suffering too with fear.

Thirty-five yards into the grass the big lion lay flattened out along the ground. His ears were back and his only movement was a slight twitching up and down of his long, black-tufted tail. He had turned at bay as soon as he had reached this cover and he was sick with the wound through his full belly, and   480 weakening with the wound through his lungs that brought a thin foamy red to his mouth each time he breathed. His flanks were wet and hot and flies were on the little openings the solid bullets had made in his tawny hide, and his big yellow eyes, narrowed with hate, looked straight ahead, only blinking when the pain came as he breathed, and his claws dug in the soft baked earth. All of him, pain, sickness, hatred and all of his remaining strength, was tightening into an absolute concentration for a rush. He could hear the men talking and he waited, gathering all of himself into this preparation for a charge as soon as the men would come into the grass. As he heard their voices his tail stiffened to twitch up and down, and, as they came into the edge of the grass, he made a coughing grunt and   490 charged.

Kongoni, the old gun-bearer, in the lead watching the blood spoor, Wilson watching the grass for any movement, his big gun ready, the second gun-bearer looking ahead and listening, Macomber close to Wilson, his rifle cocked, they had just moved into the grass when Macomber heard the blood-choked coughing grunt, and saw the swishing rush in the grass. The next thing he knew he was running; running wildly, in panic in the open, running toward the stream.

He heard the *ca-ra-wong!* of Wilson's big rifle, and again in a second crashing *carawong!* and turning saw the lion, horrible-looking now, with half his head seeming to be gone, crawling toward Wilson in the edge of the tall grass while the   500 red-faced man worked the bolt on the short ugly rifle and aimed carefully as another blasting *carawong!* came from the muzzle, and the crawling, heavy, yellow bulk of the lion stiffened and the huge, mutilated head slid forward and Macomber, standing by himself in the clearing where he had run, holding a loaded rifle, while two black men and a white man looked back at him in contempt, knew the lion was dead. He came toward Wilson, his tallness all seeming a naked reproach, and Wilson looked at him and said:

"Want to take pictures?"

"No," he said.

That was all any one had said until they reached the motor car. Then Wilson had said:

"Hell of a fine lion. Boys will skin him out. We might as well stay here in the shade."

Macomber's wife had not looked at him nor he at her and he had sat by her in the back seat with Wilson sitting in the front seat. Once he had reached over and taken his wife's hand without looking at her and she had removed her hand from his. Looking across the stream to where the gun-bearers were skinning out the lion he could see that she had been able to see the whole thing. While they sat there his wife had reached forward and put her hand on Wilson's shoulder. He turned and she had leaned forward over the seat and kissed him on the mouth.

"Oh, I say," said Wilson, going redder than his natural baked color.

"Mr. Robert Wilson," she said. "The beautiful red-faced Mr. Robert Wilson."

Then she sat down beside Macomber again and looked away across the stream to where the lion lay, with uplifted, white-muscled, tendon-marked naked forearms, and white bloating belly, as the black men fleshed away the skin. Finally the gun-bearers brought the skin over, wet and heavy, and climbed in behind with it, rolling it up before they got in, and the motor car started. No one had said anything more until they were back in camp.

That was the story of the lion. Macomber did not know how the lion had felt before he started his rush, nor during it when the unbelievable smash of the .505 with a muzzle velocity of two tons had hit him in the mouth, nor what kept him coming after that, when the second ripping crash had smashed his hind quarters and he had come crawling on toward the crashing, blasting thing that had destroyed him. Wilson knew something about it and only expressed it by saying, "Damned fine lion," but Macomber did not know how Wilson felt about things either. He did not know how his wife felt except that she was through with him.

His wife had been through with him before but it never lasted. He was very wealthy, and would be much wealthier, and he knew she would not leave him ever now. That was one of the few things that he really knew. He knew about that, about motorcycles—that was earliest—about motor cars, about duck-shooting, about fishing, trout, salmon and big-sea, about sex in books, many books, too many books, about all court games, about dogs, not much about horses, about hanging on to his money, about most of the other things his world dealt in, and about his wife not leaving him. His wife had been a great beauty and she was still a great beauty in Africa, but she was not a great enough beauty any more at home to be able to leave him and better herself and she knew it and he knew it. She had missed the chance to leave him and he knew it. If he had been better with women she would probably have started to worry about him getting another new, beautiful wife; but she knew too much about him to worry about him either. Also, he had always had a great tolerance which seemed the nicest thing about him if it were not the most sinister.

All in all they were known as a comparatively happily married couple, one of those whose disruption is often rumored but never occurs, and as the society columnist put it, they were adding more than a spice of *adventure* to their much envied and everenduring *Romance* by a *Safari* in what was known as *Darkest Africa* until the Martin Johnsons lighted it on so many silver screens where they were pursuing *Old Simba* the lion, the buffalo, *Tembo* the elephant and as well collecting specimens for the Museum of Natural History. This same columnist had reported them *on the verge* at least three times in the past and they had been. But they always made it up. They had a sound basis of union. Margot was too beautiful for Macomber to divorce her and Macomber had too much money for Margot ever to leave him.

It was now about three o'clock in the morning and Francis Macomber, who had been asleep a little while after he had stopped thinking about the lion, wakened and then slept again, woke suddenly, frightened in a dream of the bloodyheaded lion standing over him, and listening while his heart pounded, he realized that his wife was not in the other cot in the tent. He lay awake with that knowledge for two hours.

At the end of that time his wife came into the tent, lifted her mosquito bar and crawled cozily into bed.

"Where have you been?" Macomber asked in the darkness.

"Hello," she said. "Are you awake?"

"Where have you been?"

"I just went out to get a breath of fresh air."

"You did, like hell."

"What do you want me to say, darling?"

"Where have you been?"

"Out to get a breath of air."

"That's a new name for it. You *are* a bitch."

"Well, you're a coward."

"All right," he said. "What of it?"

"Nothing as far as I'm concerned. But please let's not talk, darling, because I'm very sleepy."

"You think that I'll take anything."

"I know you will, sweet."

"Well, I won't."

"Please, darling, let's not talk. I'm so very sleepy."

"There wasn't going to be any of that. You promised there wouldn't be."

"Well, there is now," she said sweetly.

"You said if we made this trip that there would be none of that. You promised."

"Yes, darling. That's the way I meant it to be. But the trip was spoiled yesterday. We don't have to talk about it, do we?"

"You don't wait long when you have an advantage, do you?"

"Please let's not talk. I'm so sleepy, darling."

"I'm going to talk."

"Don't mind me then, because I'm going to sleep." And she did.

At breakfast they were all three at the table before daylight and Francis

Macomber found that, of all the many men that he had hated, he hated Robert
Wilson the most.   600

"Sleep well?" Wilson asked in his throaty voice, filling a pipe.

"Did you?"

"Topping," the white hunter told him.

You bastard, thought Macomber, you insolent bastard.

So she woke him when she came in, Wilson thought, looking at them both
with his flat, cold eyes. Well, why doesn't he keep his wife where she belongs?
What does he think I am, a bloody plaster saint? Let him keep her where she belongs. It's his own fault.

"Do you think we'll find buffalo?" Margot asked, pushing away a dish of
apricots.   610

"Chance of it," Wilson said and smiled at her. "Why don't you stay in camp?"

"Not for anything," she told him.

"Why not order her to stay in camp?" Wilson said to Macomber.

"You order her," said Macomber coldly.

"Let's not have any ordering, nor," turning to Macomber, "any silliness,
Francis," Margot said quite pleasantly.

"Are you ready to start?" Macomber asked.

"Any time," Wilson told him. "Do you want the Memsahib to go?"

"Does it make any difference whether I do or not?"

The hell with it, thought Robert Wilson. The utter complete hell with it. So   620
this is what it's going to be like. Well, this is what it's going to be like, then.

"Makes no difference," he said.

"You're sure you wouldn't like to stay in camp with her yourself and let me
go out and hunt the buffalo?" Macomber asked.

"Can't do that," said Wilson. "Wouldn't talk rot if I were you."

"I'm not talking rot. I'm disgusted."

"Bad word, disgusted."

"Francis, will you please try to speak sensibly?" his wife said.

"I speak too damned sensibly," Macomber said. "Did you ever eat such filthy
food?"   630

"Something wrong with the food?" asked Wilson quietly.

"No more than with everything else."

"I'd pull yourself together, laddybuck," Wilson said very quietly. "There's a
boy waits at table that understands a little English."

"The hell with him."

Wilson stood up and puffing on his pipe strolled away, speaking a few words
in Swahili to one of the gun-bearers who was standing waiting for him. Macomber
and his wife sat on at the table. He was staring at his coffee cup.

"If you make a scene I'll leave you darling," Margot said quietly.

"No, you won't."   640

"You can try it and see."

"You won't leave me."

"No," she said. "I won't leave you and you'll behave yourself."

"Behave myself? That's a way to talk. Behave myself."

"Yes. Behave yourself."

"Why don't *you* try behaving?"

"I've tried it so long. So very long."

"I hate that red-faced swine," Macomber said. "I loathe the sight of him."

"He's really *very* nice."

"Oh, *shut up,*" Macomber almost shouted. Just then the car came up and 650 stopped in front of the dining tent and the driver and the two gun-bearers got out. Wilson walked over and looked at the husband and wife sitting there at the table.

"Going shooting?" he asked.

"Yes," said Macomber, standing up. "Yes."

"Better bring a woolly. It will be cool in the car," Wilson said.

"I'll get my leather jacket," Margot said.

"The boy has it," Wilson told her. He climbed into the front with the driver and Francis Macomber and his wife sat, not speaking, in the back seat.

Hope the silly beggar doesn't take a notion to blow the back of my head off, Wilson thought to himself. Women *are* a nuisance on safari.   660

The car was grinding down to cross the river at a pebbly ford in the gray daylight and then climbed, angling up the steep bank, where Wilson had ordered a way shovelled out the day before so they could reach the parklike wooded rolling country on the far side.

It was a good morning, Wilson thought. There was a heavy dew and as the wheels went through the grass and low bushes he could smell the odor of the crushed fronds. It was an odor like verbena and he liked this early morning smell of the dew, the crushed bracken and the look of the tree trunks showing black through the early morning mist, as the car made its way through the untracked, parklike country. He had put the two in the back seat out of his mind now and 670 was thinking about buffalo. The buffalo that he was after stayed in the daytime in a thick swamp where it was impossible to get a shot, but in the night they fed out into an open stretch of country and if he could come between them and their swamp with the car, Macomber would have good chance at them in the open. He did not want to hunt buff with Macomber in thick cover. He did not want to hunt buff or anything with Macomber at all, but he was a professional hunter and he had hunted with some rare ones in his time. If they got buff today there would only be rhino to come and the poor man would have gone through his dangerous game and things might pick up. He'd have nothing more to do with the woman and Macomber would get over that too. He must have gone through plenty of that 680 before by the look of things. Poor beggar. He must have a way of getting over it. Well, it was the poor sod's own bloody fault.

He, Robert Wilson, carried a double size cot on safari to accommodate any windfalls he might receive. He had hunted for a certain clientele, the international, fast, sporting set, where the women did not feel they were getting their money's worth unless they had shared the cot with the white hunter. He despised them when he was away from them although he liked some of them well enough at the time, but he made his living by them; and their standards were his standards as long as they were hiring him.

They were his standards in all except the shooting. He had his own stan- 690 dards about the killing and they could live up to them or get some one else to hunt them. He knew, too, that they all respected him for this. This Macomber was an odd one though. Damned if he wasn't. Now the wife. Well, the wife. Yes, the wife. Hm, the wife. Well he'd dropped all that. He looked around at them. Macomber sat grim and furious. Margot smiled at him. She looked younger today, more innocent and fresher and not so professionally beautiful. What's in her heart God knows, Wilson thought. She hadn't talked much last night. At that it was a pleasure to see her.

The motor car climbed up a slight rise and went on through the trees and then out into a grassy prairie-like opening and kept in the shelter of the trees 700 along the edge, the driver going slowly and Wilson looking carefully out across the prairie and along its far side. He stopped the car and studied the opening with his field glasses. Then he motioned to the driver to go on and the car moved slowly along, the driver avoiding wart-hog holes and driving around the mud castles ants had built. Then, looking across the opening, Wilson suddenly turned and said,

"By God, there they are!"

And looking where he pointed, while the car jumped forward and Wilson spoke in rapid Swahili to the driver, Macomber saw three huge, black animals looking almost cylindrical in their long heaviness, like big black tank cars, moving at a gallop across the far edge of the open prairie. They moved at a stiff-necked, 710 stiff bodied gallop and he could see the upswept wide black horns on their heads as they galloped heads out; the heads not moving.

"They're three old bulls," Wilson said. "We'll cut them off before they get to the swamp."

The car was going a wild forty-five miles an hour across the open and as Macomber watched, the buffalo got bigger and bigger until he could see the gray, hairless, scabby look of one huge bull and how his neck was a part of his shoulders and the shiny black of his horns as he galloped a little behind the others that were strung out in that steady plunging gait; and then, the car swaying as though it had just jumped a road, they drew up close and he could see the plunging huge- 720 ness of the bull, and the dust in his sparsely haired hide, the side boss of horn and his outstretched, wide-nostrilled muzzle, and he was raising his rifle when Wilson shouted, "Not from the car, you fool!" and he had no fear, only hatred of Wilson, while the brakes clamped on and the car skidded, plowing sideways to an almost stop and Wilson was out on one side and he on the other, stumbling as his feet hit the still speeding-by of the earth, and then he was shooting at the bull as he moved away, hearing the bullets whunk into him, emptying his rifle at him as he moved steadily away, finally remembering to get his shots forward into the shoulder, and as he fumbled to re-load, he saw the bull was down. Down on his knees, his big head tossing, and seeing the other two still galloping he shot at the leader 730 and hit him. He shot again and missed and he heard the *carawonging* roar as Wilson shot and saw the leading bull slide forward onto his nose.

"Get that other," Wilson said. "Now you're shooting!"

But the other bull was moving steadily at the same gallop and he missed, throwing a spout of dirt, and Wilson missed and the dust rose in a cloud and Wilson shouted, "Come on. He's too far!" and grabbed his arm and they were in

the car again, Macomber and Wilson hanging on the sides and rocketing sway-
ingly over the uneven ground, drawing up on the steady, plunging, heavy-necked,
straight-moving gallop of the bull.

They were behind him and Macomber was filling his rifle, dropping shells 740
onto the ground, jamming it, clearing the jam, then they were almost up with the
bull when Wilson yelled "Stop," and the car skidded so that it almost swung over
and Macomber fell forward onto his feet, slammed his bolt forward and fired as far
forward as he could aim into the galloping, rounded black back, aimed and shot
again, then again, then again, and the bullets, all of them hitting, had no effect on
the buffalo that he could see. Then Wilson shot, the roar deafening him, and he
could see the bull stagger. Macomber shot again, aiming carefully, and down he
came onto his knees.

"All right," Wilson said. "Nice work. That's the three."

Macomber felt drunken elation.   750

"How many times did you shoot?" he asked.

"Just three," Wilson said. "You killed the first bull. The biggest one. I helped
you finish the other two. Afraid they might have got into cover. You had them
killed. I was just mopping up a little. You shot damn well."

"Let's go to the car," said Macomber. "I want a drink."

"Got to finish off that buff first," Wilson told him. The buffalo was on his
knees and he jerked his head furiously and bellowed in pig-eyed, roaring rage as
they came toward him.

"Watch he doesn't get up," Wilson said. Then, "Get a little broadside and
take him in the neck just behind the ear."   760

Macomber aimed carefully at the center of the huge, jerking, rage-driven
neck and shot. At the shot the head dropped forward.

"That does it," said Wilson. "Got the spine. They're a hell of a looking thing,
aren't they?"

"Let's get the drink," said Macomber. In his life he had never felt so good.

In the car Macomber's wife sat very white faced. "You were marvellous, darling," she said to Macomber. "What a ride."

"Was it rough?" Wilson asked.

"It was frightful. I've never been more frightened in my life."

"Let's all have a drink," Macomber said.   770

"By all means," said Wilson. "Give it to the Memsahib." She drank the neat
whisky from the flask and shuddered a little when she swallowed. She handed the
flask to Macomber who handed it to Wilson.

"It was frightfully exciting," she said. "It's given me a dreadful headache. I
didn't know you were allowed to shoot them from cars though."

"No one shot from cars," said Wilson coldly.

"I mean chase them from cars."

"Wouldn't ordinarily," Wilson said. "Seemed sporting enough to me though
while we were doing it. Taking more chance driving that way across the plain full
of holes and one thing and another than hunting on foot. Buffalo could have 780
charged us each time we shot if he liked. Gave him every chance. Wouldn't mention it to any one though. It's illegal if that's what you mean."

"It seemed very unfair to me," Margot said, "chasing those big helpless things in a motor car."

"Did it?" said Wilson.

"What would happen if they heard about it in Nairobi?"

"I'd lose my license for one thing. Other unpleasantnesses," Wilson said, taking a drink from the flask. "I'd be out of business."

"Really?"

"Well," said Macomber, and he smiled for the first time all day. "Now she has something on you." 790

"You have such a pretty way of putting things, Francis," Margot Macomber said. Wilson looked at them both. If a four-letter man marries a five-letter woman, he was thinking, what number of letters would their children be? What he said was, "We lost a gun-bearer. Did you notice it?"

"My God, no," Macomber said.

"Here he comes," Wilson said. "He's all right. He must have fallen off when we left the first bull."

Approaching them was the middle-aged gun-bearer, limping along in his knitted cap, khaki tunic, shorts and rubber sandals, gloomy-faced and disgusted 800 looking. As he came up he called out to Wilson in Swahili and they all saw the change in the white hunter's face.

"What does he say?" asked Margot.

"He says the first bull got up and went into the bush," Wilson said with no expression in his voice.

"Oh," said Macomber blankly.

"Then it's going to be just like the lion," said Margot, full of anticipation.

"It's not going to be a damned bit like the lion," Wilson told her. "Did you want another drink, Macomber?"

"Thanks, yes," Macomber said. He expected the feeling he had had about the 810 lion to come back but it did not. For the first time in his life he really felt wholly without fear. Instead of fear he had a feeling of definite elation.

"We'll go and have a look at the second bull," Wilson said. "I'll tell the driver to put the car in the shade."

"What are you going to do?" asked Margaret Macomber.

"Take a look at the buff," Wilson said.

"I'll come."

"Come along."

The three of them walked over to where the second buffalo bulked blackly in the open, head forward on the grass, the massive horns swung wide. 820

"He's a very good head," Wilson said. "That's close to a fifty-inch spread."

Macomber was looking at him with delight.

"He's hateful looking," said Margot. "Can't we go into the shade?"

"Of course," Wilson said. "Look," he said to Macomber, and pointed. "See that patch of bush?"

"Yes."

"That's where the first bull went in. The gun-bearer said when he fell off the bull was down. He was watching us helling along and the other two buff galloping. When he looked up there was the bull up and looking at him. Gun-bearer ran like hell and the bull went off slowly into that bush." 830

"Can we go in after him now?" asked Macomber eagerly.

Wilson looked at him appraisingly. Damned if this isn't a strange one, he thought. Yesterday he's scared sick and today he's a ruddy fire eater.

"No, we'll give him a while."

"Let's please go into the shade," Margot said. Her face was white and she looked ill.

They made their way to the car where it stood under a single, wide-spreading tree and all climbed in.

"Chances are he's dead in there," Wilson remarked. "After a little we'll have a look." 840

Macomber felt a wild unreasonable happiness that he had never known before.

"By God, that was a chase," he said. "I've never felt any such feeling. Wasn't it marvelous, Margot?"

"I hated it."

"Why?"

"I hated it," she said bitterly. "I loathed it."

"You know I don't think I'd ever be afraid of anything again," Macomber said to Wilson. "Something happened in me after we first saw the buff and started after him. Like a dam bursting. It was pure excitement." 850

"Cleans out your liver," said Wilson. "Damn funny things happen to people."

Macomber's face was shining. "You know something did happen to me," he said. "I feel absolutely different."

His wife said nothing and eyed him strangely. She was sitting far back in the seat and Macomber was sitting forward talking to Wilson who turned sideways talking over the back of the front seat.

"You know, I'd like to try another lion," Macomber said. "I'm really not afraid of them now. After all, what can they do to you?"

"That's it," said Wilson. "Worst one can do is kill you. How does it go? Shakespeare. Damned good. See if I can remember. Oh, damned good. Used to 860 quote it to myself at one time. Let's see. 'By my troth, I care not; a man can die but once; we owe God a death and let it go which way it will he that dies this year is quit for the next.' Damned fine, eh?"[3]

He was very embarrassed, having brought out this thing he had lived by, but he had seen men come of age before and it always moved him. It was not a matter of their twenty-first birthday.

It had taken a strange chance of hunting, a sudden precipitation into action without opportunity for worrying beforehand, to bring this about with Macomber, but regardless of how it had happened it had most certainly happened. Look at the beggar now, Wilson thought. It's that some of them stay little boys so long, 870 Wilson thought. Sometimes all their lives. Their figures stay boyish when they're

---

3. William Shakespeare, *Henry IV*, part 2, 3.2., 234–238.

fifty. The great American boy-men. Damned strange people. But he liked this Macomber now. Damned strange fellow. Probably meant the end of cuckoldry too. Well, that would be a damned good thing. Damned good thing. Beggar had probably been afraid all his life. Don't know what started it. But over now. Hadn't had time to be afraid with the buff. That and being angry too. Motor car too. Motor cars made it familiar. Be a damn fire eater now. He'd seen it in the war work the same way. More of a change than any loss of virginity. Fear gone like an operation. Something else grew in its place. Main thing a man had. Made him into a man. Women knew it too. No bloody fear.   880

From the far corner of the seat Margaret Macomber looked at the two of them. There was no change in Wilson. She saw Wilson as she had seen him the day before when she had first realized what his great talent was. But she saw the change in Francis Macomber now.

"Do you have that feeling of happiness about what's going to happen?" Macomber asked, still exploring his new wealth.

"You're not supposed to mention it," Wilson said, looking in the other's face. "Much more fashionable to say you're scared. Mind you, you'll be scared too, plenty of times."

"But you *have* a feeling of happiness about action to come?"   890

"Yes," said Wilson. "There's that. Doesn't do to talk too much about all this. Talk the whole thing away. No pleasure in anything if you mouth it up too much."

"You're both talking rot," said Margot. "Just because you've chased some helpless animals in a motor car you talk like heroes."

"Sorry," said Wilson. "I have been gassing too much." She's worried about it already, he thought.

"If you don't know what we're talking about why not keep out of it?" Macomber asked his wife.

"You've gotten awfully brave, awfully suddenly," his wife said contemptuously, but her contempt was not secure. She was very afraid of something.   900

Macomber laughed, a very natural hearty laugh. "You know I *have*," he said. "I really have."

"Isn't it sort of late?" Margot said bitterly. Because she had done the best she could for many years back and the way they were together now was no one person's fault.

"Not for me," said Macomber.

Margot said nothing but sat back in the corner of the seat.

"Do you think we've given him time enough?" Macomber asked Wilson cheerfully.

"We might have a look," Wilson said. "Have you any solids left?"   910

"The gun-bearer has some."

Wilson called in Swahili and the older gun-bearer, who was skinning out one of the heads, straightened up, pulled a box of solids out of his pocket and brought them over to Macomber, who filled his magazine and put the remaining shells in his pocket.

"You might as well shoot the Springfield," Wilson said. "You're used to it. We'll leave the Mannlicher in the car with the Memsahib. Your gun-bearer can

carry your heavy gun. I've this damned cannon. Now let me tell you about them."
He had saved this until the last because he did not want to worry Macomber.
"When a buff comes he comes with his head high and thrust straight out. The 920
boss of the horns covers any sort of a brain shot. The only shot is straight into the
nose. The only other shot is into his chest or, if you're to one side, into the neck or
the shoulders. After they've been hit once they take a hell of a lot of killing. Don't
try anything fancy. Take the easiest shot there is. They've finished skinning out
that head now. Should we get started?"

He called to the gun-bearers, who came up wiping their hands, and the
older one got into the back.

"I'll only take Kongoni," Wilson said. "The other can watch to keep the birds
away."

As the car moved slowly across the open space toward the island of brushy 930
trees that ran in a tongue of foliage along a dry water course that cut the open
swale, Macomber felt his heart pounding and his mouth was dry again, but it was
excitement, not fear.

"Here's where he went in," Wilson said. Then to the gun-bearer in Swahili,
"Take the blood spoor."

The car was parallel to the patch of bush. Macomber, Wilson and the gun-
bearer got down. Macomber, looking back, saw his wife, with the rifle by her side,
looking at him. He waved to her and she did not wave back.

The brush was very thick ahead and the ground was dry. The middle-aged
gun-bearer was sweating heavily and Wilson had his hat down over his eyes and 940
his red neck showed just ahead of Macomber. Suddenly the gun-bearer said something in Swahili to Wilson and ran forward.

"He's dead in there," Wilson said. "Good work," and he turned to grip
Macomber's hand and as they shook hands, grinning at each other, the gun-bearer
shouted wildly and they saw him coming out of the brush sideways, fast as a crab,
and the bull coming, nose out, mouth tight closed, blood dripping, massive head
straight out, coming in a charge, his little pig eyes bloodshot as he looked at them.
Wilson, who was ahead was kneeling shooting, and Macomber, as he fired unhear-
ing his shot in the roaring of Wilson's gun, saw fragments like slate burst from the
huge boss of the horns, and the head jerked, he shot again at the wide nostrils and 950
saw the horns jolt again and fragments fly, and he did not see Wilson now and,
aiming carefully, shot again with the buffalo's huge bulk almost on him and his
rifle almost level with the on-coming head, nose out, and he could see the little
wicked eyes and the head started to lower and he felt a sudden white-hot, blinding flash explode inside his head and that was all he ever felt.

Wilson had ducked to one side to get in a shoulder shot. Macomber had
stood solid and shot for the nose, shooting a touch high each time and hitting the
heavy horns, splintering and chipping them like hitting a slate roof, and Mrs.
Macomber, in the car, had shot at the buffalo with the 6.5 Mannlicher as it seemed
about to gore Macomber and had hit her husband about two inches up and a little 960
to one side of the base of his skull.

Francis Macomber lay now, face down, not two yards from where the buffalo
lay on his side and his wife knelt over him with Wilson beside her.

The woman was crying hysterically.

"I'd get back in the car," Wilson said. "Where's the rifle?"

She shook her head, her face contorted. The gun-bearer picked up the rifle.

"Leave it as it is," said Wilson. Then, "Go get Abdulla so that he may witness the manner of the accident."

He knelt down, took a handkerchief from his pocket, and spread it over Francis Macomber's crew-topped head where it lay. The blood sank into the dry, loose earth.

Wilson stood up and saw the buffalo on his side, his legs out, his thinly-haired belly crawling with ticks. "Hell of a good bull," his brain registered automatically. "A good fifty inches, or better. Better." He called to the driver and told him to spread a blanket over the body and stay by it. Then he walked over to the motor car where the woman sat crying in the corner.

"That was a pretty thing to do," he said in a toneless voice. "He *would* have left you too."

"Stop it," she said.

"Of course it's an accident," he said. "I know that."

"Stop it," she said.

"Don't worry," he said. "There will be a certain amount of unpleasantness but I will have some photographs taken that will be very useful at the inquest. There's the testimony of the gun-bearers and the driver too. You're perfectly all right."

"Stop it," she said.

"There's a hell of a lot to be done," he said. "And I'll have to send a truck off to the lake to wireless for a plane to take the three of us into Nairobi. Why didn't you poison him? That's what they do in England."

"Stop it. Stop it. Stop it," the woman cried.

Wilson looked at her with his flat blue eyes.

"I'm through now," he said. "I was a little angry. I'd begun to like your husband."

"Oh, please stop it," she said. "Please, please stop it."

"That's better," Wilson said. "Please is much better. Now I'll stop."   [1933]

Questions for Writing and Discussion

1. How are we to read the title of this story?

2. What conventions of the adventure story does Hemingway use? In what ways does the story depart from these conventions? What is the effect of these deviations?

3. What is Wilson's "code"?

4. Hemingway has been criticized for his depiction of women. Evaluate his portrayal of Margot.

5. Does Margot shoot her husband accidentally or on purpose? What evidence is there for either interpretation?

6. How is manhood defined in this story? Is such a definition still relevant? What would the contemporary equivalents of big-game hunting be?

7. In your view, are any of the three main characters admirable? Are any praiseworthy? Why or why not?

❧ ZORA NEALE HURSTON

(1891–1960)

The Gilded Six-Bits[1]

Zora Neale Hurston was one of the few women to emerge from the Harlem Renaissance, and although her achievement was for a long time unappreciated, she is now emerging as a major figure in American literature.

Hurston was born in the all-black community of Eatonville, Florida. Her mother was a school teacher, her father a carpenter and Baptist preacher. In spite of erratic schooling (occasioned by her mother's death), she graduated from high school in 1918 and entered Howard University. Curious to see the world, Hurston traveled to New York City in January 1925, arriving with only $1.50. The Harlem Renaissance was in full force, and Hurston soon met Claude McKay (1890–1948), Langston Hughes (1902–1967), Jean Toomer (1894–1967), and other writers and artists. "Spunk," her first professional story, appeared in *Opportunity: A Journal of Negro Life* in 1925. It led to meeting novelist Fannie Hurst (1889–1968) and philanthropist Annie Nathan Meyer, who helped her obtain a scholarship to Barnard College. At Barnard, Hurston met anthropologist Franz Boas, who encouraged her to study anthropology and collect African-American folklore. Another philanthropist supported Hurston's field research from 1927–1931, but publishing companies were not interested in the material she collected. Hurston converted some of it to successful musical reviews, but her book of folklore, *Mules and Men,* did not come out until 1935.

The 1930s and 1940s were productive ones during which "The Gilded Six-Bits" appeared in *Story* magazine, and her best novel, *Their Eyes Were Watching God* (1937) was published, as were other works. By the 1950s, however, she was living in poverty, forgotten by her early admirers and supporting herself by occasional journalism, domestic service, and library work. Hurston may have harmed herself by taking controversial and conflicting political stances, and her use of African-American folk materials has likewise been misunderstood. Feminist critics, led by Alice Walker, rescued her work from obscurity, and she is now widely regarded as central to African-American literature in this century.

I T WAS A Negro yard around a Negro house in a Negro settlement that looked to the payroll of the G and G Fertilizer works for its support.

But there was something happy about the place. The front yard was parted in the middle by a sidewalk from gate to doorstep, a sidewalk edged on either side

---

1. A bit is one-eighth of a dollar; thus, six-bits is seventy-five cents.

by quart bottles driven neck down to the ground on a slant. A mess of homey flowers planted without a plan but blooming cheerily from their helter-skelter places. The fence and house were whitewashed. The porch and steps scrubbed white.

The front door stood open to the sunshine so that the floor of the front room could finish drying after its weekly scouring. It was Saturday. Everything clean from the front gate to the privy house. Yard raked so that the strokes of the rake would make a pattern. Fresh newspaper cut in fancy-edge on the kitchen shelves. 10

Missie May was bathing herself in the galvanized washtub in the bedroom. Her dark-brown skin glistened under the soapsuds that skittered down from her wash rag. Her stiff young breasts thrust forward aggressively like broad-based cones with tips lacquered in black.

She heard men's voices in the distance and glanced at the dollar clock on the dresser.

"Humph! Ah'm way behind time t'day! Joe gointer be heah 'fore Ah git mah clothes on if Ah don't make haste." 20

She grabbed the clean meal sack at hand and dried herself hurriedly and began to dress. But before she could tie her slippers, there came the ring of singing metal on wood. Nine times.

Missie May grinned with delight. She had not seen the big tall man come stealing in the gate and creep up the walk grinning happily at the joyful mischief he was about to commit. But she knew that it was her husband throwing silver dollars in the door for her to pick up and pile beside her plate at dinner. It was this way every Saturday afternoon. The nine dollars hurled into the open door, he scurried to a hiding place behind the cape jasmine bush and waited.

Missie May promptly appeared at the door in mock alarm. 30

"Who dat chunkin' money in mah do'way?" she demanded. No answer from the yard. She leaped off the porch and began to search the shrubbery. She peeped under the porch and hung over the gate to look up and down the road. While she did this, the man behind the jasmine darted to the chinaberry tree. She spied him and gave chase.

"Nobody ain't gointer be chunkin' money at me and Ah not do'em nothin'," she shouted in mock anger. He ran around the house with Missie May at his heels. She overtook him at the kitchen door. He ran inside but could not close it after him before she crowded in and locked with him in a rough and tumble. For several minutes the two were a furious mass of male and female energy. Shouting, 40 laughing, twisting, turning, and Joe trying, but not too hard, to get away.

"Missie May, take yo' hand out mah pocket!" Joe shouted out between laughs.

"Ah ain't, Joe, not lessen you gwine gimme whateve' it is good you got in yo' pocket. Turn it go Joe, do Ah'll tear yo' clothes."

"Go on tear 'em. You de one dat pushes de needles round heah. Move yo' hand Missie May."

"Lemme git dat paper sack out yo' pocket. Ah bet its candy kisses."

"Tain't. Move yo' hand. Woman ain't got no business in a man's clothes nohow. Go 'way." 50

Missie May gouged way down and gave an upward jerk and triumphed.

"Unhhunh! Ah got it. It 'tis so candy kisses. Ah knowed you had somethin' for me in yo' clothes. Now Ah got to see whut's in every pocket you got."

Joe smiled indulgently and let his wife go through all of his pockets and take out the things that he had hidden there for her to find. She bore off the chewing gum, the cake of sweet soap, the pocket handkerchief as if she had wrested them from him, as if they had not been bought for the sake of this friendly battle.

"Whew! dat play-fight done got me all warmed up," Joe exclaimed. "Got me some water in de kittle?"

"Yo' water is on de fire and yo' clean things is cross de bed. Hurry up and 60 wash yo'self and git changed so we kin eat. Ah'm hongry." As Missie said this, she bore the steaming kettle into the bedroom.

"You ain't hongry, sugar," Joe contradicted her. "Youse jes's little empty. Ah'm de one whut's hongry. Ah could eat up camp meetin,' back off 'ssociation, and drink Jurdan dry. Have it on de table when Ah git out de tub."

"Don't you mess wid mah business, man. You git in yo' clothes. Ah'm a real wife, not no dress and breath. Ah might not look lak one, but if you burn me, you won't git a thing but wife ashes."

Joe splashed in the bedroom and Missie May fanned around in the kitchen. A fresh red and white checked cloth on the table. Big pitcher of buttermilk beaded 70 with pale drops of butter from the churn. Hot fried mullet, crackling bread, ham hocks atop a mound of string beans and new potatoes, and perched on the window-sill a pone[2] of spicy potato pudding.

Very little talk during the meal but that little consisted of banter that pretended to deny affection but in reality flaunted it. Like when Missie May reached for a second helping of the tater pone. Joe snatched it out of her reach. After Missie May had made two or three unsuccessful grabs at the pan, she begged, "Aw, Joe gimme some mo' dat tater pone."

"Nope, sweetenin' is for us men-folks. Y'all pritty li'l frail eels don't need nothin' lak dis. You too sweet already."   80

"Please, Joe."

"Naw, naw. Ah don't want you to git no sweeter than whut you is already. We goin' down de road al li'l piece t'night so you go put on yo' Sunday-go-to-meetin' things."

Missie May looked at her husband to see if he was playing some prank. "Sho' nuff, Joe?"

"Yeah, We goin' to de ice cream parlor."

"Where de ice cream parlor at, Joe?"

"A new man done come heah from Chicago and he done got a place and took and opened it up for a ice cream parlor, and bein' as it's real swell, Ah wants 90 you to be one de first ladies to walk in dere and have some set down."

"Do Jesus, Ah ain't knowed nothin' 'bout it. Who de man done it?"

"Mister Otis D. Slemmons, of spots and places—Memphis, Chicago, Jacksonville, Philadelphia and so on."

2. Pan or loaf.

"Dat heavy-set man wid his mouth full of gold teethes?"

"Yeah. Where did you see 'im at?"

"Ah went down to de sto' tuh git a box of lye and Ah seen 'im standin' on de corner talkin' to some of de mens, and Ah come on back and went to scrubbin' de floor, and he passed and tipped his hat whilst Ah was scourin' de steps. Ah thought never Ah seen *him* befo'." 100

Joe smiled pleasantly. "Yeah, he's up to date. He got de finest clothes Ah ever seen on a colored man's back."

"Aw, he don't look no better in his clothes than you do in yourn. He got a puzzlegut on 'im and he so chuckle-headed,[3] he got a pone behind his neck."

Joe looked down at his own abdomen and said wistfully, "Wisht Ah had a build on me lak he got. He ain't puzzlegutted, honey. He jes' got a corperation. Dat make 'm look lak a rich white man. All rich mens is got some belly on 'em."

"Ah seen de pitchers of Henry Ford and he's a spare-built man and Rockefeller look lak he ain't got but one gut. But Ford and Rockefeller and dis Slemmons and all de rest kin be as many-gutted as dey please, ah'm satisfied wid 110 you jes' lak you is, baby. God took pattern after a pine tree and built you noble. Youse a pritty still man, and if Ah knowed any way to make you mo' pritty still Ah'd take and do it."

Joe reached over gently and toyed with Missie May's ear. "You jes' say dat cause you love me, but Ah know Ah can't hold no light to Otis D. Slemmons. Ah ain't never been nowhere and Ah ain't got nothin' but you."

"How you know dat, Joe."

"He tole us so hisself."

"Dat don't make it so. His mouf is cut cross-ways, ain't it? Well, he kin lie jes' lak anybody els." 120

"Good Lawd, Missie! You womens sho' is hard to sense into things. He's got a five-dollar gold piece for a stick-pin and he got a ten-dollar gold piece on his watch chain and his mouf is jes' crammed full of gold teethes. Sho' wisht it wuz mine. And whut make it so cool, he got money 'cumulated. And womens give it all to 'im."

"Ah don't see whut de womens see on 'im. Ah wouldn't give 'im a wind if de sherff wuz after 'im."

"Well, he tole us how de white womens in Chicago give 'im all dat gold money. So he don't 'low nobody to touch it at all. Not even put dey finger on it. Dey tole 'im not to. You kin make 'miration at it, but don't tetch it." 130

"Whyn't he stay up dere where dey so crazy 'bout 'im?"

"Ah reckon dey done made 'im vast-rich and he wants to travel some. He say dey wouldn't leave 'im hit a lick of work. He got mo' lady people crazy 'bout him than he kin shake a stick at."

"Joe, Ah hates to see you so dumb. Dat stray nigger jes' tell y'all anything and y'all b'lieve it."

"Go 'head on now, honey and put on yo' clothes. He talkin' 'bout his pritty womens—Ah want 'im to see *mine*."

---

3. Block-headed; i.e., he has a large head.

Missie May went off to dress and Joe spent the time trying to make his stomach punch out like Slemmons' middle. He tried the rolling swagger of the stranger, but found that his tall bone-and-muscle stride fitted ill with it. He just had time to drop back into his seat before Missie May came in dressed to go.

On the way home that night Joe was exultant. "Didn't Ah say ole Otis was swell? Can't he talk Chicago talk? Wuzn't dat funny whut he said when great big fat old Ida Armstrong come in? He asted me, " 'Who is dat broad wid de forty shake?' Dat's a new word. Us always thought forty was a set of figgers but he showed us where it means a whole heap of things. Sometimes he don't say forty, he jes' say thirty-eight and two and dat mean de same thing. Know whut he tole me when Ah was payin' for our ice cream? He say, 'Ah have to hand it to you, Joe. Dat wife of yours is jes' thirty-eight and two. Yessuh, she' forty!' Ain't he killin'?"

"He'll do in case of a rush. But he sho' is got uh heap uh gold on 'im. Dat's de first time Ah ever seed gold money. It lookted good on him sho' nuff, but it'd look a whole heap better on you."

"Who, me? Missie May was youse crazy! Where would a po' man lak me git gold money from?"

Missie May was silent for a minute, then she said, "Us might find some goin' long de road some time. Us could."

"Who would be losin' gold money 'round heah? We ain't even seen none dese white folks wearin' no gold money on dey watch chain. You must be figgeren' Mister Packard or Mister Cadillac goin' pass through heah . . ."

"You don't know whut been lost 'round heah. Maybe somebody way back in memorial times lost they gold money and went on off and it ain't never been found. And then if we wuz to find it, you could wear some 'thout havin' no gang of womens lak dat Slemmons say he got."

Joe laughed and hugged her. "Don't be so wishful 'bout me. Ah'm satisfied de way Ah is. So long as Ah be yo' husband, ah don't keer 'bout nothin' else. Ah'd ruther all de other womens in de world to be dead than for you to have de toothache. Less we go to bed and git our night rest."

It was Saturday night once more before Joe could parade his wife in Slemmons' ice cream parlor again. He worked the night shift and Saturday was his only night off. Every other evening around six o'clock he left home, and dying dawn saw him hustling home around the lake where the challenging sun flung a flaming sword from east to west across the trembling water.

That was the best part of life—going home to Missie May. Their whitewashed house, the mock battle on Saturday, the dinner and ice cream parlor afterwards, church on Sunday nights when Missie outdressed any woman in town —all, everything was right.

One night around eleven the acid ran out at the G and G. The foreman knocked off the crew and let the steam die down. As Joe rounded the lake on his way home, a lean moon rode the lake in a silver boat. If anybody had asked Joe about the moon on the lake, he would have said he hadn't paid it any attention. But he saw it with his feelings. It made him yearn painfully for Missie. Creation obsessed him. He thought about children. They had been married for more than a year now. They had money put away. They ought to be making little feet for shoes. A little boy child would be about right.

He saw a dim light in the bedroom and decided to come in through the kitchen door. He could wash the fertilizer dust off himself before presenting himself to Missie May. It would be nice for her not to know that he was there until he slipped into his place in bed and hugged her back. She always liked that.

He eased the kitchen door open slowly and silently, but when he went to set his dinner bucket on the table he bumped it into a pile of dishes, and something crashed to the floor. He heard his wife gasp in fright and hurried to reassure her. 190

"Iss me, honey. Don't get skeered."

There was a quick, large movement in the bedroom. A rustle, a thud, and a stealthy silence. The light went out.

What? Robbers? Murderers? Some varmint attacking his helpless wife, perhaps. He struck a match, threw himself on guard and stepped over the door-sill into the bedroom.

The great belt on the wheel of Time slipped and eternity stood still. By the match light he could see the man's legs fighting with his breeches in his frantic desire to get them on. He had both chance and time to kill the intruder in his helpless condition—half-in and half-out of his pants—but he was too weak to take action. The shapeless enemies of humanity that live in the hours of Time had waylaid Joe. He was assaulted in his weakness. Like Samson awakening after his haircut.[4] So he just opened his mouth and laughed. 200

The match went out and he struck another and lit the lamp. A howling wind raced across his heart, but underneath its fury he heard his wife sobbing and Slemmons pleading for his life. Offering to buy it with all that he had. "Please, suh, don't kill me. Sixty-two dollars at de sto' gold money."

Joe just stood. Slemmons looked at the window, but it was screened. Joe stood out like a rough-backed mountain between him and the door. Barring him from escape, from sunrise, from life. 210

He considered a surprise attack upon the big clown that stood there laughing like a chessy cat. But before his fist could travel an inch, Joe's own rushed out to crush him like a battering ram. Then Joe stood over him.

"Git into yo' damn rags, Slemmons, and dat quick."

Slemmons scrambled to his feet and into his vest and coat. As he grabbed his hat, Joe's fury overrode his intentions and he grabbed at Slemmons with his left hand and struck at him with his right. The right landed. The left grazed the front of his vest. Slemmons was knocked a somersault into the kitchen and fled through the open door. Joe found himself alone with Missie May, with the golden watch charm clutched in his left fist. A short bit of broken chain dangled between his fingers. 220

Missie May was sobbing. Wails of weeping without words. Joe stood, and after awhile she found out that he had something in his hand. And then he stood and felt without thinking and without seeing with his natural eyes. Missie May kept on crying and Joe kept on feeling so much and not knowing what to do with all his feelings, he put Slemmons' watch charm in his pants pocket and took a good laugh and went to bed.

---

4. The biblical hero, Samson, lost his strength when Delilah cut his hair. Judges 16:18–21.

"Missie May, whut you crying for?"   230

"Cause Ah love you so hard and Ah know you don't love *me* no mo'."

Joe sank his face into the pillow for a spell then he said huskily, "You don't know de feelings of dat yet, Missie May."

"Oh Joe, honey, he said he wuz gointer gimme dat gold money and he jes' kept on after me—"

Joe was very still and silent for a long time. Then he said, "Well, don't cry no mo', Missie May. Ah got yo' gold piece for you."

The hours went past on their rusty ankles. Joe still and quiet on one bed-rail and Missie May wrung dry of sobs on the other. Finally the sun's tide crept upon the shore of night and drowned all its hours. Missie May with her face stiff and   240
streaked towards the window saw the dawn come into her yard. It was day. Nothing more. Joe wouldn't be coming home as usual. No need to fling open the front door and sweep off the porch, making it nice for Joe. Never no more break-fast to cook; no more washing and starching of Joe's jumper-jackets and pants. No more nothing. So why get up?

With this strange man in her bed, she felt embarrassed to get up and dress. She decided to wait till he had dressed and gone. Then she would get up, dress quickly and be gone forever beyond reach of Joe's looks and laughs. But he never moved. Red light turned to yellow, then white.

From beyond the no-man's land between them came a voice. A strange voice   250
that yesterday had been Joe's.

"Missie May, ain't you gonna fix me no breakfus'?"

She sprang out of bed. "Yeah, Joe. Ah didn't reckon you wuz hongry."

No need to die today. Joe needed her for a few more minutes anyhow.

Soon there was a roaring fire in the cook stove. Water bucket full and two chickens killed. Joe loved fried chicken and rice. She didn't deserve a thing and good Joe was letting her cook him some breakfast. She rushed hot biscuits to the table as Joe took his seat.

He ate with his eyes on his plate. No laughter, no banter.

"Missie May, you ain't eatin' yo' breakfus'."   260

"Ah don't choose none, Ah thank yuh."

His coffee cup was empty. She sprang to refill it. When she turned from the stove and bent to set the cup beside Joe's plate, she saw the yellow coin on the table between them.

She slumped into her seat and wept into her arms.

Presently Joe said calmly, "Missie May, you cry too much. Don't look back lak Lot's wife and turn to salt."[5]

The sun, the hero of every day, the impersonal old man that beams as brightly on death as on birth, came up every morning and raced across the blue dome and dipped into the sea of fire every evening. Water ran down hill and birds   270
nested.

---

5. Lot's wife turned to a pillar of salt when she looked back as Sodom and Gomorrah were being destroyed by God's fire. Genesis 19:24–26.

Missie knew why she didn't leave Joe. She couldn't. She loved him too much. But she couldn't understand why Joe didn't leave her. He was polite, even kind at times, but aloof.

There were no more Saturday romps. No ringing silver dollars to stack beside her plate. No pockets to rifle. In fact the yellow coin in his trousers was like a monster hiding in the cave of his pockets to destroy her.

She often wondered if he still had it, but nothing could have induced her to ask nor yet to explore his pockets to see for herself. Its shadow was in the house whether or no. 280

One night Joe came home around midnight and complained of pains in the back. He asked Missie to rub him down with liniment. It had been three months since Missie had touched his body and it all seemed strange. But she rubbed him. Grateful for the change. Before morning, youth triumphed and Missie exulted. But the next day, as she joyfully made up their bed, beneath her pillow she found the piece of money with the bit of chain attached.

Alone to herself, she looked at the thing with loathing, but look she must. She took it into her hands with trembling and saw first thing that it was no gold piece. It was a gilded half-dollar. Then she knew why Slemmons had forbidden anyone to touch his gold. He trusted village eyes at a distance not to recognize his 290 stick-pin as a gilded quarter, and his watch charm as a four-bit piece.

She was glad at first that Joe had left it there. Perhaps he was through with her punishment. They were man and wife again. Then another thought came clawing at her. He had come home to buy from her as if she were any woman in the long house. Fifty cents for her love. As if to say that he could pay as well as Slemmons. She slid the coin into his Sunday pants pocket and dressed herself and left his house.

Halfway between her house and the quarters she met her husband's mother, and after a short talk she turned and went back home. If she had not the substance of marriage, she had the outside show. Joe must leave *her.* She let him see 300 she didn't want his old gold four-bits too.

She saw no more of the coin for some time though she knew that Joe could not help finding it in his pocket. But his health kept poor, and he came home at least every ten days to be rubbed.

The sun swept around the horizon, trailing its robes of weeks and days. One morning as Joe came in from work, he found Missie May chopping wood. Without a word he took the ax and chopped a huge pile before he stopped.

"You ain't got no business choppin' wood, and you know it."

"How come? Ah been choppin' it for de last longest."

"Ah ain't blind. You makin' feet for shoes." 310

Won't you be glad to have a li'l baby chile, Joe?"

"You know dat 'thout astin' me."

"Iss gointer be a boy chile and de very spit of you."

"You reckon, Missie May?"

"Who else could it look lak?"

Joe said nothing, but he thrust his hand deep into his pocket and fingered something there.

It was almost six months later Missie May took to bed and Joe went and got his mother to come wait on the house.

Missie May delivered a fine boy. Her travail was over when Joe came in from 320 work one morning. His mother and the old women were drinking great bowls of coffee around the fire in the kitchen.

The minute Joe came into the room his mother called him aside.

"How did Missie May make out?" he asked quickly.

"Who, dat gal? She strong as a ox. She gointer have plenty mo'. We done fixed her wid de sugar and lard to sweeten her for de nex' one."

Joe stood silent awhile.

"You ain't ast 'bout de baby, Joe. You oughter be mighty proud cause he sho' is de spittin' image of yuh, son. Dat's yourn all right, if you never git another one, dat un is yourn. And you know Ah'm mighty proud too, son, cause Ah never 330 thought well of you marryin' Missie May cause her ma used tuh fan her foot 'round right smart and Ah been mighty skeered dat Missie May wuz gointer git misput on her road."

Joe said nothing. He fooled around the house till late in the day then just be-fore he went to work, he went and stood at the foot of the bed and asked his wife how she felt. He did this every day during the week.

On Saturday he went to Orlando to make his market. It had been a long time since he had done that.

Meat and lard, meal and flour, soap and starch. Cans of corn and tomatoes. All the staples. He fooled around town for awhile and bought bananas and apples. 340 Way after while he went around to the candy store.

"Hellow, Joe," the clerk greeted him. "Ain't seen you in a long time."

"Nope, Ah ain't been heah. Been 'round spots and places."

"Want some of them molasses kisses you always buy?"

"Yessuh." He threw the gilded half-dollar on the counter. "Will dat spend?"

"Whut is it, Joe? Well, I'll be doggone! A gold-plated four-bit piece. Where'd you git it, Joe?"

"Offen a stray nigger dat come through Eatonville. He had it on his watch chain for a charm—goin' 'round making out iss gold money. Ha ha! He had a quarter on his tie pin and it wuz all golded up too. Tryin' to fool people. Makin' 350 out he so rich and everything. Ha! Ha! Tryin' to tole off folkses wives from home."

"How did you git it, Joe? Did he fool you, too?"

"Who, me? Naw suh! he ain't fooled me none. Know whut Ah done? He come 'round me wid his smart talk. Ah hauled off and knocked 'im down and took his old four-bits 'way from 'im. Gointer buy my wife some good ole 'lasses kisses wid it. Gimme fifty cents worth of dem candy kisses."

"Fifty cents buys a mightly lot of candy kisses, Joe. Why don't you split it up and take some chocolate bars, too. They eat good, too."

"Yessuh, dey do, but Ah wants all dat in kisses. Ah got a li'l boy chile home now. Tain't a week old yet, but he kin suck a sugar tit and maybe eat one them 360 kisses hisself."

Joe got his candy and left the store. The clerk turned to the next customer. "Wisht I could be like these darkies. Laughin' all the time. Nothin' worries 'em."

Back in Eatonville, Joe reached his own front door. There was the ring of singing metal on wood. Fifteen times. Missie May couldn't run to the door, but she crept there as quickly as she could.

"Joe Banks, Ah hear you chunkin' money in mah do'way. You wait till Ah got mah strength back and Ah'm gointer fix you for dat." [1933]

Questions for Discussion and Writing
1. What details foreshadow Missie May's infidelity?
2. Why does Joe put the gilded half-dollar under Missie May's pillow?
3. What do the gilded coins symbolize?
4. Is this a love story? Explain.
5. Is Joe's response to Missie's infidelity believable? Would you expect a husband to react as he does? Explain.
6. What is the theme of the story? Underline or highlight specific passages that support your interpretation.

✎ RAYMOND CHANDLER
(1888–1959)

The Curtain

For many years, Raymond Chandler was dismissed as a popular writer of "hard boiled" detective fiction, but gradually his reputation has grown with that of the detective novel generally, and he is now increasingly regarded as a significant voice in American literature.

Like his heroes, Chandler felt himself an outsider. He was born in Chicago but raised in England, where his mother moved after divorcing his alcoholic father. Chandler aspired to be a lawyer but, discouraged by his family, entered the civil service. He hated the work and left England. On the ship to America, he met a couple who hired him as a bookkeeper, and in a few years he was able to bring his mother to America.

After serving in World War I, Chandler joined the Dabney Oil Syndicate and rapidly rose to Vice President, but alcohol abuse cost him his job in 1932. He turned to writing detective stories for "pulp" magazines, publishing his first story in *Black Mask* in 1933. Six years later, he reworked material from the published stories (including "The Curtain") into a novel, *The Big Sleep* (1939). Success as a novelist brought him to Hollywood in the 1940s, but he was too much a loner for the collaborative world of film. Meanwhile, his wife's failing health, his own drinking, and self-doubts about his abilities as a writer led to a suicide attempt in 1955. He died a lonely man.

Chandler contributed to but did not originate the hard-boiled school of detective fiction, which reacted against the genteel conventions of the classic "well made" whodunit. His most famous hero, Philip Marlowe, is an outsider, an urban knight-errant, at once sentimental and cynical, living in a Los Angeles that is gritty, violent, corrupt. The line between the good guys and the bad, the trustworthy and the treacherous, is rarely clear. Chandler is a master of conveying this menacing environment—the dark underside of American life.

I

THE FIRST TIME I ever saw Larry Batzel he was drunk outside Sardi's[1] in a secondhand Rolls-Royce. There was a tall blonde with him who had eyes you wouldn't forget. I helped her argue him out from under the wheel so that she could drive.

The second time I saw him he didn't have any Rolls-Royce or any blonde or any job in pictures. All he had was the jitters and a suit that needed pressing. He remembered me. He was that kind of drunk.

I bought him enough drinks to do him some good and gave him half my cigarettes. I used to see him from time to time "between pictures." I got to lending him money. I don't know just why. He was a big, handsome brute with eyes like a cow and something innocent and honest in them. Something I don't get much of in my business.

The funny part was he had been a liquor runner for a pretty hard mob before Repeal.[2] He never got anywhere in pictures, and after a while I didn't see him around any more.

Then one day out of the clear blue I got a check for all he owed me and a note that he was working on the tables—gambling not dining—at the Dardanella Club, and to come out and look him up. So I knew he was back in the rackets.

I didn't go to see him, but I found out somehow or other that Joe Mesarvey owned the place, and that Joe Mesarvey was married to the blonde with the eyes, the one Larry Batzel had been with in the Rolls that time. I still didn't go out there.

Then very early one morning there was a dim figure standing by my bed, between me and the windows. The blinds had been pulled down. That must have been what wakened me. The figure was large and had a gun.

I rolled over and rubbed my eyes.

"Okay," I said sourly. "There's twelve bucks in my pants and my wrist watch cost twenty-seven fifty. You couldn't get anything on that."

The figure went over to the window and pulled a blind aside an inch and looked down at the street. When he turned again I saw that it was Larry Batzel.

His face was drawn and tired and he needed a shave. He had dinner clothes on still and a dark double-breasted overcoat with a dwarf rose drooping in the lapel.

He sat down and held the gun on his knee for a moment before he put it away, with a puzzled frown, as if he didn't know how it got into his hand.

"You're going to drive me to Berdoo," he said. "I've got to get out of town. They've put the pencil[3] on me."

---

1. A famous restaurant in Los Angeles, catering to people connected with the movies.
2. Repeal of Prohibition, 1933.
3. Put out a "contract" on him; hired someone to kill him.

"Okay," I said. "Tell me about it."

I sat up and felt the carpet with my toes and lit a cigarette. It was a little after five-thirty.

"I jimmied your lock with a piece of celluloid," he said. "You ought to use 40 your night latch once in a while. I wasn't sure which was your flop and I didn't want to rouse the house."

"Try the mailboxes next time," I said. "But go ahead. You're not drunk, are you?"

"I'd like to be, but I've got to get away first. I'm just rattled. I'm not so tough as I used to be. You read about the O'Mara disappearance of course."

"Yeah."

"Listen, anyway. If I keep talking I won't blow up. I don't think I'm spotted here."

"One drink won't hurt either of us," I said. "The Scotch is on the table there." 50

He poured a couple of drinks quickly and handed me one. I put on a bathrobe and slippers. The glass rattled against his teeth when he drank.

He put his empty glass down and held his hands tight together.

"I used to know Dud O'Mara pretty well. We used to run stuff together down from Hueneme Point. We even carried the torch for the same girl. She's married to Joe Mesarvey now. Dud married five million dollars. He married General Dade Winslow's rickety-rackety divorcée daughter."

"I know all that," I said.

"Yeah. Just listen. She picked him out of a speak,[4] just like I'd pick up a cafeteria tray. But he didn't like the life. I guess he used to see Mona. He got wise Joe 60 Mesarvey and Lash Yeager had a hot car racket on the side. They knocked him off."

"The hell they did," I said. "Have another drink."

"No. Just listen. There's just two points. That night O'Mara pulled down the curtain—no, the night the papers got it—Mona Mesarvey disappeared too. Only she didn't. They hid her out in a shack a couple of miles beyond Realito in the orange belt. Next door to a garage run by a heel named Art Huck, a hot car drop. I found out. I trailed Joe there."

"What made it your business?" I asked.

"I'm still soft on her. I'm telling you this because you were pretty swell to me 70 once. You can make something of it after I blow. They hid her out there so it would look as if Dud had blown with her. Naturally the cops were not too dumb to see Joe after the disappearance. But they didn't find Mona. They have a system on disappearances and they play the system."

He got up and went over to the window again, looked through the side of the blind.

"There's a blue sedan down there I think I've seen before," he said. "But maybe not. There's a lot like it."

He sat down again. I didn't speak.

"This place beyond Realito is on the first side road north from the Foothill 80

4. Speakeasy—a place to buy illegal drinks during Prohibition.

Boulevard. You can't miss it. It stands all alone, the garage and the house next door. There's an old cyanide plant up above there. I'm telling you this—"

"That's point one," I said. "What was the second point?"

"The punk that used to drive for Lash Yeager lit out a couple of weeks back and went East. I lent him fifty bucks. He was broke. He told me Yeager was out to the Winslow estate the night Dud O'Mara disappeared."

I stared at him. "It's interesting, Larry. But not enough to break eggs over. After all we do have a police department."

"Yeah. Add this. I got drunk last night and told Yeager what I knew. Then I quit the job at the Dardanella. So, somebody shot at me outside where I live when   90 I got home. I've been on the dodge ever since. Now, will you drive me to Berdoo?"

I stood up. It was May but I felt cold. Larry Batzel looked cold, even with his overcoat on.

"Absolutely," I said. "But take it easy. Later will be much safer than now. Have another drink. You don't *know* they knocked O'Mara off."

"If he found out about the hot car racket, with Mona married to Joe Mesarvey, they'd have to knock him off. He was that kind of guy."

I stood up and went towards the bathroom. Larry went over to the window again.

"It's still there," he said over his shoulder. "You might get shot at riding with   100 me."

"I'd hate that," I said.

"You're a good sort of heel, Carmady. It's going to rain. I'd hate like hell to be buried in the rain, wouldn't you?"

"You talk too damn much," I said, and went into the bathroom.

It was the last time I ever spoke to him.

II

I heard him moving around while I was shaving, but not after I got under the shower, of course. When I came out he was gone. I padded over and looked into the kitchenette. He wasn't there. I grabbed a bathrobe and peeked out into the hall. It was empty except for a milkman starting down the back stairs with his   110 wiry tray of bottles, and the fresh folded papers leaning against the shut doors.

"Hey," I called out to the milkman, "did a guy just come out of here and go by you?"

He looked back at me from the corner of the wall and opened his mouth to answer. He was a nice-looking boy with fine large white teeth. I remember his teeth well, because I was looking at them when I heard the shots.

They were not very near or very far. Out back of the apartment house, by the garages, or in the alley, I thought. There were two quick, hard shots and then the riveting machine. A burst of five or six, all a good chopper should ever need. Then the roar of the car going away.   120

The milkman shut his mouth as if a winch controlled it. His eyes were huge and empty looking at me. Then he very carefully set his bottles down on the top step and leaned against the wall.

"That sounded like shots," he said.

All this took a couple of seconds and felt like half an hour. I went back into my place and threw clothes on, grabbed odds and ends off the bureau, barged out into the hall. It was still empty, even of the milkman. A siren was dying somewhere near. A bald head with a hangover under it poked out of a door and made a snuffling noise.

I went down the back stairs.   130

There were two or three people out in the lower hall. I went out back. The garages were in two rows facing each other across a cement space, then two more at the end, leaving a space to go out to the alley. A couple of kids were coming over a fence three houses away.

Larry Batzel lay on his face, with his hat a yard away from his head, and one hand flung out to within a foot of a big black automatic. His ankles were crossed, as if he had spun as he fell. Blood was thick on the side of his face, on his blond hair, especially on his neck. It was also thick on the cement yard.

Two radio cops and the milk driver and a man in a brown sweater and bibless overalls were bending over him. The man in overalls was our janitor.   140

I went up to them, about the same time the two kids from over the fence hit the yard. The milk driver look at me with a queer, strained expression. One of the cops straightened up and said: "Either of you guys know him? He's still got half his face."

He wasn't talking to me. The milk driver shook his head and kept on looking at me from the corner of his eyes. The janitor said: "He ain't a tenant here. He might of been a visitor. Kind of early for visitors, though, ain't it?"

"He's got party clothes on. You know your flophouse better'n I do," the cop said heavily. He got out a notebook.

The other cop straightened up too and shook his head and went towards the   150 house, with the janitor trotting beside him.

The cop with the notebook jerked a thumb at me and said harshly: "You was here first after these two guys. Anything from you?"

I looked at the milkman. Larry Batzel wouldn't care, and a man has a living to earn. It wasn't a story for a prowl car[5] anyway.

"I just heard the shots and came running," I said.

The cop took that for an answer. The milk driver looked up at the lowering gray sky and said nothing.

After a while I got back into my apartment and finished my dressing. When I picked my hat up off the window table by the Scotch bottle there was a small   160 rosebud lying on a piece of scrawled paper.

The note said: "You're a good guy, but I think I'll go it alone. Give the rose to Mona, if you ever should get a chance. Larry."

I put those things in my wallet, and braced myself with a drink.

III

About three o'clock that afternoon I stood in the main hallway of the Winslow place and waited for the butler to come back. I had spent most of the

5. Police car.

day not going near my office or apartment, and not meeting any homicide men. It
was only a question of time until I had to come through, but I wanted to see
General Dade Winslow first. He was hard to see.

Oil paintings hung all around me, mostly portraits. There were a couple of   170
statues and several suits of time-darkened armor on pedestals of dark wood. High
over the huge marble fireplace hung two bullet-torn—or moth-eaten—cavalry
pennants crossed in a glass case, and below them the painted likeness of a thin,
spry-looking man with a black beard and mustachios and full regimentals of about
the time of the Mexican War. This might be General Dade Winslow's father. The
general himself, though pretty ancient, couldn't be quite that old.

Then the butler came back and said General Winslow was in the orchid
house and would I follow him, please.

We went out of the french doors at the back and across the lawns to a big
glass pavilion well beyond the garages. The butler opened the door into a sort of   180
vestibule and shut it when I was inside, and it was already hot. Then he opened
the inner door and it was really hot.

The air steamed. The walls and ceiling of the greenhouse dripped. In the half
light enormous tropical plants spread their blooms and branches all over the
place, and the smell of them was almost as overpowering as the smell of boiling
alcohol.

The butler, who was old and thin and very straight and white-haired, held
branches of the plants back for me to pass, and we came to an opening in the
middle of the place. A large reddish Turkish rug was spread down on the hexago-
nal flagstones. In the middle of the rug, in a wheel chair, a very old man sat with a   190
traveling rug around his body and watched us come.

Nothing lived in his face but the eyes. Black eyes, deepset, shining, untouch-
able. The rest of his face was the leaden mask of death, sunken temples, a sharp
nose, outward-turning ear lobes, a mouth that was a thin white slit. He was
wrapped partly in a reddish and very shabby bathrobe and partly in the rug. His
hands had purple fingernails and were clasped loosely, motionless on the rug. He
had a few scattered wisps of white hair on his skull.

The butler said: "This is Mr. Carmady, General."

The old man stared at me. After a while a sharp, shrewish voice said: "Place
a chair for Mr. Carmady."   200

The butler dragged a wicker chair out and I sat down. I put my hat on the
floor. The butler picked it up.

"Brandy," the general said. "How do you like your brandy, sir?"

"Any way at all," I said.

He snorted. The butler went away. The general stared at me with his unblinking eyes. He snorted again.

"I always take champagne with mine," he said. "A third of a glass of brandy
under the champagne, and the champagne as cold as Valley Forge. Colder, if you
can get it colder."

A noise that could have been a chuckle came out of him.   210

"Not that I was at Valley Forge," he said. "Not quite that bad. You may
smoke, sir."

I thanked him and said I was tired of smoking for a while. I got a handkerchief out and mopped my face.

"Take your coat off, sir. Dud always did. Orchids require heat, Mr. Carmady—like sick old men."

I took my coat off, a raincoat I had brought along. It looked like rain. Larry Batzel had said it was going to rain.

"Dud is my son-in-law. Dudley O'Mara. I believe you had something to tell me about him."   220

"Just hearsay," I said. "I wouldn't want to go into it, unless I had your O.K., General Winslow."

The basilisk eyes stared at me. "You are a private detective. You want to be paid, I suppose."

"I'm in that line of business," I said. "But that doesn't mean I have to be paid for every breath I draw. It's just something I heard. You might like to pass it on yourself to the Missing Persons Bureau."

"I see," he said quietly. "A scandal of some sort."

The butler came back before I could answer. He wheeled a tea wagon in through the jungle, set it at my elbow and mixed me a brandy and soda. He went   230 away.

I sipped the drink. "It seems there was a girl," I said. "He knew her before he knew your daughter. She's married to a racketeer now. It seems—"

"I've heard all that," he said. "I don't give a damn. What I want to know is where he is and if he's all right. If he's happy."

I stared at him popeyed. After a moment, I said weakly: "Maybe I could find the girl, or the boys downtown could, with what I could tell them."

He plucked at the edge of his rug and moved his head about an inch. I think he was nodding. Then he said very slowly: "Probably I'm talking too much for my health, but I want to make something clear. I'm a cripple. I have two ruined legs   240 and half my lower belly. I don't eat much or sleep much. I'm a bore to myself and a damn nuisance to everybody else. So I miss Dud. He used to spend a lot of time with me. Why, God only knows."

"Well—" I began.

"Shut up. You're a young man to me, so I can be rude to you. Dud left without saying goodbye to me. That wasn't like him. He drove his car away one evening and nobody has heard from him since. If he got tired of my fool daughter and her brat, if he wanted some other woman, that's all right. He got a brainstorm and left without saying goodbye to me, and now he's sorry. That's why I don't hear from him. Find him and tell him I understand. That's all—unless he needs money.   250 If he does, he can have all he wants."

His leaden cheeks almost had a pink tinge now. His black eyes were brighter, if possible. He leaned back very slowly and closed his eyes.

I drank a lot of my drink in one long swallow. I said: "Suppose he's in a jam. Say, on account of the girl's husband. This Joe Mesarvey."

He opened his eyes and winked. "Not an O'Mara," he said. "It's the other fellow would be in a jam."

"Okay. Shall I pass on to the Bureau where I heard this girl was?"

"Certainly not. They've done nothing. Let them go on doing it. Find him yourself. I'll pay you a thousand dollars—even if you only have to walk across the 260 street. Tell him everything is all right here. The old man's doing fine and sends his love. That's all."

I couldn't tell him. Suddenly I couldn't tell him anything Larry Batzel had told me, or what had happened to Larry, or anything about it. I finished my drink and stood up and put my coat back on. I said: "That's too much money for the job, General Winslow. We can talk about that later. Have I your authority to represent you in my own way?"

He pressed a bell on his wheelchair. "Just tell him," he said. "I want to know he's all right and I want him to know that I'm all right. That's all—unless he needs money. Now you'll have to excuse me. I'm tired."   270

He closed his eyes. I went back through the jungle and the butler met me at the door with my hat.

I breathed in some cool air and said: "The general wants me to see Mrs. O'Mara."

IV

This room had a white carpet from wall to wall. Ivory drapes of immense height lay tumbled casually on the white carpet inside the many windows. The windows stared towards the dark foothills, and the air beyond the glass was dark too. It hadn't started to rain yet, but there was a feeling of pressure in the atmosphere.

Mrs. O'Mara was stretched out on a white chaise lounge with both her slip- 280 pers off and her feet in the net stockings they don't wear any more. She was tall and dark, with a sulky mouth. Handsome, but this side of beautiful.

She said: "What in the world can *I* do for you? It's all known. Too damn known. Except that I don't know you, do I?"

"Well, hardly," I said. "I'm just a private copper in a small way of business."

She reached for a glass I hadn't noticed but would have looked for in a moment, on account of her way of talking and the fact she had her slippers off. She drank languidly, flashing a ring.

"I met him in a speakeasy," she said with a sharp laugh. "A very handsome bootlegger, with thick curly hair and an Irish grin. So I married him. Out of bore- 290 dom. As for him, the bootlegging business was even then uncertain—if there were no other attractions."

She waited for me to say there were, but not as if she cared a lot whether I came through. I just said: "You didn't see him leave on the day he disappeared?"

"No. I seldom saw him leave, or come back. It was like that." She drank some more of her drink.

"Huh," I grunted. "But, of course, you didn't quarrel." They never do.

"There are so many ways of quarreling, Mr. Carmady."

"Yeah. I like your saying that. Of course you knew about the girl."

"I'm glad I'm being properly frank to an old family detective. Yes, I knew 300 about the girl." She curled a tendril of inky hair behind her ear.

"Did you know about her before he disappeared?" I asked politely.

"Certainly."

"How?"

"You're pretty direct, aren't you? Connections, as they say. I'm an old speak fancier. Or didn't you know that?"

"Did you know the bunch at the Dardanella?"

"I've been there." She didn't look startled, or even surprised. "In fact I practically lived there for a week. That's where I met Dudley O'Mara."

"Yeah. Your father married pretty late in life, didn't he?"

I watched the color fade in her cheeks. I wanted her mad, but there was nothing doing. She smiled and the color came back and she rang a push bell on a cord down in the swansdown cushions of the chaise lounge.

"Very late," she said, "if it's any of your business."

"It's not," I said.

A coy-looking maid came in and mixed a couple of drinks at a side table. She gave one to Mrs. O'Mara, put one down beside me. She went away again, showing a nice pair of legs under a short skirt.

Mrs. O'Mara watched the door shut and then said: "The whole thing has got Father into a mood. I wish Dud would wire or write or something."

I said slowly: "He's an old, old man, crippled, half buried already. One thin thread of interest held him to life. The thread snapped and nobody gives a damn. He tries to act as if he didn't give a damn himself. I don't call that a mood. I call that a pretty swell display of intestinal fortitude."

"Gallant," she said, and her eyes were daggers. "But you haven't touched your drink."

"I have to go," I said. "Thanks all the same."

She held a slim, tinted hand out and I went over and touched it. The thunder burst suddenly behind the hills and she jumped. A gust of air shook the windows.

I went down a tiled staircase to the hallway and the butler appeared out of a shadow and opened the door for me.

I looked down a succession of terraces decorated with flower beds and imported trees. At the bottom a high metal railing with gilded spearheads and a six-foot hedge inside. A sunken driveway crawled down to the main gates and a lodge inside them.

Beyond the estate the hill sloped down to the city and the old oil wells of La Brea, now partly a park, partly a deserted stretch of fenced-in wild land. Some of the wooden derricks still stood. These had made the wealth of the Winslow family and then the family had run away from them up the hill, far enough to get away from the smell of the sumps, not too far for them to look out of the front windows and see what made them rich.

I walked down brick steps between the terraced lawns. On one side of them a dark-haired, pale-faced kid of ten or eleven was throwing darts at a target hung on a tree. I went along near him.

"You young O'Mara?" I asked.

He leaned against a stone bench with four darts in his hand and looked at me with cold, slaty eyes, old eyes.

"I'm Dade Winslow Trevillyan," he said grimly.

"Oh, then Dudley O'Mara's not your dad."

"Of course not." His voice was full of scorn. "Who are you?"

"I'm a detective. I'm going to find your—I mean, Mr. O'Mara."

That didn't bring us any closer. Detectives were nothing to him. The thunder was tumbling about in the hills like a bunch of elephants playing tag. I had another idea.

"Bet you can't put four out of five into the gold at thirty feet."

He livened up sharply. "With these?"

"Uh-huh."

"How much you bet?" he snapped.

"Oh, a dollar."

He ran to the target and cleaned darts off it, came back and took a stance by the bench.

"That's not thirty feet," I said.

He gave me a sour look and went a few feet behind the bench. I grinned, then I stopped grinning.

His small hand darted so swiftly I could hardly follow it. Five darts hung in the gold center of the target in less than that many seconds. He stared at me triumphantly.

"Gosh, you're pretty good, Master Trevillyan," I grunted, and got my dollar out.

His hand snapped at it like a trout taking the fly. He had it out of sight like a flash.

"That's nothing," he chuckled. "You ought to see me on our target range back of the garages. Want to go over there and bet some more?"

I looked back up the hill and saw part of a low white building backed up to a bank.

"Well, not today," I said. "Next time I visit here maybe. So Dud O'Mara is not your dad. If I find him anyway, will it be all right with you?"

He shrugged his thin, sharp shoulders in a maroon sweater. "Sure. But what can you do the police can't do?"

"It's a thought," I said, and left him.

I went on down the brick walk to the bottom of the lawns and along inside the hedge towards the gatehouse. I could see glimpses of the street through the hedge. When I was halfway to the lodge I saw the blue sedan outside. It was a small neat car, low-slung, very clean, lighter than a police car, but about the same size. Over beyond it I could see my roadster waiting under the pepper tree.

I stood looking at the sedan through the hedge. I could see the drift of somebody's cigarette smoke against the windshield inside the car. I turned my back to the lodge and looked up the hill. The Treyvillyan kid had gone somewhere out of sight, to salt his dollar down maybe, though a dollar shouldn't have meant much to him.

I bent over and unsheathed the 7.65 Luger I was wearing that day and stuck it nose-down inside my left sock, inside my shoe. I could walk that way, if I didn't walk too fast. I went to the gates.

They kept them locked and nobody got in without identification from the house. The lodge keeper, a big husky with a gun under his arm, came out and let me through a small postern at the edge of the gates. I stood talking to him through the bars for a minute, watching the sedan.

It looked all right. There seemed to be two men in it. It was about a hundred feet along in the shadow of the high wall on the other side. It was a very narrow 400 street, without sidewalks. I didn't have to go far to go to my roadster.

I walked a little stiffly across that dark pavement and got in, grabbed quickly down into a small compartment in the front part of the seat where I kept a spare gun. It was a police Colt. I slid it inside my under-arm holster and started the car.

I eased the brake off and pulled it away. Suddenly the rain let go in big splashing drops and the sky was black as Carrie Nation's bonnet.[6] Not so black but that I saw the sedan wheel away from the curb behind me.

I started the windshield wiper and built up to forty miles an hour in a hurry. I had gone about eight blocks when they gave me the siren. That fooled me. It was a quiet street, deadly quiet. I slowed down and pulled over to the curb. The sedan 410 slid up beside me and I was looking at the black snout of a submachine gun over the sill of the rear door.

Behind it a narrow face with reddened eyes, a fixed mouth. A voice above the sound of the rain and the windshield wiper and the noise of the two motors said: "Get in here with us. Be nice, if you know what I mean."

They were not cops. It didn't matter now. I shut off the ignition, dropped my car keys on the floor and got out on the running board. The man behind the wheel of the sedan didn't look at me. The one behind kicked a door open and slid away along the seat, holding the tommy gun nicely.

I got into the sedan.   420

"Okay, Louie. The frisk."

The driver came from out from under his wheel and got behind me. He got my Colt from under my arm, tapped my hips and pockets, my belt line.

"Clean," he said, and got back into the front of the car.

The man with the tommy reached forward with his left hand and took my Colt from the driver, then lowered the tommy to the floor of the car and draped a brown rug over it. He leaned back in the corner again, smooth and relaxed, holding the Colt on his knee.

"Okay, Louie. Now let's ride."

V

We rode—idly, gently, the rain drumming on the roof and streaming down 430 the windows on one side. We wound along curving hill streets, among estates that covered acres, whose houses were distant clusters of wet gables beyond blurred trees.

A tang of cigarette smoke floated under my nose and the red-eyed man said: "What did he tell you?"

"Little enough," I said. "That Mona blew town the night the papers got it. Old Winslow knew it already."

6. Carrie Nation (1846–1911), a militant campaigner for the Temperance Movement.

"He wouldn't have to dig very deep for that," Red-eyes said. "The buttons[7] didn't. What else?"

"He said he'd been shot at. He wanted me to ride him out of town. At the   440
last moment he ran off alone. I don't know why."

"Loosen up, peeper,"[8] Red-eyes said dryly. "It's your only way out."

"That's all there is," I said, and looked out of the window at the driving rain.

"You on the case for the old guy?"

"No. He's tight."

Red-eyes laughed. The gun in my shoe felt heavy and unsteady, and very far away. I said: "That might be all there is to know about O'Mara."

The man in the front seat turned his head a little and growled: "Where the hell did you say that street was?"

"Top of Beverly Glen, stupid. Mulholland Drive."   450

"Oh, that. Jeeze, that ain't paved worth a damn."

"We'll pave it with the peeper," Red-eyes said.

The estates thinned out and scrub oak took possession of the hillsides.

"You ain't a bad guy," Red-eyes said. "You're just tight, like the old man. Don't you get the idea? We want to know *everything* he said, so we'll know whether we got to blot you or no."

"Go to hell," I said. "You wouldn't believe me anyway."

"Try us. This is just a job to us. We just do it and pass on."

"It must be nice work," I said. "While it lasts."

"You'll crack wise once too often, guy."   460

"I did—long ago, while you were still in Reform School. I'm still getting myself disliked."

Red-eyes laughed again. There seemed to be very little bluster about him.

"Far as we know you're clean with the law. Didn't make no cracks this morning. That right?"

"If I say yes, you can blot me right now. Okay."

"How about a grand pin money and forget the whole thing?"

"You wouldn't believe that either."

"Yeah, we would. Here' the idea. We do the job and pass on. We're an organization. But you live here, you got goodwill and a business. You'd play ball."   470

"Sure," I said. "I'd play ball."

"We don't," Red-eyes said softly, "never knock off a legit. Bad for the trade."

He leaned back in the corner, the gun on his right knee, and reached into an inner pocket. He spread a large tan wallet on his knee and fished two bills out of it, slid them folded along the seat. The wallet went back into his pocket.

"Yours," he said gravely. "You won't last twenty-four hours if you slip your cable."

I picked the bills up. Two five hundreds. I tucked them in my vest. "Right," I said. "I wouldn't be a legit any more then, would I?"

"Think that over, dick."[9]   480

7. The police.
8. "You'd better talk, private eye."
9. Detective.

We grinned at each other, a couple of nice lads getting along in a harsh, unfriendly world. Then Red-eyes turned his head sharply.

"Okay, Louie. Forget the Mulholland stuff. Pull up."

The car was halfway up a long bleak twist of hill. The rain drove in gray curtains down the slope. There was no ceiling, no horizon. I could see a quarter of a mile and I could see nothing outside our car that lived.

The driver edged over to the side of the bank and shut his motor off. He lit a cigarette and draped an arm on the back seat.

He smiled at me. He had a nice smile—like an alligator.

"We'll have a drink on it," Red-eyes said. "I wish I could make me a grand that easy. Just tyin' my nose to my chin."

"You ain't got no chin," Louie said, and went on smiling.

Red-eyes put the Colt down on the seat and drew a flat half-pint out of his side pocket. It looked like good stuff, green stamp, bottled in bond.[10] He unscrewed the top with his teeth, sniffed at the liquor and smacked his lips.

"No Crow McGee[11] on this, in this," he said. "This is the company spread. Tilt her."

He reached along the seat and gave me the bottle. I could have had his wrist, but there was Louie, and I was too far from my ankle.

I breathed shallowly from the top of my lungs and held the bottle near my lips, sniffed carefully. Behind the charred smell of the bourbon there was something else, very faint, a fruity odor that would have meant nothing to me in another place. Suddenly and for no reason at all I remembered something Larry Batzel had said, something like: "East of Realito, towards the mountains, near the old cyanide plant." Cyanide. That was the word.

There was a swift tightness in my temples as I put the bottle to my mouth. I could feel my skin crawling, and the air was suddenly cold on it. I held the bottle high up around the liquor level and took a long gurgling drag at it. Very hearty and relaxing. About half a teaspoonful went into my mouth and none of that stayed there.

I coughed sharply and lurched forward gagging. Red-eyes laughed.

"Don't say you're sick from just one drink, pal."

I dropped the bottle and sagged far in the seat, gagging violently. My legs slid away to the left, the left one underneath. I sprawled down on top of them, my arms limp. I had the gun.

I shot him under my left arm, almost without looking. He never touched the Colt except to knock it off the seat. The one shot was enough. I heard him lurch. I snapped a shot upward towards where Louie would be.

Louie wasn't there. He was down behind the front seat. He was silent. The whole car, the whole landscape was silent. Even the rain seemed for a moment to be utterly silent rain.

I still didn't have time to look at Red-eyes, but he wasn't doing anything. I dropped the Luger and yanked the tommy gun out from under the rug, got my

10. Legally made and taxed liquor.
11. Bootleg whiskey.

left hand on the front grip, got it set against my shoulder low down. Louie hadn't made a sound.

"Listen, Louie," I said softly, "I've got the stutter gun. How's about it?"

A shot came through the seat, a shot that Louie knew wasn't going to do any good. It starred a frame of unbreakable glass. There was more silence. Louie said thickly: "I got a pineapple[12] here. Want it?"

"Pull the pin and hold it," I said. "It will take care of both of us."   530

"Hell!" Louie said violently. "Is he croaked? I ain't got no pineapple."

I looked at Red-eyes then. He looked very comfortable in the corner of the seat, leaning back. He seemed to have three eyes, one of them redder even than the other two. For under-arm shooting that was something to be almost bashful about. It was too good.

"Yeah, Louie, he's croaked," I said. "How do we get together?"

I could hear his hard breathing now, and the rain had stopped being silent. "Get out of the heap," he growled. "I'll blow."

"You get out, Louie. I'll blow."

"Jeeze, I can't walk home from here, pal."   540

"You won't have to, Louie. I'll send a car for you."

"Jeeze, I ain't done nothing. All I done was drive."

"Then reckless driving will be the charge, Louie. You can fix that—you and your organization. Get out before I uncork this popgun."

A door latch clicked and feet thumped on the running board, then on the roadway. I straightened up suddenly with the chopper. Louie was in the road in the rain, his hands empty and the alligator smile still on his face.

I got out past the dead man's neatly shod feet, got my Colt and the Luger off the floor, laid the heavy twelve-pound tommy gun back on the car floor. I got handcuffs off my hip, motioned to Louie. He turned around sulkily and put his   550 hands behind him.

"You got nothing on me," he complained. "I got protection."

I clicked the cuffs on him and went over him for guns, much more carefully than he had gone over me. He had one besides the one he had left in the car.

I dragged Red-eyes out of the car and let him arrange himself on the wet roadway. He began to bleed again, but he was quite dead. Louie eyed him bitterly.

"He was a smart guy," he said. "Different. He liked tricks. Hello, smart guy."

I got my handcuff key out and unlocked one cuff, dragged it down and locked it to the dead man's lifted wrist.

Louie's eyes got round and horrified and at last his smile went away.   560

"Jeeze," he whined. "Holy—! Jeeze. You ain't going to leave me like this, pal?"

"Goodbye, Louie," I said. "That was a friend of mine you cut down this morning."

"Holy—!" Louie whined.

I got into the sedan and started it, drove on to a place where I could turn, drove back down the hill past him. He stood stiffly as a scorched tree, his face as

12. Hand grenade.

white as snow, with the dead man at his feet, one linked hand reaching up to Louie's hand. There was the horror of a thousand nightmares in his eyes.

I left him there in the train. 570

It was getting dark early. I left the sedan a couple of blocks from my own car and locked it up, put the keys in the oil strainer. I walked back to my roadster and drove downtown.

I called the homicide detail from a phone booth, asked for a man named Grinnell, told him quickly what had happened and where to find Louie and the sedan. I told him I thought they were the thugs that machine-gunned Larry Batzel. I didn't tell him anything about Dud O'Mara.

"Nice work," Grinnell said in a queer voice. "But you better come in fast. There's a tag[13] out for you, account of what some milk driver phoned in an hour ago." 580

"I'm all in," I said. "I've got to eat. Keep me off the air and I'll come in after a while."

"You better come in, boy. I'm sorry, but you better."

"Well, okay," I said.

I hung up and left the neighborhood without hanging around. I had to break it now. I had to, or get broken myself.

I had a meal down near the Plaza and started for Realito.

VI

At about eight o'clock two yellow vapor lamps glowed high up in the rain and a dim stencil sign strung across the highway read: "Welcome to Realito."

Frame houses on the main street, a sudden knot of stores, the lights of the 590 corner drugstore behind fogged glass, a flying-cluster of cars in front of a tiny movie palace, and a dark bank on another corner, with a knot of men standing in front of it in the rain. That was Realito. I went on. Empty fields closed in again.

This was past the orange country; nothing but the empty fields and the crouched foothills, and the rain.

It was a smart mile, more like three, before I spotted a side road and a faint light on it, as if from behind drawn blinds in a house. Just at that moment my left front tire let go with an angry hiss. That was cute. Then the right rear let go the same way.

I stopped almost exactly at the intersection. Very cute indeed. I got out, 600 turned my raincoat up a little higher, unshipped a flash, and looked at a flock of heavy galvanized tacks with heads as big as dimes. The flat shiny butt of one of them blinked at me from my tire.

Two flats and one spare. I tucked my chin down and started towards the faint light up the side road.

It was the place all right. The light came from the tilted skylight on the garage roof. Big double doors in front were shut tight, but light showed at the

13. A subpoena for his arrest as a witness.

cracks, strong white light. I tossed the beam on the flash up and read: "Art Huck—Auto Repairs and Refinishing."

Beyond the garage a house sat back from the muddy road behind a thin 610 clump of trees. That had light too. I saw a small buttoned-up coupé in front of the wooden porch.

The first thing was the tires, if it could be worked, and they didn't know me. It was a wet night for walking.

I snapped the flash out and rapped on the doors with it. The light inside went out. I stood there licking rain off my upper lip, the flash in my left hand, my right inside my coat. I had the Luger back under my arm again.

A voice spoke through the door, and didn't sound pleased.

"What you want? Who are you?"

"Open up," I said. "I've got two flat tires on the highway and only one spare. 620 I need help."

"We're closed up, mister. Realito's a mile west of here."

I started to kick the door. There was swearing inside, then another, much softer voice.

"A wise guy, huh? Open up, Art."

A bolt squealed and half of the door sagged inward. I snapped the flash again and it hit a gaunt face. Then an arm swept and knocked it out of my hand. A gun had just peeked at me from the flailing hand.

I dropped low, felt around for the flash and was still. I just didn't pull a gun.

"Kill the spot, mister. Guys get hurt that way."   630

The flash was burning down in the mud. I snapped it off, stood up with it. Light went on inside the garage, outlined a tall man in coveralls. He backed inward and his gun held on me.

"Come on in and shut the door."

I did that. "Tacks all over the end of your street," I said. "I thought you wanted the business."

"Ain't you got any sense? A bank job was pulled at Realito this afternoon."

"I'm a stranger here," I said, remembering the knot of men in front of the bank in the rain.

"Okay, okay. Well there was and the punks are hid out somewhere in the 640 hills, they say. You stepped on their tacks, huh?"

"So it seems." I looked at the other man in the garage.

He was short, heavy-set, with a cool brown face and cool brown eyes. He wore a belted raincoat of brown leather. His brown hat had the usual rakish tilt and was dry. His hands were in his pockets and he looked bored.

There was a hot sweetish smell of pyroxylin paint on the air. A big sedan over in the corner had a paint gun lying on its fender. It was a Buick, almost new. It didn't need the paint it was getting.

The man in coveralls tucked his gun out of sight through a flap in the side of his clothes. He looked at the brown man. The brown man looked at me and said 650 gently: "Where you from, stranger?"

"Seattle," I said.

"Going west—to the big city?" He had a soft voice, soft and dry, like the rustle of well-worn leather.

"Yes. How far is it?"

"About forty miles. Seems farther in this weather. Come the long way, didn't you? By Tahoe and Lone Pine?"

"Not Tahoe," I said. "Reno and Carson City."

"Still the long way." A fleeting smile touched the brown lips.

"Take a jack and get his flats, Art."   660

"Now, listen, Lash—" the man in the coveralls growled, and stopped as though his throat had been cut from ear to ear.

I could have sworn that he shivered. There was dead silence. The brown man didn't move a muscle. Something looked out of his eyes, and then his eyes lowered, almost shyly. His voice was the same soft, dry rustle of sound.

"Take two jacks. Art. He's got two flats."

The gaunt man swallowed. Then he went over to a corner and put a coat on, and a cap. He grabbed up a socket wrench and a handjack and wheeled a dolly jack over to the doors.

"Back on the highway, is it?" he asked me almost tenderly.   670

"Yeah. You can use the spare for one spot, if you're busy," I said.

"He's not busy," the brown man said and looked at his fingernails.

Art went out with his tools. The door shut again. I looked at the Buick. I didn't look at Lash Yeager. I knew it was Lash Yeager. There wouldn't be two men called Lash that came to that garage. I didn't look at him because I would be looking across the sprawled body of Larry Batzel, and it would show in my face. For a moment, anyway.

He glanced towards the Buick himself. "Just a panel job to start with," he drawled. "But the guy that owns it has dough and his driver needed a few bucks. You know the racket."   680

"Sure," I said.

The minutes passed on tiptoe. Long, sluggish minutes. Then feet crunched outside and the door was pushed open. The light hit pencils of rain and made silver wires of them. Art trundled two muddy flats in sulkily, kicked the door shut, let one of the flats fall on its side. The rain and fresh air had given him his nerve back. He looked at me savagely.

"Seattle," he snarled. "Seattle, my eye!"

The brown man lit a cigarette as if he hadn't heard. Art peeled his coat off and yanked my tire up on a rim spreader, tore it loose viciously, had the tube out and cold-patched in nothing flat. He strode scowling over to the wall near me and   690
grabbed an air hose, let enough air into the tube to give it body, and hefted it in both hands to dip it in a washtub of water.

I was a sap, but their teamwork was very good. Neither had looked at the other since Art came back with my tires.

Art tossed the air-stiffened tube up casually, caught it with both hands wide, looked it over sourly beside the washtub of water, took one short easy step and slammed it down over my head and shoulders.

He jumped behind me in a flash, leaned his weight down on the rubber, dragged it tight against my chest and arms. I could move my hands, but I couldn't get near my gun.   700

The brown man brought his right hand out of his pocket and tossed a wrapped cylinder of nickels up and down on his palm as he stepped lithely across the floor.

I heaved back hard, then suddenly threw all my weight forward. Just as suddenly Art let go of the tube, and kneed me from behind.

I sprawled, but I never knew when I reached the floor. The fist with the weighted tube of nickels met me in mid-flight. Perfectly timed, perfectly weighted, and with my own weight to help it out.

I went out like a puff of dust in a draft.

VII

It seemed there was a woman and she was sitting beside a lamp. Light shone   710
on my face, so I shut my eyes again and tried to look at her through my eyelashes. She was so platinumed that her head shone like a silver fruit bowl.

She wore a green traveling dress with a mannish cut to it and a broad white collar falling over the lapels. A sharp-angled glossy bag stood at her feet. She was smoking, and a drink was tall and pale at her elbow.

I opened my eye wider and said: "Hello there."

Her eyes were the eyes I remembered, outside Sardi's in a secondhand Rolls-Royce. Very blue eyes, very soft and lovely. Not the eyes of a hustler around the fast money boys.

"How do you feel?" Her voice was soft and lovely too.   720

"Great," I said. "Except somebody built a filling station on my jaw."

"What did you expect, Mr. Carmady? Orchids?"

"So you know my name."

"You slept well. They had plenty of time to go through your pockets. They did everything but embalm you."

"Right," I said.

I could move a little, not very much. My wrists were behind my back, handcuffed. There was a little poetic justice in that. From the cuffs a cord ran to my ankles, and tied them, and then dropped down out of sight over the end of the davenport and was tied somewhere else. I was almost as helpless as if I had been   730
screwed up in a coffin.

"What time is it?"

She looked sideways down at her wrist, beyond the spiral of her cigarette smoke.

"Ten-seventeen. Got a date?"

"Is this the house next the garage? Where are the boys—digging a grave?"

"You wouldn't care, Carmady. They'll be back."

"Unless you have the key to these brackets you might spare me a little of that drink."

She rose all in one piece and came over to me, with the tall amber glass in   740
her hand. She bent over me. Her breath was delicate. I gulped from the glass craning my neck up.

"I hope they don't hurt you," she said distantly, stepping back. "I hate killing."

"And you Joe Mesarvey's wife. Shame on you. Gimme some more of the hooch."

She gave me some more. Blood began to move in my stiffened body.

"I kind of like you," she said. "Even if your face does look like a collision mat."

"Make the most if," I said. "It won't last long even this good." 750

She looked around swiftly and seemed to listen. One of the two doors was ajar. She looked towards that. Her face seemed pale. But the sounds were only the rain.

She sat down by the lamp again.

"Why did you come here and stick your neck out?" she asked slowly, looking at the floor.

The carpet was made of red and tan squares. There were bright green pine trees on the wallpaper and the curtains were blue. The furniture, what I could see of it, looked as if it came from one of those places that advertise on bus benches.

"I had a rose for you," I said. "From Larry Batzel." 760

She lifted something off the table and twirled it slowly, the dwarf rose he had left for her.

"I got it," she said quietly. "There was a note, but they didn't show me that. Was it for me?"

"No, for me. He left it on my table before he went out and got shot."

Her face fell apart like something you see in a nightmare. Her mouth and eyes were black hollows. She didn't make a sound. And after a moment her face settled back into the same calmly beautiful lines.

"They didn't tell me that either," she said softly.

"He got shot," I said carefully, "because he found out what Joe and Lash 770 Yeager did to Dud O'Mara. Bumped him off."

That one didn't faze her at all. "Joe didn't do anything to Dud O'Mara," she said quietly. "I haven't seen Dud in two years. That was just newspaper hooey, about me seeing him."

"It wasn't in the papers," I said.

"Well, it was hooey wherever it was. Joe is in Chicago. He went yesterday by plane to sell out. If the deal goes through, Lash and I are to follow him. Joe is no killer."

I stared at her.

Her eyes got haunted again. "Is Larry—is he—?" 780

"He's dead," I said. "It was a professional job, with a tommy gun. I didn't mean they did it personally."

She took hold of her lip and held it for a moment tight between her teeth. I could hear her slow, hard breathing. She jammed her cigarette in an ashtray and stood up.

"Joe didn't do it!" she stormed. "I know damn well he didn't. He—" She stopped cold, glared at me, touched her hair, then suddenly yanked it off. It was a wig. Underneath her own hair was short like a boy's, and streaked yellow and whitish brown, with darker tints at the roots. It couldn't make her ugly.

I managed a sort of laugh. "You just came out here to molt, didn't you, 790

Silver-Wig? And I thought they were hiding you out—so it would look as if you had skipped with Dud O'Mara."

She kept on staring at me. As if she hadn't heard a word I said. Then she strode over to a wall mirror and put the wig back on, straightened it, turned and faced me.

"Joe didn't kill anybody," she said again, in a low, tight voice. "He's a heel—but not that kind of heel. He doesn't know anything more about where Dud O'Mara went than I do. And I don't know anything."

"He just got tired of the rich lady and scrammed," I said dully.

She stood near me now, her white fingers down at her sides, shining in the lamplight. Her head above me was almost in shadow. The rain drummed and my jaw felt large and hot and the nerve along the jawbone ached, ached.

"Lash has the only car that was here," she said softly. "Can you walk to Realito, if I cut the ropes?"

"Sure. Then what?"

"I've never been mixed up in a murder. I won't now. I won't ever."

She went out of the room very quickly, and came back with a long kitchen knife and sawed the cord that tied my ankles, pulled it off, cut the place where it was tied to the handcuffs. She stopped once to listen, but it was just the rain again.

I rolled up to a sitting position and stood up. My feet were numb, but that would pass. I could walk. I could run, if I had to.

"Lash has the key of the cuffs," she said dully.

"Let's go," I said. "Got a gun?"

"No. I'm not going. You beat it. He may be back any minute. They were just moving stuff out of the garage."

I went over close to her. "You're going to stay here after turning me loose? Wait for that killer? You're nuts. Come on, Silver-Wig, you're going with me."

"No."

"Suppose," I said, "he did kill O'Mara? Then he also killed Larry. It's got to be that way."

"Joe never killed anybody," she almost snarled at me.

"Well, suppose Yeager did."

"You're lying, Carmady. Just to scare me. Get out. I'm not afraid of Lash Yeager. I'm his boss's wife."

"Joe Mesarvey is a handful of mush," I snarled back. "The only time a girl like you goes for a wrong gee[14] is when he's a handful of mush. Let's drift."

"Get out!" she said hoarsely.

"Okay." I turned away from her and went through the door.

She almost ran past me into the hallway and opened the front door, looked out into the black wetness. She motioned me forward.

"Goodbye," she whispered. "I hope you find Dud. I hope you find who killed Larry. But it wasn't Joe."

14. Man.

I stepped close to her, almost pushed her against the wall with my body.
"You're still crazy, Silver-Wig. Goodbye."

She raised her hands quickly and put them on my face. Cold hands, icy cold. She kissed me swiftly on the mouth with cold lips.

"Beat it, strong guy. I'll be seeing you some more. Maybe in heaven."

I went through the door and down the dark slithery wooden steps of the porch, across gravel to the round grass plot and the clump of thin trees. I came 840 past them to the roadway, went back along it towards Foothill Boulevard. The rain touched my face with fingers of ice that were no colder than her fingers.

The curtained roadster stood just where I had left it, leaned over, the left front axle on the tarred shoulder of the highway. My spare and one stripped rim were thrown in the ditch.

They had probably searched it, but I still hoped. I crawled in backwards and banged my head on the steering post and rolled over to get the manacled hands into my little secret gun pocket. They touched the barrel. It was still there.

I got it out, got myself out of the car, got hold of the gun by the right end and looked it over. 850

I held it tight against my back to protect it a little from the rain and started back towards the house.

VIII

I was halfway there when he came back. His lights turning quickly off the highway almost caught me. I flopped into the ditch and put my nose in the mud and prayed.

The car hummed past. I heard the wet rasp of its tires shouldering the gravel in front of the house. The motor died and lights went off. The door slammed. I didn't hear the house door shut, but I caught a feeble fringe of light through the trees as it opened.

I got up on my feet and went on. I came up beside the car, a small coupé, 860 rather old. The gun was down at my side, pulled around my hip as far as the cuffs would let it come.

The coupé was empty. Water gurgled in the radiator. I listened and heard nothing from the house. No loud voices, no quarrel. Only the heavy bong-bong-bong of the raindrops hitting the elbows at the bottom of rain gutters.

Yeager was in the house. She had let me go and Yeager was in there with her. Probably she wouldn't tell him anything. She would just stand and look at him. She was his boss's wife. That would scare Yeager to death.

He wouldn't stay long, but he wouldn't leave her behind, alive or dead. He would be on his way and take her with him. What happened to her later on was 870 something else.

All I had to do was wait for him to come out. I didn't do it.

I shifted the gun into my left hand and leaned down to scoop up some gravel. I threw it against the front window. It was a weak effort. Very little even reached the glass.

I ran back behind the coupé and got its door open and saw the keys in the ignition lock. I crouched down on the running board, holding on to the door post.

The house had already gone dark, but that was all. There wasn't any sound from it. No soap. Yeager was too cagy.

I reached in with my foot and found the starter, then strained back with one 880
hand and turned the ignition key. The warm motor caught at once, throbbed gently against the pounding rain.

I got back to the ground and slid along to the rear of the car, crouched down.

The sound of the motor got him. He couldn't be left there without a car.

A darkened window slid up an inch, only some shifting of light on the glass showing it moved. Flame spouted from it, the racket of three quick shots. Glass broke in the coupé.

I screamed and let the scream die into a gurgling groan. I was getting good at that sort of thing. I let the groan die in a choked gasp. I was through, finished. He 890
had got me. Nice shooting, Yeager.

Inside the house a man laughed. Then silence again, except for the rain and the quietly throbbing motor of the coupé.

Then the house door inched open. A figure showed in it. She came out on the porch, stiffly, the white showing at her collar, the wig showing a little but not so much. She came down the steps like a wooden woman. I saw Yeager crouched behind her.

She started across the gravel. Her voice said slowly, without any tone at all:

"I can't see a thing, Lash. The windows are all misted."

She jerked a little, as if a gun had prodded her, and came on. Yeager didn't 900
speak. I could see him now past her shoulder, his hat, part of his face. But no kind of a shot for a man with cuffs on his wrists.

She stopped again, and her voice was suddenly horrified.

"He's behind the wheel!" she yelled. "Slumped over!"

He fell for it. He knocked her to one side and started to blast again. More glass jumped around. A bullet hit a tree on my side of the car. A cricket whined somewhere. The motor kept right on humming.

He was low, crouched against the black, his face a grayness without form that seemed to come back very slowly after the glare of the shots. His own fire had blinded him too—for a second. That was enough. 910

I shot him four times straining the pulsing Colt against my ribs.

He tried to turn and the gun slipped away from his hand. He half snatched for it in the air, before both his hands suddenly went against his stomach and stayed there. He sat down on the wet gravel and his harsh panting dominated every other sound of the wet night.

I watched him lie down on his side, very slowly, without taking his hands away from his stomach. The panting stopped.

It seemed like an age before Silver-Wig called out to me. Then she was beside me, grabbing my arm.

"Shut the motor off!" I yelled at her. "And get the key of these damn irons 920
out of his pocket."

"You d-darn fool," she babbled. "W-what did you come back for?"

IX

Captain Al Roof of the Missing Persons Bureau swung in his chair and looked at the sunny window. This was another day, and the rain had stopped long since.

He said gruffly: "You're making a lot of mistakes, brother. Dud O'Mara just pulled down the curtain.[15] None of those people knocked him off. The Batzel killing had nothing to do with it. They've got Mesarvey in Chicago and he looks clean. The Heeb[16] you anchored to the dead guy don't even know who they were pulling the job for. Our boys asked him enough to be sure of that."   930

"I'll bet they did," I said. "I've been in the same bucket all night and I couldn't tell them much either."

He looked at me slowly, with large, bleak, tired eyes. "Killing Yeager was all right, I guess. And the chopper. In the circumstances. Besides I'm not homicide. I couldn't link any of that to O'Mara—unless you could."

I could, but I hadn't. Not yet. "No," I said. "I guess not." I stuffed and lit my pipe. After a sleepless night it tasted better.

"That all that's worrying you?"

"I wondered why you didn't find the girl, at Realito. It couldn't have been very hard—for you."   940

"We just didn't. We should have. I admit it. We didn't. Anything else?"

I blew smoke across his desk. "I'm looking for O'Mara because the general told me to. It wasn't any use my telling him you would do everything that could be done. He could afford a man with all his time on it. I suppose you resent that."

He wasn't amused. "Not at all, if he wants to waste money. The people that resent you are behind a door marked Homicide Bureau."

He planted his feet with a slap and elbowed his desk.

"O'Mara had fifteen grand in his clothes. That's a lot of jack but O'Mara would be the boy to have it. So he could take it out and have his old pals see him with it. Only they wouldn't think it was fifteen grand of real dough. His wife says 950
it was. Now with any other guy but an ex-legger in the gravy[17] that might indicate an intention to disappear. But not O'Mara. He packed it all the time."

He bit a cigar and put a match to it. He waved a large finger. "See?"

I said I saw.

"Okay. O'Mara had fifteen grand, and a guy that pulls down the curtain can keep it down only so long as his wad lasts. Fifteen grand is a good wad. I might disappear myself, if I had that much. But after it's gone we get him. He cashes a check, lays down a marker, hits a hotel or store for credit, gives a reference, writes a letter or gets one. He's in a new town and he's got a new name, but he's got the same old appetite. He has to get back into the fiscal system one way or another. A 960
guy can't have friends everywhere, and if he had, they wouldn't all stay clammed forever. Would they?"

"No, they wouldn't," I said.

---

15. Disappeared.
16. A derogatory term for a Jew.
17. A former bootlegger with a lot of money.

"He went far," Roof said. "But the fifteen grand was all the preparation he made. No baggage, no boat or rail or plane reservation, no taxi or private rental hack to a point out of town. That's all checked. His own car was found a dozen blocks from where he lived. But that means nothing. He knew people who would ferry him several hundred miles and keep quiet about it, even in the face of a reward. Here, but not everywhere. Not new friends."

"But you'll get him," I said.   970

"When he gets hungry."

"That could take a year or two. General Winslow may not live a year. That is a matter of sentiment, not whether you have an open file when you retire."

"You attend to the sentiment, brother." His eyes moved and bushy reddish eyebrows moved with them. He didn't like me. Nobody did, in the police department, that day.

"I'd like to," I said and stood up. "Maybe I'd go pretty far to attend to that sentiment."

"Sure," Roof said, suddenly thoughtful. "Well, Winslow is a big man. Anything I can do let me know."   980

"You could find out who had Larry Batzel gunned," I said. "Even if there isn't any connection."

"We'll do that. Glad to," he guffawed and flicked ash all over his desk. "You just knock off the guys who can talk and we'll do the rest. We like to work that way."

"It was self-defense," I growled. "I couldn't help myself."

"Sure. Take the air, brother. I'm busy."

But his large bleak eyes twinkled at me as I went out.

X

The morning was all blue and gold and the birds in the ornamental trees of the Winslow estate were crazy with song after the rain.   990

The gatekeeper let me in through the postern and I walked up the driveway and along the top terrace to the huge carved Italian front door. Before I rang the bell I looked down the hill and saw the Trevillyan kid sitting on his stone bench with his head cupped in his hands, staring at nothing.

I went down the brick path to him. "No darts today, son?"

He looked up at me with his lean, slaty, sunken eyes.

"No. Did you find him?"

"Your dad? No, sonny, not yet."

He jerked his head. His nostrils flared angrily. "He's not my dad I told you. And don't talk to me as if I was four years old. My dad he's—he's in Florida or   1000 somewhere."

"Well, I haven't found him yet, whoever's dad he is," I said.

"Who smacked your jaw?" he asked, staring at me.

"Oh, a fellow with a roll of nickels in his hand."

"Nickels?"

"Yeah. That's as good as brass knuckles. Try it sometime, but not on me." I grinned.

"You won't find him," he said bitterly, staring at my jaw. "Him, I mean. My mother's husband."

"I bet I do."   1010

"How much you bet?"

"More money than even you've got in my pants."

He kicked viciously at the edge of a red brick in the walk. His voice was still sulky, but more smooth. His eyes speculated.

"Want to bet on something else? C'mon over to the range. I bet you a dollar I can knock down eight out of ten pipes in ten shots."

I looked back towards the house. Nobody seemed impatient to receive me.

"Well," I said, "we'll have to make it snappy. Let's go."

We went along the side of the house under the windows. The orchid green-house showed over the tops of some bushy trees far back. A man in neat whipcord 1020 was polishing the chromium on a big car in front of the garages. We went past there to the low white building against the bank.

The boy took a key out and unlocked the door and we went into close air that still held traces of cordite[18] fumes. The boy clicked a spring lock on the door.

"Me first," he snapped.

The place looked something like a small beach shooting gallery. There was a counter with a .22 repeating rifle on it and a long, slim target pistol. Both well oiled but dusty. About thirty feet beyond the counter was a waist-high, solid-looking partition across the building, and behind that a simple layout of clay pipes and ducks and two round white targets marked off with black rings and stained by 1030 lead bullets.

The clay pipes ran in an even line across the middle, and there was a big skylight, and a row of hooded overhead lights.

The boy pulled a cord on the wall and a thick canvas blind slid across the skylight. He turned on the hooded lights and then the place really looked like a beach shooting gallery.

He picked up the .22 rifle and loaded it quickly from a cardboard box of shells, .22 shorts.

"A dollar I get eight out of ten pipes?"

"Blast away," I said, and put my money on the counter.   1040

He took aim almost casually, fired too fast, showing off. He missed three pipes. It was pretty fancy shooting at that. He threw the rifle down on the counter.

"Gee, go set up some more. Let's not count that one. I wasn't set."

"You don't aim to lose any money, do you, son? Go set 'em up yourself. It's your range."

His narrow face got angry and his voice got shrill. "You do it! I've got to relax, see. I've got to relax."

I shrugged at him, lifted a flap in the counter and went along the white-washed side wall, squeezed past the end of the low partition. The boy clicked his reloaded rifle shut behind me.   1050

"Put that down," I growled back at him. "Never touch a gun when there's anyone in front of you."

18. Smokeless gun powder.

He put it down, looking hurt.

I bent down and grabbed a handful of clay pipes out of the sawdust in a big wooden box on the floor. I shook the yellow grains of wood off them and started to straighten up.

I stopped with my hat above the barrier, just the top of my hat. I never knew why I stopped. Blind instinct.

The .22 cracked and the lead bullet bonged into the target in front of my head. My hat stirred lazily on my head, as though a blackbird had swooped at it   1060 during the nesting season.

A nice kid. He was full of tricks, like Red-eyes. I dropped the pipes and took hold of my hat by the brim, lifted it straight up off my head a few inches. The gun cracked again. Another metallic bong on the target.

I let myself fall heavily to the wooden flooring, among the pipes.

A door opened and shut. That was all. Nothing else. The hard glare from the hooded lights beat down on me. The sun peeked in at the edges of the skylight blind. There were two bright new splashes on the nearest target, and there were four small round holes in my hat, two and two, on each side.

I crawled to the end of the barrier and peeked around it. The boy was gone.   1070 I could see the small muzzles of the two guns on the counter.

I stood up and went back along the wall, switched the lights off, turned the knob of the spring lock and went out. The Winslow chauffeur whistled at his polish job around in front of the garages.

I crushed my hat in my hand and went back along the side of the house, looking for the kid. I didn't see him. I rang the front door bell.

I asked for Mrs. O'Mara. I didn't let the butler take my hat.

XI

She was in an oyster-white something, with white fur at the cuffs and collar and around the bottom. A breakfast table on wheels was pushed to one side of her chair and she was flicking ashes among the silver.   1080

The coy-looking maid with the nice legs came and took the table out and shut the tall white door. I sat down.

Mrs. O'Mara leaned her head back against a cushion and looked tired. The line of her throat was distant, cold. She stared at me with a cool, hard look, in which there was plenty of dislike.

"You seemed rather human yesterday," she said. "But I see you are just a brute like the rest of them. Just a brutal cop."

"I came to ask you about Lash Yeager," I said.

She didn't even pretend to be amused. "And why should you think of asking me?"   1090

"Well—if you lived a week at the Dardanella Club—" I waved my crunched-together hat.

She looked at her cigarette fixedly. "Well, I did meet him, I believe. I remember the rather unusual name."

"They all have names like that, those animals," I said. "It seems that Larry

Batzel—I guess you read in your paper about him too—was a friend of Dud O'Mara's once. I didn't tell you about him yesterday. Maybe that was a mistake."

A pulse began to throb in her throat. She said softly: "I have a suspicion you are about to become very insolent, that I may even have to have you thrown out."

"Not before I've said my piece," I said. "It seems that Mr. Yeager's driver— 1100 they have drivers as well as unusual names, those animals—told Larry Batzel that Mr. Yeager was out this way the night O'Mara disappeared."

The old army blood had to be good for something in her. She didn't move a muscle. She just froze solid.

I got up and took the cigarette from between her frozen fingers and killed it in a white jade ashtray. I laid my hat carefully on her white satin knee. I sat down again.

Her eyes moved after a while. They moved down and looked at the hat. Her face flushed very slowly, in two vivid patches over the cheekbones. She fought around with her tongue and lips.   1110

"I know," I said. "It's not much of a hat. I'm not making you a present of it. But just look at the bullet holes in it once."

Her hand became alive and snatched at the hat. Her eyes became flames.

She spread the crown out, looked at the holes, and shuddered.

"Yeager?" she asked, very faintly. It was a wisp of a voice, an old voice.

I said very slowly: "Yeager wouldn't use a .22 target rifle, Mrs. O'Mara."

The flame died in her eyes. They were pools of darkness, much emptier than darkness.

"You're his mother," I said. "What do you want to do about it?"

"Merciful God! Dade! He . . . shot at you!"   1120

"Twice," I said.

"But why? . . . Oh, why?"

"You think I'm a wise guy, Mrs. O'Mara. Just another hard-eyed boy from the other side of the tracks. It would be easy in this spot, if I was. But I'm not that at all, really. Do I have to tell why he shot at me!"

She didn't speak. She nodded slowly. Her face was a mask now.

"I'd say he probably can't help it," I said. "He didn't want me to find his step-father, for one thing. Then he's a little lad that likes money. That seems small, but it's part of the picture. He almost lost a dollar to me on his shooting. It seems small, but he lives in a small world. Most of all, of course, he's a crazy little sadist 1130 with an itchy trigger finger."

"How dare you!" she flared. It didn't mean anything. She forgot it herself instantly.

"How dare I? I do dare. Let's not bother figuring why he shot at *me*. I'm not the first, am I? You wouldn't have known what I was talking about, you wouldn't have assumed he did it on purpose."

She didn't move or speak. I took a deep breath.

"So let's talk about why he shot Dud O'Mara," I said.

If I thought she would yell even this time, I fooled myself. The old man in the orchid house had put more into her than her tallness and her dark hair and 1140 her reckless eyes.

She pulled her lips back and trick to lick them, and it made her look like a scared little girl, for a second. The lines of her cheeks sharpened and her hand went up like an artificial hand moved by wires and took hold of the white fur at her throat and pulled it tight and squeezed it until her knuckles looked like bleached bone. Then she just stared at me.

Then my hat slid off her knee on to the floor, without her moving. The sound it made falling was one of the loudest sounds I had ever heard.

"Money," she said in a dry croak. "Of course you want money."

"How much money do I want?"

"Fifteen thousand dollars."   1150

I nodded, stiff-necked as a floor walker trying to see with his back.

"That would be about right. That would be the established retainer. That would be about what he had in his pockets and what Yeager got for getting rid of him."

"You're too—damned smart," she said horribly. "I could kill you myself and like it."

I tried to grin. "That's right. Smart and without a feeling in the world. It happened something like this. The boy got O'Mara where he got me, by the same simple ruse. I don't think it was a plan. He hated his stepfather, but he wouldn't exactly plan to kill him."   1160

"He hated him," she said.

"So they're in the little shooting gallery and O'Mara is dead on the floor, behind the barrier, out of sight. The shots, of course, meant nothing there. And very little blood, with a head shot, small caliber. So the boy goes out and locks the door and hides. But after a while he has to tell somebody. He has to. He tells you. You're his mother. You're the one to tell."

"Yes," she breathed. "He did just that." Her eyes had stopped hating me.

"You think about calling it an accident, which is okay, except for one thing. The boy's not a normal boy, and you know it. The general knows it, the servants know. There must be other people that know it. And the law, dumb as you think 1170 they are, are pretty smart with subnormal types. They get to handle so many of them. And I think he would have talked. I think, after a while, he would even have bragged."

"Go on," she said.

"You wouldn't risk that," I said. "Not for your son and not for the sick old man in the orchid house. You'd do any awful criminal callous thing rather than risk that. You did it. You knew Yeager and you hired him to get rid of the body. That's all—except that hiding the girl, Mona Mesarvey, helped to make it look like a deliberate disappearance."

"He took him away after dark, in Dud's own car," she said hollowly.   1180

I reached down and picked my hat off the floor. "How about the servants?"

"Norris knows. The butler. He'd die on the rack before he told."

"Yeah. Now you know why Larry Batzel was knocked off and why I was taken for a ride, don't you?"

"Blackmail," she said. "It hadn't come yet, but I was waiting for it. I would have paid anything, and he would know that."

"Bit by bit, year by year, there was a quarter of a million in it for him, easy. I don't think Joe Mesarvey was in it at all. I know the girl wasn't."

She didn't say anything. She just kept her eyes on my face.

"Why in hell," I groaned, "didn't you take the guns away from him?"   1190

"He's worse than you think. That would have started something worse. I'm—I'm almost afraid of him myself."

"Take him away," I said. "From here. From the old man. He's young enough to be cured, by the right handling. Take him to Europe. Far away. Take him now. It would kill the general out of hand to know his blood was in that."

She got up draggingly and dragged herself across to the windows. She stood motionless, almost blending into the heavy white drapes. Her hands hung at her sides, very motionless also. After a while she turned and walked past me. When she was behind me she caught her breath and sobbed just once.

"It was very vile. It was the vilest thing I ever heard of. Yet I would do it   1200 again. Father would not have done it. He would have spoken right out. It would, as you say, have killed him."

"Take him away," I pounded on. "He's hiding out there now. He thinks he got me. He's hiding somewhere like an animal. Get him. He can't help it."

"I offered you money," she said, still behind me. "That's nasty. I wasn't in love with Dudley O'Mara. That's nasty too. I can't thank you. I don't know what to say."

"Forget it," I said. "I'm just an old workhorse. Put *your* work on the boy."

"I promise. Goodbye, Mr. Carmady."

We didn't shake hands. I went back down the stairs and the butler was at the front door as usual. Nothing in his face but politeness.   1210

"You will not want to see the general today, sir?"

"Not today, Norris."

I didn't see the boy outside. I went through the postern and got into my rented Ford and drove on down the hill, past where the old oil wells were.

Around some of them, not visible from the street, there were still sumps in which waste water lay and festered with a scum of oil on top.

They would be ten or twelve feet deep, maybe more. There would be dark things in them. Perhaps in one of them—

I was glad I had killed Yeager.

On the way back downtown I stopped at a bar and had a couple of drinks. 1220 They didn't do me any good.

All they did was make me think of Silver-Wig, and I never saw her again.

                                                                    [1936]

Questions for Discussion and Writing

1. Analyze Carmady's character and values. What sort of man is he? What does he believe in, if anything? Why does he sometimes accept money and other times refuse it? Which of his actions seem believable? Which are unbelievable?

2. Analyze the violence in the story. Is it excessive, offensive, essential to the

plot, gratuitous, tastefully handled? Does it need to be as graphic as it is? Why or why not?

3. Analyze Chandler's style, particularly his use of description and figurative language. Does he handle these effectively? Explain, using specific examples.

4. How would you describe the atmosphere of the story?

5. Does this story have a theme, or is it simply meant to entertain?

6. Are all the necessary clues available to the reader? Underline or highlight all the clues relevant to solving the mystery.

7. Is Dade Trevillyan a believable eleven-year-old? Is his madness credible?

V[ICTOR] S[AWDON] PRITCHETT
(1900–1997)

Sense of Humour

V. S. Pritchett has been called England's greatest short story writer of this century, yet he continues to await the recognition many think is his due. Pritchett endured an unstable childhood as his mercurial father flitted from business to business, chasing a dream of wealth he never attained. Forced to leave school at sixteen, Pritchett entered the leather trade, but like many young men of his day, he sought self-improvement through independent reading and night courses. At twenty, he left the leather business and headed for Paris to become a writer. While working in Paris, he read voraciously, eventually became a reporter for the *Christian Science Monitor,* and began writing short stories.

Like many writers, Pritchett struggled to establish himself as a novelist while publishing short stories to survive. Although he published several novels, he never succeeded in the longer form. By the late 1930s, he had established himself as one of England's foremost writers of short stories, but the outbreak of World War II permanently altered the literary landscape in Britain. When the war ended, most of the magazines that had supported short stories were dead or dying, and the new media of radio and television were taking the place of reading as people's primary leisure activity.

Ever the individualist, Pritchett avoided all movements and literary labels. Although many of his stories show the influence of Anton Chekhov (1860–1904) and James Joyce (1882–1941), he uses traditional methods of story-telling, including a plain style, clear delineation of character, and a story structure that, while not founded on plot, uses dialogue and incident to reveal character. His characters have often been called eccentrics, but Pritchett is less interested in caricature or satire than in the ways people imagine and project themselves. His stories journey through the lives of lower middle-class

Englishmen and see through them the subterfuges and dodges that people invent to create meaning and identity in a world that seems to lack both.

IT STARTED ONE SATURDAY. I was working new ground and I decided I'd stay at the hotel the weekend and put in an appearance at church.

"All alone?" asked the girl at the cash desk.

It had been raining since ten o'clock.

"Mr. Good has gone," she said. "And Mr. Straker. He usually stays with us. But he's gone."

"That's where they make their mistake," I said. "They think they know everything because they've been on the road all their lives."

"You're a stranger here, aren't you?" she said.

"I am," I said. "And so are you."   10

"How do you know that?"

"Obvious," I said. "Way you speak."

"Let's have a light," she said.

"So's I can see you," I said.

That was how it started. The rain was pouring down on the glass roof of the office.

She'd a cup of tea steaming on the register. I said I'd have one, too. What's it going to be and I'll tell them, she said, but I said just a cup of tea.

"I'm T.T.,"[1] I said. "Too many soakers[2] on the road as it is."

I was staying there the weekend so as to be sharp on the job on Monday 20 morning. What's more, it pays in these small towns to turn up at church on Sundays, Presbyterians in the morning, Methodists in the evening. Say "Good morning" and "Good evening" to them. "Ah!" they say. "Churchgoer! Pleased to see that! T.T., too." Makes them have a second look at your lines[3] in the morning. "Did you like our service, Mr.—er—er?" "Humphrey's my name." "Mr. Humphrey." See? It pays.

"Come into the office, Mr. Humphrey," she said, bringing me a cup. "Listen to that rain."

I went inside.

"Sugar?" she said.   30

"Three," I said. We settled to a very pleasant chat. She told me all about herself, and we got on next to families.

"My father was on the railway," she said.

"'The engine gave a squeal,'" I said. "'The driver took out his pocket-knife and scraped him off the wheel.'"

"That's it," she said. "And what is your father's business? You said he had a business."

"Undertaker," I said.

1. Teetotal.
2. Drinkers.
3. The narrator is a traveling salesman; his "lines" are his products.

"Undertaker?" she said.

"Why not?" I said. "Good business. Seasonable like everything else. High-class undertaker," I said.

She was looking at me all the time wondering what to say, and suddenly she went into fits of laughter.

"Undertaker," she said, covering her face with her hands and went on laughing.

"Here," I said, "what's up?"

"Undertaker!" She laughed and laughed. Struck me as being a pretty thin joke.

"Don't mind me," she said. "I'm Irish."

"Oh, I see," I said. "That's it, is it? Got a sense of humour."

Then the bell rang and a woman called out "Muriel! Muriel!" and there was a motorbike making a row at the front door.

"All right," the girl called out. "Excuse me a moment, Mr. Humphrey," she said. "Don't think me rude. That's my boyfriend. He wants the bird[4] turning up like this."

She went out, but there was her boyfriend looking over the window ledge into the office. He had come in. He had a cape on, soaked with rain, and the rain was in beads in his hair. It was fair hair. It stood up on end. He'd been economizing on the brilliantine.[5] He didn't wear a hat. He gave me a look and I gave him a look. I didn't like the look of him. And he didn't like the look of me. A smell of oil and petrol and rain and mackintosh came off him. He had a big mouth with thick lips. They were very red. I recognized him at once as the son of the man who ran the Kounty Garage. I saw this chap when I put my car away. The firm's car. Locked up, because of the samples. Took me ten minutes to ram the idea into his head. He looked as though he'd never heard of samples. Slow—you know the way they are in the provinces. Slow on the job.

"Oh, Colin," says she. "What do you want?"

"Nothing," the chap said. "I came in to see you."

"To see me?"

"Just to see you."

"You came in this morning."

"That's right," he said. He went red. "You was busy," he said.

"Well, I'm, busy now," she said.

He bit his tongue and licked his big lips over and took a look at me. Then he started grinning.

"I got the new bike, Muriel," he said. "I've got it outside. It's just come down from the works," he said.

"The laddie wants you to look at his bike," I said. So she went out and had a look at it.

When she came back she had got rid of him.

"Listen to that rain," she said. "Lord, I'm fed up with this line," she said.

"What line?" I said. "The hotel line?"

4. He should be told off.
5. Hair oil.

"Yes," she said. "I'm fed right up to the back teeth with it."

"And you've got good teeth," I said.

"There's not the class of person there used to be in it," she said. "All our family have got good teeth."

"Not the class?"

"I've been in it five years and there's not the same class at all. You never meet any fellows."

"Well," said I, "if they're like that half-wit at the garage, they're nothing to be   90
stuck on. And you've met me."

I said it to her like that.

"Oh," says she. "It isn't as bad as that yet."

It was cold in the office. She used to sit all day in her overcoat. She was a smart girl with a big friendly chin and a second one coming, and her forehead and nose were covered with freckles. She had copper-coloured hair too. She got her shoes through the trade from Duke's traveller and her clothes, too, off the Hollenborough mantle man. I told her I could do her better stockings than the ones she'd got on. She got a good reduction on everything. Twenty-five or thirty-three and a third.[6] She had her expenses cut right back. I took her to the pictures   100
that night in the car. I made Colin get the car out for me.

"That boy wanted me to go on the back of his bike. On a night like this," she said.

"Oh," she said, when we got to the pictures. "Two shillings's too much. Let's go into the one-and-sixes[7] at the side and we can nip across into the two-shillings when the lights go down.

"Fancy your father being an undertaker," she said in the middle of the show. And she started laughing as she had laughed before.

She had her head screwed on all right. She said:

"Some girls have no pride once the lights go down."   110

Every time I went to that town I took a box of something. Samples, mostly, they didn't cost me anything.

"Don't thank me," I said. "Thank the firm."

Every time I took her out I pulled the blinds in the back seat of the car to hide the samples. That chap Colin used to give us oil and petrol. He used to give me a funny look. Fishy sort of small eyes he'd got. Always looking miserable. Then we would go off. Sunday was her free day. Not that driving's any holiday for me. And, of course, the firm paid. She used to take me down to see her family for the day. Start in the morning, and taking it you had dinner and tea there, a day's outing cost us nothing. Her father was something on the railway, retired. He had a   120
long stocking somewhere, but her sister, the one that was married, had had her share already.

He had a tumour after his wife died and they just played upon the old man's feelings. It wasn't right. She wouldn't go near her sister and I don't blame her, taking the money like that. Just played upon the old man's feelings.

Every time I was up there Colin used to come in looking for her.

6. i.e., she bought her shoes and clothes from the salesmen at a discount of 25 percent or 33-1/3 percent.

7. Seats costing one shilling six pence, rather than two shillings.

"Oh, Colin," I used to say. "Done my car yet?" He knew where he got off with me.

"No, now, I can't, Colin. I tell you I'm going out with Mr. Humphrey," she used to say to him. I heard her.   130

"He keeps on badgering me," she said to me.

"You leave him to me," I said.

"No, he's all right," she said.

"You let me know if there's any trouble with Colin," I said. "Seems to be a harum-scarum sort of half-wit to me," I said.

"And he spends every penny he makes," she said.

Well, we know that sort of thing is all right while it lasts, I told her, but the trouble is it that it doesn't last.

We were always meeting Colin on the road. I took no notice of it first of all and then I grew suspicious and awkward at always meeting him. He had a new 140 motor bicycle. It was an Indian,[8] a scarlet thing that he used to fly over the moor with, flat out. Muriel and I used to go out over the moor to Ingley Wood in the firm's Morris[9]—I had a customer out that way.

"May as well do a bit of business while you're about it," I said.

"About what?" she said.

"Ah-ha!" I said, "That's what Colin wants to know," I said.

Sure enough, coming back we'd hear him popping and backfiring close behind us, and I put out my hand to stop him and keep him following us, biting our dirt.

"I see his little game," I said. "Following us."   150

So I saw to it that he did follow. We could hear him banging away behind us, and the traffic is thick on the Ingley road in the afternoon.

"Oh, let him pass," Muriel said, "I can't stand those dirty things banging in my ears."

I waved him on and past he flew with his scarf flying out, blazing red into the traffic. "We're doing fifty-eight ourselves," she said, leaning across to look.

"Powerful buses, those," I said. "Any fool can do it if he's got the power. Watch me step on it."

But we did not catch Colin. Half an hour later he passed us coming back. Cut right in between us and a lorry—I had to brake hard. I damn nearly killed 160 him. His ears were red with the wind. He didn't wear a hat. I got after him as soon as I could, but I couldn't touch him.

Nearly every weekend I was in that town seeing my girl, that fellow was hanging round. He came into the bar on Saturday nights, he poked his head into the office on Sunday mornings. It was a sure bet that if we went out in the car he would pass us on the road. Every time we would hear that scarlet thing roar by like a horse-stinger.[10] It didn't matter where we were. He passed us on the main road, he met us down the side roads. There was a little cliff under oak trees at May Ponds, she said, where the view was pretty. And there, soon after we got there, was

---

8. A make of motorcycle popular in Britain. They were painted bright red.
9. Morris was (and is) a British manufacturer of automobiles.
10. Horse-fly.

Colin on the other side of the water, watching us. Once we found him sitting on 170
his bike, just as though he were waiting for us.

"You been here in a car?" I said.

"No, motorbike," she said, and blushed. "Cars can't follow in these tracks."

She knew a lot of places in that country. Some of the roads weren't roads at
all and were bad for tyres and I didn't want the firm's car scratched by bushes, but
you would have thought Colin could read what was in her mind. For nine times
out of ten he was there. It got on my nerves. It was a red, roaring powerful thing
and he opened it full out.

"I'm going to speak to Colin," I said. "I won't have him annoying you."

"He's not annoying me," she said. "I've got a sense of humour." 180

"Here, Colin," I said one evening when I put the car away. "What's the idea?"

He was taking off his overalls. He pretended he did not know what I was
talking about. He had a way of rolling his eyeballs, as if they had got wet and loose
in his head, while he was speaking to me, and you never knew if it was sweat or
oil on his face. It was always pale, with high colour on his cheeks and very red
lips.

"Miss MacFarlane doesn't like being followed," I said.

He dropped his jaw and gaped at me. I could not tell whether he was being
very surprised or very sly. I used to call him "Marbles" because when he spoke he
seemed to have a lot of marbles in his mouth. 190

Then he said he never went to the places we went to, except by accident. He
wasn't following us, he said, but we were following him. We never let him alone,
he said. Everywhere he went, he said, we were there. Take last Saturday, he said,
we were following him for miles down the bypass, he said. "But you passed us first
and then sat down in front," I said. "I went to Ingley Wood," he said. "And you
followed me there." No, we didn't. I said, Miss MacFarlane decided to go there.

He said he did not want to complain, but fair was fair. "I suppose you
know," he said, "that you have taken my girl off me. Well, you can leave *me* alone,
can't you?"

"Here," I said. "One minute! Not so fast! You said I've taken Miss MacFarlane 200
from you. Well, she was never your girl. She only knew you in a friendly way."

"She was my girl" was all he said.

He was pouring oil into my engine. He had some cotton wool in one hand
and the can in the other. He wiped up the green oil that had overflowed, screwed
on the cap, pulled down the bonnet[11] and whistled to himself.

I went back to Muriel and told her what Colin had said.

"I don't like trouble," I said.

"Don't you worry," she said. "I had to have someone to go to all these places
with before you came. Couldn't stick in here all day Sunday."

"Ah," I said. "That's it, is it? You've been to all these places with him?" 210

"Yes," she said. "And he keeps on going to them. He's sloppy about me."

"Good God," I said. "Sentimental memories."

I felt sorry for that fellow. He knew it was hopeless, but he loved her. I suppose he couldn't help himself. Well, it takes all sorts to make a world, as my

11. Hood.

mother used to say. If we were all alike it wouldn't do. Some men can't save money. It just runs through their fingers. He couldn't save money, so he lost her. I suppose all he thought of was love.

I could have been friends with that fellow. As it was, I put a lot of business his way. I didn't want him to get the wrong idea about me. We're all human after all.   220

We didn't have any more trouble with Colin after this until Bank Holiday.[12] I was going to take her down to see my family. The old man's getting a bit past it now and has given up living over the shop. He's living out on the Barnum Road, beyond the tram stop. We were going down in the firm's car, as per usual, but something went wrong with the mag[13] and Colin had not got it right for the holiday. I was wild about this. What's the use of a garage who can't do a rush job for the holidays! What's the use of being an old customer if they're going to let you down! I went for Colin bald-headed.

"You knew I wanted it," I said. "It's no use trying to put me off with a tale about the stuff not coming down from the works. I've heard that one before."   230

I told him he'd got to let me have another car, because he'd let me down. I told him I wouldn't pay his account. I said I'd take my business away from him. But there wasn't a car to be had in the town because of the holiday. I could have knocked the fellow down. After the way I'd sent business to him.

Then I saw through his little game. He knew Muriel and I were going to my people and he had done this to stop it. The moment I saw this I let him know that it would take more than him to stop me doing what I wanted.

I said: "Right. I shall take the account of Miss MacFarlane's train fare and my own from the account at the end of the month."

I said: "You may run a garage, but you don't run the railway service."   240

I was damned angry going by train. I felt quite lost on the railway after having a car. It was crowded with trippers too. It was slow—stopping at all the stations. The people come in, they tread all over your feet, they make you squeeze up till you're crammed against the window, and the women stick out their elbows and fidget. And then the expense! a return for two runs you into just over a couple of quid.[14] I could have murdered Colin.

We got there at last. We walked up from the tram stop. Mother was at the window and let us in.

"This is Miss MacFarlane," I said.

And Mother said: "Oh, pleased to meet you. We've heard a lot about you.   250

"Oh," Mother said to me, giving me a kiss, "are you tired? You haven't had your tea, have you? Sit down. Have this chair, dear. It's more comfortable."

"Well, my boy," my father said.

"Want a wash," my father said. "We've got a washbasin downstairs," he said. "I used not to mind about washing upstairs before. Now I couldn't do without it. Funny how your ideas change as you get older.

"How's business?" he said.

12. National holiday.
13. Magneto, coil.
14. Pounds (in money).

"Mustn't grumble," I said. "How's yours?"

"You knew," he said, "we took off the horses: except for one or two of the older families we have got motors now."[15]

But he'd told me that the last time I was there. I'd been at him for years about motor hearses.

"You've forgotten I used to drive them," I said.

"Bless me, so you did," he said.

He took me up to my room. He showed me everything he had done to the house. "Your mother likes it," he said. "The traffic's company for her. You know what your mother is for company."

Then he gives me a funny look.

"Who's the girl?" he says.

My mother came in then and said: "She's pretty, Arthur."

"Of course she's pretty," I said. "She's Irish."

"Oh," said the old man. "Irish! Got a sense of humour, eh?"

"She wouldn't be marrying me if she hadn't," I said. And then I gave *them* a look.

"Marrying her, did you say?" exclaimed my father.

"Any objection?" I said.

"Now, Ernest dear," said my mother. "Leave the boy alone. Come down while I pop the kettle on."

She was terribly excited.

"Miss MacFarlane," the old man said.

"No sugar, thank you, Mrs. Humphrey. I beg your pardon, Mr. Humphrey?"

"The Glen Hotel at Swansea, I don't suppose you know that?" my father said. "I wondered if you did, being in the catering line."

"It doesn't follow she knows every hotel," my mother said.

"Forty years ago," the old man said, "I was staying at the Glen in Swansea and the headwaiter—"

"Oh, no, not that one. I'm sure Miss MacFarlane doesn't want to hear that one," my mother said.

"How's business with you, Mr. Humphrey?" said Muriel. "We passed a large cemetery near the station."

"Dad's Ledger," I said.

"The whole business has changed so that you wouldn't know it, in my life-time," said my father. "Silver fittings have gone clean out. Everyone wants simplicity nowadays. Restraint. Dignity," my father said.

"Prices did it," my father said.

"The war," he said.

"You couldn't get the wood," he said.

"Take ordinary mahogany, just an ordinary piece of mahogany. Or teak," he said. "Take teak. Or walnut."

"You can certainly see the world go by in this room," I said to my mother.

"It never stops," she said.

Now it was all bicycles over the new concrete road from the gun factory.

---

15. Hearses had been horse-drawn but were now automobiles.

Then traction engines and cars. They came up over the hill where the A.A.[16] man stands and choked up round the tram stop. It was mostly holiday traffic. Everything with a wheel on it was out.

"On this stretch," my father told me, "they get three accidents a week." There was an ambulance station at the crossroads.

We had hardly finished talking about this—in fact, the old man was still saying that something ought to be done—when the telephone rang.

"Name of MacFarlane?" the voice said on the wire.   310

"No. Humphrey," my father said. "There is a Miss MacFarlane here."

"There's a man named Colin Mitchell lying seriously injured in an accident at the Cottage Hospital, gave me the name of MacFarlane as his nearest relative."

That was the police. On to it at once. That fellow Colin had followed us down by road.

Cry, I never heard a girl cry as Muriel cried when we came back from the hospital. He had died in the ambulance. Cutting in, the old game he used to play on me. Clean off the saddle and under the Birmingham bus. The blood was everywhere, they said. People were still looking at it when we went by. Head on. What a mess! Don't let's talk about it.   320

She wanted to see him, but they said no. There wasn't anything recognizable to see. She put her arms round my neck and cried, "Colin, Colin," as if I were Colin, and clung to me. I was feeling sick myself. I held her tight and I kissed her and I thought: Holiday ruined.

Damn fool man, I thought. Poor devil, I thought.

"I knew he'd do something like this."

"There, there," I said to her. "Don't think about Colin."

Didn't she love me, I said, and not Colin? Hadn't she got me? She said yes, she had. And she loved me. But, "Oh, Colin! Oh, Colin!" she cried. "And Colin's mother," she cried. "Oh, it's terrible." She cried and cried.   330

We put her to bed and I sat with her, and my mother kept coming in.

"Leave her to me," I said. "I understand her."

Before they went to bed they both came in and looked at her. She lay sobbing with her head in the pillow.

I could quite understand her being upset. Colin was a decent fellow. He was always doing things for her. He mended her electric lamp and he riveted the stem of a wineglass so that you couldn't see the break. He used to make things for her. He was very good with his hands.

She lay on her side with her face burning and feverish with misery and crying, scalded by the salt, and her lips shrivelled up. I put my arm under her neck and I stroked her forehead. She groaned. Sometimes she shivered and sometimes she clung to me, crying: "Oh, Colin! Colin!"   340

My arm ached with the cramp and I had a crick in my back, sitting in the awkward way I was on the bed. It was late. There was nothing to do but to ache and sit watching her and thinking. It is funny the way your mind drifts. When I was kissing her and watching her I was thinking out who I'd show our new Autumn range to first. Her hand held my wrist tight, and when I kissed her I got

16. Automobile Association.

her tears on my lips. They burned and stung. Her neck and shoulders were soft and I could feel her breath hot out of her nostrils on the back of my hand. Ever noticed how hot a woman's breath gets when she's crying? I drew out my hand and lay down beside her and "Oh, Colin, Colin," she sobbed, turning over and clinging to me. And so I lay there, listening to the traffic, staring at the ceiling, and shivering whenever the picture of Colin shooting right off that damned red thing into the bus came into my mind—until I did not hear the traffic any more, or see the ceiling any more, or think any more, but a change happened—I don't know when. This Colin thing seemed to have knocked the bottom out of everything and I had a funny feeling we were going down and down and down in a lift.[17] And the further we went, the hotter and softer she got. Perhaps it was when I found with my hands that she had very big breasts. But it was like being on the mail steamer and feeling engines start under your feet, thumping louder and louder. You can feel it in every vein of your body. Her mouth opened and her tears dried. Her breath came through her open mouth and her voice was blind and husky. Colin, Colin, Colin, she said, and her fingers were hooked into me. I got out and turned the key in the door.

In the morning I left her sleeping. It did not matter to me what my father might have heard in the night, but still I wondered. She would hardly let me touch her before that. I told her I was sorry, but she shut me up. I was afraid of her. I was afraid of mentioning Colin. I wanted to go out of the house there and then and tell someone everything. Did she love Colin all the time? Did she think I was Colin? And every time I thought of that poor devil covered over with a white sheet in the hospital mortuary, a kind of picture of her and me under the sheets with love came into my mind. I couldn't separate the two things. Just as though it had all come from Colin.

I'd rather not talk any more about that. I never talked to Muriel about it. I waited for her to say something, but she didn't. She didn't say a word.

The next day was a bad day. It was grey and hot and the air smelt of oil fumes from the road. There's always a mess to clear up when things like this happen. I had to see to it. I had the job of ringing up the boy's mother. But I got round that, thank God, by ringing up the garage and getting them to go round and see the old lady. My father is useless when things are like this. I was the whole morning on the phone: to the hospital, the police, the coroner—and he stood fussing beside me, jerking up and down like a fat indiarubber ball.

I found my mother washing up at the sink and she said: "That poor boy's mother! I can't stop thinking of her."

Then my father comes in and says—just as though I was a customer: "Of course if Mrs. Mitchell desires it we can have the remains of the deceased conveyed to his house by one of our new specially sprung motor hearses and can, if necessary, make all the funeral arrangements."

I could have hit him because Muriel came into the room when he was saying this. But she stood there as if nothing had happened.

"It's the least we can do for poor Mrs. Mitchell," she said. There were small creases of shadow under her eyes, which shone with a soft strong light I had never

17. Elevator.

seen before. She walked as if she were really still in that room with me, asleep. God, I loved that girl! God, I wanted to get all this over, this damned Colin business that had come right into the middle of everything like this, and I wanted to get married right away. I wanted to be alone with her. That's what Colin did for me.

"Yes," I said. "We must do the right thing by Colin."

"We are sometimes asked for long-distance estimates," my father said.

"It will be a little something," my mother said.   400

"Dad and I will talk it over," I said.

"Come into the office," my father said. "It occurred to me that it would be nice to do the right thing by this friend of yours."

We talked it over. We went into the cost of it. There was the return journey to reckon. We worked it out that it would come no dearer to old Mrs. Mitchell than if she took the train and buried the boy here. That is to say, my father said, if I drove it.

"It would look nice," my father said. "Saves money and it would look a bit friendly," my father said. "You've done it before."

"Well," I said. "I suppose I can get a refund on my return ticket from the   410 railway."

But it was not as simple as it looked, because Muriel wanted to come. She wanted to drive back with me and the hearse. My mother was very worried about this. It might upset Muriel, she thought. Father thought it might not look nice to see a young girl sitting by the coffin of a grown man.

"It must be dignified," my father said. "You see, if she was there, it might look as though she were just doing it for the ride—like these young women on bakers' vans."

My father took me out into the hall to tell me this because he did not want her to hear. But she would not have it. She wanted to come back with Colin.   420

"Colin loved me. It is my duty to him," she said. "Besides," she said suddenly, in her full open voice—it had seemed to be closed and carved and broken and small—"I've never been in a hearse before."

"And it will save her fare too," I said to my father.

That night I went again to her room. She was awake. I said I was sorry to disturb her, but I would go at once only I wanted to see if she was all right. She said, in the closed voice again, that she was all right.

"Are you sure?" I said.

She did not answer. I was worried. I went over to the bed.

"What is the matter? Tell me what is the matter," I said.   430

For a long time she was silent. I held her hand, I stroked her head. She was lying stiff in the bed. She would not answer. I dropped my hand to her small white shoulder. She stirred and drew up her legs and half turned and said, "I was thinking of Colin. Where is he?" she asked.

"They've brought him round. He's lying downstairs."

"In the front room?"

"Yes, ready for the morning. Now be a sensible girl and go back by train."

"No, no," she said. "I want to go with Colin. Poor Colin. He loved me and I didn't love him." And she drew my hands down to her breasts.

"Colin loved me," she whispered.   440

"Not like this," I whispered.

It was a warm grey morning like all the others when we took Colin back. They had fixed the coffin in before Muriel came out. She came down wearing the bright-blue hat she had got off Dormer's millinery man[18] and she kissed my mother and father good-bye. They were very sorry for her. "Look after her, Arthur," my mother said. Muriel got in beside me without a glance behind her at the coffin. I started the engine. They smiled at us. My father raised his hat, but whether it was to Muriel and me or to Colin, or to the three of us, I do not know. He was not, you see, wearing his top hat. I'll say this for the old boy, thirty years in the trade have taught him tact.   450

After leaving my father's house you have to go down to the tram terminus before you get on the bypass. There was always one or two drivers, conductors, or inspectors there, doing up their tickets, or changing over the trolley arms. When we passed I saw two of them drop their jaws, stick their pencils in their ears, and raise their hats. I was so surprised by this that I nearly raised mine in acknowledgement, forgetting that we had the coffin behind. I had not driven one of my father's hearses for years.

Hearses are funny things to drive. They are well-sprung, smooth-running cars, with quiet engines, and if you are used to driving a smaller car, before you know where you are, you are speeding. You know you ought to go slow, say   460 twenty-five to thirty maximum, and it's hard to keep it down. You can return empty at seventy if you like. It's like driving a fire engine. Go fast out and come back slow—only the other way round. Open out in the country, but slow down past houses. That's what it means. My father was very particular about this.

Muriel and I didn't speak very much at first. We sat listening to the engine and the occasional jerk of the coffin behind when we went over a pothole. We passed the place where poor Colin—but I didn't say anything to Muriel, and she, if she noticed—which I doubt—did not say anything to me. We went through Cox Hill, Wammering, and Yodley Mount, flat country, don't care for it myself. "There's a wonderful lot of building going on," Muriel said at last.   470

"You won't know these places in five years," I said.

But my mind kept drifting away from the road and the green fields and the dullness, and back to Colin—five days before, he had come down this way. I expected to see that Indian coming flying straight out of every corner. But it was all bent and bust up properly now. I saw the damned thing.

He had been up to his old game, following us, and that had put the end to following. But not quite; he was following us now, behind us in the coffin. Then my mind drifted off that and I thought of those nights at my parents' house, and Muriel. You never know what a woman is going to be like. I thought, too, that it had put my calculations out. I mean, supposing she had a baby. You see I had   480 reckoned on waiting eighteen months or so. I would have eight hundred then.[19] But if we had to get married at once, we should have to cut right down. Then I kept thinking it was funny her saying "Colin!" like that in the night; it was funny it

18. Hat salesman.
19. Eight hundred pounds in savings.

made her feel that way with me, and how it made me feel when she called me Colin. I'd never thought of her in that way, in what you might call the "Colin" way.

I looked at her and she looked at me and she smiled but still we did not say very much, but the smiles kept coming to both of us. The light-railway bridge at Dootheby took me by surprise and I thought the coffin gave a jump as we took it.

"Colin's still watching us," I nearly said.

There were tears in her eyes.   490

"What was the matter with Colin?" I said. "Nice chap, I thought. Why didn't you marry him?"

"Yes," she said. "He was a nice boy. But he'd no sense of humour."

"And I wanted to get out of that town," she said.

"I'm not going to stay there, at that hotel," she said.

"I want to get away," she said. "I've had enough."

She had a way of getting angry with the air, like that. "You've got to take me away," she said. We were passing slowly into Muster, there was a tram ahead and people thick on the narrow pavements, dodging out into the road. But when we got into the Market Square, where they were standing round, they saw the coffin. 500 They began to raise their hats. Suddenly she laughed. "It's like being the King and Queen," she said.

"They're raising their hats," she said.

"Not all of them," I said.

She squeezed my hand and I had to keep her from jumping about like a child on the seat as we went through.

"There they go."

"Boys always do," I said.

"And another."

"Let's see what the policeman does."   510

She started to laugh, but I shut her up. "Keep your sense of humour to your-self," I said.

Through all those towns that run into one another you might say, we caught it. We went through, as she said, like royalty. So many years since I drove a hearse, I'd forgotten what it was like.

I was proud of her, I was proud of Colin, and I was proud of myself. And after what had happened, I mean on the last two nights, it was like a wedding. And although we knew it was for Colin, it was for us too, because Colin was with both of us. It was like this all the way.

"Look at that man there. Why doesn't he raise his hat? People ought to show 520 respect for the dead," she said.   [1938]

Questions for Discussion and Writing

1. Underline or circle the numerous references to money. What part does money play in the relationship between Muriel and Mr. Humphrey?
2. Is this a love story? If so, whose love story is it?
3. Does Colin's affection for Muriel represent true love? Is he a hero or a fool? Explain.

4. In Boccaccio's "Fiametta's Tale," constancy in love is rewarded in the end, but in Pritchett's it is not. Can you account for this difference by reference to the culture that produced each story?

5. What is the significance of the title? What does Muriel mean when she says she has a sense of humor?

6. Analyze the narrator's character. Why is he telling this story? Is he trying to justify himself?

7. How do you interpret the next-to-the-last paragraph? Why is the narrator "proud" of Colin and himself? In what ways is this occasion like a wedding?

ᕈ EUDORA WELTY

(b. 1909)

Why I Live at the P.O.

Like many other Southern writers, Eudora Welty was once regarded as a regionalist, specializing in eccentrics and grotesques, but her characters and themes transcend such boundaries and limitations.

Born in Jackson, Mississippi, to middle-class parents, Welty developed an early interest in writing. As a child, she published in the children's magazine, *St. Nicholas,* and as a student wrote for the high school newspaper and college literary magazines. She began her undergraduate studies at the Mississippi State College for Women in 1925 and completed her degree at the University of Wisconsin. She also spent a year at Columbia University studying business, until her father's battle against leukemia brought her back to Jackson. She has lived there ever since.

During the 1930s, Welty wrote advertising for a radio station, contributed feature articles to the *Memphis Commercial Appeal,* and took photographs of Mississippi life for the Works Progress Administration. Her first published story, "Death of a Traveling Salesman," published in *Manuscript* in 1936, brought inquiries about a novel from New York publishing houses, but Welty preferred short stories. By 1940, she was selling stories to magazines like the *Atlantic Monthly;* her first collection appeared in 1941. Writing reviews for the *New York Times* increased her awareness of technique, and she has since written perceptively about the art of fiction, especially the short story. "Wide Net" won an O. Henry Award in 1942; her novel *The Optimist's Daughter* won the Pulitzer Prize for 1973.

Welty's stories typically combine interior and exterior action in a complex balance that invites readers to enter imaginatively into the lives of her characters. She is also a master of eccentric, slightly absurdist comedy. Often her characters struggle with separation and love, a longing for communication so intense that it may frustrate itself. "Why I Live at the P.O." is a comic master-piece; "A Still Moment" shows her lyrical, philosophical side in a story of strange, intense beauty.

I WAS GETTING ALONG fine with Mama, Papa-Daddy and Uncle Rondo until my sister Stella-Rondo just separated from her husband and came back home again. Mr. Whitaker! Of course I went with Mr. Whitaker first, when he first appeared here in China Grove, taking "Pose Yourself" photos, and Stella-Rondo broke us up. Told him I was one-sided. Bigger on one side than the other, which is a deliberate, calculated falsehood: I'm the same. Stella-Rondo is exactly twelve months to the day younger than I am and for that reason she's spoiled.

She's always had anything in the world she wanted and then she'd throw it away. Papa-Daddy gave her this gorgeous Add-a-Pearl necklace when she was eight years old and she threw it away playing baseball when she was nine, with only two pearls. 10

So as soon as she got married and moved away from home the first thing she did was separate! From Mr. Whitaker! This photographer with the popeyes she said she trusted. Came home from one of those towns up in Illinois and to our complete surprise brought this child of two.

Mama said she like to made her drop dead for a second. "Here you had this marvelous blonde child and never so much as wrote your mother a word about it," says Mama. "I'm thoroughly ashamed of you." But of course she wasn't.

Stella-Rondo just calmly takes off this *hat*, I wish you could see it. She says, "Why, Mama, Shirley-T.'s adopted, I can prove it." 20

"How?" says Mama, but all I says was, "H'm!" There I was over the hot stove, trying to stretch two chickens over five people and a completely unexpected child into the bargain, without one moment's notice.

"What do you mean—'H'm!'?" says Stella-Rondo, and Mama says, "I heard that, Sister."

I said that oh, I didn't mean a thing, only that whoever Shirley-T. was, she was the spit-image of Papa-Daddy if he'd cut off his beard, which of course he'd never do in the world. Papa-Daddy's Mama's papa and sulks.

Stella-Rondo got furious! She said, "Sister, I don't need to tell you you got a lot of nerve and always did have and I'll thank you to make no future reference to my adopted child whatsoever." 30

"Very well," I said. "Very well, very well. Of course I noticed at once she looks like Mr. Whitaker's side too. That frown. She looks like a cross between Mr. Whitaker and Papa-Daddy."

"Well, all I can say is she isn't."

"She looks exactly like Shirley Temple to me," says Mama, but Shirley-T. just ran away from her.

So the first thing Stella-Rondo did at the table was turn Papa-Daddy against me.

"Papa-Daddy," she says. He was trying to cut up his meat. "Papa-Daddy!" I was taken completely by surprise. Papa-Daddy is about a million years old, and's 40 got this long-long beard. "Papa-Daddy, Sister said she fails to understand why you don't cut off your beard."

So Papa-Daddy l-a-y-s down his knife and fork! He's real rich. Mama says he is, he says he isn't. So he says, "Have I heard correctly? You don't understand why I don't cut off my beard?"

"Why," I says, "Papa-Daddy, of course I understand, I did not say any such of a thing, the idea!"

He says, "Hussy!"

I says, "Papa-Daddy, you know I wouldn't any more want you to cut off your beard than the man in the moon. It was the farthest thing from my mind! Stella-Rondo sat there and made that up while she was eating breast of chicken."

But he says, "So the postmistress fails to understand why I don't cut off my beard. Which job I got you through my influence with the government. 'Bird's nest'—is that what you call it?"

Not that it isn't the next to smallest P.O. in the entire state of Mississippi.

I says, "Oh, Papa-Daddy," I says, "I didn't say any such of a thing, I never dreamed it was a bird's nest, I have always been grateful though this is the next to smallest P.O. in the state of Mississippi, and I do enjoy being referred to as a hussy by my own grandfather."

But Stella-Rondo says, "Yes, you did say it too. Anybody in the world could of heard you, that had ears."

"Stop right there," says Mama, looking at *me*.

So I pulled my napkin straight back through the napkin ring and left the table.

As soon as I was out of the room, Mama says, "Call her back, or she'll starve to death," but Papa-Daddy says, "This is the beard I started growing on the Coast when I was fifteen years old." He would of gone on till nightfall if Shirley-T. hadn't lost the Milky Way she ate in Cairo.

So Papa-Daddy says, "I am going out and lie in the hammock, and you can sit here and remember my words: I'll never cut off my beard as long as I live, even one inch, and I don't appreciate it in you at all." Passed right by me in the hall and went straight out and got in the hammock.

It would be a holiday. It wasn't five minutes before Uncle Rondo suddenly appeared in the hall in one of Stella-Rondo's flesh-colored kimonos, all cut on the bias, like something Mr. Whitaker probably thought was gorgeous.

"Uncle Rondo!" I says, "I didn't know who that was! Where are you going?"

"Sister," he says, "get out of my way, I'm poisoned."

"If you're poisoned stay away from Papa-Daddy," I says. "Keep out of the hammock. Papa-Daddy will certainly beat you on the head if you come within forty miles of him. He thinks I deliberately said he ought to cut off his beard after he got me the P.O., and I've told him and told him and told him, and he acts like he just don't hear me. Papa-Daddy must of gone stone deaf."

"He picked a find day to do it then," says Uncle Rondo, and before you could say "Jack Robinson" flew out in the yard.

What he'd really done, he'd drunk another bottle of that prescription. He does it every single Fourth of July as sure as shooting, and it's horribly expensive.

Then he falls over in the hammock and snores. So he insisted on zigzagging right out to the hammock, looking like a half-wit.

Papa-Daddy woke up with this horrible yell and right there without moving an inch he tried to turn Uncle Rondo against me. I heard every word he said. Oh, he told Uncle Rondo I didn't learn to read till I was eight years old and he didn't see how in the world I ever got the mail put up at the P.O., much less read it all, and he said if Uncle Rondo could only fathom the lengths he had gone to to get me that job! And he said on the other hand he thought Stella-Rondo had a brilliant mind and deserved credit for getting out of town. All the time he was just lying there swinging as pretty as you please and looping out his beard, and poor Uncle Rondo was *pleading* with him to slow down the hammock, it was making him as dizzy as a witch to watch it. But that's what Papa-Daddy likes about a hammock. So Uncle Rondo was too dizzy to get turned against me for the time being. He's Mama's only brother and is a good case of a one-track mind. Ask anybody. A certified pharmacist.

Just then I heard Stella-Rondo raising the upstairs window. While she was married she got this peculiar idea that it's cooler with the windows shut and locked. So she has to raise the window before she can make a soul hear her outdoors.

So she raises the window and says, *"Oh!"* You would have thought she was mortally wounded.

Uncle Rondo and Papa-Daddy didn't even look up, but kept right on with what they were doing. I had to laugh.

I flew up the stairs and threw the door open! I says, "What in the wide world's the matter, Stella-Rondo? You mortally wounded?"

"No," she says, "I am not mortally wounded but I wish you would do me the favor of looking out that window there and telling me what you see."

So I shade my eyes and look out the window.

"I see the front yard," I says.

"Don't you see any human beings?" she says.

"I see Uncle Rondo trying to run Papa-Daddy out of the hammock," I says. "Nothing more. Naturally, it's so suffocating-hot in the house, with all the windows shut and locked, everybody who cares to stay in their right mind will have to go out and get in the hammock before the Fourth of July is over."

"Don't you notice anything different about Uncle Rondo?" asks Stella-Rondo.

"Why, no, except he's got on some terrible looking flesh-colored contraption I wouldn't be found dead in, is all I can see," I says.

"Never mind, you won't be found dead in it, because it happens to be part of my trousseau, and Mr. Whitaker took several dozen photographs of me in it," says Stella-Rondo. "What on earth could Uncle Rondo *mean* by wearing part of my trousseau out in the broad open daylight without saying so much as 'Kiss my foot,' *knowing* I only got home this morning after my separation and hung my negligee up on the bathroom door, just as nervous as I could be?"

"I'm sure I don't know, and what do you expect me to do about it?" I says. "Jump out the window?"

"No, I expect nothing of the kind. I simply declare that Uncle Rondo looks like a fool in it, that's all," she says. "It makes me sick to my stomach."

"Well, he looks as good as he can," I says. "As good as anybody in reason could." I stood up for Uncle Rondo, please remember. And I said to Stella-Rondo, "I think I would do well not to criticize so freely if I were you and came home with a two-year-old child I had never said a word about, and no explanation whatever about my separation."

"I asked you the instant I entered this house not to refer one more time to my adopted child, and you gave me your word of honor you would not," was all Stella-Rondo would say, and started pulling out every one of her eyebrows with some cheap Kress[1] tweezers.

So I merely slammed the door behind me and went down to get some green-tomato pickle. Somebody had to do it. Of course Mama had turned both the niggers loose; she always said no earthly power could hold one anyway on the Fourth of July, so she wouldn't even try. It turned out that Jaypan fell in the lake and came within a very narrow limit of drowning.

So Mama trots in. Lifts up the lid and says, "H'm! Not very good for your Uncle Rondo in his precarious condition, I must say. Or poor little adopted Shirley-T. Shame on you!"

That made me tired. I says, "Well, Stella-Rondo had better thank her lucky stars it was her instead of me came trotting in with that very peculiar-looking child. Now if it had been me that trotted in from Illinois and brought a peculiar-looking child of two, I shudder to think of the reception I'd of got, much less controlled the diet of an entire family."

"But you must remember, Sister, that you were never married to Mr. Whitaker in the first place and didn't go up to Illinois to live," says Mama, shaking a spoon in my face. "If you had I would of been just as overjoyed to see you and your little adopted girl as I was to see Stella-Rondo, when you wound up with your separation and came on back home."

"You would not," I says.

"Don't contradict me, I would," says Mama.

But I said she couldn't convince me though she talked till she was blue in the face. Then I said, "Besides, you know as well as I do that child is not adopted."

"She most certainly is adopted," says Mama, stiff as a poker.

I says, "Why, Mama, Stella-Rondo had her just as sure as anything in this world, and just too stuck up to admit it."

"Why, Sister," said Mama. "Here I thought we were going to have a pleasant Fourth of July, and you start right out not believing a word your own baby sister tells you!"

"Just like Cousin Annie Flo. Went to her grave denying the facts of life," I remind Mama.

"I told you if you ever mentioned Annie Flo's name I'd slap your face," says Mama, and slaps my face.

"All right, you wait and see," I says.

"I," says Mama, "I prefer to take my children's word for anything when it's humanly possible." You ought to see Mama, she weighs two hundred pounds and has real tiny feet.

1. Kress, Co., a five-and-ten-cent store.

Just then something perfectly horrible occurred to me.

"Mama," I says, "can that child talk?" I simply had to whisper! "Mama, I   180
wonder if that child can be—you know—in any way? Do you realize," I says, "that
she hasn't spoken one single, solitary word to a human being up to this minute?
This is the way she looks," I says, and I looked like this.

Well, Mama and I just stood there and stared at each other. It was horrible!

"I remember well that Joe Whitaker frequently drank like a fish," says Mama.
"I believed to my soul he drank *chemicals*." And without another word she marches
to the foot of the stairs and calls Stella-Rondo.

"Stella-Rondo? O-o-o-o-o! Stella-Rondo!"

"What?" says Stella-Rondo from upstairs. Not even the grace to get up off
the bed.   190

"Can that child of yours talk?" asks Mama.

Stella-Rondo says, "Can she what?"

"Talk! Talk!" says Mama: "Burdyburdyburdyburdy!"

So Stella-Rondo yells back, "Who says she can't talk?"

"Sister says so," says Mama.

"You didn't have to tell me. I know whose word of honor don't mean a thing
in this house," says Stella-Rondo.

And in a minute the loudest Yankee voice I ever heard in my life yells out,
"OE'm Pop-OE the Sailor-r-r-r Ma-a-an!" and then somebody jumps up and down
in the upstairs hall. In another second the house would of fallen down.   200

"Not only talks, she can tap-dance!" calls Stella-Rondo. "Which is more than
some people I won't name can do."

"Why, the little precious darling thing!" Mama says, so surprised. "Just as
smart as she can be!" Starts talking baby talk right there. Then she turns on me.
"Sister, you ought to be thoroughly ashamed! Run upstairs this instant and apologize to Stella-Rondo and Shirley-T."

"Apologize for what?" I says. "I merely wondered if the child was normal,
that's all. Now that she's proved she is, why, I have nothing further to say."

But Mama just turned on her heel and flew out, furious. She ran right upstairs and hugged the baby. She believed it was adopted. Stella-Rondo hadn't done 210
a thing but turn her against me from upstairs while I stood there helpless over the
hot stove. So that made Mama, Papa-Daddy and the baby all on Stella-Rondo's
side.

Next, Uncle Rondo.

I must say that Uncle Rondo has been marvelous to me at various times in
the past and I was completely unprepared to be made to jump out of my skin, the
way it turned out. Once Stella-Rondo did something perfectly horrible to him—
broke a chain letter from Flanders Field—and he took the radio back he had given
her and gave it to me. Stella-Rondo was furious! For six months we all had to
call her Stella instead of Stella-Rondo, or she wouldn't answer. I always thought 220
Uncle Rondo had all the brains of the entire family. Another time he sent me to
Mammoth Cave, with all expenses paid.

But this would be the day he was drinking that prescription, the Fourth of
July.

So at supper Stella-Rondo speaks up and says she thinks Uncle Rondo ought to try to eat a little something. So finally Uncle Rondo said he would try a little cold biscuits and ketchup, but that was all. So *she* brought it to him.

"Do you think it wise to disport with ketchup in Stella-Rondo's flesh-colored kimono?" I says. Trying to be considerate! If Stella-Rondo couldn't watch out for her trousseau, somebody had to.

"Any objections?" asks Uncle Rondo, just about to pour out all the ketchup.

"Don't mind what she says, Uncle Rondo," says Stella-Rondo. "Sister has been devoting this solid afternoon to sneering out my bedroom window at the way you look."

"What's that?" says Uncle Rondo. Uncle Rondo has got the most terrible temper in the world. Anything is liable to make him tear the house down if it comes at the wrong time.

So Stella-Rondo says, "Sister says, 'Uncle Rondo certainly does look like a fool in that pink kimono!'"

Do you remember who it was really said that?

Uncle Rondo spills out all the ketchup and jumps out of his chair and tears off the kimono and throws it on the dirty floor and puts his foot on it. It had to be sent all the way to Jackson to the cleaners and re-pleated.

"So that's your opinion of your Uncle Rondo, is it?" he says. "I look like a fool, do I? Well, that's the last straw. A whole day in this house with nothing to do, and then to hear you come out with a remark like that behind my back!"

"I didn't say any such kind of a thing, Uncle Rondo," I says, "and I'm not saying who did, either. Why, I think you look all right. Just try to take care of yourself and not talk and eat at the same time," I says. "I think you better go lie down."

"Lie down my foot," says Uncle Rondo. I ought to of known by that he was fixing to do something perfectly horrible.

So he didn't do anything that night in the precarious state he was in—just played Casino with Mama and Stella-Rondo and Shirley-T. and gave Shirley-T. a nickel with a head on both sides. It tickled her nearly to death, and she called him "Papa." But at 6:30 A.M. the next morning, he threw a whole five-cent package of some unsold one-inch firecrackers from the store as hard as he could into my bedroom and they every one went off. Not one bad one in the string. Anybody else, there'd be one that wouldn't go off.

Well, I'm just terribly susceptible to noise of any kind, the doctor has always told me I was the most sensitive person he had ever seen in his whole life, and I was simply prostrated. I couldn't eat! People tell me they heard it as far as the cemetery, and old Aunt Jep Patterson, that had been holding her own so good, thought it was Judgment Day and she was going to meet her whole family. It's usually so quiet here.

And I'll tell you it didn't take me any longer than a minute to make up my mind what to do. There I was with the whole entire house on Stella-Rondo's side and turned against me. If I have anything at all I have pride.

So I just decided I'd go straight down to the P.O. There's plenty of room there in the back, I says to myself.

Well! I made no bones about letting the family catch on to what I was up to. I didn't try to conceal it.

The first thing they knew, I marched in where they were all playing Old
Maid and pulled the electric oscillating fan out by the plug, and everything got
real hot. Next I snatched the pillow I'd done the needlepoint on right off the davenport from behind Papa-Daddy. He went "Ugh!" I beat Stella-Rondo up the stairs
and finally found my charm bracelet in her bureau drawer under a picture of
Nelson Eddy.[2]

"So that's the way the land lies," says Uncle Rondo. There he was, piecing[3]
on the ham. "Well, Sister, I'll be glad to donate my army cot if you got any place to
set it up, providing you'll leave right this minute and let me get some peace."
Uncle Rondo was in France.

"Thank you kindly for the cot and 'peace' is hardly the word I would select if
I had to resort to firecrackers at 6:30 A.M. in a young girl's bedroom," I says back
to him. "And as to where I intend to go, you seem to forget my position as postmistress of China Grove, Mississippi," I says. "I've always got the P.O."

Well, that made them all sit up and take notice.

I went out front and started digging up some four-o'-clocks to plant around
the P.O.

"Ah-ah-ah!" says Mama, raising the window. "Those happen to be my four-
o'-clocks. Everything planted in that star is mine. I've never known you to make
anything grow in your life."

"Very well," I says. "But I'll take the fern. Even you, Mama, can't stand there
and deny that I'm the one watered that fern. And I happen to know where I can
send in a box top and get a packet of one thousand mixed seeds, no two the same
kind, free."

"Oh, where?" Mama wants to know.

But I says, "Too Late, You 'tend to your house, and I'll 'tend to mine. You
hear things like that all the time if you know how to listen to the radio. Perfectly
marvelous offers. Get anything you want free."

So I hope to tell you I marched in and got that radio, and they could of all
bit a nail in two, especially Stella-Rondo, that it used to belong to, and she well
knew she couldn't get it back, I'd sue for it like a shot. And I very politely took the
sewing-machine motor I helped pay the most on to give Mama for Christmas back
in 1929, and a good big calendar, with the first-aid remedies on it. The thermome-
ter and the Hawaiian ukulele certainly were rightfully mine, and I stood on the
step-ladder and got all my watermelon-rind preserves and every fruit and vegetable I'd put up, every jar. Then I began to pull the tacks out of the bluebird wall
vases on the archway to the dining room.

"Who told you you could have those, Miss Priss?" says Mama, fanning as
hard as she could.

"I bought 'em and I'll keep track of 'em," I says. "I'll tack 'em up one on each
side the post-office window, and you can see 'em when you come to ask me for
your mail, if you're so dead to see 'em."

"Not I! I'll never darken the door to that post office again if I live to be a

2. Popular film actor and singer in the 1930s.
3. Eating small pieces of the ham.

hundred," Mama says. "Ungrateful child! After all the money we spent on you at the Normal."[4]

"Me either," says Stella-Rondo, "You can just let my mail lie there and *rot*, for all I care. I'll never come and relieve you of a single, solitary piece."

"I should worry," I says. "And who you think's going to sit down and write 320 you all those big fat letters and postcards, by the way? Mr. Whitaker? Just because he was the only man ever dropped down in China Grove and you got him—unfairly—is he going to sit down and write you a lengthy correspondence after you come home giving no rhyme nor reason whatsoever for your separation and no explanation for the presence of that child? I may not have your brilliant mind, but I fail to see it."

So Mama says, "Sister, I've told you a thousand times that Stella-Rondo simply got homesick, and this child is far too big to be hers," and she says, "Now, why don't you all just sit down and play Casino?"

Then Shirley-T. sticks out her tongue at me in this perfectly horrible way. 330 She has no more manners than the man in the moon. I told her she was going to cross her eyes like that some day and they'd stick.

"It's too late to stop me now," I says. "You should have tried that yesterday. I'm going to the P.O. and the only way you can possibly see me is to visit me there."

So Papa-Daddy says, "You'll never catch me setting foot in that post office, even if I should take a notion into my head to write a letter some place." He says, "I won't have you reachin' out of that little old window with a pair of shears and cuttin' off any beard of mine. I'm too smart for you!"

"We all are," says Stella-Rondo.   340

But I said, "If you're so smart, where's Mr. Whitaker?"

So then Uncle Rondo says, "I'll thank you from now on to stop reading all the orders I get on postcards and telling everybody in China Grove what you think is the matter with them," but I says, "I draw my own conclusions and will continue in the future to draw them." I says, "If people want to write their inmost secrets on penny postcards, there's nothing in the wide world you can do about it, Uncle Rondo."

"And if you think we'll ever *write* another postcard you're sadly mistaken," says Mama.

"Cutting off your nose to spite your face then," I says. "But if you're all deter- 350 mined to have no more to do with the U. S. mail, think of this: What will Stella-Rondo do now, if she wants to tell Mr. Whitaker to come after her?"

"Wah!" says Stella-Rondo. I knew she'd cry. She had a conniption fit right there in the kitchen.

"It will be interesting to see how long she holds out," I says, "And now—I am leaving."

"Good-bye," says Uncle Rondo.

"Oh, I declare," says Mama, "to think that a family of mine should quarrel on the Fourth of July, or the day after, over Stella-Rondo leaving old Mr. Whitaker and having the sweetest little adopted child! It looks like we'd all be glad!" 360

4. Teacher-training college.

"Wah!" says Stella-Rondo, and has a fresh conniption fit.

"*He* left *her*—you mark my words," I says. That's Mr. Whitaker, I know Mr. Whitaker. After all, I knew him first. I said from the beginning he'd up and leave her. I foretold every single thing that's happened."

"Where did he go?" asks Mama.

"Probably to the North Pole, if he knows what's good for him," I says.

But Stella-Rondo just bawled and wouldn't say another word. She flew to her room and slammed the door.

"Now look what you've gone and done, Sister," says Mama. "You go apologize."   370

"I haven't got time, I'm leaving," I says.

"Well, what are you waiting around for?" asks Uncle Rondo.

So I just picked up the kitchen clock and marched off, without saying "Kiss my foot" or anything, and never did tell Stella-Rondo good-bye.

There was a nigger girl going along on a little wagon right in front.

"Nigger-girl," I says, "come help me haul these things down the hill. I'm going to live in the post office."

Took her nine trips in her express wagon. Uncle Rondo came out on the porch and threw her a nickel.   380

And that's the last I've laid eyes on any of my family or my family laid eyes on me for five solid days and nights. Stella-Rondo may be telling the most horrible tales in the world about Mr. Whitaker, but I haven't heard them. As I tell everybody, I draw my own conclusions.

But, oh, I like it here. It's ideal, as I've been saying. You see, I've got everything cater-cornered, the way I like it. Hear the radio? All the war news. Radio, sewing machine, book ends, ironing board and that great big piano lamp—peace, that's what I like. Butter-bean vines planted all along the front where the strings are.

Of course, there's not much mail. My family are naturally the main people in 390 China Grove, and if they prefer to vanish from the face of the earth, for all the mail they write, why, I'm not going to open my mouth.

Some of the folks here in town are taking up for me and some turned against me. I know which is which. There are always people who will quit buying stamps just to get on the right side of Papa-Daddy.

But here I am, and here I'll stay. I want the world to know I'm happy.

And if Stella-Rondo should come to me this minute, on bended knees, and *attempt* to explain the incidents of her life with Mr. Whitaker, I'd simply put my fingers in both my ears and refuse to listen.   [1941]

Questions for Discussion and Writing
1. What is the tone of the story? Underline or highlight specific passages that establish the tone.
2. Why is there so much antagonism between Sister and Stella-Rondo?

3. To whom is Sister speaking? What strategies does she use to gain the listener's sympathy?

4. Explain whether Sister is justified in feeling hurt and leaving the family or whether she is over-reacting, perhaps even bordering on mental illness?

5. What does the setting, specifically the celebration of the Fourth of July, contribute to the story?

6. What is the theme of the story? Cite specific passages in support of your interpretation.

A Still Moment

LORENZO DOW RODE the Old Natchez Trace[1] at top speed upon a race horse, and the cry of the itinerant Man of God, "I must have souls! And souls I must have!" rang in his own windy ears. He rode as if never to stop, toward his night's appointment.

It was the hour of sunset. All the souls that he had saved and all those he had not took dusky shapes in the mist that hung between the high banks, and seemed by their great number and density to block his way, and showed no signs of melting or changing back into mist, so that he feared his passage was to be difficult forever. The poor souls that were not saved were darker and more pitiful than those that were, and still there was not any of the radiance he would have   10 hoped to see in such a congregation.

"Light up, in God's name!" he called, in the pain of his disappointment.

Then a whole swarm of fireflies instantly flickered all around him, up and down, back and forth, first one golden light and then another, flashing without any of the weariness that had held back the souls. These were the signs sent from God that he had not seen the accumulated radiance of saved souls because he was not able, and that his eyes were more able to see the fire flies of the Lord than His blessed souls.

"Lord, give me the strength to see the angels when I am in Paradise," he said. "Do not let my eyes remain in this failing proportion to my loving heart always."   20

He gasped and held on. It was that day's complexity of horse-trading that had left him in the end with a Spanish race horse for which he was bound to send money in November from Georgia. Riding faster on the beast and still faster until he felt as if he were flying he sent thoughts of love with matching speed to his wife Peggy in Massachusetts. He found it effortless to love at a distance. He could look at the flowering trees and love Peggy in fullness, just as he could see his visions and love God. And Peggy, to whom he had not spoken until he could speak fateful words ("Would she accept of such an object as him?"), Peggy, the bride, with whom he had spent a few hours of time, showing of herself a small round hand-writing, declared all in one letter, her first that she felt the same as he, and that the   30 fear was never of separation, but only of death.

Lorenzo well knew that it was Death that opened underfoot, that rippled by at night, that was the silence the birds did their singing in. He was close to death,

1. A road between Natchez, Mississippi, and Nashville, Tennessee, used by pioneers.

closer than any animal or bird. On the back of one horse after another, winding[2] them all, he was always riding toward it or away from it, and the Lord sent him directions with protection in His mind.

Just then he rode into a thicket of Indians taking aim with their new guns. One stepped out and took the horse by the bridle, it stopped at a touch, and the rest made a closing circle. The guns pointed.

"Incline!" The inner voice spoke sternly and with its customary lightning- 40 quickness.

Lorenzo inclined all the way forward and put his head to the horse's silky mane, his body to its body, until a bullet meant for him would endanger the horse and make his death of no value. Prone he rode out through the circle of Indians, his obedience to the voice leaving him almost fearless, almost careless with joy.

But as he straightened and pressed ahead, care caught up with him again. Turning half-beast and half-divine, dividing himself like a heathen Centaur,[3] he had escaped his death once more. But was it to be always by some metamorphosis of himself that he escaped, some humiliation of his faith, some admission to strength and argumentation and not frailty? Each time when he acted so it was at 50 the command of an instinct that he took at once as the word of an angel, until too late, when he knew it was the word of the devil. He had roared like a tiger at Indians, he had submerged himself in water blowing the savage bubbles of the alligator, and they skirted him by. He had prostrated himself to appear dead, and deceived bears. But all the time God would have protected him in His own way, less hurried, more divine.

Even now he saw a serpent crossing the Trace, giving out knowing glances.

He cried, "I know you now!", and the serpent gave him one look out of which all the fire had been taken, and went away in two darts into the tangle.

He rode on, all expectation, and the voices in the throats of the wild beasts 60 went, almost without his noticing when, into words. "Praise God," they said. "Deliver us from one another." Birds especially sang of divine love which was the one ceaseless protection. "Peace, in peace" were their words so many times when they spoke from the briars, in a courteous sort of inflection, and he turned his countenance toward all perched creatures with a benevolence striving to match their own.

He rode on past the little intersecting trails, letting himself be guided by voices and by lights. It was battlesounds he heard most, sending him on, but sometimes ocean sounds, that long beat of waves that would make his heart pound and retreat as heavily as they, and he despaired again in his failure in 70 Ireland when he took a voyage and persuaded with the Catholics with his back against the door, and then ran away to their cries of "Mind the white hat!" But when he heard singing it was not the militant and sharp sound of Wesley's[4] hymns, but a soft, tireless and tender air that had no beginning and no end, and

2. Wearing them out by over-exertion.
3. A mythical beast, with the head of a man and the body of a horse.
4. John Wesley (1703–1791) and his brother Charles (1707–1788) founded Methodism and wrote many hymns.

the softness of distance, and he had pleaded with the Lord to find out if all this meant that it was wicked, but no answer had come.

Soon night would descend, and a camp-meeting ground ahead would fill with its sinners like the sky with its stars. How he hungered for them! He looked in prescience with a longing of love over the throng that waited while the flames of the torches threw change, change, change over their faces. How could he bring them enough, if it were not divine love and sufficient warning of all that could threaten them? He rode on faster. He was a filler of appointments, and he filled more and more, until his journeys up and down creation were nothing but a shuttle, driving back and forth upon the rich expanse of his vision. He was homeless by his own choice, he must be everywhere at some time, and somewhere soon. There hastening in the wilderness on his flying horse he gave the night's torch-lit crowd a premature benediction, he could not wait. He spread his arms out, one at a time for safety, and he wished, when they would all be gathered in by his tin horn blasts and the inspired words would go out over their heads, to brood above the entire and passionate life of the wide world, to become its rightful part.

He peered ahead. "Inhabitants of Time! the wilderness is your souls on earth!" he shouted ahead into treetops. "Look about you, if you would view the conditions of your spirit, put here by the good Lord to show you and afright you. These wild places and these trails of awesome loneliness lie nowhere, nowhere, but in your heart."

A dark man, who was James Murrell the outlaw, rode his horse out of a cane brake and began going along beside Lorenzo without looking at him. He had the alternately proud and aggrieved look of a man believing himself to be an instrument in the hands of a power, and when he was young he said at once to strangers that he was being used by Evil, or sometimes he stopped a traveler by shouting, "Stop! I'm the Devil!" He rode along now talking and drawing out his talk, by some deep control of the voice gradually slowing the speed of Lorenzo's horse down until both the horses were softly trotting. He would have wondered that nothing he said was heard, not knowing that Lorenzo listened only to voices of whose heavenly origin he was more certain.

Murrell riding along with his victim-to-be, Murrell riding, was Murrell talking. He told away at his long tales, with always a distance and a long length of time flowing through them, and all centered about a silent man. In each the silent man would have done a piece of evil, a robbery or a murder, in a place of long ago, and it was all made for the revelation in the end that the silent man was Murrell himself, and the long story had happened yesterday, and the place *here*— the Natchez Trace. It would only take one dawning look for the victim to see that all of this was another story and he himself had listened his way into it, and that he too was about to recede in time (to where the dread was forgotten) for some listener and to live for a listener in the long ago. Destroy the present!—that must have been the first thing that was whispered in Murrell's heart—the living moment and the man that lives in it must die before you can go on. It was his habit to bring the journey—which might even take days—to a close with a kind of ceremony. Turning his face at last into the face of the victim, for he had never seen him

before now, he would tower up with the sudden height of a man no longer the tale 120
teller but the speechless protagonist, silent at last, one degree nearer the hero.
Then he would murder the man.

But it would always start over. This man going forward was going backward
with talk. He saw nothing, observed no world at all. The two ends of his journey
pulled at him always and held him in a nowhere, half asleep, smiling and witty,
dangling his predicament. He was a murderer whose final stroke was over-long
postponed, who had to bring himself through the greatest tedium to act, as if the
whole wilderness, where he was born, were his impediment. But behind him and
before him he kept in sight a victim, he saw a man fixed and stayed at the point of
death—no matter how the man's eyes denied it, a victim, hands spreading to reach 130
as if for the first time for life. Contempt! That is what Murrell gave that man.

Lorenzo might have understood, if he had not been in haste, that Murrell in
laying hold of a man meant to solve his mystery of being. It was as if other men,
all but himself, would lighten their hold on the secret, upon assault, and let it fly
free at death. In his violence he was only treating of enigma. The violence shook
his own body first, like a force gathering, and now he turned in the saddle.

Lorenzo's despair had to be kindled as well as his ecstasy, and could not
come without that kindling. Before the awe-filled moment when the faces were
turned up under the flares, as though an angel hand tipped their chins, he had no
way of telling whether he would enter the sermon by sorrow or by joy. But at this 140
moment the face of Murrell was turned toward him, turning at last, all solitary, in
its full, and Lorenzo would have seized the man at once by his black coat and
shaken him like prey for a lost soul, so instantly was he certain that the false fire
was in his heart instead of the true fire. But Murrell, quick when he was quick,
had put his own hand out, a restraining hand, and laid it on the wavelike flesh of
the Spanish race horse, which quivered and shuddered at the touch.

They had come to a great live-oak tree at the edge of a low marsh-land. The
burning sun hung low, like a head lowered on folded arms, and over the long
reaches of violet trees the evening seemed still with thought. Lorenzo knew the
place from having seen it among many in dreams, and he stopped readily and 150
willingly. He drew rein, and Murrell drew rein, he dismounted and Murrell dismounted, he took a step, and Murrell was there too; and Lorenzo was not surprised at the closeness, how Murrell in his long dark coat and over it his dark face
darkening still, stood beside him like a brother seeking light.

But in that moment instead of two men coming to stop by the great forked
tree, there were three.

From far away, a student, Audubon,[5] had been approaching lightly on the
wilderness floor, disturbing nothing in his lightness. The long day of beauty had
led him this certain distance. A flock of purple finches that he tried for the first
moment to count went over his head. He made a spelling of the soft *pet* of the 160
ivory-billed woodpecker. He told himself always: remember.

---

5. John James Audubon (1785–1851), naturalist and artist. His *Birds of America* (1827–1838) is a classic of
art and science.

Coming upon the Trace, he looked at the high cedars, azure and still as distant smoke overhead, with their silver roots trailing down on either side like the veins of deepness in this place, and he noted some fact to his memory—this earth that wears but will not crumble or slide or turn to dust, they say it exists in one other spot in the world, Egypt—and then forgot it. He walked quietly. All life used this Trace, and he liked to see the animals move along it in direct, oblivious journeys, for they had begun it and made it, the buffalo and deer and the small running creatures before man ever knew where he wanted to go, and birds flew a great mirrored course above. Walking beneath them Audubon remembered how in the cities he had seen these very birds in his imagination, calling them up whenever he wished, even in the hard and glittering outer parlors where if an artist were humble enough to wait, some idle hand held up promised money. He walked lightly and he went as carefully as he had started at two that morning, crayon and paper, a gun, and a small bottle of spirits disposed about his body. (Note: "The mocking birds so gentle that they would scarcely move out of the way.") He looked with care; great abundance had ceased to startle him, and he could see things one by one. In Natchez they had told him of many strange and marvelous birds that were to be found here. Their descriptions had been exact, complete, and wildly varying, and he took them for inventions and believed that like all the worldly things that came out of Natchez, they would be disposed of and shamed by any man's excursion into the reality of Nature.

In the valley he appeared under the tree, a sure man, very sure and tender, as if the touch of all the earth rubbed upon him and the stains of the flowery swamp had made him so.

Lorenzo welcomed him and turned fond eyes upon him. To transmute a man into an angel was the hope that drove him all over the world and never let him flinch from a meeting or withhold good-byes for long. This hope insistently divided his life into only two parts, journey and rest. There could be no night and day and love and despair and longing and satisfaction to make partitions in the single ecstasy of this alternation. All things were speech.

"God created the world," said Lorenzo, "and it exists to give testimony. Life is the tongue: speak."

But instead of speech there happened a moment of deepest silence.

Audubon said nothing because he had gone without speaking a word for days. He did not regard his thoughts for the birds and animals as susceptible, in their first change, to words. His long playing on the flute was not in its origin a talking to himself. Rather than speak to order to or describe, he would always draw a deer with a stroke across it to communicate his need of venison to an Indian. He had only found words when he discovered that there is much otherwise lost that can be noted down each item in its own day, and he wrote often now in a journal, not wanting anything to be lost the way it had been, all the past, and he would write about a day, "Only sorry that the Sun Sets."

Murrell, his cheated hand hiding his gun, could only continue to smile at Lorenzo, but he remembered in malice that he had disguised himself once as an Evangelist, and his final words to this victim would have been, "One of my disguises was what you are."

Then in Murrell Audubon saw what he thought of as "acquired sorrow"—
that cumbrousness and darkness from which the naked Indian, coming just as he
was made from God's hand, was so lightly free. He noted the eyes—the dark kind   210
that loved to look through chinks, and saw neither closeness nor distance, light
nor shade, wonder nor familiarity. They were narrowed to contract the heart, narrowed to make an averting plan. Audubon knew the finest-drawn tendons of the
body and the working of their power, for he had touched them, and he supposed
then that in man the enlargement of the eye to see started a motion in the hands to
make or do, and that the narrowing of the eye stopped the hand and contracted
the heart. Now Murrell's eyes followed an ant on a blade of grass, up the blade and
down, many times in the single moment. Audubon had examined the Cave-In
Rock where one robber had lived his hiding life, and the air in the cave was the
cavelike air that enclosed this man, the same odor, flinty and dark. O secret life,   220
he thought—is it true that the secret is withdrawn from the true disclosure, that
man is a cave man, and that the openness I see, the ways through forests, the
rivers brimming light, the wide arches where the birds fly, are dreams of freedom?
If my origin is withheld from me, is my end to be unknown too? Is the radiance I
see closed into an interval between two darks, or can it not illuminate them both
and discover at last, though it cannot be spoken, what was thought hidden and
lost?

In that quiet moment a solitary snowy heron flew down not far away and
began to feed beside the marsh water.

At the single streak of flight, the ears of the race horse lifted, and the eyes of   230
both horses filled with the soft lights of sunset, which in the next instant were reflected in the eyes of the men too as they all looked into the west toward the
heron, and all eyes seemed infused with a sort of wildness.

Lorenzo gave the bird a triumphant look, such as a man may bestow upon
his own vision, and thought, Nearness is near, lighted in a marsh-land, feeding at
sunset. Praise God, His love has come visible.

Murrell, in suspicion pursuing all glances, blinking into a haze, saw only
whiteness ensconced in darkness, as if it were a little luminous shell that drew in
and held the eyesight. When he shaded his eyes, the brand "H.T." on his thumb
thrust itself into his own vision, and he looked at the bird with the whole plan of   240
the Mystic Rebellion darting from him as if in rays of the bright reflected light, and
he stood looking proudly, leader as he was bound to become of the slaves, the
brigands and outcasts of the entire Natchez country, with plans, dates, maps burning like a brand into his brain, and he saw himself proudly in a moment of
prophecy going down rank after rank of successively bowing slaves to unroll and
flaunt an awesome great picture of the Devil colored on a banner.

Audubon's eyes embraced the object in the distance and he could see it as
carefully as if he held it in his hand. It was a snowy heron alone out of its flock.
He watched it steadily, in his care noting the exact inevitable things. When it feeds
it muddles the water with its foot. . . . It was as if each detail about the heron hap-   250
pened slowly in time, and only once. He felt again the old stab of wonder—what
structure of life bridged the reptile's scale and the heron's feather? That knowledge
too had been lost. He watched without moving. The bird was defenseless in the

world except for the intensity of its life, and he wondered, how can heat of blood and speed of heart defend it? Then he thought, as always as if it were new and un-believable, it has nothing in space or time to prevent its flight. And he waited, knowing that some birds will wait for a sense of their presence to travel to men before they will fly away from them.

Fixed in its pure white profile it stood in the precipitous moment, a plumi-corn on its head, its breeding dress extended in rays, eating steadily the little water creatures. There was a little space between each man and the others, where they stood overwhelmed. No one could say the three had ever met, or that this mo-ment of intersection had ever come in their lives, or its promise fulfilled. But be-fore them the white heron rested in the grasses with the evening all around it, lighter and more serene than the evening, flight closed in its body, the circuit of its beauty closed, a bird seen and a bird still, its motion calm as if it were offered: Take my flight. . . .

What each of them had wanted was simply *all*. To save all souls, to destroy all men, to see and to record all life that filled this world—all, all—but now a sin-gle frail yearning seemed to go out of the three of them for a moment and to stretch toward this one snowy, shy bird in the marshes. It was as if three whirl-winds had drawn together at some center, to find there feeding in peace a snowy heron. Its own slow spiral of flight could take it away in its own time, but for a little it held them still, it laid quiet over them, and they stood for a moment un-burdened. . . .

Murrell wore no mask, for his face was that, a face that was aware while he was somnolent, a face that watched for him, and listened for him, alert and nearly brutal, the guard of a planner. He was quick without that he might be slow within, he staved off time, he wandered and plotted, and yet his whole desire mounted in him toward the end (was this the end—the sight of a bird feeding at dusk?), to-ward the instant of confession. His incessant deeds were thick in his heart now, and flinging himself to the ground he thought wearily, when all these trees are cut down, and the Trace lost, then my Conspiracy that is yet to spread itself will be disclosed, and all the stone-loaded bodies of murdered men will be pulled up, and all everywhere will know poor Murrell. His look pressed upon Lorenzo, who stared upward, and Audubon, who was taking out his gun, and his eyes squinted up to them in pleading, as if to say, "How soon may I speak, and how soon will you pity me?" Then he looked back to the bird, and he thought if it would look at him a dread penetration would fill and gratify his heart.

Audubon in each act of life was aware of the mysterious origin he half-con-cealed and half-sought for. People along the way asked him in their kindness or their rudeness if it were true, that he was born a prince, and was the Lost Dauphin[6] and some said it was his secret, and some said that that was what he wished to find out before he died. But if it was his identity that he wished to dis-cover, or if it was what a man had to seize beyond that, the way for him was by endless examination, by the care for every bird that flew in his path and every ser-

6. The heir to the throne of France.

pent that shone underfoot. Not one was enough; he looked deeper and deeper, on and on, as if for a particular beast or some legendary bird. Some men's eyes persisted in looking outward when they opened to look inward, and to their delight, there outflung was the astonishing world under the sky. When a man at last 300 brought himself to face some mirror-surface he still saw the world looking back at him, and if he continued to look, to look closer and closer, what then? The gaze that looks outward must be trained without rest, to be indomitable. It must see as slowly as Murrell's ant in the grass, as exhaustively as Lorenzo's angel of God, and then, Audubon dreamed, with his mind going to his pointed brush, it must see like this, and he tightened his hand on the trigger of the gun and pulled it, and his eyes went closed. In memory the heron was all its solitude, its total beauty. All its whiteness could be seen from all sides at once, its pure feathers were as if counted and known and their array one upon the other would never be lost. But it was not from that memory that he could paint.   310

His opening eyes met Lorenzo's, close and flashing, and it was on seeing horror deep in them, like fires in abysses, that he recognized it for the first time. He had never seen horror in its purity and clarity until now, in bright blue eyes. He went and picked up the bird. He had thought it to be a female, just as one sees the moon as female; and so it was. He put it in his bag, and started away. But Lorenzo had already gone on, leaning a-tilt on the horse which went slowly.

Murrell was left behind, but he was proud of the dispersal, as if he had done it, as he had always known that three men in simply being together and doing a thing can, by their obstinacy, take the pride out of one another. Each must go away alone, each send the others away alone. He himself had purposely kept to 320 the wildest country in the world, and would have sought it out, the loneliest road. He looked about with satisfaction, and hid. Travelers were forever innocent, he believed: that was his faith. He lay in wait; his faith was in innocence and his knowledge was out of ruin; and had these things been shaken? Now, what could possibly be outside his grasp? Churning all about him like a cloud about the sun was the great folding descent of his thought. Plans of deeds made his thoughts, and they rolled and mingled about his ears as if he heard a dark voice that rose up to overcome the wilderness voice, or was one with it. The night would soon come; and he had gone through the day.

Audubon, splattered and wet, turned back into the wilderness with the 330 heron warm under his hand, his head still light in a kind of trance. It was undeniable, on some Sunday mornings, when he turned over and over his drawings they seemed beautiful to him, through what was dramatic in the conflict of life, or what was exact. What he would draw, and what he had seen, became for a moment one to him then. Yet soon enough, and it seemed to come in that same moment, like Lorenzo's horror and the gun's firing, he knew that even the sight of the heron which surely he alone had appreciated, had not been all his belonging, and that never could any vision, even any simple sight, belong to him or to any man. He knew that the best he could make would be, after it was apart from his hand, a dead thing and not a live thing, never the essence, only a sum of parts; and that it 340 would always meet with a stranger's sight, and never be one with the beauty in any other man's head in the world. As he had seen the bird most purely at its moment of death, in some fatal way, in his care for looking outward, he saw his long labor most revealingly at the point where it met its limit. Still carefully, for he was trained to see well in the dark, he walked on into the deeper woods, noting all sights, all sounds, and was gentler than they as he went.

In the woods that echoed yet in his ears, Lorenzo riding slowly looked back. The hair rose on his head and his hands began to shake with cold, and suddenly it seemed to him that God Himself, just now, thought of the Idea of Separateness. For surely He had never thought of it before, when the little white heron was flying down to feed. He could understand God's giving Separateness first and then giving Love to follow and heal in its wonder; but God had reversed this, and given Love first and then Separateness, as though it did not matter to Him which came first. Perhaps it was that God never counted the moments of Time; Lorenzo did that, among his task of love. Time did not occur to God. Therefore—did He even know of it? How to explain Time and Separateness back to God, Who had never thought of them, Who could let the whole world come to grief in a scattering moment?

Lorenzo brought his cold hands together in a clasp and stared through the distance at the place where the bird had been as if he saw it still; as if nothing could really take away what had happened to him, the beautiful little vision of the feeding bird. Its beauty had been greater than he could account for. The sweat of rapture poured down from his forehead, and then he shouted into the marshes.

"Tempter!"

He whirled forward in the saddle and began to hurry the horse to its high speed. His camp ground was far away still, though even now they must be lighting the torches and gathering in the multitudes, so that at the appointed time he would duly appear in their midst, to deliver his address on the subject of "In that day when all hearts shall be disclosed."

Then the sun dropped below the trees, and the new moon, slender and white, hung shyly in the west.   [1942]

Question for Discussion and Writing

1. What do these three apparently different men have in common?
2. What doubts assail Lorenzo Dow as he rides toward his meeting? Underline or highlight specific passages.
3. Why does Murrell kill? What prevents him from killing Lorenzo Dow?
4. What effect does the snowy heron have on each man?
5. What do Audubon's perceptions add to our understanding of Dow and Murrell?
6. Why does Audubon kill the heron?
7. At the end of the story, Dow yells "Tempter!" Who or what is he calling "tempter"?
8. How does Welty combine interior perception and exterior reality. Does she combine them in new ways, ways not explored by, say, James Joyce, Katherine Mansfield, or Virginia Woolf? Explain.

✎ JORGE LUIS BORGES
(1899–1986)

The Garden of Forking Paths

(BASED ON A TRANSLATION BY DONALD A. YATES)

In the 1960s, Latin American literature experienced a creative and popular "boom," and among the writers responsible for its apparently sudden emergence was Jorge Luis Borges. Borges was born into a comfortable middle-class family in Buenos Aires, Argentina. He grew up bilingual, reading widely in both English and Spanish in his parents' library. Prosperity enabled the family to live in Europe from 1914–1921, the last two years in Spain, where Borges was introduced to advanced writers. He joined the post-avant-garde movement among Latin American authors who attempted to break away from European influence and establish a truly independent literature based on radical experiments with language. He also read voraciously on an amazing variety of subjects.

While working as a librarian, he began writing short stories in 1939, collected in the influential volumes *Ficciones* (1945) and *El Aleph* (1949). Most employ the fantastic to explore philosophical, literary, and aesthetic ideas. The dictator Juan Peron forced Borges from his library position in 1946; he was not able to return to it until 1955. Meanwhile, his eyesight had steadily deteriorated, and this condition, plus his weariness at writing fantasy stories, meant that for twenty years he wrote almost nothing. He traveled widely, taught at various universities, and enjoyed the fame that his brilliantly original fiction had earned. When he resumed writing, he produced realistic stories in the traditional manner.

In Borges's typical stories, character counts for relatively little. Philosophical ideas and plots borrowed from popular literary forms drive his characters, who are often portrayed as passive figures in events over which they have little control. The result is "intertextual" fiction; that is, it reflects other fiction, ideas, philosophical paradoxes, and elaborate games—traits now associated with Metafiction. In his originality and philosophical depth, Borges has been compared to such figures as Jonathan Swift (1667–1745) and Voltaire (1694–1778). His influence on world literature has been profound.

For Victoria Ocampo

On page 22 of Liddell Hart's *History of World War I*[1] you will read that an attack against the Serre-Montauban line by thirteen British divisions (supported by 1,400 artillery pieces), planned for the 24th of July, 1916, had

---

1. Borges's reference is accurate.

to be postponed until the morning of the 29th. The torrential rains, Captain Liddell Hart comments, caused this delay, an insignificant one, to be sure.

The following statement, dictated, reread, and signed by Dr. Yu Tsun, former professor of English at the Hochschule at Tsing-tao, throws an unsuspected light over the whole affair. The first two pages of the document are missing.

"... and I hung up the receiver. Immediately afterward, I recognized the voice that had answered in German. It was that of Captain Richard Madden. Madden's presence in Viktor Runeberg's apartment meant the end of our anxieties and—but this seemed, *or should have seemed,* very secondary to me—also the end of our lives. It meant that Runeberg had been arrested or murdered.[2] Before the sun set on that day, I would encounter the same fate. Madden was implacable. Or rather, he was obliged to be so. An Irishman at the service of England, a man accused of laxity and perhaps of treason, how could he fail to seize and be thankful for such a miraculous opportunity: the discovery, capture, maybe even the death of two agents of the German Empire? I went up to my room; absurdly I locked the door and threw myself on my back on the narrow iron cot. Through the window I saw the familiar roofs and the hazy six o'clock sun.

"It seemed incredible to me that that day without premonitions or symbols should be the one of my inexorable death. In spite of my dead father, in spite of having been a child in a symmetrical garden of Hai Feng, was I—now—going to die? Then I reflected that everything happens to a man precisely, precisely *now.* Centuries of centuries and only in the present do things happen; countless men in the air, on the face of the earth and the sea, and all that really is happening is happening to me. . . . The almost intolerable recollection of Madden's horselike face banished these thoughts. In the midst of my hatred and terror (it means nothing to me now to speak of terror, now that I have outwitted Richard Madden, now that my throat yearns for the noose) it occurred to me that that tumultuous and doubtless happy warrior did not suspect that I possessed the Secret. The name of the exact location of the new British artillery park on the River Ancre.[3] A bird streaked across the gray sky and blindly I turned it into an airplane and that airplane into many (against the French sky) annihilating the artillery station with vertical bombs. If only my mouth, before a bullet shattered it, could cry out that secret name so it could be heard in Germany. . . . My human voice was very weak. How might I make it carry to the ear of the Chief? To the ear of that sick and hateful man who knew nothing of Runeberg and me save that we were in Staffordshire[4] and who was waiting in vain for our report in his arid office in Berlin, endlessly examining newspapers. . . . I said out loud: *I must flee.* I sat up noiselessly, in a useless perfection of silence, as if Madden were already lying in wait for me. Something—perhaps the mere vain ostentation of proving my resources were nil—made me look through my pockets. I found what I knew I would find. The American watch, the nickel chain and the square coin, the key

---

2. A hypothesis both hateful and odd. The Prussian spy Hans Rabener, alias Viktor Runeberg, attacked with drawn automatic the bearer of the warrant for his arrest, Captain Richard Madden. The latter, in self-defense, inflicted the wound which brought about Runeberg's death [Borges's note as "editor"].

3. In northwest France; scene of several battles in World War I.

4. A county in the English midlands.

ring with the incriminating useless keys to Runeberg's apartment, the notebook, a
letter which I resolved to destroy immediately (and which I did not destroy), the
false passport, a crown,[5] two shillings and a few pence, the red and blue pencil,
the handkerchief, the revolver with one bullet. Absurdly, I took it in my hand and
felt its weight in order to fortify my courage. Vaguely I thought that a pistol shot
can be heard at a great distance. In ten minutes my plan had been developed. The   50
telephone book listed the name of the only person capable of transmitting the
message; he lived in a suburb of Fenton, less than a half hour away by train.

"I am a cowardly man. I say it now, now that I have carried to its conclusion
a plan whose perilous nature no one can deny. I know its execution was terrible. I
didn't do it for Germany, no. I care nothing for a barbarous country which imposed upon me the abjection of being a spy. Besides, I know of a man from
England—a modest man—who for me is no less great than Goethe.[6] I talked with
him for scarcely an hour, but during that hour he was Goethe. . . . I did it because
I sensed that the Chief somehow looked down upon people of my race—those innumerable ancestors who are merged within me. I wanted to prove to him that a   60
yellow man could save his armies. Besides, I had to flee from Captain Madden. His
hands and his voice could call at my door at any moment. I dressed silently, bade
farewell to myself in the mirror, went downstairs, scrutinized the peaceful street,
and went out. The station was not far from my home, but I judged it wise to take
a cab. I argued that in this way I ran less risk of being recognized; the fact is that
in the deserted street I felt visible and vulnerable, infinitely so. I remember that I
told the cab driver to stop a little before the main entrance. I got out with a deliberate, almost painful slowness; I was going to the village of Ashgrove but I bought
a ticket for a station further on. The train would leave within a very few minutes,
at eight-fifty. I hurried; the next one would leave at nine-thirty. There was hardly a   70
soul on the platform. I walked through the coaches; I remember a few farmers, a
woman dressed in mourning, a youth enthusiastically engrossed in the *Annals* of
Tacitus,[7] and a wounded, happy soldier. At last the train pulled out. A man whom
I recognized ran in vain to the end of the platform. It was Captain Richard
Madden. Shattered, trembling, I shrank into the far corner of the seat, away from
the dreaded window.

"From a state of annihilation, I passed into an almost abject happiness. I told
myself that the duel had already begun and that I had won the first encounter by
frustrating, even if for forty minutes, even if by a stroke of fate, the attack of my
adversary. I argued that this slightest of victories was a sign of an ultimate total vic-   80
tory. I argued that it was not so slight since were it not for that precious difference
in time that the train schedule gave me, I would be in prison or dead. I argued
(with no less sophistry) that my cowardly happiness proved that I was a man capable of carrying out the adventure successfully. From this weakness I derived
strength that never abandoned me. I foresee that man will resign himself each day
to more atrocious undertakings; soon there will be no one but warriors and ban-

5. A coin worth five shillings.
6. Johann Wolfgang von Goethe (1749–1832) German poet.
7. Cornelius Tacitus (A.D. 55–115), Roman historian.

dits; I give them this advice: *The author of an atrocious undertaking ought to imagine that he has already accomplished it, ought to impose upon himself a future as irrevocable as the past.* Thus I proceeded while my eyes of a man already dead registered the ebbing of that day, which was perhaps my last, and the diffusion of the night. 90 The train ran gently along, amid ash trees. It stopped, almost in the middle of the fields. No one shouted the name of the station. "Ashgrove?" I asked a few boys on the platform. "Ashgrove," they replied. I got off.

"A lamp lit up the platform but the faces of the boys were in the shadows. One questioned me. 'Are you going to Dr. Stephen Albert's house?' Without waiting for my answer, another said, 'The house is a long way from here, but you won't get lost if you take this road to the left and bear to the left at every crossroads.' I tossed them a coin (my last), descended a few stone steps and started down the lonely road. It went downhill, slowly. It was of plain dirt; overhead the branches were intertwined; the moon, low and round, seemed to accompany me. 100

"For an instant, I thought that Richard Madden in some way had penetrated my desperate plan. Very quickly, I understood that that was impossible. The instructions to turn always to the left reminded me that such was the common procedure for discovering the central point of certain labyrinths. I have some understanding of labyrinths: not for nothing am I the great grandson of that Ts'ui Pên who was governor of Yunnan[8] and who renounced worldly power in order to write a novel that might be even more heavily populated than the *Hung Lu Meng*[9] and to construct a labyrinth in which all men would become lost. Thirteen years he dedicated to these heterogeneous tasks, but the hand of a stranger murdered him—and his novel was incoherent and no one found the labyrinth. Beneath 110 English trees I meditated on that lost maze: I imagined it inviolate and perfect on the secret summit of a mountain; I imagined it erased by rice fields or beneath the water; I imagined it infinite, no longer composed of octagonal kiosks and dead-end paths, but of rivers and provinces and kingdoms. . . . I thought of a labyrinth of labyrinths, of one sinuous spreading labyrinth that would encompass the past and the future and in some way involve the stars. Absorbed in these illusory images, I forgot that I was ordained to be pursued. I felt myself to be, for an indeterminate period of time, an abstract spectator of the world. The vague, living countryside, the moon, the remaining hours of the day affected me, as well as the slope of the road which eliminated any possibility of weariness. The evening was 120 intimate, infinite. The road descended and forked among the now dimly seen meadows. A high-pitched, almost syllabic music kept coming and going with the shifting of the wind, muted by leaves and distance. I thought that a man might be an enemy of other men, of the moments of other men, but not of a country: not of fireflies, words, gardens, streams of water, sunsets. Thus I arrived before a high, rusty gate. Between the iron bars I made out a poplar grove and a kind of pavilion. I understood suddenly two things, the first trivial, the second almost unbelievable: the music was coming from the pavilion, and the music was Chinese. For pre-

8. Province in Southern China, bordering Viet Nam.
9. A novel by Ts'ao Chan (1715–1763), considered by many to be the greatest Chinese novel. It has over 30 main and four-hundred minor characters.

cisely that reason I had completely accepted it without paying it any attention. I
do not remember whether there was a bell, a push button, or whether I called by   130
clapping my hands. The sparkling music continued.

"But from the rear of the main house a lantern approached: a lantern that the
tree trunks sometimes striped and sometimes blotted out, a paper lantern that had
the form of a drum and the color of the moon. A tall man was carrying it. I didn't
see his face for the light blinded me. He opened the gate and said slowly, in my
own language: 'I see that the pious Hsi P'êng persists in correcting my solitude.
You no doubt wish to see the garden?'

"I recognized the name of one of our consuls and I replied, disconcerted,
'The garden?'

" 'The garden of forking paths.'   140

"Something stirred in my memory and I uttered with incomprehensible certainty, 'The garden of my ancestor Ts'ui Pên.'

" 'Your ancestor? Your illustrious ancestor? Come in.'

"The damp path zigzagged like those of my childhood. We came to a library
of Eastern and Western books. I recognized bound in yellow silk several volumes
of the Lost Encyclopedia, which was edited by the Third Emperor of the
Luminous Dynasty but which was never printed. The phonograph record was
spinning next to a bronze phoenix. I also recall a *famille rose* vase and another,
many centuries older, of that shade of blue which our craftsmen copied from the
potters of Persia. . . .   150

"Stephen Albert was observing me with a smile on his face. He was, as I have
said, very tall, sharp featured, with gray eyes and gray beard. He looked something
like a priest and also a sailor. He told me later that he had been a missionary in
Tientsin 'before aspiring to become a Sinologist.'[10]

"We sat down—I on a long, low divan, he with his back to the window and
a high circular clock. I calculated that my pursuer, Richard Madden, could not arrive for at least an hour. My irrevocable decision could wait.

" 'An astounding fate, that of Ts'ui Pên,' Stephen Albert said. 'Governor of his
native province, learned in astronomy, in astrology, and in the tireless interpretation of the canonical books, chess player, famous poet and calligrapher—he aban- 160
doned all this in order to compose a book and a maze. He renounced the
pleasures of both tyranny and justice, of his oft-frequented bed, of his banquets
and even of erudition—and shut himself up for thirteen years in the Pavilion of
the Limpid Solitude. When he died, his heirs found nothing save chaotic manuscripts. His family, as you may be aware, wished to consign them to the fire; but
his executor—a Taoist or Buddhist monk—insisted on their publication.'

" 'We descendants of Ts'ui,' I replied, 'continue to curse that monk. Their
publication was senseless. The book is an indeterminate heap of contradictory
drafts. I examined it once: in the third chapter the hero dies, in the fourth he is
alive. As for the other undertaking of Ts'ui Pên, his labyrinth. . . .'   170

" 'Here is the labyrinth,' he said, indicating a tall lacquered desk.

" 'An ivory labyrinth!' I exclaimed. 'A minimal labyrinth.'

10. An expert on China.

"'A labyrinth of symbols,' he corrected me. 'An invisible labyrinth of time. I, a barbarous Englishman, have been entrusted with the revelation of this diaphanous mystery. After more than a hundred years, the details are irretrievable; but it is not difficult to conjecture what happened. Ts'ui Pên must have said once: *I am withdrawing to write a book.* And another time: *I am withdrawing to construct a labyrinth.* Everyone imagined two works; to no one did it occur that the book and the maze were one and the same thing. The pavilion of the Limpid Solitude stood in the center of a garden that was perhaps intricate; that circumstance could have suggested the idea of a physical labyrinth. Ts'ui Pên died; no one in the vast territories that were his came upon the labyrinth; the confusion of the novel suggested to me that *it* was the maze. Two circumstances gave me the correct solution to the problem. One: the curious legend that Ts'ui Pên had planned to create a labyrinth which would be strictly infinite. The other: a fragment of a letter I discovered.'

"Albert rose. He turned his back on me a few moments; he opened a drawer of the black and gold desk. He turned around holding in his hand a sheet of paper that had once been crimson, but that was now pink and tenuous and cross sectioned. Ts'ui Pên's calligraphy was justly famous. I read, uncomprehendingly and eagerly, these words written with a minute brush by a man of my blood: *I leave to the various futures (not to all) my garden of forking paths.* Without a word, I returned the sheet. Albert continued: 'Before unearthing this letter, I had questioned myself about the ways in which a book can be infinite. I could think of nothing other than a cyclical volume, a circular one. A book whose last page was identical with the first, a book which had the possibility of continuing indefinitely. I remembered too that night which is at the middle of the 1001 Nights when Queen Scheherazade (through a magical oversight of the copyist) begins to relate word for word the story of the 1001 Nights, with the risk of coming once again to the night in which she is telling it, and thus on to infinity.[11] I also imagined a Platonic, hereditary work, transmitted from father to son, in which each new individual would add a chapter or correct with pious care the pages of his elders. These conjectures entertained me; but none seemed to correspond, not even remotely, to the contradictory chapters of Ts'ui Pên. In the midst of this perplexity, I received from Oxford the manuscript you have examined. I focused, naturally, on the sentence: *I leave to the various futures (not to all) my garden of forking paths.* Almost instantly, I understood: *the garden of forking paths* was the chaotic novel; the phrase *the various futures (not to all)* suggested to me the forking in time, not in space. A broad rereading of the work confirmed the theory. In all fictional works, each time a man is confronted with several alternatives, he chooses one and eliminates the others; in the fiction of the almost unfathomable Ts'ui Pên, he chooses—simultaneously— all of them. He *creates,* in this way, diverse futures, diverse times which themselves also proliferate and fork. Here, then, is the explanation of the novel's contradictions. Fang, let us say, has a secret; a stranger calls at his door; Fang resolves to kill him. Naturally, there are several possible outcomes: Fang can kill the intruder, the intruder can kill Fang, they both can be saved, they both can die, et cetera. In the work of Ts'ui Pên, all possible outcomes occur; each one is the point of departure

11. Fictional wife of a Sultan who strangled his brides after their wedding night. She tells the 1,001 tales collected in *The Arabian Nights Entertainments.*

for other forkings. Sometimes, the paths of this labyrinth converge: for example, you arrive at this house, but in one of the possible pasts you are my enemy, in another, my friend. If you will resign yourself to my incurable pronunciation, we shall read a few pages.'   220

"His face, within the vivid circle of the lamplight, was unquestionably that of an old man, but with something unshakable about it, even immortal. He read with slow precision two versions of the same epic chapter. In the first, an army marches into battle across a desolate mountain; the horror of the rocks and shadows makes the men attach little value to their lives and they gain an easy victory. In the second, the same army marches through a palace where a great party is taking place; the glowing battle seems to them a continuation of the party and they win the victory. I listened with proper veneration to these ancient narratives, perhaps less admirable in themselves than for the fact that they had been thought out by one of my own blood and were being restored to me by a man of a remote empire, in the   230 course of a desperate adventure, on a Western isle. I remember the final words, repeated in each version like a secret commandment: *Thus fought the heroes, tranquil their admirable hearts, violent their swords, resigned to kill and to die.*

"From that moment on, I felt around me and within my dark body an invisible, intangible swarming. Not the swarming of the two divergent, parallel and finally coalescent armies, but a more inaccessible, more intimate agitation that they in some manner prefigured. Stephen Albert continued: 'I don't think that your illustrious ancestor toyed idly with these variations. I don't find it probable that he would sacrifice thirteen years to the never ending execution of an experiment in rhetoric. In your country, the novel is an inferior genre; in those days it was a de-   240 spicable genre. Ts'ui Pên was a brilliant novelist, but he was also a man of letters who undoubtedly did not consider himself a mere novelist. The testimony of his contemporaries proclaims—and his life fully confirms—his metaphysical and mystical interests. Philosophic controversy usurps a good part of his novel. I know that of all problems, none disturbed him so greatly nor worked upon him so much as the abysmal problem of time. Now then, this is the *only* problem that does not appear in the pages of the *Garden*. He does not even use the word that signifies *time*. How do you explain this voluntary omission?'

"I proposed several solutions—all inadequate. We discussed them. Finally, Stephen Albert said to me: 'In a riddle whose answer is chess, what is the only   250 prohibited word?'

"I thought a moment and replied. 'The word *chess.*'

"'Precisely,' said Albert. '*The Garden of Forking Paths* is an enormous riddle, or parable, whose theme is time; this secret reason prohibits its being mentioned. To omit a word *always,* to resort to inept metaphors and obvious paraphrases, is perhaps the most emphatic way of stressing it. This is the tortuous method preferred by the oblique Ts'ui Pên in each of the meanderings of his indefatigable novel. I have compared hundreds of manuscripts, I have corrected the errors that the negligence of the copyists has introduced, I have conjectured the plan of this chaos, I have reestablished—I think I have reestablished—the original order, I   260 have translated the entire work: it is clear to me that not once does he employ the word 'time.' The explanation is obvious: *The Garden of Forking Paths* is an incomplete, but not false, image of the universe as Ts'ui Pên conceived it. In contrast to

Newton and Schopenhauer,[12] your ancestor did not believe in a uniform, absolute time. He believed in an infinite series of times, in a growing dizzying network of divergent, convergent and parallel times. This web of times that approach one another, fork, break off, or are unaware of each other for centuries, embraces *all* possibilities. We do not exist in the majority of these times; in some you exist, and not I; in others I, and not you; in others, both of us. In the present one, which a favorable fate has granted me, you have arrived at my house; in another, while crossing the garden, you found me dead; in still another, I utter these same words, but I am a mistake, a ghost.'

" 'In every one,' I pronounced, not without a tremor in my voice, 'I am grateful to you and revere you for your re-creation of the garden of Ts'ui Pên.'

" 'Not in all,' he murmured with a smile. 'Time forks perpetually toward innumerable futures. In one of them I am your enemy.'

"Once again I felt the swarming sensation of which I have spoken. It seemed to me that the humid garden that surrounded the house was infinitely saturated with invisible persons. Those persons were Albert and I, secretive, busy, and multiform in other dimensions of time. I raised my eyes and the tenuous nightmare dissolved. In the yellow and black garden there was only one man; but this man was as strong as a statue, but this man was walking up the path and he was Captain Richard Madden.

" 'The future already exists,' I replied, 'but I am your friend. Could I see the letter again?'

"Albert rose. Standing tall, he opened the drawer of the high desk; for a moment he turned his back to me. I had readied the revolver. I fired with extreme caution. Albert fell uncomplainingly, immediately. I swear his death was instantaneous—a lightning stroke.

"The rest is unreal, insignificant. Madden broke in, arrested me. I have been condemned to the gallows. I have won out abominably; I have communicated to Berlin the secret name of the city they must attack. They bombed it yesterday; I read it in the same papers that offered to England the mystery of the learned Sinologist Stephen Albert who was murdered by a stranger, Yu Tsun. The chief had deciphered this mystery. He knew my problem was to indicate (through the uproar of the war) the city called Albert, and that I had found no other means to do so than to kill a man of that name. He does not know (no one can know) my infinite contrition and weariness."

[1942]

Questions for Discussion and Writing

1. What conventions of the detective story does Borges use, and in what ways does he depart from these? What significance do you find in the departures from convention?

2. Analyze Borges's treatment of character, especially that of Dr. Yu Tsun. Does Borges intend his characters as "real people"? Explain.

---

12. Isaac Newton (1642–1727), English physicist, and Arthur Schopenhauer (1788–1869), German philosopher. In Newton's physics, time is absolute; whereas in Einstein's physics it is relative.

3. Does this story have a theme? Can it be understood at all, or is it intended as a riddle without a solution? Explain your reasons.

4. Consider the idea of "divergent, convergent, and parallel times." Is this simply a bizarre notion, or does the idea have validity?

5. Is fiction an appropriate medium for discussing philosophical ideas? Why or why not? What is the difference between an idea that is discussed and a theme that is dramatized?

❧ SHIRLEY JACKSON
(1919–1965)

The Lottery

Shirley Jackson was born into a working-class family in San Francisco; her father was a lithographer and her mother a housewife. Jackson began writing at an early age, winning a poetry prize when she was twelve years old. When she was fourteen, her family moved to Rochester, New York. After suffering depression at the University of Rochester, she withdrew from college and spent the next year disciplining herself to write a thousand words a day. In 1937, she entered Syracuse University, majored in English, and met Stanley Hyman, whom she married immediately upon graduation in 1940. After a year in New York City, the couple moved to North Bennington, Vermont, where she lived the rest of her life, writing and raising a family.

Jackson is best known for her short stories, but she was also an accomplished horror novelist and, more surprisingly, a children's author and humorist. Her light-hearted sketches based on family life were popular in such magazines as *Good Housekeeping* and *Women's Home Companion*.

Shirley Jackson wrote many novels, sketches, and stories over the course of her lifetime, but her name will always be associated with this one story, "The Lottery." When it was published in the *New Yorker* on June 26, 1948, it created a sensation. Hundreds of astonished readers wrote to the magazine or to Jackson, most expressing anger, bewilderment, or outrage. She was accused of everything from devil worship to witchcraft. Perhaps what shocked American readers more than anything was the story's setting—small-town America. Readers could imagine intolerance, scapegoating, mob rule, and ritual murder in "primitive" societies or in Nazi Germany, but not in rural America. Some gullible readers took the story literally and wanted details about where they could go to see such a lottery.

It is unfortunate that most readers know Shirley Jackson only through this story, for she was an accomplished writer whose explorations of the Gothic in everyday life are often moving and insightful. "The Lottery," however, deserves its fame, for even after nearly fifty years, it retains its power to shock and disturb.

T HE MORNING OF JUNE 27TH was clear and sunny, with the fresh warmth of a full-summer day; the flowers were blossoming profusely and the grass was richly green. The people of the village began to gather in the square, between the post office and the bank, around ten o'clock; in some towns there were so many people that the lottery took two days and had to be started on June 26th, but in this village, where there were only about three hundred people, the whole lottery took less than two hours, so it could begin at ten o'clock in the morning and still be through in time to allow the villagers to get home for noon dinner.

The children assembled first, of course. School was recently over for the summer, and the feeling of liberty sat uneasily on most of them; they tended to gather together quietly for a while before they broke into boisterous play, and their talk was still of the classroom and the teacher, of books and reprimands. Bobby Martin had already stuffed his pockets full of stones, and the other boys soon followed his example, selecting the smoothest and roundest stones; Bobby and Harry Jones and Dickie Delacroix—the villagers pronounced his name "Delacroy"—eventually made a great pile of stones in one corner of the square and guarded it against the raids of the other boys. The girls stood aside, talking among themselves, looking over their shoulders at the boys, and the very small children rolled in the dust or clung to the hands of their older brothers or sisters.

Soon the men began to gather, surveying their own children, speaking of planting and rain, tractors and taxes. They stood together, away from the pile of stones in the corner, and their jokes were quiet and they smiled rather than laughed. The women, wearing faded house dresses and sweaters, came shortly after their menfolk. They greeted one another and exchanged bits of gossip as they went to join their husbands. Soon the women, standing by their husbands, began to call to their children, and the children came reluctantly, having to be called four or five times. Bobby Martin ducked under his mother's grasping hand and ran, laughing, back to the pile of stones. His father spoke up sharply, and Bobby came quickly and took his place between his father and his oldest brother.

The lottery was conducted—as were the square dances, the teenage club, the Halloween program—by Mr. Summers, who had time and energy to devote to civic activities. He was a round-faced, jovial man and he ran the coal business, and people were sorry for him, because he had no children and his wife was a scold. When he arrived in the square, carrying the black wooden box, there was a murmur of conversation among the villagers, and he waved and called, "Little late today, folks." The postmaster, Mr. Graves, followed him, carrying a three-legged stool, and the stool was put in the center of the square and Mr. Summers set the black box down on it. The villagers kept their distance, leaving a space between themselves and the stool, and when Mr. Summers said, "Some of you fellows want to give me a hand?" there was a hesitation before two men, Mr. Martin and his oldest son, Baxter, came forward to hold the box steady on the stool while Mr. Summers stirred up the papers inside it.

The original paraphernalia for the lottery had been lost long ago, and the black box now resting on the stool had been put into use even before Old Man Warner, the oldest man in town, was born. Mr. Summers spoke frequently to the villagers about making a new box, but no one liked to upset even as much tradition as was represented by the black box. There was a story that the present box had been made with some pieces of the box that had preceded it, the one that had been constructed when the first people settled down to make a village here. Every year, after the lottery, Mr. Summers began talking again about a new box, but every year the subject was allowed to fade off without anything's being done. The black box grew shabbier each year; by now it was no longer completely black but splintered badly along one side to show the original wood color, and in some places faded or stained.

Mr. Martin and his oldest son, Baxter, held the black box securely on the stool until Mr. Summers had stirred the papers thoroughly with his hand. Because so much of the ritual had been forgotten or discarded, Mr. Summers had been successful in having slips of paper substituted for the chips of wood that had been used for generations. Chips of wood, Mr. Summers had argued, had been all very well when the village was tiny, but now that the population was more than three hundred and likely to keep on growing, it was necessary to use something that would fit more easily into the black box. The night before the lottery, Mr. Summers and Mr. Graves made up the slips of paper and put them in the box, and it was then taken to the safe of Mr. Summers's coal company and locked up until Mr. Summers was ready to take it to the square next morning. The rest of the year, the box was put away, sometimes one place, sometimes another; it had spent one year in Mr. Graves's barn and another year underfoot in the post office, and sometimes it was set on a shelf in the Martin grocery and left there.

There was a great deal of fussing to be done before Mr. Summers declared the lottery open. There were the lists to make up—of heads of families, heads of households in each family, members of each household in each family. There was the proper swearing-in of Mr. Summers by the postmaster, as the official of the lottery; at one time, some people remembered, there had been a recital of some sort, performed by the official of the lottery, a perfunctory, tuneless chant that had been rattled off duly each year; some people believed that the official of the lottery used to stand just so when he said or sang it, others believed that he was supposed to walk among the people, but years and years ago this part of the ritual had been allowed to lapse. There had been, also, a ritual salute, which the official of the lottery had had to use in addressing each person who came up to draw from the box, but this also had changed with time, until now it was felt necessary only for the official to speak to each person approaching. Mr. Summers was very good at all this; in his clean white shirt and blue jeans, with one hand resting carelessly on the black box, he seemed very proper and important as he talked interminably to Mr. Graves and the Martins.

Just as Mr. Summers finally left off talking and turned to the assembled villagers, Mrs. Hutchinson came hurriedly along the path to the square, her sweater thrown over her shoulders, and slid into place in the back of the crowd. "Clean forgot what day it was," she said to Mrs. Delacroix, who stood next to her, and they both laughed softly. "Thought my old man was out back stacking wood." Mrs. Hutchinson went on, "and then I looked out the window and the kids was gone, and then I remembered it was the twenty-seventh and came a-running." She dried her hands on her apron, and Mrs. Delacroix said, "You're in time, though. They're still talking away up there."

Mrs. Hutchinson craned her neck to see through the crowd and found her husband and children standing near the front. She tapped Mrs. Delacroix on the arm as a farewell and began to make her way through the crowd. The people separated good-humoredly to let her through; two or three people said, in voices just loud enough to be heard across the crowd, "Here comes your Missus, Hutchinson," and "Bill, she made it after all." Mrs. Hutchinson reached her husband, and Mr. Summers, who had been waiting, said cheerfully, "Thought we were going to have to get on without you, Tessie." Mrs. Hutchinson said, grinning, "Wouldn't have me leave m'dishes in the sink, now, would you, Joe?" and soft laughter ran through the crowd as the people stirred back into position after Mrs. Hutchinson's arrival.

"Well, now," Mr. Summers said soberly, "guess we better get started, get this over with, so's we can go back to work. Anybody ain't here?"

"Dunbar," several people said. "Dunbar, Dunbar."

Mr. Summers consulted his list. "Clyde Dunbar," he said. "That's right. He's broke his leg, hasn't he? Who's drawing for him?"

"Me, I guess," a woman said, and Mr. Summers turned to look at her. "Wife draws for her husband," Mr. Summers said. "Don't you have a grown boy to do it for you, Janey?" Although Mr. Summers and everyone else in the village knew the answer perfectly well, it was the business of the official of the lottery to ask such questions formally. Mr. Summers waited with an expression of polite interest while Mrs. Dunbar answered.

"Horace's not but sixteen yet," Mrs. Dunbar said regretfully. "Guess I gotta fill in for the old man this year."

"Right," Mr. Summers said. He made a note on the list he was holding. Then he asked, "Watson boy drawing this year?"

A tall boy in the crowd raised his hand. "Here," he said. "I'm drawing for m'mother and me." He blinked his eyes nervously and ducked his head as several voices in the crowd said things like "Good fellow, Jack," and "Glad to see your mother's got a man to do it."

"Well," Mr. Summers said, "guess that's everyone. Old Man Warner make it?"

"Here," a voice said, and Mr. Summers nodded.

A sudden hush fell on the crowd as Mr. Summers cleared his throat and looked at the list. "All ready?" he called. "Now, I'll read the names—heads of families first—and the men come up and take a paper out of the box. Keep the paper folded in your hand without looking at it until everyone has had a turn. Everything clear?"

The people had done it so many times that they only half-listened to the directions; most of them were quiet, wetting their lips, not looking around. Then Mr. Summers raised one hand high and said, "Adams." A man disengaged himself from the crowd and came forward. "Hi, Steve," Mr. Summers said, and Mr. Adams said, "Hi, Joe." They grinned at one another humorlessly and nervously. Then Mr. Adams reached into the black box and took out a folded paper. He held it firmly by one corner as he turned and went hastily back to his place in the crowd, where he stood a little apart from his family, not looking down at his hand.

"Allen," Mr. Summers said. "Anderson. . . . Bentham."

"Seems like there's no time at all between lotteries any more," Mrs. Delacroix   140
said to Mrs. Graves in the back row. "Seems like we got through with the last one
only last week."

"Time sure goes fast," Mrs. Graves said.

"Clark. . . . Delacroix."

"There goes my old man," Mrs. Delacroix said. She held her breath while her
husband went forward.

"Dunbar," Mr. Summers said, and Mrs. Dunbar went steadily to the box
while one of the women said, "Go on, Janey," and another said, "There she goes."

"We're next," Mrs. Graves said. She watched while Mr. Graves came around   150
from the side of the box, greeted Mr. Summers gravely, and selected a slip of paper
from the box. By now, all through the crowd there were men holding the small
folded papers in their large hands, turning them over and over nervously. Mrs.
Dunbar and her two sons stood together, Mrs. Dunbar holding the slip of paper.

"Harburt. . . . Hutchinson."

"Get up there, Bill," Mrs. Hutchinson said, and the people near her laughed.
"Jones."

"They do say," Mr. Adams said to Old Man Warner, who stood next to him,
"that over in the north village they're talking of giving up the lottery."

Old Man Warner snorted. "Pack of crazy fools," he said. "Listening to the
young folks, nothing's good enough for *them*. Next thing you know, they'll be   160
wanting to go back to living in caves, nobody work any more, live *that* way for a
while. Used to be a saying about 'Lottery in June, corn be heavy soon.' First thing
you know, we'd all be eating stewed chickweed and acorns. There's *always* been a
lottery," he added petulantly. "Bad enough to see young Joe Summers up there joking with everybody."

"Some places have already quit lotteries," Mrs. Adams said.

"Nothing but trouble in *that*," Old Man Warner said stoutly. "Pack of young
fools."

"Martin." And Bobby Martin watched his father go forward. "Overdyke. . . .
Percy."   170

"I wish they'd hurry," Mrs. Dunbar said to her older son. "I wish they'd
hurry."

"They're almost through," her son said.

"You get ready to run tell Dad," Mrs. Dunbar said.

Mr. Summers called his own name and then stepped forward precisely and
selected a slip from the box. Then he called, "Warner."

"Seventy-seventh year I been in the lottery," Old Man Warner said as he went
through the crowd. "Seventy-seventh time."

"Watson." The tall boy came awkwardly through the crowd. Someone said,
"Don't be nervous, Jack," and Mr. Summers said, "Take your time, son."   180

"Zanini."

After that, there was a long pause, a breathless pause, until Mr. Summers,
holding his slip of paper in the air, said, "All right, fellows." For a minute, no one
moved, and then all the slips of paper were opened. Suddenly, all the women
began to speak at once, saying, "Who is it?," "Who's got it?," "Is it the Dunbars?,"

"Is it the Watsons?" Then the voices began to say, "It's Hutchinson. It's Bill," "Bill Hutchinson's got it."

"Go tell your father," Mrs. Dunbar said to her older son.

People began to look around to see the Hutchinsons. Bill Hutchinson was standing quiet, staring down at the paper in his hand. Suddenly, Tessie Hutchinson shouted to Mr. Summers, "You didn't give him time enough to take any paper he wanted. I saw you. It wasn't fair!"

"Be a good sport, Tessie," Mrs. Delacroix called, and Mrs. Graves said, "All of us took the same chance."

"Shut up, Tessie," Bill Hutchinson said.

"Well, everyone," Mr. Summers said, "that was done pretty fast, and now we've got to be hurrying a little more to get done in time." He consulted his next list. "Bill," he said, "you draw for the Hutchinson family. You got any other households in the Hutchinsons?"

"There's Don and Eva," Mrs. Hutchinson yelled. "Make *them* take their chance!"

"Daughters draw with their husbands' families, Tessie," Mr. Summers said gently. "You know that as well as anyone else."

"It wasn't *fair*," Tessie said.

"I guess not, Joe," Bill Hutchinson said regretfully. "My daughter draws with her husband's family, that's only fair. And I've got no other family except the kids."

"Then, as far as drawing for families is concerned, it's you," Mr. Summers said in explanation," and as far as drawing for households is concerned, that's you, too. Right?"

"Right," Bill Hutchinson said.

"How many kids, Bill?" Mr. Summers asked formally.

"Three," Bill Hutchinson said. "There's Bill, Jr., and Nancy, and little Dave. And Tessie and me."

"All right, then," Mr. Summers said. "Harry, you got their tickets back?"

Mr. Graves nodded and held up the slips of paper. "Put them in the box, then," Mr. Summers directed. "Take Bill's and put it in."

"I think we ought to start over," Mrs. Hutchinson said, as quietly as she could "I tell you it wasn't *fair*. You didn't give him time enough to choose. *Every*body saw that."

Mr. Graves had selected the five slips and put them in the box, and he dropped all the papers but those onto the ground, where the breeze caught them and lifted them off.

"Listen, everybody," Mrs. Hutchinson was saying to the people around her.

"Ready, Bill?" Mr. Summers asked, and Bill Hutchinson, with one quick glance around at his wife and children, nodded.

"Remember," Mr. Summers said, "take the slips and keep them folded until each person has taken one. Harry, you help little Dave." Mr. Graves took the hand of the little boy, who came willingly with him up to the box. "Take a paper out of the box, Davy," Mr. Summers said. Davy put his hand into the box and laughed. "Take just *one* paper," Mr. Summers said. "Harry, you hold it for him." Mr. Graves took the child's hand and removed the folded paper from the tight fist and held it while little Dave stood next to him and looked up at him wonderingly.

"Nancy next," Mr. Summers said. Nancy was twelve, and her school friends breathed heavily as she went forward, switching her skirt, and took a slip daintily from the box. "Bill, Jr.," Mr. Summers said, and Billy, his face red and his feet over-large, nearly knocked the box over as he got a paper out. "Tessie," Mr. Summers said. She hesitated for a minute, looking around defiantly, and then set her lips and went up to the box. She snatched a paper out and held it behind her.

"Bill," Mr. Summers said, and Bill Hutchinson reached into the box and felt around, bringing his hand out at last with the slip of paper in it.   240

The crowd was quiet. A girl whispered, "I hope it's not Nancy," and the sound of the whisper reached the edges of the crowd.

"It's not the way it used to be," Old Man Warner said clearly. "People ain't the way they used to be."

"All right," Mr. Summers said. "Open the papers. Harry, you open little Dave's."

Mr. Graves opened the slip of paper and there was a general sigh through the crowd as he held it up and everyone could see that it was blank. Nancy and Bill, Jr., opened theirs at the same time, and both beamed and laughed, turning around to the crowd and holding their slips of paper above their heads.   250

"Tessie," Mr. Summers said. There was a pause, and then Mr. Summers looked at Bill Hutchinson, and Bill unfolded his paper and showed it. It was blank.

"It's Tessie," Mr. Summers said, and his voice was hushed. "Show us her paper, Bill."

Bill Hutchinson went over to his wife and forced the slip of paper out of her hand. It had a black spot on it, the black spot Mr. Summers had made the night before with the heavy pencil in the coal-company office. Bill Hutchinson held it up, and there was a stir in the crowd.

"All right, folks," Mr. Summers said. "Let's finish quickly."   260

Although the villagers had forgotten the ritual and lost the original black box, they still remembered to use stones. The pile of stones the boys had made earlier was ready; there were stones on the ground with the blowing scraps of paper that had come out of the box. Mrs. Delacroix selected a stone so large she had to pick it up with both hands and turned to Mrs. Dunbar. "Come on," she said. "Hurry up."

Mrs. Dunbar had small stones in both hands, and she said, gasping for breath, "I can't run at all. You'll have to go ahead and I'll catch up with you."

The children had stones already, and someone gave little Davy Hutchinson a few pebbles.   270

Tessie Hutchinson was in the center of a cleared space by now, and she held her hands out desperately as the villagers moved in on her. "It isn't fair," she said. A stone hit her on the side of the head.

Old Man Warner was saying, "Come on, come on, everyone." Steve Adams was in the front of the crowd of villagers, with Mrs. Graves beside him.

"It ain't fair, it isn't right," Mrs. Hutchinson screamed, and then they were upon her.   [1948]

Questions for Discussion and Writing

1. Underline or highlight passages that are especially effective in creating atmosphere. How does the atmosphere contribute to the story's effects?
2. Analyze carefully the use of suspense. How does Jackson both advance the plot and keep us guessing about the nature of the lottery until the very end?
3. Why does the village continue the tradition of the annual lottery?
4. What does the story seem to say about human cruelty? Is the story fair in its depiction of ordinary people, especially children? Explain.
5. Why do you think the story makes such a profound emotional impact on readers?

❧ HISAYE YAMAMOTO

(b. 1921)

Seventeen Syllables

Hisaye Yamamoto has published only one collection, *Seventeen Syllables and Other Stories,* but this work has distinguished her as an outstanding writer.

She was born in Redondo Beach, California, to immigrant parents. After Japan attacked Pearl Harbor in December 1941, she and her family, along with over a hundred thousand other Japanese-Americans, were forcibly "interned" by the United States government. Yamamoto's family was sent to Poston, Arizona. Later, in 1944, she and her brothers were separated from the family and sent to Massachusetts. In the camps, Yamamoto developed her interest in writing and wrote for the camps' newspapers. In 1945, the family was released and moved to Los Angeles, where she worked for three years for the Los Angeles *Tribune,* an African-American newspaper.

Yamamoto began publishing short stories and essays in 1948 in such journals as the *Kenyon Review, Arizona Quarterly,* and *Partisan Review.* She has also published poetry and prose in a variety of Japanese publications in the United States and Canada, while continuing her work as a journalist. In the 1950s, she wrote as a pacifist for *The Catholic Worker.*

"Seventeen Syllables" was cited as a "Distinctive Short Story" by *Best American Short Stories* and filmed for the Public Broadcasting System's *American Playhouse* series. In 1986, she received a lifetime achievement award from the Before Columbus Foundation. In this story, Yamamoto creates a sensitive portrait of a young girl's coming of age and explores the familial and cultural tensions that can divide immigrant families.

THE FIRST ROSIE knew that her mother had taken to writing poems was one evening when she finished one and read it aloud for her daughter's approval. It was about cats, and Rosie pretended to understand it thoroughly and appreciate

it no end, partly because she hesitated to disillusion her mother about the quantity
and quality of Japanese she had learned in all the years now that she had been
going to Japanese school every Saturday (and Wednesday, too, in the summer).
Even so, her mother must have been skeptical about the depth of Rosie's understanding, because she explained afterwards about the kind of poem she was trying
to write.

See, Rosie, she said, it was a *haiku,* a poem in which she must pack all her   10
meaning into seventeen syllables only, which were divided into three lines of five,
seven, and five syllables. In the one she had just read, she had tried to capture the
charm of a kitten, as well as comment on the superstition that owning a cat of
three colors meant good luck.

"Yes, yes, I understand. How utterly lovely," Rosie said, and her mother,
either satisfied or seeing through the deception and resigned, went back to composing.

The truth was that Rosie was lazy; English lay ready on the tongue but
Japanese had to be searched for and examined, and even then put forth tentatively
(probably to meet with laughter). It was so much easier to say yes, yes, even when   20
one meant no, no. Besides, this was what was in her mind to say: I was looking
through one of your magazines from Japan last night, Mother, and towards the
back I found some *haiku* in English that delighted me. There was one that made
me giggle off and on until I fell asleep—

It is morning, and lo!
I lie awake, comme il faut,[1]
sighing for some dough.

Now, how to reach her mother, how to communicate the melancholy song?
Rosie knew formal Japanese by fits and starts, her mother had even less English,
no French. It was much more possible to say yes, yes.   30

It developed that her mother was writing the *haiku* for a daily newspaper, the
Mainichi Shimbun, that was published in San Francisco. Los Angeles, to be sure,
was closer to the farming community in which the Hayashi family lived and several Japanese vernaculars were printed there, but Rosie's parents said they preferred the tone of the northern paper. Once a week, the *Mainichi* would have a
section devoted to *haiku,* and her mother became an extravagant contributor, taking for herself the blossoming pen name, Ume Hanazono.

So Rosie and her father lived for awhile with two women, her mother and
Ume Hanazono. Her mother (Tome Hayashi by name) kept house, cooked,
washed, and, along with her husband and the Carrascos, the Mexican family hired   40
for the harvest, did her ample share of picking tomatoes out in the sweltering
fields and boxing them in tidy strata in the cool packing shed. Ume Hanazono,
who came to life after the dinner dishes were done, was an earnest, muttering
stranger who often neglected speaking when spoken to and stayed busy at the par-

---

1. As is proper.

lor table as late as midnight scribbling with pencil on scratch paper or carefully copying characters on good paper with her fat, pale green Parker.

The new interest had some repercussions on the household routine. Before, Rosie had been accustomed to her parents and herself taking their hot baths early and going to bed almost immediately afterwards, unless her parents challenged each other to a game of flower cards or unless company dropped in. Now if her fa- 50 ther wanted to play cards, he had to resort to solitaire (at which he always cheated fearlessly), and if a group of friends came over, it was bound to contain someone who was also writing *haiku,* and the small assemblage would be split in two, her father entertaining the non-literary members and her mother comparing ecstatic notes with the visiting poet.

If they went out, it was more of the same thing. But Ume Hanazono's life span, even for a poet's, was very brief—perhaps three months at most.

One night they went over to see the Hayano family in the neighboring town to the west, an adventure both painful and attractive to Rosie. It was attractive because there were four Hayano girls, all lovely and each one named after a season of 60 the year (Haru, Natsu, Aki, Fuyu), painful because something had been wrong with Mrs. Hayano ever since the birth of her first child. Rosie would sometimes watch Mrs. Hayano, reputed to have been the belle of her native village, making her way about a room, stooped, slowly shuffling, violently trembling (*always* trembling), and she would be reminded that this woman, in this same condition, had carried and given issue to three babies. She would look wonderingly at Mr. Hayano, handsome, tall, and strong, and she would look at her four pretty friends. But it was not a matter she could come to any decision about.

On this visit, however, Mrs. Hayano sat all evening in the rocker, as motionless and unobtrusive as it was possible for her to be, and Rosie found the greater 70 part of the evening practically anaesthetic. Too, Rosie spent most of it in the girls' room, because Haru, the garrulous one, said almost as soon as the bows and other greetings were over, "Oh, you must see my new coat!"

It was a pale plaid of grey, sand, and blue, with an enormous collar, and Rosie, seeing nothing special in it, said, "Gee, how nice."

"Nice?" said Haru, indignantly. "Is that all you can say about it? It's gorgeous! And so cheap, too. Only seventeen-ninety-eight, because it was a sale. The saleslady said it was twenty-five dollars regular."

"Gee," said Rosie, Natsu, who never said much and when she said anything said it shyly, fingered the coat covetously and Haru pulled it away.   80

"Mine," she said, putting it on. She minced in the aisle between the two large beds and smiled happily. "Let's see how your mother likes it."

She broke into the front room and the adult conversation and went to stand in front of Rosie's mother, while the rest watched from the door. Rosie's mother was properly envious. "May I inherit it when you're through with it?"

Haru, pleased, giggled and said yes, she could, but Natsu reminded gravely from the door, "You promised me, Haru."

Everyone laughed but Natsu, who shamefacedly retreated into the bedroom. Haru came in laughing, taking off the coat. "We were only kidding, Natsu," she said. "Here, you try it on now."   90

After Natsu buttoned herself into the coat, inspected herself solemnly in the bureau mirror, and reluctantly shed it, Rosie, Aki, and Fuyu got their turns, and Fuyu, who was eight, drowned in it while her sisters and Rosie doubled up in amusement. They all went into the front room later, because Haru's mother qua-veringly called to her to fix the tea and rice cakes and open a can of sliced peaches for everybody. Rosie noticed that her mother and Mr. Hayano were talking to-gether at the little table—they were discussing a *haiku* that Mr. Hayano was plan-ning to send to the *Mainichi,* while her father was sitting at one end of the sofa looking through a copy of *Life,* the new picture magazine. Occasionally, her father would comment on a photograph, holding it toward Mrs. Hayano and speaking to 100 her as he always did—loudly, as though he thought someone such as she must surely be at least a trifle deaf also.

The five girls had their refreshments at the kitchen table, and it was while Rosie was showing the sisters her trick of swallowing peach slices without chew-ing (she chased each slippery crescent down with a swig of tea) that her father brought his empty teacup and untouched saucer to the sink and said, "Come on, Rosie, we're going home now."

"Already?" asked Rosie.

"Work tomorrow," he said.

He sounded irritated, and Rosie, puzzled, gulped one last yellow slice and 110 stood up to go, while the sisters began protesting, as was their wont.

"We have to get up at five-thirty," he told them, going into the front room quickly, so that they did not have their usual chance to hang onto his hands and plead for an extension of time.

Rosie, following, saw that her mother and Mr. Hayano were sipping tea and still talking together, while Mrs. Hayano concentrated, quivering, on raising the handleless Japanese cup to her lips with both her hands and lowering it back to her lap. Her father, saying nothing, went out the door, onto the bright porch, and down the steps. Her mother looked up and asked, "Where is he going?"

"Where is he going?" Rosie said. "He said we were going home now." 120

"Going home?" Her mother looked with embarrassment at Mr. Hayano and his absorbed wife and then forced a smile. "He must be tired," she said.

Haru was not giving up yet. "May Rosie stay overnight?" she asked, and Natsu, Aki, and Fuyu came to reinforce their sister's plea by helping her make a circle around Rosie's mother. Rosie, for once having no desire to stay, was relieved when her mother, apologizing to the perturbed Mr. and Mrs. Hayano for her fa-ther's abruptness at the same time, managed to shake her head no at the quartet, kindly but adamant, so that they broke their circle and let her go.

Rosie's father looked ahead into the windshield as the two joined him. "I'm sorry," her mother said. "You must be tired." Her father, stepping on the starter, 130 said nothing. "You know how I get when it's *haiku,*" she continued, "I forget what time it is." He only grunted.

As they rode homeward silently, Rosie, sitting between, felt a rush of hate for both—for her mother for begging, for her father for denying her mother. I wish this old Ford would crash, right now, she thought, then immediately, no, no, I wish my father would laugh, but it was too late: already the vision had passed through her mind of the green pick-up crumpled in the dark against one of the mighty eucalyptus trees they were just riding past, of the three contorted, bleeding bodies, one of them hers.

Rosie ran between two patches of tomatoes, her heart working more ram- 140
bunctiously than she had ever known it to. How lucky it was that Aunt Taka and Uncle Gimpachi had come tonight, though, how very lucky. Otherwise she might not have really kept her half-promise to meet Jesus Carrasco. Jesus was going to be a senior in September at the same school she went to, and his parents were the ones helping with the tomatoes this year. She and Jesus, who hardly remembered seeing each other at Cleveland High where there were so many other people and two whole grades between them, had become great friends this summer—he always had a joke for her when he periodically drove the loaded pick-up up from the fields to the shed where she was usually sorting while her mother and father did the packing, and they laughed a great deal together over infinitesimal repartee 150
during the afternoon break for chilled watermelon or ice cream in the shade of the shed.

What she enjoyed most was racing him to see which could finish picking a double row first. He, who could work faster, would tease her by slowing down until she thought she would surely pass him this time, then speeding up furiously to leave her several sprawling vines behind. Once he had made her screech hideously by crossing over, while her back was turned, to place atop the tomatoes in her green-stained bucket a truly monstrous, pale green worm (it had looked more like an infant snake). And it was when they had finished a contest this morning, after she had pantingly pointed a green finger at the immature tomatoes 160
evident in the lugs at the end of his row and he had returned the accusation (with justice), that he had startlingly brought up the matter of their possibly meeting outside the range of both their parents' dubious eyes.

"What for?" she had asked.

"I've got a secret I want to tell you," he said.

"Tell me now," she demanded.

"It won't be ready till tonight," he said.

She laughed. "Tell me tomorrow then."

"It'll be gone tomorrow," he threatened.

"Well, for seven hakes,[2] what is it?" she had asked, more than twice, and 170
when he had suggested that the packing shed would be an appropriate place to find out, she had cautiously answered maybe. She had not been certain she was going to keep the appointment until the arrival of mother's sister and her husband. Their coming seemed a sort of signal of permission, of grace, and she had definitely made up her mind to lie and leave as she was bowing them welcome.

So as soon as everyone appeared settled back for the evening, she announced loudly that she was going to the privy outside. "I'm going to the *benjo*!" and slipped out the door. And now that she was actually on her way, her heart pumped in such an undisciplined way that she could hear it with her ears. It's be-

2. A deliberate spoonerism (reversing the first letters) on "heaven's sake."

cause I'm running, she told herself, slowing to a walk. The shed was up ahead,   180
one more patch away, in the middle of the fields. Its bulk, looming in the dimness,
took on a sinisterness that was funny when Rosie reminded herself that it was only
a wooden frame with a canvas roof and three canvas walls that made a slapping
noise on breezy days.

Jesus was sitting on the narrow plank that was the sorting platform and she
went around to the other side and jumped backwards to seat herself on the rim of
a packing stand. "Well, tell me," she said without greeting, thinking her voice
sounded reassuringly familiar.

"I saw you coming out the door," Jesus said. "I heard you running part of the
way, too."   190

"Uh-huh," Rosie said. "Now tell me the secret."

"I was afraid you wouldn't come," he said.

Rosie delved around on the chicken-wire bottom of the stall for number two
tomatoes, ripe, which she was sitting beside, and came up with a left-over that felt
edible. She bit into it and began sucking out the pulp and seeds. "I'm here," she
pointed out.

"Rosie, are you sorry you came?"

"Sorry? What for?" she said. "You said you were going to tell me something."

"I will, I will," Jesus said, but his voice contained disappointment, and Rosie
fleetingly felt the older of the two, realizing a brand-new power which vanished   200
without category under her recognition.

"I have to go back in a mintue," she said. "My aunt and uncle are here from
Wintersburg. I told them I was going to the privy."

Jesus laughed. "You funny thing," he said. "You slay me!"

"Just because you have a bathroom *inside*," Rosie said. "Come on, tell me."

Chuckling, Jesus came around to lean on the stand facing her. They still
could not see each other very clearly, but Rosie noticed that Jesus became very
sober again as he took the hollow tomato from her hand and dropped it back into
the stall. When he took hold of her empty hand, she could find no words to
protest; her vocabulary had become distressingly constricted and she thought des-   210
perately that all that remained intact now was yes and no and oh, and even these
few sounds would not easily out. Thus, kissed by Jesus, Rosie fell for the first time
entirely victim to a helplessness delectable beyond speech. But the terrible, beautiful sensation lasted no more than a second, and the reality of Jesus' lips and
tongue and teeth and hands made her pull away with such strength that she
nearly tumbled.

Rosie stopped running as she approached the lights from the windows of
home. How long since she had left? She could not guess, but gasping yet, she
went into the privy in back and locked herself in. Her own breathing deafened her
in the dark, close space, and she sat and waited until she could hear at last the   220
nightly calling of the frogs and crickets. Even then, all she could think to say was
oh, my, and the pressure of Jesus' face against her face would not leave.

No one had missed her in the parlor, however, and Rosie walked in and
through quickly, announcing that she was next going to take a bath. "Your father's

in the bathhouse," her mother said, and Rosie, in her room, recalled that she had not seen him when she entered. There had been only Aunt Taka and Uncle Gimpachi with her mother at the table, drinking tea. She got her robe and straw sandals and crossed the parlor again to go outside. Her mother was telling them about the *haiku* competition in the *Mainichi* and the poem she had entered.

Rosie met her father coming out of the bathhouse, "Are you through, 230 Father?" she asked. "I was going to ask you to scrub my back."

"Scrub your own back," he said shortly, going toward the main house.

"What have I done now?" she yelled after him. She suddenly felt like doing a lot of yelling. But he did not answer, and she went into the bathhouse. Turning on the dangling light, she removed her denims and T-shirt and threw them in the big carton for dirty clothes standing next to the washing machine. Her other things she took with her into the bath compartment to wash after her bath. After she had scooped a basin of hot water from the square wooden tub, she sat on the grey ce- ment of the floor and soaped herself at exaggerated leisure, singing "Red Sails in the Sunset"[3] at the top of her voice and using da-da-da where she suspected her 240 words. Then, standing up, still singing, for she was possessed by the notion that any attempt now to analyze would result in spoilage and she believed that the larger her volume the less she would be able to hear herself think, she obtained more hot water and poured it on until she was free of lather. Only then did she allow herself to step into the steaming vat, one leg first, then the remainder of her body inch by inch until the water no longer stung and she could move around at will.

She took a long time soaking, afterwards remembering to go around outside to stoke the embers of the tin-lined fireplace beneath the tub and to throw on a few more sticks so that the water might keep its heat for her mother, and when 250 she finally returned to the parlor, she found her mother still talking *haiku* with her aunt and uncle, the three of them on another round of tea. Her father was nowhere in sight.

At Japanese school the next day (Wednesday, it was), Rosie was grave and giddy by turns. Preoccupied at her desk in the row for students on Book Eight, she made up for it at recess by performing wild mimicry for the benefit of her friend Chizuko. She held her nose and whined a witticism or two in what she con- sidered was the manner of Fred Allen[4], she assumed intoxication and a British ac- cent to go over the climax of the Rudy Vallee[5] recording of the pub conversation about William Ewart Gladstone;[6] she was the child Shirley Temple piping, "On the 260 Good Ship Lollipop";[7] she was the gentleman soprano of the Four Inkspots

3. A popular song of the time.
4. A well-known radio comedian.
5. Popular singer.
6. Gladstone (1890–1898), was four times prime minister of England.
7. Shirley Temple was a child film star in the 1930s; "On the Good Ship Lollipop" was one of her most famous songs.

trilling, "If I Didn't Care."[8] And she felt reasonably satisfied when Chizuko wept and gasped, "Oh, Rosie, you ought to be in the movies!"

Her father came after her at noon, bringing her sandwiches of minced ham and two nectarines to eat while she rode, so that she could pitch right into the sorting when they got home. The lugs were piling up, he said, and the ripe tomatoes in them would probably have to be taken to the cannery tomorrow if they were not ready for the produce haulers tonight. "This heat's not doing them any good. And we've got no time for a break today."

It *was* hot, probably the hottest day of the year, and Rosie's blouse stuck   270
damply to her back even under the protection of the canvas. But she worked as efficiently as a flawless machine and kept the stalls heaped, with one part of her mind listening in to the parental murmuring about the heat and the tomatoes and with another part planning the exact words she would say to Jesus when he drove up with the first load of the afternoon. But when at last she saw that the pick-up was coming, her hands went berserk and the tomatoes started falling in the wrong stalls, and her father said, "Hey, hey! Rosie, watch what you're doing!"

"Well, I have to go to the *benjo*," she said, hiding panic.

"Go in the weeds over there," he said, only half-joking.

"Oh, Father!" she protested.   280

"Oh, go on home," her mother said. "We'll make out for awhile."

In the privy Rosie peered though a knothole toward the fields, watching as much as she could of Jesus. Happily she thought she saw him look in the direction of the house from time to time before he finished unloading and went back toward the patch where his mother and father worked. As she was heading for the shed, a very presentable black car purred up the dirt driveway to the house and its driver motioned to her. Was this the Hayashi home, he wanted to know. She nodded. Was she a Hayashi? Yes, she said, thinking that he was good-looking man. He got out of the car with a huge, flat package and she saw that he warmly wore a business suit. "I have something here for your mother then," he said, in a more el- 290
egant Japanese than she was used to.

She told him where her mother was and he came along with her, patting his face with an immaculate white handkerchief and saying something about the coolness of San Francisco. To her surprised mother and father, he bowed and introduced himself as, among other things, the *haiku* editor of the *Mainichi Shimbun*, saying that since he had been coming as far as Los Angeles anyway, he had decided to bring her the first prize she had won in the recent contest.

"First prize?" her mother echoed, believing and not believing, pleased and overwhelmed. Handed the package with a bow, she bobbed her head up and down numerous times to express her utter gratitude.   300

"It is nothing much," he added, "but I hope it will serve as a token of our great appreciation for your contributions and our great admiration of your considerable talent."

"I am not worthy," she said, falling easily into his style. "It is I who should make some sign of my humble thanks for being permitted to contribute."

---

8. The Four Inkspots were a popular male quartet in the 1940s; "If I Didn't Care" was one of the group's biggest hits.

"No, no, to the contrary," he said, bowing again.

But Rosie's mother insisted, and then saying that she knew she was being un-orthodox, she asked if she might open the package because her curiosity was so great. Certainly she might. In fact, he would like her reaction to it, for personally, it was one of his favorite *Hiroshiges*.[9]

Rosie thought it was a pleasant picture, which looked to have been sketched with delicate quickness. There were pink clouds, containing some graceful callig-raphy, and a sea that was a pale blue except at the edges, containing four sam-pans[10] with indications of people in them. Pines edged the water and on the far-off beach there was a cluster of thatched huts towered over by pine-dotted mountains of grey and blue. The frame was scalloped and gilt.

After Rosie's mother pronounced it without peer and somewhat prodded her father into nodding agreement, she said Mr. Kuroda must at least have a cup of tea after coming all this way, and although Mr. Kuroda did not want to impose, he soon agreed that a cup of tea would be refreshing and went along with her to the house, carrying the picture for her.

"Ha, your mother's crazy!" Rosie's father said, and Rosie laughed uneasily as she resumed judgment on the tomatoes. She had emptied six lugs when he broke into an imaginary conversation with Jesus to tell her to go and remind her mother of the tomatoes, and she went slowly.

Mr. Kuroda was in his shirtsleeves expounding some *haiku* theory as he munched a rice cake, and her mother was rapt. Abashed in the great man's pres-ence, Rosie stood next to her mother's chair until her mother looked up inquir-ingly, and then she started to whisper the message, but her mother pushed her gently away and reproached, "You are not being very polite to our guest."

"Father says the tomatoes . . ." Rosie said aloud, smiling foolishly.

"Tell him I shall only be a minute," her mother said, speaking the language of Mr. Kuroda.

When Rosie carried the reply to her father, he did not seem to hear and she said again, "Mother says she'll be back in a minute."

"All right, all right," he nodded, and they worked again in silence. But sud-denly, her father uttered an incredible noise, exactly like the cork of a bottle pop-ping, and the next Rosie knew, he was stalking angrily toward the house, almost running in fact, and she chased after him crying, "Father! Father! What are you going to do?"

He stopped long enough to order her back to the shed. "Never mind!" he shouted. "Get on with the sorting!"

And from the place in the fields where she stood, frightened and vacillating, Rosie saw her father enter the house. Soon Mr. Kuroda came out alone, putting on his coat. Mr. Kuroda got into his car and backed out down the driveway onto the highway. Next her father emerged, also alone, something in his arms (it was the picture, she realized), and, going over to the bathhouse woodpile, he threw the picture on the ground and picked up the axe. Smashing the picture, glass and all (she heard the explosion faintly), he reached over for the kerosene that was used

9. Ando Hiroshige (1797–1858), Japanese painter.
10. A flat-bottomed Chinese row boat.

to encourage the bath fire and poured it over the wreckage. I am dreaming, Rosie 350
said to herself, I am dreaming, but her father, having made sure that his act of cre-
mation was irrevocable, was even then returning to the fields.

Rosie ran past him and toward the house. What had become of her mother?
She burst into the parlor and found her mother at the back window watching the
dying fire. They watched together until there remained only a feeble smoke under
the blazing sun. Her mother was very calm.

"Do you know why I married your father?" she said without turning.

"No," said Rosie. It was the most frightening question she had ever been
called upon to answer. Don't tell me now, she wanted to say, tell me tomorrow, tell
me next week, don't tell me today. But she knew she would be told now, that the 360
telling would combine with the other violence of the hot afternoon to level her
life, her world to the very ground.

It was like a story out of the magazines illustrated in sepia, which she had
consumed so greedily for a period until the information had somehow reached her
that those wretchedly unhappy autobiographies, offered to her as the testimonials
of living men and women, were largely inventions: Her mother, at nineteen, had
come to America and married her father as an alternative to suicide.

At eighteen she had been in love with the first son of one of the well-to-do
families in her village. The two had met whenever and wherever they could, secretly, because it would not have done for his family to see him favor her—her fa- 370
ther had no money; he was a drunkard and a gambler besides. She had learned
she was with child; an excellent match had already been arranged for her lover.
Despised by her family, she had given premature birth to a stillborn son, who
would be seventeen now. Her family did not turn her out, but she could no longer
project herself in any direction without refreshing in them the memory of her in-
discretion. She wrote to Aunt Taka, her favorite sister in America, threatening to
kill herself if Aunt Taka would not send for her. Aunt Taka hastily arranged a marriage with a young man of whom she knew, but lately arrived from Japan, a young
man of simple mind, it was said, but of kindly heart. The young man was never
told why his unseen betrothed was so eager to hasten the day of meeting.   380

The story was told perfectly, with neither groping for words nor untoward
passion. It was as though her mother had memorized it by heart, reciting it to herself so many times over that its nagging vileness had long since gone.

"I had a brother then?" Rosie asked, for this was what seemed to matter now;
she would think about the other later, she assured herself, pushing back the
illumination which threatened all that darkness that had hitherto been merely
mysterious or even glamorous. "A half-brother?"

"Yes."

"I would have liked a brother," she said.

Suddenly, her mother knelt on the floor and took her by the wrists. "Rosie," 390
she said urgently, "Promise me you will never marry!" Shocked more by the request than the revelation, Rosie stared at her mother's face. Jesus, Jesus, she called
silently, not certain whether she was invoking the help of the son of the Carrascos
or of God, until there returned sweetly the memory of Jesus' hand, how it had
touched her and where. Still her mother waited for an answer, holding her wrists

so tightly that her hands were going numb. She tried to pull free. Promise, her mother whispered fiercely, promise. Yes, yes, I promise, Rosie said. But for an instant she turned away, and her mother, hearing the familiar glib agreement, released her. Oh, you, you, you, her eyes and twisted mouth said, you fool. Rosie, covering her face, began at last to cry, and the embrace and consoling hand came 400 much later than she expected.   [1949]

Questions for Discussion and Writing

1. What conflicts does Rosie encounter? How are these resolved?
2. Why does Mr. Hayashi object to his wife's poetry? Are his reasons understandable, or are they motivated by jealousy and spite? Explain.
3. How does the visit to the Hayano family relate to the rest of the story?
4. What do you think Rosie's parents would say about her affection for Jesus Carrasco? How do you know?
5. What circumstances contribute to Mr. Hayashi's actions at the climax of the story? Do they in any way excuse his behavior? Explain.
6. Why does Mrs. Hayashi ask Rosie to promise never to marry?

❧ ISAAC BASHEVIS SINGER
(1904–1991)

TRANSLATED BY ISAAC ROSENBERG

The Little Shoemakers

Isaac Bashevis Singer's work reflects his Jewish heritage and the experiences of Jews over the past three hundred years. Central to his fiction is the moral struggle between tradition and breaking with the past.

He was born in 1904 in the small town of Leoncin, Poland, to deeply devout parents. They later moved to Warsaw, to a Jewish community where religious influences were strong and secular learning was regarded with suspicion. Singer chafed against this puritanical tradition, and when his older brother, Israel Joshua, introduced him to artists and intellectuals, young Isaac was fascinated. The tug of war between faith and skepticism seemed over when Singer left Hebrew seminary to translate and proofread for a literary magazine. During the next decade, however, both Israel Joshua and Isaac learned that they could not escape their cultural roots, even after emigrating to New York City in 1935. Singer's novel *The Family Moskat* (serialized in Yiddish, 1945–1948) ended a ten-year period of struggle to find his way as a writer. Wider recognition came when his story "Gimpel the Fool" was translated and published in *The Partisan Review* in 1953.

Singer's output is divided almost equally between novels and short stories, though he also wrote a number of children's books and several volumes of autobiography as well. His techniques are rooted in tradition. He wrote everything first in Yiddish. He resisted the experimentation and new techniques of Modernism and Postmodernism, preferring conventional plots, characterization, and style. There is often a feeling of the oral tale about his stories. Such is the power of his writing, however, that these tales seem fresh and new. In a world that carelessly discards the past and embraces the new, tradition itself may be an innovation. Singer was awarded the Nobel Prize for Literature in 1978.

I
THE SHOEMAKERS AND THEIR FAMILY TREE

THE FAMILY OF THE LITTLE shoemakers was famous not only in Frampol but in the outlying district—in Yanev, Kreshev, Bilgoray, and even in Zamoshoh.[1] Abba Shuster, the founder of the line, appeared in Frampol some time after Chmielnitzki's pogroms.[2] He brought himself a plot of ground on the stubby hill behind the butcher stalls, and there he built a house that remained standing until just the other day. Not that it was in such fine condition—the stone foundation settled, the small windows warped, and the shingled roof turned a moldy green and was hung with swallows' nests. The door, moreover, sank into the ground; the banisters became bowlegged; and instead of stepping up onto the threshold, one was obliged to step down. All the same, it did survive the innumerable fires that   10 devastated Frampol in the early days. But the rafters were so rotten that mushrooms grew on them, and when wood dust was needed to staunch the blood of a circumcision, one had only to break off a piece of the outer wall and rub it between one's fingers. The roof, pitched so steeply that the chimneysweep was unable to climb onto it to look after the chimney, was always catching fire from the sparks. It was only by the grace of God that the house was not overtaken by disaster.

The name of Abba Shuster is recorded, on parchment, in the annals of the Frampol Jewish community. It was his custom to make six pairs of shoes every year for distribution among widows and orphans; in recognition of his philan-   20 thropy the synagogue called him to the reading of the Torah under the honorific title, Murenu, meaning "our teacher."

His stone in the old cemetery had vanished, but the shoemakers knew a sign for the grave—nearby grew a hazelnut tree. According to the old wives, the tree sprang from Reb Abba's beard.

Reb Abba had five sons; they settled, all but one, in the neighboring towns; only Getzel remained in Frampol. He continued his father's charitable practice of making shoes for the poor, and he too was active in the gravediggers' brotherhood.

The annals go on to say that Getzel had a son, Godel, and that to Godel was

---

1. Villages in Eastern Poland.
2. Bogdan Chmielnitzki or Khmelnitski (1595–1657) led a Cossack uprising against the Jews in eastern Poland in 1648.

born Treitel, and to Treitel, Gimpel. The shoemaker's art was handed down from 30
one generation to the next. A principle was fast established in the family, requiring
the eldest son to remain at home and succeed his father at the workbench.

The shoemakers resembled one another. They were all short, sandy-haired,
and sound, honest workmen. The people of Frampol believed that Reb Abba, the
head of the line, had learned shoemaking from a master of the craft in Brod, who
divulged to him the secret of strengthening leather and making it durable. In the
cellar of their house the little shoemakers kept a vat for soaking hides. God knows
what strange chemicals they added to the tanning fluid. They did not disclose the
formula to outsiders, and it was handed on from father to son.

As it is not our business to deal with all the generations of the little shoe- 40
makers, we will confine ourselves to the last three. Reb Lippe remained without
heir till his old age, and it was taken for a certainty that the line would end with
him. But when he was in his late sixties his wife died and he married an overripe
virgin, a milkmaid, who bore him six children. The eldest son, Feivel, was quite
well to do. He was prominent in community affairs, attended all the important
meetings, and for years served as sexton of the tailors' synagogue. It was the custom in this synagogue to select a new sexton every Simchas Torah.[3] The man so
selected was honored by having a pumpkin placed on his head; the pumpkin was
set with lighted candles, and the lucky fellow was led about from house to house
and refreshed at each stop with wine and strudel or honey cakes. However, Reb 50
Feivel happened to die on Simchas Torah, the day of rejoicing over the Law, while
dutifully making these rounds; he fell flat in the marketplace, and there was no re-
viving him. Because Feivel had been a notable philanthropist, the rabbi who conducted his services declared that the candles he had borne on his head would light
his way to Paradise. The will found in his strongbox requested that when he was
carried to the cemetery, a hammer, an awl, and a last should be laid on the black
cloth over his coffin, in sign of the fact that he was a man of peaceful industry who
never cheated his customers. His will was done.

Feivel's eldest son was called Abba, after the founder. Like the rest of his
stock, he was short and thickset, with a broad yellow beard, and a high forehead 60
lined with wrinkles, such as only rabbis and shoemakers have. His eyes were also
yellow, and the overall impression he created was that of a sulky hen. Nevertheless, he was a clever workman, charitable like his forbears, and unequaled in
Frampol as a man of his word. He would never make a promise unless he was sure
he could fulfill it; when he was not sure he said: who knows, God willing, or
maybe. Furthermore he was a man of some learning. Every day he read a chapter
of the Torah in Yiddish translation and occupied his free time with chapbooks.
Abba never missed a single sermon of the traveling preachers who came to town,
and he was especially fond of the Biblical passages which were read in the synagogue during the winter months. When his wife, Pesha, read to him, of a Sabbath, 70
from the Yiddish translation of the stories in the Book of Genesis, he would imagine that he was Noah, and that his sons were Shem, Ham, and Japheth. Or else he
would see himself in the image of Abraham, Isaac, or Jacob. He often thought that
if the Almighty were to call on him to sacrifice his eldest son, Gimpel, he would

3. Or Simhat Torah: holiday marking the end of the year-long reading of the Pentateuch.

rise early in the morning and carry out his commands without delay.[4] Certainly he would have left Poland and the house of his birth and gone wandering over the earth where God sent him. He knew the story of Joseph and his brothers by heart, but he never tired of reading it over again. He envied the ancients because the King of the Universe revealed Himself to them and performed miracles for their sake, but consoled himself by thinking that from him, Abba, to the Patriarchs, 80 there stretched an unbroken chain of generations—as if he too were part of the Bible. He sprang from Jacob's[5] loins; he and his sons were of the seed whose number had become like the sand and the stars. He was living in exile because the Jews of the Holy Land had sinned, but he awaited the Redemption, and he would be ready when the time came.

Abba was by far the best shoemaker in Frampol. His boots were always a perfect fit, never too tight or too roomy. People who suffered from chilblains, corns, or varicose veins were especially pleased with his work, claiming that his shoes relieved them. He despised the new styles, the gimcrack boots and slippers with fancy heels and poorly stitched soles that fell apart with the first rain. His 90 customers were respectable burghers of Frampol or peasants from the surrounding villages, and they deserved the best. He took their measurements with a knotted string, as in the old days. Most of the Frampol women wore wigs, but his wife, Pesha, covered her head with a bonnet as well. She bore him seven sons, and he named them after his forefathers—Gimpel, Getzel, Treitel, Godel, Feivel, Lippe, and Chananiah. They were all short and sandy-haired like their father. Abba predicted that he would turn them into shoemakers, and as a man of his word he let them look on at the workbench while they were still quite young, and at times taught them the old maxim—good work is never wasted.

He spent sixteen hours a day at the bench, a sack spread on his knees, goug- 100 ing holes with the awl, sewing with a wire needle, tinting and polishing the leather or scraping it with a piece of glass; and while he worked he hummed snatches from the canticles of the Days of Awe. Usually the cat huddled nearby and watched the proceedings as though she were looking after him. Her mother and grandmother had caught mice, in their time, for the little shoemakers. Abba could look down the hill through the window and see the whole town and a considerable distance beyond, as far as the road to Bilgoray and the pine woods. He observed the groups of matrons who gathered every morning at the butcher stalls and the young men and idlers who went in and out of the courtyard of the synagogue; the girls going to the pump to draw water for tea, and the women hurrying 110 at dusk to the ritual bath.

Evenings, when the sun was setting, the house would be pervaded by a dusky glow. Rays of light danced in the corners, flicked across the ceiling, and set Abba's beard gleaming with the color of spun gold. Pesha, Abba's wife, would be cooking kasha[6] and soup in the kitchen, the children would be playing, neighboring women and girls would go in and out of the house. Abba would rise from his work, wash his hands, put on his long coat, and go off to the tailors' synagogue for

---

4. God commanded Abraham to sacrifice his son Isaac as a test of his faith.
5. Son of Isaac and patriarch of Israel.
6. Buckwheat porridge.

evening prayers. He knew that the wide world was full of strange cities and distant lands, that Frampol was actually no bigger than a dot in a small prayer book; but it seemed to him that his little town was the navel of the universe and that his own house stood at the very center. He often thought that when the Messiah came to lead the Jews to the Land of Israel, he, Abba, would stay behind in Frampol, in his own house, on his own hill. Only on the Sabbath and on holy days would he step into a cloud and let himself be flown to Jerusalem.

II
ABBA AND HIS SEVEN SONS

Since Gimpel was the eldest, and therefore destined to succeed his father, he came foremost in Abba's concern. He sent him to the best Hebrew teachers and even hired a tutor who taught him the elements of Yiddish, Polish, Russian, and arithmetic. Abba himself led the boy down into the cellar and showed him the formula for adding chemicals and various kinds of bark to the tanning fluid. He revealed to him that in most cases the right foot is larger than the left, and that the source of all trouble in the fitting of shoes is usually to be found in the big toes. Then he taught Gimpel the principles for cutting soles and inner soles, snub-toed and pointed shoes, high heels and low; and for fitting customers with flat feet, bunions, hammer toes, and calluses.

On Fridays, when there was always a rush to work to get out, the older boys would leave cheder[7] at ten in the morning and help their father in the shop. Pesha baked hallah and prepared their lunch. She would grasp the first loaf and carry it, hot from the oven, blowing on it all the while and tossing it from hand to hand, to show it to Abba, holding it up, front and back, till he nodded approval. Then she would return with a ladle and let him sample the fish soup, or ask him to taste a crumb of freshly baked cake. Pesha valued his judgment. When she went to buy cloth for herself or the children she brought home swatches for him to choose. Even before going to the butcher she asked his opinion—what should she get, breast or roast, flank or ribs? She consulted him not out of fear or because she had no mind of her own, but simply because she had learned that he always knew what he was talking about. Even when she was sure he was wrong, he would turn out to be right, after all. He never browbeat her, but merely cast a glance to let her know when she was being a fool. This was also the way he handled the children. A strap hung on the wall, but he seldom made use of it; he had his way by kindness. Even strangers respected him. The merchants sold him hides at a fair price and presented no objections when he asked for credit. His own customers trusted him and paid his prices without a murmur. He was always called sixth to the reading of the Torah in the tailors' synagogue—a considerable honor—and when he pledged or was assessed for money, it was never neccessary to remind him. He paid up, without fail, right after the Sabbath. The town soon learned of his virtues, and though he was nothing but a plain shoemaker and, if the truth be told, something of an ignoramus, they treated him as they would a distinguished man.

When Gimpel turned thirteen, Abba girded the boy's loins in sackcloth and

7. Hebrew school.

put him to work at the bench. After Gimpel, Getzel, Treitel, Godel, and Feivel be- 160
came apprentices. Though they were his own sons and he supported them out of
his earnings, he nevertheless paid them a wage. The two youngest boys, Lippe and
Chananiah, were still attending the elementary cheder, but they too lent a hand at
hammering pegs. Abba and Pesha were proud of them. In the morning the six
workers trooped into the kitchen for breakfast, washed their six pairs of hands
with the appropriate benediction, and their six mouths chewed the roasted groats[8]
and corn bread.

Abba loved to place his two youngest boys one on each knee, and sing an
old Frampol song to them:

A mother had
Ten little boys, 170
Oh, Lord, ten little boys!

The first one was Avremele,
The second one was Berele,
The third one was called Gimpele,
The fourth one was called Dovid'l
The fifth one was called Hershele . . .

And all the boys came in on the chorus:

Oh, Lord, Hershele!

Now that he had apprentices, Abba turned out more work, and his income
grew. Living was cheap in Frampol, and since the peasants often made him a pre- 180
sent of a measure of corn or a roll of butter, a sack of potatoes or a pot of honey, a
hen or a goose, he was able to save some money on food. As their prosperity increased, Pesha began to talk of rebuilding the house. The rooms were too narrow,
the ceiling was too low. The floor shook underfoot. Plaster was peeling off the
walls, and all sorts of maggots and worms crawled through the woodwork. They
lived in constant fear that the ceiling would fall on their heads. Even though they
kept a cat, the place was infested with mice. Pesha insisted that they tear down
this ruin and build a larger house.

Abba did not immediately say no. He told his wife he would think it over.
But after doing so, he expressed the opinion that he would rather keep things as 190
they were. First of all, he was afraid to tear down the house, because this might
bring bad luck. Second, he feared the evil eye—people were grudging and envious
enough. Third, he found it hard to part with the home in which his parents and
grandparents, and the whole family, stretching back for generations, had lived and
died. He knew every corner of the house, each crack and wrinkle. When one layer
of paint peeled off the wall, another, of a different color, was exposed; and behind
this layer, still another. The walls were like an album in which the fortunes of the
family had been recorded. The attic was stuffed with heirlooms—tables and

8. Cracked grain.

chairs, cobbler's benches and lasts, whetstones and knives, old clothes, pots, pans, bedding, salting boards, cradles. Sacks full of torn prayer books lay spilled on the 200 floor.

Abba loved to climb up to the attic on a hot summer's day. Spiders spun great webs, and the sunlight, filtering in through cracks, fell upon the threads in rainbows. Everything lay under a thick coat of dust. When he listened attentively he would hear a whispering, a murmuring and soft scratching, as of some unseen creature engaged in endless activity, conversing in an unearthly tongue. He was sure that the souls of his forefathers kept watch over the house. In much the same way he loved the ground on which it stood. The weeds were as high as a man's head. There was a dense growth of hairy and brambly vegetation all about the place—the very leaves and twigs would catch hold of one's clothing as though 210 with teeth and claws. Flies and midges swarmed in the air and the ground crawled with worms and snakes of all descriptions. Ants had raised their hills in this thicket; field mice had dug their holes. A pear tree grew in the midst of this wilderness; every year, at the time of the Feast of the Tabernacle,[9] it yielded small fruit with the taste and hardness of wood. Birds and bees flew over this jungle, great big golden-bellied flies. Toadstools sprang up after each rain. The ground was unkept, but an unseen hand guarded its fertility.

When Abba stood here looking up at the summer sky, losing himself in contemplation of the clouds, shaped like sailboats, flocks of sheep, brooms, and elephant herds, he felt the presence of God, His providence and His mercy. He could 220 virtually see the Almighty seated on His throne of glory, the earth serving Him as a footstool. Satan was vanquished; the angels sang hymns. The Book of Memory in which were recorded all the deeds of men lay open. From time to time, at sunset, it even seemed to Abba that he saw the river of fire in the nether world. Flames leaped up from the burning coals; a wave of fire rose, flooding the shores. When he listened closely he was sure he heard the muffled cries of sinners and the derisive laughter of the evil host.

No, this was good enough for Abba Shuster. There was nothing to change. Let everything stand as it had stood for ages, until he lived out his allotted time and was buried in the cemetery among his ancestors, who had shod the sacred 230 community and whose good name was preserved not only in Frampol but in the surrounding district.

III

GIMPEL EMIGRATES TO AMERICA

Therefore the proverb says: Man proposes, God disposes.

One day while Abba was working on a boot, his eldest son, Gimpel, came into the shop. His freckled face was heated, his sandy hair disheveled under the skullcap. Instead of taking his place at the bench, he stopped at his father's side, regarded him hesitantly, and at last said, "Father, I must tell you something."

"Well, I'm not stopping you," replied Abba.

"Father," he cried, "I'm going to America."

---

9. Held in the autumn.

Abba dropped his work. This was the last thing he expected to hear, and up 240
went his eyebrows.

"What happened? Did you rob someone? Did you get into a fight?"

"No, Father."

"Then why are you running away?"

"There's no future for me in Frampol."

"Why not? You know a trade. God willing, you'll marry some day. You have
everything to look forward to."

"I'm sick of small towns; I'm sick of the people. This is nothing but a stinking swamp."

"When they get around to draining it," said Abba, "there won't be any more 250
swamp."

"No, Father, that's not what I mean."

"Then what do you mean?" cried Abba angrily. "Speak up!"

The boy spoke up, but Abba couldn't understand a word of it. He laid into
synagogue and state with such venom, Abba could only imagine that the poor soul
was possessed: the Hebrew teachers beat the children; the women empty their
slop pails right outside the door; the shopkeepers loiter in the streets; there are no
toilets anywhere, and the public relieves itself as it pleases, behind the bathhouse
or out in the open, encouraging epidemics and plagues. He made fun of Ezreal the
healer and of Mecheles the marriage broker, nor did he spare the rabbinical court 260
and the bath attendant, the washerwoman and the overseer of the poorhouse, the
professions and the benevolent societies.

At first Abba was afraid that the boy had lost his mind, but the longer he
continued his harangue, the clearer it became that he had strayed from the path of
righteousness. Jacob Reifman, the atheist, used to hold forth in Shebreshin, not far
from Frampol. A pupil of his, a detractor of Israel, was in the habit of visiting an
aunt in Frampol and had gathered quite a following among the good-for-nothings.
It had never occurred to Abba that his Gimpel might fall in with this gang.

"What do you say, Father?" asked Gimpel.

Abba thought it over. He knew that there was no use arguing with Gimpel, 270
and he remembered the proverb: A rotten apple spoils the barrel. "Well," he
replied, "what can I do? If you want to go, go. I won't stop you."

And he resumed his work.

But Pesha did not give in so easily. She begged Gimpel not to go so far away;
she wept and implored him not to bring shame on the family. She even ran to the
cemetery, to the graves of her forefathers, to seek the intercession of the dead. But
she was finally convinced that Abba was right: it was no use arguing. Gimpel's face
had turned hard as leather, and a mean light showed in his yellow eyes. He had
become a stranger in his own home. He spent that night out with friends, and returned in the morning to pack his prayer shawl and phylacteries,[10] a few shirts, a 280
blanket, and some hard-boiled eggs—and he was all set to go. He had saved
enough money for passage. When his mother saw that it was settled, she urged
him to take at least a jar of preserves, a bottle of cherry juice, bedding, pillows.

---

10. A box containing passages of scripture worn on the arm or forehead.

But Gimpel refused. He was going to steal over the border into Germany, and he stood a better chance if he traveled light. In short, he kissed his mother, said goodbye to his brothers and friends, and off he went. Abba, not wanting to part with his son in anger, took him in the wagon to the station at Reivetz. The train arrived in the middle of the night with a hissing and whistling, a racket and din. Abba took the headlights of the locomotive for the eyes of a hideous devil, and shied away from the funnels with their columns of sparks and smoke and their clouds of steam. The blinding lights only intensified the darkness. Gimpel ran around with his baggage like a madman, and his father ran after him. At the last moment the boy kissed his father's hand, and Abba called after him, into the darkness, "Good luck! Don't forsake your religion!"

The train pulled out, leaving a smell of smoke in Abba's nostrils and a ringing in his ears. The earth trembled under his feet. As though the boy had been dragged off by demons! When he returned home and Pesha fell on him, weeping, he said to her, "The Lord gave and the Lord has taken away . . ."

Months passed without word from Gimpel. Abba knew that this was the way with young men when they leave home—they forget their dearest ones. As the proverb says: Out of sight, out of mind. He doubted that he would ever hear from him, but one day a letter came from America. Abba recognized his son's handwriting. Gimpel wrote that he crossed the border safely, that he saw many strange cities and spent four weeks on board ship, living on potatoes and herring because he did not want to touch improper food. The ocean was very deep and the waves as high as the sky. He saw flying fish but no mermaids or mermen, and he did not hear them singing. New York is a big city, the houses reach into the clouds. The trains go over the roofs. The Gentiles speak English. No one walks with his eyes on the ground, everybody holds his head high. He met a lot of his countrymen in New York; they all wear short coats. He too. The trade he learned at home has come in very handy. He is *all right;* he is earning a living. He will write again, a long letter. He kisses his father and mother and his brothers, and sends regards to his friends.

A friendly letter, after all.

In his second letter Gimpel announced that he had fallen in love with a girl and bought her a diamond ring. Her name is Bessie; she comes from Rumania; and she works *at dresses.* Abba put on his spectacles with the brass frames and spent a long time puzzling this out. Where did the boy learn so many English words? The third letter stated that he was married and that *a reverend* had performed the service. He enclosed a snapshot of himself and wife.

Abba could not believe it. His son was wearing a gentleman's coat and a high hat. The bride was dressed like a countess in a white dress, with train and veil; she held a bouquet of flowers in her hand. Pesha took one look at the snapshot and began to cry. Gimpel's brothers gaped. Neighbors came running, and friends from all over town: they could have sworn that Gimpel had been spirited away by magic to a land of gold, where he had taken a princess to wife—just as in the storybooks the pack merchants brought to town.

To make a long story short, Gimpel induced Getzel to come to America, and

Getzel brought over Treitel; Godel followed Treitel, and Feivel, Godel; and then all
five brothers brought the young Lippe and Chananiah across. Pesha lived only for   330
the mail. She fastened a charity box to the doorpost, and whenever a letter came
she dropped a coin through the slot. Abba worked all alone. He no longer needed
apprentices because he now had few expenses and could afford to earn less; in
fact, he could have given up work altogether, as his sons sent him money from
abroad. Nevertheless he rose at his usual early hour and remained at the bench
until late in the evening. His hammer sounded away, joined by the cricket on the
hearth, the mouse in its hole, the shingles crackling on the roof. But his mind
reeled. For generations the little shoemakers had lived in Frampol. Suddenly the
birds had flown the coop. Was this a punishment, a judgment, on him? Did it
make sense?   340

Abba bored a hole, stuck in a peg, and murmured, "So—you, Abba know
what you're doing and God does not? Shame on you, fool! His will be done.
Amen!"

IV

THE SACK OF FRAMPOL

Almost forty years went by. Pesha had long since died of cholera, during the
Austrian occupation. And Abba's sons had grown rich in America. They wrote
every week, begging him to come and join them, but he remained in Frampol, in
the same old house on the stubby hill. His own grave lay ready, next to Pesha's,
among the little shoemakers; the stone had already been raised; only the date was
missing. Abba put up a bench by the side of her grave, and on the eve of Rosh
Hashanah[11] or during fasts, he went there to pray and read Lamentations. He   350
loved it in the cemetery. The sky was so much clearer and loftier than in town, and
a great, meaningful silence rose from the consecrated ground and the old gravestone overgrown with moss. He loved to sit and look at the tall white birches,
which trembled even when no breeze blew, and at the crows balancing in the
branches, like black fruit. Before she died Pesha made him promise that he would
not remarry and that he would come regularly to her grave with news of the children. He kept his promise. He would stretch out alongside the mound and whisper into her ear, as if she were still alive, "Gimpel has another grandchild. Getzel's
youngest daughter is engaged, thank God . . ."

The house on the hill was nearly in ruins. The beams had rotted away, and   360
the roof had to be supported by stone posts. Two of the three windows were
boarded over because it was no longer possible to fit glass to the frames. The floor
was all but gone, and the bare ground lay exposed to the feet. The pear tree in the
garden had withered; the trunk and branches were covered with scales. The garden itself was now overgrown with poisonous berries and grapes, and there was a
profusion of the burrs that children throw about on Tishe b'Av. People swore they
saw strange fires burning there at night, and claimed that the attic was full of bats

---

11. The Jewish New Year.

which fly into girls' hair. Be that as it may, an owl certainly did hoot somewhere near the house. The neighbors repeatedly warned Abba to move out of this ruin before it was too late—the least wind might knock it over. They pleaded with him to give up working—his sons were showering him with money. But Abba stubbornly rose at dawn and continued at the shoemaker's bench. Although yellow hair does not readily change color, Abba's beard had turned completely white, and the white, staining, had turned yellow again. His brows had sprouted like brushes and hid his eyes, and his high forehead was like a piece of yellow parchment. But he had not lost his touch. He could still turn out a stout shoe with a broad heel, even if it did take a little longer. He bored holes with awl, stitched with the needle, hammered his pegs, and in a hoarse voice sang the old shoemaker's song:

> A mother bought a billygoat,
> The shochet killed the billygoat,
> Oh, Lord, the billygoat!
> Avremele took its ears,
> Berele took its lung,
> Gimpele took the gullet,
> And Dovid'l took the tongue,
> Hershele took the neck . . .

As there was no one to join him, he now sang the chorus alone:

> Oh, Lord, the billygoat!

His friends urged him to hire a servant, but he would not take a strange woman into the house. Occasionally one of the neighbor women came in to sweep and dust, but even this was too much for him. He got used to being alone. He learned to cook for himself and would prepare soup on the tripod, and on Fridays even put up the pudding for the Sabbath. Best of all, he liked to sit alone at the bench and follow the course of his thoughts, which had become more and more tangled with the years. Day and night he carried on conversations with himself. One voice asked questions, the other answered. Clever words came to his mind, sharp, timely expressions full of the wisdom of age, as though his grandfathers had come to life again and were conducting their endless disputations inside his head on matters pertaining to this world and the next. All his thoughts ran on one theme: What is life and what is death, what is time that goes on without stopping, and how far away is America? His eyes would close; the hammer would fall out of his hand; but he would still hear the cobbler's characteristic rapping—a soft tap, a louder one, and a third, louder still—as if a ghost sat at his side, mending unseen shoes. When one of the neighbors asked him why he did not go to join his sons, he would point to the heap on the bench and say. "Nu, and the shoes? Who will mend them?"

Years passed, and he had no idea how or where they vanished. Traveling preachers passed through Frampol with disturbing news of the outside world. In the tailors' synagogue, which Abba still attended, the young men spoke of war and anti-Semitic decrees, of Jews flocking to Palestine. Peasants who had been Abba's 410 customers for years suddenly deserted him and took their trade to Polish shoe- makers. And one day the old man heard that a new world war was imminent. Hitler—may his name vanish!—had raised his legions of barbarians and was threatening to grab up Poland. This scourge of Israel had expelled the Jews from Germany, as in the days of Spain. The old man thought of the Messiah and became terribly excited. Who knows? Perhaps this was the battle of Gog and Magog?[12] Maybe the Messiah really was coming and the dead would rise again! He saw the graves opening and the little shoemakers stepping forth—Abba, Getzel, Treitel, Gimpel, his grandfather, his own father. He called them all into his house and set out brandy and cakes. His wife, Pesha, was ashamed to find the house in such 420 condition, but "Never mind," he assured her, "we'll get someone to sweep up. As long as we're all together!" Suddenly a cloud appears, envelops the town of Frampol—synagogue, house of study, ritual bath, all the Jewish homes, his own among them—and carries the whole settlement off to the Holy Land. Imagine his amazement when he encounters his sons from America. They fall at his feet, cry- ing, "Forgive us, Father!"

When Abba pictured this event his hammer quickened in tempo. He saw the little shoemakers dress for the Sabbath in silks and satins, in flowing robes with broad sashes, and go forth rejoicing in Jerusalem. They pray in the Temple of Solomon, drink the wine of Paradise, and eat of the mighty steer and Leviathan. 430 The ancient Jochanan the shoemaker, renowned for his piety and wisdom, greets the family and engages them in a discussion of Torah and shoemaking. Sabbath over, the whole clan returns to Frampol, which has become part of the Land of Israel, and reenters the old home. Even though the house is as small as ever, it has miraculously grown roomy enough, like the hide of a deer, as it is written in the Book. They all work at one bench, Abbas, Gimpels, Getzels, Godels, the Treitels and the Lippes, sewing golden sandals for the daughters of Zion and lordly boots for the sons. The Messiah himself calls on the little shoemakers and has them take his measure for a pair of silken slippers.

One morning, while Abba was wandering among his thoughts, he heard a 440 tremendous crash. The old man shook in his bones: the blast of the Messiah's trumpet! He dropped the boot he had been working on and ran out in ecstasy. But it was not Elijah the Prophet proclaiming the Messiah. Nazi planes were bombing Frampol. Panic spread through the town. A bomb fell near the synagogue, so loud that Abba felt his brain shudder in his skull. Hell opened before him. There was a blaze of lightning, followed by a blast that illuminated all of Frampol. A black cloud rose over the courtyard of the synagogue. Flocks of birds flapped about in the sky. The forest was burning. Looking down from his hill, Abba saw the or- chards under great columns of smoke. The apple trees were blossoming and burn- ing. Several men who stood near him threw themselves down on the ground and 450 shouted to him to do the same. He did not hear them; they were moving their lips in dumbshow. Shaking with fright, his knees knocking together, he reentered the

12. Mythical warring powers, Eziekiel 38:2.

house and packed a sack with his prayer shawl and phylacteries, a shirt, his shoe-maker's tools, and the paper money he had put away in the straw mattress. Then he took up a stick, kissed the mezuzah,[13] and walked out the door. It was a mira-cle that he was not killed, the house caught fire the moment he left. The roof swung out like a lid, uncovering the attic with its treasures. The walls collapsed. Abba turned about and saw the shelf of sacred books go up in flames. The black-ened pages turned in the air, glowing with fiery letters like the Torah given to the Jews on Mount Sinai. 460

V

ACROSS THE OCEAN

From that day on, Abba's life was transformed beyond recognition—it was like a story he had read in the Bible, a fantastic tale heard from the lips of a visiting preacher. He had abandoned the house of his forefathers and the place of his birth and, staff in hand, gone wandering into the world like the Patriarch Abraham. The havoc in Frampol and the surrounding villages brought Sodom and Gomorrah to mind, burning like a fiery furnace. He spent his nights in the cemetery together with the other Jews, lying with his head on a gravestone—he too, as Jacob did at Beth-El, on the way from Beer Sheba to Haran.[14]

On Rosh Hashanah the Frampol Jews held services in the forest, with Abba leading the most solemn prayer of the Eighteen Benedictions because he was the 470 only one with a prayer shawl. He stood under a pine tree, which served as an alter, and in a hoarse voice intoned the litany of the Days of Awe. A cuckoo and wood-pecker accompanied him, and all the birds roundabout twittered, whistled, and screeched. Late summer gossamers wafted through the air and trailed onto Abba's beard. From time to time a lowing sounded through the forest, like a blast on the ram's horn. As the Day of Atonement drew near, the Jews of Frampol rose at mid-night to say the prayer of forgiveness, reciting it in fragments, whatever they could remember. The horses in the surrounding pastures whinnied and neighed, frogs croaked in the cool night. Distant gunfire sounded intermittently; the clouds shone red. Meteors fell; flashes of lightning played across the sky. Half-starved lit- 480 tle children, exhausted from crying, took sick and died in their mother's arms. There were many burials in the open fields. A woman gave birth.

Abba felt he had become his own great-great-grandfather, who had fled Chmielnitzki's pogroms, and whose name is recorded in the annals of Frampol. He was ready to offer himself in Sanctification of the Name. He dreamed of priests and Inquisitions, and when the wind blew among the branches he heard martyred Jews crying out, "Hear, O Israel, the Lord our God, the Lord is One!"

Fortunately Abba was able to help a good many Jews with his money and shoemaker's tools. With the money they hired wagons and fled south, toward Rumania; but often they had to walk long distances, and their shoes gave out. 490

13. A container fixed to a door post containing verses from Deuteronomy.
14. Jacob had his famous dream at Beth-El; he fled from Beer Sheba to Haran to avoid the wrath of his brother Esau.

Abba would stop under a tree and take up his tools. With God's help, they surmounted danger and crossed the Rumanian frontier at night. The next morning, the day before Yom Kippur,[15] an old widow took Abba into her house. A telegram was sent to Abba's sons in America, informing them that their father was safe.

You may be sure that Abba's sons moved heaven and earth to rescue the old man. When they learned of his whereabouts they ran to Washington and with great difficulty obtained a visa for him; then they wired a sum of money to the consul in Bucharest, begging him to help their father. The consul sent a courier to Abba, and he was put on the train to Bucharest. There he was held a week, then transferred to an Italian seaport where he was shorn and deloused and had his clothes steamed. He was put on board the last ship for the United States.

It was a long and severe journey. The train from Rumania to Italy dragged on, uphill and down, for thirty-six hours. He was given food, but for fear of touching anything ritually unclean he ate nothing at all. His phylacteries and prayer shawl got lost, and with them he lost all track of time and could no longer distinguish between Sabbath and weekdays. Apparently he was the only Jewish passenger on board. There was a man on the ship who spoke German, but Abba could not understand him.

It was a stormy crossing. Abba spent almost the whole time lying down, and frequently vomited gall, though he took nothing but dry crusts and water. He would doze off and awake to the sound of the engines throbbing day and night, to the long, threatening signal blasts, which reeked of fire and brimstone. The door of his cabin was constantly slamming to and fro, as though an imp were swinging on it. The glassware in the cupboard trembled and danced; the walls shook; the deck rocked like a cradle.

During the day Abba kept watch at the porthole over his bunk. The ship would leap up as if mounting the sky, and the torn sky would fall as though the world were returning to original chaos. Then the ship would plunge back into the ocean, and once again the firmament would be divided from the waters, as in the Book of Genesis. The waves were a sulphurous yellow and black. Now they would saw-tooth out to the horizon like a mountain range, reminding Abba of the psalmist's words: "The mountains skipped like rams, the little hills like lambs." Then they would come heaving back, as in the miraculous Parting of the Waters. Abba had little learning, but Biblical references ran through his mind, and he saw himself as the prophet Jonah, who fled before God. He too lay in the belly of a whale and, like Jonah, prayed to God for deliverance. Then it would seem to him that this was not ocean but limitless desert, crawling with serpents, monsters, and dragons, as it is written in Deuteronomy. He hardly slept a wink at night. When he got up to relieve himself, he would feel faint and lose his balance. With great difficulty he would regain his feet and, his knees buckling under, go wandering, lost, down the narrow, winding corridor, groaning and calling for help until a sailor led him back to the cabin. Whenever this happened he was sure that he was dying. He would not even receive decent Jewish burial, but be dumped in the ocean. And he made his confession, beating his knotty fist on his chest and exclaiming, "Forgive me, Father!"

15. Last day of ten days of atonement.

Just as he was unable to remember when he began his voyage, so he was unaware when it came to an end. The ship had already been made fast to the dock in New York Harbor, but Abba hadn't the vaguest notion of this. He saw huge buildings and towers, but mistook them for the pyramids of Egypt. A tall man in a white hat came into the cabin and shouted something at him, but he remained motionless. At last they helped him dress and led him out on deck, where his sons and daughters-in-law and grandchildren were waiting. Abba was bewildered; a crowd of Polish landowners, counts and countesses, Gentile boys and girls, leaped at him, hugged him, and kissed him, crying out in a strange language, which was both Yiddish and not Yiddish. They half-led, half-carried him away, and placed him in a car. Other cars arrived, packed with Abba's kinfolk, and they set out, speeding like shot arrows over bridges, rivers, and roofs. Buildings rose up and receded, as if by magic, some of the buildings touching the sky. Whole cities lay spread out before him; Abba thought of Pithom and Rameses.[16] The car sped so fast, it seemed to him that people in the streets were moving backward. The air was full of thunder and lightning; a banging and trumpeting, it was a wedding and a conflagration at once. The nations had gone wild, a heathen festival . . .

His sons were crowding around him. He saw them as in a fog and did not know them. Short men with white hair. They shouted, as if he were deaf.

"I'm Gimpel!"

"Getzel!"

"Feivel!"

The old man closed his eyes and made no answer. Their voices ran together; everything was turning pell-mell. topsy-turvy. Suddenly he thought of Jacob arriving in Egypt, where he was met by Pharaoh's[17] chariots. He felt, he had lived through the same experience in a previous incarnation. His beard began to tremble; a hoarse sob rose from his chest. A forgotten passage from the Bible stuck in his gullet.

Blindly he embraced one of his sons and sobbed out, "Is this you? Alive?"

He had meant to say: "Now let me die, since I have seen thy face, because thou art yet alive."

VI

THE AMERICAN HERITAGE

Abba's sons lived on the outskirts of a town in New Jersey. Their seven homes, surrounded by gardens, stood on the shore of a lake. Every day they drove to the shoe factory, owned by Gimpel, but on the day of Abba's arrival they took a holiday and prepared a feast in his honor. It was to be held in Gimpel's house, in full compliance with the dietary laws. Gimpel's wife, Bessie, whose father had been a Hebrew teacher in the old country, remembered all the rituals and observed them carefully, going so far to cover her head with a kerchief. Her sisters-in-law

---

16. Cities in Egypt where the Hebrews built storehouses for Pharoah.

17. Fleeing famine, Jacob brought his family to Egypt where his son Joseph was an important official; see Genesis 47:7.

did the same, and Abba's sons put the skullcaps they had once worn during holy days. The grandchildren and great-grandchildren, who did not know a word of Yiddish, actually learned a few phrases. They had heard the legends of Frampol and the little shoemakers and the first Abba of the family line. Even the Gentiles in the neighborhood were fairly well acquainted with this history. In the ads Gimpel published in the papers, he had proudly disclosed that his family belonged to the shoemaking aristocracy: 580

> Our experience dates back three hundred years to the Polish city of Brod,
> where our ancestor, Abba, learned the craft from a local master. The community
> of Frampol, in which our family worked at its trade for fifteen generations,
> bestowed on him the title of Master in recognition of his charitable services.
> This sense of public responsibility has always gone hand in hand with our
> devotion to the highest principles of the craft and our strict policy of honest
> dealing with our customers.

The day Abba arrived, the papers in Elizabeth carried a notice to the effect that the seven brothers of the famous shoe company were welcoming their father from Poland. Gimpel received a mass of congratulatory telegrams from rival man-   590
ufacturers, relatives, and friends.

It was an extraordinary feast. Three tables were spread in Gimpel's dining room; one for the old man, his sons, and daughters-in-law, another for the grand-children, and the third for the great-grandchildren. Although it was broad day-light, the tables were set with candles—red, blue, yellow, green—and their flames were reflected from the dishes and silverware, the crystal glasses and the wine cups, the decanters reminiscent of the Passover Seder.[18] There was an abundance of flowers in every available corner. To be sure, the daughters-in-law would have preferred to see Abba properly dressed for the occasion, but Gimpel put his foot down, and Abba was allowed to spend his first day in the familiar long coat,   600
Frampol style. Even so, Gimpel hired a photographer to take pictures of the ban-quet—for publication in the newspapers—and invited a rabbi and cantor to the feast to honor the old man with traditional song.

Abba sat in an armchair at the head of the table. Gimpel and Getzel brought in a bowl and poured water over his hands for the benediction before eating. The food was served on silver trays, carried by colored women. All sorts of fruit juices and salads were set before the old man, sweet brandies, cognac, caviar. But Pharaoh, Joseph, Potiphar's wife, the Land of Goshen, the chief baker, and the chief butler spun round and round his head. His hands trembled so that he was unable to feed himself, and Gimpel had to help him. No matter how often his sons   610
spoke to him, he still could not tell them apart. Whenever the phone rang he jumped—the Nazis were bombing Frampol. The entire house was whirling round and round like a carousel; the tables were standing on the ceiling and everyone sat upside down. His face sickly pale in the light of the candles and the electric bulbs. He fell asleep soon after the soup course, while the chicken was being served. Quickly they led him to the bedroom, undressed him, and called a doctor.

---

18. The ceremony and meal celebrating the Jews' escape from Egypt; Exodus.

He spent several weeks in bed, in and out of consciousness, fitfully dozing as in a fever. He even lacked the strength to say his prayers. There was a nurse at his bedside day and night. Eventually he recovered enough to take a few steps out-doors, in front of the house, but his senses remained disordered. He would walk 620 into clothes closets, lock himself into the bathroom and forget how to come out; the doorbell and the radio frightened him; and he suffered constant anxiety be-cause of the cars that raced past the house. One day Gimpel brought him to a syn-agogue ten miles away, but even here he was bewildered. The sexton was clean-shaven; the candelabra held electric lights; there was no courtyard, no faucet for washing one's hands, no stove to stand around. The cantor, instead of singing like a cantor should, babbled and croaked. The congregation wore tiny little prayer shawls, like scarves around their necks. Abba was sure he had been hauled into church to be converted . . .

When spring came and he was no better, the daughters-in-law began to hint 630 that it wouldn't be such a bad idea to put him in a home. But something unfore-seen took place. One day, as he happened to open a closet, he noticed a sack lying on the floor which seemed somehow familiar. He looked again and recognized his shoemaker's equipment from Frampol: last, hammer and nails, his knife and pli-ers, the file and the awl, even a broken-down shoe. Abba felt a tremor of excite-ment; he could hardly believe his eyes. He sat down on a footstool and began to poke about with fingers grown clumsy and stale. When Bessie came in and found him playing with a dirty old shoe, she burst out laughing.

"What are you doing, Father? Be careful, you'll cut yourself, God forbid!"

That day Abba did not lie in bed dozing. He worked busily till evening and 640 even ate his usual piece of chicken with greater appetite. He smiled at the grand-children when they came in to see what he was doing. The next morning, when Gimpel told his brothers how their father had returned to his old habits, they laughed and thought nothing more of it—but the activity soon proved to be the old man's salvation. He kept at it day after day without tiring, hunting up old shoes in the clothes closets and begging his sons to supply him with leather and tools. When they gave in, he mended every last pair of shoes in the house—man, woman, and child's. After the Passover holidays the brothers got together and de-cided to build a little hut in the yard. They furnished it with a cobbler's bench, a stock of leather soles and hides, nails, dyes, brushes—everything even remotely 650 useful in the craft.

Abba took on new life. His daughters-in-law cried, he looked fifteen years younger. As in the Frampol days, he now rose at dawn, said his prayers, and got right to work. Once again he used a knotted string as a measuring tape. The first pair of shoes, which he made for Bessie, became the talk of the neighborhood. She had always complained of her feet, but this pair, she insisted, were the most com-fortable shoes she had ever worn. The other girls soon followed her example and also had themselves fitted. Then came the grandchildren. Even some of the Gentile neighbors came to Abba when they heard that in sheer joy of the work he was turning out custom-made shoes. He had to communicate with them, for the 660 most part, in gestures, but they got along very well. As for the younger grandchil-dren and the great-grandchildren, they had long been in the habit of standing at the door to watch him work. Now he was earning money, and he plied them with candies and toys. He even whittled a stylus and began to instruct them in the elements of Hebrew and piety.

One Sunday, Gimpel came into the workshop and, no more than half in earnest, rolled up his sleeves and joined Abba at the bench. The other brothers were not to be outdone, and on the following Sunday eight work stools were set up in the hut. Abba's sons spread sackcloth aprons on their knees and went to work, cutting soles and shaping heels, boring holes and hammering pegs, as in the good old days. The women stood outside, laughing, but they took pride in their men, and the children were fascinated. The sun streamed in through the windows, and motes of dust danced in the light. In the high spring sky, lofting over the grass and the water, floated clouds in the form of brooms, sailboats, flocks of sheep, herds of elephants. Bird sang; flies buzzed; butterflies fluttered about.

Abba raised his dense eyebrows, and sad eyes looked around at his heirs, the seven shoemakers: Gimpel, Getzel, Treitel, Godel, Feivel, Lippe, and Chananiah. Their hair was white, though yellow streaks remained. No, praise God, they had not become idolaters in Egypt. They had not forgotten their heritage, nor had they lost themselves among the unworthy. The old man rattled and bumbled deep in his chest, and suddenly began to sing in a stifled, hoarse voice:

> *A mother had*
> *Ten little boys,*
> *Oh, Lord, ten little boys!*
>
> *The sixth one was called Velvele,*
> *The seventh one was Zeinvele,*
> *The eighth one was called Chenele,*
> *The ninth one was called Tevele,*
> *The tenth one was called Judele . . .*

And Abba's sons came in on the chorus:

> *Oh, Lord, Judele!*   [1954]

———————

Questions for Discussion and Writing

1. Abba Feivel likes to imagine himself a Biblical patriarch and in fact does resemble one in some ways. What is the effect of this comparison? What point might Singer be suggesting by this device?
2. What does the house symbolize? Can the land around it be compared to the Garden of Eden? Explain.
3. Why does Abba have so much difficulty adjusting to America?
4. Why does Abba "recover" when he begins making shoes again?
5. What values does the story uphold?
6. What does the story suggest about the nature and value of tradition?
7. Compare this story to the Book of Job.

❧ FLANNERY O'CONNOR

(1925–1964)

Good Country People

Flannery O'Connor was a devout Roman Catholic who saw her stories as parables in which she wrestled with the relation of religion to violence.

Born in Savannah, Georgia, on a large dairy farm, O'Connor's earliest memories were of a news crew sent to film her pet chicken which could walk forwards and backwards. She later admitted that the incident probably initiated her interest in the maimed and grotesque. Her father died when she was sixteen, of lupus, a hereditary disease to which O'Connor herself would later fall victim. She earned a B.A. in social science in 1945 and in 1947 completed a Master of Fine Arts degree from the Iowa Writers' Workshop. Her thesis (six short stories) won a cash prize and an option with a publisher for her first novel. In 1948, she joined the writers' colony at Yaddo in Sarasota Springs, New York, where she met Robert Lowell, Alfred Kazin, and Robert Giroux, who was to become her editor at Farrar, Straus, and Giroux. In 1951, after falling ill, she moved to a farm outside Milledgeville, Georgia.

The central critical problem with O'Connor's work is to reconcile her stated intent of writing Christian fiction with the black humor and violence of her stories. Some critics see no contradiction—accepting the violence and grotesque characters as evidence of a world in need of faith and grace. Others find such a solution unconvincing and either try to reinterpret her Christianity or emphasize the apparent contradiction between her beliefs and her stories. O'Connor herself countered by saying that violence for her was not sensationalism but a way of awakening her characters to the realities of their unexamined lives. Moreover, she often published in Catholic magazines to counter the emphasis there on simple, didactic stories that glossed over the difficulties of faith in a secular age.

"Good Country People" demonstrates the tensions and perhaps the contradictions in O'Connor's fictional world—as well as the compelling power of her vision and technique.

B ESIDES THE NEUTRAL EXPRESSION that she wore when she was alone, Mrs. Freeman had two others, forward and reverse, that she used for all her human dealings. Her forward expression was steady and driving like the advance of a heavy truck. Her eyes never swerved to left or right but turned as the story turned as if they followed a yellow line down the center of it. She seldom used the other expression because it was not often necessary for her to retract a statement, but when she did, her face came to a complete stop, there was an almost imperceptible movement of her black eyes, during which they seemed to be receding, and then the observer would see that Mrs. Freeman, though she might stand there as

real as several grain sacks thrown on top of each other, was no longer there in   10
spirit. As for getting anything across to her when this was the case, Mrs. Hopewell
had given it up. She might talk her head off. Mrs. Freeman could never be brought
to admit herself wrong on any point. She would stand there and if she could be
brought to say anything, it was something like, "Well, I wouldn't of said it was and
I wouldn't of said it wasn't," or letting her gaze range over the top kitchen shelf
where there was an assortment of dusty bottles, she might remark, "I see you ain't
ate many of them figs you put up last summer."

They carried on their most important business in the kitchen at breakfast.
Every morning Mrs. Hopewell got up at seven o'clock and lit her gas heater and
Joy's. Joy was her daughter, a large blonde girl who had an artificial leg. Mrs.   20
Hopewell thought of her as a child though she was thirty-two years old and highly
educated. Joy would get up while her mother was eating and lumber into the
bathroom and slam the door, and before long, Mrs. Freeman would arrive at the
back door. Joy would hear her mother call, "Come on in," and then they would
talk for a while in low voices that were indistinguishable in the bathroom. By the
time Joy came in, they had usually finished the weather report and were on one or
the other of Mrs. Freeman's daughters, Glynese or Carramae. Joy called them
Glycerin and Caramel. Glynese, a redhead, was eighteen and had many admirers;
Carramae, a blonde, was only fifteen but already married and pregnant. She could
not keep anything on her stomach. Every morning Mrs. Freeman told Mrs.   30
Hopewell how many times she had vomited since the last report.

Mrs. Hopewell liked to tell people that Glynese and Carramae were two of
the finest girls she knew and that Mrs. Freeman was a *lady* and that she was never
ashamed to take her anywhere or introduce her to anybody they might meet. Then
she would tell how she had happened to hire the Freemans in the first place and
how they were a godsend to her and how she had had them four years. The reason
for her keeping them so long was that they were not trash. They were good country people. She had telephoned the man whose name they had given as a reference
and he had told her that Mr. Freeman was a good farmer but that his wife was the
nosiest woman ever to walk the earth. "She's got to be into everything," the man   40
said. "If she don't get there before the dust settles, you can bet she's dead, that's all.
She'll want to know all your business. I can stand him real good," he had said,
"but me nor my wife neither could have stood that woman one more minute on
this place." That had put Mrs. Hopewell off for a few days.

She had hired them in the end because there were no other applicants but
she had made up her mind beforehand exactly how she would handle the woman.
Since she was the type who had to be into everything, then, Mrs. Hopewell had
decided, she would not only let her be into everything, she would *see to it* that she
was into everything—she would give her the responsibility of everything, she
would put her in charge. Mrs. Hopewell had no bad qualities of her own but she   50
was able to use other people's in such a constructive way that she never felt the
lack. She had hired the Freemans and she had kept them four years.

Nothing is perfect. This was one of Mrs. Hopewell's favorite sayings. Another
was: that is life! And still another, the most important, was: well, other people
have their opinions too. She would make these statements, usually at the table, in

a tone of gentle insistence as if no one held them but her, and the large hulking Joy, whose constant outrage had obliterated every expression from her face, would stare just a little to the side of her, her eyes icy blue, with the look of someone who has achieved blindness by an act of will and means to keep it.

When Mrs. Hopewell said to Mrs. Freeman that life was like that, Mrs. 60 Freeman would say, "I always said so myself." Nothing had been arrived at by anyone that had not first been arrived at by her. She was quicker than Mr. Freeman. When Mrs. Hopewell said to her after they had been on the place awhile, "You know, you're the wheel behind the wheel," and winked, Mrs. Freeman had said, "I know it. I've always been quick. It's some that are quicker than others."

"Everybody is different," Mrs. Hopewell said.

"Yes, most people is," Mrs. Freeman said.

"It takes all kinds to make the world."

"I always said it did myself."

The girl was used to this kind of dialogue for breakfast and more of it for 70 dinner; sometimes they had it for supper too. When they had no guest they ate in the kitchen because that was easier. Mrs. Freeman always managed to arrive at some point during the meal and to watch them finish it. She would stand in the doorway if it were summer but in the winter she would stand with one elbow on top of the refrigerator and look down on them, or she would stand by the gas heater, lifting the back of her skirt slightly. Occasionally she would stand against the wall and roll her head from side to side. At no time was she in any hurry to leave. All this was very trying on Mrs. Hopewell but she was a woman of great patience. She realized that nothing is perfect and that in the Freemans she had good country people and that if, in this day and age, you get good country people, you 80 had better hang onto them.

She had had plenty of experience with trash. Before the Freemans she had averaged one tenant family a year. The wives of these farmers were not the kind you would want to be around you for very long. Mrs. Hopewell, who had divorced her husband long ago, needed someone to walk over the fields with her; and when Joy had to be impressed for these services, her remarks were usually so ugly and her face so glum that Mrs. Hopewell would say, "If you can't come pleasantly, I don't want you at all," to which the girl, standing square and rigid-shouldered with her neck thrust slightly forward, would reply, "If you want me, here I am—LIKE I AM."   90

Mrs. Hopewell excused this attitude because of the leg (which had been shot off in a hunting accident when Joy was ten). It was hard for Mrs. Hopewell to realize that her child was thirty-two now and that for more than twenty years she had had only one leg. She thought of her still as a child because it tore her heart to think instead of the poor stout girl in her thirties who had never danced a step or had any *normal* good times. Her name was really Joy but as soon as she was twenty-one and away from home, she had had it legally changed. Mrs. Hopewell was certain that she had thought and thought until she had hit upon the ugliest name in any language. Then she had gone and had the beautiful name, Joy, changed without telling her mother until after she had done it. Her legal name 100 was Hulga.

When Mrs. Hopewell thought the name, Hulga, she thought of the broad blank hull of a battleship. She would not use it. She continued to call her Joy to which the girl responded but in a purely mechanical way.

Hulga had learned to tolerate Mrs. Freeman, who saved her from taking walks with her mother. Even Glynese and Carramae were useful when they occupied attention that might otherwise have been directed at her. At first she had thought she could not stand Mrs. Freeman for she had found that it was not possible to be rude to her. Mrs. Freeman would take on strange resentments and for days together she would be sullen but the source of her displeasure was always obscure; a direct attack, a positive leer, blatant ugliness to her face—these never touched her. And without warning one day, she began calling her Hulga.

She did not call her that in front of Mrs. Hopewell who would have been incensed but when she and the girl happened to be out of the house together, she would say something and add the name Hulga to the end of it, and the big spectacled Joy-Hulga would scowl and redden as if her privacy had been intruded upon. She considered the name her personal affair. She had arrived at it first purely on the basis of its ugly sound and then the full genius of its fitness had struck her. She had a vision of the name working like the ugly sweating Vulcan who stayed in the furnace and to whom, presumably, the goddess had to come when called. She saw it as the name of her highest creative act. One of her major triumphs was that her mother had not been able to turn her dust into Joy, but the greater one was that she had been able to turn it herself into Hulga. However, Mrs. Freeman's relish for using the name only irritated her. It was as if Mrs. Freeman's beady steel-pointed eyes had penetrated far enough behind her face to reach some secret fact. Something about her seemed to fascinate Mrs. Freeman and then one day Hulga realized that it was the artificial leg. Mrs. Freeman had a special fondness for the details of secret infections, hidden deformities, assaults upon children. Of diseases, she preferred the lingering or incurable. Hulga had heard Mrs. Hopewell give her the details of the hunting accident, how the leg had been literally blasted off, how she had never lost consciousness. Mrs. Freeman could listen to it any time as if it had happened an hour ago.

When Hulga stumped into the kitchen in the morning (she could walk without making the awful noise but she made it—Mrs. Hopewell was certain—because it was ugly-sounding), she glanced at them and did not speak. Mrs. Hopewell would be in her red kimono with her hair tied around her head in rags. She would be sitting at the table, finishing her breakfast and Mrs. Freeman would be hanging by her elbow outward from the refrigerator, looking down at the table. Hulga always put her eggs on the stove to boil and then stood over them with her arms folded, and Mrs. Hopewell would look at her—a kind of indirect gaze divided between her and Mrs. Freeman—and would think that if she would only keep herself up a little, she wouldn't be so bad looking. There was nothing wrong with her face that a pleasant expression wouldn't help. Mrs. Hopewell said that people who looked on the bright side of things would be beautiful even if they were not.

Whenever she looked at Joy this way, she could not help but feel that it would have been better if the child had not taken the Ph.D. It had certainly not brought her out any and now that she had it, there was no more excuse for her to go to school again. Mrs. Hopewell thought it was nice for girls to go to school to have a good time but Joy had "gone through." Anyhow, she would not have been strong enough to go again. The doctors had told Mrs. Hopewell that with the best of care, Joy might see forty-five. She had a weak heart. Joy had made it plain that if it had not been for this condition, she would be far from these red hills and good country people. She would be in a university lecturing to people who knew what she was talking about. And Mrs. Hopewell could very well picture her there, looking like a scarecrow and lecturing to more of the same. Here she went about all day in a six-year-old skirt and a yellow sweat shirt with a faded cowboy on a horse embossed on it. She thought this was funny; Mrs. Hopewell thought it was idiotic and showed simply that she was still a child. She was brilliant but she didn't have a grain of sense. It seemed to Mrs. Hopewell that every year she grew less like other people and more like herself—bloated, rude, and squint-eyed. And she said such strange things! To her own mother she had said—without warning, without excuse, standing up in the middle of a meal with her face purple and her mouth half full—"Woman! do you ever look inside? Do you ever look inside and see what you are *not*? God!" she had cried sinking down again and staring at her plate, "Malebranche[1] was right: we are not our own light. We are not our own light!" Mrs. Hopewell had no idea to this day what brought that on. She had only made the remark, hoping Joy would take it in, that a smile never hurt anyone.

The girl had taken the Ph.D. in philosophy and this left Mrs. Hopewell at a complete loss. You could say, "My daughter is a nurse," or "My daughter is a school teacher," or even, "My daughter is a chemical engineer." You could not say, "My daughter is a philosopher." That was something that had ended with the Greeks and Romans. All day Joy sat on her neck in a deep chair, reading. Sometimes she went for walks but she didn't like dogs or cats or birds or flowers or nature or nice young men. She looked at nice young men as if she could smell their stupidity.

One day Mrs. Hopewell had picked up one of the books the girl had just put down and opening it at random, she read, "Science, on the other hand, has to assert its soberness and seriousness afresh and declare that it is concerned solely with what-is. Nothing—how can it be for science anything but a horror and a phantasm? If science is right, then one thing stands firm: science wishes to know nothing of nothing. Such is after all the strictly scientific approach to Nothing. We know it by wishing to know nothing of Nothing." These words had been underlined with a blue pencil and they worked on Mrs. Hopewell like some evil incantation in gibberish. She shut the book quickly and went out of the room as if she were having a chill.

This morning when the girl came in, Mrs. Freeman was on Carramae. "She thrown up four times after supper," she said, "and was up twice in the night after three o'clock. Yesterday she didn't do nothing but ramble in the bureau drawer. All she did. Stand up there and see what she could run up on."

"She's got to eat," Mrs. Hopewell muttered, sipping her coffee, while she watched Joy's back at the stove. She was wondering what the child had said to the

1. Nicolas Malebranche (1638–1715), French philosopher.

Bible salesman. She could not imagine what kind of a conversation she could possibly have had with him.

He was a tall gaunt hatless youth who had called yesterday to sell them a
Bible. He had appeared at the door, carrying a large black suitcase that weighted
him so heavily on one side that he had to brace himself against the door facing. He
seemed on the point of collapse but he said in a cheerful voice, "Good morning,
Mrs. Cedars!" and set the suitcase down on the mat. He was not a bad-looking
young man though he had on a bright blue suit and yellow socks that were not
pulled up far enough. He had prominent face bones and a streak of sticky-looking 200
brown hair falling across his forehead.

"I'm Mrs. Hopewell," she said.

"Oh!" he said, pretending to look puzzled but with his eyes sparkling, "I saw
it said 'The Cedars,' on the mailbox so I thought you was Mrs. Cedars!" and he
burst out in a pleasant laugh. He picked up the satchel and under cover of a pant,
he fell forward into her hall. It was rather as if the suitcase had moved first, jerking him after it. "Mrs. Hopewell!" he said and grabbed her hand. "I hope you are
well!" and he laughed again and then all at once his face sobered completely. He
paused and gave her a straight earnest look and said, "Lady, I've come to speak of
serious things."   210

"Well, come in," she muttered, none too pleased because her dinner was almost ready. He came into the parlor and sat down on the edge of a straight chair
and put the suitcase between his feet and glanced around the room as if he were
sizing her up by it. Her silver gleamed on the two sideboards; she decided he had
never been in a room as elegant as this.

"Mrs. Hopewell," he began, using her name in a way that sounded almost intimate, "I know you believe in Christian service."

"Well yes," she murmured.

"I know," he said and paused, looking very wise with his head cocked on
one side, "that you're a good woman. Friends have told me."   220

Mrs. Hopewell never liked to be taken for a fool. "What are you selling?" she
asked.

"Bibles," the young man said and his eye raced around the room before he
added, "I see you have no family Bible in your parlor, I see that is the one lack you
got!"

Mrs. Hopewell could not say, "My daughter is an atheist and won't let me
keep the Bible in the parlor." She said, stiffening slightly, "I keep my Bible by my
bedside." This was not the truth. It was in the attic somewhere.

"Lady," he said, "the word of God ought to be in the parlor."

"Well, I think that's a matter of taste," she began. "I think . . .'   230

"Lady," he said, "for a Christian, the word of God ought to be in every room
in the house besides in his heart. I know you're a Christian because I can see it in
every line of your face."

She stood up and said, "Well, young man, I don't want to buy a Bible and I
smell my dinner burning."

He didn't get up. He began to twist his hands and looking down at them, he
said softly, "Well lady, I'll tell you the truth—not many people want to buy one

nowadays and besides, I know I'm real simple. I don't know how to say a thing but to say it. I'm just a country boy." He glanced up into her unfriendly face. "People like you don't like to fool with country people like me!"

"Why!" she cried, "good country people are the salt of the earth! Besides, we all have different ways of doing, it takes all kinds to make the world go 'round. That's life!"

"You said a mouthful," he said.

"Why, I think there aren't enough good country people in the world!" she said, stirred. "I think that's what's wrong with it!"

His face had brightened. "I didn't introduce myself," he said. "I'm Manley Pointer from out in the country around Willohobie, not even from a place, just from near a place."

"You wait a minute," she said. "I have to see about my dinner." She went out to the kitchen and found Joy standing near the door where she had been listening.

"Get rid of the salt of the earth," she said, "and let's eat."

Mrs. Hopewell gave her a pained look and turned the heat down under the vegetables. "I can't be rude to anybody," she murmured and went back into the parlor.

He had opened the suitcase and was sitting with a Bible on each knee.

"You might as well put those up," she told him. "I don't want one."

"I appreciate your honesty," he said. "You don't see any more real honest people unless you go way out in the country."

"I know," she said, "real genuine folks!" Through the crack in the door she heard a groan.

"I guess a lot of boys come telling you they're working their way through college," he said, "but I'm not going to tell you that. Somehow," he said, "I don't want to go to college. I want to devote my life to Christian service. See," he said, lowering his voice, "I got this heart condition. I may not live long. When you know it's something wrong with you and you may not live long, well, then, lady . . ." He paused, with his mouth open, and stared at her.

He and Joy had the same condition! She knew that her eyes were filling with tears but she collected herself quickly and murmured, "Won't you stay for dinner? We'd love to have you!" and was sorry the instant she heard herself say it.

"Yes mam," he said in an abashed voice, "I would sher love to do that!"

Joy had given him one look on being introduced to him and then throughout the meal had not glanced at him again. He had addressed several remarks to her, which she had pretended not to hear. Mrs. Hopewell could not understand deliberate rudeness, although she lived with it, and she felt she had always to overflow with hospitality to make up for Joy's lack of courtesy. She urged him to talk about himself and he did. He said he was the seventh child of twelve and that his father had been crushed under a tree when he himself was eight year old. He had been crushed very badly, in fact, almost cut in two and was practically not recognizable. His mother had got along the best she could by hard working and she had always seen that her children went to Sunday School and that they read the Bible every evening. He was now nineteen year old and he had been selling Bibles for four months. In that time he had sold seventy-seven Bibles and had the

promise of two more sales. He wanted to become a missionary because he thought
that was the way you could do the most for people. "He who losest his life shall
find it," he said simply and he was so sincere, so genuine and earnest that Mrs.
Hopewell would not for the world have smiled. He prevented his peas from sliding onto the table by blocking them with a piece of bread which he later cleaned
his plate with. She could see Joy observing sidewise how he handled his knife and
fork and she saw too that every few minutes, the boy would dart a keen appraising   290
glance at the girl as if he were trying to attract her attention.

After dinner Joy cleared the dishes off the table and disappeared and Mrs.
Hopewell was left to talk with him. He told her again about his childhood and his
father's accident and about various things that had happened to him. Every five
minutes or so she would stifle a yawn. He sat for two hours until finally she told
him she must go because she had an appointment in town. He packed his Bibles
and thanked her and prepared to leave, but in the doorway he stopped and wrung
her hand and said that not on any of his trips had he met a lady as nice as her and
he asked if he could come again. She had said she would always be happy to see
him.   300

Joy had been standing in the road, apparently looking at something in the
distance, when he came down the steps toward her, bent to the side with his
heavy valise. He stopped where she was standing and confronted her directly. Mrs.
Hopewell could not hear what he said but she trembled to think what Joy would
say to him. She could see that after a minute Joy said something and that then the
boy began to speak again, making an excited gesture with his free hand. After a
minute Joy said something else at which the boy began to speak once more. Then
to her amazement, Mrs. Hopewell saw the two of them walk off together, toward
the gate. Joy had walked all the way to the gate with him and Mrs. Hopewell
could not imagine what they had said to each other, and she had not yet dared to   310
ask.

Mrs. Freeman was insisting upon her attention. She had moved from the refrigerator to the heater so that Mrs. Hopewell had to turn and face her in order to
seem to be listening. "Glynese gone out with Harvey Hill again last night," she
said. "She had this sty."

"Hill," Mrs. Hopewell said absently, "is that the one who works in the
garage?"

"Nome, he's the one that goes to chiropracter school," Mrs. Freeman said.
"She had this sty. Been had it two days. So she says when he brought her in the
other night he says, 'Lemme get rid of that sty for you,' and she says, 'How?' and   320
he says, 'You just lay yourself down across the seat of that car and I'll show you.'
So she done it and he popped her neck. Kept on a-popping it several times until
she made him quit. This morning," Mrs. Freeman said, "she ain't got no sty. She
ain't got no traces of a sty."

"I never heard of that before," Mrs. Hopewell said.

"He ast her to marry him before the Ordinary," Mrs. Freeman went on, "and
she told him she wasn't going to be married in no *office*."

"Well, Glynese is a fine girl," Mrs. Hopewell said, "Glynese and Carramae are
both fine girls."

"Carramae said when her and Lyman was married Lyman said it sure felt sa- 330
cred to him. She said he said he wouldn't take five hundred dollars for being married by a preacher."

"How much would he take?" the girl asked from the stove.

"He said he wouldn't take five hundred dollars," Mrs. Freeman repeated.

"Well we all have work to do," Mrs. Hopewell said.

"Lyman said it just felt more sacred to him," Mrs. Freeman said. "The doctor
wants Carramae to eat prunes. Says instead of medicine. Says them cramps is
coming from pressure. You know where I think it is?"

"She'll be better in a few weeks," Mrs. Hopewell said.

"In the tube,"[2] Mrs. Freeman said. "Else she wouldn't be as sick as she is."   340

Hulga had cracked her two eggs into a saucer and was bringing them to the
table along with a cup of coffee that she had filled too full. She sat down carefully
and began to eat, meaning to keep Mrs. Freeman there by questions if for any reason she showed an inclination to leave. She could perceive her mother's eye on
her. The first roundabout question would be about the Bible salesman and she did
not wish to bring it on. "How did he pop her neck?" she asked.

Mrs. Freeman went into a description of how he had popped her neck. She
said he owned a '55 Mercury but that Glynese said she would rather marry a man
with only a '36 Plymouth who would be married by a preacher. The girl asked
what if he had a '32 Plymouth and Mrs. Freeman said what Glynese had said was   350
a '36 Plymouth.

Mrs. Hopewell said there were not many girls with Glynese's common sense.
She said what she admired in those girls was their common sense. She said that
reminded her that they had a nice visitor yesterday, a young man selling Bibles.
"Lord," she said, "he bored me to death but he was so sincere and genuine I
couldn't be rude to him. He was just good country people, you know," she said,
"—just the salt of the earth."

"I seen him walk up," Mrs. Freeman said, "and then later—I seen him walk
off," and Hulga could feel the slight shift in her voice, the slight insinuation, that
he had not walked off alone, had he? Her face remained expressionless but the   360
color rose into her neck and she seemed to swallow it down with the next spoonful of egg. Mrs. Freeman was looking at her as if they had a secret together.

"Well, it takes all kinds of people to make the world go 'round," Mrs.
Hopewell said. "It's very good we aren't all alike."

"Some people are more alike than others," Mrs. Freeman said.

Hulga got up and stumped, with about twice the noise that was necessary,
into her room and locked the door. She was to meet the Bible salesman at ten
o'clock at the gate. She had thought about it half the night. She had started thinking of it as a great joke and then she had begun to see profound implications in it.
She had lain in bed imagining dialogues for them that were insane on the surface 370
but that reached below to depths that no Bible salesman would be aware of. Their
conversation yesterday had been of this kind.

He had stopped in front of her and had simply stood there. His face was

2. The fertilized egg is in a fallopian tube.

bony and sweaty and bright, with a little pointed nose in the center of it, and his look was different from what it had been at the dinner table. He was gazing at her with open curiosity, with fascination, like a child watching a new fantastic animal at the zoo, and he was breathing as if he had run a great distance to reach her. His gaze seemed somehow familiar but she could not think where she had been regarded with it before. For almost a minute he didn't say anything. Then on what seemed an insuck of breath, he whispered, "You ever ate a chicken that was two 380 days old?"

The girl looked at him stonily. He might have just put this question up for consideration at the meeting of a philosophical association. "Yes," she presently replied as if she had considered it from all angles.

"It must have been mighty small!" he said triumphantly and shook all over with little nervous giggles, getting very red in the face, and subsiding finally into his gaze of complete admiration, while the girl's expression remained exactly the same.

"How old are you?" he asked softly.

She waited some time before she answered. Then in a flat voice she said, 390 "Seventeen."

His smiles came in succession like waves breaking on the surface of a little lake. "I see you got a wooden leg," he said. "I think you're real brave. I think you're real sweet."

The girl stood blank and solid and silent.

"Walk to the gate with me," he said. "You're a brave sweet little thing and I liked you the minute I seen you walk in the door."

Hulga began to move forward.

"What's your name?" he asked, smiling down on the top of her head.

"Hulga," she said.   400

"Hulga," he murmured, "Hulga. Hulga. I never heard of anybody name Hulga before. You're shy, aren't you, Hulga?" he asked.

She nodded, watching his large red hand on the handle of the giant valise.

"I like girls that wear glasses," he said. "I think a lot. I'm not like these people that a serious thought don't ever enter their heads. It's because I may die."

"I may die too," she said suddenly and looked up at him. His eyes were very small and brown, glittering feverishly.

"Listen," he said, "don't you think some people was meant to meet on account of what all they got in common and all? Like they both think serious thoughts and all?" He shifted the valise to his other hand so that the hand nearest 410 her was free. He caught hold of her elbow and shook it a little. "I don't work on Saturday," he said. "I like to walk in the woods and see what Mother Nature is wearing. O'er the hills and far away. Pic-nics and things. Couldn't we go on a picnic tomorrow? Say yes, Hulga," he said and gave her a dying look as if he felt his insides about to drop out of him. He had even seemed to sway slightly toward her.

During the night she had imagined that she seduced him. She imagined that the two of them walked on the place until they came to the storage barn beyond the two back fields and there, she imagined, that things came to such a pass that she very easily seduced him and that then, of course, she had to reckon with his

remorse. True genius can get an idea across even to an inferior mind. She imag- 420
ined that she took his remorse in hand and changed it into a deeper understanding of life. She took all his shame away and turned it into something useful.

She set off for the gate at exactly ten o'clock, escaping without drawing Mrs.
Hopewell's attention. She didn't take anything to eat, forgetting that food is usually
taken on a picnic. She wore a pair of slacks and a dirty white shirt, and as an afterthought, she had put some Vapex on the collar of it since she did not own any
perfume. When she reached the gate no one was there.

She looked up and down the empty highway and had the furious feeling that
she had been tricked, that he had only meant to make her walk to the gate after
the idea of him. Then suddenly he stood up, very tall, from behind a bush on the 430
opposite embankment. Smiling, he lifted his hat which was new and wide-
brimmed. He had not worn it yesterday and she wondered if he had bought it for
the occasion. It was toast-colored with a red and white band around it and was
slightly too large for him. He stepped from behind the bush still carrying the black
valise. He had on the same suit and the same yellow socks sucked down in his
shoes from walking. He crossed the highway and said, "I knew you'd come!"

The girl wondered acidly how he had known this. She pointed to the valise
and asked, "Why did you bring your Bibles?"

He took her elbow, smiling down on her as if he could not stop. "You can
never tell when you'll need the word of God, Hulga," he said. She had a moment 440
in which she doubted that this was actually happening and then they began to
climb the embankment. They went down into the pasture toward the woods. The
boy walked lightly by her side, bouncing on his toes. The valise did not seem to
be heavy today; he even swung it. They crossed half the pasture without saying
anything and then, putting his hand easily on the small of her back, he asked
softly, "Where does your wooden leg join on?"

She turned an ugly red and glared at him and for an instant the boy looked
abashed. "I didn't mean you no harm," he said. "I only meant you're so brave and
all. I guess God takes care of you."

"No," she said, looking forward and walking fast, "I don't even believe in 450
God."

At this he stopped and whistled. "No!" he exclaimed as if he were too astonished to say anything else.

She walked on and in a second he was bouncing at her side, fanning with
his hat. "That's very unusual for a girl," he remarked, watching her out of the corner of his eye. When they reached the edge of the wood, he put his hand on her
back again and drew her against him without a word and kissed her heavily.

The kiss, which had more pressure than feeling behind it, produced that
extra surge of adrenaline in the girl that enables one to carry a packed trunk out of
a burning house, but in her, the power went at once to the brain. Even before he 460
released her, her mind, clear and detached and ironic anyway, was regarding him
from a great distance, with amusement but with pity. She had never been kissed
before and she was pleased to discover that it was an unexceptional experience
and all a matter of the mind's control. Some people might enjoy drain water if they
were told it was vodka. When the boy, looking expectant but uncertain, pushed

her gently away, she turned and walked on, saying nothing as if such business, for her, were common enough.

He came along panting at her side, trying to help her when he saw a root that she might trip over. He caught and held back the long swaying blades of thorn vine until she had passed beyond them. She led the way and he came 470 breathing heavily behind her. Then they came out on a sunlit hillside, sloping softly into another one a little smaller. Beyond, they could see the rusted top of the old barn where the extra hay was stored.

The hill was sprinkled with small pink weeds. "Then you ain't saved?" he asked suddenly, stopping.

The girl smiled. It was the first time she had smiled at him at all. "In my economy," she said, "I'm saved and you are damned but I told you I didn't believe in God."

Nothing seemed to destroy the boy's look of admiration. He gazed at her now as if the fantastic animal at the zoo had put its paw through the bars and 480 given him a loving poke. She thought he looked as if he wanted to kiss her again and she walked on before he had the chance.

"Ain't there somewheres we can sit down sometime?" he murmured, his voice softening toward the end of the sentence.

"In that barn," she said.

They made for it rapidly as if it might slide away like a train. It was a large two-story barn, cool and dark inside. The boy pointed up the ladder that led into the loft and said, "It's too bad we can't go up there."

"Why can't we?" she asked.

"Yer leg," he said reverently.   490

The girl gave him a contemptuous look and putting both hands on the ladder, she climbed it while he stood below, apparently awestruck. She pulled herself expertly through the opening and then looked down at him and said, "Well, come on if you're coming," and he began to climb the ladder, awkwardly bringing the suitcase with him.

"We won't need the Bible," she observed.

"You never can tell," he said, panting. After he had got into the loft, he was a few seconds catching his breath. She had sat down in a pile of straw. A wide sheath of sunlight, filled with dust particles, slanted over her. She lay back against a bale, her face turned away, looking out the front opening of the barn where hay 500 was thrown from a wagon into the loft. The two pink-speckled hillsides lay back against a dark ridge of woods. The sky was cloudless and cold blue. The boy dropped down by her side and put one arm under her and the other over her and began methodically kissing her face, making little noises like a fish. He did not remove his hat but it was pushed far enough back not to interfere. When her glasses got in his way, he took them off of her and slipped them into his pocket.

The girl at first did not return any of the kisses but presently she began to and after she had put several on his cheek, she reached his lips and remained there, kissing him again and again as if she were trying to draw all the breath out of him. His breath was clear and sweet like a child's and the kisses were sticky like 510 a child's. He mumbled about loving her and about knowing when he first seen her that he loved her, but the mumbling was like the sleepy fretting of a child being put to sleep by his mother. Her mind, throughout this, never stopped or lost itself for a second to her feelings. "You ain't said you love me none," he whispered finally, pulling back from her. "You got to say that."

She looked away from him off into the hollow sky and then down at a black ridge and then down farther into what appeared to be two green swelling lakes. She didn't realize he had taken her glasses but this landscape could not seem exceptional to her for she seldom paid any close attention to her surroundings.

"You got to say it," he repeated. "You got to say you love me."   520

She was always careful how she committed herself. "In a sense," she began, "if you use the word loosely, you might say that. But it's not a word I use. I don't have illusions. I'm one of those people who see *through* to nothing."

The boy was frowning. "You got to say it. I said it and you got to say it," he said.

The girl looked at him almost tenderly. "You poor baby," she murmured. "It's just as well you don't understand," and she pulled him by the neck, face-down, against her. "We are all damned," she said, "but some of us have taken off our blindfolds and see that there's nothing to see. It's a kind of salvation."

The boy's astonished eyes looked blankly through the ends of her hair. 530 "Okay," he almost whined, "but do you love me or don'tcher?"

"Yes," she said and added, "in a sense. But I must tell you something. There mustn't be anything dishonest between us." She lifted his head and looked him in the eye. "I am thirty years old," she said. "I have a number of degrees."

The boy's look was irritated but dogged. "I don't care," he said. "I don't care a thing about what all you done. I just want to know if you love me or don'tcher?" and he caught her to him and wildly planted her face with kisses until she said, "Yes, yes."

"Okay then," he said, letting her go. "Prove it."

She smiled, looking dreamily out on the shifty landscape. She had seduced 540 him without even making up her mind to try. "How?" she asked, feeling that he should be delayed a little.

He leaned over and put his lips to her ear. "Show me where your wooden leg joins on," he whispered.

The girl uttered a sharp little cry and her face instantly drained of color. The obscenity of the suggestion was not what shocked her. As a child she had sometimes been subject to feelings of shame but education had removed the last traces of that as a good surgeon scrapes for cancer; she would no more have felt it over what he was asking than she would have believed in his Bible. But she was as sensitive about the artificial leg as a peacock about his tail. No one ever touched it but 550 her. She took care of it as someone else would his soul, in private and almost with her own eyes turned away. "No," she said.

"I known it," he muttered, sitting up. "You're just playing me for a sucker."

"Oh no no!" she cried. "It joins on at the knee. Only at the knee. Why do you want to see it?"

The boy gave her a long penetrating look. "Because," he said, "it's what makes you different. You ain't like anybody else."

She sat staring at him. There was nothing about her face or her round freezing-blue eyes to indicate that this had moved her; but she felt as if her heart

had stopped and left her mind to pump her blood. She decided that for the first 560
time in her life she was face to face with real innocence. This boy, with an instinct
that came from beyond wisdom, had touched the truth about her. When after a
minute, she said in a hoarse high voice, "All right," it was like surrendering to him
completely. It was like losing her own life and finding it again, miraculously, in
his.

Very gently he began to roll the slack leg up. The artificial limb, in a white
sock and brown flat shoe, was bound in a heavy material like canvas and ended in
an ugly jointure where it was attached to the stump. The boy's face and his voice
were entirely reverent as he uncovered it and said, "Now show me how to take it
off and on."   570

She took it off for him and put it back on again and then he took it off himself, handling it as tenderly as if it were a real one. "See!" he said with a delighted
child's face. "Now I can do it myself!"

"Put it back on," she said. She was thinking that she would run away with
him and that every night he would take the leg off and every morning put it back
on again. "Put it back on," she said.

"Not yet," he murmured, setting it on its foot out of her reach. "Leave it off
for a while. You got me instead."

She gave a little cry of alarm but he pushed her down and began to kiss her
again. Without the leg she felt entirely dependent on him. Her brain seemed to 580
have stopped thinking altogether and to be about some other function that it was
not very good at. Different expressions raced back and forth over her face. Every
now and then the boy, his eyes like two steel spikes, would glance behind him
where the leg stood. Finally she pushed him off and said, "Put it back on me now."

"Wait," he said. He leaned the other way and pulled the valise toward him
and opened it. It had a pale blue spotted lining and there were only two Bibles in
it. He took one of these out and opened the cover of it. It was hollow and contained a pocket flask of whiskey, a pack of cards, and a small blue box with printing on it. He laid these out in front of her one at a time in an evenly spaced row,
like one presenting offerings at the shrine of a goddess. He put the blue box in her 590
hand. THIS PRODUCT TO BE USED ONLY FOR THE PREVENTION OF DISEASE, she read, and
dropped it. The boy was unscrewing the top of the flask. He stopped and pointed,
with a smile, to the deck of cards. It was not an ordinary deck but one with an obscene picture on the back of each card. "Take a swig," he said, offering her the bottle first. He held it in front of her, but like one mesmerized, she did not move.

Her voice when she spoke had an almost pleading sound. "Aren't you," she
murmured, "aren't you just good country people?"

The boy cocked his head. He looked as if he were just beginning to understand that she might be trying to insult him. "Yeah," he said, curling his lip
slightly, "but it ain't held me back none. I'm as good as you any day in the week." 600

"Give me my leg," she said.

He pushed it farther away with his foot. "Come on now, let's begin to have us
a good time," he said coaxingly. "We ain't got to know one another good yet."

"Give me my leg!" she screamed and tried to lunge for it but he pushed her
down easily.

"What's the matter with you all of a sudden?" he asked, frowning as he screwed the top on the flask and put it quickly back inside the Bible. "You just a while ago said you didn't believe in nothing. I thought you was some girl!"

Her face was almost purple. "You're a Christian!" she hissed. "You're a fine Christian! You're just like them all—say one thing and do another. You're a perfect Christian, you're . . ." 610

The boy's mouth was set angrily. "I hope you don't think," he said in a lofty indignant tone, "that I believe in that crap!" I may sell Bibles but I know which end is up and I wasn't born yesterday and I know where I'm going!"

"Give me my leg!" she screeched. He jumped up so quickly that she barely saw him sweep the cards and the blue box back into the Bible and throw the Bible into the valise. She saw him grab the leg and then she saw it for an instant slanted forlornly across the inside of the suitcase with a Bible at either side of its opposite ends. He slammed the lid shut and snatched up the valise and swung it down the hole and then stepped through himself. 620

When all of him had passed but his head, he turned and regarded her with a look that no longer had any admiration in it. "I've gotten a lot of interesting things," he said. "One time I got a woman's glass eye this way. And you needn't to think you'll catch me because Pointer ain't really my name. I use a different name at every house I call at and don't stay nowhere long. And I'll tell you another thing, Hulga," he said, using the name as if he didn't think much of it, "you ain't so smart. I been believing in nothing ever since I was born!" and then the toast-colored hat disappeared down the hole and the girl was left, sitting on the straw in the dusty sunlight. When she turned her churning face toward the opening, she saw his blue figure struggling successfully over the green speckled lake. 630

Mrs. Hopewell and Mrs. Freeman, who were in the back pasture, digging up onions, saw him emerge a little later from the woods and head across the meadow toward the highway. "Why, that looks like that nice dull young man that tried to sell me a Bible yesterday," Mrs. Hopewell said, squinting. "He must have been selling them to the Negroes back in there. He was so simple," she said, "but I guess the world would be better off if we were all that simple."

Mrs. Freeman's gaze drove forward and just touched him before he disappeared under the hill. Then she returned her attention to the evil-smelling onion shoot she was lifting from the ground. "Some can't be that simple," she said. "I know I never could." [1955] 640

Questions for Discussion and Writing

1. What is the significance of the title?
2. Analyze Hulga. Why does she want to be ugly? Why does she believe in nothing?
3. Mrs. Hopewell and Mrs. Freeman express their beliefs in a series of cliches. Is there anything wrong with a belief system based on such conventional ideas? Explain.
4. Hulga sets out to seduce and perhaps shock Manley Pointer, but he turns the

tables on her. What is revealed to Hulga by his treachery and his belief in nothing?

5. Manley Pointer descends from a long line of tricksters and hucksters in American literature. Americans seem divided between admiration for and hatred of such characters. How do you react to Pointer?

6. Flannery O'Connor always claimed that her stories were Christian in intent. What religious idea could she be trying to communicate through a story that features mostly irreligious characters and events?

7. How might a feminist interpret this story? How might a Freudian critic interpret it?

GABRIEL GARCIA MARQUEZ
(b. 1928)

TRANSLATED BY GREGORY RABASSA

Monologue of Isabel Watching It Rain in Macondo

Gabriel Garcia Marquez is one of the best known Latin American writers and a master of the style that has come to be called Magical Realism. He combines literary inventiveness with political conviction in stories that are unsettling and subversive.

Garcia Marquez was born in the remote village of Aracatca, Colombia, into a very poor family. A scholarship enabled him to attend high school, and he went on from there to study at the Universities of Colombia and Cartagena but did not take a degree. He has said in an interview that his decision to take up writing occurred when a fellow student recommended the works of Franz Kafka. "The Metamorphosis" was a revelation, and he immediately began writing stories of his own.

Much of Garcia Marquez's career has been spent in journalism, beginning in 1948 as a reporter, then as a foreign correspondent in Paris and Rome, beginning in 1955. His support for the Cuban revolution led him to become a press agent for the Cuban government for two years. Such left-wing politics incurred disfavor with the Colombian authorities, and he went into voluntary exile in Mexico and Spain during the 1960s and 1970s, where he continued in journalism and took up screen writing. Meanwhile, his novels and stories were being published and translated, most notably *One Hundred Years of Solitude* (1967; trans. 1970) and *Love in the Time of Cholera* (1980). He was awarded the Nobel Prize in 1982 and has since returned to Colombia to live.

In "Monologue of Isabel Watching It Rain in Macondo," as in other works by Garcia Marquez, Macondo comes to stand to some degree for Colombia with its deep sources of oppression and malaise. The heavy rains, which typically fall in May and October, create a sense of desolation and lassitude.

W INTER FELL ONE SUNDAY when people were coming out of church. Saturday night had been suffocating. But even on Sunday morning nobody thought it would rain. After Mass, before we women had time to find the catches on our parasols, a thick, dark wind blew, which with one broad, round swirl swept away the dust and hard tinder of May. Someone next to me said: "It's a water wind." And I knew it even before then. From the moment we came out onto the church steps I felt shaken by a slimy feeling in my stomach. The men ran to the nearby houses with one hand on their hats and a handkerchief in the other, protecting themselves against the wind and the dust storm. Then it rained. And the sky was a gray, jellyish substance that flapped its wings a hand away from our heads. 10

During the rest of the morning my stepmother and I were sitting by the railing, happy that the rain would revive the thirsty rosemary and nard in the flowerpots after seven months of intense summer and scorching dust. At noon the reverberation of the earth stopped and a smell of turned earth, of awakened and renovated vegetation mingled with the cool and healthful odor of the rain in the rosemary. My father said at lunchtime: "When it rains in May, it's a sign that there'll be good tides." Smiling, crossed by the luminous thread of the new season, my stepmother told me: "That's what I heard in the sermon." And my father smiled. And he ate with a good appetite and even let his food digest leisurely beside the railing, silent, his eyes closed, but not sleeping, as if to think that he was 20 dreaming while awake.

It rained all afternoon in a single tone. In the uniform and peaceful intensity you could hear the water fall, the way it is when you travel all afternoon on a train. But without our noticing it, the rain was penetrating too deeply into our senses. Early Monday morning, when we closed the door to avoid the cutting, icy draft that blew in from the courtyard, our senses had been filled with rain. And on Monday morning they had overflowed. My stepmother and I went back to look at the garden. The harsh gray earth of May had been changed overnight into a dark, sticky substance like cheap soap. A trickle of water began to run off the flowerpots. "I think they had more than enough water during the night," my stepmother 30 said. And I noticed that she had stopped smiling and that her joy of the previous day had changed during the night into a lax and tedious seriousness. "I think you're right," I said. "It would be better to have the Indians put them on the veranda until it stops raining." And that was what they did, while the rain grew like an immense tree over the other trees. My father occupied the same spot where he had been on Sunday afternoon, but he didn't talk about the rain. He said: "I must have slept poorly last night because I woke up with a stiff back." And he stayed there, sitting by the railing with his feet on a chair and his head turned toward the empty garden. Only at dusk, after he had turned down lunch, did he say: "It looks as if it will never clear." And I remembered the months of heat. I remembered 40 August, those long and awesome siestas in which we dropped down to die under the weight of the hour, our clothes sticking to our bodies, hearing outside the insistent and dull buzzing of the hour that never passed. I saw the washed-down walls, the joints of the beams all puffed up by the water. I saw the small garden, empty for the first time, and the jasmine bush against the wall, faithful to the memory of my mother. I saw my father sitting in a rocker, his painful vertebrae resting on a pillow and his sad eyes lost in the labyrinth of the rain. I remembered the August nights in whose wondrous silence nothing could be heard except the millenary sound that the earth makes as it spins on its rusty, uncoiled axis. Suddenly I felt overcome by an overwhelming sadness.   50

It rained all Monday, just like Sunday. But now it seemed to be raining in another way, because something different and bitter was going on in my heart. At dusk a voice beside my chair said: "This rain is a bore." Without turning to look, I recognized Martín's voice. I knew that he was speaking in the next chair, with the same cold and awesome expression that hadn't varied, not even after that gloomy December dawn when he started being my husband. Five months had passed since then. Now I was going to have a child. And Martín was there beside me saying that the rain bored him. "Not a bore," I said. "It seems terribly sad to me, with the empty garden and those poor trees that can't come in from the courtyard." Then I turned to look at him and Martín was no longer there. It was only a voice   60 that was saying to me: "It doesn't look as if it will ever clear," and when I looked toward the voice I found only the empty chair.

On Tuesday morning we found a cow in the garden. It looked like a clay promontory in its hard and rebellious immobility, its hooves sunken in the mud and its head bent over. During the morning the Indians tried to drive it away with sticks and stones. But the cow stayed there, imperturbable in the garden, hard, inviolable, its hooves still sunken in the mud and its huge head humiliated by the rain. The Indians harassed it until my father's patient tolerance came to its defense. "Leave her alone," he said. "She'll leave the way she came."

At sundown on Tuesday the water tightened and hurt, like a shroud over the   70 heart. The coolness of the first morning began to change into a hot and sticky humidity. The temperature was neither cold nor hot; it was the temperature of a fever chill. Feet sweated inside shoes. It was hard to say what was more disagreeable, bare skin or the contact of clothing on skin. All activity had ceased in the house. We sat on the veranda but we no longer watched the rain as we did on the first day. We no longer felt it falling. We no longer saw anything except the outline of the trees in the mist, with a sad and desolate sunset which left on your lips the same taste with which you awaken after having dreamed about a stranger. I knew that it was Tuesday and I remembered the twins of Saint Jerome, the blind girls who came to the house every week to sing us simple songs, saddened by the bitter   80 and unprotected prodigy of their voices. Above the rain I heard the blind twins' little song and I imagined them at home, huddling, waiting for the rain to stop so they could go out and sing. The twins of Saint Jerome wouldn't come that day, I thought, nor would the beggar woman be on the veranda after siesta, asking, as on every Tuesday, for the eternal branch of lemon balm.

That day we lost track of meals. At siesta time my stepmother served a plate of tasteless soup and a piece of stale bread. But actually we hadn't eaten since sunset on Monday and I think that from then on we stopped thinking. We were paralyzed, drugged by the rain, given over to the collapse of nature with a peaceful and resigned attitude. Only the cow was moving in the afternoon. Suddenly a   90 deep noise shook her insides and her hooves sank into the mud with greater force. Then she stood motionless for half an hour, as if she were already dead but could not fall down because the habit of being alive prevented her, the habit of remaining in one position in the rain, until the habit grew weaker than her body. Then

she doubled her front legs (her dark and shiny haunches still raised in a last agonized effort) and sank her drooling snout into the mud, finally surrendering to the
weight of her own matter in a silent, gradual, and dignified ceremony of total
downfall. "She got that far," someone said behind me. And I turned to look and on
the threshold I saw the Tuesday beggar woman who had come through the storm
to ask for the branch of lemon balm.   100

        Perhaps on Wednesday I might have grown accustomed to that overwhelm-
ing atmosphere if on going to the living room I hadn't found the table pushed
against the wall, the furniture piled on top of it, and on the other side, on a parapet prepared during the night, trunks and boxes of household utensils. The spectacle produced a terrible feeling of emptiness in me. Something had happened
during the night. The house was in disarray; the Guajiro Indians, shirtless and
barefoot, with their pants rolled up to their knees, were carrying the furniture into
the dining room. In the men's expression, in the very diligence with which they
were working, one could see the cruelty of their frustrated rebellion, of their necessary and humiliating inferiority in the rain. I moved without direction, without 110
will. I felt changed into a desolate meadow sown with algae and lichens, with soft,
sticky toadstools, fertilized by the repugnant plants of dampness and shadows. I
was in the living room contemplating the desert spectacle of the piled-up furniture
when I heard my stepmother's voice warning me from her room that I might catch
pneumonia. Only then did I realize that the water was up to my ankles, that the
house was flooded, the floor covered by a thick surface of viscous, dead water.

        On Wednesday noon it still hadn't finished dawning. And before three
o'clock in the afternoon night had come on completely, ahead of time and sickly,
with the same slow, monotonous, and pitiless rhythm of the rain in the courtyard.
It was a premature dusk, soft and lugubrious, growing in the midst of the silence   120
of the Guajiros, who were squatting on the chairs against the walls, defeated and
impotent against the disturbance of nature. That was when news began to arrive
from outside. No one brought it to the house. It simply arrived, precise, individualized, as if led by the liquid clay that ran through the streets and dragged household items along, things and more things, the leftovers of a remote catastrophe,
rubbish and dead animals. Events that took place on Sunday, when the rain was
still the announcement of a providential season, took two days to be known at our
house. And on Wednesday the news arrived as if impelled by the very inner dy-
namism of the storm. It was learned then that the church was flooded and its collapse expected. Someone who had no reason to know said that night: "The train   130
hasn't been able to cross the bridge since Monday. It seems that the river carried
away the tracks." And it was learned that a sick woman had disappeared from her
bed and had been found that afternoon floating in the courtyard.

        Terrified, possessed by the fright and the deluge, I sat down in the rocker
with my legs tucked up and my eyes fixed on the damp darkness full of hazy foreboding. My stepmother appeared in the doorway with the lamp held high and her
head erect. She looked like a family ghost before whom I felt no fear whatever because I myself shared her supernatural condition. She came over to where I was.
She still held her head high and the lamp in the air, and she splashed through the
water on the veranda. "Now we have to pray," she said. And I noticed her dry and   140
wrinkled face, as if she had just left her tomb or as if she had been made of some

substance different from human matter. She was across from me with her rosary in her hand saying: "Now we have to pray. The water broke open the tombs and now the poor dead are floating in the cemetery."

I may have slept a little that night when I awoke with a start because of a sour and penetrating smell like that of decomposing bodies. I gave a strong shake to Martín, who was snoring beside me. "Don't you notice it?" I asked him. And he said: "What?" And I said: "The smell. It must be the dead people floating along the streets." I was terrified by that idea, but Martín turned to the wall and with a husky and sleepy voice said: "That's something you made up. Pregnant women are   150 always imagining things."

At dawn on Thursday the smells stopped, the sense of distance was lost. The notion of time, upset since the day before, disappeared completely. Then there was no Thursday. What should have been Thursday was a physical, jellylike thing that could have been parted with the hands in order to look into Friday. There were no men or women there. My stepmother, my father, the Indians were adipose and improbable bodies that moved in the marsh of winter. My father said to me: "Don't move away from here until you're told what to do," and his voice was distant and indirect and didn't seem to be perceived by the ear but by touch, which was the only sense that remained active.   160

But my father didn't return: he got lost in the weather. So when night came I called my stepmother to tell her to accompany me to my bedroom. I had a peaceful and serene sleep, which lasted all through the night. On the following day the atmosphere was still the same, colorless, odorless, and without any temperature. As soon as I awoke I jumped into a chair and remained there without moving, because something told me that there was still a region of my consciousness that hadn't awakened completely. Then I heard the train whistle. The prolonged and sad whistle of the train fleeing the storm. *It must have cleared somewhere,* I thought, and a voice behind me seemed to answer my thought. "Where?" it said. "Who's there?" I asked looking. And I saw my stepmother with a long thin arm in the di-   170 rection of the wall. "It's me," she said. And I asked her: "Can you hear it?" And she said yes, maybe it had cleared on the outskirts and they'd repaired the tracks. Then she gave me a tray with some steaming breakfast. It smelled of garlic sauce and boiled butter. It was a plate of soup. Disconcerted, I asked my stepmother what time it was. And she, calmly, with a voice that tasted of prostrated resignation, said: "It must be around two-thirty. The train isn't late after all this." I said: "Two-thirty! How could I have slept so long!" And she said: "You haven't slept very long. It can't be more than three o'clock." And I, trembling, feeling the plate slip through my fingers: "Two-thirty on Friday," I said. And she, monstrously tranquil: "Two-thirty on Thursday, child. *Still* two-thirty on Thursday."   180

I don't know how long I was sunken in that somnambulism where the senses lose their value. I only know that after many uncountable hours I heard a voice in the next room. A voice that said: "Now you can roll the bed to this side." It was a tired voice, but not the voice of a sick person, rather that of a convalescent. Then I heard the sound of the bricks in the water. I remained rigid before I realized that I was in a horizontal position. Then I felt the immense emptiness. I felt the wavering and violent silence of the house, the incredible immobility that affected everything. And suddenly I felt my heart turned into a frozen stone. *I'm dead,* I thought. *My God, I'm dead.* I gave a jump in the bed. I shouted: "Ada! Ada!" Martín's unpleasant voice answered me from the other side. "They can't hear you, they're already outside by now." Only then did I realize that it had cleared and that all around us a silence stretched out, a tranquillity, a mysterious and deep beatitude, a perfect state which must have been very much like death. Then footsteps could be heard on the veranda. A clear and completely living voice was heard. Then a cool breeze shook the panel of the door, made the doorknob squeak, and a solid and monumental body, like a ripe fruit, fell deeply into the cistern in the courtyard. Something in the air revealed the presence of an invisible person who was smiling in the darkness. *Dear Lord,* I thought then, confused by the mixup in time. *It wouldn't surprise me now if they were coming to call me to go to last Sunday's Mass.* [1955] 200

Questions for Discussion and Writing

1. Underline or circle the details that make the rain seem extraordinary—something other than a simple, natural phenomenon. Analyze these details. Look for patterns that allow you to identify the nature or source of the extraordinary quality of the rain.
2. Isabel, the narrator, is strangely affected by the rain. Trace her moods and reactions. How do her moods and reactions contribute to the overall "strangeness" of the story?
3. What does the story suggest about the nature of time and reality?
4. From this story, what sense do you get of the political, social, or intellectual atmosphere of the country?

✖ PHILIP ROTH
(b. 1933)

The Conversion of the Jews

Philip Roth has been causing controversy since his first published short story, "Defender of the Faith," was seen by Jewish readers as anti-Semitic. Roth, himself a Jew, has since claimed that for him writing is most satisfying when it meets resistance.

Born in Newark, New Jersey, he graduated from Weequahic High School and went on to Rutgers and then Bucknell University where he graduated Phi Beta Kappa in 1954. Following a year of graduate study at the University of Chicago and a stint in the U.S. Army, Roth turned to teaching and subsequently to full-time writing. He married in 1958, but his wife died ten years later. His marriage to the actress Claire Bloom in 1990 ended in divorce.

Roth's early work was in the realist tradition with a strong satirical component. His depiction of his own Jewish community as materialistic and suburban in outlook and values was controversial, as was the sexual content of his fourth

novel, the best-selling *Portnoy's Complaint* (1969), which won the National Book
Award. After this, Roth turned away from realism in some of his work and toward black humor or Postmodernism. The novels since *Portnoy* have delved
further and further into the Postmodern experiment of self-reflexivity,
Metafiction, and literary play.

Roth has published many novels, most recently *Sabbath's Theater* (1995) and
has continued to write short fiction. His only published collection of stories,
however, remains *Goodbye Columbus and Five Short Stories* (1959) from which
"The Conversion of the Jews" is taken. Ozzie, the protagonist of the story,
comes from a long line of American wise-guy rebels and humorists. Is he simply
a smart-aleck with a theological bent, or is he seriously concerned about freedom of thought? In either case, his deliciously ambiguous rebellion against
what he sees as tyranny raises questions about the individual's relation to the
community, questions that resonate with particular force in view of the
Holocaust.

"**Y**OU'RE A REAL ONE for opening your mouth in the first place," Itzie said.
"What do you open your mouth all the time for?"

"I didn't bring it up, Itz, I didn't," Ozzie said.

"What do you care about Jesus Christ for anyway?"

"I didn't bring up Jesus Christ. He did. I didn't even know what he was talking about. Jesus is historical, he kept saying. Jesus is historical." Ozzie mimicked
the monumental voice of Rabbi Binder.

"Jesus was a person that lived like you and me," Ozzie continued. "That's
what Binder said—"

"Yeah? . . . So what! What do I give two cents whether he lived or not. And   10
what do you gotta open your mouth!" Itzie Lieberman favored closed-mouthed-
ness, especially when it came to Ozzie Freedman's questions. Mrs. Freedman had
to see Rabbi Binder twice before about Ozzie's questions and this Wednesday at
four-thirty would be the third time. Itzie preferred to keep *his* mother in the
kitchen; he settled for behind-the-back subtleties such as gestures, faces, snarls
and other less delicate barnyard noises.

"He was a real person, Jesus, but he wasn't like God, and we don't believe he
is God." Slowly, Ozzie was explaining Rabbi Binder's position to Itzie, who had
been absent from Hebrew School the previous afternoon.

"The Catholics," Itzie said helpfully, "they believe in Jesus Christ, that he's   20
God." Itzie Lieberman used "the Catholics" in its broadest sense—to include the
Protestants.

Ozzie received Itzie's remark with a tiny head bob, as though it were a footnote, and went on. "His mother was Mary, and his father probably was Joseph,"
Ozzie said. "But the New Testament says his real father was God."

"His *real* father?"

"Yeah," Ozzie said, "that's the big thing, his father's supposed to be God."

"Bull."

"That's what Rabbi Binder says, that it's impossible—"

"Sure it's impossible. That stuff's all bull. To have a baby you gotta get laid," Itzie theologized. "Mary hadda get laid."

"That's what Binder says: 'The only way a woman can have a baby is to have intercourse with a man.'"

"He said *that*, Ozz?" For a moment it appeared that Itzie had put the theological question aside. "He said that, intercourse?" A little curled smile shaped itself in the lower half of Itzie's face like a pink mustache. "What you guys do, Ozz, you laugh or something?"

"I raised my hand."

"Yeah? Whatja say?"

"That's when I asked the question."

Itzie's face lit up. "Whatja ask about—intercourse?"

"No, I asked the question about God, how if He could create the heaven and earth in six days, and make all the animals and the fish and the light in six days—the light especially, that's what always gets me, that He could make the light. Making fish and animals, that's pretty good—"

"That's damn good." Itzie's appreciation was honest but unimaginative: it was as though God had just pitched a one-hitter.

"But making light . . . I mean when you think about it, it's really something," Ozzie said. "Anyway, I asked Binder if He could make all that in six days, and He could *pick* the six days he wanted right out of nowhere, why couldn't He let a woman have a baby without having intercourse."

"You said intercourse, Ozz, to Binder?"

"Yeah."

"Right in class?"

"Yeah."

Itzie smacked the side of his head.

"I mean, no kidding around," Ozzie said, "that'd really be nothing. After all that other stuff, that'd practically be nothing."

Itzie considered a moment. "What'd Binder say?"

"He started all over again explaining how Jesus was historical and how he lived like you and me but he wasn't God. So I said I under*stood* that. What I wanted to know was different."

What Ozzie wanted to know was always different. The first time he had wanted to know how Rabbi Binder could call the Jews "The Chosen People" if the Declaration of Independence claimed all men to be created equal. Rabbi Binder tried to distinguish for him between political equality and spiritual legitimacy, but what Ozzie wanted to know, he insisted vehemently, was different. That was the first time his mother had to come.

Then there was the plane crash. Fifty-eight people had been killed in a plane crash at La Guardia. In studying a casualty list in the newspaper his mother had discovered among the list of those dead eight Jewish names (his grandmother had nine but she counted Miller as a Jewish name); because of the eight she said the plane crash was "a tragedy." During free-discussion time on Wednesday Ozzie had brought to Rabbi Binder's attention this matter of "some of his relations" always picking out the Jewish names. Rabbi Binder had begun to explain cultural unity and some other things when Ozzie stood up at his seat and said that what he wanted to know was different. Rabbi Binder insisted that he sit down and it was then that Ozzie shouted that he wished all fifty-eight were Jews. That was the second time his mother came.

"And he kept explaining about Jesus being historical, and so I kept asking   80
him. No kidding, Itz, he was trying to make me look stupid."

"So what he finally do?"

"Finally he starts screaming that I was deliberately simple-minded and a wise guy, and that my mother had to come, and this was the last time. And that I'd never get bar-mitzvahed if he could help it. Then, Itz, then he starts talking in that voice like a statue, real slow and deep, and he says that I better think over what I said about the Lord. He told me to go to his office and think it over." Ozzie leaned his body towards Itzie. "Itz, I thought it over for a solid hour, and now I'm convinced God could do it."

Ozzie had planned to confess his latest transgression to his mother as soon   90
as she came home from work. But it was a Friday night in November and already dark, and when Mrs. Freedman came through the door she tossed off her coat, kissed Ozzie quickly on the face, and went to the kitchen table to light the three yellow candles, two for the Sabbath and one for Ozzie's father.

When his mother lit the candles she would move her two arms slowly towards her, dragging them through the air, as though persuading people whose minds were half made up. And her eyes would get glassy with tears. Even when his father was alive Ozzie remembered that her eyes had gotten glassy, so it didn't have anything to do with his dying. It had something to do with lighting the candles.   100

As she touched the flaming match to the unlit wick of a Sabbath candle, the phone rang, and Ozzie, standing only a foot from it, plucked it off the receiver and held it muffled to his chest. When his mother lit candles Ozzie felt there should be no noise; even breathing, if you could manage it, should be softened. Ozzie pressed the phone to his breast and watched his mother dragging whatever she was dragging, and he felt his own eyes get glassy. His mother was a round, tired, gray-haired penguin of a woman whose gray skin had begun to feel the tug of gravity and the weight of her own history. Even when she was dressed up she didn't look like a chosen person. But when she lit candles she looked like something better; like a woman who knew momentarily that God could do anything.   110

After a few mysterious minutes she was finished. Ozzie hung up the phone and walked to the kitchen table where she was beginning to lay the two places for the four-course Sabbath meal. He told her that she would have to see Rabbi Binder next Wednesday at four-thirty, and then he told her why. For the first time in their life together she hit Ozzie across the face with her hand.

All through the chopped liver and chicken soup part of the dinner Ozzie cried; he didn't have any appetite for the rest.

On Wednesday, in the largest of the three basement classrooms of the synagogue, Rabbi Marvin Binder, a tall, handsome, broad-shouldered man of thirty with thick strong-fibered black hair, removed his watch from his pocket and saw   120 that it was four o'clock. At the rear of the room Yakov Blotnik, the seventy-one-year-old custodian, slowly polished the large window, mumbling to himself, unaware that it was four o'clock or six o'clock, Monday or Wednesday. To most of the students Yakov Blotnik's mumbling, along with his brown curly beard, scythe nose, and two heel-trailing black cats, made of him an object of wonder, a foreigner, a relic, towards whom they were alternately fearful and disrespectful. To Ozzie the mumbling had always seemed a monotonous, curious prayer; what made it curious was that old Blotnik had been mumbling so steadily for so many years, Ozzie suspected he had memorized the prayers and forgotten all about God.

"It is now free-discussion time," Rabbi Binder said. "Feel free to talk about 130 any Jewish matter at all—religion, family, politics, sports—"

There was silence. It was a gusty, clouded November afternoon and it did not seem as though there ever was or could be a thing called baseball. So nobody this week said a word about that hero from the past, Hank Greenberg[1]—which limited free discussion considerably.

And the soul-battering Ozzie Freedman had just received from Rabbi Binder had imposed its limitation. When it was Ozzie's turn to read aloud from the Hebrew book the rabbi had asked him petulantly why he didn't read more rapidly. He was showing no progress. Ozzie said he could read faster but that if he did he was sure not to understand what he was reading. Nevertheless, at the rabbi's re- 140 peated suggestion Ozzie tried, and showed a great talent, but in the midst of a long passage he stopped short and said he didn't understand a word he was reading, and started in again at a drag-footed pace. Then came the soul-battering.

Consequently when free-discussion time rolled around none of the students felt too free. The rabbi's invitation was answered only by the mumbling of feeble old Blotnik.

"Isn't there anything at all you would like to discuss?" Rabbi Binder asked again, looking at his watch. "No questions or comments?"

There was a small grumble from the third row. The rabbi requested that Ozzie rise and give the rest of the class the advantage of his thought. 150

Ozzie rose. "I forget it now," he said, and sat down in his place.

Rabbi Binder advanced a seat towards Ozzie and poised himself on the edge of the desk. It was Itzie's desk and the rabbi's frame only a dagger's-length away from his face snapped him to sitting attention.

"Stand up again, Oscar," Rabbi Binder said calmly, "and try to assemble your thoughts."

Ozzie stood up. All his classmates turned in their seats and watched as he gave an unconvincing scratch to his forehead.

"I can't assemble any," he announced, and plunked himself down.

"Stand up!" Rabbi Binder advanced from Itzie's desk to the one directly in 160 front of Ozzie; when the rabbinical back was turned Itzie gave it five-fingers off the tip of his nose, causing a small titter in the room. Rabbi Binder was too absorbed in squelching Ozzie's nonsense once and for all to bother with titters. "Stand up, Oscar. What's your question about?"

Ozzie pulled a word out of the air. It was the handiest word. "Religion."

---

1. Baseball player, mainly with the Detroit Tigers (1930–1947).

"Oh, now you remember?"

"Yes."

"What is it?"

Trapped, Ozzie blurted the first thing that came to him. "Why can't He make anything He wants to make!"   170

As Rabbi Binder prepared an answer, a final answer, Itzie, ten feet behind him, raised one finger on his left hand, gestured it meaningfully towards the rabbi's back, and brought the house down.

Binder twisted quickly to see what had happened and in the midst of the commotion Ozzie shouted into the rabbi's back what he couldn't have shouted to his face. It was a loud, toneless sound that had the timbre of something stored inside for about six days.

"You don't know! You don't know anything about God!"

The rabbi spun back towards Ozzie. "What?"

"You don't know—you don't—"   180

"Apologize, Oscar, apologize!" It was a threat.

"You don't—"

Rabbi Binder's hand flicked out at Ozzie's cheek. Perhaps it had only been meant to clamp the boy's mouth shut, but Ozzie ducked and the palm caught him squarely on the nose.

The blood came in a short, red spurt on to Ozzie's shirt front.

The next moment was all confusion. Ozzie screamed, "You bastard, you bastard!" and broke for the classroom door. Rabbi Binder lurched a step backwards, as though his own blood had started flowing violently in the opposite direction, then gave a clumsy lurch forward and bolted out the door after Ozzie. The class 190 followed after the rabbi's huge blue-suited back, and before old Blotnik could turn from his window, the room was empty and everyone was headed full speed up the three flights leading to the roof.

If one should compare the light of day to the life of man: sunrise to birth; sunset—the dropping down over the edge—to death; then as Ozzie Freedman wiggled through the trapdoor of the synagogue roof, his feet kicking backwards bronco-style at Rabbi Binder's outstretched arms—at that moment the day was fifty years old. As a rule, fifty or fifty-five reflects accurately the age of late afternoons in November, for it is in that month, during those hours, that one's awareness of light seems no longer a matter of seeing, but of hearing: light begins 200 clicking away. In fact, as Ozzie locked shut the trapdoor in the rabbi's face, the sharp click of the bolt into the lock might momentarily have been mistaken for the sound of the heavier gray that had just throbbed through the sky.

With all his weight Ozzie kneeled on the locked door; any instant he was certain that Rabbi Binder's shoulder would fling it open, splintering the wood into shrapnel and catapulting his body into the sky. But the door did not move and below him he heard only the rumble of feet, first loud then dim, like thunder rolling away.

A question shot through his brain. "Can this be _me_?" For a thirteen-year-old who had just labeled his religious leader a bastard, twice, it was not an improper 210 question. Louder and louder the question came to him—"Is it me? It is me?"—

until he discovered himself no longer kneeling, but racing crazily towards the edge of the roof, his eyes crying, his throat screaming, and his arms flying every-which-way as though not his own.

"Is it me? Is it me ME ME ME ME! It has to be me—but is it!"

It is the question a thief must ask himself the night he jimmies open his first window, and it is said to be the question with which bridegrooms quiz themselves before the altar.

In the few wild seconds it took Ozzie's body to propel him to the edge of the roof, his self-examination began to grow fuzzy. Gazing down at the street, he be- 220 came confused as to the problem beneath the question: was it, is-it-me-who-called-Binder-a-bastard? or, is-it-me-prancing-around-on-the-roof? However, the scene below settled all, for there is an instant in any action when whether it is you or somebody else is academic. The thief crams the money in his pockets and scoots out the window. The bridegroom signs the hotel register for two. And the boy on the roof finds a streetful of people gaping at him, necks stretched back-wards, faces up, as though he were the ceiling of the Hayden Planetarium. Suddenly you know it's you.

"Oscar! Oscar Freedman!" A voice rose from the center of the crowd, a voice that, could it have been seen, would have looked like the writing on scroll. "Oscar 230 Freedman, get down from there. Immediately!" Rabbi Binder was pointing one arm stiffly up at him; and at the end of that arm, one finger aimed menacingly. It was the attitude of a dictator, but one—the eyes confessed all—whose personal valet had spit neatly in his face.

Ozzie didn't answer. Only for a blink's length did he look towards Rabbi Binder. Instead his eyes began to fit together the world beneath him, to sort out people from places, friends from enemies, participants from spectators. In little jagged starlike clusters his friends stood around Rabbi Binder, who was still point-ing. The topmost point on a star compounded not of angels but of five adolescent boys was Itzie. What a world it was, with those stars below, Rabbi Binder below 240 . . . Ozzie, who a moment earlier hadn't been able to control his own body, started to feel the meaning of the word control: he felt Peace and he felt Power.

"Oscar Freedman, I'll give you three to come down."

Few dictators give their subjects three to do anything; but, as always, Rabbi Binder only looked dictatorial.

"Are you ready, Oscar?"

Ozzie nodded his head yes, although he had no intention in the world—the lower one or the celestial one he'd just entered—of coming down even if Rabbi Binder should give him a million.

"All right then," said Rabbi Binder. He ran a hand through his black Samson 250 hair as though it were the gesture prescribed for uttering the first digit. Then, with his other hand cutting a circle out of the small piece of sky around him, he spoke. "One!"

There was no thunder. On the contrary, at that moment, as though "one" was the cue for which he had been waiting, the world's least thunderous person ap-peared on the synagogue steps. He did not so much come out the synagogue door as lean out, onto the darkening air. He clutched at the doorknob with one hand and looked up at the roof.

"Oy!"

Yakov Blotnik's old mind hobbled slowly, as if on crutches, and though he couldn't decide precisely what the boy was doing on the roof, he knew it wasn't 260 good—that is, it wasn't-good-for-the-Jews. For Yakov Blotnik life had fractionated itself simply: things were either good-for-the-Jews or no-good-for-the-Jews.

He smacked his free hand to his in-sucked cheek, gently. "Oy, Gut!" And then quickly as he was able, he jacked down his head and surveyed the street. There was Rabbi Binder (like a man at an auction with only three dollars in his pocket, he had just delivered a shaky "Two!"); there were the students, and that was all. So far it-wasn't-so-bad-for-the-Jews. But the boy had to come down immediately, before anybody saw. The problem: how to get the boy off the roof?

Anybody who has ever had a cat on the roof knows how to get him down. You call the fire department. Or first you call the operator and you ask her for the 270 fire department. And the next thing there is great jamming of brakes and clanging of bells and shouting of instructions. And then the cat is off the roof. You do the same thing to get a boy off the roof.

That is, you do the same thing if you are Yakov Blotnik and you once had a cat on the roof.

When the engines, all four of them, arrived, Rabbi Binder had four times given Ozzie the count of three. The big hook-and-ladder swung around the corner and one of the firemen leaped from it, plunging headlong towards the yellow fire hydrant in front of the synagogue. With a huge wrench he began to unscrew the top nozzle. Rabbi Binder raced over to him and pulled at his shoulder.   280

"There's no fire . . ."

The fireman mumbled back over his shoulder and, heatedly, continued working at the nozzle.

"But there's no fire, there's no fire . . ." Binder shouted. When the fireman mumbled again, the rabbi grasped his face with both his hands and pointed it up at the roof.

To Ozzie it looked as though Rabbi Binder was trying to tug the fireman's head out of his body, like a cork from a bottle. He had to giggle at the picture they made: it was a family portrait—rabbi in black skullcap, fireman in red fire hat, and the little yellow hydrant squatting beside like a kid brother, bareheaded. From the 290 edge of the roof Ozzie waved at the portrait, a one-handed, flapping, mocking wave; in doing it his right foot slipped from under him. Rabbi Binder covered his eyes with his hands.

Firemen work fast. Before Ozzie had even regained his balance, a big, round, yellowed net was being held on the synagogue lawn. The firemen who held it looked up at Ozzie with stern, feelingless faces.

One of the firemen turned his head towards Rabbi Binder. "What, is the kid nuts or something?"

Rabbi Binder unpeeled his hands from his eyes, slowly, painfully, as if they were tape. Then he checked: nothing on the sidewalk, no dents in the net.   300

"Is he gonna jump, or what?" the fireman shouted.

In a voice not at all like a statue, Rabbi Binder finally answered. "Yes, Yes, I think so . . . He's been threatening to . . ."

Threatening to? Why, the reason he was on the roof, Ozzie remembered, was to get away; he hadn't even thought about jumping. He had just run to get away, and the truth was that he hadn't really headed for the roof as much as he'd been chased there.

"What's his name, the kid?"

"Freedman," Rabbi Binder answered. "Oscar Freedman."

The fireman looked up at Ozzie. "What is it with you, Oscar? You gonna 310 jump, or what?"

Ozzie did not answer. Frankly, the question had just arisen.

"Look, Oscar, if you're gonna jump, jump—and if you're not gonna jump, don't jump. But don't waste our time, willya?"

Ozzie looked at the fireman and then at Rabbi Binder. He wanted to see Rabbi Binder cover his eyes one more time.

"I'm going to jump."

And then he scampered around the edge of the roof to the corner, where there was no net below, and he flapped his arms at his sides, swishing the air and smacking his palms to his trousers on the downbeat. He began screaming like 320 some kind of engine, "Wheeeee . . . wheeeeee," and leaning way out over the edge with the upper half of his body. The firemen whipped around to cover the ground with the net. Rabbi Binder mumbled a few words to Somebody and covered his eyes. Everything happened quickly, jerkily, as in a silent movie. The crowd, which had arrived with the fire engines, gave out a long, Fourth-of-July fireworks oooh-aahhh. In the excitement no one had paid the crowd much heed, except, of course, Yakov Blotnik, who swung from the doorknob counting heads. "Fier und tsvansik . . . finf und tsvantsik . . . Oy, Gut!"[2] It wasn't like this with the cat.

Rabbi Binder peeked through his fingers, checked the sidewalk and net. Empty. But there was Ozzie racing to the other corner. The firemen raced with 330 him but were unable to keep up. Whenever Ozzie wanted to he might jump and splatter himself upon the sidewalk, and by the time the firemen scooted to the spot all they could do with their net would be to cover the mess.

"Wheeeee . . . wheeeee . . ."

"Hey, Oscar," the winded fireman yelled, "What the hell is this, a game or something?"

"Wheeeee . . . wheeeee . . ."

"Hey, Oscar—"

But he was off now to the other corner, flapping his wings fiercely. Rabbi Binder couldn't take it any longer—the fire engines from nowhere, the screaming 340 suicidal boy, the net. He fell to his knees, exhausted, and with his hands curled together in front of his chest like a little dome, he pleaded, "Oscar, stop it, Oscar. Don't jump, Oscar. Please come down . . . Please don't jump."

And further back in the crowd a single voice, a single young voice, shouted a lone word to the boy on the roof.

"Jump!"

It was Itzie. Ozzie momentarily stopped flapping.

"Go ahead, Ozz—jump!" Itzie broke off his point of the star and coura-

2. "Twenty-four . . . twenty-five . . . Oh, God!"

geously, with the inspiration not of a wise-guy but of a disciple, stood alone. "Jump, Ozz, jump!"   350

Still on his knees, his hands still curled, Rabbi Binder twisted his body back. He looked at Itzie, then, agonizingly, back to Ozzie.

"Oscar, Don't jump! Please, Don't Jump . . . please please . . ."

"Jump!" This time it wasn't Itzie but another point of the star. By the time Mrs. Freedman arrived to keep her four-thirty appointment with Rabbi Binder, the whole little upside down heaven was shouting and pleading for Ozzie to jump, and Rabbi Binder no longer was pleading with him not to jump, but was crying into the dome of his hands.

Understandably Mrs. Freedman couldn't figure out what her son was doing on the roof. So she asked.   360

"Ozzie, my Ozzie, what are you doing? My Ozzie, what is it?"

Ozzie stopped wheeeeeing and slowed his arms down to a cruising flap, the kind birds use in soft winds, but he did not answer. He stood against the low, clouded, darkening sky—light clicked down swiftly now, as on a small gear—flapping softly and gazing down at the small bundle of a woman who was his mother.

"What are you doing, Ozzie?" She turned towards the kneeling Rabbi Binder and rushed so close that only a paper-thickness of dusk lay between her stomach and his shoulders.

"What is my baby doing?"

Rabbi Binder gaped up at her but he too was mute. All that moved was the   370 dome of his hands; it shook back and forth like a weak pulse.

"Rabbi, get him down! He'll kill himself. Get him down, my only baby . . ."

"I can't," Rabbi Binder said, "I can't . . ." and he turned his handsome head towards the crowd of boys behind him. "It's them. Listen to them."

And for the first time Mrs. Freedman saw the crowd of boys, and she heard what they were yelling.

"He's doing it for them. He won't listen to me. It's them." Rabbi Binder spoke like one in a trance.

"For them?"

"Yes."   380

"Why for them?"

"They want him to . . ."

Mrs. Freedman raised her two arms upward as though she were conducting the sky. "For them he's doing it!" And then in a gesture older than pyramids, older than prophets and floods, her arms came slapping down to her sides. "A martyr I have. Look!" She tilted her head to the roof. Ozzie was still flapping softly. "My martyr."

"Oscar, come down, *please*," Rabbi Binder groaned.

In a startlingly even voice Mrs. Freedman called to the boy on the roof. "Ozzie, come down, Ozzie. Don't be a martyr, my baby."   390

As though it were a litany, Rabbi Binder repeated her words. "Don't be a martyr, my baby. Don't be a martyr."

"Gawhead, Ozz—*be* a Martin!" It was Itzie. "Be a Martin, be a Martin," and all the voices joined in singing for Martindom, whatever *it* was. "Be a Martin, be a Martin . . ."

Somehow when you're on a roof the darker it gets the less you can hear. All Ozzie knew was that two groups wanted two new things: his friends were spirited and musical about what they wanted; his mother and the rabbi were even-toned, chanting, about what they didn't want. The rabbi's voice was without tears now and so was his mother's.   400

The big net stared up at Ozzie like a sightless eye. The big, clouded sky pushed down. From beneath it looked like a gray corrugated board. Suddenly, looking up into that unsympathetic sky, Ozzie realized all the strangeness of what these people, his friends, were asking: they wanted him to jump, to kill himself; they were singing about it now—it made them that happy. And there was an even greater strangeness: Rabbi Binder was on his knees, trembling. If there was a question to be asked now it was not "Is it me?" but rather "Is it us? . . . Is it us?"

Being on the roof, it turned out, was a serious thing. If he jumped would the singing become dancing? Would it? What would jumping stop? Yearningly, Ozzie wished he could rip open the sky, plunge his hands through, and pull out the sun;   410 and on the sun, like a coin, would be stamped JUMP or DON'T JUMP.

Ozzie's knees rocked and sagged a little under him as though they were setting him for a dive. His arms tightened, stiffened, froze, from shoulders to fingernails. He felt as if each part of his body were going to vote as to whether he should kill himself or not—and each part as though it were independent of *him*.

The light took an unexpected click down and the new darkness, like a gag, hushed the friends singing for this and the mother and rabbi chanting for that.

Ozzie stopped counting votes, and in a curiously high voice, like one who wasn't prepared for speech, he spoke.

"Mamma?"   420

"Yes, Oscar."

"Mamma, get down on your knees, like Rabbi Binder."

"Oscar—"

"Get down on your knees," he said, "or I'll jump."

Ozzie heard a whimper, then a quick rustling, and when he looked down where his mother had stood he saw the top of a head and beneath that a circle of dress. She was kneeling beside Rabbi Binder.

He spoke again. "Everybody kneel." There was the sound of everybody kneeling.

Ozzie looked around. With one hand he pointed towards the synagogue en- 430 trance. "Make *him* kneel."

There was a noise, not of kneeling, but of body-and-cloth stretching. Ozzie could hear Rabbi Binder saying in a gruff whisper, ". . . or he'll *kill* himself," and when next he looked there was Yakov Blotnik off the doorknob and for the first time in his life upon his knees in the Gentile posture of prayer.

As for the firemen—it is not as difficult as one might imagine to hold a net taut while you are kneeling.

Ozzie looked around again; and then he called to Rabbi Binder.

"Rabbi?"

"Yes, Oscar."   440

"Rabbi Binder, do you believe in God?"

"Yes."

"Do you believe God can do Anything?" Ozzie leaned his head out into the darkness. "Anything?"

"Oscar, I think—"

"Tell me you believe God can do Anything."

There was a second's hesitation. Then: "God can do Anything."

"Tell me you believe God can make a child without intercourse."

"He can."

"Tell me!"   450

"God," Rabbi Binder admitted, "can make a child without intercourse."

"Mamma, you tell me."

"God can make a child without intercourse," his mother said.

"Make *him* tell me." There was no doubt who *him* was.

In a few moments Ozzie heard an old comical voice say something to the increasing darkness about God.

Next, Ozzie made everybody say it. And then he made them all say they believed in Jesus Christ—first one at a time, then all together.

When the catechizing was through it was the beginning of evening. From the street it sounded as if the boy on the roof might have sighed.   460

"Ozzie?" A woman's voice dared to speak. "You'll come down now?"

There was no answer, but the woman waited, and when a voice finally did speak it was thin and crying, and exhausted as that of an old man who has just finished pulling the bells.

"Mamma, don't you see—you shouldn't hit me. He shouldn't hit me. You shouldn't hit me about God, Mamma. You should never hit anybody about God—"

"Ozzie, please come down now."

"Promise me, promise me you'll never hit anybody about God."

He had asked only his mother, but for some reason everyone kneeling in the   470
street promised he would never hit anybody about God.

Once again there was silence.

"I can come down now, Mamma," the boy on the roof finally said. He turned his head both ways as though checking the traffic lights. "Now I can come down . . ."

And he did, right into the center of the yellow net that glowed in the evening's edge like an overgrown halo.   [1959]

Questions for Discussion and Writing

1. Is Ozzie just being an obnoxious youth, or are his questions sincere? How do you know? Underline or highlight relevant passages.

2. Is Rabbi Binder really a dictator? Where is the line between legitimate authority and abuse of power?

3. Compare Ozzie's faith to Abba Feivel's in "The Little Shoemakers."
4. In what sense does Ozzie become a dictator?
5. In what ways, if any, have the Jews really been converted?
6. On the one hand, Ozzie says, "You should never hit anybody about God," but on the other he coerces everyone to agree with him about God's powers. Is he contradicting himself? Is Ozzie a hypocrite? Explain.
7. How does Roth's view of tradition differ from Singer's?

ᴥ H[ERBERT] E[RNEST] BATES
(1905–1974)

Great Uncle Crow

The work of H. E. Bates provides a fascinating study in the interplay of convention and innovation, popular and artistic or "literary" modes. Like W. S. Maugham, Bates was at once an accomplished artist and a popular story-teller. His place in British literature remains uncertain.

Bates was born in the British Midlands to a lower middle-class family with strong ties to the land. As a boy, he explored the countryside around Rushden, Northamptonshire, with his maternal grandfather and soaked up local lore and stories. A scholarship to Kettering Grammar School brought him under the influence of an English teacher who encouraged his writing. His first novel, *The Two Sisters* (1926), appeared when he was barely twenty-one, but it was World War II that catapulted him to fame through a series of stories, commissioned by the British government, about Royal Air Force pilots.

Bates's fiction can range from the fiercely Naturalistic to the lushly Romantic. His rural idylls show a deep love of nature and a talent for description influenced by D. H. Lawrence (1885–1930), Joseph Conrad (1857–1924), and Thomas Hardy (1840–1928). In more somber moods, he depicts a harsh world in which people are little more than animals driven by instinctual urges.

Bates was gifted with a sense of character and place. His writing, however, seems at times to lack "ideas." In an era that often looks to literature for its philosophy or politics, he may seem remote and unengaged. His focus on rural life has often relegated him to the backwater of "regional novelists." He pioneered no new techniques, preferring instead to follow the models of Anton Chekhov (1860–1904), D. H. Lawrence, and Guy de Maupassant (1850–1893). Nevertheless, Bates is a powerful writer whose vivid characters and vibrant natural settings find natural expression in the short story.

ONCE IN THE SUMMER time, when the water-lilies were in bloom and the wheat was new in ear, his grandfather took him on a long walk up the river, to see his Uncle Crow. He had heard so much of Uncle Crow, so much that was wonderful and to be marvelled at, and for such a long time, that he knew him to be, even before that, the most remarkable fisherman in the world.

"Masterpiece of a man, your Uncle Crow," his grandfather said. "He could git a clothes-line any day and tie a brick on it and a mossel[1] of cake and go out and catch a pike as long as your arm."

When he asked what kind of cake his grandfather seemed irritated and said it was just like a boy to ask questions of that sort.   10

"Any kind o' cake," he said. "Plum cake. Does it matter? Caraway cake. Christmas cake if you like. Anything. I shouldn't wonder if he could catch a pretty fair pike with a cold baked tater."

"Only a pike?"

"Times," his grandfather said, "I've seen him sittin' on the bank on a swelter-ing hot day like a furnace, when nobody was gittin' a bite not even off a blood-sucker. And there your Uncle Crow'd be a-pullin' 'em out by the dozen, like a man shellin' harvest beans."

"And how does he come to be my Uncle Crow," he said, "if my mother hasn't got a brother? Nor my father."   20

"Well," his grandfather said, "he's really your mother's own cousin, if every-body had their rights. But all on us call him Uncle Crow."

"And where does he live?"

"You'll see," his grandfather said. "All by hisself. In a little titty bit of a house, by the river."

The little titty bit of a house, when he first saw it, surprised him very much. It was not at all unlike a black tarred boat that had either slipped down a slope and stuck there on its way to launching or one that had been washed up and left there in a flood. The roof of brown tiles had a warp in it and the sides were mostly built, he thought, of tarred beer-barrels.   30

The two windows with their tiny panes were about as large as chessboards and Uncle Crow had nailed underneath each of them a sill of sheet tin that was still a brilliant blue, each with the words "Backache Pills" in white lettering on it, upside down.

On all sides of the house grew tall feathered reeds. They enveloped it like gi-gantic whispering corn. Some distance beyond the great reeds the river went past in a broad slow arc, on magnificent kingly currents, full of long white islands of water-lilies, as big as china breakfast cups, shining and yellow-hearted in the sun.

He thought, on the whole, that that place, the river with the water-lilies, the little titty bit of a house, and the great forest of reeds talking between soft brown 40 beards, was the nicest place he had ever seen.

"Anybody about?" his grandfather called. "Crow!—anybody at home?"

The door of the house was partly open, but at first there was no answer. His grandfather pushed open the door still farther with his foot. The reeds whispered

---

1. Morsel.

down by the river and were answered, in the house, by a sound like the creek of bed springs.

"Who is't?"

"It's me, Crow," his grandfather called. "Lukey. Brought the boy over to have a look at you."

A big gangling red-faced man with rusty hair came to the door. His trousers were black and very tight. His eyes were a smeary vivid blue, the same colour as the stripes of his shirt, and his trousers were kept up by a leather belt with brass escutcheons on it, like those on horses' harness.

"Thought very like you'd be out a-pikin'," his grandfather said.

"Too hot. How's Lukey boy? Ain't seed y' lately, Lukey boy."

His lips were thick and very pink and wet, like cow's lips. He made a wonderful erupting jolly sound somewhat between a belch and a laugh.

"Comin' in it a minute?"

In the one room of the house was an iron bed with an old red check horse-rug spread over it and a stone copper in one corner and a bare wooden table with dirty plates and cups and a tin kettle on it. Two osier baskets and a scythe stood in another corner.

Uncle Crow stretched himself full length on the bed as if he was very tired. He put his knees in the air. His belly was tight as a bladder of lard in his black trousers, which were mossy green on the knees and seat.

"How's the fishin'?" his grandfather said. "I bin tellin' the boy—"

Uncle Crow belched deeply. From where the sun struck full on the tarred wall of the house there was a hot whiff of baking tar. But when Uncle Crow belched there was a smell like the smell of yeast in the air.

"It ain't bin all that much of a summer yit," Uncle Crow said. "Ain't had the rain."

"Not like that summer you catched the big 'un down at Archer's Mill. I recollect you a-tellin' on me—"

"Too hot and dry by half," Uncle Crow said. "Gits in your gullet like chaff."

"You recollect that summer?" his grandfather said. "Nobody else a-fetching on 'em out only you—"

"Have a drop o' neck-oil," Uncle Crow said.

The boy wondered what neck-oil was and presently, to his surprise, Uncle Crow and his grandfather were drinking it. It came out of a dark-green bottle and it was a clear bright amber, like cold tea, in the two glasses.

"The medder were yeller with 'em," Uncle Crow said. "Yeller as a guinea."[2]

He smacked his lips with a marvellously juicy, fruity sound. The boy's grandfather gazed at the neck-oil and said he thought it would be a corker if it was kept a year or two, but Uncle Crow said:

"Trouble is, Lukey boy, it's a terrible job to keep it. You start tastin' on it to see if it'll keep and then you taste on it again and you go on tastin' on it until they ain't a drop left as 'll keep."

2. A gold coin worth twenty-one shillings.

Uncle Crow laughed so much that the bed springs cackled underneath his bouncing trousers.

"Why is it called neck-oil?" the boy said.   90

"Boy," Uncle Crow said, "when you git older, when you git growed-up, you know what'll happen to your gullet?"

"No."

"It'll git sort o' rusted up inside. Like a old gutter pipe. So's you can't swaller very easy. Rusty as old Harry it'll git. You know that, boy?"

"No."

"Well, it will. I'm tellin', on y'. And you know what y' got to do then?"

"No."

"Every now and then you gotta git a drop o' neck-oil down it. So's to ease it. A drop o' neck-oil every once in a while—that's what you gotta do to keep the rust 100 out."

The boy was still contemplating the curious prospect of his neck rusting up inside in later years when Uncle Crow said: "Boy, you go outside and jis' round the corner you'll see a bucket. You bring handful o' cresses out on it. I'll bet you're hungry, ain't you?"

"A little bit."

He found the watercresses in the bucket, cool in the shadow of the little house, and when he got back inside with them Uncle Crow said:

"Now you put the cresses on that there plate there and then put your nose inside that there basin and see what's inside. What is't, eh?"   110

"Eggs."

"Ought to be fourteen on 'em. Four-apiece and two over. What sort are they, boy?"

"Moor-hens'."

"You got a knowin' boy here, Lukey," Uncle Crow said. He dropped the scaly red lid of one eye like an old cockerel going to sleep. He took another drop of neck-oil and gave another fruity, juicy laugh as he heaved his body from the bed. "A very knowin' boy."

Presently he was carving slices of thick brown bread with a great horn-handled shut-knife and pasting each slice with summery golden butter. Now and 120 then he took another drink of neck-oil and once he said:

"You get the salt pot, boy, and empty a bit out on that there saucer, so's we can all dip in."

Uncle Crow slapped the last slice of bread on to the buttered pile and then said:

"Boy, you take that there jug there and go a step or two up the path and dip yourself a drop o' spring water. You'll see it. It comes out of a little bit of a wall, jist by a doddle-willer."[3]

When the boy got back with the jug of spring water Uncle Crow was opening another bottle of neck-oil and his grandfather was saying: "God a-mussy man, 130 goo steady. You'll have me agooin' one way and another—"

---

3. Willow tree.

"Man alive,' Uncle Crow said, "and what's wrong with that?"

Then the watercress, the salt, the moor-hens' eggs, the spring water, and the neck-oil were all ready. The moor-hens' eggs were hard-boiled. Uncle Crow lay on the bed and cracked them with his teeth, just like big brown nuts, and said he thought the watercress was just about as nice and tender as a young lady.

"I'm sorry we ain't got the gold plate out though. I had it out a-Sunday." He closed his old cockerel-lidded eye again and licked his tongue backwards and forwards across his lips and dipped another peeled egg in salt. "You know what I had for my dinner a-Sunday, boy?"											140

"No."

"A pussy-cat on a gold plate. Roasted with broad-beans and new taters. Did you ever heerd talk of anybody eatin' a roasted pussy-cat, boy?"

"Yes."

"You did?"

"Yes," he said, "that's a hare."

"You got a very knowin' boy here, Lukey," Uncle Crow said. "A very knowin' boy."

Then he screwed up a big dark-green bouquet of watercress and dipped it in salt until it was entirely frosted and then crammed it in one neat wholesale bite 150
into his soft pink mouth.

"But not on a gold plate?" he said.

He had to admit that.

"No, not on a gold plate," he said.

All that time he thought the fresh watercress, the moor-hens' eggs, the brown bread-and-butter, and the spring water were the most delicious, wonderful things he had ever eaten in the world. He felt that only one thing was missing. It was that whenever his grandfather spoke of fishing Uncle Crow simply took another draught of neck-oil.

"When are you goin' to take us fishing?" he said.											160

"You et up that there egg," Uncle Crow said. "That's the last one. You et that there egg up and I'll tell you what."

"What about gooin' as far as that big deep hole where the chub[4] lay?" grandfather said. "Up by the back-brook—"

"I'll tell you what, boy," Uncle Crow said, "you git your grandfather to bring you over September time, of a morning, afore the steam's off the winders. Mushroomin' time. You come over and we'll have a bit o' bacon and mushroom for breakfast and then set into the pike. You see, boy, it ain't the pikin' season now. It's too hot. Too bright. It's too bright of afternoon, and they ain't a-bitin'."

He took a long rich swig of neck-oil.											170

"Ain't that it, Lukey? That's the time, ain't it, mushroom time?"

"Thass it," his grandfather said.

"Tot out," Uncle Crow said. "Drink up. My throat's jist easin' orf a bit."

---

4. A species of fish.

He gave another wonderful belching laugh and told the boy to be sure to finish up the last of the watercress and the bread-and-butter. The little room was rich with the smell of neck-oil, and the tarry sun-baked odour of the beer-barrels that formed its walls. And through the door came, always, the sound of reeds talking in their beards, and the scent of summer meadows drifting in from beyond the great curl of the river with its kingly currents and its islands of full blown lilies, white and yellow in the sun.   180

"I see the wheat's in ear," his grandfather said. "Ain't that the time for tench, when the wheat's in ear?"

"Mushroom time," Uncle Crow said. "That's the time. You git mushroom time here, and I'll fetch you a tench out as big as a cricket bat."

He fixed the boy with an eye of wonderful watery, glassy blue and licked his lips with a lazy tongue, and said:

"You know what colour a tench is, boy?"

"Yes,' he said.

"What colour?"

"The colour of the neck-oil."   190

"Lukey," Uncle Crow said, "you got a very knowin' boy here. A very knowin' boy."

After that, when there were no more cresses or moor-hens' eggs or bread-and-butter to eat, and his grandfather said he'd get hung if he touched another drop of neck-oil, he and his grandfather walked home across the meadows.

"What work does Uncle Crow do?" he said.

"Uncle Crow? Work?—well, he ain't—Uncle Crow? Well, he works, but he ain't what you'd call a reg'lar worker—"

All they way home he could hear the reeds talking in their beards. He could see the water-lilies that reminded him so much of the gold and white inside the 200 moor-hens' eggs. He could hear the happy sound of Uncle Crow laughing and sucking at the neck-oil, and crunching the fresh salty cresses into his mouth in the tarry little room.

He felt happy, too, and the sun was a gold plate in the sky.   [1959]

Questions for Discussion and Writing

1. Compare what Grandfather says about Great Uncle Crow to what the boy actually sees. What is the source of the discrepancy? Is Grandfather lying? Explain.

2. Compare this story with Chekhov's "Easter Eve" and Woolf's "Kew Gardens." What qualities does it share with the earlier stories? How does it differ?

3. Could "Great Uncle Crow" be classed as a local color story? Why or why not?

4. Describe and analyze Bates's style. How does he use language to create the effects that he does?

5. What do you see as the point or theme of the story?

❧ GRACE PALEY
(b. 1922)

The Loudest Voice

Grace Paley's blend of traditional and postmodern techniques, social activism, and humor make her a unique and refreshing voice in contemporary literature. She was born Grace Goodside in the Bronx, New York, to parents who had emigrated from Russia. Both her mother and her father had experienced political repression and exile; both were Zionists and political activists. Her father was also a doctor and story-teller. From an early age, Grace was encouraged by her parents and older siblings to write stories and poems. She absorbed tales, characters, ideas, languages, and voices at a kitchen table that rang with political debate.

At sixteen she left high school and entered Hunter College in New York, but she left without earning a degree. In 1942, she married Jess Paley. Three years later, they separated, though they did not divorce until 1971. After working for a while as a typist and studying poetry with W. H. Auden (1907–1973) at the New School for Social Research, Paley began working with community and civil-defense protest groups in the 1950s. Meanwhile, she was also raising her children and writing poetry. It was in the short story, however, that she found her voice. *The Little Disturbances of Man* (1959), her first collection of stories, won critical acclaim and commercial success. Her second collection, *Enormous Changes at the Last Minute* (1974) brought her a new generation of fans.

Much of Paley's energy has been devoted to social and political justice. Already in the 1930s, she was concerned with women's lives and issues but feared that no one would share her interest. Anti-nuclear activities in the 1950s led to anti-Viet-Nam war protests in the 1960s and 1970s. James Joyce (1882–1941) was the most significant influence on her short stories, but she also admires Anton Chekhov (1860–1904), Gertrude Stein (1874–1946), and Virginia Woolf (1882–1941). For Paley, a story must be about "the whole of life. . . . It's got to be about everything, even if it's two pages long." Donald Barthelme called her, "a wonderful writer and troublemaker," compliments she would no doubt appreciate.

THERE IS A CERTAIN place where dumb-waiters boom, doors slam, dishes crash; every window is a mother's mouth bidding the street shut up, go skate somewhere else, come home. My voice is the loudest.

There, my own mother is still as full of breathing as me and the grocer stands up to speak to her. "Mrs. Abramowitz," he says, "people should not be afraid of their children."

"Ah, Mr. Bialik," my mother replies, "If you say to her of her father 'Ssh,' they say, 'In the grave it will be quiet.' "

"From Coney Island to the cemetery," says my papa. "It's the same subway; it's the same fare."   10

I am right next to the pickle barrel. My pinky is making tiny whirlpools in the brine. I stop a moment to announce: "Campbell's Tomato Soup. Campbell's Vegetable Beef Soup. Campbell's S-c-otch Broth. . ."

"Be quiet," the grocer says, "the labels are coming off."

"Please, Shirley, be a little quiet," my mother begs me.

In that place the whole street groans: Be quiet! Be quiet! but steals from the happy chorus of my inside self not a tittle or a jot.

There, too, but just around the corner, is a red brick building that has been old for many years. Every morning the children stand before it in double lines which must be straight. They are not insulted. They are waiting anyway.   20

I am usually among them. I am, in fact, the first, since I begin with "A."

One cold morning the monitor tapped me on the shoulder. "Go to Room 409, Shirley Abramowitz," he said. I did as I was told. I went in a hurry up a down staircase to Room 409, which contained sixth-graders. I had to wait at the desk without wiggling until Mr. Hilton, their teacher, had time to speak.

After five minutes he said, "Shirley?"

"What?" I whispered.

He said, "My! My! Shirley Abramowitz! They told me you had a particularly loud, clear voice and read with lots of expression. Could that be true?"

"Oh yes," I whispered.   30

"In that case, don't be silly; I might very well be your teacher someday. Speak up, speak up."

"Yes," I shouted.

"More like it," he said. "Now, Shirley, can you put a ribbon in your hair or a bobby pin? It's too messy."

"Yes!" I bawled.

"Now, now, calm down." He turned to the class. "Children, not a sound. Open at page 39. Read till 52. When you finish, start again. He looked me over once more. "Now, Shirley, you know, I suppose, that Christmas is coming. We are preparing a beautiful play. Most of the parts have been given out. But I still need a   40 child with a strong voice, lots of stamina. Do you know what stamina is? You do? Smart kid. You know, I heard you read 'The Lord is my shepherd' in Assembly yesterday. I was very impressed. Wonderful delivery. Mrs. Jordan, your teacher, speaks highly of you. Now listen to me, Shirley Abramowitz, if you want to take the part and be in the play, repeat after me, 'I swear to work harder than I ever did before.' "

I looked to heaven and said at once, "Oh, I swear." I kissed my pinky and looked at God.

"That is an actor's life, my dear," he explained. "Like a soldier's, never tardy or disobedient to his general, the director. Everything," he said, "absolutely every-   50 thing will depend on you."

That afternoon, all over the building, children scraped and scrubbed the turkeys and the sheaves of corn off the schoolroom windows. Goodbye

Thanksgiving. The next morning a monitor brought red paper and green paper from the office. We made new shapes and hung them on the walls and glued them to the doors.

The teachers became happier and happier. Their heads were ringing like the bells of childhood. My best friend Evie was prone to evil, but she did not get a single demerit for whispering. We learned "Holy Night" without an error. "How wonderful!" said Miss Glacé, the student teacher. "To think that some of you don't even speak the language!" We learned "Deck the Halls" and "Hark! The Herald Angels". . . . They weren't ashamed and we weren't embarrassed.

Oh, but when my mother heard about it all, she said to my father: "Misha, you don't know what's going on there. Cramer is the head of the Tickets Committee."

"Who?" asked my father. "Cramer? Oh yes, an active woman."

"Active? Active has to have a reason. Listen," she said sadly, "I'm surprised to see my neighbors making tra-la-la for Christmas."

My father couldn't think of what to say to that. Then he decided: "You're in America! Clara, you wanted to come here. In Palestine the Arabs would be eating you alive. Europe you had pogroms. Argentina is full of Indians. Here you got Christmas. . . . Some joke, ha?"

"Very funny, Misha. What is becoming of you? If we came to a new country a long time ago to run away from tyrants, and instead we fall into a creeping pogrom, that our children learn a lot of lies, so what's the joke? Ach, Misha, your idealism is going away."

"So is your sense of humor."

"That I never had, but idealism you had a lot of."

"I'm the same Misha Abramovitch, I didn't change an iota. Ask anyone."

"Only ask me," says my mama, may she rest in peace. "I got the answer."

Meanwhile the neighbors had to think of what to say too.

Marty's father said: "You know, he has a very important part, my boy."

"Mine also," said Mr. Sauerfeld.

"Not my boy!" said Mrs. Klieg. "I said to him no. The answer is no. When I say no! I mean no!"

The rabbi's wife said, "It's disgusting!" But no one listened to her. Under the narrow sky of God's great wisdom she wore a strawberry-blond wig.

Every day was noisy and full of experience. I was Right-hand Man. Mr. Hilton said: "How could I get along without you, Shirley?"

He said: "Your mother and father ought to get down on their knees every night and thank God for giving them a child like you."

He also said: "You're absolutely a pleasure to work with, my dear, dear child."

Sometimes he said: "For God's sakes, what did I do with the script? Shirley! Shirley! Find it."

Then I answered quietly: "Here it is, Mr. Hilton."

Once in a while, when he was very tired, he would cry out: "Shirley, I'm just tired of screaming at those kids. Will you tell Ira Pushkov not to come in till Lester points to that star the second time?"

Then I roared: "Ira Pushkov, what's the matter with you? Dope! Mr. Hilton told you five times already, don't come in till Lester points to that star the second time."

"Ach, Clara," my father asked, "what does she do there till six o'clock she can't even put the plates on the table?"

"Christmas," said my mother coldly.

"Ho! Ho!" my father said. "Christmas. What's the harm? After all, history teaches everyone. We learn from reading this is a holiday from pagan times also, candles, lights, even Chanukah. So we learn it's not altogether Christian. So if they think it's a private holiday, they're only ignorant, not patriotic. What belongs to history, belongs to all men. You want to go back to the Middle Ages? Is it better to   110 shave your head with a secondhand razor? Does it hurt Shirley to learn to speak up? It does not. So maybe someday she won't live between the kitchen and the shop. She's not a fool."

I thank you, Papa, for your kindness. It is true about me to this day. I am foolish but I am not a fool.

That night my father kissed me and said with great interest in my career, "Shirley, tomorrow's your big day. Congrats."

"Save it," my mother said. Then she shut all the windows in order to prevent tonsillitis.

In the morning it snowed. On the street corner a tree had been decorated for   120 us by a kind city administration. In order to miss its chilly shadow our neighbors walked three blocks east to buy a loaf of bread. The butcher pulled down black window shades to keep the colored lights from shining on his chickens. Oh, not me. On the way to school, with both my hands I tossed it a kiss of tolerance. Poor thing, it was a stranger in Egypt.

I walked straight into the auditorium past the staring children. "Go ahead, Shirley!" said the monitors. Four boys, big for their age, had already started work as propmen and stagehands.

Mr. Hilton was very nervous. He was not even happy. Whatever he started to say ended in a sideward look of sadness. He sat slumped in the middle of the first   130 row and asked me to help Miss Glacé. I did this, although she thought my voice too resonant and said, "Show-off!"

Parents began to arrive long before we were ready. They wanted to make a good impression. From among the yards of drapes I peeked out at the audience. I saw my embarrassed mother.

Ira, Lester, and Meyer were pasted to their beards by Miss Glacé. She almost forgot to thread the star on its wire, but I reminded her. I coughed a few times to clear my throat. Miss Glacé looked around and saw that everyone was in costume and on line waiting to play his part. She whispered, "All right . . ." Then:

Jackie Sauerfeld, the prettiest boy in first grade, parted the curtains with his   140 skinny elbow and in a high voice sang out:

"Parents dear
We are here
To make a Christmas play in time.
It we give

In narrative
And illustrate with pantomime."

He disappeared.
My voice burst immediately from the wings to the great shock of Ira, Lester,
and Meyer, who were waiting for it but were surprised all the same.   150
"I remember, I remember, the house where I was born . . ."
Miss Glacé yanked the curtain open and there it was, the house—an old
hayloft, where Celia Kornbluh lay in the straw with Cindy Lou, her favorite doll.
Ira, Lester, and Meyer moved slowly from the wings toward her, sometimes pointing to a moving star and sometimes ahead to Cindy Lou.
It was a long story and it was a sad story. I carefully pronounced all the
words about my lonesome childhood, while little Eddie Braunstein wandered up-
stage and down with his shepherd's stick, looking for sheep. I brought up lone-
someness again, and not being understood at all except by some women
everybody hated. Eddie was too small for that and Marty Groff took his place,   160
wearing his father's prayer shawl. I announced twelve friends, and half the boys in
the fourth grade gathered round Marty, who stood on an orange crate while my
voice harangued. Sorrowful and loud, I declaimed about love and God and Man,
but because of the terrible deceit of Abie Stock we came suddenly to a famous moment. Marty, whose remembering tongue I was, waited at the foot of the cross. He
stared desperately at the audience. I groaned, "My God, my God, why hast thou
forsaken me?" The soldiers who were sheiks grabbed poor Marty to pin him up to
die, but he wrenched free, turned again to the audience, and spread his arms aloft
to show despair and the end. I murmured at the top of my voice, "The rest is silence, but as everyone in this room, in this city—in this world—now knows, I   170
shall have life eternal."
That night Mrs. Kornbluh visited our kitchen for a glass of tea.
"How's the virgin?" asked my father with a look of concern.
"For a man with a daughter, you got a fresh mouth, Abramovitch."
"Here," said my father kindly, "Have some lemon, it'll sweeten your dispo-
sition."
They debated a little in Yiddish, then fell in a puddle of Russian and Polish.
What I understood next was my father, who said, "Still and all, it was certainly
a beautiful affair, you have to admit, introducing us to the beliefs of a different
culture."   180
"Well, yes" said Mrs. Kornbluh. "The only thing . . . you know Charlie
Turner—that cute boy in Celia's class—a couple others? They got very small parts
or no part at all. In very bad taste, it seemed to me. After all, it's their religion."
"Ach," explained my mother, "what could Mr. Hilton do? They got very
small voices; after all, why should they holler? The English language they know
from the beginning by heart. They're blond like angels. You think it's so important
they should get in the play? Christmas . . . the whole piece of goods . . . they own
it."
I listened and listened until I couldn't listen any more. Too sleepy, I climbed
out of bed and kneeled. I made a little church of my hands and said, "Hear, O   190

Israel . . ." Then I called out in Yiddish, "Please, good night, good night. Ssh." My father said, "Ssh yourself," and slammed the kitchen door.

I was happy. I fell asleep at once. I had prayed for everybody: my talking family, cousins far away, passersby, and all the lonesome Christians. I expected to be heard. My voice was certainly the loudest.   [1959]

Questions for Discussion and Writing

1. How would you describe the narrator's voice? What is its tone? Its accent?
2. Is the narrator an adult or a child? Before answering consider, "I thank you, Papa, for your kindness. It is true about me to this day. I am foolish but I am not a fool."
3. What does Shirley's refusal to be quiet tell you about her as a person? What does her loud voice symbolize or suggest?
4. Is it right for the school to sponsor a Christmas play when many if not most of the pupils are Jewish? Explain.
5. How do the various characters and families explain their participation or non-participation in the Christmas pageant?
6. How do you interpret Shirley's reaction to the Christmas tree as "a stranger in Egypt"?
7. How do you interpret the last paragraph of the story?

ERNEST J. GAINES
(b. 1933)

The Sky Is Gray

Ernest J. Gaines is an African-American writer who came to maturity in the period just before the Civil Rights movement in the early 1960s. His way was not easy. Born to sharecropper parents near Oscar, Louisiana (other sources say River Lake Plantation), he remembers digging potatoes for fifty cents a day. When Ernest was eight, his father left, and Ernest was often left to care for his paraplegic aunt, who has always remained for him an example of the strong black woman triumphing over adversity. When his mother remarried and moved to California, Ernest stayed in Louisiana to help with the younger children. Strongly motivated to get an education, he later joined his mother in Vallejo to attend high school.

During high school, Gaines began reading and found his earliest models in the Russian writers Ivan Turgenev (1818–1883), Nikolai Gogol (1809–1825), and Leo Tolstoy (1828–1910). He was drawn especially to their sympathetic but unsentimental depictions of peasants. After junior college and two years in the army, he attended San Francisco State, where he published his first story.

Upon graduation, he was awarded a Wallace Stegner fellowship to study creative writing at Stanford.

Gaines's leisurely, realistic narrative style derives from the folk and oral traditions of Louisiana's storytellers and from the influences of Mark Twain (1835–1910) and William Faulkner (1897–1962). His themes are the struggle for manhood, the value of strong role models, the importance of discipline, the need for personal dignity to confront the forces of racism, the importance of balancing tradition and change. The imaginary region of Bayonne, Louisiana, is Gaines's microcosm of America and indeed the world. The stories he tells about the people in Bayonne, like their creator, seem relaxed and gentle, but beneath the quiet surface is a toughness born of hard experience and clear thinking about ethics, values, race, and the dynamics of human interaction.

GO'N BE COMING in a few minutes, Coming 'round that bend down there full speed. And I'm go'n get out my hankercher and I'm go'n wave it down, and us go'n get on it and go.

I keep on looking for it, but Mama don't look that way no more. She looking down the road where us jest come from. It's a long old road, and far's you can see you don't see nothing but gravel. You got dry weeds on both sides, and you got trees on both sides, and fences on both sides, too. And you got cows in the pastures and they standing close together. An when us was coming out yer to catch the bus I seen the smoke coming out o' the cow's nose.

I look at my mama and I know what she thinking. I been with Mama so much, jest me and her, I know what she thinking all the time. Right now it's home—Auntie and them. She thinking if they got 'nough wood—if she left 'nough there to keep 'em warm till us get back. She thinking if it go'n rain and if any of 'em go'n have to go out in the rain. She thinking 'bout the hog—if he go'n get out, and if Ty and Val be able to get him back in. She always worry like that when she leave the house. She don't worry too much if she leave me there with the smaller ones 'cause she know I'm go'n look after 'em and look after Auntie and everything else. I'm the oldest and she say I'm the man.

I look at my mama and I love my mama. She wearing that black coat and that black hat and she looking sad. I love my mama and I want put my arm 'round her and tell her. But I'm not s'pose to do that. She say that's weakness and that's cry-baby stuff, and she don't want no cry-baby 'round her. She don't want you to be scared neither. 'Cause Ty scared of ghosts and she always whipping him. I'm scared of the dark, too. But I make 'tend I ain't. I make 'tend I ain't 'cause I'm the oldest, and I got to set a good sample for the rest. I can't ever be scared and I can't ever cry. And that's the reason I didn't never say nothing 'bout my teef. It been hurting me and hurting me close to a month now. But I didn't say it. I didn't say it 'cause I didn't want act like no cry-baby, and 'cause I know us didn't have 'nough money to have it pulled. But, Lord, it been hurting me. And look like it won't start till at night when you trying to get little sleep. Then soon's you shet your eyes— umm-umm, Lord, Look like it go right down to your heart string.

"Hurting, hanh?" Ty'd say.

I'd shake my head, but I wouldn't open my mouth for nothing. You open your mouth and let that wind in, and it almost kill you.

I'd just lay there and listen to 'em snore. Ty, there, right 'side me, and Auntie and Val over by the fireplace. Val younger 'an me and Ty, and he sleep with Auntie. Mama sleep 'round the other side with Louis and Walker.

I'd just lay there and listen to em, and listen to that wind out there, and listen to that fire in the fireplace. Sometime it'd stop long enough to let me get little rest. Sometime it just hurt, hurt, hurt. Lord, have mercy.   40

II

Auntie knowed it was hurting me. I didn't tell nobody but Ty, 'cause us buddies and he ain't go'n tell nobody. But some kind o' way Auntie found out. When she asked me, I told her no, nothing was wrong. But she knowed it all the time. She told me to mash up a piece o' aspirin and wrap it in some cotton and jugg it down in that hole. I did it, but it didn't do no good. It stopped for a little while, and started right back again. She wanted to tell Mama, but I told her Uh-uh. 'Cause I knowed it didn't have no money, and it jest was go'n make her mad again. So she told Monsieur Bayonne, and Monsieur Bayonne came to the house and told me to kneel down 'side him on the fireplace. He put his finger in his mouth and made the sign of the Cross on my jaw. The tip of Monsieur Bayonne finger is some   50 hard, 'cause he always playing on that guitar. If us sit outside at night us can always hear Monsieur Bayonne playing on his guitar. Sometime us leave him out there playing on the guitar.

He made the Sign of the Cross over and over on my jaw, but that didn't do no good. Even when he prayed and told me to pray some, too, that teef still hurt.

"How you feeling?" he say.

"Same," I say.

He kept on praying and making the Sign of the Cross and I kept on praying, too.

"Still hurting?" he say.   60

"Yes, sir."

Monsieur Bayonne mashed harder and harder on my jaw. He mashed so hard he almost pushed me on Ty. But then he stopped.

"What kind o' prayers you praying, boy?" he say.

"Baptist," I say.

"Well, I'll be—no wonder that teef still killing him. I'm going one way and he going the other. Boy, don't you know any Catholic prayers?"

"Hail Mary," I say.

"Then you better start saying it."

"Yes, sir."   70

He started mashing again, and I could hear him praying at the same time. And, sure 'nough, afterwhile it stopped.

Me and Ty went outside where Monsieur Bayonne two hounds was, and us started playing with 'em. "Let's go hunting," Ty say. "All right," I say; and us went on back in the pasture. Soon the hounds got on a trail, and me and Ty followed 'em all cross the pasture and then back in the woods, too. And then they cornered this little old rabbit and killed him, and me and Ty made 'em get back, and us picked up the rabbit and started on back home. But it had started hurting me again. It was hurting me plenty now, but I wouldn't tell Monsieur Bayonne. That night I didn't sleep a bit, and first thing in the morning Auntie told me go back 80 and let Monsieur Bayonne pray over me some more. Monsieur Bayonne was in his kitchen making coffee when I got there. Soon's he seen me, he knowed what was wrong.

"All right, kneel down there 'side that stove," he say. "And this time pray Catholic. I don't know nothing 'bout Baptist, and don't want know nothing 'bout him."

III

Last night Mama say: "Tomorrow us going to town." "It ain't hurting me no more," I say. "I can eat anything on it."

"Tomorrow us going to town," she say.

And after she finished eating, she got up and went to bed. She always go to 90 bed early now. 'Fore Daddy went in the Army, she used to stay up late. All o' us sitting out on the gallery or 'round the fire. But now, look like soon's she finish eating she go to bed.

This morning when I woke up, her and Auntie was standing 'fore the fireplace. She say: " 'Nough to get there and back. Dollar and a half to have it pulled. Twenty-five for me to go, twenty-five for him. Twenty-five for me to come back, twenty-five for him. Fifty cents left. Guess I get a little piece o' salt meat with that."

"Sure can use a piece," Auntie say. "White beans and no salt meat ain't white beans."

"I do the best I can," Mama say.   100

They was quiet after that, and I made 'tend I was still sleep.

"James, hit the floor," Auntie say.

I still made 'tend I was sleep. I didn't want 'em to know I was listening.

"All right," Auntie say, shaking me by the shoulder. "Come on. Today's the day."

I pushed the cover down to get out, and Ty grabbed it and pulled it back.

"You, too, Ty," Auntie say.

"I ain't getting no teef pulled," Ty say.

"Don't mean it ain't time to get up," Auntie say. "Hit it, Ty."

Ty got up grumbling.   110

"James, you hurry up and get in your clothes and eat your food," Auntie say. "What time y'all coming back?" she say to Mama.

"That 'leven o'clock bus," Mama say. "Got to get back in that field this evening."

"Get a move on you, James," Auntie say.

I went in the kitchen and washed my face, then I ate my breakfast. I was having bread and syrup. The bread was warm and hard and tasted good. And I tried to make it last a long time.

Ty came back there, grumbling and mad at me.

"Got to get up," he say. "I ain't having no teef pulled. What I got to be getting   120
up for."

Ty poured some syrup in his pan and got a piece of bread. He didn't wash
his hands, neither his face, and I could see that white stuff in his eyes.

"You the one getting a teef pulled," he say. "What I got to get up for. I bet
you if I was getting a teef pulled, you wouldn't be getting up. Shucks; syrup again.
I'm getting tired of this old syrup. Syrup, syrup, syrup. I want me some bacon
sometime."

"Go out in the field and work and you can have bacon," Auntie say. She
stood in the middle door looking at Ty. "You better be glad you got syrup. Some
people ain't got that—hard's time is."   130

"Shucks," Ty say. "How can I be strong."

"I don't know too much 'bout your strength," Auntie say; "but I know where
you go'n be hot, you keep that grumbling up. James, get a move on you; your
mama waiting."

I ate my last piece of bread and went in the front room. Mama was standing
'fore the fireplace warming her hands. I put on my coat and my cap, and us left
the house.

IV

I look down there again, but it still ain't coming. I almost say, "It ain't coming, yet," but I keep my mouth shet. 'Cause that's something else she don't like.
She don't like for you to say something just for nothing. She can see it ain't com-   140
ing, I can see it ain't coming, so why say it ain't coming. I don't say it, and I turn
and look at the river that's back o' us. It so cold the smoke just raising up from the
water. I see a bunch of pull-doos[1] not too far out—jest on the other side the lilies.
I'm wondering if you can eat pull-doos. I ain't too sure, 'cause I ain't never ate
none. But I done ate owls and black birds, and I done ate red birds, too. I didn't
want kill the red birds, but she made me kill 'em. They had two of 'em back there.
One in my trap, one in Ty trap. Me and Ty was go'n play with 'em and let 'em go.
But she made me kill 'em 'cause us needed the food.

"I can't, I say. "I can't."

"Here," she say. "Take it."   150

"I can't," I say. "I can't. I can't kill him, Mama. Please."

"Here," she say. "Take this fork, James."

"Please, Mama, I can't kill him," I say.

I could tell she was go'n hit me. And I jecked back, but I didn't jeck back
soon enough.

"Take it," she say.

I took it and reached in for him, but he kept hopping to the back.

"I can't, Mama," I say. The water just kept running down my face. "I can't."

"Get him out o' there," she say.

I reached in for him and he kept hopping to the back. Then I reached in far-   160
ther, and he pecked me on the hand.

1. Coots, a species of water bird.

"I can't, Mama," I say.

She slapped me again.

I reached in again, but he kept hopping out my way. Then he hopped to one side, and I reached there. The fork got him on the leg and I heard his leg pop. I pulled my hand out 'cause I had hurt him.

"Give it here," she say, and jecked the fork out my hand.

She reached and got the little bird right in the neck. I heard the fork go in his neck, and I heard it go in the ground. She brought him out and helt him right in front o' me.   170

"That's one," she say. She shook him off and gived me the fork. "Get the other one."

"I can't, Mama. I do anything. But I can't do that."

She went to the corner o' the fence and broke the biggest switch over there. I knelt 'side the trap crying.

"Get him out o' there," she say.

"I can't, Mama."

She started hitting me cross the back. I went down on the ground crying.

"Get him," she say

"Octavia," Auntie say.   180

'Cause she had come out o' the house and she was standing by the tree looking at us.

"Get him out o' there," Mama say.

"Octavia," Auntie say; "explain to him. Explain to him. Jest don't beat him. Explain to him."

But she hit me and hit me and hit me.

I'm still young. I ain't no more'an eight. But I know now. I know why I had to. (They was so little, though. They was so little, I 'member how I picked the feathers off 'em and cleaned 'em and helt 'em over the fire. Then us all ate 'em. Ain't had but little bitty piece, but us all had little bitty piece, and ever'body jest   190 looked at me, 'cause they was so proud.) S'pose she had to go away? That's why I had to do it. S'pose she had to go away like Daddy went away? Then who was go'n look after us? They had to be somebody left to carry on. I didn't know it then, but I know it now. Auntie and Monsieur Bayonne talked to me and made me see.

V

Time I see it, I get out my hankercher and start waving. It sill 'way down there, but I keep waving anyhow. Then it come closer and stop and me and Mama get on. Mama tell me go sit in the back while she pay. I do like she say, and the people look at me. When I pass the little sign that say White and Colored, I start looking for a seat. I jest see one of 'em back there, but I don't take it, 'cause I want my mama to sit down herself. She come in the back and sit down, and I lean on   200 the seat. They got seats in the front, but I know I can't sit there, 'cause I have to sit back o' the sign. Anyhow, I don't want sit there if my mama go'n sit back here.

They got a lady sitting 'side my mama and she look at me and grin little bit. I grin back, but I don't open my mouth, 'cause the wind'll get in and make that teef hurt. The lady take out a pack o' gum and reach me a slice, but I shake my head.

She reach Mama a slice, and Mama shake her head. The lady jest can't understand why a little boy'll turn down gum, and she reached me a slice again. This time I point to my jaw. The lady understand and grin little bit, and I grin little bit, but I don't open my mouth, though.

They got a girl sitting 'cross from me. She got on a red overcoat, and her hair plaited in one big plait. First, I make 'tend I don't even see her. But then I start looking at her little bit. She make 'tend she don't see me neither, but I catch her looking that way. She got a cold, and ever' now and then she hist that little hankercher to her nose. She ought to blow it, but she don't. Must think she too much a lady or something.

Ever' time she hist that little hankercher, the lady 'side her say something in her yer. She shake her head and lay her hands in her lap again. Then I catch her kind o' looking where I'm at. I grin at her. But think she'll grin back? No. She turn up her little old nose like I got some snot on my face or something. Well, I show her both o' us can turn us head. I turn mine, too, and look out at the river.

The river is gray. The sky is gray. They have pull-doos on the water. The water is wavey, and the pull-doos go up and down. The bus go 'round a turn, and you got plenty trees hiding the river. Then the bus go 'round another turn, and I can see the river again.

I look to the front where all the white people sitting. Then I look at that little old gal again. I don't look right at her, 'cause I don't want all them people to know I love her. I jest look at her little bit, like I'm looking out that window over there. But she know I'm looking that way, and she kind o' look at me, too. The lady sitting 'side her catch her this time, and she lean over and say something in her yer.

"I don't love him nothing," that little old gal say out loud.

Ever'body back there yer her mouth, and all of 'em look at us and laugh.

"I don't love you, neither," I say. "So you don't have to turn up your nose, Miss."

"You the one looking," she say.

"I wasn't looking at you," I say. "I was looking out that window, there."

"Out that window, my foot," she say. "I seen you. Ever' time I turn 'round you look at me."

"You must o' been looking yourself if you seen me all them times," I say.

"Shucks," she say. "I got me all kind o' boyfriends."

"I got girlfriends, too," I say.

"Well, I just don' want you to get your hopes up," she say.

I don't say no more to that little old gal, 'cause I don't want have to bust her in the mouth. I lean on the seat where Mama sitting, and I don' even look that way no more. When us get to Bayonne, she jugg her little old tongue out at me. I make 'tend I'm go'n hit her, and she duck down side her mama. And all the people laugh at us again.

VI

Me and Mama get off and start walking in town. Bayonne is a little bitty town. Baton Rouge is a hundred times bigger 'an Bayonne. I went to Baton Rouge once—me, Ty, Mama, and Daddy. But that was 'way back yonder—'fore he went in

the Army. I wonder when us go'n see him again. I wonder when. Look like he ain't 250
ever coming home. . . . Even the pavement all cracked in Bayonne. Got grass
shooting right out the sidewalk. Got weeds in the ditch, too; jest like they got
home.

It some cold in Bayonne. Look like it colder 'an it is home. The wind blow in
my face, and I feel that stuff running down my nose. I sniff. Mama say use that
hankercher. I blow my nose and put it back.

Us pass a school and I see them white children playing in the yard. Big old
red school, and them children jest running and playing. Then us pass a café, and I
see a bunch of 'em in there eating. I wish I was in there 'cause I'm cold. Mama tell
me keep my eyes in front where they blonks.   260

Us pass stores that got dummies, and us pass another café, and then us pass
a shoe shop, and that baldheaded man in there fixing on a shoe. I look at him and
I butt into that white lady, and Mama jeck me in front and tell me stay there.

Us come to the courthouse, and I see the flag waving there. This one yer ain't
like the one us got at school. This one yer ain't got but a handful of stars. One at
school got a big pile of stars—one for ever' state. Us pass it and us turn and there
it is—the dentist office. Me and Mama go in, and they got people sitting ever'
where you look. They even got a little boy in there younger 'an me.

Me and Mama sit on that bench, and a white lady come in there and ask me
what my name. Mama tell her, and the white lady go back. Then I yer somebody 270
hollering in there. And soon's that little boy hear him hollering, he start hollering,
too. His mama pat him and pat him, trying to make him hush up, but he ain't
thinking 'bout her.

The man that was hollering in there come out holding his jaw.

"Got it, hanh?" another man say.

The man shake his head.

"Man, I thought they was killing you in there," the other man say. "Hollering
like a pig under a gate."

The man don't say nothing. He jest head for the door, and the other man
follow him.   280

"John Lee," the white lady say. "John Lee Williams."

The little boy jugg his head down in his mama lap and holler more now. His
mama tell him go with the nurse, but he ain't thinking 'bout her. His mama tell
him again, but he don't even yer. His mama pick him up and take him in there,
and even when the white lady shet the door I can still hear him hollering.

"I often wonder why the Lord let a child like that suffer," a lady say to my
mama. The lady's sitting right in front o' us on another bench. She got on a white
dress and a black sweater. She must be a nurse or something herself, I reckoned.

"Not us to question," a man say.

"Sometimes I don't know if we shouldn't," the lady say.   290

"I know definitely we shouldn't," the man say. The man look like a preacher.
He big and fat and he got on a black suit. He got a gold chain, too.

"Why?" the lady say.

"Why anything?" the preacher say.

"Yes," the lady say. "Why anything?"

"Not us to question," the preacher say.

The lady look at the preacher a little while and look at Mama again.

"And look like it's the poor who do most the suffering," she say. "I don't understand it."

"Best not to even try," the preacher say. "He works in mysterious ways. 300 Wonders to perform."

Right then Little John Lee bust out hollering, and ever'body turn they head.

"He's not a good dentist," the lady say. "Dr. Robillard is much better. But more expensive. That's why most of the colored people come here. The white people go to Dr. Robillard. Y'all from Bayonne?"

"Down the river," my mama say. And that's all she go'n say, 'cause she don't talk much. But the lady keep on looking at her, and so she say: "Near Morgan."

"I see," the lady say.

VII

"That's the trouble with the black people in this country today," somebody 310 else say. This one yer sitting on the same side me and Mama sitting, and he kind o'sitting in front of that preacher. He look like a teacher or somebody that go to college. He got on a suit, and he got a book that he been reading. "We don't question is exactly the trouble," he say. "We should question and question and question. Question everything."

The preacher jest look at him a long time. He done put a toothpick or something in his mouth, and he jest keep turning it and turning it. You can see he don't like that boy with that book.

"Maybe you can explain what you mean," he say.

"I said what I meant," the boy say. "Question everything. Every stripe, every 320 star, every word spoken. Everything."

"It 'pears to me this young lady and I was talking 'bout God, young man" the preacher say.

"Question Him, too," the boy say.

"Wait," the preacher say. "Wait now."

"You heard me right," the boy say. "His existence as well as everything else. Everything."

The preacher jest look cross the room at the boy. You can see he getting madder and madder. But mad or no mad, the boy ain't thinking 'bout him. He look at the preacher jest's hard's the preacher look at him. 330

"Is this what they coming to?' the preacher say. "Is this what we educating them for?"

"You're not educating me," the boy say. "I wash dishes at night to go to school in the day. So even the words you spoke need questioning."

The preacher jest look at him and shake his head.

"When I come in this room and seen you there with your book, I said to myself, There's an intelligent man. How wrong a person can be."

"Show me one reason to believe in the existence of a God," the boy say.

"My heart tell me, " the preacher say.

"My heart tells me," the boy say. "My heart tells me. Sure, my heart tells me. 340

And as long as you listen to what your heart tells you, you will have only what the white man gives you and nothing more. Me, I don't listen to my heart. The purpose of the heart is to pump blood throughout the body, and nothing else."

"Who's your paw, boy?" the preacher say.

"Why?"

"Who is he?"

"He's dead."

"And your mom?"

"She's in Charity Hospital with pneumonia. Half killed herself working for nothing." 350

"And 'cause he's dead and she sick, you mad at the world?"

"I'm not mad at the world. I'm questioning the world. I'm questioning it with cold logic, sir. What do words like Freedom, Liberty, God, White, Colored mean? I want to know. That's why *you* are sending us to school, to read and to ask questions. And because we ask these questions, you call us mad. No, sir, it is not us who are mad."

"You keep saying 'us'?"

" 'Us' . . . why not? I'm not alone."

The preacher jest shake his head. Then he look at ever'body in the room— ever'body. Some of the people look down at the floor, keep from looking at him. I 360 kind o' look 'way myself, but soon's I know he done turn his head, I look that way again.

"I'm sorry for you," he say.

"Why?" the boy say. "Why not be sorry for yourself? Why are you so much better off than I am? Why aren't you sorry for these other people in here? Why not be sorry for the lady who had to drag her child into the dentist office? Why not be sorry for the lady sitting on that bench over there? Be sorry for them. Not for me. Some way or other I'm going to make it."

"No, I'm sorry for you," the preacher say.

"Of course. Of course," the boy say, shaking his head. "You're sorry for me 370 because I rock that pillar you're leaning on."

"You can't ever rock the pillar I'm leaning on, young man. It's stronger than anything man can ever do."

"You believe in God because a man told you to believe in God. A white man told you to believe in God. And why? To keep you ignorant, so he can keep you under his feet."

"So now, we the ignorant?"

"Yes," the boy say. "Yes." And he open his book again.

The preacher jest look at him there. The boy done forgot all about him. Ever'body else make 'tend they done forgot 'bout the squabble, too. 380

Then I see that preacher getting up real slow. Preacher a great big old man, and he got to brace hisself to get up. He come 'cross the room where the boy is. He jest stand there looking at him, but the boy don't raise his head.

"Stand up, boy," preacher say.

The boy look up at him, then he shet his book real slow and stand up. Preacher jest draw back and hit him in the face. The boy fall 'gainst the wall, but he straighten hisself up and look right back at that preacher.

"You forgot the other cheek," he say.

The preacher hit him again on the other side. But this time the boy don't fall.

"That hasn't changed a thing," he say.

The preacher jest look at the boy. The preacher breathing real hard like he   390
jest run up a hill. The boy sit down and open his book again.

"I feel sorry for you," the preacher say. "I never felt so sorry for a man
before."

The boy make 'tend he don't even hear that preacher. He keep on reading his
book. The preacher go back and get his hat off the chair.

"Excuse me," he say to us. "I'll come back some other time. Y'all, please excuse me."

And he look at the boy and go out the room. The boy hist his hand up to his
mouth one time, to wipe 'way some blood. All the rest o' the time he keep on
reading.   400

VIII

The lady and her little boy come out the dentist, and the nurse call somebody else in. Then little bit later they come out, and the nurse call another name.
But fast's she call somebody in there, somebody else come in the place where we
at, and the room stay full.

The people coming in now, all of 'em wearing big coats. One of 'em say
something 'bout sleeting, and another one say he hope not. Another one say he
think it ain't nothing but rain. 'Cause, he say, rain can get awful cold this time o'
year.

All 'cross the room they talking. Some of 'em talking to people right by 'em,
some of 'em talking to people clare 'cross the room, some of 'em talking to any-   410
body'll listen. It's a little bitty room, no bigger 'an us kitchen, and I can see ever'-
body in there. The little old room's full of smoke, 'cause you got two old men
smoking pipes. I think I feel my teef thumping me some, and I hold my breath
and wait. I wait and wait, but it don't thump me no more. Thank God for that.

I feel like going to sleep, and I lean back 'gainst the wall. But I'm scared to
go to sleep: Scared 'cause the nurse might call my name and I won' t hear her. And
Mama might go to sleep, too, and she be mad if neither us heard the nurse.

I look up at Mama. I love my mama. I love my mama. And when cotton
come I'm go'n get her a newer coat. And I ain't go'n get a black one neither. I think
I'm go'n get her a red one.   420

"They got some books over there," I say. "Want read one of 'em?"

Mama look at the books, but she don't answer me.

"You got yourself a little man there," the lady say.

Mama don't say nothing to the lady, but she must 'a' grin a little bit, 'cause I
seen the lady grinning back. The lady look at me a little while, like she feeling
sorry for me.

"You sure got that preacher out here in a hurry," she say to that other boy.

The boy look up at her and look in his book again. When I grow up I want
be jest like him. I want clothes like that and I want keep a book with me, too.

"You really don't believe in God?" the lady say.   430

"No," he say.

"But why?" the lady say.

"Because the wind is pink," he say.

"What?" the lady say.

The boy don't answer her no more. He jest read in his book.

"Talking 'bout the wind is pink," that old lady say. She sitting on the same bench with the boy, and she trying to look in his face. The boy make 'tend the old lady ain't even there. He jest keep reading. "Wind is pink," she say again. "Eh, Lord, what children go'n be saying next?"

The lady 'cross from us bust out laughing. 440

"That's a good one," she say. "The wind is pink. Yes, sir, that's a good one." "Don't you believe the wind is pink?" the boy say. He keep his head down in the book.

"Course I believe it, Honey," the lady say. "Course I do." She look at us and wink her eye. "And what color is grass, Honey?"

"Grass? Grass is black."

She bust out laughing again. The boy look at her.

"Don't you believe grass is black?" he say.

The lady quit laughing and look at him. Ever'body else look at him now. The place quiet, quiet. 450

"Grass is green, Honey," the lady say. "It was green yesterday, it's green today, and it's go'n be green tomorrow."

"How do you know it's green?"

"I know because I know."

"You don't know it's green. You believe it's green because someone told you it was green. If someone had told you it was black you'd believe it was black."

"It's green," the lady say. "I know green when I see green."

"Prove it's green."

"Surely, now," the lady say. Don't tell me it's coming to that?"

"It's coming to just that," the boy say. "Words mean nothing. One means no 460 more than the other."

"That's what it all coming to?" that old lady say. That old lady got on a turban and she got on two sweaters. She got a green sweater under a black sweater. I can see the green sweater 'cause some of the buttons on the other sweater missing.

"Yes, ma'am," the boy say. "Words mean nothing. Action is the only thing. Doing. That' the only thing.

"Other words, you want the Lord to come down here and show Hisself to you?" she say.

"Exactly, ma'am."

"You don't mean that, I'm sure?" 470

"I do, ma'am."

"Done, Jesus," the old lady say, shaking her head.

"I didn't go 'long with that preacher at first," the other lady say; "but now—I don't know. When a person say the grass is black, he's either a lunatic or something wrong."

"Prove to me that it's green."

"It's green because the people say it's green."

"Those same people say we're citizens of the United States."

"I think I'm a citizen."

"Citizens have certain rights. Name me one right that you have. One right, 480 granted by the Constitution, that you can exercise in Bayonne."

The lady don't answer him. She jest look at him like she don't know what he talking 'bout. I know I don't.

"Things changing," she say.

"Things are changing because some black men have begun to follow their brains instead of their hearts."

"You trying to say these people don't believe in God?"

"I'm sure some of them do. Maybe most of them do. But they don't believe that God is going to touch these white people's hearts and change them tomorrow. Things change through action. By no other way." 490

Ever'body sit quiet and look at the boy. Nobody say a thing. Then the lady 'cross from me and Mama jest shake her head.

"Let's hope that not all your generation feel the same way you do," she say.

"Think what you please, it doesn't matter," the boy say. "But it will be men who listen to their heads and not their hearts who will see that your children have a better chance than you had."

"Let's hope they ain't all like you, though," the old lady say. "Done forgot the heart absolutely."

"Yes, ma'am, I hope they aren't all like me," the boy say. "Unfortunately I was born too late to believe in your God. Let's hope that the ones who come after will 500 have your faith—if not in your God, then in something else, something definitely that they can lean on. I haven't anything. For me, the wind is pink; the grass is black."

IX

The nurse came in the room where us all sitting and waiting and say the doctor won't take no more patients till one o'clock this evening. My mama jump up off the bench and go up to the white lady.

"Nurse, I have to go back in the field this evening," she say.

"The doctor is treating his last patient now," the nurse say. "One o'clock this evening."

"Can I at least speak to the doctor?" my mama say. 510

"I'm his nurse," the lady say.

"My little boy sick," my mama say. "Right now his teef almost killing him."

The nurse look at me. She trying to make up her mind if to let me come in. I look at her real pitiful. The teef ain't hurting me a tall, but Mama say it is, so I make 'tend for her sake.

"This evening," the nurse say, and go back in the office.

"Don't feel 'jected, Honey," the lady say to Mama. "I been 'round 'em a long time—they take you when they want to. If you was white, that's something else; but you the wrong shade."

Mama don't say nothing to the lady, and me and her go outside and stand 520 'gainst the wall. It's cold out there. I can feel that wind going through my coat.

Some of the other people come out of the room and go up the street. Me and Mama stand there a little while and start to walking. I don't know where us going. When us come to the other street us jest stand there.

"You don't have to make water, do you?" Mama say.

"No, ma'am," I say.

Us go up the street. Walking real slow. I can tell Mama don't know where she going. When us come to a store us stand there and look at the dummies. I look at a little boy with a brown overcoat. He got on brown shoes, too. I look at my old shoes and look at his'n again. You wait till summer, I say. 530

Me and Mama walk away. Us come up to another store and us stop and look at them dummies, too. Then us go again. Us pass a café where the white people in there eating. Mama tell me keep my eyes in front where they blonks, but I can't help from seeing them people eat. My stomach start to growling 'cause I'm hungry. When I see people eating, I get hungry; when I see a coat, I get cold.

A man whistle at my mama when us go by a filling station. She make 'tend she don't even see him. I look back and I feel like hitting him in the mouth. If I were bigger, I say. If I was bigger, you see.

Us keep on going. I'm getting colder and colder, but I don't say nothing. I feel that stuff running down my nose and I sniff. 540

"That rag," she say.

I git it out and wipe my nose. I'm getting cold all over now—my face, my hands, my feet, ever'thing. Us pass another little café, but this'n for white people, too, and us can't go in there neither. So us jest walk. I'm so cold now, I'm 'bout ready to say it. If I knowed where us was going, I wouldn't be so cold, but I don't know where us going. Us go, us go, us go. Us walk clean out o' Bayonne. Then us cross the street and us come back. Same thing I seen when I got off the bus. Same old trees, same old walk, same old weeds, same old cracked pave—same old ever'thing.

I sniff again. 550

"That rag," she say.

I wipe my nose real fast and jugg that hankercher back in my pocket 'fore my hand get too cold. I raise my head and I can see David hardware store. When us come up to it, us go in. I don't know why, but I'm glad.

It warm in there. It so warm in there you don't want ever leave. I look for the heater, and I see it over by them ba'ls. Three white men standing 'round the heater talking in Creole.[2] One of 'em come to see what Mama want.

"Got any ax handle?" she say.

Me, Mama, and the white man start to the back, but Mama stop me when us come to the heater. Her and the white man go on. I hold my hand over the heater 560 and look at 'em. They go all the way in the back, and I see the white man point to the ax handle 'gainst the wall. Mama take one of 'em and shake it like she trying to figure how much it weigh. Then she rub her hand over it from one end to the other end. She turn it over and look at the other side, then she shake it again, and shake her head and put it back. She get another one and she do it jest like she did the first one, then she shake her head. Then she get a brown one and do it that,

2. Mixture of French and Spanish spoken in Louisiana.

too. But she don't like this one neither. Then she get another one, but 'fore she shake it or anything, she look at me. Look like she trying to say something to me, but I don't know what it is. All I know is I done got warm now and I'm feeling right smart better. Mama shake this ax handle jest like she done the others, and shake her head and say something to the white man. The white man jest look at his pile of ax handle, and when Mama pass by him to come to the front, the white man jest scratch his head and follow her. She tell me come on, and us go on out and start walking again.

Us walk and walk, and no time at all I'm cold again. Look like I'm colder now 'cause I can still remember how good it was back there. My stomach growl and I suck it in to keep Mama from yering it. She walking right 'side me, and it growl so loud you can yer it a mile. But Mama don't say a word.

X

When us come up to the courthouse, I look at the clock. It got quarter to twelve. Mean us got another hour and a quarter to be out yer in the cold. Us go and stand side a building. Something hit my cap and I look up at the sky. Sleet falling.

I look at Mama standing there. I want stand close 'side her, but she don't like that. She say that's cry-baby stuff. She say you got to stand for yourself, by yourself.

"Let's go back to that office," she say.

Us cross the street. When us get to the dentist I try to open the door, but I can't. Mama push me on the side and she twist the knob. But she can't open it neither. She twist it some more, harder, but she can't open it. She turn 'way from the door. I look at her, but I don't move and I don't say nothing. I done seen her like this before and I'm scared.

"You hungry?" she say. She say it like she mad at me, like I'm the one cause of ever'thing.

"No, ma'am," I say.

"You want eat and walk back, or you rather don't eat and ride?"

"I ain't hungry," I say.

I ain't jest hungry, but I'm cold, too. I'm so hungry and I'm so cold I want cry. And look like I'm getting colder and colder. My feet done got numb. I try to work my toes, but I can't. Look like I'm go'n die. Look like I'm go'n stand right here and freeze to death. I think about home. I think about Val and Auntie and Ty and Louis and Walker. It 'bout twelve o'clock and I know they eating dinner. I can hear Ty making jokes. That's Ty. Always trying to make some kind o' joke. I wish I was right there listening to him. Give anything in the world if I was home 'round the fire.

"Come on," Mama say.

Us start walking again. My feet so numb I can't hardly feel 'em. Us turn the corner and go back up the street. The clock start hitting for twelve.

The sleet's coming down plenty now. They hit the pave and bounce like rice. Oh, Lord; oh, Lord, I pray. Don't let me die. Don't let me die. Don't let me die, Lord.

XI

Now I know where us going. Us going back o' town where the colored people eat. I don't care if I don't eat. I been hungry before. I can stand it. But I can't stand the cold.

I can see us go'n have a long walk. It 'bout a mile down there. But I don't mind. I know when I get there I'm go'n warm myself. I think I can hold out. My hands numb in my pockets and my feet numb, too, but if I keep moving I can hold out. Jest don't stop no more, that's all.

The sky's gray. The sleet keep falling. Falling like rain now—plenty, plenty. You can hear it hitting the pave. You can see it bouncing. Sometime it bounce two times 'fore it settle.   620

Us keep going. Us don't say nothing. Us jest keep going, keep going.

I wonder what Mama thinking. I hope she ain't mad with me. When summer come I'm go'n pick plenty cotton and get her a coat. I'm go'n get her a red one.

I hope they make it summer all the time. I be glad if it was summer all the time—but it ain't. Us got to have winter, too. Lord, I hate the winter. I guess ever'-body hate the winter.

I don't sniff this time. I get out my hankercher and wipe my nose. My hand so cold I can hardly hold the handkercher.

I think us getting close, but us ain't there yet. I wonder where ever'body is. 630 Can't see nobody but us. Look like us the only two people moving 'round today. Must be too cold for the rest of the people to move 'round.

I can hear my teefes. I hope they don't knock together too hard and make that bad one hurt. Lord, that's all I need, for that bad one to start off.

I hear a church bell somewhere. But today ain't Sunday. They must be ringing for a funeral or something.

I wonder what they doing at home. They must be eating. Monsieur Bayonne might be there with his guitar. One day Ty played with Monsieur Bayonne guitar and broke one o' the string. Monsieur Bayonne got some mad with Ty. He say Ty ain' go'n never 'mount to nothing. Ty can go jest like him when he ain't there. Ty 640 can make ever'body laugh mocking Monsieur Bayonne.

I used to like to be with Mama and Daddy. Us used to be happy. But they took him in the Army. Now, nobody happy no more. . . . I be glad when he come back.

Monsieur Bayonne say it wasn't fair for 'em to take Daddy and give Mama nothing and give us nothing. Auntie say, Shhh, Etienne. Don't let 'em yer you talk like that. Monsieur Bayonne say, It's God truth. What they giving his children? They have to walk three and a half mile to school hot or cold. That's anything to give for a paw? She got to work in the field rain or shine jest to make ends meet. That's anything to give for a husband? Auntie say, Shhh, Etienne, shhh. Yes, you 650 right, Monsieur Bayonne say. Best don't say it in front of 'em now. But one day they go'n find out. One day. Yes, s'pose so, Auntie say. Then what Rose Mary? Monsieur Bayonne say. I don't know, Etienne, Auntie say. All us can do is us job, and leave ever'thing else in His hand. . . .

Us getting closer, now. Us getting closer. I can see the railroad tracks.

Us cross the tracks, and now I see the café. Jest to get in there, I say. Jest to get in there. Already I'm starting to feel little better.

XII

Us go in. Ahh, it good. I look for the heater; there 'gainst the wall. One of them little brown ones. I jest stand there and hold my hand over it. I can't open my hands too wide 'cause they almost froze.

Mama standing right 'side me. She done unbuttoned her coat. Smoke rise out the coat, and the coat smell like a wet dog.

I move to the side so Mama can have more room. She open out her hands and rub 'em together. I rub mine together, too, 'cause this keep 'em from hurting. If you let 'em warm too fast, they hurt you sure. But if you let 'em warm jest little bit at a time, and you keep rubbing 'em, they be all right ever'time.

They got jest two more people in the café. A lady back o' the counter, and a man on this side the counter. They been watching us ever since us come in.

Mama get out the hankercher and count the money. Both o' us know how much money she got there. Three dollars. No, she ain't got three dollars. 'Cause she had to pay us way up here. She ain't got but two dollars and a half left. Dollar and a half to get my teef pulled, and fifty cents for us to back on, and fifty cents worse o' salt meat.

She stir the money 'round with her finger. Most o' the money is change 'cause I can hear it rubbing together. She stir it and stir it. Then she look at the door. It still sleeting. I can yer it hitting 'gainst the wall like rice.

"I ain't hungry, Mama," I say.

"Got to pay 'em something for they heat," she say.

She take a quarter out the hankercher and tie the hankercher up again. She look over the shoulder at the people, but she still don't move. I hope she don't spend the money. I don't want her spend it on me. I'm hungry, I'm almost starving I'm so hungry, but I don't want her spending the money on me.

She flip the quarter over like she thinking. She must be thinking 'bout us walking back home. Lord, I sure don't want walk home. If I thought it done any good to say something, I say it. But my mama make up her own mind.

She turn way from the heater right fast, like she better hurry up and do it 'fore she change her mind. I turn to look at her go to the counter. The man and the lady look at her, too. She tell the lady something and the lady walk away. The man keep on looking at her. Her back turn to the man, and Mama don't even know he standing there.

The lady put some cakes and a glass o' milk on the counter. Then she pour up a cup o' coffee and set it side the other stuff. Mama pay her for the things and come back where I'm at. She tell me sit down at that table 'gainst the wall.

The milk and the cakes for me. The coffee for my mama. I eat slow, and I look at her. She looking outside at the sleet. She looking real sad. I say to myself, I'm go'n make all this up one day. You see, one day, I'm go'n make all this up. I want to say it now. I want to tell how I feel right now. But Mama don't like for us to talk like that.

"I can't eat all this," I say.

They got just three little cakes there. And I'm so hungry right now, the Lord 700
know I can eat a hundred times three. But I want her to have one.

She don't even look my way. She know I'm hungry. She know I want it. I let
it stay there a while, then I get it and eat it. I eat jest on my front teefs, 'cause if it
tech that back teef I know what'll happen. Thank God it ain't hurt me a tall today.

After I finish eating I see the man go to the juke box. He drop a nickel in it,
then he jest stand there looking at the record. Mama tell me keep my eyes in front
where they blonks. I turn my head like she say, but then I yer the man coming towards us.

"Dance, Pretty?" he say.

Mama get up to dance with him. But 'fore you know it, she done grabbed 710
the little man and done throwed him 'side the wall. He hit the wall so hard he stop
the juke box from playing.

"Some pimp," the lady back o' the counter say. "Some pimp."

The little man jump up off the floor and start towards my mama. 'Fore you
know it, Mama done sprung open her knife and she waiting for him.

"Come on," she say. "Come on. I'll cut you from your neighbo to your throat.
Come on."

I go up to the little man to hit him, but Mama make me come and stand 'side
her. The little man look at me and Mama and go back to the counter.

"Some pimp," the lady back o' the counter say. "Some pimp." She start 720
laughing at the little man. "Yes, sir, you a pimp, all right. Yes, sir."

XIII

"Fasten that coat. Let's go," Mama say.

"You don't have to leave," the lady say.

Mama don't answer the lady, and us right out in the cold again. I'm warm
right now—my hands, my yers, my feet—but I know this ain't go'n last too long.
It done sleet so much now you got ice ever'where.

Us cross the railroad tracks, and soon's us do, I get cold. That wind go
through this little old coat like it ain't nothing. I got a shirt and a sweater under it,
but that wind don't pay 'em no mind. I look up and I can see us got a long way to
go. I wonder if us go'n make it 'fore I get too cold.   730

Us cross over to walk on the sidewalk. They got jest one sidewalk back here.
It's over there.

After us go jest a little piece, I smell bread cooking. I look, then I see a baker
shop. When us get closer, I can smell it more better. I shet my eyes and make 'tend
I'm eating. But I keep 'em shet too long and I butt up 'gainst a telephone post.
Mama grab me and see if I'm hurt. I ain't bleeding or nothing and she turn me
loose.

I can feel I'm getting colder and colder, and I look up to see how far us still
got to go. Uptown is 'way up yonder. A half mile, I reckoned. I try to think of
something. They say think and you won't get cold. I think of that poem, *Annabel* 740
Lee.[3] I ain't been to school in so long—this bad weather—I reckoned they done

3. Poem by Edgar Allan Poe.

passed *Annabel Lee*. But passed it or not, I'm sure Miss Walker go'n make me recite it when I get there. That woman don't never forget nothing. I ain't never seen nobody like that.

I'm still getting cold. *Annabel Lee* or no *Annabel Lee*, I'm still getting cold. But I can see us getting closer. Us getting there gradually.

Soon's us turn the corner, I see a little old white lady up in front o' us. She the only lady on the street. She all in black and she got a long black rag over her head.

"Stop," she say.   750

Me and Mama stop and look at her. She must be crazy to be out in all this sleet. Ain't got but a few other people out there, and all of 'em men.

"Yall done ate?" she say.

"Jest finished," Mama say.

"Yall must be cold then?" she say.

"Us headed for the dentist," Mama say. "Us'll warm up when us get there."

"What dentist?" the old lady say. "Mr. Bassett?"

"Yes, ma'am," Mama say.

"Come on in," the old lady say. "I'll telephone him and tell him yall coming."

Me and Mama follow the old lady in the store. It's a little bitty store, and it   760
don't have much in there. The old lady take off her head piece and fold it up.

"Helena?" somebody call from the back.

"Yes, Alnest?" the old lady say.

"Did you see them?"

"They're here. Standing beside me."

"Good. Now you can stay inside."

The old lady look at Mama. Mama waiting to hear what she brought us in here for. I'm waiting for that, too.

"I saw yall each time you went by," she say. "I came out to catch you, but you were gone."   770

"Us went back o' town," Mama say.

"Did you eat?"

"Yes, ma'am."

The old lady look at Mama a long time, like she thinking Mama might be jest saying that. Mama look right back at her. The old lady look at me to see what I got to say. I don't say nothing. I sure ain't going 'gainst my mama.

"There's food in the kitchen," she say to Mama. "I've been keeping it warm."

Mama turn right around and start for the door.

"Just a minute," the old lady say. Mama stop. "The boy'll have to work for it. It isn't free."   780

"Us don't take no handout," Mama say.

"I'm not handing out anything," the old lady say. "I need my garbage moved to the front. Ernest has a bad cold and can't go out there."

"James'll move it for you," Mama say.

"Not unless you eat," the old lady say. "I'm old, but I have my pride, too, you know."

Mama can see she ain't go'n beat this old lady down, so she jest shake her head.

"All right," the old lady say. "Come into the kitchen."

She lead the way with that rag in her hand. The kitchen is a little bitty little 790 thing, too. The table and the stove jest about fill it up. They got a little room to the side. Somebody in there laying cross the bed. Must be the person she was talking with: Alnest or Ernest—I forget what she call him.

"Sit down," the old lady say to Mama. "Not you," she say to me. "You have to move the cans."

"Helena?" somebody say in the other room.

"Yes, Alnest?" the old lady say.

"Are you going out there again?"

"I must show the boy where the garbage is," the old lady say.

"Keep that shawl over your head," the old man say.   800

"You don't have to remind me. Come, boy," the old lady say.

Us go out in the yard. Little old back yard ain't no bigger 'an the store or the kitchen. But it can sleet here jest like it can sleet in any big back yard. And 'fore you know it I'm trembling.

"There," the old lady say, pointing to the cans. I pick up one of the cans. The can so light I put it back down to look inside o' it.

"Here," the old lady says. "Leave that cap alone."

I look at her in the door. She got that black rag wrapped 'round her shoulders, and she pointing one of her fingers at me.

"Pick it up and carry it to the front," she say. I go by her with the can. I'm 810 sure the thing's empty. She could 'a' carried the thing by herself, I'm sure. "Set it on the sidewalk by the door and come back for the other one," she say.

I go and come back, Mama look at me when I pass her. I get the other can and take it to the front. It don't feel no heavier 'an the other one. I tell myself to look inside and see just what I been hauling. First, I look up and down the street. Nobody coming. Then I look over my shoulder. Little old lady done slipped there jest 's quiet 's mouse, watching me. Look like she knowed I was go'n try that.

"Ehh, Lord," she say. "Children, children. Come in here, boy, and go wash your hands."

I follow her into the kitchen, and she point, and I go to the bathroom. When 820 I come out, the old lady done dished up the food. Rice, gravy, meat, and she even got some lettuce and tomato in a saucer. She even got a glass 'o milk and a piece 'o cake there, too. It look so good. I almost start eating 'fore I say my blessing.

"Helena?" the old man say.

"Yes, Alnest?" she say.

"Are they eating?"

"Yes," she say.

"Good," he say. "Now you'll stay inside."

The old lady go in there where he is and I can hear 'em talking. I look at Mama. She eating slow like she thinking. I wonder what 's the matter now. I reck- 830 oned she think 'bout home.

The old lady come back in the kitchen.

"I talked to Dr. Bassett's nurse," she say. "Dr. Bassett will take you as soon as you get there."

"Thank you, ma'am," Mama say.

"Perfectly all right," the old lady say. "Which one is it?"

Mama nod towards me. The old lady look at me real sad. I look sad, too.

"You're not afraid, are you?" she say.

"No'm," I say.

"That's a good boy," the old lady say. "Nothing to be afraid of."   840

When me and Mama get through eating, us thank the old lady again.

"Helena, are they leaving?" the old man say.

"Yes, Alnest."

"Tell them I say good-by."

"They can hear you, Alnest."

"Good-by both mother and son," the old man say. "And may God be with you."

Me and Mama tell the old man good-by, and us follow the old lady in the front. Mama open the door to go out, but she stop and come back in the store.

"You sell salt meat?" she say.   850

"Yes."

"Give me two bits worse."[4]

"That isn't very much salt meat," the old lady say.

"That's all I have," Mama say.

The old lady go back o' the counter and cut a big piece off the chunk. Then she wrap it and put it in a paper bag.

"Two bits," she say.

"That look like awful lot of meat for a quarter," Mama say.

"Two bits," the old lady say. "I've been selling salt meat behind this counter twenty-five years. I think I know what I'm doing."   860

"You got a scale there," Mama say.

"What?" the old lady say.

"Weigh it," Mama say.

"What?" the old lady say. "Are you telling me how to run my business?"

"Thanks very much for the food," Mama say.

"Just a minute," the old lady say.

"James," Mama say to me. I move towards the door.

"Just one minute, I said," the old lady say.

Me and Mama stop again and look at her. The old lady take the meat out the bag and unwrap it and cut 'bout half o' it off. Then she wrap it up again and jugg 870
it back in the bag and give it to Mama. Mama lay the quarter on the counter.

"Your kindness will never be forgotten," she say. "James," she say to me.

Us go out, and the old lady come to the door to look at us. After us go a little piece I look back, and she still there watching us.

The sleet's coming down heavy, heavy now, and I turn up my collar to keep my neck warm. My mama tell me turn it right back down.

"You not a bum," she say. "You a man."   [1963]

------

4. Twenty-five cents' worth.

Questions for Discussion and Writing

1. Discuss whether James's mother is right to force him to kill the bird. What is she really trying to teach him?
2. What is the purpose of the scene in the dentist's office? How does it relate to the rest of the story?
3. What is Mama's purpose in entering the hardware store? If she has no intention of buying an ax handle, why does she spend so much time looking?
4. What is the significance of the title?
5. What, if anything, does the journey motif contribute to the story?
6. What does James learn during the course of the story?
7. What does Mama mean when she says, "You not a bum. You a man." How does she define manhood?

✍ YASUNARI KAWABATA

(1899–1972)

J. MARTIN HOLMAN

Immortality

Yasunari Kawabata's *Palm-of-the-Hand Stories* are aptly named, for they are brief yet highly suggestive. Kawabata was born in Osaka, Japan. Orphaned by age three, he endured a sad and lonely childhood but was fortunate to receive an excellent education at local schools and to attend Tokyo Imperial University, graduating with a degree in Japanese literature in 1924. He also studied English literature and was greatly influenced by James Joyce's *Ulysses* (1922) and its stream-of-consciousness technique. With other writers, he helped to found a literary journal, *The Age of Literary Arts,* which featured experimental writing of the Modernist movement. *The Izu Dancer,* his first major novel, appeared in 1925. By the mid-1930s, Kawabata had abandoned Western-style experiments to return to traditional Japanese methods.

During World War II, Kawabata fled to Manchuria to avoid confronting Japan's militaristic regime. He returned to his homeland after the war but remained aloof from its politics, preferring to write and to read traditional literature. His only active social involvement was to serve as president of Japan's chapter of Poets, Essayists, and Novelists (PEN, an international writers' organization) and to speak out publicly against Communist China's Cultural Revolution in 1968.

Kawabata received every one of Japan's major literary awards, and in 1968, he became the first Japanese writer to win the Nobel Prize for Literature. He took his own life in 1972 for unknown reasons.

Kawabata's stories vary greatly in theme and method, but many are built on only the slightest story line, embellished with poetic descriptions, nuanced dialogue, and a juxtaposition of events and moods that suggests a deep and mystical meaning. Some, like "Immortality," contain aspects of magical realism, integrating the normal and the supernatural. The brevity and apparent simplicity of the stories seems consistent with Japanese art forms that attempt to distill complex experiences into the simplest forms, but in these stories there is also the influence of Western Modernism, with its symbolism and subtle use of figurative language.

A<small>N OLD MAN AND</small> a young girl were walking together.
There were a number of curious things about them. They nestled close together like lovers, as if they did not feel the sixty years' difference in their ages. The old man was hard of hearing. He could not understand most of what the girl said. The girl wore maroon *hakama* with a purple-and-white kimono in a fine arrow pattern. The sleeves were rather long. The old man was wearing clothes like those a girl would wear to pull weeds from a rice field, except that he wore no leggings. His tight sleeves and trousers gathered at the ankles looked like a woman's. His clothes hung loose at his thin waist.

They walked across a lawn. A tall wire net stood in front of them. The lovers   10
did not seem to notice that they would run into it if they kept walking. They did not stop, but walked right through the net as a spring breeze might blow through it.

After they passed through, the girl noticed the net. "Oh." She looked at the man. "Shintarō, did you pass through the net, too?"

The old man did not hear, but he grabbed the wire net. "You bastard. You bastard," he said as he shook it. He pulled too hard, and in a moment, the huge net moved away from him. The old man staggered and fell holding onto it.

"Watch out, Shintarō! What happened?" The girl put her arms around him and propped him up.

"Let go of the net . . . Oh, you've lost so much weight," the girl said.   20

The old man finally stood up. He heaved as he spoke. "Thank you." He grasped the net again, but this time lightly, with only one hand. Then in the loud voice of a deaf person he said, "I used to have to pick up balls from behind a net day after day. For seventeen long years."

"Seventeen years is a long time? . . . It's short."

"They just hit the balls as they pleased. They made an awful sound when they struck the wire net. Before I got used to it, I'd flinch. It's because of the sound of those balls that I became deaf."

It was a metal net to protect the ball boys at a golf driving range. There were wheels on the bottom so they could move forward and back and right and left.   30
The driving range and golf course next to it were separated by some trees. Originally it had been a grove of all kinds of trees, but they had been cut until only an irregular row remained.

The two walked on, the net behind them.

"What pleasant memories it brings back to hear the sound of the ocean." Wanting the old man to hear these words, the girl put her mouth to his ear. "I can hear the sound of the ocean."

"What?" The old man closed his eyes. "Ah, Misako. It's your sweet breath. Just as it was long ago."

"Can't you hear the sound of the ocean? Doesn't it bring back fond memo- 40 ries?"

"The ocean . . . Did you say the ocean? Fond memories? How could the ocean, where you drowned yourself, bring back fond memories?"

"Well, it does. This is the first time I've been back to my hometown in fifty-five years. And you've come back here, too. This brings back memories." The old man could not hear, but she went on. "I'm glad I drowned myself. That way I can think about you forever, just as I was doing at the moment I drowned myself. Besides, the only memories and reminiscences I have are those up to the time I was eighteen. You are eternally young to me. And it's the same for you. If I hadn't drowned myself and you came to the village now to see me, I'd be an old woman. 50 How disgusting. I wouldn't want you to see me like that."

The old man spoke. It was a deaf man's monologue. "I went to Tokyo and failed. And now, decrepit with age, I've returned to the village. There was a girl who grieved that we were forced to part. She had drowned herself in the ocean, so I asked for a job at a driving range overlooking the ocean. I begged them to give me the job . . . if only out of pity."

"This area where we are walking is the woods that belonged to your family."

"I couldn't do anything but pick up balls. I hurt my back from bending over all the time . . . But there was a girl who had killed herself for me. The rock cliffs were right beside me, so I could jump even if I were tottering. That's what I 60 thought."

"No. You must keep living. If you were to die, there wouldn't be anyone on earth who would remember me. I would die completely." The girl clung to him. The old man could not hear, but he embraced her.

"That's it. Let's die together. This time . . . You came for me, didn't you."

"Together? But you must live. Live for my sake, Shintarō." She gasped as she looked over his shoulder. "Oh, those big trees are still there. All three . . . just like long ago." The girl pointed, so the old man turned his eyes toward the trees.

"The golfers are afraid of those trees. They keep telling us to cut them down. When they hit a ball, they say it curves to the right as though sucked in by the 70 magic of those trees."

"Those golfers will die in due time—long before those trees. Those trees are already hundreds of years old. Those golfers talk that way, but they don't understand the life span of a man," the girl said.

"Those are trees my ancestors have looked after for hundreds of years, so I had the buyer promise not to cut the trees when I sold the land to him."

"Let's go." The girl tugged at the old man's hand. They tottered toward the great trees.

The girl passed easily through the tree trunk. The old man did the same.

"What?" The girl stared at the old man and marveled. "Are you dead too, 80 Shintarō? Are you? When did you die?"

He did not answer.

"You *have* died . . . Haven't you? How strange I didn't meet you in the world of the dead. Well, try walking through the tree trunk once more to test whether you're dead or alive. If you are dead we can go inside the tree and stay."

They disappeared inside the tree. Neither the old man nor the young girl appeared again.

The color of evening began to drift onto the small saplings behind the great trees. The sky beyond turned a faint red where the ocean sounded.   [1963]

Questions for Discussion and Writing

1. Reconstruct the past lives of the two characters from information provided by the story.
2. Underline or highlight passages that convey the supernatural. Are these passages convincing? Why or why not? Is this a ghost story?
3. Does the story emphasize the importance of life or its lack of importance? Explain your answer.
4. What kind of immortality does the story depict?
5. What part does nature play in the lives of the people in this story? What part do people play in nature?

✒ JOYCE CAROL OATES

(b.1938)

Where Are You Going, Where Have You Been?

Joyce Carol Oates is a one-woman publishing phenomenon, who at last count had produced thirty volumes of short stories, twenty-four novels, and ten plays, in addition to poetry, essays, and criticism. She has even written a book on boxing.

She was born into an Irish-Catholic working-class family in Millersport, New York, a town so small that it still had a one-room school. Oates graduated Phi Beta Kappa from Syracuse University in 1956 and went on to earn an M.A. in English from the University of Wisconsin. After marriage in 1961, she taught for five years at the University of Detroit and then ten years at the University of Windsor in Canada. Since 1978 she has been writer-in-residence and distinguished professor at Princeton, where she and her husband produce the *Ontario Review* and run the Ontario Press.

Generalizing about an output as vast and varied as Oates's is risky, but typically she writes more in the Realistic mode than the Postmodern. Among her thematic concerns are characters who attempt to impose a vision or ideology on life and then disintegrate when reality fails to conform to their vision of it. She is an avowed enemy of the solipsism that she sees in much of contemporary writing, a vision of the world in which the self rather than the common vision of the whole is the standard and arbiter of reality and morality.

Critics frequently remark on the violence in her work—often of the most horrible kinds: incest, rape, murder, infanticide, self-mutilation, animal mutilation, and wife abuse. While these atrocities do occur in real life, unfortunately, at times Oates's fascination with such acts seems gratuitous.

In "Where Are You Going, Where Have You Been?" there is no violence as such; just a sense of menace from a young man who at first seems a harmless adolescent in the James Dean mold but who looks increasingly like a demon lover of folktale or myth or a malevolent criminal.

H ER NAME WAS Connie. She was fifteen and she had a quick, nervous giggling habit of craning her neck to glance into mirrors or checking other people's faces to make sure her own was all right. Her mother, who noticed everything and knew everything and who hadn't much reason any longer to look at her own face, always scolded Connie about it. "Stop gawking at yourself. Who are you? You think you're so pretty?" she would say. Connie would raise her eyebrows at these familiar old complaints and look right through her mother, into a shadowy vision of herself as she was right at that moment: she knew she was pretty and that was everything. Her mother had been pretty once too, if you could believe those old snapshots in the album, but now her looks were gone and that was why she was always after Connie.

"Why don't you keep your room clean like your sister? How've you got your hair fixed—what the hell stinks? Hair spray? You don't see your sister using that junk."

Her sister June was twenty-four and still lived at home. She was a secretary in the high school Connie attended, and if that wasn't bad enough—with her in the same building—she was so plain and chunky and steady that Connie had to hear her praised all the time by her mother and her mother's sisters. June did this, June did that, she saved money and helped clean the house and cooked and Connie couldn't do a thing, her mind was all filled with trashy daydreams. Their father was away at work most of the time and when he came home he wanted supper and he read the newspaper at supper and after supper he went to bed. He didn't bother talking much to them, but around his bent head Connie's mother kept picking at her until Connie wished her mother was dead and she herself was dead and it was all over. "She makes me want to throw up sometimes," she complained to her friends. She had a high, breathless, amused voice that made everything she said sound a little forced, whether it was sincere or not.

There was one good thing: June went places with girl friends of hers, girls who were just as plain and steady as she, and so when Connie wanted to do that her mother had no objections. The father of Connie's best girl friend drove the girls the three miles to town and left them at a shopping plaza so they could walk through the stores or go to a movie, and when he came to pick them up again at eleven he never bothered to ask what they had done.

They must have been familiar sights, walking around the shopping plaza in their shorts and flat ballerina slippers that always scuffed the sidewalk, with charm bracelets jingling on their thin wrists; they would lean together to whisper and laugh secretly if someone passed who amused or interested them. Connie had

long dark blond hair that drew anyone's eye to it, and she wore part of it pulled up
on her head and puffed out; and the rest of it she let fall down her back. She wore
a pull-over jersey blouse that looked one way when she was at home and another 40
way when she was away from home. Everything about her had two sides to it, one
for home and one for anywhere that was not home: her walk, which could be
childlike and bobbing, or languid enough to make anyone think she was hearing
music in her head; her mouth, which was pale and smirking most of the time, but
bright and pink on these evenings out; her laugh, which was cynical and drawling
at home—"Ha, ha, very funny,"—but high-pitched and nervous anywhere else,
like the jingling of the charms on her bracelet.

Sometimes they did go shopping or to a movie, but sometimes they went
across the highway, ducking fast across the busy road, to a drive-in restaurant
where older kids hung out. The restaurant was shaped like a big bottle, though 50
squatter than a real bottle, and on its cap was a revolving figure of a grinning boy
holding a hamburger aloft. One night in midsummer they ran across, breathless
with daring, and right away someone leaned out a car window and invited them
over, but it was just a boy from high school they didn't like. It made them feel
good to be able to ignore him. They went up through the maze of parked and
cruising cars to the bright-lit, fly-infested restaurant, their faces pleased and expectant as if they were entering a sacred building that loomed up out of the night to
give them what haven and blessing they yearned for. They sat at the counter and
crossed their legs at the ankles, their thin shoulders rigid with excitement, and listened to the music that made everything so good: the music was always in the 60
background, like music at a church service; it was something to depend upon.

A boy named Eddie came in to talk with them. He sat backwards on his
stool, turning himself jerkily around in semicircles and then stopping and turning
back again, and after a while he asked Connie if she would like something to eat.
She said she would and so she tapped her friend's arm on her way out—her friend
pulled her face up into a brave, droll look—and Connie said she would meet her
at eleven, across the way. "I just hate to leave her like that," Connie said earnestly,
but the boy said that she wouldn't be alone for long. So they went out to his car,
and on the way Connie couldn't help but let her eyes wander over the windshields
and faces all around her, her face gleaming with a joy that had nothing to do with 70
Eddie or even this place; it might have been the music. She drew her shoulders up
and sucked in her breath with the pure pleasure of being alive, and just at that
moment she happened to glance at a face just a few feet from hers. It was a boy
with shaggy black hair, in a convertible jalopy painted gold. He stared at her and
then his lips widened into a grin. Connie slit her eyes at him and turned away, but
she couldn't help glancing back and there he was, still watching her. He wagged a
finger and laughed and said, "Gonna get you, baby," and Connie turned away
again without Eddie noticing anything.

She spent three hours with him, at the restaurant where they ate hamburgers
and drank Cokes in wax cups that were always sweating, and then down an alley a 80
mile or so away, and when he left her off at five to eleven only the movie house
was still open at the plaza. Her girl friend was there, talking with a boy. When
Connie came up, the two girls smiled at each other and Connie said, "How was

the movie?" and the girl said, "*You* should know." They rode off the with girl's father, sleepy and pleased, and Connie couldn't help but look back at the darkened shopping plaza with its big empty parking lot and its signs that were faded and ghostly now, and over at the drive-in restaurant where cars were still circling tirelessly. She couldn't hear the music at this distance.

Next morning June asked her how the movie was and Connie said, "So-so."

She and that girl and another girl went out several times a week, and the rest of the time Connie spent around the house—it was summer vacation—getting in her mother's way and thinking, dreaming about the boys she met. But all the boys fell back and dissolved into a single face that was not even a face but an idea, a feeling, mixed up with the urgent insistent pounding of the music and the humid night air of July. Connie's mother kept dragging her back to the daylight by finding things for her to do or saying suddenly, "What's this about the Pettinger girl?"

And Connie would say nervously, "Oh, her. That dope." She always drew thick clear lines between herself and such girls, and her mother was simple and kind enough to believe it. Her mother was so simple, Connie thought, that it was maybe cruel to fool her so much. Her mother went scuffling around the house in old bedroom slippers and complained over the telephone to one sister about the other, then the other called up and the two of them complained about the third one. If June's name was mentioned her mother's tone was approving, and if Connie's name was mentioned it was disapproving. This did not really mean she disliked Connie, and actually Connie thought that her mother preferred her to June just because she was prettier, but the two of them kept up a pretense of exasperation, a sense that they were tugging and struggling over something of little value to either of them. Sometimes, over coffee, they were almost friends, but something would come up—some vexation that was like a fly buzzing suddenly around their heads—and their faces went hard with contempt.

One Sunday Connie got up at eleven—none of them bothered with church—and washed her hair so that it could dry all day long in the sun. Her parents and sister were going to a barbeque at an aunt's house and Connie said no, she wasn't interested, rolling her eyes to let her mother know just what she thought of it. "Stay home alone then," her mother said sharply. Connie sat out back in a lawn chair and watched them drive away, her father quiet and bald, hunched around so that he could back the car out, her mother with a look that was still angry and not at all softened through the windshield, and in the back seat poor old June, all dressed up as if she didn't know what a barbeque was, with all the running yelling kids and the flies. Connie sat with her eyes closed in the sun, dreaming and dazed with the warmth about her as if this were a kind of love, the caresses of love, and her mind slipped over onto thoughts of the boy she had been with the night before and how nice he had been, how sweet it always was, not the way someone like June would suppose but sweet, gentle, the way it was in movies and promised in songs; and when she opened her eyes she hardly knew where she was, the back yard ran off into weeds and a fence-like line of trees and behind it the sky was perfectly blue and still. The asbestos "ranch house" that was now three years old startled her—it looked small. She shook her head as if to get awake.

It was too hot. She went inside the house and turned on the radio to drown

out the quiet. She sat on the edge of her bed, barefoot, and listened for an hour   130
and a half to a program called XYZ Sunday Jamboree, record after record of hard,
fast, shrieking songs she sang along with, interspersed by exclamations from
"Bobby King": "An' look here, you girls at Napoleon's—Son and Charley want you
to pay real close attention to this song coming up."

And Connie paid close attention herself, bathed in a glow of slow-pulsed joy
that seemed to rise mysteriously out of the music itself and lay languidly about the
airless little room, breathed in and breathed out with each gentle rise and fall of
her chest.

After a while she heard a car coming up the drive. She sat up at once, startled, because it couldn't be her father so soon. The gravel kept crunching all the   140
way in from the road—the driveway was long—and Connie ran to the window. It
was a car she didn't know. It was an open jalopy, painted a bright gold that caught
the sunlight opaquely. Her heart began to pound and her fingers snatched at her
hair, checking it, and she whispered, "Christ. Christ," wondering how bad she
looked. The car came to a stop at the side door and the horn sounded four short
taps, as if this were a signal Connie knew.

She went into the kitchen and approached the door slowly, then hung out
the screen door, her bare toes curling down off the step. There were two boys in
the car and now she recognized the driver: he had shaggy, shabby black hair that
looked crazy as a wig and he was grinning at her.   150

"I ain't late, am I?" he said.

"Who the hell do you think you are?" Connie said.

"Toldja I'd be out, didn't I?"

"I don't even know who you are."

She spoke sullenly, careful to show no interest or pleasure, and he spoke in a
fast, bright monotone. Connie looked past him to the other boy, taking her time.
He had fair brown hair, with a lock that fell onto his forehead. His sideburns gave
him a fierce, embarrassed look, but so far he hadn't even bothered to glance at her.
Both boys wore sunglasses. The driver's glasses were metallic and mirrored everything in miniature.   160

"You wanta come for a ride?" he said.

Connie smirked and let her hair fall loose over one shoulder.

"Don'tcha like my car? New paint job," he said. "Hey."

"What?"

"You're cute."

She pretended to fidget, chasing flies away from the door.

"Don'tcha believe me, or what?" he said.

"Look, I don't even know who you are," Connie said in disgust.

"Hey, Ellie's got a radio, see. Mine broke down." He lifted his friend's arm
and showed her the little transistor radio the boy was holding, and now Connie   170
began to hear the music. It was the same program that was playing inside the
house.

"Bobby King?" she said.

"I listen to him all the time. I think he's great."

"He's kind of great," Connie said reluctantly.

"Listen, that guy's *great*. He knows where the action is."

Connie blushed a little, because the glasses made it impossible for her to see just what this boy was looking at. She couldn't decide if she liked him or if he was a jerk, and so she dawdled in the doorway and wouldn't come down or go back inside. She said, "What's all that stuff painted on your car?"   180

"Can'tcha read it?" He opened the door very carefully, as if he were afraid it might fall off. He slid out just as carefully, planting his feet firmly on the ground, the tiny metallic world in his glasses slowing down like gelatine hardening, and in the midst of it Connie's bright green blouse. "This here is my name, to begin with," he said. ARNOLD FRIEND was written in tarlike black letters on the side, with a drawing of a round, grinning face that reminded Connie of a pumpkin, except it wore sunglasses. "I wanta introduce myself, I'm Arnold Friend and that's my real name and I'm gonna be your friend, honey, and inside the car's Ellie Oscar, he's kinda shy." Ellie brought his transistor radio up to his shoulder and balanced it there. "Now, these numbers are a secret code, honey," Arnold Friend explained. He   190 read off the numbers 33, 19, 17 and raised his eyebrows at her to see what she thought of that, but she didn't think much of it. The left rear fender had been smashed and around it was written, on the gleaming gold background: DONE BY CRAZY WOMAN DRIVER. Connie had to laugh at that. Arnold Friend was pleased at her laughter and looked up at her. "Around the other side's a lot more—you wanta come and see them?"

"No."

"Why not?"

"Why should I?"

"Don'tcha wanta see what's on the car? Don'tcha wanta go for a ride?"   200

"I don't know."

"Why not?"

"I got things to do."

"Like what?"

"Things."

He laughed as if she had said something funny. He slapped his thighs. He was standing in a strange way, leaning back against the car as if he were balancing himself. He wasn't tall, only an inch or so taller than she would be if she came down to him. Connie liked the way he was dressed, which was the way all of them dressed: tight faded jeans stuffed into black, scuffed boots, a belt that pulled his   210 waist in and showed how lean he was, and a white pull-over shirt that was a little soiled and showed the hard small muscles of his arms and shoulders. He looked as if he probably did hard work, lifting and carrying things. Even his neck looked muscular. And his face was a familiar face, somehow: the jaw and chin and cheeks slightly darkened because he hadn't shaved for a day or two, and the nose long and hawklike, sniffing as if she were a treat he was going to gobble up and it was all a joke.

"Connie, you ain't telling the truth. This is your day set aside for a ride with me and you know it," he said, still laughing. The way he straightened and recovered from his fit of laughing showed that it had been all fake.   220

"How do you know what my name is?" she said suspiciously.

"It's Connie."

"Maybe and maybe not."

"I know my Connie," he said, wagging his finger. Now she remembered him even better, back at the restaurant, and her cheeks warmed at the thought of how she had sucked in her breath just at the moment she passed him—how she must have looked to him. And he had remembered her. "Ellie and I come here especially for you," he said. "Ellie can sit in back. How about it?"

"Where?"

"Where what?" 230

"Where're we going?"

He looked at her. He took off the sunglasses and she saw how pale the skin around his eyes was, like holes that were not in shadow but instead in light. His eyes were like chips of broken glass that catch the light in an amiable way. He smiled. It was as if the idea of going for a ride somewhere, to someplace, was a new idea to him.

"Just for a ride, Connie sweetheart."

"I never said my name was Connie," she said.

"But I know what it is. I know your name and all about you, lots of things," Arnold Friend said. He had not moved yet but stood still leaning back against the 240 side of his jalopy. "I took a special interest in you, such a pretty girl, and found out all about you—like I know your parents and sister are gone somewheres and I know where and how long they're going to be gone, and I know who you were with last night, and your best girl friend's name is Betty. Right?"

He spoke in a simple lilting voice, exactly as if he were reciting the words to a song. His smile assured her that everything was fine. In the car Ellie turned up the volume on his radio and did not bother to look around at them.

"Ellie can sit in the back seat," Arnold Friend said. He indicated his friend with a casual jerk of his chin, as if Ellie did not count and she should not bother with him. 250

"How'd you find out all that stuff?" Connie said.

"Listen: Betty Schultz and Tony Fitch and Jimmy Pettinger and Nancy Pettinger," he said in a chant. "Raymond Stanley and Bob Hutter—"

"Do you know all those kids?"

"I know everybody."

"Look, you're kidding. You're not from around here."

"Sure."

"But—how come we never saw you before?"

"Sure you saw me before," he said. He looked down at his boots, as if he were a little offended. "You just don't remember." 260

"I guess I'd remember you," Connie said.

"Yeah?" He looked up at this beaming. He was pleased. He began to mark time with the music from Ellie's radio, tapping his fists lightly together. Connie looked away from his smile to the car, which was painted so bright it almost hurt her eyes to look at it. She looked at that name, ARNOLD FRIEND. And up at the front fender was an expression that was familiar—MAN THE FLYING SAUCERS. It was an expression kids had used the year before but didn't use this year. She looked at it for a while as if the words meant something to her that she did not yet know.

"What're you thinking about? Huh?" Arnold Friend demanded. "Not worried about your hair blowing around in the car, are you?"   270

"No."

"Think I maybe can't drive good."

"How do I know?"

"You're a hard girl to handle. How come?" he said. "Don't you know I'm your friend? Didn't you see me put my sign in the air when you walked by?"

"What sign?"

"My sign." And he drew an X in the air, leaning out toward her. They were maybe ten feet apart. After his hand fell back to his side the X was still in the air, almost visible. Connie let the screen door close and stood perfectly still inside it, listening to the music from her radio and the boy's blend together. She stared at   280 Arnold Friend. He stood there so stiffly relaxed, pretending to be relaxed, with one hand idly on the door handle as if he were keeping himself up that way and had no intention of ever moving again. She recognized most things about him, the tight jeans that showed his thighs and buttocks and the greasy leather boots and the tight shirt, and even that slippery friendly smile of his, that sleepy dreamy smile that all the boys used to get across ideas they didn't want to put into words. She recognized all this and also the singsong way he talked, slightly mocking, kidding, but serious and a little melancholy, and she recognized the way he tapped one fist against the other in homage to the perpetual music behind him. But all these things did not come together.   290

She said suddenly, "Hey, how old are you?"

His smile faded. She could see then that he wasn't a kid, he was much older—thirty, maybe more. At this knowledge her heart began to pound faster.

"That's a crazy thing to ask. Can'tcha see I'm your own age?"

"Like hell you are."

"Or maybe a coupla years older. I'm eighteen."

"Eighteen?" she said doubtfully.

He grinned to reassure her and lines appeared at the corners of his mouth. His teeth were big and white. He grinned so broadly his eyes became slits and she saw how thick the lashes were, thick and black as if painted with a black tarlike   300 material. Then, abruptly, he seemed to become embarrassed and looked over his shoulder at Ellie. "*Him*, he's crazy," he said. "Ain't he a riot? He's a nut, a real character." Ellie was still listening to the music. His sunglasses told nothing about what he was thinking. He wore a bright orange shirt unbuttoned halfway to show his chest, which was a pale, bluish chest and not muscular like Arnold Friend's. His shirt collar was turned up all around and the very tips of the collar pointed out past his chin as if they were protecting him. He was pressing the transistor radio up against his ear and sat there in a kind of daze, right in the sun.

"He's kinda strange," Connie said.

"Hey, she says you're kinda strange! Kinda strange!" Arnold Friend cried. He   310 pounded on the car to get Ellie's attention. Ellie turned for the first time and Connie saw with shock that he wasn't a kid either—he had a fair, hairless face, cheeks reddened slightly as if the veins grew too close to the surface of his skin, the face of a forty-year-old baby. Connie felt a wave of dizziness rise in her at this sight and she stared at him as if waiting for something to change the shock of the moment, make it all right again. Ellie's lips kept shaping words, mumbling along with the words blasting in his ear.

"Maybe you two better go away," Connie said faintly.

"What? How come?" Arnold Friend cried. "We come out here to take you for a ride. It's Sunday." He had the voice of the man on the radio now. It was the same   320 voice, Connie thought. "Don'tcha know it's Sunday all day? And honey, no matter who you were with last night, today you're with Arnold Friend and don't you forget it! Maybe you better step out here," he said, and this last was in a different voice. It was a little flatter, as if the heat was finally getting to him.

"No. I got things to do."

"Hey."

"You two better leave."

"We ain't leaving until you come with us."

"Like hell I am—"

"Connie, don't fool around with me. I mean—I mean, don't fool *around*," he   330 said, shaking his head. He laughed incredulously. He placed his sunglasses on top of his head, carefully, as if he were indeed wearing a wig, and brought the stems down behind his ears. Connie stared at him, another wave of dizziness and fear rising in her so that for a moment he wasn't even in focus but was just a blur standing there against his gold car, and she had the idea that he had driven up the driveway all right but had come from nowhere before that and belonged nowhere and that everything about him and even about the music that was so familiar to her was only half real.

"If my father comes and sees you—"

"He ain't coming. He's at a barbecue."   340

"How do you know that?"

"Aunt Tillie's. Right now they're—uh—they're drinking. Sitting around," he said vaguely, squinting as if he were staring all the way to town and over to Aunt Tillie's back yard. Then the vision seemed to get clear and he nodded energetically. "Yeah. Sitting around. There's your sister in a blue dress, huh? And high heels, the poor sad bitch—nothing like you, sweetheart! And your mother's helping some fat woman with the corn—they're cleaning the corn—husking the corn—"

"What fat woman?" Connie cried.

"How do I know what fat woman, I don't know every goddamn fat woman in the world!" Arnold Friend laughed.   350

"Oh, that's Mrs. Hornsby. . . . Who invited her?" Connie said. She felt a little lightheaded. Her breath was coming quickly.

"She's too fat. I don't like them fat. I like them the way you are, honey," he said, smiling sleepily at her. They stared at each other for a while through the screen door. He said softly, "Now, what you're going to do is this: you're going to come out that door. You're going to sit up front with me and Ellie's going to sit in the back, the hell with Ellie, right? This isn't Ellie's date. You're my date. I'm your lover, honey."

"What? You're crazy—"

"Yes, I'm your lover. You don't know what that is but you will," he said. "I   360 know that too. I know all about you. But look: it's real nice and you couldn't ask for nobody better than me, or more polite. I always keep my word. I'll tell you how it is, I'm always nice at first, the first time. I'll hold you so tight you won't think you have to try to get away or pretend anything because you'll know you can't. And I'll come inside you where's it's all secret and you'll give in to me and you'll love me—"

"Shut up! You're crazy!" Connie said. She backed away from the door. She put her hands up against her ears as if she'd heard something terrible, something not meant for her. "People don't talk like that, you're crazy," she muttered. Her heart was almost too big now for her chest and its pumping made sweat break out all over her. She looked out to see Arnold Friend pause and then take a step toward the porch, lurching. He almost fell. But, like a clever drunken man, he managed to catch his balance. He wobbled in his high boots and grabbed hold of one of the porch posts.

"Honey?" he said. "You still listening?"

"Get the hell out of here!"

"Be nice, honey. Listen."

"I'm going to call the police—"

He wobbled again and out of the side of his mouth came a fast spat curse, an aside not meant for her to hear. But even this "Christ!" sounded forced. Then he began to smile again. She watched this smile come, awkward as if he were smiling from inside a mask. His whole face was a mask, she thought wildly, tanned down to his throat but then running out as if he had plastered make-up on his face but had forgotten about his throat.

"Honey—?" Listen, here's how it is. I always tell the truth and I promise you this: I ain't coming in that house after you."

"You better not! I'm going to call the police if you—if you don't—"

"Honey," he said, talking right through her voice, "honey, I'm not coming in there but you are coming out here. You know why?"

She was panting. The kitchen looked like a place she had never seen before, some room she had run inside but that wasn't good enough, wasn't going to help her. The kitchen window had never had a curtain, after three years, and there were dishes in the sink for her to do—probably—and if you ran your hand across the table you'd probably feel something sticky there.

"You listening, honey? Hey?"

"—going to call the police—"

"Soon as you touch the phone I don't need to keep my promise and can come inside. You won't want that."

She rushed forward and tried to lock the door. Her fingers were shaking. "But why lock it," Arnold Friend said gently, talking right into her face. "It's just a screen door. It's just nothing." One of his boots was at a strange angle, as if his foot wasn't in it. It pointed out to the left, bent at the ankle. "I mean, anybody can break through a screen door and glass and wood and iron or anything else if he needs to, anybody at all, and specially Arnold Friend. If the place got lit up with fire, honey, you'd come runnin' out into my arms, right into my arms an' safe at home—like you knew I was your lover and'd stopped fooling around. I don't mind a nice shy girl but I don't like no fooling around." Part of those words were spoken with a slight rhythmic lilt, and Connie somehow recognized them—the echo of a song from last year, about a girl rushing into her boy friend's arms and coming home again—   410

Connie stood barefoot on the linoleum floor, staring at him. "What do you want?" she whispered.

"I want you," he said.

"What?"

"Seen you that night and thought, that's the one, yes sir. I never needed to look anymore."

"But my father's coming back. He's coming to get me. I had to wash my hair first—" She spoke in a dry, rapid voice, hardly raising it for him to hear.

"No, your daddy is not coming and yes, you had to wash your hair and you washed it for me. It's nice and shining and all for me. I thank you sweetheart," he   420
said with a mock bow, but again he almost lost his balance. He had to bend and adjust his boots. Evidently his feet did not go all the way down; the boots must have been stuffed with something so that he would seem taller. Connie stared out at him and behind him at Ellie in the car, who seemed to be looking off toward Connie's right, into nothing. This Ellie said, pulling the words out of the air one after another as if he were just discovering them, "You want me to pull out the phone?"

"Shut your mouth and keep it shut," Arnold Friend said, his face red from bending over or maybe from embarrassment because Connie had seen his boots. "This ain't none of your business."   430

"What—what are you doing? What do you want?" Connie said. "If I call the police they'll get you, they'll arrest you—"

"Promise was not to come in unless you touch that phone, and I'll keep that promise," he said. He resumed his erect position and tried to force his shoulders back. He sounded like a hero in a movie, declaring something important. But he spoke too loudly and it was as if he were speaking to someone behind Connie. "I ain't made plans for coming in that house where I don't belong but just for you to come out to me, the way you should. Don't you know who I am?"

"You're crazy," she whispered. She backed away from the door but did not want to go into another part of the house, as if this would give him permission to   440
come through the door. "What do you. . . you're crazy, you. . . ."

"Huh? What're you saying, honey?"

Her eyes darted everywhere in the kitchen. She could not remember what it was, this room.

"This is how it is, honey: you come out and we'll drive away, have a nice ride. But if you don't come out we're gonna wait till your people come home and then they're all going to get it."

"You want that telephone pulled out?" Ellie said. He held the radio away from his ear and grimaced, as if without the radio the air was too much for him.

"I toldja shut up, Ellie," Arnold Friend said, "you're deaf, get a hearing aid,   450
right? Fix yourself up. This little girl's no trouble and's gonna be nice to me, so Ellie keep to yourself, this ain't your date—right? Don't hem in on me, don't hog, don't crush, don't bird dog, don't trail me," he said in a rapid, meaningless voice, as if he were running through all the expressions he'd learned but was no longer

sure which of them was in style, then rushing on to new ones, making them up with his eyes closed. "Don't crawl under my fence, don't squeeze in my chipmunk hole, don't sniff my glue, suck my popsicle, keep your own greasy fingers on yourself!" He shaded his eyes and peered in at Connie, who was backed against the kitchen table. "Don't mind him, honey, he's just a creep. He's a dope. Right? I'm the boy for you and like I said, you come out here nice like a lady and give me your hand, and nobody else gets hurt, I mean, your nice old bald-headed daddy and your mummy and your sister in her high heels. Because listen: why bring them in this?"

"Leave me alone," Connie whispered.

"Hey, you know that old woman down the road, the one with the chickens and stuff—you know her?"

"She's dead!"

"Dead? What? You know her?" Arnold Friend said.

"She's dead—"

"Don't you like her?"

"She's dead—she's—she isn't here any more—"

"But don't you like her, I mean, you got something against her? Some grudge or something?" Then his voice dipped as if he were conscious of a rudeness. He touched the sunglasses perched up on top of his head as if to make sure they were still there. "Now, you be a good girl."

"What are you going to do?"

"Just two things, or maybe three," Arnold Friend said. "But I promise it won't last long and you'll like me the way you get to like people you're close to. You will. It's all over for you here, so come on out. You don't want your people in any trouble, do you?"

She turned and bumped against a chair or something, hurting her leg, but she ran into the back room and picked up the telephone. Something roared in her ear, a tiny roaring, and she was so sick with fear that she could do nothing but listen to it—the telephone was clammy and very heavy and her fingers groped down to the dial but were too weak to touch it. She began to scream into the phone, into the roaring. She cried out, she cried for her mother, she felt her breath start jerking back and forth in her lungs as if it were something Arnold Friend was stabbing her with again and again with no tenderness. A noisy sorrowful wailing rose all about her and she was locked inside it the way she was locked inside this house.

After a while she could hear again. She was sitting on the floor with her wet back against the wall.

Arnold Friend was saying from the door, "That's a good girl. Put the phone back."

She kicked the phone away from her.

"No, honey. Pick it up. Put it back right."

She picked it up and put it back. The dial tone stopped.

"That's a good girl. Now, you come outside."

She was hollow with what had been fear but what was now just an emptiness. All that screaming had blasted it out of her. She sat, one leg cramped under her, and deep inside her brain was something like a pinpoint of light that kept going and would not let her relax. She thought, I'm not going to see my mother again. She thought, I'm not going to sleep in my bed again. Her bright green blouse was all wet.

Arnold Friend said, in a gentle-loud voice that was like a stage voice, "The place where you came from ain't there any more, and where you had in mind to go is cancelled out. This place you are now—inside your daddy's house—is nothing but a cardboard box I can knock down any time. You know that and always did know it. You hear me?"

She thought, I have got to think. I have got to know what to do.

"We'll go out to a nice field, out in the country here where it smells so nice 510 and it's sunny," Arnold Friend said. "I'll have my arms tight around you so you won't need to try to get away and I'll show you what love is like, what it does. The hell with this house! It looks solid all right," he said. He ran a fingernail down the screen and the noise did not make Connie shiver, as it would have the day before. "Now, put your hand on your heart, honey. Feel that? That feels solid too but we know better. Be nice to me, be sweet like you can because what else is there for a girl like you but to be sweet and pretty and give in?—and get away before her people come back?"

She felt her pounding heart. Her hand seemed to enclose it. She thought for the first time in her life that it was nothing that was hers, that belonged to her, but 520 just a pounding, living thing inside this body that wasn't really hers either.

"You don't want them to get hurt," Arnold Friend went on. "Now, get up, honey. Get up all by yourself."

She stood.

"Now, turn this way. That's right. Come over here to me.—Ellie, put that away, didn't I tell you? You dope. You miserable creepy dope," Arnold Friend said. His words were not angry but only part of an incantation. The incantation was kindly. "Now, come out through the kitchen to me, honey, and let's see a smile, try it, you're a brave, sweet little girl and now they're eating corn and hot dogs cooked to bursting over an outdoor fire, and they don't know one thing about you and 530 never did and honey, you're better than them because not a one of them would have done this for you."

Connie felt the linoleum under her feet; it was cool. She brushed her hair back out of her eyes. Arnold Friend let go of the post tentatively and opened his arms for her, his elbows pointing in toward each other and his wrists limp, to show that this was an embarrassed embrace and a little mocking, he didn't want to make her self-conscious.

She put out her hand against the screen. She watched herself push the door slowly open as if she were back safe somewhere in the other doorway, watching this body and this head of long hair moving out into the sunlight where Arnold 540 Friend waited.

"My sweet little blue-eyed girl," he said in a half-sung sigh that had nothing to do with her brown eyes but was taken up just the same by the vast sunlit reaches of the land behind him and on all sides of him—so much land that Connie had never seen before and did not recognize except to know that she was going to it.   [1965]

Questions for Discussion and Writing

1. Analyze Connie's character. How does she see herself? Explain how we as readers see her differently from the way she sees herself.

2. Who or what is Arnold Friend? Why does he seem sinister, even supernatural?

3. Will Connie go with Arnold at the end of the story? If so, where is she going? What will happen to her?

4. Is this an initiation story, similar to "My Kinsman, Major Molineaux"? Or, is something far more threatening occurring? Support your answer.

ᴖ DORIS LESSING
(b. 1919)

The Black Madonna

In spite of all attempts to define her, Doris Lessing (née Doris May Taylor) escapes easy description and categorization. The range and quantity of her fiction is enormous—traditional realism, Postmodern experimentalism, science fiction and fantasy—and she has also written plays, poetry, and essays.

Born in Iran of British parents, she grew up in Rhodesia (now Zimbabwe). After two marriages ended in divorce, she moved to England in 1949, where she has lived ever since. Her first works were in the reformist tradition of nineteenth-century women writers like Harriet Beecher Stowe (1811–1896) and Elizabeth Gaskell (1810–1865); her manner was traditional realism and her chief targets were white colonialism and racism.

Her most famous work, *The Golden Notebook* (1962) is a feminist manifesto and an attack on the inadequacies of Marxism, Freudianism, and the limits of the traditional novel. *The Children of Violence* series of novels was capped by *The Four-Gated City* (1969), in which she turns to Sufi mysticism (a form of Islam influenced by Indian religious thought) as a framework for a new beginning. Much of her fiction explores the interior world of women's lives, the constraints faced by women who seek to step over the traditional boundaries, and the psychic cost of rebellion and freedom. Whatever the subject or setting, Lessing continually seeks to understand through fiction the world we experience and how we might respond to its constantly changing realities. These explorations have led to numerous shifts in philosophy and politics, but Lessing is more interested in responding to changing conditions than in following any orthodoxy or system.

"Black Madonna" is a product of her African experiences and the racial politics encountered there, but it also raises fascinating questions about the nature of art and reality and illustrates what can happen when value systems and cultures come in conflict.

T HERE ARE SOME COUNTRIES in which the arts, let alone Art, cannot be said to
flourish. Why this should be so it is hard to say, although of course we all
have our theories about it. For sometimes it is the most barren soil that sends up
gardens of those flowers which we all agree are the crown and justification of life,
and it is this fact which makes it hard to say, finally, why the soil of Zambesia[1]
should produce such reluctant plants.

Zambesia is a tough, sunburnt, virile, positive country contemptuous of subtleties and sensibility: yet there have been States with these qualities which have
produced art, though perhaps with the left hand. Zambesia is, to put it mildly, unsympathetic to those ideas so long taken for granted in other parts of the world, to   10
do with liberty, fraternity and the rest. Yet there are those, and some of the finest
souls among them, who maintain that art is impossible without a minority whose
leisure is guaranteed by a hard-working majority. And whatever Zambesia's comfortable minority may lack, it is not leisure.

Zambesia—but enough; out of respect for ourselves and for scientific accuracy, we should refrain from jumping to conclusions. Particularly when one remembers the almost wistful respect Zambesians show when an artist does appear
in their midst.

Consider, for instance, the case of Michele.

He came out of the internment camp at the time when Italy was made a sort   20
of honorary ally, during the Second World War.[2] It was a time of strain for the authorities, because it is one thing to be responsible for thousands of prisoners of
war whom one must treat according to certain recognized standards; it is another
to be faced, and from one day to the next, with these same thousands transformed
by some international legerdemain into comrades in arms. Some of the thousands
stayed where they were in the camps; they were fed and housed there at least.
Others went as farm labourers, though not many; for while the farmers were as always short of labour, they did not know how to handle farm labourers who were
also white men: such a phenomenon had never happened in Zambesia before.
Some did odd jobs around the towns, keeping a sharp eye out for the trade   30
unions, who would neither admit them as members nor agree to their working.

Hard, hard, the lot of these men, but fortunately not for long, for soon the
war ended and they were able to go home.

Hard, too, the lot of the authorities, as has been pointed out; and for that
reason they were doubly willing to take what advantages they could from the situation; and that Michele was such an advantage there could be no doubt.

His talents were first discovered when he was still a prisoner of war. A
church was built in the camp, and Michele decorated its interior. It became a
show-place, that little tin-roofed church in the prisoners' camp, with its whitewashed walls covered all over with frescoes depicting swarthy peasants gathering   40
grapes for the vintage, beautiful Italian girls dancing, plump dark-eyed children.
Amid crowded scenes of Italian life, appeared the Virgin and her Child, smiling
and beneficent, happy to move familiarly among her people.

1. Lessing's fictional name for Rhodesia, now Zimbabwe.
2. Italy was Germany's ally in World War II, but was defeated by the Allies in 1943; hence, the part of Italy
   that was not in German hands joined the Allies. Rhodesia, as a British colony, supported the Allies.

Culture-loving ladies who had bribed the authorities to be taken inside the camp would say, "Poor thing, how homesick he must be." And they would beg to be allowed to leave half a crown[3] for the artist. Some were indignant. He was a prisoner, after all, captured in the very act of fighting against justice and democracy, and what right had he to protest?—for they felt these paintings as a sort of protest. What was there in Italy that we did not have right here in Westonville, which was the capital and hub of Zambesia? Were there not sunshine and moun- 50 tains and fat babies and pretty girls here? Did we not grow—if not grapes, at least lemons and oranges and flowers in plenty?

People were upset—the desperation of nostalgia came from the painted white walls of that simple church, and affected everyone according to his temperament.

But when Michele was free, his talent was remembered. He was spoken of as "that Italian artist." As a matter of fact, he was a bricklayer. And the virtues of those frescoes might very well have been exaggerated. It is possible they would have been overlooked altogether in a country where picture-covered walls were more common. 60

When one of the visiting ladies came rushing out to the camp in her own car, to ask him to paint her children, he said he was not qualified to do so. But at last he agreed. He took a room in the town and made some nice likenesses of the children. Then he painted the children of a great number of the first lady's friends. He charged ten shillings a time. Then one of the ladies wanted a portrait of herself. He asked ten pounds for it; it had taken him a month to do. She was annoyed, but paid.

And Michele went off to his room with a friend and stayed there drinking red wine from the Cape and talking about home. While the money lasted he could not be persuaded to do any more portraits. 70

There was a good deal of talk among the ladies about the dignity of labour, a subject in which they were well versed; and one felt they might almost go so far as to compare a white man with a kaffir[4] who did not understand the dignity of labour either.

He was felt to lack gratitude. One of the ladies tracked him down, found him lying on a camp-bed under a tree with a bottle of wine, and spoke to him severely about the barbarity of Mussolini and the fecklessness of the Italian temperament. Then she demanded that he should instantly paint a picture of herself in her new evening dress. He refused, and she went home very angry.

It happened that she was the wife of one of our most important citizens, a 80 General or something of that kind, who was at that time engaged in planning a military tattoo or show for the benefit of the civilian population. The whole of Westonville had been discussing this show for weeks. We were all bored to extinction by dances, fancy-dress balls, fairs, lotteries and other charitable entertainments. It is not too much to say that while some were dying for freedom, others were dancing for it. There comes a limit to everything. Though, of course, when the end of the war actually came and the thousands of troops stationed in the

3. Two shillings, six pence (British money).
4. An obsolete and generally derogatory term for a member of a Bantu-speaking tribe of southern Africa.

country had to go home—in short, when enjoying ourselves would no longer be a duty, many were heard to exclaim that life would never be the same again.

In the meantime, the Tattoo[5] would make a nice change for us all. The military gentlemen responsible for the idea did not think of it in these terms. They thought to improve morale by giving us some idea of what war was really like. Headlines in the newspaper were not enough. And in order to bring it all home to us, they planned to destroy a village by shell-fire before our very eyes.

First, the village had to be built.

It appears that the General and his subordinates stood around in the red dust of the parade-ground under a burning sun for the whole of one day, surrounded by building materials, while hordes of African labourers ran around with boards and nails, trying to make something that looked like a village. It became evident that they would have to build a proper village in order to destroy it; and this would cost more than was allowed for the whole entertainment. The General went home in a bad temper, and his wife said what they needed was an artist, they needed Michele. This was not because she wanted to do Michele a good turn; she could not endure the thought of him lying around singing while there was work to be done. She refused to undertake any delicate diplomatic missions when her husband said he would be damned if he would ask favours of any little Wop. She solved the problem for him in her own way: a certain Captain Stocker was sent out to fetch him.

The Captain found him on the same camp-bed under the same tree, in rolled-up trousers, and an uncollared shirt; unshaven, mildly drunk, with a bottle of wine standing beside him on the earth. He was singing an air so wild, so sad, that the Captain was uneasy. He stood at ten paces from the disreputable fellow and felt the indignities of his position. A year ago, this man had been a mortal enemy to be shot at sight. Six months ago, he had been an enemy prisoner. Now he lay with his knees up, in an untidy shirt that had certainly once been military. For the Captain, the situation crystallized in a desire that Michele should salute him.

"Piselli!" he said sharply.

Michele turned his head and looked at the Captain from the horizontal. "Good morning," he said affably.

"You are wanted," said the Captain.

"Who?" said Michele. He sat up, a fattish, olive-skinned little man. His eyes were resentful.

"The authorities."

"The war is over?"

The Captain, who was already stiff and shiny enough in his laundered khaki, jerked his head back frowning, chin out. He was a large man, blond, and wherever his flesh showed, it was brick-red. His eyes were small and blue and angry. His red hands, covered all over with fine yellow bristles, clenched by his side. Then he saw the disappointment in Michele's eyes, and the hands unclenched. "No it is not over," he said. "Your assistance is required."

"For the war?"

5. A military exercise or display for the purpose of entertainment.

"For the war effort. I take it you are interested in defeating the Germans?"

Michele looked at the Captain. The little dark-eyed artisan looked at the great blond officer with his cold blue eyes, his narrow mouth, his hands like bristle-covered steaks. He looked and said: "I am very interested in the end of the war."

"Well?" said the Captain between his teeth.

"The pay?" said Michele.

"You will be paid."

Michele stood up. He lifted the bottle against the sun, then took a gulp. He rinsed his mouth out with wine and spat. Then he poured what was left on the red earth, where it made a bubbling purple stain.

"I am ready," he said. He went with the Captain to the waiting lorry,[6] where he climbed in beside the driver's seat and not, as the Captain had expected, into the back of the lorry. When they had arrived at the parade-ground the officers had left a message that the Captain would be personally responsible for Michele and for the village. Also for the hundred or so labourers who were sitting around on the grass verges waiting for orders.

The Captain explained what was wanted. Michele nodded. Then he waved his hand at the Africans. "I do not want these," he said.

"You will do it yourself—a village?"

"Yes."

"With no help?"

Michele smiled for the first time. "I will do it."

The Captain hesitated. He disapproved on principle of white men doing heavy manual labour. He said: "I will keep six to do the heavy work."

Michele shrugged; and the captain went over and dismissed all but six of the Africans. He came back with them to Michele.

"It is hot," said Michele.

"Very," said the Captain. They were standing in the middle of the parade-ground. Around its edge trees, grass, gulfs of shadow. Here, nothing but reddish dust, drifting and lifting in a low hot breeze.

"I am thirsty," said Michele. He grinned. The Captain felt his stiff lips loosen unwillingly in reply. The two pairs of eyes met. It was a moment of understanding. For the Captain, the little Italian had suddenly become human. "I will arrange it," he said, and went off down-town. By the time he had explained the position to the right people, filled in forms and made arrangements, it was late afternoon. He returned to the parade-ground with a case of Cape brandy, to find Michele and the six black men seated together under a tree. Michele was singing an Italian song to them, and they were harmonizing with him. The sight affected the Captain like an attack of nausea. He came up, and the Africans stood to attention. Michele continued to sit.

"You said you would do the work yourself?"

"Yes, I said so."

The Captain then dismissed the Africans. They departed, with friendly looks

6. Truck.

towards Michele, who waved at them. The Captain was beef-red with anger. "You have not started yet?"

"How long have I?"

"Three weeks." 180

"Then there is plenty of time," said Michele, looking at the bottle of brandy in the Captain's hand. In the other were two glasses. "It is evening," he pointed out. The Captain stood frowning for a moment. Then he sat down on the grass, and poured out two brandies.

"Ciao," said Michele.

"Cheers," said the Captain. Three weeks, he was thinking. Three weeks with this damned little Itie! He drained his glass and refilled it, and set it in the grass. The grass was cool and soft. A tree was flowering somewhere close—hot waves of perfume came on the breeze.

"It is nice here," said Michele. "We will have a good time together. Even in a 190 war, there are times of happiness. And of friendship, I drink to the end of the war."

Next day, the Captain did not arrive at the parade-ground until after lunch. He found Michele under the trees with a bottle. Sheets of ceiling board had been erected at one end of the parade-ground in such a way that they formed two walls and part of a third, and a slant of steep roof supported on struts.

"What's that?" said the Captain, furious.

"The church," said Michele.

"Wha-at?"

"You will see. Later. It is very hot." He looked at the brandy bottle that lay on 200 its side on the ground. The Captain went to the lorry and returned with the case of brandy. They drank. Time passed. It was a long time since the Captain had sat on grass under a tree. It was a long time, for that matter, since he had drunk so much. He always drank a great deal, but it was regulated to the times and seasons. He was a disciplined man. Here, sitting on the grass beside this little man whom he still could not help thinking of as an enemy, it was not that he let his self-discipline go, but that he felt himself to be something different: he was temporarily set outside his normal behaviour. Michele did not count. He listened to Michele talking about Italy, and it seemed to him he was listening to a savage speaking: as if he heard tales from the mythical South Sea islands where a man 210 like himself might very well go just once in his life. He found himself saying he would like to make a trip to Italy after the war. Actually, he was attracted only by the North and by Northern people. He had visited Germany, under Hitler, and though it was not the time to say so, had found it very satisfactory. Then Michele sang him some Italian songs. He sang Michele some English songs. Then Michele took out photographs of his wife and children, who lived in a village in the mountains of North Italy. He asked the Captain if he were married. The Captain never spoke about his private affairs.

He had spent all his life in one or other of the African colonies as a police-man, magistrate, native commissioner, or in some other useful capacity. When the 220 war started, military life came easily to him. But he hated city life, and had his own reasons for wishing the war over. Mostly, he had been in bush-stations with one or two other white men, or by himself, far from the rigours of civilization. He had relations with native women; and from time to time visited the city where his wife lived with her parents and the children. He was always tormented by the idea that she was unfaithful to him. Recently he had even appointed a private detective to watch her; he was convinced the detective was inefficient. Army friends coming from L—— where his wife was, spoke of her at parties, enjoying herself. When the war ended, she would not find it so easy to have a good time. And why did he not simply live with her and be done with it? The fact was, he could not. And his long exile to remote bush-stations was because he needed the excuse not to. He could not bear to think of his wife for too long; she was that part of his life he had never been able, so to speak, to bring to heel.

Yet he spoke of her now to Michele, and of his favourite bushwife, Nadya. He told Michele the story of his life, until he realized that the shadows from the trees they sat under had stretched right across the parade-ground to the grandstand. He got unsteadily to his feet, and said: "There is work to be done. You are being paid to work."

"I will show you my church when the light goes."

The sun dropped, darkness fell, and Michele made the Captain drive his lorry on to the parade-ground a couple of hundred yards away and switch on his lights. Instantly, a white church sprang up from the shapes and shadows of the bits of board.

"Tomorrow, some houses," said Michele cheerfully.

At the end of a week, the space at the end of the parade-ground had crazy gawky constructions of lath and board over it, that looked in the sunlight like nothing on this earth. Privately, it upset the Captain; it was like a nightmare that these skeleton-like shapes should be able to persuade him, with the illusions of light and dark, that they were a village. At night, the Captain drove up his lorry, switched on the lights, and there it was, the village, solid and real against a background of full green trees. Then, in the morning sunlight, there was nothing there, just bits of board stuck in the sand.

"It is finished," said Michele.

"You were engaged for three weeks," said the Captain. He did not want it to end, this holiday for himself.

Michele shrugged. "The army is rich," he said. Now, to avoid curious eyes, they sat inside the shade of the church, with the case of brandy between them. The Captain talked, talked endlessly, about his wife, about women. He could not stop talking.

Michele listened. Once he said: "When I go home—when I go home—I shall open my arms . . ." He opened them, wide. He closed his eyes. Tears ran down his cheeks. "I shall take my wife in my arms, and I shall ask nothing, nothing. I do not care. It is enough to be together. That is what the war has taught me. It is enough, it is enough. I shall ask no questions and I shall be happy."

The Captain stared before him, suffering. He thought how he dreaded his wife. She was a scornful creature, gay and hard, who laughed at him. She had been laughing at him ever since they married. Since the war, she had taken to calling him names like Little Hitler, and Storm-trooper. "Go ahead, my little Hitler," she had cried last time they met. "Go ahead, my Storm-trooper. If you want to waste your money on private detectives, go ahead. But don't think I don't know what *you* do when you're in the bush. I don't care what you do, but remember that I know it . . ."

The Captain remembered her saying it. And there sat Michele on his packing-case saying: "It's a pleasure for the rich, my friend, detectives and the law. Even jealousy is a pleasure I don't want any more. Ah, my friend, to be together with my wife again, and the children, that is all I ask of life. That and wine and food and singing in the evenings." And the tears wetted his cheeks and splashed on to his shirt.

That a man should cry, good lord! thought the Captain. And without shame! He seized the bottle and drank.   280

Three days before the great occasion, some high-ranking officers came strolling through the dust, and found Michele and the Captain sitting together on the packing-case, singing. The Captain's shirt was open down the front, and there were stains on it.

The Captain stood to attention with the bottle in his hand, and Michele stood to attention too, out of sympathy with his friend. Then the officers drew the Captain aside—they were all cronies of his—and said, what the hell did he think he was doing? And why wasn't the village finished?

Then they went away.

"Tell them it is finished," said Michele. "Tell them I want to go."   290

"No," said the Captain, "no. Michele, what would you do if your wife . . . "

"This world is a good place. We should be happy—that is all."

"Michele . . . "

"I want to go. There is nothing to do. They paid me yesterday."

"Sit down, Michele. Three more days, and then it's finished."

"Then I shall paint the inside of the church as I painted the one in the camp."

The Captain laid himself down on some boards and went to sleep. When he woke, Michele was surrounded by the pots of paint he had used on the outside of the village. Just in front of the Captain was a picture of a black girl. She was young   300 and plump. She wore a patterned blue dress and her shoulders came soft and bare out of it. On her back was a baby slung in a band of red stuff. Her face was turned towards the Captain and she was smiling.

"That's Nadya," said the Captain. "Nadya . . . " He groaned loudly.

He looked at the black child and shut his eyes. He opened them, and mother and child were still there. Michele was very carefully drawing thin yellow circles around the heads of the black girl and her child.

"Good God," said the Captain, "you can't do that."

"Why not?"

"You can't have a black Madonna."   310

"She was a peasant. This is a peasant. Black peasant Madonna for black country."

"This is a German village," said the Captain.

"This is my Madonna," said Michele angrily. "Your German village and my Madonna. I paint this picture as an offering to the Madonna. She is pleased—I feel it."

The Captain lay down again. He was feeling ill. He went back to sleep.

When he woke for the second time it was dark. Michele had brought in a flaring paraffin lamp, and by its light was working on the long wall. A bottle of brandy stood beside him. He painted until long after midnight, and the Captain lay on his 320 side and watched, as passive as a man suffering a dream. Then they both went to sleep on the boards. The whole of the next day Michele stood painting black Madonnas, black saints, black angels. Outside, troops were practising in the sunlight, bands were blaring and motor cyclists roared up and down. But Michele painted on, drunk and oblivious. The Captain lay on his back, drinking and muttering about his wife. Then he would say "Nadya, Nadya," and burst into sobs.

Towards nightfall the troops went away. The officers came back, and the Captain went off with them to show how the village sprang into being when the great lights at the end of the parade-ground were switched on. They all looked at the village in silence. They switched the lights off, and there were only the tall an- 330 gular boards leaning like gravestones in the moonlight. On went the lights—and there was the village. They were silent, as if suspicious. Like the Captain, they seemed to feel it was not right. Uncanny it certainly was, but *that* was not it. Unfair—that was the word. It was cheating. And profoundly disturbing.

"Clever chap, that Italian of yours," said the General.

The Captain, who had been woodenly correct until this moment, suddenly came rocking up to the General, and steadied himself by laying his hand on the august shoulder. "Bloody Wops," he said. "Bloody kaffirs. Bloody . . . Tell you what, though, there's one Itie that's some good. Yes, there is. I'm telling you. He's a friend of mine, actually."   340

The General looked at him. Then he nodded at his underlings. The Captain was taken away for disciplinary purposes. It was decided, however, that he must be ill, nothing else could account for such behavior. He was put to bed in his own room with a nurse to watch him.

He woke twenty-four hours later, sober for the first time in weeks. He slowly remembered what had happened. Then he sprang out of bed and rushed into his clothes. The nurse was just in time to see him run down the path and leap into his lorry.

He drove at top speed to the parade-ground, which was flooded with light in such a way that the village did not exist. Everything was in full swing. The cars 350 were three deep around the square, with people on the running-boards and even the roofs. The grandstand was packed. Women dressed up as gipsies, country girls, Elizabethan court dames, and so on, wandered about with trays of ginger beer and sausage-rolls and programmes at five shillings each in aid of the war effort. On the square, troops deployed, obsolete machine-guns were being dragged up and down, bands played, and motor cyclists roared through flames.

As the Captain parked the lorry, all this activity ceased, and the lights went out. The Captain began running around the outside of the square to reach the place where the guns were hidden in a mess of net and branches. He was sobbing with the effort. He was a big man, and unused to exercise, and sodden with 360 brandy. He had only one idea in his mind—to stop the guns firing, to stop them at all costs.

Luckily, there seemed to be a hitch. The lights were still out. The unearthly graveyard at the end of the square glittered white in the moonlight. Then the lights briefly switched on, and the village sprang into existence for just long enough to show large red crosses all over a white building beside the church. Then moonlight flooded everything again, and the crosses vanished. "Oh, the bloody fool!" sobbed the Captain, running, running as if for his life. He was no longer trying to reach the guns. He was cutting across a corner of the square direct to the church. He could hear some officers cursing behind him: "Who put those red crosses there? Who? We can't fire on the Red Cross." 370

The Captain reached the church as the searchlights burst on. Inside, Michele was kneeling on the earth looking at his first Madonna. "They are going to kill my Madonna," he said miserably.

"Come away, Michele, come away."

"They're going to . . . "

The Captain grabbed his arm and pulled. Michele wrenched himself free and grabbed a saw. He began hacking at the ceiling board. There was a dead silence outside. They heard a voice booming through the loudspeakers: "The village that is about to be shelled is an English village, not as represented on the programme, a German village. Repeat, the village that is about to be shelled is . . . " 380

Michele had cut through two sides of a square around the Madonna.

"Michele," sobbed the Captain, *"get out of here."*

Michele dropped the saw, took hold of the raw edges of the board and tugged. As he did so, the church began to quiver and lean. An irregular patch of board ripped out and Michele staggered back into the Captain's arms. There was a roar. The church seemed to dissolve around them into flame. Then they were running away from it, the Captain holding Michele tight by the arm. "Get down," he shouted suddenly, and threw Michele to the earth. He flung himself down beside him. Looking from under the crook of his arm, he heard the explosion, saw a great pillar of smoke and flame, and the village disintegrated in a flying mass of debris. 390 Michele was on his knees gazing at his Madonna in the light from the flames. She was unrecognizable, blotted out with dust. He looked horrible, quite white and a trickle of blood soaked from his hair down one cheek.

"They shelled my Madonna," he said.

"Oh, damn it, you can paint another one," said the Captain. His own voice seemed to him strange, like a dream voice. He was certainly crazy, as mad as Michele himself . . . He got up, pulled Michele to his feet, and marched him towards the edge of the field. There they were met by the ambulance people. Michele was taken off to hospital, and the Captain was sent back to bed. 400

A week passed. The Captain was in a darkened room. That he was having some kind of a breakdown was clear, and two nurses stood guard over him. Sometimes he lay quiet. Sometimes he muttered to himself. Sometimes he sang in a thick clumsy voice bits out of opera, fragments from Italian songs, and—over and over again—There's a Long Long Trail. He was not thinking of anything at all. He shied away from the thought of Michele as if it were dangerous. When, therefore, a cheerful female voice announced that a friend had come to cheer him up, and it would do him good to have some company, and he saw a white bandage moving towards him in the gloom, he turned sharp over on to his side, face to the wall. 410

"Go away," he said. "Go away, Michele."

"I have come to see you," said Michele. "I have brought you a present."

The Captain slowly turned over. There was Michele, a cheerful ghost in the dark room. "You fool," he said. "You messed everything up. What did you paint those crosses for?"

"It was a hospital," said Michele. "In a village there is a hospital, and on the hospital the Red Cross, the beautiful Red Cross—no?"

"I was nearly court-martialled."

"It was my fault," said Michele. "I was drunk."

"I was responsible."

"How could you be responsible when I did it? But it is all over. Are you better?"

"Well, I suppose those crosses saved your life."

"I did not think," said Michele. "I was remembering the kindness of the Red Cross people when we were prisoners."

"Oh shut up, shut up, shut up."

"I have brought you a present."

The Captain peered through the dark. Michele was holding up a picture. It was of a native woman with a baby on her back smiling sideways out of the frame.

Michele said: "You did not like the haloes. So this time, no haloes. For the Captain—no Madonna." He laughed. "You like it? It is for you. I painted it for you."

"God damn you!" said the Captain.

"You do not like it?" said Michele, very hurt.

The Captain closed his eyes. "What are going to do next?" he asked tiredly.

Michele laughed again. "Mrs Pannerhurst, the lady of the General, she wants me to paint her picture in her white dress. So I paint it."

"You should be proud to."

"Silly bitch. She thinks I am good. They know nothing—savages. Barbarians. Not you, Captain, you are my friend. But these people they know nothing."

The Captain lay quiet. Fury was gathering in him. He thought of the General's wife. He disliked her, but he had known her well enough.

"These people," said Michele. "They do not know a good picture from a bad picture. I paint, I paint, this way, that way. There is the picture—I look and laugh inside myself." Michele laughed out loud. They say, he is a Michelangelo, this one, and try to cheat me out of my price. Michele—Michelangelo—that is a joke, no?"

The Captain said nothing.

"But for you I painted this picture to remind you of our good times with the village. You are my friend. I will always remember you."

The Captain turned his eyes sideways in his head and stared at the black girl. Her smile at him was half innocence, half malice.

"Get out," he said suddenly.

Michele came closer and bent to see the Captain's face. "You wish me to go?" He sounded unhappy. "You saved my life. I was a fool that night. But I was thinking of my offering to the Madonna—I was a fool, I say it myself. I was drunk, we are fools when we are drunk."

"Get out of here," said the Captain again.

For a moment the white bandage remained motionless. Then it swept down-wards in a bow.

Michele turned towards the door.   460

"And take that bloody picture with you."

Silence. Then, in the dim light, the Captain saw Michele reach out for the picture, his white head bowed in profound obeisance. He straightened himself and stood to attention, holding the picture with one hand, and keeping the other stiff down his side. Then he saluted the Captain.

"Yes, *sir,*" he said, and he turned and went out of the door with the picture.

The Captain lay still. He felt—what did he feel? There was a pain under his ribs. It hurt to breathe. He realized he was unhappy. Yes, a terrible unhappiness was filling him, slowly, slowly. He was unhappy because Michele had gone. Nothing had ever hurt the Captain in all his life as much as that mocking, *Yes, sir.*   470 Nothing. He turned his face to the wall and wept. But silently. Not a sound es-caped him, for the fear the nurses might hear.   [1965]

Questions for Discussing and Writing

1. How can it be that in one light Michele's village looks like a ramshackle col-lection of boards but in another light like a real village? Is this a realistic de-tail or a metaphorical one? Explain.
2. Analyze the characters of the Captain and Michele. What are their differences in culture, personality, philosophy of life?
3. The ladies talk about the dignity of labor. Is labor dignified? Is painting (or any sort of creativity) a form of labor? Explain.
4. Compare the Captain in Lessing's story to the Officer in Lawrence's "The Prussian Officer." Are they military stereotypes? Explain.
5. Why does the Captain refuse Michele's picture?
6. What does the story suggest about racism and colonialism?
7. What does the story suggest about art?

❧ YUKIO MISHIMA (KIMITAKE HIRAOKA)
(1925–1970)

TRANSLATED BY IVAN MORRIS

Swaddling Clothes

Yukio Mishima at once dazzles and infuriates, inspires and puzzles. Although he sometimes claimed to be descended from samurai warriors, he was in fact born in Tokyo into a middle-class family. His father was a civil servant. His childhood was dominated by his paternal grandmother, who protected him obsessively from the outside world, keeping him a virtual invalid and prisoner until he was twelve. When Mishima tried to enlist for military service, he was turned down because of physical problems; as a result, he spent the rest of his life in a vigorous program of physical conditioning, becoming expert in karate and swordsmanship.

Japan's defeat in World War II and its subsequent westernization heightened cultural tensions already evident before the war. Mishima himself was torn between the attractions of Western institutions and ideas, and traditional Japanese culture, particularly its samurai militarism. While often living a Western life, he formed the Shield Society whose purpose was to preserve Japan's martial spirit and traditional culture.

Mishima published dozens of novels and collections of stories and became well known internationally as a political activist and movie star. His most controversial and widely publicized act, however, was the last one of his life. On November 25, 1970, he and a few of his followers seized a defense department building near Tokyo. From a balcony, Mishima harangued skeptical soldiers on the glories of Japan's military past and its present impotence as a country prohibited by its constitution from engaging in war. Then, in a final act of defiance, Mishima ritually disemboweled himself and was decapitated by one of his followers, who was in turn beheaded by another. Needless to say, the episode threw Japan into a turmoil of cultural debate.

"Swaddling Clothes" compresses many of Mishima's concerns into a taut, dramatic story of a young woman's confrontation with the realities of Japanese life and her own (masochistic?) response to these realities.

HE WAS ALWAYS BUSY, Toshiko's husband. Even tonight he had to dash off to an appointment, leaving her to go home alone by taxi. But what else could a woman expect when she married an actor—an attractive one? No doubt she had been foolish to hope that he would spend the evening with her. And yet he must have known how she dreaded going back to their house, unhomely with its Western-style furniture and with the bloodstains still showing on the floor.

Toshiko had been oversensitive since girlhood: that was her nature. As the result of constant worrying she never put on weight, and now, an adult woman, she looked more like a transparent picture than a creature of flesh and blood. Her delicacy of spirit was evident to her most casual acquaintance.   10

Earlier that evening, when she had joined her husband at a night club, she had been shocked to find him entertaining friends with an account of "the incident." Sitting there in his American-style suit, puffing at a cigarette, he had seemed to her almost a stranger.

"It's a fantastic story," he was saying, gesturing flamboyantly as if in an attempt to outweigh the attractions of the dance band. "Here this new nurse for our baby arrives from the employment agency, and the very first thing I notice about her is her stomach. It's enormous—as if she had a pillow stuck under her kimono! No wonder, I thought, for I soon saw that she could eat more than the rest of us

put together. She polished off the contents of our rice bin like that. . . ." He   20
snapped his fingers. "'Gastric dilation'—that's how she explained her girth and her
appetite. Well, the day before yesterday we heard groans and moans coming from
the nursery. We rushed in and found her squatting on the floor, holding her stomach in her two hands, and moaning like a cow. Next to her our baby lay in his cot,
scared out of his wits and crying at the top of his lungs. A pretty scene, I can tell
you!"

"So the cat was out of the bag?" suggested one of their friends, a film actor
like Toshiko's husband.

"Indeed it was! And it gave me the shock of my life. You see, I'd completely
swallowed that story about 'gastric dilation.' Well, I didn't waste any time. I res-   30
cued our good rug from the floor and spread a blanket for her to lie on. The whole
time the girl was yelling like a stuck pig. By the time the doctor from the maternity clinic arrived, the baby had already been born. But our sitting room was a
pretty shambles!"

"Oh, that I'm sure of!" said another of their friends, and the whole company
burst into laughter.

Toshiko was dumbfounded to hear her husband discussing the horrifying
happening as though it were no more than an amusing incident which they
chanced to have witnessed. She shut her eyes for a moment and all at once she
saw the newborn baby lying before her: on the parquet floor the infant lay, and his   40
frail body was wrapped in bloodstained newspapers.

Toshiko was sure that the doctor had done the whole thing out of spite. As if
to emphasize his scorn for this mother who had given birth to a bastard under
such sordid conditions, he had told his assistant to wrap the baby in some loose
newspapers, rather than proper swaddling. This callous treatment of the newborn
child had offended Toshiko. Overcoming her disgust at the entire scene, she had
fetched a brand-new piece of flannel from her cupboard and, having swaddled the
baby in it, had laid him carefully in an armchair.

This all had taken place in the evening after her husband had left the house.
Toshiko had told him nothing of it, fearing that he would think her oversoft, over-   50
sentimental; yet the scene had engraved itself deeply in her mind. Tonight she sat
silently thinking back on it, while the jazz orchestra brayed and her husband chatted cheerfully with his friends. She knew that she would never forget the sight of
the baby, wrapped in stained newspapers and lying on the floor—it was a scene fit
for a butchershop. Toshiko, whose own life had been spent in solid comfort,
poignantly felt the wretchedness of the illegitimate baby.

I am the only person to have witnessed its shame, the thought occurred to
her. The mother never saw her child lying there in its newspaper wrappings, and
the baby itself of course didn't know. I alone shall have to preserve that terrible
scene in my memory. When the baby grows up and wants to find out about his   60
birth, there will be no one to tell him, so long as I preserve silence. How strange
that I should have this feeling of guilt! After all, it was I who took him up from the
floor, swathed him properly in flannel, and laid him down to sleep in the armchair.

They left the night club and Toshiko stepped into the taxi that her husband
had called for her. "Take this lady to Ushi-gomé," he told the driver and shut the

door from the outside. Toshiko gazed through the window at her husband's smiling face and noticed his strong, white teeth. Then she leaned back in the seat, oppressed by the knowledge that their life together was in some way too easy, too
painless. It would have been difficult for her to put her thoughts into words.   70
Through the rear window of the taxi she took a last look at her husband. He was
striding along the street toward his Nash car, and soon the back of his rather gar-
ish tweed coat had blended with the figures of the passers-by.

The taxi drove off, passed down a street dotted with bars and then by a theatre, in front of which the throngs of people jostled each other on the pavement.
Although the performance had only just ended, the lights had already been turned
out and in the half dark outside it was depressingly obvious that the cherry blossoms decorating the front of the theatre were merely scraps of white paper.

Even if that baby should grow up in ignorance of the secret of his birth, he
can never become a respectable citizen, reflected Toshiko, pursuing the same train   80
of thoughts. Those soiled newspaper swaddling clothes will be the symbol of his
entire life. But why should I keep worrying about him so much? Is it because I feel
uneasy about the future of my own child? Say twenty years from now, when our
boy will have grown up into a fine, carefully educated young man, one day by a
quirk of fate he meets that other boy, who then will also have turned twenty. And
say that the other boy, who has been sinned against, savagely stabs him with a
knife. . . .

It was a warm, overcast April night, but thoughts of the future made Toshiko
feel cold and miserable. She shivered on the back seat of the car.

No, when the time comes I shall take my son's place, she told herself sud-   90
denly. Twenty years from now I shall be forty-three. I shall go to that young man
and tell him straight out about everything—about his newspaper swaddling
clothes, and about how I went and wrapped him in flannel.

The taxi ran along the dark wide road that was bordered by the park and by
the Imperial Palace moat. In the distance Toshiko noticed the pinpricks of light
which came from the blocks of tall office buildings.

Twenty years from now that wretched child will be in utter misery. He will
be living a desolate, hopeless, poverty-stricken existence—a lonely rat. What else
could happen to a baby who has had such a birth? He'll be wandering through the
streets by himself, cursing his father, loathing his mother.   100

No doubt Toshiko derived a certain satisfaction from her somber thoughts:
she tortured herself with them without cease. The taxi approached Hanzomon and
drove past the compound of the British Embassy. At that point the famous rows of
cherry trees were spread out before Toshiko in all their purity. On the spur of the
moment she decided to go and view the blossoms by herself in the dark night. It
was a strange decision for a timid and unadventurous young woman, but then she
was in a strange state of mind and she dreaded the return home. That evening all
sorts of unsettling fancies had burst open in her mind.

She crossed the wide street—a slim, solitary figure in the darkness. As a rule
when she walked in the traffic Toshiko used to cling fearfully to her companion,   110
but tonight she darted alone between the cars and a moment later had reached the
long narrow park that borders the Palace moat. Chidorigafuchi, it is called—the
Abyss of the Thousand Birds.

Tonight the whole park had become a grove of blossoming cherry trees. Under the calm cloudy sky the blossoms formed a mass of solid whiteness. The paper lanterns that hung from wires between the trees had been put out; in their place electric light bulbs, red, yellow, and green, shone dully beneath the blossoms. It was well past ten o'clock and most of the flower-viewers had gone home. As the occasional passers-by strolled through the park, they would automatically kick aside the empty bottles or crush the waste paper beneath their feet.   120

Newspapers, thought Toshiko, her mind going back once again to those happenings. Bloodstained newspapers. If a man were ever to hear of that piteous birth and know that it was he who had lain there, it would ruin his entire life. To think that I, a perfect stranger, should from now on have to keep such a secret— the secret of a man's whole existence. . . .

Lost in these thoughts, Toshiko walked on through the park. Most of the people still remaining there were quiet couples; no one paid her any attention. She noticed two people sitting on a stone bench beside the moat, not looking at the blossoms, but gazing silently at the water. Pitch black it was, and swathed in heavy shadows. Beyond the moat the somber forest of the Imperial Palace blocked her   130 view. The trees reached up, to form a solid dark mass against the night sky. Toshiko walked slowly along the path beneath the blossoms hanging heavily overhead.

On a stone bench, slightly apart from the others, she noticed a pale object— not, as she had at first imagined, a pile of cherry blossoms, nor a garment forgotten by one of the visitors to the park. Only when she came closer did she see that it was a human form lying on the bench. Was it, she wondered, one of those miserable drunks often to be seen sleeping in public places? Obviously not, for the body had been systematically covered with newspapers, and it was the whiteness of those papers that had attracted Toshiko's attention. Standing by the bench, she   140 gazed down at the sleeping figure.

It was a man in a brown jersey who lay there, curled up on layers of newspapers, other newspapers covering him. No doubt this had become his normal night residence now that spring had arrived. Toshiko gazed down at the man's dirty, unkempt hair, which in places had become hopelessly matted. As she observed the sleeping figure wrapped in its newspapers, she was inevitably reminded of the baby who had lain on the floor in its wretched swaddling clothes. The shoulder of the man's jersey rose and fell in the darkness in time with his heavy breathing.

It seemed to Toshiko that all her fears and premonitions had suddenly taken concrete form. In the darkness the man's pale forehead stood out, and it was a   150 young forehead, though carved with the wrinkles of long poverty and hardship. His khaki trousers had been slightly pulled up; on his sockless feet he wore a pair of battered gym shoes. She could not see his face and suddenly had an overmastering desire to get one glimpse of it.

She walked to the head of the bench and looked down. The man's head was half buried in his arms, but Toshiko could see that he was surprisingly young. She noticed the thick eyebrows and the fine bridge of his nose. His slightly open mouth was alive with youth.

But Toshiko had approached too close. In the silent night the newspaper bedding rustled, and abruptly the man opened his eyes. Seeing the young woman   160 standing directly beside him, he raised himself with a jerk, and his eyes lit up. A second later a powerful hand reached out and seized Toshiko by her slender wrist.

She did not feel in the least afraid and made no effort to free herself. In a flash the thought had struck her, Ah, so the twenty years have already gone by! The forest of the Imperial Palace was pitch dark and utterly silent.   [1966[

Questions for Discussion and Writing

1. In most societies, at least in the past, illegitimacy has been regarded as shameful, and strong social sanctions may be directed at both mother and child. Why is birth outside of marriage considered shameful? Should it be? Why is the father of such a child seldom punished?
2. Why or why not are Toshiko's fears for the child's future justified?
3. How do you interpret the end of the story?
4. What would you need to know about Japanese society in order to interpret the story as a Japanese reader might? Is it possible for members of one culture to read the stories of another culture with proper understanding? Why or why not?
5. How might a feminist critic interpret the story? Discuss whether it would be appropriate to apply a Western, feminist reading to a story that probably was not written with western or feminist ideas in mind?

✐ DONALD BARTHELME
(1931–1989)

The Balloon

Photographs of Donald Barthelme show a man in a full but well-trimmed beard, with a naughty twinkle in the eye, like a merry troll. The photographs provide a clue to the writer who helped shake up the American short story in the 1960s.

Barthelme was born in Philadelphia but grew up in Texas, listening to country and western music and jazz. His father was a forward-looking architect, his mother had, in his words, a "wicked wit": both were big influences on their son. He attended the University of Houston, wrote for a while for a Houston newspaper, and then was drafted in 1953 to serve in Korea. In the early 1960s his stories began appearing in the *New Yorker,* where they gained an immediate and devoted following.

Barthelme's stories are sometimes classed as Metafiction, for they have little interest in mirroring the outside world or in making a thematic comment on it. His true subject is often language, particularly the way in which its abuse by politicians, bureaucrats, and advertisers has robbed it of power and meaning. He also writes about the city and the rag-tag, jaded lives of those who live in it. But Barthelme's stories do not so much reflect on the business of making fiction as they do on presenting a witty verbal surface, a pastiche of words that mocks official language and jolts us into awareness of its banalities. The result is not so much a story in the traditional sense as a verbal object which the reader is invited to explore for insights into the chaos of modern culture. The story's world is like a Hollywood movie set: it looks real enough from the outside, but behind the facade, there is nothing there. If this approach leads to a feeling that Barthelme's works lack a coherent image of the world, he might have replied that there is no coherence, only a world of surfaces and fragments beheld by a jangled consciousness.

THE BALLOON, BEGINNING at a point on Fourteenth Street, the exact location of which I cannot reveal, expanded northward all one night, while people were sleeping, until it reached the Park. There, I stopped it; at dawn the northernmost edges lay over the Plaza; the free-hanging motion was frivolous and gentle. But experiencing a faint irritation at stopping, even to protect the trees, and seeing no reason the balloon should not be allowed to expand upward, over the parts of the city it was already covering, into the "air space" to be found there, I asked the engineers to see to it. This expansion took place throughout the morning, soft imperceptible sighing of gas through the valves. The balloon then covered forty-five blocks north-south and an irregular area east-west, as many as six crosstown blocks on either side of the Avenue in some places. That was the situation, then.

But it is wrong to speak of "situations," implying sets of circumstances leading to some resolution, some escape of tension; there were no situations, simply the balloon hanging there—muted heavy grays and browns for the most part, contrasting with walnut and soft yellows. A deliberate lack of finish, enhanced by skillful installation, gave the surface a rough, forgotten quality; sliding weights on the inside, carefully adjusted, anchored the great, vari-shaped mass at a number of points. Now we have had a flood of original ideas in all media, works of singular beauty as well as significant milestones in the history of inflation, but at that moment there was only *this balloon,* concrete particular, hanging there.

There were reactions. Some people found the balloon "interesting." As a response this seemed inadequate to the immensity of the balloon, the suddenness of its appearance over the city; on the other hand, in the absence of hysteria or other societally induced anxiety, it must be judged a calm, "mature" one. There was a certain amount of initial argumentation about the "meaning" of the balloon; this subsided, because we have learned not to insist on meanings, and they are rarely even looked for now, except in cases involving the simplest, safest phenomena. It was agreed that since the meaning of the balloon could never be known absolutely, extended discussion was pointless, or at least less purposeful than the activities of those who, for example, hung green and blue paper lanterns from the warm gray underside, in certain streets, or seized the occasion to write messages on the surface, announcing the availability for the performance of unnatural acts, or the availability of acquaintances.

Daring children jumped, especially at those points where the balloon hovered close to a building, so that the gap between balloon and building was a matter of a few inches, or points where the balloon actually made contact, exerting an ever-so-slight pressure against the side of a building, so that balloon and building seemed a unity. The upper surface was so structured that a "landscape" was presented, small valleys as well as slight knolls, or mounds; once atop the balloon, a stroll was possible, or even a trip, from one place to another. There was pleasure 40 in being able to run down an incline, then up the opposing slope, both gently graded, or in making a leap from one side to the other. Bouncing was possible, because of the pneumaticity of the surface, and even falling, if that was your wish. That all these varied motions, as well as others, were within one's possibilities, in experiencing the "up" side of the balloon, was extremely exciting for children, accustomed to the city's flat, hard skin. But the purpose of the balloon was not to amuse children.

Too, the number of people, children and adults, who took advantage of the opportunities described was not so large as it might have been: a certain timidity, lack of trust in the balloon, was seen. There was, furthermore, some hostility. 50 Because we had hidden the pumps, which fed helium to the interior, and because the surface was so vast that the authorities could not determine the point of entry—that is, the point at which the gas was injected—a degree of frustration was evidenced by those city officers into whose province such manifestations normally fell. The apparent purposelessness of the balloon was vexing (as was the fact that it was "there" at all). Had we painted, in great letters, "LABORATORY TESTS PROVE" or "18% MORE EFFECTIVE" on the sides of the balloon, this difficulty would have been circumvented. But I could not bear to do so. On the whole, these officers were remarkably tolerant, considering the dimensions of the anomaly, this tolerance being the result of, first, secret tests conducted by night that convinced 60 them that little or nothing could be done in the way of removing or destroying the balloon, and, secondly, a public warmth that arose (not uncolored by touches of the aforementioned hostility) toward the balloon, from ordinary citizens.

As a single balloon must stand for a lifetime of thinking about balloons, so each citizen expressed, in the attitude he chose, a complex of attitudes. One man might consider that the balloon had to do with the notion *sullied,* as in the sentence *The big balloon sullied the otherwise clear and radiant Manhattan sky.* That is, the balloon was, in this man's view, an imposture, something inferior to the sky that had formerly been there, something interposed between the people and their "sky." But in fact it was January, the sky was dark and ugly; it was not a sky you 70 could look up into, lying on your back in the street, with pleasure, unless pleasure, for you, proceeded from having been threatened, from having been misused. And the underside of the balloon was a pleasure to look up into, we had seen to that, muted grays and browns for the most part, contrasted with walnut and soft, forgotten yellows. And so, while this man was thinking *sullied,* still there was an admixture of pleasurable cognition in his thinking, struggling with the original perception.

Another man, on the other hand, might view the balloon as if it were part of a system of unanticipated rewards, as when one's employer walks in and says, "Here, Henry, take this package of money I have wrapped for you, because we 80 have been doing so well in the business here, and I admire the way you bruise the tulips, without which bruising your department would not be a success, or at least not the success that it is." For this man the balloon might be a brilliantly heroic "muscle and pluck" experience, even if an experience poorly understood.

Another man might say, "Without the example of————, it is doubtful that————would exist today in its present form," and find many to agree with him, or to argue with him. Ideas of "bloat" and "float" were introduced, as well as concepts of dream and responsibility. Others engaged in remarkably detailed fantasies having to do with a wish either to lose themselves in the balloon, or to engorge it. The private character of these wishes, of their origins, deeply buried and 90 unknown, was such that they were not much spoken of; yet there is evidence that they were widespread. It was also argued that what was important was what you felt when you stood under the balloon; some people claimed that they felt sheltered, warmed, as never before, while enemies of the balloon felt, or reported feeling, constrained, a "heavy" feeling.

Critical opinion was divided:

"monstrous pourings"

                                                                        "harp"

XXXXXXX "certain contrasts with darker portions"
        "inner joy"   100
"large, square corners"
"conservative eclecticism that has so far governed
    modern balloon design"
                ::::::: "abnormal vigor"
        "warm, soft lazy passages"
"Has unity been sacrificed for a sprawling quality?"
    "*Quelle catastrophe!*"
        "munching"

People began, in a curious way, to locate themselves in relation to aspects of the balloon: "I'll be at that place where it dips down into Forty-seventh Street al- 110 most to the sidewalk, near the Alamo Chile House," or, "Why don't we go stand on top, and take the air, and maybe walk about a bit, where it forms a tight, curving line with the façade of the Gallery of Modern Art—" Marginal intersections offered entrances within a given time duration, as well as "warm, soft, lazy passages" in which . . . But it is wrong to speak of "marginal intersections," each intersection was crucial, none could be ignored (as if, walking there, you might not find someone capable of turning your attention, in a flash, from old exercises to new exercises, risks and escalations). Each intersection was crucial, meeting of balloon and building, meeting of balloon and man, meeting of balloon and balloon.

It was suggested that what was admired about the balloon was finally this: 120 that it was not limited, or defined. Sometimes a bulge, blister, or sub-section would carry all the way east to the river on its own initiative, in the manner of an army's movements on a map, as seen in a headquarters remote from the fighting. Then that part would be, as it were, thrown back again, or would withdraw into new dispositions; the next morning, that part would have made another sortie, or disappeared altogether. This ability of the balloon to shift its shape, to change, was very pleasing, especially to people whose lives were rather rigidly patterned, persons to whom change, although desired, was not available. The balloon, for the twenty-two days of its existence, offered the possibility, in its randomness, of mislocation of the self, in contradistinction to the grid of precise, rectangular pathways under our feet. The amount of specialized training currently needed, and the consequent desirability of long-term commitments, has been occasioned by the steadily growing importance of complex machinery, in virtually all kinds of operations as this tendency increases, more and more people will turn, in bewildered inadequacy, to solutions for which the balloon may stand as a prototype, or "rough draft." 130

I met you under the balloon, on the occasion of your return from Norway; you asked if it was mine; I said it was. The balloon, I said, is a spontaneous autobiographical disclosure, having to do with the unease I felt at your absence, and with sexual deprivation, but now that your visit to Bergen has been terminated, it 140 is no longer necessary or appropriate. Removal of the balloon was easy; trailer trucks carried away the depleted fabric, which is now stored in West Virginia, awaiting some other time of unhappiness, some time, perhaps, when we are angry with one another.   [1966]

Questions for Discussion and Writing

1. What does the narrator mean when he says, "We have learned not to insist on meanings"?
2. Does the narrator contradict the above statement when he says, "But the purpose of the balloon was not to amuse children"? What is the difference between purpose and meaning?
3. Analyze people's reactions to the balloon. Are these reactions typical of how people react to any new phenomenon? To a work of art? Explain.
4. At one point the narrator contrasts the ability of the balloon to change shape with the rigidity of the city beneath it. What does this contrast suggest to you?
5. How do you interpret the last paragraph? Does it suggest that the balloon exists only in the mind of the narrator?
6. How do you respond to the story? Is it, in your view, a delightful fantasy, an allegory, social commentary, other? Explain.

ROBERT COOVER
(b. 1932)

The Babysitter

Robert Coover is an important member of a small group of American writers who helped to rejuvenate the American short story after World War II, overturning both its Modernist and Realist conventions and making it a new creative outlet for the Postmodern generation.

Coover is a product of the American Midwest. He was born in Iowa and

moved to Indiana at age nine, where his father was a newspaper reporter.
Coover developed an early interest in writing, wrote for his school newspaper,
and sometimes accompanied his father on journalistic assignments. Indeed, his
first published story, "Blackdamp," was inspired by a mining accident he covered with his father. It was later expanded into his first novel, *The Origin of the
Brunists* (1966). He graduated from Indiana University in 1953 and immediately
afterward served in the Navy for four years. While studying philosophy and
history (and later painting) at the University of Chicago, he began publishing
poems in literary magazines. In the 1960s and 1970s, he lived in England and
Spain, where he married a Spanish woman he had met while in the Navy.

Although Coover has written a number of highly inventive novels, he is best
known for his ingenious and influential short stories, *Pricksongs and Descants*
(1969) and *A Night at the Movies; or, You Must Remember This* (1987). Like
Angela Carter, whose work he greatly admires, Coover often uses classical
myths and materials from popular culture to emphasize his idea that truth and
history are human constructs, not independent entities. He has also been influential in the Metafictional school of Postmodernism, which forces readers to
confront their expectations for convention and entertainment. "The Babysitter"
mixes urban folklore about babysitters with television images, fantasy, interior
monologue, and a series of interlocking but not necessarily coherent narratives
to produce one of the best-known Postmodern fictions of our time.

S HE ARRIVES AT 7:40, ten minutes late, but the children, Jimmy and Bitsy, are still
eating supper, and their parents are not ready to go yet. From other rooms
come the sounds of a baby screaming, water running, a television musical (no
words: probably a dance number—patterns of gliding figures come to mind). Mrs.
Tucker sweeps into the kitchen, fussing with her hair, and snatches a baby bottle
full of milk out of a pan of warm water, rushes out again. "Harry!" she calls. "The
babysitter's here already!"

o o o

That's My Desire? I'll Be Around? He smiles toothily, beckons faintly with his head,
rubs his fast balding pate. Bewitched, maybe? Or, What's the Reason? He pulls on
his shorts, gives his hips a slap. The baby goes silent in mid-scream. Isn't this the   10
one who used their tub last time? Who's Sorry Now,[1] that's it.

o o o

Jack is wandering around town, not knowing what to do. His girlfriend is babysitting at the Tuckers', and later, when she's got the kids in bed, maybe he'll drop
over there. Sometimes he watches TV with her when she's babysitting, it's about
the only chance he gets to make out a little since he doesn't own wheels, but they
have to be careful because most people don't like their sitters to have boyfriends

1. Titles of popular songs.

over. Just kissing her makes her nervous. She won't close her eyes because she has to be watching the door all the time. Married people really have it good, he thinks.

o   o   o

"Hi," the babysitter says to the children, and puts her books on top of the refrigerator. "What's for supper?" The little girl, Bitsy, only stares at her obliquely. She joins them at the end of the kitchen table. "I don't have to go to bed until nine," the boy announces flatly, and stuffs his mouth full of potato chips. The babysitter catches a glimpse of Mr. Tucker hurrying out of the bathroom in his underwear.

o   o   o

Her tummy. Under her arms. And her feet. Those are the best places. She'll spank him, she says sometimes. Let her.

o   o   o

That sweet odor that girls have. The softness of her blouse. He catches a glimpse of the gentle shadows amid her thighs, as she curls her legs up under her. He stares hard at her. He has a lot of meaning packed into that stare, but she's not even looking. She's popping her gum and watching television. She's sitting right there, inches away, soft, fragrant, and ready: but what's his next move? He notices his buddy Mark in the drugstore, playing the pinball machine, and joins him. "Hey, this mama's cold, Jack baby! She needs your touch!"

o   o   o

Mrs. Tucker appears at the kitchen doorway, holding a rolled-up diaper. "Now, don't just eat potato chips, Jimmy! See that he eats his hamburger, dear." She hurries away to the bathroom. The boy glares sullenly at the babysitter, silently daring her to carry out the order. "How about a little of that good hamburger now, Jimmy?" she says perfunctorily. He lets half of it drop to the floor. The baby is silent and a man is singing a love song on the TV. The children crunch chips.

o   o   o

He loves her. She loves him. They whirl airily, stirring a light breeze, through a magical landscape of rose and emerald and deep blue. Her light brown hair coils and wisps softly in the breeze, and the soft folds of her white gown tug at her body and then float away. He smiles in a pulsing crescendo of sincerity and song.

o   o   o

"You mean she's alone?" Mark asks. "Well, there's two or three kids," Jack says. He slides the coin in. There's a rumble of steel balls tumbling, lining up. He pushes a plunger with his thumb, and one ball pops up in place, hard and glittering with promise. His stare? to say he loves her. That he cares for her and would protect her, would shield her, if need be, with his own body. Grinning, he bends over the ball to take careful aim: he and Mark have studied this machine and have it figured out, but still it's not that easy to beat.

o   o   o

On the drive to the party, his mind is partly on the girl, partly on his own high- ₅₀
school days, long past. Sitting at the end of the kitchen table there with his children, she had seemed to be self-consciously arching her back, jutting her pert
breasts, twitching her thighs: and for whom if not for him? So she'd seen him
coming out of there, after all. He smiles. Yet what could he ever do about it? Those
good times are gone, old man. He glances over at his wife, who, readjusting a
garter, asks: "What do you think of our babysitter?"

◦ ◦ ◦

He loves her. She loves him. And then the babies come. And dirty diapers and one
goddamn meal after another. Dishes. Noise. Clutter. And fat. Not just tight, her
girdle actually hurts. Somewhere recently she's read about women getting heart at-
tacks or cancer or something from too-tight girdles. Dolly pulls the car door shut ₆₀
with a grunt, strangely irritated, not knowing why. Party mood. Why is her husband humming, "Who's Sorry Now?" Pulling out of the drive, she glances back at
the lighted kitchen window. "What do you think of our babysitter?" she asks.
While her husband stumbles all over himself trying to answer, she pulls a stocking
tight, biting deeper with the garters.

◦ ◦ ◦

"Stop it!" she laughs. Bitsy is pulling on her skirt and he is tickling her in the ribs.
"Jimmy! Don't!" But she is laughing too much to stop him. He leaps on her, wrapping his legs around her waist, and they all fall to the carpet in front of the TV,
where just now a man in a tuxedo and a little girl in a flouncy white dress are
doing a tapdance together. The babysitter's blouse is pulling out of her skirt, show- ₇₀
ing a patch of bare tummy: the target. "I'll spank!"

◦ ◦ ◦

Jack pushes the plunger, thrusting up a steel ball, and bends studiously over the
machine. "You getting any off her?" Mark asks, and clears his throat, flicks ash
from his cigarette. "Well, not exactly, not yet," Jack says, grinning awkwardly, but
trying to suggest more than he admits to, and fires. He heaves his weight gently
against the machine as the ball bounds off a rubber bumper. He can feel her
warming up under his hands, the flippers suddenly coming alive, delicate rapid-
fire patterns emerging in the flashing of the lights. 1000 WHEN LIT: *now!* "Got my
hand on it, that's about all." Mark glances up from the machine, cigarette dangling
from his lip. "Maybe you need some help," he suggests with a wry one-sided grin. ₈₀
"Like maybe together, man, we could do it."

◦ ◦ ◦

She likes the big tub. She uses the Tuckers' bath salts, and loves to sink into the
hot fragrant suds. She can stretch out, submerged, up to her chin. It gives her a
good sleepy tingly feeling.

◦ ◦ ◦

"What do you think of our babysitter?" Dolly asks, adjusting a garter. "Oh, I
hardly noticed," he says. "Cute girl. She seems to get along fine with the kids.

Why?" "I don't know." His wife tugs her skirt down, glances at a lighted window they are passing, adding: "I'm not sure I trust her completely, that's all. With the baby, I mean. She seems a little careless. And the other time, I'm almost sure she had a boyfriend over." He grins, claps one hand on his wife's broad gartered thigh. 90 "What's wrong with that?" he asks. Still in anklets, too. Bare thighs, no girdles, nothing up there but a flimsy pair of panties and soft adolescent flesh. He's flooded with vague remembrances of football rallies and movie balconies.

∘ ∘ ∘

How tiny and rubbery it is! she thinks, soaping between the boy's legs, giving him his bath. Just a funny jiggly little thing that looks like it shouldn't even be there at all. Is that what all the songs are about?

∘ ∘ ∘

Jack watches Mark lunge and twist against the machine. Got her running now, racking them up. He's not too excited about the idea of Mark fooling around with his girlfriend, but Mark's a cooler operator than he is, and maybe, doing it together this once, he'd get over his own timidity. And if she didn't like it, there were other 100 girls around. If Mark went too far, he could cut him off, too. He feels his shoulders tense: enough's enough, man . . . but sees the flesh, too. "Maybe I'll call her later," he says.

∘ ∘ ∘

"Hey, Harry! Dolly! Glad you could make it!" "I hope we're not late." "No, no, you're one of the first, come on in! By golly, Dolly, you're looking younger every day! How do you do it? Give my wife your secret, will you?" He pats her on her girdled bottom behind Mr. Tucker's back, leads them in for drinks.

∘ ∘ ∘

8:00. The babysitter runs water in the tub, combs her hair in front of the bathroom mirror. There's a western on television, so she lets Jimmy watch it while she gives Bitsy her bath. But Bitsy doesn't want a bath. She's angry and crying because she 110 has to be first. The babysitter tells her if she'll take her bath quickly, she'll let her watch television while Jimmy takes his bath, but it does no good. The little girl fights to get out of the bathroom, and the babysitter has to squat with her back against the door and forcibly undress the child. There are better places to babysit. Both children mind badly, and then, sooner or later, the baby is sure to wake up for a diaper change and more bottle. The Tuckers do have a good color TV, though, and she hopes things will be settled down enough to catch the 8:30 program. She thrusts the child into the tub, but she's still screaming and thrashing around. "Stop it now, Bitsy, or you'll wake the baby!" "I have to go potty!" the child wails, switching tactics. The babysitter sighs, lifts the girl out of the tub and onto 120 the toilet, getting her skirt and blouse all wet in the process. She glances at herself in the mirror. Before she knows it, the girl is off the seat and out of the bathroom. "Bitsy! Come back here!"

∘ ∘ ∘

"Okay, that's enough!" Her skirt is ripped and she's flushed and crying. "Who says?" "I do, man!" The bastard goes for her, but he tackles him. They roll and tumble. Tables tip, lights topple, the TV crashes to the floor. He slams a hard right to the guy's gut, clips his chin with a rolling left.

o o o

"We hope it's a girl." That's hardly surprising, since they already have four boys. Dolly congratulates the woman like everybody else, but she doesn't envy her, not a bit. That's all she needs about now. She stares across the room at Harry, who is slapping backs and getting loud, as usual. He's spreading out through the middle, so why the hell does he have to complain about her all the time? "Dolly, you're looking younger every day!" was the nice greeting she got tonight. "What's your secret?" And Harry: "It's all those calories. She's getting back her baby fat." "Haw haw! Harry, have a heart!"   130

o o o

"Get her feet!" he hollers at Bitsy, his fingers in her ribs, running over her naked tummy, tangling in the underbrush of straps and strange clothing. "Get her shoes off!" He holds her pinned by pressing his head against her soft chest. "No! No, Jimmy! Bitsy, stop!" But though she kicks and twists and rolls around, she doesn't get up, she can't get up, she's laughing too hard, and the shoes come off, and he grabs a stockinged foot and scratches the sole ruthlessly, and she raises up her legs, trying to pitch him off, she's wild, boy, but he hangs on, and she's laughing, and on the screen there's a rattle of hooves, and he and Bitsy are rolling around and around on the floor in a crazy rodeo of long bucking legs.   140

o o o

He slips the coin in. There's a metallic fall and a sharp click as the dial tone begins. "I hope the Tuckers have gone," he says. "Don't worry, they're at our place," Mark says. "They're always the first ones to come and the last ones to go home. My old man's always bitching about them." Jack laughs nervously and dials the number. "Tell her we're coming over to protect her from getting raped," Mark suggests, and lights a cigarette. Jack grins, leaning casually against the door jamb of the phone-booth, chewing gum, one hand in his pocket. He's really uneasy, though. He has the feeling he's somehow messing up a good thing.   150

o o o

Bitsy runs naked into the livingroom, keeping a hassock between herself and the babysitter. "Bitsy . . . !" the babysitter threatens. Artificial reds and greens and pur-ples flicker over the child's wet body, as hooves clatter, guns crackle, and stage-coach wheels thunder over rutted terrain. "Get outa the way, Bitsy!" the boy complains. "I can't see!" Bitsy streaks past and the babysitter chases, cornering the girl in the back bedroom. Bitsy throws something that hits her softly in the face: a pair of men's undershorts. She grabs the girl scampering by, carries her struggling to the bathroom, and with a smart crack on her glistening bottom, pops her back into the tub. In spite, Bitsy peepees in the bathwater.   160

o o o

Mr. Tucker stirs a little water into his bourbon and kids with his host and another man, just arrived, about their golf games. They set up a match for the weekend, a threesome looking for a fourth. Holding his drink in his right hand, Mr. Tucker swings his left through the motion of a tee-shot. "You'll have to give me a stroke a hole," he says. "I'll give you a stroke!" says his host: "Bend over!" Laughing, the other man asks: "Where's your boy Mark tonight?" "I don't know," replies the host, gathering up a trayful of drinks. Then he adds in a low growl: "Out chasing tail probably." They chuckle loosely at that, then shrug in commiseration and return to the livingroom to join their women. 170

o o o

Shades pulled. Door locked. Watching the TV. Under a blanket maybe. Yes, that's right, under a blanket. Her eyes close when he kisses her. Her breasts, under both their hands, are soft and yielding.

o o o

A hard blow to the belly. The face. The dark beardy one staggers. The lean-jawed sheriff moves in, but gets a spurred boot in his face. The dark one hurls himself forward, drives his shoulder into the sheriff's hard midriff, her own tummy tightens, withstands, as the sheriff smashes the dark man's nose, slams him up against a wall, slugs him again! and again! The dark man grunts rhythmically, backs off, then plunges suicidally forward—her own knees draw up protectively—the sheriff staggers! caught low! but instead of following through, the other man steps 180 back—a pistol! the dark one has a pistol! the sheriff draws! shoots from the hip! explosions! she clutches her hands between her thighs—no! the sheriff spins! wounded! the dark man hesitates, aims, her legs stiffen toward the set, the sheriff rolls desperately in the straw, fires: dead! the dark man is dead! groans, crumples, his pistol drooping in his collapsing hand, dropping, he drops. The sheriff, spent, nicked, watches weakly from the floor where he lies. Oh, to be whole! to be good and strong and right! to embrace and be embraced by harmony and wholeness! The sheriff, drawing himself painfully up on one elbow, rubs his bruised mouth with the back of his other hand.

o o o

"Well, we just sorta thought we'd drop over," he says, and winks broadly at Mark. 190 "Who's we?" "Oh, me and Mark here." "Tell her, good thing like her, gotta pass it around," whispers Mark, dragging on his smoke, then flicking the butt over under the pinball machine. "What's that?" she asks. "Oh, Mark and I were just saying, like two's company, three's an orgy," Jack says, and winks again. She giggles. "Oh, Jack!" Behind her, he can hear shouts and gunfire. "Well, okay, for just a little while, if you'll both be good." Way to go, man.

o o o

Probably some damn kid over there right now. Wrestling around on the couch in front of his TV. Maybe he should drop back to the house. Just to check. None of that stuff, she was there to do a job! Park the car a couple doors down, slip in the front door before she knows it. He sees the disarray of clothing, the young thighs 200

exposed to the flickering television light, hears his baby crying. "Hey, what's going
on here! Get outa here, son, before I call the police!" Of course, they haven't really
been doing anything. They probably don't even know how. He stares benignly
down upon the girl, her skirt rumpled loosely around her thighs. Flushed, frightened, yet excited, she stares back at him. He smiles. His finger touches a knee, approaches the hem. Another couple arrives. Filling up here with people. He
wouldn't be missed. Just slip out, stop back casually to pick up something or other
he forgot, never mind what. He remembers that the other time they had this
babysitter, she took a bath in their house. She had a date afterwards, and she'd just
come from cheerleading practice or something. Aspirin maybe. Just drop quietly   210
and casually into the bathroom to pick up some aspirin. "Oh, excuse me, dear! I
only . . . !" She gazes back at him, astonished, yet strangely moved. Her soft wet
breasts rise and fall in the water, and her tummy looks pale and ripply. He recalls
that her pubic hairs, left in the tub, were brown. Light brown.

                                    o o o

She's no more than stepped into the tub for a quick bath, when Jimmy announces
from outside the door that he has to go to the bathroom. She sighs: just an excuse, she knows. "You'll have to wait." The little nuisance. "I can't wait." "Okay,
then come ahead, but I'm taking a bath." She supposes that will stop him, but it
doesn't. In he comes. She slides down into the suds until she's eye-level with the
edge of the tub. He hesitates. "Go ahead, if you have to," she says, a little awk-   220
wardly, "but I'm not getting out." "Don't look," he says. She: "I will if I want to."

                                    o o o

She's crying. Mark is rubbing his jaw where he's just slugged him. A lamp lies shattered. "Enough's enough, Mark! Now get outa here!" Her skirt is ripped to the
waist, her bare hip bruised. Her panties lie on the floor like a broken balloon.
Later, he'll wash her wounds, help her dress, he'll take care of her. Pity washes
through him, giving him a sudden hard-on. Mark laughs at it, pointing. Jack
crouches, waiting, ready for anything.

                                    o o o

Laughing, they roll and tumble. Their little hands are all over her, digging and
pinching. She struggles to her hands and knees, but Bitsy leaps astride her neck,
bowing her head to the carpet. "Spank her, Jimmy!" His swats sting: is her skirt   230
up? The phone rings. "The cavalry to the rescue!" she laughs, and throws them off
to go answer.

                                    o o o

Kissing Mark, her eyes closed, her hips nudge toward Jack. He stares at the TV
screen, unsure of himself, one hand slipping cautiously under her skirt. Her hand
touches his arm as though to resist, then brushes on by to rub his leg. This blanket they're under was a good idea. "Hi! This is Jack!"

                                    o o o

Bitsy's out and the water's running. "Come on, Jimmy, your turn!" Last time, he
told her he took his own baths, but she came in anyway. "I'm not gonna take a

bath," he announces, eyes glued on the set. He readies for the struggle. "But I've already run your water. Come on, Jimmy, please!" He shakes his head. She can't make him, he's sure he's as strong as she is. She sighs. "Well, it's up to you. I'll use the water myself then," she says. He waits until he's pretty sure she's not going to change her mind, then sneaks in and peeks through the keyhole in the bathroom door: just in time to see her big bottom as she bends over to stir in the bubble-bath. Then she disappears. Trying to see as far down as the keyhole will allow, he bumps his head on the knob. "Jimmy, is that you?" "I—I have to go to the bath-room!" he stammers.

o o o

Not actually in the tub, just getting in. One foot on the mat, the other in the water. Bent over slightly, buttocks flexed, teats swaying, holding on to the edge of the tub. "Oh, excuse me! I only wanted . . . !" He passes over her astonishment, the awkward excuses, moves quickly to the part where he reaches out to— "What on earth are you doing, Harry?" his wife asks, staring at his hand. His host, passing, laughs. "He's practicing his swing for Sunday, Dolly, but it's not going to do him a damn bit of good!" Mr. Tucker laughs, sweeps his right hand on through the air as though lifting a seven-iron shot onto the green. He makes a *dok!* sound with his tongue. "In there!"

o o o

"No, Jack, I don't think you'd better." "Well, we just called, we just, uh, thought we'd, you know, stop by for a minute, watch television for thirty minutes, or, or something." "Who's we?" "Well, Mark's here, I'm with him, and he said he'd like to, you know, like if it's all right, just—" "Well, it's *not* all right. The Tuckers said no." "Yeah, but if we only—" "And they seemed awfully suspicious about last time." "Why? We didn't—I mean, I just thought—" "No, Jack, and that's period." She hangs up. She returns to the TV, but the commercial is on. Anyway, she's missed most of the show. She decides maybe she'll take a quick bath. Jack might come by anyway, it'd make her mad, that'd be the end as far as he was concerned, but if he should, she doesn't want to be all sweaty. And besides, she likes the big tub the Tuckers have.

o o o

He is self-conscious and stands with his back to her, his little neck flushed. It takes him forever to get started, and when it finally does come, it's just a tiny trickle. "See, it was just an excuse," she scolds, but she's giggling inwardly at the boy's embarrassment. "You're just a nuisance, Jimmy." At the door, his hand on the knob, he hesitates, staring timidly down on his shoes. "Jimmy?" She peeks at him over the edge of the tub, trying to keep a straight face, as he sneaks a nervous glance back over his shoulder. "As long as you bothered me," she says, "you might as well soap my back."

o o o

"The aspirin . . ." They embrace. She huddles in his arms like a child. Lovingly, pa-ternally, knowledgeably, he wraps her nakedness. How compact, how tight and small her body is! Kissing her ear, he stares down past her rump at the still clear water. "I'll join you," he whispers hoarsely.

o o o

She picks up the shorts Bitsy threw at her. Men's underwear. She holds them in   280
front of her, looks at herself in the bedroom mirror. About twenty sizes too big for her, of course. She runs her hand inside the opening in front, pulls out her thumb. How funny it must feel!

o o o

"Well, man, I say we just go rape her," Mark says flatly, and swings his weight against the pinball machine. "Uff! Ahh! Get in there, you mother! Look at that! Hah! Man, I'm gonna turn this baby over!" Jack is embarrassed about the phone conversation. Mark just snorted in disgust when he hung up. He cracks down hard on his gum, angry that he's such a chicken. "Well, I'm game if you are," he says coldly.

o o o

8:30. "Okay, come on, Jimmy, it's time." He ignores her. The western gives way to a   290
spy show. Bitsy, in pajamas, pads into the livingroom. "No, Bitsy, it's time to go to bed." "You said I could watch!" the girl whines, and starts to throw another tantrum. "But you were too slow and it's late. Jimmy, you get in that bathroom, and right now!" Jimmy stares sullenly at the set, unmoving. The babysitter tries to catch the opening scene of the television program so she can follow it later, since Jimmy gives himself his own baths. When the commercial interrupts, she turns off the sound, stands in front of the screen. "Okay, into the tub, Jimmy Tucker, or I'll take you in there and give you your bath myself!" "Just try it," he says, "and see what happens."

o o o

They stand outside, in the dark, crouched in the bushes, peeking in. She's on the   300
floor, playing with the kids. Too early. They seem to be tickling her. She gets to her hands and knees, but the little girl leaps on her head, pressing her face to the floor. There's an obvious target, and the little boy proceeds to beat on it. "Hey, look at that kid go!" whispers Mark, laughing and snapping his fingers softly. Jack feels uneasy out here. Too many neighbors, too many cars going by, too many people in the world. That little boy in there is one up on him, though: he's never thought about tickling her as a starter.

o o o

His little hand, clutching the bar of soap, lathers shyly a narrow space between her shoulderblades. She is doubled forward against her knees, buried in rich suds, peeking at him over the edge of her shoulder. The soap slithers out of his grip and   310
plunks into the water. "I . . . I dropped the soap," he whispers. She: "Find it."

o o o

"I dream of Jeannie with the light brown pubic hair!" "Harry! Stop that! You're drunk!" But they're laughing, they're all laughing, damn! he's feeling pretty goddamn good at that, and now he just knows he needs that aspirin. Watching her there, her thighs spread for him, on the couch, in the tub, hell, on the kitchen table for that matter, he tees off on the Number Nine, and—whap!—swats his host's wife on the bottom. "Hole in one!" he shouts. "Harry!" why can't his goddamn wife Dolly ever get happy-drunk instead of sour-drunk all the time? "Gonna be tough Sunday, old buddy!" "You're pretty tough right now, Harry," says his host.

o o o

The babysitter lunges forward, grabs the boy by the arms and hauls him off the 320 couch, pulling two cushions with him, and drags him toward the bathroom. He lashes out, knocking over an endtable full of magazines and ashtrays. "You leave my brother alone!" Bitsy cries and grabs the sitter around the waist. Jimmy jumps on her and down they all go. On the silent screen, there's a fade-in to a dark passageway in an old apartment building in some foreign country. She kicks out and somebody falls between her legs. Some body else is sitting on her face. "Jimmy! Stop that!" the babysitter laughs, her voice muffled.

o o o

She's watching television. All alone. It seems like a good time to go in. Just remember: really, no matter what she says, she wants it. They're standing in the bushes, trying to get up the nerve. "We'll tell her to be good," Mark whispers, "and 330 if she's not good, we'll spank her." Jack giggles softly, but his knees are weak. She stands. They freeze. She looks right at them. "She can't see us," Mark whispers tersely. "Is she coming out?" "No," says Mark, "she's going into—that must be the bathroom!" Jack takes a deep breath, his heart pounding. "Hey, is there a window back there?" Mark asks.

o o o

The phone rings. She leaves the tub, wrapped in a towel. Bitsy gives a tug on the towel. "Hey, Jimmy, get the towel!" she squeals. "Now stop that, Bitsy!" the babysitter hisses, but too late: with one hand on the phone, the other isn't enough to hang on to the towel. Her sudden nakedness awes them and it takes a moment to remember about tickling her. By then, she's in the towel again. "I hope you got 340 a good look," she says angrily. She feels chilled and oddly a little frightened. "Hello?" No answer. She glances at the window—is somebody out there? Something, she saw something, and a rustling—footsteps?

o o o

"Okay, I don't care, Jimmy, don't take a bath," she says irritably. Her blouse is pulled out and wrinkled, her hair is all mussed, and she feels sweaty. There's about a million things she'd rather be doing than babysitting these two. Three: at least the baby's sleeping. She knocks on the overturned endtable for good luck, rights it, replaces the magazines and ashtrays. The one thing that really makes her feel sick is a dirty diaper. "Just go on to bed." "I don't have to go to bed until nine," he re-

minds her. Really, she couldn't care less. She turns up the volume on the TV, set- 350
tles down on the couch, poking her blouse back into her skirt, pushing her hair
out of her eyes. Jimmy and Bitsy watch from the floor. Maybe, once they're in bed,
she'll take a quick bath. She wishes Jack would come by. The man, no doubt the
spy, is following a woman, but she doesn't know why. The woman passes another
man. Something seems to happen, but it's not clear what. She's probably already
missed too much. The phone rings.

o o o

Mark is kissing her. Jack is under the blanket, easing her panties down over her
squirming hips. Her hand is in his pants, pulling it out, pulling it hard. She knew
just where it was! Mark is stripping, too. God, it's really happening! he thinks with
a kind of pious joy, and notices the open door. "Hey! What's going on here?"   360

o o o

He soaps her back, smooth and slippery under his hand. She is doubled over,
against her knees, between his legs. Her light brown hair, reaching to her gleaming
shoulders, is wet at the edges. The soap slips, falls between his legs. He fishes for
it, finds it, slips it behind him. "Help me find it," he whispers in her ear. "Sure,
Harry," says his host, going around behind him. "What'd you lose?"

o o o

Soon be nine, time to pack the kids off to bed. She clears the table, dumps paper
plates and leftover hamburgers into the garbage, puts glasses and silverware into
the sink, and then the mayonnaise, mustard, and ketchup in the refrigerator.
Neither child has eaten much supper finally, mostly potato chips and ice cream,
but it's really not her problem. She glances at the books on the refrigerator. Not 370
much chance she'll get to them, she's already pretty worn out. Maybe she'd feel
better if she had a quick bath. She runs water into the tub, tosses in bubblebath
salts, undresses. Before pushing down her panties, she stares for a moment at the
smooth silken panel across her tummy, fingers the place where the opening would
be if there were one. Then she steps quickly out of them, feeling somehow
ashamed, unhooks her brassiere. She weighs her breasts in the palms of her
hands, watching herself in the bathroom mirror, where, in the open window behind her, she sees a face. She screams.

o o o

She screams: "Jimmy! Give me that!" "What's the matter?" asks Jack on the other
end. "Jimmy! give me my towel! Right now!" "Hello? Hey, are you still there?" "I'm 380
sorry, Jack," she says, panting. "You caught me in the tub. I'm just wrapped in a
towel and these silly kids grabbed it away!" "Gee, I wish I'd been there!" "Jack—!"
"To protect you, I mean." "Oh, sure," she says, giggling. "Well, what do you think,
can I come over and watch TV with you?" "Well, not right this minute," she says.
He laughs lightly. He feels very cool. "Jack?" "Yeah?" "Jack, I . . . I think there's
somebody outside the window!"

o o o

She carries him, fighting all the way, to the tub, Bitsy pummeling her in the back and kicking her ankles. She can't hang on to him and undress him at the same time. "I'll throw you in, clothes and all, Jimmy Tucker!" she gasps. "You better not!" he cries. She sits on the toilet seat, locks her legs around him, whips his shirt 390 up over his head before he knows what's happening. The pants are easier. Like all little boys his age, he has almost no hips at all. He hangs on desperately to his underpants, but when she succeeds in snapping these down out of his grip, too, he gives up, starts to bawl, and beats her wildly in the face with his fists. She ducks her head, laughing hysterically, oddly entranced by the spectacle of that pale little thing down there, bobbing and bouncing rubberily about with the boy's helpless fury and anguish.

o   o   o

"Aspirin? Whaddaya want aspirin for, Harry? I'm sure they got aspirin here, if you—" "Did I say aspirin? I mean, uh, my glasses. And, you know, I thought, well, I'd sorta check to see if everything was okay at home." Why the hell is it his 400 mouth feels like it's got about six sets of teeth packed in there, and a tongue the size of that liverwurst his host's wife is passing around? "Whaddya want your glasses for, Harry? I don't understand you at all!" "Aw, well, honey, I was feeling kind of dizzy or something, and I thought—" "Dizzy is right. If you want to check on the kids, why don't you just call on the phone?"

o   o   o

They can tell she's naked and about to get into the tub, but the bathroom window is frosted glass, and they can't see anything clearly. "I got an idea," Mark whispers. "One of us goes and calls her on the phone, and the other watches when she comes out." "Okay, but who calls?" "Both of us, we'll do it twice. Or more."

o   o   o

Down forbidden alleys. Into secret passageways. Unlocking the world's terrible se- 410 crets. Sudden shocks: a trapdoor! a fall! or the stunning report of a rifle shot, the *whaaii-ii-iing!* of the bullet biting concrete by your ear! Careful! Then edge forward once more, avoiding the light, inch at a time, now a quick dash for an open door-way—*look out!* there's a knife! a struggle! no! the long blade glistens! jerks! thrusts! *stabbed!* No, no it missed! The assailant's down, yes! the spy's on top, pinning him, a terrific thrashing about, the spy rips off the assailant's mask: *a woman!*

o   o   o

Fumbling behind her, she finds it, wraps her hand around it, tugs. "Oh!" she gasps, pulling her hand back quickly, her ears turning crimson. "I . . . I thought it was the soap! He squeezes her close between his thighs, pulls her back toward him, one hand sliding down her tummy between her legs. I Dream of Jeannie—"I 420 have to go to the bathroom!" says someone outside the door.

o   o   o

She's combing her hair in the bathroom when the phone rings. She hurries to answer it before it wakes the baby. "Hello, Tuckers." There's no answer. "Hello?" A

soft click. Strange. She feels suddenly alone in the big house, and goes in to watch
TV with the children.

∘ ∘ ∘

"Stop it!" she screams. "Please, stop!" She's on her hands and knees, trying to get
up, but they're too strong for her. Mark holds her head down. "Now, baby, we're
gonna teach you how to be a nice girl," he says coldly, and nods at Jack. When
she's doubled over like that, her skirt rides up her thighs to the leg bands of her
panties. "C'mon, man, go! This baby's cold! She needs your touch!"   430

∘ ∘ ∘

Parks the car a couple blocks away. Slips up to the house, glances in his window.
Just like he's expected. Her blouse is off and the kid's shirt is unbuttoned. He
watches, while slowly, clumsily, childishly, they fumble with each other's clothes.
My God, it takes them forever. "Some party!" "You said it!" When they're more or
less naked, he walks in. "Hey! What's going on here?" They go as white as bleu
cheese. Haw haw! "What's that little thing you got sticking out there, boy?" "Harry,
behave yourself!" No, he doesn't let the kid get dressed, he sends him home bareassed. "Bareassed!" He drinks to that. "Promises, promises," says his host's wife.
"I'll mail you your clothes, son!" He gazes down on the naked little girl on his
couch. "Looks like you and me, we got a little secret to keep, honey," he says   440
coolly. "Less you wanna go home the same way your boyfriend did!" He chuckles
at his easy wit, leans down over her, and unbuckles his belt. "Might as well make
it two secrets, right?" "What in God's name are you talking about, Harry?" He staggers out of there, drink in hand, and goes to look for his car.

∘ ∘ ∘

"Hey! What's going on here? They huddle half-naked under the blanket, caught
utterly unawares. On television: the clickety-click of frightened running feet on
foreign pavements. Jack is fumbling for his shorts, tangled somehow around his
ankles. The blanket is snatched away. "On your feet there!" Mr. Tucker, Mrs.
Tucker, Mark's mom and dad, the police, the neighbors, everybody comes crowding in. Hopelessly, he has a terrific erection. So hard it hurts. Everybody stares   450
down at it.

∘ ∘ ∘

Bitsy's sleeping on the floor. The babysitter is taking a bath. For more than an hour
now, he's had to use the bathroom. He doesn't know how much longer he can
wait. Finally, he goes to knock on the bathroom door. "I have to use the bathroom." "Well, come ahead, if you have to." "Not while you're in there." She sighs
loudly. "Okay, okay, just a minute," she says, "but you're a real nuisance, Jimmy!"
He's holding on, pinching it as tight as he can. *"Hurry!"* He holds his breath,
squeezing shut his eyes. No. Too late. At last, she opens the door. "Jimmy!" "I *told*
you to hurry!" he sobs. She drags him into the bathroom and pulls his pants
down.   460

∘ ∘ ∘

He arrives just in time to see her emerge from the bathroom, wrapped in a towel, to answer the phone. His two kids sneak up behind her and pull the towel away. She's trying to hang on to the phone and get the towel back at the same time. It's quite a picture. She's got a sweet ass. Standing there in the bushes, pawing himself with one hand, he lifts his glass with the other and toasts her sweet ass, which his son now swats. Haw, haw, maybe that boy's gonna shape up, after all.

o o o

They're in the bushes, arguing about their next move, when she comes out of the bathroom, wrapped in a towel. They can hear the baby crying. Then it stops. They see her running, naked, back to the bathroom like she's scared or something. "I'm going in after her, man, whether you're with me or not!" Mark whispers, and he starts out of the bushes. But just then, a light comes sweeping up through the yard, as a car swings in the drive. They hit the dirt, hearts pounding. "Is it the cops?" "I don't know!" "Do you think they saw us?" "Sshh!" A man comes staggering up the walk from the drive, a drink in his hand, stumbles on in the kitchen door and then straight into the bathroom. "It's Mr. Tucker!" Mark whispers. A scream. "Let's get outa here, man!" 470

o o o

9:00. Having missed most of the spy show anyway and having little else to do, the babysitter has washed the dishes and cleaned the kitchen up a little. The books on the refrigerator remind her of her better intentions, but she decides that first she'll see what's next on TV. In the livingroom, she finds little Bitsy sound asleep on the floor. She lifts her gently, carries her into her bed, and tucks her in. "Okay, Jimmy, it's nine o'clock, I've let you stay up, now be a good boy." Sullenly, his sleepy eyes glued still to the set, the boy backs out of the room toward his bedroom. A drama comes on. She switches channels. A ballgame and a murder mystery. She switches back to the drama. It's a love story of some kind. A man married to an aging invalid wife, but in love with a younger girl. "Use the bathroom and brush your teeth before going to bed, Jimmy!" she calls, but as quickly regrets it, for she hears the baby stir in its crib. 480

o o o

Two of them are talking about mothers they've salted away in rest homes. Oh boy, that's just wonderful, this is one helluva party. She leaves them to use the john, takes advantage of the retreat to ease her girdle down awhile, get a few good deep breaths. She has this picture of her three kids carting her off to a rest home. In a wheelbarrow. That sure is something to look forward to, all right. When she pulls her girdle back up, she can't seem to squeeze into it. The host looks in. "Hey, Dolly, are you all right?" "Yeah, I just can't get into my damn girdle, that's all." "Here, let me help." 490

o o o

She pulls them on, over her own, standing in front of the bedroom mirror, holding her skirt bundled up around the waist. About twenty sizes too big for her, of course. She pulls them tight from behind, runs her hand inside the opening in

front, pulls out her thumb. "And what a good boy am I!" She giggles: how funny it 500
must feel! Then, in the mirror, she sees him: in the doorway behind her, sullenly
watching. "Jimmy! You're supposed to be in bed!" "Those are my daddy's!" the boy
says. "I'm gonna tell!"

o   o   o

"Jimmy!" She drags him into the bathroom and pulls his pants down. "Even your
shoes are wet! Get them off!" She soaps up a warm washcloth she's had with her in
the bathtub, scrubs him from the waist down with it. Bitsy stands in the doorway,
staring. "Get out! Get out!" the boy screams at his sister. "Go back to bed, Bitsy. It's
just an accident." "Get out!" The baby wakes and starts to howl.

o   o   o

The young lover feels sorry for her rival, the invalid wife; she believes the man has
a duty toward the poor woman and insists she is willing to wait. But the man ar- 510
gues that he also has a duty toward himself: his life, too, is short, and he could
not love his wife now even were she well. He embraces the young girl feverishly;
she twists away in anguish. The door opens. They stand there grinning, looking
devilish, but pretty silly at the same time. "Jack! I thought I told you not to come!"
She's angry, but she's also glad in a way: she was beginning to feel a little too alone
in the big house, with the children all sleeping. She should have taken that bath,
after all. "We just came to see if you were being a good girl," Jack says and
blushes. The boys glance at each other nervously.

o   o   o

She's just sunk down into the tubful of warm fragrant suds, ready for a nice long
soaking, when the phone rings. Wrapping a towel around her, she goes to answer: 520
no one there. But now the baby's awake and bawling. She wonders if that's Jack
bothering her all the time. If it is, brother, that's the end. Maybe it's the end anyway. She tries to calm the baby with the half-empty bottle, not wanting to change
it until she's finished her bath. The bathroom's where the dirty diapers go, and
they make it stink to high heaven. "Shush, shush!" she whispers, rocking the crib.
The towel slips away, leaving an airy empty tingle up and down her backside.
Even before she stoops for the towel, even before she turns around, she knows
there's somebody behind her.

o   o   o

"We just came by to see if you were being a good girl," Jack says, grinning down at
her. She's flushed and silent, her mouth half open. "Lean over," says Mark amiably. 530
"We'll soap your back, as long as we're here." But she just huddles there, down in
the suds, staring up at them with big eyes.

o   o   o

"Hey! What's going on here?" It's Mr. Tucker, stumbling through the door with a
drink in his hand. She looks up from the TV. "What's the matter, Mr. Tucker?"
"Oh, uh, I'm sorry, I got lost—no, I mean, I had to get some aspirin. Excuse me!"

And he rushes past her into the bathroom, caroming off the livingroom door jamb on the way. The baby wakes.

∘ ∘ ∘

"Okay, get off her, Mr. Tucker!" "Jack!" she cries, "what are *you* doing here?" He stares hard at them a moment: so that's where it goes. Then, as Mr. Tucker swings heavily off, he leans into the bastard with a hard right to the belly. Next thing he   540 knows, though, he's got a face full of an old man's fist. He's not sure, as the lights go out, if that's his girlfriend screaming or the baby . . .

∘ ∘ ∘

Her host pushes down on her fat fanny and tugs with all his might on her girdle, while she bawls on her shoulder: "I don't *wanna* go to a rest home!" "Now, now, take it easy, Dolly, nobody's gonna make you—" "Ouch! Hey, you're hurting!" "You should buy a bigger girdle, Dolly." "You're telling me?" Some other guy pokes his head in. "Whatsamatter? Dolly fall in?" "No, she fell out. Give me a hand."

∘ ∘ ∘

By the time she's chased Jack and Mark out of there, she's lost track of the program she's been watching on television. There's another woman in the story now for some reason. The guy lives a very complicated life. Impatiently, she switches chan-   550 nels. She hates ballgames, so she settles for the murder mystery. She switches just in time, too: there's a dead man sprawled out on the floor of what looks like an office or a study or something. A heavyset detective gazes up from his crouch over the body: "He's been strangled." Maybe she'll take the bath, after all.

∘ ∘ ∘

She drags him into the bathroom and pulls his pants down. She soaps up a warm washcloth she's had in the tub with her, but just as she reaches between his legs, it starts to spurt, spraying her arms and hands. "Oh, Jimmy! I thought you were done!" she cries, pulling him toward the toilet and aiming it into the bowl. How moist and rubbery it is! And you can turn it every which way. How funny it must feel!   560

∘ ∘ ∘

"Stop it!" she screams. "Please stop!" She's on her hands and knees and Jack is holding her head down. "Now we're gonna teach you how to be a nice girl," Mark says and lifts her skirt. "Well, I'll be damned!" "What's the matter?" asks Jack, his heart pounding. "Look at this big pair of men's underpants she's got on!" "Those are my daddy's!" says Jimmy, watching them from the doorway. "I'm gonna tell!"

∘ ∘ ∘

People are shooting at each other in the murder mystery, but she's so mixed up, she doesn't know which ones are the good guys. She switches back to the love story. Something seems to have happened, because now the man is kissing his in-

valid wife tenderly. Maybe she's finally dying. The baby wakes, begins to scream.
Let it. She turns up the volume on the TV.   570

∘ ∘ ∘

Leaning down over her, unbuckling his belt. It's all happening just like he's known
it would. Beautiful! The kid is gone, though his pants, poor lad, remain. "Looks
like you and me, we got a secret to keep, child." But he's cramped on the couch
and everything is too slippery and small. "Lift your legs up, honey. Put them
around my back." But instead, she screams. He rolls off, crashing to the floor.
There they all come, through the front door. On television, somebody is saying:
"Am I a burden to you, darling?" "Dolly! My God! Dolly, I can explain . . . ?"

∘ ∘ ∘

The game of the night is Get Dolly Tucker Back in Her Girdle Again. They've got
her down on her belly in the livingroom and the whole damn crowd is working
on her. Several of them are stretching the girdle, while others try to jam the fat in-   580
side. "I think we made a couple inches on this side! Roll her over!" Harry?

∘ ∘ ∘

She's just stepped into the tub, when the phone rings, waking the baby. She sinks
down in the suds, trying not to hear. But that baby doesn't cry, it screams. Angrily,
she wraps a towel around herself, stamps peevishly into the baby's room, just letting the phone jangle. She tosses the baby down on its back, unpins its diapers
hastily, and gets yellowish baby stool all over her hands. Her towel drops away.
She turns to find Jimmy staring at her like a little idiot. She slaps him in the face
with her dirty hand, while the baby screams, the phone rings, and nagging voices
argue on the TV. There are better things she might be doing.

∘ ∘ ∘

What's happening? Now there's a young guy in it. Is he after the young girl or the   590
old invalid? To tell the truth, it looks like he's after the same man the women are.
In disgust, she switches channels. "The strangler again," growls the fat detective,
hands on hips, staring down at the body of a half-naked girl. She's considering either switching back to the love story or taking a quick bath, when a hand suddenly clutches her mouth.

∘ ∘ ∘

"You're both chicken," she says, staring up at them. "But what if Mr. Tucker comes
home?" Mark asks nervously.

∘ ∘ ∘

How did he get here? He's standing pissing in his own goddamn bathroom, his
wife is still back at the party, the three of them are, like good kids, sitting in there
in the livingroom watching TV. One of them is his host's boy Mark. "It's a good   600
murder mystery, Mr. Tucker," Mark said, when he came staggering in on them a
minute ago. "Sit still!" he shouted, "I'm just home for a moment!" Then whump

thump on into the bathroom. Long hike for a weewee, Mister. But something keeps bothering him. Then it hits him: the girl's panties, hanging like a broken balloon from the rabbit-ear antennae on the TV! He barges back in there, giving his shoulder a helluva crack on the livingroom door jamb on the way—but they're not hanging there any more. Maybe he's only imagined it. "Hey, Mr. Tucker," Mark says flatly. "Your fly's open."

o o o

The baby's dirty. Stinks to high heaven. She hurries back to the livingroom, hear- 610 ing sirens and gunshots. The detective is crouched outside a house, peering in. Already, she's completely lost. The baby screams at the top of its lungs. She turns up the volume. But it's all confused. She hurries back in there, claps an angry hand to the baby's mouth. "Shut up!" she cries. She throws the baby down on its back, starts to unpin the diaper, as the baby tunes up again. The phone rings. She answers it, one eye on the TV. "What?" The baby cries so hard it starts to choke. Let it. "I said, hi, this is Jack!" Then it hits her: oh no! the diaper pin!

o o o

"The aspirin . . ." But she's already in the tub. Way down in the tub. Staring at him through the water. Her tummy looks pale and ripply. He hears sirens, people on the porch.

o o o

Jimmy gets up to go to the bathroom and gets his face slapped and smeared with 620 baby poop. Then she hauls him off to the bathroom, yanks off his pajamas, and throws him into the tub. That's okay, but next she gets naked and acts like she's gonna get in the tub, too. The baby's screaming and the phone's ringing like crazy and in walks his dad. Saved! he thinks, but, no, his dad grabs him right back out of the tub and whales the dickens out of him, no questions asked, while she watches, then sends him—whack!—back to bed. So he's lying there, wet and dirty and naked and sore, and he still has to go to the bathroom, and outside his win- dow he hears two older guys talking. "Listen, you know where to do it if we get her pinned?" "No! Don't you?"

o o o

"Yo ho heave ho! Ugh!" Dolly's on her back and they're working on the belly side. 630 Somebody got the great idea of buttering her down first. Not to lose the ground they've gained, they've shot it inside with a basting syringe. But now suddenly there's this big tug-of-war under way between those who want to stuff her in and those who want to let her out. Something rips, but she feels better. The odor of hot butter makes her think of movie theaters and popcorn. "Hey, has anybody seen Harry?" she asks. "Where's Harry?"

o o o

Somebody's getting chased. She switches back to the love story, and now the man's back kissing the young lover again. What's going on? She gives it up, decides to

take a quick bath. She's just stepping into the tub, one foot in, one foot out, when
Mr. Tucker walks in. "Oh, excuse me! I only wanted some aspirin . . ." She grabs   640
for a towel, but he yanks it away. "Now, that's not how it's supposed to happen,
child," he scolds. "Please! Mr. Tucker . . . !" He embraces her savagely, his cal-
loused old hands clutching roughly at her backside. "Mr. Tucker!" she cries,
squirming. "Your wife called—!" He's pushing something between her legs, hurting her. She slips, they both slip—something cold and hard slams her in the back,
cracks her skull, she seems to be sinking into a sea. . .

o o o

They've got her over the hassock, skirt up and pants down. "Give her a little lesson, there, Jack baby!" The television lights flicker and flash over her glossy flesh.
1000 WHEN LIT. Whack! Slap! Bumper to bumper! He leans into her, feeling her
come alive.   650

o o o

The phone rings, waking the baby. "Jack, is that you? Now, you listen to me—!"
"No, dear, this is Mrs. Tucker. Isn't the TV awfully loud?" "Oh, I'm sorry, Mrs.
Tucker! I've been getting—" "I tried to call you before, but I couldn't hang on. To
the phone, I mean. I'm sorry, dear." "Just a minute, Mrs. Tucker, the baby's—"
"Honey, listen! Is Harry there? Is Mr. Tucker there, dear?"

o o o

"Stop it!" she screams and claps a hand over the baby's mouth. "Stop it! Stop it!
Stop it!" Her other hand is full of baby stool and she's afraid she's going to be sick.
The phone rings. "No!" she cries. She's hanging on to the baby, leaning woozily
away, listening to the phone ring. "Okay, okay," she sighs, getting ahold of herself.
But when she lets go of the baby, it isn't screaming any more. She shakes it. Oh   660
no . . .

o o o

"Hello?" No answer. Strange. She hangs up and, wrapped only in a towel, stares
out the window at the cold face staring in—she screams!

o o o

She screams, scaring the hell out of him. He leaps out of the tub, glances up at the
window she's gaping at just in time to see two faces duck away, then slips on the
bathroom tiles, and crashes to his ass, whacking his head on the sink on the way
down. She stares down at him, trembling, a towel over her narrow shoulders. "Mr.
Tucker! Mr. Tucker, are you all right . . . ?" "Who's Sorry Now? Yessir, whose back is
breaking with each . . . He stares up at the little tufted locus of all his woes, and
passes out, dreaming of Jeannie . . .

o o o

The phone rings. "Dolly! It's for you!" "Hello?" "Hello, Mrs. Tucker?" "Yes, speak-   670
ing." "Mrs. Tucker, this is the police calling . . ."

o o o

It's cramped and awkward and slippery, but he's pretty sure he got it in her, once anyway. When he gets the suds out of his eyes, he sees her staring up at them. Through the water. "Hey, Mark! Let her up!"

o   o   o

Down in the suds. Feeling sleepy. The phone rings, startling her. Wrapped in a towel, she goes to answer. "No, he's not here, Mrs. Tucker." Strange. Married people act pretty funny sometimes. The baby is awake and screaming. Dirty, a real mess. Oh boy, there's a lot of things she'd rather be doing than babysitting in this madhouse. She decides to wash the baby off in her own bathwater. She removes her towel, unplugs the tub, lowers the water level so the baby can sit. Glancing 680 back over her shoulder, she sees Jimmy staring at her. "Go back to bed, Jimmy." "I have to go to the bathroom." "Good grief, Jimmy! It looks like you already have!" The phone rings. She doesn't bother with the towel—what can Jimmy see he hasn't already seen?—and goes to answer. "No, Jack, and that's final." Sirens, on the TV, as the police move in. But wasn't that the channel with the love story? Ambulance maybe. Get this over with so she can at least catch the news. "Get those wet pajamas off, Jimmy, and I'll find clean ones. Maybe you better get in the tub, too." "I think something's wrong with the baby," he says. "It's down in the water and it's not swimming or anything."

o   o   o

She's staring up at them from the rug. They slap her. Nothing happens. "You just 690 tilted her, man!" Mark says softly. "We gotta get outta here!" Two little kids are standing wide-eyed in the doorway. Mark looks hard at Jack. "No, Mark, they're just little kids. . . ?" "We gotta, man, or we're dead."

o   o   o

"Dolly! My God! Dolly, I can explain!" She glowers down at them, her ripped girdle around her ankles. "What are the four of you doing in the bathtub with *my* babysitter?" she says sourly. "I can hardly wait!"

o   o   o

Police sirens wail, lights flash. "I heard the scream!" somebody shouts. "There were two boys!" "I saw a man!" "She was running with the baby!" "My God!" somebody screams, "they're *all* dead!" Crowds come running. Spotlights probe the bushes.   700

o   o   o

"Harry, where the hell you been?" his wife whines, glaring blearily up at him from the carpet. "I can explain," he says. "Hey, whatsamatter, Harry?" his host asks, smeared with butter for some goddamn reason. "You look like you just seen a ghost!" Where did he leave his drink? Everybody's laughing, everybody except Dolly, whose cheeks are streaked with tears. "Hey, Harry, you won't let them take me to a rest home, will you, Harry?"

o   o   o

10:00. The dishes done, children to bed, her books read, she watches the news on television. Sleepy. The man's voice is gentle, soothing. She dozes—awakes with a start: a babysitter? Did the announcer say something about a babysitter?

o o o

"Just want to catch the weather," the host says, switching on the TV. Most of the 710 guests are leaving, but the Tuckers stay to watch the news. As it comes on, the announcer is saying something about a babysitter. The host switches channels. "They got a better weatherman on four," he explains. "Wait!" says Mrs. Tucker. "There was something about a babysitter . . . !" The host switches back. "Details have not yet been released by the police," the announcer says. "Harry, maybe we'd better go . . ."

o o o

They stroll casually out of the drugstore, run into a buddy of theirs. "Hey! Did you hear about the babysitter?" the guy asks. Mark grunts, glances at Jack. "Got a smoke?" he asks the guy.

o o o

"I think I hear the baby screaming!" Mrs. Tucker cries, running across the lawn 720 from the drive.

o o o

She wakes, startled, to find Mr. Tucker hovering over her. "I must have dozed off!" she exclaims. "Did you hear the news about the babysitter?" Mrs. Tucker asks. "Part of it," she says, rising. "Too bad, wasn't it?" Mr. Tucker is watching the report of the ball scores and golf tournaments. "I'll drive you home in just a minute, dear," he says. "Why, how nice!" Mrs. Tucker exclaims from the kitchen. "The dishes are all done!"

o o o

"What can I say, Dolly?" the host says with a sigh, twisting the buttered strands of her ripped girdle between his fingers. "Your children are murdered, your husband gone, a corpse in your bathtub, and your house is wrecked. I'm sorry. But what 730 can I say?" On the TV, the news is over, and they're selling aspirin. "Hell, I don't know," she says. "Let's see what's on the late late movie."   [1969]

Questions for Discussion and Writing
1. Outline the events of the story as they pertain to Mark and Jack. Mr. Tucker, Mrs. Tucker, Jimmy, and The Babysitter, respectively. Is it always possible to do this? Why or why not?
2. Compare this story to the ideas expressed in Borges's "The Garden of the Forking Paths." What similarities do you find?
3. How do the various television programs and images relate to the events of the story?

4. What conventions of Metafiction are used in this story?

5. What conventions of Realism are used in this story?

6. How does the story portray males? Is Coover's portraits of males accurate? Explain.

7. What social comments or criticisms are implied by the story?

✌ OCTAVIO PAZ
(b. 1914)

TRANSLATED BY ELIOT WEINBERGER

The Blue Bouquet

Octavio Paz is one of Mexico's most important men of letters. As a poet, essayist, political activist, and critic, he has shaped Mexico's intellectual movements in the second half of this century and as a writer provides a link between the first generation of Modernist authors and those of the Latin American literary resurgence of the 1960s.

Paz was born into an influential but impoverished family. His grandfather was an important politician and writer; his father a prominent journalist. At school, Paz read widely in contemporary and classic poetry. He had already served on the staff of two literary magazines when, in 1937, he left Mexico City to work with peasants in the Yucatan peninsula, where he was deeply impressed both by the peasants' suffering and by the rich archaeological heritage he found there. In 1938 (during the Spanish Civil War), he was invited to attend the Second International Antifascist Writers Conference in Republican Spain. What he saw there made him want to write politically committed poetry but without blind allegiance to any party or system.

From 1938 to 1943, Paz edited poetry magazines and spent two years in America, partly on a Guggenheim Fellowship. In 1945, he joined Mexico's diplomatic corps, in which he worked for the next twenty-three years while continuing to write poetry, essays, and criticism. In 1968, however, he resigned in protest over the government's massacre of student protestors.

Paz's incisive and influential thinking combines an almost utopian desire for a society that will develop the whole person with an uncompromising honesty about the problems and failings of all current governments and ideologies. His achievements as a poet and humanitarian won him the 1990 Nobel Prize for literature, the first Mexican to be so honored.

I WOKE COVERED WITH SWEAT. Hot steam rose from the newly sprayed, red-brick pavement. A gray-winged butterfly, dazzled, circled the yellow light. I jumped from my hammock and crossed the room barefoot, careful not to step on some scorpion leaving his hideout for a bit of fresh air. I went to the little window and inhaled the country air. One could hear the breathing of the night, feminine, enormous. I returned to the center of the room, emptied water from a jar into a pewter basin, and wet my towel. I rubbed my chest and legs with the soaked cloth, dried myself a little, and, making sure that no bugs were hidden in the folds of my clothes, got dressed. I ran down the green stairway. At the door of the boarding-house I bumped into the owner, a one-eyed taciturn fellow. Sitting on a wicker   10 stool, he smoked, his eye half closed. In a hoarse voice, he asked:

"Where are you going?"

"To take a walk. It's too hot."

"Hmmm—everything's closed. And no streetlights around here. You'd better stay put."

I shrugged my shoulders, muttered "back soon," and plunged into the darkness. At first I couldn't see anything. I fumbled along the cobblestone street. I lit a cigarette. Suddenly the moon appeared from behind a black cloud, lighting a white wall that was crumbled in places. I stopped, blinded by such whiteness. Wind whistled slightly. I breathed the air of the tamarinds.[1] The night hummed,   20 full of leaves and insects. Crickets bivouacked in the tall grass. I raised my head: up there the stars too had set up camp. I thought that the universe was a vast system of signs, a conversation between giant beings. My actions, the cricket's saw, the star's blink, were nothing but pauses and syllables, scattered phrases from that dialogue. What word could it be, of which I was only a syllable? Who speaks the word? To whom is it spoken? I threw my cigarette down on the sidewalk. Falling, it drew a shining curve, shooting out brief sparks like a tiny comet.

I walked a long time, slowly. I felt free, secure between the lips that were at that moment speaking me with such happiness. The night was a garden of eyes. As I crossed the street, I heard someone come out of a doorway. I turned around,   30 but could not distinguish anything. I hurried on. A few moments later I heard the dull shuffle of sandals on the hot stone. I didn't want to turn around, although I felt the shadow getting closer with every step. I tried to run. I couldn't. Suddenly I stopped short. Before I could defend myself, I felt the point of a knife in my back, and a sweet voice:

"Don't move, mister, or I'll stick it in."

Without turning, I asked:

"What do you want?"

"Your eyes, mister," answered the soft, almost painful voice.

"My eyes? What do you want with my eyes? Look, I've got some money. Not   40 much, but it's something. I'll give you everything I have if you let me go. Don't kill me."

"Don't be afraid, mister. I won't kill you. I'm only going to take your eyes."

"But why do you want my eyes?" I asked again.

"My girlfriend has this whim. She wants a bouquet of blue eyes. And around here they're hard to find."

"My eyes won't help you. They're brown, not blue."

"Don't try to fool me, mister. I know very well that yours are blue."

"Don't take the eyes of a fellow man. I'll give you something else."

1. Tropical trees bearing a pod-shaped fruit.

"Don't play saint with me," he said harshly. "Turn around."   50

I turned. He was small and fragile. His palm sombrero covered half his face. In his right hand he held a country machete that shone in the moonlight.

"Let me see your face."

I struck a match and put it close to my face. The brightness made me squint. He opened my eyelids with a firm hand. He couldn't see very well. Standing on tiptoe, he stared at me intensely. The flame burned my fingers. I dropped it. A silent moment passed.

"Are you convinced now? They're not blue."

"Pretty clever, aren't you?" he answered. "Let's see. Light another one."

I struck another match, and put it near my eyes. Grabbing my sleeve, he or-   60 dered:

"Kneel down."

I knelt. With one hand he grabbed me by the hair, pulling my head back. He bent over me, curious and tense, while his matchete slowly dropped until it grazed my eyelids. I closed my eyes.

"Keep them open," he ordered.

I opened my eyes. The flame burned my lashes. All of a sudden he let me go.

"All right, they're not blue. Beat it."

He vanished. I leaned against the wall, my head in my hands. I pulled myself together. Stumbling, falling, trying to get up again. I ran for an hour through the   70 deserted town. When I got to the plaza, I saw the owner of the boardinghouse, still sitting in the front of the door. I went in without saying a word. The next day I left town.   [1969]

Questions for Discussion and Writing

1. Is this story the record of a dream? Discuss whether thinking of it as a dream increases or decreases its significance.

2. What is the meaning of the narrator's vision of the universe as a dialogue?

3. What is the significance of the encounter with the thief? What does the desire for a bouquet of blue eyes suggest or symbolize?

4. One could read the story as a cautionary tale or fable warning us not to go out at night. What supports such a reading? What contradicts such a reading?

✎ MARGARET LAURENCE
(1926–1987)

To Set Our House in Order

One of the most important and influential Canadian voices of this century belongs to Margaret Laurence. Her childhood in Neepawa, Manitoba, the town where she was born, was marked by loss. Her mother died when she was only four, her father five years later. A scholarship enabled her to attend United

College in Winnipeg. After college, she married and went with her husband to
Africa, where she began writing by re-telling the folktales and poems of Somalia
and Ghana. After seven years, Laurence and her husband returned to Canada,
but when the marriage broke up in 1962, she moved to England.

By this time she was writing her own fiction. Her first collection of stories,
The Tomorrow-Tamers (1963), grew out of her African experiences, but her true
métier was to recreate her home town under the guise of Manawaka and to
make it a microcosm for Canada and the world at large.

Most of Laurence's protagonists are women who feel acutely the limits placed
upon them by the strict conventions of Manawaka's Scottish inheritance. These
same pressures to conform, however, also give her people strength. They have a
work ethic and sense of purpose that enables them to achieve. Like Canada
itself, her characters struggle against odds to find identities and their own
voices. Laurence creates memorable and sympathetic characters—"ordinary
people"—whose lives seem to matter. She has an unfailing sense of place and an
ear for everyday speech. Her women express the perennial concerns of those
striving to discover themselves and to find the strength to battle quietly against
the odds.

WHEN THE BABY was almost ready to be born, something went wrong and my
mother had to go into hospital two weeks before the expected time. I was
wakened by her crying in the night, and then I heard my father's footsteps as he
went downstairs to phone. I stood in the doorway of my room, shivering and listening, wanting to go to my mother but afraid to go lest there be some sight there
more terrifying than I could bear.

"Hello—Paul?" my father said, and I knew he was talking to Dr. Cates. "It's
Beth. The waters have broken, and the fetal position doesn't seem quite—well, I'm
only thinking of what happened the last time, and another like that would be—I
wish she were a little huskier, damn it—she's so—no, don't worry, I'm quite all   10
right. Yes, I think that would be the best thing. Okay, make it as soon as you can,
will you?"

He came back upstairs, looking bony and dishevelled in his pyjamas, and running his fingers through his sand-coloured hair. At the top of the stairs, he came
face to face with Grandmother MacLeod, who was standing there in her quilted
black satin dressing gown, her slight figure held straight and poised, as though
she were unaware that her hair was bound grotesquely like white-feathered
wings in the snare of her coarse night-time hairnet.

"What is it, Ewen?"

"It's all right, Mother. Beth's having—a little trouble. I'm going to take her   20
into the hospital. You go back to bed."

"I told you," Grandmother MacLeod said in her clear voice, never loud, but
distinct and ringing like the tap of a sterling teaspoon on a crystal goblet, "I did
tell you, Ewen, did I not, that you should have got a girl in to help her with the
housework? She would have rested more."

"I couldn't afford to get anyone in," my father said. "If you thought she should've rested more, why didn't you ever—oh God, I'm out of my mind tonight—just go back to bed, Mother, please. I must get back to Beth."

When my father went down to the front door to let Dr. Cates in, my need overcame my fear and I slipped into my parents' room. My mother's black hair, so neatly pinned up during the day, was startlingly spread across the white pillowcase. I stared at her, not speaking, and then she smiled and I rushed from the doorway and buried my head upon her.

"It's all right, honey," she said. "Listen, Vanessa, the baby's just going to come a little early, that's all. You'll be all right. Grandmother MacLeod will be here."

"How can she get the meals?" I wailed, fixing on the first thing that came to mind. "She never cooks. She doesn't know how."

"Yes, she does," my mother said. "She can cook as well as anyone when she has to. She's just never had to very much, that's all. Don't worry—she'll keep everything in order, and then some."

My father and Dr. Cates came in, and I had to go, without ever saying anything I had wanted to say. I went back to my own room and lay with the shadows all around me. I listened to the night murmurings that always went on in that house, sounds which never had a source, rafters, and beams contracting in the dry air, perhaps, or mice in the walls, or a sparrow that had flown into the attic through the broken skylight there. After a while, although I would not have believed it possible, I slept.

The next morning I questioned my father. I believed him to be not only the best doctor in Manawaka, but also the best doctor in the whole of Manitoba, if not in the entire world, and the fact that he was not the one who was looking after my mother seemed to have something sinister about it.

"But it's always done that way, Vanessa," he explained. "Doctors never attend members of their own family. It's because they care so much about them, you see, and—"

"And what?" I insisted, alarmed at the way he had broken off. But my father did not reply. He stood there, and then he put on that difficult smile with which adults seek to conceal pain from children. I felt terrified, and ran to him, and he held me tightly.

"She's going to be fine," he said. "Honestly, she is. Nessa, don't cry—"

Grandmother MacLeod appeared beside us, steel-spined despite her apparent fragility. She was wearing a purple silk dress and her ivory pendant. She looked as though she were all ready to go out for afternoon tea.

"Ewen, you're only encouraging the child to give way," she said. "Vanessa, big girls of ten don't make such a fuss about things. Come and get your breakfast. Now, Ewen, you're not to worry. I'll see to everything."

Summer holidays were not quite over, but I did not feel like going out to play with any of the kids. I was very superstitious, and I had the feeling that if I left the house, even for a few hours, some disaster would overtake my mother. I did not, of course, mention this feeling to Grandmother MacLeod, for she did not believe in the existence of fear, or if she did, she never let on. I spent the morning morbidly, in seeking hidden places in the house. There were many of these—odd-shaped nooks under the stairs, small and loosely nailed-up doors at the back of clothes closets, leading to dusty tunnels and forgotten recesses in the heart of the house where the only things actually to be seen were drab oil paintings stacked upon the rafters, and trunks full of outmoded clothing and old photograph albums. But the unseen presences in these secret places I knew to be those of every person, young or old, who had ever belonged to the house and had died, including Uncle Roderick who got killed on the Somme,[1] and the baby who would have been my sister if only she had managed to come to life. Grandfather MacLeod, who had died a year after I was born, was present in the house in more tangible form. At the top of the main stairs hung the mammoth picture of a darkly uniformed man riding upon a horse whose prancing stance and dilated nostrils suggested that the battle was not yet over, that it might indeed continue until Judgment Day. The stern man was actually the Duke of Wellington, but at the time I believed him to be my grandfather MacLeod, still keeping an eye on things.

We had moved in with Grandmother MacLeod when the Depression[2] got bad and she could no longer afford a housekeeper, but the MacLeod house never seemed like home to me. Its dark red brick was grown over at the front with Virginia creeper that turned crimson in the fall, until you could hardly tell brick from leaves. It boasted a small tower in which Grandmother MacLeod kept a weedy collection of anaemic ferns. The verandah was embellished with a profusion of wrought-iron scrolls, and the circular rose-window upstairs contained glass of many colours which permitted an outlooking eye to see the world as a place of absolute sapphire or emerald, or if one wished to look with a jaundiced eye, a hateful yellow. In Grandmother MacLeod's opinion, their features gave the house style.

Inside, a multitude of doors led to rooms where my presence, if not actually forbidden, was not encouraged. One was Grandmother MacLeod's bedroom, with its stale and old-smelling air, the dim reek of medicines and lavender sachets. Here resided her monogrammed dresser silver, brush and mirror, nail-buffer and button hook and scissors, none of which must even be fingered by me now, for she meant to leave them to me in her will and intended to hand them over in the same flawless and unused condition in which they had always been kept. Here, too, were the silver-framed photographs of Uncle Roderick—as a child, as a boy, as a man in his Army uniform. The massive walnut spool bed had obviously been designed for queens or giants, and my tiny grandmother used to lie within it all day when she had migraine, contriving somehow to look like a giant queen.

The living room was another alien territory where I had to tread warily, for many valuable objects sat just-so on tables and mantelpiece, and dirt must not be tracked in upon the blue Chinese carpet with its birds in eternal motionless flight and its water-lily buds caught forever just before the point of opening. My mother was always nervous when I was in this room.

"Vanessa, honey," she would say, half apologetically, "why don't you go and play in the den, or upstairs?"

1. The River Somme in France was the site of some of the heaviest fighting during World War I.
2. Severe drought in the Great Plains caused a farming Depression in the U.S. and Canada even before the Stock Market crash in 1929.

"Can't you leave her, Beth?" my father would say. "She's not doing any harm."

"I'm only thinking of the rug," my mother would say, glancing at Grandmother MacLeod, "and yesterday she nearly knocked the Dresden shepherdess off the mantel. I mean, she can't help it, Ewen, she has to run around—"

"Goddamn it, I know she can't help it," my father would growl, glaring at the smirking face of the Dresden shepherdess.

"I see no need to blaspheme, Ewen," Grandmother MacLeod would say quietly, and then my father would say he was sorry, and I would leave.

The day my mother went to the hospital, Grandmother MacLeod called me at lunch-time, and when I appeared, smudged with dust from the attic, she looked at me distastefully as though I had been a cockroach that had just crawled impertinently out of the woodwork.

"For mercy's sake, Vanessa, what have you been doing with yourself? Run and get washed this minute. Here, not that way—you use the back stairs, young lady. Get along now. Oh—your father phoned."

I swung around. "What did he say? How is she? Is the baby born?"

"Curiosity killed a cat," Grandmother MacLeod said, frowning. "I cannot understand Beth and Ewen telling you all these things, at your age. What sort of vulgar person you'll grow up to be, I dare not think. No it's not born yet. Your mother's just the same. No change."

I looked at my grandmother, not wanting to appeal to her, but unable to stop myself. "Will she—will she be all right?"

Grandmother MacLeod straightened her already-straight back. "If I said definitely yes, Vanessa, that would be a lie, and the MacLeods do not tell lies, as I have tried to impress upon you before. What happens is God's will. The Lord giveth, and the Lord taketh away."

Appalled, I turned away so she would not see my face and my eyes. Surprisingly, I heard her sigh and left her papery white and perfectly manicured hand upon my shoulder.

"When your Uncle Roderick got killed," she said, "I thought I would die. But I didn't die, Vanessa."

At lunch, she chatted animatedly, and I realised she was trying to cheer me in the only way she knew.

"When I married your Grandfather MacLeod," she related, "he said to me, 'Eleanor, don't think because we're going to the prairies that I expect you to live roughly. You're used to a proper house, and you shall have one.' He was as good as his word. Before we'd been in Manawaka three years, he'd had this place built. He earned a good deal of money in his time, your grandfather. He soon had more patients than either of the other doctors. We ordered our dinner service and all our silver from Birks' in Toronto. We had resident help in those days, of course, and never had less than twelve guests for dinner parties. When I had a tea, it would always be twenty or thirty. Never any less than half a dozen different kinds of cake were ever served in this house. Well, no one seems to bother much these days. Too lazy, I suppose."

"Too broke," I suggested. "That's what Dad says."

"I can't bear slang," Grandmother MacLeod said. "If you mean hard up, why don't you say so? It's mainly a question of management, anyway. My accounts were always in good order, and so was my house. No unexpected expenses that couldn't be met, no fruit cellar running out of preserves before the winter was over. Do you know what my father used to say to me when I was a girl?"

"No," I said. "What?"

"God loves Order," Grandmother MacLeod replied with emphasis. "You remember that, Vanessa. God loves Order—he wants each one of us to set our house in order. I've never forgotten those words of my father's. I was a MacInnes before I got married. The MacInnes is a very ancient clan, the lairds of Morven and the constables of the Castle of Kinlochaline. Did you finish that book I gave you?"

"Yes," I said. Then, feeling some additional comment to be called for, "It was a swell book, Grandmother."

This was somewhat short of the truth. I had been hoping for her cairngorm[3] brooch on my tenth birthday, and had received instead the plaid-bound volume entitled *The Clans and Tartans of Scotland*. Most of it was too boring to read, but I had looked up the motto of my own family and those of some of my friends' families. *Be then a wall of brass. Learn to suffer. Consider the end. Go carefully.* I had not found any of these slogans reassuring. What with Mavis Duncan learning to suffer, and Laura Kennedy considering the end, and Patsy Drummond going carefully, and I spending my time in being a wall of brass, it did not seem to me that any of us were going to lead very interesting lives. I did not say this to Grandmother MacLeod.

"The MacInnes motto is *Pleasure Arises from Work*," I said.

"Yes," she agreed proudly. "And an excellent motto it is, too. One to bear in mind."

She rose from the table, rearranging on her bosom the looped ivory beads that held the pendant on which a fullblown ivory rose was stiffly carved.

"I hope Ewen will be pleased," she said.

"What at?"

"Didn't I tell you?" Grandmother MacLeod said. "I hired a girl this morning, for the housework. She's to start tomorrow."

When my father got home that evening, Grandmother MacLeod told him her good news. He ran one hand distractedly across his forehead.

"I'm sorry, Mother, but you'll just have to unhire her. I can't possibly pay anyone."

"It seems distinctly odd," Grandmother MacLeod snapped, "that you can afford to eat chicken four times a week."

"Those chickens," my father said in an exasperated voice, "are how people are paying their bills. The same with the eggs and the milk. That scrawny turkey that arrived yesterday was for Logan MacCardney's appendix, if you must know. We probably eat better than any family in Manawaka, except Niall Cameron's. People can't entirely dispense with doctors or undertakers. That doesn't mean to say I've got any cash. Look, Mother, I don't know what's happening with Beth. Paul thinks he may have to do a Cesarean. Can't we leave all this? Just leave the house alone. Don't touch it. What does it matter?"

3. Yellow or dark red rock crystal especially associated with jewelry in the Scottish highlands.

"I have never lived in a messy house, Ewen," Grandmother MacLeod said, "and I don't intend to begin now."

"Oh Lord," my father said. "Well, I'll phone Edna, I guess, and see if she can give us a hand, although God knows she's got enough, with the Connor house and her parents to look after."

"I don't fancy having Edna Connor in to help," Grandmother MacLeod objected.

"Why not?" my father shouted. "She's Beth's sister, isn't she?"

"She speaks in such a slangy way," Grandmother MacLeod said. "I have never believed she was a good influence on Vanessa. And there is no need for you to raise your voice to me, Ewen, if you please."

I could barely control my rage. I thought my father would surely rise to Aunt Edna's defence. But he did not.

"It'll be all right," he soothed her. "She'd only be here for part of the day, Mother. You could stay in your room."

Aunt Edna strode in the next morning. The sight of her bobbed black hair and her grin made me feel better at once. She hauled out the carpet sweeper and the weighted polisher and got to work. I dusted while she polished and swept, and we got through the living room and front hall in next to no time.

"Where's her royal highness kiddo?" she enquired.

"In her room," I said. "She's reading the catalogue from Robinson & Cleaver."

"Good Glory, not again?" Aunt Edna cried. "The last time she ordered three linen tea-clothes and two dozen serviettes. It came to fourteen dollars. Your mother was absolutely frantic. I guess I shouldn't be saying this."

"I knew anyway," I assured her. "She was at the lace handkerchiefs sections when I took up her coffee."

"Let's hope she stays there. Heaven forbid she should get onto the banqueting cloths. Well, at least she believes the Irish are good for two things—manual labor and linen-making. She's never forgotten Father used to be a blacksmith, before he got the hardware store. Can you beat it? I wish it didn't bother Beth."

"Does it?" I asked, and immediately realised this was a wrong move, for Aunt Edna was suddenly scrutinising me.

"We're making you grow up before your time," she said. "Don't pay any attention to me, Nessa. I must've got up on the wrong side of the bed this morning."

But I was unwilling to leave the subject.

"All the same," I said thoughtfully. "Grandmother MacLeod's family were the lairds of Morven and the constables of the Castle of Kinlochaline. I bet you didn't know that."

Aunt Edna snorted. "Castle, my foot. She was born in Ontario, just like your Grandfather Connor, and her father was a horse doctor. Come on, kiddo, we'd better shut up and get down to business here."

We worked in silence for a while.

"Aunt Edna—" I said at last, "what about Mother? Why won't they let me go and see her?"

"Kids aren't allowed to visit maternity patients. It's tough for you, I know that. Look, Nessa, don't worry. If it doesn't start tonight, they're going to do the operation. She's getting the best of care."

I stood there, holding the feather duster like a dead bird in my hands. I was not aware that I was going to speak until the words came out.

"I'm scared," I said.

Aunt Edna put her arms around me, and her face looked all at once stricken and empty of defences.

"Oh, honey, I'm scared, too," she said.

It was this way that Grandmother MacLeod found us when she came step- 260 ping lightly down into the front hall with the order in her hand for two dozen lace-bordered handkerchiefs of pure Irish linen.

I could not sleep that night, and when I went downstairs, I found my father in the den. I sat down on the hassock beside his chair, and he told me about the operation my mother was to have the next morning. He kept on saying it was not serious nowadays.

"But you're worried," I put in, as though seeking to explain why I was.

"I should at least have been able to keep from burdening you with it," he said in a distant voice, as though to himself. "If only the baby hadn't got itself twisted around—"   270

"Will it be born dead, like the little girl?"

"I don't know," my father said. "I hope not."

"She'd be disappointed, wouldn't she, if it was?" I said bleakly, wondering why I was not enough for her.

"Yes, she would," my father replied. "She won't be able to have any more, after this. It's partly on your account that she wants this one, Nessa. She doesn't want you to grow up without a brother or sister."

"As far as I'm concerned, she didn't need to bother," I retorted angrily.

My father laughed. "Well, let's talk about something else, and then maybe you'll be able to sleep. How did you and Grandmother make out today?"   280

"Oh, fine, I guess. What was Grandfather MacLeod like, Dad?"

"What did she tell you about him?"

"She said he made a lot of money in his time."

"Well, he wasn't any millionaire," my father said, "but I suppose he did quite well. That's not what I associate with him, though."

He reached across to the bookshelf, took out a small leather-bound volume and opened it. On the pages were mysterious marks, like doodling, only much neater and more patterned.

"What is it?" I asked.

"Greek," my father explained. "This is a play called *Antigone*. See, here's the 290 title in English. There's a whole stack of them on the shelves there. *Oedipus Rex.* *Electra. Medea.* They belonged to your Grandfather MacLeod. He used to read them often."

"Why?" I enquired, unable to understand why anyone would pore over those undecipherable signs.

"He was interested in them," my father said. "He must have been a lonely man, although it never struck me that way at the time. Sometimes a thing only hits you a long time afterwards."

"Why would he be lonely?" I wanted to know.

"He was the only person in Manawaka who could read these plays in the original Greek," my father said. "I don't suppose many people, if anyone, had even read them in English translations. Maybe he would have liked to be a classical scholar—I don't know. But his father was a doctor, so that's what he was. Maybe he would have liked to talk to somebody about these plays. They must have meant a lot to him."

It seemed to me that my father was talking oddly. There was a sadness in his voice that I had never heard before, and I longed to say something that would make him feel better, but I could not, because I did not know what was the matter.

"Can you read this kind of writing?" I asked hesitantly.

My father shook his head. "Nope. I was never very intellectual, I guess. Rod was always brighter than I, in school, but even he wasn't interested in learning Greek. Perhaps he would've been later, if he'd lived. As a kid, all I ever wanted to do was go into the merchant marine."

"Why didn't you, then?"

"Oh well," my father said offhandedly, "a kid who'd never seen the sea wouldn't have made much of a sailor. I might have turned out to be the seasick type."

I had lost interest now that he was speaking once more like himself.

"Grandmother MacLeod was pretty cross today about the girl," I remarked.

"I know," my father nodded. "Well, we must be as nice as we can to her, Nessa, and after a while she'll be all right."

Suddenly I did not care what I said.

"Why can't she be nice to us for a change?" I burst out. "We're always the ones who have to be nice to her."

My father put his hand down and slowly tilted my head until I was forced to look at him.

"Vanessa," he said, "she's had troubles in her life which you really don't know much about. That's why she gets migraine sometimes and has to go to bed. It's not easy for her these days, either—the house is still the same, so she thinks other things should be too. It hurts her when she finds they aren't."

"I don't see—" I began.

"Listen," my father said, "you know we were talking about what people are interested in, like Grandfather MacLeod being interested in Greek plays? Well, your grandmother was interested in being a lady, Nessa, and for a long time it seemed to her that she was one."

I thought of the Castle of Kinlochaline, and of horse doctors in Ontario.

"I didn't know—" I stammered.

"That's usually the trouble with most of us," my father said. "You go on up to bed now. I'll phone tomorrow from the hospital as soon as the operation's over."

I did sleep at last, and in my dreams I could hear the caught sparrow fluttering in the attic, and the sound of my mother crying, and the voices of the dead children.

My father did not phone until afternoon. Grandmother MacLeod said I was being silly, for you could hear the phone ringing all over the house, but nevertheless I refused to move out of the den. I had never before examined my father's books, but now, at a loss for something to do, I took them out one by one and read snatches here and there. After I had been doing this for several hours, it dawned on me that most of the books were of the same kind. I looked again at the titles.   350

Seven-League Boots. Arabia Deserta. The Seven Pillars of Wisdom. Travels in Tibet. Count Lucknor the Sea Devil. And a hundred more. On a shelf by themselves were copies of the *National Geographic* magazine, which I looked at often enough, but never before with the puzzling compulsion which I felt now, as though I were on the verge of some discovery, something which I had to find out and yet did not want to know. I riffled through the picture-filled pages. Hibiscus and wild orchids grew in a soft-petalled confusion. The Himalayas stood lofty as gods, with the morning sun on their peaks of snow. Leopards snarled from the vined depths of a thousand jungles. Schooners buffeted their white sails like the wings of giant angels against the great sea winds.   360

"What on earth are you doing?" Grandmother MacLeod enquired waspishly, from the doorway. "You've got everything scattered all over the place. Pick it all up this minute, Vanessa, do you hear?"

So I picked up the books and magazines, and put them all neatly away, as I had been told to do.

When the telephone finally rang, I was afraid to answer it. At last I picked it up. My father sounded faraway, and the relief in his voice made it unsteady.

"It's okay, honey. Everything's fine. The boy was born alive and kicking after all. Your mother's pretty weak, but she's going to be all right."

I could hardly believe it. I did not want to talk to anyone. I wanted to be by   370
myself, to assimilate the presence of my brother, towards whom, without ever having seen him yet, I felt such tenderness and such resentment.

That evening, Grandmother MacLeod approached my father, who, still dazed with the unexpected gift of neither life now being threatened, at first did not take her seriously when she asked what they planned to call the child.

"Oh, I don't know. Hank, maybe, or Joe. Fauntleroy, perhaps."

She ignored his levity.

"Ewen," she said, "I wish you would call him Roderick."

My father's face changed. "I'd rather not."

"I think you should," Grandmother MacLeod insisted, very quietly, but in a   380
voice as pointed and precise as her silver nail-scissors.

"Don't you think Beth ought to decide?" my father asked.

"Beth will agree if you do."

My father did not bother to deny something that even I knew to be true. He did not say anything. Then Grandmother MacLeod's voice, astonishingly, faltered a little.

"It would mean a great deal to me," she said.

I remembered what she had told me—*When your Uncle Roderick got killed, I thought I would die. But I didn't die.* All at once, her feeling for that unknown dead man became a reality for me. And yet I held it against her, as well, for I could see   390
that it had enabled her to win now.

"All right," my father said tiredly. "We'll call him Roderick."

Then, alarmingly, he threw back his head and laughed.

"Roderick Dhu!" he cried. "That's what you'll call him, isn't it? Black Roderick. Like before. Don't you remember? As though he were a character out of Sir Walter Scott,[4] instead of an ordinary kid who—"

He broke off, and looked at her with a kind of desolation in his face.

"God, I'm sorry, Mother," he said. "I had no right to say that."

Grandmother MacLeod did not flinch, or tremble, or indicate that she felt anything at all.

"I accept your apology, Ewen," she said.

My mother had to stay in bed for several weeks after she arrived home. The baby's cot was kept in my parents' room, and I could go in and look at the small creature who lay there with his tightly closed fists and his feathery black hair. Aunt Edna came in to help each morning, and when she had finished the housework, she would have coffee with my mother. They kept the door closed, but this did not prevent me from eavesdropping, for there was an air register in the floor of the spare room, which was linked somehow with the register in my parents' room. If you put your ear to the iron grille, it was almost like a radio.

"Did you mind very much, Beth?" Aunt Edna was saying.

"Oh, it's not the name I mind," my mother replied. "It's just the fact that Ewen felt he had to. You know that Rod had only had the sight of one eye, didn't you?"

"Sure, I knew. So what?"

"There was only a year and a half between Ewen and Rod," my mother said, "so they often went around together when they were youngsters. It was Ewen's air-rifle that did it."

"Oh Lord," Aunt Edna said heavily. "I suppose she always blamed him?"

"No, I don't think it was so much that, really. It was how he felt himself. I think he even used to wonder sometimes if—but people shouldn't let themselves think like that, or they'd go crazy. Accidents do happen, after all. When the war came, Ewen joined up first. Rod should never have been in the Army at all, but he couldn't wait to get in. He must have lied about his eyesight. It wasn't so very noticeable unless you looked at him closely, and I don't suppose the medicals were very thorough in those days. He got in as a gunner, and Ewen applied to have him in the same company. He thought he might be able to watch out for him, I guess, Rod being—at a disadvantage. They were both only kids. Ewen was nineteen and Rod was eighteen when they went to France. And then the Somme. I don't know, Edna, I think Ewen felt that if Rod had had proper sight, or if he hadn't been in the same outfit and had been sent somewhere else—you know how people always think these things afterwards, not that it's ever a bit of use. Ewen wasn't there when Rod got hit. They'd lost each other somehow, and Ewen was looking for him, not bothering about anything else, you know, just frantically looking. Then he stumbled across him quite by chance. Rod was still alive, but—"

4. Romantic Scottish novelist (1771–1832).

"Stop it, Beth," Aunt Edna said. "You're only upsetting yourself."

"Ewen never spoke of it to me," my mother went on, "until once his mother showed me the letter he'd written to her at the time. It was a peculiar letter, almost formal, saying how gallantly Rod had died, and all that. I guess I shouldn't have, but I told him she'd shown it to me. He was very angry that she had. And then, as though for some reason he were terribly ashamed, he said——*I had to write some-* 440 *thing to her, but men don't really die like that, Beth. It wasn't that way at all.* It was only after the war that he decided to come back and study medicine and go into practice with his father."

"Had Rod meant to?" Aunt Edna asked.

"I don't know," my mother said slowly. "I never felt I should ask Ewen that."

Aunt Edna was gathering up the coffee things, for I could hear the clash of cups and saucers being stacked on the tray.

"You know what I heard her say to Vanessa once, Beth? *The MacLeods never tell lies.* Those were her exact words. Even then, I didn't know whether to laugh or cry." 450

"Please, Edna—" my mother sounded worn out now. "Don't."

"Oh Glory," Aunt Edna said remorsefully. "I've got all the delicacy of a two-ton truck. I didn't mean Ewen, for heaven's sake. That wasn't what I meant at all. Here, let me plump up your pillows for you."

Then the baby began to cry, so I could not hear anything more of interest. I took my bike and went out beyond Manawaka, riding aimlessly along the gravel highway. It was late summer, and the wheat had changed colour, but instead of being high and bronzed in the fields, it was stunted and desiccated, for there had been no rain again this year. But in the bluff where I stopped and crawled under 460 the barbed wire fence and lay stretched out on the grass, the plentiful poplar leaves were turning to a luminous yellow and shone like church windows in the sun. I put my head down very close to the earth and looked at what was going on there. Grasshoppers with enormous eyes ticked and twitched around me, as though the dry air were perfect for their purposes. A ladybird[5] laboured mightily to climb a blade of grass, fell off, and started all over again, seeming to be unaware that she possessed wings and could have flown up.

I thought of the accidents that might easily happen to a person—or, of course, might not happen, might happen to somebody else. I thought of the dead baby, my sister, who might as easily been I. Would she, then, have been lying here in my place, the sharp grass making its small toothmarks on her brown arms, the 470 sun warming her to the heart? I thought of the leather-bound volumes of Greek, and the six different kinds of iced cakes that used to be offered always in the MacLeod house, and the pictures of leopards and green seas. I thought of my brother, who had been born alive after all, and now had been given his life's name.

I could not really comprehend these things, but I sensed their strangeness, their disarray. I felt that whatever God might love in this world, it was certainly not order.   [1970]

---

5. Ladybug.

Questions for Discussion and Writing

1. Analyze Grandmother MacLeod's value system. In what ways do her values and ideas help her and her family? When do they seem misguided or unhelpful?

2. Is Grandmother McLeod honest with herself and her past?

3. Like any child, Vanessa is curious about the adult world. What does she learn about it through the events of the story? What did she mean in the last paragraph when she said, "Whatever might God love in this world, it was certainly not order"?

4. What is Aunt Edna's role in the story?

5. What are the conflicts in the story? Are they resolved?

6. Discuss whether this is a unified story or a series of loosely related incidents? What ideas or themes unify the story?

⁊ AMA ATA AIDOO
(b. 1942)

No Sweetness Here

Playwright, poet, novelist, and short story writer, Ama Ata Aidoo has emerged as one of Africa's most renowned voices, speaking out on such issues as the legacy of colonialism, clashes in value systems, and the place of women in Africa's post-colonial societies.

Aidoo was born near Saltpond, Ghana, into an aristocratic family. While she absorbed traditional tribal lore and language, she also received a typical English education at Wesley School in Cape Coast and from there attended the University of Ghana. At university, she participated in a drama workshop, producing experimental plays of her own, before graduating with honors in 1964. She later received a fellowship to study creative writing at Stanford University.

Like many African intellectuals, Aidoo combines an academic and literary career with a life in practical politics. She has been Minister of Education and also a lecturer at the University of Ghana. Although her literary output has been so far relatively small—two novels, two collections of poetry, and one collection of short stories—her influence has been significant, for her work explores the complexities of contemporary African society in ways that are both true to her roots and accessible to non-Africans.

HE WAS BEAUTIFUL, but that was not important. Beauty does not play such a vital role in a man's life as it does in a woman's, especially if that man is a Fanti. If a man's beauty is so ill-mannered as to be noticeable, people discreetly ignore its existence. Only an immodest girl like me would dare comment on a boy's beauty. "Kwesi is so handsome," I was always telling his mother. "If ever I am transferred from this place, I will kidnap him." I enjoyed teasing the dear woman and she enjoyed being teased about him. She would look scandalised, pleased and alarmed all in one fleeting moment.

"Ei, Chicha." She called me the Fanticised version of "teacher." "You should not say such things. The boy is not very handsome really." But she knew she was 10 lying. "Besides, Chicha, who cares whether a boy is handsome or not?" Again she knew that at least she cared, for, after all, didn't the boy's wonderful personality throw a warm light on the mother's lively though already waning beauty? Then gingerly, but in a remarkably matter-of-fact tone, she would voice out her gnawing fear. "Please Chicha, I always know you are just making fun of me, but please, promise me you won't take Kwesi away with you." Almost at once her tiny mouth would quiver and she would hide her eyes in her cloth as if ashamed of her great love and her fears. But I understood. "O, Maami, don't cry, you know I don't mean it."

"Chicha I am sorry, and I trust you. Only I can't help fearing, can I? What 20 will I do, Chicha, what would I do, should something happen to my child?" She would raise her pretty eyes, glistening with unshed tears.

"Nothing will happen to him," I would assure her. "He is a good boy. He does not fight and therefore there is no chance of anyone beating him. He is not dull, at least not too dull which means he does not get more cane-lashes than the rest of his mates. . . ."

"Chicha, I shall willingly submit to your canes if he gets his sums wrong," she would hastily intervene.

"Don't be funny. A little warming-up on a cold morning wouldn't do him any harm. But if you say so, I won't object to hitting that soft flesh of yours." At this, 30 the tension would break and both of us begin laughing. Yet I always went away with the image of her quivering mouth and unshed tears in my mind.

Maami Ama loved her son; and this is a statement silly, as silly as saying Maami Ama is a woman. Which mother would not? At the time of this story, he had just turned ten years old. He was in Primary Class Four and quite tall for his age. His skin was as smooth as shea-butter[1] and as dark as charcoal. His black hair was as soft as his mother's. His eyes were of the kind that always remind one of a long dream on a hot afternoon. It is indecent to dwell on a boy's physical appearance, but then Kwesi's beauty was indecent.

The evening was not yet come. My watch read 4.15 P.M., that ambiguous 40 time of the day, which the Fantis, despite their great ancient astronomic knowledge, have always failed to identify. For the very young and very old, it is certainly evening, for they've stayed at home all day and they begin to persuade themselves that the day is ending. Bored with their own company, they sprawl in the marketplace or by their own walls. The children begin to whimper for their mothers, for they are tired with playing "house." Fancying themselves starving, they go back to what was left of their lunch, but really they only pray that mother will come home

---

1. Butter-like food made from the kernels of the si tree.

from the farm soon. The very old certainly do not go back on lunch remains but they do bite back at old conversational topics which were fresh at ten o'clock.

"I say, Kwame, as I was saying this morning, my first wife was a most beauti- 50 ful woman," old Kofi would say.

"Oh! yes, yes, she was an unusually beautiful girl. I remember her." Old Kwame would nod his head but the truth was he was tired of the story and he was sleepy. "It's high time the young people came back from the farm."

But I was a teacher, and I went the white man's way. School was over. Maami Ama's hut was at one end of the village and the school was at the other. Nevertheless it was not a long walk from the school to her place because Bamso is not really a big village. I had left my books to little Grace Ason to take home for me; so I had only my little clock in my hand and I was walking in a leisurely way. As I passed the old people, they shouted their greetings. Here too it was always 60 the Fanticised form of the English.

"Kudiimin-o, Chicha." Then I would answer, "Kudiimin, Nana." When I greeted first, the response was "Tanchiw," that is "Thank you."

"Chicha, how are you?"

"Nana, I am well."

"And how are the children?"

"Nana, they are well."

"*Yoo,* that is good." When an old man felt inclined to be talkative, especially if he had more than me for audience, he would compliment me on the work I was doing. Then he would go on to the assets of education, especially female educa- 70 tion, ending up with quoting Dr. Aggrey.

So this evening too, I was delayed: but it was as well, for when I arrived at the hut, Maami Ama had just arrived from the farm. The door opened, facing the village, and so I could see her. Oh, that picture is still vivid in my mind. She was sitting on a low stool with her load before her. Like all the loads the other women would bring from the farms into their homes, it was colourful with miscellaneous articles. At the very bottom of the wide wooden tray were the cassava and yam tubers, rich muddy brown, the colour of the earth. Next were the plantain, of the green colour of the woods from which they came. Then there were the gay vegeta- bles, the scarlet pepper, garden eggs, golden pawpaw and crimson tomatoes. Over 80 this riot of colours the little woman's eyes were fixed, absorbed, while the tiny hands delicately picked the pepper. I made a scratchy noise at the door. She looked up and smiled. Her smile was a wonderful flashing whiteness.

"Oh Chicha, I have just arrived."

"So I see. *Ayekoo.*"

"*Yaa,* my own. And how are you, my child?"

"Very well, Mother."

"And you?"

"Tanchiw. Do sit down, there's a stool in that corner. Sit down. Mmmm. . . . Life is a battle. What can we do? We are just trying, my daughter." 90

"Why were you longer at the farm today?"

"After weeding that plot I told you about last week, I thought I would go for one or two yams."

"Ah!" I cried.

"You know tomorrow is Ahobaa. Even if one does not feel happy, one must have some yam for old Ahor."

"Yes. So I understand. The old saviour deserves it. After all it is not often that a man offers himself a sacrifice to the gods to save his people from a pestilence."

"No, Chicha, we Fantis were so lucky."

"But Maami Ama, why do you look so sad? After all, the yams are quite big." 100 She gave me a small grin, looking at the yams she had now packed at the corner.

"Do you think so? Well, they are the best of the lot. My daughter, when life fails you, it fails you totally. One's yams reflect the total sum of one's life. And mine look wretched enough."

"O, Maami, why are you always speaking in this way? Look at Kwesi, how many mothers can boast of such a son? Even though he is only one, consider those who have none at all. Perhaps some woman is sitting at some corner envying you."

"She chuckled. "What an unhappy woman she must be who would envy Ama! But thank you, I should be grateful for Kwesi." 110

After that we were quiet for a while. I always loved to see her moving quietly about her work. Having finished unpacking, she knocked the dirt out of the tray and started making fire to prepare the evening meal. She started humming a religious lyric. She was a Methodist.

We are fighting
We are fighting
We are fighting for Canaan, the Heavenly Kingdom above.

I watched her and my eyes became misty, she looked so much like my own 120 mother. Presently, the fire began to smoke. She turned round. "Chicha."

"Maami Ama."

"Do you know that tomorrow I am going to have a formal divorce?"

"Oh! And I could not help the dismay in my voice.

I had heard, soon after my arrival in the village, that the parents of that most beautiful boy were as good as divorced. I had hoped they would come to a respectful understanding for the boy's sake. Later on when I got to know his mother, I had wished for this, for her own sweet self's sake. But as time went on I had realised this could not be or was not even desirable. Kodjo Fi was a selfish and bullying man, whom no decent woman ought to have married. He got on 130 marvellously with his two other wives but they were three of a feather. Yet I was sorry to hear Maami was going to have a final breach with him.

"Yes, I am," she went on. "I should. What am I going on like this for? What is man struggling after? Seven years is a long time to bear ill-usage from a man coupled with contempt and insults from his wives. What have I done to deserve the abuse of his sisters? And his mother!"

"Does she insult you too?" I exclaimed.

"Why not? Don't you think she would? Considering that I don't buy her the most expensive cloths on the market and I don't give her the best fish from my soup, like her daughters-in-law do."

140

I laughed. "The mean old witch!"

"Chicha, don't laugh. I am quite sure she wanted to eat Kwesi but I baptised him and she couldn't."

"Oh, don't say that Maami. I am quite sure they all like you, only you don't know."

"My child, they don't. They hate me."

"But what happened?" I asked the question I had wanted to ask for so long.

"You would ask, Chicha! I don't know. They suddenly began hating me when Kwesi was barely two. Kodjo Fi reduced my housekeeping money and sometimes he refused to give me anything at all. He wouldn't eat my food. At first, 150 I used to ask him why. He always replied, "It is nothing." If I had not been such an unlucky woman, his mother and sisters might have taken my side, but for me there was no one. That planting time, although I was his first wife, he allotted to me the smallest, thorniest plot."

"Ei, what did you say about it?"

"What could I say? At that time my mother was alive, though my father was already dead. When I complained to her about the treatment I was getting from my husband, she told me that in marriage, a woman must sometimes be a fool. But I have been a fool for far too long a time."

"Oh!" I frowned. 160

"Mother has died and left me and I was an only child too. My aunts are very busy looking after the affairs of their own daughters. I've told my uncles several times but they never take me seriously. They feel I am only a discontented woman."

"You?" I asked in surprise.

"Perhaps you would not think so. But there are several who do feel like that in this village."

She paused for a while, while she stared at the floor.

"You don't know, but I've been the topic of gossip for many years. Now, I only want to live on my own looking after my child. I don't think I will ever get 170 any more children. Chicha, our people say a bad marriage kills the soul. Mine is fit for burial."

"Maami, don't grieve."

"My daughter, my mother and father who brought me to this world have left me alone and I've stopped grieving for them. When death summoned them, they were glad to lay down their tools and go to their parents. Yes, they loved me all right but even they had to leave me. Why should I make myself unhappy about a man for whom I ceased to exist a long time ago?"

She went to the big basket, took out some cassava and plantain, and sitting down began peeling them. Remembering she had forgotten the wooden bowl into 180 which she would put the food, she got up to go for it. She looked like an orphan indeed.

"In this case," I continued the conversation, "what will happen to Kwesi?"

"What will happen to him?" she asked in surprise. "This is no problem. They may tell me to give him to his father."

"And would you?"

"No, I wouldn't."

"And would you succeed in keeping him if his father insisted?"

"Well, I would struggle, for my son is his father's child but he belongs to my family."   190

I sat there listening to these references to the age-old customs of my people of which I had been ignorant. I was surprised. She washed the food, now cut into lumps, and arranged it in the cooking-pot. She added water and put it on the fire. She blew at it and it burst into flames.

"Maami Ama, has not your husband got a right to take Kwesi from you?" I asked her.

"He has, I suppose, but not entirely. Anyway, if the elders who would make the divorce settlement ask me to let him go and stay with his father, I wouldn't refuse."

"You are a brave woman."   200

"Life has taught me to be brave," she said, looking at me and smiling, "By the way, what is the time?"

I told her, "It is six minutes to six o'clock."

"And Kwesi has not yet come home?" she exclaimed.

"Mama, here I am," a piping voice announced.

"My husband, my brother, my father, my all-in-all, where are you?" And there he was. All at once, for the care-worn village woman, the sun might well have been rising from the east instead of setting behind the coconut palms. Her eyes shone. Kwesi saluted me and then his mother. He was a little shy of me and he ran away to the inner chamber. There was a thud which meant he had thrown 210 his books down.

"Kwesi," his mother called out to him. "I have always told you to put your books down gently. I did not buy them with sand, and you ought to be careful with them."

He returned to where we were. I looked at him. He was very dirty. There was sand in his hair, ears and eyes. His uniform was smeared with mud, crayon and berry-juice. His braces were hanging down on one side. His mother gave an affectionate frown. "Kwesi, you are very dirty, just look at yourself. You are a disgrace to me. Anyone would think your mother does not look after you well." I was very much amused, for I knew she meant this for my ears. Kwesi just stood there, with- 220 out a care in the world.

"Can't you play without putting sand in your hair?" his mother persisted.

"I am hungry," he announced. I laughed.

"Shame, shame, and your chicha is here. Chicha, you see? He does not fetch me water. He does not fetch me firewood. He does not weed my farm on Saturdays as other schoolboys do for their mothers. He only eats and eats." I looked at him; he fled again into the inner chamber for shame. We both started laughing at him. After a time I got up to go.

"Chicha, I would have liked you to eat before you went away; that's why I am hurrying up with the food." Maami tried to detain me.   230

"Oh, it does not matter. You know I eat here when I come, but today I must go away. I have the children's books to mark."

"Then I must not keep you away from your work."

"Tomorrow I will come to see you," I promised.

"Yoo, thank you."

"Sleep well, Maami."

"Sleep well, my daughter." I stepped into the open air. The sun was far receding. I walked slowly away. Just before I was out of earshot, Maami shouted after me, "And remember, if Kwesi gets his sums wrong, I will come to school to receive his lashes, if only you would tell me."   240

"*Yoo,*" I shouted back. Then I went away.

The next day was Ahobaada. It was a day of rejoicing for everyone. In the morning, old family quarrels were being patched up. In Maami Ama's family all became peaceful. Her aunts had—or thought they had—reconciled themselves to the fact that, when Maami Ama's mother was dying, she had instructed her sisters, much to their chagrin, to give all her jewels to her only child. This had been one of the reasons why the aunts and cousins had left Ama so much to her own devices. "After all, she has her mother's goods, what else does she need?" they were often saying. However, today, aunts, cousins and nieces have come to a better understanding. Ahobaa is a season of goodwill! Nevertheless, Ama is going to have a   250
formal divorce today. . . .

It had not been laid down anywhere in the Education Ordinance that schoolchildren were to be given holidays during local festivals. And so no matter how much I sympathised with the kids, I could not give them a holiday, although Ahobaa was such an important occasion for them they naturally felt it a grievance to be forced to go to school while their friends at home were eating too much yam and meat. But they had their revenge on me. They fidgeted the whole day. What was worse, the schoolroom was actually just one big shed. When I left the Class One chicks to look at the older ones, they chattered; when I turned to them, Class Two and Class Three began shouting. Oh, it was a fine situation. In the afternoon,   260
after having gone home to taste the festive dishes, they nearly drove me mad. So I was relieved when it was three o'clock. Feeling no sense of guilt, I turned them all out to play. They rushed out to the field. I packed my books on the table for little Grace to take home. My intention was to go and see the divorce proceedings which had begun at one o'clock and then come back at four to dismiss them. These divorce cases took hours to settle, and I hoped I would hear some of it.

As I walked down between the rows of desks, I hit my leg against one. The books on it tumbled down. As I picked them up I saw they belonged to Kwesi. It was the desk he shared with a little girl. I began thinking about him and the unhappy connection he had with what was going on at that moment down in the vil-   270
lage. I remembered every word of the conversation I had had with his mother the previous evening. I became sad at the prospect of a possible separation from the mother who loved him so much and whom he loved. From his infancy they had known only each other, a lonely mother and a lonely son. Through the hot sun, she had carried him on her back as she weeded her cornfield. How could she dare to put him down under a tree in the shade when there was no one to look after him? Other women had their own younger sisters or those of their husbands to help with the baby; but she had had no one. The only face the little one had known was his mother's. And now . . .

"But," I told myself, "I am sure it will be all right with him."   280

"Will it?" I asked myself.

"Why not? He is a happy child."

"Does that solve the problem?"

"Not all together, but . . ."

"No buts; one should think of the house into which he would be taken now. He may not be a favourite there."

But my other voice told me that a child need not be a favourite to be happy.

I had to bring the one-man argument to an end. I had to hurry. Passing by the field, I saw some of the boys playing football. At the goal at the further end was a headful of hair shining in the afternoon sun. I knew the body to which it be- 290 longed. A goalkeeper is a dubious character in infant soccer. He is either a good goalkeeper and that is why he is at the goal, which is usually difficult to know in a child, or he is a bad player. If he is a bad player, he might as well be in the goal as anywhere else. Kwesi loved football, that was certain, and he was always the goal-keeper. Whether he was good or not I had never been able to see. Just as I passed, he caught a ball and his team clapped. I heard him give the little squeaky noise that passed for his laugh. No doubt he was a happy child.

Now I really ran into the village. I immediately made my way to Nana Kum's house, for the case was going on there. There was a great crowd in front of the house. Why were there so many people about? Then I remembered that it being a 300 holiday, everyone was at home. And of course, after the eating and the drinking of palm-wine in the morning and midday, divorce proceedings certainly provide an agreeable diversion, especially when other people are involved and not ourselves.

The courtyard was a long one and as I jostled to where Maami Ama was sit-ting, pieces of comments floated into my ears. "The elders certainly have settled the case fairly," someone was saying. "But it seemed as if Kodjo Fi had no strong proofs for his arguments," another was saying. "Well, they both have been sensi-ble. If one feels one can't live with a woman, one might as well divorce her. And I hate a woman who cringes to a man," a third said. Finally I reached her side. Around her were her family, her two aunts, Esi and Ama, her two cousins and the 310 two uncles. To the right were the elders who were judging the case; opposite were Kodjo Fi and his family.

"I have come, Maami Ama," I announced myself.

She looked at me. "You ought to have been here earlier, the case has been settled already."

"And how are things?" I inquired.

"I am a divorced woman."

"What were his grounds for wanting to divorce you?"

"He said I had done nothing, he only wanted to . . ."

"Eh! Only the two of you know what went wrong," the younger aunt cried 320 out, reproachfully. "If after his saying that, you had refused to be divorced, he would have had to pay the Ejecting Fee, but now he has got the better of you."

"But aunt," Maami protested, "how could I refuse to be divorced?"

"It's up to you. I know it's your own affair, only I wouldn't like your mother's ghost to think that we haven't looked after you well."

"I agree with you," the elder aunt said.

"Maami Ama, what was your debt?" I asked her.

"It is quite a big sum."

"I hope you too had something to reckon against him?"

"I did. He reckoned the dowry, the ten cloths he gave me, the Knocking 330 Fee. . . ."

All this had been heard by Kodjo Fi and his family and soon they made us aware of it.

"Kodjo," his youngest sister burst out, "you forgot to reckon the Knife Fee."

"No. Yaa, I did not forget," Kodjo Fi told her. "She had no brothers to whom I would give the fee."

"It's all right then," his second sister added.

But the rest of his womenfolk took this to be a signal for more free comments.

"She is a bad woman and I think you are well rid of her," one aunt screamed. 340

"I think she is a witch," the youngest sister said.

"Oh, that she is. Anyway, only witches have no brothers or sisters. They eat them in the mother's womb long before they are born."

Ama's aunts and cousins had said nothing so far. They were inclined to believe Ama was a witch too. But Maami sat still. When the comments had gone down a bit, she resumed the conversation with me.

"As I was saying, Chicha, he also reckoned the price of the trunk he had given me and all the cost of the medicine he gave me to make me have more children. There was only the Cooking Cost for me to reckon against his."

"Have you got money to pay the debt?" I asked her. 350

"No, but I am not going to pay it. My uncles will pay it out of the family fund and put the debt down against my name."

"Oh!"

"But you are a fool," Maami Ama's eldest aunt shouted at her.

"I say you are a fool," she insisted.

"But aunt . . ." Maami Ama began to protest.

"Yes! And I hope you are not going to answer back. I was born before your mother and now that she is dead, I'm your mother! Besides, when she was alive I could scold her when she went wrong, and now I say you are a fool. For seven years you have struggled to look after a child. Whether he ate or not was your af- 360 fair alone. Whether he had any cloth or not did not concern any other person. When Kwesi was a child he had no father. When he nearly died of measles, no grandmother looked in. As for aunts, he began getting them when he started going to school. And now you are allowing them to take him away from you. Now that he is grown enough to be counted among the living, a father knows he has got a son."

"So, so!" Kodjo Fi's mother sneered at her. "What did you think? That Kodjo would give his son as a present to you, eh? The boy belongs to his family, but he must be of some service to his father too."

"Have I called your name?" Ama's aunt asked the old woman. 370

"You have not called her name but you were speaking against her son." This again was from Kodjo Fi's youngest sister.

"And who are you to answer my mother back?" Ama's two cousins demanded of her.

"Go away. But who are you people?"

"Go away, too, you greedy lot."

"It is you who are greedy, witches."

"You are always calling other people witches. Only a witch can know a witch."

Soon everyone was shouting at everyone else. The people who have come 380 started going home, and only the most curious ones stood by to listen. Maami Ama was murmuring something under her breath which I could not hear. I persuaded her to come with me. All that time no word had passed between her and her ex-husband. As we turned to go, Kodjo Fi's mother shouted at her, "You are hurt. But that is what you deserve. We will get the child. We will! What did you want to do with him?"

Maami Ama turned round to look at her. "What are you putting yourself to so much trouble for? When Nana Kum said the boy ought to go and stay with his father, did I make any objection? He is at the school. Go and fetch him. Tomorrow, you can send your carriers to come and fetch his belongings from my hut." These 390 words were said quietly.

Then I remembered suddenly that I had to hurry to school to dismiss the children. I told Maami Ama to go home but that I would try to see her before night.

This time I did not go by the main street. I took the back door through back streets and lanes. It was past four already. As I hurried along, I heard a loud roaring sound which I took to be echoes of the quarrel, so I went my way. When I reached the school, I did not like what I saw. There was not a single childish soul anywhere. But everyone's books were there. The shed was as untidy as ever. Little Grace had left my books too. Of course I was more than puzzled. "How naughty 400 these children are. How did they dare to disobey me when I had told them to wait here until I came to dismiss them?" It was no use looking around the place. They were not there. "They need discipline," I threatened to the empty shed. I picked up my books and clock. Then I noticed that Kwesi's desk was clean of all his books. Nothing need be queer about this; he had probably taken his home. As I was descending the hill the second time that afternoon, I saw that the whole school was at the other end of the main street. What were the children doing so near Maami Ama's place? I ran towards them.

I was not prepared for what I saw. As if intentionally, the children had formed a circle. When some of them saw me, they all began to tell me what had 410 happened. But I did not hear a word. In the middle of the circle, Kwesi was lying flat on his back. His shirt was off. His right arm was swollen to the size of his head. I simply stood there with my mouth open. From the back yard, Maami Ama screamed, "I am drowning, people of Bamso, come and save me!" Soon the whole village was there.

What is the matter? What has happened? Kwesi has been bitten by a snake. Where? When? At school. He was playing football. Where? What has happened? Bitten by a snake, a snake, a snake.

Questions and answers were tossed from mouth to mouth in the shocked evening air. Meanwhile, those who knew about snake-bites were giving the names 420 of different cures. Kwesi's father was looking anxiously at his son. That strong powerful man was almost stupid with shock and alarm. Dose upon dose was forced down the reluctant throat but nothing seemed to have any effect. Women paced up and down around the hut, totally oblivious of the fact that they had left their festive meals half prepared. Each one was trying to imagine how she would have felt if Kwesi had been her child, and in imagination they suffered more than the suffering mother. "The gods and spirits of our fathers protect us from calamity!"

After what seemed an unbearably long time, the messenger who had been earlier sent to Surdo, the village next to Bamso, to summon the chief medicine man arrived, followed by the eminent doctor himself. He was renowned for his cure of snake-bites. When he appeared, everyone gave a sigh of relief. They all remembered someone, perhaps a father, brother or husband, he had snatched from the jaws of death. When he gave his potion to the boy, he would be violently sick, and then of course, he would be out of danger. The potion was given. Thirty minutes; an hour; two hours; three, four hours. He had not retched. Before midnight, he was dead. No grown-up in Bamso village slept that night. Kwesi was the first boy to have died since the school was inaugurated some six years previously. "And he was his mother's only child. She has no one now. We do not understand it. Life is not sweet!" This was their verdict.

The morning was very beautiful. It seemed as if every natural object in and around the village had kept vigil too. So they too were tired. I was tired too. I had gone to bed at about five o'clock in the morning and since it was a Saturday I could have a long sleep. At ten o'clock, I was suddenly roused from sleep by shouting. I opened my window but I could not see the speakers. Presently Kweku Sam, one of the young men in the village, came past my window. "Good morning, Chicha." He shouted his greeting to me.

"Good morning, Kweku," I responded. "What is the shouting about?"

"They are quarrelling."

"And what are they quarrelling about now?"

"Each is accusing the other of having been responsible for the boy's death."

"How?"

"Chicha, I don't know. Only women make too much trouble for themselves. It seems as if they are never content to sit quiet but they must always hurl abuse at each other. What has happened is too serious to be a subject for quarrels. Perhaps the village has displeased the gods in some unknown way and that is why they have taken away this boy." He sighed. I could not say anything to that. I could not explain it myself, and if the villagers believed there was something more in Kwesi's death than the ordinary human mind could explain, who was I to argue?

"Is Maami Ama herself there?"

"No, I have not seen her there."

He was quiet and I was quiet.

"Chicha, I think I should go away now. I have just heard that my sister has given birth to a girl."

"So," I smiled to myself. "Give her my congratulations and tell her I will come to see her tomorrow."

"*Yoo.*"

He walked away to greet his new niece. I stood for a long time at the window staring at nothing, while I heard snatches of words and phrases from the quarrel. And these were mingled with weeping. Then I turned from the window. Looking into the little mirror on the wall, I was not surprised to see my whole face bathed in unconscious tears. I did not feel like going to bed. I did not feel like doing anything at all. I toyed with the idea of going to see Maami Ama and then finally decided against it. I could not bear to face her; at least, not yet. So I sat down thinking about him. I went over the most presumptuous daydreams I had indulged in on his account. "I would have taken him away with me in spite of his mother's protests." She was just being absurd. "The child is a boy, and sooner or later, she must learn to live without him. The highest class here is Primary Six and when I am going away, I will take him. I will give him a secondary education. 480 Perhaps, who knows, one day he may win a scholarship to the university." In my daydreams, I had never determined what career he would have followed, but he would be famous, that was certain. Devastatingly handsome, he would be the idol of women and the envy of every man. He would visit Britain, America and all these countries we have heard so much about. He would see all the seven wonders of the world. "Maami shall be happy in the end," I had told myself. "People will flock to see the mother of such an illustrious man. Although she has not had many children, she will be surrounded by her grandchildren. Of course, away from the village." In all these reveries his father never had a place, but there was I, and there was Maami Ama, and there was his father, and he, that bone of contention, was 490 lost to all three. I saw the highest castles I had built for him come tumbling down, noiselessly and swiftly.

He was buried at four o'clock. I had taken the schoolchildren to where he lay in state. When his different relatives saw the little uniformed figure they all forgot their differences and burst into loud lamentations. "Chicha, O Chicha, what shall I do now that Kwesi is dead?" His grandmother addressed me. "Kwesi, my Beauty, Kwesi my Master, Kwesi-my-own-Kwesi," one aunt was chanting, "Father Death has done me an ill turn."

"Chicha," the grandmother continued, "my washing days are over, for who will give me water? My eating days are over, for who will give me food?" I stood 500 there, saying nothing. I had let the children sing "Saviour Blessed Saviour." And we had gone to the cemetery with him.

After the funeral, I went to the House of Mourning as one should do after a burial. No one was supposed to weep again for the rest of the day. I sat there listening to visitors who had come from the neighbouring villages.

"This is certainly sad, and it is most strange. School has become like business; those who found it earlier for their children are eating more than the children themselves. To have a schoolboy snatched away like this is unbearable indeed," one woman said.

"Ah, do not speak," his father's youngest sister broke in. "We have lost a trea- 510 sure."

"My daughter," said the grandmother again, "Kwesi is gone, gone for ever to our forefathers. And what can we do?"

"What can we do indeed? When flour is scattered in the sand, who can sift it? But this is the saddest I've heard, that he was his mother's only one."

"Is that so?" another visitor cried. "I always thought she had other children.

What does one do, when one's only water-pot breaks?" she whispered. The question was left hanging in the air. No one dared say anything more.

    I went out. I never knew how I got there, but I saw myself approaching 520 Maami Ama's hut. As usual, the door was open. I entered the outer room. She was not there. Only sheep and goats from the village were busy munching at the cassava and the yams. I looked into the inner chamber. She was there. Still clad in the cloth she had worn to the divorce proceedings, she was not sitting, standing or lying down. She was kneeling, and like one drowning who catches at a straw, she was clutching Kwesi's books and school uniform to her breast. "Maami Ama, Maami Ama," I called out to her. She did not move. I left her alone. Having driven the sheep and goats away, I went out, shutting the door behind me. "I must go home now," I spoke to myself once more. The sun was sinking behind the coconut palm. I looked at my watch. It was six o'clock; but this time, I did not run.   530

[1971]

Questions for Discussion and Reading

1. Stories from other cultures contain values, ideas, and customs that may seem unfamiliar, even strange. List the cultural differences you see in the story.
2. Western culture has its own ways of dealing with separation, single parenthood, divorce, and death. How would a Western woman deal with the problems and losses Maami Ama endures?
3. What gender inequalities does Maami Ama face?
4. What role does the narrator play in the story? In what ways is her position in the community important to her vision of events in the story?
5. The death of an only child is tragic in any situation. What circumstances or cultural ideas make Kwesi's death particularly painful?

☞ TONI CADE BAMBARA
(1939–1995)

Gorilla, My Love

When Toni Cade Bambara's collection of stories *Gorilla, My Love* appeared in 1972, America knew that a fresh, vibrant, new voice had arrived. She was born Mirkin Cade in New York City and took her present surname (changed legally in 1970) from a signature she found on a sketchbook in a trunk belonging to her great-grandmother. She spent her childhood in Harlem, Bedford-Stuyvesant, Queens, New York, and Jersey City, New Jersey, writing stories on scraps of paper. After earning a bachelor's degree from Queens College in 1959, Bambara studied in Florence and Paris, then completed a master's degree in English at City College of New York in 1964. During this period, she wrote fiction in the pre-dawn hours, the only time she could find to spare from formal study.

Bambara's interests and talents were multiple. She studied not only literature but also dance, film, and African-American studies. As a community activist, she was a social worker (1956–1959), a director and advisor to the Theater of the Black Experience (1965–1969), and the founder and director of the Pamoja Writers Collective (1976–1985). In the 1970s, she traveled illegally to Viet Nam and Cuba, where she became convinced of the political power of writing. Her major publications include *The Black Woman* (1970), *Tales and Stories for Black Folk* (1971), *The Sea Birds Are Still Alive* (stories, 1977), and *The Salt Eaters* (1980), a novel that won the American Book Award.

Bambara's writing is deliberately political, aimed at revealing the oppression of African-Americans and women. Women and children are frequently her protagonists, and their voices, often angry and funny at the same time, vividly convey the texture and political contexts of their lives. Her characters, like Hazel in "Gorilla, My Love," seem to leap off the page, fully alive.

T HAT WAS THE YEAR Hunca Bubba changed his name. Not a change up, but a change back, since Jefferson Winston Vale was the name in the first place. Which was news to me cause he'd been my Hunca Bubba my whole lifetime, since I couldn't manage Uncle to save my life. So far as I was concerned it was a change completely to somethin soundin very geographical weatherlike to me, like somethin you'd find in a almanac. Or somethin you'd run across when you sittin in the navigator seat with a wet thumb on the map crinkly in your lap, watchin the roads and signs so when Granddaddy Vale say "Which way, Scout," you got sense enough to say take the next exit or take a left or whatever it is. Not that Scout's my name. Just the name Granddaddy call whoever sittin in the navigator seat. Which 10 is usually me cause I don't feature sittin in the back with the pecans. Now, you figure pecans all right to be sittin with. If you thinks so, that's your business. But they dusty sometime and make you cough. And they got a way of slidin around and dippin down sudden, like maybe a rat in the buckets. So if you scary like me, you sleep with the lights on and blame it on Baby Jason and, so as not to waste good electric, you study the maps. And that's how come I'm in the navigator seat most times and get to be called Scout.

So Hunca Bubba in the back with the pecans and Baby Jason, and he in love. And we got to hear all this stuff about this woman he in love with an all. Which really ain't enough to keep the mind alive, though Baby Jason got no better sense 20 than to give his undivided attention and keep grabbin at the photograph which is just a picture of some skinny woman in a countrified dress with her hand shot up to her face like she shame fore cameras. But there's a movie house in the background which I ax about. Cause I am a movie freak from way back, even though it do get me in trouble sometime.

Like when me and Big Brood and Baby Jason was on our own last Easter and couldn't go to the Dorset cause we'd seen all the Three Stooges they was. And the RKO Hamilton was closed readying up for the Easter Pageant that night. And the West End, the Regun and the Sunset was too far, less we had grownups with us

which we didn't. So we walk up Amsterdam Avenue to the Washington and 30
Gorilla, My Love playin, they say, which suit me just fine, though the "my love"
part kinda drag Big Brood some. As for Baby Jason, shoot, like Granddaddy say,
he'd follow me into the fiery furnace if I say come on. So we go in and get three
bags of Havmore potato chips which not only are the best potato chips but the
best bags for blowin up and bustin real loud so the matron come trottin down the
aisle with her chunky self, flashin that flashlight dead in your eye so you can give
her some lip, and if she answer back and you already finish seein the show anyway, why then you just turn the place out. Which I love to do, no lie. With Baby
Jason kickin at the seat in front, egging me on, and Big Brood mumblin bout what
fiercesome things we goin do. Which means me. Like when the big boys come up 40
on us talking bout Lemme a nickel. It's me that hide the money. Or when the bad
boys in the park take Big Brood's Spaudeen[1] way from him. It's me that jump on
they back and fight awhile. And it's me that turns out the show if the matron get
too salty.

   So the movie can come on and right away it's this churchy music and clearly
not about no gorilla. Bout Jesus. And I am ready to kill, not cause I got anything
gainst Jesus. Just that when you fixed to watch a gorilla picture you don't wanna
get messed around with Sunday School stuff. So I am mad. Besides, we see this
raggedy old brown film *King of Kings* every year and enough's enough. Grownups
figure they can treat you just anyhow. Which burns me up. There I am, my feet up 50
and my Havmore potato chips really salty and crispy and two jawbreakers in my
lap and the money safe in my shoe from the big boys, and here comes this Jesus
stuff. So we all go wild. Yellin, booin, stompin and carryin on. Really to wake the
man in the booth up there who musta went to sleep and put on the wrong reels.
But no, cause he holler down to shut up and then he turn the sound up so we really gotta holler like crazy to even hear ourselves good. And the matron ropes off
the children section and flashes her light all over the place and we yell some more
and some kids slip under the rope and run up and down the aisle just to show it
take more than some dusty ole velvet rope to tie us down. And I'm flingin the kid
in front of me's popcorn. And Baby Jason kickin seats. And it's really somethin. 60
Then here come the big and bad matron, the one they let out in case of emergency.
And she totin that flashlight like she gonna use it on somebody. This here the colored matron Brandy and her friends call Thunderbuns. She do not play. She do
not smile. So we shut up and watch the simple ass picture.

   Which is not so simple as it is stupid. Cause I realize that just about anybody
in my family is better than this god they always talkin about. My daddy wouldn't
stand for nobody treatin any of us that way. My mama specially. And I can just see
it now, Big Brood up there on the cross talkin about Forgive them Daddy cause
they don't know what they doin. And my Mama say Get on down from there you
big fool, whatcha think this is, playtime? And my Daddy yellin to Granddaddy to 70
get him a ladder cause Big Brood actin the fool, his mother side of the family
showin up. And my mama and her sister Daisy jumpin on them Romans beatin
them with they pocketbooks. And Hunca Bubba tellin them folks on they knees
they better get out the way and go get some help or they goin to get trampled on.

1. A rubber ball used in the game of stickball.

And Granddaddy Vale saying Leave the boy alone, if that's what he wants to do
with his life we ain't got nothin to say about it. Then Aunt Daisy givin him a taste
of that pocketbook, fussin bout what a damn fool old man Granddaddy is. Then
everybody jumpin in his chest like the time Uncle Clayton went in the army and
come back with only one leg and Granddaddy say somethin stupid about that's
life. And by this time Big Brood off the cross and in the park playin handball or
skully or somethin. And the family in the kitchen throwin dishes at each other,
screamin bout if you hadn't done this I wouldn't had to do that. And me in the
parlor trying to do my arithmetic yellin Shut it off.

Which is what I was yellin all by myself which make me a sittin target for
Thunderbuns. But when I yell We want our money back, that gets everybody in
chorus. And the movie windin up with this heavenly cloud music and the smart-
ass up there in his hole in the wall turns up the sound again to drown us out.
Then there comes Bugs Bunny which we already seen so we know we been had.
No gorilla my nuthin. And Big Brood say Awwww sheeet, we goin to see the manager and get our money back. And I know from this we business. So I brush the
potato chips out of my hair which is where Baby Jason like to put em, and I march
myself up the aisle to deal with the manager who is a crook in the first place for
lyin out there sayin Gorilla, My Love playin. And I never did like the man cause he
oily and pasty at the same time like the bad guy in the serial,[2] the one that got a
hideout behind a push-button bookcase and play "Moonlight Sonata" with gloves
on. I knock on the door and I am furious. And I am alone, too. Cause Big Brood
suddenly got to go so bad even though my mama told us bout goin in them nasty
bathrooms. And I hear him sigh like he disgusted when he get to the door and see
only a little kid there. And now I'm really furious cause I get so tired grownups
messin over kids just cause they little and can't take em to court. What is it, he say
to me like I lost my mittens or wet on myself or am somebody's retarded child.
When in reality I am the smartest kid P.S. 186 ever had in its whole lifetime and
you can ax anybody. Even them teachers that don't like me cause I won't sing
them Southern songs or back off when they tell me my questions are out of order.
And cause my Mama come up there in a minute when them teachers start playin
the dozens[3] behind colored folks. She stalk in with her hat pulled down bad and
that Persian lamb coat draped back over one hip on account of she got her fist
planted there so she can talk that talk which gets us all hypnotized, and teacher be
comin undone cause she know this could be her job and her behind cause Mama
got pull with the Board and bad by her own self anyhow.

So I kick the door open wider and just walk right by him and sit down and
tell the man about himself and that I want my money back and that goes for Baby
Jason and Big Brood too. And he still trying to shuffle me out the door even
though I'm sittin which shows him for the fool he is. Just like them teachers do
fore they realize Mama like a stone on that spot and ain't backin up. So he ain't
gettin up off the money. So I was forced to leave, takin the matches from under his
ashtray, and set a fire under the candy stand, which closed the raggedy ole

2. Movies shown in weekly segments, usually before the feature film, containing sensational plots and
   stereotyped characters.
3. An African-American game of trading insults; here it suggests unfair criticism.

Washington down for a week. My Daddy had the suspect it was me cause Big Brood got a big mouth. But I explained right quick what the whole thing was about and I figured it was even-steven. Cause if you say Gorilla, My Love, you suppose to mean it. Just like when you say you goin to give me a party on my birthday, you gotta mean it. And if you say me and Baby Jason can go South pecan haulin with Granddaddy Vale, you better not be comin up with no stuff about the weather look uncertain or did you mop the bathroom or any other trickified business. I mean even gangsters in the movies say My word is my bond. So don't no-body get away with nothin far as I'm concerned. So Daddy put his belt back on. Cause that's the way I was raised. Like my Mama say in one of them situations when I won't back down, Okay Badbird, you right. Your point is well-taken. Not that Badbird my name, just what she say when she tired arguin and know I'm right. And Aunt Jo, who is the hardest head in the family and worse even than Aunt Daisy, she say, You absolutely right Miss Muffin, which also ain't my real name but the name she gave me one time when I got some medicine shot in my behind and wouldn't get up off her pillows for nothin. And even Granddaddy Vale—who got no memory to speak of, so sometime you can just plain lie to him, if you want to be like that—he say, Well if that's what I said, then that's it. But this name business was different they said. It wasn't like Hunca Bubba had gone back on his word or anything. Just that he was thinkin bout gettin married and was usin his real name now. Which ain't the way I saw it at all.

So there I am in the navigator seat. And I turn to him and just plain ole ax him. I mean I come right on out with it. No sense goin all around that barn the old folks talk about. And like my mama say, Hazel—which is my real name and what she remembers to call me when she bein serious—when you got somethin on your mind, speak up and let the chips fall where they may. And if anybody don't like it, tell em to come see your mama. And Daddy look up from the paper and say, You hear your mama good, Hazel. And tell em to come see me first. Like that. That's how I was raised.

So I turn clear round in the navigator seat and say, "Look here, Hunca Bubba or Jefferson Windsong Vale or whatever your name is, you gonna marry this girl?"

"Sure am," he say, all grins.

And I say, "Member that time you was baby-sittin me when we lived at four-o-nine and there was this big snow and Mamma and Daddy got held up in the country so you had to stay for two days?"

And he say, "Sure do."

"Well. You remember how you told me I was the cutest thing that ever walked the earth?"

"Oh, you were real cute when you were little," he say, which is suppose to be funny. I am not laughin.

"Well. You remember what you said?"

And Granddaddy Vale squintin over the wheel and axin Which way, Scout. But Scout is busy and don't care if we all get lost for days.

"Watcha mean, Peaches?"

"My name is Hazel. And what I mean is you said you were going to marry me when I grew up. You were going to wait. That's what I mean, my dear Uncle Jefferson." And he don't say nuthin. Just look at me real strange like he never saw me before in life. Like he lost in some weird town in the middle of night and lookin for directions and there's no one to ask. Like it was me that messed up the maps and turned the road posts round. "Well, you said it, didn't you?" And Baby Jason lookin back and forth like we playin ping-pong. Only I ain't playin. I'm hurtin and I can hear that I am screamin. And Granddaddy Vale mumblin how we never gonna get to where we goin if I don't turn around that take my navigator job 170 serious.

"Well, for cryin out loud, Hazel, you just a little girl. And I was just teasin."

" 'And I was just teasin,' " I say back just how he said it so he can hear what a terrible thing it is. Then I don't say nuthin. And he don't say nuthin. And Baby Jason don't say nuthin nohow. Then Granddaddy Vale speak up. "Look here, Precious, it was Hunca Bubba what told you them things. This here, Jefferson Winston Vale." And Hunca Bubba say, "That's right. That was somebody else. I'm a new somebody."

"You a lyin dawg," I say, when I meant to say treacherous dog, but just couldn't get hold of the world. It slipped away from me. And I'm crying and 180 crumplin down in the seat and just don't care. And Granddaddy say to hush and steps on the gas. And I'm losin my bearins and don't even know where to look on the map cause I can't see for cryin. And Baby Jason cryin too. Cause he is my blood brother and understands that we must stick together or be forever lost, what with grownups playin change-up and turnin you round every which way so bad. And don't even say they sorry.   [1971]

Questions for Discussion and Writing

1. Analyze the narrative voice. How does it help to characterize the narrator?
2. How does Hazel regard adults and adult authority?
3. Analyze Hazel's rendition of the Jesus story. What is it like? How does it function in the story?
4. Is Granddaddy just playing with words when he says it was Hunca Bubba who promised to marry Hazel and not Jefferson Winston Value? Are Hunca Bubba and Jefferson Winston Vale different people?
5. What is the significance of the title, and how does it relate to the story's theme? The original title was "I Ain't Playin, I'm Hurtin." Which is the better title? Why?

✄ CHINUA ACHEBE
(b. 1930)

Vengeful Creditor

Chinua Achebe is the first great West African novelist to write in English and thus reach a broad audience outside of his native Nigeria. His reputation rests on four linked novels that constitute a history of his country from the 1890s to

Nigeria's civil war (1967–1970). Chief among these is the first, *Things Fall Apart* (1958).

He was born Albert Chinualumogu Achebe in Ogidi, Nigeria, in 1930. At age eight, he began learning English. His father, Isaiah Okofor Achebe, was a lay minister in the Church Missionary Society and therefore forbade his son to participate in Igbo (Ibo) tribal ceremonies or even to eat in the homes of those not converted to Christianity. Achebe turned this social disadvantage into an asset in his fiction, for he adopts the double vision of one who is both an insider and an outsider—a partisan of his people but one who is aware of the faults as well as the virtues of traditional life. One of the virtues of *Things Fall Apart* is that it acknowledges both the strengths and weaknesses of precolonial African society.

Achebe was educated at Government College, Umuahia, one of the best schools in West Africa. He was then chosen to be among the first entering class at University College, Ibadan, essentially an extension of the University of London. He began studying medicine but switched to literature and graduated in 1953. In 1954, he began a distinguished career in radio broadcasting that lasted until 1967. When the Nigerian Civil War broke out in 1967, he became chairman of Citadel Books and Research Fellow at the University of Nigeria, rising rapidly to Professor. In addition to his teaching and writing, he has served on scores of committees and commissions in support of African literature and the arts. In a reversal of the usual pattern, he turned to poetry and short stories after succeeding as a novelist, in part because of the crisis of the civil war made novel writing impossible.

Achebe's writing is widely read not only because he gives voice to the legitimate grievances of black Africa, but also because he sees the complexities of the political and social problems facing his country and his continent. He is, by his own admission, a political writer, but he is not a dogmatic one. His ultimate aim is to promote mutual respect among all people.

"MADAME, THIS WAY," sang the alert, high-wigged salesgirl minding one of a row of cash machines in the supermarket. Mrs. Emenike veered her full-stacked trolley ever so lightly to the girl.

"Madame, you were coming to me," complained the cheated girl at the next machine.

"Ah, sorry my dear. Next time."

"Good afternoon, Madame," sang the sweet-voiced girl already unloading Madame's purchases onto her counter.

"Cash or account, Madame?"

"Cash."   10

She punched the prices as fast as lightning and announced the verdict. Nine pounds fifteen and six. Mrs. Emenike opened her handbag, brought out from it a wallet, unzipped it and held out two clean and crisp five-pound notes. The girl punched again and the machine released a tray of cash. She put Madame's money away and gave her her change and a foot-long receipt. Mrs. Emenike glanced at the bottom of the long strip of paper where the polite machine had registered her total spending with the words THANK YOU COME AGAIN, and nodded.

It was at this point that the first hitch occurred. There seemed to be nobody around to load Madame's purchases into a carton and take them to her car outside.

"Where are these boys?" said the girl almost in distress. "Sorry, Madame. 20 Many of our carriers have gone away because of this free primary[1] . . . John!" she called out, as she caught sight of one of the remaining few, "Come and pack Madame's things!"

John was a limping forty-year-old boy sweating profusely even in the air-conditioned comfort of the supermarket. As he put the things into an empty carton he grumbled aloud.

"I don talk say make una tell Manager e go fin' more people for dis monkey work."

"You never hear say everybody don go to free primary?" asked the wigged girl, jovially.   30

"All right-o. But I no go kill myself for sake of free primary."

Out in the car-park he stowed the carton away in the boot of Mrs. Emenike's grey Mercedes and then straightened up to wait while she opened her handbag and then her wallet and stirred a lot of coins there with one finger until she found a three-penny piece, pulled it out between two fingers and dropped it into the carrier's palm. He hesitated for a while and then limped away without saying a word.

Mrs. Emenike never cared for these old men running little boys' errands. No matter what you gave them they never seemed satisfied. Look at this grumbling cripple. How much did he expect to be given for carrying a tiny carton a few yards? That was what free primary education had brought. It had brought even 40 worse to the homes. Mrs. Emenike had lost three servants including her baby-nurse since the beginning of the school year. The baby-nurse problem was of course the worst. What was a working woman with a seven-month-old baby supposed to do?

However the problem did not last. After only a term of free education the government withdrew the scheme for fear of going bankrupt. It would seem that on the advice of its experts the Education Ministry had planned initially for eight hundred thousand children. In the event one million and a half turned up on the first day of school. Where did all the rest of them come from? Had the experts misled the government? The chief statistician, interviewed on the radio, said it was 50 nonsense to talk about a miscalculation. The trouble was simply that children from neighboring states had been brought in in thousands and registered dishonestly by unscrupulous people, a clear case of sabotage.

Whatever the reason the government cancelled the scheme. The *New Age* wrote an editorial praising the Prime Minister for his statesmanship and courage but pointing out that the whole dismal affair could have been avoided if the government had listened in the first place to the warning of many knowledgeable and

---

1. Free primary education.

responsible citizens. Which was true enough, for these citizens had written on the pages of the *New Age* to express their doubt and reservation about free education. The newspaper, on throwing open its pages to a thorough airing of views on the matter, had pointed out that it did so in the national cause and, mounting an old hobby-horse, challenged those of its critics who could see no merit whatever in a newspaper owned by foreign capital to come forward and demonstrate an equal or a higher order of national commitment and patriotism, a challenge that none of those critics took up. The offer of space by the *New Age* was taken up eagerly and in the course of ten days at the rate of two or even three articles a day a large number of responsible citizens—lawyers, doctors, merchants, engineers, salesmen, insurance brokers, university lecturers, etc.—had written in criticism of the scheme. No one was against education for the kids, they said, but free education was premature. Someone said that not even the United States of America in all its wealth and power had introduced it yet, how much less . . .

Mr. Emenike read the various contributions with boyish excitement. "I wish civil servants were free to write to the papers," he told his wife at least on three occasions during those ten days.

"This is not bad, but he should have mentioned that this country has made tremendous strides in education since independence because parents know the value of education and will make any sacrifice to find school fees for their children. We are not a nation of Oliver Twists."[2]

His wife was not really interested in all the argument at that stage, because somehow it all seemed to hang in the air. She had some vague, personal doubts about free education, that was all.

"Have you looked at the paper? Mike has written on this thing," said her husband on another occasion.

"Who is Mike?"

"Mike Ogudu."

"Oh, what does he say?"

"I haven't read it yet . . . Oh yes, you can trust Mike to call a spade a spade. See how he begins: 'Free primary education is tantamount to naked Communism'? That's not quite true but that's Mike all over. He thinks someone might come up to nationalize his shipping line. He is so scared of Communism."

"But who wants Communism here?"

"Nobody. That's what I told him the other evening at the Club. But he is so scared. You know one thing? Too much money is bad-o."

The discussion in the Emenike family remained at this intellectual level until one day their "Small Boy," a very bright lad of twelve helping out the cook and understudying the steward, announced he must go home to see his sick father.

"How did you know your Father was sick?" asked Madame.

"My brodder come tell me."

"When did your brother come?"

"Yesterday for evening-time."

"Why didn't you bring him to see me?"

"I no no say Madame go wan see am."

2. Poor orphans; after Charles Dickens's *Oliver Twist* (1838).

"Why you no talk since yesterday?" asked Mr. Emenike looking up from his newspaper.

"At first I tink say no go go home. But today one mind tell me say make you go see-am-o; perhaps e de sick too much. So derefore . . ."

"All right. You can go but make sure you are back by tomorrow afternoon otherwise . . ."

"I must return back by morning-time sef."

He didn't come back. Mrs. Emenike was particularly angry because of the lies. She didn't like being outwitted by servants. Look at that little rat imagining himself clever. She should have suspected something from the way he had been carrying on of late. Now he had gone with a full month's pay which he should lose in lieu of notice. It went to show that kindness to these people did not pay in the least.

A week later the gardener gave notice. He didn't try to hide anything. His elder brother had sent him a message to return to their village and register for free education. Mr. Emenike tried to laugh him out of this ridiculous piece of village ignorance.

"Free primary education is for children. Nobody is going to admit an old man like you. How old are you?"

"I am fifteen years of old, sir."

"You are three," sneered Mrs. Emenike. "Come and suck breast."

"You are not fifteen," said Mr. Emenike. "You are at least twenty and no headmaster will admit you into a primary school. If you want to go and try, by all means do. But don't come back here when you've gone and failed."

"I no go fail, oga," said the gardener. "One man for our village wey old pass my fader sef done register everyting finish. He just go for Magistrate Court and pay dem five shilling and dey swear-am for Court juju wey no de kill porson; e no fit kill rat sef."

"Well it's certainly up to you. Your work here has been good but . . ."

"Mark, what is all that long talk for? He wants to go, let him go."

"Madame, no be say I wan go like dat. But my senior brodder . . ."

"We have heard. You can go now."

"But I no de go today. I wan give one week notice. And I fit find anoder gardener for Madame."

"Don't worry about notice or gardener. Just go away."

"I fit get my pay now or I go come back for afternoon-time?"

"What pay?"

"Madame, for dis ten days I don work for dis mont."

"Don't annoy me any further. Just go away."

But real annoyance was yet to come for Mrs. Emenike. Abigail, the baby-nurse, came up to her two mornings later as she was getting ready for work and dumped the baby in her lap and took off. Abigail of all people! After all she had done for her. Abigail who came to her full of craw-craw,[3] who used rags for sanitary towels, who was so ignorant she gave the baby a full bowl of water to stop it

---

3. A skin disease characterized by pustules and severe itching.

crying and dropped some through its nose. Now Abigail was a lady; she could sew and bake, wear a bra and clean pants, put on powder and perfumes and stretch her hair; and she was ready to go.

From that day Mrs. Emenike hated the words "free primary" which had sud- 150 denly became part of everyday language, especially in the villages where they called it "free primadu." She was particularly angry when people made jokes about it and had a strong urge to hit them on the head for a lack of feeling and good taste. And she hated the Americans and the embassies (but particularly the Americans) who threw their money around and enticed the few remaining servants away from Africans. This began when she learnt later that her gardener had not gone to school at all but to a Ford Foundation man who had offered him seven pounds and bought him a bicycle and a Singer sewing-machine for his wife.

"Why do they do it?" she asked. She didn't really want or need an answer but her husband gave one all the same. 160

"Because," said he, "back home in America they couldn't possibly afford a servant. So when they come out here and find them so cheap they go crazy. That's why."

Three months later free primary school ended and school fees were brought back. The government was persuaded by then that its "piece of hare-brained socialism" as the *New Age* called it was unworkable in African conditions. This was a jibe at the Minister of Education who was notorious for his leftist sympathies and was perpetually at war with the formidible Minister of Finance.

"We cannot go through with this scheme unless we are prepared to impose new taxes," said the Finance Minister at a Cabinet Meeting. 170

"Well, then, let's impose the taxes," said the Minister of Education, which provoked derisive laughter from all his colleagues and even from Permanent Secretaries like Mr. Emenike who were in attendance and who in strict protocol should not participate in debate or laughter.

"We can't," said the Finance Minister indulgently with laughter still in his mouth. "I know my right honourable friend here doesn't worry whether or not this government lasts its full term, but some of us others do. At least I want to be here long enough to retire my election debts . . ."

This was greeted with hilarious laughter and cries of "Hear! Hear!" In debating skill Education was no match for Finance. In fact Finance had no equal in the 180 entire Cabinet, the Prime Minister included.

"Let us make no mistake about it," he continued with a face and tone now serious, "if anyone is so foolish as to impose new taxes now on our long-suffering masses . . ."

"I thought we didn't have masses in Africa," interrupted the Minister of Education starting a meagre laughter that was taken up in good sport by one or two others.

"I am sorry to trespass in my right honourable friend's territory; communist slogans are so infectious. But as I was saying we should not talk lightly about new taxes unless we are prepared to bring the Army out to quell tax riots. One simple 190 fact of life which we have come to learn rather painfully and reluctantly—and I'm not so sure even now that we have all learnt it—is that people do riot against taxes but not against school fees. The reason is simple. Everybody, even a motor-park tout,[4] knows what school fees are for. He can see his child going to school in the morning and coming back in the afternoon. But you go and tell him about general taxation and he immediately thinks that government is stealing his money from him. One other point, if a man doesn't want to pay school fees he doesn't have to, after all this is a democratic society. The worst that can happen is that his child stays at home which he probably doesn't mind at all. But taxes are different; everybody must pay whether they want to or not. The difference is pretty sharp. That's why mobs riot." A few people said "Hear! Hear!" Others just let out exhalations of relief or agreement. Mr. Emenike who had an unrestrainable admiration for the Finance Minister and had been nodding like a lizard through his speech shouted his "Hear! Hear!" too loud and got a scorching look from the Prime Minister.

A few desultory speeches followed and the government took its decision not to abolish free primary education but to suspend it until all the relevant factors had been thoroughly examined.

One little girl of ten, named Veronica, was brokenhearted. She had come to love school as an escape from the drabness and arduous demands of home. Her mother, a near-destitute widow who spent all hours of the day in the farm and, on market days, in the market left Vero to carry the burden of caring for the younger children. Actually only the youngest, aged one, needed much looking after. The other two, aged seven and four, being old enough to fend for themselves, picking palm-kernels and catching grasshoppers to eat, were no problem at all to Vero. But Mary was different. She cried a lot even after she had been fed her midmorning foo-foo[5] and soup saved for her (with a little addition of water to the soup) from breakfast which was itself a diluted left-over from last night's supper. Mary could not manage palm-kernels on her own account yet so Vero half-chewed them first before passing them on to her. But even after the food and the kernels and grasshoppers and the bowls of water Mary was rarely satisfied, even though her belly would be big and tight like a drum and shine like a mirror.

Their widowed mother, Martha, was a hard-luck woman. She had had an auspicious beginning long, long ago as a pioneer pupil at St. Monica's, then newly founded by white women-missionaries to train the future wives of native evangelists. Most of her schoolmates of those days had married young teachers and were now wives of pastors and one or two even of bishops. But Martha, encouraged by her teacher, Miss Robinson, had married a young carpenter trained by white artisan-missionaries at the Onitsha Industrial Mission, a trade school founded in the fervent belief that if the black man was to be redeemed, he needed to learn the Bible alongside manual skills. (Miss Robinson was very keen on the Industrial Mission whose Principal she herself later married.) But in spite of the bright hopes of those early evangelical days carpentry never developed very much in the way teaching and clerical jobs were to develop. So when Martha's husband died (or as those missionary artisans who taught him long ago might have put it—when he was called to higher service in the heavenly mansions by Him who was Himself

---

4. Salesman.
5. Dough made of plantains, fruit resembling bananas.

once a Carpenter on earth) he left her in complete ruins. It had been a bad-luck marriage from the start. To begin with she had had to wait twenty whole years after the marriage for her first child to be born, so that now she was virtually an old woman with little children to care for and little strength left for her task. Not that she was bitter about that. She was simply too overjoyed that God in His mercy had lifted her curse of barrenness to feel a need to grumble. What she nearly did grumble about was the disease that struck her husband and paralysed his right arm for five years before his death. It was a trial too heavy and unfair.

Soon after Vero withdrew from school Mr. Mark Emenike, the big government man of their village who lived in the capital, called on Martha. His Mercedes 220S pulled up on the side of the main road and he walked the 500 yards or so of a narrow unmotorable path to the widow's hut. Martha was perplexed at the visit of such a great man and as she bustled about for kolanut she kept wondering. Soon the great man himself in the hurried style of modern people cleared up the mystery.

"We have been looking for a girl to take care of our new baby and today someone told me to inquire about your girl . . ."

At first Martha was reluctant, but when the great man offered her £5 for the girl's services in the first year—plus feeding and clothing and other things—she began to soften.

"Of course it is not money I am concerned about," she said, "but whether my daughter will be well cared for."

"You don't have to worry about that, Ma. She will be treated just like one of our own children. My wife is a Social Welfare Officer and she knows what it means to care for children. Your daughter will all be happy in our home, I can tell you that. All she will be required to do is carry the little baby and give it its milk while my wife is away at the office and the older children at school."

"Vero and her sister Joy were also at school last term," said Martha without knowing why she said it.

"Yes, I know. That thing the government did is bad, very bad. But my belief is that a child who will be somebody will be somebody whether he goes to school or not. It is all written here, in the palm of the hand."

Martha gazed steadily at the floor and then spoke without raising her eyes. "When I married I said to myself: My daughters will do better than I did. I read Standard Three in those days and I said they will all go to College. Now they will not have even the little I had thirty years ago. When I think of it my heart wants to burst."

"Ma, don't let it trouble you too much. As I said before, what anyone of us is going to be is all written here, no matter what the difficulties."

"Yes. I pray God that what is written for these children will be better than what He wrote for me and my husband."

"Amen! . . . And as for this girl if she is obedient and good in my house what stops my wife and me sending her to school when the baby is big enough to go about on his own? Nothing. And she is still a small girl. How old is she?"

"She is ten."

"You see? She is only a baby. There is plenty of time for her to go to school."

He knew that the part about sending her to school was only a manner of speaking. And Martha knew too. But Vero who had been listening to everything from a dark corner of the adjoining room did not. She actually worked out in her mind the time it would take the baby to go about on his own and it came out quite short. So she went happily to live in the capital in a great man's family and looked after a baby who would soon be big enough to go about on his own and then she would have a chance to go to school.

Vero was a good girl and very sharp. Mr. Emenike and his wife were very   290 pleased with her. She had the sense of a girl twice her age and was amazingly quick to learn.

Mrs. Emenike, who had almost turned sour over her recent difficulty in getting good servants, was now her old self again. She could now laugh about the fiasco of free primadu. She told her friends that now she could go anywhere and stay as long as she liked without worrying about her little man. She was so happy with Vero's work and manners that she affectionately nicknamed her "Little Madame." The nightmare of the months following Abigail's departure was mercifully at an end. She had sought high and low then for another baby-nurse and just couldn't find one. One rather over-ripe young lady had presented herself and   300 asked for seven pounds a month. But it wasn't just the money. It was her general air—a kind of labour-exchange attitude which knew all the rights in the labour code, including presumably the right to have abortions in your servants' quarters and even have a go at your husband. Not that Mark was that way but the girl just wasn't right. After her no other person had turned up until now.

Every morning the older Emenike children—three girls and a boy—were leaving for school in their father's Mercedes or their mother's little noisy Fiat, Vero would bring the baby out to the steps to say bye-bye. She liked their fine dresses and shoes—she'd never worn any shoes in her life—but what she envied them   310 most was simply the going away every morning, going away from home, from familiar things and tasks. In the first months this envy was very, very mild. It lay beneath the joy of the big going away from the village, from her mother's drab hut, from eating palm-kernels that twisted the intestines at midday, from bitter-leaf soup without fish. That going away was something enormous. But as the months passed the hunger grew for these other little daily departures in fine dresses and shoes and sandwiches and biscuits wrapped in beautiful paper-napkins in dainty little school bags. One morning, as the Fiat took the children away and little Goddy began to cry on Vero's back, a song sprang into her mind to quieten him:

                                                                              320

> Little noisy motor-car
> If you're going to the school
> Please carry me
> Pee—pee—pee!—poh—poh—poh!

All morning she sang her little song and was pleased with it. When Mr. Emenike dropped the other children home at one o'clock and took off again Vero taught them her new song. They all liked it and for days it supplanted "Baa Baa Black Sheep" and "Simple Simon" and the other songs they brought home from school.   330

"That girl is a genius," said Mr. Emenike when the new song finally got to him. His wife who heard it first had nearly died from laughter. She had called Vero and said to her, "So you make fun of my car, naughty girl." Vero was happy because she saw not anger but laughter in the woman's eyes.

"She is a genius," said her husband. "And she hasn't been to school."

"And besides she knows you ought to buy me a new car."

"Never mind, dear. Another year and you can have that sports car."

"Na so."

"So you don't believe me? Just you wait and see."

More weeks and months passed and little Goddy was beginning to say a few 340 words but still no one spoke about Vero's going to school. She decided it was Goddy's fault, that he wasn't growing fast enough. And he was becoming rather too fond of riding on her back even though he could walk perfectly well. In fact his favourite words were "Cayi me." Vero made a song about that too and it showed her mounting impatience:

> Carry you! Carry you!
> Every time I carry you!
> If you no wan grow again
> I mus leave you and go school 350
> Because Vero e don tire!
> Tire, tire e don tire!

She sang it all morning until the other children returned from school and then she stopped. She only sang this one when she was alone with Goddy.

One afternoon Mrs. Emenike returned from work and noticed a redness on Vero's lips.

"Come here," she said, thinking of her expensive lipstick. "What is that?"

It turned out, however, not to be lipstick at all, only her husband's red ink. 360 She couldn't help a smile then.

"And look at her finger-nails! And toes too! So, Little Madame, that's what you do when we go out and leave you at home to mind the baby? You dump him somewhere and begin to paint yourself. Don't ever let me catch you with that kind of nonsense again; do you hear?" It occurred to her to strengthen her warning somehow if only to neutralize the smile she had smiled at the beginning.

"Do you know that red ink is poisonous? You want to kill yourself. Well, little lady you have to wait till you leave my house and return to your mother."

That did it, she thought in glowing self-satisfaction. She could see that Vero was suitably frightened. Throughout the rest of that afternoon she walked about 370 like a shadow.

When Mr. Emenike came home she told him the story as he ate a late lunch. And she called Vero for him to see.

"Show him your finger-nails," she said. "And your toes, Little Madame!"

"I see," he said waving Vero away. "She's learning fast. Do you know the proverb which says that when mother-cow chews giant grass her little calves watch her mouth?"

"Who is a cow? You rhinoceros!"

"It is only a proverb, my dear."

A week or so later Mrs. Emenike just home from work noticed that the dress 380
she had put on the baby in the morning had been changed into something much
too warm.

"What happened to the dress I put on him?"

"He fell down and soiled it. So I changed him," said Vero. But there was
something very strange in her manner. Mrs. Emenike's first thought was that the
child must have had a bad fall.

"Where did he fall?" she asked in alarm. "Where did he hit the ground?
Bring him to me! What is all this? Blood? No? What is it? My God has killed me!
Go and bring me the dress. At once!"

"I washed it," said Vero beginning to cry, a thing she had never done before. 390
Mrs. Emenike rushed out to the line and brought down the blue dress and the
white vest both heavily stained red!

She seized Vero and beat her in a mad frenzy with both hands. Then she got
a whip and broke it all on her until her face and hands ran with blood. Only then
did Vero admit making the child drink a bottle of red ink. Mrs. Emenike collapsed
into a chair and began to cry.

Mr. Emenike did not wait to have lunch. They bundled Vero into the
Mercedes and drove her the forty miles to her mother in the village. He had
wanted to go alone but his wife insisted on coming, and taking the baby too. He
stopped on the main road as usual. But he didn't go in with the girl. He just 400
opened the door of the car, pulled her out and his wife threw her little bundle of
clothes after her. And they drove away again.

Martha returned from the farm tired and grimy. Her children rushed out to
meet her and tell her that Vero was back and was crying in their bedroom. She
practically dropped her basket and went to see; but she couldn't make any sense
of her story.

"You gave the baby red ink? Why? So that you can go to school? How? Come
on. Let's go to their place. Perhaps they will stay in the village overnight. Or else
they will have told somebody there what happened. I don't understand your story. 410
Perhaps you stole something. Not so?"

"Please Mama don't take me back there. They will kill me."

"Come on, since you won't tell me what you did."

She seized her wrist and dragged her outside. Then in the open she saw all
the congealed blood on whip-marks all over her head, face, neck and arms. She
swallowed hard.

"Who did this?"

"My Madame."

"And what did you say you did? You must tell me."

"I gave the baby red ink."   420

"All right, then let's go."

Vero began to wail louder. Martha seized her by the wrist again and they set
off. She neither changed her work clothes nor even washed her face and hands.
Every woman—and sometimes the men too—they passed on the way screamed

on seeing Vero's whip-marks and wanted to know who did it. Martha's reply to all was "I don't know yet. I am going to find out."

She was lucky. Mr. Emenike's big car was there, so they had not returned to the capital. She knocked at their front door and walked in. Mrs. Emenike was sitting there in the parlour giving bottled food to the baby but she ignored the visitors completely neither saying a word to them nor even looking in their direction. It was her husband who descended the stairs a little later who told the story. As soon as the meaning dawned on Martha—that the red ink was given to the baby *to drink* and that the motive was to encompass its death—she screamed, with two fingers plugging her ears, that she wanted to hear no more. At the same time she rushed outside, tore a twig off a flowering shrub and by clamping her thumb and forefinger at one end and running them firmly along its full length stripped it of its leaves in one quick movement. Armed with the whip she rushed back to the house crying "I have heard an abomination!" Vero was now screaming and running round the room.

"Don't touch her here in my house," said Mrs. Emenike, cold and stern as an oracle, noticing her visitors for the first time. "Take her away from here at once. You want to show me your shock. Well I don't want to see. Go and show your anger in your own house. Your daughter did not learn murder here in my house."

This stung Martha deep in her spirit and froze her in mid-stride. She stood rooted to the spot, her whip-hand lifeless by her side. "My Daughter," she said finally addressing the younger woman, "as you see me here I am poor and wretched but I am not a murderer. If my daughter Vero is to become a murderer God knows she cannot say she learnt from me."

"Perhaps it's from me she learnt," said Mrs. Emenike showing her faultless teeth in a terrible false smile, "or maybe she snatched it from the air. That's right, she snatched it from the air. Look woman, take your daughter and leave my house."

"Vero, let's go; come, let's go!"

"Yes, please go!"

Mr. Emenike who had been trying vainly to find an opening for the clearly needed male intervention now spoke.

"It is the work of the devil," he said. "I have always known that the craze for education in this country will one day ruin all of us. Now even children will commit murder in order to go to school."

This clumsy effort to mollify all sides at once stung Martha even more. As she jerked Vero homewards by the hand she clutched her unused whip in her other hand. At first she rained abuses on the girl, called her an evil child that entered her mother's womb by the back of the house.

"Oh God, what have I done?" Her tears began to flow now. "If I had had a child with other women my age, that girl that calls me murderer might have been no older than my daughter. And now she spits in my face. That's what you brought me to," she said to the crown of Vero's head, and jerked her along more violently.

"I will kill you today. Let's go home first."

Then a strange revolt, vague, undirected began to well up at first slowly inside her. "And that thing that calls himself a man talks to me about the craze for education. All his children go to school, even the one that is only two years; but that is no craze. Rich people have no craze. It is only when the children of poor widows like me want to go with the rest that it becomes a craze. What is this life? To God, what is it? And now my child thinks she must kill the baby she is hired to tend before she can get a chance. Who put such an abomination into her belly? God, you know I did not."

She threw away the whip and with her freed hand wiped her tears.   [1973]

Questions for Discussion and Reading

1. Who or what is the vengeful creditor?
2. What does the story say about colonialism?
3. How does the inequality between whites and Africans affect the whites? Point to specific passages in framing your answer.
4. How do you interpret Vero's attempt to poison the baby? Why does she do it? Are her motives justified? Understandable? Vicious? Explain.
5. Analyze the reasons given for abolishing free primary education. Are they the real reasons? How do you know?
6. Why does Martha throw away the whip? What does this gesture suggest?

❧ PATRICIA GRACE
(b. 1937)

At the River

Patricia Grace is a member of the Maori tribe of New Zealand, the indigenous people of the island who have become second-class citizens since the arrival of *pakehas* (Europeans). She is, in fact, the first woman of her tribe to publish a volume of stories.

Born in Wellington, New Zealand, she attended primary school there, St. Mary's College, and then Wellington Teachers' College. After marrying Karchi Waiarike G, she spent twenty years teaching in rural schools and raising seven children. She later taught English as a second language at Porirua College, Wellington.

Acutely conscious that she lives in a society dominated by European culture and ideas, Grace has had to walk a fine line in her fiction between an honest portrayal of the plight of her people and the need to appeal to white readers. As a result, she sometimes avoids the most controversial aspects of the clash be-tween the two cultures, but at the same time she provides accurate and sensitive portraits of her people and their values. Maori culture respects nature, values spirituality and social integration, and sees time as the coming and going of generations. Stressing the strengths of these values and the traditional ways of her people, Grace often shows how Maori people have difficulty adjusting to or interacting with white culture. Technically, as in "At the River," she also attempts to capture the rhythms and patterns of Maori speech—something difficult to do in another language.

Grace's three volumes of stories, *Waiariki* (1975), *The Dream Sleepers and Other Stories* (1980), and *Electric City and Other Stories* (1988), in addition to her novels, have gained her a worldwide following and enabled her to write full time since 1985 and to serve as writer in residence at Victoria University.

The generational conflict of "At the River" transcends boundaries of language, time, and culture, but Grace treats this ancient theme in a unique and poignant way.

The morepork is the native owl of New Zealand whose night call sounds like "more pork."

S AD I WAIT, and see them come slow back from the river. The torches move slow. To the tent to rest after they had gone to the river, and while asleep the dream came. A dream of death. He came to me in the dream, not sadly but smiling, with hand on heart and said, I go but do not weep. No weeping, it is my time.

Woke then and out into the night to watch for them with sadness on me, sadness from the dream. And waiting, there came a morepork with soft wingbeat and rested above my head. "Go," I said to the bird. "He comes not with you tonight. He is well and strong. His time is not here."

But it cried, the morepork. Its call went out. Out and out until the tears were on my face. And now I wait and I see the torches come, they move slow back from 10 the river. Slow and sad they move and I think of him. Many times have we come to this place for eels. Every year we come at this time. Our children come and now our grandchildren, his and mine. This is the river for eels and this the time of year.

A long way we have travelled with our tents and food stores, our lamps and bedding and our big eel drums. Much work for us today preparing our camp. But now our camp is ready and they have gone with the torches downriver to the best eel place. And this old lady stays behind with her old kerosene lamp and the campfire dying, and the little ones sleeping in their beds. Too tired for the river tonight, too old for the work of catching eels. But not he. He is well and strong. No aching back or tired arms he. No bending, no sadness on him or thoughts of 20 death like this old one.

His wish but not mine to come here this year. "Too old," I said to him. "Let the young ones go. Stay back we two and tend our sweet potatoes and corn."

"This old body," he said. "It hungers for the taste of eel."

"The drums will be full when they return," I said. "Let them bring the eels to us, as they would wish to do."

"Ah no," he said. "Always these hands have fetched the food for the stomach. The eels taste sweeter when the body has worked in fetching."

"Go then," I said, and we prepared.

I think of him now as I await their return. "My time is here," he said in the 30 dream, and now the bird calls out. And I think too of the young ones who spoke to him today in a new way, a way I did not like.

Before the night came they worked, all of them, to make their torches for the river. Long sticks from the tea-tree, long and straight. Tins tied at the tops of the sticks, and in the tins rags soaked in oil. A good light they made as they left tonight for the river. Happy and singing they went with their torches. But I see the lights return now, dim. Dim and slow they come and sadly I await them.

And the young ones, they made their eel hooks. Straight sticks with strong hooks tied for catching eels. He smiled to see the eel hooks, the straight sticks with the strong hooks tied.   40

"Your hooks," he said. "They work for the hands?" But the young ones did not speak, instead bent heads to the work of tying hooks.

Then off, the young ones, to the hills for hare bait as the sun went down. Happy they went with the gun. Two shots went out and we awaited their return. The young ones, they came back laughing. Happy they came with the hare. "Good bait this," they said. "Good bait and good hooks. Lots of eels for us tonight."

But their nanny said to them, "A hook is good for the eel but bad for the leg. Many will be there at the river tonight, your uncles, aunties, big cousins, your nanny too. Your hooks may take a leg in place of an eel. The old way, with the stick, and the bait tied is a safe way and a good way. You waste your time with   50 hooks."

But the young ones rolled on the ground. "Ho, Grandpa," they called, "You better watch your leg tonight. The hook might get your leg, Grandpa."

"And watch your hand, Grandpa, the eel might get your hand."

"Bite your hand off, Grandpa. You better watch out."

Did not like their way of talking to their nanny but he has patience with the young.

"You'll see," he said. "You want to know how to get eels then you watch your grandpa."

They did not keep quiet, the young ones after that. Called out to him in a   60 way I did not like, but he is patient.

"Ah, Grandpa, that old way of yours is no good. That way is old like you, Grandpa."

"You might end up in the river with your old way of catching eels."

Spoke sharply to them then in our own language.

"Not for you to speak in this manner. Not our way to speak like this. It is a new thing you are doing. It is a bad thing you have learned."

No more talk from these two then, but laughing still, and he spoke up for them.

"They make their torches, the boys, and they make the hooks, and then they   70 go to the hills for hare. They think of the river and the eels in the river, and then they punch each other and roll on the ground. Shout and laugh waiting for the night to come. The funny talk it means nothing."

"Enough to shout and fight," I said. "Enough to roll on the ground and punch each other, but the talk needs to stay in the mouth."

Put my head down then not pleased, and worked at my task of kneading the bread for morning.

Now I wait and stir the ashes round the oven while the morning bread cooks, and on the ashes I see my tears fall. The babies sleep behind me in the tent, and above me the bird cries.   80

Much to do after a night of eeling when the drum is full. From the fire we scrape away the dead ashes to put into the drum of eels. All night our eels stay there in the drum of ashes to make easier the task of scraping. Scrape off the ashes and with it comes the sticky eel slime. Cut the eels, and open them out then ready for smoking. The men collect green wood from the tea-tree for our smoke drum. Best wood this, to make a good smoke. Good and clear. All day our smoke house goes. Then wrap our smoked eel carefully and pack away before night comes and time for the river again.

But no eels for us this night. No scraping and smoking and packing this time. Tonight our camp comes down and we return. The dim lights come and 90 they bring him back from the river. Slow they bring him.

Now I see two lights come near. The two have come to bring me sad news of him. But before them the bird came, and before the bird the dream—he in the dream with hand on heart.

And now they stand before me, the boys, heads down. By the dim torchlight I see the tears on their faces, they do not speak.

"They bring your nanny back," I say. "Back from the river." But they do not speak.

"Hear the morepork," I say to them. "It calls from the trees. Out and out it cries. They bring him back from the river, I see your tears."   100

"We saw him standing by the river," they say. "Saw him bend, looking into the water, and then we saw him fall."

They stand, the young ones in the dim torchlight with tears on their faces, the tears fall. And now they come to me, kneeling by me, weeping.

"We spoke bad to him," they say. "They were bad things we said. Now he has fallen and we have said bad things to him."

So I speak to them to comfort them. "He came to me tonight with hand on heart. 'Do not weep,' he said. 'It is my time.' Not your words that made him fall. His hand was on his heart. Hear the morepork cry. His time is here."

And now we weep together, this old lady and these two young ones by her. 110 No weeping he said. But we will weep a little while for him and for ourselves. He was our strength.

We weep and they return. His children and mine return from the river bearing him. Sad they come in the dim light of torches. The young ones help me to my feet, weeping still, and I go toward them as they come.

And in my throat I feel a cry well up. Lonely it sounds across the night. Lonely it sounds, the cry that comes from in me.   [1975]

Questions for Discussion and Writing

1. What does the morepork suggest or symbolize?
2. Who is the narrator? How do you know?
3. What unusual linguistic devices does the narrator use? What is their purpose or function?
4. What are the conflicts in this story? How are they revealed?

❧ RUTH PRAWER JHABVALA
(b. 1927)

In the Mountains

The life and work of Ruth Prawer Jhabvala illustrate important trends in literature during this century: its movement toward multiculturalism and its interac-
tions with other art forms, especially television and film.

Although as her name and many of her works suggest, Jhabvala is an Indian
writer, she was born Ruth Prawer in Cologne, Germany, of Polish parents. At
the outbreak of war in 1939, her family fled to England, where she continued
her schooling and eventually earned a master's degree in English literature in
1951. That same year she married C. S. H. Jhabvala and moved to India—a
profound experience both personally and artistically.

Like many encountering India for the first time, Jhabvala was at first en-
thralled with its exotic culture, and her position on the edge of Indian life and
society has given her a unique view of its social dynamics. Her early works were
entirely Indian in setting and character. In 1975, however, Jhabvala moved to
New York City, where yet again she was an outsider. Her fiction began exploring the problems immigrants still face in the "new world." Likewise, her methods vary from traditional realism to various forms of experimentation.

Much of Jhabvala's recent work has been in writing for the screen, most
prominently with such Merchant-Ivory productions as *A Room With a View*, for
which she won an Oscar in 1987, and the highly successful *Howard's End*. These
and other films have demonstrated the commercial and artistic possibilities of
well made, highly literary movies.

"In the Mountains" presents one of Jhabvala's recurring situations: the character in quest of identity and fulfillment outside the conventional roles dictated
by society.

WHEN ONE LIVES alone for most of the time and meets almost nobody, then
care for one's outward appearance tends to drop away. That was what happened to Pritam. As the years went by and she continued living by herself, her appearance became rougher and shabbier, and though she was still in her thirties,
she completely forgot to care for herself or think about herself as a physical person.

Her mother was just the opposite. She was plump and pampered, loved pas-
tries and silk saris, and always smelled of lavender. Pritam smelled of—what was
it? Her mother, enfolded in Pritam's embrace after a separation of many months,
found herself sniffing in an attempt to identify the odour emanating from her.   10
Perhaps it was from Pritam's clothes, which she probably did not change as frequently as was desirable. Tears came to the mother's eyes. They were partly for
what her daughter had become and partly for the happiness of being with her
again.

Pritam thumped her on the back. Her mother always cried at their meetings and at their partings. Pritam usually could not help being touched by these tears, even though she was aware of the mixed causes that evoked them. Now, to hide her own feelings, she became gruffer and more manly, and even gave the old lady a push toward a chair. "Go on, sit down," she said. "I suppose you are dying for your cup of tea." She had it all ready, and the mother took it gratefully, for she loved and needed tea, and the journey up from the plains had greatly tired her.

But she could not drink with enjoyment. Pritam's tea was always too strong for her—a black country brew such as peasants drank, and the milk was also that of peasants, too newly rich and warm from the buffalo. And they were in this rough and barely furnished room in the rough stone house perched on the mountainside. And there was Pritam herself. The mother had to concentrate all her energies on struggling against more tears.

"I suppose you don't like the tea," Pritam said challengingly. She watched severely while the mother proved herself by drinking it up to the last drop, and Pritam refilled the cup. She asked, "How is everybody? Same as usual? Eating, making money?"

"No, no," said the mother, not so much denying the fact that this was what the family was doing as protesting against Pritam's saying so.

"Aren't they going up to Simla[1] this year?"

"On Thursday," the mother said, and shifted uncomfortably.

"And stopping here?"

"Yes. For lunch."

The mother kept her eyes lowered. She said nothing more, though there was more to say. It would have to wait till a better hour. Let Pritam first get over the prospect of entertaining members of her family for a few hours on Thursday. It was nothing new or unexpected, for some of them stopped by every year on their way farther up the mountains. However much they may have desired to do so, they couldn't just drive past; it wouldn't be decent. But the prospect of meeting held no pleasure for anyone. Quite often there was a quarrel, and then Pritam cursed them as they drove away, and they sighed at the necessity of keeping up family relationships, instead of having their lunch comfortably in the hotel a few miles farther on.

Pritam said, "I suppose you will be going with them," and went on at once, "Naturally, why should you stay? What is there for you here?"

"I want to stay."

"No, you love to be in Simla. It's so nice and jolly, and meeting everyone walking on the Mall, and tea in Davico's. Nothing like that here. You even hate my tea."

"I want to stay with you."

"But I don't want you!" Pritam was laughing, not angry. "You will be in my way, and then how will I carry on all my big love affairs?"

"What, what?"

Pritam clapped her hands in delight. "Oh no. I'm telling you nothing, be-

---

1. A summer resort in the Himalayas.

cause then you will want to stay and you will scare everyone away." She gave her
mother a sly look and added, "You will scare poor Doctor Sahib away."   60

"Oh, Doctor Sahib," said the old lady, relieved to find it had all been a joke.
But she continued with disapproval, "Does he still come here?"

"Well, what do you think?" Pritam stopped laughing now and became offended. "If he doesn't come, then who will come? Except some goats and monkeys, perhaps. I know he is not good enough for you. You don't like him to come
here. You would prefer me to know only goats and monkeys. And the family, of
course."

"When did I say I don't like him?" the mother said.

"People don't have to say. And other people are quite capable of feeling without anyone saying. Here." Pritam snatched up her mother's cup and filled it, with   70
rather a vengeful air, for the third time.

Actually, it wasn't true that the mother disliked Doctor Sahib. He came to
visit the next morning, and as soon as she saw him she had her usual sentiment
about him—not dislike but disapproval. He certainly did not look like a person fit
to be on terms of social intercourse with any member of her family. He was a tiny
man, shabby and even dirty. He wore a kind of suit, but it was in a terrible condition and so were his shoes. One eye of his spectacles, for some reason, was
blacked out with a piece of cardboard.

"Ah!" he exclaimed when he saw her. "Mother has come!" And he was so
genuinely happy that her disapproval could not stand up to him—at least, not en- 80
tirely.

"Mother brings us tidings and good cheer from the great world outside,"
Doctor Sahib went on. "What are we but two mountain hermits? Or I could even
say two mountain bears."

He sat at a respectful distance away from the mother, who was ensconced in
a basket chair. She had come to sit in the garden. There was a magnificent view
from here of the plains below and the mountains above; however, she had not
come out to enjoy the scenery but to get the benefit of the morning sun. Although
it was the height of summer, she always felt freezing cold inside the house, which
seemed like a stone tomb.   90

"Has Madam told you about our winter?" Doctor Sahib said. "Oh, what these
two bears have gone through! Ask her."

"His roof fell in," Pritam said.

"One night I was sleeping in my bed. Suddenly—what shall I tell you—
crash, bang! Boom and bang! To me it seemed that all the mountains were falling
and, let alone the mountains, heaven itself was coming down into my poor house.
I said, 'Doctor Sahib, your hour has come.' "

"I told him, I told him all summer, 'The first snowfall and your roof will fall
in.' And when it happened all he could do was stand there and wring his hands.
What an idiot!"   100

"If it hadn't been for Madam, God knows what would have become of me.
But she took me in and all winter she allowed me to have my corner by her own
fireside."

The mother looked at them with startled eyes.

"Oh yes, all winter," Pritam said, mocking her. "And all alone, just the two of us. Why did you have to tell her?" she reproached Doctor Sahib. "Now she is shocked. Just look at her face. She is thinking we are two guilty lovers."

The mother flushed, and so did Doctor Sahib. An expression of bashfulness came into his face, mixed with regret, with melancholy. He was silent for some time, his head lowered. Then he said to the mother, "Look, can you see it?" He pointed at his house, which nestled farther down the mountainside, some way below Pritam's. It was a tiny house, not much more than a hut. "All hale and hearty again. Madam had the roof fixed, and now I am snug and safe once more in my own little kingdom."

Pritam said, "One day the whole place is going to come down, not just the roof, and then what will you do?"

He spread his arms in acceptance and resignation. He had no choice as to place of residence. His family had brought him here and installed him in the house; they gave him a tiny allowance but only on condition that he wouldn't return to Delhi. As was evident from his fluent English, Doctor Sahib was an educated man, though it was not quite clear whether he really had qualified as a doctor. If he had, he may have done something disreputable and been struck off the register. Some such air hung about him. He was a great embarrassment to his family. Unable to make a living, he had gone around scrounging from family friends, and at one point had sat on the pavement in New Delhi's most fashionable shopping district and attempted to sell cigarettes and matches.

Later, when he had gone, Pritam said, "Don't you think I've got a dashing lover?"

"I know it's not true," the mother said, defending herself. "But other people, what will they think—alone with him in the house all winter? You know how people are."

"What people?"

It was true. There weren't any. To the mother, this was a cause for regret. She looked at the mountains stretching away into the distance—a scene of desolation. But Pritam's eyes were half shut with satisfaction as she gazed across the empty spaces and saw birds cleaving through the mist, afloat in the pure mountain sky.

"I was waiting for you all winter," the mother said. "I had your room ready, and every day we went in there to dust and change the flowers." She broke out, "Why didn't you come? Why stay in this place when you can be at home and lead a proper life like everybody else?"

Pritam laughed. "Oh but I'm not like everybody else! That's the last thing!"

The mother was silent. She could not deny that Pritam was different. When she was a girl, they had worried about her and yet they had also been proud of her. She had been a big, handsome girl with independent views. People admired her and thought it a fine thing that a girl could be so emancipated in India and lead a free life, just as in other places.

Now the mother decided to break her news. She said, "He is coming with them on Thursday."

"Who is coming with them?"

"Sarla's husband." She did not look at Pritam after saying this.

After a moment's silence Pritam cried, "So let him come! They can all come—everyone welcome. My goodness, what's so special about him that you should make such a face? What's so special about any of them? They may come, they may eat, they may go away again, and goodbye. Why should I care for anyone? I don't care. And also you! You also may go—right now, this minute, if you like—and I will stand here and wave to you and laugh!"

In an attempt to stop her, the mother asked, "What will you cook for them on Thursday?"

That did bring her up short. For a moment she gazed at her mother wildly, as if she were mad herself or thought her mother mad. Then she said, "My God, 160 do you ever think of anything except food?"

"I eat too much," the old lady gladly admitted. "Dr. Puri says I must reduce."

Pritam didn't sleep well that night. She felt hot, and tossed about heavily, and finally got up and turned on the light and wandered around the house in her nightclothes. Then she unlatched the door and let herself out. The night air was crisp, and it refreshed her at once. She loved being out in all this immense silence. Moonlight lay on top of the mountains, so that even those that were green looked as if they were covered in snow.

There was only one light—a very human little speck, in all that darkness. It 170 came from Doctor Sahib's house, some way below hers. She wondered if he had fallen asleep with the light on. It happened sometimes that he dozed off where he was sitting and when he woke up again it was morning. But other times he really did stay awake all night, too excited by his reading and thinking to be able to sleep. Pritam decided to go down and investigate. The path was very steep, but she picked her way down, as sure and steady as a mountain goat. She peered in at his window. He was awake, sitting at his table with his head supported on his hand, and reading by the light of a kerosene lamp. His house had once had electricity, but after the disaster last winter it could not be got to work again. Pritam was quite glad about that, for the wiring had always been uncertain, and he had 180 been in constant danger of being electrocuted.

She rapped on the glass to rouse him, then went round to let herself in by the door. At the sound of her knock, he had jumped to his feet; he was startled, and no less so when he discovered who his visitor was. He stared at her through his one glass lens, and his lower lip trembled in agitation.

She was irritated. "If you're so frightened, why don't you lock your door? You should lock it. Any kind of person can come in and do anything he wants." It struck her how much like a murder victim he looked. He was so small and weak—one blow on the head would do it. Some morning she would come down and find him lying huddled on the floor. 190

But there he was, alive, and, now that he had got over the shock, laughing and flustered and happy to see her. He fussed around and invited her to sit on his only chair, dusting the seat with his hand and drawing it out for her in so courtly a manner that she became instinctively graceful as she settled herself on it and pulled her nightdress over her knees.

"Look at me, in my nightie," she said, laughing. "I suppose you're shocked. If Mother knew. If she could see me! But of course she is fast asleep and snoring in her bed. Why are you awake? Reading one of your stupid books—what stuff you cram into your head day and night. Anyone would go crazy."

Doctor Sahib was very fond of reading. He read mostly historical romances and was influenced and even inspired by them. He believed very strongly in past births, and these books helped him to learn about the historical eras through which he might have passed.

"A fascinating story," he said. "There is a married lady—a queen, as a matter of fact—who falls hopelessly in love with a monk."

"Goodness! Hopelessly?"

"You see, these monks—naturally—they were under a vow of chastity and that means—well—you know . . ."

"Of course I know."

"So there was great anguish on both sides. Because he also felt burning love for the lady and endured horrible penances in order to subdue himself. Would you like me to read to you? There are some sublime passages."

"What is the use? These are not things to read in books but to experience in life. Have you ever been hopelessly in love?"

He turned away his face, so that now only his cardboard lens was looking at her. However, it seemed not blank but full of expression.

She said, "There are people in the world whose feelings are much stronger than other people's. Of course they must suffer. If you are not satisfied only with eating and drinking but want something else . . . You should see my family. They care for nothing—only physical things, only enjoyment."

"Mine exactly the same."

"There is one cousin, Sarla—I have nothing against her, she is not a bad person. But I tell you it would be just as well to be born an animal. Perhaps I shouldn't talk like this, but it's true."

"It is true. And in previous births these people really were animals."

"Do you think so?"

"Or some very low form of human being. But the queens and the really great people, they become—well, they become like you. Please don't laugh! I have told you before what you were in your last birth."

She went on laughing. "You've told me so many things," she said.

"All true. Because you have passed through many incarnations. And in each one you were a very outstanding personality, a highly developed soul, but each time you also had a difficult life, marked by sorrow and suffering."

Pritam had stopped laughing. She gazed sadly at the blank wall over his head.

"It is the fate of all highly developed souls," he said. "It is the price to be paid."

"I know." She fetched a sigh from her innermost being.

"I think a lot about this problem. Just tonight, before you came, I sat here reading my book. I'm not ashamed to admit that tears came streaming from my eyes, so that I couldn't go on reading, on account of not being able to see the print. Then I looked up and I asked, 'Oh, Lord, why must these good and noble souls endure such torment, while others, less good and noble, can enjoy themselves freely?' "

"Yes, why?" Pritam asked.

"I shall tell you. I shall explain." He was excited, inspired now. He looked at her fully, and even his cardboard lens seemed radiant. "Now, as I was reading about this monk—a saint, by the way—and how he struggled and battled against nature, then I could not but think of my own self. Yes, I too, though not a saint, struggle and battle here alone in my small hut. I cry out in anguish, and the suf- 250 fering endured is terrible but also—oh, Madam—glorious! A privilege."

Pritam looked at a crack that ran right across the wall and seemed to be splitting it apart. One more heavy snowfall, she thought, and the whole hut would come down. Meanwhile he sat here and talked nonsense and she listened to him. She got up abruptly.

He cried, "I have talked too much! You are bored!"

"Look at the time," she said. The window was milk-white with dawn. She turned down the kerosene lamp and opened the door. Trees and mountains were floating in a pale mist, attempting to surface like swimmers through water. "Oh my God," she said, "it's time to get up. And I'm going to have such a day today, 260 with all of them coming."

"They are coming today?"

"Yes, and you needn't bother to visit. They are not your type at all. Not one bit."

He laughed. "All right."

"Not mine, either," she said, beginning the upward climb back to her house.

Pritam loved to cook and was very good at it. Her kitchen was a primitive little outbuilding in which she bustled about. Her hair fell into her face and stuck to her forehead; several times she tried to push it back with her elbow but only 270 succeeded in leaving a black soot mark. When her mother pointed this out to her, she laughed and smeared at it and made it worse.

Her good humour carried her successfully over the arrival of the relatives. They came in three carloads, and suddenly the house was full of fashionably dressed people with loud voices. Pritam came dashing out of the kitchen just as she was and embraced everyone indiscriminately, including Sarla and her husband, Bobby. In the bustle of arrival and the excitement of many people, the meeting went off easily. The mother was relieved. Pritam and Bobby hadn't met for eight years—in fact, not since Bobby had been married to Sarla.

Soon Pritam was serving a vast, superbly cooked meal. She went around pil- 280 ing their plates, urging them to take, take more, glad at seeing them enjoy her food. She still hadn't changed her clothes, and the smear of soot was still on her face. The mother—whose main fear had been that Pritam would be surly and difficult—was not relieved but upset by Pritam's good mood. She thought to herself, why should she be like that with them—what have they ever done for her that she should show them such affection and be like a servant to them? She even looked like their servant. The old lady's temper mounted, and when she saw Pritam piling rice onto Bobby's plate—when she saw her serving *him* like a servant, and the way he turned round to compliment her about the food, making Pritam proud and shy and pleased—then the mother could not bear any more. She went into the bed- 290 room and lay down on the bed. She felt ill; her blood pressure had risen and all her pulses throbbed. She shut her eyes and tried to shut out the merry, sociable sounds coming from the next room.

After a while, Pritam came in and said, "Why aren't you eating?"

The old lady didn't answer.

"What's the matter?"

"Go. Go away. Go to your guests."

"Oh my God, she is sulking!" Pritam said, and laughed out loud—not to annoy her mother but to rally her, the way she would a child. But the mother continued to lie there with her eyes shut.   300

Pritam said, "Should I get you some food?"

"I don't want it," the mother said. But suddenly she opened her eyes and sat up. She said, "You should give food to him. He also should be invited. Or perhaps you think he is not good enough for your guests?"

"Who?"

"Who. You know very well. You should know. You were with him the whole night."

Pritam gave a quick glance over her shoulder at the open door, then advanced toward her mother. "So you have been spying on me," she said. The mother shrank back. "You pretended to be asleep, and all the time you were spy-   310 ing on me."

"Not like that, Daughter—"

"And now you are having filthy thoughts about me."

"Not like that!"

"Yes, like that!"

Both were shouting. The conversation in the next room had died down. The mother whispered, "Shut the door," and Pritam did so.

Then the mother said in a gentle, loving voice, "I'm glad he is here with you. He is a good friend to you." She looked into Pritam's face, but it did not lighten, and she went on, "That is why I said he should be invited. When other friends   320 come, we should not neglect our old friends who have stood by us in our hour of need."

Pritam snorted scornfully.

"And he would have enjoyed the food so much," the mother said. "I think he doesn't often eat well."

Pritam laughed. "You should see what he eats!" she said. "But he is lucky to get even that. At least his family send him money now. Before he came here, do you want to hear what he did? He has told me himself. He used to go to the kitchens of the restaurants and beg for food. And they gave him scraps and he ate them—he has told me himself. He ate leftover scraps from other people's plates   330 like a sweeper or a dog. And you want such a person to be my friend."

She turned away from her mother's startled, suffering face. She ran out of the room and out through the next room, past all the guests. She climbed up a path that ran from the back of her house to a little cleared plateau. She lay down in the grass, which was alive with insects; she was level with the tops of trees and with the birds that pecked and called from inside them. She often came here. She looked down at the view but didn't see it, it was so familiar to her. The only unusual sight was the three cars parked outside her house. A chauffeur was wiping a windscreen. Then someone came out of the house and, reaching inside a car door, emerged with a bottle. It was Bobby.   340

Pritam watched him, and when he was about to go back into the house, she aimed a pebble that fell at his feet. He looked up. He smiled. "Hi, there!" he called.

She beckoned him to climb up to her. He hesitated for a moment, looking at the bottle and toward the house, but then gave the toss of his head that she knew well, and began to pick his way along the path. She put her hand over her mouth to cover a laugh as she watched him crawl up toward her on all fours. When finally he arrived, he was out of breath and dishevelled, and there was a little blood on his hand where he had grazed it. He flung himself on the grass beside her and gave a great "Whoof!" of relief.

She hadn't seen him for eight years, and her whole life had changed in the 350 meantime, but it didn't seem to her that he had changed all that much. Perhaps he was a little heavier, but it suited him, made him look more manly than ever. He was lying face down on the grass, and she watched his shoulder-blades twitch inside his finely striped shirt as he breathed in exhaustion.

"You are in very poor condition," she said.

"Isn't it terrible?"

"Don't you play tennis any more?"

"Mostly golf now."

He sat up and put the bottle to his mouth and tilted back his head. She watched his throat moving as the liquid glided down. He finished with a sound of 360 satisfaction and passed the bottle to her, and without wiping it she put her lips where his had been and drank. The whisky leaped up in her like fire. They had often sat like this together, passing a bottle of Scotch between them.

He seemed to be perfectly content to be there with her. He sat with his knees drawn up and let his eyes linger appreciatively over the view. It was the way she had often seen him look at attractive girls. "Nice," he said, as he had said on those occasions. She laughed, and then she too looked and tried to imagine how he was seeing it.

"A nice place," he said. "I like it. I wish I could live here."

"You!" She laughed again. 370

He made a serious face. "I love peace and solitude. You don't know me. I've changed a lot." He turned right round toward her, still very solemn, and for the first time she felt him gazing full into her face. She put up her hand and said quickly, "I've been cooking all day."

He looked away, as if wanting to spare her, and this delicacy hurt her more than anything. She said heavily, "I've changed."

"Oh no!" he said in haste. "You are just the same. As soon as I saw you, I thought: Look at Priti, she is just the same." And again he turned toward her to allow her to see his eyes, stretching them wide open for her benefit. It was a habit of his she knew well; he would always challenge the person to whom he was lying 380 to read anything but complete honesty in his eyes.

She said, "You had better go. Everyone will wonder where you are."

"Let them." And when she shook her head, he said, in his wheedling voice, "Let me stay with you. It has been such a long time. Shall I tell you something? I was so excited yesterday thinking: Tomorrow I shall see her again. I couldn't sleep all night. No, really—it's true."

Of course she knew it wasn't. He slept like a bear; nothing could disturb that. The thought amused her, and her mouth corners twitched. Encouraged, he moved in closer. "I think about you very often," he said. "I remember so many things—you have no idea. All the discussions we had about our terrible social system. It was great." 390

Once they had had a very fine talk about free love. They had gone to a place they knew about, by a lake. At first they were quite frivolous, sitting on a ledge overlooking the lake, but as they got deeper into their conversation about free love (they both, it turned out, believed in it) they became more and more serious and, after that, very quiet, until in the end they had nothing more to say. Then they only sat there, and though it was very still and the water had nothing but tiny ripples in it, like wrinkles in silk, they felt as if they were in a storm. But of course it was their hearts beating and their blood rushing. It was the most marvellous experience they had ever had in their whole lives. After that, they often returned there 400 or went to other similar places that they found, and as soon as they were alone together that same storm broke out.

Now Bobby heaved a sigh. To make himself feel better, he took another drink from his bottle and then passed it to her. "It's funny," he said. "I have this fantastic social life. I meet such a lot of people, but there isn't one person I can talk with the way I talk with you. I mean, about serious subjects."

"And with Sarla?"

"Sarla is all right, but she isn't really interested in serious subjects. I don't think she ever thinks about them. But I do."

To prove it, he again assumed a very solemn expression and turned his face 410 toward her, so that she could study it. How little he had changed!

"Give me another drink," she said, needing it.

He passed her the bottle. "People think I'm an extrovert type, and of course I do have to lead a very extrovert sort of life," he said. "And there is the business too—ever since Daddy had his stroke, I have to spend a lot of time in the office. But very often, you know what I like to do? Just lie on my bed and listen to nice tunes on my cassette. And then I have a lot of thoughts."

"What about?"

"Oh, all sorts of things. You would be surprised."

She was filled with sensations she had thought she would never have again. 420 No doubt they were partly due to the whisky; she hadn't drunk in a long time. She thought he must be feeling the way she did; in the past they had always felt the same. She put out her hand to touch him—first his cheek, which was rough and manly, and then his neck, which was soft and smooth. He had been talking, but when she touched him he fell silent. She left her hand lying on his neck, loving to touch it. He remained silent, and there was something strange. For a moment, she didn't remove her hand—she was embarrassed to do so—and when at last she did she noticed that he looked at it. She looked at it too. The skin was rough and not too clean, and neither were her nails, and one of them was broken. She hid her hands behind her back. 430

Now he was talking again, and talking quite fast. "Honestly, Priti, I think you're really lucky to be living here," he said. "No one to bother you, no worries, and all this fantastic scenery." He turned his head again to admire it and made his eyes sparkle with appreciation. He also took a deep breath.

"And such marvellous air," he said. "No wonder you keep fit and healthy. Who lives there?" He pointed at Doctor Sahib's house below.

Pritam answered eagerly. "Oh, I'm very lucky—he is such an interesting personality. If only you could meet him."

"What a pity," Bobby said politely. Down below, there was a lot of activity around the three cars. Things were being rolled up and stowed away in prepara- 440 tion for departure.

"Yes, you don't meet such people every day. He is a doctor, not only of medicine but all sorts of other things too. He does a lot of research and thinking, and that is why he lives up here. Because it is so quiet."

Now people could be seen coming out of Pritam's house. They turned this way and that, looking up and calling Pritam's name.

"They are looking for you," Bobby said. He replaced the cap of his whisky bottle and got up and waited for her to get up too. But she took her time.

"You see, for serious thinking you have to have absolute peace and quiet," she said. "I mean, if you are a real thinker, a sort of philosopher type." 450

She got up. She stood and looked down at the people searching and calling for her. "Whenever I wake up at night, I can see his light on. He is always with some book, studying, studying."

"Fantastic," Bobby said, though his attention was distracted by the people below.

"He knows all about past lives. He can tell you exactly what you were in all your previous births."

"Really?" Bobby said, turning toward her again.

"He has told me all about my incarnations."

"Really? Would he know about me too?" 460

"Perhaps. If you were an interesting personality. Yes all right, coming!" she called down at last.

She began the steep climb down, but it was so easy for her that she could look back at him over her shoulder and continue talking. "He is only interested in studying highly developed souls, so unless you were someone really quite special in a previous birth he wouldn't be able to tell you anything."

"What were you?" Bobby said. He had begun to follow her. Although the conversation was interesting to him, he could not concentrate on it, because he had to keep looking down at the path and place his feet with caution.

"I don't think I can tell you," she said, walking on ahead. "It is something 470 you are supposed to know only in your innermost self."

"What?" he said, but just then he slipped, and it was all he could do to save himself from falling.

"In your innermost self!" she repeated in a louder voice, though without looking back. Nimbly, she ran down the remainder of the path and was soon among the people who had been calling her.

They were relieved to see her. It seemed the old lady was being very troublesome. She refused to have her bag packed, refused to get into the car and be driven up to Simla. She said she wanted to stay with Pritam. 480

"So let her," Pritam said.

Her relatives exchanged exasperated glances. Some of the ladies were so tired of the whole thing that they had given up and sat on the steps of the veran-dah, fanning themselves. Others, more patient, explained to Pritam that it was all very well for her to say let her stay, but how was she going to look after her? The old lady needed so many things—a masseuse in the morning, a cup of Horlicks[2] at eleven and another at three, and one never knew when the doctor would have to be called for her blood pressure. None of these facilities was available in Pritam's house, and they knew exactly what would happen—after a day, or at the most two, Pritam would send them an SOS, and they would have to come back all the 490 way from Simla to fetch her away.

Pritam went into the bedroom, shutting the door behind her. The mother was lying on her bed, with her face to the wall. She didn't move or turn round or give any sign of life until Pritam said, "It's me." Then her mother said, "I'm not going with them."

Pritam said, "You will have to have a cold bath every day, because I'm not going to keep lighting the boiler for you. Do you know who has to chop the wood? Me, Pritam."

"I don't need hot water. If you don't need it, I don't."

"And there is no Horlicks."   500

"Tcha!" said her mother. She was still lying on the bed, though she had turned round now and was facing Pritam. She did not look very well. Her face seemed puffed and flushed.

"And your blood pressure?" Pritam asked.

"It is quite all right."

"Yes, and what if it isn't? There is no Dr. Puri here, or anyone like that."

The mother shut her eyes, as if it were a great effort. After a time, she found the strength to say, "There is a doctor."

"God help us!" Pritam said, and laughed out loud.

"He *is* a doctor." The mother compressed her little mouth stubbornly over 510 her dentures. Pritam did not contradict her, though she was still laughing to her-self. They were both silent together but not in disagreement. Pritam opened the door to leave.

"Did you keep any food for him?" the mother said.

"There is enough to last him a week."

She went out and told the others that her mother was staying. She wouldn't listen to any arguments, and after a while they gave up. All they wanted was to get away as quickly as possible. They piled into their cars and waved at her from the windows. She waved back. When she was out of sight, they sank back against the car upholstery with sighs of relief. They felt it had gone off quite well this time. At 520 least there had been no quarrel. They discussed her for a while and felt that she was improving; perhaps she was quietening down with middle age.

Pritam waited for the cars to reach the bend below and then—quite without malice but with excellent aim—she threw three stones. Each one squarely hit the roof of a different car as they passed, one after the other. She could hear the sound faintly from up here. She thought how amazed they would be inside their cars,

---

2. Malted milk.

wondering what had hit them, and how they would crane out of the windows but not be able to see anything. They would decide that it was just some stones crumbling off the hillside—perhaps the beginning of a landslide; you never could tell in the mountains.   530

She picked up another stone and flung it all the way down at Doctor Sahib's corrugated tin roof. It landed with a terrific clatter, and he came running out. He looked straight up to where she was standing, and his one lens glittered at her in the sun.

She put her hands to her mouth and called, "Food!" He gave a sign of joyful assent and straightaway, as nimble as herself, began the familiar climb up. [1976]

Questions for Discussion and Writing

1. Why does Pritam live in this isolated place? Is she escaping from something or to something? Explain.
2. What tensions or conflicts are revealed? Are any of them resolved? Be specific.
3. What is the relationship between Pritam and Dr. Sahib? How does their relationship pertain to the rest of the story?
4. Judging from this story, what Western customs and ideas have entered Indian society? What is Jhabvala's attitude to this mixing of cultures? Does she approve or condemn? How do you know?
5. Is Pritam's withdrawal from her family a feminist gesture? Why or why not?

⚓ LYDIA DAVIS
(b. 1947)

A Few Things Wrong With Me

Lydia Davis is a versatile writer and translator whose ceaseless experiments with the short story form are helping to lead it in new directions.

Davis was born into a family interested in literature and writing. Her father is a literary scholar and writer, and her mother has published a collection of stories. Lydia was an avid reader as a child and began writing stories at age twelve. She attended Brearly School in New York City, then the Putney School in Vermont, where she studied violin. In 1965, she entered Barnard College to major in English and while there attended a writing workshop under Grace Paley.

Before graduating, Davis spent a year in London as a messenger for the *Manchester Guardian*. Returning to college, she published the first of many translations from the French in the *Columbia Review*. After college, she worked a year for a publisher and traveled widely, experimenting with poetry and short stories. During 1973 and 1974, she lived in Paris, supporting herself by trans-lating art books and catalogs. Her first collection of stories, *The Thirteenth Woman and Other Stories,* appeared in 1976.

Davis's experimentation makes it difficult to generalize about her stories. Critics have noted a variety of characteristics: humor, a style at once clear and unsettling, and a poetic, minimalistic quality in the writing. She herself claims to find perpetual inspiration in the work of Samuel Beckett (1906–1989) and Franz Kafka (1883–1924).

"A Few Things Wrong With Me" is at once simple and complex, a disturbing portrait of a woman trying to understand herself and her relations to men.

HE SAID THERE WERE things about me that he hadn't liked from the very beginning. He didn't say this unkindly. He's not an unkind person, at least not intentionally. He said it because I was trying to get him to explain why he changed his mind about me so suddenly.

I may ask his friends what they think about this, because they know him better than I do. They've known him for more than fifteen years, whereas I've only known him for about ten months. I like them, and they seem to like me, though we don't know each other very well. What I want to do is to have a meal or a drink with at least two of them and talk about him until I begin to get a better picture of him.

It's easy to come to the wrong conclusions about people. I see now that all these past months I kept coming to the wrong conclusions about him. For example, when I thought he would be unkind to me, he was kind. Then when I thought he would be effusive he was merely polite. When I thought he would be annoyed to hear my voice on the telephone he was pleased. When I thought he would turn against me because I had treated him rather coldly, he was more anxious than ever to be with me and went to great trouble and expense so that we could spend a little time together. Then when I made up my mind that he was the man for me, he suddenly called the whole thing off.

It seemed sudden to me even though for the last month I could feel him drawing away. For instance, he didn't write as often as he had before, and then when we were together he said more unkind things to me than he ever had before. When he left, I knew he was thinking it over. He took a month to think it over, and I knew it was fifty-fifty he would come to the point of saying what he did.

I suppose it seemed sudden because of the hopes I had for him and me by then, and the dreams I had about us—some of the usual dreams about a nice house and nice babies and the two of us together in the house working in the evening while the babies were asleep, and then some other dreams, about how we would travel together, and about how I would learn to play the banjo or the mandolin so that I could play with him, because he has a lovely tenor voice. Now, when I picture myself playing the banjo or the mandolin, the idea seems silly.

The way it all ended was that he called me up on a day he didn't usually call me and said he had finally come to a decision. Then he said that because he had had trouble figuring all this out, he had made some notes about what he was going to say and he asked me if I would mind if he read them. I said I would mind very much. He said he would at least have to look at them now and then as he talked.

Then he talked in a very reasonable way about how bad the chances were for us to be happy together, and about changing over to a friendship now before it was too late. I said he was talking about me as though I were an old tire that might blow out on the highway. He thought that was funny. 40

We talked about how he had felt about me at various times, and how I had felt about him at various times, and it seemed that these feelings hadn't matched very well. Then, when I wanted to know exactly how he had felt about me from the very beginning, trying to find out, really, what was the most he had ever felt, he made this very plain statement about how there were things about me that he hadn't liked from the very beginning. He wasn't trying to be unkind, but just very clear. I told him I wouldn't ask him what these things were but I knew I would have to go and think about it.

I didn't like hearing there were things about me that bothered him. It was shocking to hear that someone I loved had never liked certain things about me. Of 50 course there were a few things I didn't like about him too, for instance an affectation in his manner involving the introduction of foreign phrases into his conversation, but although I had noticed these things, I had never said it to him in quite this way. But if I try to be logical, I have to think that after all there may be a few things wrong with me. Then the problem is to figure out what these things are.

For several days, after we talked, I tried to think about this, and I came up with some possibilities. Maybe I didn't talk enough. He likes to talk a lot and he likes other people to talk a lot. I'm not very talkative, or at least not in the way he probably likes. I have some good ideas from time to time, but not much informa- tion. I can only talk for a long time when it's about something boring. Maybe I 60 talked too much about which foods he should be eating. I worry about the way people eat and tell them what they should eat, which is a tiresome thing to do, something my ex-husband never liked either. Maybe I mentioned my ex-husband too often, so that he thought my ex-husband was still on my mind, which wasn't true. He might have been irritated by the fact that he couldn't kiss me in the street for fear of getting poked in the eye by my glasses—or maybe he didn't even like being with a woman who wore glasses, maybe he didn't like always having to look at my eyes through this blue-tinted glass. Or maybe he doesn't like people who write things on index cards, diet plans on little index cards and plot summaries on big index cards. I don't like it much myself, and I don't do it all the time. It's just a 70 way I have of trying to get my life in order. But he might have come across some of those index cards.

I couldn't think of much else that would have bothered him from the very beginning. Then I decided I would never be able to think of the things about me that bothered him. Whatever I thought of would probably not be the same things. And anyway, I wasn't going to go on trying to identify these things, because even if I knew what they were I wouldn't be able to do anything about them.

Late in the conversation, he tried to tell me how excited he was about his new plan for the summer. Now that he wasn't going to be with me, he thought he would travel down to Venezuela, to visit some friends who were doing anthropo- 80 logical work in the jungle. I told him I didn't want to hear about that.

While we talked on the phone, I was drinking some wine left over from a large party I had given. After we hung up I immediately picked up the phone again and made a series of phone calls, and while I talked, I finished one of the leftover bottles of wine and started on another that was sweeter than the first, and then finished that one too. First I called a few people here in the city, then when it got too late for that I called a few people in California, and when it got too late to go on calling California I called someone in England who had just woken up and was not in a very good mood.

Between one phone call and the next I would sometimes walk by the window and look up at the moon, which was in its first quarter but remarkably bright, and think of him and then wonder when I would stop thinking of him every time I saw the moon. The reason I thought of him when I saw the moon was that during the five days and four nights he and I were first together, the moon was waxing and then full, the nights were clear, we were in the country, where you notice the sky more, and every night, early or late, we would walk outdoors together, partly to get away from the various members of our families who were in the house and partly just to take pleasure in the meadows and the woods under the moonlight. The dirt road that sloped up away from the house into the woods was full of ruts and rocks, so that we kept stumbling against each other and more tightly into each other's arms. We talked about how nice it would be to bring a bed out into the meadow and lie down on it in the moonlight.

The next time the moon was full, I was back in the city, and I saw it out the window of a new apartment. I thought to myself that a month had passed since he and I were together, and that it had passed very slowly. After that, every time the moon was full, shining on the leafy, tall trees in the back yards here, and on the flat tar roofs, and then on the bare trees and snowy ground in the winter, I would think to myself that another month had passed, sometimes quickly and sometimes slowly. I liked counting the months that way.

He and I always seemed to be counting the time as it passed and waiting for it to pass so that the day would come when we would be together again. That was one reason he said he couldn't go on with it. And maybe he's right, it isn't too late, we will change over to a friendship, and he will talk to me now and then long distance, mostly about his work or my work, and give me good advice or a plan of action when I need one, then call himself something like my *"éminence grise."*[1]

When I stopped making my phone calls, I was too dizzy to go to sleep, because of the wine, so I turned on the television and watched some police dramas, some old situation comedies, and finally a show about unusual people across the country. I turned the set off at five in the morning when the sky was light, and I fell asleep right away.

It's true that by the time the night was over I wasn't worrying anymore about what was wrong with me. At that hour of the morning I can usually get myself out to the end of something like a long dock with water all around where I'm not touched by such worries. But there will always come a time later that day or a day or two after when I ask myself that difficult question once, or over and over again,

---

1. Literally a gray eminence—an advisor or power behind the throne. Coming from a young man, the reference is intentionally ironic.

a useless question, really, since I'm not the one who can answer it and anyone else who tries will come up with a different answer, though of course all the answers together may add up to the right one, if there is such a thing as a right answer to a question like that.   [1976]

Questions for Discussion and Writing

1. How well do the man and the narrator know each other? How unhappy is the narrator over the end of their relationship?
2. How do you assess the tone of the story?
3. Is this a love story? What features of a conventional love story does it have? What conventions does it lack? What innovations does it have?
4. The narrator ponders the man's comment that there were things about her he had not liked from the beginning; she speculates at length by herself and considers discussing the matter with his friends. Why did she not want to ask the man what these things were when they were talking on the phone?
5. Does the story reveal anything "wrong" with the narrator? With the man?
6. What, according to the story, is the potential to know others? to know oneself? for love to be mutual or reciprocal?

❧ JAMAICA KINCAID
(b. 1949)

At the Bottom of the River

Jamaica Kincaid's experiments in the lyrical short story and her controversial novels have earned her a large following. She was born Elaine Potter Richardson in St. John's Antigua, West Indies. She remembers the first nine years of her childhood as an ideally happy time, for as an only child, she enjoyed the full attention of her parents, especially her mother. When her younger brothers were born, however, Jamaica was suddenly thrust into the background, a difficult "betrayal."

Kincaid excelled in school and read voraciously (her favorite novel was *Jane Eyre*), but she was never encouraged either by her family or teachers to pursue further education. Frustrated with the lack of opportunities at home, she persuaded her parents to let her go to Scarsdale, New York, at age sixteen to serve as an au pair for a wealthy family. Later, she moved to New York City and, after earning a high school diploma, received a scholarship to study photography at Franconia College in New Hampshire. Returning to New York, she worked in various jobs, often outraging her bosses by flaunting "punk" styles before punk existed. Meanwhile, she was publishing articles in magazines for teenage girls. When the *New Yorker* accepted an essay, she formed a friendship with an editor, who encouraged her to continue writing. "Girl," was accepted by the *New Yorker* in 1978, and her collection of stories *At the Bottom of the River* (1983) made her an overnight celebrity.

Stories like "At the Bottom of the River" are sometimes criticized for being obscure. Certainly the story challenges comfortable expectations about what a story should be by using techniques usually associated with the essay. Nevertheless, in their stylistic virtuosity and honesty of feeling, Kincaid's stories repay the attentive reader with a wealth of poetry and insight.

THIS, THEN, IS the terrain. The steepest mountains, thickly covered, where huge, sharp rocks might pose the greatest danger and where only the bravest, surest, most deeply arched of human feet will venture, where a large stream might flow, and, flowing perilously, having only a deep ambition to see itself mighty and powerful, bends and curves and dips in many directions, making a welcome and easy path for each idle rill and babbling brook, each trickle of rain fallen on land that lies sloping; and that stream, at last swelled to a great, fast, flowing body of water, falls over a ledge with a roar, a loudness that is more than the opposite of complete silence, then rushes over dry, flat land in imperfect curves—curves as if made by a small boy playfully dragging a toy behind him—then hugs closely to 10 the paths made, ruthlessly conquering the flat plain, the steep ridge, the grassy bed; all day, all day, a stream might flow so, and then it winds its way to a gorge in the earth, a basin of measurable depth and breadth, and so collects itself in a pool: now comes the gloaming, for day will end, and the stream, its flow stilled and gathered up, so that trees growing firmly on its banks, their barks white, their trunks bent, their branches covered with leaves and reaching up, up, are reflected in the depths, awaits the eye, the hand, the foot that shall then give all this a meaning.

But what shall that be? For now here is a man who lives in a world bereft of its very nature. He lies on his bed as if alone in a small room, waiting and waiting 20 and waiting. For what does he wait? He is not yet complete, so he cannot conceive of what it is he waits for. He cannot conceive of the fields of wheat, their kernels ripe and almost bursting, and how happy the sight will make someone. He cannot conceive of the union of opposites, or, for that matter, their very existence. He cannot conceive of flocks of birds in migratory flight, or that night will follow day and season follow season in a seemingly endless cycle, and the beauty and the pleasure and the purpose that might come from all this. He cannot conceive of the wind that ravages the coastline, casting asunder men and cargo, temporarily interrupting the smooth flow of commerce. He cannot conceive of the individual who, on looking up from some dreary, everyday task, is struck just then by the com- 30 pleteness of the above and the below and his own spirit resting in between; or how that same individual, suddenly rounding a corner, catches his own reflection, transparent and suspended in a pane of glass, and so smiles to himself with shy admiration. He cannot conceive of the woman and the child at play—an image so often regarded as a symbol of human contentment; or how calamity will attract the cold and disinterested gaze of children. He cannot conceive of a Sunday: the peal of church bells, the sound of seraphic voices in harmony, the closeness of congregation, the soothing words of praise and the much longed for presence of an unearthly glory. He cannot conceive of how emotions, varying in color and in-

tensity, will rapidly heighten, reach an unbearable pitch, then finally explode in   40
the silence of the evening air. He cannot conceive of the chance invention that
changes again and again and forever the great turbulence that is human history.
Not for him can thought crash over thought in random and violent succession,
leaving his brain suffused in contradiction. He sits in nothing, this man: not in a
full space, not in emptiness, not in darkness, not in light or glimmer of. He sits in
nothing, in nothing, in nothing.

Look! A man steps out of bed, a good half hour after his wife, and washes
himself. He sits down on a chair and at a table that he made with his own hands
(the tips of his fingers are stained a thin chocolate brown from nicotine). His wife   50
places before him a bowl of porridge, some cheese, some bread that has been buttered, two boiled eggs, a large cup of tea. He eats. The goats, the sheep, the cows
are driven to pasture. A dog barks. His child now enters the room. Walking over,
she bends to kiss his hand, which is resting on his knee, and he, waiting for her
head to come up, kisses her on the forehead with lips he has purposely moistened.
"Sir, it is wet," she says. And he laughs at her as she dries her forehead with the
back of her hand. Now, clasping his wife to him, he bids her goodbye, opens the
door, and stops. For what does he stop? What does he see? He sees before him
himself, standing in sawdust, measuring a hole, just dug, in the ground, putting
decorative grooves in a bannister, erecting columns, carving the head of a cherub   60
over a door, lighting a cigarette, pursing his lips, holding newly planed wood at an
angle and looking at it with one eye closed; standing with both hands in his pockets, the thumbs out, and rocking back and forth on his heels, he surveys a small
accomplishment—a last nail driven in just so. Crossing and recrossing the threshold, he watches the sun, a violent red, set on the horizon, he hears the birds fly
home, he sees the insects dancing in the last warmth of the day's light, he hears
himself sing out loud:

> Now the day is over,
> Night is drawing nigh;   70
> Shadows of the evening
> Steal across the sky.

All this he sees (and hears). And who is this man, really? So solitary, his eyes
sometimes aglow, his heart beating at an abnormal rate with a joy he cannot identify or explain. What is the virtue in him? And then again, what can it matter? For
tomorrow the oak will be felled, the trestle will break, the cow's hooves will be
made into glue.

But so he stands, forever, crossing and recrossing the threshold, his head
lifted up, held aloft and stiff with vanity; then his eyes shift and he sees and he   80
sees, and he is weighed down. First lifted up, then weighed down—always he is
so. Shall he seek comfort now? And in what? He seeks out the living fossils. There
is the shell of the pearly nautilus lying amidst colored chalk and powdered ink
and India rubber in an old tin can, in memory of a day spent blissfully at the sea.
The flatworm is now a parasite. Reflect. There is the earth, its surface apparently
stilled, its atmosphere hospitable. And yet here stand pile upon pile of rocks of an

enormous size, riven and worn down from the pressure of the great seas, now receded. And here the large veins of gold, the bubbling sulfurous fountains, the mountains covered with hot lava; at the bottom of some caves lies the black dust, and below that rich clay sediment, and trapped between the layers are filaments of winged beasts and remnants of invertebrates. "And where shall I be?" asks this man. Then he says, "My body, my soul." But quickly he averts his eyes and feels himself now, hands pressed tightly against his chest. He is standing on the threshold once again, and, looking up, he sees his wife holding out toward him his brown felt hat (he had forgotten it); his child crossing the street, joining the throng of children on their way to school, a mixture of broken sentences, mispronounced words, laughter, budding malice, and energy abundant. He looks at the house he has built with his own hands, the books he has read standing on shelves, the fruit-bearing trees that he nursed from seedlings, the larder filled with food that he has provided. He shifts the weight of his body from one foot to the other, in uncertainty but also weighing, weighing . . . He imagines that in one hand he holds emptiness and yearning and in the other desire fulfilled. He thinks of tenderness and love and faith and hope and, yes, goodness. He contemplates the beauty in the common thing: the sun rising up out of the huge, shimmering expanse of water that is the sea; it rises up each day as if made anew, as if for the first time. "Sing again. Sing now," he says in his heart, for he feels the cool breeze at the back of his neck. But again and again he feels the futility in all that. For stretching out before him is a silence so dreadful, a vastness, its length and breadth and depth immeasurable. Nothing.

The branches were dead; a fly hung dead on the branches, its fragile body fluttering in the wind as if it were remnants of a beautiful gown; a beetle had fed on the body of the fly but now lay dead, too. Death on death on death. Dead lay everything. The ground stretching out from the river no longer a verdant pasture but parched and cracked with tiny fissures running up and down and into each other; and, seen from high above, the fissures presented beauty: not a pleasure to the eye but beauty all the same; still, dead, dead it was. Dead lay everything that had lived and dead also lay everything that would live. All had had or would have its season. And what should it matter that its season lasted five billion years or five minutes? There it is now, dead, vanished into darkness, banished from life. First living briefly, then dead in eternity. How vainly I struggle against this. Toil, toil, night and day. Here a house is built. Here a monument is erected to commemorate something called a good deed, or even in remembrance of a woman with exceptional qualities, and all that she loved and all that she did. Here are some children, and immeasurable is the love and special attention lavished on them. Vanished now is the house. Vanished now is the monument. Silent now are the children. I recall the house, I recall the monument, I summon up the children from the eternity of darkness, and sometimes, briefly, they appear, though always slightly shrouded, always as if they had emerged from mounds of ashes, chipped, tarnished, in fragments, or large parts missing: the ribbons, for instance, gone from the children's hair. These children whom I loved best—better than the monument, better than the house—once were so beautiful that they were thought unearthly. Dead is the past. Dead shall the future be. And what stands before my eyes, as soon as I turn my back, dead is that, too. Shall I shed tears? Sorrow is bound to death. Grief is bound to death. Each moment is not as fragile and fleeting as I once thought. Each moment is hard and lasting and so holds much that I must mourn for. And so what a bitter thing to say to me: that life is the intrusion, that to embrace a thing as beauty is the intrusion, that to believe a thing true and therefore undeniable, that is the intrusion; and, yes, false are all appearances. What a bitter thing to say to me, I who for time uncountable have always seen myself as newly 140 born, filled with a truth and a beauty that could not be denied, living in a world of light that I called eternal, a world that can know no end. I now know regret. And that, too, is bound to death. And what do I regret? Surely not that I stand in the knowledge of the presence of death. For knowledge is a good thing; you have said that. What I regret is that in the face of death and all that it is and all that it shall be I stand powerless, that in the face of death my will, to which everything I have ever known bends, stands as if it were nothing more than a string caught in the early-morning wind.

Now! There lived a small creature, and it lived as both male and female inside a mound that it made on the ground, its body wholly covered with short fur, 150 broadly striped, in the colors field-yellow and field-blue. It hunted a honeybee once, and when the bee, in bee anger and fright, stung the creature on the corner of the mouth, the pain was so unbearably delicious that never did this creature hunt a honeybee again. It walked over and over the wide space that surrounded the mound in which it lived. As it walked over and over the wide ground that surrounded the mound in which it lived, it watched its own feet sink into the grass and heard the ever so slight sound the grass made as it gave way to the pressure, and as it saw and heard, it felt a pleasure unbearably delicious, and, each time, the pleasure unbearably delicious was new to this creature. It lived so, banking up each unbearably delicious pleasure in deep, dark memory unspeakable, hoping to 160 perhaps one day throw the memories into a dungeon, or burn them on an ancient pyre, or banish them to land barren, but now it kept them in this way. Then all its unbearably delicious pleasure it kept free, each thing taken, time in, time out, as if it were new, just born. It lived so in a length of time that may be measured to be no less than the blink of an eye, or no more than one hundred millenniums. This creature lived inside and outside its mound, remembering and forgetting, pain and pleasure so equally balanced, each assigned to what it judged a natural conclusion, yet one day it did vanish, leaving no sign of its existence, except for a small spot, which glowed faintly in the darkness that surrounded it. I divined this, and how natural to me that has become. I divined this, and it is not a specter but something 170 that stood here. I show it to you. I yearn to build a monument to it, something of dust, since I now know—and so soon, so soon—what dust really is.

"Death is natural," you said to me, in such a flat, matter-of-fact way, and then you laughed—a laugh so piercing that I felt my eardrums shred, I felt myself mocked. Yet I can see that a tree is natural, that the sea is natural, that the twitter of a twittering bird is natural to a twittering bird. I can see with my own eyes the tree; it stands with limbs spread wide and laden with ripe fruit, its roots planted firmly in the rich soil, and that seems natural to me. I can see with my own eyes the sea, now with a neap tide, its surface smooth and calm; then in the next moment comes a breeze, soft, and small ripples turn into wavelets conquering 180 wavelets, and that seems natural to me again. And the twittering bird twitters away, and that bears a special irritation, though not the irritation of the sting of the evening fly, and that special irritation is mostly ignored, and what could be more natural than that? But death bears no relation to the tree, the sea, the twittering bird. How much more like the earth spinning on its invisible axis death is, and so I might want to reach out with my hand and make the earth stand still, as if it were a bicycle standing on its handlebars upside down, the wheels spun in passing by a pair of idle hands, then stilled in passing by yet another pair of idle hands. Inevitable to life is death and not inevitable to death is life. Inevitable. How the word weighs on my tongue. I glean this: a worm winds its way between furrow and furrow in a garden, its miserable form shuddering, dreading the sharp open beak of any common bird winging its way overhead; the bird, then taking to the open air, spreads its wings in majestic flight, and how noble and triumphant is this bird in flight; but look now, there comes a boy on horseback, his body taut and eager, his hand holding bow and arrow, his aim pointed and definite, and in this way is the bird made dead. The worm, the bird, the boy. And what of the boy? His ends are numberless. I glean again the death in life. 190

Is life, then, a violent burst of light, like flint struck sharply in the dark? If so, I must continually strive to exist between the day and the day. I see myself as I was as a child. How much I was loved and how much I loved. No small turn of my head, no wrinkle on my brow, no parting of my lips is lost to me. How much I loved myself and how much I was loved by my mother. My mother made up elaborate tales of the origins of ordinary food, just so that I would eat it. My mother sat on some stone steps, her voluminous skirt draped in folds and falling down between her parted legs, and I, playing some distance away, glanced over my shoulder and saw her face—a face that was to me of such wondrous beauty: the lips like a moon in its first and last quarter, a nose with a bony bridge and wide nostrils that flared out and trembled visibly in excitement, ears the lobes of which were large and soft and silk-like; and what pleasure it gave me to press them between my thumb and forefinger. How I worshipped this beauty, and in my childish heart I would always say to it, "Yes, yes, yes." And, glancing over my shoulder, yet again I would silently send to her words of love and adoration, and I would receive from her, in turn and in silence, words of love and adoration. Once, I stood on a platform with three dozen girls, arranged in rows of twelve, all wearing identical white linen dresses with corded sashes of green tied around the waist, all with faces the color of stones found lying on the beach of volcanic islands, singing with the utmost earnestness, in as nearly perfect a harmony as could be managed, minds blank of interpretation: 200

210

220

> In our deep vaulted cell
> The charm we'll prepare
> Too dreadful a practice
> For this open air.

Time and time again, I am filled up with all that I thought life might be— glorious moment upon glorious moment of contentment and joy and love running into each other and forming an extraordinary chain: a hymn sung in rounds. Oh, the fields in which I have walked and gazed and gazed at the small cuplike flowers, in wanton hues of red and gold and blue, swaying in the day breeze, and from which I had no trouble tearing myself away, since their end was unknown to me.

I walked to the mouth of the river, and it was then still in the old place near the lime-tree grove. The water was clear and still. I looked in, and at the bottom of the river I could see a house, and it was a house of only one room, with an A-shaped roof. The house was made of rough, heavy planks of unpainted wood, and the roof was of galvanized iron and was painted red. The house had four windows on each of its four sides, and one door. Though the door and the windows were all open, I could not see anything inside and I had no desire to see what was inside. All around the house was a wide stretch of green—green grass freshly mowed a uniform length. The green, green grass of uniform length extended from the house for a distance I could not measure or know just from looking at it. Beyond the green, green grass were lots of pebbles, and they were a white-gray, as if they had been in water for many years and then placed in the sun to dry. They, too, were of a uniform size, and as they lay together they seemed to form a direct contrast to the grass. Then, at the line where the grass ended and the pebbles began, there were flowers: yellow and blue irises, red poppies, daffodils, marigolds. They grew as if wild, intertwined, as if no hand had ever offered guidance or restraint. There were no other living things in the water—no birds, no vertebrates or invertebrates, no fragile insects—and even though the water flowed in the natural way of a river, none of the things that I could see at the bottom moved. The grass, in little wisps, didn't bend slightly; the petals of the flowers didn't tremble. Everything was so true, though—that is, true to itself—and I had no doubt that the things I saw were themselves and not resemblances or representatives. The grass was the grass, and it was the grass without qualification. The green of the grass was green, and I knew it to be so and not partially green, or a kind of green, but green, and the green from which all other greens might come. And it was so with everything else that lay so still at the bottom of the river. It all lay there not like a picture but like a true thing and a different kind of true thing: one that I had never known before. Then I noticed something new: it was the way everything lit up. It was as if the sun shone not from where I stood but from a place way beyond and beneath the ground of the grass and the pebbles. How strange the light was, how it filled up everything, and yet nothing cast a shadow. I looked and looked at what was before me in wonderment and curiosity. What should this mean to me? And what should I do on knowing its meaning? A woman now appeared at the one door. She wore no clothes. Her hair was long and so very black, and it stood out in a straight line away from her head, as if she had commanded it to be that way. I could not see her face. I could see her feet, and I saw that her insteps were high, as if she had been used to climbing high mountains. Her skin was the color of brown clay, and she looked like a statue, liquid and gleaming, just before it is to be put in a kiln. She walked toward the place where the grass ended and the pebbles began. Perhaps it was a great distance, it took such a long time, and yet she never tired. When she got to the place where the green grass ended and the pebbles began, she stopped, then raised her right hand to her forehead, as if to guard her eyes against a far-off glare. She stood on tiptoe, her body swaying from side to side, and she looked at something that was far, far away from where she stood. I got down on my knees and I looked, too. It was a long time before I could see what it was that she saw.

I saw a world in which the sun and the moon shone at the same time. They appeared in a way I had never seen before: the sun was The Sun, a creation of Benevolence and Purpose and not a star among many stars, with a predictable cycle and a predictable end; the moon, too, was The Moon, and it was the creation of Beauty and Purpose and not a body subject to a theory of planetary evolution. The sun and the moon shone uniformly onto everything. Together, they made up the light, and the light fell on everything, and everything seemed transparent, as if the light went through each thing, so that nothing could be hidden. The light shone and shone and fell and fell, but there were no shadows. In this world, on this terrain, there was no day and there was no night. And there were no seasons, and so no storms or cold from which to take shelter. And in this world were many things blessed with unquestionable truth and purpose and beauty. There were steep mountains, there were valleys, there were seas, there were plains of grass, there were deserts, there were rivers, there were forests, there were vertebrates and invertebrates, there were mammals, there were reptiles, there were creatures of the dry land and the water, and there were birds. And they lived in this world not yet divided, not yet examined, not yet numbered, and not yet dead. I looked at this world as it revealed itself to me—how new, how new—and I longed to go there.

I stood above the land and the sea and looked back up at myself as I stood on the bank of the mouth of the river. I saw that my face was round in shape, that my irises took up almost all the space in my eyes, and that my eyes were brown, with yellow-colored and black-colored flecks; that my mouth was large and closed; that my nose, too, was large and my nostrils broken circles; my arms were long, my hands large, the veins pushing up against my skin; my legs were long, and, judging from the shape of them, I was used to running long distances. I saw that my hair grew out long from my head and in a disorderly way, as if I were a strange tree, with many branches. I saw my skin, and it was red. It was the red of flames when a fire is properly fed, the red of flames when a fire burns alone in a darkened place, and not the red of flames when a fire is burning in a cozy room. I saw myself clearly, as if I were looking through a pane of glass.

I stood above the land and the sea, and I felt that I was not myself as I had once known myself to be: I was not made up of flesh and blood and muscles and bones and tissue and cells and vital organs but was made up of my will, and over my will I had complete dominion. I entered the sea then. The sea was without color, and it was without anything that I had known before. It was still, having no currents. It was as warm as freshly spilled blood, and I moved through it as if I had always done so, as if it were a perfectly natural element to me. I moved through deep caverns, but they were without darkness and sudden shifts and turns. I stepped over great ridges and huge bulges of stones, I stooped down and touched the deepest bottom; I stretched myself out and covered end to end a vast crystal plane. Nothing lived here. No plant grew here, no huge sharp-toothed creature with an ancestral memory of hunter and prey searching furiously for food, no sudden shift of wind to disturb the water. How good this water was. How good that I should know no fear. I sat on the edge of a basin. I felt myself swing my feet back and forth in a carefree manner, as if I were a child who had just spent the whole day head bent over sums but now sat in a garden filled with flowers in bloom colored vermillion and gold, the sounds of birds chirping, goats bleating, home from the pasture, the smell of vanilla from the kitchen, which should surely mean pudding with dinner, eyes darting here and there but resting on nothing in particular, a mind conscious of nothing—not happiness, not contentment, and not the memory of night, which soon would come.

I stood up on the edge of the basin and felt myself move. But what self? For I had no feet, or hands, or head, or heart. It was as if those things—my feet, my hands, my head, my heart—having once been there, were now stripped away, as if I had been dipped again and again, over and over, in a large vat filled with some precious elements and were now reduced to something I yet had no name for. I had no name for the thing I had become, so new was it to me, except that I did not exist in pain or pleasure, east or west or north or south, or up or down, or past or present or future, or real or not real. I stood as if I were a prism, many-sided and transparent, refracting and reflecting light as it reached me, light that never could be destroyed. And how beautiful I became. Yet this beauty was not in the way of an ancient city seen after many centuries in ruins, or a woman who has just brushed her hair, or a man who searches for a treasure, or a child who cries immediately on being born, or an apple just picked standing alone on a gleaming white plate, or tiny beads of water left over from a sudden downpour of rain, per-haps—hanging delicately from the bare limbs of trees—or the sound the hum-mingbird makes with its wings as it propels itself through the earthly air.

Yet what was that light in which I stood? How singly then will the heart de-sire and pursue the small glowing thing resting in the distance, surrounded by darkness; how, then, if on conquering the distance the heart embraces the small glowing thing until heart and glowing thing are indistinguishable and in this way the darkness is made less? For now a door might suddenly be pushed open and the morning light might rush in, revealing to me creation and a force whose na-ture is implacable, unmindful of any of the individual needs of existence, and without knowledge of future or past. I might then come to believe in a being whose impartiality I cannot now or ever fully understand and accept. I ask, When shall I, too, be extinguished, so that I cannot be recognized even from my bones? I covet the rocks and the mountains their silence. And so, emerging from my pit, the one I sealed up securely, the one to which I have consigned all my deeds that I care not to reveal—emerging from this pit, I step into a room and I see that the lamp is lit. In the light of the lamp, I see some books, I see a chair, I see a table, I see a pen; I see a bowl of ripe fruit, a bottle of milk, a flute made of wood, the clothes that I will wear. And as I see these things in the light of the lamp, all per-ishable and transient, how bound up I know I am to all that is human endeavor, to all that is past and to all that shall be, to all that shall be lost and leave no trace. I claim these things then—mine—and now feel myself grow solid and complete, my name filling up my mouth.   [1975]

Questions for Writing and Discussion

1. Who is the "I" who narrates the story?
2. What conflicts or tensions are in the story? How are they resolved?
3. Analyze the contrast between the general and the particular, the abstract and the concrete. How do these contrasts relate to the conflicts and tensions in the story?
4. Is there any order or structure to the events of the story, or are they arranged arbitrarily? Could the order be changed without affecting the story? Explain.
5. Describe and analyze the author's style and use of language in this story. What is your opinion of the style? What effect does it have on you? How does Kincaid achieve her effects?

✒ ANGELA CARTER
(1940–1992)

The Bloody Chamber

Angela Carter's ideas are often worked out through rewritten myths and fairy tales, where the elements of magic, violence, innocence, and sexuality are already present. These are not merely retellings of familiar stories, however, but daringly original renditions that completely transform familiar material.

She was born Angela Stalker in Eastbourne, Sussex, and later moved with her mother to a village in South Yorkshire to avoid the Blitz of World War II. Like her father, she worked as a journalist for a time before marrying and then entering university at Bristol, where she specialized in medieval literature. Her first novel was written while still a student, and her second, *The Magic Toyshop* won the Rhys Memorial prize for 1967. This novel earned for her a reputation as a Magical Realist for its combination of fantasy and gothic horror. Winning a Somerset Maugham award in 1979 enabled her to spend two years in Japan, where she wrote a series of perceptive essays on Japanese and Western cultures. A non-fiction work, *The Sadeian Woman* (1979), shows the strongly feminist views that were to mark her work from then on.

Carter's style explodes with energetic, original language: passionate, metaphorical, at times almost overripe. It is the perfect medium for the sense of claustrophobia and perversion that runs through many of her stories.

I REMEMBER HOW, that night, I lay awake in the wagon-lit[1] in a tender, delicious ecstasy of excitement, my burning cheek pressed against the impeccable linen of the pillow and the pounding of my heart mimicking that of the great pistons ceaselessly thrusting the train that bore me through the night, away from Paris,

---

1. A railroad sleeping car.

away from girlhood, away from the white, enclosed quietude of my mother's apartment, into the unguessable country of marriage.

And I remember I tenderly imagined how, at this very moment, my mother
would be moving slowly about the narrow bedroom I had left behind for ever,
folding up and putting away all my little relics, the tumbled garments I would not
need any more, the scores for which there had been no room in my trunks, the 10
concert programmes I'd abandoned; she would linger over this torn ribbon and
that faded photograph with all the half-joyous, half-sorrowful emotions of a
woman on her daughter's wedding day. And, in the midst of my bridal triumph, I
felt a pang of loss as if, when he put the gold band on my finger, I had, in some
way, ceased to be her child in becoming his wife.

Are you sure, she'd said when they delivered the gigantic box that held the
wedding dress he'd bought me, wrapped up in tissue paper and red ribbon like a
Christmas gift of crystallized fruit. Are you sure you love him? There was a dress
for her, too; black silk, with the dull, prismatic sheen of oil on water, finer than
anything she'd worn since that adventurous girlhood in Indo-China, daughter of a 20
rich tea planter. My eagle-featured, indomitable mother; what other student at the
Conservatoire could boast that her mother had outfaced a junkful of Chinese pi-
rates, nursed a village through a visitation of the plague, shot a man-eating tiger
with her own hand and all before she was as old as I?

"Are you sure you love him?"

"I'm sure I want to marry him," I said.

And would say no more. She sighed, as if it was with reluctance that she
might at last banish the spectre of poverty from its habitual place at our meagre
table. For my mother herself had gladly, scandalously, defiantly beggared herself
for love; and, one fine day, her gallant soldier never returned from the wars, leav- 30
ing his wife and child a legacy of tears that never quite dried, a cigar box full of
medals and the antique service revolver that my mother, grown magnificently eccentric in hardship, kept always in her reticule, in case—how I teased her—she
was surprised by footpads[2] on her way home from the grocer's shop.

Now and then a starburst of lights spattered the drawn blinds as if the railway company had lit up all the stations through which we passed in celebration of
the bride. My satin nightdress had just been shaken from its wrappings; it had
slipped over my young girl's pointed breasts and shoulders, supple as a garment of
heavy water, and now teasingly caressed me, egregious, insinuating, nudging between my thighs as I shifted restlessly in my narrow berth. His kiss, his kiss with 40
tongue and teeth in it and a rasp of beard, had hinted to me, though with the
same exquisite tact as this nightdress he'd given me, of the wedding night, which
would be voluptuously deferred until we lay in his great ancestral bed in the sea-
girt, pinnacled domain that lay, still, beyond the grasp of my imagination . . . that
magic place, the fairy castle whose walls were made of foam, that legendary habi-
tation in which he had been born. To which, one day, I might bear an heir. Our
destination, my destiny.

Above the syncopated roar of the train, I could hear his even, steady breathing. Only the communicating door kept me from my husband and it stood open.

_____
2. Thieves; muggers.

If I rose up on my elbow, I could see the dark, leonine shape of his head and my nostrils caught a whiff of the opulent male scent of leather and spices that always accompanied him and sometimes, during his courtship, had been the only hint he gave me that he had come into my mother's sitting room, for, though he was a big man, he moved as softly as if all his shoes had soles of velvet, as if his footfall turned the carpet into snow.

He had loved to surprise me in my abstracted solitude at the piano. He would tell them not to announce him, then soundlessly open the door and softly creep up behind me with his bouquet of hot-house flowers or his box of marrons glacés, lay his offering upon the keys and clasp his hands over my eyes as I was lost in a Debussy prelude. But that perfume of spiced leather always betrayed him; after my first shock, I was forced always to mimic surprise, so that he would not be disappointed.

He was older than I. He was much older than I; there were streaks of pure silver in his dark mane. But his strange, heavy, almost waxen face was not lined by experience. Rather, experience seemed to have washed it perfectly smooth, like a stone on a beach whose fissures have been eroded by successive tides. And sometimes that face, in stillness when he listened to me playing, with the heavy eyelids folded over eyes that always disturbed me by their absolute absence of light, seemed to me like a mask, as if his real face, the face that truly reflected all the life he had led in the world before he met me, before, even, I was born, as though that face lay underneath this mask. Or else, elsewhere. As though he had laid by the face in which he had lived for so long in order to offer my youth a face unsigned by the years.

And, elsewhere, I might see him plain. Elsewhere. But, where?

In, perhaps, that castle to which the train now took us, that marvellous castle in which he had been born.

Even when he asked me to marry him, and I said: "Yes," still he did not lose that heavy, fleshy composure of his. I know it must seem a curious analogy, a man with a flower, but sometimes he seemed to me like a lily. Yes. A lily. Possessed of that strange, ominous calm of a sentient vegetable, like one of those cobra-headed, funereal lilies whose white sheaths are curled out of a flesh as thick and tensely yielding to the touch as vellum. When I said that I would marry him, not one muscle in his face stirred, but he let out a long, extinguished sigh. I thought: Oh! how he must want me! And it was as though the imponderable weight of his desire was a force I might not withstand, not by virtue of its violence but because of its very gravity.

He had the ring ready in a leather box lined with crimson velvet, a fire opal the size of a pigeon's egg set in a complicated circle of dark antique gold. My old nurse, who still lived with my mother and me, squinted at the ring askance: opals are bad luck, she said. But this opal had been his own mother's ring, and his grandmother's, and her mother's before that, given to an ancestor by Catherine de Medici . . . every bride that came to the castle wore it, time out of mind. And did he give it to his other wives and have it back from them? asked the old woman rudely; yet she was a snob. She hid her incredulous joy at my marital coup—her little Marquise—behind a façade of fault-finding. But, here, she touched me. I shrugged and turned my back pettishly on her. I did not want to remember how he had loved other women before me, but the knowledge often teased me in the threadbare self-confidence of the small hours.

I was seventeen and knew nothing of the world; my Marquis had been married before, more than once, and I remained a little bemused that, after those others, he should now have chosen me. Indeed, was he not still in mourning for his last wife? Tsk, tsk, went my old nurse. And even my mother had been reluctant to see her girl whisked off by a man so recently bereaved. A Romanian countess, a lady of high fashion. Dead just three short months before I met him, a boating accident, at his home, in Brittany. They never found her body but I rummaged through the back copies of the society magazines my old nanny kept in a trunk under her bed and tracked down her photograph. The sharp muzzle of a pretty, witty, naughty monkey; such potent and bizarre charm, of a dark, bright, wild yet worldly thing whose natural habitat must have been some luxurious interior decorator's jungle filled with potted palms and tame, squawking parakeets.

Before that? *Her* face is common property; everyone painted her but the Redon engraving I liked best, *The Evening Star Walking on the Rim of Night*. To see her skeletal, enigmatic grace, you would never think she had been a barmaid in a café in Montmartre until Puvis de Chavannes saw her and had her expose her flat breasts and elongated thighs to his brush. And yet it was the absinthe doomed her, or so they said.

The first of all his ladies? That sumptuous diva; I had heard her sing Isolde, precociously musical child that I was, taken to the opera for a birthday treat. My first opera; I had heard her sing Isolde. With what white-hot passion had she burned from the stage! So that you could tell she would die young. We sat high up, halfway to heaven in the gods, yet she half-blinded me. And my father, still alive (oh, so long ago), took hold of my sticky little hand, to comfort me, in the last act, yet all I heard was the glory of her voice.

Married three times within my own brief lifetime to three different graces, now, as if to demonstrate the eclecticism of his taste, he had invited me to join this gallery of beautiful women, I, the poor widow's child with my mouse-coloured hair that still bore the kinks of the plaits from which it had so recently been freed, my bony hips, my nervous, pianist's fingers.

He was rich as Croesus. The night before our wedding—a simple affair, at the Mairie, because his countess was so recently gone—he took my mother and me, curious coincidence, to see *Tristan*. And, do you know, my heart swelled and ached so during the Liebestod that I thought I must truly love him. Yes. I did. On his arm, all eyes were upon me. The whispering crowd in the foyer parted like the Red Sea to let us through. My skin crisped at his touch.

How my circumstances had changed since the first time I heard those voluptuous chords that carry such a charge of deathly passion in them! Now, we sat in a loge, in red velvet armchairs, and a braided, bewigged flunkey brought us a silver bucket of iced champagne in the interval. The froth spilled over the rim of my glass and drenched my hands, I thought: My cup runneth over. And I had on a Poiret dress. He had prevailed upon my reluctant mother to let him buy my trousseau; what would I have gone to him in, otherwise? Twice-darned underwear, faded gingham, serge skirts, hand-me-downs. So, for the opera, I wore a sinuous shift of white muslin tied with a silk string under the breasts. And everyone stared at me. And at his wedding gift.

His wedding gift, clasped round my throat. A choker of rubies, two inches wide, like an extraordinarily precious slit throat.

After the Terror, in the early days of the Directory,[3] the aristos who'd escaped the guillotine had an ironic fad of tying a red ribbon round their necks at just the point where the blade would have sliced it through, a red ribbon like the memory of a wound. And his grandmother, taken with the notion, had her ribbon made up in rubies; such a gesture of luxurious defiance! That night at the opera comes back to me even now . . . the white dress; the frail child within it; and the flashing crimson jewels round her throat, bright as arterial blood.

I saw him watching me in the gilded mirrors with the assessing eye of a connoisseur inspecting horseflesh, or even of a housewife in the market, inspecting cuts on the slab. I'd never seen, or else had never acknowledged, that regard of his before, the sheer carnal avarice of it; and it was strangely magnified by the monocle lodged in his left eye. When I saw him look at me with lust, I dropped my eyes but, in glancing away from him, I caught sight of myself in the mirror. And I saw myself, suddenly, as he saw me, my pale face, the way the muscles in my neck stuck out like thin wire. I saw how much that cruel necklace became me. And, for the first time in my innocent and confined life, I sensed in myself a potentiality for corruption that took my breath away.

The next day, we were married.

The train slowed, shuddered to a halt. Lights; clank of metal; a voice declaring the name of an unknown, never-to-be visited station; silence of the night; the rhythm of his breathing, that I should sleep with, now, for the rest of my life. And I could not sleep. I stealthily sat up, raised the blind a little and huddled against the cold window that misted over with the warmth of my breathing, gazing out at the dark platform towards those rectangles of domestic lamplight that promised warmth, company, a supper of sausages hissing in a pan on the stove for the station master, his children tucked up in bed asleep in the brick house with the painted shutters . . . all the paraphernalia of the everyday world from which I, with my stunning marriage, had exiled myself.

Into marriage, into exile; I sensed it, I knew it—that, henceforth, I would always be lonely. Yet that was part of the already familiar weight of the fire opal that glimmered like a gypsy's magic ball, so that I could not take my eyes off it when I played the piano. This ring, the bloody bandage of rubies, the wardrobe of clothes from Poiret and Worth, his scent of Russian leather—all had conspired to seduce me so utterly that I could not say I felt one single twinge of regret for the world of tartines and maman[4] that now receded from me as if drawn away on a string, like a child's toy, as the train began to throb again as if in delighted anticipation of the distance it would take me.

3. The Reign of Terror, part of the French Revolution, took place in 1793–1794; the Directory ruled France from 1795 to 1799.
4. Tartine: bread and butter covered with jam; *maman,* mother. Together they suggest childhood.

The first grey streamers of the dawn now flew in the sky and an eldritch half-light seeped into the railway carriage. I heard no change in his breathing but my heightened, excited senses told me he was awake and gazing at me. A huge man, an enormous man, and his eyes, dark and motionless as those eyes the ancient Egyptians painted upon their sarcophagi, fixed upon me. I felt a certain tension in the pit of my stomach, to be so watched, in such silence. A match struck. He was igniting a Romeo y Julieta⁵ fat as a baby's arm.   190

"Soon," he said in his resonant voice that was like the tolling of a bell and I felt, all at once, a sharp premonition of dread that lasted only as long as the match flared and I could see his white, broad face as if it were hovering, disembodied, above the sheets, illuminated from below like a grotesque carnival head. Then the flame died, the cigar glowed and filled the compartment with a remembered fragrance that made me think of my father, how he would hug me in a warm fug of Havana, when I was a little girl, before he kissed me and left me and died.

As soon as my husband handed me down from the high step of the train, I smelled the amniotic salinity of the ocean. It was November; the trees, stunted by the Atlantic gales, were bare and the lonely halt was deserted but for his leather- 200 gaitered chauffeur waiting meekly beside the sleek black motor car. It was cold; I drew my furs about me, a wrap of white and black, broad stripes of ermine and sable, with a collar from which my head rose like the calyx of a wildflower. (I swear to you, I had never been vain until I met him.) The bell clanged; the straining train leapt its leash and left us at that lonely wayside halt where only he and I had descended. Oh, the wonder of it; how all that might of iron and steam had paused only to suit his convenience. The richest man in France.

"Madame."

The chauffeur eyed me; was he comparing me, invidiously, to the countess, the artist's model, the opera singer? I hid behind my furs as if they were a system 210 of soft shields. My husband liked me to wear my opal over my kid glove, a showy, theatrical trick—but the moment the ironic chauffeur glimpsed its simmering flash he smiled, as though it was proof positive I was his master's wife. And we drove towards the widening dawn, that now streaked half the sky with a wintry bouquet of pink of roses, orange of tiger-lilies, as if my husband had ordered me a sky from a florist. The day broke around me like a cool dream.

Sea; sand; a sky that melts into the sea—a landscape of misty pastels with a look about it of being continuously on the point of melting. A landscape with all the deliquescent harmonies of Debussy, of the études I played for him, the reverie I'd been playing that afternoon in the salon of the princess where I'd first met him, 220 among the teacups and the little cakes, I, the orphan, hired out of charity to give them their digestive of music.

And, ah! his castle. The faery solitude of the place; with its turrets of misty blue, its courtyard, its spiked gate, his castle that lay on the very bosom of the sea with seabirds mewing about its attics, the casements opening on to the green and purple, evanescent departures of the ocean, cut off by the tide from land for half a day . . . that castle, at home neither on the land nor on the water, a mysterious, amphibious place, contravening the materiality of both earth and the waves, with

5. A brand of cigar.

the melancholy of a mermaiden who perches on her rock and waits, endlessly, for a lover who had drowned far away, long ago. That lovely, sad, sea-siren of a place! 230

The tide was low; at this hour, so early in the morning, the causeway rose up out of the sea. As the car turned on to the wet cobbles between the slow margins of water, he reached out for my hand that had his sultry, witchy ring on it, pressed my fingers, kissed my palm with extraordinary tenderness. His face was as still as ever I'd seen it, still as a pond iced thickly over, yet his lips, that always looked so strangely red and naked between the black fringes of his beard, now curved a little. He smiled; he welcomed his bride home.

No room, no corridor that did not rustle with the sound of the sea and all the ceilings, the walls on which his ancestors in the stern regalia of rank lined up with their dark eyes and white faces, were stippled with refracted light from the 240 waves which were always in motion; that luminous, murmurous castle of which I was the châtelaine, I, the little music student whose mother had sold all her jewellery, even her wedding ring, to pay the fees at the Conservatoire.

First of all, there was the small ordeal of my initial interview with the housekeeper, who kept this extraordinary machine, this anchored, castellated ocean liner, in smooth running order no matter who stood on the bridge; how tenuous, I thought, might be my authority here! She had a bland, pale, impassive, dislikeable face beneath the impeccably starched white linen head-dress of the region. Her greeting, correct but lifeless, chilled me; daydreaming, I dared presume too much on my status . . . briefly wondered how I might install my old nurse, so much 250 loved, however cozily incompetent, in her place. Ill-considered schemings! He told me this one had been his foster mother; was bound to his family in the utmost feudal complicity, "as much part of the house as I am, my dear." Now her thin lips offered me a proud little smile. She would be my ally as long as I was his. And with that, I must be content.

But, here, it would be easy to be content. In the turret suite he had given me for my very own, I could gaze out over the tumultuous Atlantic and imagine myself the Queen of the Sea. There was a Bechstein[6] for me in the music room and, on the wall, another wedding present—an early Flemish primitive of Saint Cecilia[7] at her celestial organ. In the prim charm of this saint, with her plump, sallow 260 cheeks and crinkled brown hair, I saw myself as I could have wished to be. I warmed to a loving sensitivity I had not hitherto suspected in him. Then he led me up a delicate spiral staircase to my bedroom; before she discreetly vanished, the housekeeper set him chuckling with some, I dare say, lewd blessing for newlyweds in her native Breton. That I did not understand. That he, smiling, refused to interpret.

And there lay the grand, hereditary matrimonial bed, itself the size, almost, of my little room at home, with the gargoyles carved on its surfaces of ebony, vermilion lacquer, gold leaf; and its white gauze curtains, billowing in the sea breeze. Our bed. And surrounded by so many mirrors! Mirrors on all the walls, in stately 270 frames of contorted gold, that reflected more white lilies than I'd ever seen in my

6. An expensive German-made piano.
7. Patron saint of music.

life before. He'd filled the room with them, to greet the bride, the young bride. The young bride, who had become that multitude of girls I saw in the mirrors, identical in their chic navy blue tailor-mades, for travelling, madame, or walking. A maid had dealt with the furs. Henceforth, a maid would deal with everything.

"See," he said, gesturing towards those elegant girls. "I have acquired a whole harem for myself!"

I found that I was trembling. My breath came thickly. I could not meet his eye and turned my head away, out of pride, out of shyness, and watched a dozen husbands approach me in a dozen mirrors and slowly, methodically, teasingly, un- 280 fasten the buttons of my jacket and slip it from my shoulders. Enough! No; more! Off comes the skirt; and, next, the blouse of apricot linen that cost more than the dress I had for first communion. The play of the waves outside in the cold sun glittered on his monocle; his movements seemed to me deliberately coarse, vulgar. The blood rushed to my face again, and stayed there.

And yet, you see, I guessed it might be so—that we should have a formal disrobing of the bride, a ritual from the brothel. Sheltered as my life had been, how could I have failed, even in the world of prim bohemia in which I lived, to have heard hints of *his* world?

He stripped me, gourmand that he was, as if he were stripping the leaves off 290 an artichoke—but do not imagine much finesse about it; this artichoke was no particular treat for the diner nor was he yet in any greedy haste. He approached his familiar treat with a weary appetite. And when nothing but my scarlet, palpitating core remained, I saw, in the mirror, the living image of an etching by Rops from the collection he had shown me when our engagement permitted us to be alone together . . . the child with her sticklike limbs, naked but for her button boots, her gloves, shielding her face with her hand as though her face were the last repository of her modesty; and the old, monocled lecher who examined her, limb by limb. He in his London tailoring; she, bare as a lamb chop. Most pornographic of all confrontations. And so my purchaser unwrapped his bargain. And, as at the 300 opera, when I had first seen my flesh in his eyes, I was aghast to feel myself stirring.

At once he closed my legs like a book and I saw again the rare movement of his lips that meant he smiled.

Not yet. Later. Anticipation is the greater part of pleasure, my little love.

And I began to shudder, like a racehorse before a race, yet also with a kind of fear, for I felt both a strange, impersonal arousal at the thought of love and at the same time a repugnance I could not stifle for his white, heavy flesh that had too much in common with the armfuls of arum lilies that filled my bedroom in great glass jars, those undertakers' lilies with the heavy pollen that powders your 310 fingers as if you had dipped them in turmeric. The lilies I always associate with him; that are white. And stain you.

This scene from a voluptuary's life was now abruptly terminated. It turns out he has business to attend to; his estates, his companies—even on your honeymoon? Even then, said the red lips that kissed me before he left me alone with my bewildered senses—a wet, silken brush from his beard; a hint of the pointed tip of the tongue. Disgruntled, I wrapped a négligé of antique lace around me to sip the little breakfast of hot chocolate the maid brought me; after that, since it was second nature to me, there was nowhere to go but the music room and soon I settled down at my piano.

Yet only a series of subtle discords flowed from beneath my fingers: out of tune . . . only a little out of tune; but I'd been blessed with perfect pitch and could not bear to play any more. Sea breezes are bad for pianos; we shall need a resident piano-tuner on the premises if I'm to continue with my studies! I flung down the lid in a little fury of disappointment; what should I do now, how shall I pass the long, sea-lit hours until my husband beds me?

I shivered to think of *that*.

His library seemed the source of his habitual odour of Russian leather. Row upon row of calf-bound volumes, brown and olive, with gilt lettering on their spines, the octavo in brilliant scarlet morocco. A deep-buttoned leather sofa to recline on. A lectern, carved like a spread eagle, that held open upon it an edition of Huysmans's *Là-bas*, from some over-exquisite private press; it had been bound like a missal, in brass, with gems of coloured glass. The rugs on the floor, deep, pulsing blues of heaven and red of the heart's dearest blood, came from Isfahan and Bokhara; the dark panelling gleamed; there was the lulling music of the sea and a fire of apple logs. The flames flickered along the spines inside a glass-fronted case that held books still crisp and new. Eliphas Levy; the name meant nothing to me. I squinted at a title or two: *The Initiation, The Key of Mysteries, The Secret of Pandora's Box,* and yawned. Nothing, here, to detain a seventeen-year-old girl waiting for her first embrace. I should have liked, best of all, a novel in yellow paper; I wanted to curl up on the rug before the blazing fire, lose myself in a cheap novel, munch sticky liqueur chocolates. If I rang for them, a maid would bring me chocolates.

Nevertheless, I opened the doors of that bookcase idly to browse. And I think I knew, I knew by some tingling of the fingertips, even before I opened that slim volume with no title at all on the spine, what I should find inside it. When he showed me the Rops, newly bought, dearly prized, had he not hinted that he was a connoisseur of such things? Yet I had not bargained for this, the girl with tears hanging on her cheeks like stuck pearls, her cunt a split fig below the great globes of her buttocks on which the knotted tails of the cat were about to descend, while a man in a black mask fingered with his free hand his prick, that curved upwards like the scimitar he held. The picture had a caption: "Reproof of curiosity." My mother, with all the precision of her eccentricity, had told me what it was that lovers did; I was innocent but not naïve. *The Adventures of Eulalie at the Harem of the Grand Turk* had been printed, according to the flyleaf, in Amsterdam in 1748, a rare collector's piece. Had some ancestor brought it back himself from that northern city? Or had my husband bought it for himself, from one of those dusty little bookshops on the Left Bank where an old man peers at you through spectacles an inch thick, daring you to inspect his wares . . . I turned the pages in the anticipation of fear; the print was rusty. Here was another steel engraving: "Immolation of the wives of the Sultan." I knew enough for what I saw in that book to make me gasp.

There was a pungent intensification of the odour of leather that suffused his library; his shadow fell across the massacre.

"My little nun has found the prayerbooks, has she?" he demanded, with a curious mixture of mockery and relish; then, seeing my painful, furious bewilderment, he laughed at me aloud, snatched the book from my hands and put it down on the sofa.

"Have the nasty pictures scared Baby? Baby mustn't play with grownups' toys until she's learned how to handle them, must she?"

Then he kissed me. And with, this time, no reticence. He kissed me and laid his hand imperatively upon my breast, beneath the sheath of ancient lace. I stumbled on the winding stair that led to the bedroom, to the carved, gilded bed on which he had been conceived. I stammered foolishly: We've not taken luncheon yet; and, besides, it is broad daylight . . .

All the better to see you.

He made me put on my choker, the family heirloom of one woman who had escaped the blade. With trembling fingers, I fastened the thing about my neck. It was cold as ice and chilled me. He twined my hair into a rope and lifted it off my shoulders so that he could the better kiss the downy furrows below my ears; that made me shudder. And he kissed those blazing rubies, too. He kissed them before he kissed my mouth. Rapt, he intoned: "Of her apparel she retains/Only her sonorous jewellery."

A dozen husbands impaled a dozen brides while the mewing gulls swung on invisible trapezes in the empty air outside.

I was brought to my senses by the insistent shrilling of the telephone. He lay beside me, felled like an oak, breathing stertorously, as if he had been fighting with me. In the course of that one-sided struggle, I had seen his deathly composure shatter like a porcelain vase flung against a wall; I had heard him shriek and blaspheme at the orgasm; I had bled. And perhaps I had seen his face without its mask; and perhaps I had not. Yet I had been infinitely dishevelled by the loss of my virginity.

I gathered myself together, reached into the cloisonné cupboard beside the bed that concealed the telephone and addressed the mouthpiece. His agent in New York. Urgent.

I shook him awake and rolled over on my side, cradling my spent body in my arms. His voice buzzed like a hive of distant bees. My husband. My husband, who, with so much love, filled my bedroom with lilies until it looked like an embalming parlour. Those somnolent lilies, that wave their heavy heads, distributing their lush, insolent incense reminiscent of pampered flesh.

When he'd finished with the agent, he turned to me and stroked the ruby necklace that bit into my neck, but with such tenderness now, that I ceased flinching and he caressed my breasts. My dear one, my little love, my child, did it hurt her? He's so sorry for it, such impetuousness, he could not help himself; you see, he loves her so . . . and this lover's recitative of his brought my tears in a flood. I clung to him as though only the one who had inflicted the pain could comfort me for suffering it. For a while, he murmured to me in a voice I'd never heard before, a voice like the soft consolations of the sea. But then he unwound the tendrils of my hair from the buttons of his smoking jacket, kissed my cheek briskly and told me the agent from New York had called with such urgent business that he must

leave as soon as the tide was low enough. Leave the castle? Leave France! And   410
would be away for at least six weeks.

"But it is our honeymoon!"

A deal, an enterprise of hazard and chance involving several millions, lay in
the balance, he said. He drew away from me into that waxworks stillness of his; I
was only a little girl, I did not understand. And, he said unspoken to my wounded
vanity, I have had too many honeymoons to find them in the least pressing commitments. I know quite well that this child I've bought with a handful of coloured
stones and the pelts of dead beasts won't run away. But, after he'd called his Paris
agent to book a passage for the States next day—just one tiny call, my little one—
we should have time for dinner together.   420

And I had to be content with that.

A Mexican dish of pheasant with hazelnuts and chocolate; salad; white,
voluptuous cheese; a sorbet of muscat grapes and Asti spumante. A celebration of
Krug[8] exploded festively. And then acrid black coffee in precious little cups so fine
it shadowed the birds with which they were painted. I had cointreau, he had cognac in the library, with the purple velvet curtains drawn against the night, where
he took me to perch on his knee in a leather armchair beside the flickering log
fire. He had made me change into that chaste little Poiret shift of white muslin; he
seemed especially fond of it, my breasts showed through the flimsy stuff, he said,
like little soft white doves that sleep, each one, with a pink eye open. But he   430
would not let me take off my ruby choker, although it was growing very uncomfortable, nor fasten up my descending hair, the sign of a virginity so recently rup-
tured that still remained a wounded presence between us. He twined his fingers in
my hair until I winced; I said, I remember, very little.

"The maid will have changed our sheets already," he said. "We do not hang
the bloody sheets out of the window to prove to the whole of Brittany you are a
virgin, not in these civilized times. But I should tell you it would have been the
first time in all my married lives I could shown my interested tenants such a flag."

Then I realized, with a shock of surprise, how it must have been my innocence that captivated him—the silent music, he said, of my unknowingness, like   440
La Terrasse des audiences au clair de lune[9] played upon a piano with keys of ether.
You must remember how ill at ease I was in that luxurious place, how unease had
been my constant companion during the whole length of my courtship by this
grave satyr who now gently martyrized my hair. To know that my naïvety gave
him some pleasure made me take heart. Courage! I shall act the fine lady to the
manner born one day, if only by virtue of default.

Then, slowly yet teasingly, as if he were giving a child a great, mysterious
treat, he took out a bunch of keys from some interior hidey-hole in his jacket—
key after key, a key, he said, for every lock in the house. Keys of all kinds—huge,
ancient things of black iron; others slender, delicate, almost baroque; wafer-thin   450
Yale keys for safes and boxes. And, during his absence, it was I who must take care
of them all.

I eyed the heavy bunch with circumspection. Until that moment, I had not

8. A brand of champagne.
9. Piano work by Claude Debussy (1862–1918).

given a single thought to the practical aspects of marriage with a great house, great wealth, a great man, whose key ring was as crowded as that of a prison warder. Here were the clumsy and archaic keys for the dungeons, for dungeons we had in plenty although they had been converted to cellars for his wines; the dusty bottles inhabited in racks all those deep holes of pain in the rock on which the castle was built. These are the keys to the kitchens, this is the key to the picture gallery, a treasure house filled by five centuries of avid collectors—ah! he foresaw I would spend hours there.   460

He had amply indulged his taste for the Symbolists, he told me with a glint of greed. There was Moreau's great portrait of his first wife, the famous *Sacrificial Victim* with the imprint of the lacelike chains on her pellucid skin. Did I know the story of the painting of that picture? How, when she took off her clothes for him for the first time, she fresh from her bar in Montmartre, she had robed herself involuntarily in a blush that reddened her breasts, her shoulders, her arms, her whole body? He had thought of that story, of that dear girl, when first he had undressed me . . . Ensor, the great Ensor, his monolithic canvas: *The Foolish Virgins.* Two or three late Gauguins, his special favourite the one of the tranced brown girl   470 in the deserted house which was called: *Out of the Night We Come, Into the Night We Go.* And, besides the additions he had made himself, his marvellous inheritance of Watteaus, Poussins and a pair of very special Fragonards, commissioned for a licentious ancestor who, it was said, had posed for the master's brush himself with his own two daughters . . . He broke off his catalogue of treasures abruptly.

Your thin white face, chérie; he said, as if he saw it for the first time. Your thin white face, with its promise of debauchery only a connoisseur could detect.

A log fell in the fire, instigating a shower of sparks; the opal on my finger spurted green flame. I felt as giddy as if I were on the edge of a precipice; I was afraid, not so much of him, of his monstrous presence, heavy as if he had been   480 gifted at birth with more specific *gravity* than the rest of us, the presence that, even when I thought myself most in love with him, always subtly oppressed me . . . No. I was not afraid of him; but of myself. I seemed reborn in his unreflective eyes, reborn in unfamiliar shapes. I hardly recognized myself from his descriptions of me and yet, and yet—might there not be a grain of beastly truth in them? And, in the red firelight, I blushed again, unnoticed, to think he might have chosen me because, in my innocence, he sensed a rare talent for corruption.

Here is the key to the china cabinet—don't laugh, my darling; there's a king's ransom in Sèvres in that closet, and a queen's ransom in Limoges. And a key to the locked, barred room where five generations of plate were kept.   490

Keys, keys, keys. He would trust me with the keys to his office, although I was only a baby; and the keys to his safes, where he kept the jewels I should wear, he promised me, when we returned to Paris. Such jewels! Why, I would be able to change my earrings and necklaces three times a day, just as the Empress Josephine used to change her underwear. He doubted, he said, with that hollow, knocking sound that served him for a chuckle, I would be quite so interested in his share certificates although they, of course, were worth infinitely more.

Outside our firelit privacy, I could hear the sound of the tide drawing back from the pebbles of the foreshore; it was nearly time for him to leave me. One sin-

gle key remained unaccounted for on the ring and he hesitated over it; for a mo- 500
ment, I thought he was going to unfasten it from its brothers, slip it back into his
pocket and take it away with him.

"What is *that* key?" I demanded, for his chaffing had made me bold. "The
key to your heart? Give it me!"

He dangled the key tantalizingly above my head, out of reach of my straining
fingers; those bare red lips of his cracked sidelong in a smile.

"Ah, no," he said. "Not the key to my heart. Rather, the key to my enfer."[10]

He left it on the ring, fastened the ring together, shook it musically, like a
carillon. Then threw the keys in a jingling heap in my lap. I could feel the cold
metal chilling my thighs through my thin muslin frock. He bent over me to drop a 510
beard-masked kiss on my forehead.

"Every man must have one secret, even if only one, from his wife," he said.
"Promise me this, my whey-faced piano-player; promise me you'll use all the keys
on the ring except that last little one I showed you. Play with anything you find,
jewels, silver plate; make toy boats of my share certificates, if it pleases you, and
send them sailing off to America after me. All is yours, everywhere is open to
you—except the lock that this single key fits. Yet all it is is the key to a little room
at the foot of the west tower, behind the still-room, at the end of a dark little corridor full of horrid cobwebs that would get into your hair and frighten you if you
ventured there. Oh, and you'd find it such a dull little room! But you must 520
promise me, if you love me, to leave it well alone. It is only a private study, a hideaway, a 'den', as the English say, where I can go, sometimes, on those infrequent
yet inevitable occasions when the yoke of marriage seems to weigh too heavily on
my shoulders. There I can go, you understand, to savour the rare pleasure of
imagining myself wifeless."

There was a little thin starlight in the courtyard as, wrapped in my furs, I
saw him to his car. His last words were, that he had telephoned the mainland and
taken a piano-tuner on to the staff; this man would arrive to take up his duties the
next day. He pressed me to his vicuña[11] breast, once, and then drove away.

I had drowsed away that afternoon and now I could not sleep. I lay tossing 530
and turning in his ancestral bed until another daybreak discoloured the dozen
mirrors that were iridescent with the reflections of the sea. The perfume of the
lilies weighed on my senses; when I thought that, henceforth, I would always
share these sheets with a man whose skin, as theirs did, contained that toad-like,
clammy hint of moisture, I felt a vague desolation that within me, now my female
wound had healed, there had awoken a certain queasy craving like the cravings of
pregnant women for the taste of coal or chalk or tainted food, for the renewal of
his caresses. Had he not hinted to me, in his flesh as in his speech and looks, of
the thousand, thousand baroque intersections of flesh upon flesh? I lay in our
wide bed accompanied by, a sleepless companion, my dark newborn curiosity.   540

I lay in bed alone. And I longed for him. And he disgusted me.

10. Lower regions; hell.
11. A fine wool made from the vicuna, similar to a llama and alpaca.

Were there jewels enough in all his safes to recompense me for this predicament? Did all that castle hold enough riches to recompense me for the company of the libertine with whom I must share it? And what, precisely, was the nature of my desirous dread for this mysterious being who, to show his mastery over me, had abandoned me on my wedding night?

Then I sat straight up in bed, under the sardonic masks of the gargoyles carved above me, riven by a wild surmise. Might he have left me, not for Wall Street but for an importunate mistress tucked away God knows where who knew how to pleasure him far better than a girl whose fingers had been exercised, hith- 550 erto, only by the practice of scales and arpeggios? And, slowly, soothed, I sank back on to the heaping pillows; I acknowledged that the jealous scare I'd just given myself was not unmixed with a little tincture of relief.

At last I drifted into slumber, as daylight filled the room and chased bad dreams away. But the last thing I remembered, before I slept, was the tall jar of lilies beside the bed, how the thick glass distorted their fat stems so they looked like arms, dismembered arms, drifting drowned in greenish water.

Coffee and croissants to console this bridal, solitary waking. Delicious. Honey, too, in a section of comb on a glass saucer. The maid squeezed the aromatic juice from an orange into a chilled goblet while I watched her as I lay in the 560 lazy, midday bed of the rich. Yet nothing, this morning, gave me more than a fleeting pleasure except to hear that the piano-tuner had been at work already. When the maid told me that, I sprang out of bed and pulled on my old serge skirt and flannel blouse, costume of a student, in which I felt far more at ease with myself than in any of my fine new clothes.

After my three hours of practice, I called the piano-tuner in, to thank him. He was blind, of course; but young, with a gentle mouth and grey eyes that fixed upon me although they could not see me. He was a blacksmith's son from the village across the causeway; a chorister in the church whom the good priest had taught a trade so that he could make a living. All most satisfactory. Yes. He 570 thought he would be happy here. And if, he added shyly, he might sometimes be allowed to hear me play . . . for, you see, he loved music. Yes. Of course, I said. Certainly. He seemed to know that I had smiled.

After I dismissed him, even though I'd woken so late, it was still barely time for my "five o'clock." The housekeeper, who, thoughtfully forewarned by my husband, had restrained herself from interrupting my music, now made me a solemn visitation with a lengthy menu for a late luncheon. When I told her I did not need it, she looked at me obliquely, along her nose. I understood at once that one of my principal functions as châtelaine was to provide work for the staff. But, all the same, I asserted myself and said I would wait until dinner-time, although I looked 580 forward nervously to the solitary meal. Then I found I had to tell her what I would like to have prepared for me; my imagination, still that of a schoolgirl, ran riot. A fowl in cream—or should I anticipate Christmas with a varnished turkey? No; I have decided. Avocado and shrimp, lots of it, followed by no entrée at all. But surprise me for dessert with every ice-cream in the ice box. She noted all down but sniffed; I'd shocked her. Such tastes! Child that I was, I giggled when she left me.

But, now . . . what shall I do, now?

I could have spent a happy hour unpacking the trunks that contained my trousseau but the maid had done that already, the dresses, the tailor-mades hung in the wardrobe in my dressing room, the hats on wooden heads to keep their shape, the shoes on wooden feet as if all these inanimate objects were imitating the appearance of life, to mock me. I did not like to linger in my overcrowded dressing room, nor in my lugubriously lily-scented bedroom. How shall I pass the time?

I shall take a bath in my own bathroom! And found the taps were little dolphins made of gold, with chips of turquoise for eyes. And there was a tank of goldfish, who swam in and out of moving fronds of weeds, as bored, I thought, as I was. How I wished he had not left me. How I wished it were possible to chat with, say, a maid; or, the piano-tuner . . . but I knew already my new rank forbade overtures of friendship to the staff.

I had been hoping to defer the call as long as I could, so that I should have something to look forward to in the dead waste of time I foresaw before me, after my dinner was done with, but, at a quarter before seven, when darkness already surrounded the castle, I could contain myself no longer. I telephoned my mother. And astonished myself by bursting into tears when I heard her voice.

No, nothing was the matter. Mother, I have gold bath taps.

I said, gold bath taps!

No; I suppose that's nothing to cry about, Mother.

The line was bad, I could hardly make out her congratulations, her questions, her concerns, but I was a little comforted when I put the receiver down.

Yet there still remained one whole hour to dinner and the whole, unimaginable desert of the rest of the evening.

The bunch of keys lay, where he had left them, on the rug before the library fire which had warmed their metal so that they no longer felt cold to the touch but warm, almost, as my own skin. How careless I was; a maid, tending the logs, eyed me reproachfully as if I'd set a trap for her as I picked up the clinking bundle of keys, the keys to the interior doors of this lovely prison of which I was both the inmate and the mistress and had scarcely seen. When I remembered that, I felt the exhilaration of the explorer.

Lights! More lights!

At the touch of a switch, the dreaming library was brilliantly illuminated. I ran crazily about the castle, switching on every light I could find—I ordered the servants to light up all their quarters, too, so the castle would shine like a seaborne birthday cake lit with a thousand candles, one for every year of its life, and everybody on shore would wonder at it. When everything was lit as brightly as the café in the Gare du Nord, the significance of the possessions implied by that bunch of keys no longer intimidated me, for I was determined, now, to search through them all for evidence of my husband's true nature.

His office first, evidently.

A mahogany desk half a mile wide, with an impeccable blotter and a bank of telephones. I allowed myself the luxury of opening the safe that contained the jewellery and delved sufficiently among the leather boxes to find out how my marriage had given me access to a jinn's treasury—parures, bracelets, rings . . . While I was thus surrounded by diamonds, a maid knocked on the door and entered before I spoke; a subtle discourtesy. I would speak to my husband about it. She eyed my serge skirt superciliously; did madame plan to dress for dinner?

She made a moue of disdain when I laughed to hear that, she was far more the lady than I. But, imagine—to dress up in one of my Poiret extravaganzas, with the jewelled turban and aigrette on my head, roped with pearl to the navel, to sit down all alone in the baronial dining hall at the head of that massive board at which King Mark[12] was reputed to have fed his knights . . . I grew calmer under the cold eye of her disapproval. I adopted the crisp inflections of an officer's daughter. No, I would not dress for dinner. Furthermore, I was not hungry enough for dinner itself. She must tell the housekeeper to cancel the dormitory feast I'd ordered. Could they leave me sandwiches and a flask of coffee in my music room? And would they all dismiss for the night?

Mais oui, madame.

I knew by her bereft intonation I had let them down again but I did not care; I was armed against them by the brilliance of his hoard. But I would not find his heart amongst the glittering stones; as soon as she had gone, I began a systematic search of the drawers of his desk.

All was in order, so I found nothing. Not a random doodle on an old envelope, nor the faded photograph of a woman. Only the files of business correspondence, the bills from the home farms, the invoices from tailors, the billets-doux from international financiers. Nothing. And this absence of the evidence of his real life began to impress me strangely; there must, I thought, be a great deal to conceal if he takes such pains to hide it.

His office was a singularly impersonal room, facing inwards, on to the courtyard, as though he wanted to turn his back on the siren sea in order to keep a clear head while he bankrupted a small businessman in Amsterdam or—I noticed with a thrill of distaste—engaged in some business in Laos that must, from certain cryptic references to his amateur botanist's enthusiasm for rare poppies, be to do with opium. Was he not rich enough to do without crime? Or was the crime itself his profit? And yet I saw enough to appreciate his zeal for secrecy.

Now I had ransacked his desk, I must spend a cool-headed quarter of an hour putting every last letter back where I had found it, and, as I covered the traces of my visit, by some chance, as I reached inside a little drawer that had stuck fast, I must have touched a hidden spring, for a secret drawer flew open within that drawer itself; and this secret drawer contained—at last!—a file marked: *Personal.*

I was alone, but for my reflection in the uncurtained window.

I had the brief notion that his heart, pressed flat as a flower, crimson and thin as tissue paper, lay in this file. It was a very thin one.

I could have wished, perhaps, I had not found that touching, ill-spelt note, on a paper napkin marked *La Coupole,* that began: "My darling, I cannot wait for the moment when you may make me yours completely." The diva had sent him a

12. Husband of Queen Isolde or Iseult, lover of Tristan.

page of the score of *Tristan,* the Liebestod, with the single, cryptic word: "Until . . ." scrawled across it. But the strangest of all these love letters was a postcard with a view of a village graveyard, among mountains, where some black-coated ghoul enthusiastically dug at a grave; this little scene, executed with the lurid exu- berance of Grand Guignol, was captioned: "Typical Transylvanian Scene— Midnight, All Hallows." And, on the other side, the message: "On the occasion of this marriage to the descendant of Dracula—always remember, 'the supreme and unique pleasure of love is the certainty that one is doing evil.' Toutes amitiés, C."

A joke? A joke in the worst possible taste; for had he not been married to a Romanian countess. And then I remembered her pretty, witty face, and her name—Carmilla. My most recent predecessor in this castle had been, it would seem, the most sophisticated.

I put away the file, sobered. Nothing in my life of family love and music had prepared me for these grown-up games and yet these were clues to his self that showed me, at least, how much he had been loved, even if they did not reveal any good reason for it. But I wanted to know still more; and, as I closed the office door and locked it, the means to discover more fell in my way.

Fell, indeed; and with the clatter of a dropped canteen of cutlery, for, as I turned the slick Yale lock, I contrived, somehow, to open up the key ring itself, so that all the keys tumbled loose on the floor. And the very first key I picked out of that pile was, as luck or ill fortune had it, the key to the room he had forbidden me, the room he would keep for his own so that he could go there when he wished to feel himself once more a bachelor.

I made my decision to explore it before I felt a faint resurgence of my ill- defined fear of his waxen stillness. Perhaps I half-imagined, then, that I might find his real self in his den, waiting there to see if indeed I had obeyed him; that he had sent a moving figure of himself to New York, the enigmatic, self-sustaining cara- pace of his public person, while the real man, whose face I had glimpsed in the storm of orgasm, occupied himself with pressing private business in the study at the foot of the west tower, behind the still-room. Yet, if that were so, it was imper- ative that I should find him, should know him; and I was too deluded by his ap- parent taste for me to think my disobedience might truly offend him.

I took the forbidden key from the heap and left the others lying there.

It was now very late and the castle was adrift, as far as it could go from the land, in the middle of the silent ocean where, at my orders, it floated, like a gar- land of light. And all silent, all still, but for the murmuring of the waves.

I felt no fear, no intimation of dread. Now I walked as firmly as I had done in my mother's house.

Not a narrow, dusty little passage at all; why had he lied to me? But an ill- lit one, certainly; the electricity, for some reason, did not extend here, so I re- treated to the still-room and found a bundle of waxed tapers in a cupboard, stored there with matches to light the oak board at grand dinners. I put a match to my little taper and advanced with it in my hand, like a penitent, along the corridor hung with heavy, I think Venetian, tapestries. The flame picked out, here, the head of a man, there, the rich breast of a woman spilling through a rent in her dress— the Rape of the Sabines, perhaps? The naked swords and immolated horses suggested some grisly mythological subject. The corridor wound downwards; there was an almost imperceptible ramp to the thickly carpeted floor. The heavy hangings on the wall muffled my footsteps, even my breathing. For some reason, it grew very warm; the sweat sprang out in beads on my brow. I could no longer hear the sound of the sea.

A long, a winding corridor, as if I were in the viscera of the castle; and this corridor led to a door of worm-eaten oak, low, round-topped, barred with black iron.   730

And still I felt no fear, no raising of the hairs on the back of the neck, no prickling of the thumbs.

The key slid into the new lock as easily as a hot knife into butter.

No fear; but a hesitation, a holding of the spiritual breath.

If I had found some traces of his heart in a file marked: *Personal,* perhaps, here, in his subterranean privacy, I might find a little of his soul. It was the consciousness of the possibility of such a discovery, of its possible strangeness, that kept me for a moment motionless, before, in the foolhardiness of my already subtly tainted innocence, I turned the key and the door creaked slowly back.

"There is a striking resemblance between the act of love and the ministra- 740 tions of a torturer," opined my husband's favourite poet; I had learned something of the nature of that similarity on my marriage bed. And now my taper showed me the outlines of a rack. There was also a great wheel, like the ones I had seen in woodcuts of the martyrdoms of the saints, in my old nurse's little store of holy books. And—just one glimpse of it before my little flame caved in and I was left in absolute darkness—a metal figure, hinged at the side, which I knew to be spiked on the inside and to have the name: the Iron Maiden.[13]

Absolute darkness. And, about me, the instruments of mutilation.

Until that moment, this spoiled child did not know she had inherited nerves and a will from the mother who had defied the yellow outlaws of Indo-China. My 750 mother's spirit drove me on, into that dreadful place, in a cold ecstasy to know the very worst. I fumbled for the matches in my pocket; what a dim, lugubrious light they gave! And yet, enough, oh, more than enough, to see a room designed for desecration and some dark night of unimaginable lovers whose embraces were annihilation.

The walls of this stark torture chamber were the naked rock; they gleamed as if they were sweating with fright. At the four corners of the room were funerary urns, of great antiquity, Etruscan, perhaps, and, on three-legged ebony stands, the bowls of incense he had left burning which filled the room with a sacerdotal reek. Wheel, rack and Iron Maiden were, I saw, displayed as grandly as if they were 760 items of statuary and I was almost consoled, then, and almost persuaded myself that I might have stumbled only upon a little museum of his perversity, that he had installed these monstrous items here only for contemplation.

Yet at the centre of the room lay a catafalque, a doomed, ominous bier of

---

13. Instrument of torture.

Renaissance workmanship, surrounded by long white candles and, at its foot, an armful of the same lilies with which he had filled my bedroom, stowed in a four-foot-high jar glazed with a sombre Chinese red. I scarcely dared examine this catafalque and its occupant more closely; yet I knew I must.

Each time I struck a match to light those candles round her bed, it seemed a garment of that innocence of mine for which he had lusted fell away from me.

The opera singer lay, quite naked, under a thin sheet of very rare and precious linen, such as the princes of Italy used to shroud those whom they had poisoned. I touched her, very gently, on the white breast; she was cool, he had embalmed her. On her throat I could see the blue imprint of his strangler's fingers. The cool, sad flame of the candles flickered on her white, closed eyelids. The worst thing was, the dead lips smiled.

Beyond the catafalque, in the middle of the shadows, a white, nacreous glimmer; as my eyes accustomed themselves to the gathering darkness, I at last—oh, horrors!—made out a skull; yes, a skull, so utterly denuded, now, of flesh that it scarcely seemed possible the stark bone had once been richly upholstered with life. And this skull was strung up by a system of unseen cords, so that it appeared to hang, disembodied, in the still, heavy air, and it had been crowned with a wreath of white roses, and a veil of lace, the final image of his bride.

Yet the skull was still so beautiful, had shaped with its sheer planes so imperiously the face that had once existed above it, that I recognized her the moment I saw her; face of the evening star walking on the rim of night. One false step, oh, my poor, dear girl, next in the fated sisterhood of his wives; one false step and into the abyss of the dark you stumbled.

And where was she, the latest dead, the Romanian countess who might have thought her blood would survive his depredations? I knew she must be here, in the place that had wound me through the castle towards it on a spool of inexorability. But, at first, I could see no sign of her. Then, for some reason—perhaps some change of atmosphere wrought by my presence—the metal shell of the Iron Maiden emitted a ghostly twang; my feverish imagination might have guessed its occupant was trying to clamber out, though, even in the midst of my rising hysteria, I knew she must be dead to find a home there.

With trembling fingers, I prised open the front of the upright coffin, with its sculpted face caught in a rictus of pain. Then, overcome, I dropped the key I still held in my other hand. It dropped into the forming pool of her blood.

She was pierced, not by one but by a hundred spikes, this child of the land of the vampires who seemed so newly dead, so full of blood . . . oh God! how recently had he become a widower? How long had he kept her in this obscene cell? Had it been all the time he had courted me, in the clear light of Paris?

I closed the lid of her coffin very gently and burst into a tumult of sobbing that contained both pity for his other victims and also a dreadful anguish to know I, too, was one of them.

The candles flared, as if in a draught from a door to elsewhere. The light caught the fire opal on my hand so that it flashed, once, with a baleful light, as if to tell me the eye of God—his eye—was upon me. My first thought, when I saw the ring for which I had sold myself to this fate, was, how to escape it.

I retained sufficient presence of mind to snuff out the candles round the bier with my fingers, to gather up my taper, to look around, although shuddering, to ensure I had left behind me no traces of my visit.

I retrieved the key from the pool of blood, wrapped it in my handkerchief to keep my hands clean, and fled the room, slamming the door behind me.

It crashed to with a juddering reverberation, like the door of hell.

I could not take refuge in my bedroom, for that retained the memory of his presence trapped in the fathomless silvering of his mirrors. My music room seemed the safest place, although I looked at the picture of Saint Cecilia with a faint dread; what had been the nature of her martyrdom? My mind was in a tu- 820 mult; schemes for flight jostled with one another . . . as soon as the tide receded from the causeway, I would make for the mainland—on foot, running, stumbling; I did not trust that leather-clad chauffeur, nor the well-behaved housekeeper, and I dared not take any of the pale, ghostly maids into my confidence, either, since they were his creatures, all. Once at the village, I would fling myself directly on the mercy of the gendarmerie.

But—could I trust them, either? His forefathers had ruled this coast for eight centuries, from this castle whose moat was the Atlantic. Might not the police, the advocates, even the judge, all be in his service, turning a common blind eye to his vices since he was milord whose word must be obeyed? Who, on this distant 830 coast, would believe the white-faced girl from Paris who came running to them with a shuddering tale of blood, of fear, of the ogre murmuring in the shadows? Or, rather, they would immediately know it to be true. But were all honour-bound to let me carry it no further.

Assistance. My mother. I ran to the telephone; and the line, of course, was dead.

Dead as his wives.

A thick darkness, unlit by any star, still glazed the windows. Every lamp in my room burned, to keep the dark outside, yet it seemed still to encroach on me, to be present beside me but as if masked by my lights, the night like a permeable 840 substance that could seep into my skin. I looked at the precious little clock made from hypocritically innocent flowers long ago, in Dresden; the hands had scarcely moved one single hour forward from when I first descended to that private slaughterhouse of his. Time was his servant, too; it would trap me, here, in a night that would last until he came back to me, like a black sun on a hopeless morning.

And yet the time might still be my friend; at that hour, that very hour, he set sail for New York.

To know that, in a few moments, my husband would have left France calmed my agitation a little. My reason told me I had nothing to fear; the tide that would take him away to the New World would let me out of the imprisonment of 850 the castle. Surely I could easily evade the servants. Anybody can buy a ticket at a railway station. Yet I was still filled with unease. I opened the lid of the piano; perhaps I thought my own particular magic might help me, now, that I could create a pentacle out of music that would keep me from harm for, if my music had first ensnared him, then might it not also give me the power to free myself from him?

Mechanically, I began to play but my fingers were stiff and shaking. At first, I could manage nothing better than the exercises of Czerny but simply the act of playing soothed me and, for solace, for the sake of the harmonious rationality of its sublime mathematics, I searched among his scores until I found *The Well-Tempered Clavier.* I set myself the therapeutic task of playing all Bach's equations, every one, and, I told myself, if I played them all through without a single mistake—then the morning would find me once more a virgin.

Crash of a dropped stick.

His silver-headed cane! What else? Sly, cunning, he had returned; he was waiting for me outside the door!

I rose to my feet; fear gave me strength. I flung back my head defiantly.

"Come in!" My voice astonished me by its firmness, its clarity.

The door slowly, nervously opened and I saw, not the massive, irredeemable bulk of my husband but the slight, stooping figure of the piano-tuner, and he looked far more terrified of me than my mother's daughter would have been of the Devil himself. In the torture chamber, it seemed to me that I would never laugh again; now, helplessly, laugh I did, with relief, and, after a moment's hesitation, the boy's face softened and he smiled a little, almost in shame. Though they were blind, his eyes were singularly sweet.

"Forgive me," said Jean-Yves. "I know I've given you grounds for dismissing me, that I should be crouching outside your door at midnight . . . but I heard you walking about, up and down—I sleep in a room at the foot of the west tower— and some intuition told me you could not sleep and might, perhaps, pass the insomniac hours at your piano. And I could not resist that. Besides, I stumbled over these—"

And he displayed the ring of keys I'd dropped outside my husband's office door, the ring from which one key was missing. I took them from him, looked round for a place to stow them, fixed on the piano stool as if to hide them would protect me. Still he stood smiling at me. How hard it was to make everyday conversation.

"It's perfect," I said. "The piano. Perfectly in tune."

But he was full of the loquacity of embarrassment, as though I would only forgive him for his impudence if he explained the cause of it thoroughly.

"When I heard you play this afternoon, I thought I'd never heard such a touch. Such technique. A treat for me, to hear a virtuoso! So I crept up to your door now, humbly as a little dog might, madame, and put my ear to the keyhole and listened, and listened—until my stick fell to the floor through a momentary clumsiness of mine, and I was discovered."

He had the most touchingly ingenuous smile.

"Perfectly in tune," I repeated. To my surprise, now I had said it, I found I could not say anything else. I could only repeat: "In tune . . . perfect . . . in tune," over and over again. I saw a dawning surprise in his face. My head throbbed. To see him, in his lovely, blind humanity, seemed to hurt me very piercingly, somewhere inside my breast; his figure blurred, the room swayed about me. After the dreadful revelation of that bloody chamber, it was his tender look that made me faint.

When I recovered consciousness, I found I was lying in the piano-tuner's arms and he was tucking the satin cushion from the piano-stool under my head.

"You are in some great distress," he said. "No bride should suffer so much, so early in her marriage."

His speech had the rhythms of the countryside, the rhythms of the tides.

"Any bride brought to this castle should come ready dressed in mourning, should bring a priest and a coffin with her," I said.

"What's this?"

It was too late to keep silent; and if he, too, were one of my husband's crea- 910 tures, then at least he had been kind to me. So I told him everything, the keys, the interdiction, my disobedience, the room, the rack, the skull, the corpses, the blood.

"I can scarcely believe it," he said, wondering. "That man . . . so rich; so well-born."

"Here's proof," I said and tumbled the fatal key out of my handkerchief on to the silken rug.

"Oh God," he said. "I can smell the blood."

He took my hand; he pressed his arms about me. Although he was scarcely more than a boy, I felt a great strength flow into me from his touch.   920

"We whisper all manner of strange tales up and down the coast," he said. "There was a Marquis, once, who used to hunt young girls on the mainland; he hunted them with dogs, as though they were foxes. My grandfather had it from his grandfather, how the Marquis pulled a head out of his saddle bag and showed it to the blacksmith while the man was shoeing his horse. 'A fine specimen of the genus, brunette, eh, Guillaume?' And it was the head of the blacksmith's wife."

But, in these more democratic times, my husband must travel as far as Paris to do his hunting in the salons. Jean-Yves knew the moment I shuddered.

"Oh, madame! I thought all these were old wives' tales, chattering of fools, spooks to scare bad children into good behaviour! Yet how could you know, a 930 stranger, that the old name for this place is the Castle of Murder?"

How could I know, indeed? Except that, in my heart, I'd always known its lord would be the death of me.

"Hark!" said my friend suddenly. "The sea has changed key; it must be near morning, the tide is going down."

He helped me up. I looked from the window, towards the mainland, along the causeway where the stones gleamed wetly in the thin light of the end of the night and, with an almost unimaginable horror, a horror the intensity of which I cannot transmit to you, I saw, in the distance, still far away yet drawing moment by moment inexorably nearer, the twin headlamps of his great black car, gouging 940 tunnels through the shifting mist.

My husband had indeed returned; this time, it was no fancy.

"The key!" said Jean-Yves. "It must go back on the ring, with the others. As though nothing had happened."

But the key was still caked with wet blood and I ran to my bathroom and held it under the hot tap. Crimson water swirled down the basin but, as if the key itself were hurt, the bloody token stuck. The turquoise eyes of the dolphin taps

winked at me derisively; they knew my husband had been too clever for me! I
scrubbed the stain with my nail brush but still it would not budge. I thought how
the car would be rolling silently towards the closed courtyard gate; the more I   950
scrubbed the key, the more vivid grew the stain.

The bell in the gatehouse would jangle. The porter's drowsy son would push
back the patchwork quilt, yawning, pull the shirt over his head, thrust his feet
into his sabots . . . slowly, slowly; open the door for your master as slowly as you
can . . .

And still the bloodstain mocked the fresh water that spilled from the mouth
of the leering dolphin.

"You have no more time," said Jean-Yves. "He is here. I know it. I must stay
with you."

"You shall not!" I said. "Go back to your room, now. Please."   960

He hesitated. I put an edge of steel in my voice, for I knew I must meet my
lord alone.

"Leave me!"

As soon as he had gone, I dealt with the keys and went to my bedroom. The
causeway was empty; Jean-Yves was correct, my husband had already entered the
castle. I pulled the curtains close, stripped off my clothes and pulled the bedcur-
tains round me as a pungent aroma of Russian leather assured me my husband
was once again beside me.

"Dearest!"

With the most treacherous, lascivious tenderness, he kissed my eyes, and,   970
mimicking the new bride newly wakened, I flung my arms around him, for on my
seeming acquiescence depended my salvation.

"Da Silva of Rio outwitted me," he said wryly. "My New York agent
telegraphed Le Havre and saved me a wasted journey. So we may resume our interrupted pleasures, my love."

I did not believe one word of it. I knew I had behaved exactly according to
his desires; had he not bought me so that I should do so? I had been tricked into
my own betrayal to that illimitable darkness whose source I had been compelled
to seek in his absence and, now that I had met that shadowed reality of his that
came to life only in the presence of its own atrocities, I must pay the price of my   980
new knowledge. The secret of Pandora's box; but he had given me the box, himself, knowing I must learn the secret. I had played a game in which every move
was governed by a destiny as oppressive and omnipotent as himself, since that
destiny was himself; and I had lost. Lost at that charade of innocence and vice in
which he had engaged me. Lost, as the victim loses to the executioner.

His hand brushed my breast, beneath the sheet. I strained my nerves yet
could not help but flinch from the intimate touch, for it made me think of the
piercing embrace of the Iron Maiden and of his lost lovers in the vault. When he
saw my reluctance, his eyes veiled over and yet his appetite did not diminish. His
tongue ran over red lips already wet. Silent, mysterious, he moved away from me   990
to draw off his jacket. He took the gold watch from his waistcoat and laid it on the
dressing table, like a good bourgeois; scooped out his rattling loose change and
now—oh God!—makes a great play of patting his pockets officiously, puzzled lips

pursed, searching for something that has been mislaid. Then turns to me with a ghastly, a triumphant smile.

"But of course! I gave the keys to you!"

"Your keys? Why, of course. Here, they're under the pillow; wait a moment—what—Ah! No . . . now, where can I have left them? I was whiling away the evening without you at the piano, I remember. Of course! The music room!"

Brusquely he flung my negligée of antique lace on the bed.   1000

"Go and get them."

"Now? At this moment? Can't it wait until morning, my darling?"

I forced myself to be seductive. I saw myself, pale, pliant as a plant that begs to be trampled underfoot, a dozen vulnerable, appealing girls reflected in as many mirrors, and I saw how he almost failed to resist me. If he had come to me in bed, I would have strangled him, then.

But he half-snarled: "No. It won't wait. Now."

The unearthly light of dawn filled the room; had only one previous dawn broken upon me in that vile place? And there was nothing for it but to go and fetch the keys from the music stool and pray he would not examine them too   1010 closely, pray to God his eyes would fail him, that he might be struck blind.

When I came back into the bedroom carrying the bunch of keys that jangled at every step like a curious musical instrument, he was sitting on the bed in his immaculate shirtsleeves, his head sunk in his hands.

And it seemed to me he was in despair.

Strange. In spite of my fear of him, that made me whiter than my wrap, I felt there emanate from him, at that moment, a stench of absolute despair, rank and ghastly, as if the lilies that surrounded him had all at once begun to fester, or the Russian leather of his scent were reverting to the elements of flayed hide and excrement of which it was composed. The chthonic gravity of his presence exerted a   1020 tremendous pressure on the room, so that the blood pounded in my ears as if we had been precipitated to the bottom of the sea, beneath the waves that pounded against the shore.

I held my life in my hands amongst those keys and, in a moment, would place it between his well-manicured fingers. The evidence of that bloody chamber had showed me I could expect no mercy. Yet, when he raised his head and stared at me with his blind, shuttered eyes as though he did not recognize me, I felt a terrified pity for him, for this man who lived in such strange, secret places that, if I loved him enough to follow him, I should have to die.

The atrocious loneliness of that monster!   1030

The monocle had fallen from his face. His curling mane was disordered, as if he had run his hands through it in his distraction. I saw how he had lost his impassivity and was now filled with suppressed excitement. The hand he stretched out for those counters in his game of love and death shook a little; the face that turned towards me contained a sombre delirium that seemed to me compounded of a ghastly, yes, shame but also of a terrible, guilty joy as he slowly ascertained how I had sinned.

That tell-tale stain had resolved itself into a mark the shape and brilliance of the heart on a playing card. He disengaged the key from the ring and looked at it for a while, solitary, brooding.   1040

"It is the key that leads to the kingdom of the unimaginable," he said. His voice was low and had in it the timbre of certain great cathedral organs that seem, when they are played, to be conversing with God.

I could not restrain a sob.

"Oh, my love, my little love who brought me a white gift of music," he said, almost as if grieving. "My little love, you'll never know how much I hate daylight!"

Then he sharply ordered: "Kneel!"

I knelt before him and he pressed the key lightly to my forehead, held it there for a moment. I felt a faint tingling of the skin and, when I involuntarily glanced at myself in the mirror, I saw the heart-shaped stain had transferred itself to my forehead, to the space between the eyebrows, like the caste mark of a brahmin woman. Or the mark of Cain.[14] And now the key gleamed as freshly as if it had just been cut. He clipped it back on the ring, emitting that same, heavy sigh as he had done when I said that I would marry him.

"My virgin of the arpeggios, prepare yourself for martyrdom."

"What form shall it take?" I said.

"Decapitation," he whispered, almost voluptuously. "Go and bathe yourself; put on that white dress you wore to hear *Tristan* and the necklace that prefigures your end. And I shall take myself off to the armoury, my dear, to sharpen my great-grandfather's ceremonial sword."

"The servants?"

"We shall have absolute privacy for our last rites; I have already dismissed them. If you look out of the window you can see them going to the mainland."

It was now the full, pale light of morning; the weather was grey, indeterminate, the sea had an oily, sinister look, a gloomy day on which to die. Along the causeway I could see trouping every maid and scullion, every pot-boy and panscourer, valet, laundress and vassal who worked in that great house, most on foot, a few on bicycles. The faceless housekeeper trudged along with a great basket in which, I guessed, she'd stowed as much as she could ransack from the larder. The Marquis must have given the chauffeur leave to borrow the motor for the day, for it went last of all, at a stately pace, as though the procession were a cortège and the car already bore my coffin to the mainland for burial.

But I knew no good Breton earth would cover me, like a last, faithful lover; I had another fate.

"I have given them all a day's holiday, to celebrate our wedding," he said. And smiled.

However hard I stared at the receding company, I could see no sign of Jean-Yves, our latest servant, hired but the preceding morning.

"Go, now. Bathe yourself; dress yourself. The lustratory ritual and the ceremonial robing; after that, the sacrifice. Wait in the music room until I telephone for you. No, my dear!" And he smiled, as I started, recalling the line was dead. "One may call inside the castle just as much as one pleases; but, outside—never."

I scrubbed my forehead with the nail brush as I had scrubbed the key but

---

14. In Hindu society, brahmins made up the highest caste; after Cain killed Abel, he was forced to wander by God but was marked so that no one would kill him. Genesis 4:15.

this red mark would not go away, either, no matter what I did, and I knew I should wear it until I died, though that would not be long. Then I went to my dressing room and put on that white muslin shift, costume of a victim of an auto-da-fé, he had bought me to listen to the Liebestod in. Twelve young women combed out twelve listless sheaves of brown hair in the mirrors; soon, there would be none. The mass of lilies that surrounded me exhaled, now, the odour of their withering. They looked like the trumpets of the angels of death.   1090

On the dressing table, coiled like a snake about to strike, lay the ruby choker.

Already almost lifeless, cold at heart, I descended the spiral staircase to the music room but there I found I had not been abandoned.

"I can be of some comfort to you," the boy said. "Though not much use."

We pushed the piano stool in front of the open window so that, for as long as I could, I would be able to smell the ancient, reconciling smell of the sea that, in time, will cleanse everything, scour the old bones white, wash away all the stains. The last little chambermaid had trotted along the causeway long ago and now the tide, fated as I, came tumbling in, the crisp wavelets splashing on the old   1100 stones.

"You do not deserve this," he said.

"Who can say what I deserve or no?" I said. "I've done nothing; but that may be sufficient reason for condemning me."

"You disobeyed him," he said. "That is sufficient reason for him to punish you."

"I only did what he knew I would."

"Like Eve," he said.

The telephone rang a shrill imperative. Let it ring. But my lover lifted me up and set me on my feet; I knew I must answer it. The receiver felt heavy as earth.   1110

"The courtyard. Immediately."

My lover kissed me, he took my hand. He would come with me if I would lead him. Courage. When I thought of courage, I thought of my mother. Then I saw a muscle in my lover's face quiver.

"Hoofbeats!" he said.

I cast one last, desperate glance from the window and, like a miracle, I saw a horse and rider galloping at a vertiginous speed along the causeway, though the waves crashed, now, high as the horse's fetlocks. A rider, her black skirts tucked up around her waist so she could ride hard and fast, a crazy, magnificent horse-woman in widow's weeds.   1120

As the telephone rang again.

"Am I to wait all morning?"

Every moment, my mother drew nearer.

"She will be too late," Jean-Yves said and yet he could not restrain a note of hope that, though it must be so, yet it might not be so.

The third, intransigent call.

"Shall I come up to heaven to fetch you down, Saint Cecilia? You wicked woman, do you wish me to compound my crimes by desecrating the marriage bed?"

So I must go to the courtyard where my husband waited in his London-   1130 tailored trousers and the shirt from Turnbull and Asser, beside the mounting block, with, in his hand, the sword which his great-grandfather had presented to the little corporal, in token of surrender to the Republic, before he shot himself. The heavy sword, unsheathed, grey as that November morning, sharp as childbirth, mortal.

When my husband saw my companion, he observed: "Let the blind lead the blind, eh? But does even a youth as besotted as you are think she was truly blind to her own desires when she took my ring? Give it me back, whore!"

The fires in the opal had all died down. I gladly slipped it from my finger and, even in that dolorous place, my heart was lighter for the lack of it. My husband took it lovingly and lodged it on the tip of his little finger; it would go no further.

"It will serve me for a dozen more fiancées," he said. "To the block, woman. No—leave the boy; I shall deal with him later, utilizing a less exalted instrument than the one with which I do my wife the honour of her immolation, for do not fear that in death you will be divided."

Slowly, slowly, one foot before the other, I crossed the cobbles. The longer I dawdled over my execution, the more time it gave the avenging angel to descend . . .

"Don't loiter, girl! Do you think I shall lose appetite for the meal if you are so long about serving it? No; I shall grow hungrier, more ravenous with each moment, more cruel . . . Run to me, run! I have a place prepared for your exquisite corpse in my display of flesh!"

He raised the sword and cut bright segments from the air with it, but still I lingered although my hopes, so recently raised, now began to flag. If she is not here by now, her horse must have stumbled on the causeway, have plunged into the sea . . . One thing only made me glad; that my lover would not see me die.

My husband laid my branded forehead on the stone and, as he had done once before, twisted my hair into a rope and drew it away from my neck.

"Such a pretty neck," he said with what seemed to be a genuine, retrospective tenderness. "A neck like the stem of a young plant."

I felt the silken bristle of his beard and the wet touch of his lips as he kissed my nape. And, once again, of my apparel I must retain only my gems; the sharp blade ripped my dress in two and it fell from me. A little green moss, growing in the crevices of the mounting block, would be the last thing I should see in all the world.

The whizz of that heavy sword.

And—a great battering and pounding at the gate, the jangling of the bell, the frenzied neighing of a horse! The unholy silence of the place shattered in an instant. The blade did *not* descend, the necklace did *not* sever, my head did *not* roll. For, for an instant, the beast wavered in his stroke, a sufficient split second of astonished indecision to let me spring upright and dart to the assistance of my lover as he struggled sightlessly with the great bolts that kept her out.

The Marquis stood transfixed, utterly dazed, at a loss. It must have been as if he had been watching his beloved *Tristan* for the twelfth, the thirteenth time and Tristan stirred, then leapt from his bier in the last act, announced in a jaunty aria interposed from Verdi that bygones were bygones, crying over spilt milk did nobody any good and, as for himself, he proposed to live happily ever after. The puppet master, open-mouthed, wide-eyed, impotent at the last, saw his dolls break free of their strings, abandon the rituals he had ordained for them since time began and start to live for themselves; the king, aghast, witnesses the revolt of his pawns. 1180

You never saw such a wild thing as my mother, her hat seized by the winds and blown out to sea so that her hair was her white mane, her black lisle legs exposed to the thigh, her skirts tucked round her waist, one hand on the reins of the rearing horse while the other clasped my father's service revolver and, behind her, the breakers of the savage, indifferent sea, like the witnesses of a furious justice. And my husband stood stock-still, as if she had been Medusa, the sword still raised over his head as in those clockwork tableaux of Bluebeard that you see in glass cases at fairs. 1190

And then it was as though a curious child pushed his centime into the slot and set all in motion. The heavy, bearded figure roared out aloud, braying with fury, and, wielding the honourable sword as if it were a matter of death or glory, charged us, all three.

On her eighteenth birthday, my mother had disposed of a man-eating tiger that had ravaged the villages in the hills north of Hanoi. Now, without a moment's hesitation, she raised my father's gun, took aim and put a single, irreproachable bullet through my husband's head.

We lead a quiet life, the three of us. I inherited, of course, enormous wealth but we have given most of it away to various charities. The castle is now a school 1200 for the blind, though I pray that the children who live there are not haunted by any sad ghosts looking for, crying for, the husband who will never return to the bloody chamber, the contents of which are buried or burned, the door sealed.

I felt I had a right to retain sufficient funds to start a little music school here, on the outskirts of Paris, and we do well enough. Sometimes we can even afford to go to the Opéra, though never to sit in a box, of course. We know we are the source of many whisperings and much gossip but the three of us know the truth of it and mere chatter can never harm us. I can only bless the—what shall I call it?—the *maternal telepathy* that sent my mother running headlong from the telephone to the station after I had called her, that night. I never heard you cry before, 1210 she said, by way of explanation. Not when you were happy. And who ever cried because of gold bath taps?

The night train, the one I had taken; she lay in her berth, sleepless as I had been. When she could not find a taxi at that lonely halt, she borrowed old Dobbin from a bemused farmer, for some internal urgency told her that she must reach me before the incoming tide sealed me away from her for ever. My poor old nurse, left scandalized at home—what? interrupt milord on his honeymoon?—she died soon after. She had taken so much secret pleasure in the fact that her little girl had become a marquise; and now here I was, scarcely a penny the richer, widowed at seventeen in the most dubious circumstances and busily engaged in setting up 1220 house with a piano-tuner. Poor thing, she passed away in a sorry state of disillusion! But I do believe my mother loves him as much as I do.

No paint or powder, no matter how thick or white, can mask that red mark on my forehead; I am glad he cannot see it—not for fear of his revulsion, since I know he sees me clearly with his heart—but, because it spares my shame. [1979]

Questions for Discussion and Writing

1. How does knowledge of the Bluebeard story affect the story's suspense?
2. Carter has transformed the Bluebeard story from a fairy tale to a Gothic horror story. How does this change of conventions suit her purposes? What do the Gothic conventions enable her to do that she could not do within the fairy tale conventions?
3. Fairy tale characters often seem directed by fate or destiny rather than motivated by internal psychology. Is this true of Carter's characters, or has she provided motivations consistent with their actions? Consider the Marquis, the mother, and the narrator in your answer.
4. Why does the heroine retain the mark of "sin" on her forehead? In what way has she sinned? Against whom or what?
5. Why is it the mother, rather than the brothers, who rescues the heroine? What point does Carter make by this change?

ꝏ CARLOS FUENTES
(b. 1928)

TRANSLATED BY MARGARET SAYERS PEDEN

These Were Palaces

Diplomat and author, Carlos Fuentes played an important role in the upsurge of interest in Latin American literature in the 1960s. He was born in Panama City, where his father, a Mexican diplomat, was serving. From 1934 to 1940 he attended school in Washington, D.C. During this time, Mexico's President Lazaro Cardenas appropriated American-owned oil wells. Overnight, Americans who had been his friends became hostile. After leaving America, Fuentes followed his father to various Latin American capitals, including Montevideo and Rio de Janeiro, absorbing a wide variety of cultures.

His first publication, *The Masked Days* (1954), was translated in 1980 as part of his famous novel, *Burnt Water* (1980). This was followed by *Where the Air Is Clear* (1958, trans. 1960), a novel that makes use of an innovative and influential mix of anthropology, film, painting, and music. In 1956, Fuentes helped to found the *Mexican Review of Literature*, and in the following year took up the first of several diplomatic posts.

Fuentes calls his style symbolic realism and focuses his attention on problems of intercultural understanding, particularly between the United States and Mexico. He is also dedicated to Mexican cultural identity and to awakening the

Mexican middle classes to their materialism and status seeking. "These Were Palaces" suggests, among other ideas, the richness of Mexico's past in contrast to its present poverty.

N O ONE BELIEVED HER when she began saying that the dogs were coming closer, batty old bag, crazy old loon she was, muttering to herself all day long, what nightmares she must have; after what she'd done to her daughter she couldn't help but have bad nights. Besides, old people's brains get drier and drier until there's nothing left but a shriveled little nut rattling around like a marble in their hollow heads. But Doña Manuelita is so virtuous, she doesn't just water her own flowers, she waters all the flowers on the second floor, every morning you can see her carrying her green gasoline tin, her yellowed fingers sprinkling water over the big clay pots of geraniums lining the iron railing, every evening you see her slipping the covers over the bird cages so the canaries can sleep in quiet.   10

Some say, isn't Doña Manuelita the most peaceful person you've ever known? What makes people say bad things about her? Old, and all alone, she never does anything out of the ordinary, never calls attention to herself. The flowerpots in the morning, the bird cages in the evening. About nine, she goes out to do her shopping at La Merced market, and on the way back she stops in the big square of the Zócalo and goes into the Cathedral to pray for a while. Then she comes back to the old palace, a tenement now, and fixes her meal. Fried beans, warmed-over tortillas, fresh tomatoes, mint and onion, shredded chilis: the odors wafting out of Señora Manuela's kitchen are the same as those borne on the smoke from all the meals cooked over old charcoal-burning braziers. All alone, she eats, and stares at   20 the black grate awhile, and rests, she must rest. They say she's earned it. All those years a servant in a rich man's house, a lifetime, you might say.

After the siesta, about dusk, she goes out again, all stooped over, her basket filled with dry tortillas, and that's when the dogs begin to gather. It's only natural. As she walks along she throws them the tortillas, and the dogs know it and follow her. When she can get enough together to buy a chicken, she saves the bones and throws them to the dogs as they follow her down La Moneda Street. The butcher says she shouldn't do it, chicken bones are bad for dogs, they can choke on them, chicken bones splinter and pierce the intestines. Then all the badmouths say that's proof that Doña Manuelita is an evil woman, look at that, luring the dogs just to   30 kill them.

She returns about seven, soaked to the bone in the rainy season, her shoes gray with dust when it's dry. That's how everyone always thinks of her, bone-white, shrouded in dust between October and April, and between May and September a soppy mess, her shawl plastered to her head, raindrops dripping from her nose and trickling down the furrows of her eyes and cheeks and off the white hairs on her chin. She comes back from her adventures in the black blouse and flapping skirts and black stockings she always hangs out in the night air to dry. She's the only one who dares to dry her clothes at night. What did I tell you, she's mad as a hatter, what if it rains, then what good does it do? There's no sun at   40 night. And there are thieves. Never you mind. She hangs her soaked rags on the communal clotheslines that stretch in all directions across the patio of the building. I'll let them hang in the night air, the gossips imagine Doña Manuelita saying. Because the truth is, no one's ever heard her speak. And no one's ever seen her sleep. Suppositions. Doña Manuela's clothes disappear from the clothesline before anyone's up. She's never been seen at the washtubs, kneeling beside the other women, scrubbing, soaping, gossiping.

"She reminds me of a lonely old queen, forgotten by everyone," little Luisito used to say before he'd been forbidden to see her, or even speak to her.

"When she's coming up the stone staircase, I can imagine how this was a 50 great palace, Mother, how a long time ago very powerful and wealthy gentlemen lived here."

"I don't want you to have anything to do with her any more. Remember what happened to her daughter. You, more than anyone, ought to remember."

"I never knew her daughter."

"She wants you to take her place. I won't have that, that would be the last straw, the old witch."

"She's the only one who ever takes me out. Everyone else is always too busy."

"Your little sister's big enough now. She can take you."

So, following his directions, Rosa María pushed little Luisito in his wheel- 60 chair, wherever he wanted to go. Toward Tacuba Street if what he wanted to see were the old stone and volcanic rock palaces of the Viceregency, wide porticos studded with nail heads as big as coins, balconies of wrought iron, niches shelter- ing stone Virgins, high gutters and drains of verdigris copper. Toward the squat, faded little houses along Jesús Carranza Street if, on the other hand, it was his whim to think about Doña Manuelita. He was the only one who'd ever been in the old woman's room and kitchen, the only one who could describe them. There wasn't much to describe, that was the interesting thing. Behind the doors that were also windows—the wooden kitchen door hung with sheer curtains, the door to her room covered by a sheet strung on copper rods—there was nothing worthy 70 of comment. Just a cot. Everyone else decorated their rooms with calendars, altars, religious prints, newspaper clippings, flowers, soccer pennants and bullfight posters, paper Mexican flags, snapshots taken at fairs, at the Shrine of the Guadalupe. But not Manuelita. Nothing. A kitchen with clay utensils, a bag of charcoal, food for her daily meal, and the one room with its cot. Nothing more.

"You've been there. What does she have there? What's she hiding?"

"Nothing."

"What does she do?"

"Nothing. Everything she does she does outside her room. Anyone can see her—the flowerpots, the shopping, the dogs and the canaries. Besides, if you don't 80 trust her, why do you let her water your geraniums and cover your birds for the night? Aren't you afraid your flowers will wither and your little birds will die?"

It's hard to believe how slowly the outings with Rosa María go. She's thirteen years old but not half as strong as Doña Manuelita. At every street corner she has to ask for help to get the wheelchair onto the sidewalk. The old woman had been able to do it by herself. With her, if they went down Tacuba, Donceles, and Gonzales Obregón to the Plaza of Santo Domingo, it was little Luisito who did the talking, it was he who imagined the city as it had been in colonial times, it was he

who told the old woman how the Spanish city had been constructed, laid out like
a chessboard above the ruins of the Aztec capital. As a little boy, he told Doña   90
Manuelita, they'd sent him to school, it had been torture, the cruel jokes, the invalid, the cripple, his wheelchair tipped over, the cowards laughing and running
away, he lying there waiting for his teachers to pick him up. That's why he'd asked
them not to send him, to let him stay home, kids can be cruel, it was true, it
wasn't just a saying, he'd learned that lesson, now they left him alone reading at
home, the rest of them went out to work, except his mother, Doña Lourdes, and
his sister Rosa María, all he wanted was to be left to read by himself, to educate
himself, please, for the love of God. His legs weren't going to get well in any
school, he swore he'd study better by himself, honest, couldn't they take up a collection to buy him his books, later he'd go to a vocational school, he promised,   100
but only when it could be among men you could talk to and ask for a little compassion. Children don't know what compassion is.

But Doña Manuelita knew, yes, she knew. When she pushed his wheelchair
toward the ugly parts of their neighborhood, toward the empty lots along Canal
del Norte, turning right at the traffic circle of Peralvillo, it was she who did the
talking, and pointed out the dogs to him, there were more dogs than men in these
parts, stray dogs without masters, without collars, dogs born God knows where,
born of a fleeting encounter between dogs exactly like each other, a male and a
bitch locked together after the humping, strung together like two links of a
scabrous chain, while the children of the neighborhood laughed and threw stones 110
at them, and then, separated forever, forever, forever, how was the bitch to remember her mate, when alone, in one of a hundred empty lots, she whelped a litter of pups abandoned the day after they were born? How could the bitch
remember her own children?

"Imagine, little Luis, imagine if dogs could remember one another, imagine
what would happen . . ."

A secret shiver filled with cold pleasure ran down little Luisito's spine when
he watched the boys of Paralvillo stoning the dogs, chasing them, provoking angry
barking, then howls of pain, finally, whimpering, as, heads bloody, tails between
their legs, eyes yellow, hides mangy, they fled into the distance until they were lost 120
in the vacant lots beneath the burning sun of all the mornings of Mexico. The
dogs, the boys, all lacerated by the sun. Where did they eat? Where did they
sleep?

"You see, little Luis, if you're hungry, you can ask for food. A dog can't ask. A
dog must take his food anywhere he can find it."

But it was painful for little Luis to ask, and he did have to ask. They took up
the collection and bought his books. He knew that a long time ago in the big
house in Orizaba they'd had more books than they could ever read, books his
great-grandfather had ordered from Europe and then gone to Veracruz to wait for,
a shipment of illustrated magazines and huge books of adventure tales that he'd 130
read to his children during the long nights of the tropical rainy season. As the family grew poor, everything had been sold, and finally they'd ended up in Mexico
City because there were more opportunities there than in Orizaba, and because his
father'd been given a place as archivist at the Ministry of Finance. The building

where they lived was close to the National Palace and his father could walk every day and save the bus fare. Almost everyone who worked in the office wasted two or three hours a day coming to the Zócalo from their houses in remote suburbs and returning after work. Little Luis watched how the memories, the family traditions, faded away with the years. His older brothers hadn't graduated from secondary school, they didn't read, one worked for the Department of the Federal District and the other in the shoe department at the Palacio de Hierro. Of course, among them they made enough money to move to a little house in Lindavista, but that was a long way away, and besides, here in the old building on La Moneda they had the best rooms, a living room and three bedrooms, more than anyone else had. And in a place that had been a palace centuries ago little Luis found it easier to imagine things, and remember.

If only dogs could remember each other, Doña Manuelita said. But we forget, too, we forget other people and forget about our own family, little Luisito replied. At dinnertime he liked to remember the big house in Orizaba, the white façade with wrought-iron work at the windows, the ground behind the house plunging toward a decaying ravine odorous of mangrove and banana trees. In the depths of the ravine you could hear the constant sound of a rushing stream, and beyond, high above, you could see the huge mountains ringing Orizaba, looming so close they frightened you. It was like living beside a giant crowned with fog. And how it rained. It never stopped raining.

The others looked at him strangely; his father, Don Raúl, lowered his head, his mother sighed and shook hers, one brother laughed aloud, the other made a circling motion at his brow with his index finger. Little Luisito was "touched," where did he get such ideas, why he'd never been in Orizaba, he was born and bred in Mexico City, after all, the family'd come to the city forty years ago. Rosa María hadn't even heard him, she just kept eating, her shoe-button eyes were as hard as stone, and held no memories. How it pained little Luisito to beg for everything, for books and for memories. I don't forget, I collect postcards, there's the trunk filled with old snapshots, it's used as a chest, I know everything that's inside.

Doña Manuela knew all this, too, because little Luisito had told her, before they'd forbidden her to take him out for a walk. When she was alone in her room, lying on her cot, she tried to communicate silently with the boy, remembering the same things he remembered.

"Just imagine, Manuelita, how this building must have looked before."

That was little Luisito's other memory, as if the past of that big house now shared by twelve families complemented the memory of the one and only house, the house in Orizaba, the house that belonged to only one family, his family, when they'd had an important name.

"Just imagine, these were palaces."

The old woman made a great effort to remember everything the boy told her and then imagine, as he did and when he did, a majestic palace: the entryway before there was a lottery stand, the carved marble façade stripped of cheap clothing stores, the bridal shop, the photographer's shop, and the soft-drinks stand, free of the advertisements that disfigured the ancient nobility of the building. A clean,

austere, noble palace, a murmuring fountain in the center of the patio instead of
the clotheslines and washtubs, the great stone stairway, the ground floor reserved
for the servants, the horses, the kitchens, the grain storerooms, and the smell of
straw and jelly.

And on the main floor, what did the boy remember? Oh, great salons
smelling of wax and varnish, harpsichords, he said, balls and banquets, bedcham-
bers with cool brick floors, beds draped with mosquito netting, mirrored
wardrobes, oil lamps. This is the way that Doña Manuelita, alone in her room,
spoke with little Luis, after they'd been separated. This is the way she communicated with him, by remembering the things he remembered and forgetting about   190
her own past, the house where she'd worked all her life until she was an old
woman, General Vergara's house in the Roma district, twenty-five years of service,
until they'd moved out to Pedregal. There hadn't been time to win the friendship
of young Plutarco; the new mistress, Señora Evangelina, had died only a few years
after marrying the General's son, and her mistress Clotilde before that; Manuela
had been only fifty when she was fired, she reminded the General of too many
things, that's why he fired her. But he was generous. He continued to pay her rent
in the tenement on La Moneda.

"Live your last years in peace, Manuela," General Vergara had said to her.
"Every time I see you I think of my Clotilde. Goodbye."   200

Doña Manuelita chewed on a yellowed, knotted finger as she remembered
her employer's words, those memories kept intruding into the memories she
shared with little Luisito, they had nothing to do with them, Doña Clotilde was
dead, she was a saint, the General had been influential in Calle's[1] government, so
in the midst of the religious persecution Mass was celebrated in the cellar of the
house; every day Doña Clotilde, the servant Manuelita, and Manuelita's daughter,
Lupe Lupita, went to confession and received Communion. The priest would arrive at the house in lay clothes, carrying a kit like a doctor's bag containing his
vestments, the ciborium,[2] the wine and the hosts, a Father Téllez, a young priest, a
saint, whom the sainted Doña Clotilde had saved from death, giving him refuge   210
when all his friends had gone before the firing wall, shot in the early morning with
their arms opened out in a cross; she'd seen the photographs in El Universal.

That's why she'd felt so bad when the General fired her, it was as if he'd
wanted to kill her. She'd survived Doña Clotilde, she remembered too many
things, the General wanted to be left alone with his past. Maybe he was right,
maybe it was better for both of them, the employer and the servant, to go their
own ways with their secret memories, without serving as the other's witness, better
that way. She again gnawed at her finger. The General still had his son and grandson, but Manuelita had lost her daughter, she would never see her again, all because she'd brought her to this accursed tenement, she'd had to break her little   220
Lupita's solitude, in her employer's home she'd never seen anyone, she had no reason ever to leave the ground floor, she could get around quite easily in her wheelchair. But in this building there was no escape, all the overhelpful people, all the

1. Elias Calles, President of Mexico, 1924–1928.
2. A receptacle for Communion bread.

nosy people, everyone carrying her up and down stairs, let her get some sun, let her get some air, let her get out on the street, they took her from me, they stole her from me, they'll pay for it. Doña Manuela's few remaining teeth drew blood. She must think about little Luisito. She was never going to see Lupe Lupita again.

"Take me out to the empty lots where all the dogs gather," little Luisito directed Rosa María.

Some masons were constructing a wall on the vacant lot along Canal del 230 Norte. But they'd just begun to raise the cement partition on one side of the lot, and little Luisito told Rosa María to go down the other side, away from the workmen. There were no children today, but a gang of teenagers in jeans and striped jerseys, all laughing, they'd caught a dog as gray as the wall. The workmen were watching from a distance, wielding trowels and mortar, watching and elbowing one another from time to time. Beyond them, the sound of the armada of trucks choking the traffic circle of Peralvillo: buses, building-supply trucks, open exhausts, smoke, desperate horns, implacable noise. It had been in Peralvillo that little Luisito had been hit by the tram. The last streetcar in Mexico City, and it had to hit him. The teenagers clamped the dog's muzzle shut; while a few held its legs, 240 one of them laboriously cut off its tail, a mass of blood and gray hairs, better to have chopped it off with a machete, quick and clean.

They hacked at the ragged stump, leaving threads of flesh and a jet of blood spurting into the animal's throbbing anus. But the other dogs of this pack that gathered every morning on the empty lots where the workmen had begun the wall hadn't run away. They were all there, all the dogs together, at a distance, but together, watching the gray dog's torture, silent, muzzles frothing, dogs of the sun, look, Rosa María, they're not running away, and they're not just standing there stupefied waiting for it to happen to them next, no, Rosa María, look, they're looking at each other, they're telling each other something, they're remembering what's 250 happening to one of their own, Doña Manuelita's right, these dogs are going to remember the pain of one of their own pack, how one of them suffered at the hands of a bunch of cowardly teenagers, but Rosa María's shoe-button eyes were like stone, without memory.

About one o'clock Doña Manuelita peered through the curtains on her door as the girl returned, pushing her brother in his chair. Even from a distance she could see the dust on the girl's shoes and she knew that they'd gone to the empty lots where the dogs gathered. In the late afternoon the old woman covered her head with her shawl, filled her shopping bag with dry tortillas and old rags, and went out to the street.   260

A dog was waiting for her in the doorway. It stared at her with its glassy eyes and whined, asking her to follow. When they reached the corner of Vidal Alcocer, she was joined by five more dogs, and all along Guatemala, by dogs of every breed, brown, spotted, black, about twenty of them, milling around Doña Manuelita as she portioned out pieces of dry tortilla, already turning green. They surrounded her and then preceded her, showing her the way, they followed her, nudging her softly with their muzzles, their ears erect, until they reached the iron fence before the Sagrario, the chapel of the Metropolitan Cathedral. From a distance, the old woman could see the gray dog lying beside the carved wooden door beneath the baroque eaves of the portal.   270

Doña Manuela and her dogs stepped into the great stone-floored atrium, she sat beside the injured dog, you're the one they call Cloudy, aren't you, poor half-blind fellow, well, just be thankful you have that one blind eye as blue as the sky and you can see only half the world, dear God, just look what they've done to you, come here, Cloudy, here on my lap, let me bandage your tail, bastards, picking on you for their fun, sons of your poor bitching mothers, just because dogs can't defend themselves or talk or call for help, I don't know any more whether they do these things to dumb animals to keep from doing them to each other or whether they're only practicing what they plan to do tomorrow, who knows, who knows, let's see now, Cloudy, poor old puppy, why I've known you since the day   280 you were born, left on a rubbish heap, blind in that eye since birth, your mother didn't have time to lick you clean, right away you were tossed into the garbage and that's where I found you, there now, is that better? poor fellow, the cowards would pick on you, on you the most helpless of all my dogs, let's go give thanks, let's go pray for the well-being of all dogs, let's go pray, there, in the house of the Lord our God, Creator of all things.

Quietly, bent over, petting the dogs, more stooped than usual, with sweet words, Doña Manuela entered the Cathedral of Mexico that afternoon with her twenty dogs surrounding her; they managed to reach the main altar, it was the best hour, no one around but a few devout old women and two or three peasants   290 staring at the ceiling with their arms uplifted. Doña Manuelita knelt before the altar, praying aloud, a miracle, God, give my dogs a voice, give them some way to defend themselves, give them some way to remember each other and remember those who have tortured them, God, you who suffered on the cross, have mercy on these dumb animals, do not forsake them, give them the strength to defend themselves, since you did not give men mercy or teach them to treat these poor animals with tenderness. Oh, God, my Jesus, God and True Man, show that you are all of these, and give equally to all your creatures, not the same riches, no, not that, I'm not asking that much, only equal mercy so they can understand each other, or if not that, equal strength to defend themselves, don't give more love to   300 some of your creatures than to others, God, because those you have loved least will love you less, and they will say you are the devil.

Several of the women praying shushed her and one exasperatedly asked for silence and another cried, Respect the House of God, and then acolytes and two priests came running toward the altar, aghast, what sacrilege, a mad woman and a pack of mangy dogs. None of this had any effect on Doña Manuela, she'd never experienced such exaltation, she'd never spoken such beautiful and heartfelt words, almost as beautiful as those her daughter, Lupe, knew how to speak. The old woman stood there, so happy, more than bathed, feeling embalmed in the afternoon light filtering down from the highest domes, multiplied in reflections   310 from silver organ pipes, golden frames, humble vigil lights, and the glowing varnish of the rows of pews. And God, to whom she'd been speaking, was answering her, He was saying:

"Manuela, you must believe in me in spite of the fact that the world is cruel and unjust. That is the trial I send you. If the world were perfect, you would have no need to believe in me, do you understand?"

But now the priests and acolytes were dragging her away from the altar, shooing the dogs; one maddened acolyte was beating the animals with a crucifix and another was dousing them with incense to stupefy them. All the dogs began barking at once and Doña Manuela, pushed and pummeled, looked at the crystal 320 coffins wherein lay the wax statues of Christs more ill-treated than she or the dog Cloudy. Blood from your thorns, blood from your side, blood from your feet and hands, blood from your eyes, Christ of my heart, look what they have done to you, what are our sufferings compared to yours? Then why won't you allow me and my dogs to speak of our little pains here in your house that was built large enough to hold all your pain and ours?

Flung to her knees on the flat stones of the atrium, surrounded by her dogs, she was humiliated because she'd been unable to explain the truth to the priests and the acolytes, and then she was ashamed as she looked up and met the staring, uncomprehending eyes of little Luisito and Rosa María. Their mother, Señora 330 Lourdes, was with them. But her eyes, oh yes, her eyes had something to say: look! that's the proof of what kind of woman old Manuela is, just what I've always said, we'll have to cast her from our building the way the priest cast her from the temple. In the shocked recrimination of those eyes Doña Manuelita saw menace, gossip, everyone remembering once again what she'd been able to forget and make others forget by her discretion, her decency, her helpful everyday chores, watering the geraniums, covering the canaries' cages.

Luisito looked quickly from his mother's eyes to Señora Manuela's. With both hands on the wheels he pushed his chair to where the old woman lay sprawled. He held out his hand, offering her a handkerchief.   340

"Here, Manuela. You've hurt your forehead."

"Thank you, but don't get yourself in trouble over me. Go back to your mother. Look at the terrible way she's staring at us."

"It doesn't matter. Please forgive me."

"But for what, child?"

"Every time I go out to the vacant lots and see how they treat the dogs, I feel good."

"But, Luis, child."

"I think to myself, if it weren't for them I'd be the one getting the beating. As if the dogs stood between those boys and me, suffering in my place. I'm the 350 biggest coward of all, aren't I, Manuela?"

"Who knows," the stunned woman murmured as she dried the blood from her head with Luis's handkerchief; who knows, as laboriously she struggled to her feet, placing one hand on the ground and the other on her knee, then crossing them over her bulging belly and then on the arm of the wheelchair, rising like a statue of rags fallen from the highest niche of the Sagrario; who knows, is there anything you can do to make the dogs forgive you?

I'm fourteen, almost fifteen, I can talk to them like a man, they always will call me little Luis because I'll never grow very big, I'll be stuck in my chair getting smaller and smaller until I die, but today I'm fourteen, almost fifteen, and I can 360 talk to them like a man and they'll have to listen to me. He repeated these words over and over that night as before supper he pored over the photographs and postcards and letters stored in the trunk that now served as a chest, since everything had to do double duty in these tenements that used to be palaces and now sheltered down-on-their-luck families who lived there with former servants, they who'd been wealthy in Orizaba, and Manuelita, who had never been more than a servant in a wealthy house. Little Luis repeated those words to himself, sitting at his usual place at the table that was used for preparing and eating their meals, as well as for schoolwork and the extra accounting his father brought home so as to pay the bills every month. 370

Sitting in silence, waiting for someone to speak first, staring intently at his mother, daring her to begin, to tell here at the dinner table what had happened to Doña Manuela that afternoon, so yes, the gossip would begin here and tomorrow everyone in the building would know: they beat her and chased her from the Cathedral along with all her dogs. No one was saying anything, because, when she wished, Señora Lourdes knew how to impose an icy silence, to make clear to everyone that it was no time for joking, that she was reserving the right to announce something very serious.

She directed a bitter smile to each of them—to her husband, Raúl, to her two older sons, who were waiting impatiently to go to the movies with their 380 sweethearts, to Rosa María, who could hardly keep awake—but she waited until everyone had served himself the simple rice with peas to tell again the same story, the one she always dragged out to prove how bad Doña Manuelita was, how she'd made her own daughter, Lupe Lupita, believe that when she was a little girl she'd had a bad fall and that she'd been crippled and would always have to be in a wheelchair, nothing but lies, why there was nothing wrong with her at all, nothing but the selfishness and evil of Doña Manuela, who wanted to keep the girl with her forever so she'd never be alone, even if it meant ruining her own daughter's life.

"Thanks to you, Pepe," Doña Lourdes said to her oldest son. "You suspected 390 something and convinced her to get out of the wheelchair and try to walk, and you showed her how, thanks to you, my son, Lupe Lupita was saved from her mother's clutches."

"For God's sake, Mother, that's all over now, don't keep bringing it up, please," Pepe said, blushing, as he always did when his mother told the story, and stroking his thin black mustache.

"That's why I've forbidden Luis to have anything to do with Manuela. And now, this very afternoon . . ."

"Mother," Luis interrupted, "I'm almost fifteen, I'm fourteen years old, Mother, I can talk to you like a man." He looked at his father's face, drained by fa- 400 tigue, at the sleepy face of Rosa María, a girl without memories, at the stupid faces of his brothers, at the impossible pride, the haughty apprehension of his mother's beautiful face, none of them had inherited those high, hard, everlasting bones.

"Mama, that time I fell down the staircase . . ."

"It was an accident. No one was to blame."

"I know that, Mother, that isn't the point. But what I remember is how everyone in the building peeked out to see what was going on. I cried out. I was so afraid. But everyone stayed right where they were, staring, even you. She was the only one who came running to help me. She hugged me, she looked to see if I

was hurt, and ruffled my hair. I could see all their faces, Mother. I didn't see a sin- 410
gle face that wanted to help me. Just the opposite, Mother. In that moment, everyone wanted me dead, everyone wished it, I guess, out of compassion—poor little
fellow, take him out of his misery, it's better that way, what can life offer him? Even
you, Mother."

"That isn't true, Luis, how could you make up such a vicious lie?"

"I'm not very bright, Mother. I'm sorry. You're right. Doña Manuela needs me
because she lost her Lupe Lupita. She wants me to take her place."

"Of course she does. Have you just realized that?"

"No. I've always known it, but I couldn't find the words to say it until now.
It's good to know you're needed, it's good to know that if it weren't for you another 420
person would be terribly lonely. It's good to need someone, like Manuela needed
her daughter, like I need Manuela, like you need someone, Mother, everyone does . . . Like Manuela and her dogs need each other, like all of us need something, need to do something, tell something, even if it isn't true, write letters and
say that things haven't been going too badly for us, in fact that we're living in Las
Lomas, isn't that right, and that Papa has a factory, that my brothers are lawyers,
and that Rosa María is in boarding school in Canada, and I'm your pride and joy,
Mother, first in my class, a champion horseback rider, yes, me, Mother . . ."

Don Raúl laughed quietly, nodding his head. "That's what you always
wanted, Lourdes, how well your son knows you."   430

The mother's eyes, proud and despairing, did not leave little Luis's face,
denying, denying, with all the intensity her silence could muster. His father was
shaking his head: "What a shame that I couldn't give you any of that."

"You've never heard me complain, Raúl."

"No," the father said, "never. But once, way back at the beginning, you told
me the things you'd like to have had, only once, more than twenty years ago, but
I've never forgotten, though you never said it again."

"I never said it again, I've never reproached you for anything." And Señora
Lourdes's eyes were on little Luis, in wild supplication.

But the boy was talking about Orizaba now, about the big house, the pho- 440
tographs and postcards, he'd never been there, so he had to imagine it all, the balconies, the rain, the mountains, the ravine, the furniture in that once-opulent
house, the friends of a family like that, the suitors, why do you choose one person
over another to marry, Mother, aren't you ever sorry, don't you ever dream what
life could have been like with another man, and then you write letters to make
him think everything worked out, that you'd made the right choice? I'm fourteen,
I can speak like a man . . ."

"I don't know," said Don Raúl, as if coming back from a dream, as if he
hadn't followed the conversation too closely. "The Revolution got us all off the
track, some for the better and others for the worse. There was one way to be rich 450
before the Revolution, and a different way after. We knew how to be rich in the
good old days, but we were left behind, what can you do?" He laughed softly, the
way he always laughed.

"I never mailed those letters, you know that very well," Doña Lourdes said to
little Luis in a tight voice as she helped him to bed, as she did every night, the
same bed beside Rosa María, who'd fallen asleep at the table.

"Thank you, Mother, thank you for not saying anything about Manuela and her dogs."

He kissed her affectionately.

All next day Doña Manuelita expected the worst and went around watching 460 for signs of hostility. That's probably why, very early, as she was gathering up her clothing and then watering the geraniums, she knew many eyes were watching her, curtains were silently drawn back, half-opened shutters were hastily shut, dozens of dark eyes, some veiled by the drooping lids of age, some young and round and liquid, were watching her in secret, were waiting for her without saying so, were approving of those tasks she was doing as if seeking forgiveness for what had happened with Lupe Lupita. Doña Manuela finally realized that she was doing these chores so they would be grateful to her, so they would never again throw the business of Lupe in her face. More than ever, that day, she realized that, she knew the arrangement was of long standing, that everyone had come to an understand- 470 ing without any need for words, they were grateful that she watered the flowers and covered the bird cages, no one was going to say anything about what happened in the Cathedral, no one would humiliate her, everyone would forgive her for everything.

Doña Manuela spent the whole day in her room. She'd convinced herself that nothing was going to happen, but experience had taught her to be wary, alert, keep on your toes, Doña Manuela, best to sleep with one eye open, eh? Brooding in her single room and her kitchen, she fell prey to a strange bitterness, something foreign to her. If they no longer thought ill of her, why hadn't they shown it before? Why, only now that she'd been humiliated in the Cathedral, did everyone in 480 the building respect her? She didn't understand, she just didn't understand. Was it because the Señora Lourdes, Luis and Rosa María's mother, hadn't done any gossiping?

She lay on her cot, staring at the bare walls and thinking about her dogs, how thanks to her, through her, they transmitted their news, how they talked to one another and to her, Cloudy's been hurt, he's curled up by the Sagrario in bad shape, poor thing, let's go pray to God Our Savior and ask Him to keep them from chasing us or abusing us any more, Doña Manuela.

It was the same with her and little Luisito, each could sense what the other felt, if she knew what he was feeling, he must know as well what she felt, they had 490 so many things in common, especially the wheelchair, Luisito's and Lupe Lupita's. Young Pepe, little Luis's brother, took Lupe Lupita from her wheelchair. Manuela had put her there to protect her, not because she herself needed a companion, a servant is always lonely by virtue of being a servant, no, that wasn't it, it was to save her from their appetites, the way they would look at her. General Vergara with his bad reputation, his son Tín, always chasing after servant girls, no, she didn't want them to lay a hand on her Lupe Lupita, no one would try anything with a cripple, they'd feel too disgusted or too ashamed, anyone should know that . . .

"I'm telling you this now, daughter, now that you've gone forever, it was to 500 save you, I tried to save you from the terrible fate that lies in store for a servant's daughter when she is beautiful, ever since you were a little girl I tried to save you,

that's why I named you as I did, twice Lupe, Lupe Lupita, twice virgin, twice protected, my little girl."

It was a very long day, but Doña Manuelita knew there was nothing to do
but wait. The moment would come. She would receive a sign. She'd let herself feel
what her friend Luisito was feeling. They had so much in common, the wheelchair, his brother Pepe, who'd ruined La Lupita, and left her with only one of her
names, her little girl was gone forever.

"I'm telling you this now, Lupe, now that I'll never see you again . . . I tried 510
to protect you because you were all your father left me. I loved that bastard more
than I loved you, and when I lost him I loved you as I'd loved him."

Then she heard the first barking in the patio. It was after eleven but Doña
Manuela hadn't eaten, lost as she'd been in her thoughts. Never, but never, had
one of her dogs come into the patio, they knew all too well the dangers that
awaited them there. Another barking joined the first. The old woman covered her
head with her black shawl and hurried from the room. The canaries were restless.
She'd forgotten to cover them so they could sleep. They stirred uneasily, not daring to sing, not daring to sleep, as during the eclipses that had occurred twice in
Manuela's life. The moment the sun had disappeared, the animals and birds had 520
fallen silent.

Tonight, on the other hand, there was a moon and spring-like warmth.
Increasingly certain of the meaning of her life, of the role that was hers to play as
she waited for death, Doña Manuelita carefully placed the canvas covers over the
bird cages.

"There, sleep quiet, this isn't your night, this is my night, sleep now."

She completed the chore that everyone was grateful to her for performing,
the chore she did so they would be grateful and could live in peace, and then she
walked to the top of the great stone staircase. As she had known he would, little
Luis was there in his wheelchair, waiting for her.   530

It was all so natural. There was no reason it should be otherwise. Little Luis
rose from his chair and offered his arm to Doña Manuela. He stumbled a little, but
the old woman was strong, she lent him all her support. He was taller than either
of them had supposed, fourteen, going on fifteen, a young man. Together they descended the staircase, little Luisito twice supported—by the stone balustrade and
Manuelita's arm. These were the palaces of New Spain, Manuela, imagine the parties, the music, the liveried servants holding aloft sputtering candelabra, preceding
the guests on nights of great balls, the scalding wax burning their hands and never
a word of complaint. Come with me, Manuela, we'll go together, child.

Señora Manuelita's twenty dogs were in the patio, barking in unison, barking 540
with joy, all of them, Cloudy, the mangy ones, the hungry ones, the bitches
swollen with worms or with pregnancy, who knows, time would tell, the bitches
who'd recently given birth to more dogs, teats dragging, more dogs to populate
the city with orphans, with bastards, with little sons of the Virgin huddling beneath the baroque eaves of the Sagrario. Doña Manuela grasped little Luisito by his
belt and took his hand, the dogs barked happily, looking at the moon as if the
moonlit night was the first night of the world, before pain, before cruelty, and
Manuela led Luisito, the dogs were barking, but the servant and the boy heard
music, old old music, music heard centuries ago in this palace. Look at the stars,

little Luisito, Lupe Lupita always asked, when do the stars go out? Would she still 550 be asking, wherever she is? Of course she is, Manuela, of course she's asking, dance, Manuela, tell it all to me as we dance together, we're just alike, your daughter and I, Lupe Lupita and Luisito, isn't that right? Yes, yes, it's true, I see the two of you, yes, I see you now, a moonlit, starlit night just like this, dancing a waltz, the two of you together, just alike, waiting for what never comes, what never happens, children in a dream, caught in a dream: don't leave, my son, don't come out to look, stay there, it's better, stay there; but Lupita has gone, Manuela, you and I are left here in the building, it isn't Lupita and I, it's you and I, waiting, what are you waiting for, Manuela? What are you waiting for besides death?

How the dogs bark, that's why the moon's come out tonight, that's the only 560 reason it came out, so the dogs would bark, and listen, Luisito, listen to the music and let me hold you up, how well you dance, child, forget it's me, pretend you're dancing with my beautiful Lupe Lupita, that you have your arm around her waist, and as you're dancing you smell her perfume, you hear her laughter, you look into her startled doe's eyes, and I'll pretend that I still know how to remember love, my only love, Lupe's father, a servant's love, in the dark, groping, rejected, the dark of the night, love that's a single word repeated a thousand times.

"No . . . no . . . no . . . no. . . . . ."

Dazed by the dancing, intoxicated by her memories, Doña Manuelita lost her footing and fell. Little Luisito fell with her, their arms about each other, laughing, 570 as the music faded and the barking increased.

"Shall we promise to help the dogs, little Luisito?"

"Let's promise, Manuela."

"You can speak up. The dogs can't. The dogs have to take what they can."

"Don't worry. We'll look after them always."

"It isn't true what they say, that I love the dogs because I didn't love my daughter. That isn't true."

"Of course it isn't, Manuela."

And only then did Doña Manuelita ask herself why in the midst of all the uproar of barking and music and laughter no one had looked out, no door had 580 opened, no voice had protested. Did she also owe that to her friend little Luis? Did that mean no one was ever going to bother her again, not ever?

"Thank you, child, thank you."

"Imagine, Manuela, just think. Centuries ago these were palaces, great palaces, beautiful palaces, very wealthy people lived here, very important people, like us, Manuela."

Around midnight he felt very hungry and got out of bed without waking anyone. He went to the kitchen and, fumbling, found a hard roll. He smeared it with fresh cream and began to eat. Then suddenly he stopped, honor or duty, he didn't know which stopped him. Always before, he'd asked. Even for a roll spread 590 thick with cream. This was the first time he'd taken without asking. He took the dry leftover tortillas and went out to the patio to throw them to the dogs. But they were not there any longer, nor Manuelita, nor the moon, nor the music, nor anything.   [1980]

Questions for Discussion and Writing

1. Underline or circle the various instances of cruelty depicted in the story. Why does the author place so much emphasis on cruelty?
2. Why do so many people mistrust or even despise Doña Manuela? Are their suspicions justified? Explain.
3. Why are the dogs included in the story? What purpose(s) do they serve?
4. Discuss whether Doña Manuela commits a sacrilege when she takes the dogs into the church.
5. How do the various characters regard the past? Whose ideas about the past does the author endorse? How do you know?
6. What social or political statement does the story make?
7. How do you interpret the final paragraph?

✒ PAULÉ BARTÓN

(1916–1974)

TRANSLATED BY HOWARD NORMAN

Emilie Plead Choose One Egg

Paulé Bartón spent most of his life as a goatherd in his native Haiti in an obscurity which did not prevent his being arrested and persecuted by the regimes of François "Papa Doc" Duvalier (1907–1971), dictator of Haiti from 1957 to 1971, and of his son, Jean-Claude, who succeeded his father and ruled until 1986.

Bartón's style is distinctively oral, and many of his stories are retellings of traditional tales. He often uses the rhythm and humor of the Creoles. His characters endure hardships with dignity and humor, often using language as a weapon.

"Emilie Plead Choose One Egg" at first seems disconcerting in its broken English, repetition, and elusive simplicity, but beneath its surface oddities a reader can glimpse familiar ideas and problems. A deft use of suggestive images makes the story radiate beyond its setting on an island noted more for its poverty and violence than its literature.

E MILIE WAS TALKING with Bélem while looking at the gathered loud of nesting birds. "Which bird going to hatch today's woe, guess that?" Emilie said, she said, "I'll carry that egg to the man who took my donkey for my debt, I'll give him that a breakfast gift!"

"The tax man?" Bélem said.

Emilie said, "That's it, you guessing good today," she said. "Now guess which egg woe is in."

Bélem said, "How can I guess? Look how many eggs there look!"

"Got to make choices in this life," Emilie said, "Each morning a riddle to untie the knot of it, and then use that rope to tie up back luck thinking to any tree here." 10

Bélem sang, "*Tie up bad luck thinking to a tree here, Fry that woe egg up for the debt man dear,*" then he said, "That makes a good song!" he laughed then.

Emilie she said, "I'll sing it on the way over to his hut, I'll sing it to my donkey too. But now guess which egg!"

But Bélem said, "I sigh. There's too many eggs out there! I tell you my eyes worrying over each one, they look the same all," he said more.

Emilie then, "Got to make a choice hurry! That debt man yawning toward his breakfast table hurry!" Emilie said.

"You asking me something hard here I tell you. You ask a very tight riddle knot, you talking a mystery under just one bird!" Bélem said. 20

"Got to make a choice! The debt man now sitting at the table now." Emilie said.

Bélem said, "It's like asking does water from the same well taste more better after carried in buckets to your thirsty mouth by a donkey or an ox, which one? It's like asking which of two sticks the same size to knock a lemon down with, which one?" he said.

Emilie said, "Make a choice my friend. You get to taste the drinking water in your throat whoever brings it anyway. You get to squeeze the lemon on your tongue whatever stick knocks it down anyway. That debt man choose my donkey instead my table and chair to take, yes he make that choice one over the other, you know this?" 30

Bélem said, "O.K. I say all the eggs got woe today's woe in them, how's that if I say that, there I say that!" he said.

Emilie said, "That's no choice, oh my that's no choice! Now the donkey and ox both spilling water, empty gone, now the lemons shriveling up to yellow lizard eyes on the trees, now the debt man thinking greedy want of my table and chair. Which egg will stop all this, friend?" Emilie plead him to choose one egg quick.

But Bélem could not choose, so Emilie hid her table and chair then. Emilie says, "All right Bélem friend, it's all right," she soothes that way. 40

Bélem he had a wound he felt then somewhere on him, but he couldn't find it. He said, "Emilie, I hurt on me somewhere, can you see the wound?"

Emilie said, "No," she covers the table and chairs with fronds.

Bélem he says, "The salt sea will find this wound on me, it always does when I swim in it, always clean my wound." But Emilie knew the wound of confusion and no-choice was too deep inside for the salt sea to sting it clean for Bélem right now.

Questions for Discussion and Writing

1. What appears to have happened between Emilie and the tax man? Point to specific details to support your answer.
2. Is Emilie's request, "Which bird going to hatch today's woe, guess that?" meant literally or figuratively or both? Explain your answer.

3. What does she mean by "the wound of confusion and no-choice"?
4. Sum up in your words what you see as the real subject of this story.

RAYMOND CARVER
(1938–1988)

Cathedral

In Raymond Carver's relatively short life, he helped revitalize the American short story. He was born in Klatskanie, Oregon, and grew up in Yakima, Washington. His father was a saw filer in lumber mills who loved telling stories—and drinking. After graduating from high school, Raymond worked in the sawmills and a year later married Maryann Burk, only sixteen at the time. In 1958, they moved to California and Carver enrolled at Chico State College. In 1963, he won a stipend to attend the Iowa Writer's Workshop, but after six months had to leave to support his family.

For three years, Carver worked as a janitor and then as an editor, writing when he had finished his duties. A breakthrough came when one of his first published stories, "Will You Please Be Quiet, Please," was included in the *Best American Short Stories of 1967*.

Winning a National Endowment for the Arts grant enabled him to write full time, resulting in an O. Henry prize story for three successive years, 1973–1975, and invitations to teach at various universities. In 1975, he declared bankruptcy and for the next two years was frequently hospitalized for alcohol abuse. After his marriage to Maryann broke up, he began living with poet Tess Gallagher and teaching creative writing at Syracuse University.

Carter often writes from a working-class perspective. Using a technique called Minimalism by some and K-Mart Realism by others, his early stories chronicled the lives of Americans for whom despair seemed the only possible choice. *Cathedral* (1983) won a National Book Critics award and marked a turning point in his fiction, from despair to a sense that people could do more than merely survive.

Unfortunately, within a few years, Carver's health was failing. In 1988, a cancerous lung was removed, but the malignancy had spread to his brain. He married Tess Gallagher in Reno, Nevada, on June 17 and died on August 2 in Los Angeles.

THIS BLIND MAN, an old friend of my wife's, he was on his way to spend the night. His wife had died. So he was visiting the dead wife's relatives in Connecticut. He called my wife from his in-laws'. Arrangements were made. He would come by train, a five-hour trip, and my wife would meet him at the station.

She hadn't seen him since she worked for him one summer in Seattle ten years ago. But she and the blind man had kept in touch. They made tapes and mailed them back and forth. I wasn't enthusiastic about his visit. He was no one I knew. And his being blind bothered me. My idea of blindness came from the movies. In the movies, the blind moved slowly and never laughed. Sometimes they were led by seeing-eye dogs. A blind man in my house was not something I looked forward to.   10

That summer in Seattle she had needed a job. She didn't have any money. The man she was going to marry at the end of the summer was in officers' training school. He didn't have any money, either. But she was in love with the guy, and he was in love with her, etc. She'd seen something in the paper: HELP WANTED— *Reading to Blind Man,* and a telephone number. She phoned and went over, was hired on the spot. She'd worked with this blind man all summer. She read stuff to him, case studies, reports, that sort of thing. She helped him organize his little office in the county social-service department. They'd become good friends, my wife and the blind man. How do I know these things? She told me. And she told me   20 something else. On her last day in the office, the blind man asked if he could touch her face. She agreed to this. She told me he touched his fingers to every part of her face, her nose—even her neck! She never forgot it. She even tried to write a poem about it. She was always trying to write a poem. She wrote a poem or two every year, usually after something really important had happened to her.

When we first started going out together, she showed me the poem. In the poem, she recalled his fingers and the way they had moved around over her face. In the poem, she talked about what she had felt at the time, about what went through her mind when the blind man touched her nose and lips. I can remember I didn't think much of the poem. Of course, I didn't tell her that. Maybe I just   30 don't understand poetry. I admit it's not the first thing I reach for when I pick up something to read.

Anyway, this man who'd first enjoyed her favors, the officer-to-be, he'd been her childhood sweetheart. So okay. I'm saying that at the end of the summer she let the blind man run his hands over her face, said good-bye to him, married her childhood etc., who was now a commissioned officer, and she moved away from Seattle. But they'd kept in touch, she and the blind man. She made the first contact after a year or so. She called him up one night from an Air Force base in Alabama. She wanted to talk. They talked. He asked her to send him a tape and tell him about her life. She did this. She sent the tape. On the tape, she told the   40 blind man about her husband and about their life together in the military. She told the blind man she loved her husband but she didn't like it where they lived and she didn't like it that he was a part of the military-industrial thing. She told the blind man she'd written a poem and he was in it. She told him that she was writing a poem about what it was like to be an Air Force officer's wife. The poem wasn't finished yet. She was still writing it. The blind man made a tape. He sent her the tape. She made a tape. This went on for years. My wife's officer was posted to one base and then another. She sent tapes from Moody AFB, McGuire, McConnell, and finally Travis, near Sacramento, where one night she got to feeling lonely and cut off from people she kept losing in that moving-around life. She got   50 to feeling she couldn't go it another step. She went in and swallowed all the pills and capsules in the medicine chest and washed them down with a bottle of gin. Then she got into a hot bath and passed out.

But instead of dying, she got sick. She threw up. Her officer—why should he have a name? he was the childhood sweetheart, and what more does he want?—came home from somewhere, found her, and called the ambulance. In time, she put it all on a tape and sent the tape to the blind man. Over the years, she put all kinds of stuff on tapes and sent the tapes off lickety-split. Next to writing a poem every year, I think it was her chief means of recreation. On one tape, she told the blind man she'd decided to live away from her officer for a time. On another tape, she told him about her divorce. She and I began going out, and of course she told her blind man about it. She told him everything, or so it seemed to me. Once she asked me if I'd like to hear the latest tape from the blind man. This was a year ago. I was on the tape, she said. So I said okay, I'd listen to it. I got us drinks and we settled down in the living room. We made ready to listen. First she inserted the tape into the player and adjusted a couple of dials. Then she pushed a lever. The tape squeaked and someone began to talk in this loud voice. She lowered the volume. After a few minutes of harmless chitchat, I heard my own name in the mouth of this stranger, this blind man I didn't even know! And then this: "From all you've said about him, I can only conclude—" But we were interrupted, a knock at the door, something, and we didn't ever get back to the tape. Maybe it was just as well. I'd heard all I wanted to.

Now this same blind man was coming to sleep in my house.

"Maybe I could take him bowling," I said to my wife. She was at the draining board doing scalloped potatoes. She put down the knife she was using and turned around.

"If you love me," she said, "you can do this for me. If you don't love me, okay. But if you had a friend, any friend, and the friend came to visit, I'd make him feel comfortable." She wiped her hands with the dish towel.

"I don't have any blind friends," I said.

"You don't have *any* friends," she said. "Period. Besides," she said, "goddamn it, his wife's just died! Don't you understand that? The man's lost his wife!"

I didn't answer. She'd told me a little about the blind man's wife. Her name was Beulah. Beulah! That's a name for a colored woman.

"Was his wife a Negro?" I asked.

"Are you crazy?" my wife said. "Have you just flipped or something?" She picked up a potato. I saw it hit the floor, then roll under the stove. "What's wrong with you?" she said. "Are you drunk?"

"I'm just asking," I said.

Right then my wife filled me in with more detail than I cared to know. I made a drink and sat at the kitchen table to listen. Pieces of the story began to fall into place.

Beulah had gone to work for the blind man the summer after my wife had stopped working for him. Pretty soon Beulah and the blind man had themselves a church wedding. It was a little wedding—who'd want to go to such a wedding in the first place?—just the two of them, plus the minister and the minister's wife. But it was a church wedding just the same. It was what Beulah had wanted, he'd said. But even then Beulah must have been carrying the cancer in her glands. After

they had been inseparable for eight years—my wife's word, *inseparable*—Beulah's
health went into a rapid decline. She died in a Seattle hospital room, the blind   100
man sitting beside the bed and holding on to her hand. They'd married, lived and
worked together, slept together—had sex, sure—and then the blind man had to
bury her. All this without his having ever seen what the goddamned woman
looked like. It was beyond my understanding. Hearing this, I felt sorry for the
blind man for a little bit. And then I found myself thinking what a pitiful life this
woman must have led. Imagine a woman who could never see herself as she was
seen in the eyes of her loved one. A woman who could go on day after day and
never receive the smallest compliment from her beloved. A woman whose husband could never read the expression on her face, be it misery or something better. Someone who could wear makeup or not—what difference to him? She could,   110
if she wanted, wear green eye-shadow around one eye, a straight pin in her nostril,
yellow slacks, and purple shoes, no matter. And then to slip off into death, the
blind man's hand on her hand, his blind eyes streaming tears—I'm imagining
now—her last thought maybe this: that he never even knew what she looked like,
and she on an express to the grave. Robert was left with a small insurance policy
and half of a twenty-peso Mexican coin. The other half of the coin went into the
box with her. Pathetic.

So when the time rolled around, my wife went to the depot to pick him up.
With nothing to do but wait—sure, I blamed him for that—I was having a drink
and watching the TV when I heard the car pull into the drive. I got up from the   120
sofa with my drink and went to the window to have a look.

I saw my wife laughing as she parked the car. I saw her get out of the car and
shut the door. She was still wearing a smile. Just amazing. She went around to the
other side of the car to where the blind man was already starting to get out. This
blind man, feature this, he was wearing a full beard! A beard on a blind man! Too
much, I say. The blind man reached into the backseat and dragged out a suitcase.
My wife took his arm, shut the car door, and, talking all the way, moved him
down the drive and then up the steps to the front porch. I turned off the TV. I finished my drink, rinsed the glass, dried my hands. Then I went to the door.

My wife said, "I want you to meet Robert. Robert, this is my husband. I've   130
told you all about him." She was beaming. She had this blind man by his coat
sleeve.

The blind man let go of his suitcase and up came his hand.

I took it. He squeezed hard, held my hand, and then he let it go.

"I feel like we've already met," he boomed.

"Likewise," I said. I didn't know what else to say. Then I said, "Welcome. I've
heard a lot about you." We began to move then, a little group, from the porch into
the living room, my wife guiding him by the arm. The blind man was carrying his
suitcase in his other hand. My wife said things like, "To your left here, Robert.
That's right. Now watch it, there's a chair. That's it. Sit down right here. This is the   140
sofa. We just bought this sofa two weeks ago."

I started to say something about the old sofa. I'd liked that old sofa. But I
didn't say anything. Then I wanted to say something else, small-talk, about the
scenic ride along the Hudson. How going *to* New York, you should sit on the
right-hand side of the train, and coming *from* New York, the left-hand side.

"Did you have a good train ride?" I said. "Which side of the train did you sit on, by the way?"

"What a question, which side!" my wife said. "What's it matter which side?" she said.

"I just asked," I said.

"Right side," the blind man said. "I hadn't been on a train in nearly forty years. Not since I was a kid. With my folks. That's been a long time. I'd nearly forgotten the sensation. I have winter in my beard now," he said. "So I've been told, anyway. Do I look distinguished, my dear?" the blind man said to my wife.

"You look distinguished, Robert," she said. "Robert," she said. "Robert, it's just so good to see you."

My wife finally took her eyes off the blind man and looked at me. I had the feeling she didn't like what she saw. I shrugged.

I've never met, or personally known, anyone who was blind. This blind man was late forties, a heavy-set, balding man with stooped shoulders, as if he carried a great weight there. He wore brown slacks, brown shoes, a light-brown shirt, a tie, a sports coat. Spiffy. He also had this full beard. But he didn't use a cane and he didn't wear dark glasses. I'd always thought dark glasses were a must for the blind. Fact was, I wished he had a pair. At first glance, his eyes looked like anyone else's eyes. But if you looked close, there was something different about them. Too much white in the iris, for one thing, and the pupils seemed to move around in the sockets without his knowing it or being able to stop it. Creepy. As I stared at his face, I saw the left pupil turn in toward his nose while the other made an effort to keep in one place. But it was only an effort, for that eye was on the roam without his knowing it or wanting it to be.

I said, "Let me get you a drink. What's your pleasure? We have a little of everything. It's one of our pastimes."

"Bub, I'm a Scotch man myself," he said fast enough in this big voice.

"Right," I said. Bub! "Sure you are. I knew it."

He let his fingers touch his suitcase, which was sitting alongside the sofa. He was taking his bearings. I didn't blame him for that.

"I'll move that up to your room," my wife said.

"No, that's fine," the blind man said loudly. "It can go up when I go up."

"A little water with the Scotch?" I said.

"Very little," he said.

"I knew it," I said.

He said, "Just a tad. The Irish actor, Barry Fitzgerald? I'm like that fellow. When I drink water, Fitzgerald said, I drink water. When I drink whiskey, I drink whiskey." My wife laughed. The blind man brought his hand up under his beard. He lifted his beard slowly and let it drop.

I did the drinks, three big glasses of Scotch with a splash of water in each. Then we made ourselves comfortable and talked about Robert's travels. First the long flight from the West Coast to Connecticut, we covered that. Then from Connecticut up here by train. We had another drink concerning that leg of the trip.

I remembered having read somewhere that the blind didn't smoke because, as speculation had it, they couldn't see the smoke they exhaled. I thought I knew that much and that much only about blind people. But this blind man smoked his cigarette down to the nubbin and then lit another one. This blind man filled his ashtray and my wife emptied it.

When we sat down at the table for dinner, we had another drink. My wife heaped Robert's plate with cube steak, scalloped potatoes, green beans. I buttered him up two slices of bread. I said, "Here's bread and butter for you." I swallowed some of my drink. "Now let us pray," I said, and the blind man lowered his head. My wife looked at me, her mouth agape. "Pray the phone won't ring and the food 200 doesn't get cold," I said.

We dug in. We ate everything there was to eat on the table. We ate like there was no tomorrow. We didn't talk. We ate. We scarfed. We grazed that table. We were into serious eating. The blind man had right away located his foods, he knew just where everything was on his plate. I watched with admiration as he used his knife and fork on the meat. He'd cut two pieces of meat, fork the meat into his mouth, and then go all out for the scalloped potatoes, the beans next, and then he'd tear off a hunk of buttered bread and eat that. He'd follow this up with a big drink of milk. It didn't seem to bother him to use his fingers once in a while, either.   210

We finished everything, including half a strawberry pie. For a few moments, we sat as if stunned. Sweat beaded on our faces. Finally, we got up from the table and left the dirty plates. We didn't look back. We took ourselves into the living room and sank into our places again. Robert and my wife sat on the sofa. I took the big chair. We had us two or three more drinks while they talked about the major things that had come to pass for them in the past ten years. For the most part, I just listened. Now and then I joined in. I didn't want him to think I'd left the room, and I didn't want her to think I was feeling left out. They talked of things that had happened to them—to them!—these past ten years. I waited in vain to hear my name on my wife's sweet lips: "And then my dear husband came 220 into my life"—something like that. But I heard nothing of the sort. More talk of Robert. Robert had done a little of everything, it seemed, a regular blind jack-of-all-trades. But most recently he and his wife had had an Amway distributorship, from which, I gathered, they'd earned a living, such as it was. The blind man was also a ham radio operator. He talked in his loud voice about conversations he'd had with fellow operators in Guam, in the Philippines, in Alaska, and even in Tahiti. He said he'd have a lot of friends there if he ever wanted to go visit those places. From time to time, he'd turn his blind face toward me, put his hand under his beard, ask me something. How long had I been in my present position? (Three years.) Did I like my work? (I didn't.) Was I going to stay with it? (What were the 230 options?) Finally, when I thought he was beginning to run down, I got up and turned on the TV.

My wife looked at me with irritation. She was heading toward a boil. Then she looked at the blind man and said, "Robert, do you have a TV?"

The blind man said, "My dear, I have two TVs. I have a color set and a black-and-white thing, an old relic. It's funny, but if I turn the TV on, and I'm always turning it on, I turn on the color set. It's funny, don't you think?"

I didn't know what to say to that. I had absolutely nothing to say to that. No

opinion. So I watched the news program and tried to listen to what the announcer
was saying.   240

"This is a color TV," the blind man said. "Don't ask me how, but I can tell."

"We traded up a while ago," I said.

The blind man had another taste of his drink. He lifted his beard, sniffed it,
and let it fall. He leaned forward on the sofa. He positioned his ashtray on the coffee table, then put the lighter to his cigarette. He leaned back on the sofa and
crossed his legs at the ankles.

My wife covered her mouth, and then she yawned. She stretched. She said,
"I think I'll go upstairs and put on my robe. I think I'll change into something else.
Robert, you make yourself comfortable," she said.

"I'm comfortable," the blind man said.   250

"I want you to feel comfortable in this house," she said.

"I am comfortable," the blind man said.

After she'd left the room, he and I listened to the weather report and then to
the sports roundup. By that time, she'd been gone so long I didn't know if she was
going to come back. I thought she might have gone to bed. I wished she'd come
back downstairs. I didn't want to be left alone with a blind man. I asked him if he
wanted another drink, and he said sure. Then I asked if he wanted to smoke some
dope with me. I said I'd just rolled a number. I hadn't, but I planned to do so in
about two shakes.

"I'll try some with you," he said.   260

"Damn right," I said. "That's the stuff."

I got our drinks and sat down on the sofa with him. Then I rolled us two fat
numbers. I lit one and passed it. I brought it to his fingers. He took it and inhaled.

"Hold it as long as you can," I said. I could tell he didn't know the first thing.

My wife came back downstairs wearing her pink robe and her pink slippers.

"What do I smell?" she said.

"We thought we'd have us some cannabis," I said.

My wife gave me a savage look. Then she looked at the blind man and said,
"Robert, I didn't know you smoked."

He said, "I do now, my dear. There's a first time for everything. But I don't   270
feel anything yet."

"This stuff is pretty mellow," I said. "This stuff is mild. It's dope you can reason with," I said. "It doesn't mess you up."

"Not much it doesn't, bub," he said, and laughed.

My wife sat on the sofa between the blind man and me. I passed her the
number. She took it and toked and then passed it back to me. "Which way is this
going?" she said. Then she said, "I shouldn't be smoking this. I can hardly keep
my eyes open as it is. That dinner did me in. I shouldn't have eaten so much."

"It was the strawberry pie," the blind man said. "That's what did it," he said,
and he laughed his big laugh. Then he shook his head.   280

"There's more strawberry pie," I said.

"Do you want some more, Robert?" my wife said.

"Maybe in a little while," he said.

We gave our attention to the TV. My wife yawned again. She said, "Your bed is made up when you feel like going to bed, Robert. I know you must have had a long day. When you're ready to go to bed, say so."

She pulled his arm. "Robert?"

He came to and said, "I've had a real nice time. This beats tapes, doesn't it?"

I said, "Coming at you," and I put the number between his fingers. He inhaled, held the smoke, and then let it go. It was like he'd been doing it since he was nine years old.   290

"Thanks, bub," he said. "But I think this is all for me. I think I'm beginning to feel it," he said. He held the burning roach out for my wife.

"Same here," she said. "Ditto. Me, too." She took the roach and passed it to me. "I may just sit here for a while between you two guys with my eyes closed. But don't let me bother you, okay? Either one of you. If it bothers you, say so. Otherwise, I may just sit here with my eyes closed until you're ready to go to bed," she said. "Your bed's made up, Robert, when you're ready. It's right next to our room at the top of the stairs. We'll show you up when you're ready. You wake me up now, you guys, if I fall asleep." She said that and then she closed her eyes and   300 went to sleep.

The news program ended. I got up and changed the channel. I sat back down on the sofa. I wished my wife hadn't pooped out. Her head lay across the back of the sofa, her mouth open. She'd turned so that her robe had slipped away from her legs, exposing a juicy thigh. I reached to draw her robe back over her, and it was then that I glanced at the blind man. What the hell! I flipped the robe open again.

"You say when you want some strawberry pie," I said.

"I will," he said.

I said, "Are you tired? Do you want me to take you up to your bed? Are you   310 ready to hit the hay?"

"Not yet," he said. "No, I'll stay up with you, bub. If that's all right. I'll stay up until you're ready to turn in. We haven't had a chance to talk. Know what I mean? I feel like me and her monopolized the evening." He lifted his beard and he let it fall. He picked up his cigarettes and his lighter.

"That's all right," I said. Then I said, "I'm glad for the company."

And I guess I was. Every night I smoked dope and stayed up as long as I could before I fell asleep. My wife and I hardly ever went to bed at the same time. When I did go to sleep, I had these dreams. Sometimes I'd wake up from one of them, my heart going crazy.   320

Something about the church and the Middle Ages was on the TV. Not your run-of-the-mill TV fare. I wanted to watch something else. I turned to the other channels. But there was nothing on them, either. So I turned back to the first channel and apologized.

"Bub, it's all right," the blind man said. "It's fine with me. Whatever you want to watch is okay. I'm always learning something. Learning never ends. It won't hurt me to learn something tonight. I got ears," he said.

We didn't say anything for a time. He was leaning forward with his head turned at me, his right ear aimed in the direction of the set. Very disconcerting.

Now and then his eyelids drooped and then they snapped open again. Now and then he put his fingers into his beard and tugged, like he was thinking about something he was hearing on the television.

On the screen, a group of men wearing cowls was being set upon and tormented by men dressed in skeleton costumes and men dressed as devils. The men dressed as devils wore devil masks, horns, and long tails. This pageant was part of a procession. The Englishman who was narrating the thing said it took place in Spain once a year. I tried to explain to the blind man what was happening.

"Skeletons," he said. "I know about skeletons," he said, and he nodded.

The TV showed this one cathedral. Then there was a long, slow look at another one. Finally, the picture switched to the famous one in Paris, with its flying buttresses and its spires reaching up to the clouds. The camera pulled away to show the whole of the cathedral rising above the skyline.

There were times when the Englishman who was telling the thing would shut up, would simply let the camera move around over the cathedrals. Or else the camera would tour the countryside, men in fields walking behind oxen. I waited as long as I could. Then I felt I had to say something. I said, "They're showing the outside of this cathedral now. Gargoyles. Little statues carved to look like monsters. Now I guess they're in Italy. Yeah, they're in Italy. There's paintings on the walls of this one church."

"Are those fresco paintings, bub?" he asked, and he sipped from his drink.

I reached for my glass. But it was empty. I tried to remember what I could remember. "You're asking me are those frescoes?" I said. "That's a good question. I don't know."

The camera moved to a cathedral outside Lisbon. The differences in the Portuguese cathedral compared with the French and Italian were not that great. But they were there. Mostly the interior stuff. Then something occurred to me, and I said, "Something has occurred to me. Do you have any idea what a cathedral is? What they look like, that is? Do you follow me? If somebody says cathedral to you, do you have any notion what they're talking about? Do you know the difference between that and a Baptist church, say?"

He let the smoke dribble from his mouth. "I know they took hundreds of workers fifty or a hundred years to build," he said. "I just heard the man say that, of course. I know generations of the same families worked on a cathedral. I heard him say that, too. The men who began their life's work on them, they never lived to see the completion of their work. In that wise, bub, they're no different from the rest of us, right?" He laughed. Then his eyelids drooped again. His head nodded. He seemed to be snoozing. Maybe he was imagining himself in Portugal. The TV was showing another cathedral now. This one was in Germany. The Englishman's voice droned on. "Cathedrals," the blind man said. He sat up and rolled his head back and forth. "If you want the truth, bub, that's about all I know. What I just said. What I heard him say. But maybe you could describe one to me? I wish you'd do it. I'd like that. If you want to know, I really don't have a good idea."

I stared hard at the shot of the cathedral on the TV. How could I even begin to describe it? But say my life depended on it. Say my life was being threatened by an insane guy who said I had to do it or else.

I stared some more at the cathedral before the picture flipped off into the countryside. There was no use. I turned to the blind man and said, "To begin with, they're very tall." I was looking around the room for clues. "They reach way up. Up and up. Toward the sky. They're so big, some of them, they have to have these supports. To help hold them up, so to speak. These supports are called buttresses. They remind me of viaducts, for some reason. But maybe you don't know viaducts, either? Sometimes the cathedrals have devils and such carved into the front. Sometimes lords and ladies. Don't ask me why this is," I said.

He was nodding. The whole upper part of his body seemed to be moving back and forth.

"I'm not doing so good, am I?" I said.

He stopped nodding and leaned forward on the edge of the sofa. As he listened to me, he was running his fingers through his beard. I wasn't getting through to him, I could see that. But he waited for me to go on just the same. He nodded, like he was trying to encourage me. I tried to think what else to say. "They're really big," I said. "They're massive. They're built of stone. Marble, too, sometimes. In those olden days, when they built cathedrals, men wanted to be close to God. In those olden days, God was an important part of everyone's life. You could tell this from their cathedral-building. I'm sorry," I said, "but it looks like that's the best I can do for you. I'm just no good at it."

"That's all right, bub," the blind man said. "Hey, listen. I hope you don't mind my asking you. Can I ask you something? Let me ask you a simple question, yes or no. I'm just curious and there's no offense. You're my host. But let me ask if you are in any way religious? You don't mind my asking?"

I shook my head. He couldn't see that, though. A wink is the same as a nod to a blind man. "I guess I don't believe in it. In anything. Sometimes it's hard. You know what I'm saying?"

"Sure, I do," he said.

"Right," I said.

The Englishman was still holding forth. My wife sighed in her sleep. She drew a long breath and went on with her sleeping.

"You'll have to forgive me," I said. "But I can't tell you what a cathedral looks like. It just isn't in me to do it. I can't do any more than I've done."

The blind man sat very still, his head down, as he listened to me.

I said, "The truth is, cathedrals don't mean anything special to me. Nothing. Cathedrals. They're something to look at on late-night TV. That's all they are."

It was then that the blind man cleared his throat. He brought something up. He took a handkerchief from his back pocket. Then he said, "I get it, bub. It's okay. It happens. Don't worry about it," he said. "Hey, listen to me. Will you do me a favor? I got an idea. Why don't you find us some heavy paper? And a pen. We'll do something. We'll draw one together. Get us a pen and some heavy paper. Go on, bub, get the stuff," he said.

So I went upstairs. My legs felt like they didn't have any strength in them. They felt like they did after I'd done some running. In my wife's room, I looked around. I found some ballpoints in a little basket on her table. And then I tried to think where to look for the kind of paper he was talking about.

Downstairs, in the kitchen, I found a shopping bag with onion skins in the bottom of the bag. I emptied the bag and shook it. I brought it into the living room and sat down with it near his legs. I moved some things, smoothed the wrinkles from the bag, spread it out on the coffee table.

The blind man got down from the sofa and sat next to me on the carpet.

He ran his fingers over the paper. He went up and down the sides of the paper. The edges, even the edges. He fingered the corners.

"All right," he said. "All right, let's do her."   430

He found my hand, the hand with the pen. He closed his hand over my hand. "Go ahead, bub, draw," he said. "Draw. You'll see. I'll follow along with you. It'll be okay. Just begin now like I'm telling you. You'll see. Draw," the blind man said.

So I began. First I drew a box that looked like a house. It could have been the house I lived in. Then I put a roof on it. At either end of the roof, I drew spires. Crazy.

"Swell," he said. "Terrific. You're doing fine," he said. "Never thought anything like this could happen in your lifetime, did you, bub? Well, it's a strange life, we all know that. Go on now. Keep it up."

I put in windows with arches. I drew flying buttresses. I hung great doors. I   440 couldn't stop. The TV station went off the air. I put down the pen and closed and opened my fingers. The blind man felt around over the paper. He moved the tips of his fingers over the paper, all over what I had drawn, and he nodded.

"Doing fine," the blind man said.

I took up the pen again, and he found my hand. I kept at it. I'm no artist. But I kept drawing just the same.

My wife opened up her eyes and gazed at us. She sat up on the sofa, her robe hanging open. She said, "What are you doing? Tell me, I want to know."

I didn't answer her.

The blind man said, "We're drawing a cathedral. Me and him are working on   450 it. Press hard," he said to me. "That's right. That's good," he said. "Sure. You got it, bub. I can tell. You didn't think you could. But you can, can't you? You're cooking with gas now. You know what I'm saying? We're going to really have us something here in a minute. How's the old arm?" he said. "Put some people in there now. What's a cathedral without people?"

My wife said, "What's going on? Robert, what are you doing? What's going on?"

"It's all right," he said to her. "Close your eyes now," the blind man said to me.

I did it. I closed them just like he said.   460

"Are they closed?" he said. "Don't fudge."

"They're closed," I said.

"Keep them that way," he said. He said, "Don't stop now. Draw."

So we kept on with it. His fingers rode my fingers as my hand went over the paper. It was like nothing else in my life up to now.

Then he said, "I think that's it. I think you got it," he said. "Take a look. What do you think?"

But I had my eyes closed. I thought I'd keep them that way for a little longer. I thought it was something I ought to do.

"Well?" he said. "Are you looking?"   470

My eyes were still closed. I was in my house. I knew that. But I didn't feel like I was inside anything.

"It's really something," I said.   [1981]

Questions for Discussion and Writing

1. Describe the narrator's situation and character, especially as revealed in the beginning of the story. Can he be considered a typical contemporary person? Why or why not?

2. Analyze the narrator's style and tone. What do they reveal about him?

3. Analyze the character of the narrator's wife. How does she differ from her husband?

4. What is the difference between experiencing a cathedral (or anything else) directly and seeing one on television? Is it fair to say, as many critics do, that today we tend to get our experiences indirectly, through the media, rather than directly? Explain.

5. When the narrator and Robert draw the cathedral together, the narrator says, "It was like nothing else in my life up to now." What does he mean? What has he experienced or felt that is new?

❧ ALICE WALKER
(b. 1944)

Nineteen Fifty-Five

Alice Walker confronts social and human issues through characters who are struggling to survive not as members of a racial, gender, or economic group but as whole people. She was born in Eatonton, Georgia, the youngest of eight children. When she was eight, Alice was accidentally blinded in the right eye by a BB gun, and for six years refused to raise her head because of the disfiguring scar. At age fourteen, her brother paid to have the scar removed, and Alice emerged from her shell, but six years of reading and writing poems had set the course for her life.

Encouraged to make the most of her education, Walker was the valedictorian of her high school class and won a scholarship to attend Spelman College in Atlanta. After two years, she transferred to Sarah Lawrence and was appalled that no black women writers were studied in the English curriculum—a situation hardly unique at that time. After graduation in 1965, Walker was a social worker in New York City and worked with her husband, Melvyn Leventhal, on a voter registration drive in Mississippi at a time when interracial marriage was illegal in that state. Walker's first short story, "To Hell With Dying," appeared in *Best American Short Stories* for 1967. In 1972, at Wellesley College, Walker taught one of the first courses ever in African-American women writers. She has continued as a champion of black women writers and almost single-handedly rescued Zora Neale Hurston (1891–1960) from oblivion. "Nineteen Fifty-Five" explores the importance of black culture and language as instruments of self-expression and sources of courage.

1955

THE CAR IS a brandnew red Thunderbird convertible, and it's passed the house more than once. It slows down real slow now, and stops at the curb. An older gentleman dressed like a Baptist deacon gets out on the side near the house, and a young fellow who looks about sixteen gets out on the driver's side. They are white, and I wonder what in the world they doing in this neighborhood.

Well, I say to J. T., put your shirt on, anyway, and let me clean these glasses offa the table.

We had been watching the ballgame on TV. I wasn't actually watching, I was sort of daydreaming, with my foots up in J. T.'s lap.   10

I seen 'em coming on up the walk, brisk, like they coming to sell something, and then they rung the bell, and J. T. declined to put on a shirt but instead disappeared into the bedroom where the other television is. I turned down the one in the living room; I figured I'd be rid of these two double quick and J. T. could come back out again.

Are you Gracie Mae Still? asked the old guy, when I opened the door and put my hand on the lock inside the screen.

And I don't need to buy a thing, said I.

What makes you think we're sellin'? he asks, in that hearty Southern way that makes my eyeballs ache.   20

Well, one way or another and they're inside the house and the first thing the young fellow does is raise the TV a couple of decibels. He's about five feet nine, sort of womanish looking, with real dark white skin and a red pouting mouth. His hair is black and curly and he looks like a Loosianna creole.

About one of your songs, says the deacon. He is maybe sixty, with white hair and beard, white silk shirt, black linen suit, black tie and black shoes. His cold gray eyes look like they're sweating.

One of my songs?

Traynor here just *loves* your songs. Don't you, Traynor? He nudges Traynor with his elbow. Traynor blinks, says something I can't catch in a pitch I don't reg-   30 ister.

The boy learned to sing and dance livin' round you people out in the country. Practically cut his teeth on you.

Traynor looks up at me and bites his thumbnail.

I laugh.

Well, one way or another they leave with my agreement that they can record one of my songs. The deacon writes me a check for five hundred dollars, the boy grunts his awareness of the transaction, and I am laughing all over myself by the time I rejoin J. T.

Just as I am snuggling down beside him though I hear the front door bell 40 going off again.

Forgit his hat? asks J. T.

I hope not, I say.

The deacon stands there leaning on the door frame and once again I'm thinking of those sweaty-looking eyeballs of his. I wonder if sweat makes your eyeballs pink because his are sure pink. Pink and gray and it strikes me that nobody I'd care to know is behind them.

I forgot one little thing, he says pleasantly. I forgot to tell you Traynor and I would like to buy up all of those records you made of the song. I tell you we sure do love it.   50

Well, love it or not, I'm not so stupid as to let them do that without making 'em pay. So I says, Well, that's gonna cost you. Because, really, that song never did sell all that good, so I was glad they was going to buy it up. But on the other hand, them two listening to my song by themselves, and nobody else getting to hear me sing it, give me a pause.

Well, one way or another the deacon showed me where I would come out ahead on any deal he had proposed so far. Didn't I give you five hundred dollars? he asked. What white man—and don't even need to mention colored—would give you more? We buy up all your records of that particular song: first, you git royal- 60 ties. Let me ask you, how much you sell that song for in the first place? Fifty dollars? A hundred, I say. And no royalties from it yet, right? Right. Well, when we buy up all of them records you gonna git royalties. And that's gonna make all them race record shops sit up and take notice of Gracie Mae Still. And they gonna push all them other records of yourn they got. And you no doubt will become one of the big name colored recording artists. And then we can offer you another five hundred dollars for letting us do all this for you. And by God you'll be sittin' pretty! You can go out and buy you the kind of outfit a star should have. Plenty sequins and yards of red satin.

I had done unlocked the screen when I saw I could get some more money out of him. Now I held it wide open while he squeezed through the opening be- 70 tween me and the door. He whipped out another piece of paper and I signed it.

He sort of trotted out to the car and slid in beside Traynor, whose head was back against the seat. They swung around in a u-turn in front of the house and then they was gone.

J. T. was putting his shirt on when I got back to the bedroom. Yankees beat the Orioles 10–6, he said. I believe I'll drive out to Paschal's pond and go fishing. Wanta go?

While I was putting on my pants J. T. was holding the two checks.

I'm real proud of a woman that can make cash money without leavin' home, he said. And I said *Umph*. Because we met on the road with me singing in first one 80 little low-life jook after another, making ten dollars a night for myself if I was lucky, and sometimes bringin' home nothing but my life. And J. T. just loved them times. The way I was fast and flashy and always on the go from one town to another. He loved the way my singin' made the dirt farmers cry like babies and the womens shout Honey, hush! But that's mens. They loves any style to which you can get 'em accustomed.

1956

My little grandbaby called me one night on the phone: Little Mama, Little Mama, there's a white man on the television singing one of your songs! Turn on channel 5.

Lord, if it wasn't Traynor. Still looking half asleep from the neck up, but kind of awake in a nasty way from the waist down. He wasn't doing too bad with my song either, but it wasn't just the song the people in the audience was screeching and screaming over, it was that nasty little jerk he was doing from the waist down.

Well, Lord have mercy, I said, listening to him. If I'da closed my eyes, it could have been me. He had followed every turning of my voice, side streets, avenues, red lights, train crossings and all. It give me a chill.

Everywhere I went I heard Traynor singing my song, and all the little white girls just eating it up. I never had so many ponytails switched across my line of vision in my life. They was so *proud*. He was a *genius*.

Well, all that year I was trying to lose weight anyway and that and high blood pressure and sugar kept me pretty well occupied. Traynor had made a smash from a song of mine, I still had seven hundred dollars of the original one thousand dollars in the bank, and I felt if I could just bring my weight down, life would be sweet.

1957

I lost ten pounds in 1956. That's what I give myself for Christmas. And J. T. and me and the children and their friends and grandkids of all description had just finished dinner—over which I had put on nine and a half of my lost ten—when who should appear at the front door but Traynor. Little Mama, Little Mama! It's that white man who sings ———. The children didn't call it my song anymore. Nobody did. It was funny how that happened. Traynor and the deacon had bought up all my records, true, but on his record he had put "written by Gracie Mae Still." But that was just another name on the label, like "produced by Apex Records."

On the TV he was inclined to dress like the deacon told him. But now he looked presentable.

Merry Christmas, said he.

And same to you, Son.

I don't know why I called him Son. Well, one way or another they're all our sons. The only requirement is that they be younger than us. But then again, Traynor seemed to be aging by the minute.

You looks tired, I said. Come on in and have a glass of Christmas cheer.

J. T. ain't never in his life been able to act decent to a white man he wasn't working for, but he poured Traynor a glass of bourbon and water, then he took all the children and grandkids and friends and whatnot out to the den. After while I heard Traynor's voice singing the song, coming from the stereo console. It was just the kind of Christmas present my kids would consider cute.

I looked at Traynor, complicit. But he looked like it was the last thing in the world he wanted to hear. His head was pitched forward over his lap, his hands   130 holding his glass and his elbows on his knees.

I done sung that song seem like a million times this year, he said. I sung it on the Grand Ole Opry, I sung it on the Ed Sullivan show. I sung it on Mike Douglas, I sung it at the Cotton Bowl, the Orange Bowl. I sung it at Festivals. I sung it at Fairs. I sung it overseas in Rome, Italy, and once in a submarine *underseas*. I've sung it and sung it, and I'm making forty thousand dollars a day offa it, and you know what, I don't have the faintest notion what that song means.

Whatchumean, what do it mean? It mean what it says. All I could think was: These suckers is making forty thousand a *day* offa my song and now they gonna come back and try to swindle me out of the original thousand.   140

It's just a song, I said. Cagey. When you fool around with a lot of no count mens you sing a bunch of 'em. I shrugged.

Oh, he said. Well. He started brightening up. I just come by to tell you I think you are a great singer.

He didn't blush, saying that. Just said it straight out.

And I brought you a little Christmas present too. Now you take this little box and you hold it until I drive off. Then you take it outside under that first streetlight back up the street aways in front of that green house. Then you open the box and see . . . Well, just *see*.

What had come over this boy, I wondered, holding the box. I looked out the   150 window in time to see another white man come up and get in the car with him and then two more cars full of white mens start out behind him. They was all in long black cars that looked like a funeral procession.

Little Mama, Little Mama, what it is? One of my grandkids come running up and started pulling at the box. It was wrapped in gay Christmas paper—the thick, rich kind that it's hard to picture folks making just to throw away.

J. T. and the rest of the crowd followed me out the house, up the street to the streetlight and in front of the green house. Nothing was there but somebody's gold-grilled white Cadillac. Brandnew and most distracting. We got to looking at it so till I almost forgot the little box in my hand. While the others were busy mak-   160 ing 'miration I carefully took off the paper and ribbon and folded them up and put them in my pants pocket. What should I see but a pair of genuine solid gold caddy keys.

Dangling the keys in front of everybody's nose, I unlocked the caddy, motioned for J.T. to git in on the other side, and us didn't come back home for two days.

1960

Well, the boy was sure nuff famous by now. He was still a mite shy of twenty but already they was calling him the Emperor of Rock and Roll.

Then what should happen but the draft.   170

Well, says J. T. There goes all this Emperor of Rock and Roll business.

But even in the army the womens was on him like white on rice. We watched it on the News.

Dear Gracie Mae [he wrote from Germany],

> *How you? Fine I hope as this leaves me doing real well. Before I come in the army I was gaining a lot of weight and gitting jittery from making all them dumb movies. But now I exercise and eat right and get plenty of rest. I'm more awake then I been in ten years.*
>
> *I wonder if you are writing any more songs?*

Sincerely,   180
Traynor

I wrote him back:

Dear Son,

> *We is all fine in the Lord's good grace and hope this finds you the same. J. T. and me be out all times of the day and night in that car you give me—which you know you didn't have to do. Oh, and I do appreciate the mink and the new self-cleaning oven. But if you send anymore stuff to eat from Germany I'm going to have to open up a store in the neighborhood just to get rid of it. Really, we have more than enough of everything. The Lord is good to us and we don't know Want.*
>
> *Glad to here you is well and gitting your right rest. There ain't nothing like exercis-* 190 *ing to help that along. J. T. and me work some part of every day that we don't go fishing in the garden.*
>
> *Well, so long Soldier.*

Sincerely,
Gracie Mae

He wrote:

Dear Gracie Mae,

> *I hope you and J. T. like that automatic power tiller I had one of the stores back home send you. I went through a mountain of catalogs looking for it—I wanted something that even a woman could use.* 200
>
> *I've been thinking about writing some songs of my own but every time I finish one it don't seem to be about nothing I've actually lived myself. My agent keeps sending me other people's songs but they just sound mooney. I can hardly git through 'em without gagging.*
>
> *Everybody still loves that song of yours. They ask me all the time what do I think it*

means, really. I mean, they want to know just what I want to know. Where out of your life did it come from?

Sincerely,
Traynor

1968   210

I didn't see the boy for seven years. No. Eight. Because just about everybody was dead when I saw him again. Malcolm X, King, the president and his brother,[1] and even J. T. J. T. died of a head cold. It just settled in his head like a block of ice, he said, and nothing we did moved it until one day he just leaned out the bed and died.

His good friend Horace helped me put him away, and then about a year later Horace and me started going together. We was sitting out on the front porch swing one summer night, dusk-dark, and I saw this great procession of lights winding to a stop.

Holy Toledo! said Horace. (He's got a real sexy voice like Ray Charles.) Look   220
at it. He meant the long line of flashy cars and the white men in white summer suits jumping out on the drivers' sides and standing at attention. With wings they could pass for angels, with hoods they could be the Klan.

Traynor comes waddling up the walk.

And suddenly I know what it is he could pass for. An Arab like the ones you see in storybooks. Plump and soft and with never a care about weight. Because with so much money, who cares? Traynor is almost dressed like someone from a storybook too. He has on, I swear, about ten necklaces. Two sets of bracelets on his arms, at least one ring on every finger, and some kind of shining buckles on his shoes, so that when he walks you get quite a few twinkling lights.   230

Gracie Mae, he says, coming up to give me a hug. J. T.

I explain that J. T. passed. That this is Horace.

Horace, he says, puzzled but polite, sort of rocking back on his heels, Horace.

That's it for Horace. He goes in the house and don't come back.

Looks like you and me is gained a few, I say.

He laughs. The first time I ever heard him laugh. It don't sound much like a laugh and I can't swear that it's better than no laugh a'tall.

He's gitting fat for sure, but he's still slim compared to me. I'll never see three hundred pounds again and I've just about said (excuse me) fuck it. I got to think-   240
ing about it one day an' I thought: aside from the fact that they say it's unhealthy, my fat ain't never been no trouble. Mens always have loved me. My kids ain't never complained. Plus they's fat. And fat like I is I looks distinguished. You see me coming and know somebody's *there*.

Gracie Mae, he says, I've come with a personal invitation to you to my house tomorrow for dinner. He laughed. What did it sound like? I couldn't place it. See

1. Malcolm X, the Reverend Martin Luther King, Jr., John F. Kennedy, and his brother Robert were all assassinated between 1963 and 1968.

them men out there? he asked me. I'm sick and tired of eating with them. They don't never have nothing to talk about. That's why I eat so much. But if you come to dinner tomorrow we can talk about the old days. You can tell me about that farm I bought you.   250

I sold it, I said.

You did?

Yeah, I said, I did. Just cause I said I liked to exercise by working in a garden didn't mean I wanted five hundred acres! Anyhow, I'm a city girl now. Raised in the country it's true. Dirt poor—the whole bit—but that's all behind me now.

Oh well, he said, I didn't mean to offend you.

We sat a few minutes listening to the crickets.

Then he said: You wrote that song while you was still on the farm, didn't you, or was it right after you left?

You had somebody spying on me? I asked.   260

You and Bessie Smith got into a fight over it once, he said.

You *is* been spying on me!

But I don't know what the fight was about, he said. Just like I don't know what happened to your second husband. Your first one died in the Texas electric chair. Did you know that? Your third one beat you up, stole your touring costumes and your car and retired with a chorine to Tuskegee. He laughed. He's still there.

I had been mad, but suddenly I calmed down. Traynor was talking very dreamily. It was dark but seems like I could tell his eyes weren't right. It was like some*thing* was sitting there talking to me but not necessarily with a person behind it.   270

You gave up on marrying and seem happier for it. He laughed again. I married but it never went like it was supposed to. I never could squeeze any of my own life either into it or out of it. It was like singing somebody else's record. I copied the way it was sposed to be *exactly* but I never had a clue what marriage meant.

I bought her a diamond ring big as your fist. I bought her clothes. I built her a mansion. But right away she didn't want the boys to stay there. Said they smoked up the bottom floor. Hell, there were *five* floors.

No need to grieve, I said. No need to. Plenty more where she come from.

He perked up. That's part of what that song means, ain't it? No need to   280
grieve. Whatever it is, there's plenty more down the line.

I never really believed that way back when I wrote that song, I said. It was all bluffing then. The trick is to live long enough to put your young bluffs to use. Now if I was to sing that song today I'd tear it up. 'Cause I done lived long enough to know it's *true*. Them words could hold me up.

I ain't lived that long, he said.

Look like you on your way, I said. I don't know why, but the boy seemed to need some encouraging. And I don't know, seem like one way or another you talk to rich white folks and you end up reassuring *them*. But what the hell, by now I feel something for the boy. I wouldn't be in his bed all alone in the middle of the   290
night for nothing. Couldn't be nothing worse than being famous the world over for something you don't even understand. That's what I tried to tell Bessie. She

wanted that same song. Overheard me practicing it one day, said, with her hands on her hips: Gracie Mae, I'ma sing your song tonight. I *likes* it.

Your lips be too swole to sing, I said. She was mean and she was strong, but I trounced her.

Ain't you famous enough with your own stuff? I said. Leave mine alone. Later on, she thanked me. By then she was Miss Bessie Smith to the World, and I was still Miss Gracie Mae Nobody from Notasulga.

The next day all these limousines arrived to pick me up. Five cars and 300 twelve bodyguards. Horace picked that morning to start painting the kitchen.

Don't paint the kitchen, fool, I said. The only reason that dumb boy of ours is going to show me his mansion is because he intends to present us with a new house.

What you gonna do with it? he asked me, standing there in his shirtsleeves stirring the paint.

Sell it. Give it to the children. Live in it on weekends. It don't matter what I do. He sure don't care.

Horace just stood there shaking his head. Mama you sure looks *good,* he says. Wake me up when you git back.   310

Fool, I say, and pat my wig in front of the mirror.

The boy's house is something else. First you come to this mountain, and then you commence to drive and drive up this road that's lined with magnolias. Do magnolias grow on mountains? I was wondering. And you come to lakes and you come to ponds and you come to deer and you come up on some sheep. And I figure these two is sposed to represent England and Wales. Or something out of Europe. And you just keep on coming to stuff. And it's all pretty. Only the man driving my car don't look at nothing but the road. Fool. And then *finally,* after all this time, you begin to go up the driveway. And there's more magnolias—only they're not in such good shape. It's sort of cool up this high and I don't think 320 they're gonna make it. And then I see this building that looks like if it had a name it would be The Tara Hotel.[2] Columns and steps and outdoor chandeliers and rocking chairs. Rocking chairs? Well, and there's the boy on the steps dressed in a dark green satin jacket like you see folks wearing on TV late at night, and he looks sort of like a fat dracula with all that house rising behind him, and standing beside him there's this little white vision of loveliness that he introduces as his wife.

He's nervous when he introduces us and he says to her: This is Gracie Mae Still, I want you to know me. I mean . . . and she gives him a look that would fry meat.

Won't you come in, Gracie Mae, she says, and that's the last I see of her.   330

He fishes around for something to say or do and decides to escort me to the kitchen. We go through the entry and the parlor and the breakfast room and the dining room and the servants' passage and finally get there. The first thing I notice is that, altogether, there are five stoves. He looks about to introduce me to one.

---

2. Tara is the name of Scarlett O'Hara's plantation in Margaret Mitchell's *Gone with the Wind.*

Wait a minute, I say. Kitchens don't do nothing for me. Let's go sit on the front porch.

Well, we hike back and we sit in the rocking chairs rocking until dinner.

Gracie Mae, he says down the table, taking a piece of fried chicken from the woman standing over him, I got a little surprise for you.

It's a house, ain't it? I ask, spearing a chitlin.   340

You're getting *spoiled,* he says. And the way he says *spoiled* sounds funny. He slurs it. It sounds like his tongue is too thick for his mouth. Just that quick he's finished the chicken and is now eating chitlins *and* a pork chop. *Me* spoiled, I'm thinking.

I already got a house. Horace is right this minute painting the kitchen. I bought that house. My kids feel comfortable in that house.

But this one I bought you is just like mine. Only a little smaller.

I still don't need no house. And anyway who would clean it?

He looks surprised.

Really, I think, some peoples advance *so* slowly.   350

I hadn't thought of that. But what the hell, I'll get you somebody to live in.

I don't want other folks living 'round me. Makes me nervous.

You *don't?* It *do?*

What I want to wake up and see folks I don't even know for?

He just sits there downtable staring at me. Some of that feeling is in the song, ain't it? Not the words, the *feeling.* What I want to wake up and see folks I don't even know for? But I see twenty folks a day I don't even know, including my wife.

This food wouldn't be bad to wake up to though, I said. The boy had found the genius of corn bread.   360

He looked at me real hard. He laughed. Short. They want what you got but they don't want you. They want what I got only it ain't mine. That's what makes 'em so hungry for me when I sing. They getting the flavor of something but they ain't getting the thing itself. They like a pack of hound dogs trying to gobble up a scent.

You talking 'bout your fans?

Right. Right. He says.

Don't worry 'bout your fans, I say. They don't know their asses from a hole in the ground. I doubt there's a honest one in the bunch.

That's the point. Dammit, that's the point! He hits the table with his fist. It's 370 so solid it don't even quiver. You need a honest audience! You can't have folks that's just gonna lie right back to you.

Yeah, I say, it was small compared to yours, but I had one. It would have been worth my life to try to sing 'em somebody else's stuff that I didn't know nothing about.

He must have pressed a buzzer under the table. One of his flunkies zombies up.

Git Johnny Carson,[3] he says.

3. Former host of the "Tonight Show."

On the phone? asks the zombie.

On the phone, says Traynor, what you think I mean, git him offa the front   380
porch? Move your ass.

So two weeks later we's on the Johnny Carson show.

Traynor is all corseted down nice and looks a little bit fat but mostly good.
And all the women that grew up on him and my song squeal and squeal. Traynor
says: The lady who wrote my first hit record is here with us tonight, and she's
agreed to sing it for all of us, just like she sung it forty-five years ago. Ladies and
Gentlemen, the great Gracie Mae Still!

Well, I had tried to lose a couple of pounds my own self, but failing that I
had me a very big dress made. So I sort of rolls over next to Traynor, who is
dwarfted by me, so that when he puts his arm around back of me to try to hug me   390
it looks funny to the audience and they laugh.

I can see this pisses him off. But I smile out there at 'em. Imagine squealing
for twenty years and not knowing why you're squealing? No more sense of endings and beginnings than hogs.

It don't matter, Son, I say. Don't fret none over me.

I commence to sing. And I sound—wonderful. Being able to sing good ain't
all about having a good singing voice a'tall. A good singing voice helps. But when
you come up in the Hard Shell Baptist church like I did you understand early that
the fellow that sings is the singer. Them that waits for programs and arrangements
and letters from home is just good voices occupying body space.   400

So there I am singing my own song, my own way. And I give it all I got and
enjoy every minute of it. When I finish Traynor is standing up clapping and clapping and beaming at first me and then the audience like I'm his mama for true.
The audience claps politely for about two seconds.

Traynor looks disgusted.

He comes over and tries to hug me again. The audience laughs.

Johnny Carson looks at us like we both weird.

Traynor is mad as hell. He's supposed to sing something called a love ballad.
But instead he takes the mike, turns to me and says: Now see if my imitation still
holds up. He goes into the same song, *our* song, I think, looking out at his flaky   410
audience. And he sings it just the way he always did. My voice, my tone, my inflection, everything. But he forgets a couple of lines. Even before he's finished the
matronly squeals begin.

He sits down next to me looking whipped.

It don't matter, Son, I say, patting his hand. You don't even know those people. Try to make the people you know happy.

Is that in the song? he asks.

Maybe. I say.

1977
For a few years I hear from him, then nothing. But trying to lose weight takes all   420
the attention I got to spare. I finally faced up to the fact that my fat is the hurt I
don't admit, not even to myself, and that I been trying to bury it from the day I

was born. But also when you git real old, to tell the truth, it ain't as pleasant. It gits lumpy and slack. Yuck. So one day I said to Horace, I'ma git this shit offa me.

And he fell in with the program like he always try to do and Lord such a procession of salads and cottage cheese and fruit juice!

One night I dreamed Traynor had split up with his fifteenth wife. He said: *You meet 'em for no reason. You date 'em for no reason. You marry 'em for no reason. I do it all but I swear it's just like somebody else doing it. I feel like I can't remember Life.*

The boy's in trouble, I said to Horace.   430

You've always said that, he said.

I have?

Yeah. You always said he looked asleep. You can't sleep through life if you wants to live it.

You not such a fool after all, I said, pushing myself up with my cane and hobbling over to where he was. Let me sit down on your lap, I said, while this salad I ate takes effect.

In the morning we heard Traynor was dead. Some said fat, some said heart, some said alcohol, some said drugs. One of the children called from Detroit. Them dumb fans of his is on a crying rampage, she said. You just ought to turn on the   440 t.v.

But I didn't want to see 'em. They was crying and crying and didn't even know what they was crying for. One day this is going to be a pitiful country, I thought.   [1982]

Questions for Discussion and Writing

1. Who is the real-life model of Traynor?
2. What is the story satirizing?
3. What is the role of money in this story? How important or unimportant is it shown to be?
4. Why doesn't Traynor understand Gracie Mae's songs?
5. What is the significance of what happens on the Johnny Carson show?
6. What does Gracie Mae mean in the last paragraph of the story? Why does she think America will one day be "a pitiful country"?
7. Is the story an indictment of popular culture? Why or why not?

❧ NAGUIB MAHFOUZ
(b. 1911?)

The Time and the Place

Naguib Mahfouz is widely considered the most important Middle Eastern writer of this century. He is known for his exploration of social and political issues, often delivered indirectly through symbolism and allegory. He was awarded the Nobel Prize for literature in 1988.

Mahfouz was born in Cairo to a merchant father who remained aloof from his children. Closeness to his mother relieved an otherwise lonely childhood. After attending Islamic elementary and high schools, he studied philosophy at Cairo University, taking a bachelor's degree in 1934. Following postgraduate study in philosophy, he became a secretary at the University. In 1939, however, he entered the Egyptian civil service, where he served successfully for many years. From 1959 to 1969 he was Director of the Foundation for Support of the Cinema; he served as a consultant on cinema to the Ministry of Culture, from 1969 to 1971.

As a young man, Mahfouz supported Gamal Abdel Nasser, Egypt's president from 1956 to 1970, who led Egypt's break from England's domination. As Nasser's promised reforms did not materialize, Mahfouz became disillusioned and expressed his disappointment in a series of controversial novels and stories that offended both Nasser's supporters and Muslim fundamentalists. Over the years, Mahfouz has become increasingly disheartened by the hardening of attitudes on all political sides in the Middle East, by the decline of tolerance and civility, and by Egypt's repressive government. His unpopular and outspoken positions were probably responsible for an attempt on his life.

Mahfouz's short stories often resemble fairy tales from the *Arabian Nights*, but they are anything but escapist entertainment. What begins as fantasy becomes social and political commentary in the vein of Franz Kafka (1883–1924). Mahfouz's stories protest the alienation, repression, and soullessness of twentieth-century life.

I T HAPPENED ON MY last night in the old house, or rather on the night that it had been agreed was to be the last. Despite being old and clearly out of place in a contemporary setting, the house possessed a character of its own. It had become, as it were, an ancient monument, and this was further accentuated by a location that gave one a view of a square born the same year as the city of Cairo itself. By virtue of having inherited the house, we had been brought up there. Then, by reason of the discord of different generations, a feeling of antipathy had grown up between us and the house, and we found ourselves aspiring to the bright new milieux, far distant from the stone walls that lay embedded in narrow alleyways.

I was sitting in the spacious living room, on a dilapidated couch, which it 10 had been decided to dispose of, under a skylight firmly closed against the caprices of the autumn weather. I was sipping at a glass of cinnamon tea and gazing at a small brass ewer standing on a table in front of me; out of it protruded a stick of Javanese incense, slowly giving out a thread of fragrant smoke that coiled and curled under the lamplight in the silence of leave-taking. For no reason a listlessness gripped at my feeling of well-being, after which I was overcome by a mysterious sense of unease. I steeled myself to fight against it, but the whole of life piled up before my eyes in a fleeting flash, like a ball of light flung forward with cosmic speed; in no time it was extinguished, giving itself up to the unknown, submerged in its endless depths. 20

I told myself that I was acquainted with such tricks and that the departure tomorrow, so arbitrarily fixed, was reminding me of one's final departure, when the cameleer raises his voice to intone the very last song. I began to seek distraction from the sorrows of leave-taking by imagining the new abode in the wide street under the densely growing branches of mimosa lebbek trees, and the new life that gave promise of immeasurable sophisticated delights. No sooner had the cinnamon tea come to rest inside me that I made a sudden and gigantic leap that transferred me from one actuality into another. From deep within me rose a call that with boundless confidence invited me to open doors, to pull aside the screen, to invade space, and grab hold of approval and forgiveness from the atmosphere   30 so fragrant with incense. Cares, anxieties, and thoughts of annihilation all faded away, drowned in a flood of energy and a sense of enchantment and ecstasy, and my heart quivered in a wonderful dance brought into being by passionate exuberance.

Within me flashed a light, which assumed the form of a person. Presenting me with a glass of wine filled to overflowing, he said to me amiably, "Accept the gift of a miracle." I expected something to happen and it did: dissolving into nothingness, the living room was replaced by a vast courtyard that extended far into the distance until it met its boundary with the square in a thick white wall. The courtyard was covered with grassy rounds and crescents, with a well in the mid-   40 dle. At a short distance from the well was a lofty palm tree. I found myself wavering between two sensations: a feeling that told me I was witnessing a scene I had never viewed before, and another that told me that there was nothing strange about it, that I had both seen it and was remembering it. I made a violent movement with my head so as to bring myself back to the present, if in fact my mind had been wandering. The scene merely became clearer, more dominating, while between the palm tree and the well a human being took shape. This person, though concealed within a black gibba[1] and a tall green turban, was none other than myself; despite the flowing beard, the face was mine. Once again, I moved my head, but the scene merely became even clearer and sharper; the tawny light   50 indicated that the sun was setting. There also took shape, between the well and the date palm, a middle-aged man who was dressed similarly to myself. I saw him handing me a small box and saying, "These are days of insecurity. You must hide it under the ground until you return to it in due time."

"Wouldn't it be best," I asked him, "for me to have a look at it before hiding it?"

"No, no," he said firmly, "that would cause you to be hasty in taking action before a year is up, and you would perish."

"Have I to wait a year?"

"At least, then follow that which it enjoins." He was silent for a while, then   60 he continued. "These are days of insecurity," he cautioned, "and your house is liable to be searched. You must therefore hide it deep down." And the two of them set about digging close by the date palm. Having buried the box, they heaped earth on top of it and carefully leveled the surface. Then the middle-aged man

---

1. Long outer garment with sleeves nearly to the wrist worn by Egyptian Muslims.

said, "I'll leave you in the care of the Almighty. Be cautious—these are days of insecurity."

At this the scene vanished as though it had never been. The living room of the old house returned, and there was still some of the stick of incense left. Quickly I started to awaken from my state of elation and to revert to reality in all its material solidity, though for a long time I was in a state of agitated excitement. Could it have been a figment of the imagination? This was the obvious explanation, but how could I accept that and forget the scene that had assumed such concrete form, a scene that in all its dimensions had exuded such verisimilitude? I had lived some past reality that was no less solid than the reality of the present, and had seen myself—or one of my forebears—and part of an era that had passed away. It was not possible for me to doubt that without doubting my mind and senses. Naturally, I did not know how it had come about, but I knew for a fact that it had. One question forced itself upon me: Why had it happened? And why had it happened on this, my last night in the old house? All at once I felt that I was being required to do something, something from which there was no escape.

Could it be that "the other one" had taken out the box after the expiration of a year and had done that which he was directed to do? Had he reached the end of his patience and, acting too hastily, perished? Had his plan turned against him in those days of insecurity? How unrelentingly insistent was the desire to know! A strange thought occurred to me, which was that the past had been manifested to me only because "the other one" had been prevented from getting at the box and that I was being called upon to dig it up and to put into effect what was directed should be done, after it had been unknown, overlooked for such a long period of time. It was ordering me not to leave the old house so that I might act on some ancient command, the time for whose implementation had not yet arrived. Despite the fact that the whole situation was garbed in a wrapping woven of dreams, and wholly at odds with reason, it nonetheless took control of me with a despotic force. My heart became filled with the delights and pains of living in expectation.

That whole night I did not sleep a single moment, as my imagination went roaming through the vastness of time that comprised past, present, and future together, drunk with the intoxication that total freedom brings. The idea of departure was out of the question. I was overwhelmed by the desire to excavate the unknown past in the hope of coming across the word of command that had so long lain dormant. Then I pondered what should be done next. By comparing the scene that had passed away with the one that lay before me, I calculated that the old site of the date palm was where the small stairway led up to the living room. Digging, therefore, must start at a short distance from it, adjacent to the living room window.

I was then faced with the difficulty of informing my brother and sister that I had changed my mind about leaving, after having agreed with them to do so. We were still at university; I was in my last year at the Faculty of Law, while my brother, a year my junior, was studying engineering, and my sister, two years younger than I, was studying medicine. Both of them protested at my sudden change of mind, finding none of my reasons convincing, while at the same time insisting on making the move on their own and expressing the hope that I would soon join them. Before leaving, they reminded me that we had agreed to put the house up for sale so as to profit from the rise in property prices, and I raised no objection. Thus we separated for the first time in our lives, having thought that only marriage or death would ever come between us.

Nothing remained but to start work. I was in truth frightened of the possibility that it would reveal nothing, but I was driven by a force that would not let me turn back, and I made up my mind to dig on my own at night in utter secrecy. I went to work with an axe, a shovel, a basket, and tireless zeal, and soon I was stained with dust and my lungs were filled with it. There lodged in my nostrils a smell full of nostalgia of bygone days. I continued till I had dug down to a depth of my own height, helped by nothing but a feeling that I was drawing near to the truth. Then a blow from the axe gave back an unfamiliar sound that bespoke the presence of an unfamiliar substance. My heart beat so wildly that I found myself trembling all over. In the candlelight I saw the box staring up at me with a face dusty yet alive, as though reproaching me for my long delay, rebuking me for the loss of those many years, and making plain its displeasure at having kept imprisoned a word that should have been made known. At the same time I was being presented with a truth in a concrete form that was undeniable, an embodied miracle, a victory scored against time.

I brought the box up to the surface, then hurried off to the living room, carrying with me the evidence that had ferried me across from a state of dreaming to that of reality and had made a mockery of all accepted concepts. I brushed away the dust, opened the box, and found inside a letter folded up in a wrapping of ragged linen. I spread it out carefully and proceeded to read.

> O my son, may God Almighty protect you.
> The year has gone by and each has come to know his path.
> Leave not your house for it is the most beautiful in Cairo, besides which, the Believers know no other house, no other safe refuge.
> The time has come for you to meet the Guardian of the Sanctuary, our Master Arif al-Baqallani, so go to his house, which is the third one to the right as you enter Aram Gour Alley, and mention to him the password, which is: If I am absent He appears, and if He appears He will cause me to be absent.
> Thus will you discharge your duty, and fortune will smile upon you, and you will obtain that which the Believers wish for you, also that which you wish for yourself.

I read the letter so many times that the reading became mechanical and meaningless. As for my old associate, I had no knowledge as to what his fate had been. I was nevertheless certain that the house was no longer the most beautiful in Cairo, nor a safe refuge for the Believers, and that Arif el-Baqallani, Guardian of the Sanctuary, no longer existed. Wherefore, then, the vision? And wherefore the labor? Was it possible that a miracle of such magnitude could occur for no reason? Was it not conceivable that it was demanding that I go to the third house in Aram Gour Alley so that something might be bestowed upon me that I had not foreseen? Did I have it in me to stop myself from going there, drawn as I was by an avid curiosity and a longing that rejected the idea of my unique miracle ending in a futile jest? Under cover of night I set off, several hundred years late for my appointment. I found the alley lying supine under a darkness from whose depths showed the glimmer of a lamp. Except for a few individuals who quickly crossed to the main road, I saw no sign of human life. I passed by the first house and reached the second. At the third I came to a stop. I turned toward it like someone walking in a dream. I perceived that it possessed a small courtyard lying behind a low wall and that there were indistinct human forms. Before I was able to back away, the door was opened and two tall men in European dress came out. With a quickly executed flanking movement, they barred my path. Then one of them said, "Go inside and meet the person you've come to meet." 160

Taken by surprise, I said, "I didn't come to meet anyone, but I'd be glad to know the name of the person living in the house."

"Really! And why?"

Pushing aside a feeling of apprehension, I said, "I'd like to know if the person living here is from the al-Baqallani family."

"Enough of al-Baqallani—just continue your journey to its end." 170

It occurred to me that the two of them were security men, and I was seized with alarm and confusion. "There's no journey, no meeting," I said.

"You'll change your mind."

Each seized me by an arm, and despite my struggles, herded me inside. Torn from a dream, I was thrust into a nightmare. I was taken into a lighted reception room in the center of which stood a person in a white galabeya,[2] handcuffed. Round about the room I saw several men of the same type as the two who had herded me inside. One of the two men said, "He was coming to meet his friend."

A man—I guessed him to be the leader of the group—turned to the man under arrest. "One of your comrades?" he asked him. 180

"I've not seen him before," answered the young man sullenly.

Looking toward me, the leader asked, "Are you going to repeat the same story, or will you save yourself and us the trouble and confess?"

"I swear by Almighty God," I exclaimed vehemently, "that I have no connection with anything you may suspect."

He stretched out his hand. "Your identity card." I gave him the card. He read it, then asked me, "What brought you here?"

I pointed to the two men and said in an aggrieved tone, "They brought me here by force."

"They hunted you out from off the streets?" 190

"I came to the alley to ask about the al-Baqallani family."

"And what should cause you to ask about them?"

Utterly confused, I was conscious of the wariness inevitably felt by anyone under questioning. "I read about them in a history," I said, "I read that they used to live in the third house to the right as you enter this alley."

"Tell me of the work in which you read that."

I became even more confused and made no answer.

"Lying won't do any good, in fact it'll do you more harm."

"What do you want of me?" I asked in near despair.

"We're taking you in for questioning," he said quietly. 200

"You won't believe me if I tell you the truth," I shouted.

"What might this truth be?"

---

2. A smock-like garment worn in the Middle East.

I gave a sigh; there was dust in my spittle. Then I started to talk. "I was sitting alone in the living room of my house . . ." And I divulged my secret under their stern and derisive gazes. When I had finished, the man said coldly, "Pretending to be mad also won't do any good."

Taking the letter from my pocket, I called out joyfully, "Here's the proof for you."

He scrutinized it, then muttered to himself, "A strange piece of paper whose secret we shall shortly discover." He began carefully reading the lines of writing, 210 and his lips parted in a scornful smile. "An obvious code," he mumbled. Then he looked toward the owner of the house, who was under arrest, and asked him, "Would you be Arif al-Baqallani? Is that your code name?"

"I have no code name," said the young man contemptuously, "and this stranger is nothing but one of your stooges you've brought along so as to trump up a charge against me, but I'm well aware of such tricks."

"Wouldn't it be best," one of the assistants inquired of the leader, "to stay on in case some others turn up and fall into the trap?"

"We'll wait until dawn," said the leader, and he gestured to the two men holding me, at which, disregarding my protests, they began putting handcuffs on 220 me. I could not believe how things had turned out. How could they begin with a wonderful miracle and end up with such a reversal of fortune? I neither believed it could be nor gave way to despair. I was for certain up to my ears in trouble, yet the vision had not been revealed to me for mere jest. I must admit my childish error, I must reconsider things, I must put trust in time.

A heavy silence enclosed us. I brought to mind my brother and sister in the new house, and the gaping hole in the old. The situation presented itself to me from the point of view of someone standing outside it and I could not help but give a laugh. But no one turned to me, no one broke the silence.   [1982]

Questions for Discussion and Writing

1. Why is the narrator reluctant to leave the home of his ancestors?
2. What do you expect to happen after the narrator digs up the box with its strange message?
3. A central concern in the story is the relation between past and present, tradition and innovation. When he decides to search for Arif al-Baqallani, what is the narrator assuming about the relation between past and present?
4. Why does the narrator laugh at the end?

ﾞ MARGARET ATWOOD
(b. 1939)

Bluebeard's Egg

In the last twenty years, Canadian literature has emerged from obscurity to a prominent place on the world's cultural scene, and among its leaders is

Margaret Atwood—poet, novelist, short-story writer, critic, and literary historian.

Although born in Ottawa and raised in Toronto, Atwood absorbed a love of nature from her father, an entomologist, who took the family with him on his summer research expeditions into the Canadian bush. As an adolescent, Atwood was struck by the contrast between people's avowed religiousness and the grasping materialism of suburban life—a theme later explored in her fiction. She earned a B.A. in English at the University of Toronto and pursued graduate work at Radcliffe and Harvard. She was awarded the Companion of the Order of Canada in 1981 and is a Member of the Order of Ontario (1990).

For Atwood, a prominent feature of life in the late twentieth century is the tendency for people to defend themselves against chaos and violence by retreating into orthodoxies, religious or otherwise. One function of literature, therefore, is to explore the realities that lie beneath these surface conventions and orthodoxies. Another concern is linked to her feminism, a fear of power and the ways it is used (chiefly, but not only, by men) to oppress others. Her female characters are often in search of means of self-fulfillment as well and self-understanding. The power they search for, however, is not political but creative. In search of their creativity, they must connect with the mythological structures that give life coherence.

S ALLY STANDS AT the kitchen window, waiting for the sauce she's reducing to come to a simmer, looking out. Past the garage the lot sweeps downwards, into the ravine; it's a wilderness there, of bushes and branches and what Sally thinks of as vines. It was her idea to have a kind of terrace, built of old railroad ties, with wild flowers growing between them, but Edward says he likes it the way it is. There's a playhouse down at the bottom, near the fence; from here she can just see the roof. It has nothing to do with Edward's kids, in their earlier incarnations, before Sally's time; it's more ancient than that, and falling apart. Sally would like it cleared away. She thinks drunks sleep in it, the men who live under the bridges down there, who occasionally wander over the fence (which is broken down, from 10 where they step on it) and up the hill, to emerge squinting like moles into the light of Sally's well-kept back lawn.

Off to the left is Ed, in his windbreaker; it's officially spring, Sally's blue scylla is in flower, but it's chilly for this time of year. Ed's windbreaker is an old one he won't throw out; it still says WILDCATS, relic of some team he was on in high school, an era so prehistoric Sally can barely imagine it; though picturing Ed at high school is not all that difficult. Girls would have had crushes on him, he would have been unconscious of it; things like that don't change. He's puttering around the rock garden now; some of the rocks stick out too far and are in danger of grazing the side of Sally's Peugeot, on its way to the garage, and he's moving 20 them around. He likes doing things like that, puttering, humming to himself. He won't wear work gloves, though she keeps telling him he could squash his fingers.

Watching his bent back with its frayed, poignant lettering, Sally dissolves;

which is not infrequent with her. *My darling Edward,* she thinks. *Edward Bear, of little brain.*[1] *How I love you.* At times like this she feels very protective of him.

Sally knows for a fact that dumb blondes were loved, not because they were blondes, but because they were dumb. It was their helplessness and confusion that were so sexually attractive, once; not their hair. It wasn't false, the rush of tenderness men must have felt for such women. Sally understands it.

For it must be admitted: Sally is in love with Ed because of his stupidity, his monumental and almost energetic stupidity: energetic, because Ed's stupidity is not passive. He's no mere blockhead; you'd have to be working at it to be that stupid. Does it make Sally feel smug, or smarter than he is, or even smarter than she really is herself? No; on the contrary, it makes her humble. It fills her with wonder that the world can contain such marvels as Ed's colossal and endearing thickness. He is just so *stupid.* Every time he gives her another piece of evidence, another tile that she can glue into place in the vast mosaic of his stupidity she's continually piecing together, she wants to hug him, and often does; and he is so stupid he can never figure out what for.

Because Ed is so stupid he doesn't even know he's stupid. He's a child of luck, a third son who, armed with nothing but a certain feeble-minded amiability, manages to make it through the forest with all its witches and traps and pitfalls and end up with the princess, who is Sally, of course. It helps that he's handsome.

On good days she sees his stupidity as innocence, lamb-like, shining with the light of (for instance) green daisied meadows in the sun. (When Sally starts thinking this way about Ed, in terms of the calendar art from the service-station washrooms of her childhood, dredging up images of a boy with curly golden hair, his arm thrown around the neck of an Irish setter—a notorious brainless beast, she reminds herself—she knows she is sliding over the edge, into a ghastly kind of sentimentality, and that she must stop at once, or Ed will vanish, to be replaced by a stuffed facsimile, useful for little else but an umbrella stand. Ed is a real person, with a lot more to him than these simplistic renditions allow for; which sometimes worries her.) On bad days though, she sees his stupidity as wilfulness, a stubborn determination to shut things out. His obtuseness is a wall, within which he can go about his business, humming to himself, while Sally, locked outside, must hack her way through the brambles with hardly so much as a transparent raincoat between them and her skin.

Why did she choose him (or, to be precise, as she tries to be with herself and sometimes is even out loud, *hunt him down*), when it's clear to everyone she had other options? To Marylynn, who is her best though most recent friend, she's explained it by saying she was spoiled when young by reading too many Agatha Christie murder mysteries, of the kind in which the clever and witty heroine passes over the equally clever and witty first-lead male, who's helped solve the crime, in order to marry the second-lead male, the stupid one, the one who would have been arrested and condemned and executed if it hadn't been for her cleverness. Maybe this is how she sees Ed: if it weren't for her, his blundering too-many-thumbs kindness would get him into all sorts of quagmires, all sorts of sink-holes he'd never be able to get himself out of, and then he'd be done for.

---

1. The reference is to A. A. Milne's *Winnie the Pooh.*

"Sink-hole" and "quagmire" are not flattering ways of speaking about other women, but this is what is at the back of Sally's mind; specifically, Ed's two previ- 70
ous wives. Sally didn't exactly extricate him from their clutches. She's never even met the first one, who moved to the west coast fourteen years ago and sends Christmas cards, and the second one was middle-aged and already in the act of severing herself from Ed before Sally came along. (For Sally, "middle-aged" means anyone five years older than she is. It has always meant this. She applies it only to women, however. She doesn't think of Ed as middle-aged, although the gap be- tween them is considerably more than five years.)

Ed doesn't know what happened with these marriages, what went wrong. His protestations of ignorance, his refusal to discuss the finer points, is frustrating to Sally, because she would like to hear the whole story. But it's also cause for anx- 80
iety: if he doesn't know what happened with the other two, maybe the same thing could be happening with her and he doesn't know about that, either. Stupidity like Ed's can be a health hazard, for other people. What if he wakes up one day and decides that she isn't the true bride after all, but the false one? Then she will be put into a barrel stuck full of nails and rolled downhill, endlessly, while he is sitting in yet another bridal bed, drinking champagne. She remembers the brand name, because she bought it herself. Champagne isn't the sort of finishing touch that would occur to Ed, though he enjoyed it enough at the time.

But outwardly Sally makes a joke of all this. "He doesn't *know*," she says to Marylynn, laughing a little, and they shake their heads. If it were them, they'd 90
know, all right. Marylynn is in fact divorced, and she can list every single thing that went wrong, item by item. After doing this, she adds that her divorce was one of the best things that ever happened to her. "I was just a nothing before," she says. "It made me pull myself together."

Sally, looking across the kitchen table at Marylynn, has to agree that she is far from being a nothing now. She started out re-doing people's closets, and has worked that up into her own interior-design firm. She does the houses of the newly rich, those who lack ancestral furniture and the confidence to be shabby, and who wish their interiors to reflect a personal taste they do not in reality pos- sess.   100

"What they want are mausoleums," Marylynn says, "or hotels," and she cheerfully supplies them. "Right down to the ash-trays. Imagine having someone else pick out your ash-trays for you."

By saying this, Marylynn lets Sally know that she's not including her in that category, though Sally did in fact hire her, at the very first, to help with a few de- tails around the house. It was Marylynn who redesigned the wall of closets in the master bedroom and who found Sally's massive Chinese mahogany table, which cost her another seven hundred dollars to have stripped. But it turned out to be perfect, as Marylynn said it would. Now she's dug up a nineteenth-century key- hole desk, which both she and Sally know will be exactly right for the bay- 110
windowed alcove off the living room. "Why do you need it?" Ed said in his puz- zled way. "I thought you worked in your study." Sally admitted this, but said they could keep the telephone bills in it, which appeared to satisfy him. She knows ex- actly what she needs it for: she needs it to sit at, in something flowing, backlit by the morning sunlight, gracefully dashing off notes. She saw a 1940's advertisement

for coffee like this once; and the husband was standing behind the chair, leaning over, with a worshipful expression on his face.

Marylynn is the kind of friend Sally does not have to explain any of this to, because it's assumed between them. Her intelligence is the kind Sally respects.

Marylynn is tall and elegant, and makes anything she is wearing seem fash- 120 ionable. Her hair is prematurely grey and she leaves it that way. She goes in for loose blouses in cream-coloured silk, and eccentric scarves gathered from interesting shops and odd corners of the world, thrown carelessly around her neck and over one shoulder. (Sally has tried this toss in the mirror, but it doesn't work.) Marylynn has a large collection of unusual shoes; she says they're unusual because her feet are so big, but Sally knows better. Sally, who used to think of herself as pretty enough and now thinks of herself as doing quite well for her age, envies Marylynn her bone structure, which will serve her well when the inevitable happens.

Whenever Marylynn is coming to dinner, as she is today—she's bringing the 130 desk, too—Sally takes especial care with her clothes and make-up. Marylynn, she knows, is her real audience for such things, since no changes she effects in herself seem to affect Ed one way or the other, or even to register with him. "You look fine to me" is all he says, no matter how she really looks. (But does she want him to see her more clearly, or not? Most likely not. If he did he would notice the incipient wrinkles, the small pouches of flesh that are not quite there yet, the network forming beneath her eyes. It's better as it is.)

Sally has repeated this remark of Ed's to Marylynn, adding that he said it the day the Jacuzzi overflowed because the smoke alarm went off, because an English muffin she was heating to eat in the bathtub got stuck in the toaster, and she had 140 to spend an hour putting down newspaper and mopping up, and only had half an hour to dress for a dinner they were going to. "Really I looked like the wrath of God," said Sally. These days she finds herself repeating to Marylynn many of the things Ed says: the stupid things. Marylynn is the only one of Sally's friends she has confided in to this extent.

"Ed is cute as a button," Marylynn said. "In fact, he's just like a button: he's so bright and shiny. If he were mine, I'd get him bronzed and keep him on the mantelpiece."

Marylynn is even better than Sally at concocting formulations for Ed's particular brand of stupidity, which can irritate Sally: coming from herself, this sort of 150 comment appears to her indulgent and loving, but from Marylynn it borders on the patronizing. So then she sticks up for Ed, who is by no means stupid about everything. When you narrow it down, there's only one area of life he's hopeless about. The rest of the time he's intelligent enough, some even say brilliant: otherwise, how could he be so successful?

Ed is a heart man, one of the best, and the irony of this is not lost on Sally: who could possibly know less about the workings of hearts, real hearts, the kind symbolized by red satin surrounded by lace and topped by pink bows, than Ed? Hearts with arrows in them. At the same time, the fact that he's a heart man is a large part of his allure. Women corner him on sofas, trap him in bay-windows at 160 cocktail parties, mutter to him in confidential voices at dinner parties. They behave this way right in front of Sally, under her very nose, as if she's invisible, and

Ed lets them do it. This would never happen if he were in banking or construction.

As it is, everywhere he goes he is beset by sirens. They want him to fix their hearts. Each of them seems to have a little something wrong—a murmur, a whisper. Or they faint a lot and want him to tell them why. This is always what the conversations are about, according to Ed, and Sally believes it. Once she'd wanted it herself, that mirage. What had she invented for him, in the beginning? A heavy heart, that beat too hard after meals. And he'd been so sweet, looking at her with   170
those stunned brown eyes of his, as if her heart were the genuine topic, listening to her gravely as if he'd never heard any of this twaddle before, advising her to drink less coffee. And she'd felt such triumph, to have carried off her imposture, pried out of him that minuscule token of concern.

Thinking back on this incident makes her uneasy, now that she's seen her own performance repeated so many times, including the hand placed lightly on the heart, to call attention of course to the breasts. Some of these women have been within inches of getting Ed to put his head down on their chests, right there in Sally's living room. Watching all this out of the corners of her eyes while serving the liqueurs, Sally feels the Aztec rise within her. *Trouble with your heart? Get it re-*   180
moved, she thinks. *Then you'll have no more problems.*

Sometimes Sally worries that she's a nothing, the way Marylynn was before she got a divorce and a job. But Sally isn't a nothing; therefore, she doesn't need a divorce to stop being one. And she's always had a job of some sort; in fact she has one now. Luckily Ed has no objection; he doesn't have much of an objection to anything she does.

Her job is supposed to be full-time, but in effect it's part-time, because Sally can take a lot of the work away and do it at home, and, as she says, with one arm tied behind her back. When Sally is being ornery, when she's playing the dull wife of a fascinating heart man—she does this with people she can't be bothered   190
with—she says she works in a bank, nothing important. Then she watches their eyes dismiss her. When, on the other hand, she's trying to impress, she says she's in P.R. In reality she runs the in-house organ for a trust company, a medium-sized one. This is a thin magazine, nicely printed, which is supposed to make the employees feel that some of the boys are doing worthwhile things out there and are human beings as well. It's still the boys, though the few women in anything resembling key positions are wheeled out regularly, bloused and suited and smiling brightly, with what they hope will come across as confidence rather than aggression.

This is the latest in a string of such jobs Sally has held over the years: comfortable enough jobs that engage only half of her cogs and wheels, and that end up   200
leading nowhere. Technically she's second-in-command: over her is a man who wasn't working out in management, but who couldn't be fired because his wife was related to the chairman of the board. He goes out for long alcoholic lunches and plays a lot of golf, and Sally runs the show. This man gets the official credit for everything Sally does right, but the senior executives in the company take Sally aside when no one is looking and tell her what a great gal she is and what a whiz she is at holding up her end.

The real pay-off for Sally, though, is that her boss provides her with an end-

less supply of anecdotes. She dines out on stories about his dim-wittedness and
pomposity, his lobotomized suggestions about what the two of them should cook
up for the magazine; *the organ,* as she says he always calls it. "He says we need
some fresh blood to perk up the organ," Sally says, and the heart men grin at her.
"He actually said that?" Talking like this about her boss would be reckless—you
never know what might get back to him, with the world as small as it is—if Sally
were afraid of losing her job, but she isn't. There's an unspoken agreement between her and this man: they both know that if she goes, he goes, because who
else would put up with him? Sally might angle for his job, if she were stupid
enough to disregard his family connections, if she coveted the trappings of power.
But she's just fine where she is. Jokingly, she says she's reached her level of incom-
petence. She says she suffers from fear of success.

Her boss is white-haired, slender, and tanned, and looks like an English gin
ad. Despite his vapidity he's outwardly distinguished, she allows him that. In truth
she pampers him outrageously, indulges him, covers up for him at every turn,
though she stops short of behaving like a secretary: she doesn't bring him coffee.
They both have a secretary who does that anyway. The one time he made a pass at
her, when he came in from lunch visibly reeling, Sally was kind about it.

Occasionally, though not often, Sally has to travel in connection with her
job. She's sent off to places like Edmonton, where they have a branch. She interviews the boys at the middle and senior levels; they have lunch, and the boys talk
about ups and downs in oil or the slump in the real-estate market. Then she gets
taken on tours of shopping plazas under construction. It's always windy, and grit
blows into her face. She comes back to home base and writes a piece on the
youthfulness and vitality of the West.

She teases Ed, while she packs, saying she's going off for a rendezvous with a
dashing financier or two. Ed isn't threatened; he tells her to enjoy herself, and she
hugs him and tells him how much she will miss him. He's so dumb it doesn't
occur to him she might not be joking. In point of fact, it would have been quite
possible for Sally to have had an affair, or at least a one- or two-night stand, on
several of these occasions: she knows when those chalk lines are being drawn,
when she's being dared to step over them. But she isn't interested in having an affair with anyone but Ed.

She doesn't eat much on the planes; she doesn't like the food. But on the return trip, she invariably saves the pre-packaged parts of the meal, the cheese in its
plastic wrap, the miniature chocolate bar, the bag of pretzels. She ferrets them
away in her purse. She thinks of them as supplies, that she may need if she gets
stuck in a strange airport, if they have to change course because of snow or fog,
for instance. All kinds of things could happen, although they never have. When
she gets home she takes the things from her purse and throws them out.

Outside the window Ed straightens up and wipes his earth-smeared hands
down the sides of his pants. He begins to turn, and Sally moves back from the
window so he won't see that she's watching. She doesn't like it to be too obvious.
She shifts her attention to the sauce: it's in the second stage of a *sauce suprême,*
which will make all the difference to the chicken. When Sally was learning this
sauce, her cooking instructor quoted one of the great chefs, to the effect that the

chicken was merely a canvas. He meant as in painting, but Sally, in an undertone to the woman next to her, turned it around. "Mine's canvas anyway, sauce or no sauce," or words to that effect.

Gourmet cooking was the third night course Sally has taken. At the moment she's on her fifth, which is called *Forms of Narrative Fiction.* It's half reading and half writing assignments—the instructor doesn't believe you can understand an art form without at least trying it yourself—and Sally purports to be enjoying it. She tells her friends she takes night courses to keep her brain from atrophying, and her friends find this amusing: whatever else may become of Sally's brain, they say, they don't see atrophying as an option. Sally knows better, but in any case there's always room for improvement. She may have begun taking the courses in the belief that this would make her more interesting to Ed, but she soon gave up on that idea: she appears to be neither more nor less interesting to Ed now than she was before.

Most of the food for tonight is already made. Sally tries to be well organized: the overflowing Jacuzzi was an aberration. The cold watercress soup with walnuts is chilling in the refrigerator, the chocolate mousse ditto. Ed, being Ed, prefers meatloaf to sweetbreads with pine nuts, butterscotch pudding made from a package to chestnut purée topped with whipped cream. (Sally burnt her fingers peeling the chestnuts. She couldn't do it the easy way and buy it tinned.) Sally says Ed's preference for this type of food comes from being pre-programmed by hospital cafeterias when he was younger: show him a burned sausage and a scoop of instant mashed potatoes and he salivates. So it's only for company that she can unfurl her *boeuf en daube* and her salmon *en papillote,* spread them forth to be savoured and praised.

What she likes best about these dinners though is setting the table, deciding who will sit where and, when she's feeling mischievous, even what they are likely to say. Then she can sit and listen to them say it. Occasionally she prompts a little.

Tonight will not be very challenging, since it's only the heart men and their wives, and Marylynn, whom Sally hopes will dilute them. The heart men are forbidden to talk shop at Sally's dinner table, but they do it anyway. "Not what you really want to listen to while you're eating," says Sally. "All those tubes and valves." Privately she thinks they're a conceited lot, all except Ed. She can't resist needling them from time to time.

"I mean," she said to one of the leading surgeons, "basically it's just an exalted form of dress-making, don't you think?"

"Come again?" said the surgeon, smiling. The heart men think Sally is one hell of a tease.

"It's really just cutting and sewing, isn't it?" Sally murmured. The surgeon laughed.

"There's more to it than that," Ed said, unexpectedly, solemnly.

"What more, Ed?" said the surgeon. "You could say there's a lot of embroidery, but that's in the billing." He chuckled at himself.

Sally held her breath. She could hear Ed's verbal thought processes lurching into gear. He was delectable.

"Good judgement," Ed said. His earnestness hit the table like a wet fish. The surgeon hastily downed his wine.

Sally smiled. This was supposed to be a reprimand to her, she knew, for not taking things seriously enough. *Oh, come on, Ed,* she could say. But she knows also, most of the time, when to keep her trap shut. She should have a light-up JOKE sign on her forehead, so Ed would be able to tell the difference.

The heart men do well. Most of them appear to be doing better than Ed, but that's only because they have, on the whole, more expensive tastes and fewer wives. Sally can calculate these things and she figures Ed is about par.

These days there's much talk about advanced technologies, which Sally tries to keep up on, since they interest Ed. A few years ago the heart men got themselves a new facility. Ed was so revved up that he told Sally about it, which was unusual for him. A week later Sally said she would drop by the hospital at the end of the day and pick Ed up and take him out for dinner; she didn't feel like cooking, she said. Really she wanted to check out the facility; she likes to check out anything that causes the line on Ed's excitement chart to move above level.

At first Ed said he was tired, that when the day came to an end he didn't want to prolong it. But Sally wheedled and was respectful, and finally Ed took her to see his new gizmo. It was in a cramped, darkened room with an examining table in it. The thing itself looked like a television screen hooked up to some complicated hardware. Ed said that they could wire a patient up and bounce sound waves off the heart and pick up the echoes, and they would get a picture on the screen, an actual picture, of the heart in motion. It was a thousand times better than an electrocardiogram, he said: they could see the faults, the thickenings and cloggings, much more clearly.

"Colour?" said Sally.

"Black and white," said Ed.

Then Sally was possessed by a desire to see her own heart, in motion, in black and white, on the screen. At the dentist's she always wants to see the X-rays of her teeth, too, solid and glittering in her cloudy head. "Do it," she said, "I want to see how it works," and though this was the kind of thing Ed would ordinarily evade or tell her she was being silly about, he didn't need much persuading. He was fascinated by the thing himself, and he wanted to show it off.

He checked to make sure there was nobody real booked for the room. Then he told Sally to slip out of her clothes, the top half, brassière and all. He gave her a paper gown and turned his back modestly while she slipped it on, as if he didn't see her body every night of the week. He attached electrodes to her, the ankles and one wrist, and turned a switch and fiddled with the dials. Really a technician was supposed to do this, he told her, but he knew how to run the machine himself. He was good with small appliances.

Sally lay prone on the table, feeling strangely naked. "What do I do?" she said.

"Just lie there," said Ed. He came over to her and tore a hole in the paper gown, above her left breast. Then he started running a probe over her skin. It was wet and slippery and cold, and felt like the roller on a roll-on deodorant.

"There," he said, and Sally turned her head. On the screen was a large grey object, like a giant fig, paler in the middle, a dark line running down the centre. The sides moved in and out; two wings fluttered in it, like an uncertain moth's.

"That's it?" said Sally dubiously. Her heart looked so insubstantial, like a bag of gelatin, something that would melt, fade, disintegrate, if you squeezed it even a little.   350

Ed moved the probe, and they looked at the heart from the bottom, then the top. Then he stopped the frame, then changed it from a positive to a negative image. Sally began to shiver.

"That's wonderful," she said. He seemed so distant, absorbed in his machine, taking the measure of her heart, which was beating over there all by itself, detached from her, exposed and under his control.

Ed unwired her and she put on her clothes again, neutrally, as if he were actually a doctor. Nevertheless this transaction, this whole room, was sexual in a way she didn't quite understand; it was clearly a dangerous place. It was like a massage parlour, only for women. Put a batch of women in there with Ed and they would   360 never want to come out. They'd want to stay in there while he ran his probe over their wet skins and pointed out to them the defects of their beating hearts.

"Thank you," said Sally.

Sally hears the back door open and close. She feels Ed approaching, coming through the passages of the house towards her, like a small wind or a ball of static electricity. The hair stands up on her arms. Sometimes he makes her so happy she thinks she's about to burst; other times she thinks she's about to burst anyway.

He comes into the kitchen, and she pretends not to notice. He puts his arms around her from behind, kisses her on the neck. She leans back, pressing herself into him. What they should do now is go into the bedroom (or even the living   370 room, even the den) and make love, but it wouldn't occur to Ed to make love in the middle of the day. Sally often comes across articles in magazines about how to improve your sex life, which leave her feeling disappointed, or reminiscent: Ed is not Sally's first and only man. But she knows she shouldn't expect too much of Ed. If Ed were more experimental, more interested in variety, he would be a different kind of man altogether: slyer, more devious, more observant, harder to deal with.

As it is, Ed makes love in the same way, time after time, each movement following the others in an exact order. But it seems to satisfy him. Of course it satisfies him: you can always tell when men are satisfied. It's Sally who lies awake, afterwards, watching the pictures unroll across her closed eyes.   380

Sally steps away from Ed, smiles at him. "How did you make out with the women today?" she says.

"What women?" says Ed absently, going towards the sink. He knows what women.

"The ones out there, hiding in the forsythia," says Sally. "I counted at least ten. They were just waiting for a chance."

She teases him frequently about these troops of women, which follow him around everywhere, which are invisible to Ed but which she can see as plain as day.

"I bet they hang around outside the front door of the hospital," she will say,   390 "just waiting till you come out. I bet they hide in the linen closets and jump out at you from behind, and then pretend to be lost so you'll take them by the short cut.

It's the white coat that does it. None of those women can resist the white coats. They've been conditioned by Young Doctor Kildare."[2]

"Don't be silly," says Ed today, with equanimity. Is he blushing, is he embarrassed? Sally examines his face closely, like a geologist with an aerial photograph, looking for telltale signs of mineral treasure: markings, bumps, hollows. Everything about Ed means something, though it's difficult at times to say what.

Now he's washing his hands at the sink, to get the earth off. In a minute he'll wipe them on the dish towel instead of using the hand towel the way he's sup- 400
posed to. Is that complacency, in the back turned to her? Maybe there really are these hordes of women, even though she's made them up. Maybe they really do behave that way. His shoulders are slightly drawn up: is he shutting her out?

"I know what they want," she goes on. "They want to get into that little dark room of yours and climb up onto your table. They think you're delicious. They'll gobble you up. They'll chew you into tiny pieces. There won't be anything left of you at all, only a stethoscope and a couple of shoelaces."

Once Ed would have laughed at this, but today he doesn't. Maybe she's said it, or something like it, a few times too often. He smiles though, wipes his hands on the dish towel, peers into the fridge. He likes to snack.   410

"There's some cold roast beef," Sally says, baffled.

Sally takes the sauce off the stove and sets it aside for later: she'll do the last steps just before serving. It's only two-thirty. Ed has disappeared into the cellar, where Sally knows he will be safe for a while. She goes into her study, which used to be one of the kids' bedrooms, and sits down at her desk. The room has never been completely redecorated: there's still a bed in it, a dressing table with a blue flowered flounce Sally helped pick out, long before the kids went off to university: "flew the coop," as Ed puts it.

Sally doesn't comment on the expression, though she would like to say that it wasn't the first coop they flew. Her house isn't even the real coop, since neither 420
of the kids is hers. She'd hoped for a baby of her own when she married Ed, but she didn't want to force the issue. Ed didn't object to the idea, exactly, but he was neutral about it, and Sally got the feeling he'd had enough babies already. Anyway, the other two wives had babies, and look what happened to them. Since their actual fates have always been vague to Sally, she's free to imagine all kinds of things, from drug addiction to madness. Whatever it was resulted in Sally having to bring up their kids, at least from puberty onwards. The way it was presented by the first wife was that it was Ed's turn now. The second wife was more oblique: she said that the child wanted to spend some time with her father. Sally was left out of both these equations, as if the house wasn't a place she lived in, not really, so she 430
couldn't be expected to have any opinion.

Considering everything, she hasn't done badly. She likes the kids and tries to be a friend to them, since she can hardly pretend to be a mother. She describes the three of them as having an easy relationship. Ed wasn't around much for the kids,

2. Popular television physician in the 1960s.

but it's him they want approval from, not Sally; it's him they respect. Sally is more like a confederate, helping them get what they want from Ed.

When the kids were younger, Sally used to play Monopoly with them, up at the summer place in Muskoka Ed owned then but has since sold. Ed would play too, on his vacations and on the weekends when he could make it up. These games would all proceed along the same lines. Sally would have an initial run of luck and would buy up everything she had a chance at. She didn't care whether it was classy real estate, like Boardwalk or Park Place, or those dingy little houses on the other side of the tracks; she would even buy train stations, which the kids would pass over, preferring to save their cash reserves for better investments. Ed, on the other hand, would plod along, getting a little here, a little there. Then, when Sally was feeling flush, she would blow her money on next-to-useless luxuries such as the electric light company; and when the kids started to lose, as they invariably did, Sally would lend them money at cheap rates or trade them things of her own, at a loss. Why not? She could afford it.

Ed meanwhile would be hedging his bets, building up blocks of property, sticking houses and hotels on them. He preferred the middle range, respectable streets but not flashy. Sally would land on his spaces and have to shell out hard cash. Ed never offered deals, and never accepted them. He played a lone game, and won more often than not. Then Sally would feel thwarted. She would say she guessed she lacked the killer instinct; or she would say that for herself she didn't care, because after all it was only a game, but he ought to allow the kids to win, once in a while. Ed couldn't grasp the concept of allowing other people to win. He said it would be condescending towards the children, and anyway you couldn't arrange to have a dice game turn out the way you wanted it to, since it was partly a matter of chance. If it was chance, Sally would think, why were the games so similar to one another? At the end, there would be Ed, counting up his paper cash, sorting it out into piles of bills of varying denominations, and Sally, her vast holdings dwindled to a few shoddy blocks on Baltic Avenue, doomed to foreclosure: extravagant, generous, bankrupt.

On these nights, after the kids were asleep, Sally would have two or three more rye-and-gingers than were good for her. Ed would go to bed early—winning made him satisfied and drowsy—and Sally would ramble about the house or read the endings of murder mysteries she had already read once before, and finally she would slip into bed and wake Ed up and stroke him into arousal, seeking comfort.

* * *

Sally has almost forgotten these games. Right now the kids are receding, fading like old ink; Ed on the contrary looms larger and larger, the outlines around him darkening. He's constantly developing, like a Polaroid print, new colours emerging, but the result remains the same: Ed is a surface, one she has trouble getting beneath.

"Explore your inner world," said Sally's instructor in *Forms of Narrative Fiction,* a middle-aged woman of scant fame who goes in for astrology and the Tarot pack and writes short stories, which are not published in any of the magazines Sally reads. "Then there's your outer one," Sally said afterwards, to her friends. "For instance, she should really get something done about her hair." She made this trivial and mean remark because she's fed up with her inner world; she 480 doesn't need to explore it. In her inner world is Ed, like a doll within a Russian wooden doll, and in Ed is Ed's inner world, which she can't get at.

She takes a crack at it anyway: Ed's inner world is a forest, which looks something like the bottom part of their ravine lot, but without the fence. He wanders around in there, among the trees, not heading in any special direction. Every once in a while he comes upon a strange-looking plant, a sickly plant choked with weeds and briars. Ed kneels, clears a space around it, does some pruning, a little skilful snipping and cutting, props it up. The plant revives, flushes with health, sends out a grateful red blossom. Ed continues on his way. Or it may be a conked-out squirrel, which he restores with a drop from his flask of magic elixir. At set in- 490 tervals an angel appears, bringing him food. It's always meatloaf. That's fine with Ed, who hardly notices what he eats, but the angel is getting tired of being an angel. Now Sally begins thinking about the angel: why are its wings frayed and dingy grey around the edges, why is it looking so withered and frantic? This is where all Sally's attempts to explore Ed's inner world end up.

She knows she thinks about Ed too much. She knows she should stop. She knows she shouldn't ask, "Do you still love me?" in the plaintive tone that sets even her own teeth on edge. All it achieves is that Ed shakes his head, as if not understanding why she would ask this, and pats her hand. "Sally, Sally," he says, and everything proceeds as usual; except for the dread that seeps into things, the most 500 ordinary things, such as rearranging the chairs and changing the burnt-out lightbulbs. But what is it she's afraid of? She has what they call everything: Ed, their wonderful house on a ravine lot, something she's always wanted. (But the hill is jungly, and the house is made of ice. It's held together only by Sally, who sits in the middle of it, working on a puzzle. The puzzle is Ed. If she should ever solve it, if she should ever fit the last cold splinter into place, the house will melt and flow away down the hill, and then . . .) It's a bad habit, fooling around with her head this way. It does no good. She knows that if she could quit she'd be happier. She ought to be able to: she's given up smoking.

She needs to concentrate her attention on other things. This is the real rea- 510 son for the night courses, which she picks almost at random, to coincide with the evenings Ed isn't in. He has meetings, he's on the boards of charities, he has trouble saying no. She runs the courses past herself, mediaeval history, cooking, anthropology, hoping her mind will snag on something; she's even taken a course in geology, which was fascinating, she told her friends, all that magma. That's just it: everything is fascinating, but nothing enters her. She's always a star pupil, she does well on the exams and impresses the teachers, for which she despises them. She is familiar with her brightness, her techniques; she's surprised other people are still taken in by them.

Forms of Narrative Fiction started out the same way. Sally was full of good 520 ideas, brimming with helpful suggestions. The workshop part of it was anyway just like a committee meeting, and Sally knew how to run those, from behind, without seeming to run them: she'd done it lots of times at work. Bertha, the instructor, told Sally she had a vivid imagination and a lot of untapped creative energy. "No wonder she never gets anywhere, with a name like Bertha," Sally said, while having coffee afterwards with two of the other night-coursers. "It goes with her outfits, though." (Bertha sports the macramé look, with health-food sandals and bulky-knit sweaters and hand-weave skirts that don't do a thing for her square figure, and too many Mexican rings on her hands, which she doesn't wash often enough.) Bertha goes in for assignments, which she calls learning by doing. Sally likes assignments: she likes things that can be completed and then discarded, and for which she gets marks. 530

The first thing Bertha assigned was The Epic. They read *The Odyssey* (selected passages, in translation, with a plot summary of the rest); then they poked around in James Joyce's *Ulysses,* to see how Joyce had adapted the epic form to the modern-day novel. Bertha had them keep a Toronto notebook, in which they had to pick out various spots around town as the ports of call in *The Odyssey,* and say why they had chosen them. The notebooks were read out loud in class, and it was a scream to see who had chosen what for Hades. (The Mount Pleasant Cemetery, McDonald's, where, if you eat the forbidden food, you never get back to the land 540 of the living, the University Club with its dead ancestral souls, and so forth.) Sally's was the hospital, of course; she had no difficulty with the trench filled with blood, and she put the ghosts in wheelchairs.

After that they did The Ballad, and read gruesome accounts of murders and betrayed love. Bertha played them tapes of wheezy old men singing traditionally, in the Doric mode, and assigned a newspaper scrapbook, in which you had to clip and paste up-to-the-minute equivalents. The *Sun* was the best newspaper for these. The fiction that turned out to go with this kind of plot was the kind Sally liked anyway, and she had no difficulty concocting a five-page murder mystery, complete with revenge. 550

But now they are on Folk Tales and the Oral Tradition, and Sally is having trouble. This time, Bertha wouldn't let them read anything. Instead she read to them, in a voice, Sally said, that was like a gravel truck and was not conducive to reverie. Since it was the Oral Tradition, they weren't even allowed to take notes; Bertha said the original hearers of these stories couldn't read, so the stories were memorized. "To re-create the atmosphere," said Bertha, "I should turn out the lights. These stories were always told at night." "To make them creepier?" someone offered. "No" said Bertha. "In the days, they worked." She didn't do that, though she did make them sit in a circle.

"You should have seen us," Sally said afterwards to Ed, "sitting in a circle, lis- 560 tening to fairy stories. It was just like kindergarten. Some of them even had their mouths open. I kept expecting her to say, 'If you need to go, put up your hand.'" She was meaning to be funny, to amuse Ed with this account of Bertha's eccentricity and the foolish appearance of the students, most of them middle-aged, sitting in a circle as if they had never grown up at all. She was also intending to belittle the course, just slightly. She always did this with her night courses, so Ed wouldn't get the idea there was anything in her life that was even remotely as important as he was. But Ed didn't seem to need this amusement or this belittlement. He took her information earnestly, gravely, as if Bertha's behaviour was, after all, only the procedure of a specialist. No one knew better than he did that the procedures of 570 specialists often looked bizarre or incomprehensible to onlookers. "She probably has her reasons," was all he would say.

The first stories Bertha read them, for warm-ups ("No memorizing for *her,*" said Sally), were about princes who got amnesia and forgot about their true loves and married girls their mothers had picked out for them. Then they had to be rescued, with the aid of magic. The stories didn't say what happened to the women the princes had already married, though Sally wondered about it. Then Bertha read them another story, and this time they were supposed to remember the features that stood out for them and write a five-page transposition, set in the present and cast in the realistic mode. ("In other words," said Bertha, "no real magic.") They couldn't 580 use the Universal Narrator, however: they had done that in their Ballad assignment. This time they had to choose a point of view. It could be the point of view of anyone or anything in the story, but they were limited to one only. The story she was about to read, she said, was a variant of the Bluebeard motif, much earlier than Perrault's sentimental rewriting of it. In Perrault, said Bertha, the girl has to be rescued by her brothers; but in the earlier version things were quite otherwise.

This is what Bertha read, as far as Sally can remember:

There were once three young sisters. One day a beggar with a large basket on his back came to the door and asked for some bread. The eldest sister brought him some, but no sooner had she touched him than she was compelled to jump 590 into his basket, for the beggar was really a wizard in disguise. ("So much for United Appeal," Sally murmured. "She should have said, 'I gave at the office.'") The wizard carried her away to his house in the forest, which was large and richly furnished. "Here you will be happy with me, my darling," said the wizard, "for you will have everything your heart could desire."

This lasted for a few days. Then the wizard gave the girl an egg and a bunch of keys. "I must go away on a journey," he said, "and I am leaving the house in your charge. Preserve this egg for me, and carry it about with you everywhere; for a great misfortune will follow from its loss. The keys open every room in the house. You may go into each of them and enjoy what you find there, but do not go 600 into the small room at the top of the house, on pain of death." The girl promised, and the wizard disappeared.

At first the girl contented herself with exploring the rooms, which contained many treasures. But finally her curiosity would not let her alone. She sought out the smallest key, and, with beating heart, opened the little door at the top of the house. Inside it was a large basin full of blood, within which were the bodies of many women, which had been cut to pieces; nearby were a chopping block and an axe. In her horror, she let go of the egg, which fell into the basin of blood. In vain did she try to wipe away the stain: every time she succeeded in removing it, back it would come. 610

The wizard returned, and in a stern voice asked for the egg and the keys. When he saw the egg, he knew at once she had disobeyed him and gone into the forbidden room. "Since you have gone into the room against my will," he said, "you shall go back into it against your own." Despite her pleas he threw her down, dragged her by the hair into the little room, hacked her into pieces and threw her body into the basin with the others.

Then he went for the second girl, who fared no better than her sister. But the third was clever and wily. As soon as the wizard had gone, she set the egg on a shelf, out of harm's way, and then went immediately and opened the forbidden

door. Imagine her distress when she saw the cut-up bodies of her two beloved sis- 620
ters; but she set the parts in order, and they joined together and her sisters stood
up and moved, and were living and well. They embraced each other, and the third
sister hid the other two in a cupboard.

When the wizard returned he at once asked for the egg. This time it was
spotless. "You have passed the test," he said to the third sister. "You shall be my
bride." ("And second prize," said Sally, to herself this time, "is *two* weeks in
Niagara Falls.") The wizard no longer had any power over her, and had to do
whatever she asked. There was more, about how the wizard met his come-uppance
and was burned to death, but Sally already knew which features stood out for her.

At first she thought the most important thing in the story was the forbidden 630
room. What would she put in the forbidden room, in her present-day realistic version? Certainly not chopped-up women. It wasn't that they were too unrealistic,
but they were certainly too sick, as well as being too obvious. She wanted to do
something more clever. She thought it might be a good idea to have the curious
woman open the door and find nothing there at all, but after mulling it over she
set this notion aside. It would leave her with the problem of why the wizard
would have a forbidden room in which he kept nothing.

That was the way she was thinking right after she got the assignment, which
was a full two weeks ago. So far she's written nothing. The great temptation is to
cast herself in the role of the cunning heroine, but again it's too predictable. And 640
Ed certainly isn't the wizard; he's nowhere near sinister enough. If Ed were the
wizard, the room would contain a forest, some ailing plants and feeble squirrels,
and Ed himself, fixing them up; but then, if it were Ed the room wouldn't even be
locked, and there would be no story.

Now, as she sits at her desk, fiddling with her felt-tip pen, it comes to Sally
that the intriguing thing about the story, the thing she should fasten on, is the egg.
Why an egg? From the night course in Comparative Folklore she took four years
ago, she remembers that the egg can be a fertility symbol, or a necessary object in
African spells, or something the world hatched out of. Maybe in this story it's a
symbol of virginity, and that is why the wizard requires it unbloodied. Women 650
with dirty eggs get murdered, those with clean ones get married.

But this isn't useful either. The concept is so outmoded. Sally doesn't see
how she can transpose it into real life without making it ridiculous, unless she sets
the story in, for instance, an immigrant Portuguese family, and what would she
know about that?

Sally opens the drawer of her desk and hunts around in it for her nail file. As
she's doing this, she gets the brilliant idea of writing the story from the point of
view of the egg. Other people will do the other things: the clever girl, the wizard,
the two blundering sisters, who weren't smart enough to lie, and who will have
problems afterwards, because of the thin red lines running all over their bodies, 660
from where their parts joined together. But no one will think of the egg. How does
it feel, to be the innocent and passive cause of so much misfortune?

(Ed isn't the Bluebeard: Ed is the egg. Edd Egg, blank and pristine and
lovely. Stupid, too. Boiled, probably. Sally smiles fondly.)

But how can there be a story from the egg's point of view, if the egg is so closed and unaware? Sally ponders this, doodling on her pad of lined paper. Then she resumes the search for her nail file. Already it's time to begin getting ready for her dinner party. She can sleep on the problem of the egg and finish the assignment tomorrow, which is Sunday. It's due on Monday, but Sally's mother used to say she was a whiz at getting things done at the last minute.   670

After painting her nails with *Nuit Magique,* Sally takes a bath, eating her habitual toasted English muffin while she lies in the tub. She begins to dress, dawdling; she has plenty of time. She hears Ed coming up out of the cellar; then she hears him in the bathroom, which he has entered from the hall door. Sally goes in through the other door, still in her slip. Ed is standing at the sink with his shirt off, shaving. On the weekends he leaves it until necessary, or until Sally tells him he's too scratchy.

Sally slides her hands around his waist, nuzzling against his naked back. He has very smooth skin, for a man. Sally smiles to herself: she can't stop thinking of him as an egg.   680

"Mmm," says Ed. It could be appreciation, or the answer to a question Sally hasn't asked and he hasn't heard, or just an acknowledgement that she's there.

"Don't you ever wonder what I think about?" Sally says. She's said this more than once, in bed or at the dinner table, after dessert. She stands behind him, watching the swaths the razor cuts in the white of his face, looking at her own face reflected in the mirror, just the eyes visible above his naked shoulder. Ed, lathered, is Assyrian, sterner than usual; or a frost-covered Arctic explorer; or demi-human, a white-bearded forest mutant. He scrapes away at himself, methodically destroying the illusion.

"But I already know what you think about," says Ed.   690

"How?" Sally says, taken aback.

"You're always telling me," Ed says, with what might be resignation or sadness; or maybe this is only a simple statement of fact.

Sally is relieved. If that's all he's going on, she's safe.

* * *

Marylynn arrives half an hour early, her pearl-coloured Porsche leading two men in a delivery truck up the driveway. The men install the keyhole desk, while Marylynn supervises: it looks, in the alcove, exactly as Marylynn has said it would, and Sally is delighted. She sits at it to write the cheque. Then she and Marylynn go into the kitchen, where Sally is finishing up her sauce, and Sally pours them each a Kir. She's glad Marylynn is here: it will keep her from dithering, as she tends to   700 do just before people arrive. Though it's only the heart men, she's still a bit nervous. Ed is more likely to notice when things are wrong than when they're exactly right.

Marylynn sits at the kitchen table, one arm draped over the chairback, her chin on the other hand; she's in soft grey, which makes her hair look silver, and Sally feels once again how banal it is to have ordinary dark hair like her own, however well-cut, however shiny. It's the confidence she envies, the negligence. Marylynn doesn't seem to be trying at all, ever.

"Guess what Ed said today?" Sally says.

Marylynn leans further forward. "What?" she says, with the eagerness of one   710
joining in a familiar game.

"He said, 'Some of these femininists go too far,'" Sally reports. "'*Femininists.*'
Isn't that sweet?"

Marylynn holds the pause too long, and Sally has a sudden awful thought:
maybe Marylynn thinks she's showing off, about Ed. Marylynn has always said
she's not ready for another marriage yet; still, Sally should watch herself, not rub
her nose in it. But then Marylynn laughs indulgently, and Sally, relieved, joins in.

"Ed is unbelievable," says Marylynn. "You should pin his mittens to his
sleeves when he goes out in the morning."

"He shouldn't be let out alone," says Sally.   720

"You should get him a seeing-eye dog," says Marylynn, "to bark at women."

"Why?" says Sally, still laughing but alert now, the cold beginning at the ends
of her fingers. Maybe Marylynn knows something she doesn't; maybe the house is
beginning to crumble, after all.

"Because he can't see them coming," says Marylynn. "That's what you're always telling me."

She sips her Kir; Sally stirs the sauce. "I bet he thinks I'm a femininist," says
Marylynn.

"You?" says Sally. "Never." She would like to add that Ed has given no indication of thinking anything at all about Marylynn, but she doesn't. She doesn't want   730
to take the risk of hurting her feelings.

The wives of the heart men admire Sally's sauce; the heart men talk shop, all
except Walter Morly, who is good at by-passes. He's sitting beside Marylynn, and
paying far too much attention to her for Sally's comfort. Mrs. Morly is at the other
end of the table, not saying much of anything, which Marylynn appears not to notice. She keeps on talking to Walter about St. Lucia, where they've both been.

So after dinner, when Sally has herded them all into the living room for coffee and liqueurs, she takes Marylynn by the elbow. "Ed hasn't seen our desk yet,"
she says, "not up close. Take him away and give him your lecture on nineteenth-
century antiques. Show him all the pigeon-holes. Ed loves pigeon-holes." Ed ap-   740
pears not to get this.

Marylynn knows exactly what Sally is up to. "Don't worry," she says, "I won't
rape Dr. Morly; the poor creature would never survive the shock," but she allows
herself to be shunted off to the side with Ed.

Sally moves from guest to guest, smiling, making sure everything is in order.
Although she never looks directly, she's always conscious of Ed's presence in the
room, any room; she perceives him as a shadow, a shape seen dimly at the edge of
her field of vision, recognizable by the outline. She likes to know where he is,
that's all. Some people are on their second cup of coffee. She walks towards the alcove: they must have finished with the desk by now.   750

But they haven't, they're still in there. Marylynn is bending forward, one
hand on the veneer. Ed is standing too close to her, and as Sally comes up behind
them she sees his left arm, held close to his side, the back of it pressed against

Marylynn, her shimmering upper thigh, her ass to be exact. Marylynn does not move away.

It's a split second, and then Ed sees Sally and the hand is gone; there it is, on top of the desk, reaching for a liqueur glass.

"Marylynn needs more Tia Maria," he says. "I just told her that people who drink a little now and again live longer." His voice is even, his face is as level as ever, a flat plain with no signposts.   760

Marylynn laughs. "I once had a dentist who I swear drilled tiny holes in my teeth, so he could fix them later," she says.

Sally sees Ed's hand outstretched towards her, holding the empty glass. She takes it, smiling, and turns away. There's a roaring sound at the back of her head; blackness appears around the edges of the picture she is seeing, like a television screen going dead. She walks into the kitchen and puts her cheek against the re-frigerator and her arms around it, as far as they will go. She remains that way, hug-ging it; it hums steadily, with a sound like comfort. After a while she lets go of it and touches her hair, and walks back into the living room with the filled glass.

Marylynn is over by the french doors, talking with Walter Morly. Ed is stand- 770
ing by himself, in front of the fireplace, one arm on the mantelpiece, his left hand out of sight in his pocket.

Sally goes to Marylynn, hands her the glass. "Is that enough?" she says.

Marylynn is unchanged. "Thanks, Sally," she says, and goes on to listening to Walter, who has dragged out his usual piece of mischief: some day, when they've perfected it, he says, all hearts will be plastic, and this will be a vast improvement on the current model. It's an obscure form of flirtation. Marylynn winks at Sally, to show that she knows he's tedious. Sally, after a pause, winks back.

She looks over at Ed, who is staring off into space, like a robot which has been parked and switched off. Now she isn't sure whether she really saw what she 780
thought she saw. Even if she did, what does it mean? Maybe it's just that Ed, in a wayward intoxicated moment, put his hand on the nearest buttock, and Marylynn refrained from a shriek or a flinch out of good breeding or the desire not to offend him. Things like this have happened to Sally.

Or it could mean something more sinister: a familiarity between them, an understanding. If this is it, Sally has been wrong about Ed, for years, forever. Her version of Ed is not something she's perceived but something that's been perpe-trated on her, by Ed himself, for reasons of his own. Possibly Ed is not stupid. Possibly he's enormously clever. She thinks of moment after moment when this cleverness, this cunning, would have shown itself if it were there, but didn't. She 790
has watched him so carefully. She remembers playing Pick Up Sticks, with the kids, Ed's kids, years ago: how if you moved one stick in the tangle, even slightly, everything else moved also.

She won't say anything with him. She can't say anything: she can't afford to be wrong, or to be right either. She goes back into the kitchen and begins to scrape the plates. This is unlike her—usually she sticks right with the party until it's over—and after a while Ed wanders out. He stands silently, watching her. Sally concentrates on the scraping: dollops of *sauce suprême* slide into the plastic bag, shreds of lettuce, rice, congealed and lumpy. What is left of her afternoon.

"What are you doing out here?" Ed asks at last. 800

"Scraping the plates," Sally says, cheerful, neutral. "I just thought I'd get a head start on tidying up."

"Leave it," says Ed. "The woman can do that in the morning." That's how he refers to Mrs. Rudge, although she's been with them for three years now: *the woman*. And Mrs. Bird before her, as though they are interchangeable. This has never bothered Sally before. "Go on out there and have a good time."

Sally puts down the spatula, wipes her hands on the hand towel, puts her arms around him, holds on tighter than she should. Ed pats her shoulder. "What's up?" he says; then, "Sally, Sally." If she looks up, she will see him shaking his head a little, as if he doesn't know what to do about her. She doesn't look up. 810

Ed has gone to bed. Sally roams the house, fidgeting with the debris left by the party. She collects empty glasses, picks up peanuts from the rug. After a while she realizes that she's down on her knees, looking under a chair, and she's forgotten what for. She goes upstairs, creams off her make-up, does her teeth, undresses in the darkened bedroom and slides into bed beside Ed, who is breathing deeply as if asleep. *As if.*

Sally lies in bed with her eyes closed. What she sees is her own heart, in black and white, beating with that insubstantial moth-like flutter, a ghostly heart, torn out of her and floating in space, an animated valentine with no colour. It will go on and on forever; she has no control over it. But now she's seeing the egg, 820 which is not small and cold and white and inert but larger than a real egg and golden pink, resting in a nest of brambles, glowing softly as though there's something red and hot inside it. It's almost pulsing; Sally is afraid of it. As she looks it darkens: rose-red, crimson. This is something the story left out, Sally thinks: the egg is alive, and one day it will hatch. But what will come out of it?   [1984]

Questions for Discussion and Writing

1. Why does the narrator regard her husband as stupid? Is she using the term affectionately? Is she anti-male? Explain.

2. Sally spends a lot of time thinking about Ed, but he seems to take her for granted. Discuss whether it is true (as the narrator seems to imply) that women think about relationships and men think about their jobs.

3. Why does Sally take her jobs and her night courses so lightly? If she is neither "housewife" nor "career woman," what is she? What does she care about?

4. Why has Atwood made the incident involving Ed and Marylynn so ambiguous? Why not make it clear, one way or the other?

5. Is Ed like Bluebeard? Is Sally like the wives in the fairy tale—fatally curious?

6. Sally thinks that in the fairy tale the egg is "the innocent and passive cause of so much misfortune" and then she thinks that perhaps "Ed is the egg . . . blank and pristine and lovely. . . ." Is she right? Does Ed fit both of these descriptions? Is his passivity the cause of misfortunes?

7. What does Sally learn during the story?

Happy Endings

JOHN AND MARY MEET.
What happens next?
If you want a happy ending, try A.

A. John and Mary fall in love and get married. They both have worthwhile and remunerative jobs which they find stimulating and challenging. They buy a
   charming house. Real estate values go up. Eventually, when they can afford
   live-in help, they have two children, to whom they are devoted. The children
   turn out well. John and Mary have a stimulating and challenging sex life and
   worthwhile friends. They go on fun vacations together. They retire. They both
   have hobbies which they find stimulating and challenging. Eventually they die.   10
   This is the end of the story.

B. Mary falls in love with John but John doesn't fall in love with Mary. He merely
   uses her body for selfish pleasure and ego gratification of a tepid kind. He
   comes to her apartment twice a week and she cooks him dinner, you'll notice
   that he doesn't even consider her worth the price of a dinner out, and after he's
   eaten the dinner he fucks her and after that he falls asleep, while she does the
   dishes so he won't think she's untidy, having all those dirty dishes lying
   around, and puts on fresh lipstick so she'll look good when he wakes up, but
   when he wakes up he doesn't even notice, he puts on his socks and his shorts
   and his pants and his shirt and his tie and his shoes, the reverse order from the   20
   one in which he took them off. He doesn't take off Mary's clothes, she takes
   them off herself, she acts as if she's dying for it every time, not because she
   likes sex exactly, she doesn't, but she wants John to think she does because if
   they do it often enough surely he'll get used to her, he'll come to depend on
   her and they will get married, but John goes out the door with hardly so much
   as a good-night and three days later he turns up at six o'clock and they do the
   whole thing over again.
       Mary gets run-down. Crying is bad for your face, everyone knows that
   and so does Mary but she can't stop. People at work notice. Her friends tell her
   John is a rat, a pig, a dog, he isn't good enough for her, but she can't believe it.   30
   Inside John, she thinks, is another John, who is much nicer. This other John
   will emerge like a butterfly from a cocoon, a Jack from a box, a pit from a
   prune, if the first John is only squeezed enough.
       One evening John complains about the food. He has never complained
   about the food before. Mary is hurt.
       Her friends tell her they've seen him in a restaurant with another woman,
   whose name is Madge. It's not even Madge that finally gets to Mary: it's the
   restaurant. John has never taken Mary to a restaurant. Mary collects all the
   sleeping pills and aspirins she can find, and takes them and half a bottle of
   sherry. You can see what kind of a woman she is by the fact that it's not even   40

whiskey. She leaves a note for John. She hopes he'll discover her and get her to the hospital in time and repent and then they can get married, but this fails to happen and she dies.

John marries Madge and everything continues as in A.

C. John, who is an older man, falls in love with Mary, and Mary, who is only twenty-two, feels sorry for him because he's worried about his hair falling out. She sleeps with him even though she's not in love with him. She met him at work. She's in love with someone called James, who is twenty-two also and not yet ready to settle down.

John on the contrary settled down long ago: this is what is bothering him. John has a steady, respectable job and is getting ahead in his field, but Mary isn't impressed by him, she's impressed by James, who has a motorcycle and a fabulous record collection. But James is often away on his motorcycle, being free. Freedom isn't the same for girls, so in the meantime Mary spends Thursday evenings with John. Thursdays are the only days John can get away.

John is married to a woman called Madge and they have two children, a charming house which they bought just before the real estate values went up, and hobbies which they find stimulating and challenging, when they have the time. John tells Mary how important she is to him, but of course he can't leave his wife because a commitment is a commitment. He goes on about this more than is necessary and Mary finds it boring, but older men can keep it up longer so on the whole she has a fairly good time.

One day James breezes in on his motorcycle with some top-grade California hybrid and James and Mary get higher than you'd believe possible and they climb into bed. Everything becomes very underwater, but along comes John, who has a key to Mary's apartment. He finds them stoned and en-twined. He's hardly in any position to be jealous, considering Madge, but nevertheless he's overcome with despair. Finally he's middle-aged, in two years he'll be bald as an egg and he can't stand it. He purchases a handgun, saying he needs it for target practice—this is the thin part of the plot, but it can be dealt with later—and shoots the two of them and himself.

Madge, after a suitable period of mourning, marries an understanding man called Fred and everything continues as in A, but under different names.

D. Fred and Madge have no problems. They get along exceptionally well and are good at working out any little difficulties that may arise. But their charming house is by the seashore and one day a giant tidal wave approaches. Real estate values go down. The rest of the story is about what caused the tidal wave and how they escape from it. They do, though thousands drown, but Fred and Madge are virtuous and lucky. Finally on high ground they clasp each other, wet and dripping and grateful, and continue as in A.

E. Yes, but Fred has a bad heart. The rest of the story is about how kind and un-derstanding they both are until Fred dies. Then Madge devotes herself to charity work until the end of A. If you like, it can be "Madge, " "cancer," "guilty and confused," and "bird watching."

F. If you think this is all too bourgeois, make John a revolutionary and Mary a counterespionage agent and see how far that gets you. Remember, this is Canada. You'll still end up with A, though in between you may get a lustful brawling saga of passionate involvement, a chronicle of our times, sort of.

You'll have to face it, the endings are the same however you slice it. Don't be deluded by any other endings, they're all fake, either deliberately fake, with malicious intent to deceive, or just motivated by excessive optimism if not by downright sentimentality. 90

The only authentic ending is the one provided here:

John and Mary die. John and Mary die. John and Mary die.

So much for endings. Beginnings are always more fun. True connoisseurs, however, are known to favor the stretch in between, since it's the hardest to do anything with.

That's about all that can be said for plots, which anyway are just one thing after another, a what and a what and a what.

Now try How and Why.   [1983] 100

Questions for Discussion and Writing

1. What is this story satirizing?
2. Are John and Mary characters in the usual sense? Why or why not?
3. What does Atwood mean when she says plots are just "one thing after another"?
4. What is the importance of "how" and "why" in a story? Explain.

✎ ALICE MUNRO

(b. 1931)

The Progress of Love

Alice Munro is a winner of nearly every award Canada has to bestow and is recognized throughout the English-speaking world as one of its great short-story writers. She has made her own town of Wingham, Ontario, a place recognized as home by legions of readers.

Alice Laidlaw was born during the Great Depression. Her father was trying to make his fortune raising silver foxes. At school, she led a "double life." Part of her was the ordinary girl who wanted to be asked to dances; the other part of her secretly wrote stories and longed for fame. Scholarships enabled her to attend university in 1949, but after two years she married and moved with her husband to Vancouver. In 1953, she gave birth to their first child and sold her first story. For the next fifteen years, she was full-time homemaker and wife and part-time professional writer. Her big breakthrough came in 1968 when *Dance of the Happy Shades* won the Governor-General's Award for fiction.

In 1973, the Munros' marriage broke up and Alice returned to Ontario, at first to write and teach at York University and the University of Western Ontario, finally to settle just twenty miles from the town of her birth with her new husband. Since then, the books and awards have appeared in steady procession, culminating in the 1990 Canada Council Molson prize for her "outstanding lifetime contribution to the cultural and intellectual life of Canada."

Characters in Munro's stories are outwardly ordinary; only in their internal probing for the truth about themselves and others do they become extraordinary; and even then they may remain unappealing or unsympathetic. Often the stories involve some contrast or opposition—parent versus child, wife against husband, or sister against brother—but these dissolve as the narrator reaches a more complex insight. Readers of Munro's stories discover, often with a shock of recognition, some hitherto hidden aspect of themselves or the world around them.

I GOT A CALL at work and it was my father. This was not long after I was divorced and started in the real estate office. Both of my boys were in school. It was a hot enough day in September.

My father was so polite, even in the family. He took time to ask me how I was. Country manners. Even if somebody phones up to tell you your house is burning down, they ask first how you are.

"I'm fine," I said. "How are you?"

"Not so good, I guess," said my father, in his old way—apologetic but self-respecting. "I think your mother's gone."

I knew that "gone" meant "dead." I knew that. But for a second or so I saw   10
my mother in her black straw hat setting off down the lane. The word "gone" seemed full of nothing but a deep relief and even an excitement—the excitement you feel when a door closes and your house sinks back to normal and you let yourself loose into all the free space around you. That was in my father's voice, too—behind the apology, a queer sound like a gulped breath. But my mother hadn't been a burden—she hadn't been sick a day—and far from feeling relieved at her death, my father took it hard. He never got used to living alone, he said. He went into the Netterfield County Home quite willingly.

He told me how he found my mother on the couch in the kitchen when he came in at noon. She had picked a few tomatoes, and was setting them on the   20
windowsill to ripen; then she must have felt weak, and lain down. Now, telling this, his voice went wobbly—meandering, as you would expect—in his amazement. I saw in my mind the couch, the old quilt that protected it, right under the phone.

"So I thought I'd better call you," my father said, and he waited for me to say what he should do now.

My mother prayed on her knees at midday, at night, and first thing in the morning. Every day opened up to her to have God's will done in it. Every night she totted up what she'd done and said and thought, to see how it squared with Him. That kind of life is dreary, people think, but they're missing the point. For one thing, such a life can never be boring. And nothing can happen to you that you can't make use of. Even if you're racked by troubles, and sick and poor and ugly, you've got your soul to carry through life like a treasure on a platter. Going upstairs to pray after the noon meal, my mother would be full of energy and expectation, seriously smiling.

She was saved at a camp meeting when she was fourteen. That was the same summer that her own mother—my grandmother—died. For a few years, my mother went to meetings with a lot of other people who'd been saved, some who'd been saved over and over again, enthusiastic old sinners. She could tell stories about what went on at those meetings, the singing and hollering and wildness. She told about one old man getting up and shouting, "Come down, O Lord, come down among us now! Come down through the roof and I'll pay for the shingles!"

She was back to being just an Anglican, a serious one, by the time she got married. She was twenty-five then, and my father was thirty-eight. A tall good-looking couple, good dancers, good card-players, sociable. But serious people—that's how I would try to describe them. Serious the way hardly anybody is anymore. My father was not religious in the way my mother was. He was an Anglican, an Orangeman,[1] a Conservative, because that's what he had been brought up to be. He was the son who got left on the farm with his parents and took care of them till they died. He met my mother, he waited for her, they married; he thought himself lucky then to have a family to work for. (I have two brothers, and I had a baby sister who died.) I have a feeling that my father never slept with any woman before my mother, and never with her until he married her. And he had to wait, because my mother wouldn't get married until she had paid back to her own father every cent he had spent on her since her mother died. She had kept track of everything—board, books, clothes—so that she could pay it back. When she married, she had no nest egg, as teachers usually did, no hope chest, sheets, or dishes. My father used to say, with a somber, joking face, that he had hoped to get a woman with money in the bank. "But you take the money in the bank, you have to take the face that goes with it," he said, "and sometimes that's no bargain."

The house we lived in had big, high rooms, with dark-green blinds on the windows. When the blinds were pulled down against the sun, I used to like to move my head and catch the light flashing through the holes and cracks. Another thing I liked looking at was chimney stains, old or fresh, which I could turn into animals, people's faces, even distant cities. I told my own two boys about that, and their father, Dan Casey, said, "See, your mom's folks were so poor, they couldn't af-

---

1. Supporters of Protestant, British rule in Ireland, named after William of Orange, (William III, 1650–1702).

ford TV, so they got these stains on the ceiling—your mom had to watch the stains on the ceiling!" He always liked to kid me about thinking poor was anything great.

When my father was very old, I figured out that he didn't mind people doing new sorts of things—for instance, my getting divorced—as much as he minded 70 them having new sorts of reasons for doing them.

Thank God he never had to know about the commune.

"The Lord never intended," he used to say. Sitting around with the other old men in the Home, in the long, dim porch behind the spirea bushes, he talked about how the Lord never intended for people to tear around the country on motorbikes and snowmobiles.

And how the Lord never intended for nurses' uniforms to be pants. The nurses didn't mind at all. They called him "Handsome," and told me he was a real old sweetheart, a real old religious gentleman. They marvelled at his thick black hair, which he kept until he died. They washed and combed it beautifully, wet- 80 waved it with their fingers.

Sometimes, with all their care, he was a little unhappy. He wanted to go home. He worried about the cows, the fences, about who was getting up to light the fire. A few flashes of meanness—very few. Once, he gave me a sneaky, unfriendly look when I went in; he said, "I'm surprised you haven't worn all the skin off your knees by now."

I laughed. I said, "What doing? Scrubbing floors?"

"Praying!" he said, in a voice like spitting.

He didn't know who he was talking to.

I don't remember my mother's hair being anything but white. My mother 90 went white in her twenties, and never saved any of her young hair, which had been brown. I used to try to get her to tell what color brown.

"Dark."

"Like Brent, or like Dolly?" Those were two workhorses we had, a team.

"I don't know. It wasn't horsehair."

"Was it like chocolate?"

"Something like."

"Weren't you sad when it went white?"

"No. I was glad."

"Why?"   100

"I was glad that I wouldn't have hair anymore that was the same color as my father's."

Hatred is always a sin, my mother told me. Remember that. One drop of hatred in your soul will spread and discolor everything like a drop of black ink in white milk. I was struck by that and meant to try it, but I knew I shouldn't waste the milk.

All these things I remember. All the things I know, or have been told, about people I never even saw. I was named Euphemia, after my mother's mother. A terrible name, such as nobody has nowadays. At home they called me Phemie, but when I started to work, I called myself Fame. My husband, Dan Casey, called me 110 Fame. Then in the bar of the Shamrock Hotel, years later, after my divorce, when I was going out, a man said to me, "Fame, I've been meaning to ask you, just what is it you are famous for?"

"I don't know," I told him. "I don't know, unless it's for wasting my time talking to jerks like you."

After that I thought of changing it altogether, to something like Joan, but unless I moved away from here, how could I do that?

In the summer of 1947, when I was twelve, I helped my mother paper the downstairs bedroom, the spare room. My mother's sister, Beryl, was coming to visit us. These two sisters hadn't seen each other for years. Very soon after their 120 mother died, their father married again. He went to live in Minneapolis, then in Seattle, with his new wife and his younger daughter, Beryl. My mother wouldn't go with them. She stayed on in the town of Ramsay, where they had been living. She was boarded with a childless couple who had been neighbors. She and Beryl had met only once or twice since they were grown up. Beryl lived in California.

The paper had a design of cornflowers on a white ground. My mother had got it at a reduced price, because it was the end of a lot. This meant we had trouble matching the pattern, and behind the door we had to do some tricky fitting with scraps and strips. This was before the days of pre-pasted wallpaper. We had a trestle table set up in the front room, and we mixed the paste and swept it onto 130 the back of the paper with wide brushes, watching for lumps. We worked with the windows up, screens fitted under them, the front door open, the screen door closed. The country we could see through the mesh of screens and the wavery old window glass was all hot and flowering—milkweed and wild carrot in the pastures, mustard rampaging in the clover, some fields creamy with the buckwheat people grew then. My mother sang. She sang a song she said her own mother used to sing when she and Beryl were little girls.

"I once had a sweetheart, but now I have none.
He's gone and he's left me to weep and to mourn.
He's gone and he's left me, but contented I'll be,   140
For I'll get another one, better than he!"

I was excited because Beryl was coming, a visitor, all the way from California. Also, because I had gone to town in late June to write the Entrance Examinations, and was hoping to hear soon that I had passed with honors. Everybody who had finished Grade 8 in the country schools had to go into town to write those examinations. I loved that—the rustling sheets of foolscap, the important silence, the big stone high-school building, all the old initials carved in the desks, darkened with varnish. The first burst of summer outside, the green and yellow light, the townlike chestnut trees, and honeysuckle. And all it was was this same town, where I have lived now more than half my life. I wondered at it. And 150 at myself, drawing maps with ease and solving problems, knowing quantities of answers. I thought I was so clever. But I wasn't clever enough to understand the simplest thing. I didn't even understand that examinations made no difference in my case. I wouldn't be going to high school. How could I? That was before there were school buses; you had to board in town. My parents didn't have the money. They operated on very little cash, as many farmers did then. The payments from the cheese factory were about all that came in regularly. And they didn't think of my life going in that direction, the high-school direction. They thought that I would stay at home and help my mother, maybe hire out to help women in the neighborhood who were sick or having a baby. Until such time as I got married. 160 That was what they were waiting to tell me when I got the results of the examinations.

You would think my mother might have a different idea, since she had been a schoolteacher herself. But she said God didn't care. God isn't interested in what kind of job or what kind of education anybody has, she told me. He doesn't care two hoots about that, and it's what He cares about that matters.

This was the first time I understood how God could become a real opponent, not just some kind of nuisance or large decoration.

My mother's name as a child was Marietta. That continued to be her name, of course, but until Beryl came I never heard her called by it. My father always 170 said Mother. I had a childish notion—I knew it was childish—that Mother suited my mother better than it did other mothers. Mother, not Mama. When I was away from her, I could not think what my mother's face was like, and this frightened me. Sitting in school, just over a hill from home, I would try to picture my mother's face. Sometimes I thought that if I couldn't do it, that might mean my mother was dead. But I had a sense of her all the time, and would be reminded of her by the most unlikely things—an upright piano, or a tall white loaf of bread. That's ridiculous, but true.

Marietta, in my mind, was separate, not swallowed up in my mother's grownup body. Marietta was still running around loose up in her town of Ramsay, 180 on the Ottawa River. In that town, the streets were full of horses and puddles, and darkened by men who came in from the bush on weekends. Loggers. There were eleven hotels on the main street, where the loggers stayed, and drank.

The house Marietta lived in was halfway up a steep street climbing from the river. It was a double house, with two bay windows in front, and a wooden trellis that separated the two front porches. In the other half of the house lived the Sutcliffes, the people Marietta was to board with after her mother died and her father left town. Mr. Sutcliffe was an Englishman, a telegraph operator. His wife was German. She always made coffee instead of tea. She made strudel. The dough for the strudel hung down over the edges of the table like a fine cloth. It sometimes 190 looked to Marietta like a skin.

Mrs. Sutcliffe was the one who talked Marietta's mother out of hanging herself.

Marietta was home from school that day, because it was Saturday. She woke up late and heard the silence in the house. She was always scared of that—a silent house—and as soon as she opened the door after school she would call, "Mama! Mama!" Often her mother wouldn't answer. But she would be there. Marietta would hear with relief the rattle of the stove grate or the steady slap of the iron.

That morning, she didn't hear anything. She came downstairs, and got herself a slice of bread and butter and molasses, folded over. She opened the cellar 200 door and called. She went into the front room and peered out the window, through the bridal fern. She saw her little sister, Beryl, and some other neighborhood children rolling down the bit of grassy terrace to the sidewalk, picking themselves up and scrambling to the top and rolling down again.

"Mama?" called Marietta. She walked through the house to the back yard. It was late spring, the day was cloudy and mild. In the sprouting vegetable gardens, the earth was damp, and the leaves on the trees seemed suddenly full-sized, letting down drops of water left over from the rain of the night before.

"Mama?" calls Marietta under the trees, under the clothesline.

At the end of the yard is a small barn, where they keep firewood, and some 210 tools and old furniture. A chair, a straight-backed wooden chair can be seen through the open doorway. On the chair, Marietta sees her mother's feet, her mother's black laced shoes. Then the long, printed cotton summer work dress, the apron, the rolled-up sleeves. Her mother's shiny-looking white arms, and neck, and face.

Her mother stood on the chair and didn't answer. She didn't look at Marietta, but smiled and tapped her foot, as if to say, "Here I am, then. What are you going to do about it?" Something looked wrong about her, beyond the fact that she was standing on a chair and smiling in this queer, tight way. Standing on an old chair with back rungs missing, which she had pulled out to the middle of 220 the barn floor, where it teetered on the bumpy earth. There was a shadow on her neck.

The shadow was a rope, a noose on the end of the rope that hung down from a beam overhead.

"Mama?" says Marietta, in a fainter voice. "Mama. Come down, please." Her voice is faint because she fears that any yell or cry might jolt her mother into movement, cause her to step off the chair and throw her weight on the rope. But even if Marietta wanted to yell she couldn't. Nothing but this pitiful thread of a voice is left to her—just as in a dream when a beast or a machine is bearing down on you.   230

"Go and get your father."

That was what her mother told her to do, and Marietta obeyed. With terror in her legs, she ran. In her nightgown, in the middle of a Saturday morning, she ran. She ran past Beryl and the other children, still tumbling down the slope. She ran along the sidewalk, which was at that time a boardwalk, then on the unpaved street, full of last night's puddles. The street crossed the railway tracks. At the foot of the hill, it intersected the main street of the town. Between the main street and the river were some warehouses and the buildings of small manufacturers. That was where Marietta's father had his carriage works. Wagons, buggies, sleds were made there. In fact, Marietta's father had invented a new sort of sled to carry logs 240 in the bush. It had been patented. He was just getting started in Ramsay. (Later on, in the States, he made money. A man fond of hotel bars, barbershops, harness races, women, but not afraid of work—give him credit.)

Marietta did not find him at work that day. The office was empty. She ran out into the yard where the men were working. She stumbled in the fresh sawdust. The men laughed and shook their heads at her. No. Not here. Not a-here right now. No. Why don't you try upstreet? Wait. Wait a minute. Hadn't you better get some clothes on first?

They didn't mean any harm. They didn't have the sense to see that something must be wrong. But Marietta never could stand men laughing. There were always places she hated to go past, let alone into, and that was the reason. Men laughing. Because of that, she hated barbershops, hated their smell. (When she started going to dances later on with my father, she asked him not to put any dressing on his hair, because the smell reminded her.) A bunch of men standing out in the street, outside a hotel, seemed to Marietta like a clot of poison. You tried not to hear what they were saying, but you could be sure it was vile. If they didn't say anything, they laughed and vileness spread out from them—poison—just the same. It was only after Marietta was saved that she could walk right past them. Armed by God, she walked through their midst and nothing stuck to her, nothing scorched her; she was safe as Daniel.[2]

Now she turned and ran, straight back the way she had come. Up the hill, running to get home. She thought she had made a mistake leaving her mother. Why did her mother tell her to go? Why did she want her father? Quite possibly so that she could greet him with the sight of her own warm body swinging on the end of a rope. Marietta should have stayed—she should have stayed and talked her mother out of it. She should have run to Mrs. Sutcliffe, or any neighbor, not wasted time this way. She hadn't thought who could help, who could even believe what she was talking about. She had the idea that all families except her own lived in peace, that threats and miseries didn't exist in other people's houses, and couldn't be explained there.

A train was coming into town. Marietta had to wait. Passengers looked out at her from its windows. She broke out wailing in the faces of those strangers. When the train passed, she continued up the hill—a spectacle, with her hair uncombed, her feet bare and muddy, in her nightgown, with a wild, wet face. By the time she ran into her own yard, in sight of the barn, she was howling. "Mama!" She was howling. "Mama!"

Nobody was there. The chair was standing just where it had been before. The rope was dangling over the back of it. Marietta was sure that her mother had gone ahead and done it. Her mother was already dead—she had been cut down and taken away.

But warm, fat hands settled down on her shoulders, and Mrs. Sutcliffe said, "Marietta, stop the noise. Marietta. Child. Stop the crying. Come inside. She is well, Marietta. Come inside and you will see."

Mrs. Sutcliffe's foreign voice said, "Mari-et-cha," giving the name a rich, important sound. She was as kind as could be. When Marietta lived with the Sutcliffes later, she was treated as the daughter of the household, and it was a

---

2. Daniel was thrown to the lions by King Darius but protected by God. Daniel: 6.

household just as peaceful and comfortable as she had imagined other households to be. But she never felt like a daughter there.

In Mrs. Sutcliffe's kitchen, Beryl sat on the floor eating a raisin cookie and playing with the black-and-white cat, whose name was Dickie. Marietta's mother 290 sat at the table, with a cup of coffee in front of her.

"She was silly," Mrs. Sutcliffe said. Did she mean Marietta's mother or Marietta herself? She didn't have many English words to describe things.

Marietta's mother laughed, and Marietta blacked out. She fainted, after running all that way uphill, howling, in the warm, damp morning. Next thing she knew, she was taking black, sweet coffee from a spoon held by Mrs. Sutcliffe. Beryl picked Dickie up by the front legs and offered him as a cheering present. Marietta's mother was still sitting at the table.

Her heart was broken. That was what I always heard my mother say. That was the end of it. Those words lifted up the story and sealed it shut. I never asked. 300 Who broke it? I never asked, What was the men's poison talk? What was the meaning of the word "vile"?

Marietta's mother laughed after not hanging herself. She sat at Mrs. Sutcliffe's kitchen table long ago and laughed. Her heart was broken.

I always had a feeling, with my mother's talk and stories, of something swelling out behind. Like a cloud you couldn't see through, or get to the end of. There was a cloud, a poison, that had touched my mother's life. And when I grieved my mother, I became part of it. Then I would beat my head against my mother's stomach and breasts, against her tall, firm front, demanding to be forgiven. My mother would tell me to ask God. But it wasn't God, it was my mother I 310 had to get straight with. It seemed as if she knew something about me that was worse, far worse, than ordinary lies and tricks and meanness; it was a really sickening shame. I beat against my mother's front to make her forget that.

My brothers weren't bothered by any of this. I don't think so. They seemed to me like cheerful savages, running around free, not having to learn much. And when I just had the two boys myself, no daughters, I felt as if something could stop now—the stories, and griefs, the old puzzles you can't resist or solve.

Aunt Beryl said not to call her Aunt. "I'm not used to being anybody's aunt, honey. I'm not even anybody's momma. I'm just me. Call me Beryl."

Beryl had started out as a stenographer, and now she had her own typing 320 and bookkeeping business, which employed many girls. She had arrived with a man friend, whose name was Mr. Florence. Her letter had said that she would be getting a ride with a friend, but she hadn't said whether the friend would be staying or going on. She hadn't even said if it was a man or a woman.

Mr. Florence was staying. He was a tall, thin man with a long, tanned face, very light-colored eyes, and a way of twitching the corner of his mouth that might have been a smile.

He was the one who got to sleep in the room that my mother and I had papered, because he was the stranger, and a man. Beryl had to sleep with me. At first we thought that Mr. Florence was quite rude, because he wasn't used to our way 330 of talking and we weren't used to his. The first morning, my father said to Mr.

Florence, "Well, I hope you got some kind of a sleep on that old bed in there?" (The spare-room bed was heavenly, with a feather tick.) This was Mr. Florence's cue to say that he had never slept better.

Mr. Florence twitched. He said, "I slept on worse."

His favorite place to be was in his car. His car was a royal-blue Chrysler, from the first batch turned out after the war. Inside it, the upholstery and floor covering and roof and door padding were all pearl gray. Mr. Florence kept the names of those colors in mind and corrected you if you said just "blue" or "gray."

"Mouse skin is what it looks like to me," said Beryl rambunctiously. "I tell him it's just mouse skin!"

The car was parked at the side of the house, under the locust trees. Mr. Florence sat inside with the windows rolled up, smoking, in the rich new-car smell.

"I'm afraid we're not doing much to entertain your friend," my mother said.

"I wouldn't worry about him," said Beryl. She always spoke about Mr. Florence as if there was a joke about him that only she appreciated. I wondered long afterward if he had a bottle in the glove compartment and took a nip from time to time to keep his spirits up. He kept his hat on.

Beryl herself was being entertained enough for two. Instead of staying in the house and talking to my mother, as a lady visitor usually did, she demanded to be shown everything there was to see on a farm. She said that I was to take her around and explain things, and see that she didn't fall into any manure piles.

I didn't know what to show. I took Beryl to the icehouse, where chunks of ice the size of dresser drawers, or bigger, lay buried in sawdust. Every few days, my father would chop off a piece of ice and carry it to the kitchen, where it melted in a tin-lined box and cooled the milk and butter.

Beryl said she never had any idea ice came in pieces that big. She seemed intent on finding things strange, or horrible, or funny.

"Where in the world do you get ice that big?"

I couldn't tell if that was a joke.

"Off of the lake," I said.

"Off of the lake! Do you have lakes up here that have ice on them all summer?"

I told her how my father cut the ice on the lake every winter and hauled it home, and buried it in sawdust, and that kept it from melting.

Beryl said, "That's amazing!"

"Well, it melts a little," I said. I was deeply disappointed in Beryl.

"That's really amazing."

Beryl went along when I went to get the cows. A scarecrow in white slacks (this was what my father called her afterward), with a white sun hat tied under her chin by a flaunting red ribbon. Her fingernails and toenails—she wore sandals— were painted to match the ribbon. She wore the small, dark sunglasses people wore at that time. (Not the people I knew—they didn't own sunglasses.) She had a big red mouth, a loud laugh, hair of an unnatural color and a high gloss, like cherry wood. She was so noisy and shiny, so glamourously got up, that it was hard to tell whether she was good-looking, or happy, or anything.

We didn't have any conversation along the cowpath, because Beryl kept her distance from the cows and was busy watching where she stepped. Once I had them all tied in their stalls, she came closer. She lit a cigarette. Nobody smoked in the barn. My father and other farmers chewed tobacco there instead. I didn't see how I could ask Beryl to chew tobacco.

"Can you get the milk out of them or does your father have to?" Beryl said. "Is it hard to do?"

I pulled some milk down through the cow's teat. One of the barn cats came over and waited. I shot a thin stream into its mouth. The cat and I were both showing off.

"Doesn't that hurt?" said Beryl. "Think if it was you."

I had never thought of a cow's teat as corresponding to any part of myself, and was shaken by this indecency. In fact, I could never grasp a warm, warty teat in such a firm and casual way again.

Beryl slept in a peach-colored rayon nightgown trimmed with écru lace. She had a robe to match. She was just as careful about the word "écru" as Mr. Florence was about his royal blue and pearl gray.

I managed to get undressed and put on my nightgown without any part of me being exposed at any time. An awkward business. I left my underpants on, and hoped that Beryl had done the same. The idea of sharing my bed with a grownup was a torment to me. But I did get to see the contents of what Beryl called her beauty kit. Hand-painted glass jars contained puffs of cotton wool, talcum powder, milky lotion, ice-blue astringent. Little pots of red and mauve rouge—rather greasy-looking. Blue and black pencils. Emery boards, a pumice stone, nail polish with an overpowering smell of bananas, face powder in a celluloid box shaped like a shell, with the name of a dessert—Apricot Delight.

I had heated some water on the coal-oil stove we used in summertime. Beryl scrubbed her face clean, and there was such a change that I almost expected to see makeup lying in strips in the washbowl, like the old wallpaper we had soaked and peeled. Beryl's skin was pale now, covered with fine cracks, rather like the shiny mud at the bottom of puddles drying up in early summer.

"Look what happened to my skin," she said. "Dieting. I weighed a hundred and sixty-nine pounds once, and I took it off too fast and my face fell in on me. Now I've got this cream, though. It's made from a secret formula and you can't even buy it commercially. Smell it. See, it doesn't smell all perfumy. It smells serious."

She was patting the cream on her face with puffs of cotton wool, patting away until there was nothing to be seen on the surface.

"It smells like lard," I said.

"Christ Almighty, I hope I haven't been paying that kind of money to rub lard on my face. Don't tell your mother I swear."

She poured clean water into the drinking glass and wet her comb, then combed her hair wet and twisted each strand round her finger, clamping the twisted strand to her head with two crossed pins. I would be doing the same myself, a couple of years later.

"Always do your hair wet, else it's no good doing it up at all," Beryl said. "And always roll it under even if you want it to flip up. See?"

When I was doing my hair up—as I did for years—I sometimes thought of this, and thought that of all the pieces of advice people had given me, this was the one I had followed most carefully.

We put the lamp out and got into bed, and Beryl said, "I never knew it could get so dark. I've never known a dark that was as dark as this." She was whispering. I was slow to understand that she was comparing country nights to city nights, and I wondered if the darkness in Netterfield County could really be greater than that in California.   430

"Honey?" whispered Beryl. "Are there any animals outside?"

"Cows," I said.

"Yes, but wild animals? Are there bears?"

"Yes," I said. My father had once found bear tracks and droppings in the bush, and the apples had all been torn off a wild apple tree. That was years ago, when he was a young man.

Beryl moaned and giggled. "Think if Mr. Florence had to go out in the night and he ran into a bear!"   440

Next day was Sunday. Beryl and Mr. Florence drove my brothers and me to Sunday school in the Chrysler. That was at ten o'clock in the morning. They came back at eleven to bring my parents to church.

"Hop in," Beryl said to me. "You, too," she said to the boys. "We're going for a drive."

Beryl was dressed up in a satiny ivory dress with red dots, and a red-lined frill over the hips, and red high-heeled shoes. Mr. Florence wore a pale-blue summer suit.

"Aren't you going to church?" I said. That was what people dressed up for, in my experience.   450

Beryl laughed. "Honey, this isn't Mr. Florence's kind of religion."

I was used to going straight from Sunday school into church, and sitting for another hour and a half. In summer, the open windows let in the cedary smell of the graveyard and the occasional, almost sacrilegious sound of a car swooshing by on the road. Today we spent this time driving through country I had never seen before. I had never seen it, though it was less than twenty miles from home. Our truck went to the cheese factory, to church, and to town on Saturday nights. The nearest thing to a drive was when it went to the dump. I had seen the near end of Bell's Lake, because that was where my father cut the ice in winter. You couldn't get close to it in summer; the shoreline was all choked up with bulrushes. I had   460 thought that the other end of the lake would look pretty much the same, but when we drove there today, I saw cottages, docks and boats, dark water reflecting the trees. All this and I hadn't known about it. This, too, was Bell's Lake. I was glad to have seen it at last, but in some way not altogether glad of the surprise.

Finally, a white frame building appeared, with verandas and potted flowers, and some twinkling poplar trees in front. The Wildwood Inn. Today the same building is covered with stucco and done up with Tudor beams and called the Hideaway. The poplar trees have been cut down for a parking lot.

On the way back to the church to pick up my parents, Mr. Florence turned in to the farm next to ours, which belonged to the McAllisters. The McAllisters were Catholics. Our two families were neighborly but not close.

"Come on, boys, out you get," said Beryl to my brothers. "Not you," she said to me. "You stay put." She herded the little boys up to the porch, where some McAllisters were watching. They were in their raggedy home clothes, because their church, or Mass, or whatever it was, got out early. Mrs. McAllister came out and stood listening, rather dumbfounded, to Beryl's laughing talk.

Beryl came back to the car by herself. "There," she said. "They're going to play with the neighbor children."

Play with McAllisters? Besides being Catholics, all but the baby were girls.

"They've still got their good clothes on," I said.

"So what? Can't they have a good time with their good clothes on? I do!"

My parents were taken by surprise as well. Beryl got out and told my father he was to ride in the front seat, for the legroom. She got into the back, with my mother and me. Mr. Florence turned again onto the Bell's Lake road, and Beryl announced that we were all going to the Wildwood Inn for dinner.

"You're all dressed up, why not take advantage?" she said. "We dropped the boys off with your neighbors. I thought they might be too young to appreciate it. The neighbors were happy to have them." She said with a further emphasis that it was to be their treat. Hers and Mr. Florence's.

"Well, now," said my father. He probably didn't have five dollars in his pocket. "Well, now. I wonder do they let the farmers in?"

He made various jokes along this line. In the hotel dining room, which was all in white—white tablecloths, white painted chairs—with sweating glass water pitchers and high, whirring fans, he picked up a table napkin the size of a diaper and spoke to me in a loud whisper, "Can you tell me what to do with this thing? Can I put it on my head to keep the draft off?"

Of course he had eaten in hotel dining rooms before. He knew about table napkins and pie forks. And my mother knew—she wasn't even a country woman, to begin with. Nevertheless this was a huge event. Not exactly a pleasure—as Beryl must have meant it to be—but a huge, unsettling event. Eating a meal in public, only a few miles from home, eating in a big room full of people you didn't know, the food served by a stranger, a snippy-looking girl who was probably a college student working at a summer job.

"I'd like the rooster," my father said. "How long has he been in the pot?" It was only good manners, as he knew it, to joke with people who waited on him.

"Beg your pardon?" the girl said.

"Roast chicken," said Beryl. "Is that okay for everybody?"

Mr. Florence was looking gloomy. Perhaps he didn't care for jokes when it was his money that was being spent. Perhaps he had counted on something better than ice water to fill up the glasses.

The waitress put down a dish of celery and olives, and my mother said, "Just a minute while I give thanks." She bowed her head and said quietly but audibly, "Lord, bless this food to our use, and us to Thy service, for Christ's sake. Amen." Refreshed, she sat up straight and passed the dish to me, saying, "Mind the olives. There's stones in them."

Beryl was smiling around at the room.

The waitress came back with a basket of rolls.

"Parker House!" Beryl leaned over and breathed in their smell. "Eat them while they're hot enough to melt the butter!"

Mr. Florence twitched, and peered into the butter dish. "Is that what this is—butter? I thought it was Shirley Temple's curls." 520

His face was hardly less gloomy than before, but it was a joke, and his making it seemed to convey to us something of the very thing that had just been publicly asked for—a blessing.

"When he says something funny," said Beryl—who often referred to Mr. Florence as "he" even when he was right there—"you notice how he always keeps a straight face? That reminds me of Mama. I mean of our mama, Marietta's and mine. Daddy, when he made a joke you could see it coming a mile away—he couldn't keep it off his face—but Mama was another story. She could look so sour. But she could joke on her deathbed. In fact, she did that very thing. Marietta, re- 530 member when she was in bed in the front room the spring before she died?"

"I remember she was in bed in that room," my mother said. "Yes."

"Well, Daddy came in and she was lying there in her clean nightgown, with the covers off, because the German lady from next door had just been helping her take a wash, and she was still there tidying up the bed. So Daddy wanted to be cheerful, and he said, 'Spring must be coming. I saw a crow today.' This must have been in March. And Mama said quick as a shot, 'Well, you better cover me up then, before it looks in that window and gets any ideas!' The German lady—Daddy said she just about dropped the basin. Because it was true, Mama was skin and bones; she was dying. But she could joke." 540

Mr. Florence said, "Might as well when there's no use to cry."

But she could carry a joke too far, Mama could. One time, one time, she wanted to give Daddy a scare. He was supposed to be interested in some girl that kept coming around to the works. Well, he was a big good-looking man. So Mama said, 'Well, I'll just do away with myself, and you can get on with her and see how you like it when I come back and haunt you.' He told her not to be so stupid, and he went off downtown. And Mama went out to the barn and climbed on a chair and put a rope around her neck. Didn't she, Marietta? Marietta went looking for her and she found her like that!"

My mother bent her head and put her hands in her lap, almost as if she was 550 getting ready to say another grace.

"Daddy told me all about it, but I can remember anyway. I remember Marietta tearing off down the hill in her nightie, and I guess the German lady saw her go, and she came out and was looking for Mama, and somehow we all ended up in the barn—me, too, and some kids I was playing with—and there was Mama up on a chair preparing to give Daddy the fright of his life. She'd sent Marietta after him. And the German lady starts wailing. 'Oh, Missus, come down Missus, think of your little *kindren*'—'kindren' is the German for 'children'—'think of your *kindren*,' and so on. Until it was me standing there—I was just a little squirt, but I was the one noticed that rope. My eyes followed that rope up and up and I saw it 560 was just hanging over the beam, just flung there—it wasn't tied at all! Marietta hadn't noticed that, the German lady hadn't noticed it. But I just spoke up and said, "Mama, how are you going to manage to hang yourself without that rope tied around the beam?' "

Mr. Florence said, "That'd be a tough one."

"I spoiled her game. The German lady made coffee and we went over there and had a few treats, and, Marietta, you couldn't find Daddy after all, could you? You could hear Marietta howling, coming up the hill, a block away."

"Natural for her to be upset," my father said.

"Sure it was. Mama went too far."

"She meant it," my mother said. "She meant it more than you give her credit for."

"She meant to get a rise out of Daddy. That was their whole life together. He always said she was a hard woman to live with, but she had a lot of character. I believe he missed that, with Gladys."

"I wouldn't know," my mother said, in the particularly steady voice with which she always spoke of her father. "What he did say or didn't say."

"People are dead now," said my father. "It isn't up to us to judge."

"I know," said Beryl. "I know Marietta's always had a different view."

My mother looked at Mr. Florence and smiled quite easily and radiantly. "I'm sure you don't know what to make of all these family matters."

The one time that I visited Beryl, when Beryl was an old woman, all knobby and twisted up with arthritis, Beryl said, "Marietta got all Daddy's looks. And she never did a thing with herself. Remember her wearing that old navy-blue crêpe dress when we went to the hotel that time? Of course, I know it was probably all she had, but did it have to be all she had? You know, I was scared of her somehow. I couldn't stay in a room alone with her. But she had outstanding looks." Trying to remember an occasion when I had noticed my mother's looks, I thought of the time in the hotel, my mother's pale-olive skin against the heavy white, coiled hair, her open, handsome face smiling at Mr. Florence—as if he was the one to be forgiven.

I didn't have a problem right away with Beryl's story. For one thing, I was hungry and greedy, and a lot of my attention went to the roast chicken and gravy and mashed potatoes laid on the plate with an ice-cream scoop and the bright diced vegetables out of a can, which I thought much superior to those fresh from the garden. For dessert, I had a butterscotch sundae, an agonizing choice over chocolate. The others had plain vanilla ice cream.

Why shouldn't Beryl's version of the same event be different from my mother's? Beryl was strange in every way—everything about her was slanted, seen from a new angle. It was my mother's version that held, for a time. It absorbed Beryl's story, closed over it. But Beryl's story didn't vanish; it stayed sealed off for years, but it wasn't gone. It was like the knowledge of that hotel and dining room. I knew about it now, though I didn't think of it as a place to go back to. And indeed, without Beryl's or Mr. Florence's money, I couldn't. But I knew it was there.

The next time I was in the Wildwood Inn, in fact, was after I was married. The Lions Club had a banquet and dance there. The man I had married, Dan Casey, was a Lion. You could get a drink there by that time. Dan Casey wouldn't have gone anywhere you couldn't. Then the place was remodelled into the

Hideaway, and now they have strippers every night but Sunday. On Thursday
nights, they have a male stripper. I go there with people from the real-estate office   610
to celebrate birthdays or other big events.

The farm was sold for five thousand dollars in 1965. A man from Toronto
bought it, for a hobby farm or just an investment. After a couple of years, he rented
it to a commune. They stayed there, different people drifting on and off, for a dozen
years or so. They raised goats and sold the milk to the health-food store that had
opened up in town. They painted a rainbow across the side of the barn that faced
the road. They hung tie-dyed sheets over the windows, and let the long grass and
flowering weeds reclaim the yard. My parents had finally got electricity in, but
these people didn't use it. They preferred oil lamps and the wood stove, and taking
their dirty clothes to town. People said they wouldn't know how to handle lamps or   620
wood fires, and they would burn the place down. But they didn't. In fact, they
didn't manage badly. They kept the house and barn in some sort of repair and they
worked a big garden. They even dusted their potatoes against blight—though I
heard that there was some sort of row about this and some of the stricter members
left. The place actually looked a lot better than many of the farms around about
that were still in the hands of the original families. The McAllister son had started a
wrecking business on their place. My own brothers were long gone.
   I knew I was not being reasonable, but I had the feeling that I'd rather see
the farm suffer outright neglect—I'd sooner see it in the hands of hoodlums and
scroungers—than see that rainbow on the barn, and some letters that looked   630
Egyptian painted on the wall of the house. That seemed a mockery. I even disliked
the sight of those people when they came to town—the men with their hair in
ponytails, and with holes in their overalls that I believed were cut on purpose, and
the women with long hair and no makeup and their meek, superior expressions.
What do you know about life, I felt like asking them. What makes you think you
can come here and mock my father and mother and their life and their poverty?
But when I thought of the rainbow and those letters, I knew they weren't trying to
mock or imitate my parents' life. They had displaced that life, hardly knowing it
existed. They had set up in its place these beliefs and customs of their own, which
I hoped would fail them.   640
   That happened, more or less. The commune disintegrated. The goats disappeared. Some of the women moved to town, cut their hair, put on makeup, and
got jobs as waitresses or cashiers to support their children. The Toronto man put
the place up for sale, and after about a year it was sold for more than ten times
what he had paid for it. A young couple from Ottawa bought it. They have painted
the outside a pale gray with oyster trim, and have put in skylights and a handsome
front door with carriage lamps on either side. Inside, they've changed it around so
much that I've been told I'd never recognize it.
   I did get in once, before this happened, during the year that the house was
empty and for sale. The company I work for was handling it, and I had a key,   650
though the house was being shown by another agent. I let myself in on a Sunday
afternoon. I had a man with me, not a client but a friend—Bob Marks, whom I
was seeing a lot at the time.

"This is that hippie place," Bob Marks said when I stopped the car. "I've been by here before."

He was a lawyer, a Catholic, separated from his wife. He thought he wanted to settle down and start up a practice here in town. But there already was one Catholic lawyer. Business was slow. A couple of times a week, Bob Marks would be fairly drunk before supper.

"It's more than that," I said. "It's where I was born. Where I grew up." We walked through the weeds, and I unlocked the door.

He said that he had thought, from the way I talked, that it would be farther out.

"It seemed farther then."

All the rooms were bare, and the floors swept clean. The woodwork was freshly painted—I was surprised to see no smudges on the glass. Some new panes, some old wavy ones. Some of the walls had been stripped of their paper and painted. A wall in the kitchen was painted a deep blue, with an enormous dove on it. On a wall in the front room, giant sunflowers appeared, and a butterfly of almost the same size.

Bob Marks whistled. "Somebody was an artist."

"If that's what you want to call it," I said, and turned back to the kitchen. The same wood stove was there. "My mother once burned up three thousand dollars," I said. "She burned three thousand dollars in that stove."

He whistled again, differently. "What do you mean? She threw in a check?"

"No, no. It was in bills. She did it deliberately. She went into town to the bank and she had them give it all to her, in a shoebox. She brought it home and put it in the stove. She put it in just a few bills at a time, so it wouldn't make too big a blaze. My father stood and watched her."

"What are you talking about?" said Bob Marks. "I thought you were so poor."

"We were. We were very poor."

"So how come she had three thousand dollars? That would be like thirty thousand today. Easily. More than thirty thousand today."

"It was her legacy," I said. "It was what she got from her father. Her father died in Seattle and left her three thousand dollars, and she burned it up because she hated him. She didn't want his money. She hated him."

"That's a lot of hate," Bob Marks said.

"That isn't the point. Her hating him, or whether he was bad enough for her to have a right to hate him. Not likely he was. That isn't the point."

"Money," he said. "Money's always the point."

"No. My father letting her do it is the point. To me it is. My father stood and watched and he never protested. If anybody had tried to stop her, he would have protected her. I consider that love."

"Some people would consider it lunacy."

I remember that that had been Beryl's opinion, exactly.

I went into the front room and stared at the butterfly, with its pink-and-orange wings. Then I went into the front bedroom and found two human figures painted on the wall. A man and a woman holding hands and facing straight ahead. They were naked, and larger than life size.

"It reminds me of that John Lennon and Yoko Ono picture," I said to Bob   700
Marks, who had come in behind me. "That record cover, wasn't it?" I didn't want
him to think that anything he had said in the kitchen had upset me.

Bob Marks said, "Different color hair."

That was true. Both figures had yellow hair painted in a solid mass, the way
they do it in the comic strips. Horsetails of yellow hair curling over their shoulders
and little pigs' tails of yellow hair decorating their not so private parts. Their skin
was a flat beige pink and their eyes a staring blue, the same blue that was on the
kitchen wall.

I noticed that they hadn't quite finished peeling the wallpaper away before
making this painting. In the corner, there was some paper left that matched the   710
paper on the other walls—a modernistic design of intersecting pink and gray and
mauve bubbles. The man from Toronto must have put that on. The paper underneath hadn't been stripped off when this new paper went on. I could see an edge
of it, the cornflowers on a white ground.

"I guess this was where they carried on their sexual shenanigans," Bob Marks
said, in a tone familiar to me. That thickened, sad, uneasy, but determined tone.
The not particularly friendly lust of middle-aged respectable men.

I didn't say anything. I worked away some of the bubble paper to see more
of the cornflowers. Suddenly I hit a loose spot, and ripped away a big swatch of it.
But the cornflower paper came too, and a little shower of dried plaster.   720

"Why is it?" I said. "Just tell me, why is it that no man can mention a place
like this without getting around to the subject of sex in about two seconds flat?
Just say the words 'hippie' or 'commune' and all you guys can think about is
screwing! As if there wasn't anything at all behind it but orgies and fancy combi-
nations and non-stop screwing! I get so sick of that—it's all so stupid it just makes
me sick!"

In the car, on the way home from the hotel, we sat as before—the men in the
front seat, the women in the back. I was in the middle, Beryl and my mother on
either side of me. Their heated bodies pressed against me, through cloth; their
smells crowded out the smells of the cedar bush we passed through, and the pock-   730
ets of bog, where Beryl exclaimed at the water lilies. Beryl smelled of all those
things in pots and bottles. My mother smelled of flour and hard soap and the
warm crêpe of her good dress and the kerosene she had used to take the spots off.

"A lovely meal," my mother said. "Thank you, Beryl. Thank you, Mr.
Florence."

"I don't know who is going to be fit to do the milking," my father said. "Now
that we've all ate in such style."

"Speaking of money," said Beryl—though nobody actually had been—"do
you mind my asking what you did with yours? I put mine in real estate. Real estate in California—you can't lose. I was thinking you could get an electric stove, so   740
you wouldn't have to bother with a fire in summer or fool with that coal-oil thing,
either one."

All the other people in the car laughed, even Mr. Florence.

"That's a good idea, Beryl," said my father. "We could use it to set things on
till we get the electricity."

"Oh, Lord," said Beryl. "How stupid can I get?"

"And we don't actually have the money, either," my mother said cheerfully, as if she was continuing the joke.

But Beryl spoke sharply. "You wrote me you got it. You got the same as me."

My father half turned in his seat. "What money are you talking about?" he said. "What's this money?"

"From Daddy's will," Beryl said. "That you got last year. Look, maybe I shouldn't have asked. If you had to pay something off, that's still a good use, isn't it? It doesn't matter. We're all family here. Practically."

"We didn't have to use it to pay anything off," my mother said. "I burned it."

Then she told how she went into town in the truck, one day almost a year ago, and got them to give her the money in a box she had brought along for the purpose. She took it home, and put it in the stove and burned it.

My father turned around and faced the road ahead.

I could feel Beryl twisting beside me while my mother talked. She was twisting, and moaning a little, as if she had a pain she couldn't suppress. At the end of the story, she let out a sound of astonishment and suffering, an angry groan.

"So you burned up money!" she said. "You burned up money in the stove."

My mother was still cheerful. "You sound as if I'd burned up one of my children."

"You burned their chances. You burned up everything the money could have got for them."

"The last thing my children need is money. None of us need his money."

"That's criminal," Beryl said harshly. She pitched her voice into the front seat: "Why did you let her?"

"He wasn't there," my mother said. "Nobody was there."

My father said, "It was her money, Beryl."

"Never mind," Beryl said. "That's criminal."

"Criminal is for when you call in the police," Mr. Florence said. Like other things he had said that day, this created a little island of surprise and a peculiar gratitude.

Gratitude not felt by all.

"Don't you pretend this isn't the craziest thing you ever heard of," Beryl shouted into the front seat. "Don't you pretend you don't think so! Because it is, and you do. You think just the same as me!"

My father did not stand in the kitchen watching my mother feed the money into the flames. It wouldn't appear so. He did not know about it—it seems fairly clear, if I remember everything, that he did not know about it until that Sunday afternoon in Mr. Florence's Chrysler, when my mother told them all together. Why, then, can I see the scene so clearly, just as I described it to Bob Marks (and to others—he was not the first)? I see my father standing by the table in the middle of the room—the table with the drawer in it for knives and forks, and the scrubbed oilcloth on top—and there is the box of money on the table. My mother is carefully dropping the bills into the fire. She holds the stove lid by the blackened lifter in one hand. And my father, standing by, seems not just to be permitting her to do this but to be protecting her. A solemn scene, but not crazy. People doing something that seems to them natural and necessary. At least, one of them is doing what seems natural and necessary, and the other believes that the important thing is for that person to be free, to go ahead. They understand that other people might not think so. They do not care.

How hard it is for me to believe that I made that up. It seems so much the truth it is the truth; it's what I believe about them. I haven't stopped believing it. But I have stopped telling that story. I never told it to anyone again after telling it to Bob Marks. I don't think so. I didn't stop just because it wasn't, strictly speaking, true. I stopped because I saw that I have to give up expecting people to see it 800 the way I did. I had to give up expecting them to approve of any part of what was done. How could I even say that I approved of it myself? If I had been the sort of person who approved of that, who could do it, I wouldn't have done all I have done—run away from home to work in a restaurant in town when I was fifteen, gone to night school to learn typing and bookkeeping, got into the real-estate of-fice, and finally become a licensed agent. I wouldn't be divorced. My father wouldn't have died in the county home. My hair would be white, as it has been naturally for years, instead of a color called Copper Sunrise. And not one of these things would I change, not really, if I could.

Bob Marks was a decent man—good-hearted, sometimes with imagination. 810 After I had lashed out at him like that, he said, "You don't need to be so tough on us." In a moment, he said, "Was this your room when you were a little girl?" He thought that was why the mention of the sexual shenanigans had upset me.

And I thought it would be just as well to let him think that. I said yes, yes, it was my room when I was a little girl. It was just as well to make up right away. Moments of kindness and reconciliation are worth having, even if the parting has to come sooner or later. I wonder if those moments aren't more valued, and delib-erately gone after, in the setups some people like myself have now, than they were in those old marriages, where love and grudges could be growing underground, so confused and stubborn, it must have seemed they had forever.   [1986] 820

Questions for Discussion and Writing

1. What does the title mean? How does it fit the story?
2. What conflicts and tensions are there in the various marriages?
3. What part does memory play? Pay particular attention to the two episodes— the attempted suicide and the burning of the money—where there are differ-ent versions of the incidents.
4. Why does the narrator Fame say "But it wasn't God, it was my mother I had to get straight with" p. 1069? What is the nature of the conflict between mother and daughter in this story?
5. What part does Beryl play in the story?
6. Why does the narrator want to believe that her father watched and approved of her mother's burning the $3,000?
7. Analyze the last paragraph carefully. What evidence is there in the story to support the conclusions the narrator draws about "love and grudges"?

✒ LOUISE ERDRICH

(b. 1954)

Snares

Louise Erdrich's stories combine traditional Native American lore with her own experiences and a distinctly modern style and technique. Her fiction often concerns the mixing of Native and European cultures, religious tensions, Native American spirituality, the presence of history, and the "medicine" of women who bring retribution on those who violate them in some way.

Erdrich was born in Little Falls, Minnesota, where her father (of German descent) was a teacher with the Bureau of Indian Affairs and her mother (a member of the Chippewa or Ojibwa nation) also worked for the Bureau. Having access to neither television nor movies, Erdrich listened to the oral tales spun by her grandfather and others and from an early age wrote stories of her own. Her father sometimes paid her a nickel, and her mother "published" them in home-made books. In 1972, she entered Dartmouth College, where she published in the student literary magazine and won an American Academy of Poets Prize in 1975.

After graduation, Erdrich worked for the Arts Council in North Dakota and then in a variety of jobs: waiting tables, weighing trucks, working as a flagger on construction crews, weeding crops, delivering papers, managing a book distribution-company. In 1979 she entered Johns Hopkins University, from which she earned an M.F.A. While giving a poetry reading at Dartmouth, she met Michael Dorris, a professor in the Native American Studies Department. They married three years later and began collaborating on stories. "The World's Greatest Fisherman" became the best-selling novel *Love Medicine* (1984). Many Native Americans who read the novel wrote her to say that her novel was the first one they had read that accurately captured their speech. A Guggenheim Fellowship in 1985 enabled her to produce *The Beet Queen* (1986). "Snares," first written as a short story, became Chapter 5 of that novel.

IT BEGAN AFTER CHURCH with Margaret and her small granddaughter, Lulu, and was not to end until the long days of Lent and a hard-packed snow. There were factions on the reservation, a treaty settlement in the Agent's hands. There were Chippewa[1] who signed their names in the year 1924, and there were Chippewa who saw the cash offered as a flimsy bait. I was one and Fleur Pillager, Lulu's mother, was another who would not lift her hand to sign. It was said that all the power to witch, harm, or cure lay in Fleur, the lone survivor of the old Pillager clan. But as much as people feared Fleur, they listened to Margaret Kashpaw. She

---

1. The European name for the Ojibwa, whose lands bordered Lake Superior and Lake Huron.

was the ringleader of the holdouts, a fierce, one-minded widow with a vinegar
tongue.   10

Margaret Kashpaw had knots of muscles in her arms. Her braids were thin,
gray as iron, and usually tied strictly behind her back so they wouldn't swing. She
was plump as a basket below and tough as roots on top. Her face was gnarled
around a beautiful sharp nose. Two shell earrings caught the light and flashed
whenever she turned her head. She had become increasingly religious in the years
after her loss, and finally succeeded in dragging me to the Benediction Mass,
where I was greeted by Father Damien, from whom I occasionally won small sums
at dice.

"Grandfather Nanapush," he smiled, "at last."

"These benches are a hardship for an old man," I complained. "If you spread 20
them with soft pine-needle cushions I'd have come before."

Father Damien stared thoughtfully at the rough pews, folded his hands inside the sleeves of his robe.

"You must think of their unyielding surfaces as helpful," he offered. "God
sometimes enters the soul through the humblest parts of our anatomies, if they are
sensitized to suffering."

"A god who enters through the rear door," I countered, "is no better than a
thief."

Father Damien was used to me, and smiled as he walked to the altar. I adjusted my old bones, longing for some relief, trying not to rustle for fear of 30
Margaret's jabbing elbow. The time was long. Lulu probed all my pockets with her
fingers until she found a piece of hard candy. I felt no great presence in this cold
place and decided, as my back end ached and my shoulders stiffened, that our
original gods were better, the Chippewa characters who were not exactly perfect
but at least did not require sitting on hard boards.

When Mass was over and the smell of incense was thick in all our clothes,
Margaret, Lulu, and I went out into the starry cold, the snow and stubble fields,
and began the long walk to our homes. It was dusk. On either side of us the heavy
trees stood motionless and blue. Our footsteps squeaked against the dry snow, the
only sound to hear. We spoke very little, and even Lulu ceased her singing when 40
the moon rose to half, poised like a balanced cup. We knew the very moment
someone else stepped upon the road.

We had turned a bend and the footfalls came unevenly, just out of sight.
There were two men, one mixed-blood or white, from the drop of his hard boot
soles, and the other one quiet, an Indian. Not long and I heard them talking close
behind us. From the rough, quick tension of the Indian's language, I recognized
Lazarre. And the mixed-blood must be Clarence Morrissey. The two had signed
the treaty and spoke in its favor to anyone they could collar at the store. They
even came to people's houses to beg and argue that this was our one chance, our
good chance, that the government would withdraw the offer. But wherever 50
Margaret was, she slapped down their words like mosquitoes and said the only
thing that lasts life to life is land. Money burns like tinder, flows like water. And as
for promises, the wind is steadier. It is no wonder that, because she spoke so well,
Lazarre and Clarence Morrissey wished to silence her. I sensed their bad intent as
they passed us, an unpleasant edge of excitement in their looks and greetings.

They went on, disappeared in the dark brush.

"Margaret," I said, "we are going to cut back." My house was close, but Margaret kept walking forward as if she hadn't heard.

I took her arm, caught the little girl close, and started to turn us, but Margaret would have none of this and called me a coward. She grabbed the girl to her. Lulu, who did not mind getting tossed between us, laughed, tucked her hand into her grandma's pocket, and never missed a step. Two years ago she had tired of being carried, got up, walked. She had the balance of a little mink. She was slippery and clever, too, which was good because when the men jumped from the darkest area of brush and grappled with us half a mile on, Lulu slipped free and scrambled into the trees.

They were occupied with Margaret and me, at any rate. We were old enough to snap in two, our limbs dry as dead branches, but we fought as though our enemies were the Nadouissouix kidnappers of our childhood. Margaret uttered a war cry that had not been heard for fifty years, and bit Lazarre's hand to the bone, giving a wound which would later prove the death of him. As for Clarence, he had all he could do to wrestle me to the ground and knock me half unconscious. When he'd accomplished that, he tied me and tossed me into a wheelbarrow, which was hidden near the road for the purpose of lugging us to the Morrissey barn.

I came to my senses trussed to a manger, sitting on a bale. Margaret was roped to another bale across from me, staring straight forward in a rage, a line of froth caught between her lips. On either side of her, shaggy cows chewed and shifted their thumping hooves. I rose and staggered, the weight of the manger on my back. I planned on Margaret biting through my ropes with her strong teeth, but then the two men entered.

I'm a talker, a fast-mouth who can't keep his thoughts straight, but lets fly with words and marvels at what he hears from his own mouth. I'm a smart one. I always was a devil for convincing women. And I wasn't too bad a shot, in other ways, at convincing men. But I had never been tied up before.

"*Booshoo*," I said. "Children, let us loose, your game is too rough!"

They stood between us, puffed with their secrets.

"Empty old windbag," said Clarence.

"I have a bargain for you," I said, looking for an opening. "Let us go and we won't tell Pukwan." Edgar Pukwan was the tribal police. "Boys get drunk sometimes and don't know what they're doing."

Lazarre laughed once, hard and loud. "We're not drunk," he said. "Just wanting what's coming to us, some justice, money out of it."

"Kill us," said Margaret. "We won't sign."

"Wait," I said. "My cousin Pukwan will find you boys, and have no mercy. Let us go. I'll sign and get it over with, and I'll persuade the old widow."

I signaled Margaret to keep her mouth shut. She blew air into her cheeks. Clarence looked expectantly at Lazarre, as if the show were over, but Lazarre folded his arms and was convinced of nothing.

"You lie when it suits, skinny old dog," he said, wiping at his lips as if in hunger. "It's her we want, anyway. We'll shame her so she shuts her mouth."

"Easy enough," I said, smooth, "now that you've got her tied. She's plump and good looking. Eyes like a doe! But you forget that we're together, almost man and wife."

This wasn't true at all, and Margaret's face went rigid with tumbling fury and confusion. I kept talking.

"So of course if you do what you're thinking of doing you'll have to kill me afterward, and that will make my cousin Pukwan twice as angry, since I owe him a fat payment for a gun which he lent me and I never returned. All the same," I went on—their heads were spinning—"I'll forget you bad boys ever considered such a crime, something so terrible that Father Damien would nail you on boards just like in the example on the wall in church." 110

"Quit jabbering." Lazarre stopped me in a deadly voice.

It was throwing pebbles in a dry lake. My words left no ripple. I saw in his eyes that he intended us great harm. I saw his greed. It was like watching an ugly design of bruises come clear for a moment and reconstructing the evil blows that made them.

I played my last card.

"Whatever you do to Margaret you are doing to the Pillager woman!" I dropped my voice. "The witch, Fleur Pillager, is her own son's wife."

Clarence was too young to be frightened, but his mouth hung in interested puzzlement. My words had a different effect on Lazarre, as a sudden light shone, a consequence he hadn't considered. 120

I cried out, seeing this, "Don't you think she can think about you hard enough to stop your heart?" Lazarre was still deciding. He raised his fist and swung it casually and tapped my face. It was worse not to be hit full on.

"Come near!" crooned Margaret in the old language. "Let me teach you how to die."

But she was trapped like a fox. Her earrings glinted and spun as she hissed her death song over and over, which signaled something to Lazarre, for he shook himself angrily and drew a razor from his jacket. He stropped it with fast, vicious movements while Margaret sang shriller, so full of hate that the ropes should have burned, shriveled, fallen from her body. My struggle set the manger cracking against the barn walls and further confused the cows, who bumped each other and complained. At a sign from Lazarre, Clarence sighed, rose, and smashed me. The last I saw before I blacked out, through the tiny closing pinhole of light, was Lazarre approaching Margaret with the blade. 130

When I woke, minutes later, it was to worse shock. For Lazarre had sliced Margaret's long braids off and was now, carefully, shaving her scalp. He started almost tenderly at the wide part, and then pulled the edge down each side of her skull. He did a clean job. He shed not one drop of blood. 140

And I could not even speak to curse them. For pressing my jaw down, thick above my tongue, her braids, never cut in this life till now, were tied to silence me. Powerless, I tasted their flat, animal perfume.

It wasn't much later, or else it was forever, that we walked out into the night again. Speechless, we made our way in fierce pain down the road. I was damaged in spirit, more so than Margaret. For now she tucked her shawl over her naked head and forgot her own bad treatment. She called out in dread each foot of the way, for Lulu. But the smart, bold girl had hidden till all was clear and then run to Margaret's house. We opened the door and found her sitting by the stove in a litter of scorched matches and kindling. She had not the skill to start a fire, but she was dry-eyed. Though very cold, she was alert and then captured with wonder when Margaret slipped off her shawl. 150

"Where is your hair?" she asked.

I took my hand from my pocket. "Here's what's left of it. I grabbed this when they cut me loose." I was shamed by how pitiful I had been, relieved when Margaret snatched the thin gray braids from me and coiled them round her fist.

"I knew you would save them, clever man!" There was satisfaction in her voice.

I set the fire blazing. It was strange how generous this woman was to me, never blaming me or mentioning my failure. Margaret stowed her braids inside a 160 birchbark box and merely instructed me to lay it in her grave, when that time occurred. Then she came near the stove with a broken mirror from beside her washstand and looked at her own image.

"My," she pondered, "my." She put the mirror down. "I'll take a knife to them."

And I was thinking too. I was thinking I would have to kill them.

But how does an aching and half-starved grandfather attack a young, well-fed Morrissey and a tall, sly Lazarre? Later, I rolled up in blankets in the corner by Margaret's stove, and I put my mind to this question throughout that night until, exhausted, I slept. And I thought of it first thing next morning, too, and still noth- 170 ing came. It was only after we had some hot *gaulette* and walked Lulu back to her mother that an idea began to grow.

Fleur let us in, hugged Lulu into her arms, and looked at Margaret, who took off her scarf and stood bald, face burning again with smoldered fire. She told Fleur all of what happened, sparing no detail. The two women's eyes held, but Fleur said nothing. She put Lulu down, smoothed the front of her calico shirt, flipped her heavy braids over her shoulders, tapped one finger on her perfect lips. And then, calm, she went to the washstand and scraped the edge of her hunting knife keen as glass. Margaret and Lulu and I watched as Fleur cut her braids off, shaved her own head, and folded the hair into a quilled skin pouch. Then she 180 went out, hunting, and didn't bother to wait for night to cover her tracks.

I would have to go out hunting too.

I had no gun, but anyway that was a white man's revenge. I knew how to wound with barbs of words, but had never wielded a skinning knife against a human, much less two young men. Whomever I missed would kill me, and I did not want to die by their lowly hands.

In fact, I didn't think that after Margaret's interesting kindness I wanted to leave this life at all. Her head, smooth as an egg, was ridged delicately with bone, and gleamed as if it had been buffed with a flannel cloth. Maybe it was the strangeness that attracted me. She looked forbidding, but the absence of hair also 190 set off her eyes, so black and full of lights. She reminded me of that queen from England, of a water snake or a shrewd young bird. The earrings, which seemed part of her, mirrored her moods like water, and when they were still rounds of green lights against her throat I seemed, again, to taste her smooth, smoky braids in my mouth.

I had better things to do than fight. So I decided to accomplish revenge as quickly as possible. I was a talker who used my brains as my weapon. When I hunted, I preferred to let my game catch itself.

Snares demand clever fingers and a scheming mind, and snares had never failed me. Snares are quiet, and best of all snares are slow. I wanted to give Lazarre 200 and Morrissey time to consider why they had to strangle. I thought hard. One- or two-foot deadfalls are required beneath a snare so that a man can't put his hand up and loosen the knot. The snares I had in mind also required something stronger than a cord, which could be broken, and finer than a rope, which even Lazarre might see and avoid. I pondered this closely, yet even so I might never have found the solution had I not gone to Mass with Margaret and grown curious about the workings of Father Damien's pride and joy, the piano in the back of the church, the instrument whose keys he breathed on, polished, then played after services, and sometimes alone. I had noticed that his hands usually stayed near the middle of the keyboard, so I took the wires from either end.   210

In the meantime, I was not the only one concerned with punishing Lazarre and Clarence Morrissey. Fleur was seen in town. Her thick skirts brushed the snow into clouds behind her. Though it was cold she left her head bare so every-one could see the frigid sun glare off her skull. The light reflected in the eyes of Lazarre and Clarence, who were standing at the door of the pool hall. They dropped their cue sticks in the slush and ran back to Morrissey land. Fleur walked the four streets, once in each direction, then followed.

The two men told of her visit, how she passed through the Morrissey house touching here, touching there, sprinkling powders that ignited and stank on the hot stove. How Clarence swayed on his feet, blinked hard, and chewed his fingers. 220 How Fleur stepped up to him, drew her knife. He smiled foolishly and asked her for supper. She reached forward and trimmed off a hank of his hair. Then she stalked from the house, leaving a taste of cold wind, and then chased Lazarre to the barn.

She made a black silhouette against the light from the door. Lazarre pressed against the wood of the walls, watching, hypnotized by the sight of Fleur's head and the quiet blade. He did not defend himself when she approached, reached for him, gently and efficiently cut bits of his hair, held his hands, one at a time, and trimmed the nails. She waved the razor-edged knife before his eyes and swept a few eyelashes into a white square of flour sacking that she then carefully folded 230 into her blouse.

For days after, Lazarre babbled and wept. Fleur was murdering him by use of bad medicine, he said. He showed his hand, the bite that Margaret had dealt him, and the dark streak from the wound, along his wrist and inching up his arm. He even used that bound hand to scratch his name from the treaty, but it did no good.

I figured that the two men were doomed at least three ways now. Margaret won the debate with her Catholic training and decided to damn her soul by taking up the ax, since no one else had destroyed her enemies. I begged her to wait for another week, all during which it snowed and thawed and snowed again. It took 240 me that long to arrange the snare to my satisfaction, near Lazarre's shack, on a path both men took to town.

I set it out one morning before anyone stirred, and watched from an old pine twisted along the ground. I waited while the smoke rose in a silky feather from the tiny tin spout on Lazarre's roof. I had to sit half a day before Lazarre came outside, and even then it was just for wood, nowhere near the path. I had a hard time to keep my blood flowing, my stomach still. I ate a handful of dry berries Margaret had given me, and a bit of pounded meat. I doled it to myself and waited until finally Clarence showed. He walked the trail like a blind ghost and stepped straight into my noose.   250

It was perfect, or would have been if I had made the deadfall two inches wider, for in falling Clarence somehow managed to spread his legs and straddle the deep hole I'd cut. It had been invisible, covered with snow, and yet in one foot-pedaling instant, the certain knowledge of its construction sprang into Clarence's brain and told his legs to reach for the sides. I don't know how he did it, but there he was poised. I waited, did not show myself. The noose jerked enough to cut slightly into the fool's neck, a too-snug fit. He was spread-eagled and on tiptoe, his arms straight out. If he twitched a finger, lost the least control, even tried to yell, one foot would go, the noose constrict.

But Clarence did not move. I could see from behind my branches that he 260 didn't even dare to change the expression on his face. His mouth stayed frozen in shock. Only his eyes shifted, darted fiercely and wildly, side to side, showing all the agitation he must not release, searching desperately for a means of escape. They focused only when I finally stepped toward him, quiet, from the pine.

We were in full view of Lazarre's house, face to face. I stood before the boy. Just a touch, a sudden kick, perhaps no more than a word, was all that it would take. But I looked into his eyes and saw the knowledge of his situation. Pity entered me. Even for Margaret's shame, I couldn't do the thing I might have done.

I turned away and left Morrissey still balanced on the ledge of snow.

What money I did have, I took to the trading store next day. I bought the 270 best bonnet on the reservation. It was black as a coal scuttle, large, and shaped the same.

"It sets off my doe eyes," Margaret said and stared me down.

She wore it every day, and always to Mass. Not long before Lent and voices could be heard: "There goes Old Lady Coal-bucket." Nonetheless, she was proud, and softening day by day, I could tell. By the time we got our foreheads crossed with ashes,[2] she consented to be married.

---

2. On Ash Wednesday, the first day of Lent, penitent Christians are marked on the forehead with a cross of ashes.

"I hear you're thinking of exchanging the vows," said Father Damien as I shook his hand on our way out the door.

"I'm having relations with Margaret already," I told him, "that's the way we   280 do things."

This had happened to him before, so he was not even stumped as to what remedy he should use.

"Make a confession, at any rate," he said, motioning us back into the church.

So I stepped into the little box and knelt. Father Damien slid aside the shadowy door. I told him what I had been doing with Margaret and he stopped me partway through.

"No more details. Pray to Our Lady."

"There is one more thing."

"Yes?"   290

"Clarence Morrissey, he wears a scarf to church around his neck each week. I snared him like a rabbit."

Father Damien let the silence fill him.

"And the last thing," I went on. "I stole the wire from your piano."

The silence spilled over into my stall, and I was held in its grip until the priest spoke.

"Discord is hateful to God. You have offended his ear." Almost as an afterthought, Damien added, "And his commandment. The violence among you must cease."

"You can have the wire back," I said. I had used only one long strand. I also   300 agreed that I would never use my snares on humans, an easy promise. Lazarre was already caught.

Just two days later, while Margaret and I stood with Lulu and her mother inside the trading store, Lazarre entered, gesturing, his eyes rolled to the skull. He stretched forth his arm and pointed along its deepest black vein and dropped his jaw wide. Then he stepped backward into a row of traps that the trader had set to show us how they worked. Fleur's eye lit, her white scarf caught the sun as she turned. All the whispers were true. Fleur had scratched Lazarre's figure into a piece of birchbark, drawn his insides, and rubbed a bit of rouge up his arm until the red stain reached his heart. There was no sound as he fell, no cry, no word,   310 and the traps of all types that clattered down around his body jumped and met for a long time, snapping air.

                                                                                                            [1987]

_____

Questions for Discussion and Writing

1. What is the conflict between the two factions? Why is it so fierce? What is at stake?
2. What cultural tensions do the characters feel? Underline or highlight those passages that indicate specific tensions.
3. What is the relationship between the narrator and Margaret? Does their engagement come as a surprise? Why or why not?

4. What is the significance of the title? What does it refer to besides the snare set by the narrator?
5. Why does Lazarre die? What do the others think is killing him?
6. Does this story have a theme, or does it simply recount an episode from history? Explain your answer by citing evidence from the story.

☞ LORRIE MOORE
(b. 1957)

You're Ugly, Too

Lorrie Moore is a successful contemporary writer whose work is well attuned to today's culture. She was born in Glens Falls, New York. Her father was an insurance executive, her mother a housewife. After high school, she attended St. Lawrence University. While a student, she won *Seventeen Magazine's* fiction contest in 1976 with a story entitled "Raspberries." After earning a B.A. in 1978, she went to Cornell University, earning an M.F.A. in creative writing in 1982. The next year, she won an Associated Writing Programs award for her collection of stories *Self Help* while teaching at Cornell.

Moore's early stories were experiments in using the second person point of view, addressing the reader as "you" as in a self-help manual, parodying this popular form in the process. Her second collection was less innovative in form but no less refreshing in point of view. Moore's characters are usually highly intelligent people caught in contemporary dilemmas and predicaments. Unfortunately, their intelligence, self-knowledge, and devastating wit can turn out to be handicaps rather than assets, and some "self-destruct" in the face of life's difficulties. "You're Ugly, Too" deals with the loneliness that sometimes occurs when a person's life does not, for whatever reason, follow the conventional love and marriage route.

You HAD TO GET out of them occasionally, those Illinois towns with the funny names: Paris, Oblong, Normal. Once, when the Dow-Jones dipped two hundred points, the Paris paper boasted a banner headline: NORMAL MAN MARRIES OB-LONG WOMAN. They knew what was important. They did! But you had to get out once in a while, even if it was just across the border to Terre Haute, for a movie.

Outside of Paris, in the middle of a large field, was a scatter of brick buildings, a small liberal arts college with the improbable name of Hilldale-Versailles. Zoë Hendricks had been teaching American History there for three years. She taught "The Revolution and Beyond" to freshmen and sophomores, and every third semester she had the Senior Seminar for Majors, and although her student evaluations had been slipping in the last year and a half—*Professor Hendricks is often late for class and usually arrives with a cup of hot chocolate, which she offers the* 10 *class sips of*—generally, the department of nine men was pleased to have her. They felt she added some needed feminine touch to the corridors—that faint trace of Obsession and sweat, the light, fast clicking of heels. Plus they had had a sex-discrimination suit, and the dean had said, well, it was time.

The situation was not easy for her, they knew. Once, at the start of last semester, she had skipped into her lecture hall singing "Getting to Know You"— both verses. At the request of the dean, the chairman had called her into his office, but did not ask her for an explanation, not really. He asked her how she was and then smiled in an avuncular way. She said, "Fine," and he studied the way she said it, her front teeth catching on the inside of her lower lip. She was almost pretty, but her face showed the strain and ambition of always having been close but not quite. There was too much effort with the eyeliner, and her earrings, worn no doubt for the drama her features lacked, were a little frightening, jutting out from the side of her head like antennae.

"I'm going out of my mind," said Zoë to her younger sister, Evan, in Manhattan. *Professor Hendricks seems to know the entire sound track to* The King and I. *Is this history?* Zoë phoned her every Tuesday.

"You always say that," said Evan, "but then you go on your trips and vacations and then you settle back into things and then you're quiet for a while and then you say you're fine, you're busy, and then after a while you say you're going crazy again, and you start all over." Evan was a part-time food designer for photo shoots. She cooked vegetables in green dye. She propped up beef stew with a bed of marbles and shopped for new kinds of silicone sprays and plastic ice cubes. She thought her life was "OK." She was living with her boyfriend of many years, who was independently wealthy and had an amusing little job in book publishing. They were five years out of college, and they lived in a luxury midtown high-rise with a balcony and access to a pool. "It's not the same as having your own pool," Evan was always sighing, as if to let Zoë know that, as with Zoë, there were still things she, Evan, had to do without.

"Illinois. It makes me sarcastic to be here," said Zoë on the phone. She used to insist it was irony, something gently layered and sophisticated, something alien to the Midwest, but her students kept calling it sarcasm, something they felt qualified to recognize, and now she had to agree. It wasn't irony. *What is your perfume?* a student once asked her. *Room freshener,* she said. She smiled, but he looked at her, unnerved.

Her students were by and large Midwesterners, spacey with estrogen from large quantities of meat and cheese. They shared their parents' suburban values; their parents had given them things, things, things. They were complacent. They had been purchased. They were armed with a healthy vagueness about anything historical or geographic. They seemed actually to know very little about anything, but they were extremely good-natured about it. "All those states in the East are so tiny and jagged and bunched up," complained one of her undergraduates the week she was lecturing on "The Turning Point of Independence: The Battle at Saratoga." "Professor Hendricks, you're from Delaware originally, right?" the student asked her.

"Maryland," corrected Zoë.

"Aw," he said, waving his hand dismissively. "New England."

Her articles—chapters toward a book called *Hearing the One About: Uses of* 60
Humor in the American Presidency—were generally well received, though they came
slowly for her. She liked her pieces to have something from every time of day in
them—she didn't trust things written in the morning only—so she reread and
rewrote painstakingly. No part of a day, its moods, its light, was allowed to dominate. She hung on to a piece for over a year sometimes, revising at all hours, until
the entirety of a day had registered there.

The job she'd had before the one at Hilldale-Versailles had been at a small
college in New Geneva, Minnesota, Land of the Dying Shopping Mall. Everyone
was so blond there that brunettes were often presumed to be from foreign countries. *Just because Professor Hendricks is from Spain doesn't give her the right to be so* 70
negative about our country. There was a general emphasis on cheerfulness. In New
Geneva you weren't supposed to be critical or complain. You weren't supposed to
notice that the town had overextended and that its shopping malls were raggedy
and going under. You were never to say you weren't fine thank you and yourself.
You were supposed to be Heidi.[1] You were supposed to lug goat milk up the hills
and not think twice. Heidi did not complain. Heidi did not do things like stand in
front of the new IBM photocopier, saying, "If this fucking Xerox machine breaks
on me one more time, I'm going to slit my wrists."

But now, in her second job, in her fourth year of teaching in the Midwest,
Zoë was discovering something she never suspected she had: a crusty edge, brittle 80
and pointed. Once she had pampered her students, singing them songs, letting
them call her at home, even, and ask personal questions. Now she was losing sympathy. They were beginning to seem different. They were beginning to seem demanding and spoiled.

"You act," said one of her Senior Seminar students at a scheduled conference,
"like your opinion is worth more than everybody else's in the class."

Zoë's eyes widened. "I *am* the teacher," she said. "I *do* get paid to act like
that." She narrowed her gaze at the student, who was wearing a big leather bow in
her hair, like a cowgirl in a TV ranch show. "I mean, otherwise *everybody* in the
class would have little offices and office hours." *Sometimes Professor Hendricks will* 90
take up the class's time just talking about movies she's seen. She stared at the student
some more, then added, "I bet you'd like that."

"Maybe I sound whiny to you," said the girl, "but I simply want my history
major to mean something."

"Well, there's your problem," said Zoë, and with a smile, she showed the student to the door. "I like your bow," she added.

Zoë lived for the mail, for the postman, that handsome blue jay, and when
she got a real letter, with a real full-price stamp, from someplace else, she took it
to bed with her and read it over and over. She also watched television until all
hours and had her set in the bedroom, a bad sign. *Professor Hendricks has said crit-* 100
ical things about Fawn Hall,[2] the Catholic religion, and the whole state of Illinois. It is
unbelievable. At Christmastime she gave twenty-dollar tips to the mailman and to

1. Adolescent heroine of the sentimental novel by Swiss author Johanna Spiri (1827–1901).
2. Secretary of Oliver North, who was involved in the Iran-Contra scandal of the Ronald Reagan administration.

Jerry, the only cabbie in town, whom she had gotten to know from all her rides to
and from the Terre Haute airport, and who, since he realized such rides were an
extravagance, often gave her cut rates.

"I'm flying in to visit you this weekend," announced Zoë.

"I was hoping you would," said Evan. "Charlie and I are having a party for
Halloween. It'll be fun."

"I have a costume already. It's a bonehead. It's this thing that looks like a
giant bone going through your head."   110

"Great," said Evan.

"It is, it's great."

"Alls I have is my moon mask from last year and the year before. I'll probably end up getting married in it."

"Are you and Charlie getting *married*?" Foreboding filled her voice.

"Hmmmmmmnnno, not immediately."

"Don't get married."

"Why?"

"Just not yet. You're too young."

"You're only saying that because you're five years older than I am and *you're*   120
not married."

"*I'm* not married? Oh, my God," said Zoë. "I forgot to get married."

Zoë had been out with three men since she'd come to Hilldale-Versailles.
One of them was a man in the Paris municipal bureaucracy who had fixed a parking ticket she'd brought in to protest and who then asked her to coffee. At first she
thought he was amazing—at last, someone who did not want Heidi! But soon she
came to realize that all men, deep down, wanted Heidi. Heidi with cleavage. Heidi
with outfits. The parking ticket bureaucrat soon became tired and intermittent.
One cool day, in his snazzy, impractical convertible, when she asked him what was
wrong, he said, "You would not be ill-served by new clothes, you know." She wore 130
a lot of gray-green corduroy. She had been under the impression that it brought
out her eyes, those shy stars. She flicked an ant from her sleeve.

"Did you have to brush that off in the car?" he said, driving. He glanced
down at his own pectorals, giving first the left, then the right, a quick survey. He
was wearing a tight shirt.

"Excuse me?"

He slowed down at a yellow light and frowned. "Couldn't you have picked it
up and thrown it outside?"

"The ant? It might have bitten me. I mean, what difference does it make?"

"It might have bitten you! Ha! How ridiculous! Now it's going to lay eggs in 140
my car!"

The second guy was sweeter, lunkier, though not insensitive to certain paintings and songs, but too often, too, things he'd do or say would startle her. Once,
in a restaurant, he stole the garnishes off her dinner plate and waited for her to
notice. When she didn't, he finally thrust his fist across the table and said, "Look,"
and when he opened it, there was her parsley sprig and her orange slice, crumpled
to a wad. Another time he described to her his recent trip to the Louvre. "And
there I was in front of Géricault's *Raft of the Medusa,* and everyone else had wandered off, so I had my own private audience with it, all those painted, drowning

bodies splayed in every direction, and there's this motion in that painting that   150
starts at the bottom left, swirling and building, and building, and building, and
going up to the right-hand corner, where there's this guy waving a flag, and on the
horizon in the distance you could see this teeny tiny boat. . . ." He was breathless
in the telling. She found this touching and smiled in encouragement. "A painting
like that," he said, shaking his head. "It just makes you shit."

"I have to ask you something," said Evan. "I know every woman complains
about not meeting men, but really, on my shoots, I meet a lot of men. And they're
not all gay, either." She paused. "Not anymore."

"What are you asking?"

The third guy was a political science professor named Murray Peterson, who   160
liked to go out on double dates with colleagues whose wives he was attracted to.
Usually the wives would consent to flirt with him. Under the table sometimes
there was footsie, and once there was even kneesie. Zoë and the husband would
be left to their food, staring into their water glasses, chewing like goats. "Oh,
Murray," said the wife, who had never finished her master's in physical therapy
and wore great clothes. "You know, I know everything about you: your birthday,
your license plate number. I have everything memorized. But then that's the kind
of mind I have. Once at a dinner party I amazed the host by getting up and saying
good-bye to every single person there, first *and* last names."

"I knew a dog who could do that," said Zoë, with her mouth full. Murray   170
and the wife looked at her with vexed and rebuking expressions, but the husband
seemed suddenly twinkling and amused. Zoë swallowed. "It was a Talking Lab,
and after about ten minutes of listening to the dinner conversation this dog knew
everyone's name. You could say, 'Bring this knife to Murray Peterson,' and it
would."

"Really," said the wife, frowning, and Murray Peterson never called again.

"Are you seeing anyone?" said Evan. "I'm asking for a particular reason, I'm
not just being like mom."

"I'm seeing my house. I'm tending to it when it wets, when it cries, when it
throws up." Zoë had bought a mint-green ranch house near campus, though now   180
she was thinking that maybe she shouldn't have. It was hard to live in a house.
She kept wandering in and out of the rooms, wondering where she had put
things. She went downstairs into the basement for no reason at all except that it
amused her to own a basement. It also amused her to own a tree. The day she
moved in, she had tacked to her tree a small paper sign that said *Zoë's Tree.*

Her parents, in Maryland, had been very pleased that one of their children
had at last been able to afford real estate, and when she closed on the house they
sent her flowers with a Congratulations card. Her mother had even UPS'd a box of
old decorating magazines saved over the years, photographs of beautiful rooms her
mother used to moon over, since there never had been any money to redecorate. It   190
was like getting her mother's pornography, that box, inheriting her drooled-upon
fantasies, the endless wish and tease that had been her life. But to her mother it was
a rite of passage that pleased her. "Maybe you will get some ideas from these," she
had written. And when Zoë looked at the photographs, at the bold and beautiful
living rooms, she was filled with longing. Ideas and ideas of longing.

Right now Zoë's house was rather empty. The previous owner had wallpa-

pered around the furniture, leaving strange gaps and silhouettes on the walls, and
Zoë hadn't done much about that yet. She had bought furniture, then taken it
back, furnishing and unfurnishing, preparing and shedding, like a womb. She had
bought several plain pine chests to use as love seats or boot boxes, but they came   200
to look to her more and more like children's coffins, so she returned them. And
she had recently bought an Oriental rug for the living room, with Chinese symbols
on it she didn't understand. The salesgirl had kept saying she was sure they meant
Peace and *Eternal Life,* but when Zoë got the rug home, she worried. What if they
didn't mean *Peace* and *Eternal Life*? What if they meant, say, *Bruce Springsteen.* And
the more she thought about it, the more she became convinced she had a rug that
said *Bruce Springsteen,* and so she returned that, too.

     She had also bought a little baroque mirror for the front entryway, which she
had been told, by Murray Peterson, would keep away evil spirits. The mirror,
however, tended to frighten *her,* startling her with an image of a woman she never   210
recognized. Sometimes she looked puffier and plainer than she remembered.
Sometimes shifty and dark. Most times she just looked vague. *You look like someone
I know,* she had been told twice in the last year by strangers in restaurants in Terre
Haute. In fact, sometimes she seemed not to have a look of her own, or any look
whatsoever, and it began to amaze her that her students and colleagues were able
to recognize her at all. How did they know? When she walked into a room, how
did she look so that they knew it was her? Like this? Did she look like this? And
so she returned the mirror.

     "The reason I'm asking is that I know a man I think you should meet," said
Evan. "He's fun. He's straight. He's single. That's all I'm going to say."   220
     "I think I'm too old for fun," said Zoë. She had a dark bristly hair in her
chin, and she could feel it now with her finger. Perhaps when you had been without the opposite sex for too long, you began to resemble them. In an act of desperate invention, you began to grow your own. "I just want to come, wear my
bonehead, visit with Charlie's tropical fish, ask you about your food shoots."

     She thought about all the papers on "Our Constitution: How It Affects Us"
she was going to have to correct. She thought about how she was going in for ul-
trasound tests on Friday, because, according to her doctor and her doctor's assistant, she had a large, mysterious growth in her abdomen. Gallbladder, they kept
saying. Or ovaries or colon. "You guys practice medicine?" asked Zoë, aloud, after   230
they had left the room. Once, as a girl, she brought her dog to a vet, who had told
her, "Well, either your dog has worms or cancer or else it was hit by a car."

     She was looking forward to New York.

     "Well, whatever. We'll just play it cool. I can't wait to see you, hon. Don't for-
get your bonehead," said Evan.

     "A bonehead you don't forget," said Zoë.

     "I suppose," said Evan.

     The ultrasound Zoë was keeping a secret, even from Evan. "I feel like I'm
dying," Zoë had hinted just once on the phone.

     "You're not dying," said Evan. "You're just annoyed."   240

     "Ultrasound," Zoë now said jokingly to the technician who put the cold jelly
on her bare stomach. "Does that sound like a really great stereo system, or what?"
She had not had anyone make this much fuss over her bare stomach since her

boyfriend in graduate school, who had hovered over her whenever she felt ill, waved his arms, pressed his hands upon her navel, and drawled evangelically, "Heal! Heal for thy Baby Jesus' sake!" Zoë would laugh and they would make love, both secretly hoping she would get pregnant. Later they would worry together, and he would sink a cheek to her belly and ask whether she was late, was she late, was she sure, she might be late, and when after two years she had not gotten pregnant, they took to quarreling and drifted apart.

"OK," said the technician absently.

The monitor was in place, and Zoë's insides came on the screen in all their gray and ribbony hollowness. They were marbled in the finest gradations of black and white, like stone in an old church or a picture of the moon. "Do you suppose," she babbled at the technician, "that the rise in infertility among so many couples in this country is due to completely different species trying to reproduce?" The technician moved the scanner around and took more pictures. On one view in particular, on Zoë's right side, the technician became suddenly alert, the machine he was operating clicking away.

Zoë stared at the screen. "That must be the growth you found there," suggested Zoë.

"I can't tell you anything," said the technician rigidly. "Your doctor will get the radiologist's report this afternoon and will phone you then."

"I'll be out of town," said Zoë.

"I'm sorry," said the technician.

Driving home, Zoë looked in the rearview mirror and decided she looked— well, how would one describe it? A little wan. She thought of the joke about the guy who visits his doctor and the doctor says, "Well, I'm sorry to say you've got six weeks to live."

"I want a second opinion," says the guy. *You act like your opinion is worth more than everyone else's in the class.*

"You want a second opinion? OK," says the doctor. "You're ugly, too." She liked that joke. She thought it was terribly, terribly funny.

She took a cab to the airport, Jerry the cabbie happy to see her.

"Have fun in New York," he said, getting her bag out of the trunk. He liked her, or at least he always acted as if he did. She called him "Jare."

"Thanks, Jare."

"You know, I'll tell you a secret: I've never been to New York. I'll tell you two secrets: I've never been on a plane." And he waved at her sadly as she pushed her way in through the terminal door. "Or an escalator!" he shouted.

The trick to flying safe, Zoë always said, was never to buy a discount ticket and to tell yourself you had nothing to live for anyway, so that when the plane crashed it was no big deal. Then, when it didn't crash, when you had succeeded in keeping it aloft with your own worthlessness, all you had to do was stagger off, locate your luggage, and, by the time a cab arrived, come up with a persuasive reason to go on living.

"You're here!" shrieked Evan over the doorbell, before she even opened the door. Then she opened it wide. Zoë set her bags on the hall floor and hugged Evan hard. When she was little, Evan had always been affectionate and devoted. Zoë

had always taken care of her, advising, reassuring, until recently, when it seemed   290
Evan had started advising and reassuring *her.* It startled Zoë. She suspected it had
something to do with Zoë's being alone. It made people uncomfortable. "How *are*
you?"

"I threw up on the plane. Besides that, I'm OK."

"Can I get you something? Here, let me take your suitcase. Sick on the plane.
Eeeyew."

"It was into one of those sickness bags," said Zoë, just in case Evan thought
she'd lost it in the aisle. "I was very quiet."

The apartment was spacious and bright, with a view all the way downtown
along the East Side. There was a balcony and sliding glass doors. "I keep forgetting   300
how nice this apartment is. Twentieth floor, doorman . . ." Zoë could work her
whole life and never have an apartment like this. So could Evan. It was Charlie's
apartment. He and Evan lived in it like two kids in a dorm, beer cans and clothes
strewn around. Evan put Zoë's bag away from the mess, over by the fish tank. "I'm
so glad you're here," she said. "Now what can I get you?"

Evan made them a snack—soup from a can, and saltines.

"I don't know about Charlie," she said, after they had finished. "I feel like
we've gone all sexless and middle-aged already."

"Hmmm," said Zoë. She leaned back into Evan's sofa and stared out the window at the dark tops of the buildings. It seemed a little unnatural to live up in the   310
sky like this, like birds that out of some wrongheaded derring-do had nested too
high. She nodded toward the lighted fish tanks and giggled. "I feel like a bird," she
said, "with my own personal supply of fish."

Evan sighed. "He comes home and just sacks out on the sofa, watching fuzzy
football. He's wearing the psychic cold cream and curlers, if you know what I
mean."

Zoë sat up, readjusted the sofa cushions. "What's fuzzy football?"

"We haven't gotten cable yet. Everything comes in fuzzy. Charlie just watches
it that way."

"Hmmm, yeah, that's a little depressing," Zoë said. She looked at her hands.   320
"Especially the part about not having cable."

"This is how he gets into bed at night." Evan stood up to demonstrate. "He
whips all his clothes off, and when he gets to his underwear, he lets it drop to one
ankle. Then he kicks up his leg and flips the underwear in the air and catches it. I,
of course, watch from the bed. There's nothing else. There's just that."

"Maybe you should get it over with and get married."

"Really?"

"Yeah. I mean, you guys probably think living together like this is the best of
both worlds, but . . ." Zoë tried to sound like an older sister; an older sister was
supposed to be the parent you could never have, the hip, cool mom. ". . . I've al-   330
ways found that as soon as you think you've got the best of both worlds"—she
thought now of herself, alone in her house; of the toad-faced cicadas that flew
around like little caped men at night; landing on her screens, staring; of the size
fourteen shoes she placed at the doorstep, to scare off intruders; of the ridiculous
inflatable blow-up doll someone had told her to keep propped up at the breakfast
table—"it can suddenly twist and become the worst of both worlds."

"Really?" Evan was beaming. "Oh, Zoë. I have something to tell you. Charlie and I *are* getting married."

"Really." Zoë felt confused.

"I didn't know how to tell you."   340

"Yes, well, I guess the part about fuzzy football misled me a little."

"I was hoping you'd be my maid of honor," said Evan, waiting. "Aren't you happy for me?"

"Yes," said Zoë, and she began to tell Evan a story about an award-winning violinist at Hilldale-Versailles, how the violinist had come home from a competition in Europe and taken up with a local man, who made her go to all his summer softball games, made her cheer for him from the stands, with the wives, until she later killed herself. But when she got halfway through, to the part about cheering at the softball games, Zoë stopped.

"What?" said Evan. "So what happened?"   350

"Actually, nothing," said Zoë lightly. "She just really got into softball. I mean, really. You should have seen her."

Zoë decided to go to a late-afternoon movie, leaving Evan to chores she needed to do before the party—*I have to do them alone,* she said, a little tense after the violinist story. Zoë thought about going to an art museum, but women alone in art museums had to look good. They always did. Chic and serious, moving languidly, with a great handbag. Instead, she walked over and down through Kips Bay, past an earring boutique called Stick It in Your Ear, past a beauty salon called Dorian Gray's. That was the funny thing about *beauty,* thought Zoë. Look it up in the yellow pages, and you found a hundred entries, hostile with wit, cutesy with   360 warning. But look up *truth*—ha! There was nothing at all.

Zoë thought about Evan getting married. Would Evan turn into Peter Pumpkin Eater's wife? Mrs. Eater? At the wedding would she make Zoë wear some flouncy lavender dress, identical with the other maids'? Zoë hated uniforms, had even, in the first grade, refused to join Elf Girls, because she didn't want to wear the same dress as everyone else. Now she might have to. But maybe she could distinguish it. Hitch it up on one side with a clothespin. Wear surgical gauze at the waist. Clip to her bodice one of those pins that said in loud letters, SHIT HAPPENS.

At the movie—*Death by Number*—she bought strands of red licorice to tug and chew. She took a seat off to one side in the theater. She felt strangely self-   370 conscious sitting alone and hoped for the place to darken fast. When it did, and the coming attractions came on, she reached inside her purse for her glasses. They were in a Baggie. Her Kleenex was also in a Baggie. So was her pen and her aspirin and her mints. Everything was in Baggies. This was what she'd become: *a woman alone at the movies with everything in a Baggie.*

At the halloween party, there were about two dozen people. There were people with ape heads and large hairy hands. There was someone dressed as a leprechaun. There was someone dressed as a frozen dinner. Some man had brought his two small daughters: a ballerina and a ballerina's sister, also dressed as a ballerina. There was a gaggle of sexy witches—women dressed entirely in black, beau-   380 tifully made up and jeweled. "I hate those sexy witches. It's not in the spirit of

Halloween," said Evan. Evan had abandoned the moon mask and dolled herself up as a hausfrau, in curlers and an apron, a decision she now regretted. Charlie, because he liked fish, because he owned fish, collected fish, had decided to go as a fish. He had fins and eyes on the side of his head. "Zoë! How are you! I'm sorry I wasn't here when you first arrived!" He spent the rest of his time chatting up the sexy witches.

"Isn't there something I can help you with here?" Zoë asked her sister. "You've been running yourself ragged." She rubbed her sister's arm, gently, as if she wished they were alone.   390

"Oh, God, not at all," said Evan, arranging stuffed mushrooms on a plate. The timer went off, and she pulled another sheetful out of the oven. "Actually, you know what you can do?"

"What?" Zoë put on her bonehead.

"Meet Earl. He's the guy I had in mind for you. When he gets here, just talk to him a little. He's nice. He's fun. He's going through a divorce."

"I'll try." Zoë groaned. "OK? I'll try." She looked at her watch.

When Earl arrived, he was dressed as a naked woman, steel wool glued strategically to a body stocking, and large rubber breasts protruding like hams.

"Zoë, this is Earl," said Evan.   400

"Good to meet you," said Earl, circling Evan to shake Zoë's hand. He stared at the top of Zoë's head. "Great bone."

Zoë nodded. "Great tits," she said. She looked past him, out the window at the city thrown glitteringly up against the sky; people were saying the usual things: how it looked like jewels, like bracelets and necklaces unstrung. You could see Grand Central station, the clock on the Con Ed building, the red-and-gold-capped Empire State, the Chrysler like a rocket ship dreamed up in a depression. Far west you could glimpse the Astor Plaza, its flying white roof like a nun's habit. "There's beer out on the balcony, Earl—can I get you one?" Zoë asked.

"Sure, uh, I'll come along. Hey, Charlie, how's it going?"   410

Charlie grinned and whistled. People turned to look. "Hey, Earl," someone called, from across the room. "Va-va-va-voom."

They squeezed their way past the other guests, past the apes and the sexy witches. The suction of the sliding door gave way in a whoosh, and Zoë and Earl stepped out onto the balcony, a bonehead and a naked woman, the night air roaring and smoky cool. Another couple was out here, too, murmuring privately. They were not wearing costumes. They smiled at Zoë and Earl. "Hi," said Zoë. She found the plastic-foam cooler, dug into it, and retrieved two beers.

"Thanks," said Earl. His rubber breasts folded inward, dimpled and dented, as he twisted open the bottle.   420

"Well," sighed Zoë anxiously. She had to learn not be afraid of a man, the way, in your childhood, you learned not to be afraid of an earthworm or a bug. Often, when she spoke to men at parties, she rushed things in her mind. As the man politely blathered on, she would fall in love, marry, then find herself in a bitter custody battle with him for the kids and hoping for a reconciliation, so that despite all his betrayals she might no longer despise him, and in the few minutes remaining, learn, perhaps, what his last name was and what he did for a living, though probably there was already too much history between them. She would nod, blush, turn away.

"Evan tells me you're a professor. Where do you teach?"   430

"Just over the Indiana border into Illinois."

He looked a little shocked. "I guess Evan didn't tell me that part."

"She didn't?"

"No."

"Well, that's Evan for you. When we were kids we both had speech impediments."

"That can be tough," said Earl. One of his breasts was hidden behind his drinking arm, but the other shone low and pink, full as a strawberry moon.

"Yes, well, it wasn't a total loss. We used to go to what we called peach pearapy. For about ten years of my life I had to map out every sentence in my mind,   440
way ahead, before I said it. That was the only way I could get a coherent sentence out."

Earl drank from his beer. "How did you do that? I mean, how did you get through?"

"I told a lot of jokes. Jokes you know the lines to already—you can just say them. I love jokes. Jokes and songs."

Earl smiled. He had on lipstick, a deep shade of red, but it was wearing off from the beer. "What's your favorite joke?"

"Uh, my favorite joke is probably . . . OK, all right. This guy goes into a doctor's office and—"   450

"I think I know this one," interrupted Earl, eagerly. He wanted to tell it himself. "A guy goes into a doctor's office, and the doctor tells him he's got some good news and some bad news—that one, right?"

"I'm not sure," said Zoë. "This might be a different version."

"So the guy said, 'Give me the bad news first,' and the doctor says, 'OK. You've got three weeks to live.' And the guy cries, 'Three weeks to live! Doctor, what is the good news?' And the doctor says, 'Did you see that secretary out front? I finally fucked her.' "

Zoë frowned.

"That's not the one you were thinking of?"   460

"No." There was an accusation in her voice. "Mine was different."

"Oh," said Earl. He looked away and then back again. "You teach history, right? What kind of history do you teach?"

"I teach American, mostly—eighteenth and nineteenth century." In graduate school, at bars, the pickup line was always: "So what's your century?"

"Occasionally I teach a special theme course," she added. "say, 'Humor and Personality in the White House.' That's what my book's on." She thought of something someone once told her about bowerbirds, how they build elaborate structures before mating.

"Your book's on *humor*?"   470

"Yeah, and, well, when I teach a theme course like that, I do all the centuries." *So what's your century?*

"All three of them."

"Pardon?" The breeze glistened her eyes. Traffic revved beneath them. She felt high and puny, like someone lifted into heaven by mistake and then spurned.

"Three. There's only three."

"Well, four, really." She was thinking of Jamestown, and of the Pilgrims coming here with buckles and witch hats to say their prayers.

"I'm a photographer," said Earl. His face was starting to gleam, his rouge smearing in a sunset beneath his eyes.

"Do you like that?"

"Well, actually I'm starting to feel it's a little dangerous."

"Really?"

"Spending all your time in a darkroom with that red light and all those chemicals. There's links with Parkinson's, you know."

"No, I didn't."

"I suppose I should wear rubber gloves, but I don't like to. Unless I'm touching it directly, I don't think of it as real."

"Hmmm," said Zoë. Alarm buzzed through her, mildly, like a tea.

"Sometimes, when I have a cut or something, I feel the sting and think, *Shit.* I wash constantly and just hope. I don't like rubber over the skin like that."

"Really."

"I mean, the physical contact. That's what you want, or why bother?"

"I guess," said Zoë. She wished she could think of a joke, something slow and deliberate, with the end in sight. She thought of gorillas, how when they had been kept too long alone in cages, they would smack each other in the head instead of mating.

"Are you . . . in a relationship?" Earl suddenly blurted.

"Now? As we speak?"

"Well, I mean, I'm sure you have a relationship to your *work.*" A smile, a weird one, nestled in his mouth like an egg. She thought of zoos in parks, how when cities were under siege, during world wars, people ate the animals. "But I mean, with a *man.*"

"No, I'm not in a relationship with a *man.*" She rubbed her chin with her hand and could feel the one bristly hair there. "But my last relationship was with a very sweet man," she said. She made something up. "From Switzerland. He was a botanist—a weed expert. His name was Jerry. I called him 'Jare.' He was so funny. You'd go to the movies with him and all he would notice were the plants. He would never pay attention to the plot. Once, in a jungle movie, he started rattling off all these Latin names, out loud. It was very exciting for him." She paused, caught her breath. "Eventually he went back to Europe to, uh, study the edelweiss." She looked at Earl. "Are you involved in a relationship? With a *woman?*"

Earl shifted his weight, and the creases in his body stocking changed, splintering outward like something broken. His pubic hair slid over to one hip, like a corsage on a saloon girl. "No," he said, clearing his throat. The steel wool in his underarms was inching toward his biceps. "I've just gotten out of a marriage that was full of bad dialogue, like 'You want more *space?* I'll give you more space!' *Clonk.* Your basic Three Stooges."

Zoë looked at him sympathetically. "I suppose it's hard for love to recover after that."

His eyes lit up. He wanted to talk about love. "But *I* keep thinking love should be like a tree. You look at trees and they've got bumps and scars from tumors, infestations, what have you, but they're still growing. Despite the bumps and bruises, they're . . . *straight*."

"Yeah, well," said Zoë, "where I'm from, they're all married or gay. Did you see that movie *Death by Number*?"

Earl looked at her, a little lost. She was getting away from him. "No," he said.

One of his breasts had slipped under his arm, tucked there like a baguette. She kept thinking of trees, of gorillas and parks, of people in wartime eating the zebras. She felt a stabbing pain in her abdomen.   530

"Want some hors d'oeuvres?" Evan came pushing through the sliding door. She was smiling, though her curlers were coming out, hanging bedraggled at the ends of her hair like Christmas decorations, like food put out for the birds. She thrust forward a plate of stuffed mushrooms.

"Are you asking for donations or giving them away," said Earl, wittily. He liked Evan, and he put his arm around her.

"You know, I'll be right back," said Zoë.

"Oh," said Evan, looking concerned.

"Right back. I promise."

Zoë hurried inside, across the living room, into the bedroom, to the adjoin-   540
ing bath. It was empty; most of the guests were using the half bath near the kitchen. She flicked on the light and closed the door. The pain had stopped and she didn't really have to go to the bathroom, but she stayed there anyway, resting. In the mirror above the sink she looked haggard beneath her bonehead, violet grays showing under the skin like a plucked and pocky bird. She leaned closer, raising her chin a little to find the bristly hair. It was there, at the end of the jaw, sharp and dark as a wire. She opened the medicine cabinet, pawed through it until she found some tweezers. She lifted her head again and poked at her face with the metal tips, grasping and pinching and missing. Outside the door she could hear two people talking low. They had come into the bedroom and were discussing   550
something. They were sitting on the bed. One of them giggled in a false way. She stabbed again at her chin, and it started to bleed a little. She pulled the skin tight along the jawbone, gripped the tweezers hard around what she hoped was the hair, and tugged. A tiny square of skin came away with it, but the hair remained, blood bright at the root of it. Zoë clenched her teeth. "Come on," she whispered. The couple outside in the bedroom were now telling stories, softly, and laughing. There was a bounce and squeak of mattress, and the sound of a chair being moved out of the way. Zoë aimed the tweezers carefully, pinched, then pulled gently away, and this time the hair came, too, with a slight twinge of pain and then a great flood of relief. "Yeah!" breathed Zoë. She grabbed some toilet paper and dabbed at   560
her chin. It came away spotted with blood, and she tore off some more and pressed hard until it stopped. Then she turned off the light and opened the door, to return to the party. "Excuse me," she said to the couple in the bedroom. They were the couple from the balcony, and they looked at her, a bit surprised. They had their arms around each other, and they were eating candy bars.

Earl was still on the balcony, alone, and Zoë rejoined him there.

"Hi," she said. He turned around and smiled. He had straightened his cos-

tume out a bit, though all the secondary sex characteristics seemed slightly
doomed, destined to shift and slip and zip around again any moment.

"Are you OK?" he asked. He had opened another beer and was chugging.   570

"Oh, yeah. I just had to go to the bathroom." She paused. "Actually I have
been going to a lot of doctors recently."

"What's wrong?" asked Earl.

"Oh, probably nothing. But they're putting me through tests." She sighed.
"I've had sonograms, I've had mammograms. Next week I'm going in for a candy-
gram." He looked at her worriedly. "I've had too many gram words," she said.

"Here, I saved you these." He held out a napkin with two stuffed mushroom
caps. They were cold and leaving oil marks on the napkin.

"Thanks," said Zoë, and pushed them both in her mouth. "Watch," she said,
with her mouth full. "With my luck, it'll be a gallbladder operation."   580

Earl made a face. "So your sister's getting married," he said, changing the
subject. "Tell me, really, what you think about love."

"*Love?*" Hadn't they done this already? "I don't know." She chewed thoughtfully and swallowed. "All right. I'll tell you what I think about love. Here is a love
story. This friend of mine—"

"You've got something on your chin," said Earl, and he reached over to touch it.

"*What?*" said Zoë, stepping back. She turned her face away and grabbed at
her chin. A piece of toilet paper peeled off it, like tape. "It's nothing," she said. "It's
just—it's nothing."

Earl stared at her.   590

"At any rate," she continued, "this friend of mine was this award winning violinist. She traveled all over Europe and won competitions; she made records, she
gave concerts, she got famous. But she had no social life. So one day she threw
herself at the feet of this conductor she had a terrible crush on. He picked her up,
scolded her gently, and sent her back to her hotel room. After that she came home
from Europe. She went back to her old hometown, stopped playing the violin, and
took up with a local boy. This was in Illinois. He took her to some Big Ten bar
every night to drink with his buddies from the team. He used to say things like
"Katrina here likes to play the violin," and then he'd pinch her cheek. When she
once suggested that they go home, he said, 'What, you think you're too famous for   600
a place like this? Well, let me tell you something. You may think you're famous,
but you're not *famous* famous.' Two famouses. 'No one here's ever heard of you.'
Then he went up and bought a round of drinks for everyone but her. She got her
coat, went home, and shot a gun through her head."

Earl was silent.

"That's the end of my love story," said Zoë.

"You're not at all like your sister," said Earl.

"Ho, really," said Zoë. The air had gotten colder, the wind singing minor and
thick as a dirge.

"No." He didn't want to talk about love anymore. "You know, you should   610
wear a lot of blue—blue and white—around your face. It would bring out your
coloring." He reached an arm out to show her how the blue bracelet he was wearing might look against her skin, but she swatted it away.

"Tell me, Earl. Does the word *fag* mean anything to you?"

He stepped back, away from her. He shook his head in disbelief. "You know, I just shouldn't try to go out with career women. You're all stricken. A guy can really tell what life has done to you. I do better with women who have part-time jobs."

"Oh, yes?" said Zoë. She had once read an article entitled "Professional Women and the Demographics of Grief." Or no, it was a poem: *If there were a lake,* the moonlight would dance across it in conniptions. She remembered that line. But perhaps the title was "The Empty House: Aesthetics of Barrenness." Or maybe "Space Gypsies: Girls in Academe." She had forgotten.

Earl turned and leaned on the railing of the balcony. It was getting late. Inside the party guests were beginning to leave. The sexy witches were already gone. "Live and learn," Earl murmured.

"Live and get dumb," replied Zoë. Beneath them on Lexington there were no cars, just the gold rush of an occasional cab. He leaned hard on his elbows, brooding.

"Look at those few people down there," he said. "They look like bugs. You know how bugs are kept under control? They're sprayed with bug hormones, female bug hormones. The male bugs get so crazy in the presence of this hormone, they're screwing everything in sight: trees, rocks—everything but female bugs. Population control. That's what's happening in the country," he said drunkenly. "Hormones sprayed around, and now men are screwing rocks. Rocks!"

In the back the Magic Marker line of his buttocks spread wide, a sketchy black on pink like a funnies page. Zoë came up, slow, from behind and gave him a shove. His arms slipped forward, off the railing, out over the city below. Beer spilled out of his bottle, raining twenty stories down to the street.

"Hey, what are you doing?!" he said, whipping around. He stood straight and readied and moved away from the railing, sidestepping Zoë. "What the *hell* are you doing?"

"Just kidding," she said. "I was just kidding." But he gazed at her, appalled and frightened, his Magic Marker buttocks turned away now toward all of downtown, a naked pseudowoman with a blue bracelet at the wrist, trapped out on a balcony with—with *what*? *"Really, I was just kidding!"* Zoë shouted. The wind lifted the hair up off her head, skyward in spines behind the bone. If there were a lake, the moonlight would dance across it in conniptions. She smiled at him, and wondered how she looked.   [1988]

Questions for Discussion and Writing

1. Zoë seems to be out of place in most situations. Why? Is there something wrong with her, or is there something wrong with the people around her? Explain.
2. Would Zoë's problems be solved by marriage and children? Why or why not?
3. Other people in the story—the students, the men, for example—expect things from Zoë that she seems unable to give. What do they want from her?
4. Why is Zoë always cracking jokes? Is the story itself an elaborate joke, or does it have something serious to say about contemporary life? Explain.
5. Why does Zoë shove Earl? Is she just kidding? Explain.

6. What does Zoë's Halloween costume say about her? Is she a bonehead? What does Earl's costume say about him?

7. Why do you think the author selected the title she did—the punch line of a doctor joke—for this story?

8. Why does Zoë tell the story of the violinist to her sister and to Earl? Why do you think the anecdote seems so significant to Zoë?

❧ AMY TAN

(b. 1952)

Two Kinds

Amy Tan was born in Oakland, California, in 1952. Her father, who was educated in Beijing and worked for the United States Information Service after the war, immigrated to America in 1947. Her mother came to the United States in 1949, shortly before the Communists seized control of Shanghai; she was forced to leave behind three daughters from a previous marriage.

Ms. Tan grew up in Fresno, Oakland, and Berkeley, as well as the suburbs of the San Francisco Bay Area. When she was fourteen, her father and older brother both died of brain tumors. Following this double tragedy, her mother took Amy and her younger brother to live in Europe, where she graduated from high school in Montreux, Switzerland, in 1969. From 1969 to 1976, Ms. Tan attended five colleges: Linfield College in McMinnville, Oregon, where she met her husband, Lou DeMattei; San Jose City College; San Jose State University, from which she received a B.A. with a double major in English and Linguistics; University of California Santa Cruz; and UC Berkeley.

Prior to writing fiction, Ms. Tan worked as a language development consultant to programs serving developmentally disabled children. In 1983, she became a freelance business writer for various companies, such as IBM, AT&T, and Apple Computers.

In 1985, Ms. Tan attended a writing workshop, for which she wrote the story "Rules of the Game," which later became part of *The Joy Luck Club*. Her first work of fiction, *The Joy Luck Club*, was published by G. P. Putnam's Sons in 1989, and became one of the longest running best-sellers on *The New York Times* best-seller list in 1989. It was also a finalist for the National Book Award and the National Book Critics Circle Award. It received the Bay Area Book Reviewers Award for Fiction and the Commonwealth Club Gold Award. The book has been translated into more than 20 languages, including Chinese.

Her second book, a novel, *The Kitchen God's Wife*, was published in 1991, and was soon the number-one best-seller on *The New York Times* hardcover list. It also appeared on the Canadian, British, Australian, Danish, Spanish, Norwegian, and German best-seller lists.

In 1995, Putnam published Ms. Tan's novel *The Hundred Secret Senses*. It appeared immediately on *The New York Times* best-seller list, where it remained for several months. It was short-listed for the Bay Area Book Reviewers' prize.

Ms. Tan's stories have appeared in *The Atlantic, Grand Street, Lear's, McCall's, Ladies Home Journal, The New Yorker,* and other magazines, as well as numerous anthologies. Her essay "Mother Tongue" was published in *The Threepenny Review* and was selected for the 1991 edition of *Best American Essays.* Her books are assigned reading in many high schools and colleges. *The Joy Luck Club* was selected for the literature portion of the 1992–3 Academic Decathlon, a national scholastic competition for high school students.

Amy Tan and illustrator Gretchen Schields have published two books for children, *The Moon Lady* and *The Siamese Cat.* Ms. Tan co-wrote the screenplay to *The Joy Luck Club* with Ron Bass, and co-produced the Disney/Hollywood Pictures film with Mr. Bass and director Wayne Wang. Ms. Tan has been a resident at the Yaddo Colony, and is a council member of PEN American Center and the Squaw Valley Community of Writers. She lives in San Francisco and New York.

(Biographical information provided by Putnam Publishing Group.)

M Y MOTHER BELIEVED you could be anything you wanted to be in America. You could open a restaurant. You could work for the government and get good retirement. You could buy a house with almost no money down. You could become rich. You could become instantly famous.

"Of course you can be prodigy, too," my mother told me when I was nine. "You can be best anything. What does Auntie Lindo know? Her daughter, she is only best tricky."

America was where all my mother's hopes lay. She had come here in 1949 after losing everything in China: her mother and father, her family home, her first husband, and two daughters, twin baby girls. But she never looked back with re- 10 gret. There were so many ways for things to get better.

We didn't immediately pick the right kind of prodigy. At first my mother thought I could be a Chinese Shirley Temple.[1] We'd watch Shirley's old movies on TV as though they were training films. My mother would poke my arm and say, "Ni Kan"—You watch. And I would see Shirley tapping her feet, or singing a sailor song, or pursing her lips into a very round O while saying "Oh my goodness."

"Ni Kan," said my mother as Shirley's eyes flooded with tears. "You already know how. Don't need talent for crying!"

Soon after my mother got this idea about Shirley Temple, she took me to a beauty training school in the Mission district and put me in the hands of a student 20 who could barely hold the scissors without shaking. Instead of getting big fat curls, I emerged with an uneven mass of crinkly black fuzz. My mother dragged me off to the bathroom and tried to wet down my hair.

"You look like Negro Chinese," she lamented, as if I had done this on purpose.

The instructor of the beauty training school had to lop off these soggy clumps to make my hair even again. "Peter Pan is very popular these days," the in-

---

1. A child film star of the 1930s.

structor assured my mother. I now had hair the length of a boy's, with straight-across bangs that hung at a slant two inches above my eyebrows. I liked the hair-cut and it made me actually look forward to my future fame.

In fact, in the beginning, I was just as excited as my mother, maybe even more so. I pictured this prodigy part of me as many different images, trying each one on for size. I was a dainty ballerina girl standing by the curtains, waiting to hear the right music that would send me floating on my tiptoes. I was like the Christ child lifted out of the straw manger, crying with holy indignity. I was Cinderella stepping from her pumpkin carriage with sparkly cartoon music filling the air.

In all of my imaginings, I was filled with a sense that I would soon become *perfect.* My mother and father would adore me. I would be beyond reproach. I would never feel the need to sulk for anything.

But sometimes the prodigy in me became impatient. "If you don't hurry up and get out of here, I'm disappearing for good," it warned. "And then you'll always be nothing."

Every night after dinner, my mother and I would sit at the Formica kitchen table. She would present new tests, taking her examples from stories of amazing children she had read in *Ripley's Believe It or Not,* or *Good Housekeeping, Reader's Digest,* and a dozen other magazines she kept in a pile in our bathroom. My mother got these magazines from people whose houses she cleaned. And since she cleaned many houses each week, we had a great assortment. She would look through them all, searching for stories about remarkable children.

The first night she brought out a story about a three-year old boy who knew the capitals of all the states and even most of the European countries. A teacher was quoted as saying the little boy could also pronounce the names of the foreign cities correctly.

"What's the capital of Finland?" my mother asked me, looking at the maga-zine story.

All I knew was the capital of California, because Sacramento was the name of the street we lived on in Chinatown. "Nairobi!" I guessed, saying the most for-eign word I could think of. She checked to see if that was possibly one way to pro-nounce "Helsinki" before showing the answer.

The tests got harder—multiplying numbers in my head, finding the queen of hearts in a deck of cards, trying to stand on my head without using my hands, predicting the daily temperatures in Los Angeles, New York, and London.

One night I had to look at a page from the Bible for three minutes and then report everything I could remember. "Now Jehoshaphat had riches and honor in abundance and . . . that's all I remember, Ma," I said.

And after seeing my mother's disappointed face once again, something inside of me began to die. I hated the tests, the raised hopes and failed expectations. Before going to bed that night I looked in the mirror above the bathroom sink and when I saw only my face staring back—and that it would always be this ordinary face—I began to cry. Such a sad, ugly girl! I made high-pitched noises like a crazed animal, trying to scratch out the face in the mirror.

And then I saw what seemed to be the prodigy side of me—because I had never seen that face before. I looked at my reflection, blinking so I could see more clearly. The girl staring back at me was angry, powerful. This girl and I were the same. I had new thoughts, willful thoughts, or rather thoughts filled with lots of won'ts. I won't let her change me, I promised myself. I won't be what I'm not.

So now on nights when my mother presented her tests, I performed listlessly, my head propped on one arm. I pretended to be bored. And I was. I got so bored I started counting the bellows of the foghorns out on the bay while my mother drilled me in other areas. The sound was comforting and reminded me of the cow jumping over the moon. And the next day, I played a game with myself, seeing if my mother would give up on me before eight bellows. After a while I usually counted only one, maybe two bellows at most. At last she was beginning to give up hope.

Two or three months had gone by without any mention of my being a prodigy again. And then one day my mother was watching *The Ed Sullivan Show*[2] on TV. The TV was old and the sound kept shorting out. Every time my mother got halfway up from the sofa to adjust the set, the sound would go back on and Ed would be talking. As soon as she sat down, Ed would go silent again. She got up, the TV broke into loud piano music. She sat down. Silence. Up and down, back and forth, quiet and loud. It was like a stiff embraceless dance between her and the TV set. Finally she stood by the set with her hand on the sound dial.

She seemed entranced by the music, a little frenzied piano piece with this mesmerizing quality, sort of quick passages and then teasing lilting ones before it returned to the quick playful parts.

"*Ni kan*," my mother said, calling me over with hurried hand gestures, "Look here."

I could see why my mother was fascinated by the music. It was being pounded out by a little Chinese girl, about nine years old, with a Peter Pan haircut. The girl had the sauciness of a Shirley Temple. She was proudly modest like a proper Chinese child. And she also did this fancy sweep of a curtsy, so that the fluffy skirt of her white dress cascaded slowly to the floor like the petals of a large carnation.

In spite of these warning signs, I wasn't worried. Our family had no piano and we couldn't afford to buy one, let alone reams of sheet music and piano lessons. So I could be generous in my comments when my mother bad-mouthed the little girl on TV.

"Play note right, but doesn't sound good! No singing sound," complained my mother.

"What are you picking on her for?" I said carelessly, "She's pretty good. Maybe she's not the best, but she's trying hard." I knew almost immediately I would be sorry I said that.

"Just like you," she said. "Not the best. Because you not trying." She gave a little huff as she let go of the sound dial and sat down on the sofa.

The little Chinese girl sat down also to play an encore of "Anitra's Dance" by Grieg. I remember the song, because later on I had to learn how to play it.

Three days after watching *The Ed Sullivan Show*, my mother told me what my schedule would be for piano lessons and piano practice. She had talked to Mr.

2. A weekly variety show.

Chong, who lived on the first floor of our apartment building. Mr. Chong was a retired piano teacher and my mother had traded housecleaning services for weekly lessons and a piano for me to practice on every day, two hours a day, from four until six.   120

When my mother told me this, I felt as though I had been sent to hell. I whined and then kicked my foot a little when I couldn't stand it anymore.

"Why don't you like me that way I am? I'm *not* a genius! I can't play piano. And even if I could, I wouldn't go on TV if you paid me a million dollars!" I cried.

My mother slapped me. "Who ask you be genius?" she shouted. "Only ask you be your best. For you sake. You think I want you be genius? Hnnh! What for! Who ask you!"

"So ungrateful," I heard her mutter in Chinese. "If she had as much talent as she has temper, she would be famous now."

Mr. Chong, whom I secretly nicknamed Old Chong, was very strange, always 130 tapping his fingers to the silent music of an invisible orchestra. He looked ancient in my eyes. He had lost most of the hair on top of his head and he wore thick glasses and had eyes that always looked tired and sleepy. But he must have been younger than I thought, since he lived with his mother and was not yet married.

I met Old Lady Chong once and that was enough. She had this peculiar smell like a baby that had done something in its pants. And her fingers felt like a dead person's, like an old peach I once found in the back of the refrigerator; the skin just slid off the meat when I picked it up.

I soon found out why Old Chong had retired from teaching piano. He was deaf. "Like Beethoven!" he shouted to me. "We're both listening only in our head!" 140 And he would start to conduct his frantic silent sonatas.

Our lessons went like this. He would open the book and point to different things, explaining their purpose: "Key! Treble! Bass! No sharps or flats! So this is C major! Listen now and play after me!"

And then he would play the C scale a few times, a simple chord, and then, as if inspired by an old, unreachable itch, he gradually added more notes and running trills and a pounding bass until the music was really something quite grand.

I would play after him, the simple scale, the simple chord, and then I just played some nonsense that sounded like a cat running up and down on top of garbage cans. Old Chong smiled and applauded and then said, "Very good! But 150 now you must learn to keep time!"

So that's how I discovered that Old Chong's eyes were too slow to keep up with the wrong notes I was playing. He went through the motions in half-time. To help me keep rhythm, he stood behind me, pushing down on my right shoulder for every beat. He balanced pennies on top of my wrists so I would keep them still as I slowly played scales and arpeggios. He had me curve my hand around an apple and keep that shape when playing chords. He marched stiffly to show me how to make each finger dance up and down, staccato like an obedient little soldier.

He taught me all these things, and that was how I also learned I could be lazy and get away with mistakes, lots of mistakes. If I hit the wrong notes because 160 I hadn't practiced enough, I never corrected myself. I just kept playing in rhythm. And Old Chong kept conducting his own private reverie.

So maybe I never really gave myself a fair chance. I did pick up the basics pretty quickly, and I might have become a good pianist at that young age. But I was so determined not to try, not to be anybody different, that I learned to play only the most ear-splitting preludes, the most discordant hymns.

Over the next year, I practiced like this, dutifully in my own way. And then one day I heard my mother and her friend Lindo Jong both talking in a loud bragging tone of voice so others could hear. It was after church, and I was leaning against the brick wall wearing a dress with stiff white petticoats. Auntie Lindo's daughter, Waverly, who was about my age, was standing farther down the wall about five feet away. We had grown up together and shared all the closeness of two sisters squabbling over crayons and dolls. In other words, for the most part, we hated each other. I thought she was snotty. Waverly Jong had gained a certain amount of fame as "Chinatown's Littlest Chinese Chess Champion."

"She bring home too many trophy," lamented Auntie Lindo that Sunday. "All day she play chess. All day I have no time do nothing but dust off her winnings." She threw a scolding look at Waverly, who pretended not to see her.

"You lucky you don't have this problem," said Auntie Lindo with a sigh to my mother.

And my mother squared her shoulders and bragged: "Our problem worser than yours. If we ask Jing-mei wash dish, she hear nothing but music. It's like you can't stop this natural talent."

And right then, I was determined to put a stop to her foolish pride.

A few weeks later, Old Chong and my mother conspired to have me play in a talent show which would be held in the church hall. By then, my parents had saved up enough to buy me a secondhand piano, a black Wurlitzer spinet with a scarred bench. It was the showpiece of our living room.

For the talent show, I was to play a piece called "Pleading Child" from Schumann's *Scenes from Childhood*. It was a simple, moody piece that sounded more difficult than it was. I was supposed to memorize the whole thing, playing the repeat parts twice to make the piece sound longer. But I dawdled over it, playing a few bars and then cheating, looking up to see what notes followed. I never really listened to what I was playing. I daydreamed about being somewhere else, about being someone else.

The part I liked to practice best was the fancy curtsy: right foot out, touch the rose on the carpet with a pointed foot, sweep to the side, left leg bends, look up and smile.

My parents invited all the couples from the Joy Luck Club to witness my debut. Auntie Lindo and Uncle Tin were there. Waverly and her two older brothers had also come. The first two rows were filled with children both younger and older than I was. The littlest ones got to go first. They recited simple nursery rhymes, squawked out tunes on miniature violins, twirled Hula Hoops, pranced in pink ballet tutus, and when they bowed or curtsied, the audience would sigh in unison, "Awww," and then clap enthusiastically.

When my turn came, I was very confident. I remember my childish excitement. It was as if I knew, without a doubt, that the prodigy side of me really did exist. I had no fear whatsoever, no nervousness. I remember thinking to myself, This is it! This is it! I looked out over the audience, at my mother's blank face, my father's yawn, Auntie Lindo's stiff-lipped smile, Waverly's sulky expression. I had on a white dress layered with sheets of lace, and a pink bow in my Peter Pan haircut. As I sat down I envisioned people jumping to their feet and Ed Sullivan rushing up to introduce me to everyone on TV.

And I started to play. It was so beautiful. I was so caught up in how lovely I looked that at first I didn't worry how I would sound. So it was a surprise to me when I hit the first wrong note and I realized something didn't sound quite right. And then I hit another and another followed that. A chill started at the top of my head and began to trickle down. Yet I couldn't stop playing, as though my hands were bewitched. I kept thinking my fingers would adjust themselves back, like a train switching to the right track. I played this strange jumble through two re-   220
peats, the sour notes staying with me all the way to the end.

When I stood up, I discovered my legs were shaking. Maybe I had just been nervous and the audience like Old Chong had seen me go through the right motions and had not heard anything wrong at all. I swept my right foot out, went down on my knee, looked up and smiled. The room was quiet, except for Old Chong, who was beaming and shouting, "Bravo! Bravo! Well done!" But then I saw my mother's face, her stricken face. The audience clapped weakly, and as I walked back to my chair, with my whole face quivering as I tried not to cry, I heard a little boy whisper loudly to his mother, "That was awful," and the mother whispered back, "Well, she certainly tried."   230

And now I realized how many people were in the audience, the whole world it seemed. I was aware of eyes burning into my back. I felt the shame of my mother and father as they sat stiffly throughout the rest of the show.

We could have escaped during intermission. Pride and some strange sense of honor must have anchored my parents to their chairs. And so we watched it all: the eighteen-year-old boy with a fake mustache who did a magic show and juggled flaming hoops while riding a unicycle. The breasted girl with white makeup who sang from *Madame Butterfly*[3], and got honorable mention. And the eleven-year-old boy who won first prize playing a tricky violin song that sounded like a busy bee.

After the show, The Hsus, the Jongs, and the St. Clairs from the Joy Luck   240
Club came up to my mother and father.

"Lots of talented kids," Auntie Lindo said vaguely, smiling broadly.

"That was somethin' else," said my father and I wondered if he was referring to me in a humorous way, or whether he even remembered what I had done.

Waverly looked at me and shrugged her shoulders. "You aren't a genius like me," she said matter-of-factly. And if I hadn't felt so bad, I would have pulled her braids and punched her stomach.

But my mother's expression was what devastated me: a quiet blank look that said she had lost everything. I felt the same way, and it seemed as if everybody were now coming up, like gawkers at the scene of an accident, to see what parts   250
were actually missing. When we got on the bus to go home, my father was humming the busy-bee tune and my mother was silent. I kept thinking she wanted to wait until we got home before shouting at me. But when my father unlocked the door to our apartment, my mother walked in and then went to the back, into the bedroom. No accusations. No blame. And in a way, I felt disappointed. I had been waiting for her to start shouting, so I could shout back and cry and blame her for all my misery.

---

3. An opera by Giacomo Puccini (1858–1904).

I assumed my talent-show fiasco meant I never had to play the piano again. But two days later, after school, my mother came out of the kitchen and saw me watching TV.

"Four clock," she reminded me as if it were any other day. I was stunned, as though, she were asking me to go through the talent-show torture again. I wedged myself more tightly in front of the TV.

"Turn off TV," she called from the kitchen five minutes later.

I didn't budge. And then I decided. I didn't have to do what my mother said anymore. I wasn't her slave. This wasn't China. I had listened to her before and look what happened. She was the stupid one.

She came out from the kitchen and stood in the arched entryway of the living room. "Four clock," she said once again, louder.

"I'm not going to play anymore," I said nonchalantly. "Why should I? I'm not a genius."

She walked over and stood in front of the TV. I saw her chest was heaving up and down in an angry way.

"No!" I said, and I now felt stronger, as if my true self had finally emerged. So this was what had been inside me all along.

"No! I won't!" I screamed.

She yanked me by the arm, pulled me off the floor, snapped off the TV. She was frighteningly strong, half pulling, half carrying me toward the piano as I kicked the throw rugs under my feet. She lifted me up and onto the hard bench. I was sobbing by now, looking at her bitterly. Her chest was heaving even more and her mouth was open, smiling crazily as if she were pleased I was crying.

"You want me to be someone that I'm not!" I sobbed. "I'll never be the kind of daughter you want me to be!"

"Only two kinds of daughters," she shouted in Chinese. "Those who are obedient and those who follow their own mind! Only one kind of daughter can live in this house. Obedient daughter!"

"Then I wish I wasn't your daughter. I wish you weren't my mother," I shouted. As I said these things I got scared. It felt like worms and toads and slimy things crawling out of my chest, but it also felt good, as if this awful side of me had surfaced, at last.

"Too late change this," said my mother shrilly.

And I could sense her anger rising to its breaking point. I wanted to see it spill over. And that's when I remembered the babies she had lost in China, the ones we never talked about. "Then I wish I'd never been born!" I shouted. "I wish I were dead! Like them."

It was as if I had said the magic words. Alakazam!—and her face went blank, her mouth closed, her arms went slack, and she backed out of the room, stunned, as if she were blowing away like a small brown leaf, thin, brittle, lifeless.

It was not the only disappointment my mother felt in me. In the years that followed, I failed her so many times, each time asserting my own will, my right to fall short of expectations. I didn't get straight As. I didn't become class president. I didn't get into Stanford. I dropped out of college.

For unlike my mother, I did not believe I could be anything I wanted to be. I could only be me.

And for all those years, we never talked about the disaster at the recital or my terrible accusations afterward at the piano bench. All that remained unchecked, like a betrayal that was now unspeakable. So I never found a way to ask her why she had hoped for something so large that failure was inevitable.

And even worse, I never asked her what frightened her the most: Why had she given up hope?   310

For after our struggle at the piano, she never mentioned my playing again. The lessons stopped. The lid to the piano was closed, shutting out the dust, my misery, and her dreams.

So she surprised me. A few years ago, she offered to give me the piano, for my thirtieth birthday. I had not played in all those years. I saw the offer as a sign of forgiveness, a tremendous burden removed.

"Are you sure?" I asked shyly. "I mean won't you and Dad miss it?"

"No, this your piano," she said firmly. "Always your piano. You only one can play."

"Well, I probably can't play anymore," I said. "It's been years."   320

"You pick up fast," said my mother, as if she knew this was certain. "You have natural talent. You could been genius if you want to."

"No I couldn't."

"You just not trying," said my mother. And she was neither angry nor sad. She said it as if to announce a fact that could never be disproved. "Take it," she said.

But I didn't at first. It was enough that she had offered it to me. And after that, every time I saw it in my parents' living room, standing in front of the bay windows, it made me feel proud, as if it were a shiny trophy I had won back.

Last week I sent a tuner over to my parents' apartment and had the piano re-conditioned, for purely sentimental reasons. My mother had died a few months   330 before and I had been getting things in order for my father, a little bit at a time. I put the jewelry in special silk pouches. The sweaters she had knitted in yellow, pink, bright orange—all the colors I hated—I put those in moth-proof boxes. I found some old Chinese silk dresses, the kind with little slits up the sides. I rubbed the old silk against my skin, then wrapped them in tissue and decided to take them home with me.

After I had the piano tuned, I opened the lid and touched the keys. It sounded even richer than I remembered. Really, it was a very good piano. Inside the bench were the same exercise notes with handwritten scales, the same second-hand music books with their covers held together with yellow tape.   340

I opened up the Schumann book to the dark little piece I had played at the recital. It was on the left-hand side of the page, "Pleading Child." It looked more difficult than I remembered. I played a few bars, surprised at how easily the notes came back to me.

And for the first time, or so it seemed, I noticed the piece on the right-hand side. It was called "Perfectly Contented." I tried to play this one as well. It had a lighter melody but the same flowing rhythm and turned out to be quite easy. "Pleading Child" was shorter but slower, "Perfectly Contented" was longer, but faster. And after I played them both a few times, I realized they were two halves of the same song.   [1989]   350

For Discussion and Writing

1. Why does the narrator's mother want her to excel at something?
2. Is the narrator right to ask her mother, "Why don't you like me the way I am? I'm *not* a genius"? Explain.
3. Is the mother right to say, "Who ask you be genius? . . . Only ask you be your best. For you sake"?
4. The narrator says she doesn't try to learn the piano because she was determined "not to be anybody different." Does this sound like a plausible motive? Why or why not?
5. Why does the narrator say of the piano, "And after that, every time I saw it in my parents' living room, standing in front of the bay windows, it made me feel proud, as if it were a shiny trophy I had won back"?
6. What does the ending mean? In what way are "Pleading Child" and "Perfectly Contented" two halves of the same song?

✒ ISABEL ALLENDE

(b. 1942)

TRANSLATED BY MARGARET SAYERS PEDEN

And of Clay We Are Created

With the publication of *House of Spirits* (1982, translated into English, 1985), Isabel Allende burst onto the international literary scene. She has since become Latin America's best known and most widely read woman author.

Allende was born in Lima, Peru, where her father, a cousin of the Chilean President Salvadore Allende, was serving as a diplomat. Two years later, her parents divorced, but her mother married another diplomat, with the result that Isabel spent her childhood and youth in Europe and the Middle East, as well as in Latin America. After high school, Allende worked as a secretary for America's Food and Agricultural Organization and then turned to journalism, rising rapidly to become editor of an influential women's magazine and a television host in Chile.

The turning point in her life, as she herself says, occurred when a U.S-backed coup assassinated her uncle and replaced him with a military dictator. For a time, Allende retained her positions and worked with those opposing Pinochet's oppressive government, but in 1975 she was forced to flee Chile and work in Venezuela. Her first novel began as a letter to her dying grandfather in Chile and was repeatedly rejected until a publisher in Spain agreed to release it in 1982. Since then, all four of her novels have been international best-sellers.

Allende's novels are strongly political and feminist in nature; her short stories somewhat less so. For Allende, writing is not only an act of defiance against political and sexual oppression, but also an act of hope—a way to use language to preserve love and a living sense of the past.

T HEY DISCOVERED the girl's head protruding from the mudpit, eyes wide open, 10
calling soundlessly. She had a First Communion name, Azucena. Lily. In that
vast cemetery where the odor of death was already attracting vultures from far
away, and where the weeping of orphans and wails of the injured filled the air, the
little girl obstinately clinging to life became the symbol of the tragedy. The television cameras transmitted so often the unbearable image of the head budding like a
black squash from the clay that there was no one who did not recognize her and
know her name. And every time we saw her on the screen, right behind her was
Rolf Carlé, who had gone there on assignment, never suspecting that he would
find a fragment of his past, lost thirty years before.

First a subterranean sob rocked the cotton fields, curling them like waves of 20
foam. Geologists had set up their seismographs weeks before and knew that the
mountain had awakened again. For some time they had predicted that the heat of
the eruption could detach the eternal ice from the slopes of the volcano, but no
one heeded their warnings; they sounded like the tales of frightened old women.
The towns in the valley went about their daily life, deaf to the moaning of the
earth, until that fateful Wednesday night in November when a prolonged roar announced the end of the world, and walls of snow broke loose, rolling in an
avalanche of clay, stones, and water that descended on the villages and buried
them beneath unfathomable meters of telluric[1] vomit. As soon as the survivors
emerged from the paralysis of that first awful terror, they could see that houses, 30
plazas, churches, white cotton plantations, dark coffee forests, cattle pastures—all
had disappeared. Much later, after soldiers and volunteers had arrived to rescue
the living and try to assess the magnitude of the cataclysm, it was calculated that
beneath the mud lay more than twenty thousand human beings and an indefinite
number of animals putrefying in a viscous soup. Forests and rivers had also been
swept away, and there was nothing to be seen but an immense desert of mire.

When the station called before dawn, Rolf Carlé and I were together. I
crawled out of bed, dazed with sleep, and went to prepare coffee while he hurriedly dressed. He stuffed his gear in the green canvas backpack he always carried,
and we said goodbye, as we had so many times before. I had no presentiments. I 40
sat in the kitchen, sipping my coffee and planning the long hours without him,
sure that he would be back the next day.

He was one of the first to reach the scene, because while other reporters
were fighting their way to the edges of that morass in jeeps, bicycles, or on foot,
each getting there however he could, Rolf Carlé had the advantage of the television
helicopter, which flew him over the avalanche. We watched on our screens the
footage captured by his assistant's camera, in which he was up to his knees in
muck, a microphone in his hand, in the midst of a bedlam of lost children,
wounded survivors, corpses, and devastation. The story came to us in his calm
voice. For years he had been a familiar figure in newscasts, reporting live at the 50
scene of battles and catastrophes with awesome tenacity. Nothing could stop him,
and I was always amazed at his equanimity in the face of danger and suffering; it

---

1. Arising from beneath the earth's surface.

seemed as if nothing could shake his fortitude or deter his curiosity. Fear seemed never to touch him, although he had confessed to me that he was not a courageous man, far from it. I believe that the lens of the camera had a strange effect on him; it was as if it transported him to a different time from which he could watch events without actually participating in them. When I knew him better, I came to realize that this fictive distance seemed to protect him from his own emotions.

Rolf Carlé was in on the story of Azucena from the beginning. He filmed the volunteers who discovered her, and the first persons who tried to reach her; his camera zoomed in on the girl, her dark face, her large desolate eyes, the plastered-down tangle of her hair. The mud was like quicksand around her, and anyone attempting to reach her was in danger of sinking. They threw a rope to her that she made no effort to grasp until they shouted to her to catch it; then she pulled a hand from the mire and tried to move, but immediately sank a little deeper. Rolf threw down his knapsack and the rest of his equipment and waded into the quagmire, commenting for his assistant's microphone that it was cold and that one could begin to smell the stench of corpses.

"What's your name?" he asked the girl, and she told him her flower name. "Don't move, Azucena," Rolf Carlé directed, and kept talking to her, without a thought for what he was saying, just to distract her, while slowly he worked his way forward in mud up to his waist. The air around him seemed as murky as the mud.

It was impossible to reach her from the approach he was attempting, so he retreated and circled around where there seemed to be firmer footing. When finally he was close enough, he took the rope and tied it beneath her arms, so they could pull her out. He smiled at her with that smile that crinkles his eyes and makes him look like a little boy; he told her that everything was fine, that he was here with her now, that soon they would have her out. He signaled the others to pull, but as soon as the cord tensed, the girl screamed. They tried again, and her shoulders and arms appeared, but they could move her no farther; she was trapped. Someone suggested that her legs might be caught in the collapsed walls of her house, but she said it was not just rubble, that she was also held by the bodies of her brothers and sisters clinging to her legs.

"Don't worry, we'll get you out of here," Rolf promised. Despite the quality of the transmission, I could hear his voice break, and I loved him more than ever. Azucena looked at him, but said nothing.

During those first hours Rolf Carlé exhausted all the resources of his ingenuity to rescue her. He struggled with poles and ropes, but every tug was an intolerable torture for the imprisoned girl. It occurred to him to use one of the poles as a lever but got no result and had to abandon the idea. He talked a couple of soldiers into working with him for a while, but they had to leave because so many other victims were calling for help. The girl could not move, she barely could breathe, but she did not seem desperate, as if an ancestral resignation allowed her to accept her fate. The reporter, on the other hand, was determined to snatch her from death. Someone brought him a tire, which he placed beneath her arms like a life buoy, and then laid a plank near the hole to hold his weight and allow him to stay closer to her. As it was impossible to remove the rubble blindly, he tried once or

twice to dive toward her feet, but emerged frustrated, covered with mud, and spit-
ting gravel. He concluded that he would have to have a pump to drain the water,   100
and radioed a request for one, but received in return a message that there was no
available transport and it could not be sent until the next morning.

"We can't wait that long!" Rolf Carlé shouted, but in the pandemonium no
one stopped to commiserate. Many more hours would go by before he accepted
that time had stagnated and reality had been irreparably distorted.

A military doctor came to examine the girl, and observed that her heart was
functioning well and that if she did not get too cold she could survive the night.

"Hang on, Azucena, we'll have the pump tomorrow," Rolf Carlé tried to con-
sole her.

"Don't leave me alone," she begged.   110

"No, of course I won't leave you."

Someone brought him coffee, and he helped the girl drink it, sip by sip. The
warm liquid revived her and she began telling him about her small life, about her
family and her school, about how things were in that little bit of world before the
volcano had erupted. She was thirteen, and she had never been outside her vil-
lage. Rolf Carlé, buoyed by a premature optimism, was convinced that everything
would end well: the pump would arrive, they would drain the water, move the
rubble, and Azucena would be transported by helicopter to a hospital where she
would recover rapidly and where he could visit her and bring her gifts. He
thought, She's already too old for dolls, and I don't know what would please her; 120
maybe a dress. I don't know much about women, he concluded, amused, reflect-
ing that although he had known many women in his lifetime, none had taught
him these details. To pass the hours he began to tell Azucena about his travels and
adventures as a newshound, and when he exhausted his memory, he called upon
imagination, inventing things he thought might entertain her. From time to time
she dozed, but he kept talking in the darkness, to assure her that he was still there
and to overcome the menace of uncertainty.

That was a long night.

Many miles away, I watched Rolf Carlé and the girl on a television screen. I
could not bear the wait at home, so I went to National Television, where I often   130
spent entire nights with Rolf editing programs. There, I was near his world, and I
could at least get a feeling of what he lived through during those three decisive
days. I called all the important people in the city, senators, commanders of the
armed forces, the North American ambassador, and the president of National
Petroleum, begging them for a pump to remove the silt, but obtained only vague
promises. I began to ask for urgent help on radio and television, to see if there
wasn't *someone* who could help us. Between calls I would run to the newsroom to
monitor the satellite transmissions that periodically brought new details of the cat-
astrophe. While reporters selected scenes with most impact for the news report, I
searched for footage that featured Azucena's mudpit. The screen reduced the disas- 140
ter to a single plane and accentuated the tremendous distance that separated me
from Rolf Carlé; nonetheless, I was there with him. The child's every suffering hurt
me as it did him; I felt his frustration, his impotence. Faced with the impossibility

of communicating with him, the fantastic idea came to me that if I tried, I could reach him by force of mind and in that way give him encouragement. I concentrated until I was dizzy—a frenzied and futile activity. At times I would be overcome with compassion and burst out crying; at other times, I was so drained I felt as if I were staring through a telescope at the light of a star dead for a million years.

I watched that hell on the first morning broadcast, cadavers of people and animals awash in the current of new rivers formed overnight from melted snow. Above the mud rose the tops of trees and the bell towers of a church where several people had taken refuge and were patiently awaiting rescue teams. Hundreds of soldiers and volunteers from the Civil Defense were clawing through rubble searching for survivors, while long rows of ragged specters awaited their turn for a cup of hot broth. Radio networks announced that their phones were jammed with calls from families offering shelter to orphaned children. Drinking water was in scarce supply, along with gasoline and food. Doctors, resigned to amputating arms and legs without anesthesia, pled that at least they be sent serum and painkillers and antibiotics; most of the roads, however, were impassable, and worse were the bureaucratic obstacles that stood in the way. To top it all, the clay contaminated by decomposing bodies threatened the living with an outbreak of epidemics.

Azucena was shivering inside the tire that held her above the surface. Immobility and tension had greatly weakened her, but she was conscious and could still be heard when a microphone was held out to her. Her tone was humble, as if apologizing for all the fuss. Rolf Carlé had a growth of beard, and dark circles beneath his eyes; he looked near exhaustion. Even from that enormous distance I could sense the quality of his weariness, so different from the fatigue of other adventures. He had completely forgotten the camera; he could not look at the girl through a lens any longer. The pictures we were receiving were not his assistant's but those of other reporters who had appropriated Azucena, bestowing on her the pathetic responsibility of embodying the horror of what had happened in that place. With the first light Rolf tried again to dislodge the obstacles that held the girl in her tomb, but he had only his hands to work with; he did not dare use a tool for fear of injuring her. He fed Azucena a cup of the cornmeal mush and bananas the Army was distributing, but she immediately vomited it up. A doctor stated that she had a fever, but added that there was little he could do: antibiotics were being reserved for cases of gangrene. A priest also passed by and blessed her, hanging a medal of the Virgin around her neck. By evening a gentle, persistent drizzle began to fall.

"The sky is weeping," Azucena murmured, and she, too, began to cry.

"Don't be afraid," Rolf begged. "You have to keep your strength up and be calm. Everything will be fine. I'm with you, and I'll get you out somehow."

Reporters returned to photograph Azucena and ask her the same questions, which she no longer tried to answer. In the meanwhile, more television and movie teams arrived with spools of cable, tapes, film, videos, precision lenses, recorders, sound consoles, lights, reflecting screens, auxiliary motors, cartons of supplies, electricians, sound technicians, and cameramen: Azucena's face was beamed to millions of screens around the world. And all the while Rolf Carlé kept pleading

for a pump. The improved technical facilities bore results, and National Television 190
began receiving sharper pictures and clearer sound; the distance seemed suddenly
compressed, and I had the horrible sensation that Azucena and Rolf were by my
side, separated from me by impenetrable glass. I was able to follow events hour by
hour; I knew everything my love did to wrest the girl from her prison and help
her endure her suffering; I overheard fragments of what they said to one another
and could guess the rest; I was present when she taught Rolf to pray, and when he
distracted her with the stories I had told him in a thousand and one nights beneath the white mosquito netting of our bed.

When darkness came on the second day, Rolf tried to sing Azucena to sleep
with old Austrian folk songs he had learned from his mother, but she was far be- 200
yond sleep. They spent most of the night talking, each in a stupor of exhaustion
and hunger, and shaking with cold. That night, imperceptibly, the unyielding
floodgates that had contained Rolf Carlé's past for so many years began to open,
and the torrent of all that had lain hidden in the deepest and most secret layers of
memory poured out, leveling before it the obstacles that had blocked his consciousness for so long. He could not tell it all to Azucena; she perhaps did not
know there was a world beyond the sea or time previous to her own; she was not
capable of imagining Europe in the years of the war. So he could not tell her of defeat, nor of the afternoon the Russians had led them to the concentration camp to
bury prisoners dead from starvation. Why should he describe to her how the 210
naked bodies piled like a mountain of firewood resembled fragile china? How
could he tell this dying child about ovens and gallows? Nor did he mention the
night that he had seen his mother naked, shod in stiletto-heeled red boots, sobbing with humiliation. There was much he did not tell, but in those hours he re-
lived for the first time all the things his mind had tried to erase. Azucena had
surrendered her fear to him and so, without wishing it, had obliged Rolf to confront his own. There, beside that hellhole of mud, it was impossible for Rolf to flee
from himself any longer, and the visceral terror he had lived as a boy suddenly invaded him. He reverted to the years when he was the age of Azucena, and
younger, and, like her, found himself trapped in a pit without escape, buried in 220
life, his head barely above ground; he saw before his eyes the boots and legs of his
father, who had removed his belt and was whipping it in the air with the never-
forgotten hiss of a viper coiled to strike. Sorrow flooded through him, intact and
precise, as if it had lain always in his mind, waiting. He was once again in the ar-
moire where his father locked him to punish him for imagined misbehavior, there
where for eternal hours he had crouched with his eyes closed, not to see the darkness, with his hands over his ears, to shut out the beating of his heart, trembling,
huddled like a cornered animal. Wandering in the mist of his memories he found
his sister Katharina, a sweet, retarded child who spent her life hiding, with the
hope that her father would forget the disgrace of her having been born. With 230
Katharina, Rolf crawled beneath the dining room table, and with her hid there
under the long white tablecloth, two children forever embraced, alert to footsteps
and voices. Katharina's scent melded with his own sweat, with aromas of cooking,
garlic, soup, freshly baked bread, and the unexpected odor of putrescent clay. His
sister's hand in his, her frightened breathing, her silk hair against his cheek, the

candid gaze of her eyes. Katharina . . . Katharina materialized before him, floating on the air like a flag, clothed in the white tablecloth, now a winding sheet, and at last he could weep for her death and for the guilt of having abandoned her. He understood then that all his exploits as a reporter, the feats that had won him such recognition and fame, were merely an attempt to keep his most ancient fears at bay, a stratagem for taking refuge behind a lens to test whether reality was more tolerable from that perspective. He took excessive risks as an exercise of courage, training by day to conquer the monsters that tormented him by night. But he had come face to face with the moment of truth; he could not continue to escape his past. He *was* Azucena; he was buried in the clayey mud; his terror was not the distant emotion of an almost forgotten childhood, it was a claw sunk in his throat. In the flush of his tears he saw his mother, dressed in black and clutching her imitation-crocodile pocketbook to her bosom, just as he had last seen her on the dock when she had come to put him on the boat to South America. She had not come to dry his tears, but to tell him to pick up a shovel: the war was over and now they must bury the dead.

"Don't cry. I don't hurt anymore. I'm fine," Azucena said when dawn came.

"I'm not crying for you," Rolf Carlé smiled. "I'm crying for myself. I hurt all over."

The third day in the valley of the cataclysm began with a pale light filtering through storm clouds. The President of the Republic visited the area in his tailored safari jacket to confirm that this was the worst catastrophe of the century; the country was in mourning; sister nations had offered aid; he had ordered a state of siege; the Armed Forces would be merciless, anyone caught stealing or committing other offenses would be shot on sight. He added that it was impossible to remove all the dead corpses or count the thousands who had disappeared; the entire valley would be declared holy ground, and bishops would come to celebrate a solemn mass for the souls of the victims. He went to the Army field tents to offer relief in the form of vague promises to crowds of the rescued, then to the improvised hospital to offer a word of encouragement to doctors and nurses worn down from so many hours of tribulations. Then he asked to be taken to see Azucena, the little girl the whole world had seen. He waved to her with a limp statesman's hand, and microphones recorded his emotional voice and paternal tone as he told her that her courage had served as an example to the nation. Rolf Carlé interrupted to ask for a pump, and the President assured him that he personally would attend to the matter. I caught a glimpse of Rolf for a few seconds kneeling beside the mudpit. On the evening news broadcast, he was still in the same position; and I, glued to the screen like a fortuneteller to her crystal ball, could tell that something fundamental had changed in him. I knew somehow that during the night his defenses had crumbled and he had given in to grief; finally he was vulnerable. The girl had touched a part of him that he himself had no access to, a part he had never shared with me. Rolf had wanted to console her, but it was Azucena who had given him consolation.

I recognized the precise moment at which Rolf gave up the fight and surrendered to the torture of watching the girl die. I was with them, three days and two nights, spying on them from the other side of life. I was there when she told him that in all her thirteen years no boy had ever loved her and that it was a pity to leave this world without knowing love. Rolf assured her that he loved her more than he could ever love anyone, more than he loved his mother, more than his sister, more than all the women who had slept in his arms, more than he loved me, his life companion, who would have given anything to be trapped in that well in her place, who would have exchanged her life for Azucena's, and I watched as he leaned down to kiss her poor forehead, consumed by a sweet, sad emotion he could not name. I felt how in that instant both were saved from despair, how they were freed from the clay, how they rose above the vultures and helicopters, how 290 together they flew above the vast swamp of corruption and laments. How, finally, they were able to accept death. Rolf Carlé prayed in silence that she would die quickly, because such pain cannot be borne.

By then I had obtained a pump and was in touch with a general who had agreed to ship it the next morning on a military cargo plane. But on the night of that third day, beneath the unblinking focus of quartz lamps and the lens of a hundred cameras, Azucena gave up, her eyes locked with those of the friend who had sustained her to the end. Rolf Carlé removed the life buoy, closed her eyelids, held her to his chest for a few moments, and then let her go. She sank slowly, a flower in the mud.   300

You are back with me, but you are not the same man. I often accompany you to the station and we watch the videos of Azucena again; you study them intently, looking for something you could have done to save her, something you did not think of in time. Or maybe you study them to see yourself as if in a mirror, naked. Your cameras lie forgotten in a closet; you do not write or sing; you sit long hours before the window, staring at the mountains. Beside you, I wait for you to complete the voyage into yourself, for the old wounds to heal. I know that when you return from your nightmares, we shall again walk hand in hand, as before. [1991]

Questions for Discussion and Writing

1. Should the title of this story be read literally or ironically? Is it only clay of which we are created?

2. Why in a disaster of such magnitude does the fate of one person become the focus of attention? Discuss whether this is simply a trick of the media.

3. Discuss whether Azucena is exploited by the media and politicians, or whether they are genuinely concerned for her.

4. Azucena's predicament becomes a metaphor for Rolf Carlé's life. How might this be a metaphor for everyone's life?

5. Why is the story told by Rolf's "life companion" rather than by Rolf himself? What is gained by this narrative stance?

6. Why does Azucena's death affect Rolf so greatly?

7. Is the narrator right to be optimistic in the last sentence, or is she fooling herself? Explain.

ᴥ NADINE GORDIMER
(b. 1923)

Spoils

Nadine Gordimer believes in literature's ability to act as a nation's conscience and moral voice. She was born in Springs, Transvaal, a region of northeast South Africa, into a family of middle-class wealth and privilege. She began reading widely at a young age and by fifteen had already published a short story. She spent only a year at the University of Witwatersrand, married disastrously in 1949, and remarried five years later. Her first collection of stories, *Face to Face,* appeared in 1949, followed by a steady stream of novels and story collections. *The Conservationist* (1974) won the Booker Prize. She was staunch and vocal in her opposition to the now-abolished apartheid system.

Unlike Doris Lessing, Gordimer does not experiment with fictional form or technique; she essentially continues the Realist tradition of using fiction to investigate and comment on the society around her. Caught herself in the moral bind of the white liberal who hates but cannot alter the prevailing political system, she has made this dilemma her subject. Her characters are often in an ethical and political quandary, benefiting from an unjust system that they may work to overthrow but cannot. Moral failure may be paralleled by failure in love.

She effectively uses clear and simple writing, informed by acute observation and inventive metaphor.

The fall of apartheid has done nothing to undermine the power and relevance of Gordimer's novels and stories, for whatever the political system, the man or woman of privilege and conscience faces the same dilemmas. Liberal humanism in Gordimer's view is inadequate to solve these problems, but she has no alternative with which to replace it. The moral force of her writing springs from the honesty and conviction she brings to her characters and the lives they struggle to live and understand.

"Spoils" is like a story by Chekhov in its apparently aimless movement, trivial incidents, and banal dialogue. The reader has to listen intently and observe the details carefully to catch its implications.

I N THE WARMTH of the bed your own fart brings to your nostrils the smell of rotting flesh: the lamb chops you devoured last night. Seasoned with rosemary and with an undertaker's paper frill on the severed rib-bones. Another corpse digested.

"Become a vegetarian, then." She's heard it all too many times before; sick of it, sick of my being sick of it. Sick of the things I say, that surface now and then.

"I want no part of it."

We are listening to the news.

"What? What are you going on about. *What?* "

What indeed. No: which. Which is it I choose to be no part of, the boy who
threw a stone at the police, had both his arms broken by them, was sodomized by   10
prisoners into whose cell he was thrown, the kidnapped diplomat and the group
(men, as I am a man, women, as she is a woman) who sent his fourth finger by
mail to his family, the girl doused with petrol and burned alive as a traitor, those
starved by drought or those drowned by flood, far away, the nineteen-year-old son
of Mr and Mrs killed by the tremendous elemental thrill of 220 volts while using
an electric spray gun on his motorbike, near by. The planned, devised, executed
by people like myself, or the haphazard, the indifferent, executed senselessly by elemental forces. *Senselessly.* Why is there more sense in the conscious acts that
make corpses? Consciousness is self-deception. Intelligence is a liar.

"You're not having great thoughts. That's life."   20

Her beauty-salon philosophy. Stale, animal, passive. Whether I choose or
not; can't choose, can't want *no part.*

The daily necrophilia.

"Become a vegetarian, then!"

Among other people no one would ever think there was anything wrong. He
is aware of that; she is aware of his being aware, taking some kind of pride in appearing exactly as they have him in their minds, contributing to their gathering
exactly what his place in it expects of him. The weekend party invited to a lodge
on a private game reserve will include the practical, improvising man, the clown
who burns his fingers at the camp fire and gets a laugh out of it, the woman who 30
spends her time preparing to feed everyone, the pretty girl who perks up the company sexually, the good-timer who keeps everyone drinking until late, the quiet
one who sits apart contemplating the bush, one or two newcomers, for ballast,
who may or may not provide a measure of serious conversation. Why not accept?
No? *Well.* What else has he in mind that will please him better? Just say.

Nothing.

There you are!

He, in contrast to the clown, is the charmer, the wit. He knows almost everyone's foibles, he sets the anecdotes flowing, he provides the gentle jibes that make
people feel themselves to be characters.   40

Whatever their temperaments, all are nature lovers. That is nothing to be
ashamed of—surely, even for him. Their love of the wild brings them together—
the wealthy couple who own the reserve and lodge rather than racehorses or a
yacht, the pretty girl who models or works in public relations, the good-timer director of a mining house, the adventurous stockbroker, the young doctor who
works for a clerk's salary in a hospital for blacks, the clowning antique dealer . . .
And he has no right to feel himself superior—in seriousness, morality (he knows
that)—in this company, for it includes a young man who has been in political detention. That one is not censorious of the playground indulgences of his fellow
whites, so long as the regime he has risked his freedom to destroy, will kill to de-   50
stroy, lasts. That's life.

Behaving—undetectably—as what is expected of one is also a protection
against fear of what one really is, now. Perhaps what is seen to be, is himself, the

witty charmer. How can he know? he does it so well. His wife sees him barefoot, his arms round his knees on the viewing deck from which the company watches buffalo trampling the reeds down at the river, hears the amusing asides he makes while gazing through field-glasses, notices the way he has left his shirt unbuttoned in healthy confidence of the sun-flushed manliness of his breast—is the silence, the incomprehensible statements that come from it, alone with her, a way of tormenting her? Does he do it only to annoy, to punish? And what has she done to deserve what he doesn't mete out to others? Let him keep it to himself. Take a Valium. Anything. Become a vegetarian. In the heat of the afternoon everyone goes to their rooms or their makeshift beds on the shaded part of the deck, to sleep off the lunch-time wine. Even in the room allotted to them, he keeps up, out of sight of the company (but they are only a wall away, he knows they are there), what is expected. It is so hot he and she have stripped to their briefs. He passes a hand over her damp breasts, gives a lazy sigh, and is asleep on his back. Would he have wanted to take her nipples in his mouth, commit himself to love-making, if he hadn't fallen asleep, or was his a gesture from the wings just in case the audience might catch a glimpse of a slump to an off-stage presence?

The house party is like the fire the servant makes at dusk within the reed stockade beside the lodge. One never knows when a fire outdoors will smoke or take flame cleanly and make a grand blaze, as this one does. One never knows when a small gathering will remain disparate, unresponsive, or when, as this time, men and women will ignite and make a bright company. The ceremony of the evening meal was a bit ridiculous, but perhaps intended as such, and fun. A parody of old colonial times: the stockade against the wild beasts, the black man beating a drum to announce the meal, the chairs placed carefully by him in a missionary prayer-meeting circle well away from the fire, the whisky and wine set out, the smell of charred flesh from the cooking grids. Look up: the first star in the haze is the mast-light of a ship moving out, slipping moorings, breaking with this world. Look down: the blue flames are nothing but burning fat, there are gnawed bones on the swept earth. He's been drinking a lot—she noticed: so that he could stomach it all, no doubt he tells himself.

The fire twitches under ash and the dinner orchestra of insects whose string instruments are their own bodies, legs scraping against legs, wings scraping against carapace, has been silenced by the rising of the moon. But laughter continues. In the huge night, not reduced to scale by buildings, tangled by no pylons and wires, hollowed out by no street- and window-lights into habitable enclosures, the laughter, the voices are vagrant sound that one moment flies right up boldly into space, the next makes a wave so faint it dies out almost as it leaves the lips. Everyone interrupts everyone else, argues, teases. There are moments of acerbity; the grapes they are eating pop into sharp juice as they are bitten. One of the quiet guests has become communicative as will the kind who never risk ideas or opinions of their own but can reproduce, when a subject brings the opportunity, information they have read and stored. Bats; the twirling rags darker against the dark—someone suggested, as a woman cowered, that fear of them comes from the fact that they can't be heard approaching.

"If your eyes are closed, and a bird flies overhead, you'll hear the resistance of air to its wings."

"And also, you can't make out what a bat's like, where its head is—just a *thing,* ugh!"

The quiet guest was already explaining, no, bats will not bump into you, but not, as this is popularly believed, because they have an inbuilt radar system; their system is sonar, or echolocation—

"—I wear a leopard skin coat!"

The defiant soprano statement from a sub-conversation breaks through his monologue and loses him attention.

It is the pretty girl; she has greased her face against the day's exposure to the sun and her bone-structure elegantly reflects the frail light coming from the half 110 moon, the occasional waver of flame roused in the fire, or the halo of a cigarette lighter. She is almost beautiful. "—D'you hear that!" "Glynis, where did you find this girl?" "Shall we put her out to be eaten by her prey, expose her on a rock?"

"No leopards here, unfortunately."

"The coat would look much better on the leopard than on you." The wit did not live up to his reputation, merely repeated in sharper, more personal paraphrase what had been well said no one remembered by whom. He spoke directly to the girl, whereas the others were playfully half-indignant around her presence. But the inference, neither entirely conservationist nor aesthetic, seemed to excite the girl's interest in this man. She was aware of him, in the real sense, for the first 120 time.

"Wait till you see me in it." Just the right touch of independence, hostility.

"That could be arranged."

This was a sub-exchange, now, under the talk of the others; he was doing the right thing, responding with the innuendo by which men and women acknowledge chemical correspondences stirring between them. And then she said it, was guided to it like a bat, by echolocation or whatever-it-is, something vibrating from the disgusts in him. "Would you prefer me to wear a sheepskin one? You eat lamb, I suppose?"

It is easy to lose her in the crisscross of talk and laughter, to enter it at some 130 other level and let fall the one on which she took him up. He is drawn elsewhere—there is refuge, maybe, rock to touch in the ex-political prisoner. The prisoner holds the hand of his pale girl with her big nervously-exposed teeth; no beauty, all love. The last place to look for love is in beauty, beauty is only a skin, the creature's own or that of another animal, over what decays. Love is found in prison, this no-beauty has loved him while his body was not present; and he has loved his brothers—he's talking about them, not using the word, but the sense is there so strongly—although they live shut in with their own pails of dirt, he loves even the murderers whose night-long death songs he heard before they were taken to be hanged in the morning.   140

"Common criminals? In this country? Under laws like ours?"

"Oh yes, we politicals were kept apart, but with time (I was there ten months) we managed to communicate. (There are so many ways you don't think of, outside, when you don't need to.) One of them—young, my age—he was already declared a habitual criminal, inside for an indeterminate sentence. Detention's also an indeterminate sentence, in a way, so I could have some idea . . . "

"You hadn't killed, robbed—he must have done that over and over."

"Oh he had. But I hadn't been born the bastard of a kitchen maid who had no home but her room in a white woman's back yard, I hadn't been sent to a 'homeland' where the woman who was supposed to take care of me was starving 150 and followed her man to a squatter camp in Cape Town to look for work. I hadn't begged in the streets, stolen what I needed to eat, sniffed glue for comfort. He had his first new clothes, his first real bed when he joined a gang of car thieves. Common lot; common criminal."

Common sob story.

"If he had met you outside prison he would have knifed you for your watch."

"Possibly! Can you say 'That's mine' to people whose land was taken from them by conquest, a gigantic hold-up at the point of imperial guns?"

And the bombs in the streets, in the cars, in the supermarkets, that kill with 160 a moral, necessary end, to criminal intent (yes, to be criminal is to kill for self-gain)—these don't confuse *him,* make carrion of brotherhood. He's brave enough to swallow it. No gagging.

Voices and laughter are cut off. You don't come to the bush to talk politics. It is one of the alert silences called for now and then by someone who's heard, be-yond human voices, a cry. *Shhhhh* . . . Once it was the mean complaining of jack-als, and—nearer—a nasal howl from a hyena, that creature of big nostrils made to scent spilt blood. Then a squeal no one could identify: a hare pounced on by a wheeling owl? A warthog attacked by—whom? What's going on, among them, that other order, of the beasts, in their night? "They live twenty-four hours, we 170 waste the dark." "Norbert—you used to be such a nightclub bird!" And the young doctor offers: "They hunt for their living in shifts, just like us. Some sleep during the day." "Oh but they're *designed as* different species, in order to use actively all twenty-four hours. We are one species, designed for daylight only. It's not so many generations since—pre-industrial times, that's all—we went to bed at nightfall. If the world's energy supplies should run out, we'd be back to that. No electricity. No night shifts. There isn't a variety in our species that has night vision." The bat ex-pert takes up this new cue. "There are experiments with devices that may provide night vision, they're based on—"

"*Shhhhh* . . ." 180

Laughter like the small explosion of a glass dropped.

"Shut up, Claire!"

All listen, with a glisten of eye movements alone, dead still.

It is difficult for them to decide on what it is they are eavesdropping. A straining that barely becomes a grunt. A belching stir; scuffling, scuffling—but it could be a breeze in dead leaves, it is not the straw crepitation of the reeds at the river, it comes from the other direction, behind the lodge. There is a gathering, an-other gathering somewhere there. There is communication their ears are not tuned to, their comprehension cannot decode; some event outside theirs. Even the ex-political prisoner does not know what he hears; he who has heard through prison 190 walls, he who has comprehended and decoded so much the others have not. His is only human knowledge, after all; he is not a twenty-four-hour creature, either.

Into this subdued hush breaks the black man jangling a tray of glasses he has washed. The host signals: be quiet, go away, stop fussing among dirty plates.

He comes over with the smile of one who knows he has something to offer. "Lions. They kill one, two maybe. Zebras."

Everyone bursts the silence like schoolchildren let out of class.

"Where?"

"How does he know?"

"What's he say?"   200

He keeps them waiting a moment, his hand is raised, palm up, pink from immersion in the washing-up. He is wiping it on his apron. "My wives hear it, there in my house. Zebra, and now they eating. That side, there, behind."

The black man's name is too unfamiliar to pronounce. But he is no longer nameless, he is the organizer of an expedition; they pick up a shortened version of the name from their host. Siza has brought the old truck, four-wheel drive, adapted as a large station wagon, from out of its shed next to his house. Everybody is game, this is part of the entertainment the host hoped but certainly could not promise to be lucky enough to provide; all troop by torchlight the hun-   210 dred yards from the lodge, under the Mopane trees, past the bed of cannas out- lined with whitewashed stones (the host never has had the heart to tell Siza this kind of white man's house does not need a white man's kind of garden) to Siza's wives' pumpkin and tomato patch. Siza is repairing a door-handle of the vehicle with a piece of wire, commanding, in his own language, this and that from his family standing by. A little boy gets underfoot and he lifts and dumps him out of the way. Two women wear traditional turbans but the one has a T-shirt with an ad- vertising logo; girl children hang on their arms, jabbering. Boys are quietly jump- ing with excitement.

Siza's status in this situation is clear when the two wives and children do not see the white party off but climb into the vehicle among them, the dry-soled hard   220 little feet of the children nimbly finding space among the guests' shoes, their knobbly heads with knitted capping of hair unfamiliar to the touch, flesh to flesh, into which all in the vehicle are crowded. Beside the girl with her oiled face and hard slender body perfumed to smell like a lily there is the soft bulk of one of the wives, smelling of woodsmoke. "Everybody in? Everybody okay?" No, no, wait— someone has gone back for a forgotten flash-bulb. Siza has started up the engine; the whole vehicle jerks and shakes.

Wit is not called for, nor flirtation. He does what is expected: runs to the lodge to fetch a sweater, in case his wife gets chilly. There is barely room for him to squeeze by; she attempts to take a black child on her lap, but the child is too shy.   230 He lowers himself somehow into what space there is. The vehicle moves, all bod- ies, familiar and unfamiliar, are pressed together, swaying, congealed, breathing in contact. She smiles at him, dipping her head sideways, commenting lightly on the human press, as if he were someone else: "In for the kill."

It is not possible to get out.

Everyone will be quite safe if they stay in the car and please roll up the win- dows, says the host. The headlights of the old vehicle have shown Siza trees like other trees, bushes like other bushes that are, to him, signposts. The blundering of the vehicle through bush and over treestumps, anthills, and dongas has been along his highway; he has stopped suddenly, and there they are, shadow-shapes 240 and sudden phosphorescent slits in the dim arch of trees that the limit of the headlights' reach only just creates, as a candle, held up, feebly makes a cave of its own aura. Siza drives with slow-motion rocking and heaving of the human load, steadily nearer. Four shapes come forward along the beams; and stop. He stops. Motes of dust, scraps of leaf and bark knocked off the vegetation float blurring the beams surrounding four lionesses who stand, not ten yards away. Their eyes are wide, now, gem-yellow, expanded by the glare they face, and never blink. Their jaws hang open and their heads shake with panting, their bodies are bellows expanding and contracting between stiff-hipped haunches and heavy narrow shoulders that support the heads. Their tongues lie exposed, the edges rucked up on 250 either side, like red cloth, by long white incisors.

They are dirtied with blood and to human eyes de-sexed, their kind of femaleness without femininity, their kind of threat and strength out of place, associated with the male. They have no beauty except in the almighty purpose of their stance. There is nothing else in their gaunt faces: nothing but the fact, behind them, of half-grown and younger cubs in the rib-cage of a zebra, pulling and sucking at bloody scraps.

The legs and head are intact in dandyish dress of black and white. The beast has been, is being eaten out. Its innards are missing; half-digested grasses that were in its stomach have been emptied on the ground, they can be seen—some- 260 one points this out in a whisper. But even the undertone is a transgression. The lionesses don't give forth the roar that would make their menace recognizable, something to deal with. Utterances are not the medium for this confrontation. Watching. That is all. The breathing mass, the beating hearts in the vehicle— watching the cubs jostling for places within the cadaver; the breathing mass, the beating hearts in the vehicle—being watched by the lionesses. The beasts have no time, it will be measured by their fill. For the others, time suddenly begins again when the young doctor's girl-friend begins to cry soundlessly and the black children look away from the scene and see the tears shining on her cheeks, and stare at her fear. The young doctor asks to be taken to the lodge; the compact is broken, 270 people protest, why, oh no, they want to stay and see what happens, one of the lionesses has broken ranks and turns on a greedy cub, cuffing it out of the gouged prey. Quite safe; the car is perfectly safe, don't open a window to photograph. But the doctor is insistent: "This old truck's chassis is cracked right through, we're overloaded, we could be stuck here all night."

"Unreal." Back in the room, the wife comes out with one of the catch-alls that have been emptied of dictionary meaning so that they may fit any experience the speaker won't take the trouble to define. When he doesn't respond she stands a moment, in the doorway, her bedclothes in her arms, smiling, gives her head a little shake to show how overwhelming her impression has been.   280

Oh well. What can she expect. Why come, anyway? Should have stayed at home. So he doesn't want to sleep in the open, on the deck. Under the stars. All right. No stars, then.

He lies alone and the mosquitoes are waiting for his blood, upside-down on the white board ceiling.

No. Real. *Real.* Alone, he can keep it intact, exactly that: the stasis, the existence without time and without time there is no connection, the state in which he really need have, has no part, could have no part, there in the eyes of the lionesses. Between the beasts and the human load, the void. It is more desired and awful than could ever be conceived; he does not know whether he is sleeping, or 290 dead.

There is still Sunday. The entertainment is not over. Someone has heard lions round the lodge in the middle of the night. The scepticism with which this claim is greeted is quickly disproved when distinct pugs are found in the dust that surrounds the small swimming-pool which, like amniotic fluid, steeps the guests at their own body temperature. The host is not surprised; it has happened before: the lionesses must have come down to quench the thirst their feasting had given them. And the scent of humans, sleeping so near, up on the deck, the sweat of humans in the humid night, their sighs and sleep noises? Their pleasure- and anxiety-emanating dreams? 300

"As far as the lions are concerned, we didn't exist." From the pretty girl, the remark is a half-question that trails off.

"When your stomach is full you don't smell blood."

The ex-prisoner is perhaps extrapolating into the class war?—the wit puts in, and the ex-prisoner himself is the one who is most appreciatively amused.

After the mosquitoes had had their fill sleep came as indifferently as those other bodily states, hunger and thirst. A good appetite for fresh pawpaw and bacon, boerewors and eggs. Hungry, like everybody else. His wife offers him a second helping, perhaps he needs feeding up, there is a theory that all morbid symptoms are in fact of physical origin. Obsession with injustice—what's wrong with 310 the world is a disease you, an individual, can't cure, that's life. The one who went to prison may be suffering from a lack of something—amino acids, vitamins; or an excess of something, overfeeding when a child or hyperactive thyroid gland. Research is being done.

Siza confirms that the lionesses came to drink. They passed his house; he heard them. He tells with the dry, knowing smile of one who is aware of a secret to-and-fro between bedrooms. After breakfast he is going to take the party to see in daylight where the kill took place last night.

"But is there anything to see?"

Siza is patient. "They not eat all. Is too much. So they leave some, tonight 320 they come back for eat finish."

"No thanks! I don't think we should disturb them again." But nobody wants the young doctor and his girl-friend to come, anyway, and spoil the outing.

"The lions they sleeping now. They gone away. Come back tonight. Is not there now."

The wife is watching to see if she and her husband are going along. Yes, he's climbing, limber, into the old vehicle with the cracked chassis, he's giving a hand up to the hostess, he's said something that makes her laugh and purse her mouth.

The black women are thumping washing at an outdoor tub. Neither they nor their children come on this expedition. There is room to breathe without contact, this time. Everything is different in daylight. It is true that the lionesses are absent; the state that he achieved last night is absent in the same way, like them, drugged down by daylight.

Not a lion to be seen. Siza has stopped the vehicle, got out, but waved the passengers to stay put. The scrub forest is quiet, fragile pods that burst and sow their seed by wind-dispersion spiral slowly. Everybody chatters. The stockbroker leaves the vehicle and everybody shouts at him. All right. Taking his time, to show his lack of fear, he climbs aboard. "Lions are not bulls and bears, Fred." They laugh at this mild jeer which is the kind expected to sustain the wit's image—all are amused except the stockbroker himself, who knows the remark, in turn, refers to his image of himself as one whom no one would guess to be a stockbroker.

Siza comes back and beckons. The vehicle is quickly quit. And now the emptiness of the scrub forest is untrustworthy, all around, you can't see what's behind dead brush, fallen logs and the screens of layered branches that confine vision to ten feet. They talk only softly, in the sense of being stalked. The black man is leading them along what looks almost like a swept path; but it has been swept by a large body being dragged through dust and dead leaves: there is the carcass of the zebra, half-hidden in a thicket.

"No tyre-tracks, we didn't drive right into here! This can't be the place."

"They pull him here for when they come back tonight."

"What! To keep the meat fresh?"

"For the birds mustn't see." Siza gives a name in his language.

"He means vultures. Vultures, eh, Siza." A mime of the vultures' hunched posture.

"Yes, those big birds. Come look here—" The tour continues, he takes them a few paces from the carcass and stands beside a mound over which earth has been scratched or kicked. Flies whose backs spark tinny green and gold are settled on it. The black man has his audience: taking up a stick, he prods the mound and it stirs under dust like flour-coated meat moved by a fork.

"Christ, the intestines! Look at the size of that liver or spleen!"

"You mean lions can do that? Store things covered? How do they do it, just with their paws?"

"It's exactly the way my cat covers its business in the garden, scratches up earth. They're cats, too."

The young jailbird and his girl and the antique dealer have made a discovery for themselves, having, in the confidence of excitement, retraced for a short distance the way along which the kill was approached. They have found the very pile of the contents of the zebra's stomach that someone noticed last night.

It is another mound. He has come over from the mound of guts they are marvelling at. There is nothing to watch in dead flesh, it is prodded and it falls back and is still. But this mound of steaming grass that smells sweetly of cud (it has been heated by the sun as it was once heated by the body that contained it) is not dead to human perception. What's going on here is a visible transformation of an inert mass. It is literally being carried away by distinctly different species of beetles who know how to live by decay, the waste of the digestive tract. The scarabs with their armoured heads burrow right into the base of the mound, and come out backwards, rolling their ball of dung between their strong, tined legs. The tunnels they have mined collapse and spread the mound more thinly on its periphery; smaller beetles are flying in steadily to settle there, where their lighter equipment can function. They fly away carrying their appropriate load in a sac— or between their front legs, he can't quite make out. A third species, middle-sized but with a noisy buzz, function like helicopters, hovering and scooping off the top of the mound. They are flattening it perfectly evenly, who can say how or why they bother with form? That's life. If every beetle has its place, how is refusal possible. And if refusal is possible, what place is there. No question mark. These are statements. That is why there is no point in making them to anyone. There is no possible response.

The mound is slowly going to disappear; maybe the vehicle is about to take the party back to the lodge, the weekend is going to be over. He is walking back to the rest of the party, still gathered round the carcass and the black man. For the space of a few yards he is alone, for a few seconds he is equidistant between those at the dung mound and those up ahead, part of neither one nor the other. A sensation that can't be held long; now he is with the group at the kill, again. There is some special stir of attentiveness in them, they crowd round and then herd back a step, where Siza, the black man, is crouched on his hunkers. He is business-like, concentrated, not taking any notice of them. He has given them all he could; now he has the air of being for himself. He has a knife in his hand and the white man who has just joined the group recognizes it, it is the knife that is everywhere, nowhere without the knife, on the news, at the dark street-corners, under the light that the warders never turn out. The black man has thrust, made his incision, sliced back the black-and-white smooth pelt on the dead beast's uppermost hind leg and now is cutting a piece of the plump rump. It is not a chunk or hunk, but neatly butchered, prime—a portion.

They laugh, wondering at the skill, curious. As if they can't guess, as if they've never sunk their teeth into a steak in their lives. "What're you going to do with that, Siza?" Ah yes, put it in a doggy bag, take it home when you've already stuffed your own guts, taken the land (as the jailbird would say).

The black man is trimming it. Along with the knife, he has brought a sheet of newspaper. "For me. Eat it at my house. For my house."

"Is it good meat?"

"Yes, it's good."

One of the men chides, man to man. "But why not take a whole haunch— whole leg, Siza. Why such a small piece?"

The black man is wrapping the portion in newspaper, he knows he mustn't let it drip blood on the white people.

He does it to his satisfaction in his own time and looks up at them. "The lions, they know I must take a piece for me because I find where their meat is. They know it. It's all right. But if I take too much, they know it also. Then they will take one of my children."   [1991]

Questions for Discussion and Writing

1. This story takes place against the background of South African apartheid. Is the political situation (and the political discussion) relevant to the rest of the story? If so, in what way? If not, then why is it included?
2. What various types of people are included in the story? What is the point of including such a variety of types?
3. What is the meaning of the title?
4. Why is there tension between the man and the wife? What relevance do their problems have to the rest of the story?
5. Siza says that if he takes too much meat, the lions will take one of his children. How are we meant to understand this? Literally? Figuratively? Explain.
6. The story begins in a fragmentary, disjointed way. What possible purpose could such a beginning serve? Isn't a beginning like this likely to discourage readers from reading further?

ROBERT OLEN BUTLER, JR.
(b. 1945)

"Jealous Husband Returns in Form of Parrot"

Robert Olen Butler writes fiction that straddles the line between traditional narrative and post-modern fantasy. He was born in Granite City, Illinois, near St. Louis, where his father was a professor and his mother an executive secretary. He studied acting and playwriting at Northwestern University, graduating in 1967, and in 1969 earned an M.A. at the University of Iowa. He spent the next three years in Vietnam as a U.S. Army Intelligence officer. After completing his tour of duty, he worked as a journalist and substitute teacher, before becoming editor of the *Energy User News,* a position he liked because it kept him in touch with the real world. His early novels were written on commuter trains between New Jersey and Manhattan.

Butler's experiences in Vietnam became the basis of his trilogy, *The Alleys of Eden* (1981), *Sun Dogs* (1982), and *On Distant Ground* (1985). Four other novels have also been published to great critical acclaim, and two short story collections, including the Pulitzer Prize winning collection, *A Good Scent From a Strange Mountain* (1993). "Jealous Husband Returns in Form of Parrot" is from his latest collection, *Tabloid Dreams* (1996), all of whose stories are named with tabloid style headlines and thus involve uncanny, unusual, or even slightly mad experiences and ideas. Perhaps not surprisingly, he lists as major influences on his work the visionary prophets of the Old Testament—Daniel, Jeremiah, and Isaiah—and the gospel writer, St. Luke.

I NEVER CAN QUITE say as much as I know. I look at other parrots and I wonder if it's the same for them, if somebody is trapped in each of them paying some kind of price for living their life in a certain way. For instance, "Hello," I say, and I'm sit-

ting on a perch in a pet store in Houston and what I'm really thinking is Holy shit.
It's you. And what's happened is I'm looking at my wife.

"Hello," she says, and she comes over to me and I can't believe how beautiful
she is. Those great brown eyes, almost as dark as the center of mine. And her
nose—I don't remember her for her nose but its beauty is clear to me now. Her
nose is a little too long, but it's redeemed by the faint hook to it.

She scratches the back of my neck.   10

Her touch makes my tail flare. I feel the stretch and rustle of me back there.
I bend my head to her and she whispers, "Pretty bird."

For a moment I think she knows it's me. But she doesn't, of course. I say
"Hello" again and I will eventually pick up "pretty bird." I can tell that as soon as
she says it, but for now I can only give her another hello. Her fingertips move
through my feathers and she seems to know about birds. She knows that to pet a
bird you don't smooth his feathers down, you ruffle them.

But of course she did that in my human life, as well. It's all the same for her.
Not that I was complaining, even to myself, at that moment in the pet shop when
she found me like I presume she was supposed to. She said it again, "Pretty bird,"   20
and this brain that works like it does now could feel that tiny little voice of mine
ready to shape itself around those sounds. But before I could get them out of my
beak there was this guy at my wife's shoulder and all my feathers went slick flat
like to make me small enough not to be seen and I backed away. The pupils of my
eyes pinned and dilated and pinned again.

He circled around her. A guy that looked like a meat packer, big in the chest
and thick with hair, the kind of guy that I always sensed her eyes moving to when
I was alive. I had a bare chest and I'd look for little black hairs on the sheets when
I'd come home on a day with the whiff of somebody else in the air. She was still in
the same goddamn rut.   30

A "hello" wouldn't do, and I'd recently learned "good night" but it was the
wrong suggestion altogether, so I said nothing and the guy circled her and he was
looking at me with a smug little smile and I fluffed up all my feathers, made myself about twice as big, so big he'd see he couldn't mess with me. I waited for him
to draw close enough for me to take off the tip of his finger.

But she intervened. Those nut brown eyes were before me and she said, "I
want him."

And that's how I ended up in my own house once again. She bought me a
large black wrought-iron cage, very large, convinced by some young guy who
clerked in the bird department and who took her aside and made his voice go   40
much too soft when he was doing the selling job. The meat packer didn't like it. I
didn't either. I'd missed a lot of chances to take a bite out of this clerk in my stay
at the shop and I regretted that suddenly.

But I got my giant cage and I guess I'm happy enough about that. I can pace
as much as I want. I can hang upside down. It's full of bird toys. That dangling
thing over there with knots and strips of rawhide and a bell at the bottom needs a
good thrashing a couple of times a day and I'm the bird to do it. I look at the very
dangle of it and the thing is rough, the rawhide and the knotted rope, and I get
this restlessness back in my tail, a burning thrashing feeling, and it's like all the

times when I was sure there was a man naked with my wife. Then I go to this thing that feels so familiar and I bite and bite and it's very good.

I could have used the thing the last day I went out of this house as a man. I'd found the address of the new guy at my wife's office. He'd been there a month in the shipping department and three times she'd mentioned him. She didn't even have to work with him and three times I heard about him, just dropped into the conversation. "Oh," she'd say when a car commercial came on the television, "that car there is like the one the new man in shipping owns. Just like it." Hey, I'm not stupid. She said another thing about him and then another and right after the third one I locked myself in the bathroom because I couldn't rage about this anymore. I felt like a damn fool whenever I actually said anything about this kind of feeling and she looked at me like she could start hating me real easy and so I was working on saying nothing, even if it meant locking myself up. My goal was to hold my tongue about half the time. That would be a good start.

But this guy from shipping. I found out his name and his address and it was one of her typical Saturday afternoons of vague shopping. So I went to his house, and his car that was just like the commercial was outside. Nobody was around in the neighborhood and there was this big tree in the back of the house going up to a second floor window that was making funny little sounds. I went up. The shade was drawn but not quite all the way. I was holding on to a limb with arms and legs wrapped around it like it was her in those times when I could forget the others for a little while. But the crack in the shade was just out of view and I crawled on along till there was no limb left and I fell on my head. Thinking about that now, my wings flap and I feel myself lift up and it seems so avoidable. Though I know I'm different now. I'm a bird.

Except I'm not. That's what's confusing. It's like those times when she would tell me she loved me and I actually believed her and maybe it was true and we clung to each other in bed and at times like that I was different. I was the man in her life. I was whole with her. Except even at that moment, holding her sweetly, there was this other creature inside me who knew a lot more about it and couldn't quite put all the evidence together to speak.

My cage sits in the den. My pool table is gone and the cage is sitting in that space and if I come all the way down to one end of my perch I can see through the door and down the back hallway to the master bedroom. When she keeps the bedroom door open I can see the space at the foot of the bed but not the bed itself. That I can sense to the left, just out of sight. I watch the men go in and I hear the sounds but I can't quite see. And they drive me crazy.

I flap my wings and I squawk and I fluff up and I slick down and I throw seed and I attack that dangly toy as if it was the guy's balls, but it does no good. It never did any good in the other life either, the thrashing around I did by myself. In that other life I'd have given anything to be standing in this den with her doing this thing with some other guy just down the hall and all I had to do was walk down there and turn the corner and she couldn't deny it anymore

But now all I can do is try to let it go. I sidestep down to the opposite end of the cage and I look out the big sliding glass doors to the backyard. It's a pretty yard. There are great placid maple trees with good places to roost. There's a blue sky that plucks at the feathers on my chest. There are clouds. Other birds. Fly away. I could just fly away.

I tried once and I learned a lesson. She forgot and left the door to my cage open and I climbed beak and foot, beak and foot, along the bars and curled around to stretch sideways out the door and the vast scene of peace was there at the other end of the room. I flew.

And a pain flared through my head and I fell straight down and the room whirled around and the only good thing was she held me. She put her hands under my wings and lifted me and clutched me to her breast and I wish there hadn't been bees in my head at the time so I could have enjoyed that, but she put me back in the cage and wept awhile. That touched me, her tears. And I looked back to the wall of sky and trees. There was something invisible there between me and that dream of peace. I remembered, eventually, about glass, and I knew I'd been lucky, I knew that for the little fragile-boned skull I was doing all this thinking in, it meant death.

She wept that day but by the night she had another man. A guy with a thick Georgia truck-stop accent and pale white skin and an Adam's apple big as my seed ball. This guy has been around for a few weeks and he makes a whooping sound down the hallway, just out of my sight. At times like that I want to fly against the bars of the cage, but I don't. I have to remember how the world has changed.

She's single now, of course. Her husband, the man that I was, is dead to her. She does not understand all that is behind my "hello." I know many words, for a parrot. I am a yellow-nape Amazon, a handsome bird, I think, green with a splash of yellow at the back of my neck. I talk pretty well, but none of my words are adequate. I can't make her understand.

And what would I say if I could? I was jealous in life. I admit it. I would admit it to her. But it was because of my connection to her. I would explain that. When we held each other, I had no past at all, no present but her body, no future but to lie there and not let her go. I was an egg hatched beneath her crouching body, I entered as a chick into her wet sky of a body, and all that I wished was to sit on her shoulder and fluff my feathers and lay my head against her cheek, my neck exposed to her hand. And so the glances that I could see in her troubled me deeply, the movement of her eyes in public to other men, the laughs sent across a room, the tracking of her mind behind her blank eyes, pursuing images of others, her distraction even in our bed, the ghosts that were there of men who'd touched her, perhaps even that very day. I was not part of all those other men who were part of her. I didn't want to connect to all that. It was only her that I would fluff for but these others were there also and I couldn't put them aside. I sensed them inside her and so they were inside me. If I had the words, these are the things I would say.

But half an hour ago there was a moment that thrilled me. A word, a word we all knew in the pet shop, was just the right word after all. This guy with his cowboy belt buckle and rattlesnake boots and his pasty face and his twanging words of love trailed after my wife, through the den, past my cage, and I said, "Cracker." He even flipped his head back a little at this in surprise. He'd been called that before to his face, I realized. I said it again, "Cracker." But to him I was a bird and he let it pass. "Cracker," I said. "Hello, cracker." That was even better. They were out of sight through the hall doorway and I hustled along the perch and I caught a glimpse of them before they made the turn to the bed and I said, "Hello, cracker," and he shot me one last glance.

It made me hopeful. I eased away from that end of the cage, moved toward the scene of peace beyond the far wall. The sky is chalky blue today, blue like the brow of the blue-front Amazon who was on the perch next to me for about a week at the store. She was very sweet, but I watched her carefully for a day or two when she first came in. And it wasn't long before she nuzzled up to a cockatoo named Gordo and I knew she'd break my heart. But her color now in the sky is sweet, really. I left all those feelings behind me when my wife showed up. I am a faithful man, for all my suspicions. Too faithful, maybe. I am ready to give too much and maybe that's the problem.

The whooping began down the hall and I focused on a tree out there. A crow flapped down, his mouth open, his throat throbbing, though I could not hear his sound. I was feeling very odd. At least I'd made my point to the guy in the other room. "Pretty bird," I said, referring to myself. She called me "pretty bird" and I believed her and I told myself again, "Pretty bird."

But then something new happened, something very difficult for me. She appeared in the den naked. I have not seen her naked since I fell from the tree and had no wings to fly. She always had a certain tidiness in things. She was naked in the bedroom, clothed in the den. But now she appears from the hallway and I look at her and she is still slim and she is beautiful, I think—at least I clearly remember that as her husband I found her beautiful in this state. Now, though, she seems too naked. Plucked. I find that a sad thing. I am sorry for her and she goes by me and she disappears into the kitchen. I want to pluck some of my own feathers, the feathers from my chest, and give them to her. I love her more in that moment, seeing her terrible nakedness, than I ever have before.

And since I've had success in the last few minutes with words, when she comes back I am moved to speak. "Hello," I say, meaning, You are still connected to me, I still want only you. "Hello," I say again. Please listen to this tiny heart that beats fast at all times for you.

And she does indeed stop and she comes to me and bends to me. "Pretty bird," I say and I am saying, You are beautiful, my wife, and your beauty cries out for protection. "Pretty." I want to cover you with my own nakedness. "Bad bird," I say. If there are others in your life, even in your mind, then there is nothing I can do. "Bad." Your nakedness is touched from inside by the others. "Open," I say. How can we be whole together if you are not empty in the place that I am to fill?

She smiles at this and she opens the door to my cage. "Up," I say, meaning, Is there no place for me in this world where I can be free of this terrible sense of others?

She reaches in now and offers her hand and I climb onto it and I tremble and she says, "Poor baby."

"Poor baby," I say. You have yearned for wholeness too and somehow I failed you. I was not enough. "Bad bird," I say. I'm sorry.

And then the cracker comes around the corner. He wears only his rattlesnake boots. I take one look at his miserable, featherless body and shake my

head. We keep our sexual parts hidden, we parrots, and this man is a pitiful sight. 190
"Peanut," I say. I presume that my wife simply has not noticed. But that's foolish,
of course. This is, in fact, what she wants. Not me. And she scrapes me off her
hand onto the open cage door and she turns her naked back to me and embraces
this man and they laugh and stagger in their embrace around the corner.

For a moment I still think I've been eloquent. What I've said only needs repeating for it to have its transforming effect. "Hello," I say. "Hello. Pretty bird.
Pretty. Bad bird. Bad. Open. Up. Poor baby. Bad bird." And I am beginning to hear
myself as I really sound to her. "Peanut." I can never say what is in my heart to
her. Never.

I stand on my cage door now and my wings stir. I look at the corner to the 200
hallway and down at the end the whooping has begun again. I can fly there and
think of things to do about all this.

But I do not. I turn instead and I look at the trees moving just beyond the
other end of the room. I look at the sky the color of the brow of a blue-front
Amazon. A shadow of birds spanks across the lawn. And I spread my wings. I will
fly now. Even though I know there is something between me and that place where
I can be free of all these feelings, I will fly. I will throw myself there again and
again. Pretty bird. Bad bird. Good night.   [1996]

Questions for Discussion and Writing

1. How convincingly does Butler handle the point of view? What part does convention play in our acceptance of the point of view?
2. Much of the imagery in the story concerns barriers of various kinds.
   Underline or highlight these images. What do they contribute to the story?
3. What is the tone of this story? Humorous? Sad? Other? Give examples. If
   more than one tone exists in the story, which predominates?
4. Why does the narrator feel sorry for his wife when he sees her naked?
5. What does the narrator mean in the last paragraph of the story? Why will he
   continue to fly into the window?

PART TWO

A Brief History of the Short Story

EARLY FORMS OF SHORT FICTION: PRECURSORS TO THE SHORT STORY

This anthology contains a number of examples of antecedents to the short story—that is, early types of stories from which the modern short story developed. These contain the fictional conventions, devices, and techniques that would eventually lead to the short story as we know it today. Such precursors repay attention for a number of reasons. First, they are enjoyable and worthwhile in and of themselves; it is doubtful that they would have endured through the centuries if this were not the case. Second, they introduce and illustrate many of the common conventions of fiction. Third, these types of fiction are still prominent features of the short story and its criticism. Discussions of short stories often employ the terms tale, fable, sketch, and so on, because many short stories still resemble these ancient forms.

The types of early short fiction represented here are not the only ones that preceded the modern short story. Other precursors, such as stories from the Jewish Old Testament, oral traditions and folk tales from every region of the world, narrative poems, racy medieval tales called *fabliaux,* and medieval chivalric romances—all contributed directly or indirectly to the rise of the modern short story. The chronological arrangement of the precursor tales in this anthology is not intended to suggest that there is a steady line of progression from early oral tradition to the modern short story, nor should it be thought that each example illustrates a stage of higher development. Rather, these samples are among the various types of short fiction that were known and available to nineteenth-century writers as the modern short story emerged. They help us to understand how the short story arose, and they provide a convenient starting point for analysis.

TALE FROM THE AMERICAN INDIAN ORAL TRADITION: "GLUSKABE AND THE FOUR WISHES"

Tales from an oral tradition, like "Gluskabe and the Four Wishes," are so widespread and ancient that attempting to date them is futile. For our purposes, the importance of such stories is that they have existed for eons. Since there are a great many types of such stories, no one can be singled out as typical, but "Gluskabe and the Four Wishes" contains many familiar features. Gluskabe is a supernatural being, and even the four men seem larger than life, archetypal. Mixed with the tale are elements of the etiological story—the kind that explains how natural phenomena (in this case the pine tree and the boulder) came to be.

"Gluskabe and the Four Wishes" also illustrates four conventions of fiction: point of view, character, action, and moral. Although we seldom think about how a story is told, awareness of point of view is important to understanding fiction. Point of view refers to the way in which the story is presented; that is, whether we see the story from the outside, as when it is presented by an omniscient, third-person narrator or a detached first-person narrator, or whether we see it from the inside, as when it is presented by an involved first-person narrator or seen through the eyes of a central character. In the case of "Gluskabe and the Four Wishes," we accept without question that the omniscient narrator has somehow learned events in the distant past and can report accurately on events he or she could not possibly have observed. For purposes of the tale, we willingly suspend our disbelief and allow the narrator the privilege of such knowledge. Granting the narrator whatever authority he or she claims for purposes of the story is a convention of fiction that dates back to the earliest records.

Second, each man in "The Four Wishes" exhibits certain defining personality or character traits. The first is greedy, the second vain, the third fearful, the fourth conscientious. These characters are set in action by a common fictional device—the quest. We accept the events as "real" in some sense and also grant the author the license to select only a few scenes for the tale. What has happened before these events and what other events occurred during the time covered by the story are assumed to be irrelevant. Most importantly, we accept the selection of these events as complete and meaningful in itself.

The underlying human relevance gives the story its "moral," when the point of the story is made explicit and is expressed as a statement about how best to live. In other words, the characters are assumed to stand for typical human beings in typical situations, and their experiences are offered as a pattern for good and bad behavior. The belief that a story has meaning or significance beyond itself is a convention. There is no inherent reason why a story should have a "moral," a "meaning," or a "theme," but we have come to expect that a narrative will "go beyond itself." It will not just make one-dimensional sense on the surface but will also provide meaning—a comment on life.

AESOP'S FABLE: "THE TOWN MOUSE AND THE COUNTRY MOUSE"

The fable is one of the most enduring forms of short fiction, perhaps because the brevity and pungency of the form make it ideally suited to imparting simple morals or satirizing conduct. Moreover, using animals (as most fables do) with human characteristics adds a level of entertainment, for if animals are like humans, then humans must resemble animals.

This fable illustrates again the power of convention, for in this case we are asked to believe that the omniscient narrator is privy to the lives of mice, that mice speak in human language, and that these little rodents experience life much as humans do. And, once again, we grant to the narrator the right to tell us what the story means.

THEOPHRASTUS: "GARRULITY"

The Greek philosopher Theophrastus (372–287 B.C.) is credited with inventing the character-essay. This brief form has a moral and satiric purpose, like the fable, but it uses little or no action and focuses instead on a detailed portrait of a particular vice. In the seventeenth century, essayists expanded the genre to include depictions of virtues as well.

In "Garrulity," Theophrastus describes someone as though the only feature of the person's personality is excessive talkativeness. If applied to a real person, this would be extremely one-sided and distorting. No living person can be summarized in a word or even in a series of details illustrating a particular trait. But Theophrastus's character-essay, by describing a type in exaggerated terms, achieves a different kind of "truth" or "reality." We recognize the type from the description and may respond by comparing the fictional character to someone we know or by altering our own behavior to avoid being viewed in this way.

The character-essay illustrates some of the problems and conventions of present-ing characters. The problem may be stated thus: How can a complex person can be re-duced to a set of observable traits that can be captured in language? Since no human being can be rendered completely in words, fiction must strike a balance between over-simplification and confusing over-complexity. There must be selection of detail and emphasis on certain tendencies, facets, or traits. Contradictory and complemen-tary attributes may also be included to give the illusion of completeness or roundness, if the author so desires, but all literary characters are in the end artistic representations of human beings, not real people. This challenge has faced writers from the beginning, especially in short forms where the scope to develop characters is limited.

Short-story writers, like novelists and playwrights, have long "economized" on characterizations by employing stereotyped characters not much more complex than the garrulous man depicted by Theophrastus. The ruthless businessman, the crooked lawyer, the bored housewife, the absent-minded professor are all stock characters in the tradition of Theophrastus's garrulous man. They are drawn from life to some de-gree, but exaggerated or made one-dimensional. Because they have become familiar, we need or expect less detail about them. Much of the innovation in short-story writ-ing has been directed at finding new ways of developing and exploring character—or giving three dimensionality to stock characters—within the relatively brief space af-forded by the form.

MYTH: OVID, DAEDALUS, AND ICARUS

Myth is the general name given to narratives that arise from and give expression to re-ligious beliefs and social practices. They may also explain natural phenomena. Thus, myths express cultural and religious values and explain natural phenomena such as the origins of life or the operations of such natural forces as rain or the change of the seasons. "Myth" is sometimes used to mean a story that is untrue, and so it may be in a literal sense, but beneath the literal story lies a truth or belief of profound impor-tance. The Old Testament stories of creation and the flood are myths, as is the puritan idea that hard work and moral uprightness guarantee success.

Ovid's *Metamorphoses* (meaning stories about changing from one state to another) is one of the monuments of Western literature. Like many other great collections of stories, it does not invent but re-tells already well-known tales. Characters are seldom well developed; the emphasis is on action, swiftly and gracefully rendered. Thus, Daedalus is the inventor and engineer, Icarus the youth who fails to heed the voice of caution.

Ovid is the consummate detached, omniscient narrator. His comments are re-stricted to simple observations, "Fooling around, the way a boy will, always," and he never judges his characters. Ovid has rejected the author's right to draw a moral and, except for noting that Icarus gave his name to the land near where he fell, allowed the story to speak for itself. For subsequent generations, *Metamorphoses* was the "Bible" of Greek and Roman mythology, and like the Bible it attracted scores of commentators and interpreters. The Middle Ages and Renaissance allegorized the myth of Daedalus, seeing in Icarus a representation of the sin of pride. Today, we might see Daedalus as the archetypal inventor or scientist, creating something of great potential benefit (flight) that ironically leads to death and destruction. Freudian critics might interpret the tension between father and son as a classic Oedipal conflict. Over the years, this simple story has lent itself to many readings, each purporting to elucidate the true "theme" of the story—that is, to explain its unifying idea and, in the process, its continuing interest and relevance.

What is the difference between "moral" and "theme"? As we have seen, a moral tends to be unitary, singular, and directed at personal behavior or belief. Thus, Aesop's fable, "The Town Mouse and the Country Mouse" explicitly states that the simple country life of security and peace is better than luxury surrounded by fear. The writer's finger seems pointed at us, warning against the temptations of material possessions bought at the price of anxiety. A theme, on the other hand, is a unifying idea that runs through a story. While a fable contains but one moral, a story may contain several themes; that is, it may be interpreted in a number of ways. A theme may be an ethical or moral issue, an idea about the nature of reality or history, the possibility of knowledge, the complex emotions that accompany an experience such as falling in love or losing a parent, and so on. A great deal of the writing and discussion about short stories focuses on theme. Theme more than anything else "explains" the story, though in the end a good story evades even the most sophisticated attempts to define its theme.

PARABLE: ST. LUKE, THE GOOD SAMARITAN

At first glance, parables—stories told by Jesus and recorded in the New Testament of the Bible—may seem little different from fables, except that parables have human characters rather than animals. Indeed, the impetus toward teaching a moral lesson is often much the same. In the case of the Good Samaritan, for example, the parable is told to answer a lawyer who asks, "And who is my neighbor?" After hearing the parable, the lawyer answers his own question: the true neighbor is "The one who showed mercy on him."

If that were the end of it, then perhaps the parable could be seen as just a variation on the fable, but the fact that untold numbers of sermons have been preached on this text suggests that the story is not as simple as it seems. The inaction of the priest and the Levite, the fact that Samaritans in Jesus' time were a despised minority, and the actions of the Samaritan in helping the wounded man complicate this simple tale in fascinating ways.

The precise influence of parables on the development of the short story is impossible to assess. Like myths, they have supplied writers with "archetypal" situations to explore. Like fables, they are masterpieces of brevity. Characters in parables such as "The Good Samaritan" and "The Prodigal Son" are brilliant examples of brief, pithy characterization—at once recognizable types and particular individuals. And, of course, they have inspired writers as examples of how stories can be at once simple and complex, blatantly obvious and tantalizingly subtle.

GIOVANNI BOCCACCIO: FIAMETTA'S STORY

Boccaccio's *Decameron,* like Ovid's *Metamorphoses,* is a collection of stories already known, often long before being collected by their "author." In Boccaccio's case, the stories are not myth but folktales, orally transmitted stories passed from generation to generation, occasionally written down by an educated person. Boccaccio used these written versions in compiling his work, probably between 1349 and 1351.

The individual stories of the *Decameron* are set up by a framing device: three noble ladies and seven gentlemen gather in a succession of villas outside Florence, Italy, to escape the Plague of 1348. To pass the time, each tells one story on each of the ten days of their exile (hence the title, from *decum,* meaning "ten"). Every day, a general theme is announced. On the fifth day, when this story is told, the theme is "the happiness to which lovers have arrived after many troublous adventures." The framing device and the story within a story are common conventions in the short story—usually employed to make the story sound believable.

Boccaccio's stories are not about supernatural beings or mythical heroes like some of the characters in other precursor stories. Federigo, despite his extraordinary devotion and self-sacrifice, is a recognizable human being. Madame Giovanna, an extraordinarily beautiful woman and devoted mother, is also a believable person. Elevating daily life to the level of literature is among the notable innovations of the late Middle Ages.

Although Madame Giovanna and Federigo are ordinary human beings, their characters are not well developed or complex. Much of the story's appeal lies, therefore, in the ironic twists of its plot, particularly the pathos of Federigo's sacrifice of his beloved hawk so that he can properly entertain the woman he loves. This story illustrates the ability of short fiction to sustain a relatively complicated story line through a rather extended period of time, as long as the details are carefully selected to relate to the central theme. Admittedly, the story line relies heavily on coincidence, and the attitudes of the principal characters are perhaps too formulaic and stylized by the norm later established for the modern short story. However, we are likely to feel that Boccaccio has breathed into the narrative conventions of character, action, point of view, and theme, and that a very high order of story-telling has been achieved.

FAIRY TALE: THE BLUE BEARD

Although we all think we know what a fairy tale is, defining the form is not easy. Among folklorists, the German term *Märchen* is preferred to fairy tale and is used to designate orally transmitted stories, primarily from Western Europe, that often employ the supernatural and generally trace the rise of a poor hero or heroine from destitution and obscurity to wealth and fame. Two phrases that seem permanently linked to the genre are the opening words, "Once upon a time" and the concluding words, "They lived happily ever after."

Fairy tales have long been a source of fascination. Collections of similar stories have been traced to fifth-century India and ninth-century Persia, with the first published collection in Europe appearing in Italy in the sixteenth century. Perhaps the most influential collection in Europe was that by Charles Perrault in 1697, which contained such favorites as "Sleeping Beauty," "Little Red Riding Hood," "Cinderella," and "The Blue Beard." European and American Romantics found ancient and folk literature particularly appealing, and the first short stories in Germany and America have clear connections to folk and fairy literature.

The primary conventions of the fairy tale—the intervention of the supernatural and the rise of the hero or heroine from poverty to wealth—place certain limits on the genre, not the least of which is characterization. Heroes and heroines in fairy tales are not well developed characters. Often, they show little promise as youngsters but are endowed by fate with luck, bravery, and cleverness so that they overcome their opponents and achieve their goals. Interestingly, fairy-tale heroes and heroines are not always particularly virtuous, and there may be no observable connection between their moral character and their eventual success. This generalized approach to character often lends to fairy-tale heroes and heroines a strong symbolic, perhaps even allegorical, nature, which we recognize when we speak of a "Cinderella team" in sports or someone who is a "giant killer."

The action in fairy tales parallels the conventions of adventure stories: the hero or heroine faces a series of obstacles, sometimes from the same enemy, sometimes from a series of enemies, until he or she triumphs and attains the desired prize. Such a narrative line creates suspense, which in the fairy tales can be developed to a high degree. In "The Blue Beard," for instance, the heroine's repeated question to her sister Anne, "What do you see?" delays the threatened execution and creates expectations that help is on the way. Like any good literary rescue, this one comes at the last possible moment.

Fairy tales often make skillful use of setting and atmosphere. Thus, in "The Blue Beard," the castle and its contents are described to convey opulence, even decadence, and the secret chamber is pictured in grisly detail. In this way, fairy tales prefigure Gothic fiction, "invented" by Hugh Walpole in his immensely influential novel *The Castle of Otranto* (1764). Gothic stories, like those of E. T. A. Hoffmann and Edgar Allan Poe, deliberately exploit the appeal of "pleasing terror" by offering readers (safe in their arm chairs) a taste of the dark, violent, twisted, and bizarre.

All of the elements that we see in the precursor stories—a concentrated plot, narrative point of view, simple but symbolic or allegorical characters, the presence of the magical and marvelous, setting, and atmospheric detail—were appropriated by early writers of short stories. At almost the same time in Europe and America (in the first decades of the nineteenth century) various authors combined these elements into what we now call the modern short story.

THE SHORT STORY: A BRIEF HISTORY

PROBLEMS OF ORIGIN AND DEFINITION

Every pre-literate culture studied has a rich oral tradition of stories, suggesting that short fiction has been around as long as people have. Certainly telling stories around the communal campfire reaches back many thousands of years. The earliest written records support this conclusion; samples of what we would call short fiction have been found in ancient Egyptian papyri dating from 3000 or 4000 B.C. Such myths, legends, and fables from ancient cultures bear striking resemblances to short stories in both form and narrative technique. Much surviving literature from ancient times is found in anthologies or miscellanies resembling modern short-story collections, and two classics from the middle ages, Giovanni Boccaccio's *Decameron* (ca. 1350) and Geoffrey Chaucer's *Canterbury Tales* (ca. 1387) are in essence collections of short fiction. Renaissance anthologies of tales and jokes were commonplace, and as early as the seventeenth century, antiquarians and other scholars began systematically collecting and studying ballads, tales, and legends that had been passed down orally for generations.

In spite of this long tradition, many critics and scholars agree that the short story as we know it today differs from the stories produced before the early nineteenth century. For one thing, myths, fables, and legends do not serve the same purposes as the short story. The ancient stories were intended primarily to convey cultural values, explain origins, and convey morality; modern stories seldom carry fundamental cultural ideas. The fact of printing—which assumes an audience of readers scattered by time and space—also makes short stories different from oral forms, which presuppose a listening audience in personal contact with the narrator. Finally, the short story is a commercial product, created and sold for a profit, and in this respect contrasts sharply with tales of oral tradition and even those by earlier writers such as Chaucer and Boccaccio.

Clear differences exist, then, between the older and newer forms, but deciding when and where the first short story appeared remains difficult. One theory holds that it was invented in the early nineteenth century in America by Washington Irving (1783–1859). Other literary historians give credit to German writers E. T. A. Hoffmann (1776–1822) or Heinrich von Kleist (1777–1811); and still others maintain that Frenchman Prosper Mérimée (1803–1870) has an equally valid claim. Deciding where and when the short story arose is closely related to the question of what the short story is and how it can be distinguished from similar forms. If, for example, the short story differs from the fable, then how do we explain that difference when a modern short story deliberately incorporates elements of the fable? If the short story is different from the fairy tales or those of Boccaccio, then what exactly are those differences and why are they important? Such questions are part of short-story theory, the effort to define and understand the genre by locating its differences from other forms in length, structure, content, theme, impact on the reader, or some combination of these.

The first selections in this anthology present a number of forms of short fiction that preceded the short story and helped give rise to it. The value of these selections, apart from their intrinsic interest, is that they put the short story into context, help us to see its connections to earlier forms. They also provide a basis for investigating how, when, and where the short story arose. Moreover, many of the "elements" of short fiction—character, plot, point of view, setting, atmosphere, tone, and theme—are easily studied in these selections, thereby providing an introduction to critical analysis.

ROMANTICISM AND THE RISE OF THE SHORT STORY

DATES OF ROMANTICISM
Europe: 1770–1830
England: 1798–1832
North America: 1820–1860
Latin America: 1830–1880

The modern story is largely a product of Romanticism, a cultural phenomenon of the late eighteenth and early nineteenth centuries that began in Germany and then swept eastward through Europe and into the New World. Part of this movement was a concerted effort to recover and preserve oral folk traditions, stimulated in part by the success of Charles Perrault's *Tales of Mother Goose* (1697), translated into English in 1729. Researchers and scholars in many countries, such as Jacob (1785–1863) and Wilhelm Grimm (1786–1859) in Germany, Hans Christian Andersen (1805–1875) in Denmark, and Bishop Percy (1729–1811) and Sir Walter Scott (1771–1832) in Britain, collected and published traditional lore and tales of all kinds—fairy tales, legends, ballads, and songs. These narrative forms lent themselves to literary imitation, as for example the "fairy tales" of Ludwig Tieck (Germany, 1773–1853), and the folklore that Washington Irving used in such stories as "Rip Van Winkle." Several features of folklore in general and fairy tales in particular appealed to the late eighteenth and early nineteenth-century imagination: their closeness to ordinary people, their antiquity, their vivid and often supernatural incidents, and their emphasis on the extraordinary and even bizarre aspects of experience.

To understand this better, we need to look briefly at the artistic and intellectual movement known as Romanticism. This movement cannot be defined easily or simply, since it took different forms at different times and places. Certain recurring features may be listed, however, so long as it is understood that these do not apply equally to all authors or works that can legitimately be labeled "Romantic." The following ideas characterize Romanticism:

1. The needs and rights of the individual transcend these of society at large. The individual is a law unto him or herself. The person of genius (particularly the artist) is above ordinary mortals, and unrestrained self-expression is the right of everyone, particularly the artist.

2. Emotion, not reason, is the path to true understanding and wisdom. Moreover, strong emotions, especially feelings of the sublime and eternal, are good to seek and cultivate for their own sake. Experience is best understood subjectively, not objectively.

3. Communion with nature—especially nature unspoiled by humans—is a source of true feeling, a guide to moral conduct, and a vehicle for encountering the transcendent or the divine. Moreover, a life close to Nature is preferable to one in the "artificial" city.

4. People are by nature good, and evil results from social influences and repressions—hence, the idea of the noble savage, unspoiled by civilization, and a fascination with "primitive" people.

5. Imagination and originality, not restraint and tradition, are the key ingredients in any work of art.

6. The remote, the exotic, the medieval, the strange (including strange, warped, or dreamlike emotional or psychological states) are valued over the ordinary realities of daily life.

7. Stylistically, Romanticism prefers lush exuberance to decorum, restraint, and simplicity. Romantic prose is often rich with description; it tends toward abstract words like "tremendous" and "gorgeous"; it chooses and uses words for their maximum emotional effect.

8. The ideal, imaginary, and visionary are more important and more "real" than the mundane facts of daily life; by creating the ideal, artists become, as Shelley said, "the unacknowledged legislators of the world."

In the short story, these ideas most clearly manifest themselves in horror stories and ghost stories, in the depiction of character, in strong moralizing tendencies, and style.

Romanticism coincided, especially in England and North America, with the coming of industrialism, and was in many ways a reaction against the ugly realities of cities and the assaults on nature that industrialism caused. But industrialism also produced the means by which authors could earn a living through the sale of hundreds or even thousands of copies of a single work. Technological developments in printing and re-producing pictures gave impetus to newspapers and illustrated magazines, which pro-vided outlets for short works of many kinds—essays, reviews, articles, poems, and short stories. The combination of increased education and literacy, a ready commercial market, the need for professional authors to make money, and the aesthetic possibili-ties offered by producing short works of tight narrative and emotional unity produced what we now call the short story.

In this process, something else happened. The nature of story-telling changed, just as the nature of poetry changed when reading it on the page supplanted hearing it recited orally. Stories written by one individual to anonymous readers are no longer community property. The individual's vision replaces common experience. Oral tech-niques are replaced by individual style. Stories can be more complex and subtle be-cause readers can re-read what they don't understand the first time.

A different "delivery system" changes not only the content but also the cultural function of stories. Oral tales reflect communal values, but magazines supported by advertising are likely to reflect the social, political, and ethical ideas or preferences of those who write, edit, and distribute them. The possibility exists for fiction to become a means of social control.

THE EMERGENCE OF SHORT-STORY THEORY

Most early writers of short stories were not conscious that they were creating a new genre. Short fictional pieces had appeared in magazines and newspapers for almost a century before the short story, so there was little sense among writers that they were producing something qualitatively different from the essay, the character sketch, the fable, the tale, the abbreviated novel. The first important statement of this sense of dif-ference—of short-story theory—was Edgar Allan Poe's (1809–1849) famous definition of the short story as a prose work that could be read at a single sitting, that provided a "unity of effect," and that could reach a high level of artistic excellence:

> A skillful literary artist has constructed a tale. If wise, he has not fashioned his thoughts to accommodate his incidents; but having conceived, with deliberate care, a certain unique or single *effect* to be wrought out, he then invents such incidents—he then combines such events as may best aid him in establishing this preconceived effect. If his very initial sentence tend not to the outbringing of this effect, then he has failed in his first step. In the whole composition there should be no word written, of which the tendency, direct or indirect, is not to the one pre-established design. (Review of Hawthorne's *Twice-Told Tales*)

Because of this statement, Poe has sometimes been credited with inventing the form, but he probably does not deserve this honor. What Poe did was to define, not invent, the short story. Rather, as suggested above, the combination of Romantic ideas about literature, the demands by magazines for short, self-contained works of fiction, and the need for authors to earn money led to the birth of a new genre now called the short story.

Poe's now-famous theory was not immediately influential. Short fictions of many kinds other than those fitting Poe's definition continued to be written. In America, the work of Washington Irving, Nathaniel Hawthorne (1804–1864), and Poe was almost drowned by a tidal-wave of sentimental and formulaic fiction that appeared in magazines and annual "gift books"—anthologies designed primarily as Christmas presents for female readers. Chief among these in America was *Godey's Ladies' Book,* a monthly magazine that began in 1830 and soon reached a subscription of 40,000 per year. Its demand for self-contained short stories was an important impetus in the emergence of the American short story. Although it published such authors as Poe, Hawthorne, Henry Wadsworth Longfellow (1807–1882), Ralph Waldo Emerson (1803–1882), and Harriet Beecher Stowe (1811–1896), its mainstay was sentimental stories of love and virtue triumphant over evil, which were also published by dozens of other magazines and story papers. Overall, the conventional short story of the nineteenth century—in both Europe and America—was a tale that focused on the heroic, the bizarre, or the miraculous, or that dealt with love or action/adventure in an idealized way. Characters in such fiction tended to be extreme—paragons of vice or virtue, or gripped by some obsession or madness.

It is against this background that we can best appreciate the achievements of Hoffmann, Irving, Poe, Hawthorne, Caroline Kirkland (1801–1864), and others. They collectively invented a new form by using older materials in a new way. Moreover, they used many of the same conventions and addressed the same readers as did other writers, but they either used these conventions more effectively or went beyond them to create original and effective works of art. Poe occupies a unique place in this period, not only because he articulated a theory of the short story, but also because he showed in his stories and criticism that the form was capable of literary excellence. He also invented the modern detective story and contributed to the invention of science fiction.

REALISM AND NEW DIRECTIONS IN THE SHORT STORY

DATES FOR REALISM
Europe: 1830–1880
England: 1832–1903
North America: 1865–1900
Latin America: 1860–1910

As a force of artistic energy and innovation, Romanticism began to wane by the mid-nineteenth century, though its influence has never really died. Throughout the nineteenth century, and even into the twentieth, the public's appetite for romantic stories of love, adventure, detection, and mystery has been insatiable. But writers of one generation are seldom content to copy their elders. Even as some Romantic writers were producing their best work, younger writers were making valuable contributions by exploring new possibilities for the short story, among them Caroline Kirkland (1801–1864), Nikolai Gogol (1809–1852), Ivan Turgenev (1818–1883), Herman Melville (1819–1891), Gustave Flaubert (1821–1880), Mark Twain (1835–1910), and Henry James (1843–1916).

These writers were part of a movement in Western thought that we now call Realism. As a distinct literary movement, Realism was in part a reaction against the conventions of Romanticism, particularly its idealistic and sentimental aspects. Realists objected to the idealized characters, conventional moralizing, and the stilted, artificial diction of the sentimental style. For Realists, Romanticism was a misrepresentation, a deliberate lie that prevented people from apprehending reality and making sound moral judgments.

It was not only reaction against Romanticism that influenced the new movement. The rise of science and its apparent objectivity led many authors away from the subjectivity of Romanticism and toward a "clinically detached" attitude to narrative. Moreover, the idea that human behavior is determined by heredity, environment, or both suggested to authors like Guy de Maupassant (1850–1893), Gustave Flaubert (1821–1880), and Henry James (1843–1916) that literature should probe the forces that shape character and action. The Realist author often assumes the attitude of the neutral investigator who reports "the facts" of cause and effect without prejudice or the coloring of ideology.

Realists and Romantics also had different views of the purposes and functions of literature. Middle-class publishers, editors, and writers regarded literature as a force for moral good that presents examples of behavior—nobility, heroism, and self-sacrifice—to which readers should aspire. Realists, however, were inclined to see literature as a way of understanding how the world "really" works. The argument was neatly framed by George Eliot (Mary Ann Evans, 1819–1880) in an aside to the reader in her novel *Adam Bede* (1859), where she replies to the objections of an imaginary reader that her protagonists are not morally good people:

> It is so very rarely that the facts hit that nice medium required by our own enlightened opinions and refined taste! Perhaps you will say, "Do improve the facts a little, then; make them more accordant with those correct views which it is our privilege to possess. The world is not just what we like; do touch it up with a tasteful pencil, and make believe it is not quite such a mixed entangled affair. Let your most faulty characters always be on the wrong side, and your virtuous ones on the right. Then we shall see at a glance whom we are to condemn and whom we are to approve. . . ." [But] I am content to tell my simple story, without trying to make things seem better than they were; dreading nothing, indeed, but falsity, which, in spite of one's best efforts, there is reason to dread. Falsehood is so easy, truth so difficult.

LOCAL COLOR AND HUMOR

One movement that contributed to the transition between Romanticism and Realism, particularly in North America and also to some extent in Latin America, England, and Europe, was Local Color. Local Colorists were self-consciously regional writers who capitalized on the public's appetite for information about remote regions and "quaint" customs. In particular, Local Colorists emphasized the following:

1. The idiosyncrasies of dress, speech, attitude, and customs of the people who lived in a particular area, such as New England in the United States, the backwoods areas of Ontario, Canada, the ranches of Argentina, or the colonial outposts of India;

2. Descriptions of nature that captured the peculiarities of the local landscape;

3. Representations of the local dialect in pronunciation, vocabulary, and idiom;

4. Plots or story lines that revealed the peculiar characteristics and customs of the local people;

5. Strong, colorful characters representing the various types to be found in a specific locale.

The overriding purpose of local color stories was to convey the flavor of the people and places, often with no other thematic idea in mind. The emphasis on the unique character of a region's people could lead to sentimentality or idealization, but the Local Colorists' use of dialect and specific description was an important part of the Realist movement, and local color lent itself particularly well to short stories. In addition to Caroline Kirkland (1801–1864) and Harriet Beecher Stowe (1811–1896), are Mark Twain (1835–1910), Mary E. Wilkins Freeman (1852–1930), Kate Chopin (1851–1904), and Ivan Turgenev (1818–1883).

Regional writing, especially of the American West, was often marked by deliberate exaggeration and rough humor. Frontier humorists such as Mark Twain aimed their barbs at the pomposities and follies of "stuffed shirts" and "hypocrites" and thereby contributed to the "debunking" aspect of Realism. The purpose of such humor, besides entertainment, was to expose Romantic idealism, blind patriotism, and generally to remove the "rose-tinted glasses" encouraged by writers of the previous generation.

CHARACTERISTICS OF REALISM

Like Romanticism, Realism is not a single or unified ideology but a complicated series of tendencies or traits. Above all, it is not the opposite of Romanticism, since Realistic and Romantic traits may exist in the same work or the same author. Harriet Beecher Stowe and Ivan Turgenev (1818–1883) exhibit both local color realism and sentimentality, and even such exemplars of Realism as Gustave Flaubert (1821–1880) and Guy de Maupassant (1850–1893) have their lyrical and sentimental sides. Thus, while not all writers classed as Realists held to all of the following ideas, these beliefs or attitudes are characteristic of the group as a whole.

1. Like Romantics, Realists (especially in America) were democratic in spirit, believing in the individual. However, Realists were unlikely to believe in the perfectibility of mankind or in the idea that people behave in noble and self-sacrificing ways. They often use ordinary or even "low-life" characters but are less likely than Romantics to idealize them. In Realistic works, unlike Romantic ones, the individual seldom triumphs over society or the forces that oppose him or her.

2. Truth for realists is not discovered by feeling. Moreover, Realists are seldom interested in "absolute truth" and usually present truth as relative and multiple, rather than as absolute and singular.

3. Among Realists, nature is usually seen as hostile or indifferent to humans rather than as beneficent. Realists do not seek out nature as a source of inspiration, nor do they look to it for moral guidance, except perhaps to see in nature the "survival of the fittest." Many Realists excel at descriptions of nature, however, and these are sometimes lush and Romantic in feeling.

4. Realists generally deny the essential goodness of humans and if anything emphasize their innate depravity. Darwin and Freud were influential in suggesting the selfish and even "bestial" qualities of people.

5. Realists strive for originality, but in a different way from the Romantics' emphasis on the uniqueness of the individual's vision and the almost priest-like role of the artist. Realists judge art mimetically; that is, by its fidelity to what can be observed and is ordinarily experienced. The role of the artist is to observe and report, not to invent and imagine.

6. Realists reject the unusual and exotic in favor of the ordinary and commonplace. They attempt to describe things "as they are" and to present events and chains of events that are likely and probable rather than those that are novel or surprising.

7. Stylistically, Realists reject the highly colored rhetoric of the Romantics and strive for directness and precision, especially when creating spoken dialogue. Dialect, slang, and "bad grammar" are among the conventions used to simulate "real speech."

THE CONVENTIONS OF REALISM

"Realism" is a term that is as misunderstood and misapplied as "Romanticism." For many readers, realism is not a descriptive word but a judgmental one, for to them "realism" and literary quality are the same thing. This attitude often assumes that reality is a single, easily definable quality, which a given work of literature either has or lacks. "It's not realistic," is often issued by such readers as an irrefutable and final judgment about a piece of writing, a play, a film, or a television program.

A preference for Realism is as defensible as a taste for any other type of art, but those who use the term need to recognize that what we call realism in literature is as much a matter of convention as any other literary idea. In other words, "Realism," like other literary "isms," is made up of conventional ideas and techniques. Chief among the conventions of Realism is verisimilitude, the device of depicting the everyday world in such a way as to make it seem plausible, "real." Thus, Realists pay careful attention to observable details, such as dress, manners, furnishings, and the like. In addition, they focus on actions and events that mirror those of everyday life, excluding the miraculous, the bizarre, the fantastic. In this way, they hope to convince readers that what they are describing really exists and that the actions that occur in their stories could happen in "real life." Realists attempt to depict consistent, "believable" characters who act from clearly defined motives. Of course, Realist writers knew that people are complex and that motives are often multiple, not single, but at the core, Realistic characters are essentially knowable and stable.

The Realist approach often disguises the fact that all art is created by selection and emphasis. Even a photographer chooses to point the camera in one direction and not another. What is not photographed is every bit as real as what is, but of course it is not in the picture. Similarly, Realist writers select, emphasize, and arrange—they do not simply transcribe and report. Moreover, Realists often emphasize the negative, as if greed were somehow a more real emotion than generosity, or cowardice more real than heroism. Influenced by scientific empiricism, they also tend to ignore or deny the supernatural or spiritual, since such things cannot be observed. Characters in Realistic fiction may seem more believable than those in Romantic fiction because they talk in ways we recognize from experience, but even "realistic" dialogue is far more witty, pointed, fluent, and grammatical than everyday speech.

SOCIAL RESTRAINTS ON REALISM

In spite of their claim to describe the "real world" and how it works, Realists ignored or slighted many important subjects. In America, for example, most of them (Mark Twain and Harriet Beecher Stowe excepted) ignored the problems of slavery and of African-American life during and after Reconstruction. Most of them glossed over prostitution and played down the plight of women generally. No major North

American writer examined the lives of immigrants or looked seriously at the plight of Native Americans. Much of what Realists ignored in the society around them was dictated by the taste and mores of the day. Nineteenth-century people did not want to read about sex or other private bodily functions; most of them did not regard the experiences of minorities as important; most were content with the prevailing patriarchy. Although much Realist fiction criticized the status quo, only a few daring souls like Thomas Hardy (1840–1928) in England, Stephen Crane (1871–1900) in America, and Emile Zola (1840–1902) in France dared to deal more or less openly with taboo subjects like rape and prostitution. In short, the appearance of "Realism" does not guarantee that all of reality will be examined, nor does it guarantee literary quality or make fiction valid. High-quality writing in the Realist mode is as difficult to achieve as high-quality writing in the Romantic mode.

The subjects Realism deals with and the way it treats them may be as bound by literary and social convention as those of the Romantics. (Social convention, we should remember, was often supported by law, and the penalties for pornography or sedition could be severe.) Nevertheless, in the Americas and Europe there were courageous voices of dissent. Ivan Turgenev (1818–1883), Mark Twain, Anton Chekhov (1860–1904), and others asserted the dignity and value of ordinary, even inconsequential, people. Later, the emerging voices of women, African-Americans, Jews, and other groups affirmed the value and humanity of these hitherto silenced or stereotyped people. Charles W. Chesnutt (1858–1932) and Kate Chopin (1851–1904) were two Americans to publish short stories on new subjects. As the nineteenth century drew to a close, the short story was becoming an important vehicle for conveying the experiences of women and minorities.

DATES FOR NATURALISM
Europe: 1865–1900
North America: 1890–1910
Latin America: 1880–1910

In the last decades of the nineteenth century, another movement gained momentum along with Realism. The two schools are sometimes hard to distinguish, but Naturalism is marked by its emphasis on the most stark and harsh aspects of life and by its commitment to determinism. Under this philosophy, human beings are seen as animals in the natural world—creatures driven by forces and instincts they may not understand and cannot control. Fiction written in the Naturalist mode reflects the strict application of ideas derived from Auguste Comte (1798–1857), Charles Darwin (1809–1882), Sigmund Freud (1856–1939), and Karl Marx (1818–1883)—all of whom emphasize humankind's place in nature and its almost mechanical responses to internal and external stimuli. Guy de Maupassant, and Stephen Crane are among those closely allied with Naturalism.

GENRE FICTION

A parallel development during the late nineteenth century was the growth of genre fiction—the detective story, the ghost story, the love story, the rags-to-riches success story, the Gothic story, and science fiction, to name just a few. The importance of these forms to mass audiences, to the economic success of magazines, and to the development of the short story can hardly be overestimated. To take but a few examples: "The Overcoat" is partly a ghost story; "Chickamauga" shares aspects of the adventure tale. "The Ruby" is a fantasy; "Désirée's Baby" is part mystery; "The Lady With the Dog" a love story, and so on. Sometimes an author incorporates such popular elements wholesale, while at other times the writer may be deliberately playing off the conventions of these genres to create a new or surprising effect. In either case, genre stories provide many opportunities to write within conventions or to experiment with innovations.

THE "GOLDEN AGE" OF THE SHORT STORY

By the end of the nineteenth century, the short story had become an important literary genre. It was a staple part of hundreds of magazines in Europe and North America, ranging from highly literary, experimental "little magazines" like *The Mirror* (1893–1920) to substantial general interest magazines like *Harper's* (1850–) and the *Atlantic Monthly* (1857–) to popular, mass-circulation magazines such as the *Saturday Evening Post* (1821–1969) and *Frank Leslie's Popular Magazine* (1876–1956), to pulp magazines and story papers like *Saturday Night* and *Family Story Paper.* These last were devoted exclusively to short stories and serials of a highly romanticized, highly "unreal" nature, full of abductions, adventures, grand passions, beautiful heroines, and spotless heroes. The magazines mentioned above are all American, but the same kinds of publications and audiences were found throughout Canada, Europe, and to a lesser extent in Central and South America. The short story was simultaneously big business and high art, popular entertainment and the site of intense literary experimentation.

By the turn of the century, the popular idea of the short story had become almost standardized. An influential literary critic, Brander Matthews (1852–1929), proclaimed that the essence of the short story was plot. His "Philosophy of the Short Story," published first as an article in the *London Saturday Review* (July 5, 1884) and later expanded into book form (1901), provided a generation of editors and critics with the most influential theory of short fiction since Poe's. Although he stressed "unity of impression," as Poe had done, he went on to proclaim that "The Short-story is nothing if there is no story to tell;—one might almost say that a Short-story is nothing if it has no plot,—except that 'plot' may suggest to some readers a complication and an elaboration which are not really needful." Coming at the height of the short story's popularity in Europe and the Americas, Matthews' theory confirmed what most readers of the time intuitively felt.

Further support for this attitude came from the common practice of most short story writers of the day, particularly from one of the most popular and influential of the early twentieth century—O. Henry (William Sidney Porter [1862–1910]). O. Henry combined a realistic surface and a sense of life's ironies with sentimental ideas of character and a penchant for surprise or "trick" endings. His stories were immensely popular at the time and long after his death. For many people, the "O. Henry" short story remains the epitome of the form.

Matthews and O. Henry, however, were essentially backward-looking. Although millions of people (and the vast majority of literary editors) agreed with Matthews' precepts and the conventions they implied, new ideas about the short story were being practiced by Anton Chekhov, Katherine Mansfield (Katherine Mansfield Beauchamp, 1888–1923), James Joyce (1882–1941), and many others.

THE RISE OF THE MODERNIST MOVEMENT

DATES FOR MODERNISM
Europe: 1890–1945
England: 1914–1965
North America: 1914–1965
Latin America: 1880–1945

The last two decades of the nineteenth century, concurrent with the heyday of Realism and the emergence of Naturalism, saw the beginning of profound new stirrings in Western thought. Ever since the Renaissance, the certainties of religion, philosophy, and morality had been receding before the forces of science, secularism, relativism, and skepticism. During the nineteenth century, the writings of Charles Darwin (*The Origin of Species,* 1859), Karl Marx (*The Communist Manifesto,* 1848), Sir James Frazer (*The Golden Bough,* 1890–1915), Sigmund Freud (*The Interpretation of Dreams,* 1900), and many others called into question the authority of the Bible, the humanistic underpinnings of public and private morality, and the foundations of knowledge generally. In other words, thinkers in all fields challenged the ideas, values, and assumptions that had provided the basis of Western Civilization for centuries. Of course, movements like this one had happened before: in the seventeenth century, the poet John Donne claimed that "The new philosophy calls all in doubt." Now doubt seemed dominant on every front, however, and what is more, skepticism was no longer the province only of a small intellectual elite. Challenges to old ideas and ideologies reached all levels of society through the mass media of newspapers, magazines, and inexpensive books.

Early warning signs of the new movement can be discerned in the Aesthetic and Decadent movements in Europe and England in the 1890s, in the French Symbolist poets (1880–1895), in the self-conscious artistic sensibility of some Latin American short story writers like Rubén Darío (1867–1916), in the profound skepticism and pessimism of the poet and novelist Thomas Hardy (1840–1928), in the fictional experiments of Joseph Conrad (1857–1924), and in the bitter late works of Mark Twain (such as *The Man That Corrupted Hadleyburg,* 1900).

Other challenges to conventional authority came from new voices of women and the racial and ethnic minorities mentioned above: in Europe and England, the rebellion was led by women; in America, by women and hitherto silent minorities, such as Jews and African-Americans. Modernism received an additional impetus with the outbreak of World War I in 1914. During that war and its immediate aftermath, the conventions and pillars of the nineteenth century came crashing down. When the war finally ended in 1918, it was as though a whole generation had been shell-shocked in the trenches. The senseless slaughter of millions of soldiers and civilians, the use of science for purposes of mass murder and destruction, and the inability of any institution to curtail the conflict left many people—especially the young—in a state of valueless frenzy. Nothing seemed certain. No one could be trusted. Despair, hedonism, cynicism were the watchwords of the day, and for many young people in particular the only solaces were to be found in instant wealth, easy sex, and gin.

What emerged in those years preceding and following the Great War was an art form based on new assumptions and conventions. What it rejected was certainty and stability in any realm outside art itself. Modernism embraced a wide variety of experimentation in form, style, and content, as can be seen in the stories of early leaders in the movement: Katherine Mansfield, Virginia Woolf (1882–1941), and James Joyce in Britain; Ernest Hemingway (1899–1961), Sherwood Anderson (1876–1941), and Rubén Darío, among the North Americans. One aspect of Modernism rejected conventional morality, particularly in matters relating to sex. It insisted upon the freedom to explore previously taboo subjects and to do so in frank, direct language. In large measure, the Modernists turned against the presumed audience of middle-class readers who wanted entertainment and reinforcement of their prejudices (or at most gentle suggestions of reform). Rather than accommodating the reader's expectations in form and content, Modernists challenged them with fiction of deliberate complexity and difficulty. Sherwood Anderson spoke for many of his contemporaries when he said:

> There was a notion that ran through all story-telling in America, that stories must be built about a plot and that absurd Anglo-Saxon notion that they must point a moral, uplift the people, make better citizens, etc. The magazines were filled with these plot stories and most of the plays on our stage were plot plays. "The Poison Plot," I called it in conversation with my friends as the plot notion did seem to me to poison all story-telling. What was wanted I thought was form, not plot, an altogether more elusive and difficult thing to come at.

Again, it is impossible to summarize accurately a movement that spans fifty years (1914 to 1965) and includes a great many authors. However, the following features are generally considered to be among the most important and pervasive of the Modernist movement:

1. Modernists usually reject plot as an organizing device; most believed that plot was at best artificial and at worst a straight-jacket that hindered the exploration of character and consciousness.

2. Modernists often deal with interior rather than exterior action; conflict is not between a protagonist and antagonist but between the forces within the mind and heart of the character. Interior action, not exterior, leads some readers to complain that in a Modernist story, "nothing happens."

3. Modernists reject linear time: past and present, rational thought and irrational urge, conscious and unconscious motive, dream and reality, objective fact and subjective perception may all clash simultaneously and in the process give the impression of an eternal present. "Stream of consciousness" is the most extreme technique for expressing this inner complexity.

4. Character is unstable and in many cases unknowable because human behavior and its motivations are too complex to be formulated or captured.

5. Point of view may shift within a given work; the omniscient narrator may be replaced by several subjective points of view, none of which represents that of the author.

6. Theme relies increasingly on image and symbol as clues to meaning. The author's neutral stance leaves interpretation to the reader.

7. In the short story particularly, "open endings" are preferred over "closed endings." In other words, the reader is often left "hanging," not knowing how a situation is resolved or why it is resolved in a particular way.

Modernism affected all the arts, producing revolutionary ideas and modes of expression in painting, drama, dance, music, sculpture, architecture, interior design, film, and even fashion. In many ways, Modernism marked the culmination of the breach that had been widening for over a century between artist and audience. Romantics, of course, had often claimed the superiority of the artist over "ordinary" people, but the excesses of this claim had moderated under the influence of Victorian ideas of respectability and morality. Victorians might regard literature as in some ways a substitute for religion and the author as a prophet of sound values, but they could never countenance the Modernists' insistence on the author as a law unto him or herself, free from the dictates of society. For some Modernists, art was the only vehicle for bringing form out of chaos, for creating order (however fleetingly) in a world whose religion and morality had become meaningless and life itself absurd. In thus championing art and the artist, Modernism rudely rejected both the form and content of middle-class life and culture, and in some cases deliberately set out to shock the complacent bourgeois. One result was prolonged battles over censorship. Short stories were especially restricted until well into this century for the same reasons that film, television, video games, and the Internet are under pressure today: popular, mass circulation magazines were vehicles of "family entertainment" and were therefore more tightly controlled than books.

The other result was a greater than ever antagonism between "high art" and "popular art," or between high-brow, middle-brow, and low-brow culture. People used to the conventions of Realism want plot, stable characters, and closed endings in their fiction and drama, and perhaps above all the comforting sense that the world makes sense, that good triumphs over evil, and that traditional values like hard work and marital fidelity are worth preserving. W. Somerset Maugham spoke for many such people when he said, "I have myself a weakness for the short story that has a precise form. I like it to have a beginning, a middle, and an end. I do not want to be left in doubt about what happens. I like the author to say everything to the point that he has to say on the subject of his choice. That is the old fashioned method" (Qtd in Archer 97). Modernist artists typically rejected all of these conventions as outmoded, with the predictable result that mainstream audiences rejected or ignored Modernist artists.

In spite of the restraints placed on it, the short story was well suited to voices of protest and experiment, because of the proliferation of magazines—especially literary magazines—aimed at sophisticated audiences. A book requires a considerable outlay of capital and a well developed network of stores for distribution. Popular, "slick" magazines cater to large, middle-class audiences and are financed mainly by advertisers. Literary magazines, however, are relatively inexpensive to produce and need only a reliable postal system to reach subscribers. Hundreds of new authors found outlets for their ideas in the literary magazines that sprang up throughout Europe and North America beginning in the 1800s. Many lasted only a few issues, but others flourished for years. Their very existence encouraged experiment and frequently provided authors with the chance to gain exposure and an audience that could later lead to publication in mainstream magazines and then a contract for a novel with a publishing firm. Such magazines benefited not only experimental writers but also writers from groups that previously had been denied access to print. In America, a new wave of immigrant writers chronicled their experiences, often in the short story. Women and racial minorities also benefited from the little magazines. The African-American experience finally reached mainstream audiences, at first via magazines like *Scribner's* that published such authors as Charles W. Chesnutt (1858–1932) and later through the works of the so-called Harlem Renaissance of the 1920s, which involved not only literature but also art and music, particularly jazz.

CROSSCURRENTS IN THE MODERNIST PERIOD

The term Modernism applies to authors who consciously experimented with form and content, but many accomplished authors of the same period wrote within the broad traditions of Realism and Naturalism. The vogue of Modernism has often obscured the achievements of these more traditional artists, among them some of the black writers mentioned above. Modernism can be adapted to social protest or the exposure of prejudice, but its emphasis on interior action and psychological probing makes it ill-suited to depict social problems. Moreover, Modernist ideas and conventions do not appeal to everyone. At the same time that Modernism was claiming the field for technical innovation, many accomplished authors and enlightened readers continued to find value in traditional story telling. Langston Hughes (1902–1967), Zora Neale Hurston (1901?–1960), F. Scott Fitzgerald (1896–1940), H. E. Bates (1905–1974), and Isaac Bashevis Singer (1904–1991) adapted traditional methods to new situations and ideas. This is one reason why scholars and critics sometimes disagree over which authors are significant, since one group tends to favor style and method, while the other is more interested in content and message. A particularly strong tension existed in the Modernist period, therefore, between convention and innovation, and it occurs at many levels throughout the short story and indeed all art forms.

POST-MODERNISM

DATES FOR POST-MODERNISM
Europe: 1945–
North America: 1960–
Latin America: 1945–

By the midcentury, the conventions of Modernism were themselves under strong attack from a variety of sources, not least of which was the phenomenal growth in mass media, particularly radio, film, and television, during the first half of the century. By 1960, that most important medium for the short story, the magazine, had changed dramatically and fundamentally. Gone were most of the general-interest magazines, like *Collier's* and *Liberty* (to cite just two American examples), that had provided mass audiences for short stories. The most famous of all, *The Saturday Evening Post,* limped along until 1969. First radio, then television, supplanted the print media as sources of information and entertainment. By the 1960s only a handful of American magazines, primarily *Harper's, The Atlantic Monthly, Esquire, Playboy,* and *The New Yorker* were reaching significant numbers of readers with quality fiction. (The situation was similar in Britain and many other countries.) Genre fiction became almost exclusively the property of "pulp" detective and science fiction magazines like *Ellery Queen's* and *Amazing Stories.* Of course, some women's magazines continued to publish formulaic love stories and romances, but for the most part these were the province of second-rate writers, willing to meet the audience's expectations for escape and happy endings.

The rise of popular mass media was in direct opposition to the often "elitist" and "exclusive" nature of Modernist literature and art.

Meanwhile, the disintegration of the modern world continued apace. The horrors of the First World War had been surpassed by the nightmare of the Second (1939–1945). Reality seemed constantly to surpass fiction: concentration camps, genocide, internments of loyal civilians, mass bombings, Hiroshima and Nagasaki. Events seemed to outrun even the most fertile imaginations, and for many authors even the Modernists' insistence on art as a unifying force was destroyed by the splintering of consciousness and the impossibility of understanding. The very notion that literature, in Matthew Arnold's phrase, could "see life steadily and see it whole" seemed absurd. Fragments, individual perceptions, incoherence, even drug-induced hallucinations seemed more real and in touch with the times than any claim of stability or unity.

CHARACTERISTICS OF POST-MODERNISM

1. In Post-Modern thought, any sense of a unifying idea or philosophy such as religion or even the notion of scientific or social "progress" is rejected;

2. As a result, art cannot provide any kind of explanation or unity for experience—it cannot explain or unify experience;

3. Unlike Modernism, Post-Modernism does not look for a unified sense of self in the individual; like the world the individual is a random collection or collage of miscellaneous pieces of the external culture;

4. Similarly, art itself is a collage, a collection of fragments that create no unity; a work of art is an object, like a rock or piece of furniture, that the reader can examine or play with;

5. Fiction embraces all aspects of the present culture, from rock and roll to advertising, cartoons to ancient myths, often juxtaposing these in fantastic combination as a way of conveying the fragmentation of contemporary life;

6. In fiction, the "point" of the novel or story is about the process of making fiction—it is metafiction;

7. Satire, parody, jokes, black humor often dominate the tone of a work of fiction;

8. The writer may be able to expose and oppose the insane work of politicians and technocrats, but he or she has no alternate vision to offer, since there can be no coherent vision offered in place of the current power structure.

If Post-Modernism sounds much like Modernism, that is because in many respects the two movements are similar. In a way, Post-Modernism simply means that a new generation concluded, as its elders had done, that there are no certainties and that life has no meaning beyond what we can impose upon it. It is in technique that Post-Modernism distinguishes itself from Modernism, and in this respect no author has been more influential than Jorge Luis Borges (1899–1986). Borges extended the Modernist attack on objective reality by exploring the boundaries between reality and illusion, insisting that the two are inseparable. In "Death and the Compass," Borges parodies the detective story to show how Lönnrot's attempts to impose order through reason only lead to his destruction. Borges's explorations of the irrational and absurd are similar in many ways to another Latin American technique, Magical Realism. In this kind of fiction, the author establishes an apparently realistic situation and then injects into it a character or event that is blatantly fantastic or magical. Almost as influential has been the work of Donald Barthelme (1931–1989) and Robert Coover (b. 1932), whose fragmented "metafictions" expose the conventions and formulas of fiction itself. Metafiction deliberately calls attention to the arbitrariness and artificiality of fictional constructions and to the ways in which these attempt to impose order and meaning on what is chaotic and meaningless.

These movements have been followed by others, including Minimalism, Hyper- or K-Mart Realism, and the Anti-story. Minimalism is again nothing new—Hemingway strove to use few words and simple words—but later Minimalists go further. Their focus on exteriors and surfaces can puzzle readers who expect even simple language to reverberate with significance and to suggest meaning. Hyper-Realism emphasizes the inarticulate, pop-culture saturated world of the lower middle classes, where a kind of existential despair seems to reign by default. "Anti-story" is a term coined by Philip Stevik to describe stories that, among other things, emphasize extreme experiences and deliberately avoid stating a theme.

NEW WORLDS OF THE SHORT STORY

With the Post-Modernist movement has come the ever-increasing and widespread recognition of literatures other than those of North America and Europe. The short story has always been an international form, but in the late twentieth century, an explosion of interest has made literature from all over the world more readily available. In part, this interest has been promoted by the "global village" created by television, film, travel, and computer networking. More and more of the outpouring of new short fiction, written in many languages, is translated and distributed, bringing it to wider audiences. An anthology of this size can only begin to suggest the riches currently available.

Apart from a few large-circulation magazines that still publish one or two quality short stories per issue, most of today's short stories appear in little magazines sponsored by academic institutions. Some critics go so far as to say that the short story has become a kind of incestuous cottage industry in which everybody writes but nobody reads. Although the short story does face intense competition from nonprint media, annual collections like *The Best American Short Stories, Winter's Tales, The Pushcart Prize Stories, The O. Henry Awards,* and anthologies and collections of stories on every conceivable theme and subject help keep the genre vital and new work accessible. Collections by individual authors are regularly reviewed in general interest magazines like *Time, Newsweek,* and *The New York Times Book Review.* The ultimate goal of this anthology is to provide a sense of the rewards the short story has to offer in the hopes that you will become "hooked" on a form that has provided inspiration and satisfaction to writers and readers for nearly two hundred years. Ideally, you will continue your investigation into the short story indefinitely. Writers continue to hold up their end of the bargain by writing stories both conventional and innovative. Our end of the bargain—and a pleasurable one it is—is to reward their efforts with knowledgeable, appreciative, critical readership. A lifetime of pleasure and imaginative stimulation awaits those who enter into this continuing dialogue and its interplay of convention and innovation.

WORKS CITED

Anderson, Sherwood. *A Story Teller's Story.* New York: B. W. Heubsch, 1924.

Archer, Stanley. *W. Somerset Maugham: A Study of the Short Fiction.* New York: Twayne, 1993.

Poe, Edgar Allan. "Review of Nathaniel Hawthorne's *Twice-Told Tales.*" *The Complete Works of Edgar Allan Poe.* Ed. James A. Harrison. Vol. 11. New York: Thomas Y. Crowell and Co., 1942. 106–113.

PART THREE

Reading and Writing about Short Fiction

READING FICTION ACTIVELY

Reading is so much a part of our everyday lives that we can barely remember a time when we could not read. It is so automatic, in fact, that it is almost impossible to look at words on a sign or billboard, for instance, and *not* read them. But perhaps because reading is so automatic, we often take it for granted; it seems as effortless as breathing. We pick up a newspaper or magazine, skim articles here and there or carefully read one that interests us, and then just as easily cast it aside. A few minutes later, we may have forgotten almost everything we have read.

This kind of automatic reading may be fine as a way to cope with the barrage of words that assaults our eyes every day, but it encourages habits that are not useful on other occasions. Passive reading—that is, running our eyes over the words on a page without much reflection or analysis—is one of the mental habits a course in the short story strives to overcome. Short stories cannot be read passively if they are to be fully understood and enjoyed.

In *How To Read a Book,* Mortimer Adler points out that active reading is a lot like a good game of catch. When someone throws a ball to you, he or she is like a writer—sending out a message for you to grasp. Clearly, you can't catch a ball passively. You can't simply stand there and expect the ball to stick to you, or even just hold out a hand or glove and expect the ball to fall into it. You must react to the ball, move into position to catch it, and then actively grab it from the air. Only a child, fearfully holding out both hands and hoping that the ball Mommy or Daddy gently tosses will fall into them, can "play catch" in this passive way. Passive readers, like poor catchers, drop the ball or do not connect with it at all. They read the words, perhaps only half attentively, and at the conclusion of the story grunt approval or disapproval: "That was funny." "That was boring." "Not bad." Some readers justify their passivity by arguing, "I just want to enjoy the story. Analysis spoils it." But analysis does not spoil enjoyment of a piece of literature. It enhances it.

Mortimer Adler's analogy between playing catch and reading goes only so far, however. In Adler's comparison, the writer is like the person throwing the ball; the ball is both the work itself and the message or idea it is "intended" to impart, and the reader is like the catcher who must put himself in a position to "get the message." Contemporary theories of reading complicate Adler's simple analogy by denying that a story has *a* meaning *intended* by its author. Rather, stories (indeed all written "texts") are now seen as containing many possible messages, and the reader's role is even more active than Adler implies. In many contemporary theories of reading, meaning does not inhere in the text but is created by the interplay of story and reader. Meaning is not located, in other words, so much as created by reading. If this is true, then the need for active, alert reading is even greater than in Adler's scheme, for now the burden is on you, as reader, to create a meaning (an interpretation if you like) consistent not just with the author's intention (because this is unknowable) but with all the complexities and contradictions of the story as a whole.

Learning to read actively and critically is one of the chief aims of a course in the short story. The skills gained by the exercise of careful reading, critical analysis, and thoughtful discussion are useful well beyond the classroom, and far beyond the enjoyment of fiction. Such skills are needed in all aspects of life, from buying a car to investing money or deciding on how to vote. The ability to gather information, assimilate it, shape it into a meaningful pattern, and use that information to create a cogent argument, and then the ability to express that argument effectively and persuasively, are the skills imparted by good training in any academic field. Consider the following techniques as ways to help you get started as you develop your own method for active reading.

READING ACTIVELY: AN OUTLINE

1. Read the story carefully a first time, paying particular attention to the main character(s) and what happens to them. Ask yourself: what has changed during this story and why? It is a good idea at this stage to jot in the margins the main events of the action. Consult the questions at the end of the story for ideas about how to proceed with your second reading.

2. Re-read the story with the aim of understanding *exactly* what has happened to whom. As you read, underline key passages, circle important words or phrases, put question marks beside anything you don't understand.

3. In most stories, *what* happens is fairly clear, but *why* it happens is not. This is where analysis and interpretation come into play. Everything you can observe about the story—the characters and their motivations, the setting and its influence on events, the point of view, the narrator's comments, style, imagery, word choice, "symbols," tone—may help to explain or clarify the *why*. Here again, consulting the questions following the story may call your attention to aspects you may have overlooked.

4. Formulate a hypothesis based on your observations as to what the story is "saying"—what its theme or "wider significance" is. Support your overall hypothesis by evidence from the story itself.

5. Jot down any questions you have about points you do not understand or are not sure about.

6. At this point you are well prepared to discuss the story or to respond in writing. In either case, be prepared to support what you say with details and passages from the story itself.

READING ACTIVELY: A CASE STUDY

Below is John Updike's story, "The Lucid Eye in Silver Town" (1964). As you read through it the first time, focus particularly on what happens in the story— on what changes. Note how one student has noted the main events in the margins. Ignore, for the moment, the student's circlings and underlinings; we will return to them later.

The Lucid Eye in Silver Town

THE FIRST TIME I visited New York City, I was thirteen and went with my father. I went to meet my (Uncle Quin) and to buy a book about Vermeer. The Vermeer book was my idea, and my mother's; meeting Uncle Quin was my father's. A generation ago, my uncle had vanished in the direction of Chicago

At 13, he & father went to NY

and become, apparently, rich; in the last week he had come east on business and I had graduated from the eighth grade with perfect marks. My father claimed that I and his brother were the smartest people he had ever met— "go-getters," he called us, with perhaps more irony than at the time I gave him credit for—and in his (visionary way) he suddenly, irresistibly felt that now was the time for us to meet. New York in those days was seven dollars away; we measured everything, distance and time, in money then. World War II was almost over but we were still living in the Depression. My father and I set off with the return tickets and a five-dollar bill in his pocket. The five dollars was for the book.

[margin: Is it father who has the lucid eye?]

[margin: older narrator looking back]

My mother, on the railway platform, suddenly exclaimed, "I *hate* the Augusts." This surprised me, because we were all Augusts—I was an August, my father was an August, Uncle Quincy was an August, and she, I had thought, was an August.

[margin: Mother says she hates the Augusts]

My father gazed serenely over her head and said, "You have every reason to. I wouldn't blame you if you took a gun and shot us all. Except for Quin and your son. They're the only ones of us ever had any get up and git." Nothing was more infuriating about my father than his way of agreeing.

[margin: They arrive]

Uncle Quin didn't meet us at Pennsylvania Station. If my father was disappointed, he didn't reveal it to me. It was after one o'clock and all we had for lunch were two candy bars. By walking what seemed to me a very long way on pavements only a little broader than those of my home town, and not so clean, we reached the hotel, which seemed to sprout somehow from Grand Central Station. The lobby smelled of perfume. After the clerk had phoned Quincy August that a man who said he was his brother was at the desk, an elevator took us to the twentieth floor. Inside the room sat three men, each in a gray or blue suit with freshly pressed pants and garters peeping from under the cuffs when they crossed their legs. The men were not quite interchangeable. One had a caterpillar-shaped moustache, one had tangled blond eyebrows like my father's, and the third had a drink in his hand—the others had drinks, too, but were not gripping them so tightly.

[margin: Jay not impressed by N.Y.]

[margin: Uncle & other businessmen]

"Gentlemen, I'd like you to meet my brother Marty and his young son," Uncle Quin said.

"The kid's name is Jay," my father added, shaking hands with each of the two men, staring them in the eye. I imitated my father, and the moustached man, not expecting my firm handshake and stare, said, "Why, hello there, Jay!"

"Marty, would you and the boy like to freshen up? The facilities are through the door and to the left."

[margin: They hide in bathroom]

"Thank you, Quin. I believe we will. Excuse me, gentlemen."

"Certainly."

"Certainly."

My father and I went into the bedroom of the suite. The furniture was square and new and all the same shade of maroon. On the bed was an opened suitcase, also new. The clean, expensive smells of leather and lotion were beautiful to me. Uncle Quin's underwear looked silk and was full of fleurs-de-lis. When I was through in the lavatory, I made for the living room, to rejoin Uncle Quin and his friends.

"Hold it," my father said. "Let's wait in here."   They wait in
                                                          bedroom
"Won't that look rude?"

"No. It's what Quin wants."

"Now Daddy, don't be ridiculous. He'll think we've died in here."

"No, he won't, not my brother. He's working some deal. He doesn't want to be bothered. I know how my brother works: he got us in here so we'd stay in here."

"*Really,* Pop. You're such a schemer." But I did not want to go in there without him. I looked around the room for something to read. There was nothing, not even a newspaper, except a shiny little pamphlet about the hotel itself. I wondered when we would get a chance to look for the Vermeer book. I wondered what the men in the next room were talking about. I wondered why Uncle Quin was so short, when my father was so tall. By leaning out of the window, I could see taxicabs maneuvering like windup toys.

My father came and stood beside me. "Don't lean out too far."

I edged out inches farther and took a big bite of the high, cold air, spiced by the distant street noises. "Look at the green cab cut in front of the yellow," I said. "Should they be making U-turns on that street?"

"In New York it's OK. <u>Survival of the fittest is the only law here.</u>"   Father knows
                                                                                   New York
"Isn't that the Chrysler Building?"

"Yes, isn't it graceful though? It always reminds me of the queen of the chessboard.

"What's the one beside it?"

"I don't know. Some big gravestone. The one deep in back, from this window, is the Woolworth Building. For years it was the tallest building in the world."

As, side by side at the window, we talked, I was surprised that my father could answer so many of my questions. As a young man, before I was born, he had traveled, looking for work: this was not *his* first trip to New York. Excited by my (new respect,) <u>I longed to say something to remold that calm,</u>   Jay's atti-
<u>beaten face.</u>   tude
                                                                                           changes
"Do you really think he meant for us to stay out here?" I asked.

"Quin is a go-getter," he said, gazing over my head. "I admire him. Father says
Anything he wanted, from little on up, he went after it. Slam. Bang. His Jay & Quin
thinking is miles ahead of mine—just like your mother's. You can feel them are go-get-ters
pull out ahead of you." He moved his hands, palms down, like two taxis, the
left quickly pulling ahead of the right. "You're the same say."

"Sure, sure." My impatience was not merely embarrassment at being
praised; I was irritated that he considered Uncle Quin as smart as myself. At Youthful
that point in my life I was sure that only stupid people took an interest in arrogance
money.

When Uncle Quin finally entered the bedroom, he said, "Martin, I hoped They should
you and the boy would come out and join us." have come out?

"Hell, I didn't want to butt in. You and those men were talking business."

"Lucas and Roebuck and I? Now, Marty, it was nothing that my own
brother couldn't hear. Just a minor matter of adjustment. Both these men are
fine men. Very important in their own fields. I'm disappointed that you
couldn't see more of them. Believe me, I hadn't meant for you to hide in
here. Now what kind of drink would you like?"

"I don't care. I drink very little any more."

"Scotch-and-water, Marty?"

"Swell."

"And the boy? What about some ginger ale, young man? Or would you
like milk?"

"The ginger ale," I said.

"There was a day, you know, when your father could drink any two men Father used
under the table." to drink?

As I remember it, a waiter brought the drinks to the room, and while we
were drinking them I asked if we were going to spend all afternoon in this Jay wants to
room. Uncle Quin didn't seem to hear, but five minutes later he suggested leave
that the boy might like to look around the city—Gotham, he called it.
Baghdad-on-the-Subway. My father said that that would be a once-in-a-life-
time treat for the kid. He always called me "the kid" when I was sick or had
lost at something or was angry—when he felt sorry for me, in short. The
three of us went down in the elevator and took a taxi ride down Broadway,
or up Broadway—I wasn't sure. "This is what they call the Great White Way," They take
Uncle Quin said several times. Once he apologized, "In daytime it's just an- cab on
other street." The trip didn't seem so much designed for sightseeing as for Broadway,
getting Uncle Quin to the Pickernut Club, a little restaurant set in a block of stop at a
similar canopied places. I remember we stepped down into it and it was restaurant
dark inside. A piano was playing *There's a Small Hotel.*

"He shouldn't do that," Uncle Quin said. Then he waved to the man behind the piano. "How are you Freddie? How are the kids?"

"Fine, Mr. August, fine," Freddie said, bobbing his head and smiling and not missing a note.

"That's Quin's song," my father said to me as we wriggled our way into a dark curved seat at a round table.

I didn't say anything, but Uncle Quin, overhearing some disapproval in my silence, said "Freddie's a first-rate man. He has a boy going to Colgate this autumn." *People know Quin*

I asked, "Is that really your song?"

Uncle Quin grinned and put his warm broad hand on my shoulder; I hated, at that age, being touched. "I let them think it is," he said, oddly purring. "To me, songs are like young girls. They're all pretty."

A waiter in a red coat scurried up. "Mr. August! Back from the West? How are you, Mr. August?"

"Getting by, Jerome, getting by. Jerome, I'd like you to meet my kid brother, Martin."

"How do you do, Mr. Martin. Are you paying New York a visit? Or do you live here?"

My father quickly shook hands with Jerome, somewhat to Jerome's surprise. "I'm just up for the afternoon, thank you. I live in a hick town in Pennsylvania you never heard of." *Father shakes hands with the waiter*

"I see, sir. A quick visit."

"This is the first time in six years that I've had the chance to see my brother."

"Yes, we've seen very little of him these past years. He's a man we can never see too much of, isn't that right?"

Uncle Quin interrupted. "This is my nephew Jay."

"How do you like the big city, Jay?"

"Fine." I didn't duplicate (my father's mistake) of offering to shake hands.

"Why, Jerome," Uncle Quin said. "My brother and I would like to have a Scotch-on-the-rocks. The boy would like a ginger ale."

"No, wait," I said. "What kinds of ice cream do you have?"

"Vanilla and chocolate, sir." *Only 2 kinds of ice cream*

I hesitated. I could scarcely believe it, when the cheap drugstore at home had fifteen flavors.

"I'm afraid it's not a very big selection," Jerome said.

"I guess vanilla."

"Yes, sir. One plate of vanilla."

When my ice cream came it was a golf ball in a flat silver dish; it kept spinning away as I dug at it with my spoon. Uncle Quin watched me and asked, "Is there anything especially you'd like to do?"

"The kid'd like to get into a bookstore," my father said.

"A bookstore. What sort of book, Jay?"

I said "I'd like to look for a good book of Vermeer."

Jay & Quin talk about art

"Vermeer," Uncle Quin pronounced slowly, relishing the r's, pretending to give the matter thought. "Dutch school."

"He's Dutch, yes."

"For my own money, Jay, the French are the people to beat. We have four Degas ballet dancers in our living room in Chicago, and I could sit and look at one of them for hours. I think it's wonderful, the feeling for balance the man had."

"Yeah, but don't Degas' paintings always remind you of colored drawings? For actually *looking* at things in terms of paint, for the (lucid eye,) I think Vermeer makes Degas look sick."

Vermeer has "lucid eye"

Uncle Quin said nothing, and my father, after an anxious glance across the table, said, "That's the way he and his mother talk all the time. It's all beyond me. I can't understand a thing they say."

"Your mother is encouraging you to be a painter, is she, Jay?" Uncle Quin's smile was very wide and his cheeks were pushed out as if each held a candy.

"Sure, I suppose she is."

"Your mother is a very wonderful woman, Jay," Uncle Quin said.

It was such an embarrassing remark, and so much depended upon your definition of "wonderful," that I dug at my ice cream, and my father asked Uncle Quin about his own wife, Tessie. When we left, Uncle Quin signed the check with his name and the name of some company. It was close to five o'clock.

My uncle didn't know much about the location of bookstores in New York—his last fifteen years had been spent in Chicago—but he thought that if we went to Forty-second Street and Sixth Avenue we should find something. The cab driver let us out beside a park that acted as kind of a back-yard for the Public Library. It looked so inviting, so agreeably dusty, with the pigeons and the men nodding on the benches and the office girls in their taut summer dresses, that without thinking, I led the two men into it. Shimmering buildings arrowed upward and glinted through the treetops. This was New York, I felt: the silver town. Towers of ambition rose, crystalline, within me. "If you stand here," my father said, "you can see the

They look for a bookstore

Jay looks, ambition rises,

Empire State." I went and stood beneath my father's arm and followed with my eyes the direction of it. Something sharp and hard fell into my right eye. I ducked my head and blinked; it was painful.

"What's the trouble?" Uncle Quin's voice asked.

My father said, "The poor kid's got something into his eye. He has the worst luck that way of anybody I ever knew." *he gets something in his eye*

The thing seemed to have life. It bit. "Ow," I said, angry enough to cry.

"If we can get him out of the wind," my father's voice said, "maybe I can see it." *Pride?*

"No, now, Marty, use your head. Never fool with the eyes or ears. The hotel is within two blocks. Can you walk two blocks, Jay?" *Anger Note tone*

"I'm blind, not lame," I snapped.

"He has a ready wit," Uncle Quin said.

Between the two men, shielding my eye with a hand, I walked to the hotel. From time to time, one of them would take my other hand, or put one of theirs on my shoulder, but I would walk faster, and the hands would drop away. I hoped our entrance into the hotel lobby would not be too conspicuous; I took my hand from my eye and walked erect, defying the impulse to stoop. Except for the one lid being shut and possibly my face red, I imagined I looked passably suave. However, my guardians lost no time betraying me. Not only did they walk at my heels, as if I might topple any instant, but my father told one old bum sitting in the lobby, "Poor kid got something in his eye," and Uncle Quin, passing the desk, called "Send up a doctor to Twenty-eleven." *Return to hotel* *Tries to look "suave"* *Quin orders a doctor*

"You shouldn't have done that, Quin," my father said in the elevator. "I can get it out, now that he's out of the wind. This is happening all the time. The kid's eyes are too far front."

"Never fool with the eyes, Martin. They are your most precious tool in life."

"It'll work out," I said, though I didn't believe it would. It felt like a steel chip, deeply embedded.

Up in the room, Uncle Quin made me lie down on the bed. My father, a clean handkerchief wadded in his hand so that one corner stuck out, approached me, but it hurt so much to open the eye that I repulsed him. "Don't torment me," I said, twisting my face away. "What good does it do? The doctor'll be up."

Regretfully my father put the handkerchief back into his pocket.

The doctor was a soft-handed man with little to say to anybody; he wasn't pretending to be the family doctor. He rolled my lower eyelid on a thin stick,

jabbed with a Q-tip, and showed me, on the end of the Q-tip, an eyelash. He Doctor re-
dropped three drops of yellow fluid into the eye to remove any chance of in- moves an
fection. The fluid stung, and I shut my eyes, leaning back into the pillow, eyelash
glad it was over. When I opened them, my father was passing a bill into the
doctor's hand. The doctor thanked him, winked at me, and left. Uncle Quin
came out of the bathroom.

"Well, young man, how are you feeling now?" he asked.

"Fine."

"It was just an eyelash," my father said.

"*Just* an eyelash! Well I know how an eyelash can feel like a razor blade in They must
there. But, now that the young invalid is recovered, we can think of dinner." leave

"No, I really appreciate your kindness, Quin, but we must be getting back
to the sticks. I have an eight-o'clock meeting I should be at."

"I'm extremely sorry to hear that. What sort of meeting, Marty?"

"A church council."

"So you're still doing church work. Well, God bless you for it." condescending?

"Grace wanted me to ask you if you couldn't possibly come over some
day. We'll put you up overnight. It would be a real treat for her to see you
again."

Uncle Quin reached up and put his arm around his younger brother's
shoulders. "Martin, I'd like that better than anything in the world. But I am
solid with appointments, and I must head west this Thursday. They don't let They invite
me have a minute's repose. Nothing would please my heart better than to Quin; he says
share a quiet day with you and Grace in your home. Please give her my love, no.
and tell her what a wonderful boy she is raising. The two of you are raising."

My father promised, "I'll do that." And, after a little more fuss, we left.

"The child better?" the old man in the lobby called to us on the way out.

"It was just an eyelash, thank you, sir," my father said.

When we got outside, I wondered if there were any bookstores still open.

"We have no money."

"None at all?" No time or

"The doctor charged five dollars. That's how much it costs in New York to money for a
get something in your eye." book

"I didn't do it on purpose. Do you think I pulled out the eyelash and
stuck it in there myself? I didn't tell you to call the doctor."

"I know that."

"Couldn't we just go into a bookstore and look a minute?"

"We haven't time, Jay."

But when we reached Pennsylvania Station, it was over thirty minutes

until the next train left. As we sat on a bench, my father smiled reminis-
cently. "Boy, he's smart, isn't he? His thinking is sixty light-years ahead of
mine."

"Whose?"

"My brother. Notice the way he hid in the bathroom until the doctor was
gone? That's how to make money. The rich man collects dollar bills like the
stamp collector collects stamps. I knew he'd do it. I knew it when he told
the clerk to send up a doctor that I'd have to pay for it."

"Well, why *should* he pay for it? *You* were the person to pay for it."

"That's right. Why should he?" My father settled back, his eyes forward,
his hands crossed and limp in his lap. The skin beneath his chin was loose;
his temples seemed concave. The liquor was probably disagreeing with him.
"That's why he's where he is now, and that's why I am where I am."

The seed of my anger seemed to be a desire to recall him to himself, to
scold him out of being old and tired. "Well, why'd you bring along only five
dollars? You might have known something would happen."

"You're right, Jay. I should have brought more."

"Look. Right over there is an open bookstore. Now if you had brought *ten*
dollars—"

"Is it open? I don't think so. They just left the lights in the window on."

"What if it isn't? What does it matter to us? Anyway, what kind of art
book can you get for five dollars? Color plates cost money. How much do
you think a decent book of Vermeer costs? It'd be cheap at fifteen dollars,
even secondhand, with the pages all crummy and full of spilled coffee." I
kept on, shrilly flailing the passive and infuriating figure of my father, until
we left the city. Once we were on the homeward train, my tantrum ended; it
had been a kind of ritual for both of us, and he had endured my screams
complacently, nodding assent, like a midwife assisting at the birth of family
pride. Years passed before I needed to go to New York again.

Margin notes:
- Father admires Quin
- Jay yells at Father
- Father is infuriating, but has wisdom
- A ritual?
- Why a ritual?

The characters and events in this story are quite ordinary on the face of it. Jay
August and his father Martin travel from a "hick town in Pennsylvania" to New York
City to meet Jay's Uncle Quin and buy a book on the Dutch painter, Jan Vermeer. They
walk to the hotel, wait in the bathroom while Quin conducts his business, take a cab
to a small restaurant, and go in search of a bookstore. The only event of any real
drama occurs when Jay looks up at the New York skyline and gets something in his
eye. They return to the hotel, summon a doctor who removes an eyelash, and then return to the train station for the ride home. In exasperation at not getting to buy the
book, Jay yells at his father, blaming him for the day's disappointments.

At this point, some readers will be tempted to dismiss the story as pointless or see it as little more than an incident involving a bratty adolescent and his overly indulgent father. But good stories have a resonance that transcends their apparently trivial events. The last words of the story suggest as much: "it had been a kind of ritual, for both of us, and he had endured my screams complacently, nodding assent, like a mid-wife assisting at the birth of family pride. Years passed before I needed to go to New York again." The story, after all, is told in retrospect by a mature, first-person narrator reflecting on himself at age thirteen. Its events obviously mean something to him. What could the story "mean" to us?

Re-reading the first three paragraphs, we may note two contrasts or tensions: one is between rich Uncle Quin and the "poor" Martin, the other between the unambitious and passive father and the "go-getters," Jay (who has perfect grades in school) and his mother (who encourages the boy's interest in art). When mother suddenly exclaims that she "hates" the Augusts, Jay is perplexed, and his father reacts in his "infuriating" way by agreeing with her. Why "infuriating"? And why, we may wonder, has Updike chosen the family name "August"? If it refers to the adjective meaning "marked by ma-jestic dignity or grandeur", Updike is surely being ironic.

At this point, we can hypothesize that these tensions provide a clue to the story and proceed on that basis, underlining passages that seem significant to the hypothe-sis, circling characters' names and key words, using an asterisk or other mark to label particularly important points. Is Jay going to align himself with the money values, cor-ruption, ambition, and self-confidence of New York and Quin, or with the modest, non-materialistic, egalitarian, powerless, passive father?

Jay's first impression of New York is not favorable: the sidewalks are "only a little broader than those of my home town, and not so clean. . . ." But the hotel is impres-sive (as is Uncle Quin's silk underwear), and a taxi makes a U-turn. "Survival of the fittest is the only law here," Jay's father remarks. As the father demonstrates his knowl-edge of New York's skyline, Jay begins to see him in a new light: "Excited by my new respect, I longed to say something to remold that calm, beaten face." But father won't budge; he again draws the contrast between his own lackadaisical ways and those of "go-getters" like Jay and Quin. Jay, for his part, is offended that his father puts Uncle Quin and him on the same level; after all, only stupid people are interested in money.

At the father's suggestion, motivated as Jay notes, by pity, the three of them set out to see New York. But again, Jay is disappointed: Broadway looks like an ordinary street, and instead of sightseeing, they go straight to Quin's favorite restaurant, where the waiter knows and flatters him. Jay is embarrassed because his father shakes hands with a waiter, but he is also astonished that the restaurant offers only two choices in ice cream. New York seems, at this point anyway, as less satisfactory than the "hick town" in which the Augusts live. Against this background Jay and Uncle Quin discuss the merits of Vermeer vs. Degas, with Jay arguing, rather impolitely, that Vermeer has "the lucid eye." What does this term mean, we ask? Who in the story has the lucid eye to see clearly the best life choices and moral judgments? Again, Jay's father expresses his admiration for Jay and his mother, and chagrin at his own inadequacies.

Jay seems thoroughly exasperated and not the least impressed by New York when they finally set out in search of a bookstore. The mood changes, however, when Jay leads them into a small park and for the first time notices the grandeur of the skyline: "Shimmering buildings arrowed upward and glinted through the treetops. This was

New York, I felt: the silver town. Towers of ambition rose, crystalline, within me." At this moment, Jay gets something in his eye and has to return to the hotel, trying to look "passably suave" as he walks through the lobby. When the eyelash has been removed, Martin says they must return to "the sticks" for a church council meeting. Jay's disappointment in not buying the book and his anger at his father for spending their money on the doctor lead to one more apology by Martin for not being more successful and not foreseeing the need for more than five dollars. Jay, however, continues to rail at "the passive and infuriating figure of my father."

Throughout this second reading, we have noted two significant patterns. One is Jay's haughty, even cocky attitude, his confidence in his own judgment, and his almost contemptuous attitude toward his father, uncle, and New York City. The second is Martin's humility and self-deprecation whenever he compares himself and his achievements to those of his wife, son, or brother. He lacks ambition, but on the other hand, he knows and accepts himself and the choices he's made. He does not, for example, want to move to New York or imitate his brother. Who will Jay align himself with? It was at the moment when Jay's ambition and bonding with New York was at its height that the eyelash blinded him and sent him—defeated—back to the hotel and eventually back home, empty-handed. Noting this, we might also recall an apparently offhand remark from the first paragraph:

> My father claimed that I and his brother were the smartest people he had ever met—"go-getters," he called us, *with perhaps more irony than at the time I gave him credit for*—and in his *visionary way* he suddenly, irresistibly felt that now was the time for us to meet. [Emphasis added.]

From these details emerges at least a tentative reading of the story as a cautionary tale of initiation, in which a young person on the verge of adulthood is exposed to the larger world, and has to realize that it, like his family and his own identity, is complex. Jay may be seen as the classic case of the brash youngster from the provinces who finds the big city both less glamorous and more difficult to conquer, like, or dislike than he could have imagined. In this sense, the story is a variation on the "Town Mouse and the Country Mouse." In the process, Jay perhaps learns that he cannot scold his father "out of being old and tired" but that "old" can be synonomous with "wise," "experienced," or "self-accepting." The last sentence in the story also suggests something more positive, "the birth of family pride." This statement, too, is ambiguous. It could mean that Jay comes to appreciate the realities that defeated his father. Again referring to the eyelash that blinded Jay, we might recall the Biblical question, "Why do you see the speck that is in your brother's eye, but do not notice the log that is in your own eye?" (Matthew 7:3). Or perhaps Jay began to give his father credit for what he had accomplished in life (bringing a family through the Depression, serving on the church council). Certainly the italicized phrases from the passage cited above suggest that in hindsight the narrator sees his father with more clarity and respect than did the condescending boy of thirteen. From a vantage of greater maturity, he also sees that there is more than one way to interpret the term "go-getters." Is this, then, another re-enactment of Icarus and his fall?

The method of reading outlined above is often called "Formalist" or "New"

Criticism. It is a method that focuses on the work itself, attempting to account for all its details and explain them as a significant unity. There are, however, many more ways to read this or any story. Some of these will be explained more fully in other parts of this book, but listing them here may help you find other ways of analyzing and responding that you can develop as your study of the short story progresses.

Reader Response criticism focuses on how individual readers interpret or find meaning in what they read. It assumes that each person will read differently and that by sharing responses we arrive at a better understanding of the work and ourselves. The method does not restrict itself to general overall interpretations of or value judgments about the work as a whole, however, but traces the reader's responses to various episodes or aspects of the story. Another strategy in this method is to examine the devices the writer uses to shape readers' responses in a particular way. Someone using reader response techniques on Updike's story might examine Jay's attitudes toward his father and how these influenced his or her reaction to the story—what thoughts, emotions, ideas were generated in the reader by Jay's behavior. Or, a reader response analysis might examine the ways in which Updike's presentation of the characters and events shaped a particular reader's response.

Psychological criticism uses a specific psychological theory—usually Freud's—to analyze characters and episodes in the story or to inquire about the writer's psychological make-up. It assumes that most motivations are unconscious, buried in the id, but revealed through dreams, language, gestures, and actions. A psychological reading of "Lucid Eye" would almost certainly comment on the Oedipal struggle between Jay and his father. Perhaps Jay's contempt for his father lies in his too easily winning his mother's approval. It might also analyze the obvious sibling rivalry between the successful and unsuccessful brothers.

Historical/Biographical criticism investigates the cultural context in which a story was written or the details of the writer's life as a way of explaining what the story says or how the raw material of experience was transformed into fiction. A historical critic would examine small town life in the 1940s, ideas about New York City, the influence of the Depression on ordinary people, the influence of education and culture on social mobility, and other issues. A biographical critic would look to Updike's life, particularly his relationship with his father, as a way of explaining what the story says.

Myth or Archetypal criticism sees each story as embodying one or more recurring plots, situations, characters, or symbols, all of which occur in literature regardless of the time or place of its composition. The quest, the initiation, the descent into hell, various types of tests, seasonal motifs, and many other ideas may be used to analyze a given work. We hinted at such an interpretation above by comparing Jay's experiences to those of Icarus. In such a reading, parallels between the myth and the story would emphasize Jay's experiences as a recurrent pattern of pride and fall or perhaps of innocence and experience.

Feminist criticism looks at fiction for the ways in which it depicts women, the ways in which it shows how women have been exploited or been kept in subservient roles, or the ways in which women readers might respond to a work. Men may practice feminist criticism by reading "with a woman's eyes" or by asking the kinds of questions women would ask about the story. A feminist reading would examine the very small role played by women in this story, the ways in which Jay's mother is depicted, and perhaps the story's implicit assumption that only men's experiences are worth writing about.

Marxist criticism sees literature as evidence of the power struggle between classes within society. More recently, Marxism has turned its attention to showing how a given work of literature participates in and perpetuates the power system of a particular society. Marxist critics would look at the tension between the successful and unsuccessful brothers as indicative of the power struggle between capitalists and workers. It might also analyze Jay's interest in art as part of his attempt to use education to climb out of the social class and poverty into which he was born. In a Marxist reading, Jay's humiliation might be seen as Updike's conscious or unconscious acquiescence in the status quo, the lesson being that a young man of Jay's background cannot rise above his class because of the power of vested interests (symbolized by New York's skyscrapers).

There are many other ways to read stories in addition to these. Deconstruction, African-American criticism, New Historicism, and many other schools of literary analysis are there for students to use, and each affords different insights into the stories and their possible meanings. However, this is not to say that all readings are valid or that anyone's reading is as good as anyone else's. Every reading or interpretation is ultimately responsible to the text and must be justified by reference to the story itself. There are "wrong" readings—readings which ignore or distort the story beyond recognition. But there is plenty of room for discussion and exchange of ideas, and often ideas that at first seem "off the wall" provide surprisingly original and useful readings.

Taking some of the ideas implicit in the various critical approaches outlined above, we can extract the following questions that might be asked of any short story:

1. What is the unifying (theme) of the story? In framing your answer, consider:
   (a) what happens to whom and why (plot)
   (b) the nature of the characters and their motives (characterization)
   (c) the way in which the story is told (point of view)
   (d) the time and place in which the story is set (setting and atmosphere)
   (e) the narrator's tone and style
   (f) the author's use of figurative language.

Another way to ask this question is to consider the attitudes, values, or ideas that the story as a whole seems to advocate or attack.

2. What psychological forces motivate the characters' deeds and words? (Use whatever psychological theory you think most valid, or just your own sense of what makes people "tick.")

3. How do you personally react to the story as a whole? Being as honest as you can with the story and yourself, what does it mean to you? What specific incidents or episodes cause you to react in this way? How might the author be trying to manipulate your reactions?

4. How might a woman or a member of a racial or ethnic minority react to the story? Does it stereotype women or minorities? Does it ignore or trivialize their concerns or ways of seeing the world? Does it show you the world through the eyes of a minority group? If so, how might this vision differ from that of a member of the majority?

5. What does the story say about the society that is depicted in it? Is that society just or unjust? Who wields power and for what purposes? Who is punished or persecuted and for what reasons?

6. Take what seems to you to be the most obvious interpretation and "deconstruct" the story to show that it suggests alternative readings. In particular, analyze the ambiguity of the language to show how many passages could be read in a variety of ways.

7. How does the author handle the various fictional conventions, and what (if anything) seems new or innovative in the story?

Analysis is rewarding because it reveals what we might not otherwise see—not "hidden meanings" but subtle ones. Analysis exercises our mental and critical faculties and deepens our appreciation of what we have read. It is these habits of reading and reflection that this book and the course you are taking want to encourage and develop.

THE ELEMENTS OF FICTION

One way to analyze fiction is to break a story down into its component parts or elements and study them one at a time. Such an exercise is of course artificial, for the critic can no more isolate plot, character, or atmosphere from a short story than an anatomist can isolate the nervous system from a living organism.

Nevertheless, focusing on a particular aspect of a story is convenient, since not everything can be discussed at once, and does the story no violence, for in the end, the story remains an organic whole. Unlike the scientist, the critic need not "murder to dissect" (to borrow a phrase from the Romantic poet William Wordsworth). Moreover, just as specialists in medicine can diagnose a patient, even though they examine only the bones or the nervous system, so the critic can learn a great deal about the story as a whole by analyzing its constituent parts.

In the sections below, are ideas about analyzing the main elements of fiction: plot, character, point of view, setting, atmosphere, style, figurative language, and theme. One purpose of analysis is to discover not only what a story says (its themes), but how it makes its meaning(s). Another is to increase our understanding and appreciation of the writer's art and craft. Analyzing by elements can aid in both endeavors.

CHARACTER

Although there are some short stories in which character counts for very little, in most stories character is central to the story and what occurs in it. Analyzing and understanding character, therefore, is often critical to understanding how a story achieves its meaning.

Until quite recently, discussions of characters in literature were quite simple and straightforward. In most such discussions, it was assumed that literary characters represented real people in some sense and that the most interesting characters were those with complex psyches and personalities. As a result, literary characters were often psychoanalyzed using Freudian or other psychological theories. During the past twenty years or so, critics have questioned these assumptions about literary characters, even to the extent of denying that character is a useful concept at all. After all, it was argued, literary characters are merely words on a page—signs—not real human beings. They have no existence outside of the fictional world they inhabit and no "personality traits" or "psychological complexity."

The following discussion attempts to steer a middle course between these extremes, recognizing that while literary characters are not real people, readers often respond to them as if they were. It also acknowledges that we can only know a character through the story itself and that we cannot invent or interpolate characteristics that similar "real people" might possess.

Short stories arose at a time when ideas about literary character were changing. Most eighteenth century authors believed that the best way to communicate the essential truths about "human nature" was to portray their characters as easily recognizable types. The crooked lawyer, the greedy merchant, the vain woman, the jealous lover, and many others were standard features in the literature of that time. Theophrastus pioneered this technique in his character sketches of recognizable types: "Garrulity," for instance, attempts to capture the common traits of overly talkative people.

Romantics, however, had a different conception of personality. With their dedication to the individual and their belief that everyone is unique, they changed ideas about how literary characters could and should be presented. From the Romantic Era until the middle of this century, therefore, fiction has generally reflected the notion that the individual psyche and personality are more important and interesting than the so-called universal type. Realists extended this notion and went to great lengths to convince readers that their characters were real people captured in print, an idea that Modernists extended even further by delving deeply into the unconscious. The conventions of Realism, especially the idea that literary characters possess a consistent and knowable self, have dominated discussions of character for the past century or more. Post-Modern writers, however, have often broken with this idea and sometimes present characters who are intentionally "flat," incoherent, or contradictory. In Post-Modernism, character may be nothing more than a sign or symbol in an elaborate textual game.

Setting aside for the present the special difficulties of Post-Modern characterization, we can say that, in general, short stories present a particular challenge when it comes to characterization—the limitations of length. While novelists may develop characters at leisure, through a succession of episodes, over as long a period of time as is needed, short-story writers are much more restricted. Many times, therefore, they must resort to conventional, stereotypical, or "flat" characters. At other times, they can depict only limited aspects of complex characters. Short stories, thus, have a high percentage of characters who appear eccentric or warped, or who seem obsessed. Sometimes we need to acknowledge that a short story character is presented only partially—only as much as the story will allow.

Another way to look at this problem is to say that authors of short stories are faced with two basic ways of depicting character: one is to create characters who are basically emblems or types verging on the mythical or allegorical; the other is to depict limited aspects of "real" characters. In "The Blue Beard," for example, Blue Beard and his young wife are almost allegorical types of Cruelty and Innocence, respectively. We know nothing of Blue Beard's motivations or psychology beyond his habit of marrying young women, leaving them for a short time, and then murdering them when he finds they have disobeyed his orders. Similarly, we know little of the youngest daughter except that she responds to his displays of wealth and then is driven by curiosity to explore the forbidden room. Both characters, it may be said, act more out of the requirements of plot than under the impetus of what we might call "real" human motives. Cruelty and curiosity are, of course, genuine human traits, but the point is that we know nothing of the motives behind their cruelty or curiosity. By contrast, Akaky in Gogol's "The Overcoat," may behave in ways typical of bureaucrats in general, but he is also presented as an individual, with specific feelings and motivations that make him appear "real." He is not, of course, a real person, but as we read we feel justified in thinking that such a person might actually have existed and might really have done such things, felt such emotions, and thought such thoughts.

When trying to analyze characters in short stories, therefore, we may think of them as existing on a continuum between these two extremes: the purely allegorical or type character (including the Post-Modern variety) at one end of the scale, and the so-called real character at the other. Most characters in short stories occupy a place somewhere between these two poles—that is, they may have both symbolic or allegorical functions and traits of "real" people. This tension is much greater in the short story than in the novel because of the limitation of length. Furthermore, limits of length cause writers to use a kind of short-hand when depicting characters. Each action, gesture, thought, or speech carries proportionally more significance than in a novel. Atmosphere, setting, imagery, and symbol may bear more directly on character than they would in a novel. In short, analyzing characters in stories forces us to be especially attentive to nuance and suggestion. We must read and analyze with careful attention to detail and bear in mind that characters in stories may seem one-dimensional or obsessive in ways that characters in novels do not. But such one-dimensionality may simply be a product of focus and intensity and not an indication that the character is mentally or emotionally unbalanced or "crazy."

Beyond the limits of length, it is also important to reiterate that literary characters, even the most complicated ones, are not real people. No literary character is as subtle and complicated as a living person. Like a portrait artist, the short story writer may highlight certain features for emphasis and hence produce something akin to caricature. This is what political cartoonists do, and although writers seldom resort to the same level of exaggeration, the principle in each case is similar.

These considerations lead to two conclusions. First, judging literary characters by how well they resemble "real people" is problematic at best. For one thing, characters from earlier historical periods or other cultures may behave according to conventions and mores very different from our own. Even characters in contemporary stories may act under circumstances we have never encountered or imagined. Hence, whether a character resembles a "real person" we have encountered in life is less important than whether he or she seems convincing within the context of the story. Consistency and plausibility in context are more important than whether the character behaves as the reader would expect of someone in "real life." Second, the author may not be attempting to present a "real" character at all but may be deliberately creating a generalized type, an allegorical/mythical figure, or a linguistic "sign." Applying the wrong standard leads to distortion and misunderstanding.

Second, speculating about characters beyond what the story tells us is also futile. The vogue of "psychoanalyzing" literary characters presents a particular danger. (See Psychoanalytical Criticism, p. 466.) We are too often tempted to reason that because, say, certain childhood experiences often produce specific personality traits in real people that a literary character must have had a similar childhood experience. Literary characters have no childhoods—no anything—except what the story provides. We cannot know more about a character than what the story tells us or permits us to infer from direct evidence.

Analyzing character presents a particularly interesting and complicated instance of the interplay of convention and innovation. Type characters in every fictional medium, including film and television, are so common and often so persuasive that we are tempted to believe in the reality of "the strong, silent hero" or "the whore with the heart of gold." Moreover, we may become so accustomed to these type characters that we forget that they are literary clichés. Moreover, because we have become accustomed to type characters, we find their very familiarity comforting and appealing. Popular writers count upon such familiarity and often exploit it very skillfully to create characters that seem convincing because we have met them so many times before. Accustomed to such character types, we may actually be made uncomfortable by characters who don't perform in the conventional way and see them as "unreal" or "unconvincing" because they fail to meet our expectations. If one of the purposes and values of fiction is that it opens us to new experiences and ideas, then we need to remain open-minded about fictional characters and sensitive to the variety of characters authors depict.

ANALYZING CHARACTER

Analyzing characters means paying careful attention to the information provided by the story. Obviously, we must note what the character does, and even more importantly, why he or she acts in a particular way. Information about the "why" may come from a variety of sources: from other things the character does, from what the character says about his or her motivations, from what the author or narrator tells us, from what other characters say or how they react, from the context or circumstances out of which the character acts, and finally from the exact words and phrases used to express all of these. Not all information in a story is equally helpful or equally true, so we must emphasize those pieces of information that seems most vital, while not forgetting lesser points that add shading and nuance.

Some of the kinds of evidence we may use when analyzing character can be listed and illustrated as follows:

1. Summary statements by the narrator about the background, social position, and personality of the character:

> "In that same village, and in one of these very houses (which, to tell the precise truth, was sadly time-worn and weather-beaten) there lived many years since . . . a simple, good-natured fellow, of the name of Rip Van Winkle. "
> IRVING, "Rip Van Winkle"

"Yermolay, that carefree and good–natured fellow, treated [his wife] roughly and coarsely, assumed a threatening and severe air in his own home—and his poor wife had no idea of how to indulge him, shuddered at his glance, bought drink for him with her last kopeck and dutifully covered him with her own sheepskin coat when he, collapsing majestically on the stove, fell into a Herculean sleep."
TURGENEV, "Yermolay and the Miller's Wife"

2. Physical description of the character by the narrator:

"There was a saucy frankness of countenance, a knowing roguery of eye, a joviality and prankishness of demeanor, that was wonderfully captivating, especially to the ladies."
STOWE, "Uncle Lot"

"And so, in a *certain department* there was a *certain clerk;* a clerk of whom it cannot be said that he was very remarkable; he was short, somewhat pock-marked, with rather reddish hair and rather dim, bleary eyes, with a small bald patch on the top of his head, with wrinkles on both sides of his cheeks and the sort of complexion which is usually described as hemorrhoidal. . . ."
GOGOL, "The Overcoat"

3. What the character does on his own or in response to others:

"The young clerks jeered and made jokes at him to the best of their clerkly wit. . . . Akaky Akakievich never answered a word, however, but behaved as though there were no one there. It had no influence on his work; in the midst of all this teasing, he never made a single mistake in his copying."
GOGOL, "The Overcoat"

"Each morning, out of habit, Félicité entered Virginia's room and gazed at the walls. She missed combing her hair, lacing her shoes, tucking her in bed, and the bright face and little hand when they used to go out for a walk."
FLAUBERT, "A Simple Soul"

4. Commentary or interpretation by the narrator:

"There was something touching in the words and in the voice in which they were uttered. There was a note in it of something that aroused compassion. . . ."
GOGOL, "The Overcoat"

"Mrs. De Ropp would never, in her honestest moments, have confessed to herself that she disliked Conradin, though she might have been dimly aware that thwarting him 'for his own good' was a duty which she did not find particularly irksome."
SAKI, "Sredni Vashtar"

5. What the character says and how he or she says it:

"The sheriff too looked all around, as if to re-convince himself."

" 'Nothing here but kitchen things,' he said, with a little laugh for the insignificance of kitchen things."
GLASPELL, "A Jury of Her Peers"

"Forgiven? No. I am a bad, low woman; I despise myself and don't attempt to justify myself. It's not my husband but myself I have deceived."
Chekhov, "The Lady with the Dog"

" 'I [Grandmother MacLeod] was a MacInnes before I got married.
The MacInnes is a very ancient clan, the lairds of Morven and the constables of the Castle of Kinlochaline.' "
LAURENCE, "To Set Our House in Order"
Cf. the example in #6 below.

6. What characters in the story say about the character:

' "I will frankly confess that in my opinion all the fears and terrors of which you speak took place only in your mind and had very little to do with the true, external world. A loathsome character old Coppelius may have been, but what really led to the abhorrence you children felt stemmed from his hatred of children."
—Klara to Nathanael in "The Sandman" by von Kleist

"Aunt Edna snorted. 'Castle, my foot. She [Grandmother MacLeod] was born in Ontario, just like your Grandfather Connor, and her father was a horse doctor.' "
LAURENCE, "To Set Our House in Order"
Cf. the example in #5 above.

7. Imagery used by or about the character:

"His [Braggioni's] mouth opens round and yearns sideways, his balloon cheeks grow oily with the last labor of song. He bulges marvelously in his expensive garments. . . : over the tops of his glossy yellow shoes Braggioni swells with ominous ripeness, his mauve silk hose stretched taut, his ankles bound with the stout leather thongs of his shoes."
PORTER, "Flowering Judas"

"And his face was a familiar face, somehow: the jaw and chin and cheeks slightly darkened because he hadn't shaved for a day or two, and the nose long and hawklike, sniffing as if she were a treat he was going to gobble up and it was all a joke."
OATES, "Where Are You Going, Where Have You Been?"

BRIEF EXAMPLES OF CHARACTER ANALYSIS

NATHANAEL IN "THE SANDMAN"

The protagonist of E. T. A. Hoffmann's "The Sandman" presents a fascinating case in the problems of character analysis. Nathanael is unusual in fiction in that he is both a narrator of his own story and the subject of Lothar's story. (See the discussion of point of view, pp. 1188–1191.) Thus, we see him from two radically different points of view—as he sees himself and as he is seen by others.

From the first paragraph we are aware that Nathanael is a troubled young man: he calls his frame of mind "tormented" and exclaims that "Dark forebodings of some impending doom loom over me like black clouds. . . ." The question that quickly arises in our own minds is whether his childhood fears of the Sandman are simply "childish nonsense" as Klara believes, or whether they have objective validity. Another way of stating the problem is whether Nathanael's fears arise only from his diseased imagination or whether he is justified in feeling threatened. Is he aware of evils that others ignore? Is his very irrationality a source of insight?

We can, of course, simply dismiss Nathanael's story as the ravings and doings of a lunatic, but to do so would reduce a complex character into one who is merely deranged. For if we are alert to everything in the story, we must somehow account for the mysterious Coppelius, the enigmatic Coppola, and perhaps above all the automaton Olympia and her Dr. Frankenstein-like creator, Spalanzini. Olympia, certainly, is no figment of Nathanael's imagination, for she is seen and ridiculed by others whose sanity we never question. But why is Nathanael so attracted to her? Is she, like Klara, representative of a cool reasonableness that Nathanael cannot achieve? Or does she suggest another source of evil—technology—different from the supernatural evil suggested by Coppelius and Coppola?

As we grapple with these and many other similar questions revolving around Nathanael's character, we see more and more into the story and what it may be revealing about the nature of experience, the meaning of madness, and the reliability of perception.

ROBIN IN HAWTHORNE'S "MY KINSMAN, MAJOR MOLINEUX"

The nightmarish unreality of Nathanael's experiences is similar to events in "My Kinsman, Major Molineux." Robin's experiences while searching for his kinsman are less melodramatic than Nathanael's painful anxieties, and on the surface at least Robin appears to be a very different sort of young man. Compared to Nathanael, Robin is refreshingly normal. Or is he?

In the second paragraph of the story, Hawthorne describes the young hero as a hardy, handsome, country youth of eighteen making his first visit to town. Several times he is described as "shrewd." Most of what we learn about Robin emerges from his encounters with various townspeople as he inquires after his kinsman. In each case, Robin has his own interpretation of these encounters, but not until the end of the story do we know why these people behave so strangely in response to Robin's perfectly straightforward question. In effect, we share Robin's puzzlement, though we might not, even on first reading, assess people's motives and actions as he does. We probably chuckle at Robin's naivety in the encounter with the pretty woman in the scarlet petticoat. As the story unfolds, it becomes clear that Robin is closer to the allegorical mode than the realistic. Like a character in a fairy tale, he is in some ways an abstraction or type of innocent young man, unfamiliar with the ways of the world. His actions, therefore, and the events surrounding him, should probably be read more in the allegorical mode than as a record of events that might really have happened. However, this does not mean that we can dismiss him as a mere puppet or stick figure.

Observing Robin as he deals with his evening of "ambiguity and weariness" we share his confusion, but when Major Molineux is paraded by, and everyone—including Robin—laughs uproariously, suddenly we face an even greater puzzle. Why is Robin laughing, and what is he laughing at—himself, his kinsman, the situation? Moreover, what, if anything, will he learn from this experience? How will he change? If he undergoes a fall from innocence to experience, what exactly has he fallen into? Is this experience educational or corrupting, a salutary introduction to reality, or an unfortunate fall from a morally superior status? Searching the story for clues to the answers to these questions takes us nearer to an appreciation of Hawthorne's artistry, and at the same time may force us to confront issues that transcend the story. Analyzing character is not a simple exercise in cleverness but a way into the story, a way to confront it on a deeper and more meaningful level.

AKAKY AND GOGOL'S "THE OVERCOAT"

The sensational, perhaps even lurid, experiences of Nathanael and Robin take us into the secret springs and levers of the human mind, particularly its dark and unpleasant places. When we turn to Akaky in Gogol's "The Overcoat," we are also in the realm of the character's interior life—but what a difference we sense in tone and emphasis! Akaky is an intensely ordinary, even boring bureaucrat, and at least until the end of the story, the events, too, seem plausible and ordinary. But why, we may ask ourselves, does he become so obsessed about an overcoat? Would anyone in "real life" behave as Akaky does? To ask this, is probably to ask the wrong question, for indeed any real person whose life was as narrow and constructed as Akaky's, whose thoughts were as focused on a single object, would be considered unbalanced. Why does he never think about love or his family or his shoes for that matter?

This story illustrates both the strengths and the weaknesses of characteristics in a short story. Gogol does not have the space to explore Akaky's thoughts or experiences except as they relate to his function as a bureaucrat and his need for a new overcoat. Moreover, if he expanded his treatment of Akaky, he would dilute the effect the story has in concentrating intensely on this one aspect of Akaky's life. At this point, then, we might be wise to treat Akaky as we did Robin, as a symbolic or allegorical figure whose thoughts and actions should be read as suggestive rather than as "real." This approach requires a delicate balance: on the one hand, we can see Akaky as representative of a certain type of "real" person; on the other hand, it is dangerous to push this line of reasoning too far because normal "real" people do not become obsessed about overcoats.

Each reader will balance these opposites in slightly different ways and hence interpret Akaky's character differently. Each reader, too, will see somewhat different "symbolic" or "allegorical" suggestions in the way the story unfolds. For example, some readers may see the story as a criticism of bureaucracies generally and emphasize their soul-destroying pettiness. Others may see in Akaky himself a suggestion of humanity's tendency to over-value material objects, even necessary ones like overcoats. Still others will see in Akaky's return as a ghost, a foreshadowing of the revolution that eventually toppled the regime that so cruelly exploited its subjects. Thus, how we interpret character is directly related to our understanding of the story as a whole. Moreover, acknowledging the limitations of character development in a short story can prevent us from expecting characters to be more rounded than they can be or to behave more "realistically" than we have a right to expect.

JACK IN COOVER'S "THE BABYSITTER"

When we first meet Jack, he is described as and seems like a normal teen-aged boy, hoping to visit his girlfriend as she babysits for the Tuckers. He seems, in other words, like a realistic character. As realistic description and dialogue give way to Mark's various fantasies, however, his character begins slipping away; he becomes not one character but two or three—or perhaps one character with wildly contrasting attitudes: protectiveness and aggression, fear and longing, love and loathing. By the time Jack and Mark are standing outside the Tuckers' home, peering in the window (or are they?), whatever singleness and unity Jack's character had in the beginning has disintegrated into fragments of fantasy, possibility, and cliché. Jack has stopped being a character and become a linguistic sign that bears no resemblance to a "real person."

As the above examples demonstrate, there is no one "right" way to analyze and interpret literary characters. Authors use various conventions and devices to present characters and do not always ask us to regard them as "real" people of the kind we meet every day. Character must be analyzed in the total context of the story, using whatever clues the writer provides. Moreover, we must guard against accepting familiar, stereotyped characters as convincing simply because they are familiar. Such characters, in fact, may be merely cardboard conventions. At the other end of the scale, we need to recognize that a short story can often develop only one aspect of a complex character. The young protagonist of James Joyce's "Araby," for example, sometimes appears "obsessed" or even "perverse" to students. But the story concerns only a brief time and a single episode in the boy's life and must be seen as such. Over-emphasizing his admittedly odd behavior can blind us to what is typical and hence revealing in his character.

SETTING

The setting of a story refers to the time and place (or times and places) at which it occurs. Because we tend to take the setting for granted, we may easily overlook its importance, but the conscious use of setting for effect is one of the innovations that helps to separate the tale from the short story proper. A glance back at the early fictional forms and the short story precursors will show that time and place play little role. Fairy tales and myths happen in a timeless "Once upon a time" in places that are usually distinguished only by a simple descriptor: the forest, a castle, a village. Even if the author is somewhat more specific, as in "Daedalus and Icarus" where the Island of Crete is mentioned, the specifics of the locations are not really a part of the story's effect. The opening paragraphs of "Rip Van Winkle," however, establish beyond doubt the importance of setting in this story.

Below are the first two paragraphs of "Rip Van Winkle":

> Whoever has made a voyage up the Hudson must remember the Kaatskill mountains. They are a dismembered branch of the great Appalachian family, and are seen away to the west of the river, swelling up to a noble height, and lording it over the surrounding country. Every change of season, every change of weather, indeed every hour of the day, produces some change in the magical hues and shapes of these mountains; and they are regarded by all the good wives, far and near, as perfect barometers. When the weather is fair and settled they are clothed in blue and purple, and print their bold outlines on the clear evening sky; but sometimes, when the rest of the landscape is cloudless, they will gather

a hood of gray vapors about their summits, which, in the last rays of the setting sun, will glow and light up like a crown of glory.

At the foot of these fairy mountains the voyager may have descried the light smoke curling up from a village, whose shingle roofs gleam among the trees just where the blue tints of the upland melt away into the fresh green of the nearer landscape. It is a little village of great antiquity, having been founded by some of the Dutch colonists, in the early times of the province, just about the beginning of the government of the good Peter Stuyvesant (may he rest in peace!), and there were some of the houses of the original settlers standing within a few years, built of small yellow bricks brought from Holland, having latticed windows and gable fronts, surmounted with weathercocks.

At first glance this passage may appear as simply a piece of picturesque description, such as any writer under the influence of Romantic landscape painting may have produced. But if we look more closely, we may discern that the picture is not casually drawn. To point to just one feature, the mountains are described as having "magical hues" and are later called "these fairy mountains." These apparently innocent words prepare us for the magical events that unfold in the story of Rip's twenty-year sleep. Second, the careful historical and geographical details are a kind of rhetorical ploy. Narrators (Diedrich Knickerbocker, in this case) who later want to convince readers of the reality of something supernatural often begin by establishing a very realistic setting. In this case, however, the time is the romantic past of Peter Stuyvesant. In other words, this setting is a clever mixture of magical, romantic, and realistic details, designed to provide a suitable backdrop to the events the story will unfold.

Not every story manipulates setting as deliberately as Irving does in "Rip Van Winkle," but most do. Whether a story is set in the past or the present, in a city, small town, or the country, in a haunted house or contemporary condominium, the setting is likely to have a significant effect of the story's overall impact.

ATMOSPHERE

Atmosphere is related to setting in that it arises out of the time and place in which the story is set, but it depends not just on where and when but more importantly on how the setting is described or portrayed. Atmosphere is the overriding or prevailing tone or mood of the story (though in some stories it does change from beginning to end).

For example, note the different atmospheres of the following fictional villages. The village in "Rip Van Winkle," as we have just seen, is given to us as a sleepy, picturesque, tumbled-down place covered in the pastels of nostalgia. A village described by Harriet Beecher Stowe, however, has a different atmosphere:

Did you ever see the little village of Newbury, in New England? I dare say you never did; for it was just one of those out of the way places where nobody ever came unless they came on purpose: a green little hollow, wedged like a bird's nest between half a dozen high hills, that kept off the wind and keep out foreigners .... The inhabitants were all of that respectable old standfast family who make it a point to be born, bred, married, die, and be buried all in the selfsame spot. . . ."

The atmosphere here is brisk rather than sleepy, remote but not romantic, clean, neat, and purposeful as a "bird's nest." Thirdly, consider the village described by Hawthorne in "My Kinsman, Major Molineux":

> He now became entangled in a succession of crooked and narrow streets, which crossed each other, and meandered at no great distance from the waterside. The smell of tar was obvious to his nostrils, the masts of vessels pierced the moonlight above the tops of the buildings, and the numerous signs, which Robin paused to read, informed him that he was near the center of business. But the streets were empty, the shops were closed, and the lights were visible only in the second stories of a few dwelling-houses.

Here, the village is a sinister place of "crooked and narrow streets," a village whose outward signs of life reinforce Robin's sense of loneliness and unease.

Atmosphere is important because it colors our reaction to the story and its characters. We may not even be aware of its effects unless, as in a story by Poe, the author is at pains to make us aware of them. More often, the effect is subtle, but its precise effects and their relation to the rest of the story need, for that very reason, to be analyzed.

THEME

When we read fiction, we generally expect two rewards: one is to be entertained; the other is to be enlightened. The ancient poet Horace called these two expectations delight and instruction. Aesthetics is the branch of literary investigation that deals with the "delight" part of Horace's formula. When we analyze for plot, character, style, figurative language, structure, unity, and the like, we are engaging in aesthetic pursuits. When we are looking to discover "what the story means" or "what its message is," we are engaging in interpretation, in analysis to discover theme. (Some use the word *thesis* instead of *theme*.)

It is important not to confuse *theme* with *moral*. A moral is a direct statement appended to the end of an overtly didactic form like the fable. When Aesop says at the end of "Town Mouse and Country Mouse" that "A simple life with peace and quiet is better than faring luxuriously and being tortured by fear," he provides his story with a moral. A moral states what the reader should do or not do, believe or not believe, value or not value. A theme, on the other hand, is the idea about experience or life that grows out of the story and unifies its other elements. It is the "wider significance" of the story, the general observation or truth that is suggested by the particular experience that the story dramatizes. Reading fiction for a moral is a simplistic approach to interpretation. Most writers of short stories are interested in conveying an idea or wider significance of their story, but they are seldom interested in blatant moral teaching or didacticism. They use fiction as a way of exploring experience or of understanding the world, and they know that experience cannot be reduced to a simple moral such as "Honesty is the best policy" or "There's no place like home."

When we analyzed John Updike's "Lucid Eye in Silver Town," for example, we discovered that one way to interpret the story is by comparing it to Ovid's "Daedalus and Icarus." Like Icarus, Jay considers himself above his father and suffers humiliation as a consequence: his "lucid eye" is bleared by an eyelash; his pride takes a fall. Another part of the story, another theme one could say, cuts against the grain of this one, however. Jay's father is too humble, too lacking in self-respect—or so Jay thought at the time. The mature Jay, telling the story in retrospect, sees something he missed as an adolescent, that his father was more shrewd than he let on: "he suddenly, irresistibly felt that now was the time for us [Jay and Uncle Quin] to meet." But what exactly does Jay learn from his encounter with Uncle Quin? Is Quin the "golden mean" between the excess pride of Jay and the excess humility of his father? Is Jay's encounter with the wealthy but overly busy Quin a subtle warning about the dangers of being a "go-getter"? Is Jay meant to find his own "golden mean" between his Uncle and his father?

Confronting these and other questions by asking about the story's theme demonstrates that theme is seldom simple. There is often more than one idea or possible idea in a good story. As often as not, a story may leave us with as many questions as it provides answers. Thus theme cannot be reduced to anything as simple as a moral without falsifying the experience the story explores. Since theme means the idea or "message" the story communicates, it is expressed not as a single word like "pride," which is more properly thought of as the subject or issue of the story, but as a sentence with a subject and predicate: "In John Updike's 'Lucid Eye in Silver Town' Jay discovers that his pride and ambition may be misplaced and that success is more elusive and more complicated than he earlier believed."

Such a formulation is not perfect; it may miss some aspect of the story other readers find important. If we find a statement of theme lacking in some respect, we may want to turn back to the story to discover what is left out of such a reading; or we may want to go outside the story—to Updike's biography or other works by Updike, perhaps, or to works of history, sociology, psychoanalysis—as a way of helping to understand the story. What we should not do is throw up our hands in frustration and declare that the story means nothing at all or that it means whatever any reader thinks it means. Some contemporary critical theories—most notably Deconstruction—claim that looking for a theme is futile, since every work of literature conveys an almost infinite variety of ideas. Deconstructionists often seek to prove that traditional readings are undercut by contrary meanings. However, like any complex problem in art or life, the issue of theme deserves thoughtful consideration. It calls on us to examine the evidence in the story, use logic, watch for patterns, keep an open and receptive mind, and have a willingness to learn from others.

POINT OF VIEW

When we speak casually of someone's point of view, we mean the particular slant on life that a person has as a consequence of age, situation, occupation, or some other personal trait. "That's a pro-business point of view," we might say; or "Their point of view has changed now that they have children" or "From the point of view of a scientist." Point of view in this sense sometimes has a negative connotation, suggesting limitation, or in extreme cases, bias or prejudice.

In fiction, when we discuss the author's point of view we do not mean his or her prejudices or biases. We mean the person or voice in which the story is narrated. "Person" here has the meaning it carries in traditional grammar, the form of the pronouns and verbs used:

Person	What the Choice of Person Means	Examples Singular	Plural
First person (*I, we*)	The subject of sentence (or person telling the story) is doing the speaking.	*I observed a fire.*	*We put out the fire.*
Second person (*you*)	The subject of sentence (or reader or person telling the story) is being spoken to, is being directly addressed.	*You go up to the attic.*	*You [more than one] go down to the basement.*
Third person (*he, she, it,* and *they*; nouns; *each, one, all, anybody*; etc.)	The subject of sentence (or story) is being spoken about (by the author or person who is telling the story).	*He moved to town. She wrote a book. It was successful. Each said the same thing. Cynthia agreed.*	*They celebrated. All ordered coffee. Joy and John got the juke box going.*

Thus, a first-person narrator uses the pronoun "I" or "we" and is either an observer of or a participant in the action. The second-person almost never appears as such as a point of view in fiction, although narrators will occasionally address readers as "you." A third-person narrator stands outside the action of the story and is also called omniscient, since such a narrator may claim to know anything and everything related to the story, from what has happened in the past to what will happen in the future. An omniscient narrator can know what goes on in characters' minds or may even claim to know the mind of God or Satan. Convention allows this narrator to see everything simultaneously, omnisciently as God might. Theoretically, there is nothing about the situation or the characters that an omniscient narrator cannot tell us. In contrast, in a story with a first person narrator, everything is filtered through the consciousness of the implied narrator. Such a narrator cannot claim to know what another person is thinking, for instance, or what motives drive a character to a particular action. A first-person narrator may guess at a character's thoughts or motives, but the convention allows the narrator to know only what a real person in such a position could know or observe.

Not all omniscient narrators, however, take a sweeping and god-like view. Sometimes, an implied author may limit the point of view so that we see events not from some privileged position but in a much more limited way. An implied narrator who uses this approach is said (in a seeming contradiction) to be limited omniscient.

Another variation on the omniscient stance was invented by Modernist authors, who frequently blur the line between objective and subjective reality in a point of view called free indirect style. In this technique, the narrator slips into and out of characters' minds without using such signals as "He thought" or "She wondered." Katherine Mansfield illustrates the technique in "The Daughters of the Late Colonel":

> But, after all, it was not long now, and then she'd [Nurse Andrews] be gone for good. And there was no getting over the fact she had been very kind to father.

The first sentence could be spoken by an omniscient narrator, but such a narrator would not call the late colonel "father." Only one of the daughters would use such a term. The narrator has slid from an "objective" view to a "subjective" one.

Identifying the person of the implied narrator, however, does not exhaust the useful things we can say about point of view. Ever since the publication of Wayne Booth's *The Rhetoric of Fiction,* critics have distinguished between first-person narrators who are reliable and those who are unreliable. A reliable narrator is a trustworthy guide not only to what happens but also to the meaning or significance of what happens. Dr. Watson, the narrator of the Sherlock Holmes stories, gains our confidence from the very beginning of "The Blue Carbuncle":

> I had called upon my friend Sherlock Holmes upon the second morning after Christmas, with the intention of wishing him the compliments of the season. He was lounging upon the sofa in a purple dressing-gown, a pipe-rack within his reach upon the right, and a pile of crumpled morning papers, evidently newly studied, near at hand.

We trust Watson to narrate faithfully what he sees, and although Watson does not always understand everything as clearly as Holmes does, he freely admits his inability to interpret the clues or to apply Holmes's methods. Here, as in so many detective stories, the narrator's limitations are a clever device to make the detective appear particularly clever.

By contrast, Edgar Allan Poe's narrators are frequently unreliable, as in "The Tell-Tale Heart":

> True—nervous—very, very dreadfully nervous I had been and am; but why *will* you say that I am mad? The disease had sharpened my senses—not destroyed—not dulled them. Above all was the sense of hearing acute. I heard all things in the heaven and in the earth. I heard many things in hell. How, then, am I mad?

Such a narrator immediately arouses our suspicions and puts us on guard. We may be willing to suspend judgment on the narrator's sanity, but clearly we cannot fully trust a first-person narrator who claims to hear "all things in the heaven and in the earth" and who admits that others may regard him as insane.

Having categorized *point of view* in person, degree of omniscience, and reliability, we have not exhausted the useful things to say about the narrator's stance. We also need to determine the implied author's attitude toward the material and especially the characters in the story. This we may assess by being alert to direct comments by the

narrator and to the narrator's tone. Is the narrator being objective, sympathetic, satirical, or judgmental? In the case of a first person narrator especially, we need to ask why
the narrator is telling the story. What is his or her motive?

The question of point of view is intimately connected with how we receive the
story and hence how we understand and interpret its events. If we miss a narrator's
satire, for example, we miss the point entirely. We need to distinguish between facts
and interpretations, and to determine whether misinterpretations by the narrator are
conscious or unconscious, intended or accidental. To answer such basic questions, we
need to analyze carefully the story's point of view.

PLOT

Plot may be defined in a number of ways, but for our purposes it refers to a specific
way of organizing and presenting action in a short story. Plot involves the protagonist,
the main character in a literary work, seeking to attain a goal and opposed in that
search by an antagonist or by antagonists, which can be internal, external, or both. At
some point this conflict reaches a crisis which is resolved, either happily or unhappily
for the protagonist. Events in a plot are usually presented chronologically, in the order
in which they supposedly occurred, although there may be flashbacks or leaps forward
in time.

Central to the unity and meaning of plot is the way in which cause and effect relationships drive the action. Generally speaking, this force may be identified as the motivation within the protagonist or as the forces outside the protagonist that (with or without
the protagonist's knowledge) control his or her actions. Other components of plot include the exposition, that is, the setting forth of the situation when the story begins; the
rising action as the original situation becomes complicated by the conflict; the climax or
turning point when the conflict reaches its height; and the resolution or denouement
when the outcome of the climax brings the conflict to its tragic or comic ending.

In "The Story of Daedalus and Icarus," for example, the exposition explains that
Daedalus and his son are trapped on the island of Crete. To escape, Daedalus fashions
wings of feathers and wax. He also loves his son and thus warns Icarus against flying
too high or too close to the water. For his part, Icarus is motivated by pride or a desire
for independence to defy his father's warning. All this may be called the complication
or rising action. Action reaches its climax when Icarus flies too close to the sun and its
resolution when he plunges to his death. We say that the story ends tragically because
Daedalus loses his son and Icarus his life. Their goals have been thwarted in whole or
in part.

Cause and effect relationships in plots are often found in the motivations of characters, which in turn may be interpreted or understood in light of the reader's values.
In this case, we may conclude that while both Daedalus and Icarus were motivated by
laudable or understandable goals—physical escape on the part of Daedalus, psychological escape on the part of Icarus—each may be faulted for choosing inappropriate
means. Daedalus relies on his own ingenuity and on technology; Icarus indulges his
pride. From the combination of motivation, means, and result we extract a meaning
relating to the operation of pride. Another way to look at the motivations or cause and
effect is to see each character as deceived by thinking himself in control. In that case,
the theme may be expressed as the self-deception that comes from thinking that one is

in control of one's fate. Other stories present more complicated plots, but analyzing plot involves looking for the pattern of cause and effect relationships.

From this example, we can see the interplay of plot and character. Obviously, the two cannot be entirely separated, especially since interpreting motivation involves making judgments about characters as well as seeing cause and effect relations that drive the plot. Further, interpreting theme involves value judgments about the motivations of the characters and the legitimacy of the antagonist(s). In simple stories with clear-cut "bad guys" and "good guys," interpretation is straightforward, but most authors do not depict characters who are all good or all bad, and these characters usually act from mixed motives. Hence, differing interpretations of a story's characters and theme are possible and fictional problems and issues have some of the complexity of life.

FORM, NOT PLOT

In the historical overview of the short story, we saw that writers at the turn of the century became impatient with the conventions of plot and the limits it imposed on their ability to depict life as they saw it. Not all writers rejected plot, of course, and not all those who rejected it did so in every instance. Many, however, did either downplay this conventional aspect of story-telling or eliminate it altogether, which upset readers' expectations. Eliminating plot in favor of some other way of structuring and unifying the story often had the effect of baffling readers and leading them to complain, "There's no story here!"

A brief look at Chekhov's "The Lady with the Dog" and "Easter Eve" will illustrate two ways in which authors structure their narratives and eliminate some or all of the conventions of plot.

"The Lady with the Dog," presents a fairly conventional situation: Dmitri Gurov is dissatisfied with his wife and on the prowl for sexual excitement. Similarly, Anna Sergeyevna has come to Yalta for a holiday and to escape her "flunky" husband and their boring provincial life. As in a conventional love story, they have an affair. To this point, we may say that the conflict involves their flouting of society's rules about marital fidelity, and in Anna's case an interminable conflict over the morality of what she has done. If Dmitri has any internal conflict, it does not seem very important.

Then, however, the plot takes a twist. In spite of himself, Dmitri falls in love with Anna and finds he cannot live without her. Suddenly, there are two new conflicts: Dmitri's battle within himself and his sudden exasperation with the triviality and banality of Moscow. In desperation, he goes to visit Anna and thus renews their affair, but even though they remain in love and she visits him in Moscow whenever possible, the story reaches a climax but no resolution.

Chekhov has evaded the conventions of plot in two main ways. First, he places more emphasis on internal conflict than on external action. The real struggles in the story take place within the characters. Second, as noted above, he brings his story to an emotional climax but leaves the reader—and his characters—"hanging." The conflicts remain unresolved. For readers used to a neat resolution to such conflicts—either the triumph of love over adversity or the tragic end of lovers in death or separation—such an ending is frustrating, perhaps even exasperating. Chekhov may well have replied to such readers that life has conflicts but no plot; that problems are seldom resolved in life as neatly as they are in fiction.

"Easter Eve" has even less plot than "The Lady with the Dog." The first person-narrator describes the celebrations for Easter Eve as he waits to cross the river. Ieronim, the ferryman, eventually arrives and begins transporting the narrator across the river. In the midst of the celebrations, he announces his grief over the death of his friend, Nikolay, and goes on to describe Nikolay's qualities, especially his ability to write canticles. When the ferry reaches the other shore, the narrator mingles with the celebrating crowd and remembers Nikolay. Eventually, he gets back on the ferry and sees that Ieronim is still on duty. The story closes with the narrator's description of Ieronim's gaze on the young woman.

Most of this story is devoted to dialogue and description. There is no obvious conflict, no rising action or climax. Instead of reaching a conclusion, the story simply ends, leaving us in a wistful mood, perhaps, but also rather puzzled. What is this story "about"? What could it possibly mean? Analyzing such a story requires more delicate tools than the ability to identify "good guys" and "bad guys" and to assess punishments or rewards. Instead of such conventional markers, the narrator presents a series of contrasts: the joy of Easter and Ieronim's sorrow; Nikolay's gentle genius and the crowd's noisy vulgarity; the dark of the night and the light of the fires and fireworks; the materialism of the wealthy celebrants and the simple poverty and piety of Nikolay and Ieronim. Out of these contrasts, we may form an idea of what the experience has meant for the narrator. Perhaps Nikolay is an example of the artist, struggling for expression and appreciation in an indifferent world. Maybe the gentle piety of Nikolay and Ieronim is intended as a critique of the noisy, materialistic, celebrating crowd. Maybe the world's indifference to Ieronim's suffering is the point.

However we interpret the story, we are looking for its unifying elements, those devices and ideas that hold the story together and make it cohere in spite of its apparently shapeless and random events. Part of the effectiveness of a story like "Easter Eve" lies in its deliberate defiance of plot conventions. By frustrating our expectations, the writer calls attention to them and thereby sharpens our awareness of the artificiality of plot.

There is, of course, no particular virtue in having plot or in not having it. Both methods now have their own conventions. Being alert and sensitive readers simply means we learn to read in more than one way. There is often more to a good story than "a good story."

STYLE

Style is often referred to as if it were something separate from content, a suit of clothes hung over a mannequin. "There is no difference between the candidates," the political news-analyst says, "merely a contrast in style." To think this way is to misunderstand the nature and importance of style, at least in literature. Anyone who doubts this point might try the simple exercise of re-telling a story by Henry James, for example, in the style of Ernest Hemingway. Only parody could result.

Handbooks and dictionaries usually define style as the specific features of language that characterize an individual writer or writers of a particular group or time period. In such a definition, we may speak of Poe's style, or Alice Munro's style, or we might describe a style as "Romantic" or "Post-Modern." These are legitimate uses of the term, but they do not explain very clearly what style is or why it is important.

If we think of structure as the author's choices about handling the larger elements of a story, such as summary, description, and dialogue, we might think of style as the author's way of handling material at the level of the sentence. In this light, we might then look at such stylistic features as the length, variety, and complexity of the sentences (short, simple sentences or long, complex ones), the nature of the diction (simple, complex, Latinate), the level of formality of the language (colloquial, slangy, formal), the use of figurative language or rhetorical devices (plain, ornate, poetic, repetitious, dream-like, stream-of-consciousness, and so on), or the level of abstraction (abstract, concrete).

Labeling style in this way remains an empty exercise unless we relate what we say about style to the story's overall theme, effect, or ostensible purpose. One way to use stylistic analysis is to apply it to character. The way in which a character talks, the language he or she uses, is an important way to measure external features such as level of education or place of residence, and language gives clues to a character's inner nature as well. Style also creates tone and atmosphere. A writer of gothic thrillers, for example, piles on descriptive words to evoke a frightening or gloomy atmosphere, increase suspense, and create a sense of impending danger. By contrast, Stephen Crane's almost humorous description of the sea uses understatement to highlight danger. Crane's tone seems to mock the men, even as the personified sea does:

> A singular disadvantage of the sea lies in the fact that after successfully surmounting one wave you discover that there is another behind it just as important and just as nervously anxious to do something effective in the way of swamping boats. In a ten-foot dingey one can get an idea of the resources of the sea in the line of waves that is not probable to the average experience which is never at sea in a dingey.

Through such devices as characterization, tone, and figurative language, style affects everything about a story and shapes the way in which we understand it. In the end, however, what happens in a story cannot be separated from how the story is told; content cannot be divorced from style.

FIGURATIVE LANGUAGE

Traditionally, the figurative (non-literal) use of language was regarded as an ornament to prose or poetry, rather like the decoration on a cake or the chocolate coating on a nut: something to be savored for its beauty or cleverness, perhaps, but not essential to the meaning of the work. In the past fifty years or so, this attitude has been reversed. Imagery (the use of vivid figurative language to represent objects, actions, or ideas) has often received more attention from critics than any other aspect of fiction. In part, this is due to the belief that patterns of imagery can be largely unconscious on the author's part and hence a window into his or her deepest meanings. Conversely, figurative language can be seen as part of the deliberate choices an author makes in crafting a piece of fiction. In addition, as authors have abandoned plot for other ways of unifying fiction, imagery has been seen as the "glue" holding a work together. For any or all of these reasons, responding to the author's use of figurative language can add a great deal to the understanding and enjoyment of short stories.

In its root meaning, an image is any use of language that calls forth a mental picture by the use of words appealing to the senses. Stephen Crane uses an image, for example, when he writes, "A seat in this boat was not unlike a seat upon a bucking bronco." Chekhov describes the ill fate of two lovers by noting, "it was as though they were a pair of birds of passage, caught and forced to live in different cages."

Imagery in literature includes any figure of speech such as simile, metaphor, personification, or symbol. When critics talk about violent imagery, or images contrasting light and dark, they mean the sum total of such references, literal and non-literal. The various uses of figurative language have been minutely cataloged, but for most purposes, only a few terms are necessary:

Simile: a comparison involving the use of "like" or "as": "Cora was like a tree—once rooted, she stood, in spite of storms and strife, wind, and rocks, in the earth."—Langston Hughes.

Metaphor: an implicit comparison, not using "like" or "as": "Braggioni sits heaped upon the edge of a straight-backed chair. . . ."—Katherine Anne Porter.

Personification: giving human characteristics to a non-human object or abstraction: "The road is dead. Nobody nor anything will bring it back to life. Long, infinitely long, not even its gray skin betrays any sign of life."—Juan Bosch.

Symbol: an object that suggests an abstraction, person, or idea. Some symbols are almost universal in meaning: for example, a journey may symbolize the course of a life. Other symbols arise from the way in which an object is used or described in a particular work, such as the snow in "Silent Snow, Secret Snow" or the Judas flower in "Flowering Judas."

In addition to particular uses of figurative language, authors may create (consciously or unconsciously) patterns of recurring imagery within a passage or across an entire story. Consider, for example, the italicized words in the following passage from James Joyce's "Araby":

> We walked through the flaring streets jostled by drunken men and bargaining women, amid the curses of labourers, the shrill *litanies* of shop boys who stood on guard by the barrels of pig's cheeks, the nasal *chanting* of street singers who sang a "come-you-all" about O'Donovan Rosa or a ballad about the troubles in our native land. These noises converged in a single sensation of life for me: I imagined that I bore my *chalice* safely through a throng of foes. Her name sprang to my lips at moments in strange *prayers* and *praises* which I myself did not understand. My eyes were often full of tears (I could not tell why) and at times a flood from my heart seemed to pour itself out into my bosom. I thought little of the future. I did not know whether I would ever speak to her or not or, if I spoke to her, how I could tell her of my confused *adoration*. [Italics added.]

As many critics have noted, this passage is full of religious imagery in such words as "litanies," "chanting," "chalice," and the other italicized words. Surely, Joyce is using such terms deliberately and for effect. Moreover, the sordid context of this imagery—the barrels of pigs' cheeks, the cursing workmen, and so on—contrasts sharply with the religious images. The question for readers is how to interpret such imagery. Is Joyce being ironic or humorous in juxtaposing the sacred and the profane? Is he mocking his protagonist, or simply conveying the quality of his experience?

Figurative language not only enriches a description or provides memorable turns of phrase for readers to enjoy but also subtly affects our response to character, setting, and atmosphere. An author's use of figurative language also helps to define his or her style, while symbols and patterns of imagery may profoundly affect our interpretation of a story's theme. It is worthwhile, as a reader, to become sensitive to these poetic uses of language.

WRITING ABOUT SHORT STORIES

WRITING AND THINKING

Inexperienced writers sometimes think that writing is merely the act of writing down on paper what you already know and think about something. All the research about writing, however, suggests that it is not an act of recording but a process of discovering. The process of writing uncovers, focuses, and clarifies what is in the mind—and beyond that forces you to organize, support, and express clearly ideas that are only vague and incoherent notions until written down. Writing, then, is essential to the discipline of literature, just as problem solving is to mathematics or the case study is to the social sciences.

THE ASSIGNMENT

Since writing in a classroom situation begins with an assignment, let us assume that the instructor has asked for an essay of one thousand words (about four typed pages) on John Updike's "The Lucid Eye in Silver Town." Students may choose any aspect of the story, any critical theory, any approach. We will follow the progress one student, Shawna Curtis, as she responds to this assignment. Where does she begin, and how does she proceed?

THE WRITING PROCESS

CHOOSING A TOPIC

Perhaps the most difficult task any writer faces is choosing a topic. Sometimes you get lucky and a good topic simply springs to mind, but if inspiration doesn't strike, you don't need to wait passively for that proverbial light bulb to go on in your head.

Whatever you do, don't try to second-guess your instructor. Trying to figure out "what the teacher wants" will get you nowhere. What the teacher wants is writing that demonstrates a thoughtful, original, and sensitive response to the story. By all means consult your teacher for ideas if you can't get started (or at any other stage along the way), but the topic finally must be one that interests you.

The best place to begin when choosing a subject is with yourself and your own response to the story. Did you like it? Why? Did you dislike it? Why? Did some aspect of the story pique your curiosity, stimulate your imagination, seem particularly odd, or strike a resonant chord in your experience? Class discussions, a reading journal, or written responses to the questions at the end of the stories can be excellent sources of ideas at this stage.

Another possibility is to apply a critical theory. How would a psychoanalytical critic approach the story? Or a feminist, a Marxist, a Jungian, or a deconstructionist?

What information might a historical or biographical critic want to know, and how might such information illuminate the story?

There are also rhetorical devices to get you started. (You may have used these or something like them in your English composition course.) Questions of definition (is this story Romantic, Realistic, Modernist, etc?) and approaches involving comparison/contrast (comparing characters within the story, contrasting two stories by the same author, etc.) can be particularly useful in writing about fiction.

And finally, analyzing any of the "elements" of fiction—character, point of view, setting, atmosphere, plot, figurative language, theme, and style—can be fruitful. These may in turn be related to the overall idea of this book, convention and innovation. How is Updike relying on convention? What innovations in any of these elements can you see in the story? Looking at one of the "Sidebars" in this text may give you ideas of how to begin or what you might say.

One final note: choosing a topic is a necessary first step, not a life-time commitment. Because writing is a process of discovery, you mind find that your topic evolves as you proceed. There's nothing wrong with changing your mind. The point is to begin somewhere with an idea that interests you and to see how things develop from there.

CHOOSING A TOPIC: APPLICATION

From what has already been said, it should be obvious that dozens of different essays could be written about "The Lucid Eye in Silver Town." Referring to the notes already made (see pp. 1164–1172), Shawna sees some likely possibilities:

Jay and Icarus—a comparison

Jay's learning experience

Mrs. August—the marginalized woman

Family dynamics (Freudian approach?)

New York City as a symbol

Money and power; why Martin feels inferior

Who is the narrator? Jay as boy vs. Jay as adult

Jay's disappointment with New York. Compare to home town?

"Lucid Eye" as fable: town mouse vs. country mouse

Jay as obnoxious brat

August family reminds me of my own. Reader response

Who has a lucid eye? Anyone? No one?

Family values vs. success. Martin vs. Quin

This list could go on and on, but there are enough ideas here to get us started.

FINDING SOMETHING TO SAY

Listing steps in the writing process suggests that each stage is self-contained, but in fact they overlap. Trying to choose a suitable topic from the list above, for example, Shawna would inevitably ask herself, "What would I have to say about each one?" So at this point, she might try listing some ideas under promising topics to see whether they lead anywhere.

Mrs. August as marginalized woman—feminist approach
    Depicted as grouchy—the typical shrew?
    All other characters men
    Men's experiences count, women's don't
    Mrs. August hates "the Augusts"—no identity?
    Quin's attitudes condescending: all the young girls are pretty; "tell her what a wonderful boy she is raising"
    Martin's attitude toward wife exaggerated respect—the pedestal syndrome?
Who is the narrator? Jay as boy vs. Jay as adult
    Story written in retrospect—note first and last sentences
    Most of story seen through eyes of Jay at 13
    Mature narrator sees himself as he was: arrogant, short-tempered, overly sensitive, too sure of himself, resentful of weakness (including his own)
    Jay resents being "the kid"
    "I longed to say something to remold. . . ."
    "At that point in my life I was sure that only stupid people took an interest in money."
    "As I remember it. . . ."
    Embarrassed by his father
    Argues with his uncle about Degas vs. Vermeer
    Older narrator sees event "as a kind of ritual"; father as a "midwife assisting at the birth of family pride"
The August family—dysfunctional? Reader response
Trip to NY with father: I expected an adventure, may be a lesson for Jay
Shocked by mother's statement she hates Augusts
Father's response odd, unsettling
Puzzled by Quin's indifference to brother and nephew. Is this a family?
Jay wants to "remold" father. Shouldn't it be the other way around?
Quin out of touch with his family but knows Jerome's.
Strange values.
Lash in Jay's eye: his behavior inexcusable. No respect?
Jay's disappointment: is this the lesson?
Jay scolds father. Family is upside down.
Why "a ritual"? How could it be "birth of family pride"?

From these notes, it appears that any of the three topics would be possible, but before proceeding it may help to see what each entails. The feminist approach would suit someone who feels strongly about the issue or someone (perhaps a male) who wants to try reading from a female viewpoint. The writer would have to be careful, however, to make the essay a discussion of the story, not just an exercise in "male bashing." The second topic—the two narrators—is clearly literary, but even here the writer would have to relate the analysis to something significant about the story—the theme, perhaps. Otherwise, the analysis may be simply an empty exercise. Similarly, comparing the fictional family to your own is of no value unless the comparison illuminates the story in some way or at least explains why you react to it as you do. The purpose of writing, after all, is to say something interesting or valuable to the reader, not just to fill four pages with words.

DECIDING ON A THESIS

As before, then, steps of the process overlap, since choosing a topic and finding something to say involve giving the essay a point—a thesis or purpose. Theses for each topic outlined might be phrased as follows:

1. Feminist: John Updike's "The Lucid Eye in Silver Town" is an example of how fiction by males often (perhaps unintentionally) ignores and/or belittles women.

2. Analysis of point of view: The two narrators in Updike's "The Lucid Eye in Silver Town" create an ironic distance that underscores the story's theme of Jay's gradual maturation.

3. Reader response: I find John Updike's "The Lucid Eye in Silver Town" disturbing because of its complex family dynamics, which at many points resemble those in my own family.

Having reached this stage, Shawna is in the enviable position of having not one but three possible topics to pursue. After more "brainstorming" and making lists like the one above, Shawna finally selects the second topic and its thesis.

WRITING THE FIRST DRAFT

At this point, some students might want to compose an outline before going further, whereas others might simply begin writing. Shawna takes the second approach.

THE TWO NARRATORS IN JOHN UPDIKE'S "THE LUCID EYE IN SILVER TOWN"

By Shawna Curtis

(1) Although the point is easy to overlook John Updike's "The Lucid Eye in Silver Town" involves two narrators. The frame narrator, who speaks mainly at the begining and end of the story looks back on himself as a boy of thirteen and comments on the story's action. The main narrator is the boy Jay, its through him we see most of the action. This dual vision emphasizes the stories overall point of the trip to New York as a step in Jay's maturation.

(2) The role of the first narrator is to set the scene and comment on the action. In a way, he is like an omniscient narrator, looking back on himself as a thirteen-year-old adolescent. The backward looking aspect is evident from the first sentence and runs throughout the first paragraph, as the following quotes show:

"The first time I visited New York City, I was thirteen and went with my father." (xx)

"My father claimed that I and his brother were the smartest people he had ever met—'go-getters,' he called us, with perhaps more irony than at the time I gave him credit for. . . ." (xx)

"New York in those days was seven dollars away; we measured everything, distance and time, in money then." (xx)

(3) In the second paragraph, there is a sudden shift, and 13 year old Jay takes over as the main narrator. We see most of the rest of the events in the story through his eyes:

"By walking what seemed to me a very long way on pavements only a little broader than those of my home town, and not so clean, we reached the hotel. . . ." (xx)

"As, side by side at the window, we talked, I was surprised that my father could answer so many of my questions." (xx)

"I hesitated. I could scarcely believe it, when the cheap drugstore at home had fifteen flavors." (xx)

2

(4) This split in the storys point of view means that we are seeing events at the same time from two different perspectives. The mature narrator gives you the "long view" of an adult; the adolescent narrator gives you the immediate impressions and feelings he felt then. These immediate impressions are important to the story because they provide a sense that things are actually happening in the present tense. The reader needs to feel that the events are actually happening in the present, because most readers have little interest in the past and want to know what is going on now. The past, as we say, is "history," and most of us feel it has little relevance today.

(5) The other reason Updike uses this device is to allow Jay to characterize his own self. He does this without realizing it, because much of what he says and does portrays himself in a rather negative light. Part of this is his prideful attitude toward himself and his lack of respect for his father. "Nothing was more infuriating about my father than his way of agreeing" (xx), he comments at one point. Later, he thinks he knows better than his Dad by arguing with him about weather they should wait in the bedroom or join Uncle Quin. At the restaurant, "I didn't duplicate my father's mistake of offering to shake hands" with the waiter. The ultimate example of this prideful attitude is the way he screams at his father at the end of the story.

(6) Another aspect of Jay's character comes out when he gets something in his eye. Like when Uncle Quin asks if he can walk back to the hotel: "'I'm blind, not lame,' I snapped." (xx). On the way back to the hotel, he walks ahead of the adults, as if he can't bear to be seen with them. Once back there and laying on the bed he yells at his father again, "'Don't torment me,' I said, twisting my face away. 'What good does it do? the doctor'll be up'" (xx). Even after the incident, he shows himself to be full of resentment toward people who tried to help him, even through he was the one who got something in his eye and made a big fuss about it. This is the way adolescents often act. On the one hand they think they know everything and are all grown up, and then

3

they turn around and act like spoiled children, especially when they don't get their own way, as Jay doesn't because he doesn't get to buy the book on Vermeer.

(7) Anyway, its obvious that their is, as I said before, this split in the point of view. Which creates a kind of dual point of view on Jay. The older narrator makes us see that he now regards himself as a sort of spoiled brat, while the younger narrator condemns himself by unconsciously revealing himself as a brat.

(8) Sometimes, I think, it is hard to tell which narrator is talking; because the older one appears to jump in from time to time with comments. One of these occurs at the end of the third paragraph when Jay observes: "Nothing was more infuriating about my father than his way of agreeing" (xx). Is this remark made by the younger Jay or the older narrator. Its not clear. Another example is when Jay's father praises him for being so intelligent and compares him to Uncle Quin:

"Sure, sure." My impatience was not merely embarrassment at being praised; I was irritated that he considered Uncle Quin as smart as myself. At that point in my life I was sure that only stupid people took an interest in money. (xx)

A third example is when Quin offers to show them around New York and Martin says that it would be a treat for "the kid." "He always called me 'the kid' when I was sick or had lost at something or was angry—when he felt sorry for me, in short" (xx). As I said, the speaker in these and lots of other places I could point to is not clear. Probably it is not intended to be, and maybe it doesn't even matter, since either the older or the younger Jay could make the observation.

(9) The most important comments in terms of theme are the one's made by the mature narrator at the beginning and end of the story. The first I have already quoted in part:

My father claimed that I and his brother were the smartest people he had ever met—"go-getters" he called us, with perhaps more irony than at the time I gave him

4

credit for—and in his visionary way he suddenly, irresistibly felt that now was the time for us to meet. (xx)

The second comes at the very end of the story:

I kept on, shrilly flailing the passive and infuriating figure of my father, until we left the city. Once we were on the homeward train, my tantrum ended; it had been a kind of ritual, for both of us, and he had endured my screams complacently, nodding assent, like a midwife assisting at the birth of family pride. Years passed before I needed to go to New York again. (xx)

(10) These statements show that the older Jay sees the experience differently than he did when younger, and show that his view of his father has mellowed and matured. Although the experience was frustrating for the young Jay, it marked an important stage in his growing up. The older Jay can look back, perhaps feeling rather gilty, and expose the arrogant, cocky Jay who thought that because he had "perfect marks" in school that he knew better than his father. The older and wiser Jay knows better, this theme of the story is reinforced by the split vision of the narrators who tell it.

FIRST DRAFT: COMMENTARY

After reading through her first draft, Shawna feels quite proud of her work. Even on second reading, it seems very good: there is a clear thesis, and it is supported by well-chosen quotations from the story. When she showed the paper to her roommate, she said, "I think you spelled some words wrong, but it's really good. You'll get a B at least."

Shawna's instructor scribbled all over her last essay, however, so she takes it to the college's writing center and shows it to one of the student tutors. After reading it over, the tutor (evidently an English major) says, "Well, it's not bad, but how do you know that maturity is the theme of the story?" You don't provide any proof that it is. I've also put check marks beside lines that have errors or need proofreading."

Shawna is at first angered by this criticism and then mystified. What could the tutor mean? OK, so she misspelled some words, but isn't the theme obvious? As she reads the paper again, however, she sees that she has not shown how Jay has matured, except perhaps in his view of himself, and that the two quotations cited in support of the theme are themselves ambiguous. In fact, the more often she rereads those quotations from the beginning and ending of the story, the less sure she is of what they mean.

Now what? The paper is already long enough for the assignment, and anyway, if she takes time to argue fully the story's theme, the essay will divide into two parts—one on theme, one on point of view. Maybe this was the wrong topic after all. Maybe she should abandon this essay and go to the one on feminism or comparing Jay's family to hers.

Meanwhile, time is growing short. The essay is due tomorrow, and it seems crazy to throw away so much hard work. So, Shawna reads the essay again with a more critical eye and discovers two important things: first, not all the quotations are necessary, and second, there are at least two rather long digressions, one in paragraph four, the other in paragraph six. She also sees that the point about the blending of the two narrators in paragraph eight confuses the issue more than clarifies it. Finally, she decides that "maturity" doesn't really describe what happens to Jay. Maybe it would be more accurate to say that he sees his father in a new light. Moreover, if maturity is not a good way to describe the theme of the story, then much of what she says about Jay's immaturity isn't necessary, either. She still isn't sure about how this should be expressed, but perhaps by revising the essay, she will discover what she means.

This is how the essay looks after Shawna has crossed out the irrelevant passages and jotted some notes in the margin.

THE TWO NARRATORS IN JOHN UPDIKE'S "THE LUCID EYE IN SILVER TOWN"

By Shawna Curtis

?

(1) Although the point is easy to overlook John Updike's "The Lucid Eye in Silver Town" involves two narrators. The frame narrator, who speaks mainly at the begining and end of the story looks back on himself as a boy of thirteen and comments on the story's *rep.* action The main narrator is the boy Jay, its through him we see most of the action This dual vision em- *new* phasizes the stories overall point of the trip to New *perspective?* York as a step in Jay's ~~maturation~~ *new vision* *?*
(2) The role of the first narrator is to set the scene and comment on the action. In a way, he is like an omniscient narrator, looking back on himself as a thirteen-year-old adolescent. The backward looking aspect is evident from the first sentence and runs throughout the first paragraph, as the following quotes show:

"The first time I visited New York City, I was thirteen and went with my father." (1167)

shorten "My father claimed that I and his brother were the smartest people he had ever met—'go-getters,' he called us, with perhaps more irony than at the time I gave him credit for. . . ." (1165)

cut ~~"New York in those days was seven dollars away; we measured everything, distance and time, in money then." (1165)~~

(3) In the second paragraph, there is a sudden shift, and 13 year old Jay takes over as the main narrator. We see most of the rest of the events in the story through his eyes:

"By walking what seemed to me a very long way on pavements only a little broader than those of my home town, and not so clean, we reached the hotel. . . . (1165)

cut ~~"As, side by side at the window, we talked, I was surprised that my father could answer so many of my questions." (1166)~~

2

~~"I hesitated. I could scarcely believe it, when the cheap drugstore at home had fifteen flavors." (xx)~~

cut irrelevant

(4) This split in the storys point of view means that we are seeing events at the same time from two different perspectives. The mature narrator gives you the "long view" of an adult; the adolesent narrator gives you the immediate impressions and feelings he felt then. These immediate impressions are important to the story because they provide a sense that things are actually happening in the present tense. The reader needs to feel that the events are actually happening in the present, because most readers have little interest in the past and want to know what is going on now. The past, as we say, is "history," and most of us feel it has little relevance today.

(5) The other reason Updike uses this device is to allow Jay to characterize his own self *himself*. He does this without realizing it, because much of what he says and does portrays himself in a rather negative light. Part of this is his prideful attitude toward himself and his lack of respect for his father. "Nothing was more infuriating about my father than his way of agreeing" (1165), he comments at one point. Later, he thinks he knows better than his Dad by arguing with him about weather they should wait in the bedroom or join Uncle Quin. At the restaurant, "I didn't duplicate my father's mistake of offering to shake hands" (1168) with the waiter. The ultimate example of this prideful attitude is the way he screams at his father at the end of the story.

(6) Another aspect of Jay's character comes out when he gets something in his eye. Like when Uncle Quin asks if he can walk back to the hotel: "'I'm blind, not lame,' I snapped" (1170). On the way back to the hotel, he walks ahead of the adults, as if he can't bear to be seen with them. Once back there and laying on the bed he yells at his father again, "'Don't torment me,' I said, twisting my face away. 'What good does it do? the doctor'll be up'" (1170). Even after the incident, he shows himself to be full of resentment toward people who tried

3

to help him, even through he was the one who got some-
thing in his eye and made a big fuss about it. ~~This is the way adolescents often act. On the one hand they think they know everything and are all grown up, and then they turn around and act like spoiled children, especially when they don't get their own way, as Jay doesn't be-cause~~ he doesn't get to buy the book on Vermeer.

cut irrelevant

(7) Anyway, its obvious that their is, as I said be-fore, this split in the point of view. Which creates a kind of dual point of view on Jay. The older narrator makes us see that he now regards himself as a sort of spoiled brat, while the younger narrator condemns himself by unconsciously revealing himself as a brat.

(8) Sometimes, I think, it is hard to tell which nar-rator is talking; because the older one appears to jump in from time to time with comments. One of these occurs at the end of the third paragraph when Jay observes: "Nothing was more infuriating about my father than his way of agreeing" (1165). Is this remark made by the younger Jay or the older narrator. Its not clear. Another example is when Jay's father praises him for being so intelligent and compares him to Uncle Quin:

cut confusing

"Sure, sure." My impatience was not merely embar-rassment at being praised; I was irritated that he consid-ered Uncle Quin as smart as myself. At that point in my life I was sure that only stupid people took an interest in money. (1167)

A third example is when Quin offers to show them around New York and Martin says that it would be a treat for "the kid." "He always called me 'the kid' when I was sick or had lost at something or was angry—when he felt sorry for me, in short" (1167). As I said, the speaker in these and lots of other places I could point to is not clear. Probably it is not intended to be, and maybe it doesn't even matter, since either the older or the younger Jay could make the observation.

(9) The most important comments in terms of theme are the one's made by the mature narrator at the

4

beginning and end of the story. The first I have already
quoted in part:

> My father claimed that I and his brother were the
> smartest people he had ever met—"go-getters" he
> called us, with perhaps more irony than at the time
> I gave him credit for—and in his visionary way he
> suddenly, irresistibly felt that now was the time for
> us to meet. (1165)

The second comes at the very end of the story:

> I kept on, shrilly flailing the passive and infuriating
> figure of my father, until we left the city. Once we
> were on the homeward train, my tantrum ended; it
> had been a kind of ritual, for both of us, and he
> had endured my screams complacently, nodding as-
> sent, like a midwife assisting at the birth of family
> pride. Years passed before I needed to go to New
> York again. (1172)

(10) These statements show that the older Jay
sees the experience differently than he did when
younger, and show that his view of his father has mellowed and matured. Although the experience was frus-   ✓
trating for the young Jay, it marked an important
stage in his growing up. The older Jay can look back,
perhaps feeling rather gilty, and expose the arrogant,
cocky Jay who thought that because he had "perfect   ✓
marks" in school that he knew better than his father.
The older and wiser Jay knows better, this theme of the
story is reinforced by the split vision of the narrators
who tell it.

WRITING THE SECOND DRAFT

Having changed her mind somewhat about the thesis statement and the way to handle
supporting details, Shawna plunges into her second draft.

THE TWO NARRATORS IN JOHN UPDIKE'S "THE LUCID EYE IN SILVER TOWN"

By Shawna Curtis

(1) John Updike's "The Lucid Eye in Silver Town" is a story about changing perceptions. Young Jay, confident of his abilities almost to arrogance, condescending toward his father, opinionated, and resentful, undergoes a small but important humiliation during the story. Looking back on this experience as a mature man, he sees that his father arranged their trip to New York City "as a kind of ritual" (1172). What Jay learns first hand is how vulnerable he is, how easy it is to fall short of his goal, how circumstances can complicate and frustrate even the simplest plans. An important ingredient in this story's theme is the way in which Updike divides the point of view between young Jay's perceptions and his reflections on the incident years later. The differences between the two narrators underline the story's theme of changing perceptions.

(2) The role of the first narrator is to set the scene and comment on the action. The backward looking aspect is evident in the first sentence—"The first time I visited New York City, I was thirteen and went with my father" (1164)—and runs throughout the first paragraph as the mature narrator explains the family's situation and economic position. The fact this mature narrator sees things differently than he used to is signalled in the words, " 'go-getters,' he called us, with perhaps more irony than at the time I gave him credit for . . ." (1165). His roll as commentator is seen in the observations he makes at various points during the story, as when he says, "At that point in my life I was sure that only stupid people took an interest in money" (1167); and again when he observes, "The seed of my anger seemed to be a desire to recall him to himself, to scold him out of being old and tired" (1166).

(3) In the second paragraph, the point of view shifts and young Jay takes over as the main narrator. The rest of the story is seen through his eyes, as for example when he says, "By walking what seemed to

2

me a very long way on pavements only a little broader than those of my home town, and not so clean, we reached the hotel ..." (1165). In this way, we learn not only what happens but how young Jay felt about and reacted to the people and events he encounters in New York.

(4) This split in the stories point of view means that we see events simultaneously from two different perspectives. The mature narrator gives the "long view" of an adult; the adolescent narrator provides the immediate impressions and feelings he felt then. This device also allows Jay to characterize himself (unconsciously, of course) as an arrogant and opinionated young man with little respect for his father. "Nothing was more infuriating about my father than his way of agreeing" (xx), he comments at one point. Later, he thinks he knows better than his Dad by arguing with him about whether they should wait in the bedroom or join Uncle Quin. At the restaurant, "I didn't duplicate my father's mistake of offering to shake hands" (1167) with the waiter. The ultimate example of this prideful attitude is the way he screams at his father at the end of the story.

(5) The thematic importance of this device can be seen at the story's climax, when Jay walks into the park and looks up at the skyscrapers around him:

Shimmering buildings arrowed upward and glinted through the treetops. This was New York, I felt: the silver town. Towers of ambition rose, crystalline, within me. (1169)

At this moment, when Jay feels the lure of New York as a symbol of ambition and achievement, he suffers an almost ridiculously minor but telling humiliation. He gets something in his "lucid eye." It is the interior view into Jay, made possible by his role as narrator, that allows readers to experience the full impact of this event. From this moment to the end of the story, all his polite pretenses fall away. He resents anyone who tries to help, aims insulting remarks at

3

his father and uncle, and ends up in a temper tantrum of verbal abuse in the final paragraph, blaming his father for the day's disappointments, including their failure to buy a book about Vermeer. Unconsciously, the young narrator reveals himself to be a spoiled brat who, unlike his father, blames everyone but himself when things go wrong. Jay's father, whatever his failings, never blames anyone but himself.

(6) At this point, the mature narrator breaks in, commenting on the actions and attitudes of the young Jay and suggesting the meaning of the day's events:

I kept on, shrilly flailing the passive and infuriating figure of my father, until we left the city. Once we were on the homeward train, my tantrum ended; it had been a kind of ritual, for both of us, and he had endured my screams complacently, nodding assent, like a midwife assisting at the birth of family pride. Years passed before I needed to go to New York again (1172).

(7) This statement shows that the older Jay sees the experience differently than he did when younger and that his view of his father has mellowed and matured. Although the experience was frustrating for the young Jay, it marked an important shift in perception—or at least the beginning of such a shift. The first glimmerings of it occurred even during the story, when young Jay had noted:

As, side by side at the window, we talked, I was surprised that my father could answer so many of my questions. As a young man, before I was born, he had traveled, looking for work; this was not <u>his</u> first trip to New York. Excited by my new respect, I longed to say something to remold that calm, beaten face. (1166)

The older Jay can look back on these incidents, perhaps feeling rather guilty, and expose the arrogant, cocky boy who thought because he had "perfect marks" in school and could talk knowledgeably about

4

Vermeer that he was superior to his father. The story seems an act of affection, perhaps even atonement, toward a father who had suffered disappointments and was resigned to them.

(8) Jay's change of perception, from condescension toward his father to a measure of respect, is emphasized by Updike's handling of point of view and the contrast it allows between the angry, cock-sure young Jay and the mature frame narrator who now sees himself and his father with greater understanding.

FINAL CHECKING AND PROOFREADING

When she completed this second draft, Shawna felt confident that she had done justice to her thesis and answered the tutor's objection about clarifying the story's theme. She still had questions about the story: What exactly was it that Jay's father hoped the boy would learn by meeting Uncle Quin? Why does the narrator say in the last sentence, "Years passed before I needed to go to New York again"? But these issues would have to be addressed another time. Right now she needs to proofread the paper and get it as nearly perfect as she can.

Fortunately, her computer has a spell-check program, but she knows from experience that it can't catch all the typographical errors like "of" for "on" and mistakes involving homonyms like "there" and "their," "to" and "too." She also knows that she has trouble with punctuation. When she wrote her last paper, she asked a friend for help, but when the paper came back, it was obvious that the friend didn't know very much, so on the morning the paper is due, she makes another trip to the writing center, where a tutor puts a check mark besides passages that have problems and reviews some of the rules regarding commas.

Shawna doesn't have time to do another computer print-out before class, so she makes some changes in pen and hands the paper in, resolving next time to give herself another day for the assignment.

PART FOUR

Reference

GLOSSARY

Action. At the simplest level, whatever happens in the story, usually thought of as physical events; however, internal events, thoughts, and emotions may also be part of the action, particularly if they involve some change of attitude. *Cf.* **Plot.**

Adventure story. A story in which external action, particularly of the exciting kind, is central to the action or plot. Conventionally, the hero or heroine encounters physical or spiritual perils which must be defeated or overcome.

Aesthetic. Relating to art and ideas of what is beautiful or pleasing in an art form.

Allegory. Literally saying one thing but meaning another. As commonly used in criticism, allegory refers to characters who represent abstractions such as Faith or Evil, or to actions that suggest an internal or external moral conflict. Deliberate allegories consciously use characters and events that suggest abstract or symbolic qualities, but almost any story may be read allegorically.

Anecdote. A very short narrative, often relating an amusing incident.

Antagonist. The character or force that opposes the hero or heroine. An abstraction such as society or a physical force such as the sea may also be considered an antagonist. *Cf.* **Protagonist.**

Anticlimax. A sudden shift in the plot from action leading up to a climax to an irrelevant or distracting event that detracts from the expected climax. Alternately, any event that appears to be the climax but is not. *Cf.* **Climax, Plot.**

Antihero. A central character whose physical or moral traits are different from those we normally expect in a hero: cowardice instead of bravery, deceit instead of honesty, weakness instead of strength. Also, a character in a central role who in his or her ordinariness seems less than heroic.

Anti-story. Experimental stories of the 1960s and 1970s that deliberately rejected the conventions of character, plot, and especially theme, substituting fantastic incidents, incoherent characters, and discontinuous story lines. *Cf.* **Metafiction.**

Archetype. A term derived from the psychology of Carl Jung (1875–1961) who posited a "collective unconscious" as part of the individual psyche. Archetypes may be recurring characters, events, or symbols that are found in literature, regardless of time or place. The sun as a symbol of life, light as a symbol of truth, the struggles of a hero, and the experience of rebirth or initiation are all archetypes. *Cf.* **Motif.**

Atmosphere. Related to setting but not identical with it. Atmosphere refers to the feeling or mood that permeates the story—a sunny or gloomy atmosphere, for example. *Cf.* **Setting.** *See pp.* 1186–1187.

Biographical criticism. Criticism that attempts to explain the meaning or origin of a literary work by reference to events in the author's life. Such an approach is particularly helpful for understanding what events in the story may have meant to the author or why the author frequently uses certain characters, themes, settings, or situations.

Black humor. Humor that results from a cynical or pessimistic view of the world and often involves the violent, the grotesque, or the morbid. There is black humor throughout literature, but the term is especially associated with the **Anti-story** and **Post-modernism.**

Caricature. Deliberate distortion of a character's physical appearance or personality to produce a humorous effect and/or ridicule. Newspaper cartoonists use caricature in depicting politicians, for example, often by exaggerating a particular physical trait. In criticism, the term is often used in a pejorative sense.

Characters. The people (sometimes animals) who appear in a story or other literary work. Until recently, critics and readers assumed that characters were in some sense real people; that is, that they had personalities, motives, aspirations, etc., that corresponded to those of real human beings. As a result, characters were often judged by whether they seemed "real" or "fully developed." Post-Modern literary theory, however, has questioned the concept of character by arguing that literary characters are not real people but verbal constructs or "signs." *See pp.* 1177–1180.

Climax. In a conventionally plotted story, the point when the rising action reaches a turning point or crisis, after which it becomes clear whether the ending will be comic or tragic for the protagonist.

Closed ending. An ending that resolves most or all of a story's tensions and conflicts; e.g., the criminal is caught, the lovers reconcile, the hero survives the adventure.

Complication. That portion of the **plot** when the conflict becomes more complex.

Conflict. A conventional plot is built on a struggle or clash of some kind; often, conflict occurs when the protagonist encounters an obstacle or antagonist in the form of a person or force (nature, society, an inner resistance) that frustrates or interferes with his or her goal, wishes, desires, or ideals.

Convention. A term used to describe recurring features in a work of art, either of form or content. Repetition of these features leads to an implicit, often unconscious agreement between author and audience as to how literary meaning is conveyed. Fictional conventions of form, for example, include the authority of the narrator, the use of interior monologue, and the idea of characters. Detective, horror, love, and adventure stories all have their conventions of form. Conventions of content include what may or may not be represented fictionally—such as vulgar language, physical love, unpunished crime, and the like. In practice it is difficult to separate the two kinds of convention. All art depends on a certain amount of convention in order that communication may take place; however, the term is often used as a criticism for any work of art that is overly derivative, imitative, formulaic, or predictable.

Crisis or **Climax.** The point in a conventional plot when the conflict reaches its highest point of intensity; after the climax, the outcome of the conflict is clear.

Deconstruction. A school of literary criticism based on the philosophy of Jacques Derrida. Derrida argued that language is inherently ambiguous and hence that any text has innumerable possible meanings, independent either of the author's intent, the world to which the text ostensibly refers, or the conventions of literary criticism. Thus, deconstructive criticism attempts to show how a text undermines its own attempt to create meaning and instead makes possible an infinite number of readings or interpretations.

Denouement. In a conventional **plot**, the final unraveling or resolution of events after the climax.

Determinism. The theory that human behavior is mainly or wholly governed by heredity, environment, or a combination of the two. The primary governing forces may be psychological as in Freudianism, economic as in Marxism, or external rewards and punishment as in behaviorism. Determinism opposes the idea of free will, which assumes that people make conscious decisions. *Cf.* **Naturalism**.

Didactic. Used to describe a work that overtly attempts to teach a particular lesson. The term is often used pejoratively to describe a story in which the events seem manipulated or contrived to impart an idea. *Cf.* **Theme** and **Moral**. *See also pp.* 1187–1188.

Dramatic irony. *See* **Irony**.

Epiphany. A term coined by James Joyce to describe a moment of understanding or illumination achieved either by a character within the story or by the reader or both. Since Joyce's collection of stories *Dubliners,* short stories have frequently focused on such moments of insight.

Episodic story. A narrative whose events do not follow in logical or causal order but occur with no probable or necessary connection between them. Since Aristotle's emphasis on plot, episodic stories have usually been considered inferior to well-plotted ones and hence the term is often used pejoratively. *Cf.* **Plot**.

Existentialism. A philosophy associated with the French writer and thinker Jean-Paul Sartre and the theologian Søren Kierkegaard. Both believe that human beings have no essential "human nature" but define themselves and create their values by the decisions they freely make. Sartre's view is atheistic, emphasizing an absurd, meaningless universe; Kierkegaard's is Christian. *Cf.* **Determinism**.

Exposition. In a conventional plot, the early part of the story, which explains the situation before complications begin. Also, in any work of fiction, comments by the narrator that provide background information. *Cf.* **Plot**; *See also pp.* 1191–1192.

Fable. A brief narrative often involving animals as characters, with an explicit moral message stated at the end. Also used in short-story criticism (sometimes pejoratively) to describe a work that resembles a fable. *Cf.* **Allegory**.

Fairy tale. Also called Märchen. A short form of traditional, oral narrative (or a literary imitation) involving the supernatural and often featuring a hero or heroine who seems destined by fate to achieve some desirable goal—such as marrying a prince or princess, achieving wealth, or destroying an enemy.

Fantasy. Any form of literature that does not attempt verisimilitude or realism. Alternate worlds, visions, ghosts, supernatural beings (including gods and goddesses), the uncanny, and the marvelous may all be included in fantasy. Each fictional fantasy creates a world with its own laws, which the actors and actions in the plot should obey.

Feminist criticism. Broadly speaking, any way of reading that provides an alternative to the usual male-dominated theories and approaches. Feminist critics are concerned with expanding the literary canon to include previously neglected women writers, with analyzing literature for implicit or explicit sexism, with the relations between the sexes as they are depicted in literature, and with the impact of male-dominated literature on women readers, as well as many other related issues, such as the inherent sexism of language itself. *See pp.* 1175–1176.

Figurative language. Any non-literal use of language, such as simile, metaphor, personification, irony. Much figurative language is fixed in everyday usage, such as the leg of a table or the mouth of a river, but the literary use of figurative language seeks both originality and insight by extending the normal use of language. Patterns of figurative language or imagery are particularly important in formalist or New Criticism, which often finds thematic significance in patterns of figurative language. *See pp.* 1194–1196.

Foil. A character whose traits contrast with those of the protagonist and hence highlight one or more of the protagonist's qualities. For example, a thoroughly dishonest character might serve as a foil to a comparatively honest protagonist.

Foreshadowing. Any device or hint suggesting events that later occur in the story; for example, an argument might foreshadow a later violent confrontation.

Form. A term used in a wide variety of ways. One usage equates form with genre— e.g., the short story form, or even the detective story form. Form may also denote the structure or organization of the work; whether the narrative relies on or avoids plot; or the way in which dialogue, exposition, summary, description, and action are integrated to form the story. Since the Romantic period, it has been customary to investigate whether the form of a work is conventional or organic, the latter implying that the form grows out of the material rather than being imposed upon it. *See pp.* 1192–1193.

Formalism. Also called New Criticism, the dominant mode of critical inquiry from 1930–1960, particularly in America. Formalism reacted against biographical and historical criticism by insisting on the work of art as an autonomous object to be analyzed for its internal devices of order and meaning. Though now widely rejected by Post-Structuralist critical theories, formalist critics pioneered the habits of close reading now used by many critics, particularly Deconstructionists. *Cf.* **Historical criticism, Deconstruction**. *See also pp.* 1172–1175.

Formula. Any literary device or mode of expression that through over-use has become a cliché.

Frame narrative. A story in which one narrator gives way to another narrator, thus producing a story within a story. "Heart of Darkness," for instance, begins with a narrator who sets the scene and introduces Marlow, who then tells his own story.

Free indirect style. A way of handling point of view and the presentation of interior thoughts or sensations particularly associated with Modernist authors. An example of direct discourse would be, "She said to herself, 'I will never marry him.'" Indirect discourse would be "She said to herself that she would never marry him." Free indirect discourse reports, "She would never marry him." The method allows the narrator to maintain a third-person point of view while also gaining the immediacy of a first-person narrator. Hence, the point of view may seem to shift between omniscient and first-person without transition.

Free story. A term coined in the 1970s to describe experimental fiction that dispensed with such conventions of plot and theme. *Cf.* **Metafiction**.

Freudian criticism. A way of reading literature that depends on the psychological theories of Sigmund Freud. Typically, Freudian critics analyze literary characters for their unconscious motives as revealed indirectly or symbolically through what they say and do, and also by their dreams or fantasies. In Freud's theory, most motives spring unconsciously from the "id," which is the seat of instinctual desires and motives, particularly those relating to violence and sex.

The "ego" is the self or conscience; the "superego" is the partly internalized rules and conventions of society and the source of anxiety, guilt, and shame. The classic Freudian device is to analyze the workings of the so-called Oedipus Complex, by which a male child desires perfect union with the mother and hence resents his father and fears retaliation in the form of castration. *See pp.* 466–471.

Gothic fiction. Invented by Horace Walpole in his novel, *The Castle of Otranto: A Gothic Story* (1764). Strictly speaking, Gothic tales are set in the Middle Ages and usually revolve around a family curse or scandal. Other conventions include haunted castles, dire prophecies, secret passages, and supernatural beings. Subsequently, the term has been applied to any horror fiction that uses some of these conventions, especially the supernatural.

Hard boiled detective. Detective fiction featuring a tough, cynical, and frequently violent protagonist who inhabits a grimy, corrupt environment. Noted practitioners include Raymond Chandler and Dashiell Hammett.

Hero/heroine. A fictional protagonist who upholds values that are admired by the narrator—typically bravery, honesty, piety, virginity, etc. Also applied to any protagonist, even ones not particularly virtuous. *Cf.* **Antihero, Protagonist**.

Historical criticism. Any approach to explaining a literary work and/or its author by attempting to place it in its historical, social, or philosophical milieu. Historical criticism emphasizes the forces that produced or shaped a work of literature, such as the literary genre or conventions, the dominant ideology, the important social and political movements and events, and the like. *See p.* 1175. *Cf.* **New Historicism, Marxist criticism**.

Hyperbole. Deliberate exaggeration for rhetorical effect. *Cf.* **Figurative language**.

Id. *See* **Freudian criticism**.

Imagery. In its original sense, any language that attempts to paint a visual image in the reader's mind. More recently, the term applies to figurative language, e.g. the religious imagery in Joyce's "Araby." *See also pp.* 1194–1196. *Cf.* **Figurative language**.

Implied author. The author is the historical person (e.g., Angela Carter) who did the writing; the implied author is the largely imaginary person (more or less resembling the living author) who narrates the story. *Cf.* **Persona**.

Implied reader. The actual reader is the person reading the story who interprets it in the light of his or her experiences, ideas, etc. The implied reader is the ideal reader—one who would, for example, have the knowledge, values, and reading ability that the author imagines when writing.

Innovation. A break with literary tradition or convention in form or content. Innovation often arises when writers tire of previous conventions and intentionally experiment with new ways of expression or new ideas about what constitutes appropriate material for fiction. *Cf.* **Convention**.

Interior monologue. *See* **Stream of Consciousness**.

Intertextuality. A term deriving from theories of fiction opposed to the idea that fiction imitates or mimics reality (mimesis). Intertextuality refers to the way in which a new work of fiction depends on previous fiction to create its meaning. This is not simply a matter of genre or literary influence but of the system of signs by which fiction creates meaning. *Cf.* **Mimesis**.

Irony. Verbal irony is a figure of speech indicating a difference between appearance and reality or a direct contrast between what is said and what is meant. "I really like your tie," may mean, "I do not like your tie." Situational irony occurs when an action produces the opposite effect of what was intended or when a situation turns out differently from what might be expected. Dramatic irony refers to situations in which the audience or reader possesses information that the participants in the fiction are unaware of. Irony may also be applied to a mode of perception whereby one sees the discrepancy between appearance and reality, act and intention, words and meaning.

Limited omniscience. *See* **Point of view** and *pp.* 1188–1191.

Magical realism. Fiction in which the apparently real and the magic are treated as equally normal. The term was first applied to the visual arts, then to Latin American stories by such writers as Garcia Marquez and Borges.

Marxist criticism. The name given to various approaches to literature inspired by the ideas of Karl Marx. Marxist criticism focuses mainly on content rather than form, and in its early forms emphasized judging fiction by its historical accuracy and its usefulness to the class struggle (particularly a sympathetic portrayal of lower classes and criticism of higher classes or capitalism). More recent Marxist criticism has been interested in how modes of production influence literary works, in the "silences" or tensions within works that betray their ideological underpinnings, and in the "death of the author" idea, which sees authors as almost passive transmitters of cultural ideas current at the time. *Cf.* **New historicism**. *See p.* 1159.

Melodrama. Emotionally charged fiction that emphasizes dramatic action and usually employs stock characters and stereotypes. Usually used in a pejorative sense.

Metafiction. Fiction that deliberately calls attention to itself as fiction and thereby encourages readers not to confuse fictional conventions with reality but to see in them the ways in which fiction makes meaning. *Cf.* **Postmodernism**. *See p.* 1159.

Metaphor. Strictly speaking a figure of speech comparing two unlike things without using the words "like" or "as."

Mimesis. The idea that fiction imitates reality; verisimilitude. *Cf.* **Intertextuality**, **Realism**.

Minimalism. A contemporary fictional style that uses simple, even stark language and focuses on surface details for their own sake rather than as indicators of deeper significance. Minimalist authors often avoid thematic ideas, preferring simply to report reality as they see it without a moral or thematic purpose. *Cf.* **Postmodernism**. *See p.* 1159.

Modernism. An artistic movement beginning about 1890 in Europe, somewhat later in the United States, and ending about 1960 (although many critics would assert that it continues to the present). Modernism was a reaction against the conventions of Realism and Naturalism, which focused on exterior reality and asserted the knowability of experience. Modernism turned from exterior reality to interior consciousness, often abandoned plot in favor of other unifying devices, insisted on a more frank discussion of sexual matters, and frequently stressed the subjectivity of experience and reality. Many modernist authors experimented with both form and style in an effort to report their radically new visions of reality or to unify the multiplicity of realities through art. *Cf.* **Stream of consciousness, Post-Modernism.** *See also pp.* 1154–1159.

Moral. An ethical lesson explicitly stated or implicitly intended in a story. *Cf.* **Theme.** *See also pp.* 1187–1188.

Motif. A recurring image or pattern of action within a story or among various stories. For example, a forbidden object or desire may recur in a single work; or, we may say that various stories use the Bluebeard motif. *Cf.* **Archetype, Theme.**

Motive. A conscious or unconscious reason for an action. Literature has always been interested not only in what characters do but why they do it, but Freudian criticism has given new importance and complexity to motives by delving into unconscious motivations. In Realist fiction, motives are supposed to be consistent within a character's psychology, but in Post-Modernism, motives may often seem random and characters inconsistent. Stereotyped characters often act without convincing motive because that type of character always behaves in a certain way. *Cf.* **Freudian criticism, Character.** *See also pp.* 1177–1182.

Myth. A story invoking the supernatural to explain the origin of the universe or other natural phenomena, the source of cultural values or taboos, the personal qualities expected of good citizens, and similar phenomena. All religions employ myths, but even secular value systems such as capitalism and Marxism employ mythic ideas and structures—e.g., the myth of hard work as a path to financial success or the myth of history as an impersonal but decisive force in human affairs. The term is often used as a synonym for something not literally true, but myths are powerful conveyors of meaning and lie at the source of fiction and its power.

Narrator. The voice or character who actually tells the story, as distinct from the author as a person. *Cf.* **Implied narrator, Persona, Point of view.** *See also pp.* 1188–1191.

Naturalism. An artistic movement in Europe and the Americas in the late nineteenth century, influenced by science in general and Darwin in particular, which depicts human beings as a part of nature, driven by animal instincts they cannot control and living in a universe indifferent to their needs and desires. Naturalist authors advocate scientific objectivity and an interest in the "laws" of human behavior in fiction. *Cf.* **Realism.** *See also p.* 1152.

New criticism. *See* **Formalism.**

New Historicism. Traditional historical approaches to literature focus on literacy tradition or "background" information that places a work in its cultural context. New Historicism may accomplish these goals, too, but it also sees literature as consciously or unconsciously participating in and supporting the power structures of its time. *Cf.* **Marxist criticism.**

Omniscient. A point of view in which the narrator assumes the "god-like" power of knowing everything about the events and characters in the story. *Cf.* **Point of view.** *See also pp.* 1188–1191.

Open ending. An ending that leaves some or all of a story's tensions or conflicts unresolved, leaving the reader wondering whether the criminal is caught, the lovers reconcile, the hero survives, etc.

Parable. Stories told by Jesus in the New Testament to illustrate an ethical or theological moral. The term is now applied (sometimes pejoratively) to any story that resembles Biblical parables by teaching an obvious moral lesson. *Cf.* **Fable**, **Moral**, **Theme**.

Persona. Literally "a mask," thus a term used to describe the character of the person who tells the story. *Cf.* **Implied author**.

Personification. A figure of speech in which an inanimate object or natural force is portrayed or addressed as if a human being.

Plot. Regarded by Aristotle as the most important element of drama, consisting of a complete action with a beginning, middle, and end. Plot is driven by conflict between a protagonist and antagonist. Through a series of complications the conflict reaches a crisis, and it becomes clear whether the plot will end happily or tragically for the protagonist, after which the denouement or falling action brings the story to a close. Plot induces suspense in the reader who wonders both what will happen and why—and in the "why" often lies the clue to the theme developed through the plot. Brander Matthews considered plot essential to the short story, but the rigidity of its conventions led Modernist writers to seek formal unity through other means. *Cf.* **Episodic story**. *See also pp.* 1191–1192.

Point of View. The person or voice in which a story is narrated. When the narrator uses the pronoun "I," the point of view is first person. When the narrator speaks about other characters by name or uses the pronouns "he," "she," or "they," the point of view is third person. Second person "you" is rarely used. A third person narrator who claims to know everything about the characters and events in a story is called omniscient. A third person narrator that in some way is limited in his or her knowledge of characters and events is called limited omniscient. *Cf.* **Free-indirect style**. *See pp.* 1188–1191.

Post-Modernism. A highly controversial term applied to artistic and critical movements since World War II, often implying the end of Modernism. Like other *-isms,* Post-Modernism is difficult to define, but many who use the term emphasize that Post-Modernism rejects the idea that art can unify vision or experience. Thus, Post-Modernism dwells on the fragmentary nature of contemporary life, its chaotic mixture of cultural signs, the indeterminacy and inadequacy of language, the lack of meaning. Post-Modern fiction often resembles collage in presenting a deliberately disunified set of experiences, or it relies on Metafiction to call attention to the artificiality of fiction itself. Black humor, parody, and pastiche are also associated with Post-Modernism. Post-Modern criticism emphasizes the role of the reader in creating meaning, the multiplicity of meanings discoverable in a literary work, and the importance of Marxism and Feminism in interpretation. *Cf.* **Modernism**, **Deconstruction**, **Feminism**. *See also pp.* 1157–1159.

Post-Structuralism. The name for a wide variety of critical theories developed since the 1960s, extending and reacting to the ideas and methods of Structuralism. Post-Structuralist theories emphasize the indeterminacy of language and hence the instability of meaning in any work of literature. *Cf.* **Deconstruction**, **Structuralism**.

Protagonist. The main character in a story. Whereas a hero or heroine is usually someone admirable, a protagonist need not be. *Cf.* **Antagonist**, **Hero/heroine**.

Pulp magazines. So called because they were printed on cheap paper, pulp magazines were enormously popular in the 1920s. They were characterized by sensational covers and contained genre stories of the detective, western, science fiction, or fantasy variety, written almost exclusively by hack writers. *Cf.* **Detective stories**.

Reader-response theory. Formalist theories stressed the primacy of the literary work and challenged readers to find the meaning in it. Reader-response theorists emphasize that works must be read before they mean anything and that the reader participates actively in the creation of meaning and does not just passively receive it. Such a critic may analyze the way in which a work affects him or her, or may analyze the devices and strategies that seem calculated to produce a certain response in the reader. Reader-response critics also theorize about the strategies readers use to "decode" a text, many of which are in turn related to psychological, structuralist, or deconstructionist approaches.

Realism. In a general sense, realism is any attempt at verisimilitude—i.e., the depiction of characters, events, and places as they ordinarily appear, devoid of fantasy or the supernatural. As a literary movement, Realism was a nineteenth-century development, partly in reaction against Romanticism. It stressed careful attention to descriptive detail, consistency and plausibility in the manipulation of point of view, consistent psychology in the primary characters, accurate depictions of social manners and customs, and plausibility of plot. Realists also strove to avoid sentimentality and to confront some of the unpleasant aspects of life, especially sexuality. *See also pp.* 1148–1152.

Resolution. The last section of a conventional plot when the conflicts are resolved and brought to a close. *Cf.* **Plot**. *See also pp.* 1191–1192.

Romanticism. Any work of art that emphasizes the imaginative, fantastic, dream-like, improbable, or visionary may be termed romantic. However, Romanticism is a late eighteenth- and early nineteenth-century movement in Europe and North America in which the qualities listed above predominate. Romanticism was a reaction against the eighteenth-century stress on reason and common sense and hence stressed the emotional, subjective, and imaginative, and elevated these as primary avenues to truth. It also stressed spontaneity in thought and expression, indulgence in emotion for its own sake, idealism in moral and social thought, and the need for personal expression. Allied to these attitudes were the idea that Nature is a source of moral authority and the notion of the noble savage. *Cf.* **Realism**. *See also pp.* 1145–1147.

Satire. Any literary work that attempts to reform social institutions or personal conduct by means of ridicule. Satire implies a norm against which deviating behavior is measured and judged.

Sentimentality. Often defined as a work or passage that evokes excessive emotion. Such a definition, however, presupposes that there is an appropriate level of emotion for each kind of event—the death of a child, for example. Perhaps a better definition would focus on sentimentality as a stock emotion—exuding over kittens or puppies, for example—or the idealizing of certain kinds of emotion, such as romantic love. The term is also applied to works depicting ideal moral conduct as if it were the norm. All of these definitions suggest a false and sugary sensibility, played upon for cheap effects at the expense of truth.

Setting. Setting is the time and place in which a story occurs. It becomes important when it is treated or described in a particular way. A city park, for example, may be depicted as an oasis of natural beauty or as a place where drunks and perverts lurk in the bushes. An author's handling of setting, therefore, may be important in shaping our reaction to the characters and events portrayed. *Cf.* **Atmosphere**. *See also pp.* 1185–1186.

Short story. A short, fictional prose narrative, longer than an anecdote, shorter than a novel, ranging typically from 1,000 to 30,000 words. Various attempts have been made to differentiate the short story from the novel on the basis of some essential quality such as Poe's "single impression," but the form has proven too elastic. A short story may resemble a novel in all but length or be close in spirit to a lyric poem. While it often focuses on a single, self-contained incident, it may present only an episode or brief encounter, an overheard conversation, a moment in time, a feeling or atmosphere. *Cf.* **Tale**.

Simile. A figure of speech comparing two unlike things linked by the words "like" or "as." "My love is like a red, red rose" is a simile. *Cf.* **Figurative language**, **Metaphor**. *See also pp.* 1194–1196.

Sketch. A short, prose fictional work focusing mainly on character or atmosphere, often with an open ending. Under the influence of Brander Matthews, magazine editors early in this century often dismissed short stories in the Chekhovian manner as "mere sketches." The term retains some of these negative connotations of slightness or unimportance.

Stereotype. A conventional character of unvarying qualities; a stock character rather than a psychologically complex and probable individual. Popular fiction relies almost entirely on such characters, and literary fiction often uses them in minor roles. The wise-cracking servant, the dumb blonde, the crazy psychiatrist, the drunk at the bar are all stereotypes. *Cf.* **Character**. *See also pp.* 1177–1185.

Stream of consciousness. Also called interior monologue. A convention that attempts to represent in fiction the unmediated workings of the mind—almost as if the thoughts, sensations, and impressions that run through a character's mind were transferred directly to the page. The intent is to explore how the mind really works—not in complete sentences and coherent thoughts, but in fragments, connected if at all by association. Henry James was a pioneer in this technique; James Joyce and Virginia Woolf used it effectively in their novels, and it has since become an established technique.

Structuralism. An intellectual movement based largely on the linguistic theories of Ferdinand de Saussure and the anthropological ideas of Claude Levi-Strauss. Structuralism is concerned with language in the broadest sense; that is, with all signs or signifiers in communication, including literary conventions. Structuralist literary theory examines works to understand how they create meaning. Emphasis is on the pre-existing system that enables individual works to be read and understood. Structuralists, therefore, are less interested in what a particular work of literature says than how the literary system (for example, the short story) enables a particular short story to be read and understood. *Cf.* **Deconstruction**, **Post-structuralism**.

Style. Succinctly defined as an author's characteristic manner of expression—i.e., all those devices of language that set an author apart from others. Style may be analyzed by the author's choice of words (diction), figurative language, length and construction of sentences, rhythm, syntax, even punctuation. *See also pp.* 1193–1194.

Subplot. A secondary story that arises with the complication of the main plot and may contribute to, contrast with, or parallel the main plot. *Cf.* **Plot**.

Surrealism. A movement originating in France in the 1920s as a way of expressing the workings of the unconscious. Surrealism often uses non-logical associations (as in dreams or hallucinations), symbols, vivid juxtapositions, weird distortions, and fantastic images.

Symbol. An object, action, color, or image that stands for something else—e.g., the dove as a symbol of peace, the journey as a symbol of the course of a life, red as a symbol for sacrifice, or a description of wounds as a suggestion of Christ. Descriptive passages or recurring images may function symbolically, as for example when a description of urban decay symbolizes political corruption or recurring blood images suggest death. Most symbols are public in that they are shared by many authors, but some writers use private symbols. Symbols are important thematically because they express important ideas and concepts.

Tale. Often used, especially in the nineteenth century, as a synonym for short story, but in the twentieth century it often refers to a story possessing the characteristics of oral tradition, such as colloquial diction, loose structure, extraordinary events, simple characters, and the like.

Tall tale. A kind of folktale (or a literary imitation thereof), particularly popular in North America, featuring extraordinary characters and impossible events, presented as true, but obviously exaggerations, often for comic or satiric effect.

Theme. Traditionally defined as the unifying idea or "wider significance" of a story: the idea it communicates. Formalist criticism usually sought *the* theme in a story and attempted to show that all elements in the story contributed to this interpretation. Post-Structuralist critics, however, have focused on the multiplicity of themes or readings in any story. Theme is distinguished from moral in that a theme may be a comment on morality, politics, society, philosophy, or any issue of importance, whereas a moral is an exhortation to a particular kind of behavior.

Tone. The implied author's attitude toward his or her subject. Tone may be serious, mocking, playful, sarcastic, mock-serious, solemn, satirical, sympathetic, antagonistic, etc. Within a story, individual characters may use any or all the tones of voice encountered in daily conversation. *Cf.* **Style**, **Atmosphere**.

Tragedy. A story ends tragically when the conflict is resolved unhappily for the protagonist; the opposite of comedy.

Unreliable narrator. An implied narrator whose vision or understanding of events is open to question or whose motives or veracity may be doubted. Often, the narrator is unaware that he/she is not telling "the whole truth."

Verisimilitude. The attempt to reproduce exterior reality in fiction—"realism" in its broadest sense. *Cf.* **Realism**.

A SELECTIVE BIBLIOGRAPHY FOR STUDENTS: WORKS FOR FURTHER READING AND REFERENCE

BIBLIOGRAPHIES

Baldwin, Dean and Gregory L. Morris. *The Short Story in English, Britain and North America: An Annotated Bibliography.* Metuchen, N.J.: Scarecrow Press; and Pasadena, Cal. and Englewood Cliffs, N.J.: Salem Press, 1994.

Dictionary of Literary Biography. Columbia, S.C.: Bruccoli, Clark, Layman; and Detroit, Mich.: Gale Research. Vols. 74, 78, 86, 102, 113, 117, 130, 135, and 139 are especially relevant.

Magill, Frank N., ed. *Critical Survey of Short Fiction.* Rev. ed., 7 vols. Englewood Cliffs, N.J.: Salem Press, 1993.

Short Story Criticism: Excerpts from Criticism of the Works of Short Fiction Writers. Detroit, Mich.: Gale Research, 1988– . *Studies in Short Fiction.* "Annual Bibliography of Short Story Explication." *Studies in Short Fiction* 1 (Summer 1964–).

Thurston, Jarvis, O. B. Emerson, Carl Hartman, and Elizabeth Wright, eds. *Short Fiction Criticism: A Checklist of Interpretation Since 1925 of Stories and Novelettes (American, British Continental), 1800–1958.* Denver, Colo.: Alan Swallow, 1960.

Walker, Warren S., ed. *Twentieth-Century Short Story Explication: Interpretations, 1900–1966, of Short Fiction Since 1800.* 3rd ed. Hamden, Conn.: Shoe String Press, 1970. *Supplements to Third Edition.* Hamden, Conn.: Shoe String Press, 1980–. *New Series,* vol. 1 (1989–1990). Hamden, Conn.: Shoe String Press, 1993.

HISTORIES OF THE SHORT STORY

Allen, Walter. *The Short Story in English.* New York: Oxford University Press, 1981.

Bates, H. E. *The Modern Short Story.* 2nd ed. London: Michael Joseph, 1972.

Bayley, John. *The Short Story: Henry James to Elizabeth Bowen.* New York: St. Martin's Press, 1988.

Beachcroft, T. O. *The Modest Art: A Survey of the Short Story in English.* London: Oxford University Press, 1968.

Bone, Robert. *Down Home: A History of Afro-American Short Fiction from Its Beginnings to the End of the Harlem Renaissance.* New York: G. P. Putnam's Sons, 1975.

Flora, Joseph M., ed. *The English Short Story, 1880–1945: A Critical History.* Boston: Twayne, 1985.

O'Connor, Frank. *The Lonely Voice.* Cleveland: World Publishing, 1963; rpt. New York: Harper & Row, 1985.

Stevick, Philip, ed. *The American Short Story 1900–1945: A Critical History.* Boston: Twayne, 1984.

Vannatta, Dennis, ed. *The English Short Story, 1945–1980: A Critical History.* Boston: Twayne, 1985.

Weaver, Gordon, ed. *The American Short Story: 1945–1980.* Boston: Twayne, 1983.

SHORT STORY THEORY

Current-Garcia, Eugene, and Walton R. Patrick, eds. *What Is the Short Story?* Glenville, Ill.: Scott, Foresman, 1961.

Lohafer, Susan, and Jo Ellyn Clarey, eds. *Short Story Theory at a Crossroads.* Baton Rouge: Louisiana State University Press, 1989.

Matthews, Brander. *The Philosophy of the Short-Story.* New York: Longman, Green, 1901.

May, Charles E., ed. *Short Story Theories.* Athens, Ohio: Ohio University Press, 1976.

⚓ Acknowledgments

AESOP Fable, "Town Mouse and Country Mouse" from *Fables of Aesop*, translated by S.A. Handford (Penguin Classics, 1954). Copyright © 1954 by S.A. Hanford. Reprinted by permission.

AIDOO, AMA ATA "No Sweetness Here" by Ama Ata Aidoo. Copyright © 1970. Reprinted by permission.

AIKEN, CONRAD Conrad Aiken, "Silent Snow, Secret Snow," Copyright © 1932 by Conrad Aiken. Reprinted by permission of Brandt & Brandt Literary Agency.

ALLENDE, ISABEL Reprinted with the permission of Scribner, a Division of Simon & Schuster from *The Stories of Eva Luna* by Isabel Allende, translated by Margaret Sayers Peden. Copyright © 1989 Isabel Allende. English translation copyright © 1991 Macmillan Publishing Company.

ANON FAIRY TALE From *The Classic Fairy Tales* by Iona Opie and Peter Opie. Copyright © 1980 by Iona and Peter Opie. Used by permission of Oxford University Press, Inc.

ATWOOD, MARGARET "Bluebeard's Egg" by Margaret Atwood. Used by permission, McClelland & Stewart, Inc. The Canadian Publishers.

ATWOOD, MARGARET "Bluebeard's Egg" from *Bluebeard's Egg* by Margaret Atwood. Copyright © 1983, 1986 by O.W. Toad, Ltd. Reprinted by permission of Houghton Mifflin Company. All rights reserved.

ATWOOD, MARGARET "Happy Endings" is part of the collection *Good Bones and Simple Murders* by Margaret Atwood. Copyright © 1983, 1992, 1994 by O.W. Todd Ltd. A Nan A. Talese Book. Used by permission of Doubleday, a division of Bantam Doubleday Dell Publishing Group Inc., and the author.

BAMBARA, TONI From *Gorilla, My Love* by Toni Cade Bambara. Copyright © 1971 by Toni Cade Bambara. Reprinted by permission of Random House, Inc.

BARHELME, DONALD Donald Barhelme, "The Balloon," 1981, from *Unspeakable Practices, Unnatural Acts*. Copyright © 1968 by Donald Barhelme, reprinted by permission of The Wylie Agency, Inc.

BARTON, PAULE "Emilie Plead Choose One Egg" by Paula Barton. Copyright © 1980 by Howard A. Norman. English language translation copyright © 1980 by Howard A. Norman. Reprinted by permission of Melanie Jackson Agency.

BATES, H.E. H.E. Bates, "Great Uncle Crow," from *Seven by Five*. Copyright © 1959. Reprinted by permission of Laurence Pollinger Limited and the Estate of H.E. Bates.

BOCCACCIO "Fifth Day: Ninth Story" from *The Decameron* by Giovanni Boccaccio, translated by G. H. McWilliam (Penguin Classics, 1972). Translation © G. H. McWilliam, 1972.

BORGES, JORGE LUIS Jorge Luis Borges, translated by Donald A. Yates, from *Labyrinths*. Copyright © 1962, 1964 by New Directions Publishing Corp. Reprinted by permission of New Directions Publishing Corp.

BOSCH, JUAN "The Woman" by Juan Bosch. Translated by Gustavo Pellon. From *The Spanish American Short Story*, Seymour Menton, ed. Reprinted by permission.

BRUCHAC III, JOSEPH From *Gluskabe and the Four Wishes* by Joseph Bruchac. Copyright © 1988, 1995 by Joseph Bruchac. Used by permission of Cobblehill Books, an affiliate of Dutton Children's Books, a division of Penguin USA Inc.

BUTLER, ROBERT OLEN From *Tabloid Dreams* by Robert Olen Butler. Copyright © 1996 by Robert Olen Butler. Reprinted by permission of Henry Holt & Company, Inc.

CARTER, ANGELA "The Bloody Chamber." Copyright © Angela Carter, 1979. Reproduced by permission of the Estate of Angela Carter c/o Rogers, Coleridge & White Ltd., 20 Powis Mews, London W11 1JN

CARVER, RAYMOND From *Cathedral* by Raymond Carver. Copyright © 1981 by Raymond Carver. Reprinted by permission of Alfred A. Knopf Inc.

CHANDLER, RAYMOND "The Curtain" by Raymond Chandler. Copyright © 1936 The Estate of Raymond Chandler. Reprinted with permission of the Estate of Raymond Chandler.

KAWABATA, YASUNARI "Immortality" from *Palm-of-the-Hand Stories* by Yasunari Kawabata, translated by Lane Dunlop and J. Martin Holman. Translation copyright © 1988 by Lane Dunlop and J. Martin Holman. Reprinted by permission of North Point Press, a division of Farrar, Straus & Giroux, Inc.

KINCAID, JAMAICA "At the Bottom of the River" from *At the Bottom of the River* by Jamaica Kincaid. Copyright © 1983 by Jamaica Kincaid. Reprinted by permission of Farrar, Straus & Giroux, Inc.

LAURENCE, MARGARET "To Set Our House in Order" from *A Bird in the House* by Margaret Laurence. Copyright © 1963 by Margaret Laurence. Reprinted with the permission of New End Inc. and McClelland & Stewart.

LESSING, DORIS Reprinted with the permission of Simon & Schuster from *African Stories* by Doris Lessing. Copyright © 1957, 1958, 1962, 1963, 1964, 1965, 1972, 1981 by Doris Lessing.

MAHFOUZ, NAJIB "The Time and the Place," from *The Time and The Place and Other Stories* by Najib Mahfouz. Copyright © 1991 by the American University in Cairo Press. Used by permission of Doubleday, a division of Bantam Doubleday Dell Publishing Group, Inc.

MARQUEZ, GABRIEL GARCIA "Monologue of Isabel Watching it Rain in Macondo" from *Leaf Storm* by Gabriel Garcia Marquez and translated by Gregory Rabassa. Copyright © 1972 by Gabriel Garcia Marquez. Reprinted by permission of HarperCollins Publishers, Inc.

MAUGHAM, W. SOMERSET W. Somerset Maugham, "The Letter." Reprinted by permission of A.P. Watt Ltd. on behalf of The Royal Literary Fund.

MISHIMA, YUKIO By Yukio Mishima, translated by Ivan Morris, from *Death in Midsummer*. Copyright © 1966 by New Directions Publishing Corp. Reprinted by permission of New Directions Publishing Corp.

MOORE, LORRIE From *Like Life* by Lorrie Moore. Copyright © 1990 by Lorrie Moore. Reprinted by permission of Alfred A. Knopf Inc.

MUNRO, ALICE "The Progress of Love" by Alice Munro. Used by permission, McClelland & Stewart, Inc. The Canadian Publishers.

From *The Progress of Love* by Alice Munro. Copyright © 1986 by Alice Munro. Reprinted by permission of Alfred A. Knopf Inc.

NORMAN, HOWARD Copyright © 1980 by Howard A. Norman. English language translation copyright © 1980 by Howard A. Norman. Reprinted by permission of Melanie Jackson Agency.

O'CONNOR, FLANNERY "Good Country People" from *A Good Man is Hard to Find and Other Stories,* copyright © 1955 by Flannery O'Connor and renewed 1983 by Regina O'Connor, reprinted by permission of Harcourt Brace & Company.

OATES, JOYCE CAROL "Where Are You Going, Where Have You Been" by Joyce Carol Oates. Copyright © 1970 by Joyce Carol Oates. Reprinted by permission of John Hawkins & Associates, Inc.

OVID Ovid, from *Metamorphoses*, "The Story of Daedalus and Icarus" translated by Rolfe Humphries, ©1955. Reprinted by permission of Indiana University Press.

PALEY, GRACE Reprinted by permission of Grace Paley. From *The Little Disturbances of Man,* Penguin, 1987. Copyright © 1956, 1987 by Grace Paley. All rights reserved.

PAZ, OCTAVIO Octavio Paz, from *Eagle or Sun?* Copyright © 1976 by Octavio Paz and Eliot Weinberger. Reprinted by permission of New Directions Publishing Corp.

PORTER, KATHERINE ANNE "Flowering Judas" from *Flowering Judas and Other Stories,* copyright © 1930 and renewed 1958 by Katherine Anne Porter, reprinted by permission of Harcourt Brace & Company.

PRITCHETT, V.S. "Sense of Humor" by V.S. Pritchett. Copyright © 1938 by V.S. Pritchett. Reprinted by permission of The Peters Fraser and Dunlop Group Limited.

QUIROGA, HORACIO Reprinted from *The Exiles and Other Stories* by Horacio Quiroga, translated by J. David Danielson. Copyright © 1987 by the University of Texas Press. Reprinted by permission of the publisher.

ROTH, PHILIP "The Conversion of the Jews," *Goodbye, Columbus*. Copyright © 1959, renewed 1987 by Philip Roth. Reprinted by permission of Houghton Mifflin Company. All rights reserved.

SINGER, ISAAC BASHEVIS "The Little Shoemakers" by I. Bashevis Singer, translated by Isaac Rosenfeld, from *A Treasury of Yiddish Stories* by Irving Howe and Eliezer Greenberg. Copyright © 1953, 1954, 1989 by Viking Penguin, renewed © 1981, 1982 by Irving Howe and Eva Greenberg. Used by permission of Viking Penguin, a division of Penguin Books USA Inc.

STEELE, WILBER DANIEL "Footfalls" from *The Best Stories of Wilbur Daniel Steele*. Copyright 1929, 1956 by Wilbur Daniel Steele. Reprinted by permission of Harold Matson Co., Inc.

TAN, AMY Reprinted by permission of G.P. Putnam's Sons, a division of The Putnam Publishing Group from *The Joy Luck Club* by Amy Tan. Copyright © 1989 by Amy Tan.

THEOPHRASTUS   Reprinted by permission of the publishers and the Loeb Classical Library from Theophrastus, "Garrulity" from *Characters,* translated by Jeffrey Rusten et. al., Cambridge, Mass.: Harvard University Press, 1993.

TURGENOV, IVAN   "Yermolaï and the Miller's Wife" from *Sketches from a Hunter's Album* by Ivan Turgenov, translated by Richard Freeborn (Penguin Classics, 1967). Copyright © Richard Freeborn, 1967. Reprinted by permission.

UPDIKE, JOHN   From *Assorted Prose* by John Updike. Copyright © 1965 by John Updike. Reprinted by permission of Alfred A. Knopf Inc.

WALKER, ALICE   "Nineteen Fifty-Five" from *You Can't Keep a Good Woman Down,* copyright © 1981 by Alice Walker, reprinted by permission of Harcourt Brace & Company.

WELTY, EUDORA   "A Still Moment" from *The Wide Net and Other Stories,* copyright © 1942 and renewed 1970 by Eudora Welty, reprinted by permission of Harcourt Brace & Company. "Why I Live at the P.O." from *A Curtain of Green and Other Stories,* copyright © 1941 and renewed 1969 by Eudora Welty, reprinted by permission of Harcourt Brace & Company.

YAMAMOTO, HISAYE   "Seventeen Syllables" by Hisaye Yamamoto DeSoto, from *Seventeen Syllables* © 1988 by Hisaye Yamamoto DeSoto. Reprinted by permission of the author and of Kitchen Table: Women of Color Press, P.O. Box 40-4920, Brooklyn, NY 11240-4920. Also appeared in Partisan Review.

Author/Title Index

Continued from inside front cover